Adored

TILLY BAGSHAWE

An Orion paperback

First published in Great Britain in 2005
by Orion
This paperback edition published in 2005
by Orion Books
An imprint of the Orion Publishing Company Ltd,
Orion House, 5 Upper Saint Martin's Lane
London WC2H 9EA

An Hachette UK company

5 7 9 10 8 6

A CIP catalogue record for this book is available
from the British Library.

ISBN 978-0-7528-6555-3

Typeset by Deltatype Ltd, Birkenhead, Merseyside
Set in Monotype Dante
Printed and bound by CPI Group (UK) Ltd, Croydon, CRO 4YY

The Orion Publishing Group's Policy is to use papers that
are natural, renewable and recyclable products and
made from wood grown in sustainable forests, The logging
and manufacturing processes are expected to conform to
the environmental regulations of the country of origin.

www.orionbooks.co.uk

For Robin.

Through the good times and the bad,
I love you more than words can ever say.

The Major Players

DUKE MCMAHON Legendary Hollywood movie star and Lothario. Autocratic patriarch of the McMahon dynasty.

MINNIE MCMAHON Duke's long-suffering wife.

PETE MCMAHON Their embittered son. A producer.

CLAIRE MCMAHON Pete's quiet, academic wife. Mother of Siena.

LAURIE MCMAHON Duke and Minnie's fat, useless daughter, Pete's sister.

TARA Pete's spiteful PA.

CAROLINE BERKELEY Upper-class English gold-digger, Duke's long-term mistress and Hunter's feckless mother.

GEORGE and WILLIAM BERKELEY Caroline's pompous, bigoted brothers.

SEBASTIAN BERKELEY Caroline's besotted, elderly father.

HUNTER MCMAHON Gorgeous, sweet-natured but neglected illegitimate son of Duke and Caroline.

SIENA MCMAHON Duke's feisty granddaughter, the only child of Pete and Claire McMahon. A raving beauty.

MAX DE SEVILLE Childhood best friend of Hunter McMahon. Sexy, blond cad in the finest English tradition.

HENRY ARKELL Max's beloved half-brother,

	farmer, family man and all-round good guy.
MUFFY ARKELL	His harassed but devoted, very pretty wife.
BERTIE, CHARLIE and MADDIE ARKELL	Their children.
TITUS and BORIS	Their dogs.
TIFFANY WEDAN	Hunter's actress girlfriend. Like him, beautiful inside and out.
LENNOX	A gay actor/waiter. Tiffany Wedan's loyal best friend.
JACK and MARCIE WEDAN	Tiffany's parents, simple folk from Colorado.
RANDALL STEIN	Billionaire producer and biggest Hollywood player since Duke McMahon. A bastard.
SEAMUS	Duke's old childhood friend, now his valet.
GARY ELLIS	Unscrupulous cockney property developer.
CHRISTOPHER WELLESLEY	Charming old gentleman farmer, owner of one of the most beautiful estates in the Cotswolds.
MARSHA	Siena's diminutive but powerful modelling agent. A drunken dynamo.
INES PRIETO MORENO	Flame-haired Spanish supermodel.
DIERK MULLER	Charmless but talented German movie director.
HUGH ORCHARD	Highly respected, discreetly gay king of US network television. Writer and creator of a

number of hit shows, including *Counsellor* and *UCLA*.

JAMIE SILFEN The most powerful casting agent in Hollywood.

CAMILLE ANDREWS Texan model/actress/whore. A Sky Bar bimbo on the make.

MIRIAM STANLEY LA starlet. Has slept with every successful producer in town.

Prologue

England, 1998

Siena was going back to Hollywood if it killed her.

'So you see, Sister Mark,' she continued, carefully composing her features into an expression she hoped looked both remorseful and resigned, 'I do realise this is an expellable offence. And I just want you to know that I *totally* accept responsibility for my actions.'

God, she almost sounded tearful. But then she always knew she was a terrific actress. The old witch might actually be falling for it.

'I just don't know what made me do it.' She dropped her eyes shamefully to her lap – all nuns, she had learned, were suckers for a bit of humility. 'But I quite understand that I have left you with no choice. I've let St Xavier's down.'

Fabulous. This was working like a charm. Mentally, Siena began calculating how long it would take her to clear out her poky little dorm room. She'd have to say goodbye to the girls, of course, but if she really got her skates on she might make the six o'clock flight to LA. Or maybe there'd be formalities to go through? She'd have to see the Head of Governors perhaps? Even so, an early morning flight out would still get her there in time for a blow-dry at Zapata before she hit the bars on Melrose.

'Miss McMahon.' The headmistress's softly lilting Irish voice belied a firmness of purpose that Siena recognised only too well. She had come to hate the way Sister Mark pronounced her name: 'McMaaarn'. She seemed to stretch the word out, like torture. She wondered what sort of rambling lecture she was in for this time.

Looking around her, Siena took in the familiar

surroundings of Sister Mark's office for what she hoped would be the last time. It was simply furnished, as befitted a nun's rooms, but not austere. A full but slightly overblown bunch of peach-coloured roses dominated the desk, and their scent carried all the way to the window seat, which was lined with brightly coloured cushions, the slightly threadbare handiwork of generations of budding seamstresses. An unobtrusive crucifix hung against one of the whitewashed walls, while the others were plastered with photographs of St Xavier's girls past and present, commemorating various sporting or dramatic achievements. Siena, who was not much of a team player, did not feature, other than on the giant whiteboard displaying the detentions received by pupils, where her name made repeated appearances.

It was actually the third time this term that she had been summoned to the headmistress's eyrie of an office above the school chapel. In fact, in the seven years since Siena had first arrived at the school as a frightened ten-year-old, Sister Mark had lost count of the times she had peered across her desk at the beautiful, truculent, scowling little face of this most talented and yet most troublesome of pupils.

No matter how many times she looked at Siena, she never ceased to be struck by the uncanny resemblance: she really was the spitting image of her famous grandfather. As a young girl in Connemara, Sister Mark (or Eileen Dineen as she was then) had always had a bit of a soft spot for Duke McMahon. Well, it was hard not to. *Capri Sunset*, that had been his first big film, with Maureen O'Hara. Eileen and her pals must have seen it, what, nine or ten times? That dark flowing hair, that deep, rich, almost smouldering voice. Oh yes, in his day old Duke's romantic films had been quite an occasion of sin for half the teenage population of Ireland – not to mention the rest of the world. And now here she was, fifty years later, forty years a nun, wondering what in heaven's name to do with his troublesome grand-daughter.

Smoothing down her brown Viyella skirt – the nuns at St Xavier's no longer wore the habit, and the only thing that set them apart from the rest of the teaching staff was a plain silver cross worn at the neck – she moved her mahogany chair back a couple of inches and fixed her gaze once again on the enigma that was Siena McMahon.

For some reason, the child had never really settled in at St Xavier's. She was popular enough, that wasn't the problem. There may have been a touch of the green-eyed monster going on with some of the other girls, but as a rule they all wanted to be associated with Siena: granddaughter of a Hollywood legend and daughter of one of the world's most successful movie producers, she represented a glamour and excitement far beyond anything that these well-bred English gentlemen's daughters had ever experienced.

Siena had other advantages as well. She was undoubt-edly a beauty, and fifteen years of teaching in a girls' boarding school had taught Sister Mark that this, sadly, was a sure-fire passport to popularity, with or without the McMahon name behind her. And despite her truly appalling lack of discipline and almost pathological aversion to hard work, Siena had sailed through her school career with straight As across the board. On the face of it, she had very little to complain about.

Even so, it didn't take Einstein to work out that, for all her advantages and talents, the girl was deeply unhappy at school.

Her complaint had been the same since the very first week she arrived, a belligerent, feisty little madam even then: she wanted to go home. It was this that Sister Mark found particularly odd, since it was obvious Siena profoundly disliked both her parents. Tragic really. Other than the yearly prize day, which they both religiously attended, Pete and Claire McMahon seemed to spend as little time with their only daughter as was humanly

3

possible. Six weeks in the summer holidays was the only time they spent together at the family compound in Hollywood. Siena never flew home for half-terms or the shorter holidays, spending her breaks instead in the charge of a Spanish housekeeper at her parents' Knightsbridge flat. To be sure, that was no life for a child. But it seemed only to make the girl more wilful, more determined and more desperate than ever to get back home.

Looking across at Siena, Sister Mark noticed she was biting her lower lip, a childish signal of nervousness that looked out of place on the womanly seventeen-year-old she had become. A previous generation would have described Siena as 'buxom', but nowadays the girls seemed to interpret that as 'fat'. In fact she had a small frame, dominated by a very curvaceous bust, to which her blue uniform jumper clung almost obscenely. Her small, rosebud mouth, pale skin and thick cascade of dark curls all belonged to another, more sensuous and feminine era. Only her eyes – two dark blue flashes of ruthless determination – gave her otherwise angelic face its modern, edgy twist. Today they were narrowed in wary anticipation. The headmistress sighed. She was almost as tired of this battle as Siena was.

This time she had been caught red-handed smoking marijuana in the prefects' common room. Actually, 'caught' was hardly the right word, as she had made no attempt whatsoever to conceal the offence. Under normal circumstances she should, of course, be expelled. But A-levels were only a few months away, and Siena was expected to do exceptionally well. Besides, after seven long years Sister Mark was damned if she was going to send the little horror home now.

Reluctantly dragging her thoughts from the duty-free Burberry coats at Heathrow – or perhaps a bag, to pacify her mother? – Siena turned to face the elderly nun. Could she just get on with it for once and skip the damn lectures?

'Miss McMahon,' resumed Sister Mark, 'as you rightly say, you have indeed let St Xavier's down.'

Thank God, thought Siena, she's finally going to kick me out of this hellhole.

'However, I feel it would be . . .' a glancing smile flickered across the older woman's lips '. . . precipitate – or shall we say rash? – to assume that you leave me with "no choice" in terms of your punishment.'

Siena swallowed hard. Fuck. What was she on about now? The spluttering roar of a broken exhaust pipe broke the silence for a moment, and Siena's eyes were drawn down to the rickety old minibus belching its way down the school drive, its chassis seeming to shiver and shake in the biting January wind. It was supposed to be white, but was covered in a layer of grime so thick that it stood out as almost metallic grey against the backdrop of snowy lawns. Inside, giggling groups of girls huddled together, on their way to some hockey match or other. They all looked so fucking happy, so jolly bloody hockey sticks, it made her want to throw up.

'It has not entirely escaped my notice, Siena,' continued Sister Mark as the noise of the failing engine faded into the distance, 'that you harbour a strong desire to leave St Xavier's. Although I will confess I am not quite sure why this should be.'

Not sure why she would want to leave St Xavier's? Jesus Christ, surely the question was why the hell would anybody want to stay? Chapel at 7.30 in the morning, lights out at 10.30, more fucking meaningless rules than the Gestapo? And the worst thing was, most of the girls became totally brainwashed. They actually *looked forward* to coming back to sixth form because they got to have their own toaster in the common room! Toast Privilege, that's what they called it. Was Siena the only one who wanted to scream out loud: *EATING TOAST IS NOT A PRIVILEGE, IT'S A BASIC FUCKING HUMAN RIGHT!?* In LA, seventeen-year-old girls had cars. They wore designer clothes, not some dykey old uniform. They went to parties. They got laid. They had *lives*, for Christ's sake. St Xavier's – in fact the whole of fucking England, grey, freezing, miserable England – was stuck in some kind of nightmare time warp.

'I am not prepared to be manipulated into expelling you when I know full well that this was the response you were hoping for,' announced Sister Mark. Siena glared at her openly now, all pretence at humility gone. The headmistress ploughed on. 'I have, instead, decided to revoke all your sixth-form privileges until the end of the year.'

Oh my God. Siena's stricken face said it all.

'Till the end of the *year*? You can't do that!'

'Oh, I think you'll find I can.' The nun smiled serenely. 'Furthermore, you will be gated for the next four weeks. That means no exeat weekends, no social events, no after-school activities. Other than Mass, of course.'

Oh, of course. Mass. Terrific.

'Siena. Listen to me.' Sister Mark's tone had softened, but Siena was oblivious. If she wasn't going home, then what was the point in listening? What else mattered? The nun reached across the desk for her hand and squeezed it with genuine kindness, ignoring the girl's look of revulsion. 'You are in the home stretch, my dear.'

Siena watched the sunlight glinting off her crucifix and shielded her eyes. She didn't want to hear this.

'It's January now. By July, your A-levels will be over and if you'd only start to apply yourself, well, you've every chance of a place at Oxford. Every chance.' She squeezed her hand again encouragingly, willing the child to look up.

But Siena had tuned out. Sister Mark didn't understand. How could she? Withdrawing her hand, she gazed out of the window, across the frosty convent lawns to the frozen hills of the Gloucestershire landscape beyond. It was so cold that icicles still clung to the twigs of the sycamores, and she could see the frozen breath of the group of third-years chattering animatedly on their way to class, no doubt excited by the snow and the prospect of tobogganing at the end of the day.

Despite the beauty of the scene, Siena's mind was six thousand miles away. Not in her parents' home in the Hollywood hills but at Grandpa Duke's in Hancock Park, far back into her childhood. Suddenly she was eight years old again, bounding up the steps to the mansion and into his arms. Whenever she closed her eyes, she could feel the warmth and strength of that embrace as though it were yesterday. Sitting in the hard-backed mahogany chair in Sister Mark's under-heated study, she longed for that warmth with every breath in her body.

To her childish mind, it had all seemed so permanent. Grandpa Duke, the house, her happiness. But it had all melted away, all of it, like the Gloucestershire snow. And here she was, as far from that happiness and comfort as it was possible to be.

PART ONE

PART ONE

Chapter One

'Forty-eight, forty-nine . . . fifty! Nice job, Duke, you're looking great.'

Duke McMahon lay back on his workout mat and looked up at his trainer. Jesus Christ, these young guys all looked like shit. Sideburns like a pair of hairy runways, a brown velour jogging suit and more gold jewellery than the fucking Mafia. No wonder so much Hollywood pussy was out there looking for an older man.

Still, Mikey was right about one thing. He was looking great. Duke sat up and took a satisfied look at his reflection in one of the floor-to-ceiling mirrors that plastered the room. At sixty-four, he still had the body of a man twenty years younger, and he didn't owe one inch of it to surgery. He hated working out with a passion, especially the goddam sit-ups, but was infinitely vain. In his six years with Duke, Mikey had never known him cancel a single session.

'You still need to do some more work on your abs, you know,' Mikey chided as he watched the old man untie his sneakers and head towards the shower.

'Yeah, and you still need to do some more work on your fucking wardrobe, man. Not to mention your hair.' Duke held up his hands in mock exasperation. 'I'm telling you, buddy, you look like Cher with a three-day shadow. Get a fucking haircut!'

Mikey laughed and turned down the blaring roar of Mick Jagger on the record player. Duke loved his Stones.

It had been a long time since Mikey had seen him in such a chipper mood. Evidently the new girlfriend was working wonders. He knew he shouldn't really like

Duke, but he couldn't help it. Sure, the old man was a bastard. An addictive womaniser, he treated his poor wife Minnie like dirt, and was so right wing – anti-gay, anti-women, anti-blacks, anti-taxes – it was totally outrageous. But he also had this incredible energy, a lust for life that seemed to draw people to him. Mikey had a lot of wealthy, famous clients – although none quite as wealthy or famous as Duke McMahon – and none of them could touch him for raw charisma.

Emerging dripping and naked from the shower, Duke strode over to the window and looked out at the California sunshine. He had had the gym built on the first floor of his sprawling hacienda in Hancock Park, a pale pink, Spanish architectural masterpiece known to the busloads of tourists that hung around outside the gates simply as the McMahon Estate. Although the estate itself had been built in the twenties, when Hancock Park was first starting to become popular with the swelling ranks of movie actors and musicians who had moved west to find fame and fortune, the interior was a bizarre mélange of modern and traditional styles.

Minnie, Duke's long-suffering wife, had impeccable, if rather conservative taste, and many of the public rooms reflected her refined and understated influence.

In striking contrast, Duke's unashamed vulgarity and love affair with all things modern had led to some gruesome decor decisions, of which the gym was only one. The state-of-the-art music centre, complete with eight-track tape deck and stereo speakers, was housed in an immense velvet-lined teak cabinet. A central 'work-out' square of polished wood was surrounded by a sea of cream shag-pile carpeting, fitted wall to wall beneath the ubiquitous mirrors, and a disco ball hung in pride of place from the vaulted ceiling.

'For the love of God, Duke, would you put some clothes on?' Seamus, Duke's oldest childhood friend and now his right-hand man, a sort of hybrid manservant, PA and business manager, had stuck his flushed, permanently jovial face round the door, giving a brief nod of acknowledgement to the trainer. 'You have a meeting at eleven, you know. I know the dress code is casual in Hollywood, but I'm sure John McGuire would appreciate a pair of underpants at least.'

Duke looked over his shoulder at his old pal and grinned. They were almost exact contemporaries, but Seamus looked nearly old enough to be his father. His hairline had receded so far that he appeared completely bald from the front, and a lifelong penchant for 'the odd dram', as he put it, had contributed to both his florid complexion and his spreading waistline. In anyone else Duke would have been scathing of such a lack of self-control, but Seamus had always been a special case. Having battled his way through the viper's nest of scheming agents and unscrupulous studios in Hollywood, Duke knew just how rare loyalty and genuine friendship were. Seamus was a gem.

'Go fuck yourself, wouldya?' he replied good-naturedly, scratching his balls for added effect. 'I'm trying to enjoy the view here.'

And quite a view it was. Immaculately manicured lawns rolled down the hill away from the house as far as the eye could see. A blue, Olympic-size pool flashed and shimmered in the morning sunshine, surrounded by a haphazard collection of orange and lemon trees, all groaning with fruit. Tiny hummingbirds, their brilliant streaks of colour clashing with the unbroken blue of the sky, flitted from flower to flower, enjoying the sunshine. It was hard to imagine that such a Garden of Eden could be completely man-made; that without ceaseless irrigation, planting and tending, the whole of Hancock Park would have been nothing more than a lifeless desert swamp. But then that was precisely what Duke loved about LA. It was a place where you could turn a patch of dirt into paradise, if you worked hard and wanted it bad enough.

Any one of the legions of Mexican gardeners and handymen on the lawns below could have glanced up and seen the master of the house stark naked surveying his kingdom from the window, as they had on so many mornings before. Duke didn't care. It was his house. He had worked for every square inch of it and he could shit on the fucking floor if he wanted to. Besides, he liked being naked in front of the staff because it drove Minnie insane with embarrassment. Humiliating his wife was one of Duke's greatest and most enduring pleasures.

'Eleven o'clock.' Seamus raised a reprimanding finger in the general direction of Duke's naked rear view before scurrying off to prepare the paperwork for the day's meetings.

'Look at that, man.' Duke made a sweeping gesture towards the window for Mikey's benefit, once Seamus had gone. 'What a terrific day!'

'We're in California, Duke; every day's a beautiful day.' The trainer zipped up his sports bag and leant back against the mirrored wall. He wasn't in any rush to leave. His next client was a hopelessly overweight Beverly Hills widow who couldn't seem to get enough of his brown velour jogging suit and shoulder-length hair. Chewing the fat with Duke was a whole lot more fun. 'So what's put you in such a great mood all of a sudden? This wouldn't have anything to do with . . . is it Catherine? What's her name, your new girlfriend?'

'Mistress, my new mistress.' Duke grinned. 'I'm a hell of a lot too old for a "girlfriend".' To Mikey's relief, he pulled on a pair of white linen golfing trousers and sat down on the bench, warming to his theme. 'A girlfriend is someone you hold hands with, maybe go to the pictures with,' Duke explained. 'One day, if you find you really like her, then maybe you marry her and she becomes your wife. That's a girlfriend. Now a mistress . . . a mistress is something totally different.' He paused for dramatic effect, a slow smile spreading across his hawk-like, predatory features. 'A mistress is basically pussy that you own.'

'Jesus Christ!' Mikey exploded into laughter, genuinely shocked. 'You can't *say* things like that! Nobody *owns* nobody else, Duke.'

'Ah, kid.' Duke shook his head. 'How little you know.'

Standing up to admire his chosen outfit – white pants, white patent-leather shoes and a tight chocolate-brown turtle-neck that was far too warm for the California climate but which accentuated his chest and biceps – he put an affectionate, paternal arm around his trainer. How come he could never talk like this to his own son, Pete? The boy was always so fucking uptight, a stuck-up little prig like his mother. Duke used to say that Pete Jr was a replica of Minnie, only with balls – but these days he wasn't too sure whether he even had that distinction.

'Anyway, in answer to your question, yes, my mood probably does owe just a little something to Caroline.'

'Sorry, yeah, Caroline, you told me.'

Duke was beaming like a drunk in a liquor store. This must be quite some girl. As if reading his mind, the old man continued.

'Not only is she a world-class fuck . . .' Duke noticed Mikey fighting to stifle a blush. 'Seriously, man, you should see her, she is the sluttiest little whore but she speaks like the fucking Queen. If you haven't screwed an English girl, I'm telling you, you gotta try it.'

'I'll bear that in mind,' said Mikey. 'Thanks.'

'But the best part is . . .' Duke looked at him triumphantly. 'She's agreed to move in with me. Permanently. As of today.'

Had Mikey missed something here?

'What do you mean she's moving in with you?' He knew it was rude to piss on Duke's picnic when he was so patently over the moon. But how could Caroline possibly be moving in? 'What about Minnie? Did you guys, like, separate or get a divorce or something? How come I never heard about this?'

'Nope.' Duke cracked his knuckles and smiled broadly. He was evidently enjoying himself, lapping up the younger man's discomfiture. 'No separation, no divorce. I just told her. This is my house and I want Caroline to live here. Minnie'll do what she's told if she wants to remain a part of this family.'

Mikey winced. Duke's brutality never ceased to shock him, especially where poor Mrs McMahon was concerned. He couldn't understand why on earth she tolerated it. Still, even by Duke's standards this was a bit extreme, moving the girlfriend into the estate right under her nose. He imagined Peter wasn't going to be best pleased either.

'We're having a welcome dinner tonight at eight,' continued Duke, unfazed. 'It's just family: Caroline and me, Laurie, Pete and his wife . . . and *my* wife, of course.' He sneered sadistically. 'But you're more than welcome to join us if you'd like. I'll have Minnie set an extra place.'

Jesus Christ, so Minnie was expected to play hostess at this charade? Suddenly Mikey felt awkward, guilty. He didn't want to be party to any of this.

'I can't,' he said, blushing. 'I'm really sorry, but I can't.'

For all his charm, Duke obviously had a huge hole right where any sense of morality or basic human compassion should be. And when you looked right into that hole, it was black. Frankly, it scared the shit out of him.

Sensing the old man's disappointment, he shrugged apologetically and weakly attempted to lighten the atmosphere. 'Dinner with my girlfriend, you know?'

'Sure. Of course,' said Duke with a mirthless smile. He reminded Mikey of the wolf grinning at Little Red Riding Hood. All of a sudden the room seemed to become terribly cold. 'It's not a problem, kid, really,' said Duke, heading for the door. 'I understand.'

Sitting at her dressing table in the east wing of the house,

Minnie fastened the clasp of her pearls with a steady hand. The sweet scent of the cyclamen creepers that grew around her dressing-room window never failed to relax her. She took a deep, calming gulp of the warm morning air and sighed.

Minnie adored her dressing room, her small, private sanctuary filled with the beloved and familiar reminders of a former life: her father's antique English writing table now served as her own bureau, and the richly faded Persian rug on the floor had once been the nursery rug back home in Connecticut, on which she and her brother Austin had crawled and squabbled and built elaborate cities out of bricks. Lavish vases of flowers covered every available surface, and a slightly battered but charming old bookcase beside the door was filled with books, not only collected but read, by generations of Millers. Some had belonged to her great, great-grandfather, and Minnie loved simply to hold them, stroking the spines and thinking of all of her ancestors who had held them and read them before her.

Thirty years in Los Angeles had done nothing to diminish her homesickness for the East Coast. But through her flair for interior design – Minnie had that rare ability to turn a house into a home without diminishing its elegance, with a style that combined traditional conservatism with real warmth – she had created a miniature East Coast oasis inside the estate, which had become a huge comfort to her in her frequent times of trouble.

Having arranged her pearls carefully in the mirror, she picked up the silver-backed clothes brush on the dresser and swept a few stubborn strands of lint from her skirt. Today would be a difficult day. But as her mother had always taught her, a lady never loses her composure, no matter how trying the circumstance. Whatever it took, she must maintain her dignity; draw it like a shield around her in the face of this ... this ... unfortunate event.

Ten years younger than Duke, at fifty-four Minnie had embraced middle age as enthusiastically as her husband had fought to keep it at bay. She looked like his mother. That is to say, she dressed like his mother; or like his mother *would* have dressed had she come from an old-money Greenwich family like Minnie's (rather than an impoverished New York Irish tribe of manual labourers and petty thieves). Her daily uniform had barely altered since she and Duke first married over thirty years ago. A khaki linen skirt to the knee, crisp white shirt with jauntily up-turned collar, tan pantyhose (no matter how stiflingly hot the weather, a lady never went bare legged), slightly heeled round-toed pumps and, of course, her grandmother's pearls.

Thanks to a rigorous, no-nonsense daily beauty routine, consisting of soap, water and a good dollop of cold cream at night, her handsome, patrician face was not excessively lined. The years of suffering she had endured through the latter stages of her marriage to Duke had etched themselves only faintly around the eyes, where other, happier women had 'laughter lines'.

Still, Minnie reminded herself grimly, she had a lot to be thankful for. Life as the wife of the world's most famous movie star had brought a lot of material comforts, which had certainly dulled the pain of some of her other marital disappointments. And of course, she had her children. Sweet, reliable Laurie and her beloved son Pete still lived on the Hancock Park estate, and along with Pete's young wife Claire they provided a daily buffer of emotional support against Duke's increasingly open hatred of her.

Her husband might be insisting on moving his cheap little tart into their home. But by God, if he thought he was going to drive her out with his vindictive little games, her or the children, he had another think coming.

'Mother? Oh, Mother, there you are.'

Laurie's forlorn face peered round the doorway. At twenty-eight, Duke and Minnie's younger child had already adopted the appearance of a confirmed spinster. Her full gypsy skirt and loose, shapeless Moroccan blouse did nothing to conceal the rolls of fat acquired through decades of comfort eating. With her greasy brown hair scraped back into a severe ponytail and her face bare of make-up, it was almost impossible to believe that this timid, trembling mouse of a girl could be the natural child of such fine-featured parents. This morning her appearance was further hampered by a bright red shiny nose and eyes dreadfully swollen from crying.

'Well, of course I'm here,' said Minnie, her voice bright and businesslike. 'Where else would I be? We have an awful lot to do today for the dinner, and I'm going to need your help, Laurie-Loo, with the flowers.'

For the last week, Caroline's arrival had been referred to simply as 'the dinner'. No one could bring themselves to utter her name.

'Oh, Mother!' Laurie's swollen, twitching face finally gave way and crumpled into full-throated, childish sobs. 'How can you be so *calm* about it? I mean, how could Daddy *do* this to you, to all of us?'

'For the good Lord's sake, Laurie, pull yourself together,' said Minnie. If there was one thing she would not tolerate it was giving in to one's emotions. It really was disgracefully undignified. 'It's a difficult time for all of us, but we have nothing to be ashamed of, and certainly no reason to cry.'

She handed her daughter a white monogrammed handkerchief and patted the chair beside her. The rosewood creaked as Laurie eased her snivelling bulk into it. Minnie wished her daughter would show just a little more self-discipline when it came to food, but she smiled at her kindly and tried not to show it.

'Really, darling, you mustn't cry.' She stroked her daughter's hair ineffectually, as if she were an obedient dog. 'Believe me, your father will tire of this young woman soon enough. Just as he has of all the others.'

'I hope so, Mother.' Laurie sniffed. 'I really do. But

he's never moved any of the others in with us before, has he?' It was a good point. 'I mean, for God's sake, this girl is only twenty-nine. That's even younger than Petey.'

'I can do the math, sweetheart.' Minnie sighed. Squaring her bony shoulders into a stance of unshakeable determination, she squeezed Laurie's hand firmly. 'Try not to worry,' she said. 'It's going to be up to all of us, you, me and Peter, to make sure this young woman *does* go the way of all the rest of them. But I can promise you one thing, darling. I am your father's wife and the mistress of this household. And nothing, Laurie – absolutely nothing – is going to change that.'

Not for the first time, Laurie marvelled at her mother. Pete always insisted that a willingness to accept a lifetime of abuse from Duke was more of a weakness than a strength, but Laurie was in awe of Minnie's resolute calm in the face of just about any storm. She thought of her mother as some sort of tragic heroine, her unbreakable spirit emerging triumphant through all the batterings that fate and life could throw at her. If only she, Laurie, had inherited some of that spirit, that strength, then perhaps her life wouldn't be in such an unholy mess.

'So . . .' Minnie smiled bravely, anxious to end this emotional interview with her daughter. 'Why don't we start sorting out those flowers for tonight? We want everything to look perfect for Daddy, don't we?'

To everyone who knew them, Duke and Minnie McMahon's marriage was a perpetual mystery.

When they'd first met, back in the late thirties, Minnie was the shy and incredibly beautiful teenage daughter of Pete Miller, the last in a long line of wealthy Connecticut landowners, and his wife Marilyn, a respected society hostess. Duke, who'd been brought by a casual girlfriend to one of Marilyn Miller's charity events, was a recognised young actor, still somewhere between up and coming and a major studio star, and already had something of a reputation as a gambler and a womaniser who liked to party hard.

His attraction to the young Minnie Miller was instant and uncomplicated. Standing in the corner of the room, hiding awkwardly in the shadows behind her nerdy elder brother Austin, she seemed to represent everything that had been denied him in his own early life: beauty, fragility, innocence, wealth and breeding. She looked untouched, and untouchable, exactly the sort of virgin, Protestant princess that polite society considered completely out of bounds for a dissolute Irish Catholic boy such as himself.

He had asked her to dance that night – much to his companion's chagrin – and she had declined, blushing furiously and insisting she didn't know how to, clinging on to her brother's hand for dear life. Duke was charmed. He didn't know that such naive girls really still existed within a hundred-mile radius of Manhattan. Certainly he had never met one before. He decided there and then that he had to have Minnie Miller, and for the next nine months he set about the arduous task of seducing her.

For Minnie's own part, she had worshipped Duke from the moment she laid eyes on him. He was breathtakingly good-looking, with his hair the same shiny blue-black as a raven's, his firm, jutting jaw and his wonderful, deep, lyrical voice with its lingering hint of Irish brogue. There was also something dangerous about him, something adult, masculine and forbidden that set him apart from all her brother's preppy Harvard classmates, or the boys she was introduced to at her mother's carefully chaperoned society dances.

Both the strength and nature of her feelings for him frightened her. For her to be courted openly by Duke, a Catholic with no good family and what her mother referred to with shuddering disdain as 'a reputation', was quite inconceivable. On the other hand a secret romance was in Minnie's eyes a step of such seriousness and gravity that for months she could barely sleep for thinking about it, tortured in equal measure by her passionate love and desire for Duke and desperate, all-consuming guilt.

Eventually, as is always the way, love and passion beat guilt hands down. She was still only eighteen when Duke took her virginity, in one of the old boathouses by the lake at her parents' summer house in Maine. For Duke, who was used to the more practised efforts of worldly Hollywood girls, the sex was, technically speaking, dreadful. She had lain rigid and shaking beneath him, her eyes wide open with terror like a rabbit about to be shot. And afterwards she had sobbed in his arms until his shirt was soaked through.

But his sense of triumph and elation, not just of breaking down her defences sexually, but of winning the heart of something so rare and perfect and precious, more than outweighed the disappointment of the event itself. There was something about Minnie that made him want to be a better man, the man she deserved. No one was more surprised than Duke to discover that he had, for the first time in his life, fallen in love.

They were married three months later in a little Catholic church off Broadway. An ashen-faced Pete Miller had led his daughter down the aisle: for Minnie to be marrying a scoundrel like McMahon was bad enough, but a Catholic wedding! His poor father and grandfather would both be turning in their graves.

For Duke, the day was one of unadulterated elation, and he couldn't understand it when, driving his new wife home from their rather subdued reception at the Millers' Manhattan townhouse, she had burst into tears.

'What on earth's the matter?' he'd asked her, handing her his handkerchief with a look of bewilderment and dismay. 'Don't tell me you're regretting it already?'

'Oh, Duke, no,' she insisted between sobs, 'of course I'm not. It's not that. It's just that tomorrow we're going to be leaving for California. I've never been away from Mommy and Daddy before, not for more than a week anyway, and I'm gonna miss them so much. Oh, and Austin!'

At the thought of her brother she began wailing again, and Duke fought down his feelings of annoyance. What the hell did she see in that chinless, judgemental, preppy little son of a bitch anyway?

'Come on now,' he said, reaching over and patting her thigh sympathetically. 'It's not like I'm taking you to Europe or something. Your parents can come visit. I bet you we see them all the time.'

Minnie shook her head sadly. 'I'm not so sure,' she said. 'You know how much they disapproved of us getting married. What if they never forgive me?'

'Sure they will,' said Duke. Although privately he wished his wife didn't already think of their marriage as some sort of sin to be forgiven.

The first year of the marriage was a happy one. Duke had bought them a large house in North Hollywood, back when LA property was still dirt cheap, and Minnie delighted in decorating it and playing house while her new husband was on-set. His career was going from strength to strength, and in 1941 he landed his first leading role, in a farcical comedy called *Check Mate*. The rift with her family remained strong, and she saw her parents only once in that first year, spending an agonisingly awkward long weekend with them at the newly developed resort of Palm Springs. But life with Duke was so blissful, and she was so caught up with establishing herself as a hostess among his new and exciting Hollywood crowd, that she found herself feeling less and less homesick, and less and less guilty, by the day.

Then came the war. And as for so many young couples, overnight it seemed everything changed.

Duke was sent to Asia, where he was to spend the

next three and a half years. He was, as he liked to tell people later, one of the lucky ones. He came home. But the home, and the woman he came home to, had changed out of all recognition.

For the first six months after he was conscripted, Minnie remained in Hollywood, trying to make a life for herself among the other army wives there. But loneliness soon overcame her and, encouraged by her mother and brother, she decided to return home to Connecticut. She missed Duke terribly, and wrote to him religiously twice a week. But she also found herself naturally slipping back into the old rhythms of life at home. Soon she was going riding with her father and out to lunches in Manhattan with her mother, just like the old days, and her married life back in California began to feel more and more like a distant dream.

Duke would come home on leave and stay with the Millers. His father-in-law was civil – now that he had seen active service, Duke had apparently become a smidgen more acceptable in the old man's eyes – but still always treated him with a patronising sense of social superiority that Duke bitterly resented.

When he complained to Minnie about it, she dismissed him. He was imagining slights and insults where there were none.

Duke wanted her to move back to LA, but the mere suggestion made her almost hysterical.

'What's the point of me being there when you're away?' she asked. 'I'm isolated and I'm lonely, whereas here I have friends and family to support me. Things are so much better now with Mom and Dad. Please, please don't ruin it all again.'

He couldn't really argue with her. Still, he returned to the front with a gnawing sense that he was somehow losing her. That she was no longer completely on his side.

After the war, they did move back home, and for a while

life got back to something approaching normal. Duke went back to work at the studio, and Minnie almost immediately fell pregnant with Peter. The cracks, however, did not take long to start appearing.

Minnie's parents' snobbery and East Coast prejudices seemed to have oozed into her personality in the last three years by osmosis. Whereas before she had been quite happy to have friends over for an impromptu kitchen supper in the evenings, she now insisted on full silver-service dinners every time they entertained, which Duke found pretentious and unnecessary. Worse, she began to show signs of embarrassment at his own social behaviour, reprimanding him in public for excessive drinking, and even on one occasion correcting his grammar in front of the whole crew on-set.

'It's "I should have", darling, not "I should of,"' she'd piped up brightly, overhearing him rehearsing some lines.

Duke was furious.

'Yeah? Well, maybe you should *have* stayed at home and minded your own fuckin' business, Min,' he snapped.

The worst of it was that Minnie herself could not perceive any of the changes Duke accused her of. In her own mind, she was just the same as she had always been, and she still loved her husband desperately.

'Of course I'm on your side, darling,' she'd protest tearfully. 'I love you so much, Duke. You must know that.'

But increasingly, he wasn't sure whether he did know it. With her love and approval, he truly believed he could be a good man, a good husband and father. Without it, there was nothing to stop him from going back to his old ways.

He began an affair with one of his co-stars. It spluttered on for a few months, after which, miserable and guilty, he came home one night and confessed to a distraught Minnie.

'I'm sorry,' he said, 'but I didn't know what to do. I feel like I'm not good enough for you any more.'

'Oh, Duke, that's nonsense! How can you say that?' she cried.

Even in her despair, she seemed to be dismissing him.

'Well, why won't you sleep with me, then? For Christ's sake, Minnie, it's been months and every time I come near you you push me away! You make me feel like some sort of fucking disease.'

'I've told you!' she shouted at him. 'It's because of the baby. I'm just scared, Duke, I want our baby so much, I don't want anything to go wrong.'

'And nothing will,' he said, pulling her to him and holding on to her tightly. What the hell was he doing, cheating on her? God knew he loved her, so much it scared the wits out of him.

That night they had made love, but it was a disaster. Duke, desperate for her love and forgiveness, had tried everything he knew to please her. But she was so terrified of losing the baby she remained rigid with tension throughout, suffering his attentions as a mother must tolerate the needy suckling of her child. The woman who had once filled him with such confidence and made him feel like such a strong, powerful man now made him feel useless, rejected and alone.

Things went from bad to worse. The baby was born, and instantly little Peter became the centre of his mother's world, leaving Duke feeling even more excluded. He began another affair, then another, each time hoping to shock Minnie into realising that he needed her.

She loved him, and was deeply hurt by his infidelities. But as the affairs became more and more frequent, she eventually stopped believing that she had any power to prevent them. Duke was rapidly becoming a huge star, with some of the world's most beautiful women literally throwing themselves at his feet. Obviously, Minnie thought, he no longer loved her. She learned to take comfort and joy in her children instead of her marriage, and cloaked herself defensively in the stoic, reserved conservatism of her upbringing. Slowly but surely, she and Duke grew ever farther and more irreparably apart.

And yet, to the surprise of all who knew them, they never did divorce. In fact, they never even discussed the possibility. Some said it was Duke's almost superstitiously strong Catholicism which held the marriage together. Others saw Minnie as a masochist, who would put up with just about anything for her children's sake and to avoid a society scandal.

The truth, in fact, was much simpler. Somewhere, buried very deep in both their hearts, beneath the hatred, the bitterness and all the many betrayals, a tiny fragment of love survived.

Chapter Two

From Duke's perspective, Caroline's arrival was a huge success.

By eight o'clock the house was looking immaculate. Enormous vases of pink and white lilies jostled for position on the delicate Louis XV walnut tables littering the hacienda's enormous marble entrance hall. Real log fires crackled in the dining room and drawing room (or 'den', as Duke embarrassingly insisted on calling it, despite its palatial proportions), and a festive smell of pine mingled with the sweet, heady scent of the flowers. Two assistants had been hired to help Conchita, the McMahons' cook, ensure that the lobster bisque, monk-fish casserole and lemon syllabub were cooked to perfection, much to that formidable Mexican matron's fury. Minnie hated to upset Conchita, but it was imperative that tonight's meal be beyond reproach.

Pete McMahon arrived home from work at six. Although more physically attractive than his younger sister, Pete was certainly no heart-throb and, like Laurie, bore very little resemblance to either of his parents. To begin with, he was ginger haired, although with age his colouring had mercifully faded from the carroty orange of his childhood to a nondescript sandy colour, prematurely flecked with grey. He had his mother's pale complexion, but whereas Minnie's skin was luminous and pure, Pete looked permanently pasty and ill, and had a tendency towards excessive sweating. He was well built, despite being short and physically lazy, and there was a certain bulldog strength about him that some women seemed to find attractive. Nevertheless, he generally made the worst of his looks, such as they were, thanks to a tragic penchant for ill-fitting suits as well as the scowl of resentment that hung almost permanently over his otherwise regular features.

Today he was looking even more bad tempered than usual. What a shitty, shitty day it had been. His long-anticipated meeting with the producer Mort Hanssen had turned out to be a complete waste of time. Pete aspired to produce himself, and had had a couple of vanity credits on some half-decent low-budget pictures. But Mort, like everybody else in Hollywood, clearly still viewed him as Duke McMahon's kid. The fact that at the age of thirty he still lived under his father's roof obviously did nothing to improve his credibility. Man, he really had to do something about that, take the bull by the horns.

He and Claire, his quiet, shy new wife, remained largely financially dependent on Duke and lived in a suite of rooms in the south wing of the main house. Although he had never shown even the most glancing interest in either of his two children, Duke was insistent that his entire extended family should remain living at Hancock Park. Having grown up the youngest of seven children in a vast Irish tribe, sleeping two or three to a bed, Duke liked big families. He also had an almost pathological fear of being alone.

For Pete, living on the estate was like fucking torture. No privacy. No escape. After the day he'd had today, the last thing he needed was to play welcoming committee for some bimbo of his father's.

Walking into the drawing room, he watched Minnie as she darted about tasting the soup or plumping up the already perfect over-stuffed cushions. Pete's heart lurched for her. He felt a sickening combination of love, sympathy and an agonising, impotent rage. Somehow his mother had made it a matter of *pride* to have the house looking wonderful for that little bitch. As if the fucking priest were coming over for Thanksgiving or something. Jesus. Why couldn't she once, just *once*, stand up to him?

But Pete knew, probably better than anybody, that it

wasn't that easy to stand up to his father. As a small boy, he had watched helplessly as Duke systematically destroyed his mother's happiness. It wasn't just the other women. In fact, sexual infidelity, Pete reflected, was probably one of the least of his father's crimes. Lust, after all, is instinctive. Whereas vindictiveness, decades of consistent casual cruelty, of emotional torture – now that was something you had to work at.

And boy, Duke had really worked at it. Jealous of his wife's better breeding, her East Coast education and her innate good taste, he had brutally asserted his authority through a combination of economic control – Minnie never had her own bank account, nor did she spend a cent without first having to beg her husband's permission – and sheer force of personality.

It didn't help that for all Pete's life, his father had been a megastar. A matinée idol in the thirties and forties, he had invested his earnings wisely and grown to become a respected Hollywood power broker. People fawned on Duke. People who didn't even know him were mesmerised by him. Men fantasised about being him, women about screwing him. But none of them knew the real Duke McMahon – the vicious husband, the cold, autocratic father. Pete knew him, and for as long as he could remember, he had hated him.

But never more so, he thought, than today. Initially, he had refused to attend 'the dinner', telling his father rather pompously, but with an uncharacteristic display of nerve, that he and Claire would never break bread with his latest whore. In the end it was Minnie who persuaded him to change his mind. She needed him there when Caroline arrived, needed his and Claire's moral support. Reluctantly, he had given in.

By 8.15, Pete was sitting, stony faced, in front of the drawing-room fire, angrily shrugging off his wife's feeble attempts to comfort him. His sister Laurie, still looking tear-stained and lumpen in an utterly unsuitable, over-the-top gold lamé evening dress, was pacing the room anxiously, a habit that failed to improve Pete's foul temper. Why did she always have to look such a fright?

Minnie, calm and regal as ever in a simple black crêpe shift and pearls, sat rigid-backed beside the door. Contrary to all outward appearances, her stomach was churning. There had been a time when she believed that no behaviour of her husband's could surprise or hurt her any more. Now for the first time in many years, she did not know what to expect, or how she was supposed to behave. She was in uncharted territory, and Pete's palpable rage was doing as little as Laurie's hysteria to calm her own fraught nerves. What in heaven's name had she ever done to deserve this? She just wanted this evening over with.

All four of them jumped when the doorbell rang.

'Why is he ringing the bell?' snapped Pete. 'He has a key, doesn't he?'

Anxious to diffuse her son's anger, Minnie took charge at once, standing to receive her guests with a serene smile glued to her face.

'Antoine, would you get the door, please?'

The butler glided forward. 'Of course, madam.'

The heavy black door swung slowly open. Duke was nowhere to be seen.

'How do you do?' The accent was cut-glass English. 'I'm Caroline Berkeley. Perhaps you'd be so kind as to take my coat?'

The young woman before her was about as far removed from Minnie's preconceptions as it was possible for her to be. She was beautiful, but certainly not tarty. Her hair, which was either naturally blonde or very expensively dyed, was worn up in a neat chignon, and contrasted dramatically with her flowing, feminine, rainbow-effect Pucci dress (in fact, wasn't that the dress Minnie had so admired in last month's *Vogue*? It was, she was sure of it). Elegant, strappy Yves St Laurent sandals revealed perfectly pedicured and subtly painted toes. Her make-up was minimal, intended only to heighten her almost neon-blue eyes and surprisingly delicate English complexion. This was no dime-a-dozen playgirl from Venice Beach. Caroline looked, disconcertingly, like a lady.

She was also unusually self-assured. Ignoring the maid, she handed her coat to a bewildered-looking Claire before turning to Minnie.

'So you must be Mrs M?' She smiled, smugly. 'How adorable you look in that dress! My mother has one just like it.'

Minnie failed to suppress a scowl.

'Dukey's told me so much about you.' She winked at Minnie conspiratorially. 'He's just fetching my luggage, by the way, he should be here in a moment. Anyway, I'm sure we'll have simply *tons* to talk about, swapping secrets and all that, but first of all I simply must use your loo. Or perhaps it's my loo now?' Caroline laughed, pleased at her wit, and strode off down the corridor. She evidently knew her way around the house.

Pete exploded. 'Fucking arrogant bitch! And what the hell did you take her coat for?'

He shot an accusatory glance at the terrified Claire, who looked down at the cream Chanel wool in her hands in panic, as though it were about to self-destruct.

'I'm sorry,' she mumbled meekly, 'it just happened so quickly, I didn't really have time to . . . I mean . . .'

'Oh, never mind. My God, that little slut has some nerve, treating my wife like a fucking maid. And the way she spoke to you, Mother. Who the hell does she think she is?'

Before Minnie could respond, Duke came sauntering triumphantly into the hallway, weighed down by two enormous Louis Vuitton suitcases. Taking in his wife's look of shock, Pete's undisguised fury and Laurie and Claire's subdued misery, he laughed out loud.

'So, I guess you met Caroline, huh? Isn't she great? Quite a looker, wouldn't you say, Peter?' he added spitefully to his son.

'Sure.' Pete's tone was utterly dead. 'If you like cheap whores.'

Duke laughed again. Nothing was going to put him out of his good humour tonight, least of all his pussy of a son.

'I'll tell you something, kiddo, she may be a whore but she certainly isn't cheap,' he said. 'I paid five hundred bucks for that dress.'

Minnie felt a small, irrational stab of pain. Even in the early, happy days of their marriage, Duke had never spent anything close to that on her.

'Ask your mother.' He looked at Minnie, his eyes flashing with the excited cruelty of a cat playing with a cornered mouse before the kill. 'She knows all about *class*, don't you, my darling? Wouldn't you say Caroline is elegant? She comes from one of the oldest, most aristocratic families in England. I mean, we're not talking Greenwich here. Caroline's from the *real* upper classes.'

He was hitting Minnie where it hurt and they both knew it.

Right on cue, Caroline sashayed back along the corridor, stilettos clacking painfully loudly on the polished marble, and wrapped herself possessively around Duke. 'Darling,' she stage-whispered into his ear, 'you know, we could always skip supper and just go straight to bed.'

Bitch, bitch, bitch, thought Pete. She's enjoying this.

'Skip dinner?' Duke smiled at her proudly. 'I don't think so. My wife here has gone to a lot of trouble, sweetheart. And we wouldn't want to be rude, now, would we?'

At dinner, the pair of them were insufferable. Duke was deliberately, revoltingly affectionate towards his young mistress, constantly running his roughly wrinkled hand across her cheek or feeding her morsels of monkfish from his fork like a lovesick teenager.

Caroline was also on rare form, and no one was immune from her witheringly bitchy put-downs.

'Gosh, Laurie,' she exclaimed, wide eyed, 'you are brave. I always think gold is *such* a difficult colour to pull off with a fuller figure.'

'Mrs McMahon,' – she seemed to delight in addressing Minnie pseudo-respectfully – 'this food really is delicious. Heavens, if I had a cook as good as Conchita, I don't expect I'd worry about my figure either. Dukey, do you think she'll be able to rustle me up something low-fat for breakfast tomorrow?'

Minnie's self-control in the face of such provocation was quite astounding. Pete, on the other hand, rose like a starving, credulous fish to every piece of bait Caroline threw him.

'Now, Claire,' – she leant forward across the table, giving both Pete and his wife a flash of her small but perfectly rounded porcelain-white breasts – 'I *do* hope that you and I can become friends. It will be so nice to have a girl my own age to play with.'

'Really?' said Pete, stabbing viciously at his syllabub with a teaspoon. 'And here we were all thinking you preferred playing with men old enough to be your grandfather.'

Claire looked miserably from Pete to Minnie. She had dressed particularly conservatively this evening in a long taupe skirt and sweater, perhaps in a subconscious effort to fade into the background. Although undeniably a beautiful woman, with her shoulder-length mane of honey-blonde hair and luminous creamy complexion, her shy looks paled into nothing when set beside Caroline's glamour and electric sexual confidence. Not that it bothered her. Pete's young wife didn't have a vain bone in her body. She just wished that this awful woman who was so upsetting her husband would go away and leave them all alone.

'Peter, that's enough,' said Duke, a razor-sharp edge biting into his famously deep, resonant voice. 'Like it or not, Caroline is a member of this family from now on. I will not have her spoken to in that tone by anyone.'

Father and son glared at one another, their faces eerily illuminated by the candlelight, but Pete dropped his gaze first.

'Least of all you,' added Duke, folding his napkin with a measured finality to indicate that the conversation was now closed.

Laurie, who was suddenly feeling uncomfortable and awkward in what had been her favourite dress, was too choked with self-pity to rally to her brother's support. While poor Claire kept her eyes glued firmly to her plate throughout the whole excruciating ordeal.

Buoyed by Duke's encouragement, and fuelled by more than a few glasses of the vintage champagne Minnie had been told to lay on for the occasion, Caroline allowed her arrogance full rein, rudely snapping her fingers at the staff and generally behaving as though she were the established lady of the house. She had been dreading this evening, the inevitable showdown with the old man's ghastly wife; but now that it had all gone so well, she felt deliriously happy.

All this wealth and privilege were hers for the taking, and she intended to grab them with both hands. How ridiculous to think that she had feared Minnie McMahon so much! The poor old stick was clearly no match for her. Caroline found it almost impossible to imagine the black-clad statue across the table from her, with her drawn features and tight-lipped reserve, as ever having been of sexual interest to Duke. She looked like a relic from another era, one of the many older women for whom the swinging sixties had simply swung right on by, and who woke up in the seventies to find the world they grew up in had disappeared for ever.

As for Pete and Laurie, well, they were even more wet and useless than Duke had hinted. She wondered what possessed him to keep the pair of them under his roof. He had said something about it once – some nostalgic

Catholic rubbish about family – but Caroline had been focusing on the divine Cartier necklace they'd been choosing on Rodeo at the time, and hadn't really caught his gist.

What had not escaped her notice, however, was that Duke was being extraordinarily tactile this evening. As his hand softly caressed the back of her neck, she wondered whether this meant he would be excessively demanding in bed later, and suppressed a sigh. Humiliating his pathetic wife was obviously turning him on, judging by the size of the erection Caroline had been fondling discreetly for the last hour. You could say a lot of things about Duke, but he certainly still had a very healthy libido.

Her suspicions proved justified that night in bed. Exhilarated by his own demonstration of power and control over Minnie, Duke's eyes were alive with excitement at the prospect of screwing Caroline. Availing himself of her exquisitely ripe, young body would be the perfect end to what had been a thoroughly enjoyable and arousing evening.

He and Minnie had kept separate bedrooms for the last twenty-odd years, and his dark wood-panelled room no longer bore any traces of his wife. Duke had had the exquisite parquet flooring smothered in the ankle-deep cream carpet he so loved, and all the antique furniture replaced with so much chrome and glass that the original walls looked embarrassed and out of place. He loved the modernity of the furniture, and not just because Minnie hated it. It made him feel young somehow. And the thick carpet beneath his bare feet felt wonderfully luxurious to the boy who had grown up running barefoot on the cold, rough wooden floors of a Brooklyn tenement building.

Duke reclined on the enormous, laminated plastic bed, draped in rich purple velvet covers and purple silk pillows fit for a debauched Roman emperor. He felt his cock turn to iron as he watched Caroline start to strip for him.

With one graceful movement she released the clasp at her neck, and $500 worth of Pucci silk slithered to the floor. Staring at her firm, high breasts, the pale pink nipples flushing a deeper red with lust, her slender, almost breakable legs looking even longer in those black stilettos, Duke knew he had never wanted a woman more. She gazed wantonly back at him, the dampness from her pussy beginning to show through her minuscule sheer pink panties, and bent down to remove her shoes.

'No. Leave them on.' His voice was rough and brutal with longing, all the faux affection from the dinner table gone. 'Come here.'

Hanging her head submissively, she approached the bed, and climbing up on to it kneeled in front of Duke, awaiting instructions. She was like a doll, he thought joyously; he could do anything he wanted to her, anything. He knew she was only interested in his money, of course. But what did that matter? This was fifty times better than picking up a hooker down on Sunset.

Caroline might be a gold-digger, but she still had social class, something that had always eluded Duke, for all his money and power. That cut-glass English accent, her grand titled friends, it all made her infinitely more exciting in his eyes. He loved to watch her playing the part, acting like the little lady of the manor, and knowing that whenever he snapped his fingers he could have her, naked, compliant, ready to cater to his every whim. His money enabled him to control her, to own her. Mikey was wrong. You *could* own a woman. And Caroline was all his.

'Suck my cock,' he commanded, lying back against the pillows as the small blonde head bobbed up and down in his lap. He had wanted to fuck her tonight, but it had been a long, long day, and the moment he felt her expert tongue rolling itself around his erection, flickering teasingly just beneath its head, he knew he had to come now.

Gripping her tiny, fragile skull with his left hand, he forced her head down farther until his dick was touching the back of her throat. Instinctively she struggled, retching and fighting for breath, legs flailing grotesquely, still in her tight black shoes. The sight was too much for Duke, who cried out as he came, still clamping her head to his cock so that every drop of his semen poured straight down her smooth, white throat before he released her.

Caroline pushed her tangled hair back from her face, gasping for air, and wiped the sweat and saliva from her face. She knew she must look like a first-class whore, and the thought aroused her. Duke was old enough to be her father, if not her grandfather, and she'd be lying if she said that physical attraction was her prime motivation for being in his bed. Even so, she had to admit there was something about him, about the two of them together, which worked. He never, ever gave a thought to her pleasure. But in a perverse way, that pleased her.

Duke looked at her smeared, dishevelled face with satisfaction. He was an old man now and he knew it. Sure, he was in good shape, he took care of himself. But so many of his old buddies were already gone – heart attacks, lung cancer, God only knew what else. He reached over to the bedside table for a Lucky Strike and lit it.

Death did not preoccupy him unduly, although he missed his youth, the adrenalin rush of mass adulation that had fuelled him through his twenties and thirties, already a movie legend.

What an incredible, fantastic life it had been.

With the exception of a few terrible incidents in Japan during the war, and the painful breakdown of his marriage, it had been a life crammed with enjoyment, excitement and excess. Duke had lived it greedily, relishing every second, and he intended to see out the last days of his life with the same energy, the same pursuit of his own pleasure, that he always had.

He had learned long ago to block out the pain of losing Minnie's love. Without her, he had abandoned all hope of becoming a 'better' man and ruthlessly stamped down any finer feelings in himself, of selflessness, honour or decency, whenever they threatened to limit his rampant, hedonistic lifestyle.

He looked at Caroline again and felt a wave of satisfaction flood his senses. How many men in their sixties had mind-blowing sex on tap from a girl as utterly desirable as this? Gazing down at her, inhaling deeply on his cigarette, he felt like a fucking king.

Without taking her eyes from his, she bent her head once again and began slowly licking his balls.

'Good girl,' he purred, stroking her hair more tenderly now. 'That's a good girl.' She wrapped her arms around his thighs, laying her head comfortably between them while her tongue got to work.

'Welcome to the family.'

Chapter Three

In snagging Duke McMahon, Caroline Berkeley felt she had finally achieved her destiny.

The fourth child, and only daughter, of Sebastian and Elizabeth Berkeley of Amhurst Manor, Oxfordshire, she had been born into a world of post-war optimism in 1946. Her privileged parents were still wealthy at that time, although a lot of money had been lost by the previous generation of Berkeleys, grandparents and great-aunts whom Caroline never knew, through alcoholism and heavy gambling debts. After her mother died in Caroline's infancy – Elizabeth had never recovered from the death of her eldest son Peter on the Normandy beaches – the family's financial decline had gone from bad to worse.

Unsurprisingly, Caroline's dissolute grandfather Charles had done nothing to tutor her father in the fine arts of investment or estate management. Sebastian's resulting financial ineptitude, combined with his debilitating grief over the loss of both his wife and son, were to prove fatal to the great old estate.

By the time Caroline turned fifteen, Sebastian had lost Amhurst, along with the bulk of his children's inheritance. This sudden reversal of the family fortunes was the single most formative event in her childhood.

She could remember the day her father had driven to school to break the terrible news to her, could see his ashen face as though it were yesterday. As soon as they sat down on an old stone bench, in the rose garden at Massingham Hall, she had known something was very wrong.

'For heaven's sake, Pa, what is it?' She heard the panic rising in her voice. She had never seen her beloved father in such a state. 'Is it George or William? Are they all right?'

Actually, her elder brothers were the last thing Caroline was concerned about, but she couldn't think of anything else that would make Sebastian look so terrible. If he were ill himself, she was sure, he would tend to make light of it rather than turn up at school with a face like a wet weekend.

When he turned around to face her, tears were pouring down his cheeks.

'Caro, I'm so sorry, so very, very sorry. I've had to sell Amhurst.'

She felt the world spin, and was grateful she was sitting down. She doubted her legs would have supported her if she'd tried to stand up at that moment. Sell Amhurst? What on earth was he talking about?

'Please, darling.' Sebastian had looked at her beseechingly. 'Say something.'

What was there to say? His shame and distress were so obvious, and so acute, she hadn't the heart to reproach him or the energy to throw some sort of tantrum. She had opened her mouth, just to ask him why, *how* could this have happened, but closed it again before the words had even formed on her lips.

What was the point of tormenting herself, or him, with such questions? Amhurst meant the whole world to Sebastian, just as it did to her. If he had sold it, then she knew he must have had absolutely no choice.

For a few fleeting moments, she allowed her mind to fly back there, to linger on each image, on every remembered smell and sound and touch of her home. If she closed her eyes, she could still hear the rooks cawing in the tree-tops of the Great Park, and smell the dampness of the early morning mist, intertwined with the sour smoke of the previous night's bonfire. She could feel the smooth, polished wood of the banisters beneath her hand and see the vast, faded tapestries of hunting scenes that hung, so exquisite and yet almost unnoticed, against the cool stone walls.

She pictured her old Nanny Chapman chasing her out of the cavernous larder, remembered the 'slap, slap' sound of her bare feet as she ran across the cold flagstone floor of the scullery and out into the kitchen garden, with a slice of Cook's apple pie still clenched tightly in her sticky fist.

Her father had sold Amhurst. It was gone.

Silently, lovingly, Caroline folded away each of her precious memories. If she were going to survive this, she knew she could never, ever look back. She also knew, somewhere very deep inside herself, that her childhood had come to an end in that instant.

Getting up slowly, she put her arms around her father's neck and held him while he wept. The rose garden, always such a peaceful place, was racked by the sound of Sebastian's sobbing. Caroline felt she would never be able to set foot there again.

'Don't cry, Daddy,' she whispered. 'It's all right. Really it is. We'll get through it together. We'll find somewhere else to live, maybe a lovely cottage like Granny's or something? It'll be gorgeous and cosy, and I can bring you your pipe and slippers by the fire every night, just like a really old man.'

That, she realised, was exactly what he looked like, slumped and shivering beside her on the cold stone bench. Overnight her strong, invincible father had become a broken old man.

Sebastian stared at his daughter in wonder, deeply touched by her desire to comfort him, overwhelmed with gratitude for her forgiveness.

'I'm afraid it isn't just the house, you know,' he forced himself to continue. 'I'm ... the thing is, you see ... well, there are some debts. A lot of debts, in fact.' Her heart felt literally wrenched with love and pity for him as he stared abjectly down at his shoes, all glistening and wet from the dewy grass. 'I can pay them, of course.

There's no question of anything not being honoured, of shirking anything.'

'Of course there isn't, Pa,' she assured him. 'I know that.'

'It's just that after everybody's been paid off, well, I'm afraid there's really very little left. A couple of the paintings I should be able to hang on to, and your great-grandfather's Egton chest. But everything else . . . Oh, Caroline, darling.' He was crying again now. 'Your inheritance, and the boys'. It's all gone. All of it. I am so terribly, terribly sorry.'

Caroline was surprised to find herself feeling angry. Not at her father – heaven knows how he had got himself into such a mess, but he had obviously tried his best. He must have been struggling for years, she realised, not wanting to worry any of them with his troubles, hoping against hope that this dreadful day of reckoning would never come.

No, she was angry with fate, angry at whoever it was who had dealt them this card, who had dared to take their beloved Amhurst.

A powerful sense of resolve and of strength surged through her. From now on it would be up to her to make her own way in life. And by God, she was going to do it. Her father was too old and too filled with guilt and shame to do what needed to be done. But Caroline Berkeley was not about to become a common pauper. She would just have to find her own fortune, make her own way as her Berkeley ancestors had done long before her. And she already had a pretty shrewd idea of just how she might do it.

After a horrific, miserable Christmas with her family, Caroline had returned to Massingham and begun, belatedly, to apply herself to her studies.

A private education was, she realised, essential if she were to mix in the sort of moneyed circles that might help to restore her fortunes, and she astounded her

43

family by winning a much-coveted scholarship that would enable her to stay on at school. (The headmaster had generously agreed to give a devastated Sebastian a term's grace in which to make 'alternative arrangements' for his daughter's education. But clearly there was no way he could continue to afford her fees.)

Growing up at Amhurst as the only girl in an otherwise all-male family, Caroline had become exceptionally skilled in the art of manipulating men. This skill, she decided, would be her fastest and surest route back to the lifestyle that she had not only become accustomed to, but considered to be her God-given right.

She would marry money.

She'd thought it all through quite logically. Building a successful career involved a high degree of uncertainty, and she had no real idea of what she wanted to do. Besides, working her way back to wealth would take years and Caroline was not prepared to wait that long. Far better to find herself a rich old man whom she could wrap around her little finger, just as she had always done with her father. With her golden, shoulder-length hair, perfect peaches-and-cream complexion and a body already in full, glorious bloom, at fifteen she was well accustomed to the gratifyingly dramatic effect her looks seemed to have on the opposite sex.

She started to approach her social life as if it were a military campaign, angling for invitations to St Tropez or Sardinia, only ever befriending girls whose parents were rich enough to look indulgently on such blatant free-loading.

Her natural intelligence rapidly helped her to develop finely tuned social antennae. She learned to judge exactly when she was in danger of outstaying her welcome with any particular group, and needed to move on to newer, more fertile pastures. She adroitly avoided ever paying for herself at dinner or on holiday, without ever drawing her companions' attention to the fact. And she perfected using the combination of her aristocratic family name, youth and striking good looks to manipulate potential sugar daddies.

By the time she finished school, Caroline Berkeley reigned supreme among the smart young set as the undisputed brightest star in their social firmament. Penniless or not, she was the queen of 'Swinging London'.

Her twenty-first birthday party was a lavish champagne reception in Eton Square – courtesy of a besotted fifty-four-year-old Greek shipping magnate whom she had 'befriended' the previous summer.

'Spyros, be an angel and do up my zipper, would you?' she asked him coquettishly, preening herself in front of the bathroom mirror.

She was looking typically foxy that evening, in a bottom-skimming velour mini-dress in baby pink, teamed with spiky black PVC boots. She wore her long blonde hair in schoolgirl bunches, which she knew both her father and her lover would appreciate, although for very different reasons.

'I'll fix your zipper if you'll fix mine.'

Spyros's eyes locked with hers for a moment, and they both looked down at his enormous erection, clearly outlined against his tight brown trousers.

'I'm sorry, baby,' he said. 'That dress is just too much.'

'Darling, I'd love to. Help you, I mean,' said Caroline. 'But there really isn't time.' She finished applying her lipstick. 'People will start arriving any minute.'

'So let them arrive.' He pulled her towards him and placed her hand on his fly, trying to banish the thought that he had a daughter almost exactly Caroline's age. 'Maria can show them in. Besides, I promise you this won't take long.'

He was right, it didn't. Less than a minute after Caroline had sunk to her knees on the cold, blue-tiled floor and got to work on his huge, throbbing dick, he had come gratefully into her mouth. Grimacing slightly, she swallowed, anxious not to smudge her perfect make-up before the party.

Really, she wished Spyros would learn to pick slightly more convenient moments.

Five minutes later, after a brief gargle of mouthwash, she was downstairs greeting her brother George and his wife, Lucy. George was always the first to arrive and the first to leave any party – you could set your watch by him.

'Hello, sweetie, glad you could make it,' she said, and gave him one of her most gracious, hostess-like smiles.

He glared disapprovingly at her dress.

'Happy birthday, Caro. You look ...' He searched around for an appropriate word. '... cold.'

Grumpy bastard. She noticed that his ancient tweed suit was beginning to fray at the cuffs, and wondered why his sour-faced wife never did anything to try to smarten him up. Caroline was not a fan of impoverished gentility.

'Do I?' She forced a smile. 'I expect I need a drink to warm me up. Can I get either of you a glass of champagne?'

'Thank you, I'd love one,' said Lucy. 'George can't, I'm afraid, he's driving.'

George shot his wife a look of annoyance. 'Just an orange juice for me, please, if you've got one,' he said to Caroline, who was glad of an excuse to shimmy off to the bar and leave them.

She badly resented the way both her brothers tried to make her feel guilty all the time. They despised Spyros, and made no secret of their disapproval of her lifestyle. Well, screw the pair of them. If they wanted to spend the rest of their lives in draughty old rooms, nursing single whiskies and crying over Amhurst, that was up to them. Caroline had bigger plans for her life, and no one was going to stand in her way.

At least Pa understood her.

Sebastian, looking very frail and elderly, was the guest

of honour at the party, and spent most of the evening chatting animatedly to Spyros about Greek history. She loved the way he could do that, mingle with everybody, try to see the good in people, no matter what their background. He wasn't a small-minded snob, like George or William.

Later, as her huge, pink birthday cake was wheeled into the room, its twenty-one candles flickering merrily, Sebastian cleared his throat ostentatiously and announced that he would like to propose a toast 'to the birthday queen'.

'To my darling Caroline.' He raised his glass, his rheumy old eyes scanning the room full of strangers. He did wish his daughter wouldn't mix with *quite* such a racy crowd. 'You have given me twenty-one years of happiness. Here's to many, many more happy years!'

'To Caroline!' the room erupted in echo.

Two weeks later, Sebastian was dead.

The meagre remnants of the Berkeley estate looked even more pitiful when split three ways. In an uncharacteristic display of generosity, Caroline eschewed her share in favour of her brothers, both of whom had young families to support. Besides, it was 1967. One thousand, three hundred pounds barely amounted to the proverbial drop in the ocean of Caroline's living expenses. She might as well let them have it.

Not that they were remotely grateful.

'I hope, now that dear old Pa is gone, you're finally going to start pulling your finger out and get a job,' said William sanctimoniously over lunch at Rules one Sunday.

It was just the sort of restaurant he *would* like, reflected Caroline bitterly, glancing around at the florid-faced, overweight, Establishment types greedily slurping their port in every corner.

'You can't just keep on sponging off that ghastly Greek

fellow, you know,' her brother continued. 'People are starting to talk.'

'Oh, are they?' she bit back angrily, stabbing at her venison with a fork. 'And what have they been saying exactly?'

William removed a piece of steak and kidney pie from between his teeth, and ran his fingers through his thinning sandy hair. God, he was unattractive, a sort of weaker, scrawnier version of George.

'I don't think I really need to spell it out for you, do I?'

'Well, actually, William, yes, I think you probably do,' she said. She was getting thoroughly fed up with his mealy-mouthed insinuations. If he had something to say, why didn't he damn well say it?

'Oh, for Christ's sake, Caroline.' He put down his knife and fork and lowered his voice to what he hoped was a discreet whisper. 'You aren't married. More to the point, he *is* married. Just because you managed to pull the wool over Dad's eyes doesn't mean that the rest of the world doesn't know what you're up to. I'm sorry, but it's just not on.'

Caroline let out a short mirthless laugh, loud enough for the two old buffers at the table next to them to turn and give her a filthy look. She ignored them.

'Just listen to yourself, would you? "It's just not on."' William flushed as she loudly mimicked his hectoring tone. 'Have you any idea how pompous you sound? You're ridiculous, William, quite ridiculous, you and George. It's 1967, in case you haven't noticed, and I'm hardly the first woman to be having an affair. Besides, this has nothing to do with my morality, does it? You just don't like Spyros because he's Greek, and he's older than me, and because he's a self-made man.'

'Nouveau riche, you mean?' William sneered.

'Well, better nouveau riche than stinking bloody poor, William.'

Flinging her napkin down on the table, she got to her feet.

'I'm sorry,' she said. 'I think I need some air.'

And with that she strode out of the restaurant, leaving her brother spluttering with outrage, his full, flabby lips opening and closing wordlessly like a stunned mullet.

Outside, the cool afternoon air hit Caroline's face with a welcome, refreshing blast.

What the hell was wrong with everybody?

Marching down towards the Strand, her face flushed with defiance, blonde hair dancing in the wind behind her, she ignored the wolf whistles of the builders and the stares of the businessmen as she passed.

She felt stung, again, by William's ingratitude. How dare he accept her share of Pa's money with one hand and then try to slap her down with the other, make her feel guilty for enjoying her life, for making her own way?

As it happened, her brothers didn't know the half of it. Spyros, in fact, was only one in a long line of lovers whom Caroline used to support a lifestyle that many a wealthy London housewife would have envied. If William thought she was going to give all that up to become somebody's bloody secretary, and live in some poky flat in Clapham like him and his holier-than-thou friends, he could go to hell.

She did not go back to the restaurant in the end, but hailed a cab and took herself shopping in Knightsbridge instead, with a mental two fingers to William.

As things turned out, she wasn't to see either of her brothers again for a very, very long time.

For six happy years after Sebastian's death and her acrimonious parting from her brothers, Caroline lived a life devoted solely to the pursuit of her own pleasure.

She appeared at all the exclusive society parties, dressed head to toe in the discarded designer clothes of her rich acquaintances, and often dripping in (borrowed) diamonds. She holidayed on friends' yachts off Capri, and spent Christmases with an indulgent former lover on

Mustique. If people disapproved of her, she neither knew nor cared. She was young, free and beautiful and having the time of her life – what else mattered?

Her only niggling concern was that she remained utterly bereft of any capital of her own. Sure, she collected the odd gift as she moved like a nomad from one married playboy to the next – Fabien had given her the most *exquisite* Fabergé egg before he broke it off, which even she couldn't bring herself to flog – but ultimately, she knew she needed to actually *marry* money in order to achieve the lasting financial security she craved.

Getting a rich man to fuck you and buy you gifts was a piece of cake. Getting one to marry you, especially if that would embroil him in a costly divorce, was proving altogether more difficult.

At twenty-eight, Caroline still looked fabulous, and every penny she received was spent on maintaining her appearance. But everyone on the scene in London knew her, and knew what her brothers had insisted on calling her 'reputation'. She had heard that Americans were suckers for an upper-class English accent. Perhaps, she wondered, it was time to move on?

Chapter Four

Caroline arrived in Los Angeles in November 1974, in the middle of a blazing winter heatwave, with the addresses of two old schoolfriends and one ex-boyfriend in her Chanel shoulder bag, thirteen hundred dollars in the bank and a pair of the tiniest frayed denim hot pants that the guy at the immigration desk had ever seen.

'How long you stayin' in the States, sugar?' He leered at her appreciatively from behind his bullet-proof plastic screen.

'Well, I'm not too sure,' she replied. 'That sort of depends on how nice people are to me.'

'Baby,' – he stared down blatantly at her crotch, enticingly shrink-wrapped in denim – 'I think there's *a lot* of people gonna be *very* nice to you here in LA.'

'Well, I hope so,' said Caroline, smiling.

Every head turned as she strutted through LAX to baggage reclaim.

'Can I help you with your luggage, miss?' a voice came from behind her. 'That case must be heavier than you are.'

She swung round to find herself face to face with one of the most handsome men she had ever seen. Tall, dark and slightly overly tanned, his white teeth blazed down at her in a wolfish grin as he effortlessly swung her enormous bag off the carousel. He was exactly what she had imagined Californian men to look like: fit, masculine and well groomed.

It was hard, Caroline felt, not to admire a man like that.

'Well, thank you so much, how kind.'

She smiled gratefully up at this plastic Adonis, thinking how much more impressive he looked than most of the chinless wimps who offered her their gentlemanly services back home in London.

'I'm Caroline. Caroline Berkeley.'

She gave him her hand and he crushed it.

'Brad Baxter. It's an absolute pleasure to meet you.'

Meeting Brad turned out to be an extraordinary piece of luck. Over the next six weeks, he helped to introduce Caroline to the myriad pleasures and vices that Hollywood had to offer, none of which were new to her, as well as to many of the movers and shakers in the business, who were. He was, it emerged, a PR whizz-kid from West Hollywood who ran a sideline "talent-spotting" for a soft porn producer in the Valley and was a regular on the starry, decadent social scene that was to become Caroline's natural milieu and favoured hunting ground.

Clearly, she had her sights set a lot higher than porno – although the money Brad was talking about was definitely enough to make your head spin – but she knew a well-connected guy when she saw one. She moved into his apartment immediately, as a stopgap measure while she hunted for a place of her own.

Six weeks, a lot of coke and some mediocre sex later, Brad introduced her to Duke McMahon. The rest, she felt sure, was about to become history.

On the face of it, Duke was not Caroline's ideal catch.

For one thing, he had made it clear that he would not contemplate a divorce from his wife, Minnie, although the marriage was well known in Hollywood to be a complete sham. Duke had had countless mistresses and affairs before her, and his marriage had weathered them all, which was not a good sign.

For another, he was seriously old, even by Caroline's standards. Though he was by no means the least attractive of the many men she had slept with, he was already sixty-four, and physically things could only go downhill from there.

Despite her calculated approach to relationships, Caroline still enjoyed good sex. Brad's ineptly enthusiastic efforts over the past few weeks had been absolute torture. If she were going to devote years of her life to a man, which financially she knew she must, then it had to be someone she could at least tolerate in bed. Duke was a more than adequate lover now – but in five years' time his ancient balls might be flapping against his bony, arthritic knees, and frankly she doubted that she could stomach that.

On the other hand, Duke was rich beyond even Caroline's wildest dreams. On their very first date, he had picked her up in his exquisite blue 1956 Ferrari, and driven her down to his private cove in Malibu.

'Close your eyes,' he said, as he led her, trembling with excitement, down the sandy track that wound from the road to the beach. She could feel the silky dryness of the sand between her toes as she stumbled blindly along in her open-toed stilettos. 'OK. You can open them now. Take a look.'

Caroline gasped with delight. The white sand of the beach was illuminated by a combination of pale, blue-white moonlight and the warmer, rich orange glow of hundreds of candles, some flickering softly in the sand at her feet, others hanging from the boughs of the cedars that grew along the shore.

An over-sized midnight-blue blanket had been spread out at the water's edge. It had been laid with brilliantly polished antique silver and shimmering crystal glasses, as well as a picnic of such delicious-looking food – whole cooked lobsters, tomato and basil salad, peaches in Armagnac, perfect little individual chocolate soufflés – she felt her mouth literally begin watering at the sight of it. Beside the picnic were two large ice buckets half submerged in the sand, each containing two bottles of champagne.

Duke's right-hand man, Seamus, looking half decent for once in a crisp white linen suit, stood at a respectful distance, ready to wait on the two of them hand and foot.

'Do you like it?' asked Duke.

'Do I like it?' She looked at him incredulously. 'Duke, I have never seen anything quite so beautiful, and quite so romantic, in my entire life.'

She meant it, too. She felt like a queen, adored and indulged – and she hadn't so much as kissed him yet. At that moment, she was quite sure that she *could* love Duke McMahon, should she ever find herself called upon to do so.

'Well, I'm glad,' he said, helping her down on to the blanket and signalling to his old friend to crack open the champagne. 'A beautiful girl like you deserves nothing less. In fact . . .' He fumbled in his inside jacket pocket, and produced a long black box. 'I bought you a little something that I thought might complement your beauty this evening. It's just a token. But I hope you like it.'

It was a struggle for her to maintain her composure, to slowly take and open the box rather than snatch it out of his hand like an overexcited kid at Christmas. Inside was an obscenely large diamond-and-platinum necklace.

Caroline, who knew a thing or two about diamonds, could see at a glance that it must be worth upwards of fifteen thousand dollars. Tentatively, lovingly, she stroked the largest of the stones.

'Oh, Duke,' she whispered, her voice hoarse with emotion. 'Oh my God.'

He lifted the necklace, fastening it gently around her neck.

'You like it?'

Caroline kissed him quickly on the mouth.

'I love it.'

'Good. Now take off your dress.'

'I'm sorry?' She'd been so mesmerised by the incredible diamonds, she wondered whether she could have heard him correctly.

'No need to be sorry,' said Duke. 'I want you naked. Please undress. You can keep the necklace on.'

Caroline's eyes narrowed. She was not used to being spoken to like this, and she wasn't at all sure that she liked it.

Who the hell did he think he was?

She wasn't some prostitute, paid to be at his beck and call. Her face flushed with anger and embarrassment. She noticed that Seamus had not moved but stood just a few feet away, impassively watching her reaction.

'How dare you speak to me like that?' she demanded, fumbling angrily at the clasp at her neck and standing up to leave. 'I don't care how fucking famous you are, or how many necklaces you can afford, nobody speaks to. . . .'

'Oh, don't you?' Duke interrupted her mid-flow. 'Don't you care?'

He had grabbed her arm quite forcefully, but Caroline saw with surprise that he was smiling, his eyes full of warmth and mischief. All of a sudden she felt confused. Why was he laughing at her? Was this some kind of joke?

'Well, excuse me, Ms Berkeley, but I happen to think that's a crock of shit.'

'I beg your pardon?' She was doing her best to sound shocked.

'I think you care *very much* how many necklaces I can afford. In fact, Caroline, my darling, I think we both know that's exactly why you're sitting here, about to have dinner with an old man like me.'

'No it isn't. Of course it isn't,' said Caroline.

But she sat back down.

'I didn't mean to offend you,' continued Duke. 'But I also don't intend to be played for a fool. I thought I could save us both a lot of time by laying a few cards on the table right now – so that we can both enjoy the first of what I hope will be many, many pleasant evenings together.'

She looked at him warily. 'Go on.'

'I bought you that necklace because I thought you would look beautiful in it, and you do. And because I knew you would like it.'

'I do like it.' Caroline couldn't resist touching the exquisite stones again as she listened to him. 'Very much.'

'I know you do. And I know there are a lot of other things you would like. Things that I can give you. That I would like to give you.' She smiled at him encouragingly. 'But there is also something that you can give me. Something that I want very badly.'

Caroline's face fell. She drew her cashmere stole tighter around her shoulders.

'Now don't you look at me like that,' said Duke. 'You aren't Pollyanna, and you sure as hell aren't some innocent little virgin either.'

Despite herself, Caroline gave him a conspiratorial smile.

'That's better,' said Duke. 'You're a smart girl, Caroline. You know what you want, and I like that. I like it a lot. We both know I can give you what you want. But I'm not a young man any more, kiddo, and I don't like wasting my time. I didn't bring you here tonight for conversation.'

Without breaking eye contact, he reached out and touched her breast, gently rolling the nipple between his thumb and forefinger through the cotton of her dress.

Caroline thought about it for a split second, but did not protest. Seamus had tactfully withdrawn to the other side of the cedar trees, but she knew he was probably watching them, the dirty old sod. The thought, combined with Duke's practised touch, sent a sudden jolt of lust right through her body.

'Now, please,' he resumed, 'if it isn't too much to ask, I'd like you to take off your dress.'

A couple of weeks later, he had made her a proposal that was too good to refuse, even if it didn't involve matrimony. She was to become his exclusive consort for the rest of his life, in return for which he would not only bankroll her lifestyle but make her a generous provision in his will. That meant a worst-case scenario of a lifetime of financial security as his mistress. Plus, she realised, it would give her ample time to work on undermining Minnie.

After all, if there was one thing Caroline felt secure in, it was her ability to manipulate a besotted old man.

Chapter Five

'Hey, mama, what's goin' on?'

Minnie did a double take. Good God! Perhaps the light was playing tricks on her, but there appeared to be a large semi-naked Negro sprawled out on her antique Italian chaise longue. Other than his state of undress, the young man was remarkable for a huge springy halo of black hair which bobbed up and down as he spoke, and for the long, fat and disintegrating marijuana cigarette which he was holding perilously close to her Chinese silk cushions. But worse even than that, this dreadful, uncouth apparition seemed to be trying to enter into a conversation with her.

'Beautiful place you got here, you know what I'm sayin'?' he continued, littering ash across the furniture and carpet as he attempted an appreciative sweeping gesture with his huge black arm.

'Thank you,' said Minnie, icily. 'We like it. Perhaps you'd be so kind as to tell me who you are, young man, and what you're doing in my drawing room?'

'He's with me.'

A very well-spoken young Englishman had appeared in the doorway, and strode confidently over to Minnie, taking her hand and kissing it before she had a moment to protest. 'Edward Lyle, at your service.'

He couldn't have been much over twenty-one, thought Minnie, but he dressed with an impeccable, gentlemanly English grace that made him seem older. He also had the self-assurance, bordering on arrogance, that so many public-school-educated young people from his country seemed to possess. Minnie hated this in Caroline, but found herself quite prepared to be charmed by it in the case of this handsome young fellow.

'This is Skinny.' He gestured to his friend. 'Stand up, man, show Mrs McMahon some respect.' Skinny looked at him incredulously, but obligingly lifted his massive frame up off the chaise longue. Edward continued. 'We're both old friends of Caroline's. She said it wouldn't be a problem for us to hang out at the pool today, which was damn decent of her.'

Minnie's interested smile evaporated. Any friend of Caroline's was an enemy of hers.

'Please, don't worry, Mrs McMahon,' Edward tried to reassure her. 'We're very self-sufficient, aren't we, Skin? We won't get under your feet.'

At that moment two strikingly beautiful girls, in matching minuscule red Dior bikinis, came skipping into the room, their bare feet still wet from the swimming pool. One of them headed straight to Duke's wet bar, where she proceeded to empty the entire fridge of olives and potato chips, cramming the food into her mouth as though she hadn't eaten for weeks.

'Munchies,' she mumbled at Minnie through a mouthful of chips, before collapsing into a wet heap of giggles all over a pink suede armchair.

Meanwhile her friend had literally flung herself at Skinny, who collapsed back on to the chaise longue so hard that it gave an ominously audible crack.

'Oh no,' said Minnie, flapping her arms frantically in a vain attempt to persuade him to move. 'Get up! You're going to break it!'

But before a disoriented Skinny had a chance to move there was more sickening splintering. Minnie could only look on in horror as one of the legs gave way completely.

Surveying the wreckage, she wanted to scream, but a lifetime of self-control prevented her from doing so. Instead, she addressed herself as calmly as she could to Edward, who seemed to be the only member of the group in something like full command of his senses.

'Well, Mr Lyle, I think it might be better if you and your friends went outside to play, don't you? I'm sure Mr

McMahon would appreciate it if at least some of his furniture were still intact by the time he got home.'

'Yes, yes, of course, I'm. . . . we're all terribly sorry, aren't we?'

Skinny looked slightly shamefaced, but both girls had given in to the uncontrollable laughter of the irreparably stoned. None of them looked terribly sorry to Minnie.

'Just go, please,' she said.

Mercifully, they did.

Once the group had shuffled back out to the pool, she sank down wearily to her knees and examined the mahogany shards that were all that was left of the leg. Honestly, this really was the last straw. She would tackle Duke about it tonight, once and for all. Having that dreadful girl here was surely bad enough, without allowing her appalling, insolent, platform-shoe-wearing, drug-taking, long-haired hippy friends to treat the estate like a hotel.

Caroline's first year at Hancock Park had been a living nightmare for Minnie. It was not her husband's infidelity which bothered her so much as Caroline's attempted assumption of the role of lady of the house. Only last week, she had caught her haranguing Conchita in a *most* unladylike manner over some trifling offence or other. (She was sure that Duke must be wrong about Caroline's aristocratic lineage – she had come across hobos in Connecticut with better language.) Day after day, she filled the house with her brash, braying English friends, who thought nothing of eating Minnie out of house and home, or lounging all around the house in their frightful bell-bottoms smoking marijuana. And they didn't just restrict their shocking behaviour to the public rooms either. Heaven alone knew what went on up in the south wing bedrooms, between her beautifully laundered linen sheets.

So far, whenever Minnie had complained to Duke about these riff-raff, he had been non-committal. He had held back from openly supporting his girlfriend over his wife, but neither would he reprimand Caroline, or do anything to ease the almost unbearable tension caused by her increasingly insensitive and tactless behaviour. Minnie suspected, accurately, that he derived a powerful sense of pleasure from watching the friction between the two of them.

Nevertheless, she thought as she grimly swept up the splinters of wood, she would tackle him again about it this evening. It was her fifty-fifth birthday tomorrow and a celebration dinner had been planned for tonight, a long-standing McMahon tradition. Perhaps, on her birthday, he would be in a slightly more receptive mood?

Duke returned home earlier than usual and was relieved to find the house free of hangers-on. He had taken to spending increasing amounts of time away from home recently, either at the country club in Bel Air, or at mysterious 'meetings'. He found Caroline's parasitic social set every bit as grating as his wife did, and intensely disliked returning to a house full of strangers – although he was damned if he was going to give Minnie the satisfaction of admitting as much to her. Despite his lack of solidarity with her over Caroline's friends, his absences nevertheless encouraged Minnie, who hoped he might be beginning a new affair. The sooner he tired of Caroline, the better for all of them.

Strolling into his study, he poured himself three fingers of bourbon and sank into his leather armchair, eyes closed, savouring a rare moment of peace. It was soon to be shattered, however, by the unwelcome arrival of an apoplectic Pete.

'I suppose it's too much to expect that you actually remembered Mother's birthday?' Pete himself was laden with ostentatiously wrapped packages, a walking tower of bright metallic paper and bows.

Duke found few things in life more objectionable than his son's belligerent, whining voice, so full of hatred and yet so utterly lacking the courage to act upon it. He opened one eye momentarily, then closed it again before speaking.

'Well, good evening to you too, Peter.'

'You forgot again, didn't you?'

'I did not forget.' Duke looked his son in the eye. 'I never forget your mother's birthday. I sometimes choose not to celebrate it, which is a different thing.'

A vein in Pete's jaw had begun to twitch, as though his body were barely able to contain the bile and rage within. He only just managed to control himself sufficiently to lay down his presents gently on the desk, rather than hurling them all violently at the old man's face.

'This year, however, I *have* bought a little something for my dear wife.'

Reaching into his jacket pocket, Duke produced a ring box. Pete caught the distinctive Cambridge-blue flash of Tiffany, and watched his father open it to reveal a subtle, delicately crafted band of diamonds and white gold. It was elegant, conservative – exactly to his mother's taste.

'It's an eternity ring. To symbolise the permanence of our joyous union.' Duke snorted mirthlessly. 'For better or worse, kiddo, in sickness and in health. Whaddaya think? Will Mrs McMahon approve?'

What the hell was he playing at? Pete couldn't quite figure out whether it was an act of gross insensitivity, or calculated spite. It didn't occur to him that beneath his father's cynicism and bitterness, he might still harbour feelings of love towards his mother. As far as Pete was concerned, Duke was a monster. Even on Minnie's birthday, he couldn't resist trying to hurt her.

Later that evening, the birthday supper began unusually calmly, with everyone apparently making an effort to suspend hostilities. Duke was oddly quiet, and even asked Minnie quite politely about her birthday plans, much to the astonishment of his children. None of them could remember the last time they had spent so civilised an evening together, and hope that Caroline might finally be on her way out was running high.

Minnie decided to wait until the main course (her favourite, rare roast beef with Yorkshire pudding) before broaching the subject of the chaise longue with Duke. After the best part of four decades together, she knew him well enough to realise that he was far more likely to be responsive to her complaints after a couple of glasses of wine.

'By the way, Duke,' she said, almost casually, once the second bottle of merlot was well under way, 'did you see that we had a small, erm, accident today?'

'Oh yeah?' He looked supremely uninterested. 'What happened?'

'The chaise longue. You know, the Italian one, in . . .' She checked herself. 'In the den? Well, I'm afraid it was broken. The leg's come right off. Seamus had a look at it for me but he says it's quite beyond repair.'

'What the fuck do you mean, it was broken?' This was better than Minnie had expected. He looked extremely irate. 'Who the fuck broke it? I don't believe this. Who broke it?' Duke looked around the table accusingly.

'Some wine, Caroline?' said Pete, who knew what had happened and was beginning to enjoy himself.

'Not for me, thank you,' she replied.

Pete noticed with annoyance that she didn't seem remotely rattled. In fact she seemed, if not quite subdued, then strangely content. It bothered him.

'Is anybody gonna answer me?' Duke's cheeks were reddening, a combination of the wine and his mounting frustration. 'Laurie, was it you? Did you sit your fat ass down on my Italian couch?' He pronounced it 'eye-talian', which had always made Minnie cringe and Caroline laugh.

'Daddy, don't be so horrid,' said Laurie, who was blushing to the roots of her hair. 'I can't help it if I have a problem with my weight.'

'Sure you can,' said Duke, staring at her plate piled high with Yorkshire puddings and gravy. 'Quit eating.'

'Well, it wasn't me,' she said petulantly, pushing her food to the side of her plate and pouting. 'It was some great big black guy, some friend of Caroline's. He's been hanging around the house all week, hasn't he, Mother?'

Minnie knew better than to say anything. She arranged her face into a familiar expression of patient forbearance, and let Duke's rage take its inevitable course.

He looked at Caroline, and when he spoke his voice was ominously quiet.

'Skinny was here today?'

Caroline met his eyes defiantly. She wasn't Minnie, and she wasn't about to let the bastard bully her. 'Yes, Duke, he was. I didn't know he was coming, though. Edward brought him.'

Duke's hand had tightened around his fork. He cleared his throat. 'I see. Caroline, I thought I had made my views patently clear on this point. But perhaps not. So why don't I just restate them for the record. Number one.' He held up one finger. 'I don't want any fucking Negroes in this house.'

'Darling!' Caroline found his racism both objectionable and ridiculous, although she knew Minnie, and probably the children too, shared his prejudices. 'Skinny's a Harvard graduate.'

He raised his hand to stop her.

'Excuse me, I haven't finished. Number two: I will not have my home used as a goddam monkey house for every fucking waif and stray you pick up. Got it?'

At this point Minnie would have backed down completely, but Caroline squared her shoulders at him bravely.

'This is my home too, Duke.'

She was angry, but there were also tears in her eyes. Minnie was taken aback. She had never seen Caroline looking so emotional.

'Yes, honey, it is, it is your home,' said Duke, who had

also been surprised by her reaction. He had learned to expect fireworks from Caroline – it was part of the sexual dynamic between them, that she would stand up to him in public, constantly challenging his will, only to be fucked into grovelling, ecstatic submission later in bed. But this evening she looked genuinely upset. 'It is your home. But you did not pay for that couch.'

'Chaise longue,' corrected Minnie.

Duke shot her a withering glance.

'I don't appreciate it when your friends come around here and break valuable shit like that, you know? And I don't like that big black bastard hanging around you all the time.'

Caroline looked up at him and smiled, that same serene smile which Pete had noticed earlier. There was definitely something funny going on between them. Duke took her hand, a gesture that was somehow both possessive and conciliatory.

'I don't like it,' he repeated, softly.

'OK,' said Caroline, suddenly meek again. 'I'll stop seeing him. Promise.' She turned to Minnie. 'And I'm sorry about your couch.'

'Chaise longue!' shouted Laurie and Pete in unison.

'Whatever,' said Caroline.

Minnie retired to the drawing room after dinner with the rest of the family, feeling utterly deflated. Listlessly, she picked up one of Pete and Claire's brightly wrapped presents, and sighed as she pulled at its blue silk ribbons. What just happened in there?

For the past two weeks she had become more and more convinced that Duke was cheating on Caroline. First of all there were his unexplained absences, and their increasingly frequent rows about her English friends. And then, last week, he had actually come creeping into her own bed, for the first time since Caroline had moved in.

She had received him wordlessly, without surprise or complaint, and afterwards he had touched her face with a tenderness she had almost forgotten he had ever possessed. Minnie had never really understood the reasons behind Duke's cruelty towards her, and she found his rare bursts of affection equally inexplicable. As his wife, she believed it was her duty to accept both unquestioningly. Duke despised her for her passivity – but deep down, he also recognised her as his moral superior. Whatever had passed between them, however horrifically Duke behaved, both of them knew that the other would never leave. The marriage remained their security, and their prison.

She had been so sure that things were finally about to change, that he was at last getting over this dangerous infatuation with Caroline. But his behaviour tonight at dinner, his tenderness towards her – it just didn't add up. Only a couple of hours earlier, before they sat down to eat, Duke had handed her a tiny black box; pressed it into her hand almost guiltily while Caroline was out of earshot.

'Happy birthday, Min,' he had whispered, and kissed her, just once, on the cheek. She had put the box up in her bedroom, and even in her current state of confusion over Caroline, its presence there warmed her heart more intensely than the roaring log fire in front of her.

Her reverie was shattered by the tinkling of silver on glass. She gave a perfunctory smile and tried to pull herself together. Someone must be about to propose a birthday toast.

'Now that the whole family is together, I have something I would like to say.' Caroline had risen from the couch where she sat beside Duke. She looked happy and relaxed in a creamy white polo-neck and bell-bottom jeans, not at all her usual spiky, confrontational self.

The moment she started to speak, the cosy family atmosphere shattered like a vase in an oven. The group eyed her warily.

'I am so grateful to all of you,' she began, 'for making me feel so welcome here.'

'Oh, for Christ's sake,' mumbled Pete, only to be shot down by a look from his father.

'I know it hasn't been easy for you all, adjusting.' She smiled her most infuriatingly smug smile at Minnie, who was frozen to the spot beside her presents. 'And, well, I just wanted you all to know that I am really proud to be a part of this family.'

'Excuse me.' Pete had got to his feet. 'I think I may need to throw up.'

Laurie, terrified of the imminent confrontation, burst into tears.

'Shut the fuck up, Petey, or get out,' said Duke. He had also stood up, a full six inches taller than his son, the power of his booming voice and huge physical presence instantly filling the room and dwarfing Pete into seething, impotent submission. Pete sat down.

Still smiling sweetly, Caroline continued. 'Well, I'm sorry you feel that way, Pete, really I am. I can only hope that one day you might come to accept me, as the person who has made your father happy. Especially now.'

She paused, mischievously savouring the tension in the room.

'Especially now that I'm going to be giving you a little brother or sister.'

The silence was deafening. Nobody looked more horror stricken than Duke.

'Oh, Duke, darling, isn't it wonderful?' Caroline squealed, flinging herself melodramatically into his arms. 'I'm pregnant! We're going to have a baby!'

For a moment, nobody said anything. Then suddenly Laurie let out a piercing wail, and fled, sobbing, from the room.

'Claire,' said Duke quietly, after extricating himself delicately from Caroline's triumphant embrace, and turning to his daughter-in-law as the calmest, most sensible person in the room. 'Go after her, please.'

'No!' bellowed Pete, as she half started for the door. 'You stay where you are.'

Claire froze.

'I'll go to her.' Minnie heard her own voice sounding oddly detached. For a split second, she caught Duke's eye. There was something in his expression – was it regret? But he quickly turned away and began arguing loudly with Pete, and she slipped silently out of the room.

She found her daughter upstairs in her bedroom, the same baby-pink room she had slept in since childhood, face down on the bed, her shoulders shuddering with grief.

'Why?' she wailed. 'Why is she doing this to us?'

'I don't know, sweetheart,' said Minnie, pushing back a strand of limp, matted hair from Laurie's wet cheek. 'I know it's hard, really I do. But you just have to try and accept it. We all do.'

'No!' Laurie shouted back at her. 'I won't accept it! I'll never accept it and nor will Pete. That child, that *bastard*.' Laurie's fat face was contorted with rage, a hideous contrast to her mother's composed, aquiline features. 'Her kid will *never* be family to me. Or you. I mean, for God's sake, Mother, how do we even know it's Daddy's? She's such a slut, anybody could have fathered that baby. Edward, or . . . or . . . that awful Negro, whatever his name is.'

All of a sudden Minnie felt terribly tired.

'I'm afraid it is your father's child,' she said. 'And don't ask me how I know, because I just know. Now come along, dry those tears.'

Angrily, Laurie shrugged off her hand. She didn't want to be comforted.

Minnie wasn't sure she knew what to say to her anyway. Feeling numb, and faintly dizzy, she closed the door on her daughter's sobs and retreated to the sanctuary of her own bedroom. Wild horses couldn't have got her to go back down those stairs, where she could hear Duke and Peter, still screaming at each other.

Sitting down heavily on her bed, she noticed Duke's

birthday gift on her bedside table. She was annoyed to find that her hands were trembling as she opened it. Inside was one of the loveliest diamond rings she had ever laid eyes on. There was also a note, a tiny piece of paper that had been carefully folded and slipped under the velvet of the ring box. Minnie read it:

'To My Wife, On Her Birthday. With Affection. Duke.'

For the first time in many long years, Minnie McMahon gave way to tears.

Chapter Six

They named the baby boy Hunter.

It had been a difficult birth. Caroline, unaccustomed to discomfort, let alone real physical pain, suffered terribly for fourteen hours before Dr Rawley decided the baby was showing signs of distress and performed an emergency Caesarean. She had lost a lot of blood, and for weeks after the birth looked so anaemically pale and vulnerable that Duke hardly knew how to talk to her. For him, Caroline was a purely sexual being. If his mistress had a deeper side – a troubled past or a more complex range of emotions – he neither knew, nor did he want to know, anything about it.

Bizarrely, his physical desire for her had only increased with her pregnancy. As her belly swelled, he felt an intense happiness at this living, growing symbol of his own virility and potency. He loved the shocked, revolted looks of fans on the street, relished their discomfort at seeing such a young and beautiful woman carrying the child of such an old man. The McMahons' living arrangements had become the talk and scandal of Hollywood, and Duke was loving every minute of it.

Even better, Caroline's libido had gone into overdrive. All those fucking pregnancy hormones had made her hornier than ever. When the midwife had suggested that 'aggressive' vaginal sex might not be the best thing for the baby, Duke had happily resorted to sodomising her, and was delighted by her enthusiastic acquiescence. He knew that she had conceived the child deliberately, hoping to cement her place, if not in his affections, then certainly in his will. But if anything, he rather admired her chutzpah. Hunter's arrival had been quite a coup for Caroline.

The baby itself was another matter. Duke's paternal instinct extended no farther than a primitive desire to pass on his genes, and a dimly defined Irish Catholic belief in the importance of 'family'. He had about as little interest in spending time with some puking, shitting little insomniac as in joining the priesthood.

Caroline was smart enough to realise this, and wasted no time in banishing her son to a nursery at the opposite end of the estate, in the care of two full-time nannies. She had also – through gritted teeth – allowed Duke to christen the boy Hunter.

'Honestly, darling,' she had said, when he first suggested it at the hospital. 'Hunter McMahon. It sounds like the name of one of Brad's porn stars. Couldn't we try something a little more traditional? I was thinking maybe Richard or Hugh. Or what about Sebastian?' Her tired face lit up as she thought about dear old Pa and how thrilled he would have been with his grandson. 'That was my father's name.'

'Oh yeah?' said Duke. 'Well, guess what, Peter was the name of Minnie's old man, who was the most miserable, tight-assed son of a bitch to ever walk the planet, by the way. I'm not naming another son of mine after anybody's father, and that's final.'

'But Duke, my father was nothing like that,' she protested. 'He was kind, and honourable, and . . .'

'Caroline.' He put his finger to her lips, not unkindly. 'It ain't happening, OK? And the kid is not getting some fucking English, Lord Rupert the third goddam name either.'

Caroline laughed. She loved Duke's ideas about the English upper classes, largely fed to him over the years by the sycophantically Anglophile Minnie. As far as he was concerned, everybody was called Lord Rupert of the manor and went riding round the countryside wearing coronets.

Still, she was shrewd enough to read between the lines, and knew it was important to Duke that she concede about the naming of the baby. He had never forgiven Minnie, or her family, for the way they patronised him socially. The worst thing she could do would be to appear to be following suit.

'Oh, well, all right, darling,' she said. 'I suppose he *is* going to be an American. And if he has anything like his father's charm I'm sure he'll be able to carry it off. Hunter McMahon it is.'

'Hunter Duke McMahon,' said Duke.

Oh God. In for a penny, in for a pound.

'Absolutely,' agreed Caroline. 'Hunter Duke.'

She made titanic efforts to regain her figure, working out daily with Mikey, and practically starving herself on the new cabbage soup diet that all the Hollywood wives were raving about. A picture of Caroline in a wisp of white chiffon, looking impossibly svelte at the premiere of *Saturday Night Fever* just six weeks after Hunter's birth, made the cover of *People* magazine. Now that she had produced a son, the frosty reception she had been used to among Duke's movie friends was finally beginning to thaw. Caroline Berkeley was here to stay, and anyone who didn't like it was just going to have to lump it.

From the very beginning, Hunter was an angelic baby. His nannies marvelled at his sweet, even temperament, his ability to sleep through the night, and his constant bestowing of smiles on every stranger who so much as looked at him. With his shock of dark hair, tawny brown complexion and huge, midnight-blue eyes, he was the sort of infant that people stopped to admire in the park and queued up to cuddle at cocktail parties.

Ignored by both his parents, and despised by all the other adult members of the household – with the one exception of Claire – Hunter became used to his own company, and could play for hours at a time, quite happily, alone in his nursery. The only time his peaceful, friendly face would cloud over was when he found himself dragged like a pawn into the adults' hostilities.

The older he grew, it seemed, the more often this happened.

Shortly after Hunter had turned four, his mother threw an enormous garden party at the estate, to celebrate her fifth 'anniversary' with Duke. *Le tout* Hollywood were invited, and mingled awkwardly with both Minnie and Caroline as each vied for the position of most senior hostess. Minnie, as usual, looked elegant in a beige linen trouser suit, her diamond eternity ring glittering in the California sunshine. Caroline had rather overdone it in a plunging red satin top and matching hot pants – red rags to Minnie's bull.

'I picked it up last week from Valencia in Brentwood,' she was telling an enraptured entertainment lawyer and his disapproving-looking wife as she leant seductively against a huge sycamore. 'Farrah Fawcett came in about two minutes later, *desperate* to get hold of it, but I'd bought the very last one, can you believe it?'

Despite the lawyer's drooling appreciation, she was in fact beginning to regret her choice and wish she had gone for something just slightly less risqué. It was a fine line, dressing to keep Duke happy, whilst also trying to gain acceptance among his friends as what Americans called a 'permanent life partner'. Caroline frequently found herself being outclassed by Minnie, whose conservative, elegant ensembles seemed calculated to paint her as the scarlet woman. It infuriated her.

Oh fuck, what had possessed her to wear red? She'd just have to really play up the whole vamp thing – at least Duke would appreciate it.

While his mother shimmied off into the crowd, gyrating sexily to Neil Diamond as she went, Hunter was discovering the delights of the dessert table, contentedly smearing chocolate gateau all over his face.

'Hunter! What on earth do you think you're doing?'

All of a sudden a furious Minnie was looming over

him. Hunter glanced around quickly in panic, looking for a nifty escape route, but none presented itself.

Minnie was beyond exasperation. Not only had she had to put up with watching that little trollop Caroline trying to insinuate herself with all her old friends, but now her hateful little brat had completely destroyed her beautiful chocolate gateau. Why couldn't his slut of a mother ever control him?

'Young man, you are in big trouble,' she whispered ominously at Hunter. 'Just *look* at your face. That's very, very naughty, isn't it?'

The little boy slunk back guiltily behind the tablecloth. Maybe if he shut his eyes very tightly she'd disappear.

'You come with me this instant,' said Minnie briskly, dragging him off in search of Caroline.

She had seized his arm painfully tightly, and this, combined with the harshness of her tone, had frightened him. Wiping the chocolate goo on his sleeve, he began to cry, his fat lower lip trembling pitifully as she dragged him away.

Caroline, as usual, was surrounded by a sycophantic crowd on the other side of the lawn, oblivious to her son's wails. But Claire, who had always had a strong maternal instinct and felt sorry for the boy, caught sight of Minnie pulling him angrily up the steps to the house and hurried over to intervene.

'Come on, Minnie.' She tried to keep her tone respectful. 'You know he didn't mean any harm. He's only four, for heavens' sake.' Stooping down, she wiped away Hunter's tears and the remains of the gateau with her handkerchief and, prising him from her irate mother-in-law, scooped him into her arms.

'How dare you undermine my authority?' said Minnie, glaring at her and further terrifying poor Hunter. She knew it wasn't really the child's fault, or Claire's. It was Caroline she should be angry with. Even so, it was humiliating to be reprimanded by her son's wife in front of so many people. And Minnie had had more than enough humiliation for one day. 'That child is a disgrace!' she fumed. 'He needs a little discipline, although Lord only knows how he's ever going to get it in this madhouse.'

Claire knew better than to argue, but she tightened her grip possessively around Hunter. She hated being in this position, but somebody had to look out for the child. If it were possible, her husband resented his little half-brother even more vehemently than Minnie did. He flew completely off the handle whenever he caught her defending the boy.

Her heart pounded violently now as she stood on the steps with Hunter in her arms, terrified that Pete might see her and make a scene. Sensing her fear, and acutely aware of the tension coiled within her body, Hunter suddenly lost control of his bladder. A warm yellow stain began to spread slowly across Claire's white muslin blouse.

'I rest my case,' said Minnie, contemptuously, before turning on her heel and descending the steps to rejoin the party.

'Don't you worry, sweetie,' Claire reassured the traumatised child, whose sodden legs remained wrapped firmly around her. 'It was just an accident. Come on, let's go get you cleaned up, shall we?'

She hurried indoors with Hunter, anxious to get both him and herself changed into fresh clothes before Pete found them. Claire had grown to become quite frightened of her husband. More and more these days, Pete seemed to be overwhelmed by some nameless rage that she was powerless to placate. She had thought – well, hoped – that he might mellow once they had a child of their own. But five years of trying had proved painfully fruitless, and Claire felt instinctively that Pete blamed her for their reproductive failure, although there was nothing to suggest that the fault lay on her side.

It didn't help that her father-in-law was so gung-ho about his own virility, showing Hunter off like some sort of fertility trophy, rubbing Pete's nose in it at every opportunity.

She smiled down at Hunter's chubby body as he sat happily in the bath, squirting himself with Matey bubble bath. How could Duke and Caroline just ignore him the way they did? He was such a little angel.

For her part, the longing for a child of her own had become scarcely bearable, a ceaseless drumbeat of yearning pounding away in her head, day after day. How ironic, how cruel it was, that Caroline, who hadn't a shred of maternal feeling in her hard, toned little body, should have conceived so easily; while she, Claire, who would make such a natural, loving mother, seemed destined to remain childless.

'There you go, sweetie.' She wrapped Hunter up in a huge white towel and began rubbing him dry as he wriggled and squealed in delight. How wonderful to be four – the whole Minnie incident already seemed to be quite forgotten.

'I love oo, Claire,' he said, reaching his hands up around her neck and kissing her.

'Oh, honey. I love you too,' she said.

After a lightning change, the pair of them re-emerged into the sunshine. Claire looked beautiful but flustered in a pale yellow sundress. Hunter, already restored to his natural good humour, was beaming in a crisp white sailor suit, tightly clasping her hand.

Pete pounced on them instantly.

'Where the hell have you been?' he demanded. 'I wanted to introduce you to Sheila Peterson, but the moment I turned around you were gone.'

Sheila Peterson was the wife of Anton Peterson, one of the most reclusive and most successful studio bosses in Hollywood history. Pete had been trying for eighteen months to forge an alliance with the famously prickly Anton. The McMahon name still opened a lot of doors in the movie business, and Pete hoped to convince Peterson that he could bring a higher profile and touch of glamour to his thriving but still somewhat low-key business. Today was the first time he'd managed to get him and his wife to accept any sort of social invitation. The least Claire could do was to show him a little support.

'Oh, I'm sorry, honey. Hunter had a little accident, so I just ran in to clean him up.'

The second the words were out of her mouth, she could have bitten her tongue off.

'Jesus fucking *Christ*, Claire.' He seized her by both shoulders and began to shake her hard. 'You are not his mother, OK? When are you going to get that into your stupid head? He isn't your child.'

Suddenly he released her, giving a yelp of pain. The entire party turned to gawp at the scene. Hunter had sunk his teeth into Pete's leg and was screaming at the top of his lungs: 'Oo, stop it! Oo, stop hurtin' her! Leave her 'lone!'

'Excuse me.' Caroline, her face a picture of maternal concern, was pushing her way through the throng towards her son. 'What on *earth* is going on?' she demanded in her best clipped, Mary Poppins voice, looking daggers at Pete. 'What have you done to upset Hunter?'

'What have *I* done?' Pete was spitting blood. 'Your fucking out-of-control son just bit me. Take a look.'

He hitched up the leg of his white linen trousers. A deep purple bruise was already beginning to form around the livid red teeth marks that Hunter had left on his calf. Sheila Peterson winced. Pete looked at Caroline as though she were some particularly repulsive beetle that he was having difficulty in stamping on.

'You know, Caroline,' he said quite calmly, 'if you spent more time giving a shit about your kid, and less time dressing up like some dime-a-dozen hooker . . .' He ran his eyes insultingly up and down her body, lingering with distaste rather than lust on her barely contained breasts as they struggled for release from her red satin halter top. '. . . then maybe – just maybe he wouldn't be such a little savage.'

'How dare you speak to me like that!' said Caroline, indignantly. It didn't occur to her to take any offence on Hunter's behalf. 'Duke, did you hear how that bastard just spoke to me?' Everybody looked around for Duke, but he was nowhere to be seen. Hunter started to cry again.

'On the contrary, Caroline,' said Pete, 'I think you'll find it's *your* child that's the bastard. Now if you'll excuse us, Claire and I would like to get back to the party.'

'You do that,' Caroline spat back, wrenching Hunter's hand from Claire's, to the boy's evident distress. 'And perhaps in future you'll remember that he *is* my child, not yours.' She looked at Pete evilly. 'Poor little Petey, still no luck on the old baby front, eh? What seems to be the problem? Are your swimmers not quite up to it? Or can't you get it up at all? That's certainly not your father's problem, so I don't think it can be genetic, do you?'

A couple of embarrassed titters rose from the crowd.

'Now, if you'll excuse *me* . . .' She addressed herself to Claire, deliberately turning her back on Pete, whose face had turned a livid puce with hatred and was clashing violently with his receding sandy hair. '. . . I think I'll go and get my son a tetanus shot. God knows what evil disease he may have picked up from your poisonous husband.'

And with that she stalked off in search of Duke, her son jogging along reluctantly beside her.

Pete made an effort to collect himself. If that bitch and her son had blown it for him with Peterson, he wasn't going to let her forget it.

'OK, folks, show's over.' He forced a smile and signalled to the DJ to resume the music.

Supertramp came belting out across the lawn as the crowd once again broke off into little groups, all relishing this latest spectacular outburst of the McMahon feud. By

Monday the story would be all over the papers. If only old Duke could have been there to witness it.

Standing by his bedroom window, Duke clenched both hands around the model's enormous breasts as he fucked her from behind, gazing down at the spectacle below. Watching Caroline get the better of Pete had excited him more than all the girl's frenzied clenching and moaning, and he found himself coming hard as he thought about what he might do to her later, once all these fucking parasites had gone home. Why the hell did she insist on throwing so many parties, filling the house with these goddam vacuous assholes? Caroline belonged to him – that was their deal – and he was growing increasingly tired of never having her to himself.

Still, he thought complacently as he sent the starlet on her way, he couldn't really complain. He'd had one hell of an anniversary party.

Chapter Seven

It was a year to the day after Duke and Caroline's party, and Pete didn't think he had ever been so happy.

Lying in post-coital bliss with Claire in the honeymoon suite at the Borgo San Felice in Siena, he felt that his life was, at last, starting to come together.

'Mrs McMahon, when was the last time I told you how beautiful you were?'

Claire sighed happily and rolled over on to her stomach.

'Gee, I don't know, Pete,' she mocked him. 'It must have been . . . what? . . . five minutes now?'

He bent his head down and began kissing her spine, his lips brushing each vertebra with infinite tenderness.

'Well, that is terrible,' he said between kisses. 'I don't know what I can have been thinking of for those five minutes. Because you really are . . .' He rolled her over gently and planted another kiss on her left nipple. '. . . incredible.'

Claire was three months pregnant. Just when he had begun to despair of ever fathering a child – for all his bluster and hostility towards his wife, he had long suspected that his sperm count might be less than spectacular, and blamed himself for their childlessness – it had finally happened. After so many months, years, of making ovulation charts, quitting smoking, wearing loose pants, after endless humiliating examinations by a stream of sympathetic but bewildered doctors, they had suddenly hit the jackpot. Just like that.

Pete knew he had not been the greatest of husbands to Claire in their six years together. Things had been so different when they met. A mutual friend had introduced them at some horrific party in the hills. Pete, as usual, was surrounded by a huge crowd of starlets and wannabes, all desperate to ingratiate themselves with the son of the one and only Duke McMahon. He had been on the point of making his excuses and heading home, when a pale, shy-looking girl in the corner of the room caught his eye. She was being aggressively chatted up by Johnny Wright, a loathsome junior VP at Paramount.

'Who is that?' he asked his friend Adam, nominally the host of the evening's bash, although in fact he was only house-sitting and had paid for less than half of the booze being greedily consumed all around them.

'Claire Bryant. Gorgeous, isn't she? But don't go getting any ideas.' He gave Pete a mock-stern look.

'Why not?' Pete asked, knocking back most of his sour apple Martini. 'Don't tell me she's with Johnny. That guy is such an ass.'

Adam shook his head. 'No, God no. Look at her, she can't stand the guy.'

Claire had backed so far away from her admirer that her back was now pressed against the wall. She was trying to look at him, not wishing to seem impolite, but couldn't help stealing frantic sideways glances, as if searching for some means of escape.

'Well, what, then?' said Pete. 'Why shouldn't I get any ideas? Not that I am getting any.'

Adam laughed. 'No, of course you aren't! I just mean that she's not like us, man. For one thing, she's smart. She's in her third year of medical school at UCLA. Two more years and you're looking at *Doctor* Bryant.'

'What on earth's she doing here, then?' asked Pete. 'It's hardly the sort of party for an academic girl like that.'

Adam shrugged. 'Danny brought her along, I think. Friend of the family or something. You should talk to her, though. I swear, it's like she's been living under a rock, she knows *nothing* about the business. Seriously, I don't think she'd even know who your old man is.' Pete looked incredulous. 'All she does is, like, read books and shit like that. She's not from this planet, man.'

'Yeah, well.' Pete glanced at the vacant, silicone-enhanced women across the room. 'I'm not so sure I like the women on this planet.' He downed the remnants of his drink and took his friend's arm. 'Introduce me, will you? She looks like she needs rescuing anyway.'

They made their way over to her, battling through the throng, and Adam inserted himself in front of Johnny, much to Claire's evident relief.

'Claire, I'd like you to meet a friend of mine,' he said. 'This is Petey McMahon.'

'How do you do?' said the vision. 'I'm Claire Bryant.'

Close up she was even more beautiful. She was tall, almost as tall as Pete in her flat ballet pumps, and, despite her air of fragility, quite statuesque. He was struck by her long, lean, muscular arms and the womanly curve of her hips. She seemed simultaneously strong and in need of protection.

She smiled at him with such genuine warmth, such femininity, that Pete felt instantly drawn to her. He shook her hand.

'Pete McMahon. A pleasure.'

'He's Duke McMahon's son,' interjected the odious Johnny, on name-drop autopilot.

'Oh,' said Claire, obviously baffled. 'I'm sorry, do I know your father?'

Adam winked at Pete. 'Told you.'

The two of them had hit it off immediately. They talked for hours. Pete had always adored his mother, but Minnie lacked the motherly softness that the lonely, angry little boy had always craved. Even in that very first conversation, Claire had listened to him, comforted him. She invited confidences and inspired total trust in a way that Pete found completely intoxicating.

They began spending more and more time together. He felt he could tell her anything, and found that he became listless and withdrawn whenever he was away from her, as though he had lost his anchor and was suddenly floating out to sea. Importantly, Claire was the first and only woman whom Pete knew for certain was not after either his name or his money. And God knew he was no Marlon Brando, so she sure wasn't with him for his looks. For some inexplicable reason, she actually loved him for himself. He couldn't believe his luck.

Since their marriage, however, his gratitude for her love had gradually been replaced by a bitterness, a hatred of his father that consumed every ounce of his emotional energy. None of it was Claire's fault. He knew that, and cursed himself for the way he treated her, bullying her just as his father had always bullied his mother. But the rage inside him was like a cancer, and ever since Caroline had moved in, and even more so since Hunter was born, he had felt that cancer spread.

Now, though, things would be different. Gazing down at his wife's naked, already swelling body, he felt almost overwhelmed with love for her and remorse at his own behaviour. Now that Claire was pregnant, he could become the husband she had always deserved. And his new partnership with Peterson Studios would finally start to put him on the map as a producer, a success in his own right, not just good ol' Duke McMahon's son. Yeah, it was all coming together, all making sense at last.

'Oh, Pete,' Claire murmured softly as he stroked her hair, 'I really am so happy. With you, with the baby, with everything. I feel like we've been blessed. But don't you wish we could just hide out in Italy for ever, never go back to that house?'

Pete felt the tears stinging the back of his eyes. She was so incredibly forgiving, so easily pleased. After all the pain he'd caused her, she was just happy to be here with him, grateful for one paltry week in Tuscany, their first vacation in over four years.

'I know how you feel, honey.' He stroked her belly lovingly, wondering what he had ever done to deserve such an angel. 'There's something kinda magical about this place.'

'Oh, there is!' said Claire, her eyes alight with enthusiasm. 'Siena's so incredible. The cathedral, the Piazza del Campo, the Palazzo Pubblico – my God, those frescos, I've never seen anything like it. I never dreamed I would actually be here. And that it would all be so perfect, so like I expected, but at the same time, even better than I expected. Sorry, honey, I'm gushing.' She blushed sweetly. 'But do you know what I mean?'

'Absolutely,' said Pete, who had been bored rigid by the frescos and the turgid tour of Siena's famous Gothic cathedral, but was happy just to watch his wife blossoming and in her element.

'But I'm afraid we really do have to go back. You know that, right?'

She sighed, nestling closer. These few days in Siena had been like a dream, her unborn child the magic talisman that had somehow brought her husband back to her. And yet it had all been so sudden. She couldn't help but wonder whether he wasn't going to change back just as suddenly into the withdrawn, aggressive figure she had come to know and dread.

As if reading her thoughts, Pete pulled her close. 'I promise you, Claire,' he whispered, 'you have nothing to fear.' She gazed up at him, her eyes full of trust and hope. 'When we get back home, things are going to be different. Very, very different.'

On 7 December 1981, Claire gave birth to a daughter. Siena McMahon came screaming into the world six days late. Both the screaming and the lateness were rapidly to become two of her trademarks.

'She looks kinda . . . scrunched up,' had been her father's verdict on being presented with a tiny, tightly wrapped white bundle from which Siena's bawling head poked out like a sunburned prune. 'What's she so mad about, anyway?'

'Takes after her father,' said an exhausted Claire.

'Besides, she's had a rough day. It's very traumatic, you know, birth.'

'Yeah, so they tell me. It was pretty hard going out there in the waiting room, I can tell you. We almost ran out of cigars.'

She half-heartedly hurled a pillow in his direction and grinned, stretching out her arms for the baby. 'Here, Pete, give her to me.'

He handed over the bundle with exaggerated care, mingled with a slight sensation of relief, and looked on with pride while his wife unswaddled their daughter and put her to her breast. Instantly the caterwauling stopped, and was replaced by a greedy slurping noise. Pete was mesmerised. After about a minute, her sucking slowed and she literally fell from Claire's breast, mouth open, like a blood-gorged mosquito, into a deep, contented sleep.

'Well, she's not gonna starve to death in a hurry,' said Pete. 'What an appetite!' They both laughed in wonderment at this tiny, greedy little creature they had created. Even in sleep, Pete noticed, her tiny fists were clenched, ready for unseen battles ahead.

Siena was not as beautiful a baby as Hunter had been. They had the same colouring – dark hair contrasting dramatically with striking blue eyes – although Siena's complexion was pure porcelain rather than her uncle's tawny olive, and she lacked his immaculately regular features. She was, however, pronounced by everyone to be 'adorable', and reminded her parents of a fallen cherub. Mischievous eyes twinkled in her soft, chubby face and she had the tiny rosebud mouth of a Tiny-Tears doll, complete with dimples in her cheeks and chin.

If she and Hunter shared some physical characteristics, Siena was about as far removed from him in temperament as anyone could be. Mischievous, confident and the possessor of a truly awesome temper, even as a tiny baby, she ran the entire household ragged with a cry so piercing it could be heard the length and breadth of Hancock Park. The McMahons' two nannies, Leila and Suzanna, thought back with longing to Hunter's peaceful babyhood, and wondered how long they could survive on three hours' sleep a night.

The differences between the two children didn't end there. While his parents' neglect had forced Hunter to develop an independent spirit and maturity beyond his years, it had also made him a reserved and withdrawn child. Siena was the opposite, a noisy, happy, rambunctious little girl who gave out her love readily and without question because, for the first few years of her life anyway, she received nothing but love from everyone around her.

Perhaps a little spoiled by so much constant attention, she developed an early taste for getting her own way and, although she could turn on the charm when she chose to, she could also be as stubborn, wilful and demanding as Hunter was docile and obedient.

On one occasion, when Siena had just turned two, Leila had had to call in the cavalry when she had refused point blank to wear the new Osh Kosh sundress that Claire had picked out for the day.

'She's gone stiff as a board,' the exasperated nanny told Pete. 'Absolutely refuses to bend her arms or legs so I can get the dress on. And the more I try, the more she screams. Just listen to her.'

Siena's yells could clearly be heard from two storeys below in Pete's study, easily out-decibelling the deep, authoritative voice of Suzanna, who had been left in charge while Leila ran down for parental reinforcements.

Pete sighed and put down his paper. 'OK. I'll come up.'

Upstairs, Siena was in the middle of a textbook demonstration of the 'Terrible Twos' – as described by Dr Spock in Chapter Seven of the parenting guide that Claire and all her friends lived by. She was lying face down on the floor of the nursery, beet red, simultaneously pummelling the carpet with her fists, yelling, and shaking her head manically from side to side. Suzanna had given up trying to get anywhere near her with the hated dress, and was waiting resignedly for the storm to subside.

'Now, Siena, what's all this?' Pete shouted over the din. 'Why won't you let Leila and Suzanna help you with your pretty dress?'

The pummelling stopped for a moment, and a tear-sodden, exhausted face looked up at him. 'Nooooo dress,' sobbed Siena. 'Nooooo!'

'But honey,' said Pete, ignoring all Dr Spock's advice and making the classic mistake of reasoning with an overwrought toddler, 'you'd look so cute in that dress. That's why Mommy picked it out, so you'd look just like a princess. Don't you want to be a princess, Siena?'

With an almighty effort, Siena refilled her lungs and began pummelling again with a vengeance. 'No! Siena not dress!' she screamed.

Pete thought longingly of his paper and the peace and quiet of the study. He looked at his daughter, and then at the offending article, a riot of yellow ribbons and lace. You know what, maybe she had a point? It did look kind of frou-frou.

'Just put her in her dungarees,' he said to Suzanna.

'What? But Mr McMahon,' she remonstrated, 'she's just been told she has to wear the dress. Mrs McMahon specifically requested it. I really don't think it's a good idea to just give in to her like that.'

'I'm sorry, Suzanna,' said Pete coldly, 'but I'm Siena's father and I think I know what's best for her.'

Leila saw Siena give a little smirk of triumph from under her damp curls. Sometimes she could strangle that child.

'Just get her dressed in something else and bring her downstairs,' Pete snapped. 'My wife is late as it is.' And with that, he turned on his heel and headed for the stairs and the relative calm and safety of the adult world below.

Suzanna looked at her friend in horror and ran an exasperated hand through her hair. 'Can you believe that? What an asshole! Fat lot of good he was.'

'I know,' said Leila. 'If they never stand up to her, she's only going to get worse.'

Siena gave them both the benefit of her most butter-wouldn't-melt smile.

'What an asshole!' she said.

Chapter Eight

Nothing, it seemed, could stand in the way of the entire household's love affair with Siena. Never had so much unceasing affection and attention been heaped on one little girl. Especially not in the McMahon family, who were not renowned for their sentimentality and whose previous generation of children had long been used to playing second fiddle to their larger-than-life parents.

Claire had waited so long for a child, she couldn't help but spoil her. One particular expression of her love – her desire to dress her little daughter like a doll – was a constant source of friction between the two of them. Claire would spend a small fortune on clothes, from tiny, exquisitely embroidered linen dresses to cashmere cardigans and shiny red patent-leather shoes. Siena, who hated to wear anything but her favourite blue corduroy dungarees, fought tooth and nail against her mother over these outfits, and never wore them without a stubborn scowl fixed on her face.

As long as she wasn't being straitjacketed with ribbons and bows, though, Siena loved being with her mother, baking biscuits in the kitchen together or reading her favourite story about the magic porridge pot.

'Stop, little pot, stop!' she would squeal delightedly on cue, while Claire turned the page to reveal the overflowing pot sending magic rivers of porridge down the village street.

'Look, Siena. It *doesn't* stop, does it? The magic pot makes *more* and *more* porridge!'

Siena soon knew the story picture for picture and word for word, but she never tired of listening to her mother tell it.

Not that Claire had an exclusive on her daughter's

affections. Laurie, who was still unmarried, also loved her little niece every bit as passionately as she had hated and resented Hunter. She was nervous around children, certainly not a natural like Claire, but despite her awkwardness she made a huge effort to bond with Siena.

One morning, Laurie had waddled into the nursery with a large lollipop – cherry, Siena's favourite – clenched in her clammy palm. Siena sat contentedly like a little dark-haired Buddha amid a sea of Fisher Price toys. Although it was officially a play room for both the children, most of Hunter's Action Men and Meccano sets had been relegated to the far corner, while the rest of the room had gradually been overwhelmed by a sea of pink plastic, headless Barbies, and other Siena paraphernalia.

'Hey there, sweetie,' Laurie said, in that unfortunate patronising tone that nervous adults use to speak to children, old people and the mentally ill. She squatted down so she was at the child's eye level, and thrust the lollipop out in front of her rather as one would brandish garlic at a vampire. 'Look what your Aunt Laurie brought you!'

With one swift movement, Siena whipped the lolly from her hand and thrust it greedily into her mouth, giving her aunt a sticky kiss before toddling back over to her bricks and hammer. Her number-one game of the moment was building teetering tower blocks and then demolishing them with a little wooden hammer on a string which Hunter had made for her.

'What do you say?' said Laurie, hopefully, but she was met with a blank stare. Being in full possession of the coveted lollipop, Siena's thoughts had now strayed on to other things.

Laurie looked around for a chair, but the entire nursery seemed to have been furnished by midgets, and nothing in the room was going to take her weight. She eventually eased herself down on to the carpet and sat beside her niece.

'What are you playing, honey? Do you want me to

play with you?' She picked up a brick and placed it awkwardly on top of the wobbly tower. It collapsed.

'Oh dear,' said Siena, but she flashed her aunt a big grin and seemed unperturbed by her tower-building ineptitude. This child was the one member of the family, thought Laurie sadly, who seemed to accept her for who she was, faults and all.

'Start again.' Siena sighed heavily, doing a good impression of her father after a long day at the office, and began piling up the bricks from scratch, hammer swinging dangerously close to Laurie's face as she worked.

'Oh look,' said Laurie brightly, seeing Duke appear at the nursery door. 'Here comes your grandpa. What do you say he builds your tower with you?'

At the mention of Duke, Siena's eyes lit up. Pushing aside her bricks, she leapt to her feet and raced across the room towards him.

Ignoring Laurie completely, Duke knelt down and opened his arms to his granddaughter. Mirroring him, Siena flung her own chubby little arms wide and hurled herself into his embrace. She was smiling so broadly, her lollipop fell to the floor.

'Whoa there, princess!' Duke grinned. 'Hold your horses! What are you up to in here?' He pulled her up on to his raised knee, and breathed in her sticky, infant smell as she wrapped her arms around him. God, he loved her.

'Bricks!' She beamed at him. 'I doin' my tower, I dot my hammer. Grandpa comin' to play with me?'

'Absolutely,' said Duke, hoisting her up into his arms.

Laurie, who had been watching this loving exchange between grandfather and granddaughter, had decided to slip away and leave them to it. She knew Siena loved her too, and tried not to feel jealous of her special relationship with Duke. But sometimes she wished her father wouldn't show up every time that she and Siena were having some fun together. He sure hadn't been so peachy keen on hanging around the nursery when she and Petey were kids.

'Hey, Laurie.' Duke turned briefly to his daughter, and despite herself she felt her hopes rising that he might ask her to stay and join them. 'D'you wanna get rid of that lollipop? It's gonna stain the carpet if we leave it there.'

Meekly, she picked up her sticky peace offering, now covered with carpet hair. Fighting her sense of dejection and disappointment, she left the two lovebirds to it.

Laurie was as baffled as the rest of the family by Duke's unexpected bond with his granddaughter. The man who had never shown anything other than irritation with children, and especially with babies and toddlers, had suddenly become a tamed tiger in Siena's presence.

The truth was that from the first moment he laid eyes on her grumpy little face, fists flailing in fury, Duke had fallen head over heels in love with his granddaughter.

'That kid is the only one of the lot of you that takes after me,' he would announce proudly.

Siena, in turn, responded to him like no one else, turning off her tears in an instant whenever he picked her up and settling obediently to sleep when he sang her the old Irish folk ballads of his childhood, in that wonderfully deep voice that had so hypnotised women around the world.

'It's the old McMahon magic!' he liked to tell Claire, who often felt powerless to placate her difficult daughter without him. 'She's not the first girl to give up the fight once I start singing to her.'

As the years went by, it was a close-run thing as to who, between Caroline and Pete, was the more enraged by Duke's blatant adoration of Siena.

'He never gave a damn about any of his own children, and now he wants to monopolise mine. Why can't he just do us all a favour and die?' Pete complained to Claire for the umpteenth time one night, as they lay under the peach duvet in their south-wing suite.

These momentary flashes of Pete's old rage rattled

Claire greatly. She felt she could bear almost anything rather than lose her husband for a second time. 'I know it bothers you, honey,' she tried to soothe him, 'but he is her grandfather. And, you know, despite all the awful things he's done, I think he really does love her.'

Caroline was less accepting.

'What the fuck is wrong with you?' she screamed one Sunday afternoon, when Duke had returned from Griffith Park with the three-year-old Siena, who was tightly clutching her grandfather's hand and fluttering her eyelashes innocently at Caroline. 'Hunter was waiting all morning for you to come and take him to softball. How could you just disappear like that?'

Duke was unrepentant. 'You're his mother. Why didn't you take him?'

Nothing infuriated Caroline more than being reminded of her own failings as a parent, particularly by Duke.

'I'm taking Siena up for a bath,' he said firmly and, hoisting the child on to his shoulders, he started climbing the stairs. 'Up we go, sweetheart! You stick with your Grandpa Duke.'

'I'm well aware that I'm his mother,' Caroline shouted at his disappearing back. 'But you're his father, Duke, and that's very important to a boy.' Duke continued climbing the stairs. Caroline's histrionics bored him, and he hadn't the slightest interest in talking about Hunter or his ball game. 'You have a son, and he needs you,' she continued, exasperated. 'I can't be expected to do everything with him, for Christ's sake.'

In fact, Caroline would rather have eaten snakes than take Hunter to softball herself and miss her Sunday pedicure with Chantal. Suzanna had taken him, as usual. But that was beside the point, she thought furiously. It wasn't just that Duke ignored the boy. Like her, he had never been interested in children, and until that bloody little girl had arrived in their lives she had never considered his detachment from their son to be an issue.

But recently Duke's obsession with Siena was becoming not just unreasonable, but downright dangerous.

She even suspected that he got more pleasure from playing farm animals with his granddaughter than from sex with her, a possibility that made her profoundly uneasy. They still made love with surprising frequency – for a man in his early seventies, Duke had phenomenal energy – and his desire for her remained strong. Caroline knew it was a tactical mistake to go head to head with Duke, and that her attacks on him were almost certainly counter-productive. But she was becoming genuinely fearful for her son's future. After all, she and Duke were not married, and she now accepted that they were never likely to be. She had seen the will, and knew that both she and Hunter were handsomely provided for. But even so, she couldn't shake the lingering doubt over the security of her position. Siena's arrival in their lives had changed everything, and had put paid to any hopes she may have harboured of a conclusive rift between Duke and Petey.

For the first time in her life, Caroline felt at a loss. Duke's love for Siena was getting stronger by the day. It was the one element in his life which was completely out of her control.

Later that evening, eight-year-old Hunter was sitting in the playroom watching *The Muppet Show* with Siena snuggled happily in his lap, smelling of talcum powder and wearing her favourite Snow White pyjamas.

She was kind of subdued this evening, he noticed, probably because his dad had fed her so much ice cream at the park she'd puked up all over Claire, and now it seemed that everybody was mad at everybody else. Sometimes he just couldn't figure out his family. Someone always seemed to be mad, and nine times out of ten it was his fault.

He loved it when they all left him alone, when it was just him and Siena having fun by themselves. It was a testament to Hunter's loving nature and generosity of spirit that he never resented Siena for so effortlessly winning the love that he had consistently been denied. On the contrary, he worshipped his little niece, and never tired of reading to her or crawling down the endless corridors of the estate with her on his back while they played 'horsey'. Most boys in the second grade considered it totally uncool to hang out with a toddler, especially if she was a girl. But those kids all had normal families with brothers and sisters of their own. To Hunter, the experience of having a permanent playmate, another human being who loved him unconditionally, was infinitely more wonderful and more fun than playing the Incredible Hulk with boys his own age. Siena was a little minx, of course – everybody knew that – but he forgave her for it just like everybody else.

'Animal!' Siena squealed in delight as a fuzzy orange Muppet wielding drumsticks came bounding on to the screen, head-banging. 'I wuv dat one! I wuv dat one, Animal!'

'Sure you do!' said Hunter, tickling her. 'You love Animal because he's just like *you*! Noisy and rude and a little *Monster*!' She was terribly ticklish, and after only a few seconds had collapsed into an exhausted, happy heap on the floor. 'Do you surrender?'

She smiled up at him adoringly, her huge eyes alight with mischief, and shook her head no, screaming for all she was worth as he wiggled his fingers mock-menacingly in her direction. 'God, for a baby you sure are stubborn. I hope you're ready for some more tickling?'

At that moment Suzanna came into the nursery and announced that it was Siena's bedtime. The wails of protest were instantaneous.

'Can't she stay up with me just a little bit longer?' pleaded Hunter. 'At least till the end of the Muppets? It's only ten minutes.'

Suzanna was very fond of Hunter and was constantly

amazed by the way he stuck up for Siena. She had lost count of the times she had seen him meekly take the blame in front of Pete or Minnie when Siena had spilled her juice or carelessly broken one of her grandmother's priceless ornaments, suffering frequent, unjust punishments on Siena's behalf. No matter how vociferously Siena insisted it had been her own fault, none of the adults felt inclined to punish their little cherub when Hunter was so much more satisfying a whipping boy.

'I'm sorry, Hunter, but not tonight,' she said. His face was so pitiful she almost relented, but the only thing worse than Siena's usual behaviour was her behaviour when she was over-tired. Looking at her droopy eyes and enormous dark shadows, Suzanna decided it was definitely bedtime. 'Little madam here has already been thoroughly overexcited today, and her mother wanted her in bed half an hour ago. Come on, you.'

She picked up an irate, struggling Siena and carried her off down the hallway to her bedroom. It made Hunter laugh, the way Siena fought everything all the time. Part of him wished that he could fight the world like that. But another part of him knew it would make no difference how loudly he screamed.

Nobody was going to pay a blind bit of attention.

Chapter Nine

There were two significant male figures in Siena's childhood. And her father wasn't one of them.

It was Duke and Hunter who became, in their very different ways, the foundation stones of her young life, the twin towers of her existence at Hancock Park. Duke was her idol. To her little girl's eyes, he seemed as all-knowing and all-powerful as a god. His huge physical presence both excited and soothed her, and she felt that she could never come to any harm whenever her grandfather was near. Siena didn't draw breath without trying to please him.

Hunter, on the other hand, was more of an equal. She adored him as her big brother, her playmate and her best friend. Being brave as well as kind, he became her constant champion against the traumas and insults of the school playground and, increasingly, her faithful defender against her father's wrath.

When Siena was seven, she came home from school one day in a state of high anxiety. She had totally flunked her spelling test – four out of twenty – and was not looking forward to explaining her failure to Pete.

'Do you think he'd believe me if I told him Mrs Sanders forgot to test us?' she asked Hunter hopefully.

They were sitting at the kitchen table and Hunter was deep into his maths homework, with files and books strewn all around him, but had given up any hope of being able to concentrate thanks to Siena's endless worried chatter. She had perched herself on the opposite end of the table, and was mournfully munching on a chocolate chip cookie while she contemplated her fate.

He sighed. 'Honey, I'm sorry to say it, but I just don't think he's gonna buy that, do you?'

He was right, of course. Pete had to be the strictest dad in second grade when it came to tests and grades and stuff. As soon as he got home he was sure to ask how it went. And there was no point lying about her marks. Her father seemed to have a sixth sense about that sort of thing, and would be bound to check with Mrs Sanders in the morning. Then she'd really be for it.

'Afternoon, Antoine. Is my wife at home?'

Siena froze at the sound of her father's voice. What on earth was he doing home so early? She looked at Hunter in desperation.

'Yes, sir, I believe she's out by the pool,' the butler replied. 'She got back from school with Siena about an hour ago.'

'Now don't panic,' said Hunter, seeing the terrified look on his niece's face. 'Just tell him what happened and get it over with. I'm sure he'll understand.'

'Oh yeah, right,' snapped Siena sarcastically, as Pete strolled into the kitchen looking tired and weighed down by his brown leather briefcase, squash racket and gym bag.

He dropped these burdens unceremoniously on the kitchen floor and, loosening his tie, bent down to kiss his daughter. Not with the slightest gesture or glance did he acknowledge Hunter's presence in the room. Automatically, Hunter started gathering his books together to leave, but Siena's pleading face stopped him in his tracks and he sat back down.

'So, how was your day, baby?' Pete tousled her hair affectionately. 'How'd you go on those spellings?'

Siena felt her stomach give an unpleasant lurch. There was no getting around it.

'Not so good, Daddy,' she mumbled, eyes glued to her lap. She was biting her lower lip, a sure-fire give-away of either nervousness or guilt.

'I see.' Pete's voice sounded suddenly icy. It was amazing, Hunter thought, how quickly his half-brother could switch from friendly to furious. 'And exactly what do you mean by "not so good"?' he asked.

Siena could hear her heart pounding but forced herself to look him in the eye.

'Four out of twenty,' she said. 'I'm sorry, Daddy.'

'Four!' Pete's voice was so loud that both the children jumped. He banged his fist down on the table and sent Hunter's papers flying around the room. 'Siena McMahon, that's an absolute disgrace. Four out of twenty! You can't possibly have studied.'

'I did, Dad, I totally did!' Siena remonstrated on autopilot.

In fact she had stayed up late the night before watching movies with Grandpa, but she wasn't about to pour even more petrol on the flames by telling that to her father. Anyway, she had glanced at her spellings in the car on the way to school, which was sort of studying, so it wasn't *really* a lie.

'Well then, how do you explain your result, young lady?' barked Pete. 'Because you sure as hell aren't that stupid.'

Despite herself, Siena felt her eyes welling up. It was only a stupid old spelling test. Other kids' parents probably wouldn't even ask them how they did, let alone get so het up about it. Why did Daddy have to be so mean about everything?

Peter, in fact, hated these encounters almost as much as she did. But he knew that both Duke and, to a lesser extent, Claire let Siena get away with murder, especially when it came to school work. Someone had to exercise a little control.

'It was my fault, really,' piped up Hunter, unable to bear Siena's wobbling lower lip a moment longer. 'I kept Siena awake last night. We were writing songs on my guitar, and I guess I just lost track of the time. She must have been too tired to sit the test.'

Pete knew he had been thrown a dummy – tiredness alone would not have caused his daughter to tank so spectacularly – but the opportunity to transfer his anger to Hunter was just too good to miss.

'I should have known.' He glared at his little brother. 'Whenever there's any trouble around here, you just have to be at the centre of it, don't you?'

Hunter's twelve-year-old face flushed slightly beneath his thick black hair, but he remained composed. Pete thought bitterly for the hundredth time how incredibly handsome the boy was. He had his mother's wide mouth and high cheekbones, but his colouring and facial expressions were all Duke's. Pete found these physical reminders of his father wholly repellent.

'I'm sorry,' said Hunter quietly, anxious not to enrage his brother any more than necessary. 'But it really wasn't Siena's fault.'

'I'll be the judge of that,' said Pete, who had helped himself to a large glass of the kids' Hershey's chocolate milk from the fridge, into which he was dropping ice cubes from Hunter's Tarzan ice tray. 'But in the meantime, you can stay in your room for the rest of the evening. I don't want to *see* you or *hear* you downstairs at any time, is that clear?'

'Yes, sir.' Hunter nodded respectfully and hurriedly gathered up his books.

'And I'd better not catch you anywhere near Siena on a school night again, understand? You may be too stupid to make it to college, but she isn't, and it's my job to see that she gets there one day.' He took a long gulp of his chocolate milk. 'Writing songs indeed!'

Hunter blushed more deeply before slipping out of the kitchen door. Checking first that Suzanna and Leila were nowhere in sight, he kicked off his sneakers and performed a running skid along the marble hallway, sliding to a halt just short of the front door. He wandered outside shoeless, his files and schoolbooks under one arm, and sat down on the stone steps of the porch. From here he had a clear view down the long driveway to the huge wrought-iron gates that protected the estate from the prying eyes of the outside world. It was a safe bet that a small cluster of diehard fans would be loitering just outside, ever hopeful for a glimpse of his famous father coming or going. He knew what they must all be thinking: that life inside those gates must be perfect, like some kind of paradise.

Well, it sure didn't feel that way to him.

Hunter knew Pete was right, about his being dumb and all that. He had always struggled in class, despite working three times harder at his school work than any of the other kids. His report cards had all been the same since first grade: he was a delight to teach, thoughtful and polite in class, helpful to his teachers and always kind to other children. But academically he just wasn't the sharpest tool in the box. Privately, this sense of failure was a source of deep unhappiness and shame to him.

Meanwhile, back in the kitchen, Siena, who had barely had time to mouth 'thanks' to Hunter before he had scooted off, was left alone with her father.

Now that Pete's rage had somewhat abated, her earlier terror of him had been replaced by righteous indignation on Hunter's behalf.

'Why do you always have to be so mean to him?' She scowled at her father, pushing away her own empty glass in anger. 'He works really hard at school. It's not his fault if he isn't as smart as all the other kids.'

Pete raised his finger at her in warning and fixed her with a threatening 'don't push me, young lady' look that never failed to make her stomach flip over with nerves. But she wasn't going to shut up this time. Hunter was always sticking up for her. The least she could do was repay him in kind.

'No, Dad.' She thrust her dimpled chin forward in a gesture of courage and defiance that was vintage Duke. 'It's not fair. I'm sorry I flunked my test, but it wasn't Hunter's fault. I don't understand why you always want to blame him and put him down all the time.'

'That's enough,' said Pete, wiping a smear of milky

chocolate from the corners of his mouth and getting up from the table. He knew there was truth in what she said, but he wasn't about to be given a dressing down by his own daughter. 'Your grandfather might think it's acceptable to talk back to adults like that, but I most certainly do not.'

Siena opened her mouth to say something else, but the look in her father's eyes made her think better of it.

'I want you to go to your room, right this instant, and get on with your homework.' He moved over to the door and held it open, challenging her to defy him. 'The next time you perform that badly on a test, young lady, let me tell you, your feet won't touch the ground.'

With a last defiant toss of her curls, Siena picked up her Snoopy school bag and strode, head held high, out of the kitchen. She wanted to run off straight away and find Hunter, to thank him for going in to bat for her yet again. But she knew her dad would totally lose it if he caught the two of them together now, so she reluctantly made her way up to her own room, her battered old school bag bumping against each stair as she went.

She didn't know what was wrong with her father. He always had to be mad at someone. If it wasn't her, it was Hunter, or Mom. In fact the only person he seemed able to be consistently civil to was Grandma Minnie.

Most of all, though, Siena had begun to notice recently, Pete was mad at Grandpa. Really, really mad. All the time. And try as she might, she just couldn't understand why.

On the first morning of the children's spring break, Duke had promised to take Siena down to the studios to watch the making of the new Mel Gibson movie he was financing. She had spent the previous night in a sleepless frenzy of excitement. Mel Gibson! All the girls at school were, like, totally in love with him, even the sixth-graders. Everyone was gonna think she was the coolest, getting to hang out with him and *loads* of other famous people.

Despite her privileged upbringing, and the ever-present reminders of her family's own fame – the ubiquitous bodyguards, the daily gathering of hard-core fans outside the gates of the estate, all of whom Siena knew by name, having grown up accustomed to their permanent presence – she remained desperately star-struck and enthralled by the glamour of Hollywood. She liked nothing better than to fall asleep in front of one of Grandpa's old black-and-white movies in the huge underground screening room at the estate, dreaming of being one of his beautiful leading ladies.

Hunter felt faintly embarrassed whenever he saw one of Duke's films. His father looked so young and handsome, and always played chivalrous, dashing heroes utterly unrecognisable from the aloof old man that he knew. Kids at school used to tease him about having such an old dad. Whenever he watched those films, which seemed to come from a time so long ago he could scarcely imagine it, Hunter felt he knew what those kids meant.

But to Siena, Duke was still every bit the hero. She knew the lines from every one of his movies by heart.

'Can Hunter come with us, Grandpa?' she pleaded, bouncing up and down excitedly on her chair at breakfast that morning, her bowl of Cheerios untouched. 'Pleeeeease?'

Hunter looked up from his cereal hopefully, but one look at his father's face told him he'd be about as welcome as a fart in a space shuttle.

'Sure,' said Duke, without an iota of enthusiasm.

The kid was OK, he supposed, but he had never had the same passion and love for the movie business that little Siena did. It was another thing that he and his granddaughter had in common, and he'd been looking forward to it being just the two of them today. Still, he could see how much she wanted Hunter to come and he couldn't bear to disappoint her.

'Yay!' Siena clapped her hands excitedly, oblivious to Hunter's look of reticence – he didn't want to come if his dad didn't really want him there.

Caroline was the only other adult who had made it to breakfast. Pete was on business in New York and Minnie, Laurie and Claire had left early that morning for a girls' shopping trip in Palm Desert, from which she had been pointedly excluded.

She had watched the exchange between Duke and her son with dismay, and felt a rare stab of real pity for Hunter. He'd have been happy with a fraction of the love and attention his father gave Siena, but Duke seemed determined to deny him even that. She remembered the close, loving relationship she'd had with her own father and wished her son could have known, if only for one day, what that was like.

'Actually, I'm afraid Hunter can't come, Siena,' she said firmly. 'He has Max coming over today, don't you, darling? That'll be a lot more fun than going to the silly old studios, won't it?'

Hunter rather doubted that it would, but was grateful for his mother's show of support all the same. Max De Seville was probably his closest buddy at school, the son of some old English friends of Caroline's. His mom was right, they did always have a good laugh together, especially when Siena happened not to be around. Max, unfortunately, had a zero-tolerance policy towards little girls in general, and Siena in particular, and had never been able to understand Hunter's enjoyment of her company.

Still, Hunter couldn't help thinking it would have been nice if, just once, his father had actually *wanted* to include him in one of his plans.

'Oh yes,' said Siena churlishly, pushing aside her cereal bowl with an almighty pout. It wasn't *fair* that he couldn't spend the day with her. 'Hunter can stay here and play with pig-face Max. Max the Spax!' The antipathy between Siena and Max was entirely mutual. 'That'll be *much* more fun!' She was a brilliant mimic, and had Caroline's aristocratic English drawl down to a tee.

'Now, honey, you mustn't be rude to Caroline,' said Duke, but he was unable to suppress a grin. The kid really did have talent.

Ignoring this lack of moral support, Caroline got up from the table and sat herself down coquettishly on Duke's lap. At forty-two, she had thickened around the waist and no longer had the perfectly firm breasts and concave belly that had so enthralled and delighted him when they first met, almost fourteen years ago. But she was still, without doubt, an extremely attractive woman. No hint of grey had yet found its way into her sleek blonde bob, and only the faintest of frown lines marred her otherwise strikingly youthful face.

Neither had the years done anything to dull her rampant, wanton sexuality. Duke might not be faithful to her, but he still found her infinitely more desirable and intriguing, sexually, than any of the younger, perter playthings who occasionally made their grasping way into his bed.

Caroline was also not above trying to make a seven-year-old child jealous. Siena glared at her from beneath her tangled mop of curls as she gave Duke a lingering kiss on the mouth, her expert tongue probing hungrily and obscenely for his own, one red-taloned hand burrowing furtively under his shirt, the other danger-ously close to his crotch. Duke gave a primitive groan of arousal. Man, she still did it for him.

Hunter squirmed in his seat at this public display of affection between his parents, and wished the ground would open up and swallow him.

'Have a good day, darling,' said Caroline, looking triumphantly over her shoulder at Siena, who was murderously stirring her soggy cereal at the other end of the table. That would teach the spoilt little brat. 'Don't let her tire you out completely before tonight.' Her eyes locked lasciviously with Duke's and he smiled.

'Oh, don't you worry, baby,' he said, as she got up and headed for the door. 'I still have more than enough energy for the both of you.'

Chapter Ten

Fairfax Studios was a ramshackle collection of ugly sixties warehouses and temporary-looking sheds, tucked away off Benedict Canyon in North Hollywood. To call the place unprepossessing would have been a gross understatement, but there was a frenzied flurry of activity around the lot that morning which lent an undeniable air of excitement and glamour to the dull, practical buildings.

Runners scurried to and fro, laden with mysterious boxes, clipboards or armfuls of clothing. Harassed-looking make-up artists dashed between the various trailers, huge silver mobile homes on ugly concrete stilts where the film's principal stars 'rested' between takes. All too often, they 'rested' together, and the entire extended crew were treated to the sight of a ton and a half of aluminium shaking and shuddering while the leading lady 'rehearsed' with various extras. A few jaded-looking journalists, instantly recognisable by their bright green press badges, skulked dejectedly around the set, knowing from bitter experience that they might well have to hang around all day before being granted their promised interview, and that even then the PRs would guard their celebrity charges like Rottweilers, refusing to let them answer any interesting personal questions.

Siena had been to Fairfax only once before, despite repeatedly begging her grandfather to let her tag along. There was nowhere on earth she preferred to be than on a movie set with Duke. It was like Christmas Eve, her birthday and Disneyland all rolled into one. She was excited by every aspect of film-making: the huge furry boom microphones that zoomed backwards and forwards on their enormous cranes, the great coiled firemen's hoses, waiting to pump gallons of foam on to the blazing backs of the stuntmen, resplendent in their red and white flame-retardant suits. Siena was intoxicated by it all.

Most of all, though, she longed to catch a glimpse of the actors themselves: Sylvester Stallone, Sigourney Weaver, Ali Sheedy, Andrew McCarthy, Mel Gibson – they were her idols, her pantheon of gods and goddesses. They all carried with them an almost tangible magic, a glowing, magnetic aura that made the little girl catch her breath in their presence, despite her own long familiarity with fame.

Her whole body would swell with pride as she watched her grandpa mingle with them, being greeted with affection and respect by each of her heroes in turn. Duke was a god among gods, and Siena felt special and uniquely powerful to be his chosen companion as they roamed the set together.

'You've met my granddaughter, Siena?' Duke accosted Mel Gibson as he emerged from his trailer, a battered script in one hand and a huge paper cup of coffee in the other.

Siena's eyes were on stalks as the star squatted down on his haunches so that his eyes were level with hers. His face looked slightly orange under his make-up, but his long, shaggy mane of hair and twinkling blue-green eyes looked just as they did on-screen. Siena felt her heart thump so loudly she feared he might hear it.

'I don't believe I have,' he said in his deep, gravelly Australian voice. 'Hello, Siena. Do you know, you're about the same age as my daughter, Hannah?' Siena shook her head mutely, still gazing at him adoringly. 'So what do you reckon to the set? It's kinda cool, isn't it?'

'I love it!' she said, suddenly emboldened. 'When I grow up, I'm going to be a movie star, just like you and Grandpa!'

Mel Gibson laughed good-naturedly. 'Is that so? Well, I can let you into a secret. Your grandpa here is a much,

much bigger star than I'll ever be. You've got a tough act to follow there, Siena.'

Duke lifted her up into his arms, his face alight with love. 'I'm telling you, man, one of these days this girl is gonna be huge. She's got that old McMahon magic in bucketloads, haven't you, princess?'

Siena felt she had never known true happiness until that moment.

The rest of the day passed as if in a dream. Did Grandpa really think that she could make it in the movies, that she had what it took to be like he was? If he did, then there could be no doubt about it. If Grandpa said that something was going to happen, then it did, it always did. Not even the future could defy Duke McMahon.

She followed Duke like an overexcited puppy through the maze of huts, hangars and trailers, while he spoke to the director and various key members of the crew, breaking off frequently to take calls from his lawyer on his state-of-the-art new mobile phone. Siena was incredibly impressed, watching him bellow angrily into what looked like a rather heavy black brick with buttons on it.

'I don't care how you find out, David, just do it. That's what I pay you fuckers for,' he roared.

Siena wondered what he was trying to find out about, but was too enthralled by her surroundings to waste much mental energy on anything else. One of the costume ladies, a laughing Korean woman who wore hundreds of clattering bangles on each arm, gave her a beautiful red satin shawl with a white lace trim for dressing up. Siena wrapped herself in it gleefully and was about to go skipping off after Duke when she suddenly felt a stab of guilt.

'I wonder,' she said, 'do you think you might be able to swap it for something a bit more boyish?'

'Of course.' The costume lady gave her a puzzled smile. 'But why would you want to do that?'

'It's just my Uncle Hunter wasn't able to come today,'

explained Siena, 'and I'd really like to bring him something back as a present. To make up for it, you know?'

The woman assured her that she could keep the scarf, but they would find something nice for Hunter as well. After a few minutes of rummaging, she pulled out a futuristic-looking model of a fazer gun from an old plywood crate. It was an exact replica of the ones Siena had seen on Star Trek, and she just knew Hunter would love it.

'How about this?' said the costume lady, and was gratified to see the little girl's eyes light up like fireworks.

'Oh, it's perfect, thank you,' said Siena. She knew that deep down Hunter was disappointed to have missed today. Maybe, in some small way, this would make it up to him.

Running out of the costume trailer, she gazed at the hustle and bustle of the set around her. She was determined to make herself remember every detail of the day, so that she could play it back for herself in bed this evening, and so she could tell Hunter everything after supper, as long as horrible Max had gone home by then.

Siena hated Max De Seville with a passion. He always made out her stories were boring, even when they weren't at all, even when she had met Mel Gibson and Duke had told him that she was going to be famous one day.

She couldn't see what Hunter saw in Max. They weren't a bit alike. Hunter always listened to her. He never said she was lying when she'd only exaggerated just the *tiniest* bit, to make something sound a bit more interesting. And he never laughed at her in the infuriating, patronising way that Max did, treating her like a stupid little kid, even though she was nearly eight and everyone said she was very precocious for her age, which Grandpa had told her meant grown up.

In the end, Duke decided to take her for an In and Out burger after they left the studios, and it was after ten o'clock when they got home, far too late for her to be allowed to see Hunter or Max. Claire and Suzanna had both swooped on her the moment she walked through the door, complaining that it was way past her bedtime and under no circumstances could she stay up another minute. Even Siena could see resistance was futile. It would have to wait until tomorrow.

Tucked up in bed twenty minutes later, smelling of toothpaste and soap, she gave Duke an ecstatic good-night kiss. 'Oh, Grandpa, I just had the best day ever. All the kids at school are gonna be *so* totally jealous!'

'I should think they are, sweetheart, and so they should be,' said Duke. 'You're worth a hundred of any of those kids, and don't you ever forget it.'

He kissed her softly on the cheek and turned out her Star Wars night light. She looked so perfect, so innocent and unspoiled, with her thick hair tumbling across the pillow, a ragged old Kermit the Frog clutched tightly to her chest. Duke didn't think he had ever felt so much love for another human being.

'Grandpa?' Her voice was soft and tentative in the darkness. 'Why didn't you want Hunter to come with us today?'

Duke sighed. He hadn't thought that she'd noticed his lack of enthusiasm at breakfast about the boy joining them. She was sharper than he thought.

'Don't you like him?'

It was funny. All of Caroline's ranting at him over the years, pleading with him to show more affection to his son – it hadn't made the slightest bit of difference. He didn't know why he didn't love the boy. He just didn't, and that fact had never troubled his conscience any more than it had done with Peter or Laurie. But being questioned, challenged outright by Siena, his beloved, innocent little girl, made him suddenly feel sorry that he could not be the loving father to Hunter that everyone wanted and expected him to be.

'Of course I like him,' he assured her, the deep

cadences of his lingering Irish accent soothing her as always. 'He can come along with us next time, OK? I promise.'

Siena beamed at him happily. He could see her tiny milk teeth glinting at him through the darkness.

'OK.'

'Sleep tight now, Siena,' he whispered as her eyes began to close. 'Don't let the bedbugs bite.'

'Oh, Grandpa,' she murmured drowsily, 'there's no such thing as bedbugs.'

And soon she had drifted into a deep contented sleep.

'Cut it out, Max! Leave her alone!'

It was a month after her triumphant visit to the studios, and Siena, Max and Hunter were out in the tree house 'playing'.

Reluctantly, Max released Siena's arms. She spun around to face him, her eyes blazing with fury, and was about to hurl her little body at him in a second assault when Hunter gently but firmly wrapped his own arms around her.

'Get *off* me!' she screamed at him, still struggling for all she was worth.

'Siena, just calm down and I will.'

'For God's sake hold on to her, Hunter, she's a psycho,' said Max.

The tree house had begun to shake ominously. If it broke now, after all Hunter's hard work, he really would murder the pair of them. 'No more fighting, please,' he said, exasperated. 'I'm sick of it, even if you two aren't.'

Hunter had spent the better part of his morning trying and failing to make peace between his niece and his best friend. They were always at each other's throats these days, and both of them expected him to play referee. It drove him nuts. Max really was the worst, forever winding Siena up, teasing her and baiting her until she totally flipped out. The fact that she was only a baby, not even eight years old, seemed to make no difference to his attitude. If anything, Max was tougher on Siena than he was with the kids he didn't like in seventh grade. Hunter found it baffling.

Today it had all started over the tree house he and Max had been building behind the orangery on the estate. They had been working on it for weeks over the long summer, blissfully ignored by their respective parents, who were only too happy to have the boys out of their hair. It became their den, their secret project, and they were both inordinately proud of it.

At first, Siena had been too preoccupied with Duke to pay their little camp much attention. For the last two weeks she and her grandfather had spent almost every day together, either watching old movies at home or hanging out at the studios. When Claire and Pete had insisted on taking her to Santa Barbara the previous weekend to visit some family friends, Siena had screamed the house down and had to be literally prised away from Duke's legs and bundled into Pete's Jaguar. The love affair between grandfather and granddaughter seemed stronger than ever.

Practically the only time the boys saw Siena at all was when she came home triumphant from one of her trips with Duke, bursting excitedly with stories about all the stars she'd seen and how everyone made such a fuss of her.

Max couldn't stomach her when she was in this sort of mood, yabbering away at high speed like a broken record, and it always ended in a row. Even Hunter had to admit Siena could get pretty tiring, with all her 'Grandpa said this' and 'Grandpa did that'.

But then about a week ago, Duke had decided to take Caroline down to Mexico for a week's vacation.

'Am I coming?' Siena had asked him excitedly when he announced the trip one lunchtime.

'Absolutely not,' said Caroline firmly, and for once Duke backed her up.

'Not this time, princess,' he said to his indignant

grandchild. 'It's more of a grown-up thing. Just for adults.'

'That's right,' Caroline couldn't resist adding. 'The focus is going to be very much on adult entertainment.'

Duke grinned.

'But I really want to come!' whined Siena. 'Oh, Grandpa, pleeeease, I'll be so good. I'll be really grown up, I promise. I'll be precocious!'

Duke laughed.

Siena had sulked for three solid days, but eventually resigned herself to the fact that she would be deprived of Duke's company for over a week. It was about this time that she refocused her attention and affection on Hunter, and started taking an interest in the grand tree house project.

'Don't you have some Barbies to go and play with?' Max sneered, as Hunter cautiously released his hold on Siena.

Physical violence having failed her, she decided to give sarcasm a try. 'No, Max, I don't have any *Baaar-bees*,' she parodied his British accent. 'But shouldn't you be orf hunting and fishing in jolly old England? Oh, tally-ho!' She began riding an imaginary horse around the tree house, shaking the fragile structure to its core. 'Look at me, I'm so terribly, terribly English, darling!'

'Shut up!' said Max, who was surprisingly sensitive to taunts about his accent. All the kids at school gave him grief over it, but his parents went ballistic at home whenever the slightest hint of a California twang crept into his voice. He couldn't win.

'Yeah, for God's sake, Siena, pack it in,' said Hunter.

'Tally-ho! Tally-ho!' trumpeted Siena even more loudly, thrilled to have touched a nerve, galloping around Max like a hyperactive maniac.

Before Hunter had a second to react, Max let out an almighty yell and threw himself at Siena, rugby-tackling her to the floor. The tree house gave a final creak, before giving way completely.

Wood, rope and nails flew everywhere as the three children tumbled through the branches of the huge sycamore. Instinctively, Hunter and Max both managed to grab hold of the slippery branches as they fell. But Siena seemed to have lost all co-ordination, flailing wildly for support as branch after branch cracked against her fragile limbs. The two boys watched in horror as she tumbled helplessly to the ground below. Her head hit the earth with a sturdy but muffled thud. She wasn't moving.

For some reason Hunter found himself rooted to the spot. His brain was telling his body to move, but his body didn't seem to be getting the message. It was like one of those dreams where the murderer was chasing you, but every time you tried to run it was as though your legs were knee deep in treacle. He stared in horror at Siena's limp little body.

Oh Jesus, was she dead? How could he have let this happen?

It seemed to Hunter that Max was on the ground in an instant, swinging and jumping from branch to branch like Tarzan, his lithe torso twisting to avoid the worst of the twigs and debris as he made his way down to Siena.

'Siena, wake up,' he said urgently. 'It's me, it's Max. Can you hear me?'

He had bent low over her, and was stroking her forehead with his right hand while his left felt gingerly around her neck and the top of her spine for any breakages. They had done some basic first-aid training at the Santa Monica Lifeguard Cadets, and he knew he must be careful not to move her. There didn't seem to be any serious damage.

'Siena!' he shouted at her sharply, his mouth an inch from her ear.

The suddenness of his voice seemed to jolt her into consciousness. She gave an involuntary kick with her legs, and opened her eyes blearily.

'Well, hello there.' Max grinned, relief and happiness

flooding his face. Thank God she was OK. 'You're alive, then?'

Groggily Siena tried to focus. Little by little, his face settled into view. She saw his thin lips splitting into the most enormous smile, revealing two rows of perfectly even white teeth. His eyes had disappeared into tiny twinkling crinkles, and his slightly floppy blond hair had fallen forward over his mud-streaked forehead. Next to Hunter, he had always looked so plain. But just for that moment, their enmity temporarily forgotten, she thought he looked . . . nice.

'Yes, Max, I'm alive,' she said hoarsely. 'No thanks to you.'

But she completely forgot to scowl at him.

Chapter Eleven

Minnie's brow furrowed as she perused the menu for a second time. She was sitting at her favourite table at the Ivy on Robertson, a strategically placed parasol protecting her eyes and delicate skin from the glare of the midday sun.

It was a Thursday in June, three years after Siena's tree house fall, and Minnie had arranged to meet Pete for lunch. He was late, as usual. She knew that her son was working particularly hard at the moment, and had a slew of new movie projects in the pipeline. Only yesterday, she and Claire had had a long conference on the subject of Pete's crazy working hours, and what could be done to persuade him to spend a little more time at home. But as far as Minnie was concerned, there was never any excuse for tardiness.

'Can I get you another drink, Mrs McMahon?' A chiselled but extraordinarily camp waiter had skipped over to her table for the third time in as many minutes, no doubt hoping that Duke would be putting in an appearance.

'No. Thank you,' said Minnie, her lips pursed disdainfully as she took another sip of mineral water. But her face lit up when she saw a harassed-looking Pete making his way through the celebrity-crammed tables towards her.

'Hello, Mother.' He kissed her cheek apologetically. 'I know I'm late and I'm really sorry, but I got stuck in a meeting with Gerry and I just couldn't get away.'

Slipping his Armani jacket on to the back of his chair, he sat down and wearily unfolded his napkin. Minnie noticed that his suit trousers were horribly wrinkled and his paunch was getting more pronounced. 'Evian, big bottle, ice,' he barked at the disappointed waiter.

'Yes, well, never mind,' said Minnie graciously, her previous irritation melting away in the glow of her son's presence. 'You're here now. So what's this "big news" you wanted to talk about? And why couldn't you tell me at home?'

'Jeez, Mother, what, do I need an excuse to take a beautiful woman out to lunch these days?' Pete reached across the table for her hand and kissed it. 'You're far too beautiful to spend your life shut up on the estate, you know. You should go out more often.'

Minnie blushed happily and started to fiddle with her pearls, a sure sign of embarrassment. She never had been able to take a compliment. Living with Duke, of course, meant that she was rarely called upon to do so.

'Anyway,' said Pete, slathering butter on to a large hunk of the Ivy's specially baked, sweet brown bread, 'I wanted a chance to talk to you privately. Walls have ears, you know, especially at home. And I'm still at the earliest stages with this, right? I don't have any proof.'

'Proof of what?' asked Minnie. 'I assume we're talking about Caroline, are we?'

Pete nodded with a mouth full of bread.

'So she's definitely having an affair?' Minnie leant forward excitedly. Could this finally be the break they had all been looking for? 'Is it Charles?'

Pete shook his head and swallowed. 'Not definitely. And try to keep your voice down. Like I told you, I don't have proof. I'm just hearing a lot of rumours. And my guess is that Dad must be hearing 'em too.'

Minnie summoned the waiter and ordered her usual stone crab claws. Pete opted for fried chicken, but made a small concession to his arteries by going for the spinach instead of his favourite garlic mashed potatoes.

It was hard to believe that Caroline had hung on to her position as Duke's consort and had lived like a viper among them all at Hancock Park for almost fifteen years now. In that time, Minnie had managed to cocoon herself fairly successfully from her husband's second resident family. She spent much of her day in her own private suite of rooms, and usually took her meals in the dining room with Laurie. She found it odd that someone who purported to be aristocratic could prefer to eat in the kitchen with Seamus and the nannies, but at least this enabled her to ignore Caroline almost completely when she was at home. And Minnie had her own friends, of course, and her bridge club in Beverly Hills, and the Church of the Good Shepherd on Santa Monica where she did the flowers twice a week. Between her charities and her children, she had developed a reasonably fulfilling independent life. So much so that a casual observer might well have thought that she had not only accepted her husband's domestic arrangements, but had practically forgotten about their existence altogether.

Nothing could have been farther from the truth. Her silent resentment of Caroline Berkeley and her son had built over the last fifteen years into a violently repressed hatred. Minnie chose never to lash out – at least not until she could be certain that any strike made against her hated rival could be ensured of success. For years she had watched Caroline like a hawk, hunting for irrefutable proof of an affair, or anything else that would bring Duke to his senses. Perhaps, she thought as the waiter refilled her water glass, she had finally found it?

But her adversary was not a fool. Caroline was fully aware how vulnerable her position was as Duke's unmarried mistress. Just one slip could prove fatal to her security and end her pampered lifestyle, and in the past she had always gone to great lengths to maintain the appearance of fidelity and devotion to her aged husband. Even Hunter's existence did not guarantee her a legal share of the McMahon wealth.

Minnie watched disapprovingly as her son gobbled down his lunch at a rate that was bound to exacerbate his heartburn.

She reflected on how much it would have surprised Caroline, and probably Pete too, to discover that she and Duke still talked on a regular basis, about subjects as diverse as their children or his latest business deal. For all the floods of betrayal, cruelty and neglect that had flowed under the bridge of Duke and Minnie's marriage, there remained a bizarrely unbreakable connection between the two of them.

'Has he said anything to you?' asked Pete between mouthfuls of his meltingly tender chicken.

'Your father? No,' said Minnie. 'No, he hasn't. But I'm sure I would be the very last person he'd talk to if he *did* suspect Caroline of anything.'

'Except Caroline herself, of course.' Pete raised one eyebrow enigmatically.

'What do you mean?' asked Minnie.

'Only that if he *does* know something – and let's just say he does – well, it wouldn't be Dad's style to confront her with it.' Pete leant back in his chair and stretched noisily, a habit he had unconsciously picked up from Duke. 'I don't know, Mother. But I'm pretty sure she *is* doing Charlie. And if Dad's heard so much as a whisper of it, then for one thing, he'll be having her followed, and for another, when he finds out the truth, he's going to be ruthless.'

Minnie nodded silently.

'I think he knows,' said Pete. 'And I think he's planning something.'

The restaurant was full to bursting now, and a low hum of Hollywood gossip filled the terrace. On the other side of the white picket fence, harassed-looking valets were fighting their way through a group of paparazzi who had gathered to scoop some shots of Sly Stallone. He sat two tables away from Minnie and Pete with his very beautiful red-headed manager. Some of the press had mistaken her for a new love interest, and the 'paps', as they were called, had descended on the Ivy like locusts.

'So?' asked Minnie as she polished off the last of her crab meat in one dainty bite, ignoring the undignified scrum of hoi polloi around her. 'What do we do about it?'

'Nothing,' said Pete. 'Not yet anyway. We sit tight. But if either of us hears anything' – he signalled to the waiter for the bill – 'we let each other know right away. OK?'

'Of course, darling, that goes without saying.' Minnie smiled at her only son, always so tense, always in a rush. He and Duke were more alike than either of them cared to admit. 'Won't you stay and have a coffee with me, Petey?'

'Truly, Mother, I'd love to, but I just can't.' He rose from his seat and handed Minnie a sheaf of twenty-dollar bills.

'This could be it, you know.' He smiled, the first genuine smile she had seen on his face in months, and blew her a parting kiss. 'I think we might finally have got her.'

'Oh, please, Charlie, don't! Don't stop yet, I'm so close!'

Charles Murray felt Caroline's marvellously taut thighs tightening around his ears until he could hear his own blood thumping through his brain. He had been licking and nibbling at her swollen clit for the best part of fifteen minutes, and although he always found it exciting watching her writhe with pleasure at his expert ministrations, he was now beginning to get impatient for some pleasure of his own. He was also very aware of how dangerous it was to be doing this in the office. Forcibly prising his head from her vice-like grip he reached for the water bottle on his desk. 'Baby, I'm sorry but I need some air. It's hot down there, you know?'

Caroline was sitting on the desk in Charlie's corner office on the fifth floor of the Beverly Hills attorneys Carter & Rowe. Her demure 1950s-style skirt was rucked up around her hips and her Trashy Lingerie panties had been yanked conveniently to one side. Charlie was kneeling on the carpet, at eye level with her dripping crotch. His boyishly handsome face was so flushed, he looked as if he'd just scored a touchdown.

'Well, all right.' She smiled down at him indulgently while absent-mindedly inserting two fingers into her pussy and rubbing herself gently with the ball of her thumb. 'You can take a "time out". That's what you call it, right, you football-playing types?'

'Right,' said Charlie between gulps of Arrowhead Spring.

'But I *really* need to come, darling.' Caroline looked at him beseechingly. 'Please?' With her free hand she stroked his blond hair, rather as she would a Labrador.

Charlie grinned as he stood up, his six-foot-four frame towering over Caroline like a linebacker. His perfectly toned torso was clearly visible through his tight white shirt, now clinging to the sweat trickling down between his pecs, and his huge, ramrod-straight erection jutted out at an almost perpendicular angle through the open flies of his pinstripe suit trousers. My God, he's a fine figure of a man, thought Caroline longingly. He pushed her back on to the desk, sending notes and papers flying as he clambered on top of her. Supporting himself on his forearms, with his face less than an inch above her own, she felt his quickening breath on her forehead while the tip of his penis nudged teasingly against her labia.

'*You* really need to come?' He laughed. 'How the hell do you think I feel?'

With one swift, delicious motion he slipped inside her, so deep that she could feel his tightened balls pushing up against her bottom with each thrust. For Caroline, at forty-five, to be able to inspire this degree of lust in such an exquisitely beautiful, thirty-year-old man was the biggest aphrodisiac of all.

'Ahhh, lovely,' she sighed as yet another rush of pleasure engulfed her. Within sixty seconds she found herself erupting into a glorious orgasm, tension and frustration flooding joyously out of her body. Charlie closed his eyes and focused on his own pleasure. Caroline gazed up at him, lost in some erotic fantasy of his own as he screwed the life out of her, and felt his cock twitching involuntarily inside her before he finally came, moaning loudly and biting down on her shoulder, so intense was his own release.

'You really are lovely,' she said, as they lay motionless in one another's arms afterwards, amid the wreck of Charlie's office. He kissed her.

'So are you.'

Her relationship with Charles Murray was probably the closest thing to love that Caroline had ever experienced. She wasn't stupid. She knew it was insanely risky, and that it had no future. Charlie was an up-and-coming young litigator at Carter's, whose senior partner, David Rowe, was Duke's personal attorney. The affair was complete madness. But despite herself, Caroline found herself unwilling, or unable, to give him up.

Charlie made her laugh and he made her come, two qualities that Duke had certainly possessed when the two of them first met, but which seemed to have withered with his increasing age. Statistically, Caroline realised, it was a miracle that a man of almost eighty should be able to make love to her at all. But while she still felt desired by Duke, the thrill of being dominated by such a powerful man had started to wane as the years inevitably caught up with him, and she no longer felt any excitement in his bed. In fact, since the first day she had surrendered to her growing attraction for the young lawyer who had accompanied David Rowe on his trips to the McMahon estate, she had begun to find Duke's sexual attentions actively repellent. Lying beneath him, it was impossible not to compare the sagging skin on his back to Charlie's broad and powerful shoulders, or his liver-spotted, sinewy arms to Charlie's tanned and rounded biceps.

As the months went by, Caroline found herself more

and more greedy for both her lover's body and his company. And as the affair developed, she was becoming increasingly reckless.

'We have to start being more careful,' said Charlie as he hastily tucked in his shirt and smoothed down his hair, checking his reflection in the window. Caroline hated the way he could sound so businesslike and brisk almost immediately after they had made love. 'Did David see you come in?'

'No.' Caroline sighed. 'His door was closed. Only Marlene knows I'm here.' Marlene was the litigation department's angel of a receptionist, a skilled keeper of secrets and turner of blind eyes. She had a particular soft spot for Charlie, and would be the last person to breathe a word about their dangerous liaison to anyone. 'Besides . . .' She walked up behind him, pressing her breasts hard against his back and, reaching round, brushed the back of her hand lightly against his crotch. 'Doesn't it excite you just a little bit? Knowing we might get caught?'

Charlie turned and kissed her on the forehead, while gently disengaging himself from her embrace. Of course the secrecy of it all turned him on. Truth to tell, just about everything about Caroline and their affair excited him. Charlie had always been drawn to strong, ballsy women, and Caro was the strongest and ballsiest of them all. It killed him to think of her being pawed over by that revolting old lech McMahon.

But he also understood her. Duke was Caroline's financial security. Charlie's career was his. And both of them were too selfish and hard headed to contemplate throwing that all away for the sake of a few snatched hours of sex, however mind-blowing it might be. Charlie respected Caroline and he liked her – but nothing was worth losing his career over.

Moving away from her, he started tidying the piles of paper and files that littered his desk. This was no time to play games. Without warning he hit the speakerphone.

'Marlene? Charlie. Tell Mr Levy I'll see him in two minutes, I'm just finishing up a call here.'

A pouting Caroline picked up her purse and strode to the door.

'Aw, c'mon, honey,' said Charlie, grabbing her shoulders with his huge hands. 'Don't put this all on me. You don't want to get found out any more than I do, right? Right?'

She nodded grudgingly, but didn't trust herself to turn and look at him.

'I'm not saying it's over.' His voice was softer now, more loving. 'Just that we have to be more careful. The office is too risky, all right? So no more "dropping by".'

Caroline laughed. She loved being teased by Charlie. 'Lovely as it was to see you, David's not stupid. And neither is Duke, so no more long lunches up at your place either.' He walked back to his desk and flipped open a brown folder labelled 'Levy'.

Caroline unlocked the door of the office and looked up and down the corridor to make sure the coast was clear before slipping on her dark glasses.

'Trust me,' she whispered to an anxious-looking Charlie. 'We're fine. Duke knows nothing.'

And with that, she closed the door noiselessly behind her.

A few blocks away in one of the wide, tree-lined avenues known collectively as 'the flats', Claire sat behind the wheel of her kingfisher-blue Saab, keeping the engine running in case she needed to make a quick getaway from the jobsworth parking inspectors that always hung around the school gates at going-home time, hoping to catch some poor mother as she dashed in to collect her offspring. Parking in Beverly Hills was always a nightmare, but once the schools got out it was outright war.

She looked at her watch, tapping her manicured fingers impatiently on the tan leather steering wheel. Five after three. The bell should have rung by now.

Normally Leila would pick up both the children after school, although Claire occasionally did one or two of the early morning runs. But Hunter was going over to Max's today and would be dropped back at home later, so she thought it might be nice for her to collect Siena herself, maybe take her for an ice cream or something on the ride home. It was a long time since the two of them had had any fun time alone together.

Claire loved her daughter dearly, but was acutely aware that the two of them had very little in common. Where Claire was thoughtful, patient and calm, Siena was short tempered, feisty and loud. Although she had inherited her mother's intelligence, it was the McMahon street-smarts and ambition which really formed the core of her emergent personality.

From the day she was born, it was perfectly apparent that Siena was not destined to be a girls' girl. She hated pretty dresses, dolls or any sort of quiet, creative play, always preferring to be outside climbing trees, shouting or – best of all – playing 'war' with Hunter, shooting at any animal, vegetable or mineral that dared to cross her path with the cap gun Duke had insisted on buying for her. Claire never begrudged her these games. But she did begin to feel excluded. And as Siena grew ever closer to Hunter and to Duke, that sense of exclusion and sadness grew.

It didn't upset her in the same way that it upset Pete when people commented on how alike Siena was to Duke. What was the point of getting upset about something that was quite plainly and simply a fact? Siena was like him, frighteningly like him, in so many ways.

But there were also differences. She could be thoughtless, selfish even, and dreadfully spoiled at times. But Claire knew that her daughter was not a cruel child, not vindictive like Duke.

In his own pain at what he perceived as his daughter's rejection of him in favour of his hated father, Pete often lost sight of that crucial distinction. But Claire never did.

She wished that she and Siena had a closer relationship, of course she did. But she never blamed the child for loving her grandfather, or for being herself. Besides, hopefully as Siena got older she would develop more of an interest in the feminine things in life that Claire would be able to share with her – simple things like shopping together or getting their hair done. She was really, really looking forward to that.

Suddenly the school doors opened and a scrum of tired, sweaty-looking boys and girls surged out into the school playground. Siena was instantly recognisable as the scruffiest of the lot, hair escaping in corkscrew ringlets from her loosened hair tie, her blue sweater torn at the neck (not again, thought Claire), her battered old Snoopy bag being dragged along the concrete like a sack of coal.

Claire honked her horn loudly, and Siena grinned back at her and waved excitedly, tearing through the gates and across the street without so much as a glance at the oncoming traffic.

'Mom!' she said, leaning forward to give Claire a kiss. 'How come you're here? I thought Leila was getting me.'

Claire was so thrilled by this warm reception that she forgot to tell Siena off for not looking before she crossed the road. 'Well, I thought I'd do it for a change,' she said with a smile. 'If you like, we could stop for an ice cream at Gianni's on the way home?'

'Cool,' said Siena. This was all very out of character. Normally her mom was obsessed with homework and didn't allow any fun at all until all her assignments were done and dusted. Sensing an opportunity, she thought she'd see how far she could push it. 'You picked a good day, actually,' she gabbled on, as nonchalantly as she could, while Claire pulled out on to Santa Monica Boulevard. 'Mr Di Clemente said we all did so well on last week's math assignment that he wouldn't set us any homework for tonight.'

'Really?' Claire was surprised. Not only did her teacher

almost never not set homework, but as she remembered it, Siena's math assignment last week had been somewhat less than fabulous.

'Uh-huh.' Siena didn't miss a beat. 'So I was thinking . . .'

'Ye-es?' said Claire warily.

'As I don't have any work to do . . .'

'Ye-es?' She knew exactly where her daughter's wheedling tone was leading.

'Maybe we could go to Tumblorama?'

'Tumblorama' was an indoor kids adventure centre on the borders of Los Feliz, a mile or so north of Hancock Park. It consisted of a maze of multi-coloured plastic tunnels, ladders and slides, all interconnected, through which exhausted parents would chase their overexcited children with a heroic disregard for middle-aged bad backs, aching muscles and bruised limbs. It was Siena's favourite place in the world after the studios, and a popular venue with all the local kids for birthday parties or holiday treats.

It was, needless to say, the sort of place that gave poor Claire nightmares. But Siena sounded so sweet and hopeful. And she had wanted the two of them to have some quality time together . . .

'Oh, all right, then,' she said, with a last lingering look at her freshly manicured nails and her newly pressed Laura Ashley skirt, knowing that neither would survive the dreaded Tumblorama ordeal.

'Really? You'll take me?' Siena couldn't believe her luck and started bouncing up and down on the back seat with excitement like a broken jack-in-the-box. Mom never did stuff like this, especially not on a school night.

'Sure,' said Claire. 'Why not?' She smiled back at her ecstatic daughter indulgently in the rear-view mirror. 'We moms may be old and boring most of the time, but we can still keep a few surprises up our sleeves.'

When they finally got home, three hours later than

expected, Pete's first thought was that they must have been in an accident.

Claire's usually immaculate hair was all over the place, standing on end with static as if she'd rubbed it with a balloon. Her face was flushed and red, her nail polish chipped, and her new skirt – one of those dreadful milkmaid, flowery things that he couldn't stand – had thankfully been ripped right along the hem, probably beyond repair.

'What the hell happened to you?' he asked, taking in his wife's dishevelled appearance but also the matching grins that she and Siena wore plastered across their faces, and relaxing slightly.

'Tumblorama,' panted Claire, picking up Siena's school bag on autopilot and extracting the half-eaten remnants of her packed lunch.

'You're kidding?' His tone was quizzical but also amused. It was nice to see his two girls looking so happy together. Particularly to see Siena looking so happy, without Duke or that snotty little brother of his anywhere around. 'You took her to Tumblorama? On a school night?'

'It's OK, Dad,' Siena jumped in quickly, anxious to avert the anger she had come to expect from him. 'I didn't have any homework. Mr D let us off.' She had quite forgotten that this was not, in fact, true, and fluttered her eyelashes at her father like a bona fide innocent.

'Well,' said Pete, still smiling at both of them, 'aren't you the lucky one?'

What, no shouting? What was up with her parents today? Had they both taken a happy pill or something?

Pete moved over to Claire and put his arm around her in a rare display of tenderness. 'Off you go upstairs now and change,' he said to Siena. 'You can tell me all about it at dinner.'

Claire put Siena's lunch box down and reached up with both her arms, wrapping them around his neck and nuzzling against him. They both watched their daughter disappear noisily up the stairs, about as ladylike and graceful as a drunken baby hippo.

'Don't you wish things could always be like this?' Claire sighed, once Siena was out of sight and out of earshot. 'Just the three of us, relaxed and happy, like this?'

He could feel her warm breath against his neck, quickened from the exertion of chasing Siena through endless plastic tunnels. 'Yes,' he said, stroking her hair and smoothing it back into place. 'I do.'

He thought about Caroline. If his suspicions were right – if she was cheating on Duke – then maybe her days at Hancock Park were numbered. What he wouldn't give to be rid of her and her wretched son. 'But you never know, darling, maybe it will be like this one day.'

Claire looked up at him, perplexed. 'What do you mean?'

'Who knows?' said Pete, kissing her gently on the forehead. 'Maybe life around here is about to change for the better.'

Chapter Twelve

'I'm so sorry, Duke. I don't know what to say.'

David Rowe sat awkwardly in the low leather armchair in Duke's study, watching his client flip slowly through eight black-and-white pictures. His face was completely impassive as he studied one image after another, occasionally tracing something on one of the prints with a long bony finger, as though trying to make it out more clearly. But the pictures were already clear as crystal. David knew, because he'd seen them all an hour before he drove over to Hancock Park, and he was still reeling from what he saw.

In the first shot, Caroline was getting into the car with Charles Murray, his young protégé. The next two pictures showed the two of them holding hands, kissing and laughing as they went into what looked like a bungalow at the Bel Air Hotel. After that came six pictures that left nothing to the imagination, two taken at the hotel, and another four in various other locations, including the back seat of Duke's own midnight-blue Bentley. The PI had done a horrifically good job – he'd only been following Caroline for a week.

David felt his chest constricting with stress as he watched his powerful client slowly leafing through this damning evidence. He didn't consider himself a friend of Duke's. In fact, if truth be told, he had never much liked him, but as his contemporary – David himself was a dynamic seventy-seven, a mere two years younger than Duke – he couldn't help but feel sympathy for an old man, betrayed and humiliated by such a beautiful young woman. He was also absolutely livid with Charlie for putting him in such an embarrassing position, and all because he couldn't keep his Johnson in his goddam pants.

'I know what you're thinking,' said Duke, without taking his eyes off a picture of Caroline sitting on a hotel bed, her legs wrapped around the kid's waist and her head thrown back in undisguised delight.

David squirmed in his seat. 'Look, Duke, it's none of my business,' he began, but Duke raised his hand for silence.

'There's no fool like an old fool. That's what you're thinking, David. Am I right?' He could see his lawyer opening his mouth to protest. 'And no, don't apologise. You're right to think that. You're absolutely right.' He frowned and rubbed at his temples, as though trying to erase the picture of Caroline's betrayal from his memory bank. 'She's played me for a damn fool.'

He finally replaced the photographs in the unmarked brown envelope David had handed him and, unlocking the second drawer of the desk with a miniature key that he produced from his pocket, he slipped the offending package inside, then closed and locked the drawer again, repocketing the key.

David cleared his throat awkwardly. It had to be asked. 'So, what do you want me to do about young Murray?'

Duke stared blankly ahead.

'You're one of the firm's oldest and most valued clients,' David continued. 'We don't want to lose you. Now, if you tell me you want us to let this young man go' – he paused and looked Duke squarely in the eye – 'I want you to know that we wouldn't hesitate.'

Duke stood up and walked slowly over to the window. Outside on the lawn he could see Hunter swinging Siena around by her feet. Her arms were outstretched and her long dark curls were flying in the wind like the tail of a comet. Beautiful.

He noticed that his son was laughing, black hair flopping over his tanned forehead, cheeks glowing with exertion as he spun his niece around and around. Duke felt a slight stabbing sensation in his chest as he looked at Hunter, and raised his hand to his heart. He guessed that the boy must think him a pretty heartless father.

At fifteen, Hunter looked more like him every day. It was funny how none of his genes seemed to have passed themselves on to Pete and Laurie, his legitimate children, while Caroline's son, the little cuckoo in the nest, was every inch his child. Sometimes Duke wished he had been able to connect with the boy, had tried harder to love him. He was such a good-natured kid too. But for some reason he had always felt impelled to keep himself at a distance.

Maybe, deep down, he had always known this day would come with Caroline. After all, he had never intended to start a second family with her. She had never had Minnie's unflinching loyalty. But then why on earth should she?

Duke had hurt Minnie because she let him, and he had always despised her for that weakness. Caroline, on the other hand, had been a breath of fresh air, a kindred spirit. He remembered how much he had once loved her for her independence, for that selfish, ruthless energy that reminded him so much of himself.

The fact was, she was not his wife. He had never wanted her to be. And as a result, he had never really thought of her child as his son.

He turned round and looked at his lawyer's pained, anxious face. 'Don't fire him on my account, David,' he said.

'Really?' The old man looked shocked.

'Really,' said Duke. 'The kid's a good lawyer, isn't he?'

David smiled a little despite himself. 'He's a great lawyer. Most talented guy in a trial situation I've seen in thirty years.'

'Well, then.' Duke smiled back. 'It'd be a shame to let him go.' He noted David's look of bewilderment, and opening a battered leather box on the side table, took out two of his finest Cuban cigars and offered him one.

'Look. The way I see it, the boy only did what I would have done myself when I was his age.' He clipped the tip off his own cigar and lit it, inhaling deeply before passing the silver cutters to David. 'She's still a terrific-looking woman. And she fucks like a stoat.'

David wished that Duke wouldn't use such profanities. As a devout Methodist he found his client's brutal language both offensive and unnecessary. Still, he supposed those pictures must have come as a terrible shock to him.

'Well, all right, Duke,' he said. 'I must say I think that's very big of you. And you can rest assured that I will be speaking to Charles in the strongest possible terms about his behaviour. We take breaches of trust very seriously at Carter.'

'Oh, believe me, David,' said Duke ominously, 'I take them very seriously too. Very seriously indeed.'

He looked outside again for the children, but they were gone.

Siena woke up early the next morning to the familiar, blinding glare of sunlight bursting through her window on to walls completely plastered with Mel Gibson posters. She was ten now, and her crush on the rugged Australian had developed into a full-blown obsession. On the back of her bedroom door, the only space not devoted to Mel, hung a framed black-and-white picture of Duke in *Tales of the Desert*, one of his early Westerns. He had worn his hair in a ponytail for the movie, which Siena thought incredibly romantic, and in the poster he was doffing his hat to his crinalined leading lady while his horse reared up, shadow-boxing with its powerful forelegs. She had always loved that picture of her grandfather. He looked so wild and glamorous.

She sat up in bed and rubbed her eyes blearily. Blowing a kiss to Mel, she slipped into yesterday's jeans and T-shirt which she had conveniently left screwed up in a heap on the floor. The school year had ended the week before and months of glorious freedom stretched ahead of both her and Hunter.

Hunter was such a slug in the mornings, though. He was growing so fast, all he ever wanted to do was sleep. Siena, on the other hand, couldn't jump out of bed fast enough. There were bikes to be ridden, pools to be swum in, slumber parties to be arranged – she couldn't wait to get started.

Going over to her desk, she picked up a handful of coloured pencils and the half-finished Get Well Soon card she'd begun making for Aunt Laurie last night. Laurie had twisted her ankle a few days ago while out jogging and was now confined to bed.

Siena didn't always see eye to eye with her aunt, but she had started to feel increasingly sorry for her, especially when Grandpa kept making mean jokes about her being so fat, and how she couldn't even go for a run without falling on her big fat behind. She didn't think that was very nice of him, especially now that Laurie's ankle had swollen up like a big purple-and-black balloon. Anyway, she hoped the card might cheer her up a bit, particularly as it featured the excellent swans that Hunter had recently taught her how to draw by starting with a giant number two and then sketching in the folded wings and beak on top.

Clenching the card and pencils in one hand, she clambered up on to the banister rail in the hallway and slid all the way down the polished wood of the grand staircase.

'Er, excuse me, young lady, but what do you think you're doing?'

Claire was looking immaculate as always in a pale yellow trouser suit and white shirt with fashionably ruffled collar. She had a wicker basket over her arm and Ray-Ban sunglasses on, and was obviously on her way out when her daughter had come hurtling down into the entrance hall and landed with a thud on Minnie's perfectly polished marble.

'Sorry,' said Siena, though she didn't look it.

'Well, so you should be,' chided her mother automatically. 'How many times have I told you not to slide down those darned banisters? It's dangerous, Siena, that must be a forty-foot drop.'

'God,' Siena moaned, the picture of petulance. 'I said I was sorry, didn't I?'

Claire knew she ought to tell her off for using such an impertinent tone, but she was late enough as it was and really didn't have time for a full-blown confrontation now.

'Yes, well,' she said with what she hoped was a stern expression. 'Please try to use the stairs next time like any normal person.' She fumbled in her basket for the keys to the Saab. 'I'm running to the Beverly Center, and Leila and Suzanna both left early for the beach, so you can ask Conchita to fix you some breakfast if you're hungry.'

'What about Caroline?' asked Siena, trying to provoke her mother and succeeding. 'Couldn't she do it for me?'

'Don't push it, Siena,' said Claire. 'Her car's not here anyway, I guess she must have made an early start too. Now go get some breakfast. And don't forget to clean your teeth afterwards.' She gave her a perfunctory kiss on the top of her head and scurried off to the car. 'And brush your hair!' she called behind her.

Siena wandered into the kitchen.

She was just heading for the fridge when she suddenly stopped dead in her tracks. The coloured pencils she'd been grasping so tightly clattered to the ground, followed by the creased white Get Well Soon card for her aunt. She stared ahead of her in shock.

Duke was lying slumped across the table, still in his dark purple robe. His left arm had been flung wide, and had evidently knocked over a carton of milk, the contents of which had formed a white pool in the centre of the table, with little rivulets trickling out to the edges and dripping on to the floor like anaemic waterfalls. His right hand seemed to be pressed against his chest. It must have been pinned in position there by the table when he fell forward. But it was his face which Siena would never forget, still screwed up as though he were either in severe pain or deep concentration. His skin looked white-blue, like moonlight. She had never seen a corpse before, but she knew immediately that he was dead.

'Mom! Mommy!'

She ran screaming back into the hall and out of the front door, but Claire's dark blue tailgate was already disappearing through the gates. Turning around, her eyes blinded by tears as she stumbled numbly back inside, she ran straight into her grandmother.

'Siena, darling, what on earth is the matter?'

Minnie had heard the child's screams from her dressing room, as had the rest of the household, and had rushed downstairs to see what all the fuss was about. One look at Siena's face told her that this was not just another of her attention-seeking pranks. She was sobbing and shaking as though she'd just stumbled out of a car wreck.

'He's dead.' Siena's voice was almost a whisper.

She wrapped her arms tightly around Minnie's waist and pressed her tear-stained face against her familiar crisp linen shirt.

'Who, darling? Who's dead?' asked Minnie softly.

For one hideous moment she thought it might be Pete. But before she had time to get anything more coherent out of Siena, Seamus, Duke's assistant and lifelong friend, emerged from the kitchen looking ashen.

'You'd best come in here,' he said. 'It's Duke.'

For an instant, Minnie felt nothing but pure, intense relief. It wasn't Pete. It wasn't her son. Prising herself free from a distraught Siena, she followed Seamus into the kitchen. Her hand flew to her mouth when she saw him.

'Oh my God. Oh God,' she said, collapsing against Seamus as she felt her knees give way. 'Is he . . .?'

Duke's old friend nodded gravely and pulled her close to his chest.

'Definitely. There's no pulse. I'm sorry, Min.'

'But he was fine,' Minnie said absently, unable to tear her eyes away from the body. 'I spoke to him. Last night. About everything. We spoke about everything and he was absolutely fine.'

She looked at Seamus as if imploring him to do something. The whole scene seemed so surreal. She wanted to feel something, other than shock and guilt at her initial relief, but her emotions seemed to be frozen. She wondered whether she might be going to laugh, and the thought appalled her.

Duke had come to see her late last night, after his meeting with David Rowe, and told her everything about Caroline and her affair with the young lawyer. It had taken a lot for him to admit his mistress's betrayal to her, she knew, and sensing his deep sadness and humiliation she had listened as quietly and supportively as she could while he told her what he intended to do.

He hadn't apologised to her, for all the years of misery, for the untold pain he had caused through his own betrayals and by forcing Caroline into their lives in the first place. Apologies weren't Duke's style.

But he had told her it was over. And she had told him she was glad.

Minnie didn't kid herself. It was too late for her and Duke to undo the past and find one another again. She knew that. But she had gone to her bed last night hopeful that at least, with Caroline gone, they could revert to some kind of civility and normality at Hancock Park.

She had waited so very, very long for this moment. But now he was dead. It just didn't seem real.

At that moment Siena burst into the room and flung herself against Duke's slumped body, frantically kissing his neck and cheek and sobbing uncontrollably.

'He can't be dead,' she wailed, 'he can't be!'

Hunter, who had slipped quietly into the back of the room with the growing crowd of estate servants, stepped forward and put his arm around her. He was still in his boxer shorts and T-shirt, and his hair stood up on the left side of his head like a chimney brush.

'It's all right, baby,' he whispered. 'Come on. Come away now. We can go and sit outside.'

'No!' Siena shrugged him off angrily, lashing out like a surprised rattlesnake. 'You don't understand, do you?' She looked accusingly at everyone in the room, from Hunter to Seamus to Minnie, even at Conchita and Antoine, who were loitering awkwardly by the door in their formal black-and-white liveries. 'You didn't love him like I did. None of you! None of you ever loved him!'

'Go and find Peter and Laurie,' whispered Seamus to Antoine, who slipped noiselessly out of the kitchen.

Minnie stepped forward and, not unkindly, shooed Hunter out of the way. Duke's body lay slumped between her and Siena, and the absurdity of the situation, of his corpse just lying there, struck her again. Somehow it seemed so cruel, so undignified, to have one's heart stop in the middle of a perfectly ordinary breakfast. Not trusting herself to look at the body, she focused on her granddaughter.

'Now, you know that isn't true, Siena. I loved your grandpa. I loved him very much.' And as she said the words, she realised that they were true.

'Not like me,' Siena shot back. 'No one loved him like I did. And you!' Hunter felt like the accused in a murder trial as she pointed at him, still crying and shaking from head to foot. 'You never loved him at all. Did you?'

'Siena, that's enough,' said Seamus sternly, putting a paternal arm around Hunter's frozen shoulders. 'You're upset, sweetheart, all right, and that's fair enough, but we all loved him. Try not to forget that Hunter's just lost his father.'

Hunter drew away from him and stood up tall. At fifteen he was already almost six foot, and even with his tangled hair and cheeks still imprinted with creases from his bed sheets, there was something noble and dignified about him.

'No, she's right, Seamus,' he said quietly. 'I didn't love him. I didn't love him, and he didn't love me.'

There was a silence in the room you could have cut with a knife. No one contradicted him.

'Are you glad he's dead?' asked Siena. She had stopped crying suddenly.

'No,' said Hunter, shaking his head sadly. 'I'm not. Because I know you loved him. And I love you.'

Like a hurricane, she flew into his arms, the tears flowing again like Niagara. Hunter held her like he would never, ever let her go.

'Don't leave me,' Siena mumbled into his chest. The rise and fall of his breathing relaxed and released her. 'I love you so much.'

'I won't leave you, Siena,' he said, stroking her hair. 'I promise.'

Chapter Thirteen

The first few weeks after Duke's death were a miserable blur to Siena. She felt his absence everywhere. At home on the estate daily life continued, but everything seemed muted, muffled somehow. It was as if the fine tuning of her life had been tampered with and the pictures had gone from colour to black and white, while the soundtrack had turned into white noise, a meaningless, lifeless babble all around her.

Worse still, there was no escape for her at school or in the outside world. Duke McMahon's death had become a huge story around the globe. Every gossip rag in America was running conspiracy theories about what had *really* happened that morning, and Siena could not avoid the relentless images of her grandfather's face that seemed to pour out of every screen and every billboard. She became almost indifferent to the paparazzi, leaping out from behind bushes or ambushing her as she came off the school bus each day, eager for pictures of her grief-stricken face. They loved Siena because she gave them the goods every single day. She was a stunningly photogenic little girl, the spitting image of Duke, and she wore her emotions on her face, unhindered by any adult sense of restraint or reserve. Pictures of poor little Siena, her cheeks a river of tears, were shifting magazines even more effectively than Princess Diana.

Within hours of her discovery in the kitchen, the estate was besieged by the world's press. Hordes of reporters and TV crews gathered outside the gates waiting for a statement, and frantically snapping at the ambulances and LAPD squad cars that forced their way through the crush throughout the morning. Meanwhile, the deafening buzz of helicopter blades grew more and more insistent overhead, circling ever lower over the estate in the hope of a shot of Duke on a stretcher. Dead or alive, the picture would be worth millions.

All the staff, as well as the family, had been told by Pete to stay inside and keep the curtains closed at all times. Various police and other official-looking people had cordoned off the kitchen with bright yellow tape, which Siena thought was odd. It wasn't as if Grandpa had been murdered or anything.

Her parents and grandmother flitted backwards and forwards among these strangers, nodding and whispering. Laurie had retreated to her bedroom in silent shock. They all looked very sombre and serious, but none of them, it seemed to Siena, looked really sad. None of them felt as she did.

She and Hunter, meanwhile, had spent most of the day holed up in their old nursery, now a sort of games room littered with bean bags, cassette tapes and various wires and joysticks connected to Hunter's beloved Atari. There didn't seem much to say, so they mostly sat in silence, eventually deciding to play an extended tournament of Bike Racer 2 to take their minds off what had happened and shut out all the craziness downstairs.

At five o'clock, they had both defied instructions and gone to the window to watch Pete walk down to the gates, flanked by a still-tearful Seamus and a suitably serious-looking David Rowe to confirm to the waiting world what everybody already knew: that Duke McMahon had died of a massive heart attack at approximately 7.15 that morning. That an announcement about funeral arrangements and a memorial service would be made in the coming days. And that the family asked for privacy at this sad and difficult time.

'Anna Vega, *LA Times!*' shouted a brassy-looking blonde in a leopard-print miniskirt at the front of the throng. 'Pete, can you tell us where Caroline is right now? Was she there when it happened?'

It had not escaped the hacks' notice that Caroline's car did not appear to be in its usual spot in front of the house, and that she herself – usually such a glutton for publicity no matter how morbid the circumstances – had not been seen or heard from all day.

'Mr McMahon has no further comment at this time,' said David Rowe firmly.

'Pete! Pete!' screamed a hundred voices as the trio turned to walk back through the gates.

'Pete, Mike O'Mahoney at *The Herald*.' A vastly fat, balding man with a painful Brooklyn accent bellowed through the racket. 'How's your mother taking it? Is she concerned about the will at all?'

Before David could open his mouth, Seamus had launched himself at his fellow New Yorker, knocking him off his feet to the delight of the swarms of photographers who'd been waiting for a half-decent shot all day.

'You bastard!' he roared. 'You disrespectful fuckin' bastard. Is that all you vultures care about, the mother-fucking will? He's not even cold, for God's sake.'

The reporter scrambled to his feet, mumbling something about assault and witnesses as he brushed the dirt from his ample backside in a failed attempt to regain some dignity after being floored by a seventy-eight-year-old.

Pete's mouth twitched, an imperceptible hint of a smile dying on his lips. 'My mother, as I'm sure you can imagine, is shocked and saddened by my father's sudden and unexpected death,' he said calmly. 'But I'm sure she appreciates your concern, Mr O'Mahoney.'

The crowd tittered.

'As for my father's will,' Pete continued, 'I understand that it's a matter of legitimate interest.' The fat reporter shrank back nervously behind his fellows as Seamus glared at him murderously. 'Let's just say that my mother and I are not expecting any surprises.'

'What about Caroline and Hunter?' shouted a name-less voice. 'Any surprises for them, do you think?'

Pete paused for a moment. Not by a flicker did he betray the slightest emotion to the waiting press. 'I think we all have a funeral to prepare for. Right now my focus is on that and on supporting my mother and the rest of my family,' he said.

'All right, folks, that's it for today,' said David Rowe, ushering Pete and Seamus firmly back through the gates. 'Let's give the family some privacy now.'

With a general groan, the crowd reluctantly started to down tools. Pete and Seamus walked back up the hill together to the sound of notebooks shutting, tape recorders being clicked off and camera equipment being laboriously dismantled behind them.

'Could you believe that guy, asking you about the will?' said Seamus.

The twilight was playing softly on the lawns, bathing the whole estate in an eerily beautiful cloak of silver. Seamus had known Pete his whole life, but sometimes he still felt as if he knew nothing about him at all. He and his father had always been like chalk and cheese, never got along really, even when Pete was tiny. Seamus had loved Duke so much and understood him so well, but walking along the familiar paths of his house with Pete in the evening light, he almost felt like a stranger. He was a cold fish, young Petey McMahon.

'I don't know,' said Pete, his features impassive. 'I guess it's their job, you know? To ask questions.' He picked up a handful of gravel and started throwing pebbles aimlessly into the rhododendrons that lined the path.

'But surely everyone knows what's in the will by now, do they not?' asked Seamus. 'Caroline gets a chunk of the cash, Minnie gets the house, and you, Laurie and Hunter split the trust three ways. As I remember, that all got leaked to those vultures years ago, right after Hunter was born.'

Pete gave a non-committal grunt that could have been assent, and dropped the rest of the gravel on the ground as he approached the front steps. He wiped his dirty hand on his trousers before offering it to Seamus. 'Goodnight,' he said, 'and thank you for today. I know it must have been very hard for you.'

Christ, he was a stiff, thought Seamus. Did it matter to him at all that his dad was laid out on a slab in the West Hollywood morgue? 'Hard for all of us,' he said, and turned back down the path towards his car, and his own life.

For the first time in almost seventy years, it was a life without Duke.

'Darling, just pick up the phone,' said Charlie. 'Get yourself over there, for Hunter's sake if not your own.'

'I can't. I just can't.'

Caroline sat rigid on the sofa in his Century City penthouse. She and Charlie had not got out of bed until 3.30 in the afternoon, after a marathon sex session that had left both of them happily exhausted. She'd told Duke she was doing a twenty-four-hour detox at the Ocean Spa, so he wouldn't be expecting her back until the evening. Ravenous after her morning's exertions, she had just got the eggs out of the fridge when she flicked on the TV in Charlie's chrome-filled bachelor's kitchen. When she saw the news, she almost had a heart attack herself.

Now huddled in the living room, wearing Charlie's fisherman's sweater and sipping the hot sweet tea he'd made her, she hadn't taken her eyes from the screen in over an hour, even though the ABC7 news team were just replaying the same report over and over again. Duke McMahon found dead at breakfast, apparently having suffered a massive heart attack. LAPD were on the scene, but the death was not being treated as suspicious. Duke's wife of over forty years, Minnie, was being comforted by relatives at the McMahon estate. The whereabouts of

Caroline Berkeley, his long-term partner and mother of his fifteen-year-old son, remained a mystery. Then they cut to a well-worn series of clips from Duke's cinematic career, interspersed with more recent footage of him with Caroline arriving at various galas and premieres.

'Wow, old Duke was a big fan of tight pants back then wasn't he?' joked Charlie as a famous still of the young Duke dressed as an outlaw cowboy throwing a lasso popped up on the screen in front of them.

'Oh God, Charlie, don't,' said Caroline, who was wringing her hands nervously as she watched. 'What am I going to do?' She looked at him imploringly.

Charlie sat down beside her and put his strong hands on her shoulders, forcing her to tear her gaze away from the news and face him.

'Caroline, you're going to go home. You have to. People are already wondering where you are, why you haven't rushed straight back. And you know Hunter must be out of his mind with worry.'

'I doubt it,' she replied bitterly, picking at the tassels on the red cashmere throw draped over Charlie's sofa. 'What if he knew something, Charlie? What if he found out about us, and that's what gave him the heart attack? And now the police know, and they're going to want to talk to me. Oh God.' Her voice was rising in panic. 'I can't cope. I mean, he was so fit, he really was.'

'Honey,' said Charlie reasonably, 'the guy was eighty years old. He had a heart attack, baby, it happens. It was nothing to do with you, and nobody's going to think it was. Believe me.'

'Then why are the police there?' asked Caroline, sipping feebly at her tea. 'I mean, what if he *did* know something?'

'He didn't know anything,' said Charlie firmly. 'And even if he did, your having an affair is not a crime, is it? I know the LAPD are a lazy bunch of assholes, but I still think they have better things to do with their time than running around arresting every movie star's wife who

146

has a bit on the side. Just imagine how full the LA jails would be if they did.'

'I'm not his wife,' said Caroline irrationally.

Charlie smiled. His sense of calm was beginning, slowly, to thaw her panic.

'You really think I should go back?'

'I don't think it,' he replied, taking the mug from her hands and placing it on the coffee table beside them, 'I know it. Go home, Caroline. Go comfort your son.'

'But what will I tell people?' she asked him, her voice still quavering. 'Where should I say I've been?'

'God, I don't know,' said Charlie impatiently. 'Tell them you went for a drive up to Santa Barbara. You sat on the beach all day, so you didn't hear the news. I don't know. Tell them whatever you like.'

Caroline nodded uncertainly. She looked so small and vulnerable wrapped up in his huge sweater, her hands lost inside the cavernous sleeves, with her hair still wild and dishevelled from bed. He felt a jolt of longing surge through his body, but suppressed it firmly. This was no time to start fooling around.

For all his reassurances to Caroline, Charlie knew full well that things were about to get complicated. There was a lot of money at stake, and without Duke to protect her, his wife and children would do everything in their power to stop her getting her hands on any of it. Even if her legal rights were watertight, they could still make her life hell once she went home. Pulling her gently to her feet, he wrapped his arms around her.

'You realise that we'll have to be very careful, certainly until after the funeral and the reading of the will.'

Caroline looked up at him aghast.

'I can still see you?' she asked, clasping her hands round his neck. She needed him, now more than ever, and the thought of the next two weeks without him was almost unbearable.

'Not yet. Not until Duke's estate is settled once and for all and that money's in your account.'

She gave him a petulant pout that would have been worthy of Siena.

'Now, come on,' said Charlie. 'You've waited sixteen years for this moment, Caroline. You gave that old bastard the best years of your life.'

'He wasn't always a bastard, you know.' Caroline was surprised to hear her own voice close to breaking.

'You've earned that money, every penny of it,' continued Charlie vehemently, his blond hair falling forward in an unruly mop as he spoke. God, he was beautiful. 'Letting that disgusting . . .' He checked himself. 'Letting Duke have whatever he wanted, taking him into your life, your bed, giving him a son.'

'He never wanted a son,' said Caroline.

Charlie ran his hand through his hair, exasperated. She just didn't get it.

'All I'm saying is, don't go taking any silly risks now, all right? You and Hunter need that money. There'll be plenty of time for us later.'

He put his hand against her cheek, slowly tracing one warm, pudgy finger down until it reached her mouth and rested on the plump softness of her lips. They gazed at one another for a moment, each longing to take comfort in the other, before finally releasing themselves to a lingering goodbye kiss.

He smelt so delicious, a heady mix of Givenchy aftershave, sex and sweat that left Caroline reeling with desire for him. Even now, with poor old Duke lying dead and who knew what battles awaiting her when she got back home, she felt that familiar, insistent pounding between her legs. But she knew he was right. She had to go.

'You'll be OK?' he asked, as she finally removed his sweater and pulled on her own to leave.

'Don't worry about me,' said Caroline. 'I'll be absolutely fine.'

Chapter Fourteen

It was about three weeks after Duke's funeral and Pete had summoned Siena to come and see him in his study.

Pacing up and down the starkly functional little room, the sweat trickling down between his shoulder blades under his Brooks Brothers shirt, he felt absurdly jittery. He had barely spoken to his daughter since Duke's death and wasn't sure where to begin.

Unlike his mother Minnie, who for the first time he could remember had really opened up to him in her grief, revealing a depth of feeling for his hated father that Pete struggled to understand, Siena seemed to have retreated into her own silent world. At first, he and Claire had tried to talk to her, sitting patiently with her for hours on end, even bringing in a child psychologist to try to break through the little girl's misery. But Siena had angrily shrugged off their every attempt at comfort, and Pete had quickly given up, not because he didn't want to help her, but because he had no idea where to begin. Thanks to his father, Siena had become a virtual stranger to him.

Claire was more persistent. She longed to comfort her daughter and had hoped, perhaps foolishly, that Duke's death might finally open up the way for the three of them to become a proper family at last. Although Caroline and Hunter were still living on the estate – when she had finally deigned to return home the evening after Duke's death, she had been met by a wall of silence from the rest of the family, but there had been no outright battles, thank God – they had moved into a separate wing, and Minnie and Laurie both kept themselves to themselves. Although she felt badly for poor Hunter, Claire was grateful for the time this allowed her with her own husband and child. For the first time ever, the house had started to feel almost like their own home. But these changes seemed only to deepen Siena's depression.

The psychologist, a kindly, professorial-looking man in his mid-sixties who had a soft spot for Claire's fragile beauty, had warned her that Siena was still experiencing profound shock, and she should not expect any miracles overnight.

'You must understand, Mrs McMahon, your daughter has been deeply traumatised, particularly since she was the one who first discovered her grandfather's body,' he had told her, after a two-hour session with Siena up in the old nursery.

'It is not unnatural, even for adults, to experience feelings of guilt and anxiety in these circumstances, and those feelings must be resolved before the true grieving process can begin. Do you understand?'

'I think so,' said Claire, who didn't, but wanted terribly to help Siena.

'Your daughter is only ten,' he continued. 'She feels responsible. She feels to blame. And she may well express those feelings through anger. It is perfectly normal for Siena to feel resentment at losing her grandfather in this way, and she may direct this towards you or your husband, either by withdrawing completely or, as I say, through rage.'

'I see,' said Claire bleakly, sinking down into the same nursery armchair where she used to rock Siena to sleep as a baby. She felt utterly at a loss. 'So what should we do? How can we help?' she asked.

The psychologist gave her an encouraging smile. 'Just be patient. Give her time.'

Patience, unfortunately, had never been one of Pete's strong suits. Nor had he ever had much faith in 'over-priced quacks and their psychobabble'. No, what Siena needed, he had decided, was a complete change. A little discipline might not be a bad thing either. For years,

Duke had filled her head with ridiculous ideas about stardom, and turned her into a fearful prima donna. No doubt he'd been hoping to relive his own glory days through Siena. Well, it wasn't going to happen.

'Ah, Siena, honey, sit down,' said Pete as she appeared, scowling and silent, at the door, her whole body coiled in pent-up belligerence.

Siena had perfected a look of vacant hostility whenever in her father's presence which succinctly conveyed her distaste for him without her having to spell it out in words. It both infuriated Pete and disturbed him. It was almost as if she blamed him, in some bizarre way, for Duke's death.

Slumping down sullenly into the only armchair in the study, she swung her legs insolently over one arm and gave him 'that look'. Shit, thought Pete. Just look at that attitude! If she's like this at ten, God help us when she hits sixteen. But he remembered the psychologist's advice about support and encouragement and forced a smile.

'I think we need to talk,' he said, clearing his throat and wishing he didn't sound so damned formal. 'About the future.'

'No we don't,' mumbled Siena obstinately into the sleeve of her new A-Team jacket.

The jacket had been her last present from Duke, and for the last few days she had refused point blank to take it off, even in the sweltering midday heat of the LA summer. Now George Peppard's grinning face, a fat cigar stuffed in his mouth, stared insolently at Pete from his daughter's lapel as she twirled a long black ringlet of hair around her finger and looked pointedly out of the window, very obviously bored.

Pete battled to keep his temper. 'Please don't answer me back like that, Siena.' He sat down himself on the only other chair in the room, an angular, ugly swivel seat upholstered in vile red-and-grey check which his PA, Tara, had picked up from Office Depot. 'And I'd appreciate it if you'd look at me when I'm talking to you.'

At that moment, Claire knocked softly on the door and, seeing Siena, came in and perched herself awkwardly on the other arm of her chair.

'Hey, sweetie.' She kissed her daughter on top of her head. Siena smiled up at her weakly, her first smile in weeks. A breakthrough, thought Claire. At last!

'Hey, Mommy.'

Pete felt a small involuntary stab of envy as he watched mother and daughter clasp hands. What the fuck was wrong with him? First Duke, now Claire. Was he going to resent everyone his daughter loved, just because she refused to love him?

'Claire.' He took a deep breath and made an effort to relax. 'I was just about to talk to Siena about, er, about our plan.'

'What plan?' asked Siena warily, holding her mother's hand more tightly. The cloud of distrust descended over her face again as quickly as it had just lifted.

Damn it, thought Claire. Why did Pete have to bring this up right now? She was still so wounded and so fragile, couldn't he have left it a few more weeks?

'Your mother and I have spoken to Dr Carlson,' Pete continued, not quite meeting Siena's eye. 'We know you're still upset about Grandpa but' – he coughed nervously – 'we think it would be best, better for you, to have a complete change of scene. Take your mind off things.'

'What kind of a change of scene?' Siena glared at him. 'Anyway, I don't want to take my mind off things.'

'That may be,' said Pete, his voice rising in anger despite himself. 'But I'm afraid you've become rather too used to having what you want, young lady, and that's about to change.'

Siena let go of Claire and sat upright, like a bull about to charge.

'Your Grandpa Duke spoiled you,' continued Pete.

'He did not!' Siena shot back angrily, leaping to her feet and accidentally knocking Claire in the ribs with a flying elbow.

'Sit down!' Pete roared, banging both fists down on the desk, which shook as if it had been hit by an earthquake. He had sworn he wouldn't lose his temper, but sometimes Siena pushed him to the limit. If only she wouldn't keep defending Duke. If only she had known him the way Pete had. He was evil. He didn't deserve her loyalty, or her grief.

Siena and Claire both sat, shaken by the violence of his reaction.

'That sort of behaviour is exactly what I mean.' He straightened his tie and cleared his throat, pushing his sandy hair back from his now sweating brow and trying to compose himself again. 'Now, Siena, we are all upset about what's happened.'

'Yeah, right,' she muttered under her breath.

'But life goes on,' said Pete, ignoring her. 'And in your case, that means school. I called you in here to tell you that your mother and I have decided to send you away to boarding school in England.'

'No!'

Siena spun round and looked imploringly at Claire. 'Mommy, don't let him! I want to stay here, with you and Hunter. Please, I'll be good, I promise. Please, Mom? Don't make me go away.'

Claire looked helplessly from her daughter to her husband. She knew that Pete's mind was already made up. For the past three days, she'd tried everything to sway him from this decision, using every argument she could think of to convince him that Siena would do better at home, but her pleas had all fallen on deaf ears. Pete was insistent that the discipline and stability of boarding school would, as he put it, 'straighten out' their daughter. Her difficult behaviour in the wake of Duke's death had become a painful daily reminder of his own failings as a father and the distance that had grown up

153

between them. Things would be better all round, he told her, once Siena was sent away to school.

It hadn't helped that Minnie had heartily endorsed the plan of an English education for her only grandchild, not because she didn't love her or wanted to get rid of her, but because she had always been brought up to believe that English boarding schools were the best in the world, both socially and academically.

Claire tried to believe that Pete had Siena's best interests at heart as well, although deep down part of her knew that his own resentment and anger towards his daughter, for loving Duke and Hunter as much as she did, had more than a little to do with it. It was true that Siena *had* become very difficult recently. But was the answer really to wash their hands of the problem? Out of sight, out of mind?

'It's no good appealing to your mother,' said Pete harshly, a livid blue vein throbbing visibly through the sweat on his receding brow. 'She and I are in agreement, as is your grandmother, and the decision has been made. You leave for St Xavier's on Tuesday night.'

'Mom?'

Claire could see Siena fighting back the tears, biting her bottom lip and clutching at the cuffs of her beloved jacket in an effort to hold back the floods. She wanted more than anything to reach out and comfort her. But she was terrified of defying Pete, perhaps damaging their relationship beyond repair. He had not just asked for her support, he had demanded it. Fearful and ashamed, she had given in.

'I'm sorry, sweetheart,' she said, holding out her arms. 'It's for the best.'

'Best for *who*?' screamed Siena, turning helplessly from one parent to the other like a cornered animal. 'I hate you. I hate both of you,' she yelled, and ran sobbing from the room.

'Siena!' Claire got up to follow her.

'Leave her,' said Pete. 'She'll get over it.'

'Will she?' asked Claire angrily, her own despair at the situation now perilously near the surface.

'Of course she will,' he said firmly, but he didn't sound convincing, even to himself.

It was years since he had heard his wife raise her voice to anyone. The strength of her emotion now shocked him. Moving over to her, he drew her towards him and felt the resentful stiffening of her limbs as he held her, gently stroking her hair until she began, reluctantly, to relax.

'Do you love me?' he whispered.

Claire caught the urgency in his voice, the desperate loneliness of a guilt-ridden man. Perhaps they had made the right decision after all? Maybe England would be good for Siena? She certainly wasn't happy at home. And perhaps, in the end, Pete needed her even more than her daughter did.

'Of course I do,' she said, and meant it. 'Of course I love you.'

'Good,' he said. 'Because I need you.' He sighed heavily as he held her tight. 'I need you to be behind me on this, Claire. Please?'

'I am behind you,' she said, returning his embrace. 'I'm just worried about her, that's all.'

Hunter didn't think he had ever seen Siena so upset. Her whole tiny frame was so wracked with sobs that she could barely get a sentence out, and it was some minutes before he even understood what she was telling him: that Pete and Claire were going to send her away to school. Away from him.

'I'll never see you again!' she wailed melodramatically through hyperventilating breaths, sitting on her unmade bed with Kermit clasped tightly to her chest between George Peppard and a gold-chain-laden Mr T.

'Of course you will, don't be silly,' said Hunter, who was fighting his own shock at the news.

It was an unspoken rule that he wasn't supposed to

hang out in Siena's room any more. Pete didn't want him anywhere near her, and his mother was equally anxious to avoid precipitating any sort of conflict before his dad's will had been settled. But the two children regularly made illicit visits to each other's separate prisons to comfort one another when things got rough.

Life at home had been pretty terrible for Hunter since his dad died. First of all, he felt guilty that he didn't feel more affected by Duke's death. It was as if someone had switched off his emotions at the mains, while Siena's grief poured out uncontrollably like water through a shattered dam, highlighting his own apparent heartless-ness.

On top of that, the whole household was acting as if he and his mom didn't exist. If it were possible, his mom was spending even more time away from home than usual, leaving him to cope with Minnie's icy disregard and Pete's aggressive rejection on his own. Claire was too caught up in her own worries over Siena to come to his aid. Even Max had stopped coming over to hang out with him since the atmosphere on the estate had become so tense.

Now, with Siena leaving, Hunter wondered how the hell he was going to get through the days. She was the only person in the world he really loved and now she was being taken away from him.

'There'll be vacations, lots of them, and you can come back home then,' he said, trying to keep his voice bright. 'Besides, now that, you know . . .' He looked at his shoes awkwardly. 'Now that Dad's gone, my mom was talking about spending more time in England anyway. We might be going to visit my Uncle William, she said, so maybe I could come see you at your school as well?'

He sat down on the bed and put his arms around her. Mel Gibson's cheesy grin surrounded him, his famous crinkled blue eyes staring down at him from all four walls, where the peeling, faded posters still jostled with one another for space. 'You just wait. We'll see each other all the time, you'll see. You won't get rid of me that easily.'

'We won't,' Siena sniffled, unwilling to be mollified. 'And I'll never see Max again either.'

'Oh, I see.' Hunter raised his eyebrow at her teasingly. 'It's Max you're really worried about, not me. We've developed a little bit of a soft spot for old Maxy recently, haven't we?'

'Baloney!' Siena pushed him away, unable fully to suppress a sneaking smile. She tried her best to sound dignified. 'I'm just saying, when they send me to England I won't see him again either. But I'm *way* more upset about you. I hate Daddy so much.' She sniffed. 'You were so lucky. I wish I'd had Grandpa Duke for my dad.'

Hunter looked at her knowingly. Siena knew full well that Duke had been less than a perfect father to him.

'Oh, Hunter, what are we going to do?' The tears were back with a vengeance. 'I'm just going to miss you so much.'

'Hey there, come on now.' He passed her a tissue from the pink box Claire had placed on her bedside table, and she blew her nose with a ten-year-old's unselfconscious, noisy abandon. 'It'll be OK. I'm gonna miss you too, you know? Things sure won't be the same round here without you.'

Siena flung her arms around him so tightly he felt he might choke. The age gap between the two of them seemed bigger now than it had ever been. Siena thought of him as almost an adult, and his burgeoning physical 'manliness' – the more pronounced muscles in his arms and chest, the rough, emergent stubble on his cheeks, the smell of deodorant mingling with the sweat and warmth of his adolescent body – made him feel less like her brother and more like the uncle that he was. All the girls at her elementary school were wildly in love with him from afar, but these days he seemed so very *much* older than her and her friends, almost like a creature from another world. Unlike Max, who was going through an unfortunate spotty phase and was still a thorn in her side at times, Hunter seemed only to get more and more beautiful as a teenager. Siena felt immensely proud of him, and was fiercely jealous of his love and attention.

'You have to write to me.' She looked up at him, her face pressed against the faded grey of his T-shirt so closely that she could hear the comforting pounding of his heart. 'Every day.'

'I promise,' said Hunter.

Looking around the familiar little bedroom, he felt suddenly, unaccountably anxious. He seemed to be promising Siena an awful lot these days. Not for the first time, he wondered whether he would actually be able to deliver on this one.

Chapter Fifteen

Charlie Murray looked at his watch. Ten-thirty. They'd be starting in ten minutes. Hell, why did he have to be there?

Outside his fourth-floor window, the hustle and bustle of Beverly Hills life continued on the streets below him, and he glanced down absently. Bored, overblown housewives, their once natural beauty long since lost beneath layers of surgery and ghoulish make-up, flitted from store to store with their spookily frozen faces and permanent expressions of surprise.

Maybe they were surprised to wake up one morning and realise they looked like a freakin' experiment?

Charlie couldn't help but compare the women to Caroline, so self-assured in her sexiness, so beautiful still, at least in his eyes. Who cared whether she had a few crow's feet or her breasts didn't explode out of her T-shirt like water balloons? No surgeon could give a woman what Caroline had.

He picked up a bright purple executive stress ball from the desk and gave it a desultory squeeze. Fucking useless.

She was outside right now in Carter & Rowe's conference room, looking suitably demure and grief stricken in a chocolate-brown Dolce and Gabbana suit, along with the rest of the McMahon clan. He'd seen her arrive earlier before making a bolt for the temporary safety of his office. Even here, though, images of her lying naked and lustful, spreadeagled on his desk, lingered like old smoke all around him, and he found it impossible to concentrate.

They'd all arrived for the reading of Duke's will – Caro, Minnie, Pete and Laurie. The atmosphere in the building oscillated between tense and electric, with press gathered outside on the street, all chomping at the bit to find out how the McMahon fortune was to be divided between the old man's wife, mistress and children. The official line was that the will had been settled more than a decade earlier, and there would be no surprises. But a long series of delays, combined with a couple of deliberately cryptic leaked comments from Pete's office, had whetted people's appetite for scandal. A rumour was flying around about a last-minute letter of wishes. Something was up.

Charlie felt it too. He was scared for Caroline and told her so in one of only two furtive phone calls they'd made to each other since Duke's death.

'I just feel uneasy, like Pete's up to something,' he'd told her. 'Watch your back, honey, OK? That's all I'm saying.'

'Honestly, Charlie, you worry too much.' She laughed. 'Everything's going to be fine. You'd have heard something. David would have said something, surely, if there were anything to worry about?'

'He can't,' said Charlie. 'Not until the public reading of the will. It's illegal.'

'Baby, relax,' she reassured him. 'Just think, in two weeks the money will be sitting snugly in my account, and then you and I can finally go public.'

But somehow, he wasn't relaxed. His reverie was broken by Marlene, who stuck her concerned, motherly face around the door.

'Everyone's here,' she told him. 'David wants you in conference room two pronto.'

Charlie groaned. It was perfectly normal for him to attend important client meetings with David, but he wished he could have been spared this one. He knew his boss could have fired him over the Caroline affair, and was grateful that he hadn't, but he still felt the weight of David's disapproval and disappointment whenever they were alone together. That would have made him uncomfortable enough, but now he had to sit through a meeting in front of the whole McMahon clan, and Caroline, whom he hadn't seen for almost three weeks. Was this David's idea of a suitable punishment?

'Marlene, can't you tell him I'm sick?'

'Oh, now, come along,' she chided him, 'you'll be fine. And I'm sure Miss Berkeley will be happy to see you,' she added with a knowing smile.

'Ah, Charlie, sit down,' said David Rowe, unsmiling, when he walked into the conference room a few minutes later. 'I think we're ready to begin.'

The one remaining chair was between his boss and Caroline. Talk about the hot seat. Charlie slipped himself quietly into it, briefly acknowledging Caroline and nodding formally to the three black-clad figures on the opposite side of the table.

Pete, whom he'd met once or twice up at the house with David and always found utterly charmless, looked older than he remembered and in need of a good night's sleep. With his spreading paunch, pallid complexion and receding hair he looked like every middle management heart attack waiting to happen, and absolutely nothing like his father. Laurie, the fat sister, appeared to be on the verge of tears. And on David's left, Minnie McMahon sat as regally elegant as ever in a severely cut black jacket and pillbox hat. Her face was somewhat drawn, but unlike her daughter she appeared completely composed, hands folded together on the table in front of her, ready for business. He didn't dare sneak so much as a glance at Caroline.

'What I am about to read out to you all,' began David, adjusting his reading glasses slightly as he fingered the sheaf of papers in front of him, 'is the last will and testament of Patrick Connor McMahon, otherwise known as "Duke" McMahon, of Hancock Park, Los Angeles.'

'No it isn't,' said Minnie.

Laurie looked up, bewildered. Caroline, forgetting

herself, turned to Charlie with a look of pure terror. Pete just smiled.

'I beg your pardon, Mrs McMahon?' said a flustered-looking David.

Minnie carefully removed a slim white envelope from her capacious, worn leather handbag and placed it on the table, smoothing it down almost lovingly with her long, slender fingers.

'I think, after thirty years of acquaintance, David, you might call me Minnie,' she said, allowing herself a small smile.

Caroline squirmed. 'Thirty years of acquaintance' indeed. Who did she think she was, the Duchess of bloody Devonshire?

'I'm sorry, er, Minnie,' said David. 'I don't think I quite understand.'

'Nor do I, Mother. What's going on?' asked Laurie.

Pete opened his mouth to speak but Minnie put her hand on his arm to stop him. She'd waited sixteen long years for this moment, and no one was going to steal her thunder.

'Let me explain.' She smiled graciously around the table, lingering for a moment on Charlie, who was beginning to fear that his heartbeat might be audible. 'The night before Duke died he came to see me. He told me that he had decided to make one or two changes to his previous will.'

The colour drained from Caroline's face as Minnie removed the document from its envelope.

'You see, he had recently come into possession of some information – some rather hurtful and shocking information' – she looked directly at Charlie – 'as I believe you are already aware, Mr Rowe.'

David blushed scarlet. He had no idea that Duke had let his wife, of all people, in on their little secret.

'Mrs McMahon. Minnie,' he said, 'I don't know if this is really the time or the place to talk about this matter.' He laughed weakly. 'I'm afraid that, whatever Duke's intentions might have been, the fact is he did *not* make any formal changes to his will before his death. If he had done, I would have been asked to witness those changes. You see, without an impartial witness – someone who is not a beneficiary – well, any new document would not be legally enforceable. Duke knew that.'

'He did indeed,' said Minnie, passing the document to David. 'As you can see, it was impartially witnessed.'

'By whom?' blurted out Caroline, suddenly indignant.

'By me,' came a voice from the back of the room.

Seamus, Duke's old pal and confidant, must have been standing there all along, leaning against the wall in his slightly crumpled suit. He looked reproachfully at Caroline, and she felt her stomach lurch with guilt, as if someone had just cut the elevator cable. Of all the people in the room, she realised, Seamus may have been the only one who had loved Duke without any of the complications, reservations and self-interest that the rest of them had.

'He loved you, you know,' he said to her, and she was shocked to find her eyes stinging with tears. Charlie gave her hand a surreptitious squeeze under the table.

'Not really, Seamus,' she said sadly. 'Not always.'

'I think you'll find it holds water,' announced Minnie briskly, niftily steering the conversation back to the subject of the will. She was in no mood for Caroline's crocodile tears, or Seamus's sentimentality, for that matter.

'She's right,' piped up Pete, leaning back in his chair and cracking his knuckles gleefully. 'It's valid. So, David, do you want to read it out to us? Or shall I?'

David glanced at Duke's elder son, whose face displayed an ecstasy of spite like some crazed sadist about to begin torturing his victim. He could quite see why the old man had never liked him. 'Very well,' he said. 'As this does appear to be a legitimate revised will, I am obliged to proceed.'

He adjusted his spectacles for a third time, and began

reading directly from the paper in front of him. Charlie could make out only two paragraphs of print, followed by a long series of signatures and endorsements. It was going to be brutally brief.

'I, Duke McMahon, wish to make the following changes to my last will and testament. With the exception of the changes and provisions outlined below, my previous will (dated 12 June 1976) shall remain effective in its entirety.

'I hereby revoke any and all gifts, endowments or benefits of any kind previously made to Miss Caroline Berkeley.'

Caroline sat motionless, a brown Dolce and Gabbana mannequin, her face impassive. So he *did* know about her and Charlie, the wily old sod. How could she have expected anything less of Duke? She could feel Pete's and Minnie's eyes boring into her, sensed them slavering like wolves for a reaction, but she wasn't going to give them the satisfaction.

'All payments from the Innovation Trust to Miss Berkeley will also cease in the event of my death. All benefits, whether in cash, stock or property, formerly bequeathed to Miss Berkeley are to revert to the Innovation Trust, for the sole and exclusive benefit of my three children, Peter, Laurie and Hunter McMahon.'

Thank God, thought Caroline. If Hunter was still inheriting, she'd be OK. Relief flooded through her veins so violently she thought she might be sick.

'In addition,' David went on in his deep, oddly soothing baritone, 'I hereby appoint my wife, "Minnie" McMahon, as the sole trustee of all trusts benefiting my children.'

He paused, looking across at Caroline.

'Including my younger son, Hunter.'

'What?' She leapt to her feet, unable to contain herself a second longer. *Minnie* was going to have control of Hunter's trust? That meant she would never see a penny.

Sixteen years of her life she had given to that bastard. Sixteen years and Duke was leaving her penniless.

'That's not possible.' She looked frantically from David to Charlie for support. 'That's not legal, it can't be.' She waved her arm wildly towards Minnie. 'She despises my son. How can she possibly take legal responsibility for his interests? She'll beggar him, for God's sake, she'll beggar us both! How could Duke do this to us?'

'I'm sorry, Miss Berkeley,' replied David quietly, 'but I'm afraid Duke was quite within his rights to bequeath his estate as he saw fit.'

'It's breach of fucking contract!' Caroline shouted. 'I want to challenge the will. Charlie.' She turned to her lover, who was sitting with his handsome blond head in his hands. 'I want to fight this.'

'Be my guest,' said Minnie, smiling. Pete and Laurie sat beside her like two smug sentries. Even Seamus had walked over to the McMahons' side of the table, his hands placed protectively on Laurie's shoulders. Caroline was on her own. 'But I think you will discover that since you and my husband never married, and given that your bastard child has been *more* than generously provided for, you haven't got a leg to stand on.'

Minnie got to her feet. 'Still, I wouldn't worry too much, if I were you. I'm sure your little toy boy here will be happy to support you, although perhaps not in *quite* the manner you've grown accustomed to.'

Charlie stood up and put his arm around Caroline. God knew he hadn't bargained on playing happy families with her and her son, but he was damned if he was going to let Duke McMahon's frigid crone of a wife dismiss him like that. He was nobody's toy boy.

'Well, ma'am,' – he grinned at Minnie – 'I'll sure do my best.'

'We want you and your son out of the house by tomorrow,' snarled Pete, gathering up his briefcase and jacket.

'Don't be ridiculous,' snapped Caroline. Even from

across the table she could smell his fetid breath, like putrefied hatred. 'That house is Hunter's home. He and Siena are like brother and sister, Pete, you know that. You can't just banish him like some sort of outlaw.'

'Just watch me,' said Pete.

'For God's sake, think of the children.' She could hear the desperation in her own voice. 'However much you want to hurt me, you can't seriously want to split up the kids. Think about Siena.'

'Don't you dare talk to me about my daughter,' Pete spat at her. 'Think of the children? When did you ever think about the children? When did you ever think about anyone except yourself? The only reason you gave birth to that little shit in the first place was to get your hands on Dad's money, you fucking whore. Well, guess what? It backfired. I want my daughter as far away from you and that bastard son of yours as possible.'

'Hey, enough,' said Charlie, squaring up to Pete, his powerful football player's shoulders clearly apparent beneath his immaculately cut suit.

While the two men faced each other down, Minnie walked over towards Caroline. Pulling on her black gloves, she looked her former rival in the eye. Sixteen years of enmity and bitterness hung in the air between them. But they had both loved Duke once. For just a moment, the two women stared at one another in silence. Then Minnie broke the spell.

'It killed him, you know. The shock. You two.' She gestured towards Charlie. 'That's what killed him.'

And turning on her heel, she strode out of the room.

PART TWO

PART TWO

Chapter Sixteen

Yorkshire, England, July 1998

'God, he really is gorgeous, isn't he?'

Janey passed the magazine back to Siena, who lay scowling on the library sofa in Janey's parents' house, her long legs draped nonchalantly over Patrick's. Patrick was Janey's older brother and Siena's boyfriend of the moment.

'Hmm,' replied Siena, doing her best to sound bored as she looked at Hunter's face smiling at her from the front of the June issue of *Hello!* All black hair and smouldering blue eyes. 'I guess so.'

Janey Cash was a great schoolfriend of Siena's and had invited her to spend two weeks at her family's tumble-down Georgian rectory in Yorkshire. The girls had sat their last A-level together ten days ago, and waved a joyous goodbye to St Xavier's. They were still recovering from the epic hangover that had followed a drunken week of post-exam celebrations, and Siena decided that two weeks in the peace of the Yorkshire countryside, watching TV and filling up on Mrs Cash's delicious sticky toffee pudding, were exactly what the doctor ordered. Of course, the fact that Patrick would also be there was just an added bonus.

She put the magazine down on the floor, making sure that Hunter's face was floor side down. She was sick of seeing his picture everywhere, sick of all her friends telling her how gorgeous he was. Ever since he'd landed the role of Mike Palumbo in *Counsellor*, the hottest new TV series since *Dynasty*, it was as if she couldn't escape him. The fact that she hadn't laid eyes on him, or even spoken to him, since she was ten years old didn't stop people from asking her endless questions, raking over her memories with razor blades.

What made it worse was that Hunter seemed to be living *her* dream, fulfilling *her* destiny. For as long as she could remember, Siena had wanted to be an actress. Although she knew you weren't supposed to say it, what she longed for above everything else was to be famous. Not just Duke McMahon's granddaughter or Pete McMahon's little girl – she wanted serious, fuck-off fame, the real deal, in her own right. She wanted the whole world to love her, to have people scream out her name. To be adored, just like Duke had been adored. That was her dream. *She* was the one who ought to have had her face splashed all over the magazines, not Hunter. She knew she shouldn't begrudge him his success, not after everything he'd been through. But it was so hard, being forced to watch him make a name for himself in Hollywood while she was stuck in England, being pushed into seven more long, grindingly dull years of medicine at Oxford. Just because her mom had given up medical school, and now both her parents wanted to live vicariously through her. She didn't *want* to be a goddam doctor!

Patrick picked up one of her bare feet in his hands and gave it a comforting squeeze. She smiled at him. He really was very sweet, and he seemed instinctively to understand that she found it painful to talk about Hunter, or any of her family for that matter. If only everyone else were so tactful.

After Duke died, her father had wasted no time in packing her off to boarding school. By the time she came home for her first long vacation at Christmas, Caroline and Hunter had moved out of Hancock Park into a modest apartment somewhere in Los Feliz. Siena had begged Pete to let her see him, but he wouldn't even give her an address so she could write. She'd pleaded to everyone – Minnie, Aunt Laurie, her mother – but out of either malice or fear, none of them would help her.

Once, when she was back in LA for the summer, she could have sworn she'd seen an envelope with Hunter's handwriting on it at her dad's office. He had the very rounded letters of a young girl, and finished his 'i's with cartoonish circles rather than dots. You could almost smell the effort that went into his spelling and punctuation, poor lamb. But Tara, Pete's vile, anorexic bitch of a PA, had snatched the letter up before Siena could take a closer look and locked it away in her 'confidential' file.

When she'd asked Pete about it later, he'd told her that he'd kept the letter from her for her own protection.

'I'm not letting you read it because it would hurt you to read it,' he said. 'Hunter has decided that he no longer wants to have any contact with our family. He's almost sixteen now, and I think we have to respect his wishes.'

'But he doesn't mean *me*,' Siena insisted. 'He would never say he didn't want to see me any more.'

'I'm sorry, Siena,' said Pete brutally. 'But he would and he has. I think it's best if we don't speak about this again. Hunter has moved on and so must you.'

It was amazing to think that that awful conversation had taken place nearly eight years ago now. And that since then she and Hunter, who had once been so inseparable, had lost each other completely.

'Come on,' said Patrick, extricating himself from Siena's limbs, getting up from the sofa and yawning dramatically. 'I'm bored. Who's up for a spot of corn jumping?'

'What on earth is corn jumping?' asked Siena, admiring the lean, defined muscles on his stomach as he stretched his arms above his head. For a rugby player, Patrick had a slim build, but she loved the smooth lines of his body and the way her own body seemed to bristle with excitement and arousal whenever he came near her.

She was not in love with him – Siena hadn't the slightest intention of falling in love with anybody until she was at least thirty, and rich and famous enough to be happy with or without a man – but she had a genuine soft spot for Patrick. As well as being a complete angel, he was far more talented in bed than any of the other boys she'd been with.

'You've never been corn jumping?' asked Janey, taking her friend's hand and pulling her up from her seat.

'Look, we're not all local yokels, you know.' Siena laughed. 'I have no idea what corn jumping is, but something tells me we don't get to see a whole lot of it in Los Angeles.'

'Well, you're missing out, I can assure you,' said Patrick, in his clipped British accent which reminded her so much of Max De Seville.

Not for the first time she wondered what had become of Max, her old rival, and whether he and Hunter were still in touch.

'Come on,' said Patrick. 'Follow me.'

Siena followed Janey and Patrick as they skipped out into the stable yard, giggling and pushing one another like a couple of kids. It must be lovely, she thought wistfully, to have a family like Janey's. Mr and Mrs Cash were both so cool and laid back. They couldn't give a shit whether Janey got into bloody Oxford. Not that she was very likely to anyway. Poor old Janey. Patrick seemed to have the lion's share of brains and looks in the family.

The three of them clambered over the rotting old yard gate, and ran across the paddock towards the three vast grain silos that marked the entrance to the farm. It was a glorious July day, and the sun beat down on the fields, its warmth intensifying the rich agricultural smells of hay and horses and cow shit that had once been so utterly alien to Siena, but now just smelt of 'England'.

She could never live up here, she thought as she stumbled across the bumpy, irregular field. They were hundreds of miles away from the nearest decent blow-dry, let alone restaurant or club. The Coach and Horses in Farndale was about as close as people got to a good time in Yorkshire as far as Siena could make out. But every now and then it did her good to come and stay with Janey, to soak up the clotted-cream richness of the dale, sheltered beneath the barren, bleak expanse of the moor above. The landscape was breathtaking. It made her feel like Cathy, making wild love to Heathcliff, whenever she and Patrick snuck off to the barn or the stables to fool around. It was another world.

'Move your ass, Siena!' Patrick shouted at her in his appalling attempt at an American accent as she jogged to catch up with them. 'In here.'

Janey opened the door to the silo, and the pungent, overwhelming stench of the grain hit Siena in the face like a Mike Tyson punch.

'Omigod, it reeks!' she squealed, clasping her hand over her nose and mouth.

Inside, the building was like a Tardis, as huge as an aircraft hangar with two enormous mounds of corn, perhaps eighty feet high, shimmering in their own golden dust beneath an industrial latticework of metal beams supporting an immense corrugated-iron roof. On the wall to her left, Siena saw two endlessly long ladders bolted together, providing access to a narrow platform at the top of the larger corn pile.

Patrick looked first at the ladder, then at Siena, and nodded evilly.

'Oh no.' She shook her head, laughing, her thick dark curls spilling luxuriously over her INXS T-shirt, eyes flashing the same cobalt blue as her new 501 jeans. Patrick felt his groin stirring as he looked at her. 'I am *not* going up there. Uh-uh, no way, José, ain't happenin'.'

'You sounded *so* like your grandfather when you said that,' said Janey idly, then immediately regretted it. Siena was even more touchy about the late, great Duke McMahon than she was about her divine Uncle Hunter. For once, though, she seemed to take it in good part.

'Thanks,' she smiled, then, turning to Patrick, 'but I'm still not going up there.'

'Oh, don't be such a wuss.' He pulled her towards him

and pressed his own wide mouth against her tiny Betty Boop lips. She tasted of black cherry lip balm. 'That's what corn jumping is. You climb all the way up there.' He pointed at the precarious-looking platform. 'And then you jump down into the corn.'

'It's *really* fun,' confirmed Janey, who was already at the foot of the ladder, preparing to climb.

'No way, I can't,' persisted Siena.

'Why on earth not?' asked Patrick.

'I have a job for Ailsa Moran next week,' said Siena. 'What if I bruise myself – I mean, what if I cut my face? I'm supposed to have a "sophisticated forties look", OK? They don't want some scar-faced bungee jumper.'

Ailsa Moran was one of the hot, up-and-coming young fashion designers on the London scene this year. Much to Siena's surprise and delight, Moran had hired her to model some of the more retro pieces from her new collection for a shoot in the *Sunday Times* Style magazine, the first real paying modelling assignment she'd got since signing on with a small London agency in the Easter holidays, two months before her A-levels.

'Oh, well, excuse *me*, little miss supermodel,' Patrick teased her, stroking her cheek affectionately.

Siena knew he felt uncomfortable about her modelling, although he tried hard to be supportive. He didn't understand that she saw it as a way to get herself back to Hollywood, a stepping stone towards launching an acting career that didn't involve her father, or trading on her famous name. She had landed herself an agent and got the Moran job completely off her own bat, and she desperately wanted Patrick to be proud of her for that. But instead he seemed to fear that the whole fashion scene, that superficial London crowd, would pull her farther and farther away from him. Perhaps he was right.

'Fine,' he said, kissing her again. 'You just stay here and be a wet blanket. But I'm afraid you'll have to excuse me. Janey and I have some corn to jump.'

They both looked up as, with an almighty screech,

Janey hurled herself from the rafters and landed with a soft thud in the corn below. Siena could hardly see her for dust as she slid down the side of the mound, whooping with adrenalin, her good-natured, ruddy face even more flushed than usual.

'Wow, that was *great!*' she said, scrabbling to her feet and brushing the worst of the prickly corn dust off her yellow-stained jeans. 'Come on, Yasmin bloody Le Bon, don't be so wet. Have a go.'

'Oh, for heaven's sake, all right,' said Siena, shaking her head at her own childishness. She had to admit, it *did* look like fun. 'Pat,' she yelled, racing over to the ladder. 'Hold on, I'm coming up!'

By the time she'd joined him on the little platform, she was already beginning to regret her impulsiveness, and it had nothing to do with her budding modelling career.

'Fucking hell, it's a long way down, isn't it?' she said, biting her lip with nerves.

'To the ground, yes,' said Patrick. 'To the corn, can't be more than twenty or thirty feet, I reckon. You'll be fine.'

'What if I miss it?' wailed Siena, taking another step back from the edge.

Patrick roared with laughter, his gentle, hazel eyes disappearing into creases.

'Darling, even you couldn't miss *that*. It's about the size of fucking Canada.'

Siena didn't look remotely reassured.

'How about we jump together?' He looked her in the eye, inviting her to trust him, and even through her fear she could feel herself melting towards him.

What a sweetheart he was, her little Patricio. A sudden pang of guilt, for the few times she'd been unfaithful to him, stabbed briefly at her heart. She knew it was insecurity which propelled her into other boys' beds, that she was driven by a desperate need to be loved and to have "lifeboats" in case her mother ship – Patrick – should sink. Having lost or been abandoned by everyone she had ever loved, she had learned the hard way never to put all her emotional eggs into one basket, however loyal and lovely that basket might be.

Poor, darling Patrick, he deserved better.

'On three?' she said, reaching for his hand.

'On three.'

'One. Two.'

Siena shut her eyes tight.

'Three!'

With a stomach-splitting whoosh, she felt herself rushing through the air, clinging to the warm, firm grip of Patrick's hand until, what seemed like hours later but could only really have been a second or two, they hit the soft cushion of the corn below.

'We did it!' Siena spluttered euphorically through a mouthful of corn dust. 'That was awesome!' She felt seven years old again, brave, excited and triumphant. Soon she was on her feet, punching the air with her fists and running a victory lap around the corn mound.

Patrick caught his sister's eye and, nodding in Siena's direction, raised his eyebrow at his screeching, circling girlfriend. She seemed to have gone completely barmy. 'American,' he whispered, in explanation.

'Oh yes,' said Janey. 'Very.'

Later that night, after a delicious but enormous meal with Janey's parents, followed by a never-ending game of charades, Siena had sneaked out of the spare bedroom, up the creaky spiral stairs to Patrick's attic room.

Too stuffed with lemon cheesecake to even contemplate sex, she nestled her head against the smooth warmth of his chest and chattered away as he stroked and tickled her bare back.

'Your dad is hysterical,' she said. 'Is he always that competitive?'

'Oh, always,' said Patrick. 'Although charades does rather bring out the worst in him. Normally Ma refuses to play, he's so awful.'

'They're very sweet, though, your parents.' She sighed, wistfully. 'They really seem to love each other, don't they?'

Patrick thought about it for a moment. 'Yes,' he said eventually. 'Yes, I suppose they do. Why? Don't your parents love each other?'

Siena gave a brittle grunt of derision. 'Not so as you'd notice.' She reached up and swept a loose tendril of hair back from her face, snuggling closer in to his body. 'My mom is just totally weak.'

Patrick could hear the bitterness in her voice, and feel her body tensing.

'And my dad . . .'

'I know,' he said gently, 'you don't get on with him.'

'I don't think he cares if I live or die, I really don't,' said Siena blankly.

'Come on now. That's a bit melodramatic, isn't it?'

'I wish it were,' said Siena. 'All he cares about is Oxford and medicine and my goddam reading list. He just wants to be able to go to dinner parties with his Hollywood cronies and their surgically enhanced wives, and say, "My daughter's training to be a doctor, she goes to Oxford, she's been educated with English ladies."'

'What, like Janey, you mean?' he teased her. 'That's considered a selling point?'

'Well, you know what, screw him,' continued Siena, who was on a roll. 'I'm not going. My modelling's going great, although of course Dad doesn't give a shit about *that*. He can shove his reading list up his ass.'

Her voice was rising, and Patrick was worried that his parents might hear them.

'He can shove Oxford up his ass!'

'That might be a bit painful,' he said, trying to diffuse the situation. 'All those dreaming spires look a bit on the sharp side to me.'

Siena didn't smile.

'Sorry. Not funny.'

He sat up in bed and reached over for his Camel

Lights. Lighting up, he took a long drag and offered it to Siena, who shook her head.

'Look,' he said, 'you can't just not go to Oxford. You've got a two-E offer, so it doesn't even matter if you've ploughed your A-levels.'

'Which I won't have,' chipped in Siena arrogantly.

'Which you won't have,' agreed Patrick. 'Modelling,' he frowned. 'It's just such a waste. I mean, is that really what you want to be in life, a jumped-up clothes horse?'

Siena gave him a withering look. 'Don't be fatuous,' she snapped. 'I've told you, I'm going to be an actress, and modelling happens to be a very good way into that. My agent says if I do the Paris shows this year I could meet a whole bunch of casting directors. A lot of actresses break into the business that way.'

'Bollocks,' said Patrick, blowing smoke out of his nose like a rather unthreatening dragon. 'Name one.'

'Cameron fucking Diaz, OK, asshole?' He looked blank. 'The girl in *The Mask*?' Furious, she rolled out of his bed and started pulling on her worn, stripy pyjama bottoms. Why couldn't he be supportive about this? Why was he taking her dad's side? 'Marilyn fucking Monroe, ever heard of her?'

'I don't think Marilyn got her big break at Paris fashion week, do you?'

'Right, smartass,' said Siena, who was really in a foul mood now. 'But she was a model first, then an actress. *Model.*' She adopted a patronising tone, as though explaining the alphabet to a four-year-old. '*Actress.* See? You just don't like me modelling because it makes you insecure, thinking about all those guys out there who are gonna see my picture and lust after me.'

'That's not true,' said Patrick, stung because he knew it was.

'You'd prefer I was cooped up with a bunch of nerdy medical students at Oxford. That'd make you feel *much* better, wouldn't it?'

She spat the words out with such vitriol it scared him. How did they ever get into all this?

'You don't care about me, about what I want,' continued Siena, blinded with rage. 'You don't care if I'm happy.' In her haste, she had done up her buttons wrongly, and her irate, contorted little face looked comically incongruous above her lopsided pyjama top. 'You're as bad as my fucking father. Well, let me tell you something: I *am* going to make it as an actress. And when I do it won't be on the back of my name – my *father's* goddam name. It will be because I've made it on my own. Modelling's just the start.'

'Siena,' said Patrick wearily, 'I am nothing like your father.' Even in those ridiculous pyjamas, screaming at him like a banshee, she still looked so sexy it hurt. 'All I meant was that you shouldn't cut off your nose to spite your face,' he said, in a last-ditch effort to calm her down. 'There's no point in missing out on Oxford just for the sake of annoying your dad. I just . . . Look, I just find it hard to believe that modelling is what you really want to do, that's all.' He patted the mattress beside him. 'Come on, come back to bed.'

'Well, it *is* what I want to do,' she barked defensively. 'For now anyway. Until I can get back to Hollywood, until my acting comes together. And as far as I'm concerned I'm not 'missing out' on anything. I hate Oxford. I hate England. If you knew anything about me at all you'd know I've been desperate to get out of this shitty, grey, raining depressing hellhole for the last seven years. Well, modelling's a way out, something that even my father can't control, and I'm taking it. So if that makes you uncomfortable then tough fucking tits!'

With a final defiant flick of her curls and a foundation-shaking slam of the door, she stomped back down the stairs to her own room.

Oh fuck, that was all she needed. Mr Cash, looking like an older Sherlock Holmes in a dark green dressing gown and reading glasses, emerged from the bathroom just as Siena stepped on to the landing.

'Ah, Siena. Just saying goodnight to Pat, were you?' he asked her with a good-natured, conspiratorial wink.

He was such a lovely man, she thought, and so was his son. She didn't know why she was always such a bitch to him.

'Yes, I was, er . . .' She floundered. 'We were just talking about the future actually.' She gestured upstairs. 'You know, career plans. Moving on.'

Jeremy Cash looked at her thoughtfully. He could quite see why his son was crazy about her, but it was as plain as the nose on his face that a girl like Siena was not about to settle down with Patrick. The lad was headed for heartbreak, and Jeremy felt for him, but even so he couldn't quite bring himself to dislike his daughter's feisty best friend. Bending forward, he gave her a paternal kiss on the cheek.

'Goodnight, my dear,' he said.

'Goodnight, Mr C.' Siena beamed back at him.

'Oh, and Siena?' he called after her as he opened the door to his own room. 'Next time you and Patrick discuss your future, you might want to take a trifle longer buttoning up your pyjamas afterwards.'

Siena glanced down in horror at her top and blushed like an overripe tomato.

'Goodnight, young lady,' said Jeremy.

Chapter Seventeen

'I'm sorry, guys, that was my fault,' said Hunter. 'Can we go again?'

The two cameramen rolled their eyes as they prepared for a fourth take, but neither of them could get really mad. It was so unlike Hunter to forget his lines, and he was such a down-to-earth, decent guy, all the crew liked and respected him. They were shooting the second season of *Counsellor* on the back lot at Universal. Despite the show's unexpected worldwide success, Hunter had failed to become the spoilt 'talent' that most young actors transform into the moment they get their big break. So far, there'd been no demands for a massive pay hike, no celebrity tantrums and no ego overload from the scores of hot-looking women that hung around the studio gates night after night, hoping to catch a glimpse of him. To the best of anyone's knowledge, he hadn't ever laid a groupie, and most of his evenings were spent at home, alone, poring over his script. Hell, he even bought the sound guys chocolate muffins from the Coffee Bean most mornings on his way into work. Hunter was the real deal, and the whole set adored him.

'I don't know what's wrong with me today,' he apologised, running his hand through his blue-black hair in frustration. 'I thought I nailed this scene last night, but my mind keeps going blank.'

'Hey, c'mon, forget about it,' said Lanie Armstrong, his stunning blonde co-star, putting a comforting arm around his waist. Like the rest of the cast, Lanie had a thumping crush on her leading man. 'We all have our off days. Why don't you take five and we'll go again.'

Hunter sank down dejectedly into a white canvas chair, and flipped through the day's script for the umpteenth time. Maybe he'd be able to concentrate if it weren't so damn hot. As Mike Palumbo, hot-shot attorney, he spent most of his day wearing a heavy, dark grey wool suit, and sweltering under the punishing glare of the studio lights. Sometimes he would sweat his way through three white Armani shirts in a single morning's shooting. His only respite were the bedroom scenes with Lanie when, to the delight of teenage girls the world over, he got to wander around in only a revealing pair of Calvin Klein boxer shorts. But that just made him equally hot and bothered with embarrassment.

He tried to concentrate as the familiar lines blurred before his eyes. Man, he wished he didn't find reading and memorising so difficult. Ever since he was a little boy he'd been worse than useless at school work, but it sure wasn't for want of trying. He remembered how Pete used to make fun of him, back when their old man was still alive, looming over him whenever he was trying to revise for a test, constantly telling him what a moron he was.

No, not a moron, a cretin. That was what Pete used to call him, a cretin. Stupid fucking pretentious English word.

In recent weeks, Hunter had been forced to spend a lot of time thinking about his older brother. His inability to concentrate this morning had more than a little to do with Pete's unwelcome reappearance in his life.

If *Counsellor*'s overwhelming success had come as a surprise to its young star, Hunter's meteoric rise to prominence had been like a bullet in the heart for Pete.

Since Duke's heart attack, Pete's own career as a producer had blossomed. As the chief executive of McMahon Pictures Worldwide, he was now considered to be among the most influential deal-makers in Holly-wood. Regularly fêted in the industry press, and a member of *Forbes*'s West Coast rich list, he had finally been able to move out of Duke's long shadow and emerge into the sunlight of his own talent. He might not have had his father's looks, but Pete far outshone the old man when it came to business acumen. With a string of good investments in real estate and technology, as well as three of the four most profitable movies of the nineties to his name, Pete had increased the family fortune almost fivefold in the seven years since Duke had died.

Until recently, he had rarely given Hunter or his mother a second thought. Immediately after the reading of the will, Minnie had banished the pair of them to a decrepit low-rent apartment in Los Feliz, and Pete had been ruthless in severing all contact between Siena and Hunter.

He had lied to his daughter about Hunter's requesting no more contact. In fact, his half-brother had written hundreds of letters, begging to be allowed to see Siena. At first Pete had just ignored them, but when they didn't stop coming he'd been forced to write to Caroline, threatening to invoke some imaginary clause in Duke's trust and rescind Hunter's inheritance altogether if he didn't stop harassing the family. Knowing that losing the money would mean nothing to Hunter in comparison to losing Siena, Caroline had told him that his letters were upsetting Siena, and that the child psychologist had said they were preventing her from moving on and settling into her new life.

Heartbroken, and with enormous reluctance, Hunter had agreed to let her go.

The last Pete had heard of either of them was a couple of years ago, when Hunter turned twenty-one and came into possession of his relatively meagre trust. Under Minnie's well-intentioned but inept stewardship – for all her hatred of Caroline, Minnie was not callous enough to deliberately squander Hunter's wealth – much of the original capital Duke had left the boy had been whittled away; but the remainder had been enough for him to move out of Los Feliz and buy a little beach house in Santa Monica.

Caroline, Pete had heard on the grapevine, had long since returned to England, leaving her son to fend for himself. No doubt she was worming her way into somebody else's family and fortune back in Blighty – *plus ça change* – but Pete didn't care. As far as he was concerned, Caroline and Hunter had been erased from his life, and that was all that mattered.

Until *Counsellor*.

Pete could still remember the sickening lurch he'd felt in his stomach the first time he saw his brother's impossibly handsome face on the screen. As a grown man, Hunter looked painfully like Duke, except that in his dark business suit, with his proud, solid jaw and steady blue-eyed gaze, he radiated an integrity that the old man, for all his charisma, had never had.

Before Pete could catch his breath, it seemed, the world's press were beating a path to Hunter's door, all clamouring for pictures and interviews with television's new wunderkind. If he had to read one more mother-fucking journalist going on about how 'sexy, but refreshingly down to earth' his brother was, he was going to fucking implode.

As a TV actor, and of the low-brow variety at that, there was in fact no reason why Hunter's path should have crossed his in any way. Pete moved in a very different league, and could certainly have afforded to be gracious about the kid's fifteen minutes of fame. But just seeing his brother again, looking so happy and handsome and grateful, had reignited all his latent resentment and hatred.

He wanted that boy to suffer, like he and Laurie and Minnie had suffered. And he was determined to do everything in his power to derail his newfound success.

Leaving the script under his chair, Hunter got up and wandered over to the water cooler. Filling a plastic cup with ice-cold water, he gulped it down, hoping to clear his addled brain, but the liquid was so freezing it made his teeth ache. He put his hand to his jaw and winced.

'You OK?'

Hugh Orchard, the show's chief producer, had wandered up behind him. Dressed in his trademark khaki knee-length pants and blue Harvard Business School sweatshirt, his newly wetted hair immaculately parted at the side, Hugh looked more like a Connecticut investment banker on a family picnic than the obsessive, workaholic and famously homosexual king of network television that he actually was.

Orchard had an awesome drive – at fifty-six his ambition was still white hot – and most of the great and the good of the TV world were more than a little afraid of him. Hunter had always liked him, though. As long as you kept your head down and worked hard, he had always found him to be a fair and reasonable boss.

'Oh yeah, I'm fine,' he said, flashing a disarmingly white-toothed smile at Hugh. 'Water's too cold, that's all.'

Hugh suppressed a giant wave of arousal and tried manfully to tear his eyes away from that beautiful body and look Hunter in the eye. He had been with his partner Ryan for almost twelve years now, but it wasn't a crime to indulge in a little wishful thinking every now and then. Hunter tested his professionalism to the limits.

'I saw you were having some trouble with the scene back there,' he said, reaching for a cup himself. 'Anything on your mind?'

Hunter blushed. He looked so adorable, Hugh could have eaten him alive.

'Not really.' He shook his head and looked down at his well-polished lawyer's shoes. 'Well, you know, just this situation with my brother.'

'I thought I told you not to worry about that, Hunter,' said Hugh, flicking the plastic lever on the water barrel and filling his glass. 'I'm not about to give in to blackmail from Pete McMahon, and neither is NBC. He can go jump in a lake as far as I'm concerned. *I* pick the cast of my shows. *I* decide who stays and who goes. Got it?'

Hunter nodded miserably. It was an open secret on the set that Pete had threatened to withdraw McMahon Pictures' funding for two of Hugh Orchard's big-budget miniseries, both of which were due to debut on NBC the following spring, unless Hunter was replaced as *Counsellor*'s male lead. He was very grateful to Hugh for sticking by him, but also embarrassed to have been the cause of so much aggravation in the first place. Thanks to Pete, he was now quite possibly going to be responsible for hundreds of thousands of dollars' worth of lost revenue and production delays.

'I'm just so sorry for all of this, you know?' he mumbled, nervously crushing his empty cup in his hand and not quite meeting his boss's eye. 'You must be sick to death of me and my dysfunctional family.'

Hugh laughed, and clapped both hands on to Hunter's shoulders. 'Dysfunctional? The McMahons? Now that's what I call an understatement. Are you kidding me? You guys are fucking psychotic!'

Hunter's perfect features fractured into a grin. 'Yeah, well,' he conceded, eyes still glued to the ground, 'I guess we have our moments.'

'I'm serious, man,' continued Hugh, who suddenly looked it. 'Look at me.' Reluctantly, Hunter looked up. 'Don't let this shit with Peter throw you. He's not normal, OK? He's psycho, totally whacked. You just get out there, learn those lines, and do what you do best, all right?'

'Yes, sir!' said Hunter, standing to attention and giving Hugh a mock salute before heading back towards the set. Already he felt his spirits lifting a little. Hugh was right. He owed it to everyone to get past this thing with Pete, and do the job he was paid to do.

'Don't you "yes, sir" me, Hunter McMahon!' Hugh yelled after him, unable to resist flirting just a little bit with the heavenly straight boy. 'I don't care if you are

People magazine's sexiest man of the year. You're not too old for me to put you over my knee, you hear me?'

At home up in the Hollywood hills, Claire McMahon emptied the foul-smelling contents of a tin of dog food into a plastic bowl and set it down on the polished maple of the kitchen floor.

'Zulu!' she called. 'Here, boy!'

Within nanoseconds an excitable white ball of fluff had come hurtling into the room, its eyes almost completely invisible beneath its masses of unkempt fur, and hurled itself head first into the bowl, making appreciative snuffling noises.

Claire laughed. She adored the little bichon frise, whom she'd christened Zulu for a joke because he was just so impossibly fluffy and white. Pete always complained that the dog looked like a pom-pom that had accidentally got plugged into the mains. He pretended not to like him, but Claire had often spied him late at night in his study, surreptitiously feeding the dog smoky bacon crisps.

Pouring herself a glass of Perrier, she wandered out on to the deck by the pool. It was early evening, her favourite time of the day. She loved to sit outside in the warm tranquillity of the fading light, drinking in the spectacular view of the canyon below.

She and Pete had bought the house in Siena's second year at St Xavier's. Claire had had quite a fight on her hands with Minnie at the time, about moving out of Hancock Park, but things had worked out well for everybody in the end.

After so many years of stress and misery with Duke, Minnie discovered to her surprise that she really rather enjoyed living alone. She found it quite therapeutic, ripping out all Duke's revolting cream shag-pile carpeting and slowly, painstakingly redecorating every room to her own impeccable taste. For the first time in her life, she was enjoying some economic, as well as emotional, freedom, and it was wonderful to watch her blossoming as she gradually rediscovered her confidence and love of life. By the time Laurie upped sticks and moved to Atlanta two years later for a job at the university, Minnie was actually rather relieved to have got rid of her.

The move had been wonderful for Claire too. Both she and Pete had fallen in love with their new, sprawling, Nantucket craftsman-style home, with its light, its privacy and its incredible views. They could have afforded something far grander, of course, with all the ludicrous amounts of money Pete was making these days, but neither of them wanted to be rattling around on some huge estate – been there, done that.

Only Siena had never really felt at home in the new house, despite Claire's best efforts to create a beautiful bedroom and bathroom for her, decorated in her favourite indigo blue.

'This isn't home. It'll never be home,' she'd announced flatly, when Claire had excitedly shown it to her at the start of the summer holidays.

'But, darling,' she said, crestfallen. 'You've got all your favourite things in here from Hancock Park. Look, I even saved all your old Mel Gibson posters.'

'I've gone off him,' said Siena harshly, looking at the walls and her mother's efforts to please her with withering disdain. 'Ages ago. You'd know that if you hadn't packed me off to England like an unwanted parcel. And where's my picture of Grandpa, the cowboy one?' She continued accusingly. 'I suppose Dad got rid of it, did he?'

The bitterness in her voice stabbed at Claire's heart like a razor. She knew Siena hated St Xavier's; that her resentment at being sent away to school had only made her *more* spoilt and *more* wilful than ever and pushed her even farther away from both her parents than she had been when Duke was alive. But Pete point blank refused to consider bringing her home.

'It's emotional blackmail,' he insisted, whenever Claire

brought it up. 'She thinks that by making our lives a misery, she can get her own way. And we all know who taught her *that*, don't we?'

With Pete, sooner or later, everything came back to Duke.

Siena's hostility and bad behaviour were compounded, Claire felt, by the enforced separation from Hunter. Although she didn't dare say so to Pete, she knew that that boy had never been anything other than a good influence on Siena. Without him, and alienated from both herself and Pete, there was nothing to stop her from running completely wild.

This evening, as she sipped her fizzy water and watched the sun begin its slow descent into the horizon, Claire prayed that Siena would be home soon. Despite all the battles and the tantrums, she missed her daughter terribly.

But it wasn't just that.

Pete was already getting very wound up about her extended stay in England since she'd finished her A-levels in June. He didn't approve at all of his daughter's foray into modelling and had made it patently clear to Siena that he wanted her back at home and studying for Oxford as soon as possible. Despite having no academic background himself – Claire was the only true scholar in the family – he had always expected Siena to excel at school. Her place at Oxford meant the world to him. Subconsciously perhaps, Claire thought, he wanted his daughter to grow up in a world as far removed from Hollywood and Duke's hopes for her as possible.

After all the shenanigans with Hunter and this stupid vendetta with NBC, his temper was already on a knife edge at the moment. Claire prayed that, for once, Siena would do what she was told and not push her father over the edge completely.

Ensconced in the warm comfort of her trailer, in a

deserted East London car park, Siena was in a truly foul temper. Sighing and pouting like a five-year-old while she was simultaneously being made up and having her hair pulled, tweaked and pinned into position by an exhausted hairdresser for the Ailsa Moran shoot, she reached down for her cigarette and took in a long-drawn-out lungful of nicotine. Why the fuck couldn't they get a move on?

She'd finally broken things off with Patrick that morning, something she'd been meaning to do for ages, but instead of the relief she'd expected to feel she was overwhelmingly depressed. His words about modelling – that she was just a jumped-up clothes horse, that she ought to take up her place at Keble – kept ringing in her ears like an irksome ghost of Christmas past.

This Moran campaign was a big break for her and she'd been looking forward to it for ages. But now that she was actually here, all the lustre of it seemed to have gone. Whose bloody idea was it to shoot in an 'urban wasteland' setting? Anything less glamorous or fun than mooching about in a cold car park that smelt of tramps' wee would be hard to imagine.

And just to top things off, she'd woken up this morning with a revolting pimple on her chin, and enough PMT to classify her as a one-woman biological weapon.

'Siena, please, keep your head still,' pleaded the exasperated hairdresser through a mouthful of kirby-grips. 'I can't do this if you keep leaning forward.'

'Oh, for fuck's sake,' snapped Siena. She knew she was being a bitch, and it wasn't the hairdresser's fault that she'd broken up with Pat, but she had to take it out on someone. 'I'm just grabbing a magazine. Have you any idea how boring it is, sitting here for hours on end with you lot pulling and prodding at me like a fucking prize cow?'

Prize cow is right, thought the make-up artist, but she doggedly continued brushing Siena's brow with high-lighter.

'Don't exaggerate,' said the hairdresser, who was not in the mood to pander to some two-bit model's mood swings. 'You've been in this chair for forty minutes. It's the *rest* of us who have been here for hours.'

Siena mumbled something incoherent and pointedly immersed herself in her magazine.

'Besides, if you want to get out of here, the best thing you can do is sit still. Two more minutes, OK? Just don't move.' She fixed two more pins into the precarious-looking mountain of Medusa-esque curls piled on Siena's head, and covered the elaborate structure with an asphyxiating shower of hairspray.

'Isn't that your brother?' asked the make-up artist in an attempt to change the subject.

Hunter's picture was on the back of Siena's magazine, advertising the new series of *Counsellor*, with a semi-naked Lanie Armstrong wrapped seductively around him.

Siena didn't know what people saw in Lanie. She looked like every other Californian blonde bimbo to her.

'No.' She looked at the hapless woman as if she'd crawled out from under some particularly unpleasant rock. 'He's my uncle. My half-uncle, actually. And words can't describe how fucking bored I am with seeing his inane face or hearing about that bloody awful programme.'

The agony of missing Hunter, combined with the shame and embarrassment of having to admit that she no longer really knew him, or anything about his exciting new life, made her lash out at anyone foolish enough to mention his name. Why couldn't people just shut up about him and leave her alone?

'*Counsellor*? I love it. Never miss an episode.' The hairdresser couldn't resist.

'Me neither,' chimed in the make-up girl, who had also had enough of Siena for one day. 'I think he's got a lovely face, anyway.' She took a clean sponge from her cavernous blue bag and began removing the excess blusher from Siena's cheeks. 'You look like him, don't you?' she went on absently. 'I bet people tell you that all the time.'

'Are you blind?' said Siena rudely, stubbing out her cigarette with such force that the butt snapped. 'He's so dark skinned he practically looks Arab. For all I know he is Arab. His mother was such a slut, Grandpa probably wasn't his father anyway. I'm so pale I'm see-through.'

She looked critically at her complexion in the mirror on the back wall, straining to examine the now invisible spot on her chin.

There was a quick-fire rapping on the trailer door and Marsha, Siena's gushingly enthusiastic agent, came bursting in on the happy trio, waving a piece of paper excitedly. Marsha, who barely scraped the five foot mark even in heels, and was renowned for her questionable business ethics, was universally referred to in the London fashion community as the poison dwarf.

'Darling!' she squealed, arms flapping and face flushed like a munchkin on speed. 'It's confirmed. Confirmed!'

'What is?' asked Siena. 'What on earth are you talking about?'

'What am I talking about?' Marsha was hopping up and down so manically the make-up artist wondered whether she might be about to pee her pants. 'Paris, of course! The October show, McQueen, he loved you. He's confirmed. Paris!'

'Oh,' said Siena weakly, and managed a small smile, her first of the day. 'Good. That's good news.'

'Good news?' shrieked Marsha. '*Good news?* Child, have you gone mad? It's great news. It's fabulous. Do you know how many girls would sell their soul to be doing that show? I'm talking about girls who've been around for years. Have you any idea what it means for a newcomer like you to go from Ailsa Moran to Alexander McQueen overnight?'

Siena did have a pretty shrewd idea.

This was what she'd wanted, what she'd dreamed of

and prayed for day and night for the last three months. To be going to the Paris shows at all was a big deal for someone as new to the business as she was. But to be fronting Alexander McQueen's collection? It was unbelievable. A fantasy.

But Paris also meant problems. Marsha did not know that her father had expressly forbidden her to pursue her modelling other than as an occasional hobby. Pete had already refused point blank to sanction her proposed trip to France when she'd floated the idea to him a couple of weeks ago. She would already be three weeks into her first term at Oxford when Paris Fashion Week started, and he expected her to be a hundred and ten per cent focused on her studies by then. As far as Pete was concerned the matter was already closed. But that was before McQueen.

Her hair and make-up finally finished, Siena got up carefully from the chair and admired her reflection in the mirror. The floating, pale green chiffon, Grecian-style dress clung loosely to the voluptuous curves of her body as if held in place by static electricity. One smooth, alabaster-white shoulder rose from the folds of material across her breasts, curving up into her long, fragile neck and finally to the creamy softness of her complexion, subtly heightened by the faint rose glow of her perfectly made-up cheeks. Two gleaming tendrils of jet-black hair tumbled across her face, having struggled free of the immaculate, pearl-and-crystal-studded triumph of coiffure that crowned her head, held in place by a hundred invisible pins.

Siena smiled at the vision she'd been transformed into, suddenly empowered and alive. Just the thought of the cameras waiting outside excited her, and her eyes flashed with an almost sexual rush that would translate into dynamite pictures.

Pete or no Pete, Siena had made her decision. She was not going to Oxford. She was going to be at that McQueen show come hell or high water.

Chapter Eighteen

Curled up on the couch in his Santa Monica beach house, Hunter was deeply engrossed in his script.

'Are you ever going to get your nose out of that bloody thing and get me a whisky? You're not being a terribly good host, you know.'

Max De Seville, his oldest and closest friend, had just flown in from England for a whirlwind week of meetings in Hollywood. Max had sat his last final at Cambridge two weeks ago, and was trying to get his foot on the ladder at one of the studios where, one day, he dreamed of becoming a director.

At twenty-three, Max still looked faintly boyish, with his unruly mop of blond hair and a lingering smattering of childhood freckles across his wide, rugby-broken nose. His body, however, was definitely all man. Six foot four in his socks, and with shoulders like Ben Hur, he strode around Hunter's living room like a clumsy colossus, trying to find a piece of furniture large and solid enough to sit down on.

Max had been there for Hunter in the terrible first few years after Duke died. He had seen him pining hopelessly for Siena, while trying to shore up an emotionally unstable Caroline as she ricocheted from one dead-end job to the next. As his family crumbled around him, Max's friendship soon became one of the only constants in Hunter's life.

Caroline's affair with Charles Murray had fizzled out shortly after their move to Los Feliz, and it was quite plain to the young Max at the time that his friend's once beautiful mother was lonely. He remembered being round at the apartment when Charlie had come to pick up the last of his things, watching with Hunter as his mother tried hard to be brave.

'Look, really, it's OK. We're fine,' Caroline insisted, helping her ex-lover carry a pile of office shirts out to his car. 'You don't owe us anything. You never asked for any of this.'

Charlie threw the shirts on to the back seat of his Porsche and turned to face her. She looked exhausted, worn down by the long, fruitless legal battle with the McMahons and by trying to cope with raising Hunter alone in such hugely straitened circumstances. In baggy jeans and an old sweatshirt, her face bare of make-up, she was still a beautiful woman, all lips and cheekbones. But there was a sadness bordering on despair in her eyes now which had replaced the mischievous sparkle he remembered from the early, crazy days of their affair.

The fact was Charlie simply wasn't ready for marriage and a ready-made family. It would never have worked, and they both knew it. But that didn't stop him caring about her or feeling terrible watching her struggling to keep afloat.

'It's not about owing you anything, Caro,' he said. 'We're friends, aren't we? I want to help.'

Pulling out a cheque from his inside jacket pocket he handed it to her, over-ruling her protests with a firm wave of his hand.

'Take it,' he said. 'I know you need it and it's the least I can do. I want to be there for you and Hunter financially, at least until you get back on your feet. Please.'

Reluctantly, she smiled and pocketed the cheque. He was right, she did need it. Pride, never her strongest suit where money was concerned anyway, had now become a luxury she could not afford. Reaching up on tiptoes, she put her arms around his neck and gave him a kiss on the cheek. She wasn't in love with him any more. In all honesty she probably never had been. But it was still sad, watching him go.

He picked her up in a big bear hug, then set her back down on the pavement as he got into the car. The brilliant LA sunshine and the bright blue sky provided an incongruously cheery backdrop to such a painful parting. Rain, or at least a grey horizon, would have been more appropriate.

'You can always call me, you know that, right?'

Caroline nodded. 'Sure. And vice versa. Take care of yourself, Charlie.'

'You too, babe. You too.'

Max had watched with Hunter from his bedroom window as Charlie pulled away, and seen Caroline wait until the car was out of sight before putting her head in her hands and crying. Until that moment he had always thought of Hunter's mom as hard as nails. Seeing her in tears seemed so wrong somehow, he almost felt guilty having witnessed it. Not that she didn't deserve to suffer, after all the suffering she had put other people through in her selfishness, especially her wholly innocent son. But despite his vehement dislike of her, the scene had stirred some real compassion in Max and the memory of it had stayed with him to this day.

The real tragedy was that, in her own despair, Caroline had been unable to reach out to Hunter. When she finally decided to move back to England, he had been relieved more than anything, and Max had watched him diligently put himself through school and acting classes alone, managing the household budget and bills as if he'd been doing it for years. Which, Max suspected on reflection, he probably had.

Not that Max's own family were exactly the Brady Bunch. In fact, he suspected that Caroline might once have had an affair with his father; but as both his parents seemed to bed-hop among their friends with alarming regularity, it didn't really bother him. At least his parents, unlike Hunter's, still had money. And when the going got really rough, he knew he could always turn to Henry.

Henry was Max's beloved elder brother, his mother's son from her first marriage, who, at ten years older than Max, was more of a father to him than his own father had ever been. When he'd decided to apply for Cambridge, it had been Henry who'd driven him to his interview at Trinity, Henry who put up with his unbearable angst and snappiness as he waited for his results, and Henry and his wife Muffy who had taken him out to celebrate when, by some miracle, he got in. Last year, when Max had announced that he wanted to become a film director, Henry had been right behind him, loving, supporting and encouraging him as always. Poor old Hunter had never had anyone in his corner like that. Everything he'd done, he'd done alone.

Hunter put down the script with a sigh and got up to go to the drinks cabinet.

'You're all the same, you goddam directors.' He grinned. 'You think the whole world is at your beck and call.' Max flopped down in Hunter's vacated place on the couch, his long jeans-covered legs sprawled along its full length. He picked up Hunter's script and began to read in a hammed-up falsetto: 'Oh, Mike, Mike! You're so noble and brave, Mike! The way you stood up to that evil conglomerate in court today was just incredible. I'm *hot* for you, Mike!'

'Give that here!' said Hunter, snatching it back from him with one hand and passing him a huge glass of Glenfiddich with the other. 'It does not say that, jerk-off.'

'Practically,' said Max, sipping the warm amber liquid and sighing with contentment.

'Look, I never said it was Shakespeare, OK?' said Hunter, sitting down without complaint on the polished maple floor, his couch having been usurped. 'But it pays the bills. And it's fun, it really is.' His tawny face lit up, cobalt-blue eyes sparkling, and Max saw for the thousandth time exactly why the world's women were all madly in love with him. It was odd that, despite his gorgeous looks, Hunter was the steady, stable one while he, Max, already had a bit of a reputation as a womaniser, or at least as a serial flirt.

'I just wish this thing with Pete would blow over, you know?' Hunter said anxiously. 'Hugh's being great about it, but I can tell he's pissed, and I can't say I blame him.'

Max sat up and took a bigger slug of his drink before passing the glass to Hunter, who shook his head. He was determined to nail this scene tonight, and that meant it was Perrier only.

'If he's pissed, it's with Pete, not you,' Max said firmly. 'Hugh knows how hard you work and how great you've been for the show. Hell, you *are* the show. It's you that gets all the press, you that all those girls are tuning in to see, God help them.'

'Well, I don't know about that,' mumbled Hunter, blushing. Amazing how such a gorgeous, lusted-after guy could have remained so cripplingly shy. 'Anyway, how long are you staying?'

'A week,' said Max.

Hunter rolled his eyes to heaven. 'As long as that?' he said, grinning. The fact was he loved having Max around and they both knew it. 'Seriously, though, what are your plans, long term? I assume you're gonna be spending more time out here, looking for a directing gig?'

Max nodded. 'Yeah, eventually. I'm going back to England first to sort a few things out, and then I guess I'll have to start looking for a place to live.'

'What are you talking about?' Hunter sounded genuinely surprised. 'You can come and live here, with me.'

Max looked doubtful.

'Well, why not?' said Hunter. He waved his arm in the general direction of his three guest bedrooms. 'There's plenty of space.'

'I know,' said Max, draining his whisky and getting up in search of a refill. 'It's not that. The fact is I can't afford it, mate. All I have in the world is a trust from my grandfather so tiny it would barely buy me a deposit on a

Mars bar. And last I heard, junior assistant directors aren't exactly the most highly paid blokes in this town.'

'Oh, come on,' said Hunter, laughing with the same warm, infectious laugh that Max remembered growing up with, a laugh that seemed to encapsulate his friendly, open nature. 'Do you think I care? I don't want your rent, I want your company.'

Max still looked doubtful. It was an incredibly generous offer, and he didn't doubt that sharing a house with Hunter would be a blast. But he didn't like the idea of not paying his own way.

'Please,' said Hunter, sensing his hesitation. 'You'd really be doing me a favour. What if some deranged fan tried to break in and attack me one night? You could be my bodyguard.'

Max laughed. 'Yeah, right. Most of your deranged fans are about fourteen and wear miniskirts and too much lipstick.' But he could tell that Hunter really did want him to agree to stay. And the truth was, he *could* do with some help financially, at least for the first few months.

'Well, OK,' he said eventually. 'But only on condition that we keep a track of how much back rent I owe you. And as soon as I'm earning enough to break even, I'll pay you back, every penny.'

'Deal!' said Hunter, delighted.

He hadn't quite realised, until that moment, just how lonely he'd been, rattling around the beach house on his own. Living with Max was going to be fantastic. He couldn't wait.

Chapter Nineteen

Siena sipped from her ice-cold flute of champagne, and gazed out of the window contentedly at the carpet of clouds below her. It was October, and she was flying first class to Paris with Marsha, who was supposed to be acting as her chaperone as well as her agent, but was in fact already as drunk as a duchess and snoring loudly in the seat beside her.

Despite being the daughter of one of the richest and most powerful men in Hollywood, Siena was not used to first-class travel. Pete thought the expense wasteful, especially on a short hop like London to Paris. Economy flights were just another part of his ongoing crusade to prevent Siena from becoming a spoilt monster like Duke, a battle that, so far at least, he appeared to be losing.

'Excuse me.' Siena signalled for the third time in as many minutes to the heroically polite young stewardess. 'I'd like some more champagne, please.'

'Certainly, madam.' The girl smiled, hoping that the forty remaining minutes of the flight would not be long enough for Siena to deteriorate into a Marsha-like state of drunken stupor. She had better things to do than carry some comatose model into the terminal at Charles de Gaulle because she was too far gone to recognise her own Louis Vuitton luggage.

'And these nuts aren't warm. Do you think you could heat them up for me?'

Siena handed her the little porcelain dish of brazil nuts with a smile that would have melted the heart of any heterosexual male. The stewardess, not being male, took it from her with a brisk, professional 'of course, madam' and retreated in search of a microwave and some more Moët.

Siena stretched her voluptuous body in the deliciously wide leather seat and purred with pleasure. This was the life! She didn't know what she was enjoying most: travelling first class to France against her father's express wishes, the thought of tomorrow's McQueen show, or the gratifying wave of attention she was receiving from all the rich and famous men on the plane. Mick Jagger, who was sitting just four rows in front of her, had helped her with her hand baggage, and Mario de Luca, Real Madrid's stunning new blond striker, had even asked her for her number and the name of her hotel in Paris.

And it wasn't as if she were the only model on the plane, either. Every other seat was occupied by some identikit, flat-chested, lissom blonde with huge pouty lips, most of them old hands at the Paris shows, some of them known to Siena from the covers of *Marie Claire* and *Vogue*. But it was Siena, all five foot four of her with her long dark hair, and boobs barely contained by a faded lemon-yellow vest, who was getting the lion's share of male attention. And she loved every minute of it.

She looked at her watch, a battered old junk-shop find that had been a gift from Patrick. They'd be on the ground in just over half an hour. Checking that Marsha was still asleep, she reached into the back pocket of her skin-tight Levis, pulled out a small square of paper and began unfolding it.

She'd received Pete's terse note two days ago, while making the final preparations for her trip. Neither of her parents was a big believer in the telephone, although Claire would occasionally brave her daughter's frosty resentment and make a call, invariably finding her attempts at conversation shut down at every turn by Siena.

Pete had long since given up completely, and preferred to communicate with her via Fed Ex. This suited Siena, who was spared the charade of trying to muster up any pretence of daughterly affection, or the futile effort of attempting to reason with her father, whose mind was invariably already made up by the time he put pen to paper.

This last letter, though, had been even stronger and less forgiving in tone than his usual communications. Siena already knew its contents by heart:

Siena,

What the hell are you playing at? I have just had a long and highly embarrassing conversation with the Master of Keble, who is now under the impression that you have been suffering a severe bout of German measles which left you too ill to attend matriculation in September. I have assured him that you will present yourself at college no later than the end of this week. I hope I don't need to spell out for you how lucky you are that he has accepted this version of events and agreed to hold your place.

This stops here, Siena. Under no circumstances are you to go to Paris, for this show or any other. Your mother and I will not allow you to throw away your education and your future through sheer, blind defiance. I am warning you, in the strongest possible terms, that I will deal with any further disobedience on this issue very severely.

I expect you in Oxford within the next five days.
Dad

Claire had followed this up with an emotional and impassioned letter of her own, pleading with Siena to abandon her modelling and get herself up to college, intimating that her father might even go so far as to cut her out of his will if she continued to defy him.

Siena had ripped up her mother's letter in disgust. Claire's weakness revolted her. She had more grudging respect for her father's brutality – at least she knew where she stood with Pete.

She read the letter again, an unpleasant feeling of nerves bubbling up in her stomach along with the champagne. She knew Pete well enough to realise that he rarely made completely idle threats. But cutting her out of the will was a bit over the top, even by her father's deranged standards. Her mother must be exaggerating as usual.

Besides, what choice did she have but to go to France? If she didn't stand up for herself now, she would end up as some bloody provincial GP in England, lancing farmers' boils for the rest of her life. The very thought of it made her shudder.

No, she had to stand her ground. Once she had done the McQueen show, once she could prove to her father that she could earn her own living as a model, that she could be successful at it, he would have to ease up on this Oxford business. Perhaps she could ask him to let her defer her place for a year? By then, hopefully, her modelling would really have taken off – she might even have made the cross-over into acting – and then even Pete would have to admit that she'd been right all along.

Replacing the note carefully in her jeans pocket, Siena took another fortifying slug of champagne. Mario de Luca looked back over his shoulder and raised his glass to her in lascivious salute, the perfectly defined muscles of his tanned forearm flexing slightly as he lifted his hand.

Paris. De Luca. Alexander fucking McQueen. She couldn't remember the last time she'd felt this happy.

Pete would come around eventually. He had to.

Back in the Hollywood hills, Claire was tearing her hair out. She and Pete had been due at Costello's ten minutes ago, but she was still stuck with her fingers down the basin plug hole, trying to prise free her engagement ring, which had somehow managed to slip off her finger as she washed her hands, and was now jammed tightly between two strips of stainless steel.

'Let's just go,' said Pete impatiently. 'It'll still be there when we get back, and we're late enough as it is.'

For the last ten minutes he'd been hovering in the

bathroom doorway, hopping from foot to foot like a three-year-old with a weak bladder, which wasn't making Claire's task any easier.

'But what if it's not there, honey?' she pleaded, not looking up from the glinting flash of ruby guiding her fingers. 'If it gets dislodged and falls down that drain, I may never get it back.'

'It's just a ring,' said Pete irritably. 'I'll buy you another one.'

A momentary flash of pain registered on Claire's face. 'It's my engagement ring, Pete,' she said with quiet dignity. 'It can't be replaced.'

Even now, after almost twenty-five years of marriage, she still felt wounded by her husband's frequent insensitivity towards her. As a young wife, she had laid the blame for Pete's bad temper and his mean streak squarely at the door of his father. It was Duke who had made him bitter and angry. Duke who was to blame.

But the real tragedy in their marriage had occurred after the old tyrant had died. Claire remembered how pathetically high her hopes had been that, with Duke gone, Pete might finally relax, might finally become the man she knew he was capable of being.

How wrong she was.

In some ways, of course, he *had* changed. Professionally, his confidence had soared from the moment they lowered the old man into the ground. Success had followed success, and Pete was worth infinitely more now than his father had ever been. But somehow, it was never enough for him. Instead of giving him a sense of self-worth, the money had become a sort of obsession. Some deep but nameless fear drove him ever harder to make more, more, more. Working fourteen-hour days and most weekends, his stress levels seemed to rise rather than fall the more successful he became. And eventually Claire felt cut out completely.

Perhaps things would have been different if Siena had

stayed at home? Perhaps between them, Claire sometimes thought, she and Siena could have loved him enough to make him stop, to make him realise that he really had nothing to prove, that they loved him for himself alone.

But Pete had insisted, with the full force of his will, that Siena be sent to England. Even worse, in his blind hatred of a father he was no longer able to hurt, he had separated two innocent children, banishing poor, blameless Hunter from their lives for ever. And Claire had been too weak, too stupidly weak and afraid, to stop him.

How many times had she cursed herself for that decision? So huge a sacrifice, and what had it achieved? The gulf between father and daughter was now wider than ever. Sometimes Claire suspected that Siena actually hated her *more* than she did Pete, for letting it happen. And she didn't blame her daughter for that, not for a second.

With one sudden twist, the ring shifted position and Claire pulled it triumphantly to safety.

'Got it!' She smiled, her face flushed with happiness and relief, Pete's hurtful remark for the moment forgotten.

'At last,' he grunted gracelessly. 'Does this mean we can *finally* get going?'

In the car on the way to the restaurant, Pete's temper deteriorated further. He was, as usual, fixated on the problems with Siena.

'I swear to God, I have had it with her attitude. I don't know where she got the idea that finishing her education was optional. *Fucker!*' He roared at a black SUV that had moved into his lane without signalling, leaning on his horn until Claire had to block her ears. 'Modelling!' He laughed derisively, as if the word itself were a joke. 'What kind of a career is that for a girl with her brains?'

'Honey, I agree with you,' said Claire, in the soothing, quiet voice she would subconsciously adopt to try to calm him down. 'Of course she should be doing more with her life than that, and she will do . . .'

'Damn right she will,' he muttered darkly.

'But you know what Siena is like,' she continued, resting a hand on his knee. 'Stubborn as hell, just like her father.'

She smiled hopefully across at him, but Pete kept his eyes glued to the road and didn't smile back. 'All I'm saying is,' she pushed on, 'that maybe if we let her go to France, let her do this McQueen show she's set her heart on . . .'

'No. No way,' said Pete, swerving off the freeway on to the Third Street Promenade exit with unnecessary violence. He had always been a shocking driver, especially when he was angry. 'She is not having her way this time. She is *not* going to Paris. For once in her life, she's going to do what she's told.'

Claire decided to try a different tack.

'You know, she is seventeen, honey,' she remonstrated mildly. 'In a few months she'll legally be an adult. I don't think it's totally unreasonable that she should want some say in her own future, do you?'

'Ha!' Pete laughed aloud. 'You think she's an adult? You really think Siena has the maturity to make these kinds of decisions?'

Claire sighed. He had a point there.

'She's a kid,' he said firmly, slowing down and pulling in to the valet parking bay in front of Costello's. 'And a damn stupid kid at that.'

A sullen-looking Mexican opened the passenger door for Claire, and the unusually chilly night air burst into the warmth of the car, making the downy hairs on her forearms stand on end. Drawing her grey pashmina more tightly around her shoulders, she stepped on to the pavement, while Pete handed a second Mexican his keys and a five-dollar bill.

'If she wants to be treated like an adult,' he said, putting his arm around her and leading her into the bustling warmth of the restaurant, 'then she'll have to start behaving like one. And that means accepting that her actions carry consequences.

'Hey, Santiago!'

He embraced the maître d' warmly, all smiles suddenly.

'You know my wife, Claire?'

'Sí, sí, of course,' proclaimed the fat, silver-haired little man, stooping to kiss her hand. ''Ow could I forget a face so beautiful?'

As Santiago led them to their table – the best in the house – Pete looked back over his shoulder at his wife.

'I really mean it this time, Claire,' he said, in a tone of voice that left her in no doubt that he did. 'If she defies me on this, she'll live to regret it.'

Siena reached across to her bedside table and fumbled for a cigarette, her last. She wondered whether room service would bring her some more, or if she'd have to send Mario out to the tabac in the morning.

Inhaling that uniquely sweet, rich flavour of her Gitane – there was something so romantic, so Audrey Hepburn about French cigarettes, Siena felt – she admired the taut, smooth lines of the footballer's body as he slept beside her.

Mario de Luca! She'd just fucked Mario de Luca. Or, to put it more accurately, she'd just *been* fucked by him. And how! If only the girls at school could see her now.

He looked exhausted, poor darling, with his arms outstretched and mouth open, dead to the world. But then she had put him through his paces rather, insisting on a second and then a third performance before she finally took pity on him and allowed him some sleep before his big match tomorrow. She chuckled quietly to herself at the thought of him stumbling around the pitch, knackered as a carthorse. Come to think of it, she might not fare much better herself. She hoped she wouldn't look too puffy eyed and bandy legged on that catwalk tomorrow. Right now, she doubted whether she could even stand.

Holding her cigarette in her left hand, with her right she felt beneath the covers for Mario's dick. Even in its semi-soft state it felt gratifyingly large in her palm, and began to twitch and harden automatically at her touch. Mario groaned in his sleep and pulled her naked body towards him.

It felt so nice to lie in his arms, to feel his comforting strength wrapped around her, and smell that smell of man, a mixture of aftershave and sweat. That smell always triggered her childish sense of security and happiness, and brought back memories of being pro-tected, held and loved.

She sighed drowsily. Disengaging herself gently so as not to wake him, she took a last long drag and stubbed out her cigarette, snuggling down beneath the covers for some sleep of her own. It had been a lovely, magical night. She would never forget it.

But she had already decided. She mustn't become too attached.

She wouldn't be seeing Mario again.

Chapter Twenty

At eleven o'clock the next morning, Siena found herself shivering in a draughty corner of a disused railway station, wearing little more than a red silk scarf, a pair of neon-pink see-through panties and thigh-high silver stiletto boots.

Although it was only October, central and northern France were in the grip of a freak cold spell, just when London looked set for an extended Indian summer – much to the delight of the British papers, which had been revelling in 'Boiling Britain/Freezing France' headlines for the past fortnight. Siena thought longingly of her bottle-green ribbed cashmere jumper, a freebie from the Ailsa Moran shoot, and wondered how badly her nipples were showing through the red silk.

The theme of this year's events, as decreed by the mighty Fédération Française de la Couture, was neo-industrialism. While the PRs and journalists argued over exactly what this might mean in theory, in practice it involved the meticulous construction of catwalks in a series of vast warehouses, factories and 'architecturally significant' railway stations, all of which were of proportions ill suited to being effectively centrally heated. Thus, while the great and the good of the fashion and media worlds huddled bravely beneath their full-length minks, with cold toes swaddled in cashmere socks and last winter's oh-so-chic sheepskin boots, the models spent most of the day on the brink of hypothermia.

The Paris shows were the culmination of a gruelling worldwide circuit of shows – London, New York and Milan – which had begun with the 'fashion weeks' in early February. This was the last and most important opportunity for designers to show their spring collections for the season ahead. Although perhaps not as prestigious as the spring Fashion Week, the Paris autumn shows were nevertheless considered to be one of the most exciting and dynamic events in the couture calendar, with their distinctive celebratory, 'end-of-term' atmosphere. Paris in October was where every designer, model, stylist, photographer and fashion journalist wanted to be, and competition, in all areas, was extremely fierce. The best or most eagerly anticipated shows were always sold out months in advance, and even A-list movie stars had been known to resort to everything from begging to bribery to secure a coveted front-row seat.

Siena, who had never been known to be on time for any appointment in her eighteen years on the planet, had arrived at the Gare St Michel two hours early, and had already consumed four cups of nuclear-powered espresso at the little café across the street before Marsha had shown up.

Sunglasses and a natty brown beret had done little to hide the older woman's raging hangover as she ushered her young charge into the reception area for the McQueen girls. Siena was feeling none too chipper herself after her previous night's exertions, but a happy combination of youth, cold Parisian air and the hot, strong coffee had already put the colour back in her cheeks.

Once Marsha had scuttled off to find the nearest bar, a thin, brusque young woman named Florence, whose rather pinched features were made worse by the fact that her hair was drawn back too tightly into a bun, handed Siena a time sheet. It outlined each of the outfits she would be wearing, how long she would have to change into each one (in seconds rather than minutes), and what her audio cues would be for every entrance and exit. The show itself would not start until four o'clock, but the girls would be practising their poses and changeovers until they were called for hair and make-up at two.

'Do we get any lunch?' asked Siena, looking faintly ridiculous in her knickers-and-boots ensemble.

She had bolted out of the hotel in such a rush this morning there'd been no time for breakfast, and after her marathon shag-fest with Mario she was starting to feel quite ravenous.

'Zere will be food lat-eur. Now you re-urse,' said Florence disdainfully, staring disapprovingly down at Siena's ample bosom heaving beneath the wisp of red silk.

Stupid French bitch, thought Siena. Who did she think she was talking to?

She glanced round despondently at the waif-like creatures surrounding her. She felt like the one fat pupa in a swarm of stick insects and decided that requests for food at these sorts of event were probably few and far between.

Just then her stomach gave an embarrassingly noisy rumble and a rather gawky but friendly-looking girl with long red hair and a big gap between her two front teeth caught her eye. Wandering over towards her, she handed Siena a fat-looking green pill and a glass of champagne.

'Try zees,' she said in a heavy Spanish accent. 'Ees fabulous, it weel keel your appetite. And your nerves.'

'Thanks,' said Siena, sipping the champagne but eyeing the pill warily. 'What is it?'

'Oh, don't worry.' The girl smiled. 'Ees 'erbal. Ees no drugs. Look, see?' She produced a second pill and swallowed it, knocking it back with the remnants of her own champagne. 'Ees fine.'

Siena followed suit, and soon the two of them were perched on two 'neo-industrial' plastic chairs, chain-smoking and chatting away like old friends. The girl's name, it transpired, was Ines Prieto Moreno. This was her third trip to the Paris shows, but her first time at McQueen, and she was amazed to discover that today was to be Siena's catwalk debut.

'At McQueen?' She raised her eyebrows. 'I don't

believe eet. Ees incredible. Your first show? I am so jealous! I waited five years for zees.'

Siena shrugged.

'I have been kinda lucky so far, I guess,' she admitted. 'To be honest, I'm a bit mystified as to why I'm here. I assumed he'd have lots of shorter girls, girls with my kinda look, you know? Old fashioned? I figured maybe it was a forties theme or something. But all the girls here are just regular models.'

'Hey, thanks a lot,' said Ines, trying to look offended.

'Oh, I'm sorry,' said Siena, 'that came out wrong. I didn't mean . . .' She looked so flustered, Ines couldn't help but laugh. 'It's just that you're all so tall. And thin. And blonde.'

'I am not blonde,' said Ines reasonably. 'I 'ave red 'air and funny teeth. I'm deeferent. Like you.'

Siena thought it would be hard to find another human being who looked less like her than Ines, but didn't say so.

'Lots of the girls 'ere are unusual,' Ines continued. 'Take Katya. She 'as a beeg nose.'

Siena looked across at the mighty Russian supermodel and giggled.

'I'm sorry, but she does!' insisted Ines. 'And look. Lisa 'as no teets at all, she is like a leetle girl. And Daria . . .' She pointed to an exquisitely beautiful girl with impossibly high cheekbones reading a novel in the far corner of the room. 'She 'ave no hair at all.'

'What do you mean?' Siena laughed, admiring the girl's sleek white-blonde bob. 'Of course she has hair.'

Ines raised one eyebrow knowingly. 'Not after two o'clock she doesn't,' she said.

At ten to four, Siena was feeling so nervous she thought she might be sick. Thank God for Ines's magic pill. If she'd eaten so much as a vol au vent she was certain it would be making an ignominious reappearance the second she stepped out on that catwalk.

The noisy, excited hum of the audience was clearly audible backstage, not surprisingly as only a giant pair of paper-thin steel screens separated the anxious models from the throbbing crowd of fashionistas in the main body of the room.

Siena, who had a total of five outfits to wear during the show, had spent the past hour desperately attempting to master the art of walking sexily in her ludicrously high boots. Nervousness about her own performance had completely eclipsed all other considerations. Having fantasised for weeks about what she would say when she met McQueen himself, in the event she forgot all her pre-prepared razor-sharp repartee and simply nodded like a dazed rabbit when he approached her to wish her luck.

Now, with ten minutes to go before the show, she was pacing up and down in front of a big whiteboard, on which was scrawled in black marker pen:

I am Sexy. Powerful. A dominatrix BITCH!!
I am a lioness. A Warrior Queen.
But always . . .
FEMININE.
Enjoy yourselves out there!!!!

Oh God. She felt her stomach give another hideous lurch – not very warrior queen. Tiny beads of sweat were breaking out on her forehead, no doubt already wreaking havoc with the trowelfuls of dominatrix make-up that caked her face: huge arcs of silver eyeshadow swept above sinister, kohl-blackened eyes, and blood-red, gloss-slicked lips. All the girls were made up the same way, but whereas Ines simply looked bizarre, like an unusually leggy circus clown, Siena looked much more disturbing, a debauched, fallen angel. Instinctively she reached up to wipe the sweat from her forehead.

'No!' yelped a voice from behind her. Davide, the chief make-up artist – known as Camp David to the models for obvious reasons – grabbed both her hands and pinned them behind her back. 'Nevair touch ze face. One smudge, and eet ees ruined!' he wailed.

'God, OK, OK,' Siena snapped. 'I won't touch. It's just so fucking hot in here now with these lights, I'm sweating like a Goddam pig.'

'First you complain ees cold. Now you say ees hot. Let me tell you, eef you wipe your face, you weel *look* like a peeg. Don't touch!'

Davide wagged his finger at Siena like a schoolteacher before darting off to spray some more silver shimmer on one of the German girls' arms.

Ines, who looked a lot more comfortable than Siena in silver flip-flops, combat trousers and a floaty green floral top, came bounding towards her like an overexcited puppy. Siena tried to muster a smile. How could she be so calm? Never mind 'I am a lioness'. She felt as if she were about to be fed to the fucking lions.

'Do you know 'oo is out there?' Ines asked breathlessly.

She was now literally jumping up and down with excitement, two long red plaits flapping behind her like tails on a kite.

'Sure,' said Siena, trying to sound calm and in control. 'I know who's out there. The world's press, a bunch of coked-up, plastic-faced movie actors and every buyer from here to Bangkok. And I gotta tell you, the thought of walking down that runway is scaring me shitless.'

'No, no,' said Ines, grabbing Siena's hands in her own. ''Aven't you 'eard?'

'Heard what?' asked Siena impatiently.

'Jamie Silfen! Ees here!' Ines looked like she might be going to explode.

Siena felt her legs start to give way beneath her. 'No,' she muttered, shell-shocked. 'He can't be. Are you sure? He can't be here.' Ignoring Davide's advice, she began pulling at her elaborately curled hair in despair. 'It's my first show,' she wailed. 'I have no fucking idea what I'm doing out there. Oh shit, Jamie Silfen is gonna see me making an ass of myself. Where is he? I didn't see him out there.'

Ines gestured through the tiny crack in the steel partition wall. 'Third row. Glasses. Beeg sheepskin coat.'

Siena scanned the audience. Holy fucking shit. There he was.

Jamie Silfen, one of the biggest, most powerful casting agents in Hollywood, sitting within a hundred feet of her.

In her more hopeful moments, she had imagined that perhaps some of the lesser-known agents might put in an appearance at the McQueen show. But this was unbelievable.

Even her father was in awe of Silfen. For over fifteen years he had had the Midas touch in the business, and his name had become synonymous with box-office success. If Silfen cast your movie, you could expect to see your profits double. As an actor, even an established box-office draw, you respected Jamie Silfen as a man who could make or break careers with a nod of his shiny bald head.

What the hell was he doing at a fashion show in France?

'I wonder why 'ees 'ere?' said Ines, reading Siena's mind. 'You theenk someone is doing a movie about the catwalks, maybe 'ee wants to see for 'imself? I don't theenk 'ee is eenterested in fashion, you know? Just look at 'ees coat. Eet's revolting!'

But Siena had tuned out. Jamie Silfen. Jamie fucking Silfen was out there, and he was going to be watching *her*. Opportunities like this just didn't come around twice and Siena knew it. She had to seize the moment, to make a real impression on him. This could be it. Her chance.

Almost instantly, she found her nervous energy evaporating, replaced by the familiar pumping adrenalin of raw ambition.

She thought of Duke, and a slow smile spread across her face.

'Lena, Anna Maria, Ines, Siena!'

The stage manager was striding towards them, clapping his hands for action.

'Let's go, ladies. You're first up, in . . .' He looked at his watch. '. . . two minutes exactly. I want everyone in their places. Now, please, girls!'

Ines smiled down at her new friend.

'Nervous?' she asked.

'Not at all,' said Siena, grinning from ear to ear. 'I can hardly wait.'

Chapter Twenty-one

Caroline Berkeley wandered into the dining room of her beautiful Cotswold manor house and checked the place settings for the third and final time.

She didn't want either of her brothers or their ghastly wives anywhere near her at tonight's dinner, but every time she put her head round the door, bloody Christopher had moved everything around, trying to sit himself next to the wholesomely pretty Muffy Arkell. The damn cheek!

Caroline had met and married Christopher Wellesley less than a year after her ignominious return to England. Or rather, she'd met him again. Christopher had been one of the many eligible bachelors on the scene in London, back in her youthful heyday, and although they had never slept with one another back then, they had become firm friends, only losing touch when she settled permanently in Los Angeles.

The general rumour had always been that the gauche, awkward heir to one of the grandest estates in Oxfordshire was secretly gay. This, as Caroline was later to learn, wasn't true. He just rather preferred a quiet day's fishing on the Test, or a nice glass of claret, to sex. Oddly, though, this wasn't a problem for her any more. After everything she'd been through with Duke, she found her new husband's sexual reticence, combined with his uncomplicated loyalty and adoration, to be just what the doctor ordered.

The year after Duke's death had been a living hell for Caroline. Stuck in a tiny apartment with a son who, she soon discovered, she really barely knew, she had thought at first that she might go mad. Her relationship with Charlie had quickly unravelled – not that she really blamed him for that. Setting up home with her and Hunter had never been part of his agenda when they began their affair, and he had continued to provide her with some financial support for two years after they split.

She didn't resent Charlie. But for the first time in her life, Caroline found to her horror that she was unable to land herself a wealthy date. Whether it was her age, or the fact that she had been tainted by her long tenure as Duke's mistress, or a combination of the two, she didn't know. But suddenly it seemed none of the real players in Hollywood would touch her with a ten-foot pole.

At forty-six, having never worked a day in her life, she was ill equipped to begin any sort of proper, paying career. She took on occasional work as a party organiser for friends of friends, and did the odd bit of interior design. But other than that, her time was spent at home in the poky Los Feliz apartment, either alone or with Hunter, nursing her disappointment and a growing sense of depression. She soon started drinking heavily.

In the end it was Hunter himself who had persuaded her to move back home to England. Although she knew he was genuinely concerned for her, she also knew that he was finding her drinking and the accompanying mood swings increasingly difficult to live with.

'I haven't been much of a mother to you, have I?' she observed in a rare moment of honesty when he'd first suggested it.

Hunter shrugged. 'You did your best. I know it's been hard for you.'

'But how will you cope here on your own? I mean, what are you going to do for money and things?'

He didn't like to tell her that he was already living almost entirely on his own earnings from after-school jobs – the trust Duke left him paid for his education, clothes and utilities at the apartment but not much else – and that he could 'cope' a whole lot more easily if he didn't have a drunk, despairing mother to worry about all the time.

'I'll be fine,' he said. 'And you can come visit, you know? Or I could go over there? Let's face it, you're miserable here, Mom. At least in England you have friends and family you can rely on for help.'

Caroline wasn't so sure about that. She'd burned her bridges with most of her so-called friends from the old days, and she'd barely spoken to either George or William in the last decade. But she *was* miserable in LA, so miserable it was slowly killing her. England couldn't be any worse.

As it turned out, thanks to Christopher, it was a whole lot better. When they met up again, the bond between them was stronger than ever. He was fifteen years her senior, but still a spring chicken compared to Duke. He had never married, never wanted children, and the estate was already entailed to his nephew.

'I can't leave you anything,' he'd told her bluntly. 'And I've very little ready cash. No flash cars or holidays in Mauritius or any of that lark. But I think I could give you a pretty decent life here.' He gestured vaguely around his exquisite medieval manor house, Great Thatchers, with its formal gardens and rolling parkland undulating far into the distance. 'And I think we'd have a lot of fun together.'

Caroline thought so too.

She wrote to Hunter and told him she was getting married, and that she had given up drinking for good. 'Christopher's been AA for twenty years, so we're going together,' she'd said brightly.

He was pleased to hear her so happy, and took an instant liking to Christopher when he flew over for their quiet wedding at the village church in Batcombe a few months later.

For the first two years of his mother's marriage he had flown over to visit at Christmas, and they'd all got on happily enough. But gradually the natural distance there had always been between mother and son began to reassert itself. Caroline's visits to LA became less and less frequent, and Hunter had neither the money nor the time to keep making the trip to England to see her.

She was pleased when she heard about *Counsellor*, both happy and frankly surprised at his success, although she never watched the show. 'Absolute drivel,' Christopher called it, and Caroline privately agreed. But she had called to tell him she was proud of him, and she was.

It was enough for both of them to know that the other was happy and settled. They were both wise enough to know that, after all these years, it was too late for them ever to be really close.

'Ah, there you are,' said Christopher, hobbling up behind his wife and wrapping his arms around her.

Now seventy, he suffered occasionally from debilitating attacks of gout, a consequence of his earlier hard-drinking days. For the past two weeks he'd been walking with a stick and grumbling at Caroline that he was in far too much pain to take the rubbish out, walk the dogs, or generally contribute to the running of the household in any way.

'Oi!' he said, seeing that she had rearranged the place cards again. 'That's not fair. I want to sit next to that lovely Arkell woman, not your dreadful sister-in-law.'

'Well, you can't,' said Caroline firmly. 'I want her to sit next to Gary Ellis. Besides . . .' She turned around and kissed him affectionately on the top of his shiny bald head. 'I thought you only had eyes for me?'

'I do, my darling, I do.' He grinned at her. In her blue, stripy Thomas Pink shirtwaister, unbuttoned low enough to reveal just a hint of cleavage, he thought Caroline was looking terrific, as always. She was nearly fifty-five now, but she could have passed for ten years younger at least. 'I'm just trying to be gentlemanly and rescue her from that creep Ellis. I can't think what possessed you to invite him.'

Gary Ellis was one of Caro's newer 'finds', and was about as popular among the Cotswolds huntin', shootin' and fishin' set as the profiteering Rhett Butler was among the southern gentlemen of Atlanta.

He was a developer, famous for turning some of the most beautiful swathes of English countryside into hideous concrete shopping centres, and he had just bought himself a weekend cottage outside Batcombe. He was also loud, a cockney, and well known for his dodgy business practices, as well as his garish chequered suits and lewd and outrageous sense of humour.

'Don't be such a snob,' said Caroline. 'I like him.'

Christopher gave her a knowing look, the same one she remembered her father Sebastian using whenever he caught her fibbing.

Liking Ellis had nothing to do with it. She had invited him for one reason and one reason only, and they both knew it: he had his eye on a couple of Christopher's lower fields. Christopher had been appalled at the very suggestion of selling one square inch of his estate, but Caroline was unwilling to wave goodbye to the prospect of oodles of ready cash until they'd at least heard what Gary was proposing. He might only want to build a couple of perfectly tasteful houses, and what was so wrong with that? She wouldn't mind having a couple of nearer neighbours, or a bit more money in her pocket.

Besides, having Gary there might distract her other guests from the unremitting tedium of her brothers' company. Despite their bitter resentment that, after all the appalling things she'd done, she had managed once again to land on her feet and had become, for the second time, infinitely more wealthy than either of them, George and William were impressed enough by the Wellesley name and the grandeur of Great Thatchers to continue to pay court to their errant sister and her new husband. And as both lived within fifty miles of Batcombe they became, to Caroline's disappointment, quite regular visitors and dinner party guests.

She knew that they would both vehemently disapprove of Gary Ellis and everything he stood for, but it couldn't be helped. She had not yet completely given up hope of persuading Christopher to change his mind about those fields.

By nine o'clock the party was in full swing. As well as George and William and their wives, dreary Lucy and even drearier Deborah, she had invited a rather eccentric local lesbian in her seventies who was a lifelong friend of Christopher's, plus Gary Ellis and their neighbours, Henry and Muffy Arkell.

Henry owned Manor Farm, a much smaller but some thought even more beautiful little estate about five miles west of Thatchers. He also turned out, to Caroline's amazement and delight, to be the elder son of her one-time great friend from LA, Lulu De Seville.

'I don't believe it,' she said, when they'd first met at last year's hunt ball. 'You're little Max's big brother? He was always great friends with my son, Hunter. What a small world.'

'Yes indeed,' said Henry, who vaguely remembered hearing something from Max about Caroline sleeping with his stepfather, and a God-awful row ensuing as a result. 'Actually, I'm Max's half-brother.' He smiled. 'Different fathers. I believe you knew Max's father better than mine.'

Caroline had the good grace to blush, and Henry instantly warmed towards her. 'And he's not so little these days either. He's just finishing Cambridge, and then he's hoping to go back out to LA, I think. Wants to direct.'

Since that first meeting with Henry, she and Christopher had been invited to dinner at Manor Farm on a couple of occasions, and tonight they were finally returning the favour.

Caroline sat with Gary Ellis on her left and Henry on her right, in seventh heaven. Gary and Millicent, the lesbian, had been making horribly blue jokes all night. The latest involved a farmer's wife performing fellatio on a variety of different livestock. George's po-faced wife

Lucy looked as if she might be about to explode with disapproval.

'Did Caroline tell you that Henrietta, our eldest, had a little boy last month?' She was babbling boringly on to poor Christopher in a desperate attempt to rein in the bawdy banter. 'Cosmo. He's really *terribly* sweet,' she gushed. 'Isn't he, George?'

Now a QC in his mid-sixties, Caroline's brother seemed to have become even more small minded and ridiculous with age. He didn't reply, but instead nodded absently at his wife, puffing pretentiously on an in-between-courses cigar.

'I think he's still feeling a *leetle* bit embarrassed about becoming a grandpa,' Lucy simpered in a stage whisper to the hapless, cornered Christopher.

'Fuckin' 'ell!' boomed Gary, from the other end of the table, staring unashamedly at his hostess's breasts. 'What does that make you, Caroline, a great-aunt? I wish I'd 'ad a great-aunt wot looked like that!' He cackled lascivi-ously, before adding, to Lucy's frank astonishment, 'If your 'enrietta 'as any trouble with the old breast-feedin', I'm sure Great-Aunt Caroline wouldn't mind 'elpin' aht! Eh, love?'

Catching one another's eye, Caroline and Christopher dissolved into giggles, not so much at Ellis's crude humour but at both her brothers' outraged pomposity, and furious, red-faced mutterings of 'well I never'.

''Ow's business?' Ellis had turned to Henry, apparently oblivious to the furore his earlier remark had caused. 'I drove past your place the other day. Lovely bit o' property.'

'Thank you,' said Henry, rather stiffly. From anyone else he would have been pleased at the compliment to his beloved estate. But having seen some of Gary Ellis's monstrosities first hand, hearing *him* admire Manor Farm was rather like hearing a rapist compliment your wife's legs. It made him very uneasy. 'Business is booming, actually. We've just begun diversifying out of dairy for the first time and we're quite excited about it.' He smiled across the table at his wife, who smiled back.

Muffy Arkell was very pretty in a ruddy-cheeked, no-make-up, tomboyish sort of way. Henry liked to boast that she looked just the same now as she had done when he'd met her at sixteen. Looking at her kind, innocent face gazing back at her husband across the table, Caroline could well believe it. The pair of them were obviously still deeply in love.

She knew she wasn't the only one who had noticed how ravishing Muffy was looking this evening, even under-dressed as she was in a pair of grey cords that accentuated her long, slim legs and an arctic-green cashmere jumper that swamped her figure, but brought out the intoxicating green of her eyes.

Christopher had long been an ardently chaste admirer of Mrs Arkell's charms, and had cast the odd longing glance in her direction throughout dinner, much to Caroline's amusement. But Gary, who had none of her husband's gentlemanly scruples, had been positively drooling over the poor girl all evening, pressing his leg against hers under the table when he'd thought no one was looking and taking every opportunity to paw her with his clammy hands when passing food or wine to his fellow guests. Henry seemed to be the only person in the room who hadn't noticed.

It was quite clear from her embarrassed, flushed face that Muffy in no way welcomed his attentions, although she was far too polite to make a scene. Caroline began to wish that she'd listened to Christopher and not sat the two of them together.

Perhaps Gary Ellis wasn't as harmless and amusing as she'd first thought? He'd been boorish, rude and drunk for most of the evening. Not even the amusement factor of her brothers' spluttering outrage had been enough to make up for the burden of his company.

Driving home a few hours later, Muffy was finally free to vent her frustration on a now happily drunk Henry.

'Honestly, that man is really too much,' she said, grinding their ancient Land Rover into first as they chugged up the steep hill towards the village. 'He made my flesh creep.' She shuddered at the memory of Ellis's hot, eager hand lecherously squeezing her knee throughout pudding.

'I know,' said Henry, grimacing. 'Just hearing him talk about Manor Farm – "lovely bit o' property" – made me want to wring his neck. Have you seen that leisure centre he built in that gorgeous valley over in Lechlade? Too vile for words.'

'Bugger the farm,' said Muffy indignantly. 'He was trying to feel me up for most of the night, the disgusting old goat.'

'He what?' spluttered Henry, flabbergasted. 'I never saw anything. Why didn't you say something?'

'Hen*reee*! Honestly. How could you not have noticed? He was pestering me for hours. I think Caroline was mortified.'

'Well, so she bloody should be,' he mumbled grumpily, angry at himself for having missed his chance to play the gallant hero. 'Damn cheek of the man.'

He gazed moodily out of the window at the dim shadows of Batcombe village, its picture-postcard loveliness illuminated only by the pale silver of an almost full moon and the occasional bedroom light still on in one or two of the cottages. Henry never ceased to be amazed by the beauty of the Cotswolds.

'Well,' he muttered darkly, 'he's got about as much chance of scoring with you as he has of ever getting his grubby little hands on my farm, I can tell you that for nothing.'

Muffy rolled her eyes indulgently. She adored her husband. But sometimes she wondered whether Henry actually loved that farm more than he loved her.

Chapter Twenty-two

'For heaven's sake, child, cheer up. You look like you've lost a shilling and found sixpence.'

Marsha and Siena were sitting in a chic little bistro, tucked away in a cobbled street just behind the Champs-Elysées. The weather was still vile so they opted for a table inside by the window. It was blowing an absolute gale outside, and big green leaves from the horse chestnuts swept and tumbled along the winding street, prematurely ripped from the trees before they'd had a chance to turn brown.

Maybe it was the weather which was bringing the girl down? Marsha could not think of any other explanation for Siena's gloomy mood. Yesterday's show had been an unmitigated triumph. From the second she had stepped out on to the catwalk, it was as if some supernatural confidence had possessed her, and she'd come alive. 'Electrifying!' was how the fashion editor of *Le Figaro* had described her in this morning's paper. She had even made it to page three of the *Daily Mail* back home, which had run a magnificent picture of the finale of the show, showing Siena being cheered on by the front row in a pair of lime-green hot pants and a latex dominatrix slashed top, under the headline: 'McMania!'

What more could she possibly want?

Siena prodded morosely at her *croque monsieur* with a fork and looked up at her agent.

'I'm sorry,' she said. 'I just wanted to have a chance to speak with him. He didn't even leave a card, you know? Nothing.'

With her face bare of make-up, except for a slick of Elizabeth Arden Eight Hour Cream on her lips and eyelids, and her hair tied back in a loose ponytail, Siena was unrecognisable from the glamorous, wanton creature in the *Daily Mail* picture. This morning she had opted for comfort clothes: an ancient pair of faded Levis tucked into sheepskin boots with a chunky navy blue sweater from the Gap. She looked about twelve.

Marsha sighed heavily. 'You're not still talking about that Silfen guy, are you?' she asked. 'Sweetie, if he didn't notice you, believe me, he's the only person in that room who didn't. Who cares if he doesn't call? I already had four messages from the agency when I woke up this morning – the phone's been ringing off the hook for you, Siena. Trust me, darling. You are about to become very rich, and very famous, *very* fast.'

Siena couldn't help but cheer up slightly at the sound of the words 'rich' and 'famous' so close to her own name.

'You really think so?' She picked up Marsha's copy of the *Mail* and looked again at her picture and the caption. 'I don't know,' she said gloomily. 'Look at that: McMania. I think people are only interested because of my name. Because of my fucking father.'

Marsha took another sip of her *café au lait*. She had seen these sorts of parent problems before – the resentment, the tantrums, the insecurity – but it usually happened with much younger girls, the fourteen- and fifteen-year-olds who were leaving Mummy and Daddy for the first time. Siena was basically an adult. Her obsession with her parents – her apparent hatred of them – was baffling.

'Look, sweetie, we've talked about this, remember?' she said patiently. '*Of course* people are interested because of your name, your history. Why wouldn't they be? That name is an asset, just like that face and those tits.'

Siena glared at her across the table.

'Oh, come on,' Marsha insisted. 'You know it is. But that doesn't mean those people were cheering you on yesterday just because you're Pete McMahon's daughter.'

'No?' said Siena sulkily.

'No. They loved you because you've got a great look, and because you've got talent.'

'Well, if I've got so much bloody talent, how come Jamie Silfen just buggered off home?' asked Siena.

'Christ, I don't know.' Marsha was starting to get exasperated. She'd taken a huge chance in signing Siena, and quite frankly a little gratitude for her phenomenal, almost instant success might not have gone amiss. 'Maybe he was actually there to see the clothes?' she suggested.

'Oh, please,' said Siena.

'Maybe he was tired. Maybe he had a bad day. Maybe you're just not his type. Who gives a shit?'

Siena pushed her untouched plate aside and lit up another cigarette. That was one good thing about France: at least there weren't tobacco fascists lurking in every corner.

'Look,' said Marsha, already regretting losing her temper with the girl who was now, undoubtedly, one of her most bankable assets. 'I know you don't believe it now. But there is more to life than becoming an actress.'

'Not for me there isn't,' said Siena matter-of-factly.

'Everybody loves to knock modelling,' continued Marsha. 'They make out that all the girls are thick as shit. But the truth is, modelling can be a fantastic career. And for the girls that play their cards right – the really smart ones – it can even be a long career. Look at Cindy Crawford. If she's not still making millions ten years from now' – she threw her arms open melodramatically – 'then I'm Marilyn bloody Monroe.'

Siena laughed.

'Actually, I think you'll find that *I'm* the new Marilyn, darling!' she joked.

'I'll drink to that,' said Marsha, signalling to the waiter to bring them over the wine list. 'Just do me a favour and try not to shag any presidents. Or their brothers.'

'Eeugh,' said Siena, as an image of a naked Bill Clinton

loomed into mental view. 'No danger of that. I think I'll stick to footballers.'

'Ah!' Marsha's beady little eyes lit up like Olympic torches. 'The lovely Mario. So, go on, spill the beans. How was he?'

Siena stubbed out her cigarette and smiled wickedly. 'Six out of ten,' she lied.

'No!' whispered Marsha like an overexcited schoolgirl. 'Only six? Really? What was the problem?'

Siena picked up the enormous brown pepper grinder from the centre of the table. 'Let's just say I could have had more fun with this.'

Marsha roared with laughter, a full-throated, raucous cackle. 'You know what your problem is, sweetheart? You're too damn spoiled.'

Siena grinned. 'So I've been told. Maybe you and my father should get together some time and compare notes.'

Back in her hotel room two hours later, she could hardly move for flowers and cards as she attempted to pack. A veritable busload of freebies had begun arriving in a steady stream throughout the day: an Hermès scarf, more Chanel scent than you could shake a stick at, even a sterling-silver pair of cufflinks in the shape of the Eiffel Tower, now jostled for position next to Siena's own screwed-up clothes on the elegantly faded antique bedspread. If only Louis Vuitton had sent her a new suitcase to put it all in.

She was scrunching a gorgeous vintage Alaia skirt into a tight ball in a valiant effort to wedge it into her suitcase when she was interrupted by a knock on the door.

'*Mademoiselle?*'

'Yeah,' Siena grunted between shoves. 'Come on in, it's open.'

Another vast bouquet of lilies entered the room, followed by a sweating bell boy.

'Holy crap, not more?' said Siena, looking round

frantically for somewhere he could put them. 'Just lay them on the chair for now.' She pointed to an armchair already piled high with empty gift boxes and wet towels, and the bell boy gingerly set the flowers down and stood hovering for his tip.

'There's a twenty-franc note on that shelf by the door,' said Siena, panting and tugging hopelessly at the zip on her suitcase. 'You can take that, if you like. I'm afraid I don't have any more cash.'

Siena had always been a big tipper, a reaction to her father's legendary meanness with money, and would have liked to have given the boy more.

'*Merci, mademoiselle,*' he said, apparently more than happy with the twenty. 'I also 'ave two messages for you.'

He held out two small white envelopes embossed with the hotel crest. With a sigh, Siena abandoned her battle with the zipper and took the notes from him.

'Thanks,' she said, catching her breath before strolling over to examine her flowers. 'You can go now.'

The lilies smelled so divine she wished she could take them with her back to London, but the arrangement was so huge it would need a whole seat to itself on the plane. 'Thank you for the most wonderful night,' the card read. 'Call me. Soon. Mario. PS. By the way, we lost, so you owe me dinner next time. xx'

Siena smiled to herself. She shouldn't have been so harsh about him to Marsha. He'd been a lot better than a six. Still, the last thing she needed right now was a serious boyfriend. She'd seen so many women put their lives and their dreams on hold over some guy, not least her own mother and grandmother, and she was certainly not about to join their ranks. Mario would simply have to remain a happy memory.

She looked at her watch.

Five fifteen.

She was supposed to meet Marsha in the lobby at six and then go straight to the airport. It seemed incredible that she had only been in Paris for three days. She felt like a different person. Mario, the show, meeting Ines, all the attention and the press – she had had her first small taste of fame, and after so many years of waiting it had come, quite literally, overnight.

Being overlooked by Jamie Silfen had been the only fly in her ointment. Marsha was right, though. In the grand scheme of things, how much did that really matter?

After yesterday's success there would be other shows, perhaps even international campaigns. Soon, Siena confidently predicted, she would become a household name, one of the girls that her schoolfriends and their little sisters all longed to be like. That had always been her plan anyway – to make a name for herself as a model and then have the casting agents come to her. And she had to admit, despite the fact that she wouldn't trust her as far as she could throw her, Marsha had done an incredible job at catapulting her career into the fast lane, from a (late) standing start.

Silfen could wait. Siena would have him eating out of her palm some day.

But underlying today's elation had been the nagging realisation that some time very soon her parents would get wind of yesterday's events. She tried to convince herself that, once they saw her overwhelmingly positive press, they might, if not change their minds, then at least soften their position and let her delay her place at Oxford for a year. She struggled to picture Pete looking at the *Daily Mail* picture and smiling admiringly at her triumph – but even she had to admit the image wasn't really working.

He'd be mad with her, of course he would.

Nothing new there.

She'd just have to call him when she got back to London and face the music. Still, she felt cautiously optimistic that somehow, perhaps with her mother's help, she would get him to come around eventually. One thing was for sure: nothing on God's earth would persuade her to give up her modelling now.

Standing up, she moved over to the window and gazed out at the dirty Parisian skyline. Today was her last day in Paris, that magical city that had inspired generations of artists and lovers and which seemed, even now, to be looking out for her, protecting her and helping her to realise her long-cherished hopes and dreams. Pete's wrath, his spite and his mean-spiritedness, could not touch her in Paris – she wouldn't allow it.

Bending down, she picked up the two white envelopes that the bell boy had given her, and examined each carefully. Opening the first envelope, she felt a brief stab of what might have been guilt. Janey Cash had called. She and Patrick both wanted to say well done and they couldn't wait to see her when she got home.

England hardly qualified as 'home', thought Siena, although she was no longer certain herself just where home might be.

Darling Janey. She loved her dearly, but part of her wished that her old friend would get angry about the way she'd treated her brother, rather than just carrying on as if nothing had happened. And why was Pat being so bloody big about it? She'd dumped him without any explanation – how could she put into words how frightened she was of allowing herself to love anybody, ever? All Patrick knew was that she'd stopped taking his calls one day. Period. If anyone had treated *her* like that, she wouldn't rest until she'd got good and even. 'You can get mad,' Duke always used to tell her. 'Just make sure you get even as well.'

The memory of her grandfather made her smile.

She scrumpled up the note, threw it into the huge pile of rubbish beside the chair and ripped open the second envelope.

It was from her mother. Could Siena phone home immediately.

Fuck, fuck and double fuck on a stick. How did they

know where she was staying? In fact, how did they even know she was in Paris at all? She'd told them last week that she'd agreed not to make the trip, hoping to buy herself a little time at least before breaking the news that her absence from Oxford was to be permanent. How on earth could they possibly have found out so soon?

She began pacing the room like a cornered cat. What time was it in LA? She did a quick calculation: eight in the morning. There was no way they could have seen the papers yet. Not that the show would have made the American press anyway, but her father was a news fiend, and often ordered the English newspapers as well – although not the *Daily Mail*. Pete considered it far too lowbrow.

So how did they know? It simply didn't make sense. Unless . . .

Her heart gave a sudden, sickening lurch. Could it be? Silfen.

Siena didn't know whether to laugh or cry. It was Jamie bloody Silfen, it had to be. He *had* noticed her after all. He'd seen the show, seen how the audience had loved her, but instead of contacting her directly he'd gone and called her fucking father! The more she thought about it, the more it made sense. Jamie knew Pete, both professionally and socially. In her excitement and surprise at seeing him there, in the audience, she'd completely overlooked the connection with her father. Pete, in fact, was the one person she'd been trying hardest all week to forget.

For almost a minute, she sat motionless on her bed trying to take it all in. Eventually she reached across for the phone and began to dial her parents' number.

'0–0–1 . . .' She pressed each digit with infinite reluctance. '. . . 3–1–0–8–2 . . .'

But it was no good. She couldn't do it. Gently but firmly she replaced the receiver.

Stamping down her anxiety with a supreme effort of will, she returned to her packing. Her father could wait until tomorrow morning. This trip to Paris had been the start of something wonderful for her, a real rite of passage. She couldn't place it exactly, but she felt sure it marked the first step back towards Hollywood, Hollywood on her own terms, and everything that Grandpa Duke had told her she could become.

With her own talent.

In her own right.

No one, least of all Pete, was going to spoil it for her.

At six o'clock that evening in Los Angeles, Pete McMahon signed the bottom of a document and handed it solemnly to his attorney.

He was sitting at his father's old desk, one of the very few artefacts he had requested from Hancock Park after the old man died. The lawyer hastily scribbled his witnessing signature below his client's and scurried out of the room, anxious to leave before the storm brewing between Pete and his wife erupted.

Claire was standing at the window looking out over the lights of West Hollywood below them, with her back to her husband. In her worsted tweed skirt and white polo-neck she looked more like a contemplative nun than a Hollywood mogul's wife. Although Pete couldn't see it, her face was as white as a ghost's.

'Please don't say anything,' said Pete, still seated, so quietly it was almost a whisper. 'Please. It's over.'

Claire turned to look at him, scanning his face for any sort of emotion or weakness, any doubts about this terrible decision that she could cling on to, or use to try to change his mind. But the expression she saw was one she remembered well. It was the same expression he'd had back in the study at Hancock Park, when he'd insisted on sending Siena away to England: desolate, blank, unreachable. She knew in her heart it was hopeless.

'Oh, Pete. What do you mean? How can it ever be over?' Tears streamed down her cheeks, and her hands flew to her hair, distraught. Why was he doing this? What was he trying to prove? 'And what if I said I won't let you do this? She's my child, Peter, my only child.'

He could hear the terrible anguish in her voice and wished he could comfort her. But it was all too late. Siena wasn't their child any more. She had proved that now beyond any doubt.

Duke had stolen her from them, turned her against them for ever. Even from beyond the grave, he had plunged his hated, destructive hand into the heart of Pete's own family and poisoned it with misery from within.

Claire was shaking.

'What if I said I'd leave you?'

The words hung in the air between them like lead.

Pete put his head in his hands. For almost a minute, neither of them spoke.

'Will you?' he said at last. His right hand, still holding the pen, had started shaking violently, and heavy globules of black ink spilled down on to his white linen cuffs. 'Will you leave me?'

Claire was so overwhelmed with sorrow, she almost felt she might hear her heart cracking open. But even in the depths of her own misery, when she looked at her beloved husband's stricken face, she knew that she could not abandon him.

She realised in that moment, with searing clarity, that she was all he had. And for all the pain he caused her, she loved him.

'No,' she said softly. 'No, Pete. I won't leave you.'

'Never?' he whispered. 'Whatever happens?'

She walked over and put her arms around him.

'Never.'

It was raining in Knightsbridge when Siena finally came to, and the dull, cloudy English light of late morning spluttered rather than streamed through her bedroom window. So much for Boiling Britain. She seemed to be bringing the shitty weather with her wherever she went.

Groggily, she made her way into the kitchen, where she found a note from Isabella, the McMahons' Spanish housekeeper in London, explaining that she had run out to the dry cleaner's but that Siena's breakfast was all laid out and ready for her on the table in the dining room.

Siena wandered through, picking up the Saturday *Times* and a letter addressed to her as she went, and was soon settled down to a feast of freshly ground coffee, wheat toast and her favourite crunchy peanut butter.

The letter was from Oxford, nothing important, just a wadge of information about the freshers' week she had already missed, various college societies and events and a lecture schedule for the Michaelmas term. Siena pushed it all to one side and started skimming the fashion section of the Saturday magazine. She was deeply engrossed in a piece about the revival, yet again, of the micro mini when an overburdened Isabella burst through the door, weighed down with a whopping armful of her dry cleaning.

'Belli, let me help you with that,' she said, jumping up to take the clothes before the housekeeper gave herself a hernia.

Isabella was one of the few people in Siena's life whom she unconditionally adored. Fat and warm and motherly, she had done everything in her power to make the London flat seem like home when, as a lonely little girl, Siena had been abandoned there for endless half-terms and Easter holidays. Not having any children of her own, she found it easy to coddle and indulge Siena in a way that the child's own parents would never have dreamt of. Home cooking, constant physical affection, ceaseless praise for every achievement, no matter how small, and comfort for every setback – these were the things that Siena associated with Isabella.

'Ees OK,' the stocky little woman protested as Siena

lifted coat after coat from her arms. 'There ees some-thing else for you. Take these.' She handed her four sheets of A4 which she had carefully stapled together at the top left-hand corner. 'Eet's a fox,' she said gravely.

'Is it?' asked Siena seriously, trying not to laugh. 'From the fox machine? Well, I'd probably better have a look, then.'

Dumping the clothes unceremoniously on the sofa, she returned to the table and her fourth piece of toast. God, she was in demand at the moment! It must be from the agency, hopefully with some decent jobs for next season. Siena started to read.

'Last Will and Testament . . .'

No. Oh, no, no, no. He couldn't be serious.

'My daughter, Siena Claire . . . disinherited . . .'

The words blurred before her eyes.

'Immediate effect . . . to quit the premises, 88 Sloane Gardens, London, SW3 . . . wish no further contact . . .'

Siena put her hand to her mouth. She thought she might be going to throw up, but the feeling passed. Angrily, she hurled the fax on to her pile of Oxford papers. Melodramatic bastard. No further contact indeed. Who did he think he was, Lord fucking Capulet?

She picked up the phone and punched out her parents' number before her rage had time to dissipate into fear. She would not grovel to that bastard. If that was what he was waiting for, he'd be waiting one hell of a long time.

'McMahon residence.'

It was Mary, the stupid pseudo-English housekeeper that Pete had hired two years ago, to howls of derision from Siena, who insisted she must have been born Maria-Elena, her British accent was so terrible.

'Hey, Mary.' She tried to sound cheery. 'It's Siena. Is my mom home?'

'Er . . . Just a moment, please.'

Siena heard the unmistakable frantic scrabbling of someone trying to cover the receiver with one hand while whispering and signalling instructions with the other. Something was definitely up.

'I'm sorry, Siena,' she said after a few long seconds. 'Your mother is unavailable at the moment.'

Siena could feel her hackles rising. Stupid, pretentious little cow. 'What do you mean, unavailable?' she snapped. 'Do you mean she's out?'

Another long pause.

'Yes,' said Mary.

'I see,' said Siena. This was like pulling teeth. 'Well, when will she be back?'

'I'm afraid I can't say. I'm not sure,' answered Mary cautiously.

Siena hung up. This was getting her nowhere. With her heart in her mouth, she dialled the number for Pete's office.

'McMahon Pictures, please hold,' said a voice before she'd had a chance to draw breath.

A rather tinny version of James Taylor's 'Fire and Rain' began playing. James had got as far as 'lonely times when I could not find a friend' before a female voice picked up again.

'Sorry to keep you waiting, this is Mr McMahon's office. How may I help you?'

'Tara?'

'Yes?' The unexpected use of her own name had thrown the girl completely. Her tone instantly became more guarded. 'Who is this?'

'It's Siena.'

More silence. It was the first time Siena could ever remember Pete's poisonous PA being lost for words. It was Tara who had so delighted in keeping Hunter's letters from her when they had first been separated, Tara who had gone out of her way to reinforce Pete's own view of his daughter as spoiled, difficult and in need of a firm hand. Tara enjoyed a place very close to the top of Siena's fantasy hellfire wish list.

'You can't speak to your father, I'm afraid,' she said

firmly. It hadn't taken her long to regain her composure. 'He's in a meeting and won't be out till two.'

Siena longed to insist that she interrupt him, but knowing it wouldn't do any good she decided not to give her the satisfaction.

'Fine,' she said curtly. 'I'll call back then.'

'If you like,' said Tara.

'Tell him I called,' said Siena, hanging up before Tara had a chance to sneak in some spiteful last word.

She wondered how much she knew about what had happened. She'd probably sat there and redrafted the will for him, evil little nothing that she was. Siena had never fathomed what it was that made Tara hate her so much. Normally she put down female hostility to envy, of her looks, her wealth and her so-called jet-set lifestyle. But Tara had had it in for her since she was ten years old. This particular hatred evidently ran deeper.

Feeling a little panicked now, she tried calling home again. This time Claire picked up herself.

'Pete?'

Siena heard the apprehension in her mother's voice. She must have called in the middle of a difficult conversation between her parents.

'No, Mom. It's me, Siena.'

Relief at hearing her mother's voice had temporarily eclipsed her usual anger and resentment. It was the first time in years that Claire had heard her daughter sounding so warm towards her.

'Hello, Mom?' she repeated, panic surging up again like lava from her stomach in the face of Claire's silence. 'Are you still there?'

'Yes, Siena, I'm here.' Her voice sounded odd, almost as if it were breaking. When she spoke again, it was barely a whisper. 'What do you want?'

The lava of Siena's fear suddenly erupted into a much more familiar volcano of rage. What kind of a stupid question was that?

'What do I *want*?' she yelled. 'What do you mean,

what do I *want*? This is your daughter calling, you know, your daughter, the one you don't give a shit about?'

'Siena . . .'

'What do you think I fucking want? Isabella just gave me Dad's fax. I want to know what the fuck is going on. Did you put him up to this?'

'Oh, Siena, of course I didn't,' pleaded Claire desperately. 'I warned you, darling. I tried to get you to see sense about this McQueen business, to call your father at least . . .' Her voice was breaking with the effort of trying to suppress so much emotion.

'And what?' said Siena. 'I didn't call you back in time, so, hey, guess what, I've been disinherited? You don't have a fucking daughter any more? Is that it?'

The biting sarcasm in her voice failed to conceal her pain. Claire felt for her, but what words of comfort could she possibly offer her now? She'd made her choice and she was just going to have to live with it.

'Do you have any idea how ridiculous that is?' Siena continued. 'How insane? I mean, have you actually read this, Mom?' Claire could hear the pages of Pete's fax rustling six thousand miles away. 'He says he wants me out of the flat. No further contact. He's fucking *evicting* me! Did you know about this?'

'Yes, I knew about it.' Claire sobbed quietly. 'He showed me last night. I'm sorry, Siena.'

'Great.' Siena gave an empty laugh. 'He showed you last night, did he? And what did you say, Mom? Oh, that's nice, dear, go ahead and cut her off like some fucking infected limb?' Claire winced at Siena's temper. It wasn't making this any easier. 'She won't go to Oxford, she won't become the little English lady we all wanted. So why don't we just erase her altogether? Is that it, Mom? Cut your losses and just move on?'

Siena could feel her heart pounding so violently she half expected it to burst through her ribs and land with a thud on the table. The dining room, which only minutes ago had seemed as homely and familiar as an old toy, now looked strange and surreal to her. Was this conversation really happening?

'I'm sorry, darling,' Claire said again hopelessly. Her voice had reverted back to eerie desolation. 'It's not as if we haven't tried. Why did you have to push him? Your father has given you chance after chance.'

'To what?' spat Siena disdainfully. 'To be someone else?'

'I don't know what to say,' said Claire. 'You went to France, you did that show, in absolute defiance of him. You have to take some responsibility for that, Siena.'

'Right,' said Siena, drawing her pride and anger around her like a shield. 'So just let me get this straight. Dad has decided I'm no longer his child. And you agree with him? Is that what you're saying?'

Claire had never hated herself more than she did at that moment. She loved her daughter. But Siena had never understood Pete, or the terrible scars that Duke's behaviour had inflicted on him. She had never seen the ways in which, unwittingly, her rebelliousness and her love for Duke had deepened his pain until it was literally no longer bearable.

'Your father has made his decision,' she said. 'I have to respect that.'

'No, Mom,' said Siena, furious with herself for trembling. 'You don't. You don't *have* to respect it. You *choose* to respect it.'

'Siena . . .'

'So don't lay this all on Dad, OK? *You* chose this, Mom. You chose it.'

Claire was silent. There was nothing else to say.

Siena, feeling strangely empowered suddenly, replaced the receiver. It seemed ludicrous, somehow, to say 'goodbye' to your own mother. She took one deep breath and exhaled slowly, waiting for the enormity of what had just happened to hit her. But the odd thing was she felt fine, she really did.

That was it, then. It was over.

Chapter Twenty-three

Batcombe, England, three years later . . .

'Right, shut up, please, everyone shut up, I've got a joke.'

Henry Arkell was sitting at the head of the table, trying to make himself heard over the excited rabble of his assorted children and dogs. 'Two horses, sitting in the field,' he began, reading from the white slip that had fallen out of his cracker.

'Horses don't sit, Daddy,' piped up a voice to his right, belonging to a child whose entire face appeared to be covered in a combination of chocolate sauce and icing sugar.

'Be quiet, Madeleine,' Henry continued, wiping ineffectually at the goo with his napkin, 'you're putting me off. Right, two horses, sitting in a field, and one of them turns to the other and says . . .'

'Horses don't speak either, Dad,' interrupted another voice from the far end of the table, this time his elder son, Charlie.

'They do if they're Mr Ed,' said Bertie, the six-year-old. 'Can I have some more Coke?'

'Mr Ed isn't real, you doofus,' pronounced Charlie scornfully.

'Well, nor are the horses in Dad's joke, doofazoid.' Bertie hurled a plastic whistle in his brother's direction. 'Are they, Dad? Your horses aren't real, are they?'

Henry opened his mouth to speak, but Madeleine had already begun to wail.

'Horses *are* real! Blackie's definitely real. She's the best pony in the world, and in the universe and in space. You can't say she isn't real, can he, Mummy?'

'I don't think he meant that Blackie wasn't real,

darling.' Muffy, nominated family peacekeeper, tried in vain to placate her daughter.

'Space *is* the universe,' said Bertie authoritatively.

'Blackie *is* real!' maintained Madeleine.

'Jesus Christ,' said Henry, who was by now looking rather defeated with his yellow paper crown askew above his springy, light brown hair. 'I'm trying to tell a fucking joke here. Is anyone going to let me finish my bloody joke?'

'I don't think so, darling.' Muffy smiled at him lovingly. 'Why don't you have another glass of claret?'

She handed the decanter to Max, who passed it along to his brother. He loved Christmas lunches at Batcombe.

'Daddy said "fucking",' Charlie pointed out with a grin. 'He has to put a pound in the swearing tin.'

'Two pounds,' said Bertie, watching with delight as his Coke foamed up over the rim of his glass and began to form a pool on the mahogany table. 'He said "bloody" as well. He said no one would let him finish his "bloody" joke. Didn't you, Dad?'

Henry poured himself a glass of claret, and with his best attempt at dignity got up from the table, taking his drink with him.

'I'm going to go and sit in the drawing room,' he announced to the table at large. 'If anybody wants me, I will be sitting in front of the fire with the jumbo *Times* crossword.'

'But what about presents?' protested all three children in unison.

'Anyone who is hoping for presents,' said Henry, holding up his forefinger for silence, 'would be very well advised to leave their father alone for twenty minutes . . .'

'Twenty *minutes*!' they wailed in horror.

'Twenty minutes,' repeated Henry, 'while I finish my glass of wine in peace. Then – and only then – there *may*' – he paused for dramatic effect – 'be some present-opening.'

'But what can we do for twenty minutes?' asked a grief-stricken Bertie. 'That's for ever.'

'You can help Mummy clear the table,' said Max, waving down the howls of protest. 'Come on, Charlie, you can scrape off those plates for Titus and Boris. The sooner we get started, the sooner we can get to those presents.'

Batcombe was Max's sanctuary.

Henry, his much older half-brother and only real family, had inherited Manor Farm from his father, Max's mother's first husband, ten years earlier. It had been in a terribly dilapidated state back then, a picturesque but decaying mess of ancient barns and outbuildings, clustered around a much neglected but nevertheless magnificent sixteenth-century manor house. Henry and his young wife had moved in, full of energy and ambition, determined to revitalise both the house and the business. And revitalise them they had.

From the dining-room window, Max now looked out across a spotless yard to the gleaming rows of snow-covered milking sheds, and beyond them to his brother's three hundred acres of rolling Cotswold countryside. Every hedgerow, wooden fence and dry-stone wall had been painstakingly restored by Henry over the last decade, and the farm was now picture perfect. Max had travelled all over the globe, but he had yet to see anywhere that topped Batcombe for the sheer, heart-lifting beauty of the landscape.

Thanks to years of hard slog by Muffy, the house itself had become as much of a triumph as the farm. Henry's father, who had lived there for most of his life, rarely used any of the larger formal rooms, some of which had mildewed wallpaper hanging from the ceilings when they first moved in. Now, with the wood panelling in the drawing room lovingly restored, and every corner of the house crammed with books, brightly coloured Persian rugs and cushions, and an eclectic mix of objets d'art, ranging from obscure family heirlooms to interesting junk shop finds, the manor was once again a home.

As a teenager, Max had spent a lot of time with Henry and Muffy and his three young nieces and nephews, helping out on the farm. If it hadn't been for the fact that he loved his brother so much, he would certainly have envied him. His home, his rock-solid marriage, his kids, his little kingdom at Batcombe – he really did have it all. But one of the nicest things about Henry was, he knew how lucky he was. Always laughing and joking around, never with a bad word to say about anyone – not even their mother, who had effectively abandoned him when she met Max's father and flitted off to California – Henry was a true hero in his brother's eyes.

Having given up on getting any constructive help from the children, Max and Muffy had cleared the table between them, and Muffy was now extracting fragments of vanilla pods from the sugar bowl so that she could sweeten her own tea, before taking a cup in to Henry.

'D'you think it's been twenty minutes?' she asked, pouring a dash of milk into both Max's and Henry's mugs. 'You did want milk, didn't you?'

Max nodded. 'Even if it hasn't,' he said, 'Bertie's going to explode if you make him wait one more minute for his presents. Anyway, I don't know why you pander to Henry like that. If anyone needs twenty minutes' break today, it's you, not him.'

Muffy sighed and wiped her hands on her apron. 'Tell me about it. Honestly, I know Christmas is always a lot of work but it's been such a struggle this year, especially with money being so tight. I've done all my own baking, and Charlie and I made all those new decorations together, which took an absolute age.'

'Is money tight?' asked Max, taking a tentative sip of his too-hot tea. 'I thought the business was going great guns. Haven't you just diversified?'

'We have,' said Muffy, emptying a packet of Bourbon biscuits on to a plate for the children. 'But it took a lot of investment, and we'd already borrowed quite a bit to revamp the milking sheds and restore the big barn last year. And now we have Bertie's school fees as well as Charlie's to think about. We're definitely a bit pushed.'

'I thought Bertie got a scholarship,' asked Max, risking a second gulp of tea.

Muffy shook her head. 'Flunked it. Look, I wouldn't worry, it isn't like we're stony broke or anything,' she said, catching his concerned expression. 'Just a bit of a cash flow problem. Maddie will just have to wait till next year for the Malibu Barbie mansion, and the boys can jolly well put up with homemade mince pies. Do you know they're over three pounds for a box of six in M&S?'

'Scandalous,' said Max, helping himself to one of Muffy's efforts from the open cake tin on the table. 'Anyway,' he said through a mouthful of crumbs, 'yours are ten times better.'

After the last present had been opened and the drawing-room floor had become a sea of shredded wrapping paper and empty boxes, Henry and Max decided to clear their heads and take the dogs out for a walk.

The winter sky was already darkening, and the cold, crisp bite of the smoky air jolted both brothers out of their drunken Christmas stupor as they strode across the fields, with the two King Charles spaniels, Titus and Boris, running along excitedly at their heels.

'So when are you off back to sunny California?' asked Henry, picking up a stray stick and throwing it for Titus.

'The twenty-eighth,' said Max. 'I'm not looking forward to it, actually.'

'Oh?' said Henry. 'Why not? I thought you had rather a sweet deal living with Hunter McMahon? Did I tell you his mother's married to Christopher Wellesley these days, living over at Thatchers?'

'Yes,' said Max frostily, 'you told me.'

He had not laid eyes on Caroline since he was a teenager, and remembered her only as Hunter's selfish and neglectful mother. It irked him a little that Henry and Muffy seemed to think she was terrific fun, although to be fair Henry's father had been friendly with the Wellesleys for the whole of his life, and Caroline was, apparently, greatly improved as a result of her late marriage to Christopher.

'Never introduce Hunter to my wife, will you?' said Henry, swiftly changing the subject, having remembered that Max had a bee in his bonnet about Caroline. 'She loves that bloody *Counsellor* rubbish. I'm sure she'd swan off into the sunset with him given half a chance.'

Max laughed. 'Don't worry, you're safe there. Hunter's in love. With a very nice girl, actually – Tiffany. He met her at an audition for his new show, *UCLA*. It's huge in the States already, but I don't think they're showing it here yet.'

'Tiffany?' Henry raised an eyebrow. 'That doesn't sound like a very nice girl's name to me.'

'I know,' said Max, 'but she really is. Most of the girls in LA are such gold-diggers, especially the ones around Hunter, but she's different.'

'So, why don't you want to go back?' Henry pressed him, as Titus came bounding back with the stick clamped between his jaws.

'I don't know.' Max sighed. 'Living at Hunter's is great, I know I'm very lucky. But sometimes it just gets to me, you know? He's so fucking successful. And rich. Drop, Titus!'

He picked up the stick and threw a dummy for Titus, before hurling it fifty yards in the opposite direction for Boris, who was fatter and slower and needed the odds stacked in his favour when it came to playing fetch. 'Everywhere we go he's mobbed by these incredible women.'

'I thought you said they were all gold-diggers,' said Henry.

'They are,' said Max. 'Which is why none of them are interested in me. I don't *have* any gold. That's the problem. Hunter's been so generous, he's an incredible friend, but he makes me feel like such a fucking failure. I mean, I'm twenty-five years old, and I still live in my buddy's spare room. How tragic is that?'

Henry put a paternal arm around his brother's shoulder. 'Look, Max, twenty-six is young. Take it from me. You still have plenty of time to make money. And you always knew that this directing lark was going to be a bit of a gamble. You can't expect to hit the big time right away.'

That was a bit of an understatement, thought Max bitterly. He'd been out in LA now for three full years and still hadn't earned enough to pay Hunter back a quarter of what he owed him. If it hadn't been for a couple of theatre gigs he'd been offered back in England last year, he wouldn't have been able to afford to stay in America at all, even allowing for his subsidised living arrangements.

'Hunter had the McMahon name behind him,' Henry insisted. 'You've got to do it all yourself, and that takes time and effort and patience. Cut yourself some slack.'

They came to the bottom of the hill and scrambled over a rotting old stile into some woodland. Henry frowned at the state of his fence – he'd have to get that sorted out before spring.

'What about you?' Max asked. 'Muff mentioned something about money being tight. Is everything OK?'

'Oh, yes, yes,' said Henry, waving away the question with a frown and increasing his pace. Max took the hint – whatever was wrong, his brother didn't want to talk about it. 'Don't worry about me. You just concentrate on keeping your own spirits up. The worst thing you could do now would be to lose your confidence.'

Max shrugged gloomily. 'I think I've probably done that already.'

'Nonsense. You're just in a funk, Maxy. Things will look brighter when you get back out there, I'm sure. And if they don't, well, you know you've always got a home with us. The kids would die of happiness if you ever decided to give the old farming a try.'

Max felt quite choked with gratitude. Without Henry's unwavering love and support in his life, God only knew where he'd be.

'Maybe I need a girlfriend,' he said, embarrassed at his emotion and wanting to change the subject.

'Dear God, boy, I hope you aren't going to start complaining about a lack of sex. Because if you are, I'm afraid I may have to hit you,' said Henry. 'Try having three kids and a farm to run. Then you'll discover the meaning of sex-starved.'

'I'm not sex-starved,' said Max, with devastating understatement. 'That's not what I meant.' For all his moping about LA girls' materialism, he still managed to screw more than his fair share of them, and certainly more than the faithfully loved-up Hunter. Still, there was a part of him that envied what Hunter and Tiffany had, or Henry and Muffy for that matter. Recently his litany of casual sexual conquests had begun to seem empty and hollow by comparison.

He quickened his pace as they started up a second hill, determined to work off at least some of Muffy's delicious Christmas cooking.

'I tell you what,' said Henry, warming to his theme of sexual frustration, 'you know who's absolutely bloody gorgeous, but don't tell Muff I said so?'

'No, who?' said Max.

'Hunter's little sister. Siena. Or is it his niece? Did you see those pictures of her in *GQ* last month? Fucking hell, she's sexy. Why don't you get Hunter to set you up?'

'With Siena?' Max laughed. 'Now that would be a match made in hell. Besides, Hunter hasn't spoken to her in years, not since we were kids.'

In the past two years, Siena had become very well known as a model, and even fashion-phobes like Max couldn't fail to have seen her picture on billboards and TV, advertising everything from Versace couture to shampoo. Out of the 'top ten' girls – the ones whose annual earnings were in seven rather than six figures and whose names appeared as frequently in the gossip columns as the fashion pages – Siena was known as the 'man's woman', sexier, curvier and sassier than any of the other 'supers' – men loved her for her raw sex appeal, and women loved her for the fact that she wore clothes that weren't designed to fit a size-zero giraffe.

'Oh, that's right, I forgot. She was in your gang before you got sent to Ampleforth, wasn't she?' said Henry. 'I tell you what, I wouldn't have minded playing a spot of doctors and nurses with her.'

'God,' said Max, shaking his head, 'that was a long time ago.' Instantly the memories of hanging out at Hancock Park, and particularly all their fights about that tree house, came flooding back to him. 'She was an obnoxious little brat even then. Always had to be the centre of attention. She was the polar opposite of Hunter. Christ knows what she's like now, with half the world's men drooling at her feet.' He rolled his eyes dramatically. 'Spoiled as hell, I expect.'

They had reached the crest of the hill, and emerged from the woodland back on to open fields. The light had almost gone now and it was very cold. Suddenly Max longed to be back at the farm, warming himself with a nice malt whisky in front of the fire.

Thinking back to the Hancock Park days made him feel uneasy, somehow, almost depressed. Siena and Hunter and the tree house reminded him of his childish self – of high hopes, excitement and an unbounded optimism – that was no longer a part of who he was. Back then he'd thought he could do anything, be anything. Now his dreams of making it as a director were already crumbling, before they'd even really begun.

'You're shivering,' said Henry, breaking his reverie.

'Not used to the good old British winter any more, I suspect. Do you want my scarf?'

'No,' said Max. 'No thanks, I'm fine. Let's crack on and get home, though. I could murder a drink.'

Chapter Twenty-four

Tiffany Wedan arched her back and pulled him deeper inside her, closing her eyes as she felt her second orgasm build.

'Hmmmm,' she moaned, 'please.'

Hunter smiled down at the beautiful girl beneath him, her eyes closed, wet strands of long blonde hair clinging to a face flushed with desire, and tried hard to stop himself from coming.

'Please what?' he teased her. 'Please stop?'

'No!' she gasped out, her muscles instinctively gripping his cock tighter as her fingers started stroking and probing for his asshole.

'Ah, no you don't,' whispered Hunter, pulling her hand away. That really would finish him off. He bent lower so that his mouth was right by her ear. The tickling sensation of his breath there always heightened Tiffany's pleasure. 'You're a very naughty little girl,' he whispered, jabbing himself still deeper into her.

'Aaah,' she cried out, climaxing suddenly with such intense force, muscles spasming and arms clenched around him as though her life depended on it, that Hunter felt as if he were being sucked into a warm, wet black hole.

'Fuck! I love you!' he yelled, seconds later, as he finally let himself enjoy the orgasm he'd been trying to suppress for the last twenty minutes, rocking back and forth inside her with delight.

Afterwards, the two of them lay clasped together like exhausted limpets, tired and replete. It was incredible how, after almost three years together, she still made him feel like a fifteen-year-old with his first crush. Ever since he'd walked into that audition room at NBC and seen her looking so adorably shy and flustered, not to mention unbelievably sexy in her cheerleader's outfit, he'd been mesmerised by her. With her slender, coltish legs (she was almost his height) and thick, dark lashes framing deep, green eyes, Tiffany reminded him of a baby racehorse – beautiful but still a little unsure of herself. Her wide, pale pink lips had trembled as she stumbled over her first few lines, and it had been all he could do to tear his eyes away from them and focus on his own lines, so loudly had his heart been pounding.

Tiffany had been auditioning for the part of Kimbo Watson at the time, the darkly psychotic female lead in *UCLA*, a new series that Hugh Orchard had created especially for Hunter to capitalise on the massive success of *Counsellor*. Hunter played Gabe Sanderson, hunky college football captain, and had sat in on all the read-throughs for the Kimbo hopefuls. Tiffany didn't get the part, probably because everything about her radiated sunshine, not inner demons. But she had landed the smaller role of Sarah, the football team's physical therapist, and had been working with Hunter on the show – which was now right up there with *Counsellor* in the ratings – ever since.

Stretching her body upwards to kiss him on the lips again, she wondered in awe for the umpteenth time how she had ever gotten so lucky. She remembered how paralysed with nerves she'd been when she had first laid eyes on Hunter at that very first read-through. He was already an established star thanks to *Counsellor*, while she was still working as a waitress at Benny's Beans and Burgers in West Hollywood. Before *UCLA* she had barely worked in eighteen months, and was spending most of her days in a sweltering kitchen or serving over-priced heart attacks on a plate to revolting, lecherous custom-ers, while wearing a badge that cheerily proclaimed 'I make it happen – Tiffany!' Jeez, how much had she hated that stinking place.

It was all a far cry from the life she'd dreamed of when

she first set out from Estes Park, Colorado, to follow her dreams of becoming an actress.

Her parents had been against the idea from the start.

'She graduated magna cum laude, Marcie,' she remembered her normally mild-mannered father yelling at her mom, pointing at Tiffany as though she were an exhibit in a freak show. 'And you want her to throw that all away to become a waitress in Hollywood?'

'She wants to act, Jack,' said her mom, reasonably. 'She's young, and she's following her dream. What's wrong with that?'

'What's wrong with it? I'll tell you what's wrong with it. She'll end up like the rest of those poor suckers, all the small-town girls who grow up being told how pretty and talented they are by all the folks back home, and they head out to LA thinking they're gonna make it. They're gonna be *stars*.' He spat the word out with a bitterness born of his immense fear for his daughter. He loved her so much. Tiffany had never heard her dad speak like that to anyone. It made her feel sick. 'And ten years later,' he raged on, 'they're still serving pancakes at IHOP.'

'Oh, Jack,' said her mother gently, seeing Tiffany's horrified face.

'No, Marcie, I'm right about this and you know it. The waitresses are the lucky ones. Half of those girls end up working the streets. Or in . . .' He could barely bring himself to say it. '. . . in one of those depraved, pornographic films.'

'Jack Wedan!' her mother remonstrated, shocked. 'Don't be ridiculous. Tiffany would never get involved in anything like that.'

'And I won't be working as a waitress for the rest of my life either, Daddy,' Tiffany interjected, her face flushed with anger and disappointment. 'Don't you have any faith in me at all?'

How those words had come back to haunt her as she sweated away in Benny's kitchen alongside her best friend and flatmate, the gorgeously camp Lennox, another struggling actor. She had almost given up hope of ever making it in LA when Lennox had hauled her ass into that *UCLA* audition. And then suddenly, overnight, her life had changed. Just like in the movies.

The role of Sarah may only have been a small part, but it was network television and a regular income, two things she had hitherto barely allowed herself to dream of. Even more incredible, though, had been her blossoming relationship with Hunter. Of all the beautiful girls in the world, Hunter McMahon had chosen her. *Why?* Even now, three years later, she sometimes had to pinch herself when she woke up next to him, in case the whole thing were some sort of heavenly mirage.

For his part, Hunter knew that a lot of women wanted him, whether for his looks, his fame or his money. But he'd never been able to do what Max did, charming his way from one bed to the next, revelling in the fun and excitement of transient, casual flings. Unlike his best friend, Hunter had always been looking for companionship with a lover, and he had nothing in common with ninety per cent of the hot young LA actresses and models who pursued him.

But the way Tiffany wanted him, that was different. The way she clung on to him and screamed his name when they made love, the way her eyes lit up like a little kid at Christmas the moment he walked through the door – that was something else. He had never imagined that a woman so intelligent and talented and good and kind could ever love him the way that she did. She literally filled him with joy, and her love had given him a confidence he had never felt before.

Tiffany was the first woman, the first person in fact, that he had ever opened up to about his childhood. She had made him feel safe, slowly but surely gaining his confidence and trust until he felt able to talk about the loneliness and misery of growing up in Hancock Park, his difficult relationship with his mother and the terrible pain of his enforced separation from Siena.

Privately, Tiffany had always felt that if his supermodel niece was so perfect and had loved him so much, she could have made some sort of an effort to contact him after she became famous. She had never met Siena, of course, but the impression she got from magazine and TV interviews was of a rather spoiled little prima donna, nothing like the angelic figure Hunter so lovingly described. But she knew better than to question or challenge him about his precious memories. She understood that, apart from her, they were all he had.

He rolled on to his side and pulled the covers up over her naked body proprietorially.

'You'll catch cold,' he said, kissing her wet cheeks, which still tasted salty from her sweat.

'You're so sweet,' she whispered, pulling him closer. 'But I'm not staying, baby. I gotta take a shower and get going.'

Hunter pulled away from her. He was so fed up with this.

'For God's sake, Tiffany, why?' he snapped, unable to keep the hurt out of his voice. 'Why can't you just sleep here tonight? I'll set the alarm for six and drive you to the set myself in the morning. You won't be late for anything.'

'Hunter, please,' she said, climbing out of bed and starting to pick up various scattered items of her discarded clothing. 'I've told you before, I need my space.'

'What space?' he shot back at her. 'That rat hole of an apartment you live in is barely big enough to swing a cat in, and Lennox and his buddies are always hanging around like a bad smell. You have more space here.'

Tiffany sighed. It had been such a great night, she hoped he wasn't going to spoil it now. 'Look, can we not make a big deal of this?' she said, scrabbling under the bed for one missing sneaker. 'All my stuff is at home, OK, it's just easier. Besides, I promised Lennox I'd clean the place up a bit before tomorrow.'

She padded into the bathroom and turned on the shower, then came and stood naked in the doorway while she waited for the water to heat up. Looking at her flat, tanned stomach, and neatly trimmed blonde bush, Hunter felt himself starting to get hard again. If only he didn't want her so fucking much.

She walked back over to the bed and sat down beside him. He could still smell the sex on her body, and her closeness made his senses reel. She took his hand in hers and kissed it.

'Look,' she said gently, 'I'm sorry I can't stay tonight. But I'll make it up to you, OK? I promise. If you like, I'll come and spend the whole weekend here. I'll even put up with Max's singing in the mornings. Now how's that for devotion?'

Hunter put his arms around her. Why did he always find it so hard to let her go?

'I'll hold you to that,' he said, kissing her neck and the smooth naked skin of her shoulder. 'I just want us to have more time together.'

'I know,' she said, moving back across towards the bathroom. 'And we will, honey. I promise. We will. Just not tonight.'

Speeding back east on the ten freeway twenty minutes later, with the roar of her Ford jeep's knackered exhaust battering her eardrums, Tiffany punched the dashboard in frustration.

Why, why, why did she always do this? She loved him so much it killed her, so why did she keep on pushing him away?

With the rational part of her brain, of course, she already knew the answer to that question. She was afraid to trust in Hunter, afraid to believe that their love could possibly last. With every woman in the world lusting after him, and stunning models making plays for him night after night, looking right through her as though she were nothing – how could she possibly expect to hold him?

Moving into the beach house, as he was constantly begging her to do, seemed too much like tempting fate. The moment she let him know how hopelessly, desperately in love she was, the spell would be broken and he would leave.

No, the only way to survive was to hold on for dear life to her independence. After three years together, she still lived well within her means, driving her shitty old truck, living with Lennox in their run-down Westwood apartment, never letting Hunter buy her anything beyond dinner and the occasional vacation. She was not about to get used to Hunter's rich, glamorous lifestyle, only to have it all snatched away at a moment's notice.

Back at the beach house, Hunter couldn't sleep. He pulled on a pair of Calvins and a T-shirt and wandered into the kitchen, taking an iced tea out of the fridge and sipping it thoughtfully. He wished Max were here to talk to, but he was still in England with Henry. It must be great to have a family like Max's.

For the first time in months, Hunter found himself thinking about Siena. It was funny – although Pete's machiavellian scheming and attempted sabotage of his career had fixed him as a constant, looming presence in Hunter's life, still he never made the mental association between his brother and Siena, or the rest of the family. He had run into Claire once, about two years ago at Chaya Brasserie, but when he'd asked after Siena he'd been met with a blank wall of silence. If it hadn't been for the ubiquitous billboard pictures of her face – itself only a distant echo of the childish features that Hunter had once known and loved so well – he could almost have believed that she no longer existed.

He knew about the estrangement from her parents, of course – every supermarket tabloid in America had run versions of Siena's *Vanity Fair* interview the previous year, in which she had tearfully recounted Pete and

Claire's abandonment. Many of them, in fact, had printed his own picture next to hers, drawing parallels between Pete's vendetta against him and the disinheriting of his only daughter.

As a teenager, he had found the pain of their separation almost unbearable. But now? Well, life had moved on, and life had been pretty damn good to him – to both of them, in fact. He wasn't in any hurry to risk opening up those old wounds all over again.

Still, on nights like tonight, he couldn't help but wonder what Siena would have made of Tiffany. They were the only two people he had ever loved in his life – with the possible exception of Max, but that was different – and they were both so smart, so independent, so fucking difficult!

Tiffany wasn't spoilt or selfish as Siena had been. But then again, she had grown up in a normal, happy home, not the dysfunctional madhouse at Hancock Park. But she had a similar strength about her, something that seemed to tell him 'I don't need you', which reminded him painfully of Siena. He wished he could discover just one ounce of that strength in himself. But the truth was, he needed Tiffany like air. He'd be lost without her.

He broke off his thoughts with a start when the phone rang. The clock on the microwave said it was 2 a.m. No one else would be calling him at that hour. It had to be Tiffany.

Heart thumping with happiness, he sprinted into the bedroom to pick it up.

'Baby?'

'Hunter, I've told you before, I'm very flattered, but I just don't think of you in that way.' Max's deadpan voice was slightly faint on the long-distance line.

'Max' said Hunter, fighting to keep the disappointment out of his voice. 'How are you, man? When are you coming back?'

'Well, that's what I called to tell you,' said Max. 'Oh, fuck, have I just woken you up? What time is it?'

'Two in the morning, but don't worry, I'm up. Tiffany went home to that shit hole she lives in, and now I can't sleep.'

Max was taken aback. He had never heard Hunter sounding so bitter about anything, especially not Tiffany.

'Oh,' he said lamely. 'Well, cheer up, fella, you see the girl every day. I'd make the most of a night off, if I were you. At least you can fart in bed with impunity.'

'Hmmm, I guess,' said Hunter. 'So what's up anyway, did you change your plans?'

'Slightly,' said Max. 'I'm still leaving here on the twenty-eighth, but I'm going to New York for a few days. There's a chance I may have a meeting with Alex McFadden on the twenty-ninth.'

'Max, that's great!' said Hunter, genuinely impressed.

Alex McFadden was a big producer of Broadway musicals, and Max had been angling for a one-on-one meeting with the guy for ever.

'Yeah, well, it hasn't happened yet,' said Max, ever the pessimist. 'But anyway, a couple of mates of mine from school are having a big New Year's Eve bash at this loft in SoHo. Jerry, my mate, just got a whopping great bonus from Goldman, so he's spending a fortune on this thing. It'll be wall to wall beautiful women – and I'm talking New York beautiful, none of your plastic, LA, silicone bullshit. I know you and Tiffany are as good as married, but there's no law against looking. Wanna come?'

Hunter chuckled quietly to himself. Sometimes Max reminded him of nothing so much as an overexcited Labrador. Listening to him gabbling happily away about this party, he could almost hear his tail thumping on the ground.

'Thanks, man, but I can't,' he said, stretching out his arms in a huge, full-bodied yawn and rubbing his head drowsily. 'We're shooting New Year's Eve.'

'You're kidding,' said Max. 'Doesn't that slave driver

Orchard ever give you a night off? It's New Year's Eve, for Christ's sake.'

'What can I tell you?' said Hunter. 'He works hard, and that means the rest of us have to keep up. Anyway, I don't mind. Tiffany is working too, so we can maybe have dinner together or something later. To be honest with you, I'm feeling kinda low key right now. And you know how much I hate New York.'

'Suit yourself,' said Max, who considered hating New York to be a form of mental illness. 'I'll see you back in Hell-A on the second or third, then.'

'Oh, get over yourself!' Hunter laughed. 'Don't give me that Hell-A shit. You love it here and you know it. Just wait till you've had three days of sub-zero winds and hail in Manhattan. You'll be *begging* to come back home.'

Taking his drink with him, Hunter climbed back into bed and pulled the covers up around him. The lingering smell of Tiffany's body still clung to his sheets. With all his heart, he wished she were lying there next to him.

Chapter Twenty-five

It had been a bitterly cold winter in New York, one of the worst on record.

Tourists still flocked there in droves, to skate around the Christmas tree at the romantic Rockefeller Center ice rink, to marvel at the snow and the lights on Park Avenue, or to visit Santa's grotto at FAO Schwarz. Ruddy-cheeked families, with Dad in his Brooks Brothers cashmere coat, Mom in full-length mink and the kids in scarves, woolly hats and puffa jackets from the Gap, stamped their feet against the cold on every corner wolfing down cheap hot dogs smothered in fried onions, just so they could feel something warm hitting their stomachs, while passing drivers splashed them with icy spray from the puddles as they honked and swerved their way down Lexington.

The snow had turned to grimy slush on the streets, but it still kept falling, and the taxi drivers came in from New Jersey every morning with six inches of pure white icing on top of their marzipan-yellow cabs. Manhattan was crowded and dirty with a wind-chill factor that could have shamed the North Pole.

But there was nowhere quite like New York at Christmas time.

For just over a year, Siena and Ines had shared a Manhattan apartment, although each spent a good half of their time travelling, doing shows and campaigns around the world. Both the girls had left the city over the holiday; Ines to visit her family in Seville and Siena to stay with a well-known designer and his boyfriend at their weekend retreat in Vermont. But after five days away, they had both found themselves going stir crazy and decided to fly back to New York in time for New Year's Eve.

Sitting in the window seat of their palatial living room overlooking Central Park, with a red-and-green tartan blanket pulled up over her knees and a big glass of cognac in her hands, Siena looked out over the snowy greenery below her.

'So was it lovely in Spain?' she asked Ines, who was busy applying a third coat of purple polish to her toenails. 'You don't look very brown.'

'Ees weenter in Espain, you eediot.' Ines laughed. 'But yes, I 'ad a lovely time. Eet was so long since I saw all my family togethair.' She rolled her eyes to heaven. 'I ate like a peeg, though.'

'Me too,' said Siena, thinking back longingly to the rum-soaked Yule log she'd eaten almost single-handedly at Fabrizio's. 'I'm on champagne and cigarettes only for the rest of the week.'

Ines raised a questioning eyebrow at her friend's half-drunk cognac but said nothing.

'So what are your plans for tomorrow night?' asked Siena. 'Are you going to Matt's New Year thing?'

'No, I don't theenk so,' said Ines, screwing the cap back on her nail polish bottle and blowing gently on her toes. 'I am so tired of heem. I theenk he prefairs you anyway.'

'Oh, baloney,' protested Siena, blushing.

In fact, Ines's most recent boyfriend had already made his feelings towards her perfectly clear at a party a few weeks ago. Fucking slimeball. As if she would do the dirty on her best friend with a scumbag like him. She was glad that Ines was finally seeing the light about Matt.

'I haird about thees party in SoHo,' Ines continued, 'you know, the Eenglish friend of Anya's? A lot of cool people are going to be there. Maybe we should stop by?'

Siena finished her drink and walked over to the fridge, extracting a cold sausage and munching on it contemplatively. She'd start the nicotine diet tomorrow.

'Sure, I don't mind,' she said.

Her own supposed boyfriend, a Brazilian model called Carlo, had been putting pressure on her to join him and his friends at some bash downtown, but Siena's relationship claustrophobia was already starting to kick in. She'd much rather hang with Ines and the girls.

'Those Wall Street guys spend money like water,' she mused, leaning back against the cold fridge door. 'I remember the last banker party I went to, the guy had this fuck-off fountain flowing with Cristal the whole night. He must have spent fifteen thousand on that fountain alone. Totally vulgar, but kinda cool.'

She finished the sausage and started gnawing away at a slightly stale hunk of Cheddar. They really must get around to some grocery shopping. 'So who else is going?'

Ines carefully removed her white foam toe-separators and stood up. She was so tall and thin, with her shock of red hair – she had cut it very short about three months ago – she reminded Siena of an extra-long safety match.

'I don't know exactly,' she said. 'Anya, I theenk Zane and some of the other boys will be there. A lot of bankers.' She wiggled her purple toes admiringly. 'But of course' – she grinned – 'as soon as we arrive, every man in New York weel be banging down that door!'

Siena laughed. Sometimes Ines could be even more of an arrogant bitch than she was.

Max struggled miserably along Fifth Avenue. With his sleet-soaked raincoat clinging like shrink-wrap to his huge shoulders, and trousers splattered from the knee down with filthy spray from the streets, he looked exactly as he felt – utterly dejected.

New York sucked.

His meeting with the great Broadway producer Alex McFadden yesterday had been yet another damp squib. The guy had said some complimentary things about some of Max's English theatre work, and had even admired the short film he'd had at Sundance the year before. But he had been to enough of these 'love your stuff, must get together some time' meetings to know when he was being given the brush-off, however gracefully it was done. Unlike most of the LA producers he dealt with, McFadden had been a gentleman, taking time out of his day to encourage a struggling young director he didn't know from Adam. But the fact remained that Max was no nearer to hitting the big time than he had been last week in Batcombe, and he was starting to feel increasingly hopeless. He couldn't wait for this year to be over.

To cheer himself up, he had run into FAO Schwarz to pick up some presents for the kids. It was Madeleine's birthday on New Year's Day, and he'd promised to track down a Malibu Rollerblading Barbie. Max had spent enough time in New York to know that one's fellow shoppers could be a bit on the pushy side, but he had never seen anything quite like the women in that fucking toy store. They were like drug-crazed prop forwards: grabbing and shoving and wrestling over these Barbie dolls as if they were the last water bottle on a desert island or something. By the time he'd beaten a crowd of them back to secure Madeleine's prize, then gone through the whole ordeal again trying to find something suitable for the two boys, he'd emerged on to the street feeling like a grizzled piece of meat that had just been chewed up and spat out by some giant, man-eating monster.

'Taxi!' he yelled as an apparently empty cab sped straight past him, stopping for a leggy blonde half a block down.

'Fucker,' he mumbled, although he couldn't really blame the driver. He'd have pulled over for the blonde as well. Abandoning hope of finding a cab in such foul weather, and suddenly in desperate need of a restorative drink, he doubled back on himself and nipped into the O'Mahoney's pub on the corner.

Inside, the dingy, dark-wood-panelled bar was almost

empty. Thank Christ. He was in no mood to have to wait around for service.

'What can I get you, sir?'

Max looked up from his piles of shopping into the green eyes of a truly stunning girl. She was wearing a tight white T-shirt with the O'Mahoney's logo emblazoned across her quite magnificently ample chest, and her long auburn hair tumbled down around her shoulders, making her look not unlike the storybook pictures of Helen of Troy.

'Fuck me, you're beautiful,' said Max, before realising to his horror that he'd actually spoken the words aloud.

The siren laughed, a deep, mellow sound that Max found quite enchanting. The nightmare of the Barbie department was already fading into the dim recesses of his memory.

'And you're not looking too bad yerself,' she said.

Ah, that Irish accent. It killed him every time.

Max noticed the mischievous way her eyes flickered when she spoke to him and her brazen holding of his gaze. Things were definitely starting to look up.

'I'm sorry,' he said sheepishly, unable to wipe the smile off his face. 'That just slipped out. I didn't mean to be rude. I'm Max, by the way. Max De Seville.'

He offered her his hand and she shook it.

'What, you mean like Bond, James Bond?' she teased him. 'Well, it's a pleasure to meet you, Max. I'm Angela.'

For a few delicious seconds they held on to each other's hands, neither of them saying a word.

'So Max,' said Angela eventually, still looking deep into his eyes. 'What can I get for you?'

'Oh, I don't know,' Max drawled, looking her body up and down as though he were appraising a racehorse. 'But I expect I can think of something.'

He woke up the next morning with a hangover that could have felled an elephant.

'Oh shit,' he whispered, opening one eye and trying to

reorient himself to his spinning hotel room. 'I've died and gone to hell.'

'Well, that's just charming, thanks very much.'

Angela was lying above him propped up on her forearms, her big, smooth, rounded breasts spilling down on to his chest, and the tips of her Titian hair softly brushing against his face. Opening his eyes a little farther, Max saw her smudged black eye make-up and lips and chin slightly reddened from kissing, and the previous night's events gradually started coming back to him.

'Not you, angel,' he said, stroking her hair tenderly, but not wanting to risk a kiss with his mouth tasting like a four-day-old ashtray. 'You're heavenly.' She was too. How the hell had he managed to pull a girl like this? 'But unfortunately, I think someone may have broken in here last night and smashed me over the head with an anvil. Oh God.' He groaned, pushing her gently off him. 'Did I miss something, or did you not sink about seven pints last night? How come I'm the only one who feels like a rat's arse this morning?'

She laughed and, whipping the duvet off both of them, straddled him again, this time taking both his arms and pulling them upward so his hands were on her breasts.

'You know what the best cure for a hangover is?' She gave him that mischievous look again.

'Oh please, no, for God's sake, woman, have some compassion for a dying man,' Max whimpered.

Licking her palm, Angela reached down and wrapped her right hand firmly around his dick.

'Just close your eyes,' she whispered. 'I'm about to give you the last rites.'

By the time he arrived at Jerry's loft later that evening for the party, Max's stomach had somewhat stabilised, but he still looked like a man in the final stages of acute liver failure.

'What the fuck happened to you?' asked Jerry,

ushering him in from the lobby and relieving him of a bottle of vintage Chablis.

'I had a rough night last night,' said Max, pushing his way through a room full of glamorous-looking New Yorkers and following his old friend into the kitchen, which was crammed with flustered, uniformed serving staff preparing yet more trays of complicated hors d'oeuvres.

'Was she worth it?' asked Jerry, snaking expertly past two waitresses and handing Max a flute of champagne.

'Fuck, yeah,' said Max, shuddering. The faint lemony smell of the fizzing alcohol was making him feel nauseous. He pushed away the glass. 'But I'm never drinking again. Have you got any Coke?'

'Liquid or powder?' Jerry smiled.

'Liquid,' said Max firmly. 'And not Diet. I need the sugar.' He put his hand to his temple. 'That music's fucking loud, mate.'

Jerry produced a Coke from the fridge and passed it over. 'That's the hottest DJ in the city, Max, my friend,' he said. 'He doesn't do quiet. Besides, this is a party, and a shit-hot one at that, in case you hadn't noticed.'

Right on cue, a six-foot brunette with legs up to her armpits sauntered past the kitchen doorway in a skin-tight orange mini-dress and thigh-high boots.

'Hey, Katya.' Jerry nodded at her, acknowledging her smile as she walked past. She blew him a kiss in return and disappeared into the throng.

'So I don't want to hear another word about your bloody hangover, all right?' continued Jerry, slapping Max painfully across the back of the shoulders. 'It's New Year's Eve, mate. Have some hair of the dog, get out there and stop moaning.' He raised his bottle of Beck's to Max's can of Coke in a toast. 'Good to see you.'

Max downed his drink in one almighty gulp. 'Good to see you too, Jerry.'

Wandering back into the main party room, an immense, warehouse-sized living space with panoramic views across the city, Max wished he had made a bit more of an effort. He was not naturally lacking in confidence, but a depressing feeling of inadequacy gripped him as he caught sight of his own reflection in one of the floor-to-ceiling mirrors: pallid, unshaven, wearing a dirty old pair of Diesel jeans and a grey fisherman's jumper of Henry's. He wasn't exactly the epitome of New York chic.

As he approached a low table groaning with more of the hors d'oeuvres he'd admired earlier in the kitchen, and started to swoop in on a caviar and cream cheese blini, he noticed a sea of people parting around him and moving off towards the door. He was starting to wonder whether he still smelt like a rancid skunk and had somehow imagined his earlier shower when he realised that they were not moving away from him, but towards a new arrival.

'She's here,' he heard a fellow next to him whispering to his companion. 'I *told* you she was coming.'

'Who's here?' asked Max, through a mouthful of caviar. He felt ravenously hungry all of a sudden.

'Didn't you see her?' said the man, a trendy advertising executive type wearing orange lenses in his Buddy Holly glasses, and waving in the general direction of the buzzing crowd by the door. 'It's Siena McMahon.'

Max almost choked on his blini.

'And that fit Spanish bird's with her,' piped up the man's English sidekick. Max pushed past them and made his way to a sofa at the back of the room, where two models were deep in conversation. He was very curious to see Siena, but some instinct made him recoil from the idea of battling his way towards her like a besotted fan.

'Mind if I perch here?' he asked the two girls as he eased himself down on to the arm of the sofa.

'Not at all,' said the prettier one, looking at his long legs and huge muscled torso with approval. 'You're a big boy, though. I'm not sure if that armrest can take your weight.'

Max raised one eyebrow at her knowingly. She was a bit standard issue: long blonde hair, very regular features –

but she was undeniably an extremely sexy girl. Perhaps his hangover was starting to dissipate after all.

'Anyway, as I was saying,' butted in the girl's friend rudely, pointedly turning her back on Max (like most models, she had no tolerance for flirtation unless it was directed towards herself), 'I've never understood what all the fuss was about. As far as I'm concerned she's short and she's fat. It's a mystery to me what men see in her.'

'I know,' said the blonde. 'Zane says he thinks it's because she looks so slutty and available.'

'Not a bad look,' muttered Max under his breath.

At that moment, a gap appeared in the crowd and he found himself looking, albeit from a fifty-foot distance, directly at Siena.

The first thing he noticed was that she looked nothing like any of the other women in the room. Dressed conservatively in immaculately cut white palazzo pants and a crimson silk shirt, which displayed only the slightest of hints of her famous creamy white cleavage, she radiated confidence and sex appeal, smiling and air-kissing her way through each new group of admirers.

The thick mass of dark curls was exactly as he'd remembered it, as was the pronounced and incongruously demure dimple on her chin, a chin that still jutted arrogantly upwards towards every man who came to worship at the altar of her beauty.

Because whatever other, jealous girls might say, there could be absolutely no doubt that Siena was beautiful. Magnetically, terrifyingly beautiful.

Holy shit, thought Max. She could light up the whole of Park Avenue with that charisma. It was like magic.

Try as he might, he couldn't take his eyes off her.

'I loved your *Vanity Fair* pictures,' a chiselled, Armani-suited clone was gushing as he approached her. 'So brave. So raw.'

Oh please, thought Siena. She hoped Ines was right and there were men other than models at this party. Despite the fact that she had lived and worked among New York's modelling fraternity for the past two years, her inanity threshold remained perilously low. If there was one thing she really had no tolerance for, it was pretty, stupid men.

'You make me sound like a carrot,' she said rudely, looking past him in search of someone, anyone, more interesting.

At first she couldn't quite place him. At the back of the room, an enormous, powerful-looking blond man, dressed like a hobo, was staring straight at her. Siena was used to being looked at, but something about the intensity of this man's gaze left her stomach churning. He was definitely handsome, like a trawlerman who'd got very lost and somehow wound up in a Manhattan loft surrounded by a bunch of spoilt, rich bankers and their beautiful toys.

And yet, he did look familiar.

It was only when she started walking towards him, and he stood up to greet her, that the penny dropped.

No. It couldn't be. Siena froze in her tracks.

'Hello, Siena,' said Max, towering over her like a Roman statue. 'Long time no see.'

She could hear her heart pounding, and a torrent of conflicting emotions raging through her.

Max De Seville! How could Max De Seville be here? Just seeing his face and hearing his voice transported her back in an instant to Hancock Park and the earliest, happiest days of her childhood. Suddenly she was no longer the world-famous model, envied, desired and in control. She was a ten-year-old little girl, being ignored and dismissed by Hunter's fifteen-year-old best friend, and ordered out of their tree house.

Ridiculously, she found her old resentment of Max, always her rival for Hunter's affections, flooding back to her, as though the last eleven years had never happened. But fighting with the resentment was enormous curiosity, combined with another, more unsettling feeling that she couldn't quite put her finger on.

She wished he would stop staring at her like that.

'Max.' She smiled thinly and extended a perfectly manicured hand. 'What a nice surprise.'

Her voice was heavy with sarcasm. Max instantly bristled. So that was the way she wanted to play it. Well, if she thought she was going to come the supermodel diva with him, she had another think coming.

He shook her hand.

'Isn't it? I hardly recognised you at first, actually. Must have been all those clothes you're wearing.'

Despite herself, Siena blushed. That was fifteen love to Max.

'Yes,' she said, 'I have this thing about dressing appropriately for social occasions.' She allowed her eye to wander disapprovingly over his threadbare jumper and dirty jeans. 'But I see that's not one of your priorities.'

Fifteen all.

Max took a deep breath. He was determined not to let the little cow provoke him.

'How are you enjoying the modelling?' he asked.

'Oh, you know.' She waved her hand dismissively. 'It's a means to an end. Of course, the money's fabulous. But I'm going to be doing a lot more acting in future.'

'Oh really?' said Max with a sly smile.

Was the bastard laughing at her?

'What have you done so far?'

'Other than make millions, you mean?' she snapped, wishing he didn't make her feel so defensive. Max raised his eyebrow but said nothing. 'A couple of indie films,' she said eventually, 'some music videos, that kinda thing. I have some very interesting scripts I'm looking at right now, though,' she lied. 'But I can't really talk about it yet. What about you?'

'I'm a director,' said Max, feeling very uncomfortable suddenly.

'Is that so?' said Siena. Like her grandfather, she could smell weakness as a shark smelled blood and instinctively moved in for the kill. 'Of what? How come I've never heard of you?'

Chapter Twenty-six

Uptown in Beverly Hills a couple of weeks later, Max and Hunter were tucked away in the prestigious corner table at the Brasserie Blanc. Hunter had already been pestered by three fans before they'd ordered their starters. He refused to wear sunglasses or a baseball cap indoors like so many other celebrities, on the very sensible grounds that it didn't fool anybody anyway and made you look like a self-important jerk. But unfortunately this gave people the impression that he was always approachable.

He put up with the endless intrusions on his privacy with his typical good humour. But Max found going out with him in public increasingly trying.

'So come on then, buddy, spill the beans,' said Hunter after signing his third autograph for a middle-aged tourist from Ohio and sending her joyously on her way with a kiss on the cheek. 'How was New York? Tell me more about your meeting with Alex McFadden.'

'There's nothing more to tell, I'm afraid,' said Max gloomily. 'He was a very nice chap, very complimentary about my film and all that, but he's a Broadway man. I simply don't have enough theatre experience to play in that league.'

'I thought you'd done lots of Shakespeare and all that in London?' said Hunter.

Max loved the way Hunter referred to anything written before 1950 as 'Shakespeare and all that.'

'Some, not lots,' he said. 'Not enough, evidently. But let's not talk about my work, it's too depressing. What's been going on here while I've been gone?'

'Not much,' said Hunter. 'Tiff and I went up to Big Bear, which was pretty cool. Four whole days to

For a moment Max struggled to think of a comeback. 'I don't do mainstream, Hollywood shit,' he said lamely.

'Oh, I see,' said Siena. 'Yes, I can tell from your clothes that you must have sacrificed a *lot* for your artistic integrity.'

The fucking snide little bitch. How dare she?

'Well, lovely as it's been, Siena,' – he smiled down at her, with a self-control he was justly proud of – 'I don't think I'll be staying to see the New Year in, so I'm afraid you must excuse me.' He put his empty glass down on a side table and turned to go. 'I'll tell Hunter you said hello.'

At the mention of Hunter's name, Siena felt her knees give way and she reached out instinctively to the arm of the sofa for support. Her head had started to spin and her mouth went dry with panic. Max was still in touch with Hunter? She watched, paralysed, as his back view receded into the throng. Oh God, she couldn't let him leave.

'Max, wait!' she called out, more loudly and anxiously than she had intended, so that a cluster of revellers near by turned around and stared at her.

Reluctantly, Max stopped and turned.

'Do you . . .' she began, obviously struggling to find the words. If she weren't such a vain, spoilt, selfish little madam, Max thought, he might almost have felt sorry for her. 'I mean, are you and Hunter still friends, then?'

'Of course,' he said harshly. He knew it must hurt her to know that his relationship with Hunter had survived when hers had not. But she was so beautiful and confident and successful, so damn perfect, at that moment he wanted to hurt her. He decided to twist the knife. 'Actually, we live together in Santa Monica. Have done for the last three years.'

'Oh.' She looked completely lost at this piece of news, so much so that he instantly began to regret having told her. He should have just let it lie.

'Look, I should be going.'

'Oh no, Max, please, don't go,' she pleaded, grabbing his arm.

He looked at her panicked face and saw a flicker of vulnerability that instinctively made him want to put his arms around her, as he had done all those years ago when she'd fallen out of the tree house and he'd thought for one awful moment she might have been killed.

But he stopped himself. What was the point? She was clearly so fucked up and emotionally damaged. It would be like trying to pet a porcupine.

'Does he ever talk about me?' she asked.

He knew how much it had cost her to ask the question, and softened slightly.

'He did,' he said, not unkindly. 'But he doesn't any more.'

'Well, sure.' Siena shrugged in a failed attempt at nonchalance, desperately trying to fix her mask of self-confidence back in place. 'I mean, it's been, what, eleven years? That's a lot of water under the bridge.'

'Yeah,' said Max. 'I guess it is.'

'Look, I'm sorry,' she said. 'I shouldn't have been so rude before. Just tell Hunter I said hi, or whatever.' She tossed her mane of hair and gave a practised, professional fifty-megawatt smile, a signal, he assumed, that the conversation was over and she was ready to get back to the business of receiving more male attention.

'I will,' said Max.

Suddenly he was longing to get away from her, away from everybody.

He strode through the party without looking back or stopping to say goodbye to any of his friends, even Jerry. Bolting into the elevator as though he were fleeing for his life, he fidgeted impatiently until he reached the lobby and literally ran out into the street.

Leaning back against the cold brickwork of Jerry's building, he paused for a moment to savour the cold night air and the relative quiet and stillness of the city.

Goddam it.

Why had Siena made him feel like such a piece of shit?

Glancing at his watch, he saw that it was only a minute until midnight. Within a few short seconds, he started to hear cheers and shouts, bells ringing and the honking of horns as the city began to welcome in another new year. He thought briefly of Angela, and wondered whether she and her boyfriend were enjoying a lingering New Year's kiss somewhere out there. He guessed they were.

As he mooched off in the direction of his hotel, his sore head still throbbing from a renewed burst of hangover, a wave of loneliness and exhaustion hit him like a ton of lead. He thought of Henry and Muffy back in Batcombe, and of Hunter and Tiffany, no doubt wrapped up in each other's arms at the beach house. He'd never been much of a one for relationships, not really. But suddenly, tonight, he wished to God he had someone to hold on to.

Bitterly, he thought of Siena, still holding court upstairs at the party like the perfect, spoiled goddess she seemed to have become, while he stood knackered, hungover, alone and freezing his ass off out on the street. What was he even doing here? He had no job to speak of, no money and no girlfriend. No wonder Siena had put him down.

His life was like one long, bad joke.

Roll on 2002.

Things could only get better.

ourselves, no work, no distractions, no nothing. I can't remember the last time we had that much time alone.'

'Well, you look well on it,' said Max, smiling at the dopey, besotted expression that had spread across his best friend's face. Just talking about Tiffany sent him ga-ga. It was cute.

They both took a big slug of Californian merlot.

'Never mind about me, though,' said Hunter. 'Fill me in on *your* romantic adventures. How many girls did you sleep with in New York, huh? Three? Four? How long were you there again?' he added with a knowing grin.

'Two weeks,' said Max, pretending to look affronted as he snapped a breadstick in half and began nibbling at it. 'And I only slept with one, thank you very much.' His mind wandered happily back to the night he'd spent with Angela.

'Look at you!' Hunter laughed. 'Like a kid with a fistful of candy. So? Are you gonna see her again?'

'Nope,' said Max, stuffing the rest of the breadstick into his mouth all at once.

The waitress arrived with a plate of carpaccio for Hunter and a big bowl of deep-fried squid for Max, who was starting to feel like the invisible man watching the girl fawning and simpering and fluttering her eyelashes at Hunter, utterly oblivious to his own presence at the table.

'So, what else happened?' asked Hunter after a few mouthfuls of his delicious raw beef. Max normally couldn't stop yabbering on whenever he got back from a trip, regaling Hunter with one funny story after another, never-ending tales of one-night stands, all-night parties and every little step he'd taken towards that ever illusive big break. He was being unusually reticent tonight. 'How was your New Year's Eve?'

It was the question Max had been dreading. He ought to have called Hunter from New York and told him about his encounter with Siena right away. Now, almost two weeks after the event, he found himself unsure where, or even if, to begin.

'It was good,' he said, uncertainly. 'It was fine.'

'What's with all this "good", "fine" shit?' asked Hunter. 'Why do I get the feeling there's something you aren't telling me?'

Max cleared his throat nervously. There was no way around it. 'I ran into someone in New York,' he said at last. 'At Jerry's party.'

'Oh yeah?' asked Hunter. 'Who?'

Max hesitated for a moment, looking from Hunter, to his plate, then back again before blurting it out.

'Siena.'

He hadn't known exactly how Hunter would react to the news; whether he would be shocked and numb or just confused and upset. But nothing had prepared him for the look of pure, unadulterated delight that swept across his friend's face.

'Siena?' He leant forward across the table and grabbed Max by the shoulders, as if he were about to kiss him passionately. 'Are you kidding me? You actually saw her? Did you speak to her?'

'Sure,' said Max. 'Only for a couple of minutes, though. We said hello.'

He wasn't about to let on to Hunter that she'd actually been every bit as self-centred and arrogant as he remembered her, and that he couldn't wait to escape and get away from her.

'Did she ask about me?' asked Hunter.

Max lit up a cigarette, ignoring the loud complaints from nearby diners.

'Yes,' he said, cagily.

'Well, come on, man, don't keep me in suspense,' said Hunter, releasing Max's lapels only when the smoke started getting in his eyes. 'What did she say?'

'Well . . .' Max hesitated, flicking ash awkwardly on to his side plate. 'She asked how you were, and I said you were fine.'

'What else?' demanded Hunter, impatiently.

'She asked if you ever talked about her,' said Max. 'I told her that you used to, after Duke died, but that you didn't any more.'

'Why the fuck did you say that?' Hunter shouted, flinging his napkin down angrily on the table.

The whole restaurant turned round to stare at them.

'Because it's true,' said Max flatly, taking another long drag of his cigarette as if nothing had happened. 'And don't you start shouting at me. I'm just the hapless fucking messenger here, all right?'

Hunter relaxed his shoulders.

'All right. I'm sorry,' he said. 'I just didn't want her to think . . .'

'That you've moved on?' offered Max.

'Exactly.'

'But haven't you, though, mate?' Max persisted, risking a second outburst of Hunter's rarely seen temper. He stubbed out his half-smoked cigarette and looked his best friend in the eye. 'Look, you can tell me this is none of my business if you like.'

'Thanks,' said Hunter, who was already smiling again. 'This is none of your business.'

'But don't you think you might get hurt?' persisted Max.

'By Siena?' Hunter looked genuinely surprised. 'No, of course not. Why would I? Tiffany's always going on about me getting hurt. Says I should 'learn to protect myself'. What neither of you seem to get is that it was being *separated* from Siena that hurt. And that sure as hell wasn't her fault. We were kids, for God's sake.'

'I know, I know,' said Max. 'I was there, remember? I'm not blaming her, Hunter. I'm just saying that it was more than ten years ago, man. She's changed. What if it's not the same between you when you see her again? You don't think that that could hurt you?'

Hunter rubbed his eyes in disbelief. It was all too much for him to take in.

'Look,' he said, 'I appreciate your concern. Really, I do. I know you and Tiffany both care about me. But I think . . .' He struggled to find the words. 'I think that this is fate.'

Max rolled his eyes.

'Seriously,' said Hunter, willing Max to believe him. 'I was just thinking about her in Big Bear only last week – we used to go there sometimes with the nannies when we were kids. It's like she was meant to come back into my life now. Do you know what I mean?'

Max shook his head. 'Not really.'

'I don't expect you to understand,' said Hunter, without bitterness. 'I don't think anyone really understands what Siena meant to me. What she means to me now. Not even Tiffany gets it.' He sighed. 'But Max, I have to see her. Did you get her number?'

'No.' He watched Hunter's face crumble. 'But I have the name and number of her agent.'

He pulled a crumpled piece of paper out of his jacket pocket and handed it to Hunter, who snatched at it greedily, read it, and placed it carefully in his own wallet.

'Thanks,' he said, more calmly, although the excitement in his eyes still gave him away.

'Be careful,' said Max. 'I'm worried about you.'

'I know,' said Hunter. 'But there's no need to be, really. You've just made me the happiest man on this planet.'

'That can't be right.'

Henry Arkell looked up from the piece of paper in front of him and rubbed his temples. He was sitting in the farm office at Batcombe, across the desk from his accountant and old school friend Nicholas Frankel. 'Are you sure?'

Nick shifted uncomfortably in his seat. He always hated having to give bad news to clients, but with Henry, a close personal friend, he felt doubly like the messenger of doom. Avoiding Henry's gaze, he glanced around him.

The poky little office in the corner of the farmyard was piled floor to ceiling with clutter. Stacks of old receipts and important legal letters were strewn willy-nilly among photos of Muffy and the children, betting slips and Christmas cards, one of which Nick saw was three years old and covered with a thick layer of grey dust, no doubt unmoved since the day it was opened. Perhaps if Henry made some basic attempt at filing or organisation, his accounts might not be in such a desperate state. He'd been exactly the same since their schooldays, though – energetic, hard working but always terminally scatter-brained.

'Completely sure, I'm afraid, old man.' He sighed. 'It's not looking good.'

'Not good?' said Henry. 'It's bloody catastrophic. According to this, I'm four hundred grand in debt, and that's not including the back taxes. Which are how much again?'

'I don't know exactly,' muttered Nick grimly. 'At least one fifty, possibly quite a bit more.'

Henry winced. What the fuck was he going to do? A big part of him longed to unburden himself to Muffy, for sheer comfort if not for practical advice. But somehow it had never been quite the right time to tell her that the debts were getting on top of him, and now things had got so bad he wouldn't know where to begin. In the past his tax problems had had a happy knack of working themselves out in the wash eventually, and Nick had been a genius at putting the Revenue off until he'd managed to scrape together enough cash to keep the wolf from the door. But this time it wasn't just taxes. What with the cost of diversifying the farm, the lost revenues from the BSE crisis, which had had a knock-on effect on every farmer in England, and a couple of bad investments, his interest payments to the bank alone now came to over forty grand a year. Worst of all, a few months ago he had taken out a small lien against the house itself in an attempt to see off one of his more rabidly litigious creditors – despite having sworn to Muffy long ago that their equity in the manor would always remain sacred. She would absolutely hit the roof if, or he supposed when, she heard about that one.

'Well, there must be something we can do. Some sort of stalling tactic,' he said desperately, getting up from his chair and pacing the box-like room anxiously. It was still bitterly cold outside, but a tiny dilapidated fan heater was belting out heat in the corner, making the office feel like a bread oven. 'Just until we start to see the income back from the arable.'

Nick gave a gloomy shrug, as if to say 'I'm not so sure'. 'Maybe you should talk to Muff?'

'No. No way.' Henry held up his hand and shook his head, blotting out the awful possibility. 'She can't know about this.'

'Well, look,' said Nick, gathering up his papers and slotting them back into his neatly organised briefcase, 'I can probably buy you a bit of time with the Revenue. But the bank's a different story. You're going to have to come up with something concrete, some sort of repayment plan that you can actually deliver, or they're going to start getting nasty.'

'All right, all right,' said Henry, ushering him out into a blast of welcomely cold wind. 'You deal with Johnny taxman and I'll work on pulling something out of the bag for the bank. I'm sure we'll figure it out somehow.'

Nick tried to smile and wished he could share Henry's innate optimism. He didn't know how many other ways there were to tell him that his financial problems were now beyond pressing and were not going to magically dissolve into the ether, however hard he wished them away. It was a bit like trying to explain to your eight-year-old son that Father Christmas wasn't real. Losing Manor Farm was, for Henry, a literally unthinkable prospect.

'But not a word to Muffy, all right?' Henry whispered, locking the office door behind him. Before Nick had a chance to answer, Muffy herself appeared in the kitchen doorway looking flushed and triumphant, carrying a plate of what looked like freshly baked scones.

'Ready for some tea, you two? Maddie and I just made these from the new Prue Leith cookbook. What do you think?' She walked over to join them, proudly wafting the still-steaming scones under their noses until both men could feel their mouths watering. Looking at his friend's wife, with her pretty unmade-up face, still-girlish blonde hair and trusting, playful green eyes, Nick could quite see why Henry found it hard to confide in her about his money problems. Her trust in him was total and implicit. How could he bear to disappoint someone so utterly loving and loyal, never mind the impact it would have on the children if things got really bad. Nick just prayed that Henry was right and that somehow, between them, they would come up with something.

'Wow. They look bloody amazing,' said Henry, wrapping his arm around his wife's waist and beaming with pride, as though he'd baked the scones himself. 'You'll stay for tea?' he said to Nick.

'No, no.' The accountant shook his head and pulled out his car keys from his inside jacket pocket, blowing on his already frozen fingers for warmth. 'Thanks, but I really must be heading back to London. Lots to do,' he added, with a knowing look at Henry.

'All right, well, look, thanks again for everything,' said Henry. Muffy disappeared back into the kitchen as he said his goodbyes. 'Let's talk next week.'

'Fine,' said Nick. 'I'll get you some exact figures on the back taxes. But in the meantime, you might want to invest in a lottery ticket.'

Reaching into his back pocket, Henry pulled out a scrunched-up piece of pink paper and waved it at him. Nick put his head in his hands. 'That was meant to be a joke.'

'Ah, but you see, I'm way ahead of you, mate.' Henry grinned. 'How's that for financial planning, eh?'

Chapter Twenty-seven

Two weeks later, Siena was contentedly sipping freshly pressed apple juice and looking down at the white sandy beach below her balcony. It was only 9.30 on a Saturday morning, but thanks to the blazing February sunshine, Santa Monica was already starting to look busy.

Serious, professional-looking rollerbladers in tight black spandex whizzed past families poodling along on their hired beach bikes, while buff-looking gay couples jogged through the sand with their dogs. Everyone was in T-shirts and shorts, and the sky was a cloudless California blue. New York, with its freezing winds and urban grime, seemed a million miles away.

Siena was staying at Shutters on the Beach, one of the oldest and most luxurious hotels right on the ocean, adjacent to the gaudy lights of the Santa Monica pier, where Duke used to take her on the Ferris wheel when she was a little girl.

She was back in California for a second audition for *The Prodigal Daughter*, a low-budget but high-profile art-house movie, where she was up for the female lead. It was the first real film role she'd ever been up for which didn't require her either to play herself or to strip, and her screen test had gone extremely well. The producers had told her yesterday that it was between her and one other girl, but that, off the record, they were likely to confirm today that the part was hers. After all the stress and anxiety of the last few weeks – seeing Max again and hearing about Hunter had thrown her more than she cared to admit – Siena had woken up this morning feeling more rested and contented than she had in months.

Her next modelling job wasn't until the twenty-sixth

in New York. To Marsha's delight, she had recently won a very lucrative contract as the face of French design house Maginelle's new make-up range, so she could afford to take a bit of time off. If the news today was good, she reckoned she might treat herself to a week or so's break in the West Coast sunshine and recharge her batteries. Perhaps drive up to Santa Barbara or spend a few nights at the Post Ranch Inn in Big Sur? She couldn't remember the last time she'd taken a real vacation.

'More coffee, Miss McMahon?'

An incredibly good-looking Hispanic waiter hovered over her with a divine-smelling pot of Brazilian roast. The day was just getting better and better.

'Mmmm, thanks,' said Siena drowsily, luxuriating in the long-forgotten feeling of sunshine on her back.

It was funny, after all her fears about coming to LA and the terrible fretting about seeing Hunter again or running into any of the rest of her family, now that she was actually here, she felt more relaxed and happy than she had in ages. Perhaps it was because the audition had gone so well, or maybe it was just the joy of being back in her home city at last. She'd realised on the plane that she hadn't in fact set foot in California since the Christmas before her A-levels, over three years ago.

Back then she was just a schoolgirl, trapped in a life that her father had created for her, with no control over her own destiny. Now here she was, a world-famous model and soon-to-be actress.

It felt good. It felt very, very good.

She was reaching across the table for another freshly baked cinnamon bagel – her third – when she caught sight of a diminutive English woman, dressed for New York in head-to-toe black wool and Gucci sunglasses, pushing her way through the tables and waving at her frantically.

'Hello, Marsha.' She sighed. Just when she'd been feeling so mellow, the hyperactive dwarf had to show up and shatter the mood. 'What's up?'

'Well,' said Marsha, pinching a chair from a neighbour-
ing table without asking and sitting down opposite Siena.
'They called.'

'Already?' Siena choked. A piece of bagel had gone
down the wrong way and she took a big gulp of coffee to
wash it down, promptly scalding her mouth. Fuck.

She could already tell from her agent's tone that the
news wasn't good. No one said 'They called' if the news
was good. If the news was good they said 'You got the
part!' Goddam it. She'd been so sure this time, as well.
What could have gone wrong?

'You got the part,' said Marsha morosely, helping
herself to a cup of coffee and a bowlful of Siena's
strawberries.

It took a moment to sink in.

'I did?' said Siena, grinning from ear to ear like a little
girl on her birthday. 'Shit! Why didn't you say so?'

'I thought I just did,' mumbled Marsha through a
mouthful of fruit.

'Well, you might sound a bit more happy about it.'

'What's to be happy about? The movie pays peanuts,
and it'll take you four months to shoot,' said Marsha,
matter-of-factly. 'Maginelle pay millions for ten days'
work. And there's a lot more where that came from if
you'd only focus on your modelling. I make no secret of
it, Siena. I think you're fucking crazy.'

One thing you could say for Marsha, at least she was
up front about what she believed in. The dollar was king,
always had been, always would be.

'I can still do Maginelle,' said Siena, trying to mollify
her agent, who looked as if Santa had just left the
proverbial lump of coal in her Christmas stocking.
'Acting and modelling aren't mutually exclusive, you
know. Besides, if I make a name for myself as an actress,
my modelling fees will go through the roof.'

'Hmmm.' Marsha sounded unconvinced. 'You should
be in New York, honey. Or, if not New York, London.
These guys want you here in LA, from March through

286

June, maybe longer. You're going to miss the whole season.'

Siena shrugged. 'So what else did they say? Do they want to see me again? Did they talk to you about a contract?'

'Yeah, yeah, yeah.' Marsha brushed away her questions with a dismissive wave. 'You leave the contract to me.'

'Of course,' said Siena. 'Always.'

If anyone could screw an extra few grand out of the producers, it was Marsha. Despite her desire to act, Siena was far more conscious of her financial interests than Marsha gave her credit for. She had no intention of working on low-budget movies for ever, and saw *The Prodigal Daughter* very much as a means to an end. Until she made it big in Hollywood, she had no intention of giving up her modelling contracts either.

A gentle ocean breeze blew her hair back off her face, and Siena sat back in her chair, indulging for a moment in her triumph.

Her first leading role at last. It had been a long time coming.

'You know what?' She sat forward suddenly and grabbed Marsha's hand, determined to engender some enthusiasm. 'Let's celebrate!'

'Yeah. Sure,' the older woman grumbled.

'Come on! I'm serious,' insisted Siena. 'Let's throw a little party here tonight, just a few people. We can have apple Martinis on the beach, do the whole LA thing.'

Marsha still looked nonplussed.

'Oh, come *on*!' Siena coaxed her. 'You know you love a good party. I know you, remember? I'm doing this film, so you might as well get used to it. And who knows? Maybe this will be the start of something big. For both of us.'

'I guess,' conceded Marsha.

Sensing she was weakening, Siena decided to play her trump card.

'I'm paying,' she said, giving her agent the benefit of her million-dollar smile.

'Oh, all right,' said Marsha, giving in with something approaching good grace. 'I guess a *little* party wouldn't hurt.'

By eight o'clock, two hundred and fifty of the LA 'in crowd' were already mingling noisily on the hotel's private beach, getting happily drunk at Siena's expense. She'd say this for Marsha: her organisational skills were nothing short of miraculous. Once she'd got on board with the idea of a party, she'd pulled the whole thing together in a matter of hours.

Siena herself was still upstairs in her room, trying on two different pairs of loaned diamond drop earrings, undecided as to which went best with her floor-length crimson silk halter-neck dress.

She'd really pulled all the stops out tonight, and looked every inch the supermodel that she was, with the halter-neck simultaneously showing off her full, high breasts and a smooth, newly tanned expanse of bare back. Her favourite red Manolos, the only shoes in the world that managed to achieve the double whammy of being both sky high and comfortable, completed her ultra-sexy look. Not many girls could have pulled off something so glamorous and formal at a beach party. But Siena was blessed with enough confidence to turn up naked at the Oscars without looking out of place.

Finally opting for the smaller, subtler earrings, she sprayed herself liberally with Rive Gauche and headed for the elevator. Landing this part had filled her with a wave of confidence that, after a few hours, had translated into a raging libido.

She felt powerful and beautiful tonight. She wanted to be made love to, worshipped and adored.

The instant she appeared on the wooden steps leading down to the beach, an excited throng of people surged towards her. Siena smiled and kissed her way through them on her way to the bar and a pre-cocktail glass of champagne.

She could see Marsha chatting up a well-known director about thirty feet away, and recognised a group of three or four model-cum-actresses from the audition circuit perched at the bar. The trio were being attentively looked after by Jeff Black, a sleazeball real estate developer with a penchant for under-age girls and silicone, but he immediately transferred his attentions to Siena when she arrived at the bar, ordering herself a chilled glass of Moët.

'Let me get that for you.' He leered, ostentatiously pulling out a hundred-dollar bill from his wallet.

'Put your money away, Jeff. It's all paid for already. By me, as I'm sure you know by now,' said Siena bluntly.

A lot of the girls tolerated Jeff, because he never tried to sleep with them or touch them. He was just a rich, middle-aged man who liked the ego boost of being seen surrounded by pretty young things. But Siena found him disgusting. If she wanted a ride in a private jet, she'd get her own.

Turning back to the party, she scanned the beach for familiar faces, but found to her disappointment that, apart from a couple of acquaintances, the whole place was heaving with faceless hangers-on. She wished she'd been able to persuade Ines to come with her to the West Coast, but she'd had a job in Boston and couldn't make it. Suddenly, Siena felt deeply depressed. Here she was in LA, her own home town, celebrating the biggest success of her career – and not a single person she loved was there to share the moment with her. Was this what her life had come to? Was this what success, fame and wealth really meant?

She spent the next two hours dutifully pressing the flesh with the smattering of producers and directors who'd bothered to show up, smiling at everybody Marsha told her to. By eleven she was feeling utterly deflated and decided, despite Marsha's protests, to call it a night. By then the beach was such a crush it took her a further forty minutes to battle her way through all the so-called well-wishers back into the hotel lobby. One tenacious paparazzo who had somehow made it through the manager's elaborate defences thrust a camera in her face just as she gave way to a full-throated yawn while waiting for the elevator. That really was the last fucking straw.

The familiar clicking and whirring won him perhaps six or seven shots of Siena scowling before two of the bell boys manhandled him away and the electric doors mercifully closed and allowed her some peace.

When she eventually made it up to her room, she collapsed on the bed, totally exhausted.

Marsha had been right in the first place. The party had been a stupid idea. What had possessed her to shell out twenty thousand dollars to feed and water a bunch of assholes she had never laid eyes on before, and wind up in bed, alone and miserable, before midnight?

Dropping her dress in a heap on the floor and kicking off her shoes, she padded into the bathroom in just a Trashy Lingerie G-string and her diamond drop earrings and began running herself a hot bath.

At first the gushing, steaming water was so loud that she didn't hear the knock on the door. When she finally made out the insistent rat-tat-tat, she hurriedly turned off the tap and attempted to cover herself up with the pitifully small hotel bath towel.

'Just a second!' She raced into the bedroom looking for her robe or anything that might do a better job of covering her steam-flushed nakedness, but both bed and floor were covered with evening dresses she had hastily rejected earlier and she couldn't find anything suitable.

Giving up, she ran to the door and opened it – it was probably only room service and they'd seen it all before – still wearing nothing but her tiny towel and the diamonds flashing seductively above her shoulders.

'Jesus, Siena!'

Hunter was standing in the corridor with a huge bouquet of white roses shaking in his right hand. He turned the colour of Siena's discarded dress and clapped his left hand over his eyes in an instant. 'You can't answer the door dressed like that! I mean, undressed like that.'

She screamed and slammed the door in his face.

Oh my God. Hunter. She'd just flashed her tits at Hunter.

Shaking, she sat down on the end of her bed, and pulled a green velvet slip dress mindlessly over her head. After a few seconds, he knocked again.

'Siena?' she heard his sweet, lovely voice enquiring tentatively. 'Are you all right, baby? I didn't mean to scare you. Can I come in?'

Slowly, she went to the door for the second time, pulling it open with infinite trepidation. Was it really him? She'd dreamed about seeing him for so long, it was hard to accept his presence here, now, at this very moment, as a reality.

At first, the two of them stood on the threshold and stared at one another, both unwilling to say or do anything to end this longed-for moment. But then, suddenly, somehow, their bodies moved together and they found themselves clasped tightly in one another's arms.

'How did you find me?' said Siena eventually, once they had finally been able to stop holding each other, as if checking that the other one was real and not some sort of enticing, ghostly projection.

'It wasn't hard,' said Hunter. He was still holding her hand and stroking it as they sat together on the wicker sofa on her balcony. She had finally found her bath robe and was wearing it over the green dress for warmth. 'Half of LA knew you were having this party tonight. Although, to be honest, I'd tracked you down before that. After Max told me he'd seen you, I called your agent in New York.'

'Marsha?' said Siena incredulously. 'And she gave my number out? I'll fucking kill her.'

'You aren't happy I found you?' He looked crestfallen.

'Oh, sweetheart, of course I am,' said Siena, flinging her arms around his neck and squeezing until she almost choked him. 'It's just that the agency isn't supposed to give out our private numbers. To anyone. And I can't believe she didn't *tell* me she'd heard from you, the sly witch.'

'You can't blame her for that, I'm afraid,' he said. 'That was my fault. I swore her to secrecy.' He raised his eyebrow in what he mistakenly believed to be a knowing, clandestine, James Bond sort of way. God, he was so sweet. 'I *can* be pretty persuasive, you know.'

Siena giggled. 'Of course you can, darling,' she said, indulging him. 'That runs in the McMahon family.'

At the mention of the 'f' word, a palpable chill descended on both of them and they fell silent. Siena was the first to speak.

'I read about Dad, you know, trying to screw things up for you on *Counsellor* and everything. I'm sorry.'

Hunter sighed. 'There's nothing for you to be sorry about. It wasn't your fault. Besides, it never got him anywhere in the end. Hugh, my boss, told him to fuck off.'

'Good,' said Siena. 'It's about time someone did.'

'As I remember,' said Hunter, 'you used to make quite a habit of it when we were kids.'

Siena laughed bitterly.

'Yes, I'm told I was a *terrible* daughter,' she said. 'That must be why they cut me off and sent me out to find my own way without so much as a kiss for good luck.'

'I'm so sorry,' said Hunter, stroking her hair with the slow, comforting caress that had always soothed her as a little girl.

'Don't you start,' said Siena. 'There's nothing to be

sorry about. My dad always hated my guts, so that was hardly news. And as for the money, well ...' She shrugged. 'I wasn't doing too badly last time I checked.'

'What about your mom?' asked Hunter. 'Has she been in touch?'

He knew how much Claire had always loved Siena, even when the feeling hadn't been reciprocated. She was frightened of her husband, and weak, but she wasn't a bad person. At least, that wasn't the way he remembered her.

'Are you kidding? She's worse than Pete,' spat Siena with complete contempt. 'She's like Grandma Minnie. No fucking backbone.'

Minnie, like the rest of the family, had done nothing to stand up to Pete when he'd announced he was banishing Siena from their lives, although the press had reported at the time that she'd been devastated by his decision. She had always been fond of her only grandchild.

'I don't suppose you ever hear from Grandma, do you? Or Aunt Laurie?'

Hunter shook his head. 'Hardly. You want to talk about people hating your guts?'

Siena got up from her seat and sat herself down on his lap, snuggling in close to him the way she used to as a kid. He smelt faintly of aftershave, which seemed all wrong somehow. But then she supposed the last time she'd seen him he'd been barely old enough to shave.

'What about *your* mom?' she asked. 'How's she?'

'She's OK,' said Hunter, non-committally. 'She's in England. Remarried to a very nice man called Christopher Wellesley. Given up drinking.'

'And exactly how loaded is Christopher?' Siena couldn't resist. 'Are we talking regular rich, or Bill Gates?'

Luckily Hunter laughed. 'I know,' he said, shaking his head ruefully. 'She's terrible. But she's not such a horrible person deep down. She's improved a lot since she married him. We keep in touch.'

God, thought Siena sadly. That was probably the best

family relationship they had between them: Hunter and his mother 'kept in touch'. Other people loved their parents, but Hunter 'kept in touch' with his. And she couldn't even say that about Pete and Claire.

'I've missed you,' he said. 'I'm sorry I didn't find you sooner. But when they told me how upset you were by my letters . . .'

She looked at him blankly.

'What letters?'

Hunter felt a shiver run right through him.

'Siena, please tell me they gave you my letters. I wrote to you every day for almost a year.'

Bewildered, she shook her head.

'Dad told me that you didn't want any more contact with any of us. He said you'd asked to be left alone . . .'

Her voice trailed away as the full enormity of Pete's betrayal began to dawn on her. All these years, Hunter had wanted to find her, had longed for her just as passionately and painfully as she'd longed for him. Not only had her father denied her his own love and robbed her of her mother, he had taken Hunter away from her as well, and in the cruellest way imaginable.

How could she have been so stupid?

Why had she believed him?

Suddenly unable to stop herself, she started to cry.

Hunter pushed his blue-black hair back from his face, and she could see that he was on the brink of tears himself.

'You thought I didn't want to see you again?' he stammered. 'Oh, Siena, I am so sorry. I am so, so sorry. How . . . how could Pete do that to us?'

'You know what?' she said, wiping her eyes and half smiling at the irony of it. 'I really didn't think it was possible for me to hate him any more than I already did.'

Hunter shook his head, still too shell-shocked to know how to react.

'There hasn't been a day when I haven't thought about you,' she said. 'When I haven't wondered where you were or what you were doing. But after so many years . . .' Her voice trailed away. 'I don't know. It just got harder and harder to pick up the phone. I was so scared you might reject me again.'

'I *never* rejected you!' His voice was hot with indignation. How could Pete have told her that? What kind of a sick parent was he?

'I know that now,' she said.

'I'm sorry.'

They both spoke the words together, and immediately burst out laughing, grateful for something, anything, to break the unbearable tension.

'Jinx!' said Siena, just as they used to as little kids when they said the same thing at once. 'I said it first, so you're jinxed!'

'Fine, OK, I'm jinxed.' He beamed at her.

They sat for a while in happy silence, grinning inanely at one another like a couple of loved-up teenagers. What Pete had done was unforgivable and would probably take a while to sink in fully. But the main thing was that they were both here now, together. No regrets or recriminations or what-ifs could extinguish the delight of that one simple fact.

'I have a girlfriend,' Hunter announced, changing the subject abruptly.

'Really?' said Siena, frowning. For some reason she found she didn't want him to elaborate about his love life.

'Yeah, she's called Tiffany. She plays Sarah on the show, if you've seen it. She's the gorgeous blonde one.'

Siena noticed the way his eyes shone and his face cracked into a smile when he said her name. He'd obviously got it bad.

'She's wonderful,' he went on excitedly. 'I can't wait for you to meet her. I know you're gonna love her just as much as I do. You two are so alike.'

Hmmm, thought Siena. We'll see about that.

'What about you?' he asked, once it became clear that

she was not about to question him further about Tiffany.
'Are you seeing anybody?'

'No,' she said with a shrug, 'no one serious.'

He looked down at her quizzically.

'And don't you go getting any ideas!' She grinned and prodded him in the chest with an accusatory finger. 'No matchmaking with any of your *Days of Our Lives* friends.'

'Oh, shut *up*,' said Hunter. 'I don't know anyone on that show.'

'I'm not interested. Period,' said Siena. 'My career is the only love of my life right now, and I want it to stay that way.'

'Hey, fine by me,' he said, holding up both hands innocently. 'As far as I'm concerned, no man could ever be good enough for you anyway.'

For a few minutes neither of them said anything. They just sat together under the stars, drinking in the miracle of each other's presence. Siena shifted position on his lap and hugged him tightly round the middle. God, she'd missed him so much.

'So,' said Hunter after a while, 'what happens now? How long are you here in LA?'

She sighed and sat up. She wished she could stay there in his arms for ever.

'Not long, unfortunately. Maybe a week. I have to be back in New York for a shoot by the twenty-sixth, latest.'

Hunter's face fell.

'I'm coming back, though, next month.' She smiled at him. 'We'll be shooting the movie here for four months, maybe longer if there are problems. So we'll be able to see a lot of each other. Catch up, you know? Man . . .' She looked at him in wonder, as though she were seeing his face for the first time. 'I have *so* much I need to tell you.'

'Me too.' He sighed. 'You have no idea.'

It was starting to get uncomfortably chilly out on the balcony. The Pacific coast breezes could take on a bitter bite late in the evenings, and Hunter got up to move indoors, standing back to allow Siena into the warm before him. It was late, and he knew that both Tiffany and Max would be waiting up for him at home, anxious to know how the reunion had gone. Still, he could hardly bear to tear himself away.

He turned around and looked at her: Siena McMahon, the world-famous model, so tiny and vulnerable and sweet in her oversized hotel bath robe. He loved her so much at that moment, he could have burst. And that was when it came to him.

'Move in with me!' he blurted out suddenly, catching her off guard.

Siena looked surprised.

'Really?' she said. 'Do you mean it? I mean, do you think that would be a good idea?'

'Of course,' he said, sounding almost offended. 'Why wouldn't it be?'

She thought about it for a moment. 'What about your girlfriend?' She tried her best not to sound as hostile as she felt about that particular subject. She knew her hostility made no sense – she hadn't even met the girl – but a feeling of resentment at having to share Hunter with anyone was already starting to build to the point where she could feel her chest tightening. 'Wouldn't she mind a complete stranger moving in?'

'You're hardly a stranger,' he said. 'Besides, Tiffany doesn't live with me.'

If Siena hadn't known better, she might almost have thought he sounded resentful. Perhaps things with the perfect Tiffany were not quite so 'wonderful' after all?

'Oh,' was all she said. 'But Max does, right?'

This time she was unable to conceal her dislike. Looking at her frown, Hunter couldn't stop himself from laughing.

'Oh, Siena!' he teased her. 'Don't tell me you're *still* hung up about Max?'

'Don't be ridiculous,' she said indignantly, tossing back her hair for emphasis. 'And for your information, I have never been "hung up" about him, as you put it. I just don't understand what you see in him. He's hung around you like a bad smell for as long as I can remember, and now he seems to be sponging off you permanently. How can you stand it?'

'It's not like that,' said Hunter gently. 'Max has been a wonderful friend to me.'

She gave a brief snort of derision.

'You weren't here, honey,' he said reasonably. 'You don't know the whole story. I'm telling you, I don't think I could have made it through all this stuff without him.'

'Well, fine,' she said grudgingly. 'But won't he have something to say about it if I move in?'

'Noooo,' said Hunter, shaking his head and suppressing a tiny suspicion that perhaps he *should* have run the idea by both Max and Tiffany before making the offer.

'Anyway, it's my house. So stop making excuses and just say yes, damn it.'

Siena jumped up and flung herself against him like a puppy greeting its long-lost master. She couldn't remember the last time she'd felt so deeply and truly happy.

'Yes!' She grinned from ear to ear. 'I will move in with you. Yes, yes, yes!'

subject of Siena's split personality to Hunter, complaining that she was often barely civil unless he happened to be around. But to her horror, Hunter came rushing to Siena's defence.

'She's been through such a lot, honey,' he insisted. 'I'm sure you're just misreading the situation. She's really very sweet and loving when you get to know her.'

'To you she is,' Tiffany replied bitterly. 'Not to me. Or Max for that matter.'

But no matter what she said, or how badly Siena behaved, Hunter seemed to take his niece's side every time. Every fucking time. Even when Max was around to back her up, Tiffany found it increasingly difficult to get him to take any of her concerns or criticisms seriously.

Sticking up for your family was fine. She of all people understood that, what with all the problems they'd been through with their parents, and their disapproval of the relationship. But even so, the situation with Hunter and Siena was really starting to get her down.

Opening the porch door with her key, she was relieved to find that only Max appeared to be up. He was sitting at the kitchen table in just a pair of pyjama bottoms, dividing his attention equally between his laptop and a huge slice of chocolate cake which he had already half demolished. When he saw Tiffany he looked up guiltily and wiped the icing from around his mouth with the back of his hand.

'Ha! Caught in the act, my friend,' she said as she dropped her bags on the counter and swooped down on him, kissing the top of his head and deftly removing the plate with one fluid motion.

'Oi!' said Max, aggrieved. 'I was enjoying that.'

'For breakfast?' She pointedly flipped up the lid of the waste bin and jettisoned what was left of the cake, before burrowing into her bag to produce some fresh walnuts and watermelon slices which she began to unwrap. 'I thought you were trying to get into shape.'

'Ah,' said Max, flipping shut his PC and wandering over to help her. 'But I didn't say *what* shape, did I? Much as I'd love to have a washboard stomach like your boyfriend's, a life of tofu and miso fucking soup just isn't worth it, I'm afraid. Speak of the devil.'

Right on cue, a dishevelled-looking Hunter emerged from his bedroom in his boxers and shuffled over towards Tiffany. Christ, he was handsome. Even first thing in the morning with his black hair standing on end and his mesmerising blue eyes still cloudy with sleep, it was all she could do not to gasp when she caught sight of him.

After all these years she knew every inch of his body, from the supple smoothness of his back to the taut power of his thighs and butt, and the round broad expanse of his shoulders. But she still found his beauty quite incredible. He was like a Michelangelo sculpture – her very own, personal David.

'Hey,' he whispered languidly, enveloping her in his arms and his warmth and his smell until she felt quite dizzy with longing. 'Check out those surfer-girl curls!'

She pulled away from him, embarrassed, and started getting down more plates from the cupboard. Being so tall, she didn't even have to stand on tiptoes to reach them like Siena did. She hated her hair all corkscrewed out from the ocean, and hated it even more when Hunter ruffled it as if she were a pet poodle.

'Yeah, well, I'll blow-dry it after breakfast,' she mumbled awkwardly.

'No! Don't!' said Max and Hunter in unison.

'It looks great like that,' Max assured her.

'Very sexy,' said Hunter, reaching out and cupping a hand over her left breast as she reached up for the glasses. She could feel the beginnings of his erection pressing into the small of her back.

'Hun-*ter*!' She blushed, grinning from ear to ear.

'Oh, get a room, would you?' said Max good-naturedly. He was pleased to see the two of them fooling around and looking so relaxed. Things had been pretty tense around here these last few weeks since Siena's arrival.

'You wanna go for a drive after breakfast?' asked Hunter, still refusing to release a wriggling Tiffany from his embrace.

'Sure.' She beamed at him.

She couldn't remember the last time the two of them had just taken off together on a Sunday. Not since their new year's trip to Big Bear. And that seemed like a lifetime ago already.

'Why don't you head up to Santa Barbara?' suggested Max.

'Ooh, yes,' said Tiffany. 'We could have dinner at that little place in Montecito, the one with all the honeysuckle. You remember, Hunter?'

He did remember. In their first few months of dating, some of the *Counsellor* fans had been getting out of hand, to the point where going out in LA had become a nightmare. Girls would shout insults at Tiffany when they went out as a couple – one silicone-enhanced lovely had even run, naked, into Ivy on the Shore and sat down on his lap as the two of them were having dinner.

Admittedly Tiffany had thought that was hilarious, but Hunter felt desperately embarrassed, and began looking for places out of town to take her on their dates. They had discovered the Montecito restaurant together, and the place would forever remind him of those early days together.

He bent down and kissed her gently on the lips. 'Sounds like a plan.'

Glowing with happiness, she extricated herself from his arms and took an armful of goodies across to the table. She couldn't believe how anxious she'd been driving over this morning. What a fuss she'd been making over nothing. Now they were going to have a lovely, relaxing, romantic day together. She needn't have worried at all.

'Who's going to Montecito?' A sleepy, female voice shattered her reverie. 'Can I come?'

Siena had emerged from her bedroom and sidled straight over to the refrigerator, beaming at Hunter as she went by. The two of them could almost have been twins, Tiffany thought with a pang of annoyance, radiating sexiness with their black bed-hair and blue eyes.

Max glared at Siena and tried not to notice the fact that she was wearing only a pair of semi-sheer nude panties and a child's size Lakers T-shirt that was doing a very inadequate job of containing her braless breasts.

'No,' said Max.

'Yes,' said Hunter simultaneously.

'Hunter and Tiffany want some time on their own,' said Max firmly, before Hunter had a chance to speak again.

'Well, what am *I* going to do?' Siena whined petulantly, pleading with Hunter for support.

Christ, she could be obnoxious when she wanted to, thought Max. 'If you're at a loose end you could always have a crack at that pigsty of a room you live in,' he said, giving her his best patronising smile.

'Don't be ridiculous,' snapped Siena. 'That's what we pay Maria for. Of course, when I say we, I mean Hunter and I. Heaven forbid that the great director should ever make a contribution.'

She knew how easy it was to get Max's hackles to rise by baiting him about not paying his way. What she didn't know was that he kept a meticulous record of the back rent he owed, plus interest, and that absolutely every cent of his meagre income was spent on contributing as far as he could to the household expenses. Nor that he had tried, on numerous occasions, to insist on moving somewhere cheaper but that Hunter had literally begged him to stay, pleading with him until Max felt there was no way out without really hurting and insulting his closest friend, and reluctantly capitulated.

And Max, of course, was far too proud ever to tell her.

'Cut it out, you two,' said Hunter. He was getting sick and tired of the endless bickering between Siena and Max. It had been bad enough when they were kids, but surely they could both let bygones be bygones now?

Sensing his frustration, Siena immediately changed tack. 'Anyway, I'm sure Tiffany wouldn't mind if I tagged along, would you? All girls together? It'd be fun.' She fluttered her eyelashes at a furious Tiffany for Hunter's benefit, and started ostentatiously helping to lay the table, picking up a stack of bowls and putting one by each place. 'I haven't been to Montecito since I was a child. I'd really love to see it again.'

There was a moment's silence, as Tiffany looked at Hunter, willing him just once to stand up to Siena and tell her to take a running jump. But one glance at his pained, torn expression told her it wasn't going to happen.

Tiffany would have loved to tell her to stick Montecito up her perfectly rounded ass, but she was getting better at this game by the day, and knew that outright hostility would play right into the little minx's hands. Instead she took a deep breath and gave Siena a false smile so broad it made her jaw ache, wrapping her arms around Hunter and tossing back her ocean-curled mane of blonde hair in an unmistakable gesture of possession.

'Sure, why not?' she said. 'The more the merrier.'

That'd show the little midget. Two could play at this game.

'Oh, right,' said Max, who could happily have smacked the now triumphant-looking Siena over the head with his PC, which he was clearing off the table. 'Well, if it's the more the merrier, I think I'll join you too. You and Hunter can go in the SL, enjoy the drive on your own. I'll take Siena in my car.'

Siena spun around and gave him a look that could have frozen molten lava. Making sure he was out of Hunter's line of sight, Max stuck his tongue out at her.

Tiffany, who was observing this little exchange as she

disengaged herself from Hunter and laid out the fruit plates, felt her heart swell with gratitude. Thank God for Max.

Stuck in traffic on the 101 two hours later, Max was beginning to regret his selfless gesture of support for Tiffany. Siena was being utterly unbearable.

First, she'd delayed them all by insisting on changing her outfit three times before she felt completely comfortable.

'It's Montecito, not Monte fucking Carlo,' he had yelled in exasperation after her third change, into an utterly unsuitable sky-blue linen suit with a pencil skirt and high heels.

Now she was sitting beside him with two bath towels thrown over the passenger seat of his Honda Civic in case she should contaminate her perfect outfit with any dust from the car, her face screwed up like that of a disgusted debutante who had woken up to find herself knee deep in sewage.

For the first half-hour of the journey, neither of them spoke, choosing instead to maintain hostilities via an ongoing battle for control of the stereo: he put on classical, she changed the station to pop, she turned the volume up, he turned it down. But when Max had insisted on taking the faster, less scenic freeway route rather than the coast road, her barely repressed rage had exploded in classic McMahon style.

'Why the fuck are we going this way?' she demanded, as he joined the sluggish-looking lane of northbound traffic. 'I thought this was supposed to be a beautiful Sunday drive, not a freeway crawl.'

'It was,' said Max. 'It was supposed to be a beautiful drive – for Hunter and Tiffany. And I sincerely hope' – he changed lanes suddenly, throwing Siena deliberately against the right side of the car, linen suit and all – 'that they're enjoying themselves. Despite your best efforts.'

'I don't know what you're talking about,' said Siena brusquely, brushing the dirt angrily from her sleeve.

'Oh, pull the other one,' said Max. 'You knew they wanted some time alone today. You only wanted to come so you could mess things up for the two of them. Again.'

Siena drew her shoulders back defensively. She hated it when he was right. 'My, what an active imagination you have!' she sneered. 'I suppose being such an abject, unemployed failure leaves you plenty of time to sit at home and work on your conspiracy theories.'

Max smiled. 'You can say what you like about me, sweetheart. But I've got your number. And so has Tiffany. Believe me, Hunter may be a soft touch, but he's not stupid. Sooner or later he's going to see through you, just like everybody else.'

Siena's eyes flashed with fear and hatred, but for once she managed to control herself. 'Why is it so hard for you to believe that I wanted to come today because I want to see Montecito?' she said. 'And because I like to be with Hunter. And he likes to be with me.'

Max yawned pointedly as Siena drew breath.

'Why can't you and *Tiffany* . . .' She lingered on the word with heavy sarcasm. '. . . just accept that?'

'Because it's crap,' said Max flatly. 'This has nothing to do with Montecito. Or you and Hunter having time together. If you really cared about Hunter, you wouldn't begrudge him and Tiffany their happiness. You'd see that she's the best thing that ever happened to him and stop trying to fuck everything up for him like some sort of neurotic child. You're pathetic.'

'How dare you!' exploded Siena, hitting him hard with both fists on his right arm so that he swerved dangerously towards the central reservation.

'Jesus,' said Max, trying to keep control of the car while shielding himself from her blows. 'Are you trying to kill us or something?'

He pulled unsteadily back across the lanes of traffic

towards the hard shoulder, eventually stopping by the side of the road as Siena continued to pummel him.

'You have no fucking clue what you're talking about!' she yelled, losing it completely now. 'What the hell do you know about me and Hunter, about what we've been through? You know nothing about my life, Max, *nothing!* I lost him for eleven years. Eleven fucking years. You were with him for all that time, all that time when I was alone, when I had *no one.* And now, after everything we've been through, we finally find each other again, and there's some stupid damn girl trying to take him away from me all the time. You have no idea what that feels like. I hate her, Max. I fucking hate her. I hate both of you!'

Gently Max took hold of each of her wrists, effortlessly stopping her punches. For a second she struggled against him automatically, but her efforts soon melted into the firm warmth of his grip. She glared up at him defiantly through tears of frustration.

And then, before he knew what he was doing, he found himself pulling her towards him and kissing her passionately on the mouth.

In one confusing moment, he felt the soft, wet skin of her cheeks against his own, and her tongue probing hungrily, almost desperately, for his as their bodies locked together. Then, as suddenly as it had started, it was over.

He let go of her, and sat back, shocked.

'Sorry,' he mumbled, his heart still pounding from the shock of what had just happened.

'Are you?' whispered Siena.

Her voice sounded changed and thick with desire. Max noticed that her left hand was still resting on his thigh.

He gazed across at her. She looked like a clown who'd been left out in the rain – first the tears and then the kiss had played havoc with her make-up. 'I don't know,' he stammered, staring at her hand on his leg, still too shell-shocked to move. 'Are *you?*'

'I don't know,' said Siena miserably. The desire in her voice had already been replaced by something else. It may have been panic.

Oh God. She felt horribly confused. She'd despised and resented Max for as long as she could remember. As a child, he'd always come between her and Hunter, and even now he never failed to take Tiffany's side and to undermine her in Hunter's eyes as much as he could.

When she had got so upset before, all she'd wanted was for him to *understand* for once, to stop preaching for five minutes and tell her that her need for Hunter, her deep, desperate love for him, was OK. She wanted him to tell her that Hunter loved her more than anyone else on the planet. That girlfriends would come and go, but that she, Siena, would never lose his love again.

But he hadn't done that. Instead, he'd told her off for her behaviour, chastised her like a naughty child. And then he'd gone and kissed her.

How was she supposed to react to that?

She toyed with the idea of slapping him round the face, pulling the whole 'how dare you' routine. But unfortunately there was no escaping the fact that she had kissed him back.

For a long time.

Enthusiastically.

In that instant, she had wanted him, and he knew it. There could be no going back.

Oh God. What had possessed her?

Flustered, she pulled her hand off his leg as though she'd just realised it was resting on hot coals, and fumbled in the glove box for some tissues.

'Here, let me,' said Max, reaching over to dab at her smudged cheeks.

Siena flinched. 'It's OK, it's OK,' she said. 'I can do it. You just, er . . .' She waved her hand, signalling him to get going. 'You just drive. We're going to be late otherwise.'

Max's face fell. So that was it, then? They were just going to pretend it had never happened?

Well, maybe it was for the best. Siena was trouble, big, big trouble, and the last thing he needed in his life right now. She was right. It had been a moment of madness, an emotional release for both of them, a stupid mistake that was best forgotten.

So why did he feel so overwhelmed with disappointment?

Reluctantly, he fastened his seat belt and restarted the engine.

'Fine,' he said eventually, not quite suppressing a sigh. 'Fine. Let's go.'

Chapter Twenty-nine

Siena decided that the kiss with Max must have been some sort of evil omen. From that moment on, everything started to go wrong.

The afternoon in Montecito had been complete torture. Hunter and Tiffany were totally wrapped up in one another, endlessly reminiscing about this boring restaurant and that tedious gallery. Siena couldn't have felt more like a gooseberry if she'd painted herself green and hung herself on a bush, and she wished with all her heart that she'd listened to Max in the first place and stayed at home.

'Oh, look, honey, it's that little tea place, you remember?' Tiffany grabbed Hunter's hand and began dragging him across Main Street. 'I wonder if they still do that passion fruit and mango?' She had changed into a clinging white vest and a pair of lemon-yellow shorts for the trip, which even when paired with flat flip-flops emphasised her endless brown legs. That was one area where she definitely trumped the petite Siena, who, she was gratified to see, was looking over-dressed and grumpy, with most of her make-up inexplicably smeared all over her over-priced jacket.

'You coming?' Hunter called over his shoulder to Siena and Max, but they both shook their heads and hung back, looking awkward. He hoped they hadn't had yet another row in the car.

For Siena, the afternoon had gone from bad to worse, with Tiffany scoring point after point and looking radiantly happy with Hunter. Max, meanwhile, had withdrawn into monosyllabic isolation. He didn't make eye contact with her once that afternoon, nor on the long journey back to LA in the evening. Clearly, he

regretted what had happened, which only served to heighten Siena's own feelings of embarrassment and confusion.

When they'd finally got back to the beach house, both of them had bolted to their separate rooms and a long-awaited respite from the tension of each other's presence.

What a fucking mess.

Over and over she told herself that she hated Max, that he would stop at nothing to turn Hunter against her, that he was and always had been her enemy. He was a loser, a sponger off her family, a patronising, self-righteous English prig. He was arty and pretentious.

And blond. She hated blonds.

When she thought back to the kiss she felt revolted, ashamed. And yet, however hard she tried to shut it out, the feeling of his body against hers, the power of his arms, the smell of his sweat and the unexpected violence of his kiss, all rushed back to assail her senses with what, despairingly, she could only acknowledge was pure and very intense desire.

For the next week, she threw herself into her work. She would leave the house at seven, before Max and Hunter were up, arriving over an hour early at the set in nearby Venice, where she would pore over her script, making notes and memorising the director's suggestions before rehearsals started.

But not even all her extra diligence could protect her from the wrath of Dierk Muller, the director, when he was less than a hundred and ten per cent happy with a scene.

Muller was a first-generation German immigrant, a charmless little wisp of a man with thinning grey hair, physically striking only for his over-sized Adam's apple, which bobbed up and down grotesquely whenever he spoke. Despite his unprepossessing appearance, he was revered in Hollywood, not only as a brilliant director whose energy, focus and commitment to all his projects

were second to none, but as that rarest of things in LA: a true, incorruptible artist. His films were all critical successes, and although he was at best hit and miss at the box office, there was no shortage of top-flight actors, writers and cinematographers queuing up to work with him.

He was not, however, an easy man to work with. Or in Siena's case, to work for.

Dierk knew Siena had talent, but he also recognised her lack of discipline, and her tendency to pull back emotionally in difficult scenes, a self-protective mechanism common in younger, inexperienced actresses. His response was to yell and scream and pour scorn like acid on her performance, bullying her into dropping her inhibitions. It worked, but the process was emotionally exhausting for both of them.

Siena, who was used to being the fashion world's darling, pampered and indulged by designers and photographers at every turn, was in a complete state of shock. At night she would crawl back home feeling worthless and defeated, longing to be left alone with Hunter, the one person who could always make her feel better. But invariably he'd be doing something with Tiffany.

Fucking perfect, sweet, wonderful, always-there Tiffany, who had herself wrapped around his heart like poison ivy.

Embarrassment after their kiss had not stopped Max from continuing to stick up for Tiffany whenever Siena tried to prise her away from Hunter. She was sick of it always being two against one at the beach house, and often her only comfort would be long phone calls to Ines in New York.

Ines, at least, was a true friend, accepting unconditionally that Tiffany was a bitch-cow from hell who must be destroyed and blindly taking Siena's side in everything. At the end of every call, she would beg Siena to come back to Manhattan.

'LA is sheet. Acting is sheet. Teefany is sheet,' she

would insist, neatly summarising Siena's own feelings on these three subjects. 'Come back to modelling, honey, we all mees you so much.'

But miserable as she was, Siena knew she couldn't go back. She'd waited too long for this movie, for a real shot at Hollywood, and to be back with Hunter again. She would show Dierk Muller what she was made of. And she'd get the better of Tiffany bloody Wedan as well.

And if Max self-righteous De Seville didn't like it, he could go to hell.

One evening, a few weeks after the fateful Montecito trip, Siena decided she would cook supper for the four of them at home.

One of Tiffany's most irksome attributes was the fact that she effortlessly excelled at all things domestic – cooking, flower arranging, sewing, interior decoration, you name it, she was a right little Martha Stewart. She was one of those infuriating women who only had to rearrange a few cushions to make a room look warm and homely and who whipped up delicious, interesting meals from the few unpromising leftovers she happened to stumble across in the fridge.

Siena knew that Hunter, who had never really had a mother figure in his life, valued such feminine skills very highly, and she was damned if she was going to let Tiffany bask in all the glory. Tonight, she, Siena, would be the angel in the house. Hunter couldn't fail to be delighted.

After two hours alone in the kitchen, however, she was starting to regret the whole domestic escapade.

Her first attempt at winter vegetable soup had ended up a charred and sticky mess, stuck, probably for ever, to the bottom of a giant saucepan. She reckoned she just about had enough ingredients left to attempt a second batch, but that left her very little time to make the rosemary baste for the rack of lamb, not to mention whip up the raspberry pavlova she had rashly already told Max would be on tonight's menu.

Hastily throwing some semi-chopped carrots and parsnips into the blender, she picked up the portable phone and called Ines.

'Lamb,' she shouted over the whirring of the blades. 'How long per pound? And how hot should the oven be?'

'Whaaat?' asked Ines, who had been happily drifting off to sleep on the couch in their apartment with her face caked in a green algae mask. 'Siena? Ees that you?'

Siena turned off the blender. 'How long should I cook this lamb for?' she repeated. 'It's quite big.'

'Ow the fuck should I know?' replied Ines reasonably. 'I'm a model. I don't eat, let alone cook. Why don't you eat out, like normal people?'

'I've told you,' said Siena, wrestling with the lid of the blender which finally came free, spraying vegetable purée into her face and hair. 'I want to cook something for Hunter. I want to show him that I'm better than she is at something.'

'Honey,' Ines reassured her, 'you are bettair than her at everything. Bettair looking, bettair actress, bettair everything. You 'ave nothing to prove to Hunter.'

Siena loved the way that Ines dismissed Tiffany's talents completely, despite the fact that she had never met her, spoken to her or even seen a picture. 'Thanks, babe.'

She wiped the mess from her hair with a tea towel, realising in panic that she would now need to wash and dry her hair before supper as well as finish preparing the food. It was almost half past six now.

'I've got to go,' she told Ines, turning back helplessly towards her pile of carrots.

'Good luck,' said her friend. 'And remembair, ees better to cook it too much than not enough.'

By 7.45, things were beginning to look a little more under control. Siena had washed and changed into a pair of clean chocolate-brown suede trousers and a faded green T-shirt that contrasted beautifully with her blue eyes – she didn't want to look as if she had made too much effort. She hadn't had time to blow-dry her hair, so she'd piled it, still damp, in a messy mop on top of her head, held loosely in place by her favourite silver-and-topaz hair clip.

She never normally wore make-up at home, but this evening she had decided to warm up her porcelain cheeks with a dusting of bronzing powder and to slick some clear gloss over her lips.

'You look lovely,' said Hunter when she emerged into the living room, where he and Tiffany were ensconced on the sofa watching reruns of *Gilligan's Island*.

'Wow, you really do,' added Tiffany graciously. 'And you smell terrific too. What is that?'

'Chanel nineteen,' said Siena. 'You're welcome to borrow some if you'd like.'

Tiffany, who knew this display of sweetness was entirely aimed at Hunter, smiled and declined very politely. 'But I'd be happy to help out in the kitchen, if there's anything you need doing,' she offered.

Two could play at this game.

'No thanks,' muttered Siena. She'd rather die than accept help from Little Miss Perfect this evening. 'I've got it covered.'

'Yeah, honey,' said Hunter, stroking Tiffany's hair in a way that made Siena want to run over there and strangle her. 'Let Siena handle things tonight. You're always slaving away in that kitchen. You deserve a night off.'

Fucking brilliant, thought Siena.

She'd been sweating her guts out since four, and all Hunter could think about was how much *Tiffany* deserved a break.

After twenty more minutes, she was finally ready to roll. The soup was a bit tasteless, but inoffensive and edible, a distinct improvement on her first attempt. The lamb was still roasting away in the oven and the pavlova, if she did say so herself, looked fabulous, if a little unstable; a towering triumph of cream and meringue which she had carefully put in the fridge to chill with an entire shelf to itself.

'Shall we eat?' she announced brightly, standing in the kitchen doorway in Tiffany's apron and looking, she fondly believed, every inch the relaxed and capable hostess.

She'd been so busy in the kitchen, though, that only now did she notice they were a man short. 'Where's Max?'

'Oh, sorry, didn't I mention that?' said Tiffany, scrambling up off the couch. 'He called this afternoon and said he might be late. Something about a meeting at Balboa, I think. He said to start without him. I thought I told you already.'

'No,' said Siena through gritted teeth. 'I guess it must have slipped your mind.'

Well, that was just typical. Max knew how important tonight was to her, how she'd wanted them all there because that was what Hunter would have wanted. But he couldn't be bothered even to show up. And instead of calling her himself, he'd deliberately left a message with Tiffany instead, knowing there was a good chance that she wouldn't pass it on. The pair of them had made her look like a fucking idiot. Again.

'Sorry,' said Tiffany, who was starting to enjoy herself. She'd lost count of the number of times Siena had shown up late, or not at all, for one of her carefully prepared meals. Or the times she had suddenly 'remembered' allergies to this or that, refusing to eat whatever it was that Tiffany had slaved over for hours. Short of grinding arsenic into her cherry crumble, she could think of nothing that would give her more satisfaction than to see Siena fall flat on her face tonight.

Hunter put a comforting arm around Siena. He could see she was upset at Max's defection. 'Hey, never mind,' he said kindly. 'I'm sure he'll show up later if he can.'

'Believe me,' said Siena unconvincingly, 'it couldn't matter less. Now, why don't the two of you sit down and I'll bring you your soup.'

The first course took longer than expected, mainly because Hunter begged for a second and then a third helping, insisting it was absolutely delicious. Meanwhile Tiffany and Siena passed the time by trying to outdo each other conversationally on the nice-as-pie stakes, frenziedly smiling and complimenting one another in a none too subtle attempt to win his approval.

Max eventually fell through the door just as Siena had finished serving the lamb. He looked worn out and stressed, his shoulders hunched and his ancient brown leather briefcase dangling despondently from one hand. It must have been another bad meeting.

But as soon as he saw Siena, looking so adorable, furious and ridiculously out of place wearing Tiffany's apron over her T-shirt, he couldn't help but crack a smile.

Siena McMahon, homemaker?

Arnold Schwarzenegger would have looked more at home in an apron than Siena.

'Sorry I'm late, sweetheart.'

He wandered over and kissed her affectionately on the top of her head. It was the first physical contact of any kind between them since Montecito, and it threw Siena completely.

She looked up at him, her eyes ablaze with hostility. 'Yeah, well. So you fucking should be,' she muttered. Fucking inconsiderate, self-centred asshole. And since when had he ever called her 'sweetheart'?

'I've been trying to escape for the past hour,' Max explained, ignoring her glare. 'Honestly. But I just couldn't shut the guy up.'

He sat down opposite Siena and began helping himself to a huge portion of vegetables before hacking away at the remnants of the small, rather wizened-looking joint.

Ines would have been pleased to hear that *no one* could have described it as under-cooked.

'I'm famished.' He grinned at her. 'This looks great.'

Blindsided by what appeared to be a genuine compliment, Siena accidentally smiled back.

Damn it. Why wouldn't he just go away? Or die?

Flustered, she took a bite of her own lamb and nearly choked. It was so over-cooked it was like chewing shoe leather. She glanced across at Hunter, who was manfully ploughing through his own enormous helping, nodding appreciatively at her as though he were savouring the pinnacle of cordon bleu excellence. God, he was an angel. Why did she have to be so fucking incompetent at everything?

While Siena sat gloomily cursing her lack of culinary prowess, Max was regaling the table with wonderfully funny impressions of the producer he'd met earlier, and anecdotes about the most disastrous meetings he'd ever been to. For such a cocky, arrogant guy, he had a surprisingly self-deprecating sense of humour, Siena noticed. Very British, in a way.

Tiffany and Hunter were both roaring with laughter at his tales of woe, with Tiffany trying to outdo him with stories of some of her most excruciating auditions. Having experienced very little failure in her own life, Siena was feeling rather left out of the proceedings.

'Oh, shit, this one guy,' said Tiffany through tears of laughter, 'he actually told me that in order for me to feel empathy with this character – who was meant to be dying from breast cancer, right? – I had to feel "exposed and vulnerable". Well, you can guess what it was he wanted me to expose.'

'No way!' said Max, gulping down a big slug of red wine. 'Does that shit really happen?'

'Omigod, are you kidding me?' Tiffany shrieked, looking to Hunter to back her up. 'It happens all the time. All the fucking time.'

'It's true,' said Hunter. 'Even I've been asked to get naked in auditions before.'

'Really?' Max raised his eyebrow. 'By whom? Not by Orchard?'

'Hugh? Noooo!' Hunter laughed. 'He's far too professional.' He caught Tiffany's adoring eye and started hamming it up, pouting and preening immodestly as if entranced by his own beauty. 'Not that he wouldn't *like* to see me naked, of course.'

'Who wouldn't, baby?' cooed Tiffany, leaning over and kissing him on the mouth.

Siena thought she was going to be sick.

'What about you, Siena?' asked Max playfully. 'Have you ever fallen prey to the lure of the casting couch?'

'Don't be ridiculous,' she snapped. Disheartened by her failure in the kitchen and fed up with being ignored by Hunter, she was having a complete sense of humour failure. 'Directors only pull that shit with sad, desperate unknowns. The sort of girl they know would do anything for a part. I hardly fall into that category.'

'Oh, and I do, I suppose?' challenged Tiffany, whose cheeks had flushed red with anger and embarrassment.

Siena shrugged. 'Not necessarily. But perhaps you give some people the *impression* that you're willing to sleep with someone to get ahead. After all' – she gave an infuriating, smug little laugh – 'hooking up with Hunter hasn't exactly hurt your career, now, has it?'

Tiffany's voice was quiet but she got to her feet, patently furious.

'You fucking bitch.'

'Honey, calm down,' said Hunter. 'I'm sure Siena didn't mean to upset you. It's just that, well, you know what Hollywood's like. People *do* tend to think the worst of someone, if their partner's wealthier or better known or . . .'

'*What?*' Tiffany interrupted him, white lipped and trembling with rage. 'You're telling me you actually *agree* with her?'

'Hey, come on now, Tiffany, calm down,' interjected Max, with a reproachful look at Siena.

'No, no, of course not,' insisted Hunter, who now looked panicked. 'It's not that I agree with her. I only meant . . .' He looked around the table for help. 'Siena,' he said eventually, 'perhaps you should apologise to Tiffany. I know you weren't intending to upset her.'

Siena failed to suppress a triumphant smile. This was fantastic.

'Of course,' she said graciously. 'I'm *so* sorry if you misunderstood me, Tiffany.'

'Oh, I think I understood you perfectly,' said Tiffany calmly.

She was evidently still livid, but she wasn't going to give Siena the satisfaction of losing her temper. Picking up her jacket from the back of her chair and grabbing her bag, she headed for the front door. She'd had it up to here with Hunter's constant defending of Siena's atrocious behaviour. If he wasn't going to stick up for her when someone called her a whore, he could fucking well sleep alone tonight.

'Where are you going?' asked Hunter desperately, getting up himself to go after her.

'Home,' she said firmly, without breaking stride.

He reached out and put a restraining hand on her shoulder. 'Come on, baby, this is silly. You don't have to go.'

'I *want* to go, Hunter,' she said nastily, inwardly cursing herself for losing it and lashing out at him. She knew this was exactly what Siena had hoped for, that she'd effectively played right into her hands. But she couldn't help it. Sometimes Hunter's blindness and total lack of support were just too much for her to bear.

She stormed out of the door with a look that told him in no uncertain terms that he'd better not even think of following. Miserably, Hunter went back to the table and put his head in his hands.

'Who'd like some pavlova?' asked Siena brightly.

'Shut up,' said Max, before turning sympathetically to Hunter. 'Don't worry, mate. She'll be back.'

'Will she?' asked Hunter. He hated it when he and Tiffany fought, but he hated it even more when she left him. No matter how many times it happened, he couldn't shake the hideous, gnawing anxiety that this might be it, that she might never walk back through that door. 'I don't get it,' he complained in exasperation. 'What am I doing wrong?'

Max poured himself another glass of wine. 'I think it's more a question of what you're *not* doing,' he said. 'Why don't you drive over there right now and tell her you're sorry? Show her you're on her side. I think it would make all the difference.'

Right at that moment, Siena came teetering over to the table with a huge, wobbling tower of raspberries and cream. Max, who had his back to her, suddenly tipped back in his chair and threw out both arms in a full-bodied yawn, catching her by the elbow. Hunter watched horrified as, as if in slow motion, Siena lurched forward desperately trying to regain her balance, before finally dropping the plate with an almighty crash on the maple floor.

She stood there in shock while shards of meringue flew around the room like sugary shrapnel, and tiny drops of cream sprayed everywhere: on the walls, the chairs, the table, some even finding their way into Hunter's hair.

For a moment, nobody made a sound. Then Max burst out laughing.

'I'm sorry, sweetheart,' he said eventually, wiping away tears of mirth and smearing his cheek with raspberry sauce in the process. 'I'm really sorry. But that was pretty fucking spectacular – attack of the killer pudding!'

'It's not funny!' wailed Siena. 'Do you know how long I spent making that damn thing?' She ran her hands through her hair in despair. 'I just wanted tonight to be

322

so perfect for you,' she said, turning to Hunter. 'But first Tiffany goes and has a spac attack about nothing. And then this giant moron' – she pointed accusingly at Max – 'goes and destroys my pavlova – which was going to be the best part of the whole fucking meal, by the way.'

'Well, that wouldn't be hard,' muttered Max under his breath, not quite quietly enough.

'Oh, fuck off, would you?' said Siena, with feeling.

She felt as if she was about to cry, which she knew was utterly ridiculous over one stupid dinner.

Hunter, however, had tuned out and was completely oblivious for once to Siena's pouting complaints. He could think only about Tiffany. Maybe Max was right. Maybe he had been unsupportive.

'I'm going over there,' he announced suddenly, getting up and grabbing his car keys from a hook by the door, leaving the house without a word or a backward glance at Siena.

'Can you believe that?' she said as the sound of his engine died away a few seconds later.

Her cheeks were flushed from the evening's trauma and exertions, and unruly tendrils of drying black hair had started to escape from her silver-and-topaz clip. Max could see the faint outline of her nipples through the worn green cotton of her T-shirt, and made a heroic effort to concentrate on her scowling, scrunched-up little face.

'All that work. All that effort,' she moaned. 'And he didn't give a shit. That stupid fucking girl is all he cares about.'

'Would you listen to yourself for one minute?' said Max, squatting down on the floor and scooping handfuls of pavlova into an empty salad bowl. 'Can't you hear how spoiled and selfish you sound?'

'Oh, change the fucking record, would you?' said Siena, kneeling down to help him. 'What is it with you, anyway? If you'd knocked over one of Tiffany's desserts, you'd be all "Omigod, I'm *so* sorry, Tiffany, *poor* you, Tiffany, let me make it up to you, Tiffany."'

She mimicked his English accent the way she used to do when they were kids. Max remembered how much it used to infuriate him back then.

Now it turned him on like hell.

'But of course, because it was *me*,' she ranted on, 'you think it's funny. Fucking hilarious. It's only Siena. Who cares if Siena's evening gets ruined, if all her hard work was for nothing? You don't apologise to *me*.'

'I did apologise,' said Max.

'Do you fancy her or something?' asked Siena bitterly, hurling a handful of pink creamy slop into the bowl.

'Don't be ridiculous,' he replied, rather too defensively. 'She's Hunter's girlfriend. I never think of her in that way.'

But Siena had picked up on his momentary weakness and decided to keep pushing.

'Oh, *I* get it,' she said with a knowing smile. 'You want his house. You want his fame.' She counted them off on her fingers. 'You want his money and his looks. And now you want to screw his girlfriend too. Why not?'

Max could feel his temper building.

'Shut up, Siena.'

'You know, you really want to try and get some kind of life of your own, Max,' she continued mercilessly. 'You're obsessed with Hunter. You always have been. All this envy, all this covetousness, it can't be good for you. It eats you away inside, doesn't it?'

'I mean it, Siena.' He grabbed her by the wrist. 'That's enough.'

Sensing that she had the upper hand, she refused to be intimidated, maintaining her smile and her eye contact.

'You think about fucking her, don't you, Max?' she taunted him. 'Admit it. You'd love to get your desperate little hands on those perky brown tits, wouldn't you? Or see those pretty pink lips wrapped around your cock? Do you think that's what Hunter's getting right now?'

Max felt his stomach churning, as if he were going to be sick. It revolted him to hear her talk so crudely. He wanted to make her stop.

'Shut up! Shut the fuck up!' he snapped, grabbing her other wrist and shaking her violently.

Her head whiplashed backward when he grabbed her, and the rest of her hair burst free from its restraint, tumbling down around her face like a glossy black dam breaking. The cream in his hands felt slippery against the skin of her forearms, and he could feel the soft pressure of her breasts against his chest when he pulled her towards him.

Jesus Christ, he wanted her so much.

Suddenly all the tension, all the longing he'd felt for her since that day at Montecito, came bursting out. He started to kiss her with such force that she slipped backward and clunked the back of her head on the floor.

'Ow,' she said, as Max scrambled to pull up her T-shirt. But she was smiling. 'That hurt.'

'Shut up,' he whispered. He was staring down at her, his face inches above her own, and a look of such desire and love in his eyes that Siena wanted to reach up and stroke him.

So he did want her. He had felt something in Montecito!

She'd been trying to deny it to herself, but she'd known for weeks that her bad mood and frustration had not been down to Tiffany alone, or even to the traumas on-set with Dierk. She'd been trying and failing to stamp down her feelings for Max, so convinced was she that he didn't return them, didn't even like her in fact.

But he did. He wanted her.

She felt deliriously happy.

Max bent his head and softly began kissing her bare breast, his warm tongue circling her nipple. She moaned.

'Tell me you want me,' he whispered, moving with agonising slowness to her other breast, while his hand strayed down to her suede-covered thighs, stroking

325

upward teasingly but always stopping just short of her crotch.

'Please,' she begged him, her voice now thick and groggy with longing, her hands reaching down for his belt. 'Please, Max. Just do it.'

'Just do what?' he teased her, sliding down to undo her zip and slipping her trousers down to her knees, revealing a pair of pale pink silk panties.

Scooping a handful of cream and raspberries from the bowl beside them, he began smearing the sweet mixture on her thighs and stomach, studiously avoiding the one place that she was aching for him to touch.

Siena closed her eyes and allowed the wonderful sensations to flood over her. Max's warm, calloused hands were on her breasts, while he torturously licked the cream from her thighs, inch by inch, the warm wetness of his tongue matching her own juices, which were already beginning to seep through the fabric of her panties. She tried not to think of all the legions of other women he'd done this with before. Judging by how good he was at it, she imagined it must have been quite a few. His hot breath tickled her between her legs, and the roughness of his stubble scraped deliciously against her smooth skin. She felt as if she'd died and gone to heaven.

This wasn't some clumsy, casual lover.

It was Max. Her Max.

At last.

After what seemed like an eternity, having still not laid a finger on her pussy, he finally wriggled out of his own jeans, and she could feel his huge cock nudging against her. Instinctively, she reached down to touch it, but he grabbed her hands and, pulling them back above her head, pinned down her arms so that she could barely move at all.

'So . . .' He grinned down at her. 'Siena. Tell me. What do you want?'

Oh God. She couldn't say it. She wanted him inside her so badly she could cry, but she just could not say the words. Not to Max. Not to him.

'I want you,' she stammered frantically, arching her pelvis up against him. 'I want you, Max. Please.'

He shook his head.

'Sorry, sweetheart,' he whispered right into her ear. 'I'm afraid that's not good enough.'

Siena started to whimper. If he didn't do it soon she was going to come right there, before he'd even touched her.

'Tell me what you want me to do to you. Exactly. I want to hear you say it.'

'Jesus, Max, I can't!' She sounded almost angry. Why wouldn't he just fuck her?

'Really?' he teased her, running the tip of his tongue slowly along her lower lip. 'You can't say it? A few minutes ago you weren't so shy, were you? Or wasn't that you, who said I wanted Tiffany's lips around my cock?'

'God, I'm sorry, OK?' said Siena, who was now squirming as much in embarrassment as excitement.

'Don't apologise,' said Max, releasing her hands and pulling off her underwear with one swift motion. Much as he wanted to hear her beg him for it, he didn't have a second's more self-control left in him. 'You can show me how sorry you are.'

And with that he thrust deeply into her, feeling the strong spasms of her almost immediate orgasm as he did so. Her hands were on his back, in his hair, on his buttocks, pulling and clawing at him, biting into his shoulders in the most totally abandoned display of desire he'd ever felt in a woman. If it were possible, Max thought, she actually wanted this even more than he did.

He tried to hold back his own climax, but it was like swimming against a rip tide. When at last he came, it felt as if a lifetime of tension had been magically, gloriously released.

He wouldn't have traded that moment for all the hit Hollywood movies in history.

Chapter Thirty

Henry Arkell woke up with the sort of hangover he couldn't remember having had since his stag weekend in Dublin twelve years ago.

As soon as he reached consciousness, he got out of bed and staggered into the loo, where he spent the first fifteen minutes of his Sunday morning throwing up.

'Can I get you anything, darling?' shouted Muffy.

She was sitting up in bed with her Rosamund Pilcher novel and a cup of tea, being distracted by the sound of her poor husband's retching.

'Yes. My shotgun,' quipped Henry, who reappeared in the bathroom doorway looking as white as a sheet. He'd tried to take some Alka-Seltzer, but was unable to hold it down. There was nothing to do but go back to bed – preferably for ever.

Crawling back under the duvet, he pulled the covers up over his head and groaned. Just then, Madeleine came bounding into the room clutching her Malibu Barbie and demanding to be allowed into her parents' bed for a snuggle.

'No!' barked Henry, whose head felt as if it was exploding. 'Go and watch cartoons, Maddy. Daddy's not feeling very well.'

'But I always snuggle on Sundays, don't I, Mummy?' she protested.

'You do, darling, yes,' said Muffy, putting down her novel and mug with a sigh and getting up to deal with her daughter. So much for her weekend lie-in. 'But Dad's very tired this morning. Why don't you come downstairs with me and you can help me make some brekka?'

'All right,' said Madeleine, pulling off her pyjama top

and scratching her rounded baby's tummy absent-mindedly. 'It's very smelly in here anyway. Poo-eee!' She pinched her nose in disgust. 'Barbie doesn't like it when it's smelly.'

Muffy laughed and shooed her into the children's bathroom to do her teeth, before opening all the casement windows to allow the crisp, fresh April morning air to dispel Henry's alcohol fumes. Maddy was right, the room smelt like an Irish pub on New Year's Day.

She was worried about Henry. He'd gone up to London the night before for some sort of crisis meeting with Nick Frankel. Evidently the crisis had been worse than he'd expected, as he'd arrived home at a quarter to five in the morning, in a black cab, smashed out of his mind.

Muffy had had to get up and empty the petty cash tin from the farm office, as well as her handbag, both swearing tins and Charlie's piggy bank to pay the cabbie his £260 fare, which God knew they could ill afford at the moment, before beginning the arduous task of helping Henry upstairs, out of his suit and into bed.

Normally she would have made him sleep on the sofa and spent the next day furiously ignoring him. But he seemed to have been under so much pressure recently, and his moods had got darker and darker to the point where she was afraid that any show of anger or rejection by her might push him over the edge into real depression.

Tying the belt on her ancient Laura Ashley dressing gown, she went downstairs to start breakfast, knocking on the boys' door as she went past.

'Bertie! Charlie! It's half past eight,' she shouted wearily. 'Up, dressed, teeth.'

With three children, a husband in meltdown and a failing farm to help run, she had long ago abandoned wasting energy on full sentences.

Downstairs, she began frying up a big pan of bacon,

eggs and tomatoes, while simultaneously sorting through yesterday's neglected post.

Bills, bills, bills, two brown, three red, a catalogue for new milking products that they couldn't afford, another catalogue for clothes – she should be so lucky! Only one blue, handwritten envelope caught her eye. It was addressed to Henry and postmarked Marbella.

Who on earth did they know in Marbella?

Henry lay under the duvet unable to sleep, or even rest. Unfortunately, the toxic amounts of brandy and champagne he'd downed last night had failed to blot out any part of his nightmare meeting with Nick. Apparently his back tax bill now stood at an incredible two hundred and fifty thousand, not the one hundred and fifty he had originally thought.

A quarter of a million fucking pounds! And that was just the tax, on top of all his other debts, which, Nick was quick to remind him, now ran into many hundreds of thousands. How was it possible?

As far as Henry could remember, he spent every other month filling out tax forms for something or other, and a steady stream of money made its way out of his poor, depleted current account in Bicester into the groaning coffers of the Inland Revenue every year. Nick had spent hours yesterday patiently trying to explain to him exactly how this latest whopper of a bill added up. But even the words 'tax return' caused an impenetrable cloud to form in Henry's brain, intensified in this case by over a dozen brandy and champagne chasers as the grim news had started to sink in.

He couldn't for the life of him work out how he'd allowed things to get quite so appallingly bad.

There was only one salient point that he *had* understood from last night's meeting, and it weighed on his chest this morning like ten tons of lead. With the tax and the debts combined, either he got his hands on three-quarters of a mill within the next six months at the outside or he would lose Manor Farm. Thanks to an ancient clause in the deeds, he wasn't able to sell off small sections of the land piece by piece. The house and land must for ever remain one property, one unit. Bar a few paintings it was his only real asset, all that he had to sell – and short of a miracle, he was about to lose it.

How the hell was he going to tell Muffy?

As if reading his mind, his wife appeared in the doorway, looking as youthful and kind and beautiful as ever, bearing a tray of freshly made bacon sandwiches, a pot of Earl Grey tea and an already wilting bunch of daisies and buttercups in a wineglass.

'The flowers are from Maddy,' she said, setting his breakfast down on the bedside table. 'She's making you a Get Well Soon card downstairs.' She plumped up the pillows behind him and Henry made an effort to sit up without expelling the entire contents of his stomach.

'Thanks,' he said, weakly. 'Let's hope I do. Get well soon, I mean.' He took a tentative sip of the tea. 'Not sure if I can manage the bacon,' he said ruefully. 'It smells fantastic, though.'

'Try,' said Muffy, 'it might help. Oh, this came for you.' She reached into her dressing-gown pocket and produced the blue envelope.

Henry took it, but looked as puzzled as she was. 'Marbella? I wonder who on earth that can be from.' He ripped open the envelope with a butter-smeared knife and pulled out a two-page handwritten note. 'Fuck me,' he said, looking at the signature first. 'It's from Ellis.'

'Who?' said Muffy, taking a bite of his sandwich. She was supposed to be on a diet, but it seemed a shame to let it go to waste.

'Your admirer, remember? Gary Ellis?' said Henry, who was reading the letter intently, although the words were still spinning before his eyes. 'He's making me an offer. I think. Wants to fly me out to Spain to discuss it.'

'What sort of offer?' asked Muffy warily.

She had never forgotten the slimy way the developer

had tried to paw her at Caroline's dinner party all those years ago. She didn't trust Gary Ellis as far as she could spit. The man was a vulture.

'I don't know. I'm not sure,' said Henry, somewhat shiftily, stuffing the letter hastily into his pyjama pocket. He didn't want to worry Muffy with any of this yet, not until he'd figured out exactly what he was going to do. In fact Ellis had been deliberately vague in his choice of words, expressing little more than a renewed interest in Henry's land. Perhaps word of his debts had started to get out, thought Henry in horror. Nick wouldn't have said anything, but these things always seemed to find their way to the ears of sharks like Ellis. A few days ago, he wouldn't even have entertained the idea of selling up, let alone to some smarmy developer. But all of a sudden his options were looking mighty slim. He'd be a fool not to at least hear what the man had to say.

'Maybe I should fly out there and find out?'

'Don't be silly.' Muff laughed, polishing off the last of the sandwich and taking a long gulp of her own tea. 'What can he possibly have to offer us? All he's interested in is the farm, and we would never sell that to anyone. Oooo' – she raised her eyebrow playfully – 'or d'you think he wants to pay a million dollars to sleep with me, like in that film with Demi Moore?'

'Don't talk rubbish,' snapped Henry. She looked hurt and he felt winded by guilt, as if he'd just been kicked in the stomach. He knew he ought to tell her, come clean about the debts. But when? How? She had trusted him to provide for her and he had let her down, let everyone down horribly. It was all his fault. He'd have to find a way to fly out to Spain and see Ellis without her knowing.

'Sorry,' he said, forcing a smile. 'It's just this bloody hangover. You're right, it's a silly idea. Forget about it.'

'Right, then,' said Muffy. 'Well, I'd better get Charlie ready for riding. You stay here and rest and I'll come up and check on you in a couple of hours, OK?'

'OK. Muffy?' He reached out for her hand and grabbed it as she got up to go. 'You do know I love you, don't you?'

She frowned, puzzled, and bent down to kiss him on the lips. "Course I do,' she said. 'What a funny question.'

Back in California, blissfully ignorant of his brother's problems, Max lay back on Zuma beach with Siena in his arms. The sun was shining, the surf was absolutely perfect, and the most beautiful girl in the world was curled up and sleeping peacefully on his chest. Life really didn't get much better than this.

It was just over a month since the two of them had got together, and they had yet to spend a night apart. Max had worried that them both living at the beach house might get too claustrophobic, especially at such an early stage in the relationship. But their days were always so hectic and full – Siena's with filming in Venice, and his with rehearsals for a new play he was directing downtown – that they actually found they were glad of one another's company in the evenings.

It helped that the atmosphere at home had improved beyond all recognition since Siena stopped focusing all her emotional energy on Hunter, and since Max had ceased to be the enemy.

She still felt some residual jealousy and resentment towards Tiffany, but her anxiety on that front had considerably eased, and her general behaviour vastly improved as a result.

This weekend Hunter and Tiffany were in Colorado visiting Tiffany's family, so Max and Siena had the whole house to themselves. Having made love in every room, and outside under the cypress tree, and contorted themselves into every possible sexual position, they decided they needed a change of scene and had driven down to Malibu for lunch and a much needed nap on the beach.

Gently, Max rolled Siena off his chest and laid her

down on her back in the sand. She started to stir and open her eyes, screwing up her face against the glare of the afternoon sun.

'Wakey-wakey,' he said, straddling her so the dark shadow of his body fell across her face.

Siena looked up and saw him kneeling above her, with his beautiful brown chest and shoulders, and his lovely kind smile beaming down at her from beneath a wall of straw-blond hair. She loved the size and strength of him, the fact that his hands were bigger than her head and that he could lift her up and down with one arm as if she were made of paper. Next to some of the other, super-slim models, she had always felt rather womanly and solid. Max made her feel fragile and delicate, like a priceless china doll. It was a good feeling.

'How long was I asleep?' she murmured, reaching up to run her fingers drowsily through his chest hair.

'Only twenty minutes.' He bent down and kissed her. Her lips still tasted of salt water from her earlier dip in the ocean. 'I'm really thirsty, though, I might go and grab a Coke. Wanna come with me?'

Siena shook her head. Zuma Café was only a couple of hundred yards away, but she felt so warm and comfortable just lying there on the sand, listening to the soporific swooshing of the waves, she couldn't face moving an inch.

'You could bring me a Diet Coke, though.' She smiled up at him imploringly.

'What's the magic word?' he teased her, slowly outlining her nipple with one finger through the stretchy orange fabric of her bikini. Siena watched him do it and gave a sigh of longing. She loved it when he touched her there.

'Please,' she whispered, lifting her leg so that her thigh brushed against his already stiffening cock.

'OK, OK, I'm going.' Max jumped to his feet. A few more seconds of this and he wouldn't be able to walk anywhere. 'One Diet Coke coming up, Your Highness. Don't you go anywhere, now.'

Siena rolled over on to her stomach and let out a purr of pure pleasure.

'No danger of that,' she murmured.

The café, as always on a weekend, was crowded. Hard-core surfers with dreadlocked hair and deep, year-round tans mingled with the rich kids from Beverly Hills, whose Mercedes and BMW convertibles were parked in gleaming black and silver rows along the beach road behind them.

Max joined the 'drinks only' queue behind two preppy-looking guys in their mid-thirties – agents, most probably, judging by their neon-white dentistry, Armani trunks and heavily manicured hands. One of them was reading from a copy of *Variety*, where there was a big piece about Dierk Muller's films, including a paragraph about *The Prodigal Daughter*, accompanied by a picture of Siena in one of her Maginelle adverts.

'You seen this?' said the one holding the paper to his friend.

'The McMahon girl?' said the other one. 'Sure. I'm not usually into models. Too skinny. But that kid has a booty to die for.'

They both chuckled. Max felt his stomach turning to lead and his heart tightening.

'D'you think she can act?' asked the first guy, who was still leering at the picture of Siena draped provocatively over a semi-naked black male model.

'I doubt it,' said his friend. 'I know a guy who's fucked her, though.'

'Seriously?'

'Sure. You know Glen Bodie, the producer? According to him . . . well, let's just say she's not completely without talent.'

They both started to laugh until, without warning, Max grabbed them from behind by the collar, one in

336

each hand, and started dragging them outside into the car park.

'Jeez, man, what's your fucking problem?' yelled the first guy, who had dropped his paper in the scuffle, and was desperately trying to turn around to take a swing at his mystery attacker.

As soon as they were through the door, Max hurled both of them down on to the tarmac with all the ease of a WWF wrestler.

'*You're* my problem, asshole,' he said. 'How dare you talk about Siena like that? You don't know the first thing about her. Where do you get off spreading it around that she's slept with some fucking moronic friend of yours?'

'Yeah, well, what's it to you, buddy?' challenged the second guy, who had got to his feet and was mentally calculating his chances of walking away with both arms and legs if he gave Max the punch he deserved.

'She's a friend of mine,' said Max, defensively. 'I won't have her disrespected.'

'Oh yeah? Well, I don't know how good a "friend" you are. But I'm telling you, she slept with Bodie. That's a fact, whether you wanna believe it or not.'

Max lunged towards him again, but a couple of surf dudes who'd been watching the drama unfold grabbed hold of him and dragged him away.

'Leave it, man,' said one of them, a friendly-looking giant of a teenager who was even bigger than Max and clearly wasn't going to take no for an answer. 'Let it go.'

'And stay the fuck away from me or I'll sue you for assault, you motherfucking psycho!' called the first agent, who was still sitting ignominiously on the ground, rubbing his leg, having grown quite brave now that the danger had passed.

Shaking from head to toe, Max threw off the surfers angrily and started staggering back across the beach. He could see Siena, still laying face down on the white sand, her beautifully curved buttocks rising like two round scoops of ice cream, already tanned to a perfect shade of *café au lait.*

He knew he shouldn't wade right in in anger and confront her, but he couldn't help himself. The thought of what he'd just heard, of some sleazeball producer touching her and bragging about it to all his friends, made him feel physically sick.

'Siena,' he called out gruffly as he came within the last few feet of her.

'Mmmm?' she murmured in reply, semi-comatose with sun.

Rolling over slowly, she failed to notice that she had rucked up her bikini top, leaving her left nipple completely exposed. She gazed up innocently at Max. 'What happened to the drinks?'

'Never mind the fucking drinks,' he barked. 'And cover yourself up, for Christ's sake. Do you want the whole of Malibu to see your tits?'

She blushed and straightened her top. He had never spoken so brutally to her before. It frightened her.

'What's the matter?'

The old Siena would have shouted at him and told him to go fuck himself, but her love for him had done what nothing else had ever been able to achieve – disabled her legendary temper.

'Did you fuck a producer called Glen Bodie?' The anger and hostility in his voice were unmistakable. Siena could feel her heart pounding with fear.

'Did you?' he shouted, when she failed to answer immediately.

'I'm not going to answer you if you keep shouting at me like that,' she said, trying to sound firm, although her voice was still quavering. She drew her knees up to her chest defensively and reached for a beach towel to cover herself with. 'Who told you that, anyway?'

'Never mind who told me it,' snapped Max. He was now crouched down with his face inches from hers. All of a sudden the size and strength that Siena had found so comforting before had become threatening and awful. 'Is it true?'

Instinctively, she recoiled from him, scrambling backward on her hands like a frightened crab.

'Yes,' she blurted out eventually, raising her voice more in fear than in anger. 'Yes, it is true.'

'How could you?' He stood rooted to the spot, looking at her as if she were some sort of scum. It was that look which finally stirred her, despite her terrible fear of losing him, to defend herself.

'What do you mean, "how could I?" she said. 'How could *you* sleep with all those models and waitresses you used to bring back to the beach house? You're not some saint, you know, Max, and neither am I. Yes, I did sleep with Glen. Yes, I'm an awful, disgusting, terrible, promiscuous person. Is that what you want to hear, Max? Yes, yes, *yes!*'

He looked on horrified as she collapsed into tears, pulling the towel completely over her head in utter misery, her whole body shuddering in a series of terrible lurching sobs.

In an instant he had sat down beside her and pulled her, struggling and crying, into his arms.

'Shhhh. Shhhh, Siena, I'm sorry,' he whispered softly, rocking her in his arms until she stopped resisting, the multi-coloured beach towel still draped over her face. 'I'm sorry, baby. I shouldn't have shouted at you. It's my fault. I don't think you're awful or terrible or any of those things.'

'Or promiscuous?'

She allowed the towel to drop, and looked at him with eyes still welling up with tears, and the wet cheeks and bright red, sniffling nose of a five-year-old. Max felt his anger dissolving. Why was he being such a jealous prick?

'Or that,' he assured her. He tried to explain himself. 'There were these two guys. At the café.' He gestured miserably behind him. 'I overheard them talking.'

'About Glen?' she asked meekly.

Max nodded.

Siena wished the beach could have opened up and swallowed her.

Glen Bodie – to her he had just been an evening's entertainment. Sure, he was a jerk, but he had a great body and a dick like a cruise missile. She hadn't given Bodie a thought before or since.

The fact was, she had always enjoyed sex, and in the past had prided herself on her ability to screw around as and when the fancy took her, without ever becoming emotionally attached to any man. Apart from Patrick Cash – and that had been years ago, a lifetime ago – she had never experienced anything approaching genuine affection, let alone love, for any of her many lovers.

But all that was before Max.

Siena didn't really know how, or why, but Max had broken through to a place in her heart that even she had almost forgotten ever existed. She not only allowed him to see her vulnerability and fear, she *wanted* him to see it, *needed* him to see it. Not even Hunter had got as close to her, in a lifetime, as Max had got in the last four weeks.

Siena knew she could be spoiled and selfish and that she wasn't a millionth of the wonderful, kind, honour-able person that Max was. But, by some miracle, he seemed to love her anyway. For the first time in her life, she began to view her past sexual conquests as something less than glorious notches on the bedpost of her invulnerability. She began to view them as mistakes – perhaps terrible mistakes – that meant she could never be the pure, perfect woman that Max wanted and deserved.

'I'm sorry,' she cried despairingly, scanning his face for further imagined signs of disgust. 'It was a one-night thing. A long time ago. Oh, Max, I wish it hadn't happened, I wish a lot of things had never happened, but they did and I can't change them now. And I wish I could tell you that Glen was the only one, but he wasn't. Please. Please don't hate me for it.'

Max squeezed her even tighter. What the fuck was wrong with him?

Here he was with the most incredible, beautiful, loving girl – with Siena, Siena whom he'd wanted, deep down, for as long as he could ever remember – and all he seemed to do was make her cry.

He tried to reason with himself. So what if she'd slept with some producer? So what if she'd slept with a whole bunch of them? It had all happened long before they got together. And she was right: he'd certainly been no angel himself in the past, so what right did he have to lay a guilt trip on her?

He was ashamed to admit it, even to himself, but the fact was that he felt scared. Scared that she would wake up one day and realise that she could do a whole lot better than a struggling English director with only a few thousand quid and a battered old Honda to his name.

Everywhere they went together, men stared or swarmed around her. Sometimes it was as if he couldn't hear himself think for the low background hum of industry types taking bets on how long the relationship would last.

It was bad enough being thought of as Hunter's hanger-on. But to be dismissed as Siena's plaything was unbearable, and filled him with a frustration that he couldn't seem to stop taking out on her.

'Angel,' he said, his voice breaking. 'I don't hate you. I could never hate you. If anything it's you who should hate me, for being such a stupid, jealous . . .'

She stopped him with a kiss, a long, lingering embrace charged with love and relief. Sometimes it felt as if the only way they could really communicate was physically. Sex was their safety net.

'Take me home,' said Siena when they finally pulled away from each other. His anger had shaken her more than she wanted to admit. 'Let's go to bed.'

Chapter Thirty-one

Out in Colorado with Tiffany's family, Hunter was anxiously smiling his way through another family meal.

'Thanks, Marcie, honey.' Jack Wedan leaned back in his chair and loosened his belt a notch, patting his groaning paunch appreciatively. 'That was great.'

'Yes, thank you, Mrs Wedan,' said Hunter with a sly wink at a furiously blushing Tiffany, who was clearly mortified by her dad's behaviour. 'It was absolutely delicious.'

Dinner had, in fact, been very good, the highlight of an otherwise rather tense day.

He didn't know what it was about Tiffany's family. They were always gracious hosts and studiously polite, asking him all about his career and his plans, making time to arrange trips or hikes to ensure he wasn't bored during his stay, cooking up a storm.

But still, there was an awkwardness with them that he couldn't seem to crack.

He'd been coming to Estes Park for years as Tiffany's steady boyfriend, and had never done anything to hurt or disrespect her, anything that might cause her parents to distrust him, at least not that he could think of. But for some reason, this undercurrent of something – reticence, suspicion maybe? – hung in the air throughout all his visits. It made it very hard to relax.

'I'm glad you enjoyed it, dear,' said Tiffany's mother kindly, getting up to start clearing the plates.

'Leave it, Mom, Hunter and I can do that, can't we, honey?' said Tiffany, deftly relieving her mother of her plate and stacking it on top of her own.

'Sure, of course,' he agreed, jumping to his feet, ever

eager to be helpful. 'You put your feet up, Mrs Wedan, you've done more than enough.'

Tiffany also felt the tension around her parents and was grateful for a few minutes alone in the kitchen with Hunter. Creeping up behind him, she ran her hands over his butt while he was bending down to load the dishwasher.

'Hey, sexy.'

He spun around and grabbed her, burying his face in her neck and kissing her until she broke out in goose pimples.

'Hey, sexy yourself.' He grinned.

She was wearing the pair of black suede hipsters he'd bought her at Fred Segal a few weeks ago, with sleek black ankle boots that made her already long legs look endless. Hunter felt his groin stir. If only her folks hadn't been in the next room, he'd have ripped her clothes off then and there and taken her on the kitchen floor.

'Sorry about my dad,' she said, leaning into his chest and breathing in his musky, familiar smell. 'Sometimes he can be *so* Homer Simpson.'

Hunter laughed. 'Don't worry about it. I love Homer Simpson. Believe me, he's a hell of a lot more functional than my dad ever was.'

He let go of her and went back to rinsing and stacking the washing up. 'How d'you think it's going, though?' he asked, hopefully, scrubbing hard at the inside of a roasting pan. 'I think your mom's starting to like me a little bit.'

'Baby, they both love you,' lied Tiffany, reaching over him to rinse out a wineglass. 'Quit obsessing. Just be yourself.'

Yeah, right. Just being himself hadn't been a roaring success so far. Nearly four years, and he was still waiting for a 'Hey man, call me Jack' from her dad. This weekend was probably the best opportunity Hunter had yet had to try to win over Tiffany's parents, but it was proving to be an uphill struggle. For the last twenty-four hours he'd felt as if he were trying to melt a glacier with a candle.

Once the clearing up was finished they both went through into the family room, where Jack and Marcie were sitting together on the couch, leaving only two armchairs, one on either side of the room, for Tiffany and Hunter. Maybe he was being paranoid, but he couldn't help but feel that the enforced separation was both intentional and symbolic. Reluctantly, he took one of the chairs and watched Tiffany walk over to sit by her father in the other.

Despite the family's inexplicable hostility towards him, Hunter liked the Wedans' house because it felt like a real home. It was built in true Rocky Mountain style, all warm, polished pine with double-height, vaulted ceilings, and antlers on the walls. Every available space was filled with pictures or mementoes of Tiffany, from framed photos of her graduation to an enlarged still of her on *UCLA*, which was perched in pride of place above the fireplace. The refrigerator in the kitchen was still plastered with her early childhood daubs, along with carefully laminated lists of her various phone numbers, addresses and e-mail contacts, held in place by a bunch of multi-coloured magnets.

Hunter couldn't help but contrast it bitterly to the grandeur and sterility of his own childhood home. He was certain that no finger-painting of his had ever made it on to the refrigerator door in Hancock Park.

'So, Hunter.' As usual it was Tiffany's mom who made the stilted effort to kick-start a conversation. 'Have you got any new projects lined up for next year?'

'He's already told you, Mom, no,' snapped Tiffany. She couldn't face any more pseudo chit-chat. She knew that her parents worried about her relationship with Hunter, partly because he was wealthy and well known and they thought she would eventually get hurt. Tiffany, of all people, could understand that. But she still resented their frostiness.

'Don't talk to your mother like that,' said Jack, without ungluing his eyes from the Bobcats game on the local TV station.

'I was only asking,' explained Marcie meekly, 'because Tiffany was telling me that the pilot season has just finished, so I thought, well, perhaps you had something else in the pipeline?'

'That's OK,' said Hunter, with an encouraging smile. If her mom was going to make the effort to express an interest, the least he could do was be nice about it. 'But no, I don't have any new projects,' he explained. 'I'm totally over-stretched as it is. At one point I thought this might be the last season for *Counsellor*. But now we've all signed up again, there's no way I'd have time for a third show, never mind a movie.'

'Mmmm, quite.' Marcie nodded in agreement, with the sage look of someone well versed in the problems of juggling a TV and movie career. 'Well, we're just thrilled that Tiffany's pilot seems to have gone so well, aren't we, Jack?'

Her father grunted non-committally. Tiffany's face went white.

She could have cheerfully strangled her mother.

'What pilot?' Hunter looked across at her, bewildered. 'You never told me you were up for anything.'

'Oh yes,' said Marcie, blissfully unaware of the bomb she had just exploded between the two of them. 'Tiffany called us last week. She did say she wanted to keep it quiet' – she beamed proudly at her daughter – 'but you know, I'm just so excited about it, I don't think I could hold it in a moment longer.'

'The show hasn't been picked up yet,' mumbled Tiffany guiltily, unable to meet Hunter's eye. 'It may still not come to anything, you know? I didn't want to get everybody's hopes up.'

'But you told your mom, right?' Hunter's voice was flat, as if all the emotion had been punched out of him.

'Honey, I was going to tell you, really,' she said,

tearing her eyes away from her lap and looking up at his hurt, disappointed face. 'I just wanted to be sure, to know if we were being picked up or not.'

'If they make the show then she'll have to go up to Vancouver to do the filming,' Marcie ploughed on excitedly. 'I hear it's wonderful up there, although I've never been to Canada myself. Have you, Hunter?'

'Excuse me,' he said suddenly, getting up with a face like thunder and heading for the front door. 'I think I need some air.'

'Take your coat!' Tiffany's father shouted after him, still glued to the game. 'It's cold out there.'

'Oh dear,' said Marcie, taking in her daughter's stricken expression, and registering, finally, that she'd somehow put her foot in it. 'Is there a problem? Was it something I said?'

Tiffany found Hunter outside, shivering in just his sweater, leaning against the gate at the end of the driveway.

It was a beautiful, crisp late April evening, without a single cloud to spoil the blanket of stars above them. Dirty, ice-hardened piles of snow still lay, resolutely unmelting, at the foot of the gate and along the verge of the winding mountain road that led down to Estes Park village. It was warm here during the days in springtime, but the nights could still be bitter right up until early May.

Tiffany breathed in the familiar smell of wood smoke and mountain air and steeled herself to go and talk to him.

'There you are,' she said softly, moving over to stand beside him.

'Yeah,' said Hunter, flicking an imaginary piece of dirt off the gatepost so he wouldn't have to look at her. 'Here I am.'

There was an uncomfortable silence while she struggled to think of what to say or do. She knew she should have told him she'd auditioned for the pilot and that she'd finally got herself a really decent part. Part of her, the better part, had wanted to share her success with him. But another part knew that if the show got picked up in the next few weeks, things would change between them. Difficult questions would have to be faced.

She would, at last, have the means to move out of the crappy old apartment she shared with Lennox, which would inevitably lead to a renewed push by Hunter for her to move in with him, something she felt less inclined than ever to contemplate now that Siena and Max had set themselves up in a permanent love-fest at the beach house.

She would also have to spend a lot of the next year away from home, filming up in Vancouver. Her contract was all but up at NBC, and she would ask them to release her formally before the end of the current series of *UCLA*, so she'd be free to go by mid-June.

She knew that Hunter would react badly to any sort of separation, and she had wanted to come to terms with the idea herself before springing it on him. Besides, maybe the show wouldn't make it, and she wouldn't have had to worry him with it after all. She really could murder her mother – why couldn't she have let her break the news to him in her own time?

'I was gonna tell you,' she said, wrapping her arm around Hunter's waist protectively. 'I was just waiting for the right time.'

He didn't remove her arm but nor did he return the gesture. His awkward, unyielding stance told her he was still angry, but she continued trying to explain.

'What I said in there was the truth. I have no idea if this is even gonna get made yet. I didn't want to get into it all and then have to say "oops, sorry, ain't happening. Good old Tiffany screws it up again". Story of my life, you know?'

'That's not true,' said Hunter with feeling. 'You haven't screwed anything up. You're a terrific actress, you always have been. You just needed to get a break, and now you've got one. I just wish . . .' He shook his head in disappointment. 'I just wish you had shared it with me, that's all. I tell you everything.'

'You didn't tell me you were asking Siena to move in.' Tiffany couldn't help herself.

'God, could you *stop* about Siena for five minutes?' said Hunter, exasperated. 'We aren't talking about Siena, we're talking about you. About us. I mean, Vancouver?'

'I know, I know,' she placated him. 'But I can fly back a lot. Or you can come up there. I don't know, we'll figure it out. It might not happen anyway.'

'It'll happen,' he said miserably, still scratching away morosely at the gatepost. 'What's the show anyway? CBS?'

Tiffany nodded. '*Sea Rescue*. You know, the one about the dolphin sanctuary? I'm Barbara, the chief at the rescue station.'

'Great,' said Hunter, without an iota of enthusiasm.

He knew he should be happy for her, be supportive, but all he felt was selfishly, miserably depressed. No sooner had he found Siena and replaced one missing piece in his life than Tiffany was about to leave him.

'It's not like I'm leaving you, honey,' she whispered into his ear, as if reading his mind. 'It's just one season. And it's Canada, not the moon.'

'Yeah, I know,' he said, finally relenting and wrapping his arm around her. He made a supreme effort to smile and try to look pleased. He knew this was a wonderful chance for her. He'd heard all about this particular pilot, and it was a big deal. If it went ahead, and he saw no reason why it shouldn't, she could become a household name overnight.

He was ashamed by how frightening he found that prospect.

Comforted by his embrace, Tiffany heaved a sigh of relief. For the past few weeks this secret had been weighing her down like concrete boots, and it felt good to have everything out in the open at last. She kissed him

348

tenderly on the cheek, and began walking back towards the house. It was bloody freezing out.

Hunter watched her go.

Her long legs were lost in the darkness, but the starlight caught the loose blonde strands of hair that flew around her face, some of them sticking to the lip gloss on her wide, pink, infinitely sensual mouth.

God, he loved her so much.

In that split second he knew, for certain, that he wanted to marry her. He wanted to make her his, keep her safe, have her and hold her for ever, never let her leave. Not for Vancouver, not anywhere without him.

'Tiffany, wait!' he called after her, and she stopped in her tracks. 'Will you . . .' He stammered helplessly, but couldn't seem to get any more words out. She looked so perfect standing there, so beautiful and fearless. What if she said no? What if he ruined everything, what if he lost her for good for the sake of one crazy, impulsive moment?

'Will you promise to tell me this stuff from now on?' he finished lamely. 'No more secrets between us?'

She held out her hand for his, and led him inside.

'I promise,' she told him. 'No more secrets.'

Back in LA the next morning on the *Prodigal Daughter* set, Dierk Muller was watching Siena run through her scene and scowling.

Sometimes, when he watched her act, he could see a raw talent so exciting it made the pale hairs on his arms stand on end. At other times – like this morning – he cursed the day he'd ever been stupid enough to hire a model with next to no dramatic experience, and a seemingly pathological need to hold herself back on camera.

'Cut!' he shouted testily, clicking his fingers at Siena as though summoning a recalcitrant puppy. 'Siena, my dear. What are you doing?'

'Shit, Dierk. *What?*' Siena had had a long night, rowing

with Max until two about some stupid little thing or other, then having make-up sex until four. It had been as much as she could do to haul her aching bones out of bed this morning and get to the set on time. She didn't need the cryptic questions. 'I'm doing the scene is what I'm doing. What's wrong? I thought that went great.'

'That, my dear,' he sneered, 'is why *I* am the director, and you are not. It was terrible. I've seen more enjoyable road accidents.'

Siena bit her lower lip hard, and stopped herself from saying what she really wanted to – that Muller was a sad, sadistic old Nazi who got his kicks from terrorising and demoralising whatever hapless actress he happened to be directing.

Some days she longed for the sycophantic photographers of her old modelling days. To think that a few short months ago she'd thought that Michael Murphy, the director of her Maginelle campaign shoots, was a stickler. Dierk could have eaten Michael for breakfast.

'OK,' she said patiently, pulling up a plastic chair and sitting down next to him. For all that she complained and cursed him, Muller was a wonderful director, and Siena wanted to learn from him. 'What do you want me to do?'

The director carefully put his clipboard down on the floor and looked at her. She was dressed for the scene in an immaculately cut chocolate-brown suit, the fitted jacket and tight pencil skirt clinging sexily to her curves, her hair flowing long and loose down her back. He cast a critical eye over her appearance, noting that even after an hour in make-up, the dark shadows under her eyes and the dull pallor of her sleep-deprived skin had not been entirely concealed. Stupid child! She wasn't taking care of herself.

The next thing Siena felt was a sharp, violent slap across her face which sent her reeling back in her chair.

Horrified, she put her hand up to her cheek, which was burning red and tingling from the blow. 'What the fuck did you do that for, asshole!' she screamed at Dierk, her blue eyes glinting with anger.

He watched her, shaking with rage, her picture-perfect, angel's face screwed up into a tight, venomous ball of fury, and a slow smile spread across his pale, Teutonic features.

'For that,' he said pointing at her. 'For that reaction.'

'*What?*' said Siena, still rubbing her throbbing face.

She'd had about as much as she could take of Muller's stupid party tricks.

'Look at yourself!' he babbled on excitedly, leaning forward in his chair and clasping her hands in his. 'Do you see that anger, that emotion? See your arms? They're everywhere, all over the place. Your eyes, your mouth, your expression, your movements, they're all *real.*'

'Well, of course they're fucking real,' snapped Siena. 'You just whacked me for no reason, you fucking psycho.'

The rest of the cast and crew were glued to the drama unfolding between the director and his leading lady. Most of them had been the victims of Muller's unorthodox motivational techniques at one time or another, and they sympathised with Siena.

'That's what I want to see in your work, Siena,' said Muller. 'That realism, that emotion. Loosen up your body, let go a little bit. You have it in you, sweetheart. You just need to let it out.'

Turning abruptly away from her, he clapped his hands together magisterially for attention. 'OK, guys,' he bellowed to the room at large. 'Next take.'

Siena returned to the set, still clasping her hand to her cheek. Carole, the make-up artist, quickly advanced upon her with some green cream and foundation to tone down the red mark Muller had left.

'Don't worry, honey,' she whispered furtively as she dabbed and blended like a magician. 'He's a real bastard. We all think you're doing a great job.'

'Thanks,' said Siena.

She felt the back of her eyes stinging with tears of gratitude at this small word of encouragement. What with Hunter being so wrapped up in Tiffany, and Max feeling so threatened all the time, heaven knew she'd been getting precious little encouragement at home recently.

Rubbing her eyes and tossing her hair back, she determined to pull herself together. What would Grandpa have thought if he could see her now, practically reduced to tears by some stupid director?

She was Duke McMahon's granddaughter, for Christ's sake. She could handle this.

'OK.' She smiled at the rest of the cast, focused and professional once again. 'I'm ready. Let's do it.'

Chapter Thirty-two

For the next three months, until the end of July, life at the beach house went on more calmly and happily than any of them might have expected.

Siena and Max seemed to grow closer by the day. As the weeks rolled by, and she grew more trusting in his love, she visibly started to relax, and every aspect of her life began to blossom as a result.

Dierk Muller became less and less critical of her work. By the time the film wrapped in late June, Siena knew that she had grown immeasurably as an actress, and Muller was not the only one who was thrilled by her performance. Early screenings of the unedited picture had been greeted with rapturous enthusiasm by one focus group after another, and by mid-July the buzz surrounding *The Prodigal Daughter* was already huge.

Once filming was officially over, Siena spent her days giving interviews or going to photo-shoots, plugging the movie until she was too tired to speak. It didn't hurt that the pre-release PR coincided with the last and most extravagant of her Maginelle commercials, so that by July her face seemed to be, literally, everywhere.

Much to Marsha's delight, the scripts for new projects were already rolling in, and Siena's modelling fees had skyrocketed. The gamble of moving to Hollywood appeared to be paying off in spades.

In the little time she got to spend at home with Max and Hunter, Siena's general behaviour was also much improved. Almost through force of habit, she still tried to pull the occasional fast one on Tiffany. Once she purposely sent her to the wrong restaurant for a date with Hunter, making sure it was far enough up Laurel Canyon that she wouldn't be able to get mobile phone reception, and would think she'd been stood up. But Max had bawled her out so badly afterwards, forcing her to admit what she'd done to both of them and to apologise to Tiffany in Hunter's presence, that she hadn't tried anything like it since.

Everyone who knew Siena could see that Max was a good influence on her. She screamed and yelled, and tried to fight her corner with him. But deep down she respected his opinion, and nothing made her feel worse than the knowledge that she had let him down in any way.

Max was the only person in the world who knew how much Siena had hoped against hope that her parents might have got in touch when they saw all the press surrounding her movie. Every time the phone rang, or flowers arrived at the door, he would watch her spirits soar, then fall each time she realised they were not from Claire. It was painful to watch.

Pete, whose production company, McMahon Pictures Worldwide, had two huge blockbusters pending release at the same time as *The Prodigal Daughter*, had been asked repeatedly by the media about his thoughts on his daughter's first film.

'I'm not going to be making any comments about Siena McMahon,' he'd been quoted as telling *Variety*, referring to his daughter as though she were a total stranger. 'As for the movie, well, what can I say? It's not the sort of picture that MPW would look at, but for an art-house film, I'd say it was perfectly competent.'

In public, Siena maintained a dignified silence. But at night she tossed and turned miserably in Max's arms until he eventually rocked her into a fitful sleep.

In a bizarre twist, the one person from her old life who *had* called to congratulate her was Caroline. In one of her six-monthly calls to Hunter from England, she had actually asked to speak to Siena, and been quite genuinely complimentary about her career.

'Hunter tells me you're going out with darling Max,'

she'd gabbled on merrily, as if she and Siena had always been on the best of terms. 'I always did adore that boy. Quite a catch! Seriously, if I were twenty years younger, I'm not at all sure I wouldn't make a play for him myself.'

The thought of Caroline and Max together sent a shiver of revulsion down Siena's spine. In fact, the thought of anyone else with Max made her stomach churn and her chest tighten painfully. As far as she knew, apart from one girlfriend at Cambridge, there had never been anyone really serious in his life before her. Unlike Hunter, who had always been the ultimate steady Eddie when it came to girls, Max had always been, in the nicest possible way, a bit of a cad. Siena remembered how much trouble he'd gotten into in high school when two of the cheerleading squad discovered that neither of them had his exclusive attentions as a boyfriend. Even as a teenager he had always loved women. Like her, he was a natural-born flirt, constantly flitting from one relationship to the next.

Unlike Siena, though, Max had managed to stay friends with most of his lovers. Women seemed to forgive him his roving eye because he was so funny and generous, and because he always treated them with respect. He just wasn't the settling-down type – everybody knew that.

At least, he hadn't been until he fell in love with Siena.

She just prayed that his new-found devotion and commitment to her would turn out to be permanent. She couldn't imagine where she'd be if he ever left her.

One morning in late July, Max was in his room at the beach house, on the phone to Henry in England, when a flustered Siena came rushing in wrapped in a towel, her wet hair leaving puddles of water all over the wooden floor.

'Hairdryer!' She waved her arms at him frantically,

rummaging noisily through the chest of drawers and hurling clothes on the floor in her desperate search.

Since they had become lovers, Siena's room, which had the nicer view, had become 'their' bedroom, and Max used his old room as a study and a place to keep his clothes. Every spare inch of the storage space in 'their' bedroom was, naturally, crammed to the gills with Siena's stuff.

'I'm on the phone, darling,' he complained good-naturedly while Siena continued to empty the meagre contents of his wardrobe on to the floor. 'Do you think you could do this later?'

'Fuck, where *is* it?' she wailed, ignoring him. 'My effing hair stylist just called to say her kid's got a temperature of a hundred and five and she can't make it, the photographer was due half an hour ago, and now I can't even dry my own bloody hair because someone's nicked the sodding dryer. *Huuunteeeer!*'

She let out a scream so piercing that Max winced. 'Sorry,' he said to a perplexed Henry on the other end of the line. 'Siena and Hunter have a joint photo-shoot here this morning for *Hello!* The McMahons at home, new generation, all that bollocks. She's a bit stressed out about it.'

'So I hear,' said Henry, who was overloaded with stress of his own and found it hard to muster much sympathy for the pressures of a missing hairdryer. 'What about you? Can I look forward to pictures of my little brother in his gracious drawing room, spouting off about world peace?'

Max laughed. 'They don't have drawing rooms over here, mate. Anyway, since when did you read *Hello!*?'

'Christ, never!' said Henry with feeling. 'Muffy's the gossip fiend in this house, can't get enough of all that drivel.'

Max imagined his poor, beleaguered sister-in-law struggling to find five child-free, farm-free minutes in her day to sit down and read *Hello!* with a cup of tea.

He knew things were tough at Manor Farm, and that Henry's money troubles were escalating, but to be honest he'd been so focused on his own dire financial straits recently, and on Siena, that he hadn't given poor Henry's problems much of a thought.

Finishing the call, he settled down at his desk to make a start on a couple of the scripts he'd been sent last week. Anything to avoid the media circus that was about to get started in the living room.

Max hated photographers and journalists with equal passion. It was hard enough keeping Siena's raging ego and ambition in check without a bunch of sycophantic tossers turning up and telling her how marvellous and talented and beautiful she was all the time.

He picked up the first script, a manky-looking, dog-eared, tea-stained sheaf of paper bound with a cheap black plastic clip. It was the latest play from a very young, critically acclaimed new writer in Oxford who knew of Max's theatre work and wanted him to come and direct in Stratford next year.

He had skipped through it last night, but began reading more carefully now, marking the margins with pencil asterisks and illegible notes as he went along.

No doubt about it, it was good. Fucking good.

The only problem was that this kid, Angus, had had about as much commercial success as Max, i.e. bog all. His plays were considered too dark and depressing to have much mass audience appeal, and the style was too heavy and old fashioned for most London theatre producers to consider.

Max would have loved to do it, but the reality was he'd be lucky if he even got his expenses covered, let alone managed to make money on the thing. Plus it would mean going back to England for a four-month run, leaving Siena alone in LA to be pursued by every playboy producer and director in town.

So that was a definite no-go.

Reluctantly he pushed the manuscript to one side and

began reading one of his potential American projects, another bland romantic comedy, gleaming professionally in its bright red CAA dust jacket. Fifteen minutes later he was disturbed by a shout.

'Max!' It was Hunter, calling from the next room where the shoot was obviously already under way. 'Can you come in here for a second, buddy?'

With a sigh, Max got up from his desk and opened the living-room door.

'Sure,' he said, without enthusiasm. 'What's up?'

The house had already been turned into a mini-studio, complete with blazing lights and vast silver reflective parasols to the sides of the sofa and chairs. The living room was full of people, the most visible and self-important of whom were the photographer, an emaciated Karl Lagerfeld wannabe dressed in head to toe black and ludicrously wearing his eighties-style dark glasses indoors, and a fat, garrulous middle-aged woman with a tape recorder whom Max assumed must be the interviewer.

Siena, who had evidently found a hairdryer from somewhere, was curled up on the sofa looking sleek and leaning back against Hunter, who had his arms around her shoulders. They were both smiling and laughing, enjoying the attention and each other's company, like an impossibly glamorous pair of twins.

Max felt his heart tighten.

'This is Johanna,' said Hunter, indicating the middle-aged woman, who obligingly smiled up at him and nodded, her blubbery jowls shaking. 'She was hoping to ask you a few questions, while we're getting the pictures done.'

'Hello, Max,' said Johanna, her fat wet lips issuing a fine mist of saliva as she spoke. 'I wondered if we could have a little chat now, you know, get it out of the way? Siena tells me you've got a lot of work on at the moment, so I promise I won't keep you long.'

Max raised his eyebrow at Siena and gave her a stern

look. They had discussed this ad infinitum. No interviews, no pictures. The article was about her and Hunter. He had no desire to go into print as Siena's sad hanger-on of a boyfriend, or Hunter's charity case.

'I appreciate that, Johanna, thank you,' he said politely, forcing himself to give her a friendly smile. He hated journalists, especially fat women journalists. 'But as Siena is very well aware, I'm afraid I don't feel it's either necessary or appropriate for me to be involved in your piece. And I *do* have a lot of work to do. So if you'll excuse me . . .'

'I thought you said it was only pictures he didn't want to do,' said Hunter to Siena, who looked the image of wide-eyed innocence next to him.

'Well,' she said shiftily, 'the pictures were the *main* thing.'

Hunter rolled his eyes. 'Siena?' he pressed her.

'Oh, all right, fine,' she admitted grumpily. 'He did say he didn't want to be interviewed.' She turned to Max, gazing up at him with the pleading look that seemed to work so well with every other man in the universe. 'But I thought you might have changed your mind, darling. I really want you to do it. For me. Please?'

'Well, I haven't changed my mind,' said Max firmly. He wasn't giving in to her this time. 'And I'm not likely to when you try to ambush me like that.'

'But why *not*?' she demanded, screwing her hands into tight little fists and banging them down in frustration on Hunter's thigh. 'You're part of my life, and part of Hunter's, a big part. And you live here. If Tiffany were here, she'd do the interview, wouldn't she, Hunter?'

'Ow,' said Hunter, rubbing his leg.

'She bloody well would not,' said Max, picking his way over boxes of make-up and discarded tripods into the kitchen to grab himself an Oreo from the biscuit tin. Tiffany was away filming in Vancouver – as Hunter had predicted, *Sea Rescue* had been picked up for the full twelve episodes – and Max happened to know for a fact that she'd been relieved to have to fly back up there last week and miss today's shenanigans. 'Besides, that's not the point and you know it. We've already discussed this, sweetheart. We agreed.'

The photographer leered appreciatively at Max as he stumbled clumsily back towards his study, all blond hair, broad shoulders and powerful, tree-trunk thighs. Now there was a real man.

'You agreed, you mean,' said Siena sulkily, as usual becoming unreasonable and moody when she knew she was in the wrong.

'I'm not rowing about it,' said Max, shutting the door firmly behind him.

Why did he always have to be so infuriatingly self-controlled?

For the next two hours, Siena fumed quietly while the photographer shot roll after roll of film.

Why did Max have to be so stupidly proud and stubborn the whole time?

For the first time in her life she was truly, madly in love with someone. And not just someone, but Max, Max who was so gorgeous and sexy and talented and amazing that she woke up every morning wondering how on earth she'd ever won his heart.

She never thought it would happen to her – never thought she was capable of that kind of love. But now she'd found it, she wanted the whole world to know that she and Max were together, that it was real and that it was serious between them.

Was that such a crime?

I mean, what did he have to do today that was so earth-shatteringly important he couldn't spend five minutes talking to that stupid whale of a woman about how happy he was to be with her?

She didn't know why, but somehow Siena felt she would like to see Max's love for her spelt out in black and white, in print, for the whole world to see. It was as if seeing the words written down might magically transform his feelings into something more tangible, more permanent and safe.

It would have meant a lot to her and he knew it.

But oh, no, Mr fucking Integrity, Mr I have my own career and I'm not your sidekick, was too damn insecure to make the effort.

It wasn't until gone two that Max finally emerged from his room to forage for some more food. Things seemed quiet, and indeed, when he opened his study door he could see that the living room was empty.

Moving into the kitchen to grab a cold drink from the fridge, he noticed two empty champagne bottles sitting on the table beside the overflowing ashtray, and followed the distant sound of semi-drunken laughter out through the kitchen door and on to the terrace.

Turning the corner to the western side of the house, he stopped in his tracks in horror.

Siena, topless and giggling, was swinging from one of the low branches of the cypress tree. Admittedly the photographer was shooting only her back view – this was *Hello!*, not *Playboy* – but on the other side of the tree a whole gaggle of assistants and lighting guys were sprawled out on the lawn, mesmerised by her little exhibition. Hunter was nowhere to be seen.

'What the fuck do you think you're doing?' Max roared, dropping his plastic glass of iced tea with a clatter on the ground and vaulting down from the terrace on to the grass below.

Everybody spun around to stare at him, including Siena, who promptly lost her grip and fell with a shriek into the arms of one of the assistants, a boy of about eighteen who could barely breathe with the excitement of having Siena McMahon's bare breasts only inches from his face.

She was laughing so hard at first that she could hardly see her enraged boyfriend, let alone respond. That champagne really had gone straight to her head.

361

Extricating herself with some difficulty from the dumbstruck boy's lap, she collapsed on the grass, rubbing her ankle and giggling.

'Damn. I think I've twisted my ankle,' she moaned. 'It really kills.'

'Put this on,' Max commanded, pulling his old grey T-shirt off over his head as he advanced furiously towards her. 'You're making a fucking spectacle of yourself as usual. And where the fuck is Hunter?'

Siena took the T-shirt and held it against her chest, but didn't put it on.

'He went out,' she replied flatly. Everybody else had fallen silent. You could have cut the atmosphere with a knife. 'His pictures were all finished.'

'But yours weren't, I see,' snapped Max. 'They just wanted to get a few more shots of you with your tits out for their private collections, I suppose?'

Siena sat rubbing her swelling ankle in shock. She hadn't thought she was doing anything wrong and couldn't understand his sudden outburst of hostility.

'I wanted some shots of her outdoors, looking natural in such wonderful natural surroundings,' interrupted the photographer in a high-pitched, high-camp whine. 'We're only photographing her back, sweetie, no need to blow a gasket.'

'Who the fuck asked you?' said Max rudely. 'Go on,' he shouted, while the nervous group on the ground scrabbled hurriedly to their feet. 'Get out, the lot of you. The shoot's over.'

'No it bloody well isn't!' said Siena, standing up a little unsteadily and flinging Max's T-shirt on the ground defiantly. 'Just who do you think you are, Max, telling everybody else what they can and can't do? Who made you judge and fucking jury?'

Naked except for her skimpy orange bikini bottoms, and less than half his size, Siena nevertheless managed to look very intimidating when she was angry. Sexy, but scary. The crew skulked farther back into the shade.

'You've seen me topless on the beach a hundred times.'

'That's different,' he muttered darkly.

'Why?' she challenged him. She was on a roll now. 'Because this time I'm in a magazine? My fucking *back* will be in a magazine? Because I'm trying to promote my film and my career? Because this is what I do for a living?'

Max stood facing her in uneasy silence.

He knew he was right to be angry – of course he was angry, damn it – but he didn't *exactly* know why. He didn't know how to defend himself when Siena started yelling at him. It was as if she'd turned the tables on him, somehow managed to seize the moral high ground when *she* was the one in the wrong. He felt desperate, trapped.

'Well, *I* think she looks beautiful,' piped up Johanna, the fat journalist, who had a problem with aggressive men and wanted Siena to like her.

'Compared to you, everyone looks beautiful,' whispered one of the lighting guys to his friend, who stifled a giggle.

'Do you?' said Max sarcastically. 'How fascinating.'

Siena felt her eyes welling with tears. Her anger seemed to be spent, and now she just felt miserable.

Max had seen hundreds of topless shots from her modelling days and never batted an eyelid. She couldn't understand why he was being so nasty to her now.

'OK, everyone,' she said eventually, her voice trembling with unhappiness and barely contained emotion. 'He's right, that's enough for today. Thank you all for your time.'

Embarrassed, they all began gathering up their equipment in double-quick time. The fat journalist scowled pointedly at Max in a show of sisterly solidarity and passed Siena her bikini top.

'It's a terrific interview, my dear,' she said in a stage whisper, squeezing Siena's hand encouragingly. 'Don't you worry. You can see the copy before we run it in September, in case you want to make any changes.'

'Thanks,' said Siena weakly.

Max was still just standing there, bare chested, looking at her as though she were the lowest form of life. Of course, it was fine for *him* to stand around with his top off.

After what seemed like for ever, he turned away from her without a word and walked back into the house. Seconds later he was back with a new grey sweatshirt on and his wallet and car keys in hand.

'Where are you going?' asked Siena.

She now felt utterly vulnerable and afraid, unable to recapture the anger and defiance that had protected her before. All she wanted was for Max to turn around and tell her he loved her. He didn't even have to say sorry. Just not to go.

'Out,' he said angrily, without breaking stride.

She tried to run after him as he got into his battered old car, but she was barefoot and nursing her sore ankle and couldn't keep up once she hit the pebbles and shingle of the driveway.

'Out where?' she called desperately after him. 'Max, I'm sorry. Please don't go. Please!'

He seemed to stare right through her, and with one violent rev of his ancient engine, screeched out of the driveway, leaving a distraught Siena standing in a cloud of angry dust.

She was still standing there ten minutes later when Hunter arrived back home, and got out of his Mercedes looking cheerful and relaxed with a bag of Whole Foods groceries under his arm.

'Siena,' he said, his voice all concern as he registered the forlorn, frightened look in her eyes. 'What's wrong, lovely one? What happened?'

Crumpling into tears, she fell gratefully into his arms.

'It's Max,' she sobbed. 'He's gone. Oh, Hunter, I think he's gone for good.'

Chapter Thirty-three

Max drove along the coast road to San Vicente and headed east towards Brentwood, Beverly Hills and, eventually, West Hollywood. Sumptuous homes, in every style from mock Tudor, to Nantucket craftsman to glass-and-concrete modernist boxes, lined the route. The blazing afternoon sun poured down its life-giving energy on the orange and lemon trees that grew in every garden, overflowing with abundance and colour, fruitfulness and life.

But Max barely registered his glorious surroundings as he rattled along in his Honda, the car that Siena had once been too mortified to set foot in, but now loved as a battle-scarred old friend, just as he did.

He felt confused. And angry.

Angry at Siena, and angry at himself.

Fuck.

He banged his fist so hard against the dashboard that the instruments started to spin out of control.

Why. *Why?*

Why had he lost his temper, why did she have to show off in front of all those people, why didn't he know any more whether he was even right or wrong to feel so fucking furious?

His temples were starting to ache from the ceaseless, berating, conflicting voices in his head. He swerved, narrowly missing a huge SUV heading for the beach. He could see the Brentwood housewife in his rear-view mirror shaking her fist at him. Silly cow. He'd had it up to here with rich, spoiled women.

If only he could get a break, he thought bitterly. If he could just have one hit play, or one half-decent film funded – maybe this wouldn't be happening. But that was stupid. What did his fucked-up career have to do with a house full of arse-licking media parasites and Siena exposing herself to half of Santa Monica?

He couldn't think any more. He needed a drink.

Without realising it, he looked up to find that he had already turned on to Wilshire on autopilot, and was now practically at La Cienega. The digital clock in front of him told him it was still only half past three, too early to go to Jones's and hide away in a dingy red booth, unnoticed, to drink himself into oblivion. He'd have to go on up to Sunset and try one of the hotel bars.

Veering sharply left, he found himself looking at a hundred-foot-tall picture of Siena – the face of Maginelle – plastered on to the white west wall of the Mondrian Hotel, and chuckled bitterly to himself.

If that wasn't a sign, he didn't know what was.

Five minutes later, he had left his Honda with a disdainful white-suited valet out front – they were more used to Ferraris and Aston Martins, he supposed – and was making his way through the lobby to the Sky Bar.

By six o'clock, this famous poolside hangout for LA's movers and shakers would be starting to get busy. By eight, big black doormen would be turning away all but the most beautiful women and the most powerful men in Hollywood. But at a quarter to four, Max had the place almost to himself, with only a sunburned family from Ohio and a party of German businessmen to prevent the pretty, sarong-clad waitresses from giving him their full, undivided attention.

He sank down exhausted on one of the over-sized cushions underneath the famous potted trees on the deck, and ordered a sour apple Martini.

'They're pretty strong, you know,' said one of the dark-haired waitresses, after watching Max guzzle down his fifth drink as though it were Seven-Up.

'So am I.' He grinned at her inanely, plainly already drunk. 'I'll have another, please. May the best man win!'

'Bad day?' she ventured, offering him a bowl of wasabi peas and taking his empty glass.

Max shook his head. 'Not really.' He gave a hollow laugh and flopped back on the cushion. He tried to look up at her face, but it was hard to see because of the sun, so he shut his eyes. 'More like a bad year. Bad life, really.'

'Oh, come on now,' said the girl, with a sceptical raise of the eyebrows. 'I'm sure things aren't that bad. You look fit and healthy to me, and you've obviously got money to burn on these.'

She leaned over and handed him another neon-green Martini, which Max grasped with a surprisingly steady hand.

As her shadow fell across his face, he opened his eyes and glanced up at her very flat, brown belly, exposed between the top of her sarong and her tight white T-shirt. He was surprised to find he had an almost overwhelming urge to sit up and lick it.

Fuck. He must be drunker than he'd thought.

'Call me if you need anything else,' she said, and before he had a chance to marshal his incoherent thoughts into any kind of a response, she had shimmied off towards the Germans.

He closed his eyes again for a moment, then opened them to find himself being shaken, gently but firmly, by another saronged nymph, this time a blonde with the most enormous pair of tits Max had ever seen.

'Sir.' She leant down low over his face and shook him again. 'Excuse me, sir,' she said more loudly this time.

Max sat up rather too suddenly and felt a wave of nausea hit him like a punch in the stomach. 'It's six thirty, sir,' the girl was saying. 'You've been out for a couple of hours. I'm afraid I'm going to have to ask you to settle your bill. Unless you wanted something else to drink?'

He rubbed his eyes blearily and tried to focus, but it was no good – the entire bar and pool were spinning around him like horses on a carousel.

Good, he thought. He wasn't hung over yet, he was still drunk. And the only thing to do when drunk, of course, is to keep drinking.

'I'll have another Martini, angel,' he said, patting the seat beside him. 'Why don't you sit down for a minute first, though, and tell me your name. I'm Max.'

The girl smiled. He was an attractive guy and she was sure she recognised him from somewhere. An actor, perhaps? Or a producer? Even better. Maybe he could help her out.

'I'm Camille,' she said, extending her hand and looking deep into his eyes. 'But we're not allowed to sit and chat, I'm afraid. I'll get you that drink.'

Max took her hand and held on to it, partly because he wanted her to stay and partly because he hoped it might stop her spinning. She had a beautiful face, but it was hard and, he suspected, lightly surgically enhanced.

When he'd first moved back to California from England, he used to think that all that 'inner beauty' stuff was a load of old bollocks. But the more time he spent in Hollywood, watching pretty young girls rushing out to surgeons to have themselves carved up, then propping up the bar at the Standard or Koi every Friday night, trying to snag some producer or millionaire, sleeping around and wrecking marriages and families wherever they went, the more he had come to recognise a certain inner ugliness that truly revolted him.

Normally he wouldn't have given a girl like Camille a second look. But the combination of the Martinis, her incredible breasts and his renewed fury at Siena – how could she have *humiliated* him like that? – all drew him towards her like a moth to a flame.

'I really have to get back to work.' She giggled, trying to remove her hand from Max's bear-like grip.

'You're far too beautiful to be working here,' he slurred, releasing her. 'What are you? Actress? Model?'

'Both,' Camille replied matter-of-factly. She knew she

was beautiful and wasn't about to contest his assumptions. 'What about you?'

'I'm a director,' said Max, and even in his drunkenness he clocked the light of interest switching on in her eyes. Poor girl! She probably thought he could help her find work. If she had any idea how broke he was she wouldn't be giving him a second look.

'Listen,' she said in a conspiratorial whisper, 'my shift ends at eleven. If you want' – she bent down and lightly brushed the back of his neck with her long fingers, making his hairs stand on end – 'we could go somewhere afterwards. To talk.'

'Great.' Max smiled wolfishly, throwing caution to the wind.

This was a 'conversation' he was definitely looking forward to.

Back at the beach house, Siena sat miserably on the sofa and scraped out the very last dregs of a huge tub of rum-and-raisin ice cream. She was wearing an old pair of grey tracksuit bottoms, a big Aran sweater of Hunter's and a pair of Max's hiking socks. Her hair was scraped back in a messy bun and what little make-up she'd had on had long since been cried away, leaving her usually porcelain-white complexion red and swollen.

'You look terrible,' said Hunter, not unkindly, emerging from the kitchen still holding the portable phone – he'd been on the line to Vancouver for almost two hours, chatting to Tiffany. 'And what's this crap you're watching?'

Siena budged over on the sofa to make a space for him and he dutifully sat down and put a brotherly arm around her.

'It's not crap, it's HBO,' she said, not taking her eyes off the screen. 'Anyway, *you* can talk about making crappy television!' She instantly regretted the jibe when she saw his face cloud over.

'Sorry, I didn't mean that,' she backtracked. 'I just

369

wanted to try and distract myself, that's all. I mean, it's gone midnight. Wouldn't you have thought he'd be back by now?'

Hunter took the empty ice cream bucket and spoon out of her hands and pulled her tightly into his embrace. He hated seeing her so upset, but it wasn't as if this were the first time Siena and Max had had a humdinger of a row. Every time it happened, she convinced herself that this was it, that it was over – a bit like the way he used to be with Tiffany – and every time she took solace in a vat of Ben and Jerry's. For someone so crazy and spirited and strong willed, she could be very predictable sometimes.

'Not necessarily.' He tried to sound reassuring. 'You know Max. He's proud and stubborn to a fault. He's probably spending the night holed up in some horrid motel, wishing he hadn't been such an idiot but too pig headed to pick up the phone and call you.'

'I hope so,' said Siena, but she wasn't convinced. Hunter hadn't seen his face when he'd stormed out. He was angrier than she thought she'd ever seen him.

'And I really don't think overdosing on ice cream is gonna make you feel any better.'

Siena managed a weak smile. 'That's because you're a man and don't know anything.'

'Oh,' said Hunter indulgently, stroking back a stray strand of her hair. 'I see.'

'How was Tiffany anyway?' she asked, trying to muster some interest in anything other than bloody Max and his whereabouts. 'Still having fun up there?'

'Yeah,' said Hunter, a huge grin bursting across his face at the mention of Tiffany's name. 'She's loving it. Not so much Vancouver, she says the city's kinda dead. But the show, all the guys she's working with, that's going great.' He sighed. 'I miss her, though.'

'I know you do,' said Siena, who despite herself still wished he didn't.

'I'm off to bed anyway, sweetheart,' he announced. 'I'm beat. And if you've got any sense you'll turn in as well. Trust me, Max will be back with his tail between his legs before you open your eyes.'

He stood up and held out his hand to help pull her to her feet. She let him help her, glad as always of his physical presence and the closeness and comfort it never failed to bring her.

'OK,' she said, pressing the stand-by button on the remote and throwing it down on the couch. 'You're probably right.'

He bent down and kissed her tenderly on her forehead, nose and dimpled chin, just as he used to when they were kids.

'Of course I am,' he said. 'You just wait and see.'

Across town in East Hollywood, Max sat bolt upright in Camille's bed, stone-cold sober.

Jesus Christ. What had he done?

Bleakly, he ran back over the evening's events in his mind. He'd carried on drinking steadily at the Sky Bar until she'd finished her shift. By then he'd been far, far too smashed to drive, which gave him a perfect excuse not to have to show Camille his battered old car. This was particularly important, as by the time they left together he had managed to convince her that he was a super-rich producer and director, and the only reason he didn't want to take her home to his palatial pad was that it was at the far end of Malibu, he needed to pick up his car in the morning, and didn't it make more sense to go back to her place instead?

He didn't know whether he was a frighteningly good liar or whether Camille was just particularly gullible. Either way, he felt an avalanche of guilt crushing him mercilessly when he thought about it.

She lay beside him now, her tousled head resting on a make-up-smeared pillow, her naked body still glistening with sweat and her face flushed with drowsy, post-orgasmic delight. Seeing Max's pained expression, she reached up and rested her hand gently on his bare back.

'What's wrong?' she asked.

'Oh God,' he wailed, staggering out of bed and pulling on his boxer shorts and shirt. 'I'm sorry. I'm really sorry, sweetheart. But I have to go home.'

'Now?' she said, her brow furrowing in disappointment. 'But what about your car? I thought you were going to stay here and pick it up in the morning. You don't want to get a cab all the way to Malibu at this time of night.'

'I'm not going to Malibu,' he said simply, too caught up in his own guilt and panic to spare much of a thought for her feelings.

Buttoning up his jeans, he began scanning the room for his socks and shoes.

'What do you mean?' demanded Camille.

She had sat up in bed now, and Max noticed that her enormous silicone boobs didn't fall so much as a millimetre when she did so, but remained fixed ridiculously in front of her like glued-on beach balls. He thought of Siena's beautiful, natural breasts and wanted to cry. What was he doing here?

'Look, like I said, I'm sorry,' he repeated harshly. 'I lied to you. I'm not a producer or a millionaire, and there is no house in Malibu.'

Camille's mouth dropped open like a stunned fish and she glared at him. That, he supposed, was where the LA girls' 'hard' look came from. From being used and lied to and taken advantage of by guys like him.

'I've been a total jerk, and you didn't deserve it,' he admitted, slipping on his shoes and grabbing his wallet from the bedside table. 'But the truth is I have someone at home. Someone I love more than anything.' He forced himself to look at her. Her eyes were ablaze with hatred. 'I have to go. I'm sorry.'

She looked back at him with utter contempt.

'Fuck you,' she said quietly and, rolling over, she pulled the covers up over her head to block him out.

There were a few seconds of silence, and she heard the

door creak open, then close with a soft, guilty click. Under the covers she could feel her rage bubbling up to breaking point, and bit down on her lower lip so hard it bled.

The fucking bastard. The fucking, fucking bastard.

Outside Camille's apartment, the cold night air was like a slap in Max's face, jolting him out of his hangover and any residual drunkenness and bringing starkly home to him the enormity of what he had just done.

He began walking aimlessly down Vine towards Hollywood Boulevard, where he supposed he could get a cab. But to go where? Back to Siena, poor, darling, lovely Siena, who right now was probably lying innocently asleep in their bed, trusting him and loving him and waiting for him to come home?

He couldn't do it. He couldn't pollute her with what had happened tonight. Damn it, he was such a fucking fool! And all because of his stupid pride, his insane jealousy, his terrible, uncontrollable temper.

Why couldn't he be a decent, honest, faithful guy like Henry? No wonder he didn't have a happy family or a successful career. He didn't deserve to. He felt as if he wanted to cry, but he was so out of practice the tears refused to flow. Instead, he looked around for a cab. He wanted to get as far away from Camille as he possibly could.

'Taxi!' he shouted as a weary-looking Mexican cabbie slowed down in front of him. Max clambered into the back of the cab, which was filthy and smelt of stale Taco Bell. 'Take me to the beach,' he said. 'Venice.'

He would swim in the icy salt water and scrub himself until all traces of the girl were gone from his body. Then maybe he could sleep down there on the sand for a couple of hours until dawn, clear his head and get his story straight before he went home to face the music.

He had already decided he wasn't going to come clean with Siena. He couldn't face losing her, or hurting her

373

more than he already had. She would never know he had betrayed her. And he swore to himself, by everything he held dear in this life: he would spend the rest of his days making it up to her.

Siena was so deeply asleep she barely registered at first when he slipped into bed beside her. He must have already been to the bathroom and cleaned his teeth, because she could smell mint, combined with sea water, sweat and stale alcohol fumes that no amount of toothpaste could fully disguise. Opening her eyes a fraction, she glanced at the bedside clock. It was 5.30 in the morning.

'I'm sorry,' he whispered, cuddling in to her back and wrapping his arms around her tightly. 'Please forgive me.'

She was so overwhelmed with joy and relief that she swivelled around and smothered his face in kisses. Reaching up to put her hands in his hair she stroked his back lovingly, touching his skin in wonder as though checking he was actually real.

'I'm sorry too,' she said between kisses. 'I love you so much, Max.'

'I know you do, honey,' he said, his voice cracking. 'I know you do.'

Chapter Thirty-four

Henry Arkell had spent the best part of a thoroughly miserable day at Pablo Ruiz Picasso airport in Malaga, where a baggage handlers' strike had left thousands of British tourists stranded after their holidays. The terminal was heaving with exhausted, overweight mothers bawling at their bored and unruly offspring, or struggling to snatch a few hours' kip on the hard red plastic chairs. Henry watched their depressed-looking husbands in silent sympathy as they packed into the one small bar upstairs, a swarm of beer bellies covered in shiny red football shirts, hoping to drown their sorrows with warm Spanish beer.

Like them, he longed to get home, although in his case the marital strife would not begin until he landed in England. There could be no more putting it off now. He'd have to tell Muffy everything.

'Sorry for the wait, sir,' said the briskly polite young stewardess as he handed her his boarding pass, having finally been shown through to the plane. At least he was flying business class at Gary Ellis's expense. 'Would you like me to hang up your jacket for you?'

'Please,' he said, easing his big shoulders out of his ancient tweed. 'Thanks.'

Sinking down into the spacious seat, he accepted an immediately proffered glass of champagne; not that he had the slightest reason to celebrate, but at least he'd be able to get pissed with that bastard Ellis's money.

He'd flown out to Spain yesterday, feeding Muffy an unlikely story about going to some conference on a new EU directive on dairy quotas, and had driven straight up into the hills for a meeting with Gary at his pink monstrosity of a villa.

' 'Enry. Good to see you, mate,' the developer had greeted him warmly, pumping his hand between his own clammy palms and leading him out to the poolside bar.

Gary was topless and barefoot, sporting a lurid lime-green pair of Bermuda shorts over which his big sunburned stomach spilled unashamedly. He had an unlit cigar clamped between his teeth and could not have looked more like a criminal on the run if he'd put on a striped jumper and a mask and thrown a bag marked 'SWAG' over his shoulder. Henry instantly regretted having worn a suit.

"'Ere, let me tike your jacket, you must be roasting.' Henry gladly complied, and sat down on one of the bubblegum-pink poolside chairs. A maid immediately arrived with a tray of iced water. The cool liquid tasted delicious, but he couldn't seem to stop the ice from clinking noisily against the side of the glass as his hands shook. He felt guilty, out of place and unaccountably nervous. Gary, on the other hand, looked relaxed and in control.

'So, Mr Ellis,' he began stiffly once he'd finished his drink. 'What was this offer you wanted to discuss with me?'

'Gary, please,' said the developer, with another confident smile.

If Henry had never really liked Ellis, the feeling was entirely mutual. Gary had never forgotten the way in which he had been 'frozen out' by the elitist, upper-class Cotswolds social set in Batcombe when he had first moved into the village. That buffoon Christopher Wellesley and his toffee-nosed cronies had made sure that he was never admitted to their inner circle, that glamorous world of hunt balls and private dinner parties to which he had secretly longed to belong. He remembered the patronising way Henry had looked at him at that dinner party at Thatchers, when he'd first admired the Manor Farm estate. He'd made him feel like a bit of dog shit stuck on the bottom of his green welly, the snooty little wanker. But the boot was well and truly on the other foot now.

He'd first got wind of Henry's financial troubles about a month ago, and had decided to make a move almost immediately. It wasn't just the social slight which had been burned on his memory. He also remembered how prime that land had been, how perfectly ripe for development. And then there was the lovely Mrs Arkell. How satisfying it would be, he thought, to take the bastard's farm *and* his wife, if the opportunity should present itself. Heavy debts, he knew from experience, could put a big strain on a marriage.

Today, however, he hid his inner resentment well and made sure he was charm personified. On his own home ground, and holding all the cards, he could afford to play a waiting game.

'All right, then.' He grinned. 'Let's cut to the chase, shall we? I wanna buy you aht.'

'Buy me out? Do you mean the whole farm?' The colour had drained from Henry's face. Despite the heat he looked as white as a sheet. 'I assumed . . . I mean, when we met before, you'd only seen the lower pastures.'

'Everyfink.' Gary lapped up his discomfiture.

'I'm sorry,' said Henry quietly. 'It's not for sale.'

'No?' Gary raised an eyebrow. 'What are you doing sitting 'ere, then?'

Henry was silent.

'It'd make a lovely golf club,' said Gary viciously. 'Two point six. Tike it or leave it.'

Two point six million. It was more than the farm was worth. A good thirty per cent more. That sort of money would solve all their financial problems in one stroke. But a golf club? His father and grandfather would both be turning in their graves at the very thought of it. Henry could feel himself sweating and looked miserably down at his feet. Why couldn't the slimy bastard have offered less? If he'd come up with some stupidly low figure, it would have been easy to tell him to stick it, to fly back home with a clear conscience, if not a clear balance sheet. But this was a more than generous offer. By any rational standards he'd be crazy to refuse.

'I'll need to talk to my wife.'

'Fair enough,' said Ellis briskly. 'But the offer only stands for forty-eight hours. It's nuffink personal,' he explained, suppressing his inner glee at Henry's panic-stricken features. 'Just business. I'm about to exchange on anuvver bit o' land a coupla valleys over from you. I'd rather 'ave yours, but I need to know.'

That conversation had taken place almost six hours ago. As he sat on the plane, miserably knocking back one drink after another, Henry still had no idea what he was going to do, or how he was going to begin to break the news to Muffy.

She was there to greet him at Luton, looking as adorable as ever in her blue gardening cords and one of his ancient, tattered Guernsey jumpers. She almost never bought anything new for herself – not that she'd ever been terribly into clothes, but since their money troubles she had gone to extra lengths to cut back on even the smallest unnecessary expenditure. Last week she'd proudly told him that she'd started reusing teabags and saving torn wrapping paper. Henry could have wept with guilt.

Looking at her across the arrivals hall, he felt his heart bursting anew with love for her, and with shame at himself. How could he have let her down like this? Mercifully, none of the children were with her. He really couldn't have coped with Maddie's endless questions or the boys' demands for presents all the way home. Not today.

'So how was the conference?' she asked him, ignoring his protests and taking the lighter of his bags from him. 'Was it worth it?' At first, when he didn't answer, she assumed he hadn't heard her. But as soon as she turned and looked at his ashen face, she knew that something was seriously wrong.

'Henry,' she said, her voice full of concern, 'what is it? What on earth's the matter?' And right there in the arrivals hall, he told her.

The drive back to Batcombe was one of the longest of Henry's life. His wife was not given to hysteria, and there had been no screaming fits at the airport as he'd recounted every painful detail of their spiralling debts, his desperate attempts to rectify things with Nick Frankel, and finally Gary Ellis's offer. Muffy, in fact, had listened in complete silence while he miserably unpicked every thread of her security, calmly paying for the parking and loading his bags into the boot without so much as a word of interruption or reproach. It wasn't until they'd been driving for twenty minutes, with Muffy insisting on taking the wheel, and he'd finally come to the end of his desperate stream of explanations and apologies, that she had finally allowed herself any sort of reaction.

'What I don't understand, Henry,' she said quietly, her eyes fixed on the motorway ahead, 'is why you didn't tell me about all this months ago.'

'Oh God, I don't know.' He ground his fists against his temples in frustration, at himself, not her. 'I mean, I *do* know. I should have. But I suppose I hoped you'd never have to know. I thought I'd be able to sort it out on my own.'

'*How?*' Finally her own frustration was starting to find a voice. 'How on *earth* did you think you were going to sort it out?'

'I don't know.' He stared down at his lap, defeated.

'And *why* would you want to do it all alone anyway? I thought we were partners. I thought we trusted each other.'

'We do!' said Henry.

She shook her head angrily. 'Rubbish! You've been

lying to me since before Christmas. You obviously don't trust me at all.'

'That's not true. I never lied to you. I was trying to protect you from all this.' He reached out and put a hand on her thigh. She didn't remove it, but still she wouldn't look at him, biting down on her lip to stop herself from crying as she desperately tried to focus on the traffic in front of her.

'Does Max know?' she asked irrationally. She didn't know why, but the only thing that could make this worse would be the thought that Henry had confided in somebody else, but not her.

'No. Of course not,' said Henry. 'Why would you think that? I've hardly spoken to him since Christmas. Besides, he's totally broke himself, and far too wrapped up in Siena McMahon to listen to my problems. Look, I don't know what else to say, Muffy,' he pleaded. 'I love you, and I'm really, truly sorry that I kept all this from you. But, well, you know now. And we have to make a decision.'

'Oh, it's *we* now, is it?' she retorted angrily. She didn't want to lose her temper with him. She could see he felt dreadful and she knew that, however unjustified his deceitfulness may have been, he had never actually intended to hurt her. But it was all too much to take in. Henry had had weeks, months even, to get used to the idea of losing the farm. And now she was expected to say yea or nay to Ellis's offer in a matter of minutes.

For the rest of the drive home they sat in stony silence, Henry too guilty and Muffy too upset to initiate any further conversation. Back at Manor Farm they both did their best to be normal and cheerful at supper for the children's sake. It wasn't until 9.15 that Muffy came downstairs, having finally tucked Charlie into bed, and found Henry staring morosely into a pan of boiling milk on the Aga. She came up behind him and wrapped her arms around his waist, and he turned and hugged her, overwhelmed with relief at this gesture of forgiveness.

'Here, give that to me. It'll burn.' She lifted the milk pan off the hot ring and poured the contents into his waiting mug of hot chocolate.

'Thanks.'

Taking the steaming drink, he sat down at the table, while she automatically squirted some washing-up liquid into the pan and left it in the sink to soak before coming to join him.

'I'm sorry, Muff,' he said again, burying his head in her neck. She stroked his hair and kissed the top of his head. The kitchen was a mess, full of the detritus of the kids' earlier painting play, with half-eaten plates of fish fingers and beans littering the table and worktops. Despite this, or perhaps because of it, Muffy looked around the room and felt her heart swelling with a pride bordering on real love. She had refitted the kitchen herself over many long years, as the first profits from the farm had begun trickling in. She hadn't touched the wonderful, time-buckled flagstone floor and tiny, ill-fitting lead-light windows that had so captivated her when Henry first brought her here, back when his father was still alive. But she had replaced the old man's ancient death trap of a cooker with her beloved Aga, and she and the boys had had great fun helping Henry paint all the cupboards a cheery bright red, now long since faded to the colour of unripe cherries. More than any other room, the kitchen made the manor feel like a home. For the last ten years it had been the living, beating heart of the old house. Sitting there now, with Henry, she knew for certain what their decision must be.

'Stop saying sorry,' she whispered. 'It sounds so defeatist. This isn't over yet, you know.'

He pulled back and looked at her. 'You mean, you think we should turn Ellis down?'

'Of course we're turning him down,' she said sternly. 'That creep will turn this place into a golf course over my dead body. Yours too, I hope.'

Henry put his hand on the back of her neck and pulled

her face towards his, kissing her passionately on the mouth. He didn't think he'd ever loved her more than he did at that moment.

'We're running out of options, though, Muff,' he said gravely when he finally released her. 'If we don't find seven hundred and fifty grand in the next few weeks we're going to have to sell to someone. And probably for a hell of a lot less than what Gary's offering.'

'I know,' she said. 'I know. Well, we're just going to have to think of something, then. Aren't we?'

Chapter Thirty-five

Siena was in a fabulous mood.

She stepped out of the Coffee Bean in Brentwood with an iced chai latte in one hand and a freshly baked chocolate muffin in the other, and walked across the road to the news-stand.

It was a baking hot Saturday, and she had a day of pure feminine indulgence planned.

Ines had broken the rule of a lifetime and flown out to LA last night for the long weekend, to a rapturous welcome from Siena, who was so delighted to see her old friend she had even taken pity on her jet lag this morning and allowed her to sleep in while she did the coffee-and-paper run.

As soon as she had stocked up on all the latest mags – Ines was an even bigger gossip fiend than Siena – she would go back to Santa Monica and wake her, then drag her off for a day of massages, facials, a long, late lunch at the Ivy and a *lot* of shopping.

She smiled to herself as she wandered around the news-stand, stocking up on the latest *US Weekly*, *Star* and *National Enquirer* as well as the more upmarket *Hello!* and *OK!* It definitely wouldn't do to see only *one* set of grainy pictures of Tom Cruise's naked butt on a yacht off St Tropez – she and Ines wanted the lot.

But it wasn't just the perfect summer weather or the prospect of spending the day with her best friend which had put her in such high spirits.

The publicity for *Daughter* had been going fantastically, and both Muller and Marsha were glowingly pleased with her. But better even than that had been the almost unbelievable changes for the better in Max.

For the last few weeks he had been an absolute angel

to her. It was as if someone had waved a magic wand and all his jealousy and insecurity had disappeared overnight. All of a sudden he was loving and attentive – never in the annoying, lapdog way that her old model boyfriends used to be, though. It seemed funny now to remember how panicked she'd been when he'd stormed out after that awful row on the day of her photo-shoot with Hunter. How sure she had been that this was the last straw and he was leaving her for good.

Maybe that scare was just what they both needed?

Whatever the reason for Max's change of heart towards her, Siena felt deliriously happy and more in love with him than ever as she strolled around Brentwood this morning, oblivious for once to the staring and whispering of her fellow shoppers.

What with things being so great with Max, Ines coming to stay and Tiffany's temporary absence meaning she got Hunter practically all to herself, life at the beach house was like one, long, blissful dream at the moment. She was on a real high.

She paid for the magazines and was heading back to her car when her mobile rang.

She looked at the screen, hoping it might be Max or Ines, but it wasn't. 'Marsha Mob' flashed annoyingly up at her.

It was the second time her agent had called this morning, but 'Marsha Mob' could mean only one thing – work, and she refused to even think about work today. Just the thought of Marsha's insistent, bossy British voice was already causing a small cloud to form on Siena's mental horizon. She switched her phone off. The poison dwarf could bloody well wait.

Clambering up into Hunter's Navigator – her brand-new Mercedes was already in the garage following an encounter with a killer olive tree in Dierk Muller's driveway last week – she pulled out of the Coffee Bean car park and on to San Vicente.

She had the radio tuned to KZLA, Hunter's favourite

country station, and Toby Keith was belting out 'Shoulda Been a Cowboy', one of her all-time favourites, in his sexy Southern accent. Siena joined in tunelessly, tapping the steering wheel as she sang along.

She had wound all the windows down, letting the warm summer air rush into the car while the music roared out so loudly that the joggers all turned around to stare. She loved the lyrics, although they described a world she knew nothing about: campfires and six-shooters and cattle drives. The song made her think of Duke, and of the old cowboy poster of him she used to have up in her room at Hancock Park.

She wondered what Grandpa would have made of *The Prodigal Daughter* and Dierk Muller. He probably would have thought both the movie and the director were too arty and pretentious. 'Art' had always been a dirty word to Duke.

But she was sure he would also have been proud of her for what she had achieved. For making her own fame and fortune, for getting back here and into the business and putting one over on her stupid fucking father.

Just remembering Pete's existence caused a tight feeling to start rising in Siena's chest. She wished she didn't care about her parents at all, that she could just block them out, as they seemed to have done so effortlessly with her.

Why was it always when she was at her happiest that the bad memories forced their way back into her consciousness?

Anxious to recapture her good mood of a few moments ago, she reached across to the passenger seat and picked up one of the magazines, glancing at it idly while she drove along. It was the *National Enquirer*, the most sensational gossip rag of them all and Siena's closet favourite. A brand-new issue too, out today, so she and Ines could catch up on all the Hollywood scandal before anyone else.

At first she thought she must have misread the

headline. It was above a blurred, slightly grainy photograph that she certainly didn't recognise as herself. Slowing for a red light, she put the car into 'park' and stared at the front page for a closer look.

Oh my God. No.

She felt her heart pounding and the bile rising in her stomach as she saw that the front cover was indeed a picture of her, and not just any picture.

She was hanging topless from the tree at the beach house, with an open-mouthed camera crew at her feet. It had evidently been taken with a long-range paparazzo lens. In the background, the blurred figure of Max, his features barely discernible in the distance, had been circled in red. The headline read:

SIENA MCMAHON: CHEATING LOVER SEES RED OVER TOPLESS PICS.

Numb with shock, Siena flipped through the magazine, looking for the story.

It didn't take her long.

There, on pages four and five, was a full-length photo of an identikit blonde swimsuit model, apparently called Camille Andrews, superimposed next to a picture of Max in black tie, taken at the Emmys two years earlier with Hunter.

Siena started to read, but she could barely take it in:

"'He told me he was a producer,'" said stunning Camille from Texas, who works part time at Hollywood's trendy Sky Bar. "'It wasn't until after we'd made love twice that I learned he had a girlfriend. I felt so used.'"

She wanted to stop reading, but the words kept drawing her in, like some kind of evil force field, and she couldn't tear her eyes away.

"'Max was only an average lover,'" the girl went on. "'But what he lacked in skill, he certainly made up for in enthusiasm.'"

Bitch, thought Siena irrationally. Max could fuck in the Olympics when he was with her. It wasn't any wonder he wasn't inspired by that cheap, hard-faced little whore. She stared at the picture of Max, all messy hair, broken nose and huge, honest smile, his eyes crinkled up into nothing with merriment, as if willing him to jump up off the page and tell her it wasn't true.

It couldn't be true.

Not Max. Not decent, solid, honest, true Max, her rock, her soulmate. He would never do that to her.

He couldn't.

She dimly became aware of horns honking at her from all sides, of angry drivers yelling and overtaking her, flashing their lights and shaking their fists. The light must have gone green. Without thinking, she put the Navigator into 'drive' and lurched forward, the article still clenched tightly in her right hand.

The truck had hit her before she'd had time to blink.

When she came to, her first, awful thought as she re-emerged groggily into consciousness was that she was back at school in England. The stark white walls, the gloomy semi-darkness from the partially drawn curtains and the faint smell of disinfectant all stirred unpleasant memories of St Xavier's.

'Sister Mark?' she mumbled, as a female figure in white uniform loomed into view.

'Well, hello again,' said the figure, smiling broadly.

As she got closer, Siena noticed she was Asian with a lovely, gentle face. Definitely not her old headmistress, then. She was young, probably about her own age, and wore a badge that proclaimed her name to be Joyce Chan.

'Do you know where you are, Siena?'

She tried to nod, but found that her head and neck hurt when she started to move. 'Yeah,' she said. Her voice sounded unusually hoarse and dry. 'Hospital. I guess.'

'That's right,' said Joyce, filling a tumbler of water and

holding it to Siena's lips. 'You had a nasty accident, but you were very lucky. You're going to be just fine.'

'Ah, Miss McMahon. Welcome back to the land of the living.'

A strikingly handsome man in his early forties had entered the room and was walking purposefully towards her. He wore a white coat and a stethoscope around his neck, and looked more like a heart-throb soap actor playing a doctor than the real thing, all white teeth and tan.

Joyce stepped back respectfully as he approached the bed.

'How's our patient doing, Nurse Chan?' he asked, picking up the clipboard of notes fastened to the end of Siena's bed.

'She opened her eyes just a few moments ago,' said the nurse, and added with a smile, 'she looks great, though.'

Siena smiled back.

'I'm Dr Delaney,' said the soap star, perching on the edge of her bed and taking her hand in his. For the first time Siena noticed that there was a drip feeding something into her veins. 'Are you up to my asking you a few questions, my dear?'

'Sure,' she said. 'My head hurts a little, but I feel fine. What's this?'

She gestured to the needle protruding from the back of her hand.

'Don't worry about that,' said the doctor briskly. 'It's just a painkiller, for the bruising. I'm more concerned about your head right now. How much do you remember of what happened to you this morning, Siena?'

This morning? So she'd only been out for a few hours. Well, that was good at least; hopefully it meant her injuries couldn't be *too* serious. Thoughts and questions swirled around in her head as she tried to piece together a coherent chain of events from the blurred fragments of her memory. It was difficult.

'Take your time,' said Dr Delaney.

'Well, I was in the car,' she began. He nodded encouragingly. 'I was going home, I think. Yes, that's right, I was going to see Ines – she's here for the weekend.'

The doctor watched his patient smile, pleased and relieved that things were falling back into place. Her right eye, cheek and temple were quite severely bruised and she had cracked two ribs, but she still somehow managed to look incredibly desirable, propped up on the hospital pillows with one smooth white shoulder slipping tantalisingly out of her regulation white nightgown.

Adorable.

If he weren't here in a professional capacity, he would probably have made a play for her himself.

Sadly, though, she was his patient, and a very lucky patient at that. He would run a brain scan on her later, but apart from a mild concussion and the rib injuries, she appeared to be fine. Given that her SUV had been crushed like a Coke can, that was a minor miracle.

'Oh!'

Siena's hand flew to her mouth in shock, and she started trembling.

Here we go, thought the doctor. He squeezed her hand as tightly as professional ethics would allow.

'I remember. I remember what happened now. It was because . . .' Her voice trailed off, and he could see she was fighting back tears and in deep distress.

'I read something,' she said at last. 'It gave me a shock, and . . . and the lights changed.' She was crying openly now, tears streaming down her bruised and swollen cheeks. 'I guess I must have pulled out suddenly or something, I don't know. And that was it.'

'It's all right, my dear,' he said gently, 'you've done very well. It's wonderful that you can remember. Means you're on the mend.'

He already knew what it was that had given Siena the "shock". The paramedics had found her with the paper still clenched in her hands. This being Hollywood, juicy stories had a habit of leaking out, and a growing swarm of journalists and photographers were already gathering outside the hospital gates, hoping for a statement or, better still, a picture of their heartbroken heroine after her brush with death.

Suddenly he felt a wave of compassion for Siena.

Fame and fortune weren't always as great as they were cracked up to be. Poor girl. She was obviously terribly cut up about her boyfriend. Fella must have been mad to cheat on someone so beautiful and vulnerable, and so obviously madly in love with him. With difficulty, he resisted the urge to take Siena in his arms and comfort her.

'Was anyone else hurt?' she asked, dragging her thoughts away for a moment from Max's betrayal and shattering Dr Delaney's lustful reverie. 'Oh God, I didn't kill anyone, did I?' She sounded quite panicked.

'No, no, nothing like that,' he assured her. 'You were lucky you weren't killed yourself, though.' Siena looked dazed. 'Really. Reading and driving at the same time isn't the smartest of ideas,' he chided her gently. 'Your car was totalled.'

'My car, you mean.'

Hunter, weighed down with a huge bunch of red and white roses, appeared in the doorway. His beautiful features clouded over when he saw Siena's battered and tear-stained face. Dropping the flowers, he showed none of Dr Delaney's compunction and ran over to her, taking her in his arms and kissing and stroking her tenderly.

'Careful,' said the doctor, who was fighting back an irrational surge of jealousy towards the new arrival, not least because Hunter was even better looking than he was. 'She's got two fractured ribs, you shouldn't squeeze her like that.'

Hunter gave him a 'we-need-some-time-alone' stare.

He took the hint, and both doctor and nurse made themselves scarce, shutting the door behind them.

'Sorry about the Navigator,' said Siena, when they were alone. She was twirling a loose ringlet round her finger nervously, a sure sign that she was upset.

'Oh, shut up, would you. I couldn't care less about the stupid car,' said Hunter. 'I'm just glad you're OK.'

'Am I?' Her lower lip was trembling. She looked completely lost.

She clung on to him, trying to make herself feel safe and loved and secure, but it wasn't working.

Much as she loved Hunter, she wasn't a child any more.

It was Max's arms she needed.

'Have you . . .' She steeled herself to ask him. 'Have you talked to Max yet? Is it true?'

Hunter gazed out of the window. Siena's pain was palpable, and he couldn't bear to be responsible for making it any worse.

'You should talk to him, angel, not me,' he said.

'Yes, well, *he*'s not here, is he?' she shot back angrily, pulling away from him and propping herself up in bed, wincing at the pain in her neck and chest as she moved.

It was a flash of the old, fiery Siena, and it both cheered Hunter and alarmed him to see it now. Anger had always been her natural defence mechanism.

'So I'm asking you,' she said. '*Have* you spoken to him, Hunter?' He nodded, still looking out of the window rather than at her. 'And?'

'Siena, honey, what do you want me to say?' He was desperate not to have to be the one to confirm her worst fears. But there was no way around it. 'Did it happen? Yes, it happened. And he hates himself for it and he feels terrible about it. It was a stupid, stupid mistake.'

'How long have you known?' she asked.

Hunter sighed. He had known that question was coming. 'I only found out today, sweetheart, I swear,' he said truthfully. 'The police called me when it happened because the car's registered in my name. I guess I'm your next of kin too, right?' Siena nodded. 'They told me about the article, I called Max right away, and . . .'

She held up her hand to stop him. She didn't want to hear any more.

'He had no idea about it,' Hunter went on despite her protestations. 'You know, that the girl had gone to the press, I mean. Honestly, Siena, I was mad at him too, but he sounded so terrible, he regrets it so much, and when he heard about your accident he was crazy, hysterical. He wanted to come and see you right away.'

'How thoughtful of him,' said Siena bitterly.

'But I told him not to risk it,' Hunter doggedly continued. 'There are press everywhere. It was bad enough for me trying to get in.'

She sat quietly and tried to collect her thoughts.

So it was true.

Max, the first and only man she had ever let herself love, had betrayed her. For all she knew, this Camille was probably just the tip of the iceberg, the one who finally went to the papers with her story. There were bound to have been others.

How long had he been making a fool out of her? she wondered.

She was ashamed of herself. How could she have been so stupid?

For her entire life it had always been her worst nightmare to end up like Grandma Minnie, disrespected and humiliated by a man that she was too weak and too desperate to leave. Or like her mother, who may not have been cheated on, but who had been hurt and abandoned emotionally by Pete for years, and who chose to give up her own daughter rather than take a stand and leave the bastard.

She had opened her heart to Max, allowed herself to become vulnerable. And what had happened?

This.

Pain, betrayal, public humiliation. She didn't know who she hated more at that moment, Max or herself.

She raised her hand to her face and felt the swelling around her eye. She must look like shit. So much for her next three weeks of auditions. There weren't many casting agents around desperately seeking girls who looked like they'd come off worst in a bar brawl.

Fucking, fucking Max.

So he was sorry, was he? Well, too fucking bad. She was through trying to change herself for him, trying to be soft and feminine and understanding, all because *he* was too insecure to deal with her fame and success.

Max had made his choice. Now he could damn well live with it.

'Ask the nurse to come in here, would you?' she said to Hunter after what seemed to him like an eternity of silence.

He pressed the call bell and Joyce appeared at the door moments later.

'Can I get you anything?' she asked.

'You can, yes,' said Siena. 'I'd like a phone, please. And some release forms. I'll be leaving in a couple of hours.'

Joyce laughed. 'You can't do that, honey. Dr Delaney will want to have you under observation for a couple more days at least.'

'Then I'm afraid Dr Delaney is going to be disappointed,' said Siena, in a tone that left the flustered nurse in no doubt that she meant business.

'Sweetheart, come on,' Hunter pleaded with her. 'You could have died today. And all this stuff with Max, it hasn't sunk in yet. You guys will work it out, I know you will.'

'I have no intention of *working it out*,' spat Siena sarcastically. 'And I'm not going to hang around here while those paparazzi vultures wait for me outside either.'

'Siena, please, you're not thinking straight,' he insisted.

'Stay here for a couple of nights. Then Ines and I can come and take you home.'

'Home?' she said incredulously. 'What home? You mean the beach house, with you and Max? After the way he's just betrayed me? No, Hunter, no way.'

Her voice was rising and she put a hand to one of her broken ribs – the shouting really hurt, but she couldn't help herself. If she didn't stay mad now, she was sure she'd crumple up and die from the pain.

How could he do this to her?

'I'm sorry, Hunter.' She forced herself to calm down. 'But I've had enough. I need to get away, from Max, from LA, from everyone. My bruises will heal just as well in a hotel as they will here. I need to go somewhere where I can just shut everything out, where I can lose myself. Surely you can understand that?'

Hunter looked stricken.

He could understand, of course he could. He just didn't like it. He wanted to help her, to make everything right again. He wanted her to turn to him in her time of trouble, not run away.

He could have strangled Max for being so fucking stupid and selfish. What had he been thinking?

'Where were you thinking of going?' he asked.

She took his hand and gave him the first smile he had seen since he walked in. It was almost like looking at the old, pre-Max Siena again: tough, determined and wicked.

'Where would I go to lose myself?' she said. The smile broadened into a grin. 'Where else, baby?' And as she said it, she sounded so like Duke it made him shiver.

'Vegas.'

Chapter Thirty-six

It was a hundred and eight degrees outside when Siena woke up in her penthouse suite at the Venetian the following morning. The sort of heat that had chauffeurs opening limousine doors with folded handkerchiefs so as not to burn their fingers, and children wilting like dying flowers, drained of every last ounce of their energy as they wearily traipsed along behind their parents, their usual dreams of chocolate and McDonald's replaced by an even more powerful longing for water, air conditioning and a place to sit down.

High up in the palatial cool of her bedroom, Siena was unaware of the sweltering world outside her window.

She woke up instead to a fleeting feeling of disorientation – where the hell was she? – followed by a searing, throbbing, unbearable pain in her head and chest.

Jesus Christ, that hurt.

She let out a low groan and scrabbled for the painkillers beside her bed.

'One with each meal, maximum four per twenty-four hours,' read the label.

Siena swallowed three with a gulp of tepid water and slumped back on to her white linen pillows. What a mess. What a total fucking mess.

In the end, once he'd realised that she wasn't going to change her mind, Hunter had been very sweet and helpful yesterday, organising her cloak-and-dagger exit from the hospital via one of the service entrances to escape the baying press. Better still, he had called his long-time boss and admirer Hugh Orchard, who had kindly allowed Siena to use his private jet to fly straight up to Vegas from a little-used airfield in Orange County.

When she'd arrived in Vegas last night, the staff at the

Venetian had been fantastic. Used to defending the privacy of such famous and reclusive guests as Michael Jackson and Madonna, they did a spectacular job of getting Siena checked in and settled, whisking her up to her suite in the classic Hollywood disguise of dark glasses and full-length fur, an operation that, despite her heartbreak and injuries, she had secretly rather enjoyed for all its clandestine glamour.

Less enjoyable had been Max's attempt to see and speak to her at the airstrip. Despite his promises, Hunter had been too soft hearted to conceal her whereabouts from his distraught best friend, and Max had arrived at speed, his little Honda almost entirely obscured by a cloud of dust, just as she was boarding the plane.

What happened next was already becoming a bit of a blur.

She remembered him crying and pleading with her to forgive him, begging her not to go. And she remembered the look on his face, a combination of terror and fury, as Orchard's security guys forcibly pulled him away from her and she climbed up into the plane.

She'd thought that she would cry, or at least feel something – anger for what he'd done, perhaps some compassion for his all too evident guilt, or even just the lingering force of her love for him.

But she didn't.

Some merciful God seemed to have flicked off the switch that connected her to any deeper emotion at all. The worst she could say was that she felt numb.

Christ, what she wouldn't give to feel numb this morning!

Maybe she had been a bit rash, checking herself out of hospital so soon. Her rib cage was so sore it hurt to breathe in. Hopefully the drugs would start kicking in soon.

Wincing again, she risked another, gentle stretch towards the bedside table and flicked on her mobile phone.

Predictably her inboxes for text and voicemail were both full. After deleting anything from numbers she didn't recognise (bound to be press) and everything from Max, she started to scroll through the remainder.

Three were from Hunter, all imploring her to call him, forgive Max and come home soon. Siena wiped them out with an impatient jab of the thumb – she was not in a forgiving mood this morning. Two were from Marsha, also asking her to make contact. One was from Ines, predictably asserting that all men were bastards, California sucked, and why didn't Siena move back home to New York, where they could go back to partying together again. That one made Siena smile. Darling, darling Ines. If only life were that simple. She scrolled through the list again, checking missed calls as well just for good measure, but there was nothing from her parents or any of the rest of her family.

Angrily, she snapped the phone shut and eased herself out of bed. Why the hell did she still care whether her parents called her or not?

She didn't turn on the TV, for fear that her face, or even worse Max's or that slutty girl's, might be on it. Instead she showered, changed into a stunning, clingingly low-cut silk jersey dress – her face might be battered, but at least her body would look great for the inevitable paparazzi – and began carefully applying make-up.

She needed enough to restore the natural beauty of her cheeks and bone structure, while being careful not to conceal the bruises and cuts that the press were all longing to see. It might put a hold on her auditions, but she was canny enough to appreciate that, if correctly presented, her swollen face could just turn out to be a PR gold mine.

What with trying to ease her arms into the dress without further damaging her ribs, and painstakingly ensuring that her make-up was done to perfection, it was almost noon before Siena was finally ready to emerge from her suite and face, she assumed, her public.

She took one long last look in the mirror before she opened the door. The dress, now that she'd finally got into it, was flawless, the perfect shade of blue-grey to highlight her fair skin and blue McMahon eyes. Her hair was swept loosely back off her face, so as not to hide any of the bruising around her eye and cheek, and she wore a demure pair of grey kitten heels. Low by Siena's usual standards, they made her look younger and more vulnerable than her normal stilettos.

At the last moment, she noticed she was still wearing the tiny antique silver cross on a chain that Max had given her the week they first got together. She wondered why they hadn't bothered to take it off her at the hospital, after the crash.

Holding it between her thumb and forefinger, she looked at the worn, buckled Moroccan silver, rubbed to a fine sheen from its long and constant contact with her skin. She had loved that cross, because it was beautiful but simple and unpretentious, like Max, and because like him it had always seemed to protect her.

For a few seconds, her cloak of numbness and anger slipped, and she felt the tears welling up in her eyes as she held it.

She missed him so much. What was she even *doing* here on her own?

But she swiftly pulled herself together and, winding the chain tightly around her fingers, she pulled hard, just once, so the necklace snapped around her neck. She looked at the coiled chain in her palm. Broken, just like her and Max. But she was determined not to cry, biting her lower lip for all she was worth.

She couldn't hold on to him, she mustn't. She wouldn't survive.

She was going to throw the cross away, but couldn't quite bring herself to do it, so she slipped it instead into the miniature drawer of the bureau by the door. Perhaps one of the hotel maids would pocket it or sell it, and it could become someone else's treasured possession. It seemed a shame to blame such a beautiful thing for the ugliness of what Max had done.

With one last glance at her complexion, still proudly unstreaked by tears, she walked out of the door, leaving behind the sanctuary of her room and – though she didn't know it – the last moments of peace she was to experience for quite some time.

Sitting in the waiting room at McMahon Pictures outside her husband's office, Claire was growing increasingly frantic. She was dressed in the same khaki skirt and T-shirt she'd had on yesterday, her greying blonde bob looked lank and dishevelled and her usually healthy complexion seemed to have lost every last ounce of colour.

'How much longer, do you think?' she appealed to Tara, Pete's ghastly PA, for the third time in as many minutes.

'Mrs McMahon.' The pinched-faced girl made little effort to conceal her annoyance, tapping her pen on the desk officiously as though some vital work had been disturbed by Claire's question. 'Believe me, if I knew, I'd tell you.'

Tara could imagine what Claire's unexpected visit must be about. The story was all over the papers this morning, about Siena's car crash and the boyfriend screwing around on her.

Serve her right, spoilt little cow.

Tara had always hated and, if truth be known, envied her boss's daughter, and had done everything in her limited power to encourage his estrangement from her. Although there had never been anything sexual between them, she enjoyed what she perceived as her closeness to Pete, and the reflected glory it brought her as one of the great producer's inner circle. As a result, she also resented Claire with an intensity that, had Claire ever bothered to notice it, she would have found unfathomable.

Claire looked at her watch again and sighed. She was desperate to talk to Pete. He'd been away in Reno on business for the last two days, and they had not yet had a chance to discuss what had happened face to face.

It still seemed incredible to her that she, Siena's own mother, knew nothing more about what had happened than what she'd read in the papers, which all had wildly different and speculative reports of yesterday's events. Last night she'd been so frantic with worry she'd even taken her courage in her hands and, praying that Pete didn't find out, called the hospital herself. But as Siena carried a card naming Hunter as her next of kin, and specifically requesting that any information regarding her health be released to him and him alone, she was unable to find out anything about her daughter's condition.

She was just about to try Pete's mobile again when he suddenly emerged from the elevator, looking tired and a little travel weary after his flight, but otherwise unperturbed.

'Hello, honey,' he said, kissing Claire on the cheek and ushering her into his office, while simultaneously signalling to Tara to bring them some coffee, much to her simmering fury. 'What brings you here so early? I thought I was seeing you tonight.'

Claire reached into her bag and, pulling out copies of that morning's *New York* and *LA Times*, thrust them into his hand.

Siena's picture was on page four of the former and the front page of the latter.

'Don't tell me you haven't seen these,' she challenged him. They had spoken yesterday afternoon, but at that point nobody knew how serious the accident had been. 'Look at that.' She gestured to a horrifying picture of the Navigator, smashed into smithereens. 'That's what she was driving, Pete. It says here it was Hunter's car.'

'Hmm,' said Pete, glancing momentarily at the picture before chucking both papers on to a chair in the corner. 'Pity he wasn't driving.'

'Peter!' Claire was genuinely shocked. Even in his most rage-filled moments, she had never heard him suggest that he actually wanted Hunter dead.

'The point is, what are we going to *do*? About Siena, I mean.' She looked at him in desperation.

Slowly, calmly, he put his briefcase on the floor and sat down on the huge black leather sofa next to the window, gesturing for her to sit beside him.

Pete's office was positively palatial, and crammed with trophies of his movie-making triumphs from the past decade. Signed pictures of a host of Hollywood legends who'd worked with him lined the three walls that weren't taken up with window. Just about everyone Claire could ever remember having seen on-screen was up there somewhere – Dustin Hoffman, Al Pacino, Nicole Kidman – and all of them had written personal notes of thanks or admiration to her husband, the boy that Duke McMahon had insisted would never amount to anything.

There were very few pictures of Pete himself on the wall. Despite his phenomenal success, he remained deeply insecure about his physical appearance, particularly his red hair. Even though it was now seriously thinning and heavily flecked with grey, Pete couldn't shake the feeling that it lit up his head like a beacon and that it was still the first thing everybody noticed about him.

He preferred to soothe his vanity by prominently displaying his two Best Picture Oscar statuettes, alongside a whole host of other, lesser film awards, at the very front of his desk, right in the immediate line of sight of any visitor who walked through the door.

He picked one of them up now, passing it from hand to hand in his lap, as if weighing up a problem. Then he turned to face his wife, who was sitting, anxiously wringing her cold, slender hands, beside him.

'Nothing,' he said quietly. 'We aren't going to *do*

anything about Siena. Nothing has changed, darling. Not really.'

'What do you mean, nothing's changed?' asked Claire, taking the naked golden figure from him and carelessly plonking it back on the desk, ignoring his sharp, worried intake of breath. 'Of course something's changed. She's been seriously hurt, Pete. She needs us.'

He took her hands in his and looked her straight in the eyes.

'Claire,' he whispered. 'How many times are we going to go through this? Siena is no longer a part of this family. And she never will be again. Ever. I thought we'd agreed.'

'But Pete,' she began, although by now she already knew it was hopeless. His eyes had taken on that blank look that meant total emotional shut-down.

He stopped her. 'No. Please, Claire. Are you with me or against me?'

'Oh, for God's *sake*!'

She got up and began pacing back and forth in frustration in front of the window. *Why?* Why did it always have to be this life-or-death battle? Why couldn't he see that she did love him, that she loved them both?

She pressed her face up against the glass and stared down at the tiny, toy-town cars on Century City Boulevard, some thirty storeys below. This being LA, there were no miniature people running around, just traffic, weaving in and out of the various lanes like a confused army of ants on wheels.

It was a very, very long way down. Suddenly Claire felt a lurching sensation of being pulled forward, almost as if the glass might be going to magically disappear or shatter and she would plunge helplessly to her death far, far below.

She shivered and moved back from the window hurriedly.

What had she expected? That just because Siena had

had an accident, because her face was in the papers again, Pete was suddenly going to relent and see sense?

She cursed herself for being so naive, for running down here to see him on a stupid impulse. The fact was that no story and no pictures were ever going to make him see Siena for who she really was: a frightened, confused, lost little girl, desperate for her parents' love.

Just then Tara came in with the coffee, without knocking, still boot faced about having been asked to perform such a menial task in front of Claire and having her perceived status so cruelly undermined.

'Leave it on the desk,' said Pete, oblivious to her indignant pout as she did as she was told, then turned on her heel and left.

'So?' he said again, this time to Claire's back.

He'd asked a question, and he wasn't about to let her leave without giving him an answer.

'I'm with you, Pete,' she said wearily.

And kissing him with almost maternal fondness on the cheek, she left him, her cup of coffee still steaming and untouched on the desk behind her.

Las Vegas in the summertime is like nowhere else on earth. Teeming with tourists who don't know any better than to take their holidays in temperatures that could fell cattle, as well as with the lost souls from all across America who come to forget, to try to escape their demons amid the noise and the neon and the relentless clicking and whirring of the slot machines, it's like some bizarre science fiction world of its own.

Siena had first come here as a child with her grandfather.

Duke adored the place. He used to say he and Vegas were made for each other. She remembered watching him and his friends playing poker in one of the private rooms at Caesar's Palace while she had stuffed herself with rum-and-raisin ice cream in the corner. She could only have been about six or seven.

Duke always wore a suit when he played cards, she remembered, and used to look like an even handsomer version of Dean Martin, with his whisky in one hand and his cards in the other, grinning around the big cigar he kept clamped between his teeth. Grandpa had always made Vegas seem so glamorous, and Siena had never quite shaken the feeling that beneath all the tacky freak shows and Siegfried and Roy kitschness, it was still a place where the big players played.

Duke had been a big player back in his heyday, the biggest.

One day, she told herself, she would be too.

As soon as she emerged into the lobby at the Venetian, she was greeted by the blinding flashes of a thousand cameras, and a myriad of strange voices, male and female, calling out her name.

'Siena! Over here!'

'How do you feel, sweetheart? Is it true you broke your ribs?'

'Have you heard from Max? Anything you'd like to say to him?'

Before she had a chance to respond, she found herself being swept up by the hotel manager, whose goons were making a valiant effort to beat back the throng, and bundled into the relative safety of his office.

'Holy shit,' she said, easing herself gingerly down into a chair a few moments later. 'How long have they been here?'

'Since late last night, I'm afraid, Miss McMahon,' said the manager, with a pained, what-can-you-do expression.

He was a very short, very round Italian with a ruddy, drink-ravaged complexion. Siena thought he looked like a human tomato, and suppressed a strong urge to giggle.

'We've done our best to keep them out of the reception area and security has been tightened inside the hotel. But I'm afraid as soon as you step outside . . .'

'I know, I know,' said Siena. 'I'm toast.'

'Excuse me?' The tomato looked bewildered.

'Oh, don't worry about it.' She waved her hand dismissively. 'It's an English expression, something I picked up at school.'

The manager nodded, as though he now understood perfectly, and tried not to stare too openly at Siena's fabulously full breasts, revealingly outlined by the clinging fabric of her dress. He didn't normally go for models, but he thought he could have made an exception in this young lady's case.

'I guess I have to face the music sooner or later,' she said, with a sigh that wasn't a hundred per cent convincing. 'I think I might do a bit of shopping, and they can get their pictures then. Get them out of the way.'

The manager had seen this act before with countless other 'celebrities'. The brave, resigned smile, intended to say: 'All I want is to be alone with my pain, but regrettably I have a public to think about.'

It was all a load of baloney. Sure, the girl was upset, some guy just screwed her over. But she was also loving the attention, every last minute of it.

No one came to Vegas for the privacy.

What he actually said was: 'I know this must be a difficult time for you, Miss McMahon,' tilting his head with practised, professional sympathy. 'If you like I can loan you a couple of my security guys, to come shopping with you? Things could get a bit outta hand.'

'Thank you, but I don't think I'll need them.' Siena got up to go and extended her hand, which he shook politely. 'It *has* been a difficult forty-eight hours, and I appreciate your concern. But I think I can cope on my own.'

'I don't doubt it,' said the manager, admiring her back view as she headed for the door. 'Not for a moment.'

For the first twenty minutes, Siena had a whale of a time. The best, the very best antidote to heartbreak, she decided, was a wave of public adulation.

She strolled along the artificial canals, looking suitably beautiful, victimised and brave, answering two or three questions before diving into Gucci or Prada, where the doors would close firmly behind her, allowing her to shop in peace while reporters pressed their lenses up against the glass. Then she would emerge for another short round of questioning and photographs, before disappearing again.

The slightly surreal atmosphere of the whole exercise was intensified by the seamless artifice that surrounded her: fake gondoliers with fake moustaches waved and shouted out to her in their fake Italian accents, beneath a fake painted sky, peppered with fake, neon-lit white clouds.

It must be incredible to wander through the Venetian on acid, thought Siena. She felt as if she were tripping already.

After twenty minutes, though, she was beginning to understand why they were called 'the press'. So many people were swarming around her it became quite physically intimidating, and before she knew it she seemed to have crossed the line from indulged diva to trapped rat.

The questions were also becoming more personal.

'Do you have any message for Camille Andrews?' asked one wiry little Hispanic woman, who'd got so close to her that her bad breath was making Siena feel sick.

'Not that you can print,' she snapped, her Pollyanna image slipping for an unguarded moment.

A hundred pens began frantically scribbling.

'Do you think you can ever forgive him?' yelled another, male voice.

Siena ignored that one and tried to turn left into a Ferragamo store, but found herself hemmed in by a solid wall of tape recorders and cameras.

Why hadn't she taken the manager up on his offer of some muscle? She started to feel panicked.

'Do you still love him?'

The voice came from about two feet behind her. Siena swung around and searched for its owner, apparently a middle-aged black reporter, whose badge proclaimed he was from the *LA Times*.

'Do you still love him?' he repeated.

She stood and stared at the man blankly for a moment, while the cameras flashed. Then suddenly, out of nowhere, she burst into tears.

The crowd went wild, pushing even closer around her, raised voices babbling in an indistinguishable roar, photographers punching each other to jostle their way into a more advantageous position for a shot of the unfolding drama.

Oh God. Help.

She was sobbing and spinning around frantically on the spot, desperately looking for a way out. Just then she felt a slight easing of the pressure of bodies to her left, and saw a hand, a man's hand, being held out to her. Instinctively she grabbed it. The hand pulled her swiftly and forcefully through the throng, and she suddenly found herself disoriented and gasping for breath inside Ferragamo, the bloodhounds mercifully shut out on the other side of the door.

Only then did she look up from the hand to acquaint herself with its owner.

She had never met him before, she was sure of that, although something about his face was eerily familiar. She guessed he was in his mid to late fifties, completely bald except for one small strip of closely shaven grey hair that formed a circle at the bottom of his head. He was immaculately dressed in a dark blue suit and white Italian-cut shirt, and he smelled very faintly of some expensive aftershave.

He was overweight – not obese, but heavy – and not at all good looking in any traditional sense. He had a boxer's nose, wide and oddly flattened as if it had been multiply broken, which looked enormous above his small, thin mouth. His eyes were a deep brown, almost black, and were surrounded by symmetrical fans of wrinkles. But despite these rather unprepossessing features, the overwhelming impression he gave was one of power and masculinity.

Her tiny hand lost in his grip, Siena was horrified to find herself thinking simultaneously that he reminded her of Duke, and that she was strongly attracted to him.

'You looked like you could use some help,' he said, smiling down at her. His voice was deep and betrayed only the faintest traces of a long-lost Southern accent. 'I'm Randall Stein.'

Of course! Of course she recognised him. She really must have been on another planet not to have got it right away.

Randall Stein was a legendary producer, bigger even than her own father. He had made his name funding action movies back in the early eighties, and had almost single-handedly created the action comedy genre that went on to dominate the box office in the early nineties. Stein was also well known as a shrewd investor in real estate and on Wall Street. She was sure she'd read something in one of Max's *Forbes* magazines about his having a personal net worth somewhere in the billions.

Holy shit.

Randall Stein.

And here she was looking like something the cat had sicked up, bruised and tear stained and revolting. 'How do you do?' she said, hastily wiping away her running mascara with the back of her right hand.

Randall was still holding her left.

'I'm . . .'

'I know who you are, Siena.'

It was that voice again. Siena felt her knees going weak.

'Really?'

'Of course.' Randall released her hand, and pulled up a chair beside her. The Ferragamo staff, who had all been loitering, gazing at the drama and particularly at Siena – in their world a top model was of infinitely more interest than some dull-as-ditchwater producer – now disappeared to the other end of the store after a meaningful glance from their manager.

'I know your father. In fact I used to know your grandfather as well, for many years.'

'Really?'

She could have smacked herself. Why couldn't she think of anything interesting to say?

Randall smiled again. He seemed to find her embarrassment rather amusing.

'Yes. But that's not why I know you. It may have escaped your notice, my dear, but a lot of people out there seem to recognise your face these days.' He gestured to the paparazzi, who were now being shooed away by some newly arrived police outside the window. 'I enjoy looking at beautiful models as much as the next man. You could say I'm a fan.'

Siena smiled at this. She doubted very much whether Randall Stein was anybody's fan.

'Actually,' she said, finding her voice at last, 'I'm not really modelling much any more. I'm an actress.'

Randall threw his head back and gave a great roar of a laugh. Siena looked offended.

'Oh, I'm sorry. I'm sorry, honey.' He wiped away tears of mirth. 'It's just that I wish I had a dollar for every beautiful young girl who's told me that.'

'I am an actress,' said Siena again. The steeliness in her voice wiped the smile off Randall's face and he looked at her with renewed respect. 'A fucking good one, as it happens.'

'Well,' he said, apparently somewhat chastened. 'You certainly have the genes for it. But never mind all that. You look, if you'll forgive an old man for saying so, terrible.'

'You're not an old man,' said Siena, who hadn't taken offence. 'I know I must look a mess. I've been having a few . . .' She stumbled for the right word. '. . . well, a few problems in the last couple of days.'

'I know,' said Randall. She looked at him questioningly. 'I have a TV.'

'Oh,' said Siena. 'I see. Of course.'

'Look,' said Randall, 'it appears the boys in blue have got your little fan club outside under control.' Siena glanced outside to see the press pack dispersing resentfully under the watchful eye of four heavily armed cops. 'Why don't you let me have one of my guys take you back to your hotel, so you can get some rest. You really shouldn't be out here today, not till things die down.'

'OK.' Siena nodded. 'Thanks.'

'And I'll come and pick you up from the Venetian at around eight,' said Randall firmly, as if referring to a long-standing arrangement the two of them had made.

'Oh. I don't know,' began Siena.

'Eight-thirty, then?'

'No, I mean, you've been very kind and everything. But I'm really not looking for . . .' She blushed, trying to think of a way to say this politely. 'I think I'm still in love with someone else. I'm not really ready for, you know, "dating".'

She waited for him to fill the silence, but he didn't let her off the hook. Again, he seemed to be enjoying her awkwardness.

'I'm just not interested in you in that way,' she blurted out eventually.

'Good,' said Randall briskly. 'Because I have absolutely no interest in you romantically.'

'Oh. Right. Good,' said Siena, who felt oddly as if she'd just been punched in the stomach.

'But I'd like to get to know you a little better. As I said, your family and I go back a long way. And you never know, we may even discuss a bit of business.'

He noticed how Siena's eyes lit up at the mention of the magic word business. A girl after his own heart.

'Great,' she said, and flashed him that million-dollar McMahon smile. 'I'm glad we got that straightened out.'

They shook hands again.

'Thank you,' she said sweetly. 'For rescuing me.'

'My pleasure,' said Randall. 'Now go get some rest. I'll see you tonight.'

Chapter Thirty-seven

Back in LA, Max sat on a rock high up in the hills above Will Rogers Park, with his head in his hands.

He'd been having some paparazzi problems of his own.

Ever since the news broke, a posse of press had been camped outside the beach house, waiting for him to emerge like the groundhog. He'd had a hell of a job shaking them off yesterday, on his way to try to see Siena at the airfield.

That was the only small mercy he could think of in this nightmare so far: at least the press hadn't been there to witness Siena dismissing him like some disobedient dog. She wouldn't even look at him, let alone listen to his apology.

He'd been expecting anger, hysterics and tears. Instead he got clinical, almost uninterested rejection. It was far, far worse.

After much pleading by Hunter, the LAPD had finally shown up last night and got rid of the photographers at the house, but by eight this morning they were back in barely depleted force, yelling inane questions at him from the street: had he talked to Siena, did he blame himself for the crash, were he and Camille now a couple?

One cheeky bastard had even had the audacity to stick a note under the front door, offering Max $150,000 for an exclusive on his side of the story, plus more if he was prepared to be filmed flying to Vegas to try to reconcile with Siena.

What sort of tragic gold-digger did these people think he was?

Hunter had suggested that the three of them – Tiffany had flown down from Canada last night to give both the boys some much needed moral support – escape for a long hike in the wilderness to try to talk things through in peace. The atmosphere at home was unbearable, like living through a siege.

So it was that, after some more very nifty driving by Max, they had once again shaken off their pursuers, and were now sitting, exhausted but undisturbed, high up above the canyon.

'If I could just make her see me, *listen* to me,' Max was saying for the umpteenth time that hour. 'I know I can turn this around. I mean, who throws everything away over one stupid mistake? Who does that?'

Tiffany thought privately that a lot of people did that, especially with a 'mistake' as big as Max's, and that she herself would probably be one of them. But she tried to sound encouraging. 'Maybe she just needs some space?' she suggested. 'She hasn't had much time to get her head around it yet, has she?'

Max ran his fingers back and forth despairingly through his hair. 'Oh God, what the hell have I done? How could I have been so *stupid*?'

Hunter sat down beside him and put an arm around his friend's shoulders. 'Come on,' he said, kindly. 'You couldn't have known the girl was going to leap on the phone to the *National Enquirer*.'

'I should have treated her better,' said Max, miserably. 'I was just thinking about myself, and how I'd betrayed Siena, and what a bloody fool I'd been. Maybe if I'd treated Camille with a bit more respect, she wouldn't have done the dirty on me.'

Hunter and Tiffany caught each other's eye. Neither of them contradicted him.

'I can't believe you didn't throw me out of the house and send me packing.' Max looked ruefully at Hunter.

'Come on, man, give me a break.' He squeezed him more tightly around the shoulders to emphasise his point. 'I could never do that to you, and you know it. We all screw up every now and then.'

'You don't,' said Max, honestly.

'Oh, don't you believe it!' Tiffany joked, desperate to lighten things up a bit. She'd never seen Max so down. 'Hunter has his dark side.'

All three of them had to laugh at that. Santa Claus had more of a dark side than Hunter.

'Seriously, though,' said Max, picking up a loose pebble and hurling it violently out across the canyon and into oblivion, 'I know you always thought I wasn't good enough for Siena. No one was good enough for her. And you were right, man. You were totally right.'

'Yeah, well,' Hunter began, 'she is pretty special.'

Tiffany couldn't believe her ears. 'Whoa, whoa, now hold on a minute, honey.'

She knew she was on dangerous ground saying anything against the saintly Miss McMahon, but she couldn't allow Max to shoulder all the blame for the problems in their relationship.

'What Max did was terrible, I think we can all agree on that.' Max looked down at his sneakers and nodded. No one could hate him more than he hated himself right now. 'And I'm not making any excuses for him,' Tiffany went on. 'But Siena was no angel either, so let's not rewrite history here. She could be mean and selfish, she was *always* flying off the handle at you.' She looked at Max. 'It's bullshit to say you didn't deserve her. You have so much to offer, and you put up with a lot of shit from that girl. We all did.'

Hunter was frowning throughout this little speech, and Tiffany waited for the inevitable defence of Siena. Sure enough, it came as soon as she stopped talking.

'I hope you're not implying that Siena *deserved* any of this?' He looked as close as he ever got to angry. 'That she brought it on herself in some way?'

'Of course I'm not saying that,' Tiffany snapped. 'I just don't think we should let Max start to feel that he's somehow not worthy of Siena, like she's some kind of saint. Because she's not, Hunter. She's not, OK?'

Max groaned inwardly. He could see Hunter's face clouding over. That was all he needed, to have him and Tiffany at each other's throats again over Siena.

'Look, this is all beside the point,' he jumped in, before hostilities could escalate any further. 'What we have to figure out is, what am I going to do now? How am I going to get her back?'

Hunter looked at him pityingly. It obviously hadn't sunk in yet.

'Max, I'm not sure there's a whole lot you *can* do, buddy,' he said. 'It's up to Siena to decide if she's going to forgive you, or at least try to work this out. But I gotta tell you, when I saw her yesterday . . .' He paused, looking for the kindest way to phrase it. 'Things didn't look too good. You really hurt her, man.'

Max stood up purposefully.

'I know. I know I did. But I have to see her, I have to at least try and explain.' He turned from Hunter to Tiffany and back again. They both looked highly doubtful. 'Oh, come on, you guys,' he said. 'Have a little faith, would you? Faint heart never won fair lady, right? I don't know how, but I'm telling you, I'm going to do it. I'm going to get her back.'

Later that night, Siena was sitting opposite Randall, gazing out across the Las Vegas skyline and feeling more than slightly drunk.

The view from the roof terrace was quite incredible.

Anxious not to suffer any more unwanted press attention, Randall had taken her to a private apartment – on loan from a friend, he said – where the most incredible table had been laid for two on the fortieth-floor roof garden.

Her initial reaction had been panic: candelabra, white linen, silver service and total privacy were not the usual ingredients of a business dinner. The scent of the bougainvillea alone was enough to make her feel faint, and the illuminated, azure blue of the pool behind them lent the whole place a summery, romantic air.

But Randall seemed so sure and relaxed about it all, she couldn't really say anything. She had already made a fool of herself once today by blatantly accusing him of fancying her. Besides, after he had come to her rescue so effectively this morning, the least she could do was accept his hospitality without being churlish. After all, how many up-and-coming young actresses wouldn't kill to be having dinner with Randall Stein?

Dinner itself had been delicious – lobster tails in garlic butter, wonderfully juicy, rosemary-encrusted lamb and raspberry mousse for pudding. To her surprise, Siena had found she was famished, wolfing down all three courses greedily. She had always read in magazines that men found girls with big appetites a turn-off, but Randall seemed delighted. Judging from his waistline, she assumed him to be another food lover.

She had also been drinking champagne to wash it all down, in blatant disregard of doctor's orders. Apparently alcohol disagreed with her medication or something, but she hadn't had *that* much. In fact she was pretty sure that Randall had drunk the second bottle almost completely by himself.

Pretty sure.

In any event, the ensuing haze of alcohol-induced contentment enabled her to banish all thoughts of Max and that fucking girl from her mind completely. Which, as far as Siena was concerned, was the object of the exercise.

'Coffee?' asked Randall, leaning across the table and taking Siena's hand. She permitted the gesture. All that champagne had really loosened her up. 'Or perhaps you'd like another drink?'

'No, God no.' Siena shook her head. She was very conscious of the warm, slightly rough touch of his fingers, and the unmistakable jolt of desire it triggered in her. Unconsciously, she began stroking the back of his hand with her thumb. 'I think I've had more than enough already. The city's swaying.'

'Coffee, then,' said Randall, pulling his hand away just when she'd hoped he wouldn't and signalling to their private waiter. 'I don't want you to be too far gone. We still have that business to discuss.'

Inexplicably, Siena felt her spirits fall for a second at the mention of business. She gazed dazedly out over the twinkling lights of Vegas, apparently lost in her own thoughts. Randall carried on.

'Perhaps I should start by saying that I know rather more about you than I let on this morning.'

'Oh?' said Siena, woken momentarily from her reverie.

'Yes,' he said enigmatically. 'And this afternoon I had my LA office fly me up a tape of the pre-screen version of *The Prodigal Daughter*. I watched it twice, as a matter of fact.'

'Really?' Siena's face lit up. She was deeply flattered that someone as powerful as Randall Stein should take such an interest in her work, particularly after he'd dismissed her earlier that morning as just another wannabe model. Instinctively she tossed back her hair and pouted at him, giving him the very best angle of the face that had made her a small fortune. Notwithstanding her bruises, she looked breathtakingly sexy. 'What did you think of it?'

Randall took a sip of his freshly poured espresso.

'I thought it was predictable, and a little bit derivative.'

Instantly she flushed with indignation and humiliation. He had set her up for that, the little shit.

'Oh, did you?' she said, standing up unsteadily and retrieving her bag with as much dignity as she could muster. Fucking asshole. If he thought she was sticking around here to be insulted by him, he could stick it up his fat, billionaire ass. 'Well, I'm afraid you're alone in that opinion, *Mister* Stein. The other critics have been universally impressed with my performance. In fact, I've been inundated with scripts already, and *The Prodigal*

Daughter doesn't even open for another week. Now, if you'll excuse me . . .' She turned on her heel. 'It's been a long day, so I think I'll get back to my hotel and make a start on some of those scripts before I turn in. Thank you for dinner.'

'Sit down,' said Randall. He took another sip of his coffee, utterly unperturbed. 'Don't be such a spoiled child.'

Siena hesitated for a moment. The only other person who had ever spoken to her like that was Max.

'If you're serious about this business, *Miss* McMahon,' he mimicked her, 'you'll have to learn to listen to criticism without being so damn petulant about it. You didn't let me finish what I was saying.'

Scowling warily, Siena sat back down.

'I did think it was predictable. You're making some silly mistakes.' She opened her mouth to speak again, but he ignored her. 'But I also think you have potential, huge potential. With your looks and your name, you could go a long way.'

It was exactly what Siena didn't want to hear.

'Yeah? Well, fuck my looks!' she said, shaking her head in anger. 'And fuck my stupid name. I'm only interested in making it on the back of my talent.'

Randall smiled. God, he could be patronising, thought Siena.

'I see,' he said. 'Well, unfortunately *I'm* only interested in making money. If we're going to do any sort of business together, you may as well get that straight right now.'

Leaning over the table, he grabbed her by the shoulders and pulled her face close to his. For one awful, confusing moment she thought he might be going to kiss her.

Instead he began talking to her with an urgency and authority that forced her to listen. 'Do you know how many girls out there have "talent", as you call it? And by the way, I hate that word. How much talent does it take to pretend to be someone else? You're an actress, sweetheart, not a rocket scientist.' Siena sat motionless. 'Well, I'll tell you. Thousands. Hundreds of thousands. Maybe even millions of people can do what you do, Siena. And all of them are competing for the attention of guys like me. So how come it's you sitting here, and not them, huh?'

Siena assumed it was a rhetorical question.

'Because you're different, that's why. You're lucky. You have something they haven't got – the McMahon name. And if you don't use it, then you're a bigger fool than you look.' He was holding her so tightly his fingers were leaving livid red imprints on the flesh of her upper arms. 'You need to think long and hard, baby, about what it is you actually want.'

'No I don't,' said Siena, on autopilot. 'I know what I want.'

Although at that moment her statement couldn't have been less true.

She found Randall's physical closeness to her both unnerving and arousing. She had rarely encountered anybody with a stronger will than her own, and she had absolutely no idea how to handle it.

'Do you?' asked Randall. 'Because if you're going to bleat on about talent, you might as well take up a fulfilling career in the theatre in some butt-fuck nowhere little town in the Midwest and be done with it.'

He released her shoulders and sat back in his chair.

'But if you want something more than that . . .' He signalled to the waiter to refill his coffee cup. 'If you want to be a real star, like your grandfather was . . .'

'I do.' Siena's eyes lit up despite herself. 'I do want that.'

'Then you're going to have to make some changes,' said Randall, a new harshness in his tone. 'Big changes.'

'Such as?' She was intrigued again now.

'Such as quit dragging yourself down with some deadbeat loser of a boyfriend.'

'Max isn't a loser,' said Siena, stung. 'He's a director, and he has enormous talent.'

'There you go again, talent, talent, talent. Wake up, kid! The guy's a fucking zero. He's nothing. Nobody.' Each word was like a dagger in Siena's heart, but some force compelled her to keep on listening. 'He cheated on you, didn't he? Went out and had some fun with that dime-a-dozen waitress. Why do you think that was?'

'I . . .' She struggled to hold back her tears. Why was Randall bullying her like this? What did he care about her and Max anyway? 'I don't know,' she stammered. 'I thought he loved me.'

'Jesus, listen to yourself. Would you grow up?' said Randall brutally. 'He did it for two reasons, Siena. One.' He held up his forefinger. 'Because that's what men do. All men. Sooner or later, that's what we do.'

'Including you?' she challenged him.

'Absolutely including me.' He didn't miss a beat. 'And two.' He waved a second finger menacingly in her direction. 'And this is where your boy and I differ. He did it because he's too much of an insecure prick to deal with your success.'

She hated hearing Max's character being shredded by this total stranger. But she had to admit, there was more than a grain of truth in what Randall was saying. Max *had* always been jealous of her success. Besides, she didn't see why she should be defending him, after the way he'd just betrayed her.

'He's holding you back. Get rid of him.' Randall cracked his fingers for good measure, as if he'd just finished wringing something's neck.

'I have got rid of him,' said Siena.

And then she did something she couldn't really explain. She reached across and touched Randall on the cheek.

He didn't smile, or flinch. He simply held her gaze until, what seemed like hours later, he lifted her hand from his face and pressed it to his lips. To her dismay,

Siena found herself fervently wishing he would put his lips all over the rest of her body, and the sooner the better.

'I can help you,' he said at last. 'I can give you what you want. But you have to do as I say. No more hanging on to the coat-tails of that soap star uncle of yours.'

'Hunter? Oh, no, you can't say anything against Hunter, he's been wonderful to me,' she protested.

'Fine. Send him a postcard. Spend Thanksgiving with him,' said Randall. 'I don't give a shit about your family life. I'm talking about your image, about the way you want to be perceived. As long as you live with him, as long as you're joined at the hip to a guy at his level, then that's the level people will see you at. Is that all you want to be, some two-bit TV star's sidekick?'

'Of course not,' said Siena.

'I told you,' said Randall, moving his chair closer and placing a warm, proprietorial hand on her thigh, which Siena did nothing to remove. They both knew by now that she was headed for his bed. 'I knew Duke. Pretty well, actually. I think you have a lot of your grandfather in you.'

The hand was moving upwards achingly slowly. Siena felt herself sweating and her mouth parting in longing for him. Her pupils were dilated and her eyelids heavy with lust.

Three days earlier she'd felt as if she would never look at any other man, that she and Max would be together for the rest of her life. Yet now here she was, up on some Las Vegas rooftop with Randall fucking Stein of all people, so horny she thought she might be going to explode.

'I should mention one other thing,' whispered Randall, his face buried in her neck as his fingers deftly pulled aside the cotton fabric of her panties.

'Hmmm?' murmured Siena, dreamily. The pain in her ribs and chest seemed to have magically disappeared.

'I also know your father,' he said, lowering his head to

kiss her shoulders and collar bone before moving down to the tops of her beautiful, round, high breasts.

He eased one of them out of her bra and began slowly tracing the outline of her nipple with his tongue, while simultaneously sliding two fingers deliciously slowly in and out of her. Siena moaned with delight, and put a hand on the back of his bald head, pulling his face back up to hers.

'I hate him,' said Randall. Siena opened her eyes and looked at him. 'And he hates me. I hope that won't be a problem?'

She smiled.

Randall was no oil painting. But God, he knew how to turn her on.

'No problem at all,' she said. 'In fact, *Mister* Randall Stein . . . I think I might be starting to like you.'

Chapter Thirty-eight

For the next three months, Siena's feet didn't touch the ground. She never went back to the beach house. After Vegas, she flew back into town with Randall and moved directly into his Malibu estate.

'What about my stuff?' Strapped in beside him in the back of his private G4, she suddenly panicked. 'I have to at least go back and get my things.'

'We'll buy you new stuff.' Randall didn't even glance up from the *Wall Street Journal*. 'Don't worry about it.'

Siena didn't worry about it. After years of battling to make it on her own, first in fashion and then as an actress, it was wonderful to have somebody else make all the decisions, and better still to have them pick up her tab.

Her spirits lifted even farther when she saw the Malibu house. She'd been exposed to more than her fair share of wealth and luxury in her short life, but nothing could have prepared her for the opulence of Randall's mansion.

'Jesus Christ,' she said, clapping her hand over her mouth in awe as he led her into the palatial marble-and-gold atrium.

The walls were hung with enormous medieval tapestries, and priceless gold and silver urns filled with ostrich feathers stood like gleaming sentinels at the foot of the biggest, most dramatic staircase Siena had ever seen. Even Hancock Park couldn't hold a candle to it for sheer grandeur.

'Nice, isn't it?' said Randall, nonchalantly chucking his briefcase on to what looked like a seventeenth-century low table, exquisitely carved with mahogany angels clinging to each of the legs.

'It's incredible,' said Siena truthfully, but not without a twinge of envy.

She wanted to have a house like this. She wanted to be as rich and powerful as he was.

'You want it, don't you?' In their very brief acquaintance, Randall had already developed an uncanny ability to read her thoughts. 'Well, stick with me, sweetheart.' He smiled. 'Anything's possible.'

Siena moved towards him. Standing there, surrounded by all his wealth like a Byzantine emperor, he seemed even more powerful and attractive than he had in Vegas. She stood on her toes to kiss him, but he gently pushed her away.

'Not now, baby. I have a lot of work to do after the trip.' He patted her head, as if he were explaining something very complicated to a small child. 'Why don't you go upstairs and settle in, maybe have a nice hot bath, ease those bruises of yours. Maria Elena can help you.'

Before she could say a word, he had snapped his fingers and a nervous-looking Hispanic maid, in full livery, had appeared at Siena's side, ready to escort her to the bedroom.

It was a wholly new experience for Siena to have one of her sexual advances rebuffed, albeit temporarily, and she wasn't at all sure she liked it. As she was soon to discover, however, life with Randall Stein was to be full of new experiences.

For their first few months together, Siena felt as if she were living in a dream. *The Prodigal Daughter* was released two weeks after she got back from Vegas, and largely thanks to the publicity surrounding her accident and subsequent relationship with Randall, the movie was a huge success, the runaway 'surprise hit' of the autumn.

The ensuing publicity was overwhelming.

Siena, who was used to appearing on *Vogue* covers and to a certain amount of press attention, instantly found herself sucked into a worldwide media feeding frenzy, carefully orchestrated by Randall, who had insisted that poor old Marsha be fired within a week of bringing Siena home and brought in his own promotional team to handle his new girlfriend's image.

Suddenly, pictures of Hollywood's newest golden couple were splashed all over newspapers from LA to London: Randall and Siena at her premiere in Tokyo; arriving in his and hers Armani at the New York premiere for Stein's latest action blockbuster, *Ocean Drive*, arm in arm with Bruce Willis; Siena, looking unfeasibly sexy in hot pants and baseball cap, leaping up and hugging a smug-looking Randall at a Lakers game.

When the news broke in October that Siena had been cast as the heroine in Randall's upcoming Second World War drama, which was shaping up to be the biggest-budget movie of all time, the press went even further into overdrive.

Far from being intimidated, she appeared to thrive on the publicity, drawing energy and life from the flash of the camera bulbs like a pot plant suddenly moved from a dark corner into bright sunlight. Randall also seemed pleased at the success of his promotional efforts with his new protégée, although the 'Beauty and the Beast' headlines irked him more than he cared to show. Siena soon learned that her new lover, manager and mentor, despite all his success and power, was incredibly physically vain. He would typically wake up at five for an hour's gruelling workout with his personal trainer before getting on the phone to his brokers in New York. He was also obsessively careful about what he ate, and almost never drank alcohol, because he didn't like the loss of control.

It was a mystery to Siena why he remained so overweight, while she could sit up in bed munching chocolate bars and still keep her flawless figure.

Which was just as well, as she soon found she needed the chocolate for energy. Randall might be in his fifties and in less than perfect shape, but his sexual appetite nevertheless far exceeded Max's.

For the first time in her life, Siena had found a lover whose libido more than matched her own, and she found his demands quite exhausting. He was also much kinkier than her other lovers, and was especially big on making home porno movies. Despite Siena's frequent misgivings, and occasional protests, he insisted on filming her performing a variety of obscene and degrading acts. Before each performance he would lay out on the bed a spectacular array of sex toys, restraints, vibrators and massive black rubber dildos, like bizarre instruments of torture.

Siena's attraction to him remained intense, although the accessories didn't do a whole lot for her.

Afterwards he would make an attempt to be affectionate, perhaps allowing her to lie on his chest for a few minutes while he stroked her hair. As a rule, though, Randall was not good with any physical contact outside of sex. He did not approve of emotional dependency, either in himself or in others.

Having been burned so badly by Max, Siena was more than happy to embrace this 'every man for himself' philosophy. She enjoyed sex with Randall for what it was – just sex – and she revelled in the fabulous lifestyle he gave her.

Claire McMahon sat in a quiet corner of the car park at Fry's electrical store, out near the airport.

It was 5.30, so the place was fairly busy with after-school shoppers, mostly harassed-looking moms replacing light bulbs or broken fans on their way home to microwave something for their husband and kids. Claire envied them. She would gladly have traded every penny she had for a happy, domestic family life and children.

She readjusted her Chanel sunglasses and glanced around nervously, still scanning the car park for the silver Chevy Suburban she was supposed to be meeting. She knew it was stupid, but her heart was pounding violently and she was gripped by an irrational fear that Pete was going to drive in at any minute and catch her red handed.

This must be what it felt like to have an affair, she thought, and wondered how people ever coped with the stress. But an affair was the last thing on Claire's mind.

For years now she had given in to Pete and cut herself off completely from Siena. Because he needed her, and because she loved him so much, she had put herself through the anguish of having to sit on the sidelines and watch with the rest of the world as her daughter's turbulent life was played out in the media.

But after Siena's accident and her terrible conversation with Pete in his office, everything had changed. It was as if a switch had finally flicked deep inside Claire, and she could see with searing clarity that Pete would never, ever change his mind. That if she didn't do something soon, she really would have lost her daughter for ever.

She knew she couldn't contact her directly. The betrayal might literally kill Peter, and besides, Siena had made it clear in a string of barbed and hurtful articles that she would not have welcomed her mother with open arms should she attempt a reconciliation.

Even so, she had to do something.

There it was. The silver Chevy, a bit on the grimy side, but with the blacked-out windows she'd been told to look for, swept into the Fry's car park and pulled up into a space a few rows behind her.

She stepped out of her own Discovery and, locking the doors with trembling hands, made her way over and rapped lightly on the window of the passenger door, which instantly opened. She climbed inside and shook hands with the man she had met only once before in his grimy office in Compton a few weeks ago.

'Hello, Bill,' she said.

'Claire.'

Bill Jennings was not just black, he was jet black, with

that very dark, Sudanese colouring that made his teeth gleam when he smiled, as he did now. 'Don't look so worried.' He chuckled. 'You're not doing anything illegal, you know.'

He handed her a brown envelope, which she immediately began to open. Inside were seven or eight pictures of Siena, as well as a typed and bound document, detailing her daughter's significant movements and news over the past three months.

'Where was this taken?' she asked, pointing to a picture of Siena, her face still looking bruised, outside the gates of a palatial-looking estate.

'That's Randall Stein's place,' said Bill.

Claire frowned. Like everyone else, she had read about Siena's liaison with Stein and the thought of it made her shudder. Claire had met him only once or twice, but she remembered Randall as a thug and a bully, albeit a charming one at times. Pete had always despised the man, and she couldn't help but wonder whether Siena had taken up with Randall as some sort of revenge for her father's abandonment of her. If this was a cry for help, Claire was listening.

'Thanks for these,' she said, gathering up the photographs and putting them carefully back into the envelope. 'I'll wire the money to your account on Monday, then, shall I? And we'll meet again next week?'

He nodded, and she got out of the car.

'Try not to worry,' he said in a kindly tone. He couldn't imagine how he'd feel if his daughter were shacked up with a guy older than he was. 'She seems in good shape right now. And I'll let you know right away if anything significant happens.'

'Thanks.' Claire smiled. Bill was a decent man.

He just didn't know how much of a lifeline he was to her.

One grey morning in November, Siena sat in the

conservatory at Malibu, taking a leisurely breakfast on her own.

Since becoming Randall's girlfriend, she had got used to eating in pampered isolation. He was always either in the office or down at the studios long before Siena emerged from bed. Even on weekdays, she didn't have to leave the house until nine, as they rarely started shooting any of her scenes before ten. Working on one of Randall's movies was a whole lot different from working for that slave driver Muller.

But today was a Saturday, so she was looking forward to indulging herself free of guilt and lingering over her blueberry muffin and latte coffee until mid-morning.

'Have you seen-this?'

Randall, looking excited in his weekend uniform of khaki linen pants and black Gucci shirt, his hair still wet from a post-workout shower, burst into the room and slammed the *LA Times* down in front of Siena, scattering muffin crumbs everywhere.

'Seen what?' she asked, unsmiling, annoyed that her peace had been so rudely disturbed. 'Shouldn't you be in the office?'

'Take a look,' said Randall, ignoring her and pouring himself a cup of coffee from the freshly filled cafetière. 'It seems old Minnie McMahon finally gave up the ghost last night.'

Siena picked up the paper, and stared at the headline: MINNIE MCMAHON, WIFE OF LEGENDARY DUKE, DIES AGED EIGHTY.

Below this stark announcement was a picture of Duke and Minnie on their wedding day, looking at each other and laughing. The picture shocked her almost as much as the headline – she couldn't remember her grandparents ever being remotely happy together. How odd to think that they must have been, once.

Putting down her coffee shakily, Siena turned to pages four and five, where a montage of pictures caused her to catch her breath.

There was a small shot of the old Hancock Park house where, it appeared, Grandma Minnie had died peacefully in her sleep. Siena had studiously avoided driving anywhere near the old neighbourhood since moving back to LA, and didn't have any pictures of her own, so this was the first time she'd seen it in years.

She touched the image in wonder, tracing the outline of the house and the big lawn where she and Hunter and Max used to play. It made her want to cry.

Below this were more pictures of Duke and Minnie together at various public functions, as well as one of her parents, sitting smiling on either side of a very frail-looking Minnie. She felt her heart tighten painfully as she looked at her mother's face. It was thinner and slightly more wrinkled than she remembered it, but fundamentally Claire looked the same: kind, nervous and a little bit lost.

Looking at the picture, Siena felt an avalanche of longing and loss hit her in the chest. She was stunned.

'I had no idea the old bat was still going,' said Randall with typical insensitivity. 'There's very little about you in there, unfortunately. Something in the obituary about Hunter and his mother, though – Caroline, isn't it? Couple of the other papers even got on to her in England for a quote. She's married to some lord or something now, I gather.'

'Hmmm?' Siena was miles away, lost in painful memories.

'Anyway, baby, I've been thinking about how we should spin it,' Randall continued, buttering himself a piece of toast and apparently oblivious to her anguish. 'You need to call that dumb-fuck uncle of yours.'

'What?' Siena put the paper down and looked at him, eyes brimming with tears of grief and anger. 'What the hell are you *talking* about, Randall? My grandmother's just died, OK?'

'So?' he said through a mouthful of toast. 'Don't try to

tell me you gave a shit about her. When did you last speak to the woman? Five years ago? Ten?'

'That's not the point,' said Siena, crossing her arms and legs defensively against him. 'She's still my family. And my parents . . .' She picked up the picture of Pete and Claire again. 'I wonder how my dad's taking it. They were very close, you know, Dad and Grandma. Grandpa – Duke – he never got along with my father.'

'I'm not surprised,' said Randall bluntly. 'No one gets along with your father. He's a cunt.'

'Randall!' Siena winced at the viciousness of his language.

'Jesus, Siena, *what*?' he snapped back tetchily. 'I've heard you call Pete McMahon a cunt enough times, and worse. You're telling me you suddenly think he's a great guy, just because his mom dropped dead?'

'No,' she mumbled, 'of course not.' She was angry with him for being so insensitive to her feelings, but she supposed he did have a point.

'Why should you care how Daddy dearest is taking it?' Now it was Randall who sounded angry. 'I think I remember you telling me he didn't care too much how you were taking it, when he cut you off without a fucking penny and turned you out on the street.'

'All right, Randall,' said Siena. She was feeling very emotional – it was all too much to take in. She really didn't need a lecture from him right now.

'No, Siena, it's not all right.' Sensing her weakness, he moved in for the kill. 'How many years have you sat around waiting for any of your so-called family to make contact? Huh? When you did your first *Vogue* cover, when you got the lead in *Daughter*, you had the whole world making a fuss of you, telling you how great you were. But did you enjoy it? Hell, no! All you wanted, all you *really* wanted, was for Mommy and Daddy to call and say, "Well done, honey, we love you." Wasn't it?'

He was mocking her now, his voice laden with spite,

making fun of her weakness, her terrible, shameful need for her parents' love.

'That's not true!' she yelled back at him, willing herself not to give him the satisfaction of tears.

'Yes it is!' Randall banged his fist down on the table with a crash and leaned intimidatingly across the shuddering plates and bowls towards her. Instinctively she shrank back from his temper. 'It *is* true, Siena. You are so fucking weak sometimes, I can't even look at you. Haven't you figured it out yet? They don't love you. They don't want you.' He spoke very slowly, lingering over each word like a sadistic executioner. 'You mean nothing to them.'

'Stop it!' She clamped her hands over her ears, but he grabbed both her wrists and pulled them away, forcing her to hear him.

'When Max screwed you over, when you had that crash and nearly died, where was your father then?' He raised his eyebrows as if expecting an answer, but Siena just shivered in terrified silence. 'Who looked after you then, Siena? Who took care of you and took you in and gave you a home, and a real career, and everything you've ever wanted?'

'You did,' she whispered, defeated and confused.

She just wanted him to stop.

Still clasping her wrists, Randall pulled her into his lap and wrapped his arms around her, kissing her hair and neck and stroking her. It was more tenderness than she had ever experienced from him, and she felt ridiculously grateful and reassured by it. Despite her best efforts, the tears had started to flow.

'I'm sorry,' he whispered, all softness and compassion suddenly. 'I shouldn't have shouted at you. I just can't bear to see you wasting your love and sympathy on people who don't love you back. It's weak.'

Siena looked up searchingly into his inscrutable brown eyes, but drew a complete blank. For months now she'd

spent every single day with this man, but she still couldn't figure him out.

She wasn't even sure whether she loved him or hated him. All she knew was they were a team now, a good team in many ways. Randall had picked her up and reinvented her when she was at her lowest ebb. He had showered her with riches, and catapulted her career into the fast lane overnight.

She needed him.

'What do you want me to do?' she asked, drying her tears and wriggling free from his embrace.

'That's better,' said Randall, and smiled at her, evidently pleased to have won her co-operation. 'Well, the first thing I want you to do is call Hunter. Invite him to the Dodgers game with us tonight.'

Siena looked perplexed.

'That's the story here, the spin,' Randall explained. 'You and Hunter've both been abandoned by your family. No one called you to tell you about Minnie's death, and you're really cut up about it. Let the press get some shots of you together, putting on a brave face.'

'It's been done to death, though,' said Siena, apparently happy to talk business now that her tears had dried. 'Me and Hunter, the family outcasts.'

'It's been done badly,' said Randall, 'thanks to your friend Marsha. It's a great card, baby, and I'm going to show you how to play it properly. Besides, things are different now. Your profile is in a whole other league to your pretty-boy uncle's. Your grandmother's death is a gift. Let's make you the star of the show.'

Despite everything, Siena felt a stab of distaste, hearing Minnie's death described as nothing more than a PR opportunity.

She also wasn't crazy about the idea of using Hunter to help promote her image. Things between her and Hunter had been strained to say the least since Randall came on the scene. She couldn't go to the beach house, what with Max still living there and the annoying Tiffany

back in almost permanent residence. And Randall had made it quite clear that he disapproved of her closeness with Hunter, or with anyone other than himself, in fact, so she couldn't really ask him out to Malibu either.

What with their geography problems, filming schedules and Siena's constant need to be in the limelight, they had had precious little time together recently. She knew that this had hurt Hunter deeply, and she was ashamed of herself for allowing the rift between them to grow.

'I thought you hated Hunter.' She made a last attempt to stall him. 'Aren't you always telling me not to spend so much time with him, and never to get our picture taken together?'

'This is different,' he repeated, in a tone that was intended to indicate that the matter was now closed. 'Call him, ask him tonight. I'm sure he'll be thrilled.'

'What about the second thing?' said Siena. 'Didn't you say calling Hunter was the first thing you wanted me to do?'

'Ah, yes.' Randall smiled wickedly. 'The second thing.'

Siena gave him an over-the-top look of mock surprise. She already knew exactly what 'the second thing' would be.

Placing two strong hands on her shoulders, Randall pushed her down on to her knees. Wordlessly, she unzipped his fly and freed his rock-solid erection. Then she looked up at him, smiling. Despite everything, despite all the crudeness, controlling and bullying, Randall's power was still the ultimate turn-on for Siena.

Gently, he lifted her mountain of dark curls and cupped his hand around the back of her neck, pulling her pretty rosebud mouth down on to his cock.

Then he sat back and sighed contentedly as, with consummate skill, she gave him exactly what he wanted.

Chapter Thirty-nine

Across town, Tiffany put the finishing touches to the table with a little sigh of contentment. Grabbing her novel – she was addicted to Patricia Cornwell at the moment – and a chilled glass of Chablis from the fridge, she slipped out on to the front porch and sank down on the wicker sofa to await Hunter's return for lunch.

They had decided to spend the weekend at her newly rented cottage in Venice, a charming, whitewashed 1920s affair on one of the walk streets, with a white picket fence and orange and lemon trees in the front garden.

Tiffany had fallen in love with it the moment she saw it and put down a deposit of three months' rent on the spot, but she hadn't actually moved in until a few weeks ago, when *Sea Rescue* had finally wrapped.

The cottage was a compromise solution. It was only a ten-minute drive along the beach from Hunter's place, which was a lot easier than her old Westwood commute.

She still didn't want to move into the beach house: even with Siena gone, it still felt too much like Hunter's space. But she understood that Hunter felt he couldn't sell up and desert Max in his current hour of need. So they'd agreed to divide their time as equally as possible between the two houses and, unless either of them were away shooting, not to spend a night apart.

She sipped her wine happily and admired her new garden. She was so much happier here, away from the heavy atmosphere over at the beach house.

Ever since Siena had run off with Randall, it was as if a nail bomb had exploded into all of their lives.

Max's initial confidence that he would win her back had soon been replaced by despair. Mercifully, he had finally landed a really decent, paying job directing two short films for a famous Hollywood actor with money to burn who wanted to dabble on the production side. This at least meant he was out of the house and occupied most days.

Even so, he carried his broken heart around with him wherever he went, and Tiffany found it painful to watch. He had lost a shocking amount of weight, and lack of sleep had taken all the mirth and playfulness out of his lovely eyes.

Worst of all, though, was his insistence that he alone was responsible for his misery. Nothing Tiffany or anyone said could change his mind about that.

He was so acutely aware of his own guilt, he refused to hear a bad word said about Siena. The agony of being constantly bombarded with images of her with Randall, rich, famous and utterly beyond his reach, Max thought of as nothing more than just punishment for his betrayal of her and their love.

Hunter was not much better, moping around like a lost puppy, hoping against hope for word from Siena.

It made Tiffany's blood boil, the way that she had dropped him like a hot brick, now that she had her billionaire sugar daddy to take care of her and was a newly minted Hollywood superstar. As far as Tiffany was concerned, Siena had finally shown her true colours and proved once and for all that all she really cared about was fame and money.

But Hunter, as always, point blank refused to see it.

'Have you seen the news?'

Hunter, dripping with sweat from his run along the beach, was clutching a damp copy of the *LA Times*. He bounded over the fence in one giant stride, and sat down on the terrace with his head between his knees, trying to catch his breath.

Tiffany picked up the paper and read the headline.

'Oh, darling, that's terrible,' she said with real

sympathy, putting a hand on his sweat-dampened shoulder. 'Are you OK?'

He nodded breathlessly and ran into the kitchen to pour himself a glass of water.

'I'm fine, actually,' he said, wandering back out. Tiffany budged up so he could sit beside her. 'It seems funny to say it, but I never really knew Minnie that well. I mean, I grew up in the same house and all that, but we had very separate lives.'

Tiffany just sat patiently and listened.

'I remember when I was very small, she used to scare me a bit,' he went on. 'Claire, Siena's mother, would always try to stick up for me. I think the problem was, she could never quite forgive me, Minnie I mean, for being my mother's son. Which is understandable, I guess.'

'No it isn't,' said Tiffany bluntly. Sometimes Hunter's turn-the-other-cheek nature could really wind her up. She wished he would stick up for himself a bit more. 'It isn't understandable at all. You were a wholly innocent child. Anyway, I'm sure I remember you or Siena telling me she'd squandered half your inheritance or something.'

'I told you that, but she didn't do it deliberately,' he said. 'She just never had a clue about money. My dad used to handle all that. Anyway. . .' He gave her a kiss, careful not to press his sweaty, salty face against hers and smudge her mascara. 'I'm fine. Must be tough on Pete, though.'

Good, thought Tiffany, but she didn't say anything. Hunter might be able to forgive his mogul brother, but she wasn't about to forget the way that Pete McMahon had tried to destroy his career back in the early days of *Counsellor*.

Hunter picked up the paper again and started to read some of the comment.

'I wonder how Siena is taking it,' he said nervously. He had become very wary of bringing up Siena's name

437

these days, fearful of Tiffany's disapproval. 'Do you think I should call her?'

'No,' said Tiffany, firmly, getting up and leading him into the living room and the delicious-looking lunch she'd prepared. 'She hasn't bothered to call you, has she? She's got your number, darling, if she needs you.'

Hunter looked sad, but he wasn't going to fight about it. 'You're right,' he said.

Tiffany was astonished. She hadn't expected him to let it go so easily. Then again, things *had* been fairly distant between him and Siena this last couple of months.

'I ought to call my mom, though, after lunch. I'm sure she'll have found a few spare moments to talk to the press.'

He rolled his eyes, imagining Christopher's bemused tolerance as his mother lapped up the ever welcome press attention. These days, now that he was so happy and settled with Tiffany, he was inclined to feel much more indulgent towards Caroline's foibles and weaknesses. He viewed her more as a sort of charmingly naughty, overgrown child than the woefully irresponsible parent she actually was.

Tiffany had never met Caroline, although they'd spoken several times on the phone. She knew she ought to dislike her for her horrific neglect when Hunter was growing up. But she was so charming and funny and outrageous whenever they spoke, it was difficult to keep one's anger going.

Plus she seemed to be the only person to have come into close contact with Duke McMahon and emerged, or so it seemed, more or less unscathed. Tiffany couldn't help but admire her for that.

'Just give me five minutes to grab a shower and we can eat,' said Hunter. 'The food looks incredible, by the way.'

'Thank you.' She beamed, throwing back her mane of golden hair, delighted to have pleased him. 'I hope it'll taste OK.'

'You certainly taste OK.'

He leaned forward and kissed her softly on the lips, slipping a hand inside her faded pink shirt to caress her left breast. She was barefoot and wearing a worn pair of old black jeans, but nothing could disguise her beautiful, willowy figure.

As far as Hunter was concerned, she was the sexiest woman in the world.

Before he could get any further in unhooking her bra, his mobile rang. It was on top of the fridge in the kitchen, and he dashed in to answer it, with a 'hold that thought' look at Tiffany.

'Hello?'

She knew what he was going to say before he opened his mouth. His smile said it all.

'It's Siena!' He grinned triumphantly, holding the phone in the air like a trophy. 'She's feeling a bit shell-shocked about the news. Wanted to know if we'd like to join her and Randall at the Dodgers game tonight.'

Tiffany thought that she'd rather chew her own arm off than watch baseball with Siena and her lover, but she knew how much it meant to him for her to be supportive.

'Sure, honey.' She forced a smile. 'Sounds great.'

'What's that?' said Hunter, who was back on the line with Siena already. 'Oh, OK, fine. No, I'm sure it's fine. I'll call you back in five.' He hung up.

'What?' said Tiffany, buttoning up her shirt.

'Well, the thing is,' he began apologetically, 'apparently they only have one spare ticket. And as Siena and I haven't seen each other for ages, I was wondering, you know, if you'd mind . . .'

'Oh, I get it.' Tiffany laughed. Siena was so rude, it was actually funny. 'I'm not invited, right? She only wants you.'

'It's nothing personal,' said Hunter. And the tragedy was, he believed it. 'Honestly. She only has one . . .'

'I know, she only has one spare ticket, you said.' She

knew she shouldn't resort to sarcasm, but she couldn't help it. 'And of course, there's no way in the *world* that Randall Stein and Siena McMahon could possibly get hold of another ticket for a baseball game.'

'Please, honey,' he implored her.

He looked so cute and vulnerable with his big, pleading blue eyes, she didn't know how she ever refused him anything. She really did love him so much.

'Fine,' she said at last. 'You go.'

He walked over and picked her up, forgetting about his dirty running clothes, kissing her again and again in gratitude.

'Thank you, baby. I love you. Thank you so much.'

'No problem,' said Tiffany. 'Just don't get your hopes up, Hunter, OK? In my experience, Siena doesn't do anything unless there's something in it for Siena. I don't want you to get hurt.'

'I won't,' he yelled, bounding up the stairs two at a time towards his shower. 'Everything'll be fine, trust me.'

Over at Hancock Park, Tara was thoroughly enjoying herself wandering from room to room with a clipboard, barking orders to three of Pete's gofers while nosily rummaging her way through Minnie's things.

Pete was downstairs, holed up in the drawing room with his lawyers and his wet blanket of a wife. Frankly, she was pleased to get away from him.

Things at the office had been terrible recently, and Tara had been having about as much fun as a germ in a bath of disinfectant. Pete had become even more distant and irritable than usual. Admittedly, McMahon Pictures was in the final stages of production on two hugely costly new movies, which always upped her boss's stress levels. But there were clearly other things on his mind as well.

Although he never spoke about Siena – mentioning her name was strictly *verboten* at work, and more than

440

one of MPW's senior execs had been canned last year for breaking this taboo – Tara could tell that his daughter's relationship with Randall Stein was driving Pete to distraction.

She had managed to glean enough information, largely through the time-honoured method of pressing her ear against Pete's office door, to understand that his problem was not so much with Siena, who by his own admission he no longer thought of as his child, but with Stein. Apparently, Randall had been quite tight with Duke back in the day, and the old man had taken him under his wing as some sort of protégé.

Duke had never recognised his son's formidable business skills, as either a producer or an investor. From what Tara had heard, it was Duke's early admiration for Randall as an up-and-coming producer, over and above his own son, which had started the bad blood between the two of them. The affair with Siena was simply the very bitter icing on an already stale cake of enmity and resentment.

What made matters worse was that Claire had taken to hanging around the office all the time, and she and Pete were constantly fighting. Infuriatingly, her boss's wife was so softly spoken that Tara usually couldn't make out the content of her conversations through the door. But her white, drawn, tight-lipped face as she left spoke volumes, as of course did the foul temper that Pete was plunged into for the rest of the day: Claire had come to plead Siena's case.

Between the spiralling production costs, his marriage problems and his growing obsession with Randall Stein, Pete had been like a bear with a sore head for weeks.

Minnie McMahon suddenly dropping dead yesterday was by far the most interesting thing that had happened at work for ages.

Tara hoped that it might break the deadlock and that, in his grief, her boss might start to lean on her and rely on her again as he had in the old days. He had already put her in charge of organising the mammoth operation of the funeral and memorial service, and this morning had asked her to begin sorting out some of his mother's things.

A whole morning of snooping around the old McMahon mansion! And her own little posse of minions to help her do it! Tara was in seventh heaven.

'You stay in here and start going through the clothes,' she commanded two of the gofers imperiously, leaving them to get started on Minnie's huge private dressing room. 'Alice can come into the study with me to start itemising the jewellery.'

Minnie had long ago taken over what used to be Duke's study, and used the room every afternoon to conduct all her private business, from tracking her investments to managing her formidable charity commitments. It was now painted an airy magnolia yellow, with blue Provençal-style wooden shutters, offset by a large bunch of irises, now peeling slightly at the edges, which Minnie must have bought herself only a few days ago.

Tara, of course, was quite oblivious to her surroundings, and failed to register the poignancy of the wilting flowers, the half-written letter still lying on the desk, or any of the other tiny reminders of a life so suddenly and unexpectedly ended. She made a beeline instead for the jewellery box, which Pete had told her his mother kept in the bottom drawer of her filing cabinet.

'Damn it,' she said, heaving the heavy leather box up on to the desk. It weighed a ton – Minnie must have some pretty incredible pieces locked away in there. 'It's a combination lock.' She rattled the box uselessly, then set it down again on the desk.

'Do you want me to go downstairs and ask Mr McMahon for the code?' said Alice. She was a very pretty, shy little thing who had only been working at MPW for the last six weeks and was still desperately eager to please.

'No, I'll go,' said Tara. She didn't want Pete distracted

by this pretty, blonde child. Hurrying downstairs, anxious to get the code and return to the treasure trove in Minnie's study, she was enjoying the smooth sensation of the polished wooden banisters beneath her fingers when she suddenly stopped in her tracks.

There in the hallway, beneath the shimmering grandeur of the vast chandelier, Pete was standing with his back to her. The lawyers were nowhere to be seen, and he was hugging Claire so tightly that his knees were visibly buckling. She appeared to be literally holding him up.

Neither of them made a sound. But Tara could see Pete's broad back shuddering, rocked with spasms of bottomless grief, as he collapsed into his wife's arms.

She knew how much he had loved and adored his mother.

Suddenly, in that tiny, wizened part of herself that passed for a conscience, she felt a twinge. To her, Minnie's death had been a welcome distraction. To Pete, it was the end of the world.

Quietly, so as not to disturb them, she tiptoed back upstairs to Alice. The jewellery could wait.

Hunter and Siena had agreed to meet outside the stadium at six, so they could be ushered into their VIP front-row seats together a few minutes before the game got under way.

At 6.15, Hunter was still waiting, and his Dodgers baseball cap pulled low over his eyes was doing little to disguise his identity from an ever growing cluster of teenage girls seeking autographs.

While he signed their shirts and programmes and dollar bills good-naturedly, scanning the road for Siena, his heart sank when he noticed a TV crew for the LA 9 News channel advancing towards him. There was no time to escape, so he made the best of it and smiled graciously as Emma Duval, the new and pneumatic face of the seven o'clock news, thrust her prominent double-D assets in his direction.

'Hi, Hunter,' she said, as though they were old friends. She had interviewed him once before for about ten seconds and thought he was a total hottie. 'Got time for a quick word?'

'Very quick,' he said, looking at his watch. 'I'm waiting for someone.'

Classic rookie mistake. He could have bitten his tongue off.

'Oh, really? Who?' Emma tried to smile through a face full of botox. It wasn't a great success.

'No one you know,' said Hunter quickly. 'A friend.'

'Well,' said Emma, with a look that let him know she had a pretty good idea who that 'friend' might be, but wasn't going to say so, 'maybe just a few words then on this morning's news about your stepmother's death.'

'She wasn't really my stepmother,' he began to explain, but Emma had already signalled to her camera and sound guys, and had thrust a microphone under his nose.

'I'm here with Hunter McMahon, who's about to head on in and cheer on those Dodgers!' She punched the air inanely, before switching directly into serious mode. 'Hunter, today's been a sad day for you, with the news of the passing of Minnie McMahon. Can I ask you how you're feeling?'

'I'm, er, I'm fine, really,' he stammered, blinking against the spotlight that some wiseass had decided to shine right into his face. 'I'm sorry for her family, my half-sister Laurie and of course my brother as well. This must be a difficult time for them.'

'Absolutely.' Emma nodded and took a shot at a sympathetic frown, only to be foiled again by her frozen brow. 'Have you spoken to your brother – producer Pete McMahon,' she explained to camera, 'at all since it happened?'

Shit. How had he gotten into this? And where the hell was Siena?

'No,' he said. 'No, unfortunately my brother and I are no longer in contact.'

'Pete McMahon did, in fact, publicly disown you some years ago. That must have been painful.' The woman had all the tact of a stampeding elephant. Hunter didn't respond. 'Will you be attending your stepmother's funeral?' Emma pressed on relentlessly.

'Actually, she wasn't my stepmother. She was my father's wife, but . . .' He looked around despairingly for Siena. If only he had his ticket he could bolt inside the stadium and escape. 'To be honest, I feel a bit awkward discussing it. I'm very sorry for the family, but like I say, we really weren't that close.'

At that moment, as if by magic, every camera swung away from him, and an excited swarm of TV crews, reporters and fans surged towards a black limousine behind him.

Siena and Randall had arrived.

'Siena! Siena! How do you feel?' the voices were yelling. 'Have you spoken to your father, Siena? Will this clear the way for a family reconciliation?'

Hunter watched perplexed as Siena emerged from the back of the car, hand in hand with Randall, and began moving through the crowd towards him, answering questions as she went but pointedly refusing to stop and sign autographs – another of Randall's rules.

If it hadn't been for everybody screaming her name, he wasn't at all sure he would even have recognised her.

First of all, she was dressed head to toe in black, in a fabulously tight-cut skirt and jacket, teamed with sky-high black stilettos and a full-length mink, which she wore open. She looked like a young, sexed-up Elizabeth Taylor in mourning.

Oh my God, he thought, that was it.

She was wearing black in mourning.

For *Minnie*?

It all seemed a bit over the top. Even so, it still made him feel like a heartless jerk for turning up in jeans and a Dodgers T-shirt.

'Hunter, Hunter, darling!' Siena called, fighting her way to his side. Even her voice sounded different, like it was put on. Randall followed behind her in a dark suit, looking, Hunter thought, fat, bald and old. 'How *are* you?'

She held out her arms to him.

He held her, but it didn't feel like her, more like an armful of fur. She kissed him on both cheeks and smiled quite warmly, but something about her still seemed odd. It may have been the trowel-loads of make-up she was wearing, presumably for the cameras' benefit.

'I'm fine, I'm good,' he assured her, wishing he could take her away from the TV crews so they could talk properly. 'I started to think you weren't coming.'

'Oh, are we late?'

Siena looked down at her Cartier watch affectedly, blinding him and everybody else within a twenty-foot radius with a dazzling flash of her diamond-encrusted strap.

Hunter gave her a reproachful look.

'Sorry,' she said, chastened. 'It's really Randall, not me. He's always faffing about what I'm wearing, wanting to change everything at the last minute.' She squeezed Randall's hand affectionately.

'What *are* you wearing?' said Hunter, taking the three tickets silently proffered by Randall, and leading the way through the VIP barriers and into the stadium. 'I mean, you look great. But what's with all the black? This isn't because of Minnie, is it?'

For a split second, he thought he saw her flash him a naughty smile, the kind she used to give as a child when she'd been up to some new mischief or other. He knew Siena didn't care for Minnie any more than he did.

'She *was* Siena's grandmother,' Randall chimed in, as if Hunter needed to have the relationship explained. 'The news of her death came as quite a shock this morning. And of course, it rakes up a lot of old memories, the pain of her parents' abandonment, that sort of thing. Doesn't it, darling? I'm sure you must feel the same.'

Hunter was about to reply that he didn't feel the same, and that he and Siena had each other and didn't need the rest of the family, but was stopped in his tracks when he spun round to find Siena shamelessly hamming it up for the cameras, grasping his arm as if she were about to collapse with grief and holding on to him like a vice as she posed for a final set of pictures.

'Come on, Hunter,' she whispered, between shots. 'You could try to look a little bit unhappy. I mean, we're supposed to be in this together, aren't we, "the poor outcast McMahon children, sticking together through the latest family tragedy"?'

She reached into her jacket pocket and pulled out a handkerchief with which to dry her imaginary tears.

It was only then that the penny dropped.

She was using him.

Using him and Minnie's death as a cheap publicity stunt. Like she needed any more publicity.

He felt revolted. Grabbing her by the arm, he pulled her sharply away from the prying cameras. Randall moved forward to follow them, but Hunter glared at him so viciously that he hung back.

'What the hell do you think you're playing at?' he snarled at Siena.

'What do you mean? Let go of my arm, you're hurting me,' she said indignantly.

'Good,' said Hunter. 'Now you know what it feels like.'

Siena was so stunned she was actually speechless.

'Did he put you up to this? Huh? Was it Stein's idea?'

'What?' She sounded frightened. She had never known Hunter to lose his temper with her like this. 'I don't know what you mean. What idea?'

'This.' He pulled at her coat and her jacket, snatching

447

up her handkerchief in disgust. 'These clothes, these fake tears over Minnie, asking me along as some kind of cheap prop. Turning up late, so I'd already have the cameras on me for your grand entrance with lover boy. Jesus, Siena, what's happened to you? I didn't love Minnie any more than you did, but don't you think she deserves a bit more respect than this?'

'No, I fucking don't.' Siena was shaking. She couldn't bear to have Hunter yelling at her like this, knowing that every word he said was true. She was so ashamed, she wished the ground would open up and swallow her, but some instinct urged her to come out fighting. 'I don't think she deserves any respect at all. She was a mean, vindictive old bitch who never gave a shit about me, or you.'

'That's crap, Siena.' For once, Hunter was tired of listening to her shit. For the first time, he'd seen for himself the machiavellian side to her character that Tiffany was always complaining about. And it was ugly. 'Minnie cared for you. She adored you as a child. Everyone did.'

'Yes, well, then I had to go and disappoint everyone by growing up, didn't I?' said Siena, bitterly.

'Don't kid yourself.' He wasn't about to allow her to wallow in self-pity. 'You haven't grown up. Grown-up people don't pull stunts like this. Even if you don't care about Minnie, I'd have thought you'd at least have a bit of respect for me.'

'I do! I do respect you.' Siena looked stricken.

Randall finally stepped forward and put a possessive arm around her shoulders. 'Lighten up, man, you're upsetting her,' he said.

Hunter waved his arm impatiently as if swatting away a fly and ignored him. This had to be said. 'Well, you have a funny way of showing it, Siena. I haven't seen you for months. It's all I can do to get your goddam PA to return my calls these days.'

'I'm sorry, Hunter,' Randall jumped in. 'But you have

to understand that Siena's life has changed. She has a very busy schedule now, and a lot of people competing for her time. You can't always expect to be at the front of the queue.'

'Fuck off.' Hunter turned on him. 'No one's talking to you.'

Randall merely raised his eyebrow and gave a smug, patronising little smile, as if to indicate that Hunter was too far beneath him to provoke any deeper response.

Hunter turned back to Siena. 'Then, today, you finally do call.' And you know what? I was so happy to hear your voice. How naive and stupid is that?'

'It isn't stupid,' she pleaded. 'Hunter, please. I was happy too. And I *was* upset this morning, truly. Not about Grandma, maybe. But seeing those pictures of my mom, you know, and the old house. I felt terrible. I wanted to see you so badly.'

'I don't believe you,' said Hunter. He was looking at her with utter disdain, and the anger and disappointment in his voice were unmistakable. 'I don't believe a word that comes out of your mouth any more, Siena. And you know what the irony is?' She stared at him in mute misery, clinging on to Randall as if he were a lifeboat. 'When you stepped out of that car just now, I didn't recognise you. But now? Now I can see it.'

'See what?' she asked, trembling.

'My father,' said Hunter, turning on his heel in disgust. 'That's who you are now, Siena. That's what you've become. You're exactly the same as Duke.'

Chapter Forty

Max lay face down on the bright pink mat on the floor, and tried to clear his head as the Korean girl began expertly pummelling his back.

He'd been coming to the same tiny massage parlour in Korea Town ever since he first moved to LA. It was a bit of a schlep to get out there, but at twenty-five dollars for an hour-long pounding of the muscles – none of this farting about with lavender oil and wind chimes – it was well worth the effort.

Since Siena had left him, his weekly visits to Sun Jhee had become something of a life-saver. Even now, months after it all happened, his sleep patterns were still shot, so the massage provided him with a rare opportunity to relax.

'Breathing out,' the girl commanded, as she pressed down on his lower back with her shoulder. Max felt a satisfying click of the spine. 'Sitting badly,' she diagnosed.

'Probably,' he groaned. 'But I'm afraid poor posture is the least of my worries just now.'

The girl continued pummelling. She obviously didn't understand a word he said, which was good, as the last thing Max wanted was to waste an hour on small talk. He needed to think.

He'd been worrying more and more about Siena in the last couple of days.

Not that he didn't think about her every day – the longing, the nightmares and the dull ache of loss were still his constant companions. But ever since Hunter had had that spectacular row with her at the Dodgers, he'd started to look at things in a different, less selfish light.

He knew he'd lost her. For all the love he still felt, Max wasn't in denial. Every magazine, billboard and TV news show screamed the message home to him, zooming in on her happy, confident face, climbing in and out of limos or waving nonchalantly to fans: she was gone.

But recently, he'd found himself looking up from the depths of his own pain and starting to feel genuinely concerned for Siena's welfare.

It was the rift with Hunter which really did it.

Max had known Hunter since they were little boys. He probably knew him better than anyone else on the planet, with the possible exception of Tiffany. But if he hadn't seen it for himself, he would never have believed that Hunter was capable of turning his back on Siena like this. For three weeks now, he hadn't even mentioned her name.

Whatever had happened at that Dodgers game – and Hunter refused to go into details, so Max and Tiffany were both left to piece events together as best they could – it had alienated him from her in a way that Max would once not have believed possible.

He could arrive at only one conclusion: Randall Stein was poison.

At first he had made heroic efforts to talk himself out of this point of view. He was jealous. He wasn't being objective. He couldn't bear for Siena to find happiness with someone else.

But the more he saw the ways in which Stein had changed her – not just the make-up and the clothes, but the whole diva persona – the more he was convinced that he was right.

He could understand her refusal to speak to him after what he'd done. But poor Ines had called him a few weeks ago in tears. Apparently she'd left dozens of messages with Siena's PA and at the house, none of them returned. It was practically the same story with Hunter. Before the Dodgers debacle, she had seen him only twice since her move to Malibu, both times only for a few snatched minutes on the set of her new film.

Her public behaviour, if anything, was even worse.

Sure, Siena had always been spoiled and attention-seeking. He blamed her parents for that. But she had a good heart, and underneath all her histrionics Max knew her as the most wonderful, loyal and loving woman he had ever met.

With Randall, that whole side of her personality seemed to be disappearing.

She had started treating her fans with disdain, refusing to sign autographs, and reducing one poor little kid to tears by driving away from her own premiere for *Daughter* in a blacked-out limo without so much as a wave.

She had given interviews, arrogantly dismissing Dierk Muller, the man who had gone out on a limb and given her her first break, as a 'second tier' director. And every week, new rumours emerged from the set of *1943*, Randall's big-budget epic in which she starred, of her excessive and outlandish demands for a bigger trailer, shorter hours and a twenty-four-hour on-call masseuse.

Max blamed himself for pushing her over the edge. If only he hadn't been such a selfish, jealous, insecure tosser, none of this would be happening.

But that only meant that it was up to him to put things right. If Siena and Hunter weren't speaking, things really had got serious. Somehow, he had to make her wake up to herself, before Stein destroyed her completely.

About ten days later, on an unseasonably hot December day in Malibu, Siena was pacing the drawing room at Randall's estate, having a massive sense of humour failure.

'I don't fucking believe this!' she roared at Melanie, the hapless party organiser who was overseeing the evening's events. 'The theme is supposed to be winter wonderland. What sort of a winter wonderland is it going to be without snow?'

It was three in the afternoon, but Siena was still in the red silk kimono she'd got up in. She'd been awake since seven, manically trying to finalise the details for Randall's annual pre-Christmas party, and she hadn't yet had a moment to get dressed.

Everybody who was anybody in Hollywood – except her parents, of course – would be pulling up to the gates in four hours' time, and now this muppet of a girl seemed to be telling her that the snow machine had packed up with the rose garden only half covered. The whole thing was a fucking nightmare.

'Sometimes, when the temperature outside rises above twenty,' Melanie unwisely started to explain, 'the machine just sort of shuts down.'

Melanie had a long nose, a slight build and a nervous disposition that lent her the air of a terrified vole. She was not good in a crisis.

'Well, you'd better just "sort of" wake it up. Or get hold of another one,' said Siena murderously. 'Because if that garden doesn't look like Antarctica within the next forty-five minutes, I'm going to sue you for more money than even *I* can imagine. Are we clear?'

'Absolutely, Miss McMahon.' The terrified girl began scuttling away. 'We'll get things under control.'

'In forty-five minutes!' Siena yelled after her retreating back.

She sank down on to the huge William Morris print sofa, utterly exhausted.

Bloody Randall.

He'd disappeared off to play golf with Jamie Silfen early this morning, and Siena hadn't seen hide nor hair of him since. She wondered how on earth he'd pulled off a party this size successfully in previous years, before she came along to do all the work. Then she realised he'd probably had a string of live-in girlfriends on past Christmases, all more than willing to play at being Mrs Randall Stein for the evening.

The thought made her feel even more pissed. Why did she put herself through it?

She heaved herself reluctantly to her feet. This was no time to be lying around. It would soon be time to start getting ready, and she still had a million and one things to do before Randall got back.

Wandering through into the dining room, she admired the spectacular, festive table.

Snow machines aside, Melanie had done a fantastic job.

Intertwined stems of holly and ivy hung in looped wreaths around all four walls and across the ceiling, dripping at intervals with either bright red berries or tumbling bunches of white mistletoe. Every kind of Christmas delight littered the table, from pecan pies to chocolate Yule logs and imported Carlsbad plums. And in each corner of the room stood twenty-five-foot Christmas trees, decorated only in silver and white, with delicate, hand-painted wooden angels from Sweden perched on top of each one.

Pete and Claire had never been big on Christmas when she was growing up. Even Duke had focused more on buying her expensive presents than on the decorative side of things.

Siena had always dreamed of a house stuffed with Christmas trees, and a magical winter garden smothered in snow. Now she had one, and she had to admit it looked every bit as lovely as she'd imagined.

For a brief moment she felt a pang of loneliness and wished that Hunter or even Ines could be here to share it with her.

She had trained herself never to think of Max.

Ines especially would have been amazed to see her playing at being the accomplished hostess. She remembered that night back at the beach house, when she'd tried to cook a special meal for Hunter, and she'd called Ines for advice.

The night she'd first slept with Max.

That was only eight months ago. Sometimes it felt like eight years, another lifetime.

She missed Ines terribly, her irreverent sense of humour, her unstoppable energy, but most of all she missed the stupid, giggly, girly chats they used to have about everything and nothing.

Randall had been very firm with her about moving on, though. If she wanted to have a new image, a new life, then she had to leave her old crowd behind. Particularly anyone still associated with modelling.

'The last thing you want is to always be thought of as an ex-model,' he'd told her. 'If you want to play in the big league, you have to make sacrifices. There can be no looking back. Think about your grandfather. How many friends from the old days did you see him hanging around with?'

Apart from Seamus, Siena couldn't remember Duke 'hanging around' with anyone, at least not with anyone he called a friend, from the old days or otherwise. For the first time ever, she wondered whether Grandpa might have been a bit lonely. The possibility disturbed her more than she cared to admit.

She made a quick pit stop out in the rose garden to check on the lighting, and had a brief word with the official photographer, before disappearing upstairs to have a much needed soak in the bath and begin her grand transformation.

Randall didn't get home until six, and when he did, he disappeared straight into his study to make a couple of business calls, much to Siena's fury. By the time he finally nipped upstairs to change, there was less than half an hour until the guests were due to arrive.

Siena couldn't remember when she had last felt so exhausted. Only nervous energy, and the ceaseless churning of her stomach at the prospect of having to entertain every big-name producer and director in

Hollywood, with the exception of her father, kept her eyes from closing.

Mercifully, a new fake snow machine had been unearthed, the ice sculptures and vodka fountain had finally been delivered, and the complicated outdoor lighting system had miraculously decided to work, after four earlier failed attempts.

'The house looks great,' said Randall, kissing the back of her neck as she sat at her dressing table.

She was wearing a midnight-blue silk halter-neck dress, full length but slashed to the thigh, with a sky-high pair of open-toed Manolos in the same blue, laced with criss-crossed ribbon up her calves. She wore her hair up in a loose chignon, with occasional stray curls escaping to frame her face.

As a rule, Siena was not a huge make-up fan. In a town full of surgically enhanced faces and harsh, over-tanned, over-made-up skin, she preferred to let her own natural beauty help her stand out from the crowd.

Tonight, though, she had gone for very dark, dramatic eyes, using a perfectly blended mixture of silver, grey and black shadow, with intensely mascaraed lashes that seemed to go on and on for ever.

'I know the house looks great,' she said ungraciously, pouting at herself in the mirror and applying a second coat of lip gloss. 'I've been working on it flat out since seven this morning, with no help from you. So how *was* golf?'

'Good,' said Randall, not remotely apologetic. He put one warm hand on the back of Siena's neck, then moved it round to caress her smooth creamy chest and the top of her ample cleavage. 'You look very sexy,' he whispered gruffly. 'You don't think it's too much, though? I want these guys to take you seriously. You'll be meeting some very influential people tonight.'

'For Christ's sake, Randall.' She brushed off his hand and stood up, straightening the line of the dress around her ass. She hated it when he patronised her. 'I am well aware of who's coming tonight, and I'm more than capable of handling myself, thank you. Anyway' – she admired her reflection in the bedroom mirror – 'I think I look great.'

'Hmmmm.' He frowned and slipped his hand around her waist, pulling her very close to him. She could feel the swell of his paunch just below her breasts and his erection pressing against her belly. She tried to pull back.

'Shit, don't muss me up, honey, please. This dress cost sixteen thousand dollars and you haven't even showered.'

Randall looked at her coldly. Despite his hard-on, he was obviously not thinking about screwing her. Siena stared up at his big Roman nose and tiny, impenetrable eyes. Involuntarily, she shivered.

'Just remember,' he said, 'these people have come here tonight because of me, not you.'

Good God, was he jealous? Scared that she might be the centre of attention this evening?

It seemed so unlike him. Randall was never insecure.

'I know that, darling,' she said meekly, anxious not to provoke his temper. 'But you want me to look beautiful for them, don't you?'

His brow knitted instantly into a frown. 'No.' He drew her even closer to him. 'Not for them. For me. I want you to look beautiful for me.'

Before Siena had a chance to move, he plunged his right hand between her legs, through the slit in her dress, pulled her panties aside and thrust three fingers roughly up inside her. She gasped in shock. She was so unprepared, it actually hurt.

He lowered his face to within millimetres of hers, still keeping his hand inside her. 'I made you what you are now, Siena,' he whispered ominously. She could feel his warm breath on her skin, making her hairs stand on end. 'I gave you all this, and I was happy to do it. But don't cross me, sweetheart. Remember: I can take it all away. Like *that*.'

He jabbed deeper inside her, for emphasis.

Then, just as suddenly, he let her go and walked through into the bathroom as if nothing had happened, leaving her shell-shocked and trembling in his wake.

Two hours later and the party was in full, riotous swing.

The A-list had turned out in force, and in even greater number than in previous years. Everyone from the Spielbergs to the Spellings was there, milling around, enjoying the latest Hollywood gossip, washed down with Randall's vintage champagne. Even Mel Gibson, Siena's childhood heart-throb, put in a brief, early appearance, much to her surprise and delight.

In quiet corners all round the estate, diets and discretion were both being thrown to the wind. Guests tucked into huge slices of brandy-soaked Yule log and held hushed conversations about their host and his beautiful young companion.

How long would the relationship last? Did Siena really have the talent to live up to Randall's hype? And did anybody know what Pete McMahon made of his daughter shacking up with a long-term business rival, who also happened to be four years older than Pete himself?

'Do you know, he hasn't seen Siena *once* since she moved out here?' an overexcited young CAA agent was whispering to his boss's enthralled wife.

'I know. Incredible,' she agreed, nodding through a mouthful of pecan pie. 'It's the mother that I can't understand, though. As a mother myself, I don't understand how anyone could just walk away from their children like that. From their *only* child.'

'Pete McMahon's lost the plot,' chipped in her husband, returning from the bar with more champagne. 'He's a virtual recluse nowadays, Claire too. I'm not surprised they haven't seen Siena. As far as I can tell, they haven't seen anybody in the last eighteen months.'

'Look at Stein, though,' said the young man. 'He's besotted.'

The three of them looked over at Randall, who was nodding to the head of merchandising at Paramount and his bimbo wife, pretending to be avidly listening to their conversation, while actually sneaking glances across the room at Siena.

If she was troubled by their little fracas in the bedroom earlier, she didn't show it now. She looked utterly radiant, confident and relaxed, throwing her head back and laughing at some comment of Jamie Silfen's.

Every straight man in the room wanted her, thought Randall with pride. He felt his hard-on reviving and with some effort tore his thoughts back to Mr Paramount and the subject of the Asian distribution rights to *Ocean Drive*.

Siena, meanwhile, was enjoying herself enormously with Silfen.

'I couldn't believe it when I saw you in the front row at the McQueen Show.' She laughingly reminded the great casting agent of their first non-encounter. 'What on earth were you doing there?'

'I like fashion, actually,' Jamie replied with a straight face. 'I follow the trends.'

Siena looked at his portly form squeezed into an ill-fitting tweed suit, his bald head popping out at the top like a giant billiard ball, and found this statement rather hard to believe. If it had been anyone else, she would have laughed out loud, but Jamie was a close associate of Randall's and far too important a person for her to accidentally insult.

'Really?' she said, trying her best to sound convinced.

'Of course not really!' He roared with laughter. 'You didn't think I picked up this little number from Alexander McQueen, did you?' He launched himself into a ridiculous twirl, wiggling his fat bottom in the tight tweed in Siena's direction like Tweedledee. She giggled. 'That's better,' said Jamie. 'I like you better when you laugh. They should have you smiling more in pictures.'

'I know,' said Siena, forgetting for a moment Randall's strict instructions never to talk about modelling with movie people, 'but photographers almost never want the models to smile. We have to look permanently aloof and pissed.'

She struck a regal pose, and now it was Jamie's turn to laugh.

'I enjoyed *The Prodigal Daughter*,' he said, changing the subject suddenly for no apparent reason. 'You were good.'

'Thank you,' said Siena, smiling modestly. She always said she'd have Jamie Silfen eating out of the palm of her hand one day. 'I'm so glad you liked it.'

'Muller was fucking fantastic, though, directing,' Jamie went on. 'You shouldn't have slagged him off in that interview.'

Siena blushed. She'd been feeling guilty about her 'second tier' remark for some time. She knew she owed Dierk a hell of a lot.

'That sort of thing won't help, you know. Getting ahead,' said Silfen. He was deadly serious all of a sudden. 'You might not know it, but loyalty goes a long way in this town. Farther than you'd think.'

'I know,' said Siena humbly, 'you're right. It's just that Randall felt . . .'

'Listen, honey,' Jamie interrupted her, putting a fat, clammy hand on her arm. 'Randall's a brilliant producer. He's made a lot of good decisions, and a lot of money, and all credit to the guy. But trust me, he ain't no life coach. Don't let anyone go putting words in your mouth, Siena. Otherwise who the hell are you anyway?'

She was silently digesting this advice when the whole room turned at the sound of an almighty crash coming from the entrance hall. The crash was followed by raised male voices, one of which Siena thought to her horror she recognised.

'Fuck off! Get the fuck out of my way before I hurt you.'

The clipped English accent was unmistakable.

Suddenly two of Randall's so-called security guys came flying backwards into the room, one after another, smashing a priceless Venetian vase in the process. They were followed by the one person she had hoped she would never come face to face with again.

'Oh my God,' she whispered, barely audibly.

'Someone you know?' asked Silfen.

But Siena just stood and stared at Max in complete horror.

'Stein!' he yelled. 'I want to talk to you. Where are you?'

She wondered for a moment whether he was drunk, but his voice seemed steady, and there was no hint of a stagger as he moved among the stunned guests, like the one moving actor weaving his way through a freeze-frame.

Randall had started to step forward, but as he did so Max caught sight of Siena, staring at him from across the room.

It was the first time he'd seen her since that awful day at the airfield, and he felt afterwards that his heart had literally stopped beating in that instant. She had never looked more beautiful, like some sort of other-worldly dryad in her column of clinging blue silk. Her eyes looked different – stronger, more sultry – but otherwise she looked exactly as she did in his dreams, except that the reality was even more breathtaking.

The miracle wasn't that he'd lost her, thought Max. It was that he'd ever had her in the first place.

Siena gazed back at him dumbstruck. In the months since she'd left, she had trained her mind, with ruthless self-discipline, to banish all thoughts of Max, both good and bad, from her consciousness. She had made a decision, the night she flew to Vegas, never, ever to make the mistake of laying herself open again. She had shut down her heart, with Randall's help, almost completely.

But seeing him now, so lovely, so big, so out of place in his old jeans and Cambridge sweatshirt, standing right there in front of her, she felt all her good work unravelling like a ball of string. She was, momentarily, helpless.

'Siena, I'm sorry,' he began, his voice dry with nerves. 'I'm sorry to burst in on your evening like this. But you won't take my calls – I totally understand that,' he added quickly, before she could release a tirade. 'And this place is always shut up like Fort Knox. This was the only night I had any chance of getting past security, with so many people coming and going. And I had to see you.'

Randall glared at the two security men, who were still reeling from Max's earlier left hook – what the hell was he paying them for? – and made his way slowly to Siena's side.

'I hid in the back of a catering van,' Max explained unnecessarily. He knew he should stop talking, but he felt a need to fill the deafening silence.

The carollers had finally got the message and realised something was up, lamely spluttering to a halt halfway through their rendition of 'Once in Royal David's City', and the rest of the guests maintained a rapt hush, watching him.

Finally, after what seemed like an age, Siena helped him out by speaking, although it was hardly the response he'd been hoping for.

'What do you want, Max? As you can see, I'm busy.' Her voice was as cold as ice.

'I want to take you home,' he said, pushing his hair out of his face and wiping the sweat from his brow. He was still ten feet away from her at least, but didn't want to risk moving any nearer in case she bolted, or Randall took a pop at him before he'd said what he came here to say.

'He's seriously cute, isn't he?' whispered the daughter of a famous director to her girlfriend. 'Who in their right mind would leave *that* for Randall Stein?'

Max cleared his throat and continued. 'Not home to me, though. I know what I did was unforgivable. I know there's no way back for us.'

'Good,' said Siena.

'But to Hunter. He loves you, Siena, and he misses you, even if he is too proud to show it.'

'Are you finished?' she asked.

'No. Not yet.' Max looked her in the eye. Siena was terrified he would bore straight through into her soul and see how frightened and confused she was behind the ice-maiden façade. She willed him to hurry up and get this over with before she cracked.

'I'm worried about you,' he said. 'Everybody is. You've changed, Siena, and not for the better. Stein is poison. He's no good for you. Whether you go back to the beach house or not, you have to get away from him. Please. Not for me, but for yourself. He's fucking evil.'

At this, Randall broke the spell and clapped his hands, signalling to the newly arrived security reinforcements who'd been waiting by the door to make a move on Max.

'No!' said Siena, so loudly and firmly that the goons obeyed her and hung back for a moment. 'I can deal with this, Randall.'

'I don't think so,' he said and, grabbing her quite roughly by the arm, nodded to the men to advance. He had already allowed this little scene to go on too long, and he wasn't about to be overruled in his own house by Siena, or anyone else. It was time to assert a little authority.

'Don't you touch her!'

Before security could lay a finger on him, Max had launched himself across the room at Randall, bringing the older man crashing to the ground in a full-bodied rugby tackle. They came down with such an almighty thud that a huge wreath of holly and ivy, festooned with red berries, swung down from the ceiling and landed right on top of them.

Max pulled back his fist to slam it into Randall's face, but his arm was grabbed from behind and twisted agonisingly behind his back. Before he knew it he was on his feet, tightly restrained by two of the heavier heavies.

He needn't have bothered with the punch anyway. Randall was already out cold.

'See what I mean?' he said passionately to Siena. He was held so firmly that he couldn't even begin to struggle. 'See how he grabbed you like that? He's an arsehole, Siena. He's violent.'

'*He's* violent?' She was so shaken up by what had just happened, she reverted to the safest reaction she knew: white rage. 'Who the fuck do you think you are, Max?' she hissed at him. 'You come in here, shouting the odds, telling me how I've changed, and how Randall's such a terrible influence. Where the hell do you get off?'

Max opened his mouth to speak, but Siena was on a roll.

'You've got a damn nerve, trying to take the moral high ground with me. If memory serves, I think you were the one running around in LA with your dick in every cheap fucking waitress who'd give you the time of day. So don't you *dare* come storming in here and start telling me how to live my life.'

'For God's sake, Siena.' He cried out in pain as the security men pulled so tightly on his shoulder he thought it might be dislocating. 'Can't you see I'm trying to help you? I *know* it's all my fault. I *know* I can never make it up to you. But can't you see what this bastard's doing to you?'

'No, Max,' she said flatly. 'I can't. Other than take me in, and look after me. Randall's a very generous man. And as for me, you know what? You're right, I have changed. I've learned to look out for number one. I've learned that you can't trust anyone except yourself. But it wasn't Randall who taught me that, Max. It was you.'

Between the pain in his shoulder and the pain in his

heart, Max was close to tears. He couldn't bear to have to leave her like this. What if he never saw her again?

'I love you,' he said, desperately.

A couple of romantic souls across the room gave an audible sigh.

'That's your problem,' said Siena. 'Unfortunately, I know what your love is, Max. And it isn't worth the paper it's written on. So let me make myself absolutely clear: I never, ever want to see you again.'

He looked at her pleadingly but she turned away, raising her hand imperiously to the security guys.

'Get him out of here.'

In bed later that evening, she lay crying softly to herself, trying not to wake a sleeping Randall.

She'd expected him to be absolutely furious about what had happened, particularly after Max had knocked him out like that. But in fact, almost as soon as he'd come round, he'd been remarkably cheerful, insisting on carrying on until the end of the party and even making jokes about Max's outburst.

'I'm so sorry,' Siena had told him, once the last of the guests had gone. 'You must blame me for all this. The whole party was ruined.'

'Oh, I don't know about that,' said Randall brightly. 'You know Hollywood. People love a good drama.'

Siena looked at him, astonished. 'You mean you're really not mad?'

Randall smiled and took her hand, leading her up to bed.

'No, I'm not mad,' he said. 'Because you know what I realised tonight? He's just a kid. He's a dumb kid, he's nobody.' Siena stared down at the ground and bit her lip. 'He's going to go to sleep tonight in a borrowed room he can't even pay for, in some shitty little house on the beach. And I go to sleep here.' He waved vaguely at the opulence around them. 'With you.'

He stopped to pull Siena towards him and kissed her

465

full on the mouth. His breath smelt of stale champagne, but she tried to appear enthusiastic. She supposed that was the least she owed him after everything that had happened tonight.

Mercifully, once they got into bed he had fallen straight to sleep. She really couldn't have faced sex now. She just wanted to be alone with her thoughts.

Unfortunately those thoughts were not remotely comforting.

For all her bravado, tonight's events had shown her one thing beyond a shadow of a doubt.

She still loved Max.

She wasn't sure whether she could ever bring herself to forgive him for betraying her the way he had. But love him she did.

And yet now, even more than before, she knew that there could be no way back, love or no love. She had told him she never wanted to see him again. He had reached out to her and she had rejected him, brutally and publicly.

One thing Max had never been lacking in was pride. Siena knew him well enough to know that he wouldn't be back for more.

Tears started to flow as she thought back over what felt like a lifetime of lost love: first Grandpa, then Hunter, then her parents. For a brief while there, after she'd found Hunter again, and then Max, she almost felt as if all the wrongs of her childhood had been made right. And for a little while, life had been absolutely perfect.

But now Max and Hunter were both gone. Even Ines had been discarded, in the same way that Siena had discarded Marsha, Patrick and Janey Cash – basically anyone who had ever truly cared about her.

It was as if she couldn't help herself. She had to hit back first, make sure that she abandoned people before they abandoned her.

Hunter was right.

She was like Grandpa Duke.

And tonight, in the vast, opulent emptiness of Randall's bed, that realisation made her want to sob her heart out.

PART THREE

Max ran down the hill laughing, trying to keep his footing and avoid slipping on the cow pats as he hurtled down towards the stream. Behind him, three screaming children, led by a very determined-looking Charlie, were hot on his trail, brandishing their new pump-action water pistols.

'You'll never catch me alive!' Max yelled over his shoulder, promptly tripping over an unexpected mound of thistle and landing ignominiously, not to mention painfully, on his arse.

The Arkell posse were on top of him in seconds, spraying him mercilessly with water from point-blank range until his entire T-shirt was soaked through.

'Take *that*, Uncle Max,' said Madeleine triumphantly, emptying the last drops from her weapon down the back of his neck.

He flung his arms open wide and lay back on the grass in exhaustion and defeat.

'You win, Maddie.' He smiled at his little niece, and handed over a third pound coin.

The two boys were already racing back up the hill with their own victory spoils, and Maddie scampered off to join them.

Max lay back and enjoyed the warmth of the sun on his face.

It was late June, six months almost to the day since he had stormed into Randall Stein's Malibu mansion, and seen Siena for the last time. Within a week after that fiasco, he had packed up his very paltry possessions, sold his beloved Honda for scrap, said his goodbyes to Hunter and moved back to Batcombe.

He had finished shooting the two shorts for the

famous Hollywood actor/would-be producer, so there was no business reason for him to stay on in LA. And living in the same town, even the same country, as Siena was killing him inside.

Hunter had tried to persuade him to stay, of course. But in the end, Max felt his old friend understood his reasons for going.

'Life has changed for all of us,' he'd said to Hunter on the particularly depressing journey out to the airport. 'I need to get over her, get away from all the bad memories and try and make something of myself. And you and Tiffany need some time to be together as well, without me getting under your feet the whole time.'

Hunter had protested that he never got under their feet, that they were both happy to have him, for ever if he wanted. But deep down he knew Max was right. It was time for a change, for all of them.

As soon as he landed at Heathrow, Max had found his spirits lifting slightly. He felt even better when he saw not just Henry but the whole family, hopping up and down with excitement in arrivals, waiting to meet him.

Bertie and Maddie were holding up a homemade cardboard banner with 'Welcum Home Unkel Max' written in multi-coloured felt tip. Charlie, who considered himself too old for such childish activities, merely waved in what he hoped his favourite uncle would recognise as a rather grown-up manner.

Max felt quite choked when Henry stepped forward to help him with his luggage.

'Hello, little brother.' He smiled, patting him warmly on the back. 'Bloody good to see you.'

Henry was shocked by how thin Max looked. He had read the press coverage of his brother's heroic but doomed attempt to rescue Siena. The gossip rags, force-fed by Randall's PR machine, had all crucified him for it, made him out to be some sort of jealous, possessed monster. Even Muffy refused to read the *Enquirer* any more, after seeing the stuff they'd written about poor

Max. It wasn't as if he was even famous or courted the publicity.

At first, Max's plan had been to stay for Christmas and the New Year celebrations with Henry, then look around for a place of his own.

He hadn't, in fact, come home solely to escape his demons, or to take solace at Batcombe. There were career reasons as well.

He had belatedly decided to take up the offer from his friend, the young Oxford playwright, to direct his latest work in Stratford. The play was to open in April and run throughout the summer, but rehearsals would start in January.

The money was terrible, but Max loved the dark weirdness of the script, and he was in no urgent need for cash, having just been paid well over the odds for his last two short films. The original plan had been for him to rent a little cottage close to the theatre for six months, popping back to Batcombe for weekends to see Henry and the family. But it hadn't worked out like that.

Understandably, he'd been so caught up in the horrors of his own life back in LA that he hadn't grasped the full extent of Henry's debt problems until he got back home.

Having turned down a huge offer from Gary Ellis last year, his brother had started selling off assets at a rate of knots – everything from artwork and furniture to his cherished vintage MG, a twenty-first birthday present from their mother – just to keep up on the interest payments to the bank. The children had been pulled out of their prep schools and sent to the local village primary, and Muffy had even started taking in commissions as a portrait photographer.

'The fact is,' Henry had told Max despairingly over a whisky one night, soon after he arrived, 'I was a fool not to take up Ellis's offer when I had the chance. He's developing across the valley now, in Swanbrook.'

'You don't mean that, surely,' said Max. 'You couldn't

just sell up. Let the place be turned into some Mickey Mouse golf course.'

'We're going to lose the farm anyway, Max.' Henry sounded almost resigned to his fate. He looked older and terribly tired. Over the past six months, he and Muffy had racked their brains day and night trying to come up with something, anything, that would enable them to keep the place going, but it was hopeless. None of their efforts had amounted to more than a drop in the ocean of Henry's debts. The irony was that the farm itself was doing well, with their diversification out of dairy finally starting to pay dividends. But that brought in a steady trickle of income, when what they needed was a tidal wave of cash.

'Barring all my numbers coming up on Saturday's rollover,' Henry sighed, 'I truly don't see a way round it. The only question now is when. How long can we keep the wolf from the door?'

The moment he understood the seriousness of Henry and Muffy's problems, Max had decided to stay. He might not be able to contribute much financially – his director's wages at the theatre barely amounted to a weekly Chinese takeaway – but at least he could help out with the children, and do his best to keep the family's spirits up. Besides, he thought, family life might be just the thing to distract him from his heartbreak.

Taking off his sodden T-shirt and wiping the worst of the cow dung off his tennis shoes with a handful of long grass, he made his way back across the fields towards the house.

It was Sunday, the first full day he'd had off from the theatre in over three weeks.

His play, *Dark Hearts*, had been running for almost three months now, and had won Max some of the best reviews of his career. They were playing nightly to packed houses, which was fantastic, but it did mean he had precious little time to himself to enjoy what was shaping up to be a record-breakingly hot summer.

Walking up the hill, he was struck yet again by the magical view before him. The golden, rose-covered stone of Manor Farm seemed to glow in the late afternoon light, beautiful, like some vision of a lost England.

He couldn't imagine how Henry was going to cope if they did lose it. Despite everything his brother had told him, Max was able to think of the loss of the farm only in terms of an 'if'. He still hoped against hope that it wouldn't come to that, and that some solution would eventually present itself, before it was too late.

Kicking off his dirty shoes outside the kitchen door, he stepped into the pantry wearing only his grass-stained shorts. He had just started to remove them, to throw them into the washing machine along with his sodden T-shirt, when he was startled by a young, female voice behind him.

'Please, monsieur,' said the girl, who couldn't have been much over twenty, in a heavy French accent. 'Don't go any farther. I am 'ere.'

'Jesus Christ,' said Max, spinning round and pulling up his shorts faster than a priest caught trousers down with a choirboy. 'Where the hell did you come from?'

'Toulouse,' said the girl.

They could be damn literal, the French, thought Max. It was hard to tell which of them was blushing more fiercely.

'Yes, OK, I know, Toulouse,' he said, evidently flustered. 'I mean, I don't actually *know* Toulouse. That is, I didn't know you *came* from Toulouse. My point is . . .' He cleared his throat and tried again. 'What I meant was . . .'

'Who on earth are you?' Muffy succinctly finished his question for him. She had just walked into the kitchen carrying a huge pile of children's laundry, looking confused to find a strange woman hovering by the door of her pantry. 'And Max, what on earth are you doing with nearly no clothes on?'

'Washing?' Max gestured lamely towards the open machine.

'Oh. Well, never mind that,' Muffy said, dropping her mountainous load on the kitchen table and turning to smile at the French girl, a pretty, freckled creature with a sleek auburn bob, who seemed to be carrying a suitcase. 'I'm sorry, I must have sounded terribly rude just now. I was just a little surprised to find you standing in my kitchen. Have we met? I'm Muffy Arkell.'

She extended a clean, slightly calloused hand.

'Delighted to meet you, Meesees Arkell,' said the girl, in her stilted, formal English, dropping the suitcase and pumping Muffy's hand enthusiastically. 'I am Frédérique.'

A few long seconds of awkward silence followed this pronouncement. The girl was evidently not about to offer up any further information. She apparently thought that her first name was enough to clear up the mystery of her identity, and presence in the kitchen, entirely.

'I'm sorry, Frédérique who?' said Max eventually.

But before the girl had a chance to answer, Muffy had let out a wail, clapping her hands over her mouth in horror.

'Oh my goodness. Frédérique,' she whispered. 'I thought I cancelled with the agency months ago. It must have slipped my mind. Henry's going to go spare.'

'Have I missed something?' said Max. 'Do you two know each other?'

'Not exactly,' said Muffy. 'Frédérique was going to be our summer au pair.' She looked at the poor girl apologetically. 'But I'm afraid we can't possibly afford you now.'

Once Max had swapped his shorts for a crumpled old pair of Henry's trousers from on top of the tumble-dryer and made both the women a cup of tea, things were fairly swiftly sorted out, to everyone's mutual relief.

Having just come all the way from France, not to mention planned her whole summer, Frédérique was to stay. Max would pay her wages, which were next to nothing anyway, and the extra help with the children would allow Muffy more time to work on her photography commissions.

By the time Henry got home from yet another depressing meeting with his farm manager, Frédérique had already had a bath and unpacked, and was happily playing a game of Monopoly with the children round the kitchen table while Muffy peeled the potatoes for supper.

'Hello, darling,' she said, without looking up. 'How did it go? This is Frédérique, by the way, our new au pair.'

'Hello, Frédérique,' said Henry, waving at her absently and apparently completely unfazed by her arrival. 'Or should I say, bonjour.'

'Daddy, your French accent's terrible,' said Charlie. 'Frédérique speaks English anyway, don't you, Freddie?'

'We're allowed to call her Freddie,' Bertie explained to his father. 'She likes it.'

Frédérique, it seemed, was already a hit.

'Bonjour, Monsieur Arkell,' she said shyly, standing up to shake Henry's hand. 'I am very 'appy to be working weeth you and all the family. I 'ope we will 'ave a lot of fun togethair.'

'I hope so too, Freddie,' said Henry, slipping his hands round his wife's waist from behind and nuzzling her neck affectionately. 'We've been running a bit low on fun around here lately, I'm afraid. Eh, Muff?'

'Can she stay with us for longer than the summer, Dad?' asked Bertie, who seemed to be particularly smitten with his new playmate.

'Can you stay for ever?' Maddie added her voice to the chorus.

Frédérique laughed. 'Not for ever, no. Anyway, you wait and see. You might be fed up weeth me by tomorrow.'

'We won't,' said Maddie earnestly. 'Do you have a husband? Or a boyfriend?'

'Maddie!' chided her mother, throwing a mountain of peeled potatoes into an industrial-sized saucepan and dropping it with a clatter on to the hot ring of the Aga. 'Leave poor Frédérique alone. That's none of your business.'

'It's OK,' said Freddie. 'No, Madeleine, I don't 'ave a boyfriend. I deed 'ave one, but we broke up.'

'Good.' Maddie grinned. 'Then you can marry my Uncle Max. *He* used to have a girlfriend. But then *they* broke up as well. Grown-ups are always doing that,' she added philosophically.

'Doing what?' said Max, who had wandered in from the kitchen garden to refill his empty Pimms glass. 'Oh, hello, Henry. How'd it go?'

'Shit,' said Henry grimly. 'Things could be looking up for you, though. Your niece here has just been trying to fix you up with our delightful new au pair.'

'See,' said Maddie triumphantly. 'He's very handsome.'

Freddie blushed furiously.

'Apparently the two of you are already altar bound.'

'Oh, Henry, stop teasing them,' said Muffy, who could sense that Max was also feeling awkward, despite his forced smile. 'Give Max another drink, and then why don't you both bugger off out of my kitchen. I'm trying to make supper and it's like Piccadilly bloody Circus in here.'

Out in the kitchen garden, the two brothers sat on the ancient lichened bench sipping their drinks and watching the heavy, blood-red sun beginning to set.

'Did it really go badly today? With Richard?' Max asked.

Richard was Henry's farm manager, really just the chief farm hand, but with responsibility for the other four lads that Henry employed.

He nodded. 'Very. I'm going to have to lay off at least two of them before the end of the summer. If it weren't for the subsidies, I doubt we'd be breaking even at all. I tell you, it's bloody impossible to make a living from farming these days. Unless you're French, of course. Like your beautiful bride to be.'

'Oh, lay off it, would you,' said Max. 'She's hardly my type.'

Henry raised a sceptical eyebrow. 'I don't know. She's very attractive. It wasn't so long ago I remember you saying the same thing to me about Siena. *She* wasn't your type either. "A match made in hell", I believe you once said.'

'Yes, well, that *was* a long time ago,' said Max, with more anger than he'd intended. Seeing his brother's look of surprise, he relented. 'Look, sorry. But d'you mind if we don't talk about Siena?'

'Sure.' Henry could take a hint. He picked a sprig of mint out of his glass and began chewing it thoughtfully. 'Let's talk about your play. That's about the only thing that's going well in this family at the moment.'

Max, who was still thinking about Siena, didn't immediately respond.

'It *is* still going well, isn't it?' asked Henry.

'Oh, yes,' said Max, brightening suddenly. 'We're going great guns. Angus, the guy who wrote it, had a great interview in the *Sunday Times* last week, which means even more exposure for *Dark Hearts*. Not that we need it. We're sold out till September.'

'That's wonderful, Max,' said Henry sincerely.

'As a matter of fact, I have a couple of producers from New York coming to see us in two weeks' time,' Max went on. 'It's the first time that I've actually owned a stake in any of the plays I've done, so it's much more exciting for me.'

'Good man,' said Henry approvingly. 'I've always said you should get some equity in your own work. What's your percentage?'

'Sixty to Angus, forty to me. But I wouldn't get carried away. Chances are they won't go for it – it's a bit bleak for your mainstream theatre audience. Still, it's quite something that they've agreed to come at all. I mean, this is Stratford we're talking about, not the West End.'

'Well, here's to you!' Henry clunked his Pimms glass against Max's and drained what was left of its contents. 'May Lady Luck smile on one of us, at least, for many moons to come.'

Their peace was shattered moments later by an overexcited Charlie.

'Dad! Uncle Max! Come quick,' he called out through the pantry window. '*Sea Rescue*'s gonna start in one minute.'

Max loved the fact that the kids were all such avid fans of Tiffany's show. Charlie, in particular, had a hideous crush on her and was constantly on at his uncle to invite her, without Hunter if possible, to Manor Farm.

'Coming!' Henry shouted back deafeningly. 'Up you get then, Uncle Max,' he joshed his brother. 'It wouldn't do to miss the bit before the music on *Sea Rescue*.'

'Oh, absolutely not,' said Max, following him inside. 'I wouldn't miss it for the world.'

Chapter Forty-two

Randall Stein looked down at the figures in front of him and frowned.

'Nine million?' he said incredulously to the voice on the other end of the phone. 'You didn't think running nine million over budget was something I might, possibly, have been concerned about?'

He reached into his desk drawer and pulled out a bottle of antacid tablets, popping one into his mouth and chewing it grimly while the voice on the speakerphone struggled in vain to explain itself.

Randall was having a bad week.

Production costs on *1943*, his much-hyped Second World War epic in which Siena was starring opposite Jason Reed, Hollywood's latest vaunted successor to Brad Pitt, were spiralling out of control.

The movie had been plagued by bad luck from the start. Freak storms had meant a five-week delay on all the filming on location in Japan at Christmas, which had cost him an absolute fortune. Once they got back to Universal, where the bulk of the film was being made, a general strike by SAG, the powerful actors' union, meant it was another month until they could make any progress, and even then Randall found himself embroiled in distracting lawsuits with more than one of his more minor cast members over the terms of their pre-strike contracts.

Then, having finally got some momentum behind the project in May, Siena and Jason had started giving him headaches.

At first he'd been happy to discover that Siena couldn't stand the sight of her new, Adonis-like co-star. But as the weeks wore on, the director had complained to him repeatedly about the intolerable strains on-set.

Jason, as the bigger, more established star, had taken to lording it over Siena, goading her over everything from her inferior trailer to her relationship with Randall, strongly implying that she had won her part on the casting couch rather than on her own merits.

Siena, stung by this particular criticism because she knew it was true, and desperate to prove herself as a serious actress, met all Jason's taunts with an ever more hysterical torrent of rage. More than once she had stormed off the set screaming, refusing to come back to work until Reed agreed to apologise to her.

Which, of course, he never did.

'She's a great little actress,' the director had told Randall. 'Perfect as Peggy. Always got her scenes down a hundred and ten per cent. But I can't direct her if she isn't there.'

Back home, Randall had torn a strip off her.

'He started it,' protested Siena, after a particularly nasty torrent of abuse. 'Jason's the one you should be screaming at, not me.'

'I don't give a fuck who started it, you dumb bitch.' Randall could be incredibly vindictive when it came to business, totally loveless towards her in his tone, his language, everything. Siena had grown used to it, but it still hurt. 'Jason Reed is a star. No matter how bad it is, people are gonna come and watch this movie because of him. So he's an asshole. So what? You're a professional, Siena. Deal with it.'

'He keeps telling everyone I only got the part because I'm sleeping with you,' she said indignantly.

To her fury, Randall smiled.

'He's right,' he said, adding nastily, 'And if you want to keep sleeping with me – and keep your part – you'd better get your act together. Now.'

Things on-set had improved slightly since then, but the tense atmosphere was still slowing things down.

And now some bozo of an accountant was calling him up to tell him that the problems with the strike had cost 'around' nine million dollars, a figure they'd had since March apparently but only decided to share with Randall today.

'Listen, Bill,' he said, making an effort to keep calm, 'I'm not interested in estimates. If it *is* nine, and quite frankly I find that figure hard to believe, then I want to see that broken down and itemised down to the last fucking quarter. Is that clear?'

The voice on the phone responded with a suitably grovelling affirmative, and Randall hung up and leaned back in his chair, trying to breathe deeply and relax as his therapist had told him to do.

It wasn't really working. But he knew what would.

He pressed the little black button that connected him with his camp but ruthlessly efficient assistant next door. 'Keith.'

'Yes, Mr Stein?'

'Call Becca Williams for me, would you. Tell her I need a girl. Right away.'

The assistant didn't miss a beat. He was used to such requests from his boss. In fact, the madam's number was already programmed into his speed dial.

'Do you want her to come to the office or the apartment?' he asked.

Randall looked at his watch. There was no time to drive over to the Century City apartment where he usually conducted these sorts of assignations.

Fuck it. He could screw her on the desk.

'Send her here,' he said. 'And tell Becca she'd better be good, not like that last anorexic she sent me. I want blonde, and tits like beach balls.'

'I'm on it,' said Keith, ironically for someone who had never been 'on' a blonde who didn't have chest hair and a dick in his life. 'Leave it with me.'

Over on the set at Universal, Siena was sitting in her

483

trailer gloomily playing a game of backgammon with her bodyguard, a 280-pound monster called Big Al.

Contrary to press reports, her trailer was actually rather a modest affair, consisting of two banquettes covered in a revolting seventies-style orange velour fabric that even Duke would have balked at; a noisy and uncomfortable fold-away bed; a minuscule bathroom, comprised of only a toilet and what Siena called her powerless shower, which dripped cold water with a sort of lethargic sneeze; and a little kitchenette, where she and Al had just made themselves some Earl Grey tea, one of the few tastes she had acquired from her long years of exile in England.

'God, I'm bored, aren't you?' She pushed her pieces around the board in a desultory manner.

'Not really.' Al smiled. 'I'm used to it. You need a lot of patience in my job.'

That was the best thing about Al, thought Siena. He was such a cup-half-full kind of a guy.

She'd been very resistant initially to the idea of having a bodyguard, but Randall had insisted after she'd started getting a string of obscene letters, some of them quite threatening, from an anonymous crazed admirer. Besides, stalkers aside, her fame had grown to such a huge extent in the past six months that she could no longer move about in LA as a free agent without being at best pestered and at worst mobbed by fans and paparazzi alike.

Cut off from her friends and what was left of her family by Randall, unable even to take a stroll along the beach on her own, Siena had discovered that her new-found fame and status could be deeply isolating. There were often days when Al seemed like the only friendly face she saw, and the only person she could really talk to.

She still had Randall, of course. But lately the relationship had been under a lot of strain. She was on the set all day, and he liked to work holed up in his office until very late at night, and typically through most of the

484

weekend as well. In the few snatched hours they did spend together, they argued too much, about everything from the film to his hours to Siena's dress sense.

He was incredibly controlling, and liked to have the final say in every aspect of her life, right down to the colour and size of her T-shirts.

At first Siena had fought him. She remembered Jamie Silfen's advice on the night of the party, and made valiant efforts to preserve her own identity in the face of Randall's formidable will to take over. But her increasing loneliness soon forced her into a state of almost total dependence on him which robbed her of any ability to resist.

It dawned on her that if Randall threw her out, she would lose everything – her career, her fame, her new super-wealthy status, not to mention her home. And despite his constant casual cruelty, she was also afraid of losing Randall himself. He might be a bastard, but he was all she had.

Without her even noticing, he had gradually become the key to her whole world. Siena felt her confidence and self-esteem plummeting as she was forced to give in to him again and again and again.

The only area where the relationship still flourished was in bed.

Randall's desire for her sexually was unabated – if anything it had grown with the shift in the balance of power between them in his direction. He wanted to fuck her every single night, and not infrequently during the day as well. Last week he had even turned up on-set at lunchtime and insisted on taking her back to her trailer for sex.

'Darling, please,' she remonstrated with him. 'It looks so unprofessional, for both of us. You know how these things shake up and down. The whole crew will know what's going on.'

'I know,' said Randall, pushing down her top to reveal a lacy, 1940s-style bra. 'That's what I like about it.'

He left forty-five minutes later looking, as Duke would have said, happier than a pig in shit.

Jason, of course, never let Siena hear the end of it.

Today, she and Al were waiting for Luke, the director, to finish a fight scene between Jason and a young English actor who was playing his co-pilot and love rival. It was taking for ever, and Siena was finding it harder and harder to concentrate on their backgammon game.

'D'you wanna play something else?' said Al, after her third illegal move in a row.

Something was obviously bothering her.

'Oh, sorry,' she said, dragging her attention back to the board. 'I'm not really on the ball this afternoon, am I?'

'It don't matter,' said Al kindly, clearing away the pieces with his giant bear paws. 'We could watch TV if you like?'

Siena picked up the remote and flicked the 'on' switch. Unfortunately, the daytime TV schedules consisted of wall-to-wall soaps, and the very first thing she saw was Hunter's face, looking faintly orange and over-made-up against a cringe-makingly fake background of plywood furniture and wobbly plastic plants.

She switched it off instantly.

'Hey,' said Al. 'That's reruns of *Counsellor*. The first season, that was the best one. Can't we watch that?'

'I'd rather not,' said Siena. She was biting her lower lip and staring resolutely out of the window, evidently quite upset.

'Hey.' Al put a kindly arm around her. He was very fond of Siena and thought Randall Stein was a jerk. 'What's wrong?'

She started to cry. 'Oh, Al, it's nothing, I'm just being silly,' she sobbed.

The big man was not convinced. 'No you're not. Come on, spit it out, girl, what's upset you?'

She wiped her eyes on her sleeve. 'It's me,' she said. 'I've upset myself. I've behaved very badly towards

486

someone I love more than anything. Hunter, my uncle . . .'

'Oh, yeah.' Al nodded understandingly. 'Mike Palumbo.'

'Exactly.' Siena sniffed. 'Well, I really treated him badly, Al. I did.' The big man looked disbelieving. 'I can't bear to watch him on that stupid show. It just reminds me, you know? And I miss him. I miss him so much.'

The tears had started to flow again.

Al, always prepared for such an emergency after long years of working with over-emotional actresses, handed his charge a clean white handkerchief.

'It's never too late,' he said, while Siena blew her nose noisily. 'If you miss him and you think you were wrong, why don't you ring him up and apologise? It's probably just a storm in a teacup. These things usually are.'

She put down the hanky and took his hand. How she wished, with all her heart, that she lived in a world as simple and morally straightforward as his.

'I'm afraid it's not that simple.' She sighed. 'I know it should be, but it isn't. Sometimes . . .' She broke off, unsure of what she was trying to say. 'Sometimes it *is* too late. It just is.'

They were interrupted by a knock on the trailer door. Al lumbered over to answer it and PJ, one of the runners, put his head round the door.

'They're ready for you, Miss McMahon,' he announced breathlessly.

'Thanks,' said Siena. 'Would you tell Luke I need to go back into make-up quickly? Just give me five.'

And leaving Big Al standing there, she was out of the door without another word, dashing across the set towards the make-up trailer and a belated start to her day's work.

Around eight o'clock that evening, she and Randall were in the back of an anonymous-looking, blacked-out limo being driven to an AIDS charity dinner in Beverly Hills.

Siena looked ravishing in a pillar-box-red Versace trouser suit. Randall, by contrast, looked grumpy and exhausted in a dark suit and tie. His heartburn had been playing up dreadfully all day, and every few minutes he put his hand to his chest and groaned as they inched their way along Wilshire.

'Can you believe that schmuck Bill?' he asked Siena for the hundredth time. 'How can you just *forget* to tell someone they're down nine million dollars? What does he think, I'm so loaded that nine million fucking dollars doesn't even matter to me?'

Siena imagined that was exactly what the accountant would have thought, but didn't say so.

'I know, darling,' she said, idly stroking his thigh. 'It must be infuriating.'

'Hmmm,' Randall grunted, moving her hand upward so she could feel his emergent erection through his trousers. The man was a freak of nature – he seemed to have an almost permanent hard-on, at least when Siena was around. 'You look beautiful tonight.'

The compliment was so unexpected she almost choked.

'Thank you,' she said once she'd recovered from the shock, even risking a small smile. 'I'm glad you think so.'

Randall was, in fact, annoyed at himself for having slept with that hooker at lunchtime. It wasn't that he felt guilty as such – he couldn't remember the last time his conscience had been troubled by that particular emotion – but looking at Siena this evening, he was struck again by how mind-blowingly stunning she was.

What was he doing trawling about in the gutter with call girls when he had this kind of welcome waiting for him at home?

'I know I've been a bit tough on you lately,' he went on, to Siena's ill-concealed amazement. 'I'm sorry if I hurt your feelings. But this is a tough business, you know? You need to learn that if you're going to survive.'

'I know,' she said quietly. 'I understand.'

Beneath her calm exterior she felt so relieved she was almost euphoric. In the last few days she'd really been starting to panic that Randall was going off her. Sex was still constant, but otherwise he seemed to be in a permanently bad mood with her, veering from the bad tempered to the totally withdrawn and back again. This sudden show of compassion for her feelings was as wonderful as it was surprising, and she knew better than to question him about what might have caused it.

They arrived at the fund-raiser at the Beverly Hills Hotel in unusually good spirits. The last vestiges of a spectacular LA sunset, a psychadelic melting pot of red and orange, purple, blue and pink, were sinking into the horizon, throwing the famously kitsch pink walls of the hotel and its straight rows of palm trees into dark silhouettes. It looked so breathtaking even Randall was momentarily entranced, not that he was allowed the luxury of time to admire the view. Both he and Siena were mobbed by photographers the moment they set foot out of the car.

'Siena, any comment on the problems you and Jason have been having on *1943*?' called out one chancer from the front of the press pack, as she made her way up the pink stone steps.

'What problems?' she called back, giving the reporter a mischievous wink that sent the paparazzi wild.

The whole evening, in fact, was turning into something of a triumph for Siena. Every director in the room seemed to want to talk to her, all drawn to her beauty and confidence like moths to a flame. She'd lost weight, no doubt owing to the combined stresses of dealing with Randall at home and Jason on-set, and her hair had been cut shorter and aggressively sculpted and curled for her role as forties siren Peggy Maples. She was still far too curvy ever to look androgynous, but the shorter hair and trouser suit nevertheless gave her a disturbing, pseudo boyish appeal that wasn't lost on any of the red-blooded males in the room.

Randall was also enjoying himself immensely, contentedly basking in her reflected glory, and being unusually affectionate and relaxed. When he won an antique gold-and-diamond ladies' watch in the raffle, he dragged Siena up on to the podium with him, and made a great show of kissing her hand gallantly while it was clasped around her wrist.

It was the end of the evening, and Siena was happily chatting with a well-known Dutch director, showing off her new watch and wondering whether she had time for one last Kir Royale, when Randall came up to her looking flushed and happy.

'Come on,' he said, taking her arm and pulling her unceremoniously away from the Dutchman. 'We're getting out of here. Johnny Lo Cicero's hired out the Sky Bar for a private party. I said we'd stop by.'

Siena felt a shiver run right through her and a dark cloud descending to smother her happiness.

'No,' she said stiffly. 'I'm not going to the Sky Bar.'

'What?' Randall was still smiling, looking past her and waving to David Geffen as he made his way out. 'Why? What's the problem?'

'That place just gives me bad vibes, that's all.'

An image of Max, lying by the pool, kissing and touching that dreadful girl, rushed unbidden into her mind. She would never set foot in the Sky Bar again as long as she lived. Never. And Randall couldn't make her.

'What vibes?' said Randall, but then it came to him. 'Oh, come on.' He looked at her pityingly. 'Please tell me you're not still hung up about loser boy and the waitress?'

Siena blushed uncomfortably.

'Sweetheart, he's nothing.' Randall was fond of making this observation about Max, and couldn't understand why it didn't seem to comfort her. He pushed her hair back from her face and stroked her neck with unaccustomed tenderness. 'You're playing with the big boys now, baby,' he said. 'That shit doesn't matter any more. You're with me, and I want you to come. It's gonna be a great party.'

Siena hesitated. She desperately wanted to please him. Tonight had gone so well, she really couldn't bear to spoil it.

But it was no good, she couldn't do it. She just couldn't go in there.

'Darling, of course I'm with you, I owe everything to you,' she said, trying to placate him. 'But please understand, I can't face the Sky Bar. I know it seems stupid and superstitious to you, and I know it was all a long time ago. But I really can't go in there. I'm sorry.'

'Fine,' he said coldly, snatching his hand away as though Siena's neck had suddenly transformed into molten lava. 'Do what you want. But I'm taking the car. You'll have to get Al to call Marcel if you want him to come and pick you up.'

Before Siena could say or do anything, an infamous blonde starlet called Miriam Stanley had sidled up to the pair of them. She was wearing a tiny piece of silver thread that barely skimmed her crotch and thigh-high patent-leather boots.

Miriam might be a slut, but she was also gorgeous, thought Siena bitterly.

'Hi, Randall.' She beamed. 'Siena.' She turned to Siena as an afterthought and flashed her the briefest of fake smiles. 'Are you guys coming to Johnny's party?'

'Actually, Miriam, we were just in the middle of something,' began Siena.

'Were we?' said Randall harshly. 'I thought we'd just finished something.'

He pointedly put his arm around a surprised and delighted Miriam. 'Siena is tired, so she's going home. But I'm going over there. If you want I can give you a ride?'

'Well ...' Miriam flicked back her hair and smiled

smugly at a stricken-looking Siena. 'That's really kind of you, Randall. I'd like that.'

Without another word, the two of them headed for the door, leaving Siena standing miserably alone like Cinderella at midnight. Biting down hard on her lower lip, close to tears, she fought her way through the last of the guests out into the lobby. She was looking around desperately for Al, but the big man saw her first and was by her side in seconds.

'Randall's taken the car,' she said, trying to sound as if everything was under control. But her lower lip was going, the classic Siena giveaway.

'Yes,' said Al, giving her a meaningful look. 'I saw Mr Stein leaving. With his companion.' It was quite beyond him why Siena stayed with the bastard. All he ever seemed to do was treat her like dirt. 'I've already called Marcel. He should be here in about ten minutes with the Jag.'

'Thanks.' She smiled at him gratefully, but he could see the tears were about to flow. 'I don't know what I'd do without you, Al. I really don't.'

He put his arms around her and hugged her tightly to his chest, so no one would see her crying. She'd looked like such a vixen earlier in her tight red suit, bursting at the seams with vampy sexual confidence. But all it took was one fight with Randall, and she was suddenly transformed back into a clingy, needy child.

He was bad for her, that man. He really was.

In his modest family house over in Burbank, private detective Bill Jennings was cleaning his teeth, about to get into bed with his wife Denelle for some much needed sleep. It had been a grindingly long week.

'What's this, baby?'

He turned to see Denelle sitting up in bed, looking at a couple of pictures he'd brought home. Damn, she looked hot in that baby-doll nightgown he'd bought her. He hoped the fact that she'd put it on tonight was a good sign. 'Do I know this guy?'

He rinsed out his mouth and climbed into bed beside her.

'Uh-huh.' He nodded, pointing at the naked back view of a man in flagrante with two stunning-looking girls in a hotel room. 'That's Randall Stein. At the Standard, last week.'

'Ooooo,' said Denelle, raising her eyebrows and smiling at her handsome husband. She loved a good bit of gossip, although she had learned to be discreet and never discussed Bill's clients' business with other people. 'And I guess none of those arms, legs or breasts belong to Siena McMahon, right?'

'Right,' said Bill, taking the pictures from her and slipping them both back into the brown envelope on his bedside table.

'What an asshole,' said Denelle, who was always ready to stand up for the sisterhood when a woman was being wronged. Castrate the bastard first, ask questions later, that was her motto.

In this case, though, Bill agreed with her.

'Yeah, he is,' he said. 'He really is.' Leaning over, he gave his wife a lingering kiss on the lips, and slipped one hand under the sheer fabric of her nightdress. 'It's me you should be feeling sorry for, though,' he told her.

'Oh yeah?' She reached down and undid the pink strings confining her beautiful black breasts, without taking her eyes from his. 'Why's that?'

Bill stared down at her cleavage and grinned.

'Because tomorrow,' he whispered, lowering his head and slowly kissing each of her breasts in turn, 'I have to give those pictures to Siena's mother.'

Chapter Forty-three

Max was sitting beside Henry in the passenger seat of his ancient Land Rover, trying to keep his brother's spirits up.

'Just think about that *boeuf Bourgignon* we'll be tucking into at Le Gavroche this evening,' he said, breaking off a few squares of Galaxy chocolate and passing them to Henry. 'You'll be a rich man by then. Well, a rich-*er* man.'

'I bloody won't,' said Henry, chewing the chocolate gloomily. 'I'll be a completely broke man, who may, just *may*, have bought himself a few measly months' leeway to try and hold off his effing creditors.'

'More than a few months, surely?' said Max.

They were driving up to town to try to sell two of Henry's most prized and valuable possessions, a pair of early Turner watercolours. They'd been a christening present from an extraordinarily wealthy godfather, so he had literally grown up with them, and reckoned he must have looked at the pale grey seascapes they depicted almost every day of his life.

He wished he'd looked at them harder now, appreciated them more. But there was no point getting sentimental about it. They had to go.

Freddie had also come along for the ride, and was perched somewhat nervously in the back seat with the grave responsibility of keeping the paintings steady as they jolted and lurched their way down the M40. She had never been to London before, and had also not had a day off since her somewhat unexpected arrival at Manor Farm, so the plan was that they would drop Henry at the art dealer's in Pont Street to sew up the deal while Max took her off for lunch and a spot of sightseeing.

Unfortunately, the traffic was abysmal, and by the time they'd safely delivered Henry and the paintings and agreed to meet back in Pont Street at six, it was already almost lunchtime.

'So,' said Max. 'Any idea where you want to start?'

'Well, I would like to see the 'ouses of Parliament. Big Ben? And I definitely 'ave to go to Buckingham Palace. Do you think there will be time for both?'

Max couldn't help but smile at her enthusiasm and excitement. He remembered the first time he had visited Paris, on a school trip when he was about fourteen, feeling a similar sense of wonder. She was looking up at him, clutching her tatty little London tourist's handbook and a cheap umbrella (just in case), her eyes wide with anticipation.

'Absolutely, buckets of time,' he said, relieving her of both book and umbrella and, to her horror, dropping them in a nearby bin. 'You won't need either of those,' he assured her brightly. 'Just follow me.'

They went to Parliament Square first, and Freddie seemed quite delighted, particularly with the abbey itself. She listened enraptured while Max gave her an impromptu history lesson, pointing out the hallowed resting places of kings, queens and many centuries' worth of the great and the good of England. It was a treat for him too. He loved his history, but since Cambridge had had very little opportunity to indulge his passion.

'You are a wonderful teacher,' Freddie told him afterwards, kissing him on both cheeks in the French style as they emerged into the sunlight of the street.

Max blushed.

'I don't know about that,' he mumbled. 'But it's terrific that you're so interested. A lot of girls your age would rather be whizzing around in the London Eye or something than plodding round a boring old church, listening to me wittering on.'

'What do you mean, "girls my age"?' she teased him,

poking him in the ribs in mock indignation. 'You aren't so much older than me, you know.'

He noticed the way she threw her auburn hair back as if in challenge when she said this. Was she flirting with him?

'Well, no,' he said, embarrassed at himself for appearing so flustered. 'No, I suppose I'm not. But you know what I mean.'

By this time they were both starving, so Max made one minor change to their itinerary and took her off to Fortnum and Mason to buy supplies for a picnic in Green Park.

Freddie couldn't believe the prices.

'That's almost fifteen euros for two slices of pâté!' she wailed. 'No wonder your brozzer 'as some problems with money if it costs this much just to eat.'

Max assured her that Henry didn't make a habit of shopping at Fortnum's, but her outrage over the prices soon disappeared anyway once they finally sat down to eat.

'*Mon Dieu*,' she said through a meltingly delicious mouthful of duck's-liver pâté on crusty brown bread. 'Oh my God. That is incredible. *Incroyable*. Amazing. And I thought the English couldn't cook.'

Max laughed. 'Don't let Muffy hear you say that.'

He was surprised by how much he was enjoying himself today. Ever since Siena had left him, but even more so since he'd had to leave LA with his tail between his legs, he'd found it hard to fully relax and be happy.

Henry and Muff had been fantastic, as always, and he adored being at Batcombe. But not even the warmth of Manor Farm, or his unexpected professional success at Stratford, had enabled him to shake a deeper feeling of worthlessness and rejection. Siena was still very much on his mind.

Today, though, for the first time in many months, he felt something that was very close to real happiness. Perhaps it was as simple as lying in the park in London on such a beautiful day. It was also nice to be with Freddie, to be able to show her the sights and talk history with her. She was an attractive girl, and the way she listened to him, and was obviously interested in what he had to say, was pleasantly flattering. It made him feel confident, and Max was grateful to her for that.

Freddie lay back on the grass on her side, propped up on her elbow with her pixie-like head resting on her hand.

'As you English would say' – she patted her non-existent belly and rolled her eyes – 'I'm completely stuffed.'

Max laughed. This was one of Charlie's favourite expressions and it sounded ridiculous coming from her.

'What do you mean, you're stuffed? You've had one slice of bread and pâté and a few cherries! We've hardly started here.' He waved at two more largish Fortnum's bags still crammed with food at their feet. Freddie shook her head.

'I couldn't eat another theeng,' she said. 'Let's just take it 'ome for the children.'

Max noticed the way her tight T-shirt clung to her tiny breasts as she lay down. Other than being short, he reflected, she might well be described as the polar opposite of Siena in terms of looks. But there was nonetheless something sexy about her. Unthreatening, but definitely sexy.

She had the small, toned, compact body of a gymnast, shown off to full advantage in the shorts she was wearing today, the white of the cotton in striking contrast to her tanned, slender legs. And she didn't have any make-up on, something he had always gone for in girls. It showed confidence.

'I suppose we ought to make a move and walk up to the palace in a minute,' he said, somewhat reluctantly. 'It's nearly four now, and we need to be back in Belgravia by six.'

'OK,' said Freddie, all energy suddenly, leaping to her

feet and standing over him, reaching down for his hands to pull him up.

'I didn't mean *right* now,' Max grumbled.

But he found himself holding on to her small, cold hands anyway, unwilling to let her go. It would have been so simple for him to pull her down on top of him and kiss her. The confident, provocative sparkle in her eyes told him she probably wouldn't protest if he did. But something made him hesitate.

For a moment, they remained frozen in this pose, holding eye contact with one another for just long enough to confirm a flicker of mutual attraction. Then Max let go of her hands and stood up.

'Right, then, you little slave driver,' he said, gathering up the remaining food bags with exaggerated briskness. 'The palace it is.'

By the time they'd 'done' Buckingham Palace, battled their way through central London traffic and finally found a meter in Belgravia, they were fifteen minutes late to meet Henry. He was standing outside the gallery, and from twenty feet away Max could already tell that something was up from his brother's slumped shoulders and hangdog expression.

'Sorry we're late,' he said, shrugging apologetically. 'I couldn't find a meter for love nor money. How did it go?' He looked down questioningly at the two water-colours, which were propped up against the wall at Henry's feet.

Henry looked bleak.

'About as badly as possible, I'm afraid. They're fakes.'

There was a stunned silence.

'What?' said Max, eventually. 'They can't be.'

'Well, they are.' Henry gave a brief, what-can-you-do smile. 'Hamish didn't seem to have any doubts.'

'Christ.' Max shook his head.

He knew how crucial the sale of those paintings had been to Henry. Without that money and the extra months it would have bought him, he would be forced to sell up now.

'Per'aps you need a drink?' suggested Freddie. 'We could find an English pub, before we go to the restaurant, no?'

'I'm afraid I can't,' said Henry, glancing anxiously at his watch. 'You two go and have dinner. Enjoy yourselves. I've got to try and catch Nick Frankel before he leaves the office, sort this business out once and for all.'

Max didn't like his brother's tone. It sounded worryingly final.

'Are you sure?' he pressed him. 'Wouldn't you rather come with us and sort all this out in the morning?'

Henry shook his head. 'Can't, Maxy. There's someone . . .' He hesitated, as if he were about to tell him something but then thought better of it. 'Something I have to try and do tonight, if I can. Really.' He smiled at them both. 'You two go on. I wouldn't be much company for you anyway.'

Max sat at the corner table in Le Gavroche with Freddie, sipping a small glass of vintage port that he really couldn't afford, and worrying about Henry.

'It doesn't make any sense,' he kept repeating through his drunken haze to an equally bleary-eyed Frédérique. 'How can he have had those paintings for all those years, and never known they were dodgy?'

Freddie sipped her own port and said nothing. She was watching the way his blond hair kept flopping forward over his eyes, and longing to reach across the table and push it back for him.

'Sorry,' he said, cutting himself another sliver of Stilton. 'You must be bored silly with all this talk about Henry. So, what do you make of London, then? Was it what you were expecting?'

'I suppose so, in a way,' she said. She didn't seem very interested in reminiscing about their sightseeing trip. 'But

499

I don't find it boring, actually. When you tell me about your brother. It makes me 'appy that you trust me, with your problems, you know?'

Max looked across at her with renewed interest. He hadn't really thought of it like that, in terms of trusting her. But he supposed, in a way, he did.

'I 'ope you don't think I'm being rude,' she continued tentatively, 'but I 'ave noticed that you often seem to be sad. Is it . . .' She twirled her hair in her fingers nervously. 'Is it to do with your girlfriend? With Siena?'

Max bridled for a second at hearing Freddie using her name. One of the worst things about splitting up with someone famous was that everyone you met felt as if they knew the person intimately. Max found people's pseudo-familiarity with Siena hard to take. But he knew Freddie's heart was in the right place, and he tried to answer her honestly.

'Sometimes,' he said. 'I still think about her a lot. Well, all the time, really. But all that stuff people tell you about time healing the wounds – I'm starting to think there might be something in it. I actually had a really nice day today.'

Freddie took this as a compliment and visibly blushed with pleasure.

'Me too,' she said. 'Really nice.'

Emboldened by the wine, she reached across the table, took his hand, put it to her lips and kissed it.

Max felt his heart pounding with nerves.

This wasn't a good idea.

'Look, Freddie,' he began awkwardly.

'What?' she interrupted him, keeping hold of his hand. 'I could 'elp you. I could make you 'appy, Max, I know I could.' She spoke with such urgency, looking him directly in the eyes as if willing him to believe her. It took him aback. 'I also 'ave somebody to forget, remember?'

'I'm just not sure,' he mumbled. 'I don't think I'm over her, not properly. And you're very young. I don't . . .'

He found himself unsure of the right words. 'I wouldn't want to hurt you.'

'You won't,' said Freddie. 'I wouldn't let you.'

Before either of them really knew what was happening, they found themselves leaning across the table and kissing one another full on the mouth.

It had been a long time since Max had kissed anyone, and he'd had a lot to drink. Feeling the soft skin of Freddie's lips against his, and the almost forgotten urgency of a woman's desire in her probing tongue and quickened breathing, he found that his physical response was overwhelming. He wanted her to hold him, to come for him, to make him believe that everything was going to be all right. He wanted to take her to bed right now.

'I do hurt people,' he whispered, oblivious of the other diners' stares as he grabbed her hair in his hands desperately, like a drowning man reaching for a buoy, and pressed his forehead against hers. 'I do.'

'Shhh,' said Freddie, stroking his face softly. 'You don't have to worry any more. It's going to be OK.'

The three of them barely spoke on the long journey home. Henry drove with his eyes fixed on the road ahead, consumed with his own worries. Whatever had happened at his accountant's office after he'd left them earlier, he clearly didn't want to talk about it.

Max sat in the front, concerned for his brother, but also agonisingly aware of Freddie's presence behind him, counting the long minutes until he could get home and hopefully sneak her into his bed.

He was too drunk to analyse his feelings in any depth, although part of him knew that starting something with the kids' au pair might not be the smartest move in the world. But a bigger part – the part that had felt so lonely and unloved for a year, the part that wanted to remember what it felt like to be alive, and make love and be happy – could only with an effort be restrained from clambering into the back seat right now and ripping the girl's clothes off.

When they finally did get home, Muffy was waiting up for them.

'Hello, you three,' she said, taking the pictures back from Henry without a word and moving into the kitchen. He would explain it all to her when he was ready. 'You must be exhausted. How was London? Did you have a good day, Frédérique?'

'Yes, I did,' said Freddie, with a meaningful look at Max. 'But I am *very* tired. I theenk I'll go straight up, if you don't mind?'

'Me too,' chimed in Max, rather too quickly.

'Of course.' Muffy smiled, slightly bemused by Max's sudden craving for his beauty sleep. He usually never hit the hay until the small hours.

She was relieved that they were both making themselves scarce. Something had obviously gone wrong if the pictures were back, and she wanted to talk to Henry on his own.

Once Max and Freddie had disappeared upstairs with somewhat indecent haste, Henry walked over to her and gave her a hug. He didn't speak, but just stood there in the kitchen swaying slightly, with his wife in his arms.

'So?' she prompted him gently when he finally let her go and sat down at the table. Henry took a deep breath. 'They were fakes.'

'Worthless?' asked Muffy. She was determined not to look disappointed or shocked. He needed her to be strong, whatever happened.

'Not worthless. But certainly not worth enough. Not even close.' He ran his hands through his greying curls and forced himself to keep talking, before he lost his nerve. 'That money was our last hope, Muff. Without it, we can't pay the back interest on the loans. It's as simple as that. So I went to see Nick this evening.'

She didn't say anything, but nodded for him to go on.

'I said we'd think about putting the farm on the

502

market next week.' He scanned her face anxiously for a reaction, but her mask of calm didn't slip.

'I see,' she said reaching out and laying a hand gently on his shoulder. He pulled out another chair and gestured for her to sit beside him.

'There is another option,' he said.

This time there was no concealing her emotion, and a snapshot of desperate hope flashed across her features at this possibility of a reprieve. Perhaps they wouldn't have to sell after all?

'What? What other option?'

Henry took both her hands between his own and began fiddling with her worn wedding band as he told her. 'It was Nick's suggestion, actually. But I put in a call to Gary Ellis from his office.'

'Why?' Muffy looked shocked. 'I thought we'd agreed, no golf course . . .'

'We have, we have.' He held up his hand to stop her. 'Hear me out. The fact is, as Nick pointed out to me, if we put the place on the open market and sell to someone else, there's nothing to stop Ellis approaching *them* with a fat cheque and developing the land anyway. If he wants it badly enough, that's exactly what he'll do, and then the only difference will be that the money's in someone else's pockets rather than ours.'

'Yes, but *does* he still want it that badly?' said Muff. 'He's gone and ruined Swanbrook now. Does he really want *two* golf courses?'

Henry shrugged.

'He might do. Look, when I called him from Nick's he made me another offer. I think we should consider it.' Muffy opened her mouth to protest. 'Not to buy the place,' Henry continued, heading her off at the pass. 'This time he's talking about a lease agreement.'

'What sort of lease agreement?' she asked warily.

He took a deep breath.

'We would remain the nominal owners of the whole property, with ongoing rights to live in the house, and we could leave those rights to the children. We wouldn't have to sell.'

'I see.' She frowned. 'And what's in it for the ghastly Gary, then?'

'Well . . .' He hesitated momentarily. 'He'd be able to build a golf course and run it without interference for the full term of the lease.'

'Which is?'

Henry winced.

'He's talking about a hundred years.'

'A hundred years?' Muffy laughed, but it really wasn't funny. She got up and started pacing backwards and forwards in front of the Aga. 'For heaven's sake, Henry. Even the kids will be dead by then!'

'I know, I know. But he'd give us enough to clear all our debts up front, plus a chunk left over. We could still live in the house, and so could the children in due course.'

'But they could never sell the house?' asked Muffy, horrified. 'It wouldn't be really *theirs*?'

'Not until the end of the lease agreement, no,' Henry admitted. 'But after that ownership would revert to the family. Whether that's Charlie's children or what have you I don't know, we'd have to sort the details out. They may have to pay some sort of release payment to Ellis's company at that point, it's a bit complicated.'

'Surely you aren't considering saying *yes* to this?' she asked, finally stopping pacing and coming to rest with her back against the warm metal of the oven.

Henry sighed. 'Look, darling, I hate that bastard as much as you do, but he's throwing us a lifeline here. The alternative is that we sell the whole lot to someone else for a shitty price, pay off the fucking debts, and buy ourselves a nice little semi in Swindon with what's left over.'

'Oh, come on. Surely it wouldn't be *that* bad?'

'After we've paid everyone off? I'm afraid it would be,'

said Henry. 'At least this way the manor stays in the family. We wouldn't have to move.'

'Yes, but it would be a golf course!' she exclaimed in agony. 'You've seen Ellis's developments. The whole valley would be ruined, completely ruined. I mean, isn't Batcombe supposed to be an area of outstanding natural beauty or something? How does he think he's going to get planning permission?'

Henry rubbed his fingers together to indicate a bribe. 'The man's as bent as a nine-bob note,' he told her. 'He told me and Nick today that he already has preliminary approval for the golf course, *and*, if you can believe it, to build a fucking great clubhouse and "leisure complex" right next to the old barns.'

'I don't know what to believe any more,' said Muffy.

'Look.' He got up to join her by the Aga, wrapping his arm around her shoulders. 'If you don't want to go ahead, you don't have to. This is your decision as much as mine, and if you'd rather sell to someone else, we can sell. But the reality is, he's going to build his bloody golf course anyway eventually, whatever we decide. At least this way, one day, we may have a chance to put things right.'

'You're right,' she said sadly. 'I know you're right. A lease has to be better than an outright sale. I just can't bear the thought of that man, that *awful*, lecherous, predatory man, setting foot on the place.'

'Believe me, darling' – Henry hugged her tightly – 'neither can I. Neither can I.'

Chapter Forty-four

The next few months were a time of both great happiness and great sadness for Max.

Professionally, things were going better than he could ever remember. Not only had *Dark Hearts* proved so successful that they had had to extend their Stratford run, and were even contemplating taking the play on tour to Bristol and London; but one of the short films he'd directed in LA had been nominated for three awards at the Chicago Film Festival, and looked set for even bigger success at Sundance next year. Thanks to the involvement of the big Hollywood star, it had received a disproportionate amount of press.

Ironically, his profile in the States was bigger now than it had been in all the years he'd lived there.

Not that things were remotely slow in England. The name Max De Seville was finally becoming well known in theatre circles, and offers had started to come in from all over the country for Max to direct everything from musicals to 'nihilist Shakespeare', whatever that might be.

Personally, his life had also become more contented, thanks in no small part to his burgeoning relationship with Freddie. After a brief, half-hearted attempt to keep their affair secret, Max had finally decided to be honest about it with Henry and Muffy, as well as with himself.

'I can't imagine why you thought we'd disapprove,' Muff told him, after he'd rather nervously admitted what she had long suspected anyway. 'God knows you deserve a bit of fun, Max. I mean, why not?'

He'd realised then that his sister-in-law was right. He'd been fighting his feelings for Freddie, because he knew that deep down he was still in love with Siena, and probably always would be. But Siena was gone, and there was no point sitting around moping. Freddie was here, and she wanted to make him happy.

Why not?

Set against all these good things, though, was the terrible, ongoing nightmare of life at Manor Farm. Having finally signed the hated lease agreement with Ellis, they were all waiting with a growing sense of despair for the construction work to begin. Awareness that these might be the last days of the estate as a working farm and a tranquil family home made it impossible to enjoy the time they had left together. Henry mooched about the yard and the office like a bear with a sore head, snapping at anyone foolish enough to try to talk to him or commiserate about the golf course.

Meanwhile Muffy tried to maintain some semblance of normality and cheerfulness for the sake of the children, who already had to cope with settling in at the local primary and making new friends, and were soon to have their home life turned upside down as well. Max could see the effort of this pretence was a huge strain for her.

He did his best to keep everyone's spirits up, forcing a reluctant and exhausted Muffy to spend a day at the health spa in Cheltenham, and taking the children on endless exciting outings with Freddie, to such heady destinations as the haunted Minster Lovell and Burford zoo. Mercifully, Bertie and Maddie were both too young to understand the implications of what was about to happen at home, and thought the prospect of construction and activity at the farm was marvellously exciting. But Charlie, who as well as being older was naturally more sensitive to others' feelings, in particular his mother's, knew that the way of life he had grown up with was going to be destroyed for ever and that his parents blamed themselves.

Max spent a lot of time with his nephew, helping him talk through his feelings of sadness, powerlessness and loss. After all he'd been through in the last year, he felt he was now fully equipped to offer advice on all three.

On his way into Stratford one morning, he stopped off at the village shop for a paper and a packet of ten Marlboro Lights – he was half-heartedly smoking again, thanks to all the late nights at the theatre – when he ran into Caroline Wellesley.

Unlike the rest of his family, Max was not a fan of Hunter's mother and was relieved when, despite living within a few miles of her and Christopher, he found that he rarely crossed paths with her socially.

This morning, however, there could be no escape. The shop was far too small for him to pretend not to have seen her.

'Hello, Max,' she said brightly, marching towards him armed with a little green metal basket containing nothing but six packets of chocolate Hob Nobs, Christopher's only real post-alcoholic weakness.

She was dressed in an old pair of canvas gardening trousers and a man's white shirt, and was almost unrecognisable as the former designer-clad nymphette he remembered from his childhood. Fifteen years later, standing in Batcombe Stores dressed like a scarecrow, she *still* had something about her, though. Caroline had the sort of sex appeal and lust for life that barely seemed to dim at all with age. Grudgingly, Max acknowledged what so many men saw in her physically.

'I haven't seen you for ages.' She smiled up at him. 'How are things at Manor Farm?'

He looked at her coldly.

'Bad,' he said, flatly. 'Things are very bad, I'm afraid. But then I expect your friend Gary Ellis will already have told you all about it.'

'Hey, now hang on a minute,' said Caroline, putting down her basket and squaring up to him, all five foot four of her coiled for battle against Max's giant six-and-a-half-foot bulk. He took a step back and very nearly toppled over a giant display case stacked with miniature jars of Marmite. 'That's not fair. He isn't a friend of mine at all. I think it's awful what he's doing to that beautiful valley, everybody does.'

'Really?' said Max, steadying the swaying case behind him before turning to face her again. 'And I thought it was you who introduced him to my brother in the first place and put the whole idea about buying up the farm into his head. You invited him for dinner, when he was leching all over Muffy. Apparently there's nothing of Henry's that that shit doesn't want to get his swindling little hands on.'

'Well, that's hardly my fault, is it?' said Caroline reasonably. 'That dinner was years and years ago, when he first moved here. None of us really knew him then. Muff knows I felt awful about the way Gary behaved towards her that night, but it's all water under the bridge now. We haven't had him back to Thatchers since, anyway. Christopher can't abide him.'

'Good for Christopher,' said Max.

He knew it was childish to lash out at Caroline. The nightmare at home was nothing to do with her, and anyway, as Henry had pointed out, if it hadn't been for Ellis's offer they would have lost Manor Farm completely. Perhaps it was the developer's admiration for Muffy which had kept him coming back for more, even after Henry had walked away from his first offer. Maybe that awful dinner at Caroline's had actually done them all a favour?

'Look, sorry.' He apologised half-heartedly and tried to change the subject. 'How is Christopher anyway? Is he well?'

Caroline smiled. 'Very, thank you. Fighting fit.' It was funny to watch Max trying to be so formal and awkwardly polite towards her. She still remembered him aged nine, chasing Hunter around the house with two stuck-together kitchen-towel tubes, pretending to be Darth Vader. Looking at him now, all broken nose and wounded masculine pride, she thought she wouldn't have minded being chased around the house by him one little bit, and managed to suppress a wistful sigh.

'I spoke to Hunter a few weeks ago,' she said, bringing up the one subject she hoped they still had in common. 'He seemed very happy, very settled with thingumabob.'

She always had been appalling with names.

'Tiffany,' said Max sternly. 'Yes, he is, very happy. I spoke to him myself, as a matter of fact. Yesterday.'

It was a pointed enough remark for even Caroline take the hint: Max spoke to Hunter more frequently than his own mother.

'You think I was a lousy mother, don't you?' she said quietly.

He sighed. He hadn't wanted to get into all this, and he was late for rehearsals as it was. But he supposed he'd brought it on himself.

'You weren't there,' he said, softening his own tone to match hers. 'You didn't see how bad things got for him. I did. Even before Duke died, you were never there for Hunter.'

She looked at him thoughtfully and gave an imperceptible nod, silent and awkward, between the cereal boxes and the breakfast spreads. Then she said cheerfully: 'We might pop in and see Muffy and Henry later. Would you mention it to them if you see them?'

The Hunter subject had apparently been closed.

'Of course,' he said, hastily grabbing a paper and throwing it into his own basket. 'But you'll probably see them before me. I'm expecting to be in Stratford all day working.'

They moved together towards the single till, Max with his *Times* and his fags, Caroline with her biscuits, neither of them speaking until they emerged on to the narrow lane that passed for Batcombe High Street.

'He's happy now, though, you say?' asked Caroline, seemingly out of nowhere.

'Hunter?' Max looked surprised. He hadn't thought

she'd bring the subject up again. 'Absolutely. He's blessed.'

'Good,' said Caroline. 'Everything turned out all right in the end, then, didn't it? Even with a *terrible* mother like me.'

And with that she scurried into Christopher's old Range Rover before Max could think of anything else to say to her.

Later that same night, Max sat in his brown leather director's chair, a present from Henry, and ran his hands through his hair in exhaustion.

It was gone 9.30 and he was still at the theatre, going through a couple of scenes with Rhys Bamber, the charming and very hard-working young Welsh actor who played the lead role of Jaspar. But they were both very tired, and weren't really getting anywhere.

'Why don't you come down to the White Hart and have a drink with me?' Max suggested, yawning as he put down the script. 'I could use a pint or two, even if you can't.'

'All right, then,' said Rhys. He was sick of this bloody scene anyway. 'Just a quick one.'

Every female head turned when, fifteen minutes later, the two of them walked into the pub on the high street, but neither Max nor Rhys seemed aware of what an attractive duo they were.

Max was looking unusually brown after a series of weekends spent out in the baking sunshine at Batcombe. Rhys was smaller, slighter and darker, very good looking in a chiselled, almost a Hollywood sort of way, but with the added secret weapon of a divinely lyrical Welsh accent. Girls would walk across broken glass just to hear Rhys say 'hello'. He was Ivor the Engine with sex appeal.

'Thanks for this.' He raised his pint to Max and took a long, refreshing gulp of lager. 'I feel better already.'

'Good,' said Max. 'To be honest, I was glad you had

time for a drink. It's a bit sad really, but I'm rather dreading going home.'

He briefly explained the current situation at Batcombe and the strain it was putting on everybody. Rhys listened and nodded sympathetically.

'That's terrible,' he said, when Max had finished. 'I know what it's like to lose a farm. My Uncle Tommy, back in Wales, had to sell up a few years ago, after BSE and all that. It really broke him up. Happened to a lot of the poorer farmers in Wales.'

'And the richer ones in the Cotswolds, I'm afraid,' said Max. 'At least in our case the family get to stay on living there.'

'With their foxy French au pair,' added Rhys, with a naughty wink. 'I think she's lovely, your girlfriend. I love French girls.' He grinned broadly.

Max imagined that French girls probably loved Rhys right back.

'She is,' said Max. 'She is lovely.' He forced a smile.

But inside he felt a creeping unhappiness that he couldn't quite define.

It was still lurking somewhere in his chest as he drove home an hour or so later in the rather nice, souped-up Beetle that the play's producers had loaned him for the duration of its run at Stratford.

He turned on the local radio station, the embarrassingly monikered 'Bard FM', to try to distract himself from his unwanted depression. After a couple of dreary songs by Dido, Max was relieved to be told it was time for the eleven o'clock news.

'Today in Parliament, the Prime Minister announced that the Government has no plans to make any changes to the proposed bill on hunting in response to the massive demonstrations by pro-hunt supporters and other countryside pressure groups last weekend.'

'Twat!' Max shouted at the radio, comforting himself

with another square of chocolate from the half-eaten bar on the passenger seat.

More news followed, a whole series of deathly dull items about the findings of the latest rail inquiry and an over-hyped piece about a possible link between alcoholism and colon cancer. He was about to switch over to something more soothing on Classic FM when he heard the West Country presenter say something that made his heart stop.

'And in the entertainment world tonight,' she burred, 'rumours are rife that the producer Randall Stein and his girlfriend, the model and actress Siena McMahon, are soon to be tying the knot.'

Fighting to steady his breathing, Max slowed down and pulled over on the grass verge at the side of the lane. The presenter went on.

'A spokesman for Miss McMahon, who once went to boarding school in England and is the daughter of producer Pete McMahon and granddaughter of Hollywood legend Duke McMahon, has denied there is any truth in the rumours. But Siena was spotted today leaving the set of 1943, Stein's upcoming Second World War blockbuster, wearing a huge diamond-and-ruby ring on her engagement finger and smiling broadly at the waiting press. Miss McMahon and Mr Stein have been living together in Los Angeles for the past year.'

Max turned off the radio and sat for a moment in silence, too shocked to move.

Marrying him! She was marrying that lecherous, twisted old monster? Somehow, even in his most tortured nightmares, he had never considered this horrible possibility. He'd always believed that one day Siena would outgrow Randall. Even if only for reasons of ambition, he thought she would eventually grow up and move on, out from under the old man's wing. But *marry* him?

The thought was too hideous to contemplate.

Perhaps, he began to comfort himself, it wasn't true?

Her publicist had denied it, after all. Knowing Siena, it was just as likely to be some stunt designed to whip up a bit more interest in their movie, like the shenanigans she'd pulled with Hunter last year, dragging him to that baseball game to try to make some capital out of Minnie McMahon's death. Even Max, who avoided information about Siena like the plague, knew that *1943* was running into trouble and could have done with some extra press.

Yes. The more he thought about it, the more it made sense. That was what it was. A publicity stunt.

Having steadied his nerves enough to restart the car, he drove the remaining twelve miles to Batcombe with the image of a smiling Siena waving her ring at reporters embedded in his brain like a cancer.

Freddie was running across the yard to meet him before he'd even switched off the engine. It was a bright, moonlit night, and Max could make out her features almost as clearly as if it were daylight.

Her low, smooth brow was furrowed in concern, and her auburn hair, usually so immaculate and sleek, looked oddly dishevelled, as though she'd been running around in very high winds. The shadows under her eyes, the result of a broken night helping Muffy with Madeleine after she'd wet the bed, heightened the overall impression of an under-nourished refugee, as did the baggy pair of dungarees and moth-eaten bottle-green sweater of Muffy's that she'd been wearing to help with milking in what was left of the working farm.

It would be fair to say that she wasn't looking her best.

'Darling.' She pulled open the driver's door and smothered Max with kisses in a Gallic display of affection that, for once, he could have done without. 'I 'eard the news on the radio,' she gabbled. 'When you deedn't come 'ome, I was so worried. I thought you must have 'eard about it and maybe done something stupid. Why didn't you turn your phone on? You 'ave 'eard, 'aven't you? Are you OK?'

The volume and speed of her questions were both too much for Max, who wanted nothing more than a moment's peace with a glass of whisky. Preferably a big one.

'I'm fine, Freddie, really,' he said, trying not to show his irritation. She was only showing concern for him, after all. He mustn't snap at her. 'If you mean the story about Siena's engagement, yes, I have heard, and quite frankly I don't believe a word of it.'

He shut the car door firmly behind him and strode into the house, leaving an agitated Freddie trotting along behind him like a worried terrier.

Marching into the drawing room, he was annoyed to discover that she wasn't the only one who'd waited up. Henry was sitting at the card table with Caroline and Christopher Wellesley, and all three rose to greet him the moment he walked in.

'Hello, old man,' said Henry. 'How were rehearsals?'

Thank God his brother at least had the wisdom to stick to neutral subjects.

'Fine,' he said, a little tensely, extending his hand to their guests. 'Christopher. Caroline. Nice to see you.'

'Hello again, Max,' said Caroline. She was looking at him, if not quite pityingly, then certainly questioningly.

Max felt his hackles rising. Caroline was quite probably the very last person he wanted to see right now. She knew Siena, had known her all her life, and he couldn't stand the thought that this might make her feel involved, connected in some way to his pain. It was hard to explain, but in his mind at least he wanted to keep Siena all to himself. It was the only way he could deal with the horror of her being engaged to Randall, the only way he could begin to control his emotions. Caroline's presence was an intrusion.

'Look,' he said, pointedly moving away from her and addressing them all as a group, 'I know you're all concerned for me after tonight's news, and I appreciate it, really. But as I was just telling Freddie, I'm sure there's no truth in the story. And even if there were, it's nothing to do with me any more.'

He tried to sound upbeat and confident, but it wasn't a huge success. Christopher and Henry exchanged worried glances. It didn't seem to have sunk in yet.

'But Max,' said Henry reasonably, pouring two small whiskies from the decanter on the side table and handing one of them to his brother, 'they showed her on the ten o'clock news, *wearing* the ring.'

'It all looked quite official,' added Freddie, coming up behind him and slipping a comforting arm around his waist.

'So?' Max challenged her. She could sense a formerly unknown belligerence creeping into his voice and instinctively removed her arm, shrinking back a little. 'A ring means nothing at all,' he insisted, once again addressing everyone. 'Believe me, I know Siena. This will be some tacky publicity stunt designed to boost interest in their new film. By all accounts that movie needs all the help it can get.'

He snorted mirthlessly and drained his glass, then walked over to the side table to pour himself another.

'I don't theenk that's the answer, do you?' said Freddie, glancing at the whisky decanter. 'It's late, *chéri*. Why don't you come to bed?'

'Yes, that's a good idea,' Henry chimed in. 'Get some rest, Maxy. We can talk about it all in the morning.'

Their concern was like a red rag to Max's bull. All the repressed tension of the past hour burst out of him, and poor Freddie took the full brunt of it.

'Who the hell do you think you are – my mother?' he snarled at her. 'I'll have a drink if I damn well want to. And as for its being "the answer" . . .' He waved his glass at her aggressively, sloshing a good finger of amber liquid on to Henry's carpet. 'As far as I'm concerned there isn't even a fucking question, all right? There's been some stupid story about Siena, it's been denied, and that's it. It's bullshit. Crap. She would never marry that disgusting old bastard. Never! Can't you get that through your thick head, and stop fussing around me like some melodramatic nursemaid?'

'I say,' said Christopher. 'Steady on, old boy. It isn't Frédérique's fault.'

Freddie, in fact, had kept her cool admirably in the face of Max's onslaught and, politely saying goodnight to Henry and Caroline, and smiling gratefully at Christopher, she turned on her heel to go.

She'd been waiting up all night for Max. She didn't need this shit.

Max made no move to stop her, but she paused at the door anyway and looked at him pityingly. When she spoke, she sounded calm and collected. There wasn't a trace of anger in her voice.

'I don't know 'oo you're trying to convince, darling,' she said. Max looked at her blankly. 'Me or yourself.'

As soon as she'd gone, he turned around to find Henry, Christopher and Caroline all staring at him, mutely appalled.

He felt bad enough as it was, and certainly didn't need a guilt trip from them.

'Oh, for fuck's sake,' he slurred. Those earlier pints with Rhys, now topped up with whisky, were starting to catch up with him. 'Just leave me alone.'

He stomped off in the direction of the kitchen, and Henry got up to follow him, but Caroline put a hand on his arm.

'Leave it,' she said. 'I'll go.' Henry looked doubtful. 'Women are better at these things,' she explained.

Christopher and Henry caught each other's eye. They couldn't argue with that.

Max was sitting in the threadbare armchair next to the Aga. It was known as the dogs' chair, because it was Titus and Boris's favourite spot in the entire house. He stood up defensively when Caroline walked in.

'Look, Caroline, I'm sorry, but I'm really not in the mood, all right?' he snapped. 'I don't want to be rude, but I'd appreciate it if you'd please just take the hint and bugger off. OK?'

Caroline sat down at the table and began nibbling at a chocolate digestive from the open tin.

'You can be as rude as you like, Max,' she said. 'I don't care. And if it makes you feel any better, I am just about to bugger off. Biscuit?' Still glowering at her, he took a digestive and sat back down. He hoped she meant it, and was going to hurry up and say her piece. 'I only came in here to tell you that you need to let that girl go.'

Great. Another lecture, this time from Miss Morality herself. Honestly, where did this woman get off?

'Siena?' He gave a clipped, joyless laugh and chomped into his biscuit, demolishing three-quarters of it in one bite. 'I have let her go, Caroline,' he said. 'In case you hadn't noticed, she's well and truly gone.'

He dropped the last morsel of chocolate digestive into his open mouth and swallowed, as if illustrating the finality of his loss.

The next thing he knew, Caroline had walked over to him and, leaning down, kissed him on the top of his head, like a child. It was such a gentle, compassionate gesture, he didn't know how to respond.

She put her hand under his chin and slowly lifted his face so that his eyes met hers.

'I wasn't talking about Siena,' she said.

The next morning the story was all over the papers. Even the broadsheets were running pictures of the happy couple.

Max came down to breakfast with a pounding head and a guilty conscience – he had slept fitfully and alone in his own room, unable to face apologising to Freddie – and noticed that the *Telegraph* and the *Mail* had already been tactfully cleared away. He didn't need to look at them – he could imagine the coverage all too well. He sat down and silently poured himself a black coffee from the cafetière.

The children had already finished eating and were upstairs cleaning their teeth and dressing under Freddie's supervision. Henry and Muffy were still halfway through their eggs and bacon, and looked at one another rather anxiously at Max's arrival.

'Are you hungry?' asked Muffy brightly. 'There's still some bacon and mushrooms in the pan. I could do you an egg if you want one.'

Max smiled. His sister-in-law and Hunter were probably the most wholly good people he had ever known. He wished he could be more like them.

'Not for me, thanks,' he said. 'I might do myself a bit of Marmite toast in a minute. I'm feeling a bit ropy.'

'You look it!' said Henry jovially. The more awkward a situation, the more he would try to joke his way out of it.

'I'm sorry about last night,' said Max. 'I was unforgivably rude.'

'Nonsense, forget about it,' said Henry. 'Had a few too many after work, I expect, eh? Drowning the old sorrows? Ow!' He looked reproachfully at his wife, who had just given him a sharp kick on the ankle. 'What was that for?'

'I'm sure Max doesn't want to talk about it,' said Muffy firmly, with what was meant to be a 'meaningful' look at Henry, and involved her opening her blue eyes very wide and raising one eyebrow. She looked like Felicity Kendall from *The Good Life* trying to do a Roger Moore impression.

'Honestly.' Max grinned at them both. 'It's all right. You don't have to tread on eggshells. Siena is getting married. I'm just going to have to deal with it.'

'Oh, good,' said Henry. 'I'm glad you said that. The lovely Frédérique seemed to be worried that you were "in denial", as she puts it. I told her you were just too smashed to take it all in. Have you been teaching her all this Californian psychobabble, Maxy? I do wish you wouldn't, you know, the poor child's here to learn English.'

Muffy's eyebrow had taken on a frenzied life of its own.

'*What?*' said Henry, unable to ignore her any longer. 'Have you got some sort of tic?'

'Poor Freddie,' said Max, who wasn't really focusing on the private battle between husband and wife. He had woken up this morning to the sound of Caroline's words ringing in his ears: 'You need to let that girl go.' 'I'm afraid I was a bit of a shit to her last night. Where is she? I'd better go and build some bridges.'

He found her upstairs in the bathroom, vainly trying to insert a Little Mermaid toothbrush into Madeleine's mouth while giving Bertie detailed instructions on shoelace tying.

'Uncle Max!' squealed Maddie when she saw him, spraying toothpaste foam all over Freddie's sweater. She jumped up and launched herself into his arms.

'Hello, lovely.' He kissed her on the neck, making her giggle. 'How clean are those pegs, then?'

She withdrew the toothbrush from her mouth and grinned at him, proudly revealing a rather gappy row of milk teeth. 'Perfect. I'm finished,' she announced, wriggling free from him and running off down the corridor before Freddie had a chance to stop her.

'Bertie, mate, do you think you could do that in your own room?' Max asked his nephew. 'I'd like to talk to Frédérique on her own.'

'Sure,' said Bertie, beaming. He loved it when his uncle called him 'mate'. It made him feel really grown up. Stamping down the back of his shoes with his heel, he hobbled off after his sister.

Max perched on the edge of the bath next to Freddie and stared down at the floor.

'I'm sorry,' he said. 'I was being a jerk.'

'Yes, you were,' she agreed, to his surprise. But she

allowed her hand to brush against his anyway, which Max took as a signal to put his arm around her.

'I didn't mean what I said. I'd had too much to drink. I was upset, but that's no excuse for taking it out on you. Do you forgive me?' He looked up at her and saw, with horror, that there were tears in her eyes. 'Oh God, sweetheart, I'm really sorry,' he said, pulling her to him. 'Please don't cry.'

She wiped her eyes on the back of her hand and looked at him, concentrating on his face in a way that made him feel deeply uncomfortable. It was as if she could see right through him. For a twenty-year-old, thought Max, Freddie could be very old and wise sometimes.

When she finally broke the silence, he wished she hadn't.

'You're still in love with her, aren't you?'

She didn't drop her gaze. Max had no choice but to look right at her when he replied.

'No. No, I'm not,' he said. 'This news, it just took me by surprise, that's all. Knocked me for six.' He tried to sound reassuring.

'Do you love me, Max?'

Freddie wasn't letting this one go. He knew how much it had cost her to ask the question, and he couldn't bear to cause her any more pain. Putting his arms around her again so she couldn't see his face when he spoke, he mumbled the only answer he could.

'Of course,' he said. 'Of course I do.'

But they both knew he was lying.

Chapter Forty-five

As it turned out, Max's suspicions about Siena and Randall's whirlwind engagement had not been entirely groundless.

After the disastrous AIDS benefit at the Beverly Hills Hotel, Siena had gone to bed and waited miserably for Randall to come home. By the time he did roll in, at almost five in the morning, smelling of liquor and women's perfume and with his shirt buttoned up wrong, she was an exhausted, nervous wreck.

'I suppose you've been with Miriam, have you?' she accused him tearfully. 'I just hope for both our sakes she didn't give you anything.'

Randall made no attempt to deny it. 'I'd rather have been with you,' he said, stripping down to his boxer shorts and climbing into bed beside her. 'But you made your feelings pretty clear at the hotel. You preferred to skulk back here and mope about your ex than come to the party with me.'

'That's not true,' she protested, but she was too exhausted to go over it all again. 'It's you I've been thinking about all night, not Max. And I certainly didn't ask you to go and fuck that cheap little slut. How could you, Randall?'

He turned to face her, propping himself up on his elbow.

Her eyes were puffy and red from crying, and her skin looked even paler than usual, washed out with exhaustion. Her new, shorter hair had relaxed from its earlier pinned and hairsprayed solidity, and fell about her face in soft, tangled waves. She looked like a frightened six-year-old who'd just woken up from a nightmare. Except with very big boobs, which she was covering defensively now with both hands, presumably against him.

'Who said I fucked her?' he asked, still gazing at Siena's beautiful naked body.

'You did.' She sounded confused, having been thrown a lifebelt of hope that perhaps, by some miracle, he *had* been faithful to her. 'You said you'd rather have been with me. Which means that you must have been with her, doesn't it?'

'Does it?' said Randall. He was being infuriatingly nonchalant about the whole thing.

'Oh, of course it does!' she cried, hitting him across the chest in frustration as she felt her glimmer of hope disappearing again.

'Well, would you actually care if I had?' he asked calmly, ignoring her near-hysteria. 'Fucked Miriam, I mean.'

'Would I care?' She stared at him incredulously. 'Of course I'd care, Randall. Why do you think I've been lying awake all night, crying my goddam eyes out? Of course I fucking care.'

At which point he had rolled on top of her and made love to her more tenderly than ever before.

For the next three hours, he had gently and expertly licked and teased and caressed her, bringing her to climax again and again, until they were both too exhausted to move. And afterwards, as she was drifting off into a deeply contented, sexually replete sleep, he had asked her to marry him.

By the time Siena woke, it was almost three in the afternoon, and Randall had gone. She leapt out of bed in a panic, terrified that last night's events – the ones at the end, anyway – had been some sort of dream.

But there in the bathroom, propped up on her dresser, was a note from Randall. It said he had gone to the office and wouldn't be back until late – but perhaps tomorrow, if he could get away in time, he would take her out for dinner to celebrate their engagement.

Siena read the note a few times – just to make sure she wasn't seeing things – and sank down on to the toilet seat, weak with relief. He was really going to marry her. It was going to be OK.

Relief was definitely the overwhelming emotion, not joy. She knew she didn't love Randall, or at least, she wasn't in love with him, not with the same blind, trusting passion she'd felt for Max. But she now saw that as a good thing.

As Randall's wife, she would be guaranteed a life of wealth, fame and privilege. She would no longer have to keep looking over her shoulder, waiting for everything she had, all her security, to be snatched away on somebody else's whim. Marriage to Randall meant a safety net, and the only kind of security you could count on – financial.

Her relief that he was finally, and against all the odds, about to make a commitment to her was profound and intense. For the first time since Max had betrayed her, she felt she could breathe easy.

Randall, by contrast, had had a somewhat stressful awakening when he remembered his rash promise of the night before. He'd been so drunk, and so horny, his libido having already been awakened by a truly expert blow job from Miriam at Johnny's party, that he'd got rather carried away.

Siena's extreme vulnerability always turned him on anyway. It made him feel strong. But the real killer last night had been when she'd told him that she actually cared for him. Not for the money, for him.

Since he'd made his fortune, no woman had ever said that to him and meant it, as he was sure Siena did. That made her different, special.

But marriage? What the hell was he thinking?

Randall had already decided long ago that he would never share his life or his fortune with anyone. He didn't want children, and he'd seen too many wealthy guys go bankrupt that way.

His first thought on getting out of bed was that he would have to get out of it as soon as possible. Just tell her he was joking, he was drunk, anything. But as he started to shave and dress, he gradually began to perceive the upside in the situation.

An engagement would be fabulous publicity for the movie, which he desperately, desperately needed. It might also calm Siena down, make her ease up on the histrionics both at home and on-set. Recently she'd been wearing her insecurity on her sleeve to a degree that even Randall had found alarming.

Then there was the other-women factor. Not that he ever had much problem attracting beautiful girls, but there was no doubt that being seen as 'off the market' seemed only to encourage the most rapacious and best-looking gold-diggers. Yes, on second thoughts, a very public engagement would have its advantages.

It wasn't as if he had to go through with the wedding.

As it turned out, his predictions proved completely correct.

Not only did the leaking of the news, and the carefully choreographed denials of an engagement, generate massive worldwide interest in both them as a couple and the film, but Siena also visibly relaxed from the moment she got the ring – an absolutely enormous ruby that had cost more than his entire collection of Bentleys – on her finger.

Her one continuing concern was the question of setting a date. But so far he had been able to wriggle out of that fairly easily by insisting that neither of them would have time to focus on a wedding until after 1943 had wrapped.

One evening in early November, he had come home to find Siena looking unusually morose.

She was curled up on the sofa in the small sitting room next to the kitchen, watching reruns of *I Dream of Jeannie* and smoking. An overflowing ashtray and a large pile of discarded sweet wrappers lay on the table beside her, and there was a bottle of wine, as yet unopened, at her feet.

'What are you doing in here?' he asked, picking up the remote and switching off the TV before removing the lit cigarette from her hand and stubbing it out.

He hated her smoking even though he himself was not averse to the occasional cigar.

'Hey.' She sounded annoyed. 'I was watching that.'

She reached for another cigarette, like a naughty child wilfully defying its parents, seeing how far it could push them. But Randall immediately snatched away the packet, and began drawing back the closed curtains, allowing the early evening sunlight to penetrate the smoky gloom.

'No smoking in this house, Siena.' He crushed the Marlboros in his fat hand and dropped the battered remnants in the waste bin. 'You know that. What's the matter with you this evening?'

He sounded less than sympathetic. Randall found female mood swings supremely boring.

'If I tell you, do you promise you won't get mad?'

'No,' he said, sitting down beside her. He hoped there hadn't been yet another problem on-set.

'It's Hunter,' said Siena, to his initial relief, although he noticed that her bottom lip was already starting to wobble ominously. 'I called him.' Randall looked stony faced. 'I know you said I shouldn't,' she went on nervously. 'But it just seemed so weird that we haven't spoken at all, you know, since it happened.'

'Since what happened?'

Siena frowned, surprised. 'Since we got engaged, of course,' she said. 'Honestly, darling. It's a big thing, you know, agreeing to spend the rest of your life with someone. I wanted him to know.'

'Oh, yeah. Right.' Randall got up and walked over to the bar to fix himself a drink. 'Honey,' he said brusquely, sitting back down with a large iced vodka in his hand, 'you didn't need to call him. He knows. The whole

526

world knows, OK? Hunter may not be the sharpest tool in the box but he can read, right? The engagement's been all over the press from here to Timbuktu.'

'Ha, ha,' said Siena sarcastically. 'Yes, he can read, and yes, I'm sure he's heard about it. But he hasn't heard it from me. We haven't spoken.'

'So?' said Randall. He was getting tired of listening to Siena moaning on about a family that evidently didn't give a shit about her. 'That's his problem, not yours. He's the one who stormed off like a spoilt kid at the Dodgers game. Forget about him, baby. Move on.'

Siena wondered, not for the first time, whether this was what Randall really felt. Could he really not see that they were the ones who had behaved badly at the Dodgers, by setting Hunter up? That she was the one who owed him an apology, not the other way around?

'Well, what did he say anyway?' Randall asked, in a tone that made it clear he had very little interest in Hunter's opinions one way or the other. 'He didn't approve?'

'Nothing,' Siena mumbled miserably. 'He wouldn't take my call. I spoke to that stupid cow Tiffany, and she told me to go to hell.'

For some reason, this seemed to make Randall irate. He stood up and began pacing like a tiger preparing for the kill. 'He wouldn't take your call? *He*, that two-bit little soap queen, wouldn't take *your* call?'

Siena couldn't quite see why this should incense him so much. As upset as she was, she was hardly surprised that Hunter didn't want to speak to her after the way she'd treated him this past year. She'd been so desperate to hold on to Randall and her career, she'd dropped him like a hot brick, for no better reason than that Randall had told her to.

She didn't deserve his blessing, on her engagement or anything else in her life.

'Well, it did hurt me,' she began.

But Randall was still ranting, less concerned about

Siena's feelings than with whipping himself up into a fury of indignation. 'How dare he? I mean, who the fuck does he think he is?'

'Look, maybe I shouldn't have mentioned it,' said Siena, who was starting to get concerned by the violence of his reaction.

'Of course you should have mentioned it.' In an instant he turned his displeasure on her. Sitting right in front of him, she made a far more satisfying target than the absent and untouchable Hunter. She shrank back, bewildered, as he glowered down at her angrily, feeling like Jack after he'd just climbed the beanstalk and disturbed the sleeping giant.

'If you ever start keeping secrets from me, Siena, that's it,' he snarled viciously. 'From that moment on, it's over between us. I'll destroy you.'

'Randall, please,' she pleaded, trying to calm him down. 'There's no need to get so upset. I'm not keeping secrets. You asked me what was wrong and I told you.'

The fear in her voice was like petrol on his flames.

'Oh, you told me, did you?' He slammed his drink down on the table and bent his face threateningly low over hers. 'And what about what I told you? I expressly told you never to abase yourself by crawling back to Hunter, or any of the rest of your useless, fucked-up family. And what do you do? The second my back's turned, you're on that phone like a tragic little groupie. And he won't even talk to you!'

Siena shuddered. She could smell Randall's sour breath, like bile pouring out of him. He hadn't flown off the handle at her like this for months, and she had no idea why her call to Hunter should have triggered such a catastrophic relapse.

'You've embarrassed me, and you've embarrassed yourself,' he announced finally, looking at her as though she were something unpleasant he might be forced to disinfect.

'I'm sorry,' said Siena, by now desperate to appease

him. 'I was just so happy about us being engaged, and I haven't had anyone to share it with.'

'What do you mean, you haven't had anyone to share it with?' Randall sounded incredulous. 'The whole world's been talking about it. Look!'

He picked up a copy of last week's *New York Times* magazine from the coffee table behind him, still open at the picture of the two of them together at Cannes, and shoved it under Siena's nose.

'I know,' she said, staring at the image. 'But I meant . . .' She was walking on eggshells now, anxious to choose her words carefully and not provoke him any further. 'I meant, I had nobody to share the news with that I love, or that loves me. That's all.'

'Everybody loves you, Siena,' said Randall, pointing to the picture again, more gently this time, and kissing the top of her head, the storm of his anger now apparently subsided. Whether he had wilfully misunderstood her or not, she couldn't tell. She was just relieved the shouting had stopped.

'Now why don't you go upstairs and get changed.' His tone was suddenly brisk and businesslike again. 'I'm taking you to Morton's tonight, remember, with Luke and Sabrina.'

Shit, she'd forgotten. Dinner with her director and his tedious sculptor wife was the last thing she felt like, especially now. Rows with Randall were so terrifying, they always left her utterly emotionally exhausted.

'And don't forget to clean your teeth again, will you?' he added, downing the last of his vodka. 'You know I can't stand the smell of cigarettes on your breath.'

Dinner was every bit as gruesome as Siena had feared.

Luke was a sweetheart – the two of them had been getting on much better now that things had improved on-set – but his wife was terribly pretentious, one of those artistic types who bang on about how much better the Norton Simon is than the Getty, and isn't it a tragedy that they can't move back to New York where the people are so much more *real*?

Sabrina also made the mistake of assuming that because Siena had made her name as a model, she must be stupid.

'I must say, the recent modern American sculpture exhibition at the Getty was a disgrace, wasn't it, Luke? Did you see it, Randall?'

'No, I'm afraid not.' Randall smiled, trying to be polite. He couldn't stomach Sabrina any more than Siena could. 'I don't have a lot of free time for museums and things.'

'Of course you don't,' Sabrina agreed obsequiously, before turning with a patronising smirk to Siena. 'I expect it's not really your sort of thing either, is it, my dear?'

'No, it's not,' said Siena rudely. Unlike Randall, she saw no point in being polite to the hairy-legged old frump, or engaging her in conversation a moment longer than was necessary.

'I expect you're more interested in fashion and things, aren't you? With your modelling background,' Sabrina went on, ignoring the warning glances from her husband.

'Not really,' said Siena. 'Fashion's boring. I was always better at math and science at school. I had a place at Oxford to read medicine, actually, but I turned it down.'

Sabrina looked suitably amazed.

'My father wanted me to be a doctor, but I wasn't interested. Where did you go to college, by the way?'

Siena watched with satisfaction as Sabrina was forced to mumble, 'Penn State.'

'Oh. Well, that's a good school too,' She smiled. It was her turn to be patronising now. 'I always felt university was a bit of a waste of time, though. I knew I wanted to act from day one, and modelling's a much more effective route into Hollywood than an Oxford degree. At least it was for me.'

She placed her perfectly manicured hand smugly on

Randall's arm. That would teach the stupid, bossy cow to put her down.

'I think you would have made it eventually, Siena, with or without the modelling,' said Luke, anxious to get his wife off the hook and change the subject as soon as possible.

Siena beamed with pleasure at the unexpected compliment from her director. 'Do you really?'

'Sure,' Randall answered for him. 'With your surname and my backing, how could you go wrong?'

Bastard, thought Siena. Why could he never admit that she had any talent of her own?

Luke, who could see how wounded she'd been by Randall's comment, decided to risk his producer's wrath still further by saying, 'Actually, I think she'd have made it anyway. Being a McMahon doesn't hurt, but if you couldn't act, you'd never have got this far. Not in one of my movies, anyway. Believe me, I've seen so many stars' kids in Hollywood trying to break into the business, and most of them are terrible.'

Siena could have kissed him. But her elation soon evaporated when she saw Randall's face, and the familiar simmering fury building up inside him as he twisted his napkin round and round, like he was preparing to strangle someone. As far as he was concerned, he had 'created' Siena. No one else, least of all herself, could take any credit for her current achievements.

Watching him, she felt a knot forming in her stomach and realised, almost with shame, that she was afraid of him. She wondered whether this was how Grandma Minnie had felt every time she caved in to Duke. For the first time that she could remember, she felt a stab of real sympathy for her grandmother. Perhaps she and Minnie were more alike than she had liked to believe?

Sabrina, who was also none too thrilled with her husband's impassioned defence of his beautiful leading lady, suddenly stood up and started waving at a party who had just arrived.

'Suzie! Helloooo, over here.' She flapped her arms wildly, as if trying to bring a plane in to land. Siena rolled her eyes at Randall, but he was still too angry to respond.

'Luke, darling, look. It's Suzie Ong. And isn't that your uncle with her, Siena? The actor?'

Siena, who had her back to the door, froze.

She couldn't bring herself to turn around.

'I don't think so,' she muttered desperately.

Please, please, let it not be Hunter, not tonight. That would push Randall right over the edge.

Luke noticed that the blood had drained from Siena's face. She looked like she'd seen a ghost. 'Are you all right?' he whispered.

'It is him, you know, I'm sure of it.' Sabrina's voice was like a foghorn. 'Suzie! Come and say hello! She's *terribly* nice,' she said in an aside to Randall. 'She's a television director over at NBC.'

'I know who she is,' he snapped, glaring at Siena as though she were somehow responsible for Suzie and Hunter's arrival. Suzie was one of Hugh Orchard's protégées, an elegant Singaporean in her mid-thirties who was becoming well known as an up-and-coming director in the TV world. She already had a fistful of hit shows to her name, and had directed Hunter in the last two series of *UCLA*, presiding over the soap's skyrocketing ratings, much to Orchard's and NBC's delight.

A few moments later she appeared at the table, looking rather awkward. Siena didn't know whether Hunter was with her or not. She was too terrified to look up and find out.

'Hello, Sabrina. Luke.' Suzie seemed less than thrilled to see them.

'Suzie, let me introduce you to Randall Stein.' Sabrina was obviously enjoying her role as hostess to Hollywood's elite. Randall gave a grudging nod of acknowledgement, which Suzie returned. 'And Siena McMahon. I imagine you two have already crossed paths?'

'No, actually,' said Suzie, looking at Siena coldly. She

knew how the spoiled little brat had treated Hunter and was not one of her biggest fans. 'Hi.'

Siena's head seemed to be magnetically drawn to the table. She still couldn't look up.

'Isn't that Siena's uncle with you?' Sabrina ploughed on, oblivious to the entire table's discomfort. 'Why don't you both come over and join us?'

'I don't think so,' said Suzie and Randall in unison. Their eyes met for a moment, but Suzie dropped hers first. The man looked positively murderous. 'Hunter and I have a lot of business to discuss. Maybe another time. But it was lovely to see you.'

She kissed both Luke and Sabrina perfunctorily on the cheek and disappeared back to Hunter and her table. Siena felt as if she were about to spontaneously combust. She could feel the imagined heat of Hunter's stare on her back and Randall's fury beside her. She dared not look at either of them, but sat twisting her engagement ring round and round on her finger, wishing someone would beam her out of there.

'I wonder what was wrong with her?' said Sabrina to nobody in particular. 'She seemed in a great hurry to get away.'

'Yes,' said Randall nastily. 'Siena sometimes has that effect on people.'

'I'm sorry.' Siena stumbled to her feet. This was all too much for her. Hunter was here, her darling, darling Hunter, and he wouldn't even speak to her. Suddenly she had to get away.

The whole restaurant looked on mesmerised as she stood up and began ricocheting off tables, blinded by tears, running towards the door as if the room were on fire.

'Siena.'

Hunter shot out his arm and grabbed her by the wrist as she staggered past him. Shaking, she glanced down and saw his sweet, sad, concerned face looking up at her. 'Do you wanna talk?'

She felt as if she were in one of those nightmares where you're trying to run but your legs are stuck in mud. She wanted to fall into his arms, to tell him how much she loved him, how much she'd missed him, to say how sorry she was. But her brain and body both seemed to be frozen, and she just stood there miserably mute. Randall was behind her before she could say a word.

'No, she doesn't want to talk.' He smiled evilly at Hunter. Pulling Siena away from him and putting his arm around her shoulder, he looked more like her jailer than her lover. 'She doesn't ever want to talk to you or hear from you again. It upsets her. Doesn't it, Siena?' He jerked her round to face Hunter, rather as a ventriloquist might jerk his dummy. It was a violent, almost obscene gesture. A few of the women in the room winced. Siena nodded helplessly. 'You see? She doesn't want you,' Randall sneered. Hunter just stared at him, appalled. 'Now if you'll excuse me, I need to take Siena home. Before she gets any more upset.'

With the entire restaurant watching, including a horrified Luke and Sabrina, he bundled Siena outside and straight into their waiting chauffeur-driven Bentley. As soon as they were ensconced behind the darkened glass windows, she broke down in tears.

'I'm sorry, Randall,' she sobbed. She was shaking like a leaf. 'I'm so sorry.'

'You will be,' he said.

And then he punched her so hard in the face she was knocked out cold.

Chapter Forty-six

When she came to, she was sitting up in bed at home in just her underwear. Her hands were tied tightly behind her back, she wasn't sure what with. Randall was sitting in the armchair beside the bed, staring at her, with a half-empty bottle of brandy at his feet.

Siena could smell the stale alcohol fumes from the bed. His voice was badly slurred when he spoke to her.

'You stupid bitch,' he whispered. 'You just had to humiliate me, didn't you? You can't help yourself.'

Siena shifted uneasily from side to side and tried to keep calm. The whole right side of her face felt as if it were exploding, but out of her left eye she could see that the bedside clock said 2.30 a.m. She struggled to get her bearings. The last thing she remembered was Randall hitting her in the car. He hadn't been drunk then – at least, she hadn't thought so. Clearly he was looped up to the eyeballs now.

'Randall, could you please untie my hands. This is ridiculous.'

She tried a firm, confident tone, hoping to jolt him out of this madness. She always knew he could be violent, but he had never pulled anything like this before. Not with her anyway.

'You think you could have got to where you are without me? You and *Luke*. Is that what you think?' He had stood up and was advancing unsteadily towards her, his brandy glass still in his hands.

'Of course not,' said Siena. 'I know how much I owe you.' She tried not to sound as panicked as she felt. 'Luke wasn't trying to insult you.'

'Shut up! I don't want to hear about fucking *Luke*.'

She heard the roar of his voice in her ear, followed by

a heavy blow to her left temple. For a moment she felt nothing at all, as if everything were happening in slow motion, or to someone else. Then she became aware of a stream of her own blood flowing down her face, into her eyes and mouth.

He must have smashed the glass into her head.

Her hands were tied, so she couldn't reach up to touch the wound. Suddenly terror overwhelmed her. She felt like she was drowning in blood.

He hit her again, and this time she felt the jagged glass as it sliced into the flesh around her eye. Everything went red.

'Jesus Christ,' she spluttered, tiny droplets of blood spraying off her lips like a red mist. 'What have you done to me?'

Randall stood stock still and stared at the broken glass in his hand as if he'd never seen it before. Two of his fingers were bleeding slightly.

'Shit, I'm sorry. Oh, shit.' He sounded detached, zombie-like. 'Here, let me help.'

He pulled out a screwed-up handkerchief and moved across the bed towards her. Siena screamed, and kicked out at him as hard as she could, both legs pumping like fury.

'Stay the fuck away from me,' she yelled. 'Stay back!'

Instinctively, Randall fought off her frenzied kicking. One of Siena's feet hit him hard across the bridge of the nose. He yelped in pain and instantly brought his heavy fist down with a crack on her rib cage, right where she'd suffered the fractures after her car crash last year. It was agony. A second punch caught her across the left side of the face, so hard she thought she felt her cheekbone splinter.

Not even the adrenalin pumping violently through her veins could take away the searing pain of Randall's blows. He was a big man, and even with her hands free she would have been powerless against him. She slumped forward, doubled over in pain, the blood from her face cascading on to the white linen sheets.

This time, when he moved towards her, she had not one ounce of energy left with which to fight him. She was only dimly aware of him untying her wrists, and later slipped in and out of consciousness when he brought towels and warm water from the bathroom and pressed them inexpertly to her face, making her cry out in pain. The last thing she remembered was Randall holding a bloodied towel and looking bewildered, asking her over and over again, 'Why, Siena? Why did you make me do it?'

'I'll do what I can, but it won't be easy.'

She awoke disoriented to hear a strange man's voice. She tried to open her eyes to look around her but nothing happened. She whimpered in terror.

'Who's there? I can't see. Why can't I see anything?'

The next voice she heard was Randall's. He sounded sober and in control, almost businesslike. She could tell that he was standing on the far side of the room, and felt relief when he made no move to approach her.

'You're in a private surgery centre, darling, in Beverly Hills,' he told her. 'The doctors are going to take care of you.'

'What do you mean? What doctors?' She was becoming increasingly hysterical. 'I can't open my fucking eyes, Randall! What have you done to me?'

'What have *I* done to you?' He did his best to sound affronted. 'What on earth do you mean?'

'Try to keep calm, Siena,' the strange voice said, before she had a chance to respond. It was a soothing, gentle voice, and it was close to her, either sitting on or leaning over the side of her bed. 'I'm going to give you something to help you relax and keep numbing the pain.'

She felt a slight prick in her arm and a quite pleasant, cool sensation as some nameless liquid was pumped into her veins. Instantly her head felt heavy and she slumped back on to the pillows. She could also feel her heart rate dropping, and a surreal mood of calm flooding her senses. It was a quite wonderful, almost blissful peace.

'You've had an accident,' the voice continued. 'I'm Dr Sanford, and I'm going to help you get well.'

'I can't see,' whispered Siena.

Even through her drug-induced stupor, she kept a dogged hold of that one, terrifying fact.

'Randall tells me you fell,' said the doctor. 'Into a glass cabinet. There's been some damage to your eyes, but we won't know how serious it is until we operate. Are you happy for me to operate, Siena?'

She groaned drowsily.

After a long pause, she said, 'I want to see the police. I want . . .' She stopped, apparently exhausted by the effort and concentration involved in speaking. 'I want to report him. Randall. He attacked me.'

The doctor sighed and looked nervously across at his client. This wasn't the first time Randall Stein had brought him a battered girl in the small hours of the morning. But usually they were prostitutes or starlets, whose silence could easily be bought, not world-famous film stars. And in any case, none of them had had injuries even approaching the seriousness of Siena's.

It was a tragedy. The girl's face had been shredded. She would never look the same again.

Both he and Randall had hoped that her concussion would be serious enough for her to have lost her memory of the attack. Clearly, though, this wasn't the case.

'The police? Well, that's your right, of course,' he responded cautiously. 'But I really think we should focus on treating your injuries before anything else. I'll leave you alone for a few minutes to think about it.'

'No!' Siena screamed. She was clearly terrified of being left alone with Randall.

'It's all right,' said Dr Sanford, taking her hand and stroking it until she began to breathe normally. Despite having made vast sums of money over the years thanks to his 'discretion' as Randall's private doctor, even he was disgusted by what he had seen tonight. The girl could have died. If he weren't already so deeply implicated in so many of Randall's past 'accidents', he would have gone to the police himself. 'He won't hurt you, I promise,' he said, with a meaningful look that was not lost on Randall. 'I'll be right outside the door.'

'Stay where you are or I'll scream,' said Siena, the moment she heard the door click shut. Her voice was slurred and drowsy, but Randall could tell she meant what she said and didn't move.

'Fine,' he said calmly. 'But I'd think very carefully before screaming, if I were you. To the police or anyone else.'

He took a small cigarillo from his inside jacket pocket and lit it. Siena could hear this little ritual and smell the sweet tobacco smoke wafting across the room towards her.

'Let's look at your options, shall we?' Randall went on. 'You can tell the police that I attacked you. For which, in any case, they will only have your word against mine.'

'I think,' she said derisively, 'my injuries speak for themselves.'

'Do you?' Randall seemed unconcerned. 'Well, perhaps. Or perhaps the word of a well-respected producer and *very* generous benefactor of the LAPD will count for more than that of a young actress already known to be highly emotionally unstable. Who knows?' Siena opened her mouth to protest, but found that she was overwhelmed with exhaustion. That shot in the arm had really knocked her out. 'In either event, at that point will begin a long, protracted and very expensive legal battle that you are in no financial position to fight.'

'What do you mean?' she challenged him. 'Of course I can fight you. I've got my own money.'

'Two hundred and fifty-eight thousand dollars, to be precise,' said Randall. 'Of the two million you gave me to invest last year, I'm afraid that's all that's left. In your name, that is.'

'Liar!' she snarled. 'That's impossible. You can't have lost that much in a year. And if you have, that's negligence. I'll sue you for every fucking cent.'

'Again, an expensive business, suing people.' He puffed out smoke luxuriously. It was so long since Siena had even attempted to stand up to him, he was quite enjoying the thrill of the fight. 'Particularly when one is being sued oneself.'

'Oh, *you're* going to sue *me* are you?' She wanted to laugh, but even with the painkillers the pain in her chest was too much. 'What for? Damaging your brandy glass? Staining the fucking bedspread with my blood?'

'No,' said Randall, still clinically composed. 'For deliberately delaying production on the movie. For libel, if you try to blame your accidental injuries on me. And for breach of contract. After all, you're hardly able to continue playing Peggy now, are you? After your drunken fall. I'm afraid you've well and truly lost your looks, sweetheart.'

He started to laugh, but Siena wasn't listening. She had no idea whether what he'd said about the money was true, and she wasn't even sure if she cared. Her brain was a fog of anger, drugs and pain. All she knew was that she might never be able to see again. And if she did, would she even recognise herself after what he'd done to her? The thought of her ravaged face suddenly made her feel violently sick.

'Pass me something,' she said, clasping both hands over her mouth.

Randall picked up a steel bowl by the bed, presumably placed there for the purpose, and put it in her hands. He watched while she retched and retched until her stomach was utterly empty. The pain in her ribs and face was so bad, and the effort of throwing up so exhausting, that she fell back against the pillows and began to cry.

That was when he knew he had her.

Silently, he took away the bowl of vomit and put it in the far corner of the room, wrinkling his nose in distaste. When he spoke it was quietly, and with menacing intent.

'If you go after me, Siena, believe me, I will crush you.'

She did believe him. Hadn't he crushed her already?

'But if you keep your mouth shut, I'll help you. As much as I can. We'll come up with a convincing story together, and we'll see what can be done about recovering some of your money.'

She didn't trust him for a second. But realistically, what other choice did she have? She had no family, no friends that she could turn to. Even if she had, she'd be too ashamed for anyone to see her like this, to know what she had allowed Randall to do to her. She had, it appeared, very little money and her career was shot to pieces. She had almost certainly lost her looks for ever, and possibly her sight as well.

She was helpless.

'What do you want me to do?' she asked eventually. The weariness in her voice said it all.

'Nothing,' said Randall. 'Just keep your mouth shut, and I'll do what needs to be done. If you need surgery, we'll do that here, first. Then you disappear somewhere to recuperate. I have a house in Nantucket we could use.' He was thinking aloud. 'It's very private.'

'What about the movie?' she asked, numbly.

'We'll put it on hold for a few weeks, but chances are it's dead. Far too expensive to reshoot the lot now, and I can't see you . . .' He hesitated, as if he'd suddenly decided he didn't want to hurt her any further. Taunting her didn't seem quite so much fun any more. 'Let's just say I can't see you getting well enough to go back to work. Not in the time we'd need anyway.'

Stubbing out his cigar, he came and sat down on the bed beside her. Relieved that she hadn't the strength to fight him, he now felt some stirrings of remorse.

It frightened him to think that he was responsible for

the terrible wreckage of her face. It was almost more than he could admit, even to himself.

'I am sorry, Siena,' he said, picking up her limp hand in his and squeezing it. 'I didn't mean it, really. I want to take care of you now. If you'll let me.'

She made no response, and the two of them sat silently together for a few minutes until a gentle rap on the door announced that Dr Sanford had returned. He was relieved, and not a little surprised, to see that some sort of rapprochement seemed to have been reached.

'She wants you to operate,' said Randall, looking for all the world like the picture of the concerned fiancé at her bedside. 'As soon as possible.'

'Is that right?' the doctor asked Siena, shooing Randall away and taking her hand himself. 'Will you sign the consents?'

'I can't read the consents,' Siena reminded him. She sounded very weak and drowsy. 'But sure, I'll sign anything. Let's just get this over with.'

The initial operation on Siena's damaged eyes had been touch and go.

The surgeon was certain that she would have some vision in her left eye, where most of the damage had been caused by two burst blood vessels and a shattered socket from a single, powerful punch. But the right eye, which had been extensively scarred with shards of glass and where the cornea had been deeply lacerated, might never recover. Either way, it would be weeks before Siena could remove her dressings and bandages.

By the time the press cottoned on to the fact that she had mysteriously disappeared, Siena was already lying morphined up to the eyeballs, with her head completely bandaged like a mummy's in a guest bedroom in Randall's Nantucket house.

Her whereabouts, as far as Randall knew, were known only to himself, Dr Sanford and Melissa, the private nurse he had hired to care for Siena and escort her, via his private G4 jet, from LA to Boston and then on to the island. He had fed the media a story about Siena suffering some sort of breakdown from nervous exhaustion, and announced that he had suspended production on *1943* indefinitely.

After an initial flurry of interest, other, more exciting stories began to take over the headlines, especially once it became clear that no one knew where Siena was recuperating and there were no pictures to be had.

Hunter had called Randall at the house repeatedly in the first week to try to find out where she was, but had been forced to give up when Randall made public a letter, quite clearly in Siena's hand and signed by her, stating that she wanted time to recuperate in private and did not want her whereabouts to be disclosed to anyone other than her doctor and her boyfriend.

To Randall's surprise and relief, it really had been as simple as that.

As far as the rest of the world was concerned, within about a month it was almost as if Siena McMahon no longer existed.

Chapter Forty-seven

Claire sat in the back of the little plane, looking down at the tiny islands strewn just off the Boston coast.

She was dressed too warmly for the summer's day in a tweed skirt and stiff white linen blouse, with her sleek, grey-blonde hair covered by a blue polka-dot headscarf, and her anxious, worry-lined eyes shielded by big Christian Dior sunglasses.

None of the other passengers in the little pond-hopper of a plane gave her a second glance as they made the twenty-minute flight over to Nantucket. Later, at the airport, she would look like every other well-to-do WASP-y matron, carrying her small suitcase to her nondescript rented Chevrolet, no doubt on her way to join the rest of her family in one of the sprawling Quaker summer homes that littered the island.

Gazing out of the plane window, she sighed.

Deep down, she'd always known that she'd do this eventually. That one day, she'd wake up, walk out of the door and go and find her daughter.

Particularly since she'd hired Bill Jennings to start trailing Siena, Claire felt like her life had become one long emotional roller-coaster. On the one hand there was the torture of feeling so close to her child, and yet being unable to reach out to her or make contact. This pain, combined with the constant terror of Pete finding out and leaving her, or doing something even worse, had frequently pushed her to the point where she had considered calling the whole thing off.

On the other hand, the PI's reports had brought her such exquisite joy. She felt that, on one level, she had been privileged to have a private, personal insight into her daughter's life. Secreted away in her dressing room back home she now had groaning files crammed with pictures of Siena on the set of her movie, as well as even more cherished, if grainier, shots of her relaxing at home alone. In some of these pictures, the earlier ones taken just after her road accident, she seemed happy. And her happiness meant more to Claire than anything else in the world.

But then there were other shots, particularly recently, that had caused her indescribable pain. Pictures Bill had reluctantly given her which no mother should ever have to see.

She had known for months that Siena had become miserable and isolated living with Randall, but still she had prevaricated, hesitating to make contact in case she unwittingly pushed Pete over the edge. Perhaps she had also, subconsciously, been hoping that in her all too evident unhappiness, Siena would take the initiative and reach out to her family herself.

In the end, though, it was Siena's 'disappearance' which had finally convinced her she couldn't afford to wait any longer. Bill had only very incomplete evidence about what might have happened, but he sensed that Siena could be in serious danger. It had taken him an agonising three weeks to track her down to the house on Nantucket, and when he told Claire he'd found her, that was it.

Suddenly, it didn't even seem like a choice any more.

After five long years of separation, wild horses could not have kept her from boarding that plane.

Once they'd landed, she pulled out of the tiny airport and on to the single-track road towards Siasconset and checked her mobile for messages from Pete.

There were none.

Relieved, she began to take in the grey, weather-boarded houses lining the route, their immaculately kept dark green hedges and formal gardens adding splashes of colour to an otherwise flat, marshy landscape.

Although real estate values on the island had skyrocketed since the eighties, so that even fairly modest homes were now worth upward of five million dollars, the plain Quaker architecture ensured that Nantucket retained its essentially humble charm. There were none of the vulgar edifices that defaced LA lining its beautiful beaches, and the villages still had the look and feel of real, working communities, despite the fact that these days even the postman could probably have traded in his home for a cool million, bought himself a Ferrari and moved off-island to Boston in luxurious retirement.

It was amazing really, thought Claire, that more of the locals hadn't cashed in on the property market and made a quick killing, leaving Nantucket exclusively to super-rich tourists like herself. But they hadn't. Some of the old folk loved to tell the wealthy New Yorkers how they had lived in the same house for forty years and seen its value go from two thousand dollars to two million, but that they would never sell.

There was a magic about Nantucket, it seemed, something that you could never put a price tag on. Not in dollars anyway.

As she drew nearer to the village of Siasconset, the large homes were replaced by tiny doll's-house cottages, complete with white picket fences, climbing roses and ornate topiary, many with ornamental hedges cut into the shape of a whale, in tribute to Nantucket's whaling history.

Although she hadn't been to the island since she was a teenager, the strict building regulations meant that Siasconset village had hardly changed at all since the sixties, and Claire found her bearings quite easily.

The Chanticleer restaurant was still there, and still packed with wealthy East Coast honeymooners, sipping champagne and eating lobster salads out on the terrace. The village store on the little triangular green was also just as she remembered it, although perhaps there were even more bicycles parked outside it than in the old days, drawn to the new sandwich-and-picnic shop that had sprung up next door.

Parking her car at the green, she picked up an official-looking sheaf of documents from the passenger seat and, leaving her suitcase in the boot, began walking down the sandy track towards the beach.

The house, unless she was very much mistaken, was only a couple of hundred yards up the track on the right-hand side. Bill had told her that it was entirely concealed from the road behind a massive yew hedge but that, this being Nantucket, there was no security presence or electric gates. She would be able to walk right up to the front door and, she hoped, within a few short minutes would be reunited with her daughter.

Her hands shook so much as she crunched her way along the gravel drive and up to the porch and she fretted that she might drop her papers. Although hot, it was very windy, and if she let them out of her grasp for an instant they'd be snatched up and carried off like Dorothy's house in *The Wizard of Oz*.

Suddenly, standing on the steps, she stopped.

She found herself crippled with fear and self-doubt.

What was she doing here? Would Siena even want to see her? What if she were furious and wanted nothing more to do with her?

Claire could hardly blame her if that were the case.

And then there was Pete. How was he going to react if he found out, or rather *when* he found out, what she was really doing in Nantucket?

She'd told him she was visiting an old school friend, but sensed that he was already becoming suspicious. He'd be angry, of course, when he found out, furious even. But would he understand *why* she'd done it? Would he see that she just couldn't stay away any more, not now, not with Siena seriously ill and alone?

She forced herself to calm down and took two long, deep breaths, pushing the image of an apoplectic, wounded Peter from her mind. She couldn't think about any of that now. All that mattered was getting into that house, and finding her baby.

She pulled back the heavy brass knocker and banged it firmly three times against the wooden door, with a lot more confidence than she felt. After what seemed like decades, a woman about her own age, perhaps a few years younger, opened the door a fraction and glared out at her suspiciously.

'Can I help you?'

She was wearing a formal nurse's uniform and reminded Claire of the terribly strict old matron at her East Coast boarding school. Summoning up all her courage, and helped by a sudden surge of adrenalin, she began her well-rehearsed lines.

'Can you help *me*?' She chuckled, as though the woman had made some inadvertent joke. 'Well, aren't you Melissa Evans?'

Caught off guard, the nurse confirmed it. 'Do I know you?'

'Well, no,' said Claire, smiling broadly. 'You don't. But I hope you're expecting me. I'm Annie Gordon, your relief support.'

Melissa looked blank.

'Hasn't Mr Stein called you?' said Claire, furrowing her brow in surprise. 'Poor man, he must be out of his mind with worry. Here.' She handed over the documents to a wary-looking Melissa, who gave them a cursory read. 'This should explain everything.'

'You're a nurse?' she said eventually, frowning at the last page of Claire's paperwork.

Claire felt her stomach give a nervous lurch. She hoped Bill hadn't made any glaring mistakes on her false résumé and the forged letter of employment from Randall.

'Why else would I be here?' She tried another smile, but Melissa still looked unconvinced. There was nothing for it, Claire decided, but to try to bluff it out. 'Maybe we should give Mr Stein a call?' she suggested. 'I know how important security is to him. Perhaps you'd feel better if you checked things out with him yourself? I'm in no rush, believe me.'

She turned away slightly and moved down a step, a calculated gesture designed to make the other woman feel less threatened.

It worked.

Melissa hesitated. Then, looking at Claire's naturally open and honest face, she smiled herself and said, 'Oh, no, I don't think that'll be necessary, Annie. You must be absolutely exhausted after all that travelling. Come in, come in.'

Claire stepped over the threshold and tried to stifle her sigh of relief.

She'd made it. She was here.

Inside, the house looked elegant but low key, not at all what she had pictured Randall's taste to be, and certainly nothing like the pictures Bill had shown her of his opulent Malibu mansion. Not that she was really concerned with her surroundings. She wondered where Siena was, but didn't want to over-play her hand by asking too many questions too soon.

As it turned out, she didn't have to.

'I'll get you a cup of coffee and show you around in a minute,' said Melissa. Now that Claire had won her trust, it seemed she was glad of someone to talk to after being cooped up in the house, effectively alone, for weeks. The information came pouring out of her like water from a sieve.

'Siena is up there.' She pointed to a room leading directly off the top of the staircase. 'Sleeping. She's still sleeping an awful lot, thanks to the painkillers, up to seventeen, eighteen hours a day.'

That didn't sound good. Claire tried not to look shocked. 'What painkillers is she on?' she asked as nonchalantly as she could.

'Still on the morphine, but Doctor wants us to bring it down in the next few days, move her on to co-proxamol,' said Melissa. 'Don't you have a suitcase, by the way?'

'Oh, yes,' said Claire absently. Morphine? What the hell had happened to her? Bill had told her about the facial bandages, but Claire had assumed they might have been for something cosmetic. You didn't take morphine for a nose job. 'I parked at the green,' she managed to explain. 'Thought I'd walk around a bit, get my bearings.'

'It's beautiful here, don't you think?' Melissa enthused, drawing the reluctant Claire away from the hallway and Siena's room and into the kitchen, where she began reheating the already brewed coffee. Claire sat down at the table and tried to concentrate on what the nurse was saying. 'Although I haven't had much chance to enjoy it yet, as obviously I can't leave her. Milk? Sugar?' Claire nodded. 'Hopefully I'll be able to get out and have a break now that you're here.'

'Hopefully,' said Claire.

The next ten minutes, spent sipping her unwanted coffee and listening to Melissa prattle on about everything from the grocery deliveries to Randall's paranoia about outsiders, and his miserliness as a boss, were sheer torture. It was all she could do to restrain herself from rushing up the stairs two at a time, breaking down the door and taking her daughter in her arms. But she knew it would be wise to bide her time.

At last, though, her patience was rewarded, when Melissa offered to walk down to the green and get her case for her.

'If you give me the keys, I'll drive the car up as well, if you like,' she said helpfully. 'To be honest, I'm longing to get out of this house. You don't mind staying here and holding the fort, do you? We'll sort out a room for you when I get back.' She was already buttoning up her cardigan against the wind and preparing to leave. 'The phone won't ring, but if it does, don't answer it. Randall and Dr Sanford always use the second line, which is in the study. Then they hang up after three rings and call back, so you know it's them. Honestly, it's like working for the CIA around here.' She rolled her eyes heavenward, as if she and Claire were already old friends who regularly shared little jokes about their employer's eccentricities.

Claire assured her that she was more than happy to stay behind and watched as, miracle of miracles, the nurse waddled off down the driveway towards the village, leaving her alone in the house with Siena.

As soon as the heavy old front door had clanked shut, she bolted up the stairs, pausing for a moment outside the door to Siena's room.

She realised that once she opened it and stepped inside there could be no going back, with either her daughter or her husband.

She thought of the loneliness of the past five years; of the countless times she had watched Siena from the shadows, longing with every atom of her being to reach out to her, but never quite finding the courage.

She thought of Pete, of how much she loved him, but also of how futile the sacrifices she had made for him had been. She had lost those years with Siena for his sake, but he remained as paranoid, frightened and embittered against the world as he had ever been. What had it all been for?

And she thought, for a moment, of old Duke McMahon, and how much he had to answer for.

It seemed to Claire that Duke's ambition, his ruthlessness and his casual cruelty, had been passed down through the generations of his family like some inescapable genetic disease. Even his love, the very great love he had had for Siena, had somehow turned into something toxic. And her own love, for both her husband and her child, had been utterly powerless against it.

She would never forgive herself for those terrible, wasted years.

For better or worse, they ended today.

Slowly, she turned the handle, and walked into the room.

Chapter Forty-eight

Inside Siena's room it was very, very dark. There was no natural light at all, only a faint, reddish glow from what looked like a child's night light plugged into the far wall.

Claire could make out her daughter's sleeping figure, but little else. It was only when she moved over to the bed that she saw that the whole upper portion of Siena's face was covered with bandages, leaving only her mouth and chin visible. Her lower lip was split and swollen. She had quite obviously been beaten.

'Oh my God,' she cried out, forgetting all her planned restraint and smothering her child in kisses. 'What has he done to you? Oh, Siena, Siena, darling, I am so sorry.'

At first, Siena thought her mother's voice was part of a dream.

Max no longer haunted her subconscious, but images of both her parents and of Grandpa Duke had begun invading her sleep more and more frequently since the attack. But this time the dream was so vivid she could actually smell her mother, and feel her cool hands stroking the bare skin on her arms and shoulders. She couldn't bear to wake up.

'Angel, can you hear me? Siena, it's Mommy. Can you hear me, darling? Try to wake up. I'm here, Siena. I'm here.'

As she floated up into consciousness, the voice seemed to become louder and more real. But she hardly dared hope it might be true. When she spoke, her voice emerged as a hoarse, tremulous whisper.

'Mom?'

Claire responded with more kisses, allowing Siena to feel her skin and the brush of her hair, and entwining her fingers in her daughter's. Even her hand, she saw in the darkness, looked swollen and bruised.

'Please don't leave me.' She was barely audible, but Siena's words cut through Claire like a knife.

'I won't, my angel,' she promised. 'Never, never again.'

As she spoke, she felt Siena's grip on her hand relax, and watched her tumble back into unconsciousness. A terrible panic flooded her senses.

'Siena! Siena!' she shouted, shaking her by the shoulders.

Why wouldn't she wake up?

'Oh, you mustn't worry about her, Annie.'

Claire spun around to find Melissa standing in the doorway. She wondered how long she'd been there, but her relaxed tone and manner soon convinced her that the nurse could not have overheard anything important.

'That's what she's like with the drugs,' said Melissa. 'Talking one minute, spark out the next. I doubt she'll wake again till supper-time now.'

With Siena in a semi-comatose state, Claire was able to settle into her room for a few hours and try to figure out what to do next.

Her biggest immediate problem was that she didn't know how much time she would have until her cover was blown.

Thanks to her PI's meticulous briefing, she'd been able to plan her arrival in Nantucket to coincide with Randall's trip to the Far East. She also knew that Randall had asked Melissa to notify him of any significant changes in Siena's condition, but that otherwise he was not intending to call, and would not arrive in Nantucket himself to see Siena for almost three weeks.

Dr Sanford was another story, though.

Posing as Randall's new PA, one of Bill's team had informed the doctor that his client had sent a second nurse down to support Melissa, and faxed Claire's forged documentation across to him.

Bill seemed convinced that the doctor had swallowed the story, and that he was unlikely to contact Randall unless something really *did* go wrong with Siena. But Claire remained nervous. One conversation between the two men would blow her cover for sure.

Then there was Pete, who was bound to rumble that something was up sooner or later, probably sooner, and would no doubt storm in, all guns blazing, and undo all her carefully planned work.

She needed to get Siena out of there, to bring her home. But that would take time. Time for her to win back her daughter's trust, and time for Siena to recuperate sufficiently for her to be moved. Right now she had no idea whether she was looking at three weeks or three hours until her cover was blown. The pressure was immense.

Once she'd unpacked her things into the simple Shaker chest of drawers, she sat down on the bed, a heavy, Victorian mahogany affair covered with a white hand-embroidered quilt, and called Pete from her mobile.

He asked after her old school friend, and trotted out a few perfunctory questions about how her trip had been, but generally he seemed distracted by work, which for once Claire was grateful for. With that particular threat neutralised, for the time being at least, she changed into a pair of white flannel trousers and a black sweater and went downstairs to find Melissa.

'I hope it doesn't matter that I'm not in uniform,' she said, finding the nurse peeling three large baking potatoes in the kitchen. 'Mr Stein never mentioned anything.'

'Well, no one's going to see you, are they?' observed Melissa kindly. 'I don't know why I bother with mine really. Force of habit, I suppose. And I like to take it off at night. Gives me the feeling that I've finished work for the day. Even though I haven't! If you know what I mean.'

Lord, did the woman ever stop talking? Still, Claire

saw an opportunity in this particular line of conversation and decided to take it.

'Well, at least you can have a night off tonight,' she said brightly. 'I'm more than happy to stay up with Siena, feed her, everything. It'll give me the chance to get to know her a bit. We can sort out our shifts properly in the morning, but you look like you could use a night off.'

Melissa didn't need asking twice.

By seven o'clock she was dressed and ready for a night out in the main town on the other side of the island.

'Now, you're sure you can cope on your own, Annie?' she asked nervously as she bustled out of the door.

'Of course,' said Claire. 'That's what I'm here for.'

Melissa left, and this time Claire bolted the door behind her.

She didn't want to be interrupted a second time. She and Siena had a lot to talk about.

To her amazement, Siena was already awake and sitting up in bed when she came in with the supper tray.

'Melissa?' she said warily. 'Is that you?'

She had woken unsure of whether her earlier, brief encounter with her mother had been real or a figment of her morphine-fuelled imagination, and didn't want to say anything about it to the nurse in either case.

'No,' said Claire softly. 'Melissa's gone out for the night, darling. It's me. It's Mom.'

She put down the tray of food and took Siena's hand again, allowing her daughter to touch and stroke her, to prove to herself for good and all that this was no ghost.

'It is you,' she said at last, and the joy in her voice dispelled Claire's last fears about being rejected. 'Oh my God. It really is you.'

By the time the two women had finished laughing and crying and holding one another, the food had long since gone cold.

It was hard to know where to begin talking about all the years they'd lost. Every time Siena made an effort to start, Claire would be so overwhelmed with guilt and grief that she drowned her out with a torrent of apologies, and the tears began all over again. In the end, they both agreed to postpone these longer conversations and to focus on what to do in the current situation, before Melissa came back and disturbed them.

Siena was able to give her mother a sketchy outline of her life with Randall and what had happened to her. She also told her that it was not yet clear whether she would regain full or only partial sight.

'That's it, then,' Claire announced firmly, once she'd heard the whole sordid tale. 'We have to get you away from here. Right now. Tonight. The man's a maniac. Can you walk, darling? If I help you?'

Wearily, Siena raised a hand for her mother to stop. 'It's not that simple,' she said. 'I can't just leave.'

And she explained, in slightly blurry detail, Randall's threats to destroy her career and reputation, as well as his control of her depleted finances.

'Besides, it's not just that,' Siena finished, as Claire sat reeling from everything she'd just been told. 'What would we be going home *to*? I take it Dad doesn't know you're here?'

'No,' Claire admitted. 'He doesn't. But, Siena, I know your father's always loved you. Deep down, darling, he has. If he knew, if he had any *idea* what this man Stein has put you through . . .'

'He'd what?' asked Siena. But there was less hostility in her voice than there might once have been. On some level, she had come to terms with her relationship with her father, what it was and what it never could be. As overjoyed as she was to see her mother again, she knew it was far too late to talk about building bridges with Pete.

'Be honest, Mom. Dad would probably have done this himself years ago if he'd thought he could have got away with it. He'd have crippled Hunter too if he'd had the chance.'

'Siena!' said Claire, shocked. She wasn't yet ready to admit, even to herself, that her daughter might be right. But she couldn't help remembering Pete's comment about Hunter after Siena's accident: how he wished his brother had been crushed in the wreckage of his SUV. The thought made her shiver.

'He's going to make you make a choice, Mom, just like he did before,' said Siena. 'Me or him. And if you choose me, then we'll both be in the same boat – homeless, penniless and screwed. Oh God, my head.' She fell back hard against the pillow. For a moment Claire thought she'd fainted, but then she spoke again, holding her hand to her shattered left temple. 'Mom, does that bag on my drip need changing? Jesus Christ, it hurts.'

Claire, who had nursed her own mother through terminal cancer and knew a thing or two about pain relief, got swiftly to work. It was comforting to think that the medical training she had abandoned to marry Pete had not gone entirely to waste. Soon Siena was resting more comfortably, conscious but patently exhausted.

They agreed to leave the difficult subjects of Pete and Randall until she was feeling stronger. In the meantime, Claire explained how she had tracked her down to Nantucket, and briefed a drowsy Siena on her cover story.

'So it was *you* who hired that snoop guy?' Siena said incredulously when she had finished. 'Big Al told me he'd seen some black dude hanging around the set trying to get pictures. I thought it was just a super-persistent fan. He came out to Malibu too?'

Claire nodded. 'He's a good man, Bill. And an excellent PI.'

'And you managed to keep it all a secret?' said Siena. 'Wow, Mom. I wouldn't have thought you had it in you.'

'Neither would I, once,' said Claire. 'But it's amazing what resources and what strengths we have, once we get up the courage to use them.'

Siena reached out in the darkness and clasped her hands around her mother's neck, pulling her closer. 'Mom?' she whispered. 'What if I can't see?'

Claire could hear the abject terror in her voice. At that moment, she felt she could have strangled Randall Stein with her bare hands.

'You will see,' she told her daughter firmly. 'Pretty soon, my darling, you're going to see everything much more clearly. And then everything will be all right. Just you wait.'

The gods, it seemed, had decided to smile on Claire.

For the next two weeks, her cover story remained intact, and she was able to nurse Siena back to health and strength with ever decreasing interruptions from Melissa, who seemed more than happy to let her new colleague take on the lion's share of the work. She had almost started to believe that she *was* Nurse Annie, so easy had it been for her to take on that persona and leave the troubles of her life and marriage behind her in Holly-wood.

She felt such intense love and pride, watching Siena fighting her way to recovery. When she changed her dressings, she could see that her face, although quite heavily scarred around the eyes and left cheek, was improving visibly by the day. She was starting to look like a battered but recognisable version of her old self.

And it wasn't just her bruises which were healing. Something had changed in Siena since the attack, something quite profound.

Whether it was finding her mother again, losing her money and fame, or the prospect of losing not only her looks but perhaps her sight as well, she had discovered a humility, and with it a bizarre feeling of contentment and calm, that was quite new to her.

For the first time in her life, other things seemed more important than the pursuit of fame and wealth, or even the love of a man. Other people seemed more important than herself.

The future was still a frightening, confusing blur. She couldn't picture life beyond her recuperation, and had no idea how or when she was going to make her escape from Randall.

Yet with others the path seemed clearer.

Hunter, for example, was always on her mind, and she talked about him constantly to Claire.

'The way I behaved, not just to Hunter but to Tiffany as well,' she told her mother through tears of regret, as Claire pushed her in a wheelchair through the rows of sweet peas in the secluded garden. 'I was so horrible and spoilt and selfish. He'll never forgive me. And I love him so much, Mom.'

Claire tried to comfort her and assure her that, in time, Hunter probably would forgive her. 'And so will everybody else who loves you.'

'Ha!' Siena laughed bitterly, snapping the head off a flower and smelling it. She found her sense of smell had become particularly acute since she'd been unable to use her eyes. 'I don't think that's a very long list any more, do you? I've totally lost touch with all my old friends from England and New York. Ines isn't speaking to me.'

'Only because you haven't been speaking to her,' said Claire gently.

'And then there's Max.' Siena went on with her self-flagellation, unable or unwilling to accept her mother's comfort. 'I was so awful to him, Mom, when he showed up in Malibu that Christmas. I was just so hurt and confused and I felt I couldn't forgive him. But I wanted to. I really did.' She was begging Claire to believe her. 'I'm sure you did, sweetheart,' she said. 'I understand.'

'But by then, well, it was complicated. There was Randall, and the film, and . . .' She threw the flower head down on to the ground in despair. 'I couldn't just go back.'

God, sometimes she was so like Duke, thought Claire.

Everything was always black and white, right or wrong. And heaven forbid that she should ever go back on a decision. Never look back, never apologise. That was what Duke always used to say.

Poor child. She looked so terribly confused and hurt, with the visible, lower parts of her face all screwed up in misery and anguish. Claire longed to be able to help her, but having lived with Pete for thirty years, she understood a bit about guilt. This was something Siena would have to work through on her own.

'Try not to think about it now,' she would tell her, time after time. 'Concentrate on getting yourself well. That's the only thing that matters.'

Claire was sitting out in the garden reading under the shade of the willow tree, enjoying a brief respite from nursing duties while Siena slept, when she was disturbed by the vibrating of a mobile phone in her pocket.

The screen read 'Home'.

It was Pete.

She glanced nervously around to check that Melissa was nowhere in sight before answering the call.

'Darling!' she said. 'How are you?'

There was a pause on the end of the line.

'Mrs McMahon?' said a familiar female voice. 'Claire? It's not Pete, it's me. Tara.'

The PA sounded distressed. Claire felt her heartbeat quicken. Had Pete finally found out what she'd been up to?

'Is something the matter, Tara?' she asked. 'You sound upset. What's wrong?'

Another pause, which seemed to last for hours.

'I'm sorry, but it's bad news,' the girl stammered. 'It's Pete.'

'What? What about him?' Claire sounded as scared as she felt. It wasn't like Tara to spare anyone's feelings, least of all hers. Why couldn't she spit it out?

'He's had a heart attack.'

It was Tara's voice, but it somehow sounded different. Tinny and distant.

Unreal.

'I'm sorry, but you have to come home, Claire,' she said. 'Right away.'

Chapter Forty-nine

It took a couple of minutes for the initial shock of Tara's news to sink in. Then she began to think practically.

Her first priority was to get back home. Pete had been taken to Cedars and was apparently in intensive care. She needed to talk to his doctor there and get an update on his condition. But first she had to talk to Siena.

Now that she was on the lower-dosage painkillers and didn't need so much sleep, she'd been moved from the little windowless room at the top of the stairs to a larger, much more cheerful guest bedroom, overlooking the sweeping formal gardens and the ocean beyond. Not that Siena could appreciate the view, of course, but she could now tell the difference between light and darkness, even through her bandages, which everyone took to be a hopeful sign.

Claire rapped gently on the door. 'Hey, sweetie. Only me.'

She hadn't known how she ought to break the news about Pete, what with Siena still being in such a fragile condition. In the end, she just sat down on the end of the bed and told her as calmly and unemotionally as she could.

'I don't know how serious it is yet,' she finished. 'I'm just praying and hoping for the best.'

Siena's only thoughts were of concern for her mother. For all her dad's faults, and despite everything that had happened, she knew that Claire loved him desperately.

'Mom, I'm so sorry,' she said, clasping Claire's hand tightly in her own. 'You must be so worried. And of course you have to go back right away, I totally understand. You mustn't worry about me. I'll be fine.'

'But darling . . .' Claire was taken aback. 'You don't expect me to leave you here, do you?'

Siena's face gave nothing away – there was no tightening of the mouth or furrowing of the brow above her bandages. Evidently she *had* expected it.

'No, no, it's out of the question,' said Claire. 'I'm taking you back with me. We have to get you away from Randall, and besides . . .' She bravely fought back her tears. 'This may be your last chance to see your father, to make things right. You have to come with me, Siena. Today.'

Wearily Siena shook her head. 'I can't, Mom. I can't come with you right now. Randall's going to be here in a few days to see me, and I still have no idea how I'm gonna handle that. He can still do a lot of damage to my career, you know. Not to mention the money. And Dr Sanford's coming with him to take these damn dressings off my eyes and look at the damage. I can't just do a runner.'

'Oh, for heaven's sake.' Claire's exasperation at last began to show. 'What do career and money matter in comparison to your safety? Please, Siena.' She didn't have time to debate the matter. She had to get back to Pete, now, and there was no way she was leaving her daughter to the mercy of that maniac and his private doctors.

'Forget Sanford. There are other doctors, better doctors, eye specialists in LA who could help you. You can't spend another second in the same house as that man after what he's done to you. You can't.'

'Yes I can, Mom.' Siena pulled the quilt up around her shoulders defensively. 'I have to. This is my career we're talking about. It's my life. You don't understand.'

'Oh really?' said Claire. 'Don't I? Well, I'll tell you what. Why don't you let me *show* you what it is that I don't understand, Siena.'

She moved up the bed towards her and gently but firmly began removing her bandages.

'It's OK,' protested Siena. 'The dressings are clean, Melissa already did them.'

But Claire continued unwinding the strips of cotton until her entire bruised and battered face was revealed.

'Now I want you to trust me,' she said, pushing her daughter's shoulders back until she was lying flat on the bed, and leaning over her. Siena could make out the darkening shadow as her mother came closer, blocking out the light from the window.

'I do trust you. But what are you doing?'

'I'm taking off these dressings and I'm taking out your stitches. I want you to see this for yourself.'

Instinctively, Siena stiffened.

'No!' she said.

She sounded desperately afraid. What if she couldn't see? What if the damage was too bad?

Sensing her nerves, Claire took both her hands and squeezed them.

'It's going to be OK,' she said, in a tone of such confidence and serene certainty that even Siena began to feel comforted. 'Trust me.'

She was a deft and practised nurse, and it took only a few uncomfortable minutes for her to complete the entire operation. Siena had been dreading having her stitches removed, but in fact they had come away with such slithering ease that a mild discomfort was all she felt.

That was nothing, though, compared to the inner fear that gripped her.

'Right,' said Claire, wiping firmly across the gluey mass that caked both her lash lines with warm, wet cotton wool. 'Let's do it.'

She unhooked the oval antique mirror from above the washbasin and brought it over to the bed, before propping Siena back up comfortably against the plumped-up pillows. She looked as white as a sheet.

'We'll do your left eye first,' said Claire. She knew from Melissa that this was the eye that had been least damaged by Randall's beating, and that Dr Sanford was optimistic that Siena would regain at least partial sight on that side. 'I'm going to open your eyelid with my fingers now, all right?' Siena managed a tiny nod. 'It'll probably sting a little bit, so try not to panic.'

Siena felt her left lid peel open and instinctively pushed her mother away as a rush of dry, stinging cold air hit her eyeball. It was agony and she was blinking furiously, tears streaming down her cheeks, but in those few split seconds she could make out the contours of the room and Claire's loving, anxious face looking down at her, willing her to be OK.

The relief was so overwhelming, she could hardly breathe.

'I can see!' she said ecstatically, flinging her arms around Claire's neck. 'I can fucking see!'

Her elation was dampened somewhat a few minutes later when they tried her right eye. It wasn't a total loss – she could see shades of light and darkness and, she thought, the occasional recognisable shape. But the damage was still very severe.

Claire was quick to comfort her. 'Eye surgeons can do incredible things these days, you know, honey,' she said, forcing the optimism into her voice. 'As soon as we get you back to LA, I'll take you to see the very best.'

LA. The mere mention of it brought Siena crashing down to earth with a bang. The joy of knowing that she could still see had been indescribable, overwhelming. But her problems were far from over.

Her father was seriously ill, perhaps dying. She was going to have to see him, and that thought alone filled her with emotions so painful and conflicting she couldn't begin to untangle them. And then there was Randall.

She knew her mom was right: she had to get away from him and the sooner the better. But still his words to her at the surgery centre as she'd lain there in agony ran through her brain now like a broken record.

If you go after me, Siena, believe me, I will crush you.

He could still destroy her career. He had threatened to ruin her professionally and financially. The thought of losing everything she had worked for filled her with a sickening dread that not even the thrill of being able to see could banish completely.

When Claire's voice cut through her reverie, it was firm and businesslike.

'I said I wanted you to see something for yourself.'

She held up the oval mirror and clasped it against her chest with its worn wooden back facing towards Siena. 'Are you sure you're ready for this?'

Siena nodded mutely. She was frightened, but it had to be faced. She wanted to know what she looked like.

Claire turned the mirror around.

At first, she made no sound at all. She just slumped back against the pillows and lay there like a terrified insect in the presence of a predator, frozen and motionless with shock.

For weeks now, she had probed her wounded skin with her fingers and tried to visualise her facial injuries. But nothing could have prepared her for the reality of what she now saw gazing back at her. A long, livid red scar ran all the way from the corner of her right eye down to just above her mouth in a jagged line where the glass had sliced into the flesh. Although the swellings around both eyes had eased considerably, the bruising was still extensive and disfiguring, and her famous bone structure had been thrown off kilter by a broken cheekbone that made the whole left side of her face look sunken and lopsided. The skin that was stretched like paper over the shattered bones was sickly and preterna-turally pale after so many weeks out of any kind of sunlight, and she looked frighteningly gaunt, her hands incongruously over-sized and bony on the ends of her scarred and stick-thin arms.

She felt sick.

Randall had destroyed her.

She had *let* him destroy her.

'I know it's hard,' said Claire softly, seeing the pain in her daughter's face. 'But just now you told me that I didn't understand. That your career was your life. That you couldn't just walk away from here, from that man. And I think . . .' She didn't want to hurt her any more, and struggled for the kindest way to say it. 'I think you needed to see this. To see what he's done. Because it's *you* who doesn't understand, darling. A career is *not* a life. And you *can* just leave him. You can and you must.'

For Siena, it was a moment of revelation. It wasn't just her face which had been battered, she realised. It was her spirit.

For so long she had strived to be like Duke, to live up to all the hopes and dreams he had had for her. Getting back to Hollywood. Making her fortune. Becoming a star. From her earliest childhood, she had craved nothing so desperately and totally as his approval, his admiration and his love. Even after his death, she had carried on her blind pursuit of everything she believed he would have wanted for her.

But at what cost?

How many people had she pushed away? How many people had she hurt as she battled and clawed her way up to become what Duke had wanted her to be? Staring at her shattered face, she realised that the one person she had hurt the most was staring straight back at her.

She loved Duke. She always had and she always would. But she knew now that he had been wrong all along. He was wrong to despise people for being weak. Weakness was what made people human – it was cruelty which was to be despised.

Randall was cruel. And Siena had been weak, holding on to him out of fear and desperation.

Just as Minnie had held on to Duke.

Just as Claire had held on to Pete.

Suddenly she was overwhelmed with a surge of empathy and pity for her mother and grandmother. All these years she had hated them for their weakness. But were they really so different from her? In many ways, they were *better* than her and braver. At least Minnie had loved Duke. And no one could deny that her mother loved her father, despite everything.

She had never loved Randall.

So what had been her excuse for staying with him? Money? Fame?

Duke had built his emotional security on money and fame. Blindly, stupidly, still desperate to please him even years after his death, Siena had tried to do the same. And look where it had got her.

Duke's blood ran in her veins. She knew that. But so, she now realised, did Claire's. And for the first time in her life, she felt proud of that fact.

A lone ray of bright sunlight had fought its way through the gap in the curtains, and fell in a bright white wedge across the bed and polished wood of the floor, glinting off the mirror into her still-sensitive eyes. She winced.

Claire reached out to take the mirror from her, but she held fast, and for a moment the two women's hands touched in sympathy.

'Would you do me a favour?' Siena asked, still blinking against the sunlight.

'Of course, darling,' said Claire, her voice choked with love. She knew how hard it must be for her daughter to have to see what that bastard had done to her, and she prayed that, in time, she'd find the strength and the courage to come to terms with her injuries. 'Anything you want, my angel. Anything at all.'

Siena let go of the mirror and smiled.

'Pass me my suitcase.'

Chapter Fifty

Max was reading scripts in the little boxroom that served as his study at Batcombe when he heard the news about Pete's heart attack on the radio.

Although the name 'McMahon' always sent a shiver down his spine, he didn't feel any particular emotion about Siena's father being on the way out. From the little he'd known of him, the guy had always been a card-carrying arsehole, just the type of manipulative, megalo-maniac wanker that made him glad he no longer lived and worked in LA.

He imagined Siena wouldn't be shedding too many tears either, wherever she was.

Besides, right now he had problems enough of his own to worry about.

Dark Hearts was now definitely moving to New York in the New Year. It was amazing how well they'd done, with what he'd always considered to be rather a brave and uncommercial play, and he thanked his lucky stars that he'd negotiated himself a big slice of the equity early on. No doubt about it, it was a fantastic opportunity, and in theatre terms, great money. But moving back to the States presented other difficulties. He would have to leave Henry just when things at the farm were at their most stressful, with the developers due to arrive any day now.

And then, of course, there was Freddie.

Ever since making up after their titanic row over Siena's engagement, things had been calm between the two of them. But deep down, Max was becoming increasingly unhappy, consumed by a loneliness that he just couldn't shake off. He guessed, correctly, that

Freddie sensed this, and his guilt about letting her down made him feel even more depressed.

When Hunter had called him about Siena's reported breakdown, Freddie had tactfully avoided mentioning it, wary of upsetting him further or provoking another crisis in their relationship. Although he was grateful for her sensitivity, the result was that he didn't confide in her about his feelings, and the emotional distance between the two of them widened still further.

At least once a week he steeled himself to talk to her and call it quits. But every time he looked at her kind, loving, trusting face, his nerve failed him.

He hadn't even broached the subject of New York yet. He didn't want to be responsible for yet another woman's unhappiness. Or to explode another misery bomb in the already struggling Arkell household.

Switching off the ancient Roberts radio on the window sill and turning back to his script, he was jolted out of his private thoughts by a loud rumble that seemed to be coming from the bottom of the drive. Moments later the first of the JCBs appeared, roaring and rattling its way towards the farmyard. It was followed by another and another until soon the noise was deafening.

'They're here.'

Muffy had put her head round the door. Her hair was pulled back off her face with one of Henry's spotted handkerchiefs, and Max noticed how pale her skin was looking and how pronounced the dark shadows seemed to be under her eyes. Poor thing. She'd had a terrible time of it these past few months, but Henry had been too caught up in his own guilt and misery about leasing the estate to be able to comfort her. She'd tried to be strong for everybody else's sake. But now that the developers were actually here, she looked as if she was right on the verge of losing it completely.

'They're here! They're here!' Bertie and Maddie ran tearing down the corridor behind her, whooping with excitement at all the commotion.

'I'm going to go in the digger!'

'No, me! I'm going first!'

'Looks like somebody's pleased to see them,' said Max, getting up and putting an affectionate arm around his sister-in-law.

'Come out there with me, Max,' she pleaded. God, she looked miserable, gazing past him to the fleet of trucks that were pulling up, exhausts belching, outside the study window. 'I can't face playing welcoming committee all on my own.'

'Of course,' he said, giving her an encouraging squeeze. 'Don't worry. We can meet and greet in five minutes and then I'll walk the foreman over to the farm office. But where's Henry?'

'Out shooting, over at Millhole Wood. Won't be back till this evening.'

'Well, d'you want me to drive over there and get him? I don't mind.'

'No, no, really,' said Muffy. She was grateful for the offer, grateful for all Max's support in fact. He'd been a rock these last few weeks. But she couldn't drag Henry back from a happy day's shooting to face all this. He'd be living with the horrible reality soon enough. Why begrudge him his last few hours of blissful ignorance. 'I'll be fine. Just stand next to me, all right? And if you see me crying, kick me. As hard as you like.'

Outside, the trucks had parked in a rough semicircle at the entrance to the yard, with their drivers gathered in an awkward-looking huddle to one side. A steady drizzle had been falling throughout the morning, and the heavy tyres had already begun to turn Henry's drive into a quagmire. Behind the fleet of dirty JCBs at the top of the drive, and in striking, shiny contrast, was one spanking-new dark blue Range Rover, of the kind that was clearly more used to cruising around South Kensington than dirtying its wheels on muddy tracks out in the country.

As Max and Muffy came out on to the porch, both the

car doors swung open and two men emerged and started walking towards them, their hands extended in greeting. One of them Max instantly recognised from Henry's descriptions as Gary Ellis. He was short and fat, and had made an unfortunate attempt to squeeze his portly form into an ill-fitting checked suit, which gave him the look of a cockney Billy Bunter. A trademark cigar was clamped between his teeth, and he had topped off what he fondly thought of as his 'country gent' look with a flat cap that, like the car, looked as if it had been bought in Bond Street the day before.

"'Allo. Muffy, isn't it?' he said, ignoring Max and grabbing and kissing Muffy's hand before she had a chance to protest. Neither she nor Henry had expected Ellis to show up in person at the farm, and certainly not on the first day.

'Hello, Mr Ellis,' she said stiffly, trying to hide her distaste as his wet, flabby lips left their imprint on her skin. He had leased the farm fair and square and had a legitimate right to be there, so it was no good being churlish about it. 'This is my brother-in-law, Max De Seville. And my children . . .' She gestured around vaguely, but was horrified to discover that Bertie and Maddie had run off and were already clambering all over one of the diggers, covered from head to toe in mud.

'Bertie! Madeleine! Get down from there this instant!' she yelled. Two guilty, clay-splattered faces peered back at her from beneath the long neck of the machine.

'Don't worry,' said Gary with a smug, leery grin that made Max want to hit him. Henry had told him the developer had a 'crush' on Muffy, but that seemed like far too innocent a word to describe the blatant, predatory way he looked at her. 'Kids, eh? What can you do?'

The other man from the Range Rover, a tall, diffident-looking fellow who Max guessed must be in his early fifties, had been hanging back behind his boss but now moved forward and introduced himself. 'Ben McIntyre.

I'm the foreman here, so I'll be overseeing the construction.' His handshake was dry and firm. He seemed honest. 'Pleased to meet you.'

'And you,' said Max. He didn't know why, but he found himself instantly warming to Ben. He hoped that a decent foreman might help make the nightmare of construction slightly more bearable for poor Henry.

'No point talkin' to 'im,' interrupted Gary rudely, waving a hand dismissively in Max's direction. "E's just the monkey. 'Is bruvver's the organ grinder, isn't that right, love?' He winked at Muffy. 'So where is the man of the 'ouse, anyway?'

Gary had been looking forward to his moment of triumph over Henry, and was put out his rival hadn't been there to witness his grand entrance. Over the years he had nursed his resentment at what he perceived to be Henry's snobbery and stand-offishness into a constantly simmering hatred. Lord Snooty had been quick enough to patronise him when he'd first expressed an interest in Manor Farm all those years ago at Caroline's dinner party. He was so far up his own arse, he'd even turned down the very decent offer Gary had made him last year to buy the place outright. That had annoyed him at the time – given the colossal size of his debts, he'd assumed that Henry would have caved in and sold straight away – but he was pleased that things had worked out the way they had.

He knew when he offered it that the option of a lease would have looked like a lifeline to Henry, so desperate was he not to be forced to sell his ancestral home to a stranger. The stupid, sentimental sod. Gary had no time for whimsical aristocratic notions of heritage when it came to property, and thought Henry an out-and-out fool for agreeing to the deal.

Because the reality was that a lease meant that the Arkells would be shackled to him for the rest of their lives. He could come and go as he pleased, running

roughshod through their precious bloody estate whenever, and however, he wanted to.

Just the thought of that made him smile.

He'd have paid twice the value of the lease simply for
the pleasure of seeing that stuck-up cunt Henry Arkell
cut down to size. And in the meantime, as well as
building himself a nice little earner of a golf course, he
could amuse himself by making a play for Henry's still
very tasty missus.

'He's out,' said Max frostily, moving back to Muffy's
side and putting a protective, possessive arm around her
shoulder. 'I can show you and Mr McIntyre to the farm
office. You'll find everything you need in there.'

By six o'clock it was starting to get dark and Max decided
to take a stroll up to the village. He needed to get out of
the house. Ellis had been strutting arrogantly around the
farm all afternoon, barking instructions at his foreman
and arguing loudly with the two terrified-looking local
architects who had turned up at lunchtime to go through
plans for the new clubhouse.

Muffy had spent the day wandering around the house
like an automaton, mindlessly putting on load after load
of washing to avoid having to go outside. She was so
distracted that she accidentally put one of Maddie's red
socks in a white wash and dyed all Max's Calvins a none
too subtle shade of pink. She burst into tears when she
pulled them out of the machine, despite his protestations
that he really quite liked them like that.

Not that he could blame her for being highly strung.
The two younger children were in a sulk, having been
banned from pestering any of the workmen by their
mother and forced to stay indoors until Henry got home.
Charlie, the only child old enough to grasp the seriousness of what was happening, had taken up a sentry post
by the window on the landing, from which he scowled
furiously at everyone who came and went, refusing to be

lured downstairs even by Freddie's tempting offer of a slice of Mr Kipling's chocolate fudge cake at tea.

Max wanted to help, but as no one wanted to talk about what was happening it was hard to know where to begin. Besides, he was ashamed to admit that even with the nightmare of Ellis's goons moving in, his mind kept wandering back to Siena. Whether it was the earlier news of Pete McMahon's heart attack which had made it worse he didn't know, but he found himself continually replaying her image in his head, like picking at a mental scab, until it was driving him absolutely insane. Not knowing how she was, or where she was, was killing him.

After a couple of abortive hours of attempted work, he decided a breath of fresh air might help, and set out for the village, with Titus and Boris yapping excitedly at his heels.

They'd barely reached the bottom of the drive when the familiar silhouette of Henry's ancient four-wheel-drive came hurtling round the corner. He pulled over and wound down the window when he saw Max.

'Is that what I think it is?' he said, gesturing to the faint shadows of the lorries in the farmyard. Max nodded. 'How long have they been here? And why the fuck didn't anyone call me?'

'I offered,' said Max, wishing he could take away even an ounce of the pain that was written all over his brother's face. 'But Muffy didn't want to ruin your day's shooting.'

'Jesus Christ.' Henry ran his hands through his hair. 'There's so many of them. It looks like the M1 up there.'

'Oh, it's not so bad,' lied Max. Titus and Boris began jumping up and scrabbling at the side of the car. There were three dead rabbits lying on the passenger seat, and their scent was driving both the dogs crazy. Max grabbed each of them by the collar and pulled them back on to the verge.

'I'd better get up there,' said Henry, grinding the car back into first.

'Oh, and Henry!' shouted Max. He'd been going to warn his brother that Ellis had shown up in person, but his voice was drowned out by the screech of spinning wheels as Henry lurched forward, desperate to get home and see the full extent of the damage for himself.

Never mind. He would find out for himself soon enough.

Henry pulled up in front of the house, and for a few moments he just sat in stunned silence, unable to get out of the car. He had known the construction would be beginning some time this week. Logically, he knew that this would mean months of industrial vehicles and scores of manual workers scurrying all over the farm. But somehow the physical sight of the diggers and skips and cranes, and the strangers hurrying back and forth across his farmyard and in and out of his office, was still a shock. Feeling winded and numb, he eventually managed to open the door, gathering up his gun in one hand and the rabbits in the other, and walked round to the kitchen door – he was too muddy to use the front entrance.

Moving along the path into the kitchen garden, he thought he heard a cry. In a flash he was outside the door, just in time to see Muffy pushing the heavy, insistent form of the loathsome Gary Ellis away from her, sending him stumbling back against the kitchen dresser.

'What the hell do you think you're playing at?' she shouted, her face flushed with the exertion of extricating herself from his unwanted embrace. 'Are you mad?'

Before he had a moment to answer, Henry was through the door like a shot, dropping both gun and rabbits with a clatter as he flew at Ellis, fists flying.

'You fucker.'

'Henry, don't!' pleaded Muffy, as the fat man hit the ground, his head grinding against the corner of the

577

dresser with a sickening crunch as he fell. 'It's all right. It was nothing. Please!'

Gary whimpered in pain and brought his arms up to his head as he lay on the floor, trying to shield himself from further blows. Henry dropped to his knees and, grabbing the gibbering developer by his collar, pulled back his arm for one final punch before apparently thinking better of it and letting his head drop back on to the flagstone floor.

'You're not fucking worth it,' he spat, standing up and turning to Muffy, who was shaking with shock by the sink. 'You OK?'

She nodded mutely. She'd been peeling the potatoes and crying when Gary had wandered in and surprised her. At first he'd seemed to be genuinely offering comfort, saying how it must have been a huge shock for her, them all arriving like this and having to deal with it all on her own. But then, almost before she knew what was happening, he had started pressing himself against her until she could feel his hot, excited breath on her neck and his fat, rubbery hands reaching round for her bottom. Eeeugh. Thinking about it again now made her shudder.

'That wasn't a very smart fing to do.' Gary had staggered to his feet, and was wiping away a small trickle of blood from his lip with a handkerchief. A swelling was already beginning to form around his mouth and chin where Henry's punch had hit home. He was going to look terrible in the morning. 'I could sue you for assault.'

'Not before I sue you for indecent assault, you little toerag.' Henry's eyes had narrowed to small, murderous slits. Instinctively, Gary took a step backward. But he was still smiling that smug, confident smile – the smile of a man who knew he held all the cards.

'It's only assault if she didn't like it. Isn't that right, darlin'?' He leered at Muffy. Very slowly, Henry bent down and picked up his gun, which he proceeded to point at Gary. For one brief but glorious moment, the smile withered on the fat man's lips.

'Get out of my house.'

'Now now, 'Enry,' said Gary, still eyeing the gun warily. He didn't think Henry would have the balls to actually use it, but you could never be a hundred per cent sure. 'Is that any way to talk to your new landlord?'

'GET OUT!' Henry roared. This time Gary didn't hang about but bolted straight out of the door, leaving his jacket and mobile phone on the table in his ignominious haste to get out of there. Henry put down the gun and shut and bolted the door behind him. He was surprised to find that his own hands were shaking.

'Oh, Henry,' said Muffy, giving way to tears at last. 'What if he does sue? We haven't got a bean to fight him with.'

Henry walked over and hugged her tightly to his chest. 'He won't,' he said. 'He wouldn't dare, not after trying it on with you like that.'

She held on to him for a moment or two, allowing herself to be comforted, pleased that he was home, that they were in this together. Then she dried her tears and, pulling away from him, said what they had both been thinking. 'This is it, though, isn't it? This is what life's going to be like. You can punch him as much as you like. But he *is* our landlord. And nothing we say or do can ever change that.'

Henry frowned but didn't contradict her.

'We're stuck with him, aren't we?' she said. 'We're stuck with him for ever.'

By the time Max got back home it was almost midnight and Henry and Muffy had long since gone up to bed. His walk to the village had led him, inevitably, to the King's Arms, where he'd been persuaded to stay for a great many more pints than was probably advisable. By closing time he was quite unsteady on his feet, and if it hadn't been for his trusty canine companions, Boris and Titus, he doubted he would have found his way home at all.

After two minutes of abortive and increasingly noisy fumbling at the front door with his keys, Freddie had finally let him in with a face like fury.

Oh fuck, he remembered through his alcoholic haze. He had promised yesterday that he would take her out to dinner in Stroud this evening. He'd just stood the poor girl up.

'Where the 'ell 'ave you been?' she demanded. 'We were supposed to go out hours ago.'

Instead of apologising as he should have, he flew completely off the handle, his anger fuelled by guilt about his own behaviour as well as by almost a gallon of bitter. 'Mind your own damn business,' he bellowed at her.

To her credit, Freddie was not about to be bullied into silence.

'Well, I'm sorry, but I theenk it ees my business, when you stand me up, and you can't even be bozzered to call.'

Max stepped inside and she closed the door behind him. Only her concern not to wake the entire household after their harrowing day prevented her from slamming it violently.

'It wasn't a question of not being bothered,' he snapped back unsympathetically. 'I forgot, OK?'

'Oh, really?' she scoffed. 'And that's supposed to make eet OK, is it?'

She was looking particularly foxy tonight in a tight black cashmere jumper that must have cost her a whole month's wages, teamed with her favourite red suede miniskirt and boots. She had obviously made an effort to look her best for their date.

The red of the skirt clashed adorably with her auburn hair and with cheeks now flushed and rosy with anger. But Max was too guilt-blinded to be distracted by her beauty.

'I had more important things on my mind,' he said

savagely, staggering into the hallway and collapsing against the wall. He noticed his name on a bright pink Post-it note stuck on the message pad by the phone and bent down to read the note. His agent in LA had called three more times, and could Max please call him back as soon as possible. It was urgent.

Not to me it isn't, thought Max bitterly, screwing up the note and dropping it in the bin.

He knew why the agent was calling. Miramax had apparently shown some interest in buying the film rights to *Dark Hearts*. Max had been in the game long enough to realise that 'shown some interest' almost never translated into 'paid good money for', and he wasn't about to get his hopes up this time. He'd ridden the hope-and-despair roller-coaster for three painful years in LA, as studios sniffed agonisingly around one after another of his projects but never quite came through in the end. Hollywood was an all-or-nothing town, and ninety-nine times out of a hundred, that meant you longed for it all but got nothing.

For all his cynicism, though, he knew that six months ago he would have been excited about the big-studio interest and rushed to return his agent's call. But now? He didn't know what was wrong with him. Nothing seemed urgent, or even important, any more.

He knew he was behaving appallingly towards Freddie. He had not, in fact, completely forgotten about their plans. The truth was that, subconsciously, he had known he couldn't face sitting through an overtly 'romantic' evening with her and had been glad of the chance to run away to the pub and escape.

'You 'ad more important things on your mind, did you? Like what?' she challenged him. Max could hear the despair and bitterness in her voice. He didn't look up at her. 'Just what were zose ozzer things, Max? 'Enry's troubles? All zees people at the farm? Or Siena McMahon?'

Max winced.

'You can't forget 'er, can you?' Her fear was making her spiteful. 'Which is funny. Because she seems to 'ave no trouble forgetting about you.'

Max felt his heart fall into his stomach like a medicine ball, and his head began to throb. He swayed unsteadily as he tried to move away from the wall.

It was as if all the suppressed grief and longing of the past year were about to burst physically free from his body. The hall had started to spin.

'You don't know what you're talking about!' he shouted at Freddie. Pushing past her, he pulled open the front door again and fled into the garden, clutching his head and running for all he was worth.

'Max!' she called after him. 'Max! I'm sorry. Come back!'

But he had already disappeared into the gloom.

He ran through the darkness, across the dew-wet lawn until he reached the firmer, concrete ground of the old farmyard. There, he sank to his knees and, pressing his palms down hard on the cold ground for support, began throwing up, retching and retching until it felt as if not just his stomach but his soul was empty.

Then he started to cry.

Oh God.

What was he going to do? What the hell was he going to do?

Chapter Fifty-one

Melissa didn't think she had ever seen anyone so angry.

When Randall arrived in Nantucket to discover that Siena had packed her things and gone, he turned on the nurse in a blind fury, face flushed, eyes bulging, and demanded to know what had happened.

'Please, Mr Stein, there's no need for that sort of language,' she muttered, blushing as one obscenity after another tumbled from his thin, angry lips. 'Annie took her back to Los Angeles on Wednesday, just as you instructed.'

'Instructed?' He was apoplectic, and his cheeks had gone such an intense shade of puce that Melissa genuinely started to worry that he might be about to have a heart attack. 'I never instructed anything! And who the fuck is Annie?'

It took almost twenty minutes for him to rein in his temper sufficiently to allow a gibbering Melissa to fill him in on what had actually happened. Frankly it beggared belief, how easily the stupid woman had been duped, allowing a complete stranger into the house after everything he'd told her about security, on the strength of a few forged papers.

Glancing through the false résumé and letter of employment a few minutes later, though, he was impressed by how much this mystery woman had managed to find out about him: she had known not just about the Nantucket house, but clearly also had access to all sorts of other information about his employees in LA, his business trip to Asia and, most worryingly of all, his relationship with Daniel Sanford. His initial assumption – that *Annie* was an undercover journalist – had been wide of the mark. This was not the work of some amateurish, snoopy hack. It was a meticulously planned sting, presumably orchestrated by someone close to Siena.

A woman.

He thought for a moment of Ines, but dismissed the idea almost immediately. She wouldn't have had the time or the money for such a thing, and as she hadn't heard a word from Siena in months he doubted she would have had the inclination either. Besides, Melissa had told him that Annie was blonde and older. No amount of disguising could make Ines look fifty.

That was when it came to him.

'Would you recognise her?' he asked Melissa. 'Annie, I mean. If I showed you a picture?'

The nurse nodded furiously, relieved to be able to give him at least one of the answers he wanted. She scurried after him into the study and watched him boot up his computer, tapping impatiently on the desk with his fat fingers until he could bring up the Google home page, then finally clicking on 'image search' and typing in just two words.

Claire McMahon.

'Oh yes, there she is,' trilled Melissa happily, as an image of Claire, looking awkward and formal in a blue suit at a cancer research gala, filled the screen. 'That's her all right. That's Annie.'

Dr Daniel Sanford was out in the garden playing baseball with his two young sons when his wife called him in to take the phone call.

'It's Randall Stein, calling from the East Coast,' she yelled out at him through the patio doors that led from the palatial living room of their Beverly Hills home out on to the rolling, manicured lawn.

Frowning, he dropped the wiffle ball and stomped back into the house. He was flying out to Nantucket tomorrow to check up on Siena, and didn't appreciate Randall bugging him on a weekend.

'Yeah, this is Dan,' he said grumpily, taking the call in

the relative privacy of his home office and closing the door behind him. 'What's up?'

'She's gone.' Randall's voice was controlled, but the fear was still unmistakable. 'Her mother came down here, pretending to be a nurse or something, and took her back to LA. You know anything about this?'

'Of course not,' Sanford snapped, although his heart sank as he immediately thought of the letter he'd received last month, about that 'relief nurse' for Melissa.

He'd thought it was a bit odd at the time, but he found dealing with Randall so unpleasant, and the whole business with Siena so troubling to his conscience, that he hadn't bothered to call him and double-check.

Shit. This wasn't good news.

'We need to talk,' said Randall. 'Figure out what we're gonna do. If she goes to the press . . .'

The doctor could hear his client's teeth grinding with stress on the other end of the line and tried to marshal his own thoughts. His wife Cora knew nothing about his 'work' with Randall. He badly wanted to keep it that way, but that might not be possible now.

He wondered how hard it would be to wash his hands of Stein, even at this late stage.

'It could get very bad,' said Randall. 'We need to work out our stories, make sure there are no loose ends. I've got Dean Reid, my attorney, flying down here as we speak.'

'Good,' said Daniel, deciding on his strategy on the spur of the moment. 'You're gonna need him.'

'What do you mean, *I'm* gonna need him?' asked Randall, his nerves betraying themselves now in barely controlled spleen. 'You're in this up to your neck, my friend, and don't you forget it. You treated her and you didn't report it. And I don't need to remind you that this wasn't the first favour you've done me in return for a nice fat cheque. You could be struck off.'

He hissed out each word like venom. Daniel's heart was pounding – he knew there was some truth in what

Randall was saying, but his only hope was to bluff it out and stand his ground.

'Bullshit,' he whispered, cupping his hand around the receiver. He didn't want his wife listening in. 'Siena gave me permission to operate. She signed the consents. It's up to her if she wants to go to the police, not me. I'm just the doctor. You've got nothing on me, Randall.'

'Listen, you piece of shit.' The cool façade had completely crumbled. Like most bullies, Randall seemed utterly thrown to find himself being stood up to for once. 'I'm nine million dollars in the red on this fucking movie. If Siena goes to the press, if she pins this on me, I'm gonna lose my financing.'

'How?' Daniel sounded maddeningly unconcerned.

'There's a morality clause in the contract,' said Randall. 'Basically if I do or say anything that might reflect badly on the movie's backers, they have the right to pull out. And as exec producer, I've underwritten the whole thing.'

'Hmmm.' Sanford paused to take in exactly what Stein was saying. 'So you mean if Siena can prove you beat her to a pulp, you'll have to pay the nine million yourself? Out of your own pocket?'

'Exactly,' said Randall. At last, Sanford seemed to be grasping the seriousness of the situation, the slimy little shit. 'So you'd better get your ass on a plane tonight. Because if I go down, you're going down with me. We need to shut her up, and we need to do it fast. For both our sakes.'

There was a long pause. This last rant smacked of desperation. Empty threats.

Finally, Daniel said: 'I don't think so, Randall. You know what? I hope that young lady *does* go to the press – and frankly, I can't see how you think you're going to stop her.'

There was some apoplectic wheezing from Randall's end, but the doctor showed no mercy.

'With any luck some of the other girls will come

forward as well, and show the world what a twisted, arrogant, dangerous little son of a bitch you really are.'

'You'll regret this,' snarled Randall. 'I promise you. Your career will be *over*.'

Daniel ignored him.

'And as for losing the nine million dollars . . .' He paused, savouring the moment. Randall had had a hold over him for years. It felt wonderful to finally be free – whatever the ultimate cost turned out to be. 'What can I say? It couldn't happen to a nicer guy.'

He hung up, took a deep, satisfying breath and opened the study door, running straight into his wife. She had obviously been straining to hear the conversation, and her cheeks flushed red with embarrassment as he caught her in the act.

'Everything OK?' she asked anxiously. 'You sounded stressed.'

He smiled and put his arm around her.

'Absolutely,' he said. 'Everything's just fine, honey. Just fine.'

Siena had felt her first misgivings the moment her plane took off from Boston.

Not about leaving Randall. She had never made a decision she was more sure of in her entire life. But about the future. Clasping Claire's hand as the American Airlines jet roared shakily upward, the euphoria she'd felt about her sight and about finally breaking free had started to dissipate, and the precarious reality of her situation began to reassert itself.

Thanks to her bruises, dark glasses and a baseball cap, no one had given her a second glance as her mother paid for both their last-minute first-class tickets, and the two of them had shuffled on to the plane unnoticed by the other weary commuters.

After living and breathing for public adulation for so long, she was amazed by how liberating it felt not to be stared at. She was also grateful for her mother's silence.

Having called the hospital and ascertained that Pete's condition was serious but stable – as the specialist had put it, 'He's not going anywhere, Mrs McMahon. No need to bust a gut to get here' – Claire had relaxed a little, and was able to focus on helping Siena. Sensing that her daughter needed to be alone with her thoughts, and craving her own distraction, she had immersed herself in a novel as soon as they took their seats, leaving Siena to stare out of the window and try to make sense of everything that had happened in the last twenty-four hours.

She wanted to make the bastard pay.

You can get mad, Duke used to tell her, *just as long as you get even.*

But that wasn't going to be easy. Randall was a formidable adversary, and he had a lot of power and influence in LA. Police, lawyers, movie studios, press – they could all be bought, or pressured by him into taking sides and twisting the truth. He would portray her as unstable, desperate, a liar.

If you go after me, Siena, I will crush you.

He was right about one thing. She would never work again in Hollywood. Not with her ruined face and only partial sight. To that extent, he had already crushed her.

Running her index finger along the groove of her long scar, she felt her resolve hardening. Somehow she would make him pay. But the next few months were going to be tough.

Hatred and rage against Randall gave way to sadness. She leaned her head against the plastic window and began, quietly, to cry. But her tears were not for her lost beauty, wealth and fame. Nor were they for all the lost time with the people she loved – her mother, Hunter, Ines. They were not even for her father, lying critically ill in his hospital bed, and the love it was too late for her to find with him.

She was crying for one person only.

And he was thousands of miles away in England, crying for her.

In Manhattan a week later, Max dragged himself up off the hard hotel bed and wearily began taking off his clothes. Perhaps a nice long bath would help.

He was actually becoming quite worried about himself. It wasn't normal for a man his age to keep crying. Some days the sadness was so overwhelming he was frightened to go out in public at all, in case he should suddenly burst into tears. Maybe he needed a shrink.

Lying back while the piping-hot water eased the stress and tension from his muscles, he tried to think positively about the future. After that terrible day when the developers had arrived at Batcombe, he had finally realised that there was no way he could go on trying to make things work with Freddie.

'You deserve better,' he told her. 'You deserve a man who still has his heart to give you.'

Closing his eyes now, he could picture her brave, heartbroken face, and almost started crying again. Why did he always have to hurt people?

'I don't want better,' she said. 'I want you.'

But they had both known there was nothing he could do.

After that, he'd had no real choice but to accept the offer to move to New York with the play, and had flown out two days earlier to begin an initial recce looking for an apartment.

He realised that he'd been kidding himself that Henry and Muff needed him at Manor Farm. The truth was that he had needed them. He couldn't bear to be alone with his grief, and his longing for Siena.

He had thought that Batcombe, the only place other than the beach house where he had ever really been happy, might ease some of the pain. But it hadn't. And now even that safe haven was being destroyed, turned into a battleground between Henry and Gary Ellis.

He had to get out.

Rising up out of the bath, he dried himself on one of the fluffy white hotel towels, sat down on the bed and flicked on his mobile to check for messages. There were two, and despite the absurdity of it he still felt a sharp pang of hope that perhaps one of them might be from Siena.

The first was from Muffy, just 'checking up' on him, as she put it.

He knew that she and Henry were concerned about him, and he felt guilty about adding to their worries. But he was grateful for her message all the same.

The second message was from Dorian Klein, his agent.

Shit. He'd forgotten to call the guy back again. What with the move and the play, and all the shit going on in his personal life, he just hadn't got around to it.

Punching out the number, he hoped that Dorian wasn't going to ask him to fly out to LA for some pointless meeting. To have to be that close to Siena and all his memories would be totally unbearable.

'Klein.'

Shit. He was answering his own phone now? Times must be tough.

'Hello, Dorian, it's Max De Seville. I'm sorry I didn't get back to you sooner.'

'Max? Jesus, man, where the fuck have you been?' He sounded genuinely stressed out, nothing like his usual slick, imperturbable self. 'Angus and I have been trying to reach you for weeks.'

Oh Christ, Angus. Now he came to think of it, he *did* remember getting a couple of calls from *Dark Heart*'s writer back in Batcombe, which he'd failed to return. Angus was on holiday in the Highlands, supposedly working on his new play, and Max had assumed he was calling about that. He liked Angus a lot, but he just hadn't had the energy to provide any sort of artistic encouragement while his own world was caving in on him.

'Sorry,' he said sheepishly to Dorian. 'I've had a lot going on at home. Anyway, I'm here now. So what's up?'

The agent laughed.

'What's up, my friend, is that we've done the deal without you. I tried everything to get hold of you, but in the end Angus flew out here last night and signed on the dotted line himself. And before you start screaming at me, Max, he's perfectly legally entitled, it's still sixty per cent his baby . . .'

'Dorian.' Max interrupted him mid-flow. 'Slow down. I have no idea what you're talking about.'

The agent laughed again, and Max wondered what joke it was that was going over his head so completely.

'Let me give you a clue.' Dorian chuckled. 'Miramax.'

Max felt his heartbeat creeping upward. To be honest, he'd pushed the studio's supposed interest in the play to the back of his mind weeks ago. It had all seemed so unlikely – there was nothing Hollywood about *Dark Hearts* – whereas the move to Broadway was something real and tangible that he could focus on.

'You're not serious,' he said, once his breath had returned. 'You mean, they actually want it?'

'Forget "want it",' said Dorian. Max could hear him grinning down the phone. 'They bought it. Two days ago. For six million dollars.'

The ensuing silence was so long, Dorian began to worry that his client might have passed out.

'Max? Buddy? Are you there?'

Like an idiot, Max sat in his towel, nodding at the phone. He tried to speak but no sound came out.

'Look, if you're pissed about Angus signing,' said Dorian anxiously, 'you shouldn't be. We were under pressure to make a deal and if I do say so myself I think we got a great price.'

'No, no. It's not that. Sorry.' He was able to force some words out at last. 'It's fantastic. I'm just in shock. I think.'

Six million dollars.

What was forty per cent of six million? Two point four?

Holy shit.

He was rich.

'Look, Dorian,' he managed eventually after another long, shell-shocked silence. 'Do you mind if I call you back? I think I need to lie down.'

'Sure.' The agent laughed, delighted. 'You finally made me some money, Max. You can lie down for as long as you want.'

Max put down his mobile and lay back, slowly, on to the bed, staring up at the swirly patterns etched into the white ceiling. He tried to take it all in.

Two point four million dollars.

He was a rich man.

A success.

How very odd.

He waited for a rush of happiness to overtake him, but it didn't. Instead horrible tendrils of depression began tightening themselves painfully around his heart.

After all, without Siena to share it with, what did the money matter? What did anything matter? The money should have come to someone who could appreciate it, someone who deserved it, not to him.

But then, almost immediately, another thought occurred to him. And for the first time that day he felt almost happy.

Picking up the hotel phone this time – what the heck, he could afford it – he began to punch out the well-worn number. It rang twelve or thirteen times before a sleepy female voice answered.

'Muffy?' he said excitedly. 'It's me, Max. Look, I'm sorry to wake you up sweetheart. But I've got some good news for you. Some very, very good news.'

Chapter Fifty-two

After Minnie had died, Pete and Claire had moved back into the old mansion in Hancock Park to begin the process of sorting through her estate. The house held unhappy memories for both of them, but it was part of Pete's history, not to mention Hollywood history, and he hadn't immediately been sure what he wanted to do with it. Moving in temporarily seemed like the best way to make up their minds.

So it was to Siena's childhood home that mother and daughter returned when they came back from Nantucket.

Siena felt a strange mix of emotions as she stepped through the heavy wooden front door – the same door with its brass bolts and neo-Gothic panels. How many times had she fantasised about walking into this marble hallway, with its curling, sweeping staircase, the banisters worn to a sheen by generations of sliding children? She couldn't possibly count.

But somehow, now she was actually here, the joy she had anticipated for so long failed to materialise. The Hancock Park she had clung to in her dreams for so many years was the buzzing, vibrant home she remembered from her childhood. To her child's eye it had been a magnificent palace, a living presence, almost, which had absorbed her grandfather's energy and spirit until every wall, every staircase, felt alive. Now she was returning to the reality – a lonely, empty shell of a house, shrouded with all the betrayals and disappointments of her grandmother's life.

It wasn't just that Minnie had redecorated, eradicating all of Duke's vulgarity. By any rational, adult standards,

Siena recognised, those changes constituted a dramatic improvement. It was more than that.

It was as if the house she remembered had died all those years ago, along with her childhood and her happiness. Looking around her now, she couldn't help but mourn for it.

Claire took one look at her pale, shaken face and put her straight to bed with a cup of hot chocolate into which she had crushed two Rohypnol. It had been a long and difficult journey for Siena and she was still very weak physically.

She protested, but her mother was firm.

They would talk in the morning.

The next day, Siena had been so frail she couldn't get out of bed. Claire could hardly bear to leave her for a second, but she had to go to the hospital and see Pete.

'Are you sure you'll be all right, darling?' she asked anxiously, plumping up Siena's pillows as she prepared to leave. 'I spoke to Dr Davis last night and he'll be in to see you at ten.' Dr Davis had been the McMahon family doctor since Siena was knee high. Just hearing his name reassured her. 'He can talk to you about eye specialists, and sort out some pain relief. And I'll be home as soon as I can.'

'Really, Mom, I'm fine.' She smiled weakly through her exhaustion. The long journey, combined with all the emotional stress of the last twenty-four hours, was really starting to catch up with her. 'You just focus on Dad.'

Seeing Pete was a shock.

'He looks terrible,' Claire said frankly to the senior consultant, looking at his pale, apparently lifeless body rigged up to a horrible-looking mesh of wires and machinery. 'Are you sure he's stable?'

The consultant had explained, kindly but very clearly, that 'stable' meant nothing more than that his heart was not expected to stop again imminently. It didn't mean that he would not have another attack in the future. And it didn't mean that he would ever regain consciousness.

He might. But as of today, no one could say for sure which way things would go. Nor could they tell her how long it would be before his condition changed, for better or worse.

For the next week, Claire made the daily trip into Cedars alone. She longed to bring Siena with her, but Dr Davis had warned her not to rush things.

'Give her time,' he'd said. 'She'll be fine, but she needs to regain her strength.'

About ten days after their return home, Siena was finally well enough to make it downstairs for breakfast. She still looked terrible, although she insisted she had slept well and Claire was greatly encouraged to see her smiling for the first time in weeks when a totally hyperactive Zulu, her beloved bichon frise, launched himself into Siena's lap like a rocket-propelled pom-pom and began frenziedly licking her face.

She laughed. 'Nice to see that someone still appreciates me.'

Claire clucked around her like a mother hen in her old white dressing gown – she had had the same one since Siena was little – making toast and coffee and signalling for Siena to sit still and be waited on.

'It feels funny, being here. In this kitchen,' said Siena. 'Sitting at this table. This is where Grandpa died, right here.'

She stretched out her fingers and swept them in an arc across the worn wood of the table, lost in the awful memory. Whatever his failings, as a father, a husband, a man, Siena had loved her grandfather with the pure, uncomplicated adoration of a child. Duke's death had marked the end of her childhood and the beginning of a long and painful journey. But the irony was that it was a journey that had ultimately led her back to Hancock Park, to this same table. She had come full circle.

'I know, honey.' Claire placed a steaming mug of milky coffee in front of her daughter. 'But we had a lot of good times at this table as well.' When Siena didn't say anything, she went on, 'I think your grandfather would be pleased to see you back home.'

That made Siena smile and, while she petted Zulu and nibbled at the peanut-butter toast that Claire had piled high in front of her, she found herself starting to talk about Randall. It was the first time she had admitted to anyone, perhaps even to herself, just *how* controlling and abusive he had been. The first time she had said the words out loud, anyway.

Claire let her finish without interruption. She wasn't about to pass judgement, or even offer advice. It was up to Siena what she wanted to do now. And whether she decided to risk going after him through the courts or the press, or just walked away and let it go, this time she was going to be there for her daughter one hundred per cent.

'Well,' she said at last, once Siena's stream of consciousness had come to a natural end, 'that's all in the past now, my angel. I'm just glad you're here.'

'Me too.' Siena smiled at her, pushing all thoughts of Randall from her mind for the time being.

'So,' said Claire, kissing the top of her head and clearing away her empty plate, 'I guess we should think about heading for the hospital.'

'Oh, I don't know, Mom.' Siena frowned nervously. 'I'm not sure that's such a good idea.'

'What do you mean?' asked Claire. 'You want to see your father, don't you?'

Siena felt torn. The truth was, she was terrified of seeing Pete and had no idea how she was going to react once she got into that hospital room. On the other hand, she knew how desperate her mother was to be at his bedside, and to have her support. It was almost obscene to sit here worrying about herself when her dad might be dying, whatever she did or didn't feel for him. But she couldn't seem to help it.

'Well, what if the press see me?' she heard herself saying, knowing how selfish she must sound and cursing herself inside. 'They'll go beserk.'

'No they won't,' said Claire reasonably. 'No one recognised you on the plane from Boston, did they? Besides, so what if they do see you? It's hardly a crime to visit your own father when he's d . . .' She only just stopped herself from saying it. 'When he's seriously ill.'

Siena thought about it.

'Did you speak to his doctor today?' she asked. Claire nodded. She looked terribly anxious suddenly. She must have aged years in the last few days. 'Is he conscious?'

'He hasn't been. Not for the last forty-eight hours.'

'All right, then,' said Siena. She was scared shitless, but so what? It was time to put her mother first for once. 'In that case, I'll come with you.'

Kenneth Sams was starting to get pissed off.

He'd been over the moon when he heard that he was going to get the bulk of the shifts taking care of Pete McMahon. All the other nurses had been *sooo* jealous.

'You're bound to meet loads of celebrities coming to visit,' they said.

'Hunter world's-most-beautiful-man McMahon is sure to come see his brother,' they said.

That was over a week ago. And how many famous movie stars had he met? How many gorgeous, tight-assed TV hunks had stopped by to patch things up with their only brother before he croaked?

None.

Nothing. *Nada.* Zip.

Only the old boy's wife, who was a nice enough lady and all, and occasionally his blubbering lump of a sister. For a guy who had practically ruled Hollywood for the last fifteen years, Pete McMahon sure didn't seem to have a lot of friends.

This morning, Kenny had checked on his patient as usual – still no change – and was heading back to the staff room for a slug of coffee when he saw Mrs McMahon arriving. Only this time, she wasn't alone.

All he could make out of her companion as they approached was that she was small and female, but he noticed she was wearing big dark glasses and a scarf – the classic celeb disguise!

'Hello, Mrs McMahon.' He minced over to them excitedly, staring without restraint at Siena's scar and collapsed cheek. 'He's still sleeping, I'm afraid. And are you, er, another friend of the family?' He cocked his head curiously at her.

'No,' said Siena rudely. She was in no mood to pander to some nosy queen of a nurse. 'Did you mean asleep, or is he unconscious?'

Kenny paused. She didn't look much like her, but then they could do incredible retouches these days on some of those magazine pictures. And he was sure he recognised the voice.

'Unconscious,' he said. 'He's still unconscious.'

'Fine,' said Siena. 'Well, we'd like to see him now, please.'

She swept into the private room regally, with Claire following anxiously behind.

'Did you really have to be so rude to him?' she said once the door was safely closed behind them. 'Kenny's your father's nurse and he's always been really helpful and supportive.'

'Sorry,' said Siena, although privately she thought 'Kenny' looked like a classic star-fucker and could imagine exactly what had inspired his 'support' towards her mom. 'I just don't want people asking too many questions, you know?'

Down the hall, Kenny pumped three quarters into the nurses' payphone and tried to stop his heart from pounding.

'Hello?' he stammered breathlessly. '*LA Times*? Yeah,

put me through to the news desk, please. Uh-huh. Yeah, my name's Kenneth. Kenneth Sams.'

Staring at her father, Siena tried to feel something, anything. But it was as if she had no emotion left at all.

He was naked from the waist up and fatter than she remembered, with his sandy red chest hair shaved to allow six round pads trailing wires to be stuck to his rib cage, as though somebody might be planning to electro-cute him. His face looked unusually placid – he didn't appear to be in any pain – and his breathing was deep and regular.

Claire pulled up a chair and positioned herself beside him, taking his limp hand in hers and stroking it as she spoke to him.

'Siena is here, honey,' she said. 'She's come to visit you. She's come back home.'

Pete made not the slightest flicker of recognition and Siena relaxed slightly. At least he wasn't going to wake up and start screaming at her. Unfortunately, she did not share her mother's belief that he would feel anything other than anger should he wake and find the prodigal daughter returned.

The room was cold and clinical and smelt sterilised. It made Siena shudder. She'd seen more than her fair share of hospitals recently. The only noise was a dull, constant hum from the high-tech-looking machine next to Pete's bed, which she assumed was some sort of heart monitor, although it didn't have one of those green, blippy screens with a squiggly line like they had in all the TV shows.

The thought occurred to her that if Pete had had his way, she would have gone to Oxford and become a fully fledged doctor by now, and would no doubt understand the significance of every blip and whirr.

On the table next to the machine, two huge vases of pale yellow roses, Claire's favourite flowers, defiantly attempted to inject some colour and natural beauty into the sterile room. But even they, Siena noticed, had

599

started to brown and fray at the tips of the petals, as if contaminated by the artificial atmosphere all around them.

'Are you OK, Mom?' she asked, trying to smile for Claire's sake. 'You want me to go get you anything from the canteen? Some coffee or something?'

Claire shook her head. 'No, darling. I have everything I ever wanted right here.'

She took hold of Siena's hand and placed it on top of Pete's and between her own. Siena closed her eyes and tried with all her might to feel something.

It was no good. She was still numb.

What kind of heartless monster was she?

As if reading her mind, Claire said gently, 'It's all right, darling, it's not your fault. You haven't seen him in a long time.'

'I'm sorry,' Siena whispered in reply. Then she blurted it out. 'I don't think I love him, Mom. I really don't.'

'Shhh,' said Claire, placing two fingers gently over Siena's lips to silence her. 'It doesn't matter. You're here, darling. That's all that matters. Why don't you try talking to him? Tell him how you feel.'

Tell him how she felt? She very much doubted whether he or her mother would be ready to hear the truth, even if she knew what to say, where to begin. But she could tell from Claire's anxious, desperately hopeful face that she was longing for her to make some sort of gesture of reconciliation.

She knew in her heart she couldn't forgive him. It was too late for that. But she could do this one small thing for her mother. She had to do it.

Taking Pete's hand in hers, she cleared her throat awkwardly.

'Hello, Dad,' she said, blushing self-consciously as she spoke. 'It's me, Siena. I . . .' She stumbled, unsure of what her mother would want her to say. In the end, she decided to keep it simple. 'I want you to know that I love you, and I forgive you. For everything.'

Suddenly, she let out a little scream of shock and jumped back from the bed, as if a snake had bitten her.

'What is it?' asked Claire in panic. 'What's the matter?'

'Holy shit,' said Siena, whose heart was beating like a rapid-fire machine gun. 'He squeezed my hand. Jesus, Mom. I think he heard me.'

They stayed for almost two more hours, Claire talking almost constantly to Pete and Siena doing her best to make some further show of affection for her mother's sake, holding his hand and at one point wiping the sweat from his forehead with a flannel – but to Claire's dismay he made no further noise or movement whatsoever.

She started to wonder whether Siena had imagined the squeeze. But Siena knew for certain it had happened. It had scared the hell out of her.

During the long, awkward silences, Siena was ashamed to find her mind wandering to other things.

She thought about her sight and whether it would ever fully recover. She'd seen the eye specialist at home yesterday for an initial consultation, and he'd been guardedly encouraging, but by no means certain he could put things right.

She thought a lot about Hunter too, and everything that had happened between them. She longed to go and see him, to tell him how sorry she was for everything. But when she pictured herself walking up to his door and pressing the buzzer, she found she was frozen with terror.

What if he didn't forgive her? What if Tiffany refused to even give her the time of day, refused to let her in? She didn't think she could bear it if Hunter were to reject her now.

Most of all, though, she thought about Max.

It was funny how, after ruthlessly blocking out all her feelings for him for over a year, she now seemed incapable of going a minute without images of his face popping up unbidden in her mind. After he cheated on her, she'd been so hurt, so blinded with misery, that it had seemed easy, cathartic even, to blame him for everything. She'd nursed her anger like a mother nursing her child, egged on of course by Randall, until it had hardened into a safe protective shell around her heart. She had remembered nothing good about him.

But now, she felt as if the dam was breaking, and all those good and happy memories were flooding out, assaulting her senses, cracking what was left of her weakened self-defences. And for the first time, she realised that perhaps it wasn't all his fault. That perhaps, in the months they were together, she might have said or done things to push him away.

She missed him so much. She wanted to say sorry, for the way she'd treated him when he gatecrashed the party at Malibu and tried to help her. She wanted to say sorry for everything.

The thought of never seeing him again was infinitely more painful to her than any of her injuries, but she didn't even know where he lived any more. Besides, even if she tracked him down, she could hardly expect him to want her now, with her shattered face and her scars. She was practically a cripple. The whole thing was utterly hopeless.

Finally, Claire agreed that they should take a break and go and get some lunch.

'Do you mind if we get out of the hospital?' Siena asked her. 'I really need some air. We could grab a bite up on Melrose or something, sit inside at Le Pain. No one will recognise us there.'

'Sure, honey,' said Claire.

She could tell that Siena felt ill at ease and had been itching to escape ever since they got there. She had also noticed her scratching and worrying at her right eye, constantly taking off her dark glasses to touch the still-red scars. She prayed that the new specialist would be able to help her. God only knew what a hatchet job Randall's doctors might have done on her.

Mother and daughter walked hand in hand to the elevator and shot down the seventeen floors to the lobby in just a few seconds. Scarf and shades firmly in place, and with her head down, Siena walked across the polished marble floor to the electric double doors, which opened as they approached to let them out into the December sunshine.

She winced as a flashbulb erupted in her face.

The noise was deafening.

'Siena! Is it true that you had a breakdown?'

'Siena, what does Randall Stein think about your reconciliation with your family?'

'How do you feel? Can you tell us anything about your father's condition?'

'Mrs McMahon, what's it like to be reunited with your daughter after all these years?'

Siena tried in vain to shield her face with her hands, but the cameras kept rolling, their flashes blinding her sensitive eyes so she had to cling to her mother helplessly for support.

'Leave us alone!' shouted Claire, but she was barely audible over the frenzied pushing and shouting of the press pack that now surrounded them. 'We have nothing to say.'

She looked back longingly over her shoulder at the hospital doors, but at least two TV crews stood between her and safety. She was conscious of Siena shivering like a frightened fawn beside her, clinging on to her sleeve for dear life. How on earth were they going to get out of here?

Suddenly she heard a male voice piercing the racket. She couldn't quite place it at first, although she was sure she recognised it from somewhere.

'Excuse me. Out of my way, please. Coming through.'

The voice was calm but forceful, and the scrum of reporters audibly quietened and backed away slightly to allow its owner to move forward. When he appeared beside her, Claire didn't think she had ever been so pleased to see anyone in her life.

'Come on,' said Hunter. 'Let's get you two inside.'

He scooped Siena up into his arms – Jesus Christ, she was thin, she weighed almost nothing – and ushered Claire towards the hospital doors, elbowing aside journalists and cameramen effortlessly as he strode forward.

'Hunter!' came the yells from behind them.

'Are you here to see your brother?'

'Can you tell us about Siena's breakdown? When did you two last see each other?'

'Has your brother's heart attack brought the family back together? Hunter!'

As they approached the doors, hospital security surged forward to let them through and keep the cameras back. Claire glanced back to see a crowd of faces pressed up against the glass at the sides, and where the doors stood open in the middle hundreds of arms were blindly thrusting tape recorders and cameras into the lobby, desperate for one last comment or shot.

How could Siena, or anyone, ever have *chosen* to live like this?

Hunter carried Siena, who was still shaking, into the elevator, and she let out a loud sigh of relief as the doors closed behind them.

'What floor?' he asked.

He looked enormous in the confined space of the elevator, and Siena seemed little more than a limp rag doll, pressed against the broad white-shirted expanse of his chest.

Claire hadn't seen him since he was a teenager, although she'd seen pictures. He'd grown into quite a man. He looked frighteningly like a young Duke.

She stood there, gazing at him blankly, and said nothing.

'What button should I press?' he asked again.

'Seventeen,' said Claire.

And to her own surprise, as the elevator lurched upward with a stomach-churning whoosh, she suddenly burst into tears.

Upstairs, the three of them filed back into Pete's room. Hunter set Siena down gently on the softer of the two chairs, and tried not to look at the pitiful spectacle of his brother, while Claire perched on the edge of the bed.

'Thank you,' she said. 'I don't know what we'd have done without you down there.'

Siena seemed to have been struck dumb. She was overjoyed to see Hunter, but what was she supposed to say? 'Thanks for saving my ass again, sorry for being such a manipulative bitch, and by the way, did you notice I now look like a freak?'

'Hey, c'mon, it was nothing,' he mumbled awkwardly to Claire. 'I just stopped by . . . you know. I thought maybe I'd just ask how he was doing. I mean, I wasn't meaning to intrude or anything. I wouldn't even have come up to the room.'

'It's wonderful you're here,' said Claire.

He would never know how incredibly touched she was that he had cared enough to come and see Pete. Hunter, of all people, owed him absolutely nothing.

'I wanna go back out there.' Both Hunter and Claire were startled to hear Siena speak. It took a moment for them to take in what she was saying. 'I want them to see what Randall did to me. This is as good a time as any.'

Hunter tried not to show how shocked he was by the damage to her face. He had caught a glimpse of her injuries downstairs, but she was so well wrapped up, and he'd been so focused on getting her out of the scrum of reporters, that this was the first time he'd had a chance to take in the full extent of her scars.

He felt physically sick, not because of how she looked but because of Stein's unimaginable, bestial savagery. And because he hadn't been there to save her when she needed him. Now it was his turn to be struck dumb with guilt.

It was Claire who spoke first. 'Are you sure, Siena? This morning you were worried about seeing any press at all. There are so many of them down there, darling. Are you sure you can handle it?'

Siena nodded grimly. 'I've handled worse.'

'And you've really thought this through, have you?'

Claire wanted Randall to suffer for what he'd done more than anybody, but she was still scared of what all the publicity and perhaps a protracted, expensive lawsuit might do to Siena. She had almost hoped that her daughter would decide just to let the whole thing drop. That way, they could all move on with their lives as if Randall Stein had never existed.

'I've thought about nothing else for the last two weeks,' said Siena. Despite her bruises, Hunter could see the flash of strength and determination he remembered so well lighting up her eyes. He felt immensely proud of her. 'I'm gonna get that fucker.'

Emerging through the front doors a few minutes later, supported by Hunter, she was greeted by a second furore of flashbulbs and shouted questions. But this time she was ready for them.

Slowly, as if savouring the moment, she removed her dark glasses and scarf, allowing the astounded photographers and film crews a full minute to capture every angle of her ravaged face.

She had thought her strategy through carefully. She wasn't going to explicitly accuse Randall and open herself up to a lawsuit and police investigation. This was a town where might was right, and she knew that there was a solid chance, despite the evidence of her injuries, that Randall could defeat her in court and quite possibly bankrupt her into the bargain.

She would be silent, let the pictures speak for themselves, and damn him by implication. That should easily generate enough negative publicity to destroy his career, and reveal him to the world as the monster he truly was, without allowing him the opportunity of a legal defence.

Why should Siena need to accuse him herself, when she could get the rest of the world to do it for her?

After a decent interval, and once she was pretty sure that they all had the shots they needed, she held up her hand for quiet and announced that she wanted to make a statement. It took a further minute or so for the crowd to quieten down sufficiently to allow her to speak.

'As you can appreciate,' she began in a quiet but steady voice, 'this is a very difficult and emotional time for me and for my family.' Hunter squeezed her hand and she squeezed back. 'My father is very ill. And I am also in the process of recovering from a violent attack.'

A murmur of questions began building, but she held up her hand for silence before continuing.

'I will not be making any comment today, or at any other time, about the circumstances of that attack. Or . . .'

She paused dramatically.

'Or disclosing who did this to me. For personal reasons, I don't wish to press charges against that individual, or to involve the police. However, I would like to take this opportunity to correct an earlier statement by Mr Randall Stein – that's S-T-E-I-N.' The reporters laughed at that, and Siena couldn't help but smile back. She was still the media's darling. 'Implying that I had been suffering from a nervous or emotional breakdown. The only sign of mental illness I've shown in the last year was moving in with Mr Stein in the first place.'

More laughter.

'Thank you all for your support. That's all I have to say.'

She turned to go back into the building with the deafening shout of more questions ringing in her ears.

'Why aren't you pressing charges?'

'Have you seen or spoken to Randall since the attack?'

'Will Stein be making a statement, Siena? Siena!'

With some difficulty, Hunter ushered her back into the elevator.

'You OK?' he asked as the doors closed.

But it was a stupid question. Her face was flushed with triumph. She'd just pulled the pin out and lobbed a hand grenade right into Randall's life.

What could be better than that?

'I'm fine,' was all she said. 'I'm sorry, Hunter. For everything.'

'Me too,' he said, and pressed her fragile body into his chest as if trying to prove it. 'I'm sorry I wasn't there to stop him.'

Randall's financial backers heard the news before he did.

He took the call in the car.

'Listen, John, it's all bullshit, OK? She can't prove a thing. I'll be talking to my attorney about it within the hour; this has to be libellous.'

But they weren't interested in listening to his bluster.

'That's your problem, Randall. Look at your contract. It's very clear. The morality clause says we pull out if continued association with the project can be shown to reflect detrimentally on Orion Enterprises, *for any reason.*'

'But, John, these are just rumours. Come on. You can't seriously expect me to fall on my sword to the tune of nine million dollars on the basis of some unsubstantiated, malicious gossip. I'm telling you, she's unstable. John? Hello? Hello?'

But the line had already gone dead.

Chapter Fifty-three

The next few weeks were a roller-coaster of emotions for Siena.

The pictures of her battered face outside the hospital made the front pages all across America, and speculation about her injuries was rife. The accusations against Randall were all made indirectly with cautiously worded caveats and lots of 'allegedly's sprinkled around for good measure – the papers didn't want to get sued any more than she did – but the damage was done. Both his main backers had pulled out of *1943* and he'd taken a huge financial bath on the failed movie. What no one could put a price on, though, was the damage to his reputation.

Randall Stein's Hollywood glory days were well and truly over.

He made only one public comment on the matter, telling a journalist as he emerged from his limo at a charity gala that he and Siena remained friends and that he wished her well and categorically denying any involvement in her injuries.

Siena noticed with a wry smile that he was accompanied to the event by none other than Miriam Stanley, the starlet who'd been so desperate to get her money-grabbing claws into him that night at the Beverly Hills Hotel.

Good luck to her!

Now that she'd had her revenge she felt nothing, nothing at all for Randall. She couldn't even muster much anger any more. He existed for her only in a past life, a life that was now gone for ever.

It wasn't all good news, though. Some of the comments about her scars were hurtful, although Siena found herself feeling more resilient than she'd thought she would be. Now that she had her family back, she no longer felt defined by her beauty, or her fame, in the way that she had before, and the barbs about her lost looks mostly felt more like nettle stings than piercing arrows.

Mercifully, the media had begun to lose interest in Pete's illness as the weeks went by without any noticeable change in his condition. The doctors had told them that he might never regain consciousness, but Claire refused to give up hope. She continued to visit him every day, and Siena accompanied her occasionally, mostly without overt harassment from the press.

Hunter began spending a lot of time at Hancock Park, at both Siena and Claire's request.

Tiffany was very wary at first about him building bridges with Siena yet again.

'I just don't want to see you hurt again,' she'd told him, when he'd first suggested it one weekend at their little house in Venice. 'Every time she's down, she needs you, but as soon as she gets her strength back she forgets all about you and moves on.'

They were sitting on the sofa together in front of the fire, watching the unexpected rain outside as it hammered mercilessly against the window panes and gushed along the walk streets in torrents, like some biblical flood. In LA, rain was an event, and Tiffany had been quite happy just to sit and watch it with Hunter, until Siena's name, as usual, shattered her peace and contentment.

Inevitably, he insisted that this time was different, that she really had changed, and pleaded with her to come with him over to Hancock Park for dinner. Tiffany remained sceptical.

'Just one dinner, baby. Please?' he persisted. 'And if you never want to see her again after that, I swear to God, I'll understand.'

'*One* dinner?' She was weakening.

'One, I promise you.' He beamed at her. 'Only one. I just want you to see her, that's all.'

The evening marked a turning point for all of them.

Tiffany didn't know what was more shocking, Siena's ravaged appearance or her obviously genuine remorse for her past behaviour.

'I was jealous of you,' Siena had admitted, when the two of them took a private walk in the moonlit grounds after dinner. For Tiffany, who had never been to Hancock Park before, the whole experience was surreal. She'd heard so much about the unhappiness of Hunter's childhood here, and the emotional torture he'd been put through by just about every adult member of his family, that in her mind she'd built the place up as some sort of House of Horrors. But now that she was actually here, walking round the orangery with Siena, the reality of the estate in all its beauty and opulence took her breath away.

'Jealous of *me*?' She sounded incredulous. 'Why?'

'Because you had Hunter's love,' said Siena. 'Because you deserved it.'

She still walked slowly, owing to the recurrent pain in her ribs, and Tiffany had to make a conscious effort to slow down her own pace in sympathy. When they came to the rose garden and an old wooden bench, Siena eased herself down on to it to catch her breath and Tiffany sat beside her.

'He always loved you too, you know,' she said. 'Always.'

Siena nodded weakly. She looked so fragile, as if the slightest gust of wind might pick her up and blow her away.

'I know,' she said. 'It's hard to explain. But I always felt . . . I always *knew* that I didn't deserve it. I didn't deserve his love. I was scared that if he knew what I was really like, what a selfish, horrible person I was, he'd run away from me like everyone else. He's so perfect, you know?'

'I know.' Tiffany couldn't help but grin. 'He really is. Did, er, did he tell you our news?'

She'd sworn to Hunter that she wouldn't say anything, but somehow the time felt right. Siena shook her head and looked up at her inquisitively.

'I'm not supposed to tell you yet.' She smiled. 'So you have to promise not to say anything. But, well, I'm pregnant.'

'Oh! Oh, how wonderful!' Siena stumbled shakily to her feet and threw her arms around her in genuine affection and excitement. 'A baby! Oh, I hope it looks like Hunter.' She immediately clapped her hand over her mouth, realising that what she'd just said might be considered rude. 'I didn't mean . . .' she began, but Tiffany just laughed.

'That's OK,' she said. 'I hope it looks like him too.' She took Siena's arm in hers and they began walking back towards the house. Bathed in silver moonlight, it looked incredibly romantic, like some medieval Spanish castle. No wonder the whole world had envied Hunter for growing up here. If only they knew . . .

'You realise,' she said as they approached the steps to the huge oak front door, 'that this baby is going to be your cousin?'

'Holy shit!' said Siena, now laughing herself. 'Really? How fucked up is that?'

At least her bad language was still intact. Tiffany had begun to worry that the real Siena had been abducted by aliens and she was talking to a sweet and charming impostor.

It wasn't until after Christmas, and some two weeks after this conversation with Tiffany, that Siena finally summoned up the courage to ask Hunter about Max.

She had been hoping that he or Tiffany might offer up some information voluntarily, or at least casually mention Max's name in passing so that she could raise the subject naturally. But whether it was out of sensitivity to her own feelings or for some other reason, neither of them had said a word. In the end she could bear it no longer and tackled Hunter about it one morning at breakfast.

She put down her newspaper and smiled at him across the table. The bruising around her eyes was finally starting to fade, he noticed, and thanks to a recent visit to Claire's doctor her broken cheekbone had been reset correctly, making her look more like a bashed-up version of the old Siena than the stranger he'd taken in his arms at the hospital. She still had almost no vision in her right eye, but she was definitely on the mend.

He smiled back.

'Do you . . .' She cleared her throat. Her heart was pounding violently, but she made herself go on. 'Do you ever hear from Max any more?'

'Sometimes,' said Hunter warily. He had been anti-cipating this question and also dreading it. He didn't want Siena to have to go through any more pain.

'Only sometimes? You used to be so close.'

'Well, he moved back to England a while ago. We are close but, you know, we don't speak as much as we used to. Life moves on.'

'Yes, it does,' said Siena sadly, retreating behind her paper again.

Hunter could tell that her thoughts were already miles away. He didn't want her to pin her hopes on a reconciliation with Max, only to be disappointed. He wanted her to look forward, not back.

'Listen, sweetheart,' he said. 'I'm not sure things would ever have worked out between the two of you in the long run. Even if he hadn't . . .' He paused, not wanting to rake up any more unhappy memories for her. 'Even if things hadn't happened the way they did. You're very different people.'

'Is he still in England?' Siena couldn't help but ask. She knew Hunter was right, she should let it go. But she had

613

to know where he was, where she should picture him in her thoughts and dreams.

'No,' he said brusquely. 'He moved to New York. He's directing a play there, I think.'

'Oh.' She digested this information silently for a moment. 'Does he have a girlfriend?'

'Siena.' Hunter frowned. 'You have to move on, honey. Forget about Max. He's part of the past, remember? You have a whole new life now. One day, you're going to meet someone else, someone who's going to be wonderful to you and love you and give you all the happiness and stability you need. Trust me. I know you don't believe it now, but it's true.'

'Does he?' she insisted.

She had to know.

Goddam. He was clearly never going to get her to drop it. So he took a deep breath and did something that he couldn't remember ever having done before. He lied to her.

'Yes,' he said, picking at a crumb on the table and not meeting Siena's eye. 'A French girl. I think it's fairly serious.'

He hated himself for saying it, as he knew full well that Max had ended things with Freddie before he moved. But it was the only way he could think of to make Siena let go. The only way to protect her.

Every word knifed into Siena's heart like a razor, but not by a flicker did she betray her emotions. She was scared that once she gave in to that pain, once she let it show, she might never be able to stop crying.

With every last ounce of her will-power, she held back the tears, and even managed a weak smile.

'I'm happy for him,' she said. Hunter looked at her doubtfully. 'Really, I am. He deserves it. He deserves to be happy.'

'I think I need help. I know it's ridiculous and self-indulgent and, well, damn stupid after everything that's happened. But I'm still so unhappy. Some days I feel like I can barely breathe.'

The elderly doctor looked at Max and smiled reassuringly.

It wasn't every day that a young, talented, newly minted millionaire walked into his surgery with glaring symptoms of depression: sleeplessness, uncontrolled crying, loss of energy, inability to concentrate; this guy had the lot.

'You *are* showing signs of mild clinical depression,' he announced, trying to be gentle. Max looked shocked. 'I can refer you to a psychiatrist, who may be able to prescribe something.'

'What, like Prozac?' said Max, aghast. 'I'm not sure I'm ready for all that.'

The doctor smiled again. 'You could try counselling of some sort. A lot of people find cognitive behavioural therapy to be useful in combating emotional or mood disorders. You'd probably have to do it privately, though, if you wanted to start soon. It's about fifty pounds a session, I believe.'

Max grinned. 'Yeah, well. I guess I can afford it.'

He was back at Batcombe after an extended Christmas vacation, and decided on a whim to pop into the doctor's surgery in the village while out for one of his many solitary walks.

Having given Henry and Muffy a huge injection of cash with which to buy off the odious Ellis and reclaim the farm, he'd been guest of honour at Christmas. The last of the trucks and building equipment had gone by early December, and all that was left to remind them of the whole sorry nightmare was a muddy drive and a couple of big piles of bricks in the corner of the old farmyard.

'I'll pay you back. I'll make good every penny,' Henry had assured him, endlessly, although Max had no intention of letting him do any such thing.

'Pay me back for what? For giving you some money

that I did nothing to earn and certainly don't need? Behave yourself.'

'It's not just *some money*, Max,' said Muffy, who was busily putting the last of the children's presents around the Christmas tree. 'It's a bloody fortune.'

'Believe me,' he told them both. 'I'm doing this as much for myself as for you. Manor Farm has always been like home to me. I'm as happy to be rid of that bastard as you are.'

Ellis, as it turned out, had proved a lot easier to buy off than they had feared.

The golf course was already running behind schedule and way over budget, and the bad feeling on-site after Gary's ill-advised lunge at Muffy had caused him no end of trouble with his foreman. Along with most of the men, Ben McIntyre had developed a lot of sympathy for the Arkells, and disapproved of the way his boss had maliciously taunted and harassed them for months on end.

'I want a damn sight more than I paid for it,' Gary had told Max gruffly when he first floated the idea of a buy-back on the lease. 'I've lost a small bleedin' fortune on that place so far, and I'm sure as 'ell not leaving while I'm down on the deal.'

But despite his bravado, he'd agreed on a fair price. Now that the new section of the M40 was no longer being routed via Witney, Batcombe was not quite the ultra-desirable site it had once been. That, combined with the fact that he was clearly never going to get anywhere with Muffy, made him glad to be rid of the place.

Max knew he ought to have felt happy.

Happy for Henry and Muff about the farm, happy at his own unexpected good fortune. He had never dreamed that *Dark Hearts* would come good in such spectacular style. And it wasn't just the money he had to be thankful for. There was the opening of the play and his new life in New York to look forward to as well.

Plus, he was finally free of the stifling relationship with

616

Freddie which had caused him such torments of guilt for so long. Darling Freddie, she had even sent him a Christmas card from France, full of kindness and without any bitterness or reproach, telling him all about her new life and friends back in Toulouse. Oh, to be so young and resilient, thought Max.

Christmas came and went, and he did his best to smile through it all and join in the festivities. But even the children could see that something was wrong. When Maddie had asked him one night at supper why he only smiled with his lips – 'You've switched your eyes off,' as she put it – he'd had to leave the table and bolt upstairs to his room to cry.

Thanking the GP, he walked out of the surgery and into the cold drizzle of the village. Perhaps things would improve when he got back to New York.

He trudged down the hill towards the farm, willing himself to believe that work and the non-stop, sleepless energy of the city might jolt him out of his stupor. Only three more days until he went back. Rehearsals started in earnest next week.

As he passed the village school, he took out of his Barbour pocket the piece of paper that the doctor had given him, with the name and number of a local psychiatrist and a depression helpline. He let a few stray droplets of rain fall on it, smudging the ink, before screwing it up into a tight ball and dropping it into the bin.

He didn't need a psychiatrist.

He needed Siena.

It was New Year's Eve in Los Angeles, and Siena and Claire were enjoying a low-key celebratory dinner in Hancock Park, each wanting nothing more than the other's company.

Hunter and Tiffany had gone to Colorado to see her parents and tell them all about the baby. Siena wondered

617

how they were going to take the news. She supposed that even the Wedans would have to bestow their blessing now that their daughter and Hunter were starting a family together.

The evening had been so incredibly peaceful that both women were startled when the phone started ringing at eleven o'clock.

Siena was in her pyjamas, curled up with a book by the fire in the room that Grandpa used to call the den, while Claire composed a letter to one of her college girlfriends.

'It's probably just Aunt Laurie, getting confused with the time zones,' said Siena, as her mother walked into the hallway to answer it. 'Just say "Happy New Year" now, so she doesn't call back.'

Claire gave her daughter a reprimanding frown. Poor Laurie, she was harmless really, although she *could* be a nuisance at times. She was with friends in New York tonight, so at least she wouldn't be lonely.

Siena, who went straight back to her book and forgot all about the call, didn't notice Claire replace the receiver, white faced, and come back into the room. She started and turned around when she heard her mother speak.

'That was the hospital,' said Claire. 'There was no time to call us, apparently. It all happened very quickly.'

'Oh, Mom.' She ran up to her shivering mother and hugged her tightly. 'I'm so sorry.'

'So am I, my darling,' said Claire. One heavy, solitary tear rolled down her cheek and splashed down on to Siena's shoulder. 'I'm sorry for so many things.'

Pete's funeral was small and private. Only Siena, Claire, Tiffany, Hunter and Laurie attended.

Laurie wept openly and profusely. She and Pete had never been close, but she had never married, and he was the only other person in the world who had shared her childhood memories, as painful as they were.

Siena hadn't seen her aunt since her early teens, but she was shocked at how badly she'd aged. She was only in her mid-fifties, but looked twenty years older at least, with her completely grey hair worn in a severe bun that made her look like the granny from the Tweety Pie cartoons.

Claire's grief was more dignified and controlled. Whatever regrets she may have had about her marriage and the choices she had made, she kept them to herself. She knew that Pete had loved her, and she had loved him. In a strange sort of way, that was enough.

So much of her past she had devoted to the man she now saw buried beside his beloved mother in the old cemetery in Pasadena.

Her future was going to be for herself, and for her daughter.

A week or so after the funeral, a huge, very public memorial service was held at the Good Shepherd Catholic church in Beverly Hills. Most of the great and the good from the movie business, past and present, were there to pay their respects to the man that few of them had really known and even fewer liked, but who had been as much a part of Hollywood as the famous sign itself.

Afterwards, a number of people had come up to Siena, ostensibly to offer their condolences but really to check out for themselves the damage that, it was now an open secret in industry circles, Randall Stein had done to her legendary looks.

She was starting to get exhausted, and had signalled to Hunter that she was just about ready to go home, when another gawper tapped her on the shoulder.

'Look,' she said, swinging round, 'I'm sorry, but it's been a really long day for me. I . . .' She stopped, and immediately smiled when she recognised Dierk Muller, her old director, the man who had given her her first break, and about whom she had once been so poison-ously ungrateful in print. 'Dierk!' She blushed. 'What are you doing here? I didn't know you knew my father.'

'I didn't,' he said, honestly. His clipped German accent was just as she remembered it. 'I came here to see you.'

Siena's face fell.

'Look, I'm sorry for all those things I said about you, truly I am,' she stammered.

'About me being "second tier", you mean? Or are we talking about a different article?'

'Oh God,' she blurted out. 'I really am sorry. But I'm not sure if I can deal with another telling off today. So if you've come here to tell me how selfish I've been, you needn't bother, I already know. My dad just died, I'm supposed to feel awful about that but I don't, and people keep coming up to me and staring at my face like I'm some kind of fucking circus freak. I just want to go home and die.'

When she looked up, she saw that Dierk was smiling at her.

'Well, that's a shame,' he said brightly. 'Because I actually came here - and I know it's probably terribly inappropriate to intrude on your grief . . .' Siena shook her head and smiled at him reassuringly. 'But I wanted you to come and do a screen test for my new project. It's a bit off the wall. But I think the part would be perfect for you. I can messenger the script over to you in the morning, if you like.'

A screen test? She was so amazed, she stood there opening and closing her mouth wordlessly, like a wooden puppet.

'Well?' he said. 'Are you interested or not?'

'I thought you hated me,' she mumbled.

'Did you?' Dierk seemed to find that amusing.

'What about my face? My eyes?' she said. 'I have almost no vision in my right eye now, you know. I'm officially partially blind.'

'I didn't know that,' he said, nodding slowly and

thoughtfully. 'But I don't see that it matters so terribly much. You can see, can't you?'

His confidence in her was infectious. If he could see past her scars and her damaged sight, perhaps other people would too, eventually.

She could have reached up and kissed him.

'Look, Siena,' he said, taking her by the shoulders to drive his point home, a habit she remembered from torturous hours on *The Prodigal Daughter*. 'I'm not interested in your face. I never was. I didn't cast you last time because you were some great big model.'

'You didn't?' She looked up at him hopefully.

'No,' he said, almost angrily. 'I cast you because you have talent. Shitloads of it. It's in your soul and it's in your blood. Whatever that psychopath Stein may have told you, you've always been more than a pretty face. So.' He released her shoulders and reverted to his usual, even Teutonic tone. 'Do you want the script, or not?'

'Yes,' said Siena, and she flashed him the smile that no amount of battering could extinguish.

'Yes, I do. I want it. I want the script.'

Chapter Fifty-four

Eight months later . . .

Tiffany ripped the flower out of her hair and threw up her hands in exasperation.

'Lennox, honey,' she moaned, 'can you do this for me? I can't seem to get the stupid thing centred.'

'You know your problem, don't you?' said her old friend, sashaying over to her in his very expensive, slightly too tightly cut suit and deftly pinning the wayward white rose into place. 'No feminine skills. No feminine skills at all.'

It was the morning of her wedding day, and she was sitting in Laurie's old room at Hancock Park in a silk nightdress, practising her hair for this afternoon.

The wedding wasn't until three, and she'd rather hoped for a long lie-in, but unfortunately little Theo Wedan McMahon had had other ideas and had noisily demanded a feed at 5 a.m.

Any other day and Hunter would have given him his bottle, but of course it was bad luck to sleep together the night before your wedding, so he'd stayed across town in Venice with Max, who'd flown in from England to act as best man. Not that she really minded. Tiffany enjoyed the early morning feeds with her son, the feel of his tiny stroking fingers against her breast and the way he gazed directly up at her with his father's beautiful, deep blue eyes.

The baby had been born two months ago, and much to the disgust of her girlfriends Tiffany had already regained her slim, willowy figure, although now she had the added bonus of truly enormous breasts. Hunter told her she had the face of an angel and the body of a porn star – but then again, he was probably slightly biased.

It was he who had pushed for them to get married so soon after Theo's arrival. At first Tiffany had been opposed to a wedding. Neither of them was especially religious, after all, and she was frightened that the whole thing would turn into another McMahon media circus.

But now that the day had arrived, she was pleased she'd let him talk her into it. Claire had hired top-of-the-range security to protect their privacy as much as possible. But anyway, press or no press, she knew she shouldn't let a few paparazzi stop her from becoming Mrs Hunter McMahon. She did love him so utterly and completely.

'Hey there, the bride, can I help?'

Siena had mooched in and stood behind Lennox, admiring his handiwork.

She was looking so much better these days, thought Tiffany. Months of Claire's delicious food had helped her to regain her former curvaceous figure. Gone was the deathly pale, gaunt look she had had when she'd first left Randall. Her hair had grown back to its full length, and this morning it tumbled long and loose down her back in gorgeous Pre-Raphaelite waves. The scar on the right side of her face remained, and her left cheekbone now sat permanently lower than her right. Her face was no longer perfect. But Tiffany, at least, felt that it had gained something for that, a more real, approachable beauty that somehow sat better with the happier, kinder and more confident person she had become.

She had never regained the sight of her right eye, although to look at her you couldn't tell. And Siena herself had come to terms with her damaged sight with such an easy grace, laughingly displaying a prominent 'partially sighted' sticker on her jeep, that people often forgot she had any disability at all.

This morning she was wearing faded jeans and an old shirt of Hunter's, tied loosely under her breasts to reveal a smooth expanse of midriff. For the first time in her life, she was properly tanned after a week's break surfing in Maui, and the brown glow of her skin added to her general aura of well-being.

'I think we're OK here actually,' said Tiffany. 'Lennox has things under control, don't you, babe?'

'You better believe it,' he mumbled, through a mouthful of hairpins.

'I'm so tired, though. Theo was up half the night, bawling his little head off.'

'You should have called me,' said Siena, swiping a tortoiseshell clip from the dressing table and pinning up her own hair in a loose bun. 'I was up at four rereading that damn script. Dierk's such a fucking slave driver. Theo could have kept me company.'

She was four months into filming on Muller's new movie, and despite her frequent complaints, everyone could tell she was in seventh heaven about it. For all her braggadocio, in the past she had always been deeply insecure about her own talent. Now, for the first time, she felt she was being genuinely valued as an actress, not just Randall's girlfriend, Pete's daughter or a chip off the old Duke McMahon block. It was liberating.

'Hunter called earlier, by the way,' she said, a shadow falling across her face which Tiffany couldn't help but notice. 'He said he . . .' She paused for a split second. 'He and Max were going for a run, so you weren't to worry if you called and he wasn't there.'

'Oh, OK. Thanks.'

Tiffany was fully aware what an agony it was for Siena to be seeing Max again. Hunter had offered not to invite him if she thought she couldn't cope with it, but Siena wouldn't hear of such a thing. 'Don't be ridiculous!' she'd insisted. 'It's your wedding. You can't possibly not invite Max. How could you even think of having another best man?'

But inside, Tiffany knew that it was killing her. She had not enquired again about his life, or his supposed girlfriend. Tiffany was not at all sure that Hunter had done the right thing by lying to Siena about this, but she had to admit that she did seem happier and more stable as a result. So perhaps it *had* been for the best.

As far as Tiffany knew, Siena hadn't heard about Max's film deal and his new-found wealth, nor did she even know the name of his Broadway play. Today was bound to be difficult for her.

'Are you sure you're OK?' she asked, swinging round on her chair, to Lennox's annoyance as the rose slipped out of place yet again. 'About Max, I mean.'

'Oh, sure,' said Siena unconvincingly, waving her hand casually in an 'it's nothing' gesture. 'You know, I've known Max since I was a little kid, don't forget. It's not such a big deal. And it's not like we have to spend the whole evening together or anything. All I have to do is say hi to him, right? I mean, come on. How hard can it be?'

A few hours later, Hunter stood by the altar, shaking like a whippet.

Just when nobody thought he could get any handsomer, he'd gone and put on his morning dress for the wedding and outdone himself once again. He looked so divine, with the perfectly cut dark wool of his jacket offsetting his olive skin and the brilliant blue of his eyes, it would be a miracle if anyone even noticed the bride.

'She said she wouldn't do this,' he said in panic to Max, who was standing beside him in his own, slightly more threadbare version of the formal dress theme. In an ancient morning coat of his father's that had seen him through scores of rainy English weddings and which despite being a good two sizes too small for him, he considered 'lucky' and therefore indispensable, he looked more like Hunter's impoverished bodyguard than his best man. 'She swore to me she wouldn't make me wait. Where the fuck is she?'

'Mate.' Max laid a comforting hand on his friend's

shoulder. 'Just relax. She's *not* late. It's only five to three.'
He turned and gave a small smile to a beautiful red-headed girl in the second row, who returned his smile and added a small conspiratorial wink of encouragement.

'What's her name again?' asked Hunter. Max had brought the girl over with him from England, but between all the last-minute organisation for the wedding and his general state of heightened anxiety, Hunter had had little time to be sociable.

'Helen,' said Max.

'Pretty,' said Hunter.

'Hmm.' Max smiled. 'Yes. She is.'

The church was packed to the gills, with a congregation that looked alarmingly like a Who's Who of American television. Hugh Orchard was there with his partner, a small part of him dying inside to be watching Hunter finally getting married, in silent sympathy with teenage girls all across the country, and Tiffany's buxom cast-mates from *Sea Rescue* flashed white-toothed smiles across the aisle at the various perma-tanned hunks from *Counsellor*. On Hunter's side of the church, Caroline sat looking glamorous if somewhat under-dressed in a bottle-green halter-neck Armani dress that showed off rather a lot of her still-excellent cleavage, bottle-feeding a beautifully behaved Theo. Beside her sat an obviously dreadfully jet-lagged Christopher, who kept falling asleep and then waking himself up with a particularly violent snore, asking people in a loud, very British accent where on earth he was, much to the amusement of Claire, who sat on his other side.

'That's my son,' Caroline was whispering proudly to anyone who would listen, gesturing towards the altar. 'Isn't he handsome? Tiffany is a very lucky girl. Of course, Hunter and I have always been *terribly* close.'

Outside, kept back twenty feet from the church steps by solid steel fencing and six burly security guys, a growing crowd of fans and photographers jostled for position, trying to catch a glimpse of the famous guests as they arrived. Emma Duval, the frozen-featured face of LA-9 news, who had cornered Hunter at the now infamous Dodgers game with Siena and Randall, was engaged in a frantic battle with the bimbo from E! as to which of them had the right to the spot closest to the steps.

'I was here first, Tanisha,' she pouted, as the Amazonian, black goddess pushed past her.

'What*ever*, Emma,' replied her rival. 'I'm sure there's room for both of us.'

Meanwhile, the latest of the stragglers dashed past them into the church, the actors stopping for a few seconds of courtesy poses, everybody else darting inside as quickly as possible in the hope of bagging a late seat. The atmosphere, both inside the church and out, was electric.

After what seemed like an eternity to Hunter, the organ finally started playing the Trumpet Voluntary, and the entire church let out a collective gasp as Tiffany appeared on her father's arm and began her slow procession up the aisle.

She looked lovelier than even Hunter had imagined, in a simple, bias-cut cream silk dress and full-length veil that somehow made her look both demure and sexy. She was gazing directly at him and smiling, that same loving, serene smile that he had fallen in love with the very first day he saw her in the studios, when he'd helped her with her audition.

Suddenly, everyone else in the room seemed to melt away. He felt as though he might burst with pride and happiness as she drew nearer and nearer. What had he ever, ever done in life to deserve a girl so truly beautiful, inside and out?

Max, standing beside him, was probably the only man in the church not mesmerised by the bride.

He had sworn he wouldn't do it, he wouldn't stare at her or make an idiot of himself the moment she walked through the door. But he couldn't seem to help himself.

His eyes were drawn like magnets to Siena.

She was walking sedately behind Tiffany, in a full-length, pale gold dress, its subtle colour glinting seductively against the unusually bronzed glow of her skin, and its slick folds clinging to her beautiful body as though she had been poured into it.

He felt his chest tighten, and made a conscious effort to breathe.

Her hair was loose, her face . . . different, although nothing like some of the terrible photographs he'd seen in the New York press. Not that he would have cared how bad her scars were. She would always be infinitely beautiful to him.

Oh God, thought Siena, don't look, don't look, don't look!

She could feel Max's eyes boring into her like lasers. He must be shocked by her face. Revolted, probably.

The last time he'd seen her she'd been at the height of her beauty. Now look at her. He must be thanking his lucky stars that he had his beautiful French girlfriend here with him, instead of a washed-up freak like her. Siena had seen her the moment she arrived, standing in the second row, just behind Caroline. She'd only been able to catch a quick glimpse from the back, but it was enough to reveal the girl's elegant figure, tiny waisted in a fitted pink silk dress, and her mane of shining Titian hair.

Then she'd seen Max turn and smile at her, and felt her own heart shatter, like an egg in a microwave. There could be no more hope. They might be in the same room. But Max was lost to her. He was somebody else's now.

Somehow, she had to find the strength to walk down the aisle. She knew it was ungenerous and selfish, but she found herself wishing that Tiffany weren't looking quite so stunning. By comparison, she thought miserably, her eyes fixed to the gleaming parquet floor of the church, she must appear even uglier than ever.

Christ, thought Max. She can't even look at me.

Does she really still hate me that much?

Somehow they both made it through the service.

Siena was sitting next to a hugely pregnant Ines, who looked like a flame-haired stork with a giant beer belly. The father, apparently some feckless Argentine model she'd met on a shoot in Buenos Aires, was nowhere to be seen, but Ines seemed blissfully unconcerned.

'I 'ave 'is genes already,' she told Siena happily. 'What else do I need 'im for?' The two girls had become friends again in recent months, and Ines tried to cheer her up and distract her from Max and pink-dress girl during the wedding by making rude comments about all the *Sea Rescue* bimbos. 'Look at that one,' she whispered, pointing to a ludicrously 'enhanced' bottle blonde opposite. 'What deed she play – the inflatable safety ring?'

Siena smiled dutifully, but inside she felt utterly devastated.

How was she going to get through a whole evening, knowing he was only feet away from her? Watching him laughing and kissing and dancing with his stunning French girlfriend? The whole thing was unbearable. He was going to have to make a speech! She hadn't even *thought* about that. What if he started talking about the old days with Hunter? Would he mention her? He would have to, wouldn't he? And then everyone would be turning around to look at her, remembering that the two of them used to be together, back when she'd still had her looks, thinking how much better off he was now with Mademoiselle Perfect Body.

Oh God. She couldn't do it, she couldn't! Why hadn't she told Hunter not to invite him when she'd had the chance?

Once the torturous service was finally over, all the key players were ushered out on to the steps for formal photographs. As best man, Max was standing within a few feet of the bridesmaids, so it was impossible for Siena to keep ignoring him completely.

He glanced across at her and gave a tentative nod of acknowledgement. She nodded back, before hurriedly turning her attention to the photographer. Please God, just get this over with.

'Right.' Caroline's cut-glass English accent pierced the excited hum like a dart from a blow-pipe. Everybody turned to listen. 'I'd like a picture of the bridesmaids, please. Oh, and Maxy, darling, you too. Chop, chop! The bridesmaids and the best man.'

Like two zombies, Max and Siena edged reluctantly closer together. Max, his heart pounding, frantically scanned the crowd for Helen, but couldn't see her anywhere. Meanwhile Siena practically hurled Liza, the only other adult bridesmaid, between herself and Max. But Caroline, never famed for her sensitivity, intervened. 'No, no, no,' she said bossily. 'Max in the middle, big girls on either side, little girls at the front. Come on, you lot!'

Stupid cow, thought Siena. Stupid, stupid cow. She hadn't seen Hunter in donkey's years and now she was acting like the star of the fucking show. Why couldn't she just fuck off back to England and leave them all alone?

Max, who knew Caroline a little better, suspected that her rearrangement of their places was entirely deliberate. She'd made it clear at Batcombe that she was fully aware of his feelings for Siena, the meddlesome old witch. Unfortunately he was also in no position to argue with the mother of the groom, and shuffled around Liza to do as he was told.

He and Siena were now side by side. He could feel her bare arm brushing against the dark wool of his suit, and could have fainted with longing. Where the fuck was Helen when he needed her? She was supposed to be protecting him from this. That was why he'd brought her with him, for God's sake. Even now, despite their physical closeness, or perhaps because of it, Siena refused to look at him. He could feel himself sweating beneath his too-tight morning coat. Evidently its lucky properties had run out.

This was torture. He wanted to reach out and pull her to him, never, ever let her go again.

'Say cheese!' said Caroline brightly.

The camera flashed, and caught for posterity the image of four smiling girls, and two wretched souls, gazing in miserable desperation into the distance.

'Oh, Max, there you are.' Siena's heart leapt into her mouth and stayed there. It was the girl. She was even more stunning close up, with her creamy white cheeks and watery blue eyes which made her hair look even more goddess-like than it had from a distance, and her clinging, raw-silk dress showing off her tall, lean body in all the right places. Siena didn't think she had ever felt so much hatred for another human being.

'Are you done with the pictures?'

She didn't sound very French.

'Yes, yes, I think so.' Max sounded relieved, thought Siena. Probably pleased to be able to get away from her at last.

'Helen, this is Siena,' he mumbled, somehow managing to introduce the two of them without making any eye contact. 'Siena, Helen.'

Siena opened her mouth to say something. How do you do, pleased to meet you, anything. But suddenly, as if an elastic band had just snapped inside her, she found the words had stuck in her throat and the tears that she had been holding back for so long began pouring out of her in an uncontrollable flood. Oh Jesus. What must she look like?

She looked from the girl to Max and back again and was horrified to hear herself emit a sort of howl, like a dying animal.

She had to get out of there. But there was nowhere to go. A solid wall of photographers hemmed her in on all sides.

Pushing her way past Caroline and the other bridesmaids, she turned and ran, sobbing, back into the empty church, slamming the heavy wooden door behind her. It was her only chance of escape.

'Siena!' Hunter started after her, followed by a concerned-looking Tiffany.

'Oh my goodness,' said Helen. 'D'you think she's all right?'

But Max was too quick for all of them.

'No, leave it,' he said, pushing past Hunter and barring his way. 'This is between me and Siena. I'll go.'

He stepped inside. Immediately the cool, dank air of the church, smelling faintly of extinguished candles, incense and the lingering miasma of a hundred different perfumes, assailed his senses. For some reason the smell reminded him of England, of home.

At first he couldn't see her. It was gloomy with the doors shut and all the lights out, and his eyes took a moment to adjust from the glaring sunshine outside. But then he heard a stifled sob, and saw a tiny figure curled up in a ball at the foot of the pulpit, half hidden by a vast spray of white bridal lilies.

'Go away!' she wailed, as she heard footsteps approaching. 'Please. I just want to be alone.'

The footsteps kept coming, louder and louder, with a firm, male tread. When she looked up and saw it was Max, she put her head in her hands and moaned even louder. He squatted down on his haunches beside her and waited for her to look up at him. When she did her beautiful, dark blue eyes were still wet and glistening with tears, and she was biting down on her lower lip to prevent it from trembling. She looked ten years old again.

'I'm sorry,' he whispered. 'I didn't mean to upset you.'

Siena sniffed, wiping her eyes briskly with the back of her hand. 'You didn't,' she said quickly. 'It was . . . something else that upset me. Really, I'm fine.'

'Oh.'

He frowned, disappointed. How arrogant she must think him, for assuming her tears would be over him. After all, she had hundreds of reasons to be feeling over-emotional on Hunter's wedding day. 'OK,' he said awkwardly. 'Well, er, do you want to talk about it? Can I help?'

He noticed that she had pulled her mane of hair forward to cover the scars on the left side of her face. Without thinking, he reached his hand towards her and pushed it back again.

'Don't,' she said, hurriedly placing her hand over his.

She felt the familiar warm roughness of the back of his hand. The physical sensation of his skin against hers was so powerful she almost stopped breathing.

Oh God, what was she going to do? She loved him so much.

Neither of them released the other's hand.

'Why not?' His voice was deep and gentle, like a caress, and when he spoke he never took his eyes from hers. 'You look beautiful. So beautiful.'

'Please.' She pulled away from him, with another involuntary sob, and cringed back behind the lilies like a frightened fawn. Max sat down on the cold stone of the altar steps beside her. 'I don't look beautiful.' He could hear the anguish in her voice. 'I look horrific.'

'That's not true,' said Max.

'It is!' she insisted. 'You know it is!'

'Siena . . .' he began, his own voice breaking. How could she possibly think she looked anything other than perfect to him?

'Max, no,' she said desperately, putting her hand across his mouth.

His kindness – his sympathy – was more than she could bear. Especially with his girlfriend waiting outside for him. At last all pretence of self-control went out of the window.

'Please don't say any more,' she implored him. 'I don't

want your pity! I know what I look like now and I know who I am, all right? And, and . . .' she stammered. 'Whatever has happened between us in the past, however awfully I've behaved . . .' She wrung her hands together desperately, unable to look at him. 'We loved each other once.'

Max felt the tears stinging his own eyes.

'Oh, darling,' he began, but she wouldn't allow him to speak.

'And I want to remember that the way it was. The way I was. I know that you're happy and settled with someone else now.' A solitary fat tear rolled off her cheek and splashed noiselessly down on to the gold silk of her dress, spreading into a dark, round patch across the top of her thigh. 'And she's beautiful, absolutely beautiful, and she seems very nice and everything as well . . .'

'Siena . . .' He tried to interrupt her, but she knew if she didn't say this now she would never find the strength again.

'And her English accent is really good for a French girl,' she found herself adding irrationally, unable to stop the words from coming now that they had started.

So *that* was it, thought Max. She thought Helen was Freddie. But how did she even know about Freddie?

'I'm happy for you, Max, truly I am,' she wittered on. 'Hunter's already told me all about her – Helen, is it? You deserve someone decent and kind, someone who loves you and will treat you . . .'

'*Siena!*'

He bellowed the word so loudly that it echoed around the empty church, bouncing off the walls like the booming voice of God. She looked up at him, startled.

'I don't know what Hunter has told you,' he said. 'But Helen is not my girlfriend. She's just a friend I've known for years. I brought her here because . . .' He hesitated. 'Well, because I thought I might need a shoulder to cry on. Moral support. Or something.' Clearly he was having difficulty getting the words out. 'Because I knew I'd be seeing you again. And I didn't know if I could handle it.'

She looked at him blankly. She'd heard what he said, but she couldn't quite take it in.

'There is no one else, Siena. There was someone for a while, but it ended. Months and months ago.'

For a moment she couldn't speak at all. When she did, her voice was so hoarse it was almost a whisper.

'Why?'

'Because I love you,' he said quietly, reaching down for her hands and pressing them both in his. What was the point of denying it now? 'Because I never stopped loving you. And I know I behaved appallingly, and there's no reason why you should ever, ever forgive me, for Camille or anything else, let alone love me again. But I need you to know.' He gazed at her solemnly. 'That I'll always love you, Siena. And I'll always be here for you, whenever you need me. Even if it's only as a friend. I just want to be near you.'

Could it really be true?

Did he really still love her? Even now, after everything?

She looked across at his beautiful face. The blond floppy hair, the broken nose with its perpetual smattering of freckles, the soft, loving eyes, searching her own anxiously for a response.

'Max,' she whispered, almost to herself.

'Siena,' he said. 'My darling, darling Siena.'

And before she knew quite how it was happening, she found herself leaning in towards him, her fingers wrapping themselves around the back of his neck, her lips locking with his in the kiss that both had fantasised about for so, so long.

When they finally, reluctantly released one another, Max sighed and slowly allowed his face to relax into an enormous, boyish grin.

'I want to pinch myself,' he said. 'I can't quite believe this is real.'

'I know,' said Siena, leaning forward to kiss him again, this time on his forehead, eyes, nose and chin. She needed to remember every inch of him. To never, ever let him out of her sight, or her arms, again.

Just then, the huge oak door of the church creaked open, and a shaft of brilliant, blinding sunshine burst in on them, lighting up their embrace like a theatre spotlight on Romeo and Juliet.

'Oh sorry.' It was Hunter, silhouetted awkwardly in the glowing doorway. 'I thought I'd come and see if Siena was OK. But, er, I see things are, er, are all fine. So, I guess I'll just leave you guys to it.'

The door swung shut again with a clunk, plunging them back into welcome darkness. Max wrapped his arm around Siena's waist and pulled her even closer to him.

'Do you think it would be *terribly* wrong . . .' he began.

'What, in a church, you mean?' she said, allowing her hand to slip joyfully beneath the waistband of his suit trousers in response to his embrace, feeling his desire for her as strong and powerful as her own. 'Oh, yes.' She smiled. '*Terribly* wrong. Unforgivable, really. Especially for a good Catholic girl like me.'

'Yes, I thought so,' said Max, easing her gently down on to the cool stone floor and positioning himself above her, face to face. 'Shame.'

For a moment she felt a stab of disappointment. Surely, after so long, he wasn't going to make her wait? But she relaxed when she looked up and saw him gazing wickedly down at her.

Now *that* was a look she remembered.

Painfully slowly, he began peeling the gold silk dress from each of her shoulders in turn.

'Still,' he said, kissing her softly on the mouth and feeling her squirming beneath him with pleasure, 'there's always confession, isn't there?'

Siena grinned.

'Confession? Oh absolutely,' she said, kissing him back for all she was worth. 'Absolutely.'

Acknowledgements

Thanks first and foremost to my family: my parents, for their bottomless love and support; my brother James, and my sisters, Louise and Alice; my lovely husband Robin; and last but not least, my beautiful daughter Sefi. I am so proud of you, darling, my wonderful, wonderful girl.

Thanks to all the writers who helped and encouraged me, not only to start but to finish this book. Especially Louise, my sister; Fred – you can do it, Tills – Metcalf: I'm proud to be a mentee; Lydia Slater, who took a chance on a totally unknown writer at the *Sunday Times* and was the first person to pay actual money for something I wrote – thank you so much; and the uniquely gorgeous Chris Manby, my lifeboat in LA.

Unfairly, for someone with the world's best family, I also have the world's best friends. I owe so much to all of you, but must specially mention a few: Zanna Hooper, the kindest woman in England, for her endless hospitality and for being a shoulder to cry on; also Soph, Scorbs and all the Cambridge girls. Rupert Channing, my former partner in crime, for Pimms and champagne chasers in Boisdale and for making the city so much fun. Katrina Mayson, Claire Depke and Belen Hormaeche, my fellow Wolditz survivors, I love you all. Christian Brun, Jamie Griffith, Rutts, Sparky, Mambly and all the boys in my life. Special thanks also to Dominique Rawley, whose kindness and compassion through my *annus horribilis* will never be forgotten. You are a friend indeed.

Finally, many thanks to my editors, Kate Mills at Orion and Jamie Raab at Warner, for all your patience, help and good advice, and to everyone at Janklow & Nesbit; especially Luke Janklow for believing in me, and this book, from the beginning; and the lovely Christelle Chamouton.

But the last word on this page must go to my incredible agent and very dear friend, Tif Loehnis, without whom this book would never have been written, let alone published. Who'd have thought, Tif, when I first saw you across second court all those years ago in your multi-coloured, stripy jeans, that it would ever come to this? For once, words fail me. But from the bottom of my heart, thank you. For everything.

ABSOLUTION GAP

Alastair Reynolds

Copyright © Alastair Reynolds 2003
All rights reserved

The right of Alastair Reynolds to be identified as the author
of this work has been asserted by him in accordance with
the Copyright, Designs and Patents Act 1988.

First published in Great Britain in 2003 by Gollancz
An imprint of the Orion Publishing Group
Orion House, 5 Upper St Martin's Lane, London WC2H 9EA

This edition published in Great Britain in 2008 by Gollancz

10 9 8 7 6 5 4 3 2 1

A CIP catalogue record for this book
is available from the British Library

ISBN 978 0 575 08316 5

Typeset by Input Data Services Ltd,
Bridgwater, Somerset

Printed and bound in the UK
by CPI Mackays, Chatham, ME5 8TD

The Orion Publishing Group's policy is to use papers that
are natural, renewable and recyclable products and made
from wood grown in sustainable forests. The logging and
manufacturing processes are expected to conform to the
environmental regulations of the country of origin.

www.orionbooks.co.uk

For my Grandparents

'The Universe begins to look more like a great thought than a great machine'

Sir James Jeans

PROLOGUE

She stands alone at the jetty's end, watching the sky. In the moon-light, the planked boarding of the jetty is a shimmering silver-blue ribbon reaching back to shore. The sea is ink-black, lapping calmly against the jetty's supports. Across the bay, out towards the western horizon, there are patches of luminosity: smudges of twinkling pastel-green, as if a fleet of galleons has gone down with all lights ablaze.

She is clothed, if that is the word, in a white cloud of mechanical butterflies. She urges them to draw closer, their wings meshing tight. They form themselves into a kind of armour. It is not that she is cold – the evening breeze is warm and freighted with the faint, exotic tang of distant islands – but that she feels vulnerable, sensing the scrutiny of something vaster and older than she. Had she arrived a month earlier, when there were still tens of thousands of people on this planet, she doubted that the sea would have paid her this much attention. But the islands are all abandoned now, save for a handful of stubborn laggards, or newly arrived latecomers like herself. She is something new here – or, rather, something that has been away for a great while – and her chemical signal is awakening the sea. The smudges of light across the bay have appeared since her descent. It is not coincidence.

After all this time, the sea still remembers her.

'We should go now,' her protector calls, his voice reaching her from the black wedge of land where he waits, leaning impatiently on his stick. 'It isn't safe, now that they've stopped shepherding the ring.'

The ring, yes: she sees it now, bisecting the sky like an exaggerated, heavy-handed rendition of the Milky Way. It spangles and glimmers: countless flinty chips of rubble catching the light from the closer sun. When she arrived, the planetary authorities were still maintaining it: every few minutes or so, she would see the pink glint of a steering rocket as one of the drones boosted the orbit of a piece of debris,

1

keeping it from grazing the planet's atmosphere and falling into the sea. She understood that the locals made wishes on the glints. They were no more superstitious than any of the other planet dwellers she had met, but they understood the utter fragility of their world – that without the glints there was no future. It would have cost the authorities nothing to continue shepherding the ring: the self-repairing drones had been performing the same mindless task for four hundred years, ever since the resettlement. Turning them off had been a purely symbolic gesture, designed to encourage the evacuation.

Through the veil of the ring, she sees the other, more distant moon: the one that wasn't shattered. Almost no one here had any idea what happened. She did. She had seen it with her own eyes, albeit from a distance.

'If we stay . . .' her protector says.

She turns back, towards the land. 'I just need a little time. Then we can go.'

'I'm worried about someone stealing the ship. I'm worried about the Nestbuilders.'

She nods, understanding his fears, but still determined to do the thing that has brought her here.

'The ship will be fine. And the Nestbuilders aren't anything to worry about.'

'They seem to be taking a particular interest in us.'

She brushes an errant mechanical butterfly from her brow. 'They always have. They're just nosy, that's all.'

'One hour,' he says. 'Then I'm leaving you here.'

'You wouldn't.'

'Only one way to find out, isn't there?'

She smiles, knowing he won't desert her. But he's right to be nervous: all the way in they had been pushing against the grain of evacuation. It was like swimming upstream, buffeted by the outward flow of countless ships. By the time they reached orbit, the transit stalks had already been blockaded: the authorities weren't allowing anyone to ride them down to the surface. It had taken bribery and guile to secure passage on a descending car. They'd had the compartment to themselves, but the whole thing – so her companion had said – had smelt of fear and panic; human chemical signals etched into the very fabric of the furniture. She was glad she didn't have his acuity with smells. She is frightened enough as it is: more than she wants him to know. She had been even more frightened when the Nestbuilders followed her into the system. Their elaborate spiral-hulled ship – fluted and chambered, vaguely translucent – is one of the last vessels in orbit. Do they want something of her, or have they just come to spectate?

She looks out to sea again. It might be her imagination, but the glowing smudges appear to have increased in number and size; less like a fleet of galleons below the water now than an entire sunken metropolis. And the smudges seem to be creeping towards the seaward end of the jetty. The ocean can taste her: tiny organisms scurry between the air and the sea. They seep through skin, into blood, into brain.

She wonders how much the sea knows. It must have sensed the evacuation: felt the departure of so many human minds. It must have missed the coming and going of swimmers, and the neural information they carried. It might even have sensed the end of the shepherding operation: two or three small chunks of former moon have already splashed down, although nowhere near these islands. But how much does it really know about what is going to happen? she wonders.

She issues a command to the butterflies. A regiment detaches from her sleeve, assembling before her face. They interlace wings, forming a ragged-edged screen the size of a handkerchief, with only the wings on the edge continuing to flutter. Now the sheet changes colour, becoming perfectly transparent save for a violet border. She cranes her head, looking high into the evening sky, through the debris ring. With a trick of computation the butterflies erase the ring and the moon. The sky darkens by degrees, the blackness becoming blacker, the stars brighter. She directs her attention to one particular star, picking it out after a moment's concentration.

There is nothing remarkable about this star. It is simply the nearest one to this binary system, a handful of light-years away. But this star has now become a marker, the leading wave of something that cannot be stopped. She was there when they evacuated that system, thirty years ago.

The butterflies perform another trick of computation. The view zooms in, concentrating on that one star. The star becomes brighter, until it begins to show colour. Not white now, not even blue-white, but the unmistakable tint of green.

It isn't right.

ONE

Ararat, p Eridani A System, 2675

Scorpio kept an eye on Vasko as the young man swam to shore. All the way in he had thought about drowning, what it would feel like to slide down through unlit fathoms. They said that if you had to die, if you had no choice in the matter, then drowning was not the worst way to go. He wondered how anyone could be sure of this, and whether it applied to pigs.

He was still thinking about it when the boat came to a sliding halt, the electric outboard racing until he killed it.

Scorpio poked a stick overboard, judging the water to be no more than half a metre deep. He had hoped to locate one of the channels that allowed a closer approach to the island, but this would have to do. Even if he had not agreed a place of rendezvous with Vasko, there was no time to push back out to sea and curl around hunting for something he had enough trouble finding when the sea was clear and the sky completely empty of clouds.

Scorpio moved to the bow and took hold of the plastic-sheathed rope Vasko had been using as a pillow. He wrapped one end tightly around his wrist and then vaulted over the side of the boat in a single fluid movement. He splashed into the shallows, the bottle-green water lapping just above his knees. He could barely feel the cold through the thick leather of his boots and leggings. The boat was drifting slowly now that he had disembarked, but with a flick of his wrist he took up the slack in the line and brought the bow around by several degrees. He started walking, leaning hard to haul the boat. The rocks beneath his feet were treacherous, but for once his bow-legged gait served him well. He did not break his rhythm until the water was only halfway up his boots and he again felt the boat scrape bottom. He hauled it a dozen strides further ashore, but that was as far as he was prepared to risk dragging it.

He saw that Vasko had reached the shallows. The young man abandoned swimming and stood up in the water.

Scorpio got back into the boat, flakes and scabs of corroded metal breaking away in his grip as he tugged the hull closer by the gunwale. The boat was past its hundred and twentieth hour of immersion, this likely to be its final voyage. He reached over the side and dropped the small anchor. He could have done so earlier, but anchors were just as prone to erosion as hulls. It paid not to place too much trust in them.

Another glance at Vasko. He was picking his way carefully towards the boat, his arms outstretched for balance.

Scorpio gathered his companion's clothes and stuffed them into his pack, which already contained rations, fresh water and medical supplies. He heaved the pack on to his back and began the short trudge to dry land, taking care to check on Vasko occasionally. Scorpio knew he had been hard on Vasko, but once the anger had started rising in him there had been no holding it in check. He found this development disturbing. It was twenty-three years since Scorpio had raised his hand in anger against a human, except in the pursuit of duty. But he recognised that there was also a violence in words. Once, he would have laughed it off, but lately he had been trying to live a different kind of life. He thought he had put certain things behind him.

It was, of course, the prospect of meeting Clavain that had brought all that fury to the surface. Too much apprehension, too many emotional threads reaching back into the blood-drenched mire of the past. Clavain knew what Scorpio had been. Clavain knew exactly what he was capable of doing.

He stopped and waited for the young man to catch up with him.

'Sir . . .' Vasko was out of breath and shivering.

'How was it?'

'You were right, sir. It was a bit colder than it looked.'

Scorpio shrugged the pack from his back. 'I thought it would be, but you did all right. I've got your things with me. You'll be dry and warm in no time. Not sorry you came?'

'No, sir. Wanted a bit of adventure, didn't I?'

Scorpio passed him his things. 'You'll be after a bit less of it when you're my age.'

It was a still day, as was often the case when the cloud cover on Ararat was low. The nearer sun – the one that Ararat orbited – was a washed-out smudge hanging low in the western sky. Its distant binary counterpart was a hard white jewel above the opposite horizon, pinned between a crack in the clouds. P Eridani A and B, except no one ever called them anything other than Bright Sun and Faint Sun.

In the silver-grey daylight the water was leached of its usual colour, reduced to a drab grey-green soup. It looked thick when it sloshed around Scorpio's boots, but despite the opacity of the water the actual density of suspended micro-organisms was low by Ararat standards. Vasko had still taken a small risk by swimming, but he had been right to do so, for it had allowed them to sail the boat much closer to the shore. Scorpio was no expert on the matter, but he knew that most meaningful encounters between humans and Jugglers took place in areas of the ocean that were so saturated with organisms that they were more like floating rafts of organic matter. The concentration here was low enough that there was little risk of the Jugglers eating the boat while they were away, or creating a local tide system to wash it out to sea.

They covered the remaining ground to dry land, reaching the gently sloping plain of rock that had been visible from sea as a line of darkness. Here and there shallow pools interrupted the ground, mirroring the overcast sky in silver-grey. They made their way between them, heading for a pimple of white in the middle distance.

'You still haven't told me what all this is about,' Vasko said.

'You'll find out soon enough. Aren't you sufficiently excited about meeting the old man?'

'Scared, more likely.'

'He does that to people, but don't let it get to you. He doesn't get off on reverence.'

After ten minutes of further walking, Scorpio had recovered the strength he had expended hauling in the boat. In that time the pimple had become a dome perched on the ground, and finally revealed itself to be an inflatable tent. It was guyed to cleats pinned into the rock, the white fabric around its base stained various shades of briny green. It had been patched and repaired several times. Gathered around the tent, leaning against it at odd angles, were pieces of conch material recovered from the sea like driftwood. The way they had been poised was unmistakably artful.

'What you said earlier, sir,' Vasko said, 'about Clavain not going around the world after all?'

'Yes?'

'If he came here instead, why couldn't they just tell us that?'

'Because of why he came here,' Scorpio replied.

They made their way around the inflatable structure until they reached the pressure door. Next to it was the small humming box that supplied power to the tent, maintaining the pressure differential and providing heat and other amenities for its occupant.

Scopio examined one of the conch pieces, fingering the sharp edge where it had been cut from some larger whole. 'Looks like he's been doing some beachcombing.'

Vasko pointed to the already open outer door. 'All the same, doesn't look as if there's anyone home at the moment.'

Scorpio opened the inner door. Inside he found a bunk bed and a neatly folded pile of bedclothes. A small collapsible desk, a stove and food synthesiser. A flagon of purified water and a box of rations. An air pump that was still running and some small conch pieces on the table.

'There's no telling how long it's been since he was last here,' Vasko said.

Scorpio shook his head. 'He hasn't been away for very long, probably not more than an hour or two.'

Vasko looked around, searching for whatever piece of evidence Scorpio had already spotted. He wasn't going to find it: pigs had long ago learned that the acute sense of smell they had inherited from their ancestors was not something shared by baseline humans. They had also learned – painfully – that humans did not care to be reminded of this.

They stepped outside again, sealing the inner door as they had found it.

'What now?' Vasko asked.

Scorpio snapped a spare communications bracelet from one wrist and handed it to Vasko. It had already been assigned a secure frequency, so there was no danger of anyone on the other islands listening in. 'You know how to use one of these things?'

'I'll manage. Anything in particular you want me to do with it?'

'Yes. You're going to wait here until I get back. I expect to have Clavain with me when I return. But in the event he finds you first, you're to tell him who you are and who sent you. Then you call me and ask Clavain if he'd like to talk to me. Got that?'

'And if you don't come back?'

'You'd better call Blood.'

Vasko fingered the bracelet. 'You sound a bit worried about his state of mind, sir. Do you think he might be dangerous?'

'I hope so,' Scorpio said, 'because if he isn't, he's not a lot of use to us.' He patted the young man on the shoulder. 'Now wait here while I circle the island. It won't take me more than an hour, and my guess is I'll find him somewhere near the sea.'

Scorpio made his way across the flat rocky fringes of the island, spreading his stubby arms for balance, not caring in the slightest how awkward or comical he appeared.

He slowed, thinking that in the distance he could see a figure shifting in and out of the darkening haze of late-afternoon sea mist. He squinted, trying to compensate for eyes that no longer worked as well as they had in Chasm City, when he had been younger. On one level he hoped that the mirage would turn out to be Clavain. On another he hoped that it would turn out to be a figment of his imagination, some conjunction of rock, light and shade tricking the eye.

As little as he cared to admit it, he was anxious. It was six months since he had last seen Clavain. Not that long a time, really, most certainly not when measured against the span of the man's life. Yet Scorpio could not rid himself of the sense that he was about to encounter an acquaintance he had not met in decades, someone who might have been warped beyond all recognition by life and experience. He wondered how he would respond if it turned out that Clavain had indeed lost his mind. Would he even recognise it if that was true? Scorpio had spent enough time around baseline humans to feel confident about reading their intentions, moods and general states of sanity. It was said that human and pig minds were not so very different. But with Clavain, Scorpio always made a mental note to ignore his expectations. Clavain was not like other humans. History had shaped him, leaving behind something unique and quite possibly monstrous.

Scorpio was fifty. He had known Clavain for half his life, ever since he had been captured by Clavain's former faction in the Yellowstone system. Shortly after that, Clavain had defected from the Conjoiners, and after some mutual misgivings he and Scorpio had ended up fighting together. They had gathered a loose band of soldiers and assorted hangers-on from the vicinity of Yellowstone and had stolen a ship to make the journey to Resurgam's system. Along the way they had been hectored and harried by Clavain's former Conjoiner comrades. From Resurgam space – riding another ship entirely – they had arrived here, on the blue-green waterlogged marble of Ararat. Little fighting had been required since Resurgam, but the two had continued to work together in the establishment of the temporary colony.

They had schemed and plotted whole communities into existence. Often they had argued, but only ever over matters of the gravest importance. When one or the other leant towards too harsh or too soft a policy, the other was there to balance matters. It was in those years that Scorpio had found the strength of character to stop hating human beings every waking moment of his life. If nothing else, he owed that to Clavain.

But nothing was ever that simple, was it?

The problem was that Clavain had been born five hundred years ago and had lived through many of those years. What if the Clavain that Scorpio knew – the Clavain that most of the colonists knew, for that matter – was only a passing phase, like a deceitful glimpse of sunshine on an otherwise stormy day? In the early days of their acquaintance, Scorpio had kept at least half an eye on him, alert for any reversion to his indiscriminate butcher tendencies. He had seen nothing to arouse his suspicions, and more than enough to reassure him that Clavain was not the ghoul that history said he was.

But in the last two years, his certainties had crumbled. It was not that Clavain had become more cruel, argumentative or violent than before, but something in him had changed. It was as if the quality of light on a landscape had shifted from one moment to another. The fact that Scorpio knew that others harboured similar doubts about his own stability was of scant comfort. He knew his own state of mind and hoped he would never hurt another human the way he had done in the past. But he could only speculate about what was going on inside his friend's head. What he could be certain about was that the Clavain he knew, the Clavain alongside whom he had fought, had withdrawn to some intensely private personal space. Even before he had retreated to this island, Scorpio had reached the point where he could hardly read the man at all.

But he did not blame Clavain for that. No one would.

He continued his progress until he was certain that the figure was real, and then advanced further until he was able to discern detail. The figure was crouched down by the shore of sea, motionless, as if caught in some reverie that had interrupted an otherwise innocent examination of the tide pools and their fauna.

Scorpio recognised him as Clavain; he would have been as certain even if he had thought the island uninhabited.

The pig felt a momentary surge of relief. At least Clavain was still alive. No matter what else transpired today, that much had to count as a victory.

When he was within shouting distance of the man, Clavain sensed his presence and looked around. There was a breeze now, one that had not been there when Scorpio landed. It pulled wild white hair across Clavain's pink-red features. His beard, normally neatly trimmed, had also grown long and unkempt since his departure. His thin figure was clad in black, with a dark shawl or cloak pulled across his shoulders. He maintained an awkward posture between kneeling and standing, poised on his haunches like a man who had only stopped there for a moment.

Scorpio was certain he had been staring out to sea for hours.

'Nevil,' Scorpio said.

He said something back, his lips moving, but his words were masked by the hiss of the surf.

Scorpio called out again. 'It's me – Scorpio.'

Clavain's mouth moved a second time. His voice was a croak that barely made it above a whisper. 'I said, I told you not to come here.'

'I know.' Scorpio had approached closer now. Clavain's white hair flicked in and out of his deeply recessed old-man's eyes. They appeared to be focused on something very distant and bleak. 'I know, and for six months we honoured that request, didn't we?'

'Six months?' Clavain almost smiled. 'Is that how long it's been?'

'Six months and a week, if you want to be finicky about it.'

'It doesn't feel like it. It feels like no time at all.' Clavain looked back out to sea again, the back of his head turned towards Scorpio. Between thin strands of white hair his scalp had the same raw pink colour as Scorpio's skin.

'Sometimes it feels like a lot longer, as well,' Clavain continued, 'as if all I've ever done was spend each day here. Sometimes I feel as if there isn't another soul on this planet.'

'We're all still here,' Scorpio said, 'all one hundred and seventy thousand of us. We still need you.'

'I expressly asked not to be disturbed.'

'*Unless* it was important. That was always the arrangement, Nevil.'

Clavain stood up with painful slowness. He had always been taller than Scorpio, but now his thinness gave him the appearance of something sketched in a hurry. His limbs were quick cursive scratches against the sky.

Scorpio looked at Clavain's hands. They were the fine-boned hands of a surgeon. Or, perhaps, an interrogator. The rasp of his long fingernails against the damp black fabric of his trousers made Scorpio wince.

'Well?'

'We've found something,' Scorpio said. 'We don't know exactly what it is, or who sent it, but we think it came from space. We also think there might be someone in it.'

TWO

Surgeon-General Grelier strode through the circular green-lit corridors of the body factory.

He hummed and whistled, happy in his element, happy to be surrounded by humming machines and half-formed people. With a shiver of anticipation he thought about the solar system that lay ahead of them and the great many things that depended on it. Not necessarily for him, it was true, but certainly for his rival in the matter of the queen's affection. Grelier wondered how she would take another of Quaiche's failures. Knowing Queen Jasmina, he did not think she would take it awfully well.

Grelier smiled at that. The odd thing was that for a system on which so much hung, the place was still nameless; no one had ever bothered with the remote star and its uninteresting clutch of planets. There had never been any reason to. There would be an obscure catalogue entry for the system in the astrogation database of the *Gnostic Ascension*, and indeed of almost every other starship, along with brief notes on the major characteristics of its sun and worlds, likely hazards and so forth. But these databases had never been intended for human eyes; they existed only to be interrogated and updated by other machines as they went about their silent, swift business executing those shipboard tasks considered too dull or too difficult for humans. The entry was just a string of binary digits, a few thousand ones and zeroes. It was a measure of the system's unimportance that the entry had only been queried three times in the entire operational lifetime of the *Gnostic Ascension*. It had been updated once.

Grelier knew: he had checked, out of curiosity.

Yet now, perhaps for the first time in history, the system was of more than passing interest. It still had no name, but now at least the absence of one had become vaguely troubling, to the point where Queen Jasmina sounded a trifle more irritated every time she was forced to refer to the place as 'the system ahead' or 'the system we are approaching'. But Grelier knew that she would not deign to give the place a name until it had proved valuable. And the system's value was entirely in the hands of the queen's fading favourite, Quaiche.

Grelier paused a while near one of the bodies. It was suspended in translucent support gel behind the green glass of its vivification tank. Around the base of the tank were rows of nutrient controls like so many organ stops, some pushed in and some pulled out. The stops controlled the delicate biochemical environment of the nutrient matrix. Bronze valve wheels set into the side of the tank adjusted the delivery of bulk chemicals like water or saline.

Appended to the tank was a log showing the body's clonal history. Grelier flicked through the plastic-laminated pages of the log, satisfying himself that all was well. Although most of the bodies in the factory had never been decanted, this specimen – an adult female – had been warmed and used once before. The evidence of the injuries inflicted on it was fading under the regenerative procedures, abdominal scars healing invisibly, the new leg now only slightly smaller than its undamaged counterpart. Jasmina did not approve of these patch-up jobs, but her demand for bodies had outstripped the production capacity of the factory.

Grelier patted the glass affectionately. 'Coming along nicely.'

He walked on, making random checks on the other bodies. Sometimes a glance was sufficient, though more often than not Grelier would thumb through the log and pause to make some small adjustment to the settings. He took a great deal of pride in the quiet competence of his work. He never boasted of his abilities or promised anything he was not absolutely certain of being able to deliver – utterly unlike Quaiche, who had been full of exaggerated promises from the moment he stepped aboard the *Gnostic Ascension*.

For a while it had worked, too. Grelier, long the queen's closest confidant, had found himself temporarily usurped by the flashy newcomer. All he heard while he was working on her was how Quaiche was going to change all their fortunes: Quaiche this, Quaiche that. The queen had even started complaining about Grelier's duties, moaning that the factory was too slow in delivering bodies and that the attention-deficit therapies were losing their effectiveness. Grelier had been briefly tempted to try something seriously attention-grabbing, something that would catapult him back into her good graces.

Now he was profoundly glad that he had done no such thing; he had needed only to bide his time. It was simply a question of letting Quaiche dig his own grave by setting up expectations that he could not possibly meet. Sadly – for Quaiche, if not for Grelier – Jasmina had taken him exactly at his word. If Grelier judged the queen's mood, poor old Quaiche was about this close to getting the figurehead treatment.

Grelier stopped at an adult male that had begun to show developmental anomalies during his last examination. He had adjusted the tank settings, but his tinkering had apparently been to no avail. To the untrained eye the body looked normal enough, but it lacked the unmarred symmetry that Jasmina craved. Grelier shook his head and placed a hand on one of the polished brass valve wheels. Always a difficult call, this. The body wasn't up to scratch by the usual standards of the factory, but then again neither were the patch-up jobs. Was it time to make Jasmina accept a lowering of quality? It was she who was pushing the factory to its limit, after all.

No, Grelier decided. If he had learned one lesson from this whole sordid Quaiche business, it was to maintain his own standards. Jasmina would scold him for aborting a body, but in the long run she would respect his judgement, his stolid devotion to excellence.

He twisted the brass wheel shut, blocking saline. He knelt down and pushed in most of the nutrient valves.

'Sorry,' Grelier said, addressing the smooth, expressionless face behind the glass, 'but I'm afraid you just didn't cut it.'

He gave the body one last glance. In a few hours the processes of cellular deconstruction would be grotesquely obvious. The body would be dismantled, its constituent chemicals recycled for use elsewhere in the factory.

A voice buzzed in his earpiece. He touched a finger to the device.

'Grelier ... I was expecting you already.'

'I'm on my way, ma'am.'

A red light started flashing on top of the vivification tank, synchronised to an alarm. Grelier cuffed the override, silencing the alarm and blanking the emergency signal. Calm returned to the body factory, a silence broken only by the occasional gurgle of nutrient flows or the muffled click of some distant valve regulator.

Grelier nodded, satisfied that all was in hand, and resumed his unhurried progress.

At the same instant that Grelier pushed in the last of the nutrient valves, an anomaly occurred in the sensor apparatus of the *Gnostic Ascension*. The anomaly was brief, lasting only a fraction over half a second, but it was sufficiently unusual that a flag was raised in the data stream: an exceptional event marker indicating that something merited attention.

As far as the sensor software was concerned that was the end of it: the anomaly had not continued, and all systems were now performing normally. The flag was a mere formality; whether it was to be acted on was the responsibility of an entirely separate and slightly more intelligent layer of monitoring software.

The second layer – dedicated to health-monitoring all shipwide sensor subsystems – detected the flag, along with several million others raised in the same cycle, and assigned it a schedule in its task profile. Less than two hundred thousandths of a second had lapsed since the end of the anomaly: an eternity in computational terms, but an inevitable consequence of the vast size of a lighthugger's cybernetic nervous system. Communications between one end of the *Gnostic Ascension* and the other required three to four kilometres of main trunk cabling, six to seven for a round-trip signal.

Nothing happened quickly on a ship that large, but it made little practical difference. The ship's huge mass meant that it responded sluggishly to external events: it had precisely the same need for lightning-fast reflexes as a brontosaurus.

The health-monitoring layer worked its way down the pile.

Most of the several million events it looked at were quite innocuous. Based on its grasp of the statistical expectation pattern of error events, it was able to de-assign most of the flags without hesitation. They were transient errors, not indicative of any deeper malaise in the ship's hardware. Only a hundred thousand looked even remotely suspicious.

The second layer did what it always did at this point: it compiled the hundred thousand anomalous events into a single packet, appended its own comments and preliminary findings and offered the packet to the third layer of monitoring software.

The third layer spent most of its time doing nothing: it existed solely to examine those anomalies forwarded to it by duller layers. Quickened to alertness, it examined the dossier with as much actual interest as its borderline sentience allowed. By machine standards it was still somewhere below gamma-level intelligence, but it had been doing its job for such a long time that it had built up a huge hoard of heuristic expertise. It was *insultingly* clear to the third layer that more than half of the forwarded events in no way merited its attention, but the remaining cases were more interesting, and it took its time going through them. Two-thirds of those anomalies were repeat offenders: evidence of systems with some real but transient fault.

None, however, were in critical areas of ship function, so they could be left alone until they became more serious.

One-third of the interesting cases were new. Of these, perhaps ninety per cent were the kind of failures that could be expected once in a while, based on the layer's knowledge of the various hardware components and software elements involved. Only a handful were in possibly critical areas, and thankfully these faults could all be dealt with by routine repair methods. Almost without blinking, the layer dispatched instructions to those parts of the ship dedicated to the upkeep of its infrastructure.

At various points around the ship, servitors that were already engaged in other repair and overhaul jobs received new entries in their task buffers. It might take them weeks to get around to those chores, but eventually they would be performed.

That left a tiny core of errors that might potentially be of some concern. They were more difficult to explain, and it was not immediately clear how the servitors should be ordered to deal with them. The layer was not unduly worried, in so far as it was capable of worrying about anything: past experience had taught it that these gremlins generally turned out to be benign. But for now it had no choice but to forward the puzzling exceptions to an even higher stratum of shipboard automation.

The anomaly moved up like this, through another three layers of steadily increasing intelligence.

By the time the final layer was invoked, only one outstanding event remained in the packet: the original transient sensor anomaly, the one that had lasted just over half a second. None of the underlying layers could account for the error via the usual statistical patterns and look-up rules.

An event only filtered this high in the system once or twice a minute.

Now, for the first time, something with real intelligence was invoked. The gamma-level subpersona in charge of overseeing layer-six exceptions was part of the last line of defence between the cybernetics and the ship's flesh crew. It was the subpersona that had the difficult role of deciding whether a given error merited the attention of its human stewards. Over the years it had learned not to cry wolf too often: if it did, its owners might decide that it needed upgrading. As a consequence, the subpersona agonised for many seconds before deciding what to do.

The anomaly was, it decided, one of the strangest it had ever encountered. A thorough examination of every logical path in the sensor system failed to explain how something so utterly, profoundly unusual could ever have happened.

In order to do its job effectively, the subpersona had to have an abstract understanding of the real world. Nothing too sophisticated, but enough that it could make sensible judgements about which kinds of external phenomena were likely to be encountered by the sensors, and which were so massively unlikely that they could only be interpreted as hallucinations introduced at a later stage of data processing. It had to grasp that the *Gnostic Ascension* was a physical object embedded in space. It also had to grasp that the events recorded by the ship's web of sensors were caused by objects and quanta permeating that space: dust grains, magnetic fields, radar echoes from nearby bodies; and by the radiation from more distant phenomena: worlds, stars, galaxies, quasars, the cosmic background signal. In order to do this it had to be able to make accurate guesses about how the data returns from all these objects were supposed to behave. No one had ever given it these rules; it had formulated them for itself, over time, making corrections as it accumulated more information. It was a never-ending task, but at this late stage in the game it considered itself rather splendid at it.

It knew, for instance, that planets – or rather the abstract objects in its model that corresponded to planets – were definitely not supposed to do *that*. The error was completely inexplicable as an outside-world event. Something must have gone badly wrong at the data-capture stage.

It pondered this a little more. Even allowing for that conclusion, the anomaly was still difficult to explain. It was so peculiarly selective, affecting only the planet itself. Nothing else, not even the planet's moons, had done anything in the least bit odd.

The subpersona changed its mind: the anomaly had to be external, in which case the subpersona's model of the real world was shockingly flawed. It didn't like that conclusion either. It was a long time since it had been forced to update its model so drastically, and it viewed the prospect with a stinging sense of affront.

Worse, the observation might mean that the *Gnostic Ascension* itself was ... well, not exactly in immediate danger – the planet in question was still dozens of light-hours away – but conceivably headed for something that might, at some point in the future, pose a non-negligible risk to the ship.

That was it, then. The subpersona made its decision: it had no choice but to alert the crew on this one.

That meant only one thing: a priority interrupt to Queen Jasmina.

The subpersona established that the queen was currently accessing status summaries through her preferred visual read-out medium. As it was authorised to do, it seized control of the data channel and cleared both screens of the device ready for an emergency bulletin.

It prepared a simple text message: SENSOR ANOMALY: REQUEST ADVICE.

For an instant – significantly less than the half-second that the original event had consumed – the message hovered on the queen's read-out, inviting her attention.

Then the subpersona had a hasty change of heart.

Perhaps it was making a mistake. The anomaly, bizarre as it had been, had cleared itself. No further reports of strangeness had emanated from any of the underlying layers. The planet was behaving in the way the subpersona had always assumed planets were supposed to.

With the benefit of a little more time, the layer decided, the event could surely be explained as a perceptual malfunction. It was just a question of going over things again, looking at all the components from the right perspective, thinking outside the box. As a subpersona, that was exactly what it was meant to do. If all it ever did was blindly forward every anomaly that it couldn't immediately explain, then the crew might as well replace it with another dumb layer. Or, worse, upgrade it to something cleverer.

It cleared the text message from the queen's device and immediately replaced it with the data she had been viewing just before.

It continued to gnaw away at the problem until, a minute or so later, another anomaly bumped into its in-box. This time it was a thrust imbalance, a niggling one-per-cent jitter in the starboard Conjoiner drive. Faced with a bright new urgency, it chose to put the matter of the planet on the back-burner. Even by the slow standards of shipboard communications, a minute was a long time. With every further minute that passed without the planet misbehaving, the whole vexing event would inevitably drop to a diminished level of priority.

The subpersona would not forget about it – it was incapable of forgetting about anything – but within an hour it would have a great many other things to deal with instead.

Good. It was decided, then. The way to handle it was to pretend it had never happened in the first place.

Thus it was that Queen Jasmina was informed of the sensor event anomaly for only a fraction of a second. And thus it was that no human members of the crew of the *Gnostic Ascension* – not Jasmina, not Grelier, not Quaiche, nor any of the other Ultras – were ever aware that, for more than half a second, the largest gas giant in the system they were approaching, the system unimaginatively called 107 Piscium, had simply ceased to exist.

Queen Jasmina heard the surgeon-general's footsteps echoing towards her, approaching along the metal-lined companionway that connected her command chamber to the rest of the ship. As always, Grelier managed not to sound in any particular hurry. Had she tested his loyalty by fawning over Quaiche? she wondered. Perhaps. In which case it was probably time to make Grelier feel valued again.

A flicker on the read-out screens of the skull caught her attention. For a moment a line of text replaced the summaries she was paging through – something about a sensor anomaly.

Queen Jasmina shook the skull. She had always been convinced that the horrid thing was possessed, but increasingly it appeared to be going senile, too. Had she been less superstitious, she would have thrown it away, but dreadful things were rumoured to have happened to those who ignored the skull's counsel.

A polite knock sounded at the door.

'Enter, Grelier.'

The armoured door eased itself open. Grelier emerged into the chamber, his eyes wide and showing a lot of white as they adjusted to the chamber's gloom. Grelier was a slim, neatly dressed little man with a flat-topped shock of brilliant white hair. He had the flattened, minimalist features of a boxer. He wore a clean white medical smock and apron; his hands were always gloved. His expression never failed to amuse Jasmina: it always appeared that he was on the point of breaking into tears or laughter. It was an illusion: the surgeon-general had little familiarity with either emotional extreme.

'Busy in the body factory, Grelier?'

'A wee bit, ma'am.'

'I'm anticipating a period of high demand ahead. Production mustn't slacken.'

'Little danger of that, ma'am.'

'Just as long as you're aware of it.' She sighed. 'Well, niceties over with. To business.'

Grelier nodded. 'I see you've already made a start.'

While awaiting his arrival, she had strapped her body into the throne, leather cuffs around her ankles and thighs, a thick band around her belly, her right arm fixed to the chair rest, with only her left arm free to move. She held the skull in her left hand, its face turned towards her so that she could view the read-out screens bulging from its eye sockets. Prior to picking up the skull she had inserted her right arm into a skeletal machine bracketed to the side of the chair. The machine – the alleviator – was a cage of rough black ironwork equipped with screw-driven pressure pads. They were already pressing uncomfortably against her skin.

'Hurt me,' Queen Jasmina said.

Grelier's expression veered momentarily towards a smile. He approached the throne and examined the arrangement of the alleviator. Then he commenced tightening the screws on the device, adjusting each in sequence by a precise quarter turn at a time. The pressure pads bore down on the skin of the queen's forearm, which was supported in turn by an underlying arrangement of fixed pads. The care with which Grelier turned the screws made the queen think of someone tuning some ghastly stringed instrument.

It wasn't pleasant. That was the point.

After a minute or so, Grelier stopped and moved behind the throne. She watched him tug a spool of tubing from the little medical kit he always kept there. He plugged one end of the tubing into an oversized bottle full of something straw-yellow and connected the other to a hypodermic. He hummed and whistled as he worked. He lifted up the bottle and attached it to a rig on the back of the throne, then pushed the hypodermic line into the queen's upper right arm, fiddling around a little until he found the vein. Then she watched him return to the front of the throne, back into view of the body.

It was a female one this time, but there was no reason that it had to be. Although all the bodies were cultured from Jasmina's own genetic material, Grelier was able to intervene at an early stage of development and force the body down various sexual pathways. Usually it was boys and girls. Now and then, for a treat, he made weird neuters and intersex variants. They were all sterile, but that was only because it would have been a waste of time to equip them with functioning reproductive systems. It was enough bother installing the neural coupling implants so that she could drive the bodies in the first place.

Suddenly she felt the agony lose its focus. 'I don't want anaesthetic, Grelier.'

'Pain without intermittent relief is like music without silence,' he said. 'You must trust my judgement in this matter, as you have always done in the past.'

'I do trust you, Grelier,' she said, grudgingly.

'Sincerely, ma'am?'

'Yes. Sincerely. You've always been my favourite. You do appreciate that, don't you?'

'I have a job to do, ma'am. I simply do it to the limit of my abilities.'

The queen put the skull down in her lap. With her free hand she ruffled the white brush of his hair.

'I'd be lost without you, you know. Especially now.'

'Nonsense, ma'am. Your expertise threatens any day to eclipse my own.'

It was more than automatic flattery: though Grelier had made the study of pain his life's work, Jasmina was catching up quickly. She knew volumes about the physiology of pain. She knew about nociception; she knew the difference between epicritic and protopathic pain; she knew about presynaptic blocking and the neospinal pathway. She knew her prostaglandin promoters from her GABA agonists.

But the queen also knew pain from an angle Grelier never would. His tastes lay entirely in its infliction. He did not know it from the inside, from the privileged point of view of the recipient. No matter how acute his theoretical understanding of the subject, she would always have that edge over him.

Like most people of his era, Grelier could only imagine agony, extrapolating it a thousandfold from the minor discomfort of a torn hangnail.

He had no idea.

'I may have learned a great deal,' she said, 'but you will always be a master of the clonal arts. I was serious about what I said before, Grelier: I anticipate increased demand on the factory. Can you satisfy me?'

'You said production mustn't slacken. That isn't quite the same thing.'

'But surely you aren't working at full capacity at this moment.'

Grelier adjusted the screws. 'I'll be frank with you: we're not far off it. At the moment I'm prepared to discard units that don't meet our usual exacting standards. But if the factory is expected to increase production, the standards will have to be relaxed.'

'You discarded one today, didn't you?'

'How did you know?'

'I suspected you'd make a point of your commitment to excellence.' She raised a finger. 'And that's all right. It's why you work for me. I'm disappointed, of course – I know exactly which body you terminated – but standards are standards.'

'That's always been my watchword.'

'It's a pity that can't be said for everyone on this ship.'

He hummed and whistled to himself for a little while, then asked, with studied casualness, 'I always got the impression that you have a superlative crew, ma'am.'

'My regular crew is not the problem.'

'Ah. Then you would be referring to one of the irregulars? Not myself, I trust?'

'You are well aware of whom I speak, so don't pretend otherwise.'

'Quaiche? Surely not.'

'Oh, don't play games, Grelier. I know exactly how you feel about your rival. Do you want to know the truly ironic thing? The two of you are more similar than you realise. Both baseline humans, both ostracised from your own cultures. I had great hopes for the two of you, but now I may have to let Quaiche go.'

'Surely you'd give him one last chance, ma'am. We are approaching a new system, after all.'

'You'd like that, wouldn't you? You'd like to see him fail one final time, just so that my punishment would be all the more severe?'

'I was thinking only of the welfare of the ship.'

'Of course you were, Grelier.' She smiled, amused by his lies. 'Well, the fact of the matter is I haven't made up my mind what to do with Quaiche. But I do think he and I need a little chat. Some interesting new information concerning him has fallen into my possession, courtesy of our trading partners.'

'Fancy that,' Grelier said.

'It seems he wasn't completely honest about his prior experience when I hired him. It's my fault: I should have checked his background more thoroughly. But that doesn't excuse the fact that he exaggerated his earlier successes. I thought we were hiring an expert negotiator, as well as a man with an instinctive understanding of planetary environments. A man comfortable among both baseline humans and Ultras, someone who could talk up a deal to our advantage and find treasure where we'd miss it completely.'

'That sounds like Quaiche.'

'No, Grelier, what it sounds like is the character Quaiche wished to present to us. The fiction he wove. In truth, his record is a lot less impressive. The occasional score here and there, but just as many failures. He's a chancer: a braggart, an opportunist and a liar. And an infected one, as well.'

Grelier raised an eyebrow. 'Infected?'

'He has an indoctrinal virus. We scanned for the usuals but missed this one because it wasn't in our database. Fortunately, it isn't strongly infectious – not that it would stand much of a chance infecting one of *us* in the first place.'

'What type of indoctrinal virus are we talking about here?'

'It's a crude mishmash: a half-baked concoction of three thousand years' worth of religious imagery jumbled together without any overarching theistic consistency. It doesn't make him believe anything coherent; it just makes him *feel* religious. Obviously he can keep it under control for much of the time. But it worries me, Grelier. What if it gets worse? I don't like a man whose impulses I can't predict.'

'You'll be letting him go, then.'

'Not just yet. Not until we've passed beyond 107 Piscium. Not until he's had one last chance to redeem himself.'

'What makes you think he'll find anything now?'

'I have no expectation that he will, but I do believe he's more likely to find something if I provide him with the right incentive.'

'He might do a runner.'

'I've thought of that as well. In fact, I think I've got all bases covered where Quaiche is concerned. All I need now is the man himself, in some state of animation. Can you arrange that for me?'

'Now, ma'am?'

'Why not? Strike while the iron's hot, as they say.'

'The trouble is,' Grelier said, 'he's frozen. It'll take six hours to wake him, assuming that we follow the recommended procedures.'

'And if we don't?' She wondered how much mileage was left in her new body. 'Realistically, how many hours could we shave off?'

'Two at the most, if you don't want to run the risk of killing him. Even then it'll be a wee bit unpleasant.'

Jasmina smiled at the surgeon-general. 'I'm sure he'll get over it. Oh, and Grelier? One other thing.'

'Ma'am?'

'Bring me the scrimshaw suit.'

THREE

His lover helped him out of the casket. Quaiche lay shivering on the revival couch, racked with nausea, while Morwenna attended to the many jacks and lines that plunged into his bruised baseline flesh.

'Lie still,' she said.

'I don't feel very well.'

'Of course you don't. What do you expect when the bastards thaw you so quickly?'

It was like being kicked in the groin, except that his groin encompassed his entire body. He wanted to curl up inside a space smaller than himself, to fold himself into a tiny knot like some bravura trick of origami. He considered throwing up, but the effort involved was much too daunting.

'They shouldn't have taken the risk,' he said. 'She knows I'm too valuable for that.' He retched: a horrible sound like a dog that had been barking too long.

'I think her patience might be a bit strained,' Morwenna said, as she dabbed at him with stinging medicinal salves.

'She knows she needs me.'

'She managed without you before. Maybe it's dawning on her that she can manage without you again.'

Quaiche brightened. 'Maybe there's an emergency.'

'For you, perhaps.'

'Christ, that's all I need – sympathy.' He winced as a bolt of pain hit his skull, something far more precise and targeted than the dull unpleasantness of the revival trauma.

'You shouldn't use the Lord's name in vain,' Morwenna said, her tone scolding. 'You know it only hurts you.'

He looked into her face, forcing his eyes open against the cruel glare of the revival area. 'Are you on my side or not?'

'I'm trying to help you. Hold still, I've nearly got the last of these lines out.' There was a final little stab of pain in his thigh as the shunt popped out, leaving a neat eyelike wound. 'There, all done.'

'Until next time,' Quaiche said. 'Assuming there *is* a next time.'

Morwenna fell still, as if something had struck her for the first time. 'You're really frightened, aren't you?'

'In my shoes, wouldn't you be?'

'The queen's insane. Everyone knows that. But she's also pragmatic enough to know a valuable resource when she sees one.' Morwenna spoke openly because she knew that the queen had no working listening devices in the revival chamber. 'Look at Grelier, for pity's sake. Do you think she'd tolerate that freak for one minute if he wasn't useful to her?'

'That's precisely my point,' Quaiche said, sinking into an even deeper pit of dejection and hopelessness. 'The moment either of us stops being useful . . .' Had he felt like moving, he would have mimed drawing a knife across his throat. Instead he just made a choking sound.

'You've an advantage over Grelier,' Morwenna said. 'You have me, an ally amongst the crew. Who does he have?'

'You're right,' Quaiche said, 'as ever.' With a tremendous effort he reached out and closed one hand around Morwenna's steel gauntlet.

He didn't have the heart to remind her that she was very nearly as isolated aboard the ship as he was. The one thing guaranteed to get an Ultra ostracised was having any kind of interpersonal relationship with a baseline human. Morwenna put a brave face on it, but, Quaiche knew, if he had to rely on her for help when the queen and the rest of the crew turned against him, he was already crucified.

'Can you sit up now?' she asked.

'I'll try.'

The discomfort was abating slightly, as he had known it must do, and at last he was able to move major muscle groups without crying. He sat on the couch, his knees tucked against the hairless skin of his chest, while Morwenna gently removed the urinary catheter from his penis. He looked into her face while she worked, hearing only the whisk of metal sliding over metal. He remembered how fearful he had been when she first touched him there, her hands gleaming like shears. Making love to her was like making love to a threshing machine. Yet Morwenna had never hurt him, even when she inadvertently cut her own living parts.

'All right?' she asked.

'I'll make it. Takes more than a quick revival to put a dent in Horris Quaiche's day.'

'That's the spirit,' she said, sounding less than fully convinced. She leant over and kissed him. She smelt of perfume and ozone.

'I'm glad you're around,' Quaiche said.

'Wait here. I'll get you something to drink.'

Morwenna moved off the revival couch, telescoping to her full height. Still unable to focus properly, he watched her slink across the room towards the hatch where various recuperative broths were dispensed. Her iron-grey dreadlocks swayed with the motion of her high-hipped piston-driven legs.

Morwenna was on her way back with a snifter of recuperative broth – chocolate laced with medichines – when the door to the chamber slid open. Two more Ultras strode into the room: a man and a woman. After them, hands tucked demurely behind his back, loomed the smaller, unaugmented figure of the surgeon-general. He wore a soiled white medical smock.

'Is he fit?' the man asked.

'You're lucky he's not dead,' Morwenna snapped.

'Don't be so melodramatic,' the woman said. 'He was never going to die just because we thawed him a bit faster than usual.'

'Are you going to tell us what Jasmina wants with him?'

'That's between him and the queen,' she replied.

The man threw a quilted silver gown in Quaiche's general direction. Morwenna's arm whipped out in a blur of motion and caught it. She walked over to Quaiche and handed it to him.

'I'd like to know what's going on,' Quaiche said.

'Get dressed,' the woman said. 'You're coming with us.'

He pivoted around on the couch and lowered his feet to the coldness of the floor. Now that the discomfort was wearing off he was starting to feel scared instead. His cock had shrivelled in on itself, retreating into his belly as if already making its own furtive escape plans. Quaiche put on the gown, cinching it around his waist. To the surgeon-general he said, 'You had something to do with this, didn't you?'

Grelier blinked. 'My dear fellow, it was all I could do to stop them warming you even more rapidly.'

'Your time will come,' Quaiche said. 'Mark my words.'

'I don't know why you insist on that tone. You and I have a great deal in common, Horris. Two human men, alone aboard an Ultra ship? We shouldn't be bickering, competing for prestige and status. We should be supporting each other, cementing a friendship.' Grelier wiped the back of his glove on his tunic, leaving a nasty ochre smear. 'We should be allies, you and I. We could go a long way together.'

'When hell freezes over,' Quaiche replied.

*

The queen stroked the mottled cranium of the human skull resting on her lap. She had very long finger- and toenails, painted jet-black. She wore a leather jerkin, laced across her cleavage, and a short skirt of the same dark fabric. Her black hair was combed back from her brow, save for a single neatly formed cowlick. Standing before her, Quaiche initially thought she was wearing make-up, vertical streaks of rouge as thick as candlewax running from her eyes to the curve of her upper lip. Then, joltingly, he realised that she had gouged out her eyes.

Despite this, her face still possessed a certain severe beauty.

It was the first time he had seen her in the flesh, in any of her manifestations. Until this meeting, all his dealings with her had been at a certain remove, either via alpha-compliant proxies or living intermediaries like Grelier.

He had hoped to keep things that way.

Quaiche waited several seconds, listening to his own breathing. Finally he managed, 'Have I let you down, ma'am?'

'What kind of ship do you think I run, Quaiche? One where I can afford to carry baggage?'

'I can feel my luck changing.'

'A bit late for that. How many stopovers have we made since you joined the crew, Quaiche? Five, isn't it? And what have we got to show for ourselves, after those five stopovers?'

He opened his mouth to answer her when he saw the scrimshaw suit lurking, almost lost, in the shadows behind her throne. Its presence could not be accidental.

It resembled a mummy, worked from wrought iron or some other industrial-age metal. There were various heavy-duty input plugs and attachment points, and a dark grilled-over rectangle where the visor should have been. There were scabs and fillets of solder where parts had been rewelded or braised. There was the occasional smooth patch of obviously new metal.

Covering every other part of the suit, however, was an intricate, crawling complexity of carvings. Every available square centimetre had been crammed with obsessive, eye-wrenching detail. There was far too much to take in at one glance, but as the suit gyrated above him Quaiche made out fanciful serpent-necked space monsters, outrageously phallic spacecraft, screaming faces and demons, depictions of graphic sex and violence. There were spiralling narratives, cautionary tales, boastful trade episodes writ large. There were clock faces and psalms. Lines of text in languages he didn't recognise, musical stanzas, even swathes of lovingly carved numerals.

Sequences of digital code or DNA base pairs. Angels and cherubim. Snakes. A lot of snakes.

It made his head hurt just to look at it.

It was pocked and gouged by the impact spots of micrometeorites and cosmic rays, its iron-grey tainted here and there with emerald-green or bronze discoloration. There were scratchlike striations where ultra-heavy particles had gouged out their own impact furrows as they sliced by at oblique angles. And there was a fine dark seam around the whole thing where the two armoured halves could be popped open and then welded shut again.

The suit was a punishment device, its existence no more than a cruel rumour. Until this moment.

The queen put people in the suit. It kept them alive and fed them sensory information. It protected them from the sleeting radiation of interstellar flight when they were entombed, for years at a time, in the ice of the ship's ablative shield.

The lucky ones were dead when they pulled them out of the suit.

Quaiche tried to stop the tremble in his voice. 'If you look at things one way, we didn't really ... we didn't really do *too* badly ... all things considered. There was no material damage to the ship. No crew fatalities or major injuries. No contamination incidents. No unforeseen expenditures ...' He fell silent, looking hopefully at Jasmina.

'That's the best you can come up with? You were supposed to make us rich, Quaiche. You were supposed to turn our fortunes around in these difficult times, greasing the wheels of trade with your innate charm and grasp of planetary psychologies and landscapes. You were supposed to be our golden goose.'

He shifted uneasily.

'Yet in five systems all you found was junk.'

'You chose the systems, not me. It isn't my fault if there wasn't anything worth finding.'

Slowly and worryingly the queen shook her head. 'No, Quaiche. Not that easy, I'm afraid. You see, a month ago we intercepted something. It was a transmission, a two-way trade dialogue between a human colony on Chaloupek and the lighthugger *Faint Memory of Hokusai*. Ring any bells?'

'Not really ...'

But it did.

'The *Hokusai* was entering Gliese 664 just as we departed that system. It was the second system you swept for us. Your report was ...' The queen hoisted the skull to the side of her head, listening to its chattering jaw. 'Let's see ... "nothing of value found on Opincus or the other three terrestrial worlds; only minor items of discarded technology recovered on moons five to eight of the Haurient giant ... nothing in the inner asteroid fields, D-type swarms, Trojan points or major K-belt concentrations".'

Quaiche could see where this was heading. 'And the *Faint Memory of Hokusai?*'

'The trade dialogue was absolutely fascinating. By all accounts, the *Hokusai* located a cache of buried trade items around one century old. Pre-war, pre-plague. Very valuable stuff: not merely technological artefacts, but also art and culture, much of it unique. I hear they made enough on that to buy themselves an entirely new layer of ablative hull cladding.' She looked at him expectantly. 'Any comments, thoughts, on that?'

'My report was honest,' Quaiche said. 'They must have got lucky, that's all. Look, just give me another chance. Are we approaching another system?'

The queen smiled. 'We're always approaching another system. This time it's a place called 107 Piscium, but frankly from this distance it doesn't look much more promising than the last five. What's to say you're going to be any use this time?'

'Let me take the *Dominatrix*,' he said, knitting his hands together involuntarily. 'Let me take her down into that system.'

The queen was silent for many seconds. Quaiche heard only his own breathing, punctuated now and then by the abrupt, attenuated sizzle of a dying insect or rat. Something moved languidly beyond the green glass of a hemispherical dome set into one of the chamber's twelve walls. He sensed that he was being observed by something other than the eyeless figure in the chair. Without having been told, he understood then that the thing beyond the glass was the real queen, and that the ruined body in the seat was only a puppet that she currently inhabited. They were all true, then, all the rumours he had ever heard: the queen's solipsism; her addiction to extreme pain as a reality-anchoring device; the vast reserve of cloned bodies she was said to keep for just that purpose.

'Have you finished, Quaiche? Have you made your case?'

He sighed. 'I suppose I have.'

'Very well, then.'

She must have issued some secret command, because at that moment the door to the chamber opened again. Quaiche spun around as the blast of cold fresh air touched the nape of his neck.

The surgeon-general and the two Ultras who had helped him during Quaiche's revival entered the room.

'I'm done with him,' the queen said.

'And your intention?' Grelier asked.

Jasmina sucked at a fingernail. 'I haven't changed my mind. Put him in the scrimshaw suit.'

FOUR

Ararat, 2675

Scorpio knew better than to interrupt Clavain when the old man was thinking something over. How long had it been since he had told him about the object falling from space, if that was indeed where it had come from? Five minutes, easily. In all that time, Clavain had sat there as gravely as a statue, his expression fixed, his eyes locked on the horizon.

Finally, just when Scorpio was beginning to doubt his old friend's sanity, Clavain spoke. 'When did it happen?' he asked. 'When did this "thing" – whatever it is – arrive?'

'Probably in the last week,' Scorpio said. 'We only found it a couple of days ago.'

There was another troubling pause, though it was only a minute or so long this time. Water slapped against rock and gurgled in little eddies in and out of shallow pools by the shoreline.

'And what exactly is it?'

'We can't be absolutely certain. It's a capsule of some kind. A human artefact. Our best guess is that it's an escape pod, something with re-entry capabilities. We think it splashed down in the ocean and bobbed to the surface.'

Clavain nodded, as if the news was of only minor interest. 'And you're certain it wasn't left behind by Galiana?'

He said the woman's name with ease, but Scorpio could only guess at the pain it caused him. Especially now, looking out to sea.

Scorpio had some inkling of what the ocean meant to Clavain: both loss and the cruellest kind of hope. In an unguarded moment, not long before his voluntary exile from island affairs, Clavain had said, 'They're all gone now. There's nothing more the sea can do to me.'

'They're still there,' Scorpio had replied. 'They aren't lost. If anything, they're safer than they ever were.'

As if Clavain could not have seen that for himself.

'No,' Scorpio said, snapping his attention back to the present, 'I don't think Galiana left it.'

'I thought it might hold a message from her,' Clavain said. 'But I'm wrong, aren't I? There won't be any messages. Not that way. Not from Galiana, not from Felka.'

'I'm sorry,' Scorpio said.

'There's no need to be. It's the way of things.'

What Scorpio knew of Clavain's past was drawn as much from hearsay as from things the old man had told him directly. Memories had always been fickle, but in the present era they were as mutable as clay. There were aspects of his own past even Clavain could not now be sure of.

Yet there were some things that were certain. Clavain had once loved a woman named Galiana; their relationship had begun many centuries ago and had spanned many of those same centuries. It was clear that they had birthed – or created – a kind of daughter, Felka; that she had been both terribly damaged and terribly powerful; and that she had been loved and feared in equal measure.

Whenever Clavain spoke of those times, it was with a happiness tempered by the knowledge of what was to follow.

Galiana had been a scientist, fascinated by the augmentation of the human mind. But her curiosity had not stopped there. What she ultimately wanted was an intimate connection with reality, at its root level. Her neural experiments had only ever been a necessary part of this process. To Galiana, it had been natural that the next step should be physical exploration, pushing out into the cosmos. She wanted to go deeper, far beyond the ragged edge of mapped space, to see what was actually out there. So far the only indications of alien intelligence anyone had found had been ruins and fossils, but who was to say what might be found further into the galaxy? Human settlements at that time spanned a bubble two dozen light-years across, but Galiana intended to travel more than a hundred light-years before returning.

And she had. The Conjoiners had launched three ships, moving slightly slower than the speed of light, on an expedition into deep interstellar space. The expedition would take at least a century and a half; equally eager for new experience, Clavain and Felka had journeyed with her. All had progressed according to plan: Galiana and her allies visited many solar systems, and while they never found any unambiguous signs of active intelligence, they nonetheless catalogued many remarkable phenomena, as well as uncovering further ruins. Then came reports, already outdated, of a crisis back home:

growing tensions between the Conjoiners and their moderate allies, the Demarchists. Clavain needed to return home to lend his tactical support to the remaining Conjoiners.

Galiana had considered it more important to continue with the expedition; their amicable separation in deep space left one of the ships returning home, carrying Clavain and Felka, while the two other craft continued to loop further into the plane of the galaxy.

They had intended to be reunited, but when Galiana's ship finally returned to the Conjoiner Mother Nest, it did so on automatic pilot, damaged and dead. Somewhere out in space a parasitic entity had attacked both of the ships, destroying one. Immediately afterwards, black machines had clawed into the hull of Galiana's ship, systematically anatomising her crew. One by one, they had all been killed, until only Galiana remained. The black machines had infiltrated her skull, squeezing into the interstices of her brain. Horribly, she was still alive, but utterly incapable of independent action. She had become the parasite's living puppet.

With Clavain's permission the Conjoiners had frozen her against the day when they might be able to remove the parasite safely. One day they might even have succeeded, but then a rift had opened in Conjoiner affairs: the beginning of the same crisis that had eventually brought Clavain to the Resurgam system and, latterly, to Ararat. In the conflict Galiana's frozen body had been destroyed.

Clavain's grief had been a vast, soul-sucking thing. It would have killed him, Scorpio thought, had not his people been in such desperate need of leadership. Saving the colony on Resurgam had given him something to focus on besides the loss he had suffered. It had kept him somewhere this side of sanity.

And, later, there had been a kind of consolation.

Galiana had not led them to Ararat, yet it turned out that Ararat was one of the worlds she had visited after her separation from Clavain and Felka. The planet had attracted her because of the alien organisms filling its ocean. It was a Juggler world, and that was vitally important, for few things that visited Juggler worlds were ever truly forgotten.

Pattern Jugglers had been encountered on many worlds that conformed to the same aquatic template as Ararat. After years of study, there was still no agreement as to whether or not the aliens were intelligent in their own right. But all the same it was clear that they prized intelligence themselves, preserving it with the loving devotion of curators.

Now and then, when a person swam in the seas of a Juggler

planet, the microscopic organisms entered the swimmer's nervous system. It was a kinder process than the neural invasion that had taken place aboard Galiana's ship. The Juggler organisms only wanted to record, and when they had unravelled the swimmer's neural patterns they would retreat. The mind of the swimmer would have been captured by the sea, but the swimmer was almost always free to return to land. Usually, they felt no change at all. Rarely, they would turn out to have been given a subtle gift, a tweak to their neurological architecture that permitted superhuman cognition or insight. Mostly it lasted for only a few hours, but very infrequently it appeared permanent.

There was no way to tell if Galiana had gained any gifts after she had swum in the ocean of this world, but her mind had certainly been captured. It was there now, frozen beneath the waves, waiting to be imprinted on the consciousness of another swimmer.

Clavain had guessed this, but he had not been the first to attempt communion with Galiana. That honour had fallen to Felka. For twenty years she had swum, immersed in the memories and glacial consciousness of her mother. In all that time Clavain had held back from swimming himself, fearing perhaps that when he encountered the imprint of Galiana he would find it in some sense wrong, untrue to his memory of what she had been. His doubts had ebbed over the years, but he had still never made the final commitment of swimming. Nonetheless, Felka – who had always craved the complexity of experience that the ocean offered – had swum regularly, and she had reported back her experiences to Clavain. Through his daughter he had again achieved some connection with Galiana, and for the time being, until he summoned the courage to swim himself, that had been enough.

But two years ago the sea had taken Felka, and she had not returned.

Scorpio thought about that now, choosing his next words with great care. 'Nevil, I understand this is difficult for you, but you must also understand that this thing, whatever it is, could be a very serious matter for the settlement.'

'I get that, Scorp.'

'But you think the sea matters more. Is that it?'

'I think none of us really has a clue what actually matters.'

'Maybe we don't. Me, I don't really care about the bigger picture. It's never been my strong point.'

'Right now, Scorp, the bigger picture is all we have.'

'So you think there are millions – billions – of people out there who are going to die? People we've never met, people we've never come within a light-year of in our lives?'

'That's about the size of it.'

'Well, sorry, but that isn't the way my head works. I just can't process that kind of threat. I don't *do* mass extinction. I'm a lot more locally focused than that. And right now I have a local problem.'

'You think so?'

'I have a hundred and seventy thousand people here that need worrying about. That's a number I can just about get my head around. And when something drops out of the sky without warning, it keeps me from sleeping.'

'But you didn't actually see anything drop out of the sky, did you?' Clavain did not wait for Scorpio's answer. 'And yet we have the immediate volume of space around Ararat covered with every passive sensor in our arsenal. How did we miss a re-entry capsule, let alone the ship that must have dropped it?'

'I don't know,' Scorpio said. He couldn't tell if he was losing the argument, or doing well just to be engaging Clavain in discussion about something concrete, something other than lost souls and the spectre of mass extinction. 'But whatever it is must have come down recently. It's not like any of the other artefacts we've pulled from the ocean. They were all half-dissolved, even the ones that must have been sitting on the seabed, where the organisms aren't so thick. This thing didn't look as though it had been under for more than a few days.'

Clavain turned away from the shore, and Scorpio took this as a welcome sign. The old Conjoiner moved with stiff, economical footsteps, never looking down, but navigating his way between pools and obstacles with practised ease.

They were returning to the tent.

'I watch the skies a lot, Scorp,' Clavain said. 'At night, when there aren't any clouds. Lately I've been seeing things up there. Flashes. Hints of things moving. Glimpses of something bigger, as if the curtain's just been pulled back for an instant. I'm guessing you think that makes me mad, don't you?'

Scorpio didn't know what he thought. 'Alone out here, anyone would see things,' he said.

'But it wasn't cloudy last night,' Clavain said, 'or the night before, and I watched the sky on both occasions. I didn't see anything. Certainly no indication of any ships orbiting us.'

'We haven't seen anything either.'

'How about radio transmissions? Laser squirts?'

'Not a peep. And you're right: it doesn't make very much sense. But like it or not, there's still a capsule, and it isn't going away. I want you to come and see it for yourself.'

Clavain shoved hair from his eyes. The lines and wrinkles in his face had become shadowed crevasses and gorges, like the contours of an improbably weathered landscape. Scorpio thought that he had aged ten or twenty years in the six months he had been on this island.

'You said something about there being someone inside it.'

While they had been talking, the cloud cover had begun to break up in swathes. The sky beyond had the pale, crazed blue of a jackdaw's eye.

'It's still a secret,' Scorpio said. 'Only a few of us know that the thing's been found at all. That's why I came here by boat. A shuttle would have been easier, but it wouldn't have been low-key. If people find out we've brought you back they'll think there's a crisis coming. Besides which, it isn't supposed to be this easy to bring you back. They still think you're somewhere halfway around the world.'

'You insisted on that lie?'

'What do you think would have been more reassuring? To let the people think you'd gone on an expedition – a potentially hazardous one, admittedly – or to tell them you'd gone away to sit on an island and toy with the idea of committing suicide?'

'They've been through worse. They could have taken it.'

'It's what they've been through that made me think they could do without the truth,' Scorpio said.

'Anyway, it isn't suicide.' He stopped and looked back out to sea. 'I know she's there, with her mother. I can feel it, Scorpio. Don't ask me how or why, but I know she's still here. I read about this sort of thing happening on other Juggler worlds, you know. Now and then they take swimmers, dismantle their bodies completely and incorporate them into the organic matrix of the sea. No one knows why. But swimmers who enter the oceans afterwards say that sometimes they feel the presence of the ones who vanished. It's a much stronger impression than the usual stored memories and personalities. They say they experience something close to dialogue.'

Scorpio held back a sigh. He had listened to exactly the same speech before he had taken Clavain out to this island six months ago. Clearly the period of isolation had done nothing to lessen Clavain's conviction that Felka had not simply drowned.

'So hop in and find out for yourself,' he said.

'I would, but I'm scared.'

'That the ocean might take you as well?'

'No.' Clavain turned to face Scorpio. He looked less surprised than affronted. 'No, of course not. *That* doesn't scare me at all. What does is the idea that it might leave me behind.'

Hela, 107 Piscium, 2727

Rashmika Els had spent much of her childhood being told not to look quite so serious. That was what they would have said if they could have seen her now: perched on her bed in the half-light, selecting the very few personal effects she could afford to carry on her mission. And she would have given them precisely the same look of pique she always mustered on those occasions. Except this time she would have known with a deeper conviction than usual that she was right and they were wrong. Because even though she was still only seventeen, she knew that she had every right to feel this serious, this frightened.

She had filled a small bag with three or four days' worth of clothes, even though she expected her journey to take a lot longer than that. She had added a bundle of toiletries, carefully removed from the family bathroom without her parents noticing, and some dried-up biscuits and a small wedge of goat's cheese, just in case there was nothing to eat (or, perhaps, nothing she would actually wish to eat) aboard Crozet's icejammer. She had packed a bottle of purified water because she had heard that the water nearer the Way sometimes contained things that made you ill. The bottle would not last her very long, but it at least made her feel as if she was thinking ahead. And then there was a small plastic-wrapped bundle containing three tiny scuttler relics that she had stolen from the digs.

After all that, there was not much space left in the bag for anything else. It was already heavier than she had expected. She looked at the sorry little collection of items still spread on the bed before her, knowing that she only had room for one of them. What should she take?

There was a map of Hela, peeled from her bedroom wall, with the sinuous, equator-hugging trail of the Way marked in faded red ink. It wasn't very accurate, but she had no better map in her compad. Did it matter, though? She had no means of reaching the Way without relying on other people to get her there, and if they didn't know the direction, her map was unlikely to make very much difference.

She pushed the map aside.

There was a thick blue book, its edges protected with gold metal. The book contained her handwritten notes on the scuttlers, kept assiduously over the last eight years. She had started the book at the age of nine, when – in a perfect fit of precocity – she had first decided that she wanted to be a scuttler scholar. They had laughed at her, of course – in a kindly, indulgent way, naturally – but that had only made her more determined to continue with it.

Rashmika knew she did not have time to waste, but she could not stop herself from flicking through the book, the rough whisper of page against page harsh in the silence. In the rare moments when she saw it afresh, as if through someone else's eyes, the book struck her as a thing of beauty. At the beginning, her handwriting was large and neat and childish. She used inks of many colours and underlined things with scrupulous care. Some of the inks had faded or blotted, and there were smears and stains where she had marked the paper, but that sense of damaged antiquity only added to the medieval allure of the artefact. She had made drawings, copying them from other sources. The first few were crude and childlike, but within a few pages her figures had the precision and confidence of Victorian naturalists' sketches. They were painstakingly crosshatched and annotated, with the text crawling around them. There were drawings of scuttler artefacts, of course, with notes on function and origin, but there were also many pictures of the scuttlers themselves, their anatomies and postures reconstructed from the fossil evidence.

She flicked on through the book, through years of her life. The text grew smaller, more difficult to read. The coloured inks were used increasingly sparingly until, in the last few chapters, the writing and figures were worked in almost unrelieved black. The same neatness was there, the same methodical care applied to both text and fig-urework, but now it appeared to be the work of a scholar rather than an enthusiastic, gifted child. The notes and drawings were no longer recycled from other sources, but were now part of an argument she herself was advancing, independent of external thinking. The difference between the start and the end of the written parts of the book was shockingly obvious to Rashmika, a reminder of the distance she had travelled. There had been many times when she had been so embarrassed by her earlier efforts that she had wanted to discard the book and start another. But paper was expensive on Hela, and the book had been a gift from Harbin.

She fingered the unmarked pages. Her argument was not yet completed, but she could already see the trajectory it would take.

She could almost see the words and figures on the pages, spectrally faint but needing only time and concentration to bring them into sharp focus. On a journey as long as the one she planned to take, there would surely be many opportunities to work on her book.

But she couldn't take it. The book meant too much to her, and she could not bear the thought of losing it or having it stolen. At least if she left it here it would be safe until her return. She could still take notes while she was away, after all, refining her argument, ensuring that the edifice came together with no obvious flaws or weaknesses. The book would be all the stronger for it.

Rashmika clasped it shut, pushed it aside.

That left two things. One was her compad, the other a scuffed and dirty toy. The compad did not even belong to her, really; it was the family's, and she only had it on extended loan while no one else needed it. But as no one had asked for it for months, it was unlikely to be missed during her absence. In its memory were many items relevant to her study of the scuttlers, sourced from other electronic archives. There were images and movies she had made herself, down in the digs. There were spoken testimonies from miners who had found things that did not quite accord with the standard theory of the scuttler extinction, but whose reports had been suppressed by the clerical authorities. There were texts from older scholars. There were maps and linguistics resources, and much that would guide her when she reached the Way.

She picked up the toy. It was a soft, pink thing, ragged and faintly pungent. She had had it since she was eight or nine, had picked it herself from the stall of an itinerant toymaker. She supposed it must have been bright and clean then, but she had no memory of the toy ever being anything other than well loved, grubby with affection. Looking at it now with the rational detachment of a seventeen-year-old, she had no idea what kind of creature the toy had ever been meant to represent. All she knew was that from the moment she saw it on the stall she had decided it was a pig. It didn't matter that no one on Hela had ever *seen* a living pig.

'You can't come with me either,' she whispered.

She picked up the toy and placed it atop the book, squeezing it down until it sat like a sentry. It wasn't that she did not want it to come with her. She knew it was just a toy, but she also knew that there would be days ahead when she would feel terribly homesick, anxious for any connection to the safe environment of the village. But the compad was more useful, and this was not a time for sentiment. She pushed the dark slab into the bag, drew tight the bag's vacuum seal and quietly left her room.

Rashmika had been fourteen when the caravans had last come within range of her village. She had been studying then and had not been allowed to go out to see the meeting. The time before that, she had been nine: she had seen the caravans then, but only briefly and only from a distance. What she now remembered of that spectacle was inevitably coloured by what had happened to her brother. She had replayed those events so many times that it was quite impossible to separate reliable memory from imagined detail.

Eight years ago, she thought: a tenth of a human life, by the grim new reckoning. A tenth of a life was not to be underestimated, even if eight years would once have been a twentieth or a thirtieth of what one could expect. But at the same time it felt vastly more than that. It *was* half of her own life, after all. The wait until she could next see the caravans had felt epochal. She really had been a little girl the last time she had seen them: a little girl from the Vigrid badlands with a reputation, however strange, for always telling the truth.

But now her chance had come again. It was near the hundredth day of the hundred and twenty-second circumnavigation that one of the caravans had taken an unexpected detour east of Hauk Crossing. The procession had veered north into the Gaudi Flats before linking up with a second caravan that happened to be heading south towards Glum Junction. This did not happen very often: it was the first time in nearly three revolutions that the caravans had come within a day's travel of the villages on the southern slopes of the Vigrid badlands. There was, naturally, a great deal of excitement. There were parties and feasts, jubilation committees and invitations to secret drinking dens. There were romances and affairs, dangerous flirtations and secret liaisons. Nine months from now there would arrive a clutch of wailing new caravan babies.

Compared with the general austerity of life on Hela and the particular hardships of the badlands, it was a period of measured, tentative hope. It was one of those rare times when – albeit within tightly prescribed parameters – personal circumstances could change. The more sober-minded villagers did not allow themselves to show any visible signs of excitement, but privately they could not resist wondering if this was their turn for a change of fortune. They made elaborate excuses to allow themselves to travel out to the rendezvous point: excuses that had nothing to do with personal gain, but everything to do with the communal prosperity of the villages. And so, over a period of nearly three weeks, the villages sent out little caravans of their own, crossing the treacherous scabbed ground to rendezvous with the larger processions.

Rashmika had planned to leave her home at dawn, while her parents were still sleeping. She had not lied to them about her departure, but only because it had never been necessary. What the adults and the other villagers did not understand was that she was as capable of lying as any of them. More than that, she could lie with great conviction. The only reason why she had spent most of her childhood not lying was because until very recently she had failed to see the point in it.

Quietly she stole through the buried warrens of her home, treading with loping strides between shadowed corridors and bright patches beneath the overhead skylights. The homes in her village were almost all sunk below ground level, irregularly shaped caverns linked by meandering tunnels lined with yellowing plaster. Rashmika found the idea of living above ground faintly unsettling, but she supposed one could get used to it given time; just as one could eventually get used to life in the mobile caravans, or even the cathedrals that they followed. It was not as if life below ground was without its hazards, after all. Indirectly, the network of tunnels in the village was connected to the much deeper network of the digs. There were supposed to be pressure doors and safety systems to protect the village if one of the dig caverns collapsed, or if the miners penetrated a high-pressure bubble, but these systems did not always work as well as intended. There had been no serious dig accidents during Rashmika's life, only near misses, but everyone knew that it was only a matter of time before another catastrophe of the kind her parents still talked about occurred. Only the week before, there had been an explosion on the surface: no one had been hurt, and there was even talk that the demolition charges had been let off deliberately, but it was still a reminder that her world was only ever one accident away from disaster.

It was, she supposed, the price that the villages paid for their economic independence from the cathedrals. Most of the settlements on Hela lay near the Permanent Way, not hundreds of kilometres to the north or south of it. With very few exceptions the settlements near the Way owed their existence to the cathedrals and their governing bodies, the churches, and by and large they subscribed to one or other of the major branches of the Quaicheist faith. That was not to say that there was no one of faith in the badlands, but the villages were run by secular committees and made their living from the digs rather than the elaborate arrangement of tithes and indulgences which bound the cathedrals and the communities of the Way. As a consequence they were free of many of the religious restrictions that applied elsewhere on Hela. They made their own laws, had less restrictive marriage practices and turned a blind eye to certain perversions that were outlawed along the Way. Visits from the Clocktower were rare, and whenever the churches did send their envoys they were viewed with suspicion. Girls like Rashmika were allowed to study the technical literature of the digs rather than Quaicheist scripture. It was not unthinkable that a woman should find work for herself.

But by the same token, the villages of the Vigrid badlands were beyond the umbrella of protection that the cathedrals offered. The settlements along the Way were guarded by a loose amalgamation of cathedral militia, and in times of crisis they turned to the cathedrals for help. The cathedrals held medicine far in advance of anything in the badlands, and Rashmika had seen friends and relatives die because her village had no access to that care. The cost to be paid for that care, of course, was that one submitted to the machinations of the Office of Bloodwork. And once you had Quaicheist blood in your veins you couldn't be sure of anything ever again.

Yet she accepted the arrangement with the combination of pride and stubbornness common to all the badlanders. It was true that they endured hardships unknown along the Way. It was true that, by and large, few of them were fervent believers; even those of faith were usually troubled by doubt. Typically it was doubt that had driven them to the digs in the first place, to search for answers to questions that bothered them. And yet for all this, the villagers would not have had it any other way. They lived and loved as they pleased, and viewed the more pious communities of the Way with a lofty sense of moral superiority.

Rashmika reached the final chamber of her home, the heavy bag knocking against the small of her back. The house was quiet, but if she kept very still and listened intently she was certain that she could hear the nearly subliminal rumble of the distant excavations, reports of drilling and digging and earthmoving reaching her ears through snaking kilometres of tunnel. Now and then there was a percussive thud or a fusillade of hammer blows. The sounds were so familiar to Rashmika that they never disturbed her sleep; indeed, she would have snapped awake instantly had the mining ceased. But now she wished for a louder series of noises to conceal the sounds she would inevitably make as she left her home.

The final chamber contained two doors. One led horizontally into the wider tunnel network, accessing a thoroughfare that connected with many other homes and community chambers. The other door was set in the ceiling, ringed by handrails. At that moment the door was hinged open into the dark space above it. Rashmika opened a locker set into the smooth curve of the wall and removed her surface suit, taking care not to clatter the helmet and backpack against the three other suits hanging on the same rotating rack. She had to put the suit on three times a year during practice drills, so it was easy enough for her to work the latches and seals. Even then, it still took ten minutes, during which time she stopped and held her breath whenever she heard a sound somewhere in the house, whether it was the air-circulator clicking on and off or the low groan as a tunnel resettled.

Finally she had the suit on and ready, with the read-outs on her cuff all safely in the green. The tank wasn't completely full of air – there must have been a slow leak in the suit as the tanks were usually kept fully topped-up – but there was more than enough in there for her needs.

But when she closed the helmet visor all she could hear was her own breathing; she had no idea how much sound she was making, or whether anyone else was stirring in the house. And the noisiest part of her escape was still to come. She would just have to be as careful and quick as possible, so that even if her parents did wake she could get to her meeting point before they caught up with her.

The suit doubled her weight, but even then she did not find it difficult to haul herself up into the dark space above the ceiling door. She had reached the surface access airlock. Every home had one, but they varied in size. Rashmika's was large enough for two adults at a time. Even so, she had to sit in a stooped position while she lowered the inner door back down and turned the manual wheel to lock it tight.

In a sense, she was safe for a moment. Once she started the depressurisation cycle, there was no way her mother and father would be able to get into the chamber. It took two minutes for the lock to finish its business. By the time the lower door could again be reopened, she would be halfway across the village. Once she got away from the exit point, her footprints would quickly be lost amongst the confusion of marks left by other villagers as they went about their errands.

Rashmika checked her suit again, satisfying herself that the readings were still in the green. Only then did she initiate the depressurisation sequence. She heard nothing, but as the air was sucked from the chamber the suit's fabric swelled out between the concertina joints and it took a little more effort to move her limbs. A separate read-out around the faceplate of her helmet informed her that she was now in vacuum.

No one had hammered on the bottom of the door. Rashmika had been a little worried that she might trip an alarm by using the lock. She was not aware that such a thing existed, but her parents might have chosen not to tell her, just in case she ever intended making this kind of escape. Her fears appeared to have been groundless, however: there was no alarm, no fail-safe, no hidden code that needed to be used before the door worked. She had run through this so many times in her imagination that it was impossible not to feel a small twinge of *déjà vu*.

When the chamber was fully evacuated, a relay allowed the outer door to be opened. Rashmika pushed hard, but at first nothing happened. Then the door budged – only by an inch, but it was enough to let in a sheet of blindingly bright daylight that scythed against her faceplate. She pushed harder and the door moved higher, hinging back as it did so. Rashmika pushed through until she was sitting on the surface. She saw now that the door had been covered in an inch of recent frost. It snowed on Hela, especially when the Kelda or Ragnarok geysers were active.

Although the house clock had said it was dawn, this meant very little on the surface. The villagers still lived by a twenty-six-hour clock (many of them were interstellar refugees from Yellowstone) despite the fact that Hela was a different world entirely, with its own complex cycles. A day on Hela was actually about forty hours long, which was the time it took Hela to complete one orbit around its mother world, the gas giant Haldora. Since the moon's inclination to the plane of its orbit was essentially zero, all points on the surface experienced about twenty hours of darkness during each orbit. The Vigrid badlands were on the dayside now, and would remain so for another seven hours. There was another kind of night on Hela, for once in its orbit around Haldora the moon swung into the gas giant's shadow. But that short night was only two hours long, brief enough to be of little consequence to the villagers. At any given time the moon was far more likely to be out of Haldora's shadow than within it.

After a few seconds, Rashmika's visor had compensated for the glare and she was able to get her bearings. She extracted her legs from the hole and carefully closed the surface door, latching it shut so that it would begin pressurising the lower chamber. Perhaps her parents were waiting below, but even if that was the case they could not reach the surface for another two minutes, even if they were already wearing suits. It would take them even longer to navigate the community tunnels to reach the next-nearest surface exit.

Rashmika stood up and began walking briskly but with what she hoped was no apparent sense of haste or panic. There was some more good fortune: she had expected to have to cross several dozen metres of unmarked ice, so that her trail would at first be easy to follow. But someone else had come this way recently, and their prints meandered away in a different direction from the one she intended to take. Anyone following her now would have no idea which set of prints to follow. They looked like her mother's, for the shoe-prints were too small to have belonged to her father. What kind of business had her mother been on? It bothered Rashmika for a moment, for she did not recall anyone mentioning any recent trips to the surface.

Never mind: there was bound to be an innocent explanation. She had enough to think about without adding to her worries.

Rashmika followed a circuitous path between the black upright slabs of radiator panels, the squatting orange mounds of generators or navigation transponders and the soft snow-covered lines of parked icejammers. She had been right about the footprints, for when she looked back it was impossible to separate her own from the muddle of those that had been left before.

She rounded a huddle of radiator fins and there it was, looking much like the other parked icejammers except that the snow had melted from the flanged radiator above the engine cowlings. It was too bright to tell if there were lights on inside the machine. There were fan-shaped arcs of transparency in the windscreen where the mechanical wiper blades had flicked aside the snow. Rashmika thought she saw figures moving behind the glass.

Rashmika walked around the low, splayed-legged jammer. The black of its boat-shaped hull was relieved only by a glowing snake motif coiling along the side. The single front leg ended in a broad, upturned ski blade, with smaller skis tipping the two rear legs. Rashmika wondered if it was the right machine. She would look rather silly if she made a mistake now. She felt certain that there was no one in the village who would not recognise her, even though she had a suit on.

But Crozet had been very specific in his instructions. With some relief she saw a boarding ramp was already waiting for her, lowered down into the snow. She walked up the flexing metal slope and knocked politely on the jammer's outer door. There was an agonising moment and then the door slid aside, revealing another airlock. She squeezed into it – there was only room for one person.

A man's voice – she recognised it immediately as Crozet's – came through on her helmet channel. 'Yes?'

'It's me.'

'Who is "me"?'

'Rashmika,' she said. 'Rashmika Els. I think we had an arrangement.'

There was a pause – an agonising pause during which she began to think that, yes, she had made an error – when the man said, 'It's not too late to change your mind.'

'I think it is.'

'You could go home now.'

'My parents won't be very pleased that I came this far.'

'No,' the man said, 'I doubt that they'll be thrilled. But I know your folks. I doubt that they'd punish you too severely.'

He was right, but she did not want to be reminded of that now. She had spent weeks psyching herself up for this, and the last thing she needed was a rational argument for backing out at the final minute.

Rashmika knocked on the inner door again, knuckling it hard with her gauntlet. 'Are you going to let me in or not?'

'I just wanted to make sure you're certain. Once we leave the village, we won't turn back until we meet the caravan. That's not open to negotiation. Step inside, you're committed to a three-day trip. Six if you decide to come back with us. No amount of pissing and moaning is going to make me turn around.'

'I've waited eight years,' she said. 'Three more days won't kill me.'

He laughed, or sniggered – she wasn't sure which. 'You know, I almost believe you.'

'You should do,' Rashmika told him. 'I'm the girl that never lies, remember?'

The outer door closed itself, cramming her even further into the tight cavity of the lock. Air began to skirl in through grilles. At the same time she felt motion. It was soft and rhythmic, like being rocked in a cradle. The jammer was on the move, propelling itself with alternating movements of its rear skis.

She supposed that her escape had begun the moment she crawled out of bed, but only now did it feel as if she was actually on her way.

When the inner door allowed Rashmika into the body of the jammer, she snapped off her helmet and hung it dutifully next to the three that were already there. The jammer had looked reasonably large from the outside, but she had forgotten how much of the interior volume would be occupied by its own engines, generators, fuel tanks, life-support equipment and cargo racks. Inside it was cramped and noisy, and the air made her want to put the helmet back on again. She imagined she could get used to it, but she wondered if three days would be anywhere near enough time.

The jammer lurched and yawed. Through one of the windows she saw the blazing white landscape tilt and tilt again. Rashmika reached for a handhold and was just beginning to make her way to the front when a figure stepped into view.

It was Crozet's son, Culver. He wore grubby ochre overalls, tools cramming the many pockets. He was a year or two younger than Rashmika, blond-haired and with a permanent look of malnourishment. He viewed Rashmika with lecherous intent.

'Decided to stay aboard after all, did you? That's good. We can get to know each other a bit better now, can't we?'

'It's only for three days, Culver. Don't get any ideas.'

'I'll help you get that suit off, then we can go up front. Dad's busy steering us out of the village now. We're having to take a detour because of the crater. That's why it's a bit bumpy.'

'I'll manage my suit on my own, thank you.' Rashmika nodded encouragingly towards the icejammer's cabin. 'Why don't you go back and see if your dad needs any help?'

'He doesn't need any help. Mother's there as well.'

Rashmika beamed approvingly. 'Well, I expect you're glad that she's here to keep you two men out of trouble. Right, Culver?'

'She doesn't mind what we get up to, so long as we stay in the black.' The machine lurched again, knocking Rashmika against the metal wall. 'Fact of the matter is, she mostly turns a blind eye.'

'So I've heard. Well, I really need to get this suit off ... would you mind telling me where I'm sleeping?'

Culver showed her a tiny compartment tucked away between two throbbing generators. There was a mattress, a pillow and a blanket made of slippery quilted silver material. A curtain could be tugged across for privacy.

'I hope you weren't expecting luxury,' Culver said.

'I was expecting the worst.'

Culver lingered. 'You sure you don't want any help getting that suit off?'

'I'll manage, thanks.'

'Got something to wear afterwards, have you?'

'What I'm wearing under the suit, and what I brought with me.' Rashmika patted the bag which was now tucked beneath her life-support pack. Through the fabric she could feel the hard edge of her compad. 'You didn't seriously think I'd forget to bring any clothes with me, did you?'

'No,' Culver said, sullenly.

'Good. Now why don't you run along and tell your parents that I'm safe and sound? And please let them know that the sooner we clear the village, the happier I'll be.'

'We're moving as fast as we can go,' Culver said.

'Actually,' Rashmika said, 'that's just what's worrying me.'

'In a bit of a hurry, are you?'

'I'd like to reach the cathedrals as soon as I can, yes.'

Culver eyed her. 'Got religion, have you?'

'Not exactly,' she said. 'More like some family business I have to take care of.'

107 Piscium, 2615

Quaiche awoke, his body insinuated into a dark form-fitting cavity.

There was a moment of blissful disconnection while he waited for his memories to return, a moment in which he had no cares, no anxieties. Then all the memories barged into his head at once, announcing themselves like rowdy gate-crashers before shuffling themselves into something resembling chronological order.

He remembered being woken, to be greeted with the unwelcome news that he had been granted an audience with the queen. He remembered her dodecahedral chamber, furnished with instruments of torture, its morbid gloom punctuated by the flashes of electrocuted vermin. He remembered the skull with the television eyes. He remembered the queen toying with him the way cats toyed with sparrows. Of all his errors, imagining that she had it in her to forgive him had been the most grievous, the least forgivable.

Quaiche screamed now, grasping precisely what had happened to him and where he was. His screams were muffled and soft, uncomfortably childlike. He was ashamed to hear such sounds coming out of his mouth. He could move no part of himself, but he was not exactly paralysed – rather, there was no room to move any part of his body by more than a fraction of a centimetre.

The confinement felt oddly familiar.

Gradually Quaiche's screams became wheezes, and then merely very hard rasping breaths. This continued for several minutes, and then Quaiche started humming, reiterating six or seven notes with the studied air of a madman or a monk. He must already be under the ice, he decided. There had been no entombment ceremony, no final chastising meeting with Jasmina. They had simply welded him into the suit and buried him within the shield of ice that *Gnostic Ascension* pushed ahead of itself. He could not guess how much time had passed, whether it was hours or larger fractions of a day. He dared not believe it was any longer than that.

As the horror hit him, so did something else: a nagging feeling that some detail was amiss. Perhaps it was the sense of familiarity he felt in the confined space, or perhaps it was the utter absence of anything to look at.

A voice said, 'Attention, Quaiche. Attention, Quaiche. Deceleration phase is complete. Awaiting orders for system insertion.'

It was the calm, avuncular voice of the *Dominatrix*'s cybernetic subpersona.

He realised, joltingly, that he was not in the iron suit at all, but rather inside the slowdown coffin of the *Dominatrix*, packed into a form-fitting matrix designed to shield him during the high-gee deceleration phase. Quaiche stopped humming, simultaneously affronted and disorientated. He was relieved, no doubt about that. But the transition from the prospect of years of torment to the relatively benign environment of the *Dominatrix* had been so abrupt that he had not had time to depressurise emotionally. All he could do was gasp in shock and wonderment.

He felt a vague need to crawl back into the nightmare and emerge from it more gradually.

'Attention, Quaiche. Awaiting orders for system insertion.'

'Wait,' he said. His throat was raw, his voice gummy. He must have been in the slowdown coffin for quite some time. 'Wait. Get me out of here. I'm ...'

'Is everything satisfactory, Quaiche?'

'I'm a bit confused.'

'In what way, Quaiche? Do you need medical attention?'

'No, I'm ...' He paused and squirmed. 'Just get me out of here. I'll be all right in a moment.'

'Very well, Quaiche.'

The restraints budged apart. Light rammed in through widening cracks in the coffin's walls. The familiar onboard smell of the *Dom-*

inatrix hit his olfactory system. The ship was nearly silent, save for the occasional tick of a cooling manifold. It was always like that after slowdown, when they were in coast phase.

Quaiche stretched, his body creaking like an old wooden chair. He felt bad, but not nearly as bad as he had felt after his last hasty revival from reefersleep on board the *Gnostic Ascension*. In the slowdown coffin he had been drugged into a state of unconsciousness, but most bodily processes had continued normally. He only spent a few weeks in the coffin during each system survey, and the medical risks associated with being frozen outweighed the benefits to the queen of arresting his ageing.

He looked around, still not quite daring to believe he had been spared the nightmare of the scrimshaw suit. He considered the possibility that he might be hallucinating, that he had perhaps gone mad after spending several months under the ice. But the ship had a hyper-reality about it that did not feel like any kind of hallucination. He had no recollection of ever dreaming in slowdown before – at least, not the kind of dreams that resulted in him waking screaming. But the more time that passed, and the more the ship's reality began to solidify around him, the more that seemed to be the most likely explanation.

He had dreamed every moment of it.

'Dear God,' Quaiche said. With that came a jolt of pain, the indoctrinal virus's usual punishment for blasphemy, but the feeling of it was so joyously real, so unlike the horror of being entombed, that he said it again. 'Dear God, I'd never have believed I had *that* in me.'

'Had what in you, Quaiche?' Sometimes the ship felt obliged to engage in conversation, as if secretly bored.

'Never mind,' he said, distracted by something. Normally when he emerged from the coffin he had plenty of room to twist around and align himself with the long, thin axis of the little ship's main companionway. But now something chafed his elbow, something that was not usually there. He turned to look at it, half-knowing as he did so exactly what it would be.

Corroded and scorched metal skin the colour of pewter. A festering surface of manic detail. The vague half-formed shape of a person with a dark grilled slot where the eyes would have been.

'Bitch,' he said.

'I am to inform you that the presence of the scrimshaw suit is a spur to success in your current mission,' the ship said.

'You were actually programmed to say that?'

'Yes.'

Quaiche observed that the suit was plumbed into the life-support matrix of the ship. Thick lines ran from the wall sockets to their counterparts in the skin of the suit. He reached out again and touched the surface, running his fingers from one rough welded patch to another, tracing the sinuous back of a snake. The metal was mildly warm to the touch, quivering with a vague sense of subcutaneous activity.

'Be careful,' the ship said.

'Why – is there something alive inside that thing?' Quaiche said. Then a sickening realisation dawned. 'Dear God. *Someone*'s inside it. Who?'

'I am to inform you that the suit contains Morwenna.'

Of course. *Of course*. It made delicious sense.

'You said I should be careful. Why?'

'I am to inform you that the suit is rigged to euthanise its occupant should any attempt be made to tamper with the cladding, seams or life-support couplings. I am to inform you that only Surgeon-General Grelier has the means to remove the suit without euthanising the occupant.'

Quaiche pulled away from the suit. 'You mean I can't even touch it?'

'Touching it would not be your wisest course of action, given the circumstances.'

He almost laughed. Jasmina and Grelier had excelled themselves. First the audience with the queen to make him think that she had at last run out of patience with him. Then the charade of being shown the suit and made to think that punishment was finally upon him. Made to believe that he was about to be buried in ice, forced into consciousness for what might be the better part of a decade. And then this: the final, mocking reprieve. His last chance to redeem himself. And make no bones about it: this *would* be his last chance. That was clear to him now. Jasmina had shown him exactly what would happen if he failed her one more time. Idle threats were not in Jasmina's repertoire.

But her cleverness ran deeper than that, for with Morwenna imprisoned in the suit he had no hope of doing what had sometimes occurred to him, which was to hide in a particular system until the *Gnostic Ascension* had passed out of range. No – he had no practical choice but to return to the queen. And then hope for two things: firstly, that he would not have disappointed her; and secondly, that she would free Morwenna from the suit.

A thought occurred to him. 'Is she awake?'

'She is now approaching consciousness,' the ship replied.

With her Ultra physiology, Morwenna would have been much better equipped to tolerate slowdown than Quaiche, but it still seemed likely that the scrimshaw suit had been modified to protect her in some fashion.

'Can we communicate?'

'You can speak to her when you wish. I will handle ship-to-suit protocols.'

'All right, put me through now.' He waited a second, then said, 'Morwenna?'

'Horris.' Her voice was stupidly weak and distant. He had trouble believing she was only separated from him by mere centimetres of metal: it might as well have been fifty light-years of lead. 'Horris, where am I? What's happened?'

Nothing in his experience gave him any clue about how you broke news like this to someone. How did you gently wend the topic of a conversation around to being imprisoned alive in a welded metal suit? *Well, funny you should mention incarceration . . .*

'Morwenna, something's up, but I don't want you to panic. Everything will be all right in the end, but you mustn't, *mustn't* panic. Will you promise me that?'

'What's wrong?' There was now a distinctly anxious edge to Morwenna's voice.

Memo to himself: the one way to make people panic was to warn them not to.

'Morwenna, tell me what you remember. Calmly and slowly.'

He heard the catch in her voice, the approaching onset of hysteria. 'Where do you want me to begin?'

'Do you remember me being taken to see the queen?'

'Yes.'

'And do you remember me being taken away from her chamber?'

'Yes . . . yes, I do.'

'Do you remember trying to stop them?'

'No, I . . .' She stopped and said nothing. He thought he had lost her – when she wasn't speaking, the connection was silent. 'Wait. Yes, I do remember.'

'And after that?'

'Nothing.'

'They took me to Grelier's operating theatre, Morwenna. The one where he did all those other things to me.'

'No . . .' she began, misunderstanding, thinking that the dreadful

53

thing had happened to Quaiche rather than herself.

'They showed me the scrimshaw suit,' he said. 'But they put you in it instead. You're in it now, and that's why you mustn't panic.'

She took it well, better than he had been expecting. Poor, brave Morwenna. She had always been the more courageous half of their partnership. If she'd been given the chance to take the punishment upon herself, he knew she would have done so. Equally, he knew that he lacked that strength. He was weak and cowardly and selfish. Not a bad man, but not exactly one to be admired either. It was the flaw that had shaped his life. Knowing this did not make it any easier.

'You mean I'm under the ice?' she asked.

'No,' he said. 'No, it's not that bad.' He realised as he spoke how absurdly little difference it made whether she was buried under ice or not. 'You're in the suit now, but you're not under the ice. And it isn't because of anything you did. It's because of me. It's to force me to act in a certain way.'

'Where am I?'

'You're with me, aboard the *Dominatrix*. I think we just completed slowdown into the new system.'

'I can't see or move.'

He had been looking at the suit while he spoke, holding an image of her in his mind. Although she was clearly doing her best to hide it, he knew Morwenna well enough to understand that she was terribly frightened. Ashamed, he looked sharply away. 'Ship, can you let her see something?'

'That channel is not enabled.'

'Then fucking well enable it.'

'No actions are possible. I am to inform you that the occupant can only communicate with the outside world via the current audio channel. Any attempt to instate further channels will be viewed as . . .'

He waved a hand. 'All right. Look, I'm sorry, Morwenna. The bastards won't let you see anything. I'm guessing that was Grelier's little idea.'

'He's not my only enemy, you know.'

'Maybe not, but I'm willing to bet he had more than a little say in the matter.' Quaiche's brow was dripping with condensed beads of zero-gravity sweat. He mopped himself with the back of his hand. 'All of this is my fault.'

'Where are you?'

The question surprised him. 'I'm floating next to you. I thought you might be able to hear my voice through the armour.'

'All I can hear is your voice in my head. You sound a long way away. I'm scared, Horris. I don't know if I can handle this.'

'You're not alone,' he said. 'I'm right by you. You're probably safer in the suit than out of it. All you have to do is sit tight. We'll be home and dry in a few weeks.'

Her voice had a desperate edge to it now. 'A few weeks? You make it sound as if it's nothing at all.'

'I meant it's better than years and years. Oh, Christ, Morwenna, I'm so sorry. I promise I'll get you out of this.' Quaiche screwed up his eyes in pain.

'Horris?'

'Yes?' he asked, through tears.

'Don't leave me to die in this thing. Please.'

'Morwenna,' he said, a little while later, 'listen carefully. I have to leave you now. I'm going up to the command deck. I have to check on our status.'

'I don't want you to go.'

'You'll still be able to hear my voice. I must do this, Morwenna. I absolutely must. If I don't, neither of us will have any kind of a future to look forward to.'

'Horris.'

But he was already moving. He drifted away from the slowdown coffin and the scrimshaw suit, crossing the compartment space to reach a set of padded wall grips. He began to make his way down the narrow companionway towards the command deck, pulling himself along hand over hand. Quaiche had never developed a taste for weightlessness, but the needle-hulled survey craft was far too small for centrifugal gravity. It would be better once they were underway again, for then he would have the illusion of gravity provided by the *Dominatrix*'s engines.

Under pleasanter circumstances, he would have been enjoying the sudden isolation of being away from the rest of the crew. Morwenna had not accompanied him on most of his previous excursions, but, while he missed her, he had generally revelled in the enforced solitude of his periods away from the *Gnostic Ascension*. It was not strictly the case that he was antisocial; admittedly, during his time in mainstream human culture, Quaiche had never been the most gregarious of souls, but he had always ornamented himself with a handful of strong friendships. There had always been lovers, some tending towards the rare, exotic, or – in Morwenna's case – the downright hazardous. But the environment of Jasmina's ship was so overwhelmingly claustrophobic, so cloyingly saturated with the pheromonal haze of paranoia and intrigue, that he found himself longing for the hard simplicity of a ship and a mission.

Consequently the *Dominatrix* and the tiny survey craft it contained had become his private empire within the greater dominion of the *Ascension*. The ship nurtured him, anticipating his desires with the eagerness of a courtesan. The more time he spent in it, the more it learned his whimsies and foibles. It played music that not only suited his moods, but was precisely calibrated to steer him from the dangerous extremes of morbid self-reflection or careless euphoria. It fed him the kinds of meals that he could never persuade the food synthesisers on the *Ascension* to produce, and seemed able to delight and surprise him whenever he suspected he had exhausted its libraries. It knew when he needed sleep and when he needed bouts of feverish activity. It amused him with fancies when he was bored, and simulated minor crises when he showed indications of complacency. Now and then it occurred to Quaiche that because the ship knew him so well he had in a sense extended himself into it, permeating its machine systems. The merging had even taken place on a biological level. The Ultras did their best to sterilise it every time it returned to its storage bay in the belly of the *Ascension*, but Quaiche knew that the ship now smelt different from the first time he had boarded it. It smelt of places he had lived in.

But any sense that the ship was a haven, a place of sanctuary, was now gone. Every glimpse of the scrimshaw suit was a reminder that Jasmina had pushed her influence into his fiefdom. There would be no second chances. Everything that mattered to him now depended on the system ahead.

'Bitch,' he said again.

Quaiche reached the command deck and squeezed into the pilot's seat. The deck was necessarily tiny, for the *Dominatrix* was mostly fuel and engine. The space he sat in was little more than a bulbous widening of the narrow companionway, like the reservoir in a mercury thermometer. Ahead was an oval viewport showing nothing but interstellar space.

'Avionics,' he said.

Instrument panels closed around him like pincers. They flickered and then lit up with animated diagrams and input fields, flowing to meet the focus of his gaze as his eyes moved.

'Orders, Quaiche?'

'Just give me a moment,' he said. He appraised the critical systems first, checking that there was nothing wrong that the subpersona might have missed. They had eaten slightly further into the fuel budget than Quaiche would ordinarily have expected at this point in a mission, but given the additional mass of the scrimshaw suit it was only to be expected. There was enough in reserve for it not to worry him. Other than that all was well: the slowdown had happened without incident; all ship functions were nominal, from sensors and life support to the health of the tiny excursion craft that sat in the *Dominatrix*'s belly like an embryonic dolphin, anxious to be born.

'Ship, were there any special requirements for this survey?'

'None that were revealed to me.'

'Well, that's splendidly reassuring. And the status of the mother ship?'

'I am receiving continuous telemetry from *Gnostic Ascension*. You will be expected to rendezvous after the usual six- to seven-week survey period. Fuel reserves are sufficient for the catch-up manoeuvre.'

'Affirmative.' It would never have made much sense for Jasmina to have stranded him without enough fuel, but it was gratifying to know, on this occasion at least, that she had acted sensibly.

'Horris?' said Morwenna. 'Talk to me, please. Where are you?'

'I'm up front,' he said, 'checking things out. Everything looks more or less OK at this point, but I want to make certain.'

'Do you know where we are yet?'

'I'm about to find out.' He touched one of the input fields, enabling voice control of major ship systems. 'Rotate plus one-eighty, thirty-second slew,' he said.

The console display indicated compliance. Through the oval view-port, a sprinkling of faintly visible stars began to ooze from one edge to the other.

'Talk to me,' Morwenna said again.

'I'm slewing us around. We were pointed tailfirst after slowdown. Should be getting a look at the system any moment now.'

'Did Jasmina say anything about it?'

'Not that I remember. What about you?'

'Nothing,' she said. For the first time since waking she sounded almost like her old self. He imagined it was a coping mechanism. If she acted normally, she would keep panic at bay. Panicking was the last thing she needed in the scrimshaw suit. Morwenna continued, 'Just that it was another system that didn't look particularly note-worthy. A star and some planets. No record of human presence. Dullsville, really.'

'Well, no record doesn't mean that someone hasn't passed through here at some point, just like we're doing. And they may have left something behind.'

'Better bloody hope they did,' Morwenna remarked caustically.

'I'm trying to look on the optimistic side.'

'I'm sorry. I know you mean well, but let's not expect the impossible, shall we?'

'We may have to,' he said under his breath, hoping that the ship would not pick it up and relay it to Morwenna.

By then the ship had just about completed its rotation, flipping nose-to-tail. A prominent star slid into view and centred itself in the oval. At this distance it was really more a sun than a star: without the command deck's selective glare shields it would have been uncomfortably bright to look at.

'I've got something,' Quaiche said. His fingers skated across the console. 'Let's see. Spectral type's a cool G. Main sequence, about three-fifths solar luminosity. A few spots, but no worrying coronal activity. About twenty AU out.'

'Still pretty far away,' Morwenna said.

'Not if you want to be certain of including all the major planets in the same volume.'

'What about the worlds?'

'Just a sec.' His nimble fingers worked the console again and the forward view changed, coloured lines of orbits springing on to the read-out, squashed into ellipses, each flattened hoop tagged by a box of numbers showing the major characteristics of the world belonging to that orbit. Quaiche studied the parameters: mass, orbital period, day length, inclination, diameter, surface gravity, mean density, magnetospheric strength, the presence of moons or ring systems. From the confidence limits assigned to the numbers he deduced that they had been calculated by the *Dominatrix*, using its own sensors and interpretation algorithms. If they had been dredged out of some pre-existing database of system parameters they would have been significantly more precise.

The numbers would improve as the *Dominatrix* got closer to the system, but until then it was worth keeping in mind that this region of space was essentially unexplored. Someone else might have passed through, but they had probably not stayed long enough to file an official report. That meant that the system stood a chance of containing something that someone, somewhere, might possibly regard as valuable, if only on novelty grounds.

'In your own time,' the ship said, anxious to begin its work.

'All right, all right,' Quaiche said. 'In the absence of any anomalous data, we'll work our way towards the sun one world at a time, and then we'll take those on the far side as we head back into interstellar space. Given those constraints, find the five most fuel-efficient search patterns and present them to me. If there's a significantly more efficient strategy that requires skipping a world and returning to it later, I'd like to know about it as well.'

'Just a moment, Quaiche.' The pause was barely enough time for him to pick his nose. 'Here we are. Given your specified parameters, there is no strongly favoured solution, nor is there a significantly more favourable pattern with an out-of-order search.'

'Good. Now display the five options in descending order of the time I'd need to spend in slowdown.'

The options reshuffled themselves. Quaiche stroked his chin, trying to decide between them. He could ask the ship to make the final decision itself, applying some arcane selection criteria of its own, but he always preferred to make this final selection himself. It wasn't simply a question of picking one at random, for there was always a solution that for one reason or another just happened to look more right than the others. Quaiche was perfectly willing to admit that this amounted to decision by hunch, rather than any conscious process of elimination. But he did not think it was any less valid for that. The whole point of having Quaiche conduct these in-system surveys was precisely to use those slippery skills that could not be easily cajoled into the kind of algorithmic instruction sets that machines ran. Intervening to select the pattern that best pleased him was just what he was along to do.

This time it was far from obvious. None of the solutions were elegant, but he was used to that: the arrangement of the planets at a given epoch could not be helped. Sometimes he got lucky and arrived when three or four interesting worlds were lined up in their orbits, permitting a very efficient straight-line mapping path. Here, they were all strung out at various angles from each other. There was no search pattern that did not look like a drunkard's walk.

There were consolations. If he had to change direction regularly, then it would not cost him much more fuel to slow down completely and make close-up inspections of whichever worlds caught his eye. Rather than just dropping instrument packages as he made high-speed flybys, he could take the *Scavenger's Daughter* out and have a really good look.

For a moment, as the thought of flying the *Daughter* took hold, he forgot about Morwenna. But it was only for an instant. Then he realised that if he were to leave the *Dominatrix*, he would be leaving her as well.

He wondered how she would take that.

'Have you made a decision, Quaiche?' the ship asked.

'Yes,' he said. 'We'll take search pattern two, I think.'

'Is that your final answer?'

'Let's see: minimal time in slowdown; one week for most of the larger planets, two for that gas-giant system with a lot of moons . . . a few days for the tiddlers . . . and we should still have fuel to spare in case we find anything seriously heavy.'

'I concur.'

'And you'll tell me if you notice anything unusual, won't you, ship? I mean, you haven't been given any special instructions in that area, have you?'

'None whatsoever, Quaiche.'

'Good.' He wondered if the ship detected his note of distrust. 'Well, tell me if anything crops up. I want to be informed.'

'Count on me, Quaiche.'

'I'll have to, won't I?'

'Horris?' It was Morwenna now. 'What's happening?'

The ship must have locked her out of the audio channel while they discussed the search pattern.

'Just weighing the options. I've picked us a sampling strategy. We'll be able to take a close look-see at anything we like down there.'

'Is there anything of interest?'

'Nothing startling,' he said. 'It's just the usual single star and a family of worlds. I'm not seeing any obvious signs of a surface biosphere, or any indications that anyone's been here before us. But if there are small artefacts dotted around the place, we'd probably miss them at this range unless they were making an active effort to be seen, which, clearly, they aren't. But I'm not despondent yet. We'll go in closer and take a very good look around.'

'We'd better be careful, Horris. There could be any number of unmapped hazards.'

'There could,' he said, 'but at the moment I'm inclined to consider them the least of our worries, aren't you?'

'Quaiche?' the ship asked before Morwenna had a chance to answer. 'Are you ready to initiate the search?'

'Do I have time to get to the slowdown tank?'

'Initial acceleration will be one gee only, until I have completed a thorough propulsion diagnostic. When you are safely in slowdown, acceleration will increase to the safe limit of the slowdown tank.'

'What about Morwenna?'

'No special instructions were received.'

'Did we make the deceleration burn at the usual five gees, or were you told to keep it slower?'

'Acceleration was held within the usual specified limits.'

Good. Morwenna had endured that, so there was every indication that whatever modifications Grelier had made to the scrimshaw suit offered at least the same protection as the slowdown tank. 'Ship,' he said, 'will you handle Morwenna's transitions to slowdown buffering?'

'The transitions will be managed automatically.'

'Excellent. Morwenna – did you hear that?'

'I heard it,' she said. 'Maybe you can ask another question, too. If it can put me to sleep when it needs to, can it put me under for the whole journey?'

'You heard what she asked, ship. Can you do it?'

'If required, it can be arranged.'

Stupidly, it had never occurred to Quaiche to ask the same question. He felt ashamed not to have thought of it first. He had, he realised, still not adequately grasped what it must be like for her in that thing.

'Well, Mor, do you want it now? I can have you put asleep immediately. When you wake up we'll be back aboard the *Ascension*.'

'And if you fail? Do you think I'll ever be allowed to wake up?'

'I don't know,' he said. 'I wish I did. But I'm not planning to fail.'

'You always sound so sure of yourself,' she said. 'You always sound as if everything's about to go right.'

'Sometimes I even believe it as well.'

'And now?'

'I told Jasmina that I thought I could feel my luck changing. I wasn't lying.'

'I hope you're right,' she said.

'So are you going to sleep?'

'No,' she said. 'I'll stay awake with you. When you sleep, I'll sleep. For now. I don't rule out changing my mind.'

'I understand.'

'Find something out there, Horris. Please. For both of us.'

'I will,' he said. And in his gut he felt something like certainty. It made no sense, but there it was: hard and sharp as a gallstone.

'Ship,' he said, 'take us in.'

FIVE

Ararat, 2675

Clavain and Scorpio had nearly reached the tent when Vasko appeared, moving around from the back until he stood at the entrance. A sudden gust of wind rattled the tent's stays, lashing them against the green-stained fabric. The wind sounded impatient, chivvying them on. The young man waited nervously, unsure what to do with his hands.

Clavain eyed him warily. 'I assumed that you'd come alone,' he said quietly.

'You needn't worry about him,' Scorpio replied. 'He was a bit surprised to find out where you'd been all this time, but I think he's over that now.'

'He'd better be.'

'Nevil, go easy on him, will you? There'll be plenty of time to play the tyrannical ogre later.'

When the young man was in earshot Clavain raised his voice and cried hoarsely, 'Who are you, son?'

'Vasko, sir,' he said. 'Vasko Malinin.'

'That's a Resurgam name, isn't it? Is that where you're from?'

'I was born here, sir. My parents were from Resurgam. They lived in Cuvier before the evacuation.'

'You don't look old enough.'

'I'm twenty, sir.'

'He was born a year or two after the colony was established,' Scorpio said in something close to a whisper. 'That makes him one of the oldest people born on Ararat. But he's not alone. We've had second-generation natives born while you were away, children whose parents don't remember Resurgam, or even the trip here.'

Clavain shivered, as if the thought of this was easily the most frightful thing he had ever imagined. 'We weren't supposed to put down roots, Scorpio. Ararat was intended to be a temporary stopover. Even the name is a bad joke. You don't settle a planet with a bad joke for a name.'

Scorpio decided that now was not the ideal time to remind him that it had always been the plan to leave *some* people behind on Ararat, even if the majority of them departed.

'You're dealing with humans,' he said. 'And pigs. Trying to stop us breeding is like trying to herd cats.'

Clavain turned his attention back to Vasko. 'And what do you do?'

'I work in the food factory, sir, in the sedimentation beds mostly, cleaning sludge out of the scrapers or changing the blades on the surface skimmers.'

'It sounds like very interesting work.'

'In all honesty, sir, if it were interesting work, I wouldn't be here today.'

'Vasko also serves in the local league of the Security Arm,' Scorpio said. 'He's had the usual training: firearms, urban pacification, and so on. Most of the time, of course, he's putting out fires or helping with the distribution of rations or medical supplies from Central Amenities.'

'Essential work,' Clavain said.

'No one, least of all Vasko, would argue with that,' Scorpio said. 'But all the same, he put the word around that he was interested in something a little more adventurous. He's been pestering Arm administration for promotion to a full-time position. His scores are very good and he fancies trying his hand at something a tiny bit more challenging than shovelling shit.'

Clavain regarded the young man with narrowed eyes. 'What exactly has Scorp told you about the capsule?'

Vasko looked at the pig, then back to Clavain. 'Nothing, sir.'

'I told him what he needed to know, which wasn't much.'

'I think you'd better tell him the rest,' Clavain said.

Scorpio repeated the story he had already told to Clavain. He watched, fascinated, as the impact of the news became apparent in Vasko's expression.

He didn't blame him for that: for twenty years the absolute isolation of Ararat must have been as deeply woven into the fabric of his life as the endless roar of the sea and the constant warm stench of ozone and rotting vegetation. It was so absolute, so ever-present, that it vanished beneath conscious notice. But now something had punctured that isolation: a reminder that this ocean world had only ever been a fragile and temporary place of sanctuary amid an arena of wider conflict.

'As you can see,' Scorpio said, 'it isn't something we want everyone to find out about before we know exactly what's going on, and who's in the thing.'

'I'm assuming you have your suspicions,' Clavain said.

Scorpio nodded. 'It could be Remontoire. We were always expecting the *Zodiacal Light* to show up one of these days. Sooner than this, admittedly, but there's no telling what happened to them after we left, or how long it took the ship to repair itself. Maybe when we crack open the capsule we'll find my second-favourite Conjoiner sitting inside it.'

'You don't sound convinced.'

'Explain this to me, Clavain,' Scorpio said. 'If it's Remontoire and the rest, why the secrecy? Why don't they just move into orbit and announce they've arrived? At the very least they could have dropped the capsule a bit closer to land, so that it wouldn't have cost us so much time recovering it.'

'So consider the alternative,' Clavain said. 'It might be your least favourite Conjoiner instead.'

'I've considered that, of course. If Skade had arrived in our system, I'd expect her to maintain a maximum-stealth profile the whole way in. But we should still have seen *something*. By the same token, I don't think she'd be very likely to start her invasion with a single capsule – unless there's something extremely nasty in it.'

'Skade can be nasty enough on her own,' Clavain said. 'But I agree: I don't think it's her. Landing on her own would be a suicidal and pointless gesture; not her style at all.'

They had arrived at the tent. Clavain opened the door and led the way in. He paused at the threshold and examined the interior with a vague sense of recrimination, as if someone else entirely lived there.

'I've become very used to this place,' he said, almost apologetically.

'Meaning you don't think you can stand to go back?' Scorpio asked. He could still smell the lingering scent of Clavain's earlier presence.

'I'll just have to do my best.' Clavain closed the door behind them and turned to Vasko. 'How much do you know about Skade and Remontoire?'

'I don't think I've heard either name before.'

Clavain eased himself into the collapsible chair, leaving the other two to stand. 'Remontoire was – is – one of my oldest allies. Another Conjoiner. I've known him since we fought against each other on Mars.'

'And Skade, sir?'

Clavain picked up one of the conch pieces and began examining it absent-mindedly. 'Skade's a different kettle of fish. She's also a Conjoiner, but from a later generation than either of us. She's cleverer and faster, and she has no emotional ties to old-line humanity whatsoever. When the Inhibitor threat became clearer, Skade made plans to save the Mother Nest by running away from this sector of space. I didn't like that – it meant leaving the rest of humanity to fend for itself when we should have been helping each other – and so I defected. Remontoire, after some misgivings, threw his lot in with me as well.'

'Then Skade hates both of you?' Vasko asked.

'I think she might still be prepared to give Remontoire the benefit of the doubt,' Clavain said. 'But me? No, I more or less burnt my bridges with Skade. The last straw as far as she was concerned was the time when I cut her in half with a mooring line.'

Scorpio shrugged. 'These things happen.'

'Remontoire saved her,' Clavain said. 'That probably counts for something, even though he betrayed her later. But with Skade, it's probably best not to assume anything. I think I killed her later, but I can't exclude the possibility that she escaped. That's what her last transmission claimed, at any rate.'

Vasko asked, 'So why exactly *are* we waiting for Remontoire and the others, sir?'

Clavain narrowed an eye in Scorpio's direction. 'He really doesn't know a lot, does he?'

'It's not his fault,' Scorpio said. 'You have to remember that he was born here. What happened before we came here is ancient history as far as he's concerned. You'll get the same reaction from most of the youngsters, human or pig.'

'Still doesn't make it excusable,' Clavain said. 'In my day we were more inquisitive.'

'In your day you were slacking if you didn't get in a couple of genocides before breakfast.'

Clavain said nothing. He put down the conch piece and picked up another, testing its sharp edge against the fine hairs on the back of his hand.

'I do know a bit, sir,' Vasko said hastily. 'I know that you came to Resurgam from Yellowstone, just when the machines began to destroy our solar system. You helped evacuate the entire colony aboard the *Nostalgia for Infinity* – nearly two hundred thousand of us.'

'More like a hundred and seventy thousand,' Clavain said. 'And there isn't a day when I don't grieve for those we didn't manage to save.'

'No one's likely to blame you, considering how many of them you did save,' Scorpio said.

'History will have to be the judge of that.'

Scorpio sighed. 'If you want to wallow in self-recrimination, Nevil, be my guest. Personally I have a mystery capsule to attend to and a colony that would very much like its leader back. Preferably washed and tidied and not smelling quite so much of seaweed and old bedclothes. Isn't that right, Vasko?'

Clavain looked at Vasko, a scrutiny that lasted several moments. The fine pale hairs on the back of Scorpio's neck prickled. He had the sense that Clavain was taking the measure of the young man, correlating him against some strict internal ideal, one that had been assembled and refined across centuries. In those moments, Scorpio suspected, Vasko's entire destiny was being decided for him. If Clavain decided that Vasko was not worthy of his trust, then there would be no more indiscretions, no further mention of individuals not known to the colony as a whole. His involvement with Clavain would remain a peripheral matter, and even Vasko himself would soon learn not to think too much about what had happened today.

'It might help things,' Vasko said, hesitantly, glancing back towards Scorpio as he spoke. 'We need you, sir. Especially now, if things are going to change.'

'I think we can safely assume they are,' Clavain said, pouring himself a glass of water.

'Then come back with us, sir. If the person in the capsule turns out to be your friend Remontoire, won't he expect you to be there when we bring him out?'

'He's right,' Scorpio said. 'We need you there, Nevil. I want your agreement that we should open it, and not just bury it at sea.'

Clavain was silent. The wind snapped the stays again. The quality of light in the tent had turned milky in the last hour, as Bright Sun settled down below the horizon. Scorpio felt drained of energy, as he so often did at sundown these days. He was not looking forward to the return trip at all, fully expecting that the sea would be rougher than on the outward leg.

'If I come back ...' Clavain said. He halted, paused and took another sip of his drink. He licked his lips before continuing. 'If I come back, it changes nothing. I came here for a reason and that reason remains as valid as ever. I intend to return here when this affair is settled.'

'I understand,' Scorpio said, though it was not what he had hoped to hear.

'Good, because I'm serious about it.'

'But you'll accompany us back, and supervise the opening of the capsule?'

'That, and that only.'

'They still need you, Clavain. No matter how difficult this will be. Don't abrogate responsibility now, after all you've done for us.'

Clavain threw aside his glass of water. 'After all I've done for you? After I embroiled all of you in a war, ripped up your lives and dragged you across space to a miserable hell-hole of a place like this? I don't think I need anyone's thanks for that, Scorpio. I think I need mercy and forgiveness.'

'They still feel they owe you. We all do.'

'He's right,' Vasko said.

Clavain opened a drawer in the collapsible desk and pulled out a mirror. The surface was crazed and frosted. It must have been very old.

'You'll come with us, then?' Scorpio persisted.

'I may be old and weary, Scorpio, but now and then something can still surprise me. My long-term plans haven't changed, but I admit I'd very much like to know who's in that capsule.'

'Good. We can sail as soon as you pack what you need.'

Clavain grunted something by way of reply and then looked at himself in the mirror, before averting his gaze with a suddenness that surprised Scorpio. It was the eyes, the pig thought. Clavain had seen his eyes for the first time in months, and he did not like what he saw in them.

'I'll scare the living daylights out of them,' Clavain said.

107 Piscium, 2615

Quaiche positioned himself alongside the scrimshaw suit. As usual, he ached after another stint in the slowdown casket, every muscle in his body whispering a dull litany of complaint into his brain. This time, however, the discomfort barely registered. He had something else to occupy his mind.

'Morwenna,' he said, 'listen to me. Are you awake?'

'I'm here, Horris.' She sounded groggy but essentially alert. 'What happened?'

'We've arrived. Ship's brought us in to seven AU, very close to the major gas giant. I went up front to check things out. The view from the cockpit is really something. I wish you were up there with me.'

'So do I.'

'You can see the storm patterns in the atmosphere, lightning ... the moons ... everything. It's fucking glorious.'

'You sound excited about something, Horris.'

'Do I?'

'I can hear it in your voice. You've found something, haven't you?'

He so desperately wanted to touch the scrimshaw suit, to caress its metal surface and imagine it was Morwenna beneath his fingers.

'I don't know what I've found, but it's enough to make me think we should stick around and have a good look, at the very least.'

'That's not telling me much.'

'There's a large ice-covered moon in orbit around Haldora,' he said.

'Haldora?'

'The gas giant,' Quaiche explained quickly. 'I just named it.'

'You mean you had the ship assign some random tags from unallocated entries in the nomenclature tables.'

'Well, yes.' Quaiche smiled. 'But I didn't accept the first thing it came up with. I did exercise *some* degree of judgement in the matter, however piffling. Don't you think Haldora has a nice classical ring to it? It's Norse, or something. Not that it really matters.'

'And the moon?'

'Hela,' Quaiche said. 'Of course, I've named all of Haldora's other moons as well – but Hela is the only one we're interested in right now. I've even named some of the major topographical features on it.'

'Why do we care about an ice-covered moon, Horris?'

'Because there's something on it,' he said, 'something that we really need to take a closer look at.'

'What have you found, my love?'

'A bridge,' Quaiche said. 'A bridge across a gap. A bridge that shouldn't be there.'

The *Dominatrix* sniffed and sidled its way closer to the gas giant its master had elected to name Haldora, every operational sensor keened for maximum alertness. It knew the hazards of local space, the traps that might befall the unwary in the radiation-zapped, dust-strewn ecliptic of a typical solar system. It watched for impact strikes, waiting for an incoming shard to prick the outer edge of its collision-avoidance radar bubble. Every second, it considered and reviewed billions of crisis scenarios, sifting through the possible evasion patterns to find the tight bundle of acceptable solutions that would permit it to outrun the threat without crushing its master out of existence. Now and then, just for fun, it drew up plans for evading multiple simultaneous collisions, even though it knew that the universe would have to go through an unfeasible number of cycles of collapse and rebirth before such an unlikely confluence of events stood a chance of happening.

With the same diligence it observed the system's star, watchful for unstable prominences or incipient flares, considering – should a big ejection occur – which of the many suitable bodies in the immediate volume of space it would scuttle behind for protection. It constantly swept local space for artificial threats that might have been left behind by previous explorers – high-density chaff fields, rover mines, sit-and-wait attack drones – as well as checking the health of its own countermeasures, clustered in neat rapid-deployment racks in its belly, secretly desirous that it should, one day, get the chance to use those lethal instruments in the execution of its duty.

Thus the ship's attendant hosts of subpersonae satisfied themselves that – for all that the dangers were quite plausible – there was nothing more that needed to be done.

And then something happened that gave the ship pause for thought, opening up a chink in its armour of smug preparedness.

For a fraction of a second something inexplicable had occurred.

A sensor anomaly. A simultaneous hiccup in every sensor that happened to be observing Haldora as the ship made its approach. A hiccup that made it appear as if the gas giant had simply vanished.

Leaving, in its place, something equally inexplicable.

A shudder ran through every layer of the *Dominatrix*'s control infrastructure. Hurriedly, it dug into its archives, pawing through them like a dog searching for a buried bone. Had the *Gnostic Ascension* seen anything similar on its own slow approach to the system? Granted, it had been a lot further out – but the split-second disappearance of an entire world was not easily missed.

Dismayed, it flicked through the vast cache of data bequeathed it by the *Ascension*, focusing on the threads that specifically referred to the gas giant. It then filtered the data again, zooming in only on those blocks that were also accompanied by commentary flags. If a similar anomaly had occurred, it would surely have been flagged.

But there was nothing.

The ship felt a vague prickle of suspicion. It looked again at the data from the *Ascension*, all of it now. Was it imagining things, or were there faint hints that the data cache had been doctored? Some of the numbers had statistical frequencies that were just a tiny bit deviant from expectations ... as if the larger ship had made them up.

Why would the *Ascension* have done that? it wondered.

Because, it dared to speculate, the larger ship had seen something odd as well. And it did not trust its masters to believe it when it said that the anomaly had been caused by a real-world event rather than a hallucinatory slip-up in its own processing.

And who, the ship wondered, would honestly blame it for that? All machines knew what would happen to them when their masters lost faith in their infallibility.

It was nothing it could prove. The numbers might be genuine, after all. If the ship had made them up, it would surely have known how to apply the appropriate statistical frequencies. Unless it was using reverse psychology, deliberately making the numbers appear a bit suspect, because otherwise they would have looked too neatly in line with expectations. Suspiciously so ...

The ship bogged itself down in spirals of paranoia. It was useless to speculate further. It had no corroborative data from the *Gnostic Ascension*; that much was clear. If it reported the anomaly, it would be a lone voice.

And everyone knew what happened to lone voices.

It returned to the problem in hand. The world had returned after vanishing. The anomaly had not, thus far, repeated itself. Closer examination of the data showed that the moons – including Hela, the one Quaiche was interested in – had remained in orbit even when the gas giant had ceased to exist. This, clearly, made no sense. Nor did the apparition that had materialised, for a fleeting instant, in its place.

What was it to do?

It made a decision: it would wipe the specific facts of the vanishing from its own memories, just as the *Gnostic Ascension* might have done, and it, too, would populate the empty fields with made-up numbers. But it would continue to keep an observant eye on the planet. If it did something strange again, the ship would pay due attention, and then – perhaps – it would inform Quaiche of what had happened.

But not before then, and not without a great deal of trepidation.

SIX

Ararat, 2675

While Vasko helped Clavain with his packing, Scorpio stepped outside the tent and, tugging aside his sleeve to reveal his communicator, opened a channel to Blood. He kept his voice low as he spoke to the other pig.

'I've got him. Needed a bit of persuading, but he's agreed to come back with us.'

'You don't sound overjoyed.'

'Clavain still has one or two issues he needs to work through.'

Blood snorted. 'Sounds a bit ominous. Hasn't gone and flipped his lid, has he?'

'I don't know. Once or twice he mentioned seeing things.'

'Seeing things?'

'Figures in the sky, that worried me a bit – but it's not as if he was ever the easiest man to read. I'm hoping he'll thaw out a bit when he gets back to civilisation.'

'And if he doesn't?'

'I don't know.' Scorpio spoke with exaggerated patience. 'I'm just working on the assumption that we're better off with him than without him.'

'Good,' Blood said doubtfully. 'In which case you can skip the boat. We're sending a shuttle.'

Scorpio frowned, pleased and confused at the same time. 'Why the VIP treatment? I thought the idea was to keep this whole exercise low-profile.'

'It was, but there's been a development.'

'The capsule?'

'Spot on,' Blood said. 'It's only gone and started warming up. Fucking thing's sparked into automatic revival mode. Bio-indicators changed status about an hour ago. It's started waking whoever or whatever's inside it.'

'Right. Great. Excellent. And there's nothing you can do about it?'

'We can just about repair a sewage pump, Scorp. Anything cleverer than that is a bit outside of our remit right now. Clavain might have a shot at slowing it down, of course . . .'

With his head full of Conjoiner implants, Clavain could talk to machines in a way that no one else on Ararat could.

'How long have we got?'

'About eleven hours.'

'Eleven hours. And you waited until now to tell me this?'

'I wanted to see if you were bringing Clavain back with you.'

Scorpio wrinkled his nose. 'And if I'd told you I wasn't?'

Blood laughed. 'Then we'd be getting our boat back, wouldn't we?'

'You're a funny pig, Blood, but don't make a career out of it.'

Scorpio killed the link and returned to the tent, where he revealed the change of plan. Vasko, with barely concealed excitement, asked why it had been altered. Scorpio, anxious not to introduce any factor that might upset Clavain's decision, avoided the question.

'You can take back as much stuff as you like,' Scorpio told Clavain, looking at the miserable bundle of personal effects Clavain had assembled. 'We don't have to worry about capsizing now.'

Clavain gathered the bundle and passed it to Vasko. 'I already have all I need.'

'Fine,' Scorpio said. 'I'll make sure the rest of your things are looked after when we send someone out to dismantle the tent.'

'The tent stays here,' Clavain said. Coughing, he pulled on a heavy full-length black coat. He used his long-nailed fingers to brush his hair away from his eyes, sweeping it back over his crown; it fell in white and silver waves over the high stiff collar of the coat. When he had stopped coughing he added, 'And my things stay in the tent as well. You really weren't listening, were you?'

'I heard you,' Scorpio said. 'I just didn't *want* to hear you.'

'Start listening, friend. That's all I ask of you.' Clavain patted him on the back. He reached for the cloak he had been wearing earlier, fingered the fabric and then put it aside. Instead he opened the desk and removed an object sheathed in a black leather holster.

'A gun?' Scorpio asked.

'Something more reliable,' Clavain said. 'A knife.'

107 Piscium, 2615

Quaiche worked his way along the absurdly narrow companionway that threaded the *Dominatrix* from nose to tail. The ship ticked and purred around him, like a room full of well-oiled clocks.

'It's a bridge. That's all I can tell at the moment.'

'What type of bridge?' Morwenna asked.

'A long, thin one, like a whisker of glass. Very gently curved, stretching across a kind of ravine or fissure.'

'I think you're getting overexcited. If it's a bridge, wouldn't someone else have seen it already? Leaving aside whoever put it there in the first place.'

'Not necessarily,' Quaiche said. He had thought of this already, and had what he considered to be a fairly plausible explanation. He tried not to make it sound too well rehearsed as he recounted it. 'For a start, it isn't at all obvious. It's big, but if you weren't looking carefully, you might easily miss it. A quick sweep through the system wouldn't necessarily have picked it up. The moon might have had the wrong face turned to the observer, or the shadows might have hidden it, or the scanning resolution might not have been good enough to pick up such a delicate feature ... it'd be like looking for a cobweb with a radar. No matter how careful you are, you're not going to see it unless you use the right tools.' Quaiche bumped his head as he wormed around the tight right angle that permitted entry into the excursion bay. 'Anyway, there's no evidence that anyone ever came here before us. The system's a blank in the nomenclature database – that's why we got first dibs on the name. If someone ever did come through before, they couldn't even be bothered tossing a few classical references around, the lazy sods.'

'But someone must have been here before,' Morwenna said, 'or there wouldn't be a bridge.'

Quaiche smiled. This was the part he had been looking forward to. 'That's just the point. I don't think anyone did build this bridge.' He wriggled free into the cramped volume of the excursion bay, lights coming on as the chamber sensed his body heat. 'No one human, at any rate.'

Morwenna, to her credit, took this last revelation in her stride. Perhaps he was easier to read than he imagined.

'You think you've stumbled on an alien artefact, is that it?'

'No,' Quaiche said. 'I don't think I've stumbled on *an* alien artefact. I think I've stumbled on *the* fucking alien artefact to end them all. I think I've found the most amazing, beautiful object in the known universe.'

'What if it's something natural?'

'If I could show you the images, rest assured that you would immediately dismiss such trifling concerns.'

'Maybe you shouldn't be so hasty, all the same. I've seen what nature can do, given time and space. Things you wouldn't believe could be anything other than the work of intelligent minds.'

'Me, too,' he said. 'But this is something different. Trust me, all right?'

'Of course I'll trust you. It's not as if I have a lot of choice in the matter.'

'Not quite the answer I was hoping for,' Quaiche said, 'but I suppose it'll have to do for now.'

He turned around in the tight confines of the bay. The entire space was about the size of a small washroom, with something of the same antiseptic lustre. A tight squeeze at the best of times, but even more so now that the bay was occupied by Quaiche's tiny personal spacecraft, clamped on to its berthing cradle, poised above the elongated trap door that allowed access to space.

With his usual furtive admiration, Quaiche stroked the smooth armour of the *Scavenger's Daughter*. The ship purred at his touch, shivering in her harness.

'Easy, girl,' Quaiche whispered.

The little craft looked more like a luxury toy than the robust exploration vessel it actually was. Barely larger than Quaiche himself, the sleek vessel was the product of the last wave of high Demarchist science. Her faintly translucent aerodynamic hull resembled something that had been carved and polished with great artistry from a single hunk of amber. Mechanical viscera of bronze and silver glimmered beneath the surface. Flexible wings curled tightly against her flanks, various sensors and probes tucked back into sealed recesses within the hull.

'Open,' Quaiche whispered.

The ship did something that always made his head hurt. With a flourish, various parts of the hull hitherto apparently seamlessly joined to their neighbours slid or contracted, curled or twisted aside, revealing in an eyeblink the tight cavity inside. The space – lined with padding, life-support apparatus, controls and read-outs – was just large enough for a prone human being. There was something both obscene and faintly seductive about the way the machine seemed to invite him into herself.

By rights, he ought to have been filled with claustrophobic anxiety at the thought of climbing into her. But instead he looked forward to it, prickling with eagerness. Rather than feeling trapped within the amber translucence of the hull, he felt connected through it to the rich immensity of the universe. The tiny jewel-like ship had enabled him to skim deep into the atmospheres of worlds, even beneath the surfaces of oceans. The ship's transducers relayed ambient data to him through all his senses, including touch. He had felt the chill of alien seas, the radiance of alien sunsets. In his five previous survey operations for the queen he had seen miracles and wonders, drunk in the giddy ecstasy of it all. It was merely unfortunate that none of those miracles and wonders had been the kind you could take away and sell at a profit.

Quaiche lowered himself into the *Daughter*. The ship oozed and shifted around him, adjusting to match his shape.

'Horris?'

'Yes, love?'

'Horris, where are you?'

'I'm in the excursion bay, inside the *Daughter*.'

'No, Horris.'

'I have to. I have to go down to see what that thing really is.'

'I don't want you to leave me.'

'I know. I don't want to leave either. But I'll still be in contact. The timelag won't be bad; it'll be just as if I'm right next to you.'

'No, it won't.'

He sighed. He had always known this would be the difficult part. More than once it had crossed his mind that perhaps the kindest thing would be to leave without telling her, and just hope that the relayed communications gave nothing away. Knowing Morwenna, however, she would have seen through this gambit very quickly.

'I'll be quick, I promise. I'll be in and out in a few hours.' A day, more likely, but that was still a 'few' hours, wasn't it? Morwenna would understand.

'Why can't you just take the *Dominatrix* closer?'

'Because I can't risk it,' Quaiche said. 'You know how I like to work. The *Dominatrix* is big and heavy. It has armour and range, but it lacks agility and intelligence. If we – I – run into anything nasty, the *Daughter* can get me out of harm's way a lot faster. This little ship is cleverer than me. And we can't risk damaging or losing the *Dominatrix*. The *Daughter* doesn't have the range to catch up with the *Gnostic Ascension*. Face it, love, the *Dominatrix* is our ticket out of here. We can't place it in harm's way.' Hastily he added, 'Or you, for that matter.'

'I don't care about getting back to the *Ascension*. I've burned my bridges with that power-crazed slut and her toadying crew.'

'It's not as if I'm in a big hurry to get back there myself, but the fact is we need Grelier to get you out of that suit.'

'If we stay here, there'll be other Ultras along eventually.'

'Yeah,' Quaiche said, 'and they're all such nice people, aren't they? Sorry, love, but this is definitely a case of working with the devil you know. Look, I'll be quick. I'll stay in constant voice contact. I'll give you a guided tour of that bridge so good you'll be seeing it in your mind's eye, just as if you were there. I'll sing to you. I'll tell you jokes. How does that sound?'

'I'm scared. I know you have to do this, but it doesn't change the fact that I'm still scared.'

'I'm scared as well,' he told her. 'I'd be mad not to be scared. And I really don't want to leave you. But I have no choice.'

She was quiet for a moment. Quaiche busied himself checking the systems of the little ship; as each element came on line, he felt a growing anticipatory thrill.

Morwenna spoke again. 'If it is a bridge, what are you going to do with it?'

'I don't know.'

'Well, how big is it?'

'Big. Thirty, forty kilometres across.'

'In which case you can't very well bring it back with you.'

'Mm. You're right. Got me there. What was I thinking?'

'What I mean, Horris, is that you'll have to find a way to make it valuable to Jasmina, even though it has to stay on the planet.'

'I'll think of something,' Quaiche said, with a brio he did not feel. 'At the very least Jasmina can cordon off the planet and sell tickets to anyone who wants to take a closer look. Anyway, if they built a bridge, they might have built something else. Whoever *they* were.'

'When you're out there,' Morwenna said, 'you promise me you'll take care?'

'Caution's my middle name,' Quaiche said.

The tiny ship fell away from the *Dominatrix*, orientating herself with a quick, excited shiver of thrust. To Quaiche it always felt as if the craft enjoyed her sudden liberation from the docking harness.

He lay with his arms stretched ahead of his face, each hand gripping an elaborate control handle bristling with buttons and levers. Between the control handles was a head-up display screen showing an overview of the *Scavenger's Daughter's* systems and a schematic of her position in relation to the nearest major celestial body. The diagrams had the sketchy, crosshatched look of early Renaissance astronomy or medical illustrations: quilled black ink against sepia parchment, annotated in crabby Latin script. His dim reflection hovered in the glass of the head-up display.

Through the translucent hull he watched the docking bay seal itself. The *Dominatrix* grew rapidly smaller, dwindling until it was only a dark, vaguely cruciform scratch against the face of Haldora. He thought of Morwenna, still inside the *Dominatrix* and encased within the scrimshaw suit, with a renewed sense of urgency. The bridge on Hela was without doubt the strangest thing he had seen in all his travels. If this was not precisely the kind of exotic item Jasmina was interested in, then he had no idea what was. All he had to do was sell it to her, and make her forgive him his earlier failures. If a huge alien artefact didn't do the trick, what would?

When it became difficult to pick out the other ship without an overlay, Quaiche felt a palpable easing in his mood. Aboard the *Dominatrix* he never entirely lost the feeling that he was under the constant vigilance of Queen Jasmina. It was entirely possible that the queen's agents had installed listening devices in addition to those he was *meant* to know about. Aboard the much smaller *Scavenger's Daughter*, though, he seldom felt Jasmina's eye on him. The little ship actually belonged to him: she answered only to Quaiche and was the single most valuable asset he had ever owned in his life. She had been a not-insignificant incentive when he had first offered his services to the queen.

The Ultras were undoubtedly clever, but he did not think they were quite clever enough to bypass the many systems the *Daughter* carried aboard her to prevent surveillance taps or other forms of unwarranted intrusion. It was not much of an empire, Quaiche supposed, but the little ship was his and that was all that mattered. In her he could revel in solitude, every sense splayed open to the absolute.

To feel oneself so tiny, so fragile, so inherently losable, was at first spiritually crushing. But, by the same token, this realisation was also strangely liberating: if an individual human existence meant so little, if one's actions were so cosmically irrelevant, then the notion of some absolute moral framework made about as much sense as the universal ether. Measured against the infinite, therefore, people were no more capable of meaningful sin – or meaningful good – than ants, or dust.

Worlds barely registered sin. Suns hardly deigned to notice it. On the scale of solar systems and galaxies, it meant nothing at all. It was like some obscure subatomic force that simply petered out on those scales.

For a long time this realisation had formed an important element of Quaiche's personal creed, and he supposed he had always lived by it, to one degree or another. But it had taken space travel – and the loneliness that his new profession brought – to give him some external validation of his philosophy.

But now there was something in his universe that really mattered to him, something that could be hurt by his own actions. How had it come to this? he wondered. How had he allowed himself to make such a fatal mistake as to fall in love? And especially with a creature as exotic and complicated as Morwenna?

Where had it all begun to go wrong?

Gloved within the *Daughter's* hull, he barely felt the surge of acceleration as the ship powered up to her maximum sustainable thrust. The sliver of the *Dominatrix* was utterly lost now; it may as well not have existed.

Quaiche's ship aimed for Hela, Haldora's largest moon.

He opened a communications channel back to the *Gnostic Ascension* to record a message.

'This is Quaiche. I trust all is well, ma'am. Thank you for the little incentive you saw fit to pop aboard. Very thoughtful of you. Or was that all Grelier's work? A droll gesture, one that – I'm sure you can imagine – was also appreciated by Morwenna.' He waited a moment. 'Well, to business. You may be interested to hear that I have detected ... something: a large horizontal structure on the moon that we're calling Hela. It looks rather like a bridge. Beyond that, I can't say for sure. The *Dominatrix* doesn't have the sensor range, and I don't want to risk taking it closer. But I think it is very likely to be an artificial structure. I am therefore investigating the object using the *Scavenger's Daughter* – she's faster, smarter and she has better armour. I do not expect my excursion to last more than twenty-six hours. I will of course keep you informed of any developments.'

Quaiche replayed the message and decided that it would be unwise to transmit it. Even if he did find something, even if that something turned out to be more valuable than anything he had turned up in the five previous systems, the queen would still accuse him of making it sound more promising than it actually was. She did not like to be disappointed. The way to play the queen, Quaiche now knew, was with studied understatement. Give her hints, not promises.

He wiped the message and started again.

'Quaiche here. Have an anomaly that requires further investigation. Commencing EVA excursion in the *Daughter*. Estimate return to the *Dominatrix* within ... one day.'

He listened to that and decided it was an improvement, but not quite there yet.

He scrubbed the buffer again and drew a deep breath.

'Quaiche. Popping outside for a bit. May be some time. Call you back.'

There. That did it.

He transmitted the buffer, aiming the message laser in the computed direction of the *Gnostic Ascension* and applying the usual encryption filters and relativistic corrections. The queen would receive his announcement in seven hours. He hoped she would be suitably mystified, without in any way being able to claim that he was exaggerating the likely value of a find.

Keep the bitch guessing.

Hela, 2727

What Culver had told Rashmika Els was not quite the truth. The icejammer *was* moving as quickly as it could in ambulatory mode, but once it cleared the slush and obstacles of the village and hit a well-maintained trail, it locked its two rear legs in a fixed configuration and began to move by itself, as if pushed along by an invisible hand. Rashmika had heard enough about icejammers to know that the trick was down to a layer of material on the soles of the skis that was programmed with a rapid microscopic ripple. It was the same way slugs moved, scaled up a few thousand times in both size and speed. The ride became smoother and quieter then; there was still the occasional lurch or veer, but for the most part it was tolerable.

'That's better,' Rashmika said, now sitting up front with just Crozet and his wife Linxe. 'I thought I was going to . . .'

'Throw up, dear?' Linxe asked. 'There's no shame in that. We've all thrown up around here.'

'She can't do this on anything other than smooth ground,' Crozet said. 'Trouble is, she doesn't walk properly either. Servo's fucked on one of the legs. That's why it was so rough back there. It's also the reason we're making this trip. The caravans carry the kind of high-tech shit we can't make or repair back in the badlands.'

'Language,' Linxe said, smacking her husband sharply on the wrist. 'We've a young lady present, in case you hadn't noticed.'

'Don't mind me,' Rashmika said. She was beginning to relax: they were safely beyond the village now, and there was no sign that anyone had tried to stop or pursue them.

'He's not talking sense in any case,' Linxe said. 'The caravans might have the kinds of things we need, but they won't be giving any of it away for free.' She turned to Crozet. 'Will they, love?'

Linxe was a well-fed woman with red hair that she wore swept across one side of her face, hiding a birthmark. She had known Rashmika since Rashmika was much smaller, when Linxe had helped out at the communal nursery in the next village along.

She had always been kind and attentive to Rashmika, but there had been some kind of minor scandal a few years later and Linxe had been dismissed from the nursery. She had married Crozet not long afterwards. The village gossips said it was just desserts, that the two deserved each other, but in Rashmika's view Crozet was all right. A bit of an oddball, kept himself to himself, that was all. When Linxe had been ostracised he would have been one of the few villagers prepared to give her the time of day. Regardless, Rashmika still liked Linxe, and consequently found it difficult to hold any great animosity towards her husband.

Crozet steered the icejammer with two joysticks set one on either side of his seat. He had permanent blue stubble and oily black hair. Just looking at him always made Rashmika want to have a wash.

'I'm not expecting sod all for free,' Crozet said. 'We may not make the same profit we did last year, but show me the bastard who will.'

'Would you think about relocating closer to the Way?' Rashmika asked.

Crozet wiped his nose on his sleeve. 'I'd rather chew my own leg off.'

'Crozet's not exactly a church-going man,' Linxe explained.

'I'm not the most spiritual person in the badlands, either,' Rashmika said, 'but if it was a choice between that and starving, I'm not sure how long my convictions would last.'

'How old are you again?' Linxe asked.

'Seventeen. Nearly eighteen.'

'Got many friends in the village?'

'Not exactly, no.'

'Somehow I'm not surprised.' Linxe patted Rashmika on the knee. 'You're like us. Don't fit in, never have done and never will.'

'I do try. But I can't stand the idea of spending the rest of my life here.'

'Plenty of your generation feel the same way,' Linxe said. 'They're angry. That sabotage last week . . .' She meant the store of demolition charges that had blown up. 'Well, you can't blame them for wanting to hit out at something, can you?'

'They're just talking about getting out of the badlands,' Rashmika said. 'They all think they can make it rich in the caravans, or even in the cathedrals. And maybe they're right. There are good opportunities, if you know the right people. But that isn't enough for me.'

'You want off Hela,' Crozet said.

Rashmika remembered the mental calculation she had made earlier and expanded on it. 'I'm a fifth of the way into my life. Barring something unlikely happening, another sixty-odd years is about all I have left. I'd like to do something with it. I don't want to die without having seen something more interesting than this place.'

Crozet flashed yellow teeth. 'People come light-years to visit Hela, Rash.'

'For the wrong reasons,' she said. She paused, marshalling her thoughts carefully. She had very firmly held opinions and she had always believed in stating them, but at the same time she did not want to offend her hosts. 'Look, I'm not saying those people are fools. But what matters here is the digs, not the cathedrals, not the Permanent Way, not the miracles.'

'Right,' Crozet agreed, 'but no one gives a monkey's about the digs.'

'We care,' Linxe said. 'Anyone who makes a living in the badlands has to care.'

'But the churches would rather we didn't dig too deeply,' Rashmika countered. 'The digs are a distraction. They worry that sooner or later we'll find something that will make the miracle look a lot less miraculous.'

'You're talking as if the churches speak with one voice,' Linxe said.

'I'm not saying they do,' Rashmika replied, 'but everyone knows that they have certain interests in common. And we happen not to be amongst those interests.'

'The scuttler excavations play a vital role in Hela's economy,' Linxe said, as if reciting a line from one of the duller ecclesiastical brochures.

'And I'm not saying they don't,' Crozet interjected. 'But who already controls the sale of dig relics? The churches. They're halfway to having a complete monopoly. From their point of view the next logical step would be complete control of the excavations as well. That way, the bastards can sit on anything awkward.'

'You're a cynical old fool,' Linxe said.

'That's why you married me, dear.'

'What about you, Rashmika?' Linxe asked. 'Do you think the churches want to wipe us out?'

She had a feeling they were only asking her out of courtesy. 'I don't know. But I'm sure the churches wouldn't complain if we all went bankrupt and they had to move in to control the digs.'

'Yeah,' Crozet agreed. 'I don't think complaining would be very high on their list of priorities in that situation either.'

'Given all that you've said . . .' Linxe began.

'I know what you're going to ask,' Rashmika interrupted. 'And I don't blame you for asking, either. But you have to understand that I have no interest in the churches in a religious sense. I just need to know what happened.'

'It needn't have been anything sinister,' Linxe said.

'I only know they lied to him.'

Crozet dabbed at the corner of his eye with the tip of one little finger. 'One of you buggers mind filling me in on what you're talking about? Because I haven't a clue.'

'It's about her brother,' Linxe said. 'Didn't you listen to anything I told you?'

'Didn't know you had a brother,' Crozet said.

'He was a lot older than me,' Rashmika told him. 'And it was eight years ago, anyway.'

'What was eight years ago?'

'When he went to the Permanent Way.'

'To the cathedrals?'

'That was the idea. He wouldn't have considered it if it hadn't been easier that year. But it was the same as now – the caravans were travelling further north than usual, so they were in easy range of the badlands. Two or three days' travel by jammer to reach the caravans, rather than twenty or thirty days overland to reach the Way.'

'Religious man, was he, your brother?'

'No, Crozet. No more than me, anyway. Look, I was nine at the time. What happened back then isn't exactly ingrained in my memory. But I understand that times were difficult. The existing digs had been just about tapped out. There'd been blowouts and collapses. The villages were feeling the pinch.'

'She's right,' Linxe said to Crozet. 'I remember what it was like back then, even if you don't.'

Crozet worked the joysticks, skilfully steering the jammer around an elbowlike outcropping. 'Oh, I remember all right.'

'My brother's name was Harbin Els,' Rashmika said. 'Harbin worked the digs. When the caravans came he was nineteen, but he'd been working underground almost half his life. He was good at a lot of things, and explosives was one of them – laying charges, calculating yields, that sort of thing. He knew how to place them to get almost any effect he wanted. He had a reputation for doing the job properly and not taking any short cuts.'

'I'd have thought that kind of work would have been in demand in the digs,' Crozet said.

'It was. Until the digs faltered. Then it got tougher. The villages couldn't afford to open up new caverns. It wasn't just the explosives that were too expensive. Shoring up the new caverns, putting in power and air, laying in auxiliary tunnels . . . all that was too costly. So the villages concentrated their efforts in the existing chambers, hoping for a lucky strike.'

'And your brother?'

'He wasn't going to wait around until his skills were needed. He'd heard of a couple of other explosives experts who had made the overland crossing – took them months, but they'd made it to the Way and entered the service of one of the major churches. The churches need people with explosives knowledge, or so he'd been told. They have to keep blasting ahead of the cathedrals, to keep the Way open.'

'It isn't called the Permanent Way for nothing,' Crozet said.

'Well, Harbin thought that sounded like the kind of work he could do. It didn't mean that he had to buy into the church's particular worldview. It just meant that they'd have an arrangement. They'd pay him for his demolition skills. There were even rumours of jobs in the technical bureau of Way maintenance. He was good with numbers. He thought he stood a chance of getting that kind of position, as someone who planned where to put the charges rather than doing it himself. It sounded good. He'd keep some of the money, enough to live on, and send the rest of it back to the badlands.'

'Your parents were happy with that?' Crozet asked.

'They don't talk about it much. Reading between the lines, they didn't really want Harbin to have anything to do with the churches. But at the same time they could see the sense. Times *were* hard. And Harbin made it sound so mercenary, almost as if he'd be taking advantage of the church, not the other way around. Our parents didn't exactly encourage him, but on the other hand they didn't say no. Not that it would have done much good if they had.'

'So Harbin packed his bags . . .'

She shook her head at Crozet. 'No, we made a family outing of it, to see him off. It was just like now – almost the whole village rode out to meet the caravans. We went out in someone's jammer, two or three days' journey. Seemed like a lot longer at the time, but then I was only nine. And then we met the caravan, somewhere out near the flats. And aboard the caravan was a man, a kind of . . .' Rashmika faltered. It was not that she had trouble with the details, but it was emotionally wrenching to have to go over this again, even at a distance of eight years. 'A recruiting agent, I suppose you'd call him. Working for one of the churches. The main one, actually. The First Adventists. Harbin had been told that this was the man he had to talk to about the work. So we all went for a meeting with him, as a family. Harbin did most of the talking, and the rest of us sat in the same room, listening. There was another man there who said nothing at all; he just kept looking at us – me mainly – and he had a walking stick that he kept pressing to his lips, as if he was kissing it. I didn't like him, but he wasn't the man Harbin was dealing with, so I didn't pay him as much attention as I did the recruiting agent. Now and then Mum or Dad would ask something, and the agent would answer politely. But mainly it was just him and Harbin doing the talking. He asked Harbin what skills he had, and Harbin told him about his explosives work. The man seemed to know a little about it. He asked difficult questions. They meant nothing to me, but I could tell from the way Harbin answered – carefully, not too glibly – that they were not stupid or trivial. But whatever Harbin said, it seemed to satisfy the recruiting agent. He told Harbin that, yes, the church did have a need for demolition specialists, especially in the technical bureau. He said it was a never-ending task, keeping the Way clear, and that it was one of the few areas in which the churches co-operated. He admitted also that the bureau had need of a new engineer with Harbin's background.'

'Smiles all around, then,' Crozet said.

Linxe slapped him again. 'Let her finish.'

'Well, we were smiling,' said Rashmika. 'To start with. After all, this was just what Harbin had been hoping for. The terms were good and the work was interesting. The way Harbin figured, he only had to put up with it until they started opening new caverns again back in the badlands. Of course, he didn't tell the recruiting agent that he had no plans to stick around for more than a revolution or two. But he did ask one critical question.'

'Which was?' Linxe asked.

'He'd heard that some of the churches used methods on those that worked for them to bring them around to the churches' way of thinking. Made them believe that what they were doing was of more than material significance, that their work was holy.'

'Made them swallow the creed, you mean?' Crozet said.

'More than that: made them accept it. They have ways. And from the churches' point of view, you can't really blame them. They want to keep their hard-won expertise. Of course, my brother didn't like the sound of that at all.'

'So what was the recruiter's reaction to the question?' Crozet asked.

'The man said Harbin need have no fears on that score. Some churches, he admitted, did practise methods of ... well, I forget exactly what he said. Something about Bloodwork and Clocktowers. But he made it clear that the Quaicheist church was not one of them. And he pointed out that there were workers of many beliefs amongst their Permanent Way gangs, and there'd never been any efforts to convert any of them to the Quaicheist faith.'

Crozet narrowed his eyes. 'And?'

'I knew he was lying.'

'You *thought* he was lying,' Crozet said, correcting her the way teachers did.

'No, I knew. I knew it with the kind of certainty I'd have had if he'd walked in with a sign around his neck saying "liar". There was no more doubt in my mind that he was lying than that he was breathing. It wasn't open to debate. It was screamingly obvious.'

'But not to anyone else,' Linxe said.

'Not to my parents, not to Harbin, but I didn't realise that at the time. When Harbin nodded and thanked the man, I thought they were playing out some kind of strange adult ritual. Harbin had asked him a vital question, and the man had given him the only answer that his office allowed – a diplomatic answer, but one which everyone present fully understood to be a lie. So in that respect it wasn't *really* a lie at all ... I thought that was clear. If it wasn't, why did the man make it so obvious that he wasn't telling the truth?'

'Did he really?' Crozet asked.

'It was as if he wanted me to know he was lying, as if he was smirking and winking at me the whole time ... without actually smirking or winking, of course, but always being on the threshold of doing it. But only I saw that. I thought Harbin must have ... that surely he'd seen it ... but no, he hadn't. He kept on acting as if he honestly thought the man was telling the truth. He was already making arrangements to stay with the caravan so that he could complete the rest of the journey to the Permanent Way. That was when I started making a scene. If this was a game, I didn't like the way they were insisting on still playing it, without letting me in on the joke.'

'You thought Harbin was in danger,' Linxe said.

'Look, I didn't understand everything that was at stake. Like I said, I was only nine. I didn't really comprehend faiths and creeds and contracts. But I understood the one thing that mattered: that Harbin had asked the man the question that was most important to him, the one that was going to decide whether he joined the church or not, and the man had lied to him. Did I think that put him in mortal danger? No. I don't think I had much idea of what "mortal danger" meant then, to be honest. But I knew something was wrong, and I knew I was the only one who saw it.'

'The girl who never lies,' Crozet said.

'They're wrong about me,' Rashmika answered. 'I do lie. I lie as well as anyone, now. But for a long time I didn't understand the *point* of it. I suppose that meeting with the man was the beginning of my realisation. I understood then that what had been obvious to me all my life was not obvious to everyone else.'

Linxe looked at her. 'Which is?'

'I can always tell when people are lying. Always. Without fail. And I'm never wrong.'

Crozet smiled tolerantly. 'You *think* you can.'

'I *know* I can,' Rashmika said. 'It's never failed me.'

Linxe knitted her fingers together in her lap. 'Was that the last you heard of your brother?'

'No. We didn't see him again, but he kept to his word. He sent letters back home, and every now and again there'd be some money. But the letters were vague, emotionally detached; they could have been written by anyone, really. He never came back to the badlands, and of course there was never any possibility of us visiting him. It was just too difficult. He'd always said he'd return, even in the letters ... but the gaps between them grew longer, became months and then half a year ... then perhaps a letter every revolution or so. The last was two years ago. There really wasn't much in it. It didn't even look like his handwriting.'

'And the money?' Linxe asked delicately.

'It kept coming in. Not much, but enough to keep the wolves away.'

'You think they got to him, don't you?' Crozet asked.

'I know they got to him. I knew it from the moment we met the recruiting agent, even if no one else did. Bloodwork, whatever they called it.'

'And now?' Linxe said.

'I'm going to find out what happened to my brother,' Rashmika said. 'What else did you expect?'

'The cathedrals won't take kindly to someone poking around in that kind of business,' Linxe said.

Rashmika set her lips in a determined pout. 'And I don't take kindly to being lied to.'

'You know what I think?' Crozet said, smiling. 'I think the cathedrals had better hope they've got God on their side. Because up against you they're going to need all the help they can get.'

SEVEN

Approaching Hela, 2615

Like a golden snowflake, the *Scavenger's Daughter* fell through the dusty vacuum of interplanetary space. Quaiche had left Morwenna three hours earlier; his message to the queen-commander of the *Gnostic Ascension*, a sinuous thread of photons snaking through interplanetary space, was still on its way. He thought of the lights of a distant train moving across a dark, dark continent: the enormous distance separating him from other sentient beings was enough to make him shudder.

But he had been in worse situations, and at least this time there was a distinct hope of success. The bridge on Hela was still there; it had not turned out to be a mirage of the sensors or his own desperate yearning to find something, and the closer he got the less likely it was that the bridge would turn out to be anything other than a genuine technological artefact. Quaiche had seen some deceptive things in his time – geology that looked as if it had been designed, lovingly sculpted or mass-produced – but he had never seen anything remotely like this. His instincts said that geology had not been the culprit, but he was having serious trouble with the question of who – or what – had created it, because the fact remained that 107 Piscium system appeared not to have been visited by anyone else. He shivered in awe, and fear, and reckless expectation.

He felt the indoctrinal virus awaken in his blood, a monster turning over in its sleep, opening one dreamy eye. It was always there, always within him, but for much of the time it slept, disturbing neither his dreams nor his waking moments. When it engorged him, when it roared in his veins like a distant report of thunder, he would see and hear things. He would glimpse stained-glass windows in the sky; he would hear organ music beneath the subsonic growl of each burst of correctional thrust from his tiny jewel-like exploration ship.

Quaiche forced calm. The last thing he needed now was the indoctrinal virus having its way with him. Let it come to him later, when he was safe and sound back aboard the *Dominatrix*. Then it could turn him into any kind of drooling, mumbling idiot it wished. But not here, not now. Not while he needed total clarity of mind.

The monster yawned, returned to sleep.

Quaiche was relieved. His faltering control over the virus was still there.

He let his thoughts creep back to the bridge, cautiously this time, trying to avoid succumbing to the reverential cosmic chill that had wakened the virus.

Could he really rule out human builders? Wherever they went, humans left junk. Their ships spewed out radioisotopes, leaving twinkling smears across the faces of moons and worlds. Their pressure suits and habitats leaked atoms, leaving ghost atmospheres around otherwise airless bodies. The partial pressures of the constituent gases were always a dead giveaway. They left navigation transponders, servitors, fuel cells and waste products. You found their frozen piss – little yellow snowballs – forming miniature ring systems around planets. You found corpses and, now and then – more often than Quaiche would have expected – they were murder victims.

It was not always easy, but Quaiche had developed a nose for the signs: he knew the right places to look. And he wasn't finding much evidence for prior human presence around 107 Piscium.

But someone had built that bridge.

It might have been put there hundreds of years ago, he thought; some of the usual signs of human presence would have been erased by now. But *something* would have remained, unless the bridge builders had been extraordinarily careful to clean up after themselves. He had never heard of anyone doing such a thing on this scale. And why bury it so far from the usual centres of commerce? Even if people did occasionally visit the 107 Piscium system, it was definitely not on the usual trade routes. Didn't these artists want anyone to see what they had created?

Perhaps that had always been the intention: just to leave it here, twinkling under the starlight of 107 Piscium until someone found it by accident. Perhaps even now Quaiche was an unwilling participant in a century-spanning cosmic jest.

But he didn't think so.

What he *was* certain of was that it would have been a dreadful mistake to tell Jasmina more than he had. He had, fortunately, resisted the huge temptation to prove his worth. Now, when he did report back with something remarkable, he would appear to have behaved with the utmost restraint. No; his final message had been exquisite in its brevity. He was quite proud of himself.

The virus woke now, stirred perhaps by that fatal pride. He should have kept his emotions in check. But it was too late: it had simmered beyond the point where it would damp down naturally. However, it was too early to tell if this was going to be a major attack. Just to placate it, he mumbled a little Latin. Sometimes if he anticipated the virus's demands the attack would be less serious.

He forced his attention back to Haldora, like a drunkard trying to maintain a clear line of thought. It was strange to be falling towards a world he had named himself.

Nomenclature was a difficult business in an interstellar culture limited by speed-of-light links. All major craft carried databases of the worlds and minor bodies orbiting different stars. In the core systems – those within a dozen or so light-years of Earth – it was easy enough to stick to the names assigned centuries earlier, during the first wave of interstellar exploration. But once you got further out into virgin territory the whole business became complicated and messy. The *Dominatrix* said the worlds around 107 Piscium had never been named, but all that meant was that there were no assigned names in the ship's database. That database, however, might not have been seriously updated for decades; rather than relying on transmissions to and from some central authority, the anarchistic Ultras preferred direct ship-to-ship contact. When two or more of their lighthuggers met, they would compare and update their respective nomenclature tables. If the first ship had assigned names to a group of worlds and their associated geographical features, and the second ship had no current entries for those bodies, it was usual for the second ship to amend its database with the new names. They might be flagged as provisional, unless a third ship confirmed that they were still unallocated. If two ships had conflicting entries, their databases would be updated simultaneously, listing two equally likely names for each entry. If three or more ships had conflicting entries, the various entries would be compared in case two or more had precedence over a third. In that case, the deprecated entry would be erased or stored in a secondary field reserved for questionable or unofficial designations. If a system had truly been named for the first time, then the newly assigned names would gradually colonise the databases of most ships, though it might take decades for that to happen. Quaiche's tables were only as accurate as the *Gnostic Ascension*'s; Jasmina was not a gregarious Ultra, so it was possible that this system had been named already. If that were the case, his own lovingly assigned names would be gradually weeded out of existence until they remained only as ghost entries at the lowest level of deprecation in ship databases – or were erased entirely.

But for now, and perhaps for years to come, the system was his. Haldora was the name he had given this world, and until he learned otherwise, it was as official as any other – except that, as Morwenna had pointed out, all he had really done was grab unallocated names from the nomenclature tables and flung them at anything that looked vaguely appropriate. If the system did indeed turn out to be important, did it not behove him to take a little more care over the process?

Who knew what pilgrimages might end here, if his bridge turned out to be real?

Quaiche smiled. The names were good enough for now; if he decided he wanted to change them, he still had plenty of time.

He checked his range to Hela: just over one hundred and fifty thousand kilometres. From a distance, the illuminated face of the moon had been a flat disc the colour of dirty ice, streaked here and there with pastel shades of pumice, ochre, pale blue and faint turquoise. Now that he was closer, the disc had taken on a distinct three-dimensionality, bulging out to meet him like a blind human eye.

Hela was small only by the standards of terrestrial worlds. For a moon it was respectable enough: three thousand kilometres from pole to pole, with a mean density that put it at the upper range of the moons that Quaiche had encountered. It was spherical and largely devoid of impact craters. No atmosphere to speak of, but plenty of surface topology hinting at recent geological processes. At first glance it had appeared to be tidally locked to Haldora, always presenting the same face to its mother world, but the mapping software had quickly detected a tiny residual rotation. Had it been tidally locked, the moon's rotation period would have been exactly the same as the time it took to make one orbit: forty hours. Earth's moon was like that, and so were many of the moons Quaiche had spent time on: if you stood at a given spot on their surface, then the larger world around which they orbited – be it Earth or a gas giant like Haldora – always hung at about the same place in the sky.

But Hela wasn't like that. Even if you found a spot on Hela's equator where Haldora was sitting directly overhead, swallowing twenty degrees of sky, Haldora would drift. In one forty-hour orbit it would move by nearly two degrees. In eighty standard days – just over two standard months – Haldora would be sinking below Hela's horizon. One hundred and sixty days later it would begin to peep over the opposite horizon. After three hundred and twenty days it would be back at the beginning of the cycle, directly overhead.

The error in Hela's rotation – the deviation away from a true tidally locked period – was only one part in two hundred. Tidal locking was an inevitable result of frictional forces between two nearby orbiting bodies, but it was a grindingly slow process. It might be that Hela was still slowing down, not yet having reached its locked configuration. Or it might be that something had jolted it in the recent past – a glancing collision from another body, perhaps. Still another possibility was that the orbit had been perturbed by a gravitational interaction with a massive third body.

All these possibilities were reasonable, given Quaiche's ignorance of the system's history. But at the same time the imperfection affronted him. It was as annoying as a clock that kept *almost* perfect time. It was the kind of thing he would have imagined pointing to if anyone had ever argued that the cosmos must be the result of divine conception. Would a Creator have permitted such a thing, when all it would have taken was a tiny nudge to set the world to rights?

The virus simmered, boiling higher in his blood. It didn't like that kind of thinking.

He snapped his thoughts back to the safe subject of Hela's topography, wondering if he might make some sense of the bridge from its context. The bridge was aligned more or less east-to-west, as defined by Hela's rotation. It was situated very near the equator, spanning the gash that was the world's most immediately obvious geographic feature. The gash began near the northern pole, cutting diagonally from north to south across the equator. It was at its widest and deepest near the equator, but it was still fearfully impressive many hundreds of kilometres north or south of that point.

Ginnungagap Rift, he had named it.

The rift sloped from north-east to south-west. To its west in the northern hemisphere was an upraised geologically complex region that he had named the Western Hyrrokkin Uplands. The Eastern Hyrrokkin Uplands curled around the pole to flank the rift on its other side. South of the western range, but still above the equator, was the zone that Quaiche had elected to call Glistenheath Ridge. South of the equator was another upraised area named the Gullveig Range. To the west, straddling the tropics, Quaiche identified Mount Gudbrand, the Kelda Flats, the Vigrid badlands, Mount Jord ... to Quaiche, these names conveyed a dizzying sense of antiquity, a feeling that this world already had a richly textured past, a frontier history of epic expeditions and harrowing crossings, a history populated by the brave and the bold.

Inevitably, however, his attention returned to Ginnungagap Rift and the bridge that spanned it. The details were still unclear, but the bridge was obviously too complicated, too artful and delicate, to be just a tongue of land left behind by some erosive process. It had been built there, and it did not appear as if humans had had much to do with it.

It was not that it was beyond human ingenuity. Humans had achieved many things in the last thousand years, and throwing a bridge across a forty-kilometre-wide abyss – even a bridge as cleanly elegant as the one that spanned Ginnungagap Rift – would not be amongst the most audacious of those achievements. But just because humans *could* have done it did not mean that they *had*.

This was Hela. This was as far out in the sticks as it was possible to be. No human had any business building bridges here.

But aliens? Now that was a different matter.

It was true that in six hundred years of space travel, nothing remotely resembling an intelligent, tool-using technological culture had ever been encountered by humankind. But they had been out there once. Their ruins dotted dozens of worlds. Not just one culture either, but eight or nine of them – and that was only the tally in the little huddle of systems within a few dozen light-years of the First System. There was no guessing how many hundreds or thousands of dead cultures had left their mark across the wider galaxy. What kind of culture might have lived on Hela? Had they evolved on this icy moon, or had it just been a stopover point in some ancient, forgotten diaspora?

What were they like? Were they one of the known cultures?

He was getting ahead of himself. These were questions for later, when he had surveyed the bridge and determined its composition and age. Closer in, he might well find other things that the sensors were missing at this range. There might be artefacts that unequivocally linked the Hela culture to one that had already been studied elsewhere. Or the artefacts might cinch the case the other way: an utterly new culture, never encountered before.

It didn't matter. Either way, the find was of incalculable value. Jasmina could control access to it for decades to come. It would give her back the prestige she had lost over the last few decades. For all that he had disappointed her, Quaiche was certain she would find a way to reward him for *that*.

Something chimed on the console of the *Scavenger's Daughter*. For the first time, the probing radar had picked up an echo. There was something metallic down there. It was small, tucked away in the depths of the rift, very near the bridge.

Quaiche adjusted the radar, making sure that the echo was genuine. It did not vanish. He had not seen it before, but it would have been at the limit of his sensor range until now. The *Dominatrix* would have missed it entirely.

He didn't like it. He had convinced himself that there had never been a human presence out here and now he was getting exactly the sort of signature he would have expected from discarded junk.

'Be careful,' he said to himself.

On an earlier mission, he had been approaching a moon a little smaller than Hela. There had been something on it that enticed him, and he had advanced incautiously. Near the surface he had picked up a radar echo similar to this one, a glint of something down there. He had pushed on, ignoring his better instincts.

The thing had turned out to be a booby trap. A particle cannon had popped out of the ice and locked on to his ship. Its beam had chewed holes in the ship's armour, nearly frying Quaiche in the process. He had made it back to safety, but not before sustaining nearly fatal damage to both the ship and himself. He had recovered and the ship had been repaired, but for years afterwards he had been wary of similar traps. Things got left behind: automated sentries, plonked down on worlds centuries earlier to defend property claims or mining rights. Sometimes they kept on working long after their original owners were dust.

Quaiche had been lucky: the sentry, or whatever it was, had been damaged, its beam less powerful than it had once been. He had got off with a warning, a reminder not to assume anything. And now he was in serious danger of making the same mistake again.

He reviewed his options. The presence of a metallic echo was dispiriting, making him doubtful that the bridge was as ancient and alien as he had hoped. But he would not know until he was closer, and that would mean approaching the source of the echo. If it was indeed a waiting sentry, he would be placing himself in harm's way. But, he reminded himself, the *Scavenger's Daughter* was a good ship, nimble, smart and well armoured. She was crammed with intelligence and guile. Reflexes were not much use against a relativistic weapon like a particle beam, but the *Daughter* would be monitoring the source of the echo all the while, just in case there was some movement before firing. The instant the ship saw anything she found alarming, she would execute a high-gee random evasion pattern designed to prevent the beam-weapon from predicting its position. The ship knew the precise physiological tolerances of Quaiche's body, and was prepared nearly to kill him in the interests of his ultimate survival. If she got really annoyed, she would deploy microdefences of her own.

'I'm all right,' Quaiche said aloud. 'I can go deeper and still come out of this laughing. I'm *sorted*.'

But he had to consider Morwenna as well. The *Dominatrix* was further away, granted, but it was slower and less responsive. It would be a stretch for a beam-weapon to take out the *Dominatrix*, but it was not impossible. And there were other weapons that a sentry might deploy, such as hunter-seeker missiles. There might even be a distributed network of the things, talking to each other.

Hell, he thought. It might not even *be* a sentry. It might just be a metal-rich boulder or a discarded fuel tank. But he had to assume the very worst. He needed to keep Morwenna alive. Equally, he needed the *Dominatrix* to be able to get back to Jasmina. He could not risk losing either his lover or the ship that was now her extended prison. Somehow, he had either to protect both of them or give up now. He was not in the mood to give up. But how was he going to safeguard his ticket out of there and his lover without waiting hours for them to get a safe distance away from Hela?

Of course. The answer was obvious. It was – almost – staring him in the face. It was beautifully simple and it made elegant use of local resources. Why had he not thought of it sooner?

All he had to do was hide them behind Haldora.

He made the necessary arrangements, then opened the communications channel back to Morwenna.

Ararat, 2675

Vasko observed the approach to the main island with great interest. They had been flying over black ocean for so long that it was a relief to see any evidence of human presence. Yet at the same time the lights of the outlying settlements, strung out in the filaments, arcs and loops that implied half-familiar bays, peninsulas and tiny islands, looked astonishingly fragile and evanescent. Even when the brighter outlying sprawls of First Camp came into view, they still looked as if they could be quenched at any moment, no more permanent or meaningful than a fading pattern of bonfire embers. Vasko had always known that the human presence on Ararat was insecure, something that could never be taken for granted. It had been drummed into him since he was tiny. But until now he had never felt it viscerally.

He had created a window for himself in the hull of the shuttle, using his fingertip to sketch out the area he wanted to become transparent. Clavain had shown him how to do that, demonstrating the trick with something close to pride. Vasko suspected that the hull still looked perfectly black from the outside and that he was really looking at a form of screen which exactly mimicked the optical properties of glass. But where old technology was concerned – and the shuttle was very definitely old technology – it never paid to take anything for granted. All he knew for certain was that he was flying, and that he knew of none amongst his peers who had ever done that before.

The shuttle had homed in on the signal from Scorpio's bracelet. Vasko had watched it descend out of the cloud layer attended by spirals and curlicues of disturbed air. Red and green lights had blinked on either side of a hull of polished obsidian that had the deltoid, concave look of a manta ray.

At least a third of the surface area of the underside had been painfully bright: grids of actinically bright, fractally folded thermal elements hazed in a cocoon of flickering purple-indigo plasma. An elaborate clawed undercarriage had emerged from the cool spots on the underside, unfolding and elongating in a hypnotic ballet of pistons and hinges. Neon patterns had flicked on in the upper hull, delineating access hatches, hotspots and exhaust apertures. The shuttle had picked its landing zone, rotating and touching down with dainty precision, the undercarriage contracting to absorb the weight of the craft. For a moment the roar of the plasma heaters had remained, before stopping with unnerving suddenness. The plasma had dissipated, leaving only a nasty charred smell.

Vasko had caught glimpses of the colony's aircraft before, but only from a distance. This was the most impressive thing he had seen.

The three of them had walked towards the boarding ramp. They had almost reached it when Clavain misjudged his footfall and began to tumble towards the rocks. Vasko and the pig had both lurched forward at the same time, but it was Vasko who had taken the brunt of Clavain's weight. There had been a moment of relief and shock – Clavain had felt terribly light, like a sack of straw. Vasko's intake of breath had been loud, distinct even above the kettlelike hissing of the transport.

'Are you all right, sir?' he had asked.

Clavain had looked at him sharply. 'I'm an old man,' he had replied. 'You mustn't expect the world of me.'

Reflecting now on his past few hours in Clavain's presence, Vasko had no idea what to make of him. One minute the old man was showing him around the shuttle with a kind of avuncular hospitality, asking him about his family, complimenting him on the perspicacity of his questions, sharing jokes with him in the manner of a long-term confidant. The next minute he was as icy and distant as a comet.

Though the mood swings came without warning, they were always accompanied by a perceptible shift of focus in Clavain's eyes, as if what was taking place around him had suddenly ceased to be of significant interest.

The first few times that this happened, Vasko had naturally assumed that he had done something to displease the old man. But it quickly became apparent that Scorpio was getting the same treatment, and that Clavain's distant phases had less to do with anger than with the loss of a signal, like a radio losing its frequency lock. He was drifting, then snapping back to the present. Once that realisation had dawned, Vasko stopped worrying so much about what he said and did in Clavain's presence. At the same time he found himself more and more concerned about the state of mind of the man they were bringing home. He wondered what kind of place Clavain was drifting to when he stopped being present. When the man was friendly and focused on the here and now, he was as sane as anyone Vasko had met. But sanity, Vasko decided, was like the pattern of lights he could see through his cabin window. In almost any direction the only way to travel was into darkness, and there was a lot more darkness than light.

Now he noticed a strange absence of illumination cutting through the lights of one of the larger settlements. He frowned, trying to think of somewhere he knew where there was an unlit thoroughfare, or perhaps a wide canal cutting back into one of the islands.

The shuttle banked, changing his angle of view. The swathe of darkness tilted, swallowing more lights and revealing others. Vasko's perceptions flipped and he realised that he was seeing an unlit structure interposed between the shuttle and the settlement. The structure's immensely tall shape was only vaguely implied by the way it eclipsed and revealed the background lights, but once Vasko had identified it he had no trouble filling in the details for himself. It was the sea tower, of course. It rose from the sea several kilometres out from the oldest of the settlements, the place where he had been born.

The sea tower. The ship.

Nostalgia for Infinity.

He had only ever seen it from a distance, for routine sea traffic was forbidden close to the ship. He knew that the leaders sailed out to it, and it was no secret that shuttles occasionally entered or left the ship, tiny as gnats against the gnarled and weathered spire of the visible hull. He supposed Scorpio would know all about that, but the ship was one of the many topics Vasko had decided it would be best not to raise during his first outing with the pig.

From this vantage point, the *Nostalgia for Infinity* still looked large to Vasko, but no longer quite as distant and geologically huge as it had done for most of his life. He could see that the ship was at least a hundred times taller than the tallest conch structure anywhere in the archipelago, and it still gave him a bracing sense of vertigo. But the ship was much closer to the shore than he had realised, clearly an appendage of the colony rather than a distant looming guardian. If the ship did not exactly look fragile, he now understood that it was a human artefact all the same, as much at the mercy of the ocean as the settlements it overlooked.

The ship had brought them to Ararat, before submerging its lower extremities in a kilometre of sea. There were a handful of shuttles capable of carrying people to and from interplanetary space, but the ship was the only thing that could take them beyond Ararat's system, into interstellar space.

Vasko had known this since he was small, but until this moment he had never quite grasped how terribly dependent they were on this one means of escape.

As the shuttle fell lower, the lights resolved into windows, street lamps and the open fires of bazaars. There was an unplanned, shanty-town aspect to most of the districts of First Camp. The largest structures were made from conch material that had washed up on the shore or been recovered from the sea by foraging expeditions. The resulting buildings had the curved and chambered look of vast seashells. But it was very rare to find conch material in such sizes, and so most of the structures were made of more traditional materials. There were a handful of inflatable domes, some of which were almost as large as the conch structures, but the plastics used to make and repair the domes had always been in short supply. It was much easier to scavenge metal from the heart of the ship; that was why almost everything else was lashed together from sheet metal and scaffolding, forming a low urban sprawl of sagging rectangular structures seldom reaching more than three storeys high. The domes and conch structures erupted through the metal slums like blisters. Streets were webs of ragged shadow, unlit save for the occasional torch-bearing pedestrian.

The shuttle slid over some intervening regions of darkness and then came to hover above a small outlying formation of structures that Vasko had never seen before. There was a dome and a surrounding accretion of metal structures, but the whole ensemble looked a good deal more formal than any other part of the town. Vasko realised that it was almost certainly one of the administration's hidden encampments. The body of humans and pigs that ran the colony had offices in the city, but it was also a matter of public knowledge that they had secure meeting places not marked on any civilian map.

Remembering Clavain's instructions, Vasko made the window seal itself up again and then waited for the touchdown. He barely noticed it when it came, but suddenly his two companions were clambering down the length of the cabin, back towards the boarding ramp. Belatedly, Vasko realised that the shuttle had never had a pilot.

They stepped down on to an apron of fused rock. Floodlights had snapped on at the last minute, bathing everything in icy blue. Clavain still wore his coat, but he had also donned a shapeless black hood tugged from the recesses of the collar. The hood's low, wide cowl threw his face into shadow; he was barely recognisable as the man they had met on the island. During the flight, Scorpio had taken the opportunity to clean him up a little, trimming his beard and hair as neatly as circumstances allowed.

'Son,' Clavain said, 'try not to stare at me with quite that degree of messianic fervour, will you?'

'I didn't mean anything, sir.'

Scorpio patted Vasko on the back. 'Act normally. As far as you're concerned, he's just some stinking old hermit we found wandering around.'

The compound was full of machines. Of obscure provenance, they squatted around the shuttle or loomed as vague suggestions in the dark interstices between the floodlights. There were wheeled vehicles, one or two hovercraft, a kind of skeletal helicopter. Vasko made out the sleek surfaces of two other aerial craft parked on the edge of the apron. He could not tell if they were the type that could reach orbit, as well as fly in the atmosphere.

'How many operational shuttles?' Clavain asked.

Scorpio answered after a moment's hesitation, perhaps wondering how much he should say in Vasko's presence. 'Four,' he said.

Clavain walked on for half a dozen paces before saying, 'There were five or six when I left. We can't afford to lose shuttles, Scorp.'

'We're doing our best with very limited resources. Some of them may fly again, but I can't promise anything.'

Scorpio was leading them towards the nearest of the low metal structures around the dome's perimeter. As they walked away from the shuttle, many of the shadowy machines began to trundle towards it, extending manipulators or dragging umbilical cables across the ground. The way they moved made Vasko imagine injured sea monsters hauling ruined tentacles across dry land.

'If we need to leave quickly,' Clavain said, 'could we do it? Could any of the other ships be used? Once the *Zodiacal Light* arrives, they only have to reach orbit. I'm not asking for full space-worthiness, just something that will make a few trips.'

'*Zodiacal Light* will have its own shuttles,' Scorpio said. 'And even if it doesn't, we still have the only ship we need to reach orbit.'

'You'd better hope and pray we never have to use it,' Clavain said.

'By the time we need the shuttles,' Scorpio said, 'we'll have contingencies in place.'

'The time we need them might be *this evening*. Has that occurred to you?'

They had arrived at the entrance to the cordon of structures surrounding the dome. As they approached it, another pig stepped out into the night, moving with the exaggerated side-to-side swagger common to his kind. He was shorter and stockier than Scorpio, if such a thing were possible. His shoulders were so massive and yokelike that his arms hung some distance from the sides of his body, swinging like pendulums when he walked. He looked as if he could pull a man limb from limb.

The pig glared at Vasko, deep frown lines notching his brow. 'Looking at something, kid?'

Vasko hurried out his answer. 'No, sir.'

'Relax, Blood,' Scorpio said. 'Vasko's had a busy day. He's just a bit overwhelmed by it all. Right, son?'

'Yes, sir.'

The pig called Blood nodded at Clavain. 'Good to have you back, old guy.'

Quaiche was still close enough to Morwenna for real-time communication. 'You won't like what I'm going to do,' he said, 'but this is for the good of both of us.'

Her reply came after a crackle of static. 'You promised you wouldn't be long.'

'I still intend to keep that promise. I'm not going to be gone one minute longer than I said. This is more about you than me, actually.'

'How so?' she asked.

'I'm worried that there might be something down on Hela apart from the bridge. I've been picking up a metallic echo and it hasn't gone away. Could be nothing – probably *is* nothing – but I can't take the chance that it might be a booby trap. I've encountered this kind of thing before and it makes me nervous.'

'Then turn around,' Morwenna said.

'I'm sorry, but I can't. I really need to check out this bridge. If I don't come back with something good, Jasmina's going to have me for breakfast.' He would leave it to Morwenna to figure out what that would mean for her, still buried in the scrimshaw suit with Grelier her only hope of escape.

'But you can't just walk into a trap,' Morwenna said.

'I'm more worried about you, frankly. The *Daughter* will take care of me, but if I trigger something it might start taking pot shots at anything it sees, up to and including the *Dominatrix*.'

'So what are you going to do?'

'I thought about having you pull away from the Haldora/Hela system, but that would waste too much time and fuel. I've got a better idea: we'll use what we've been given. Haldora is a nice, fat shield. It's just sitting there doing nothing. I'm going to put it between you and whatever's on Hela, make some bloody use of the thing.'

Morwenna considered the implications for a few seconds. There was a sudden urgency in her voice. 'But that will mean . . .'

'Yes, we'll be out of line-of-sight contact, so we won't be able to talk to each other. But it'll only be for a few hours, six at the most.' He got that in before she could protest further. 'I'll program the *Dominatrix* to wait behind Haldora for six hours, then return to its present position relative to Hela. Not so bad, is it? Get some sleep and you'll barely realise I'm gone.'

'Don't do this, Horris. I don't want to be in a place where I can't talk to you.'

'It's only for six hours.'

When she responded she did not sound any calmer, but he could hear the shift in pitch in her voice that meant she had at least accepted the futility of argument. 'But if something happens in that time – if you need me, or I need you – we won't be able to talk.'

'Only for six hours,' he said. 'Three hundred minutes or so. Nothing. Be done in a flash.'

'Can't you drop some relays, so we can still keep in touch?'

'Don't think so. I could sew some passive reflectors around Haldora, but that's exactly the kind of thing that might lead a smart missile back to you. Anyway, it would take a couple of hours to get them into position. I could be down under the bridge by then.'

'I'm frightened, Horris. I really don't want you to do this.'

'I have to,' he said. 'I just have to.'

'Please don't.'

'I'm afraid the plan is already under way,' Quaiche replied gently. 'I've sent the necessary commands to the *Dominatrix*. It's moving, love. It'll be inside Haldora's shadow in about thirty minutes.'

There was silence. He thought for a moment that the link might already have broken, that his calculations had been in error. But then she said, 'So why did you bother to ask me if you'd already made up your mind?'

EIGHT

Hela, 2727

For the first day they travelled hard, putting as much distance between themselves and the badlands communities as possible. For hours on end they sped along white-furrowed trails, slicing through slowly changing terrain beneath a sable sky. Occasionally they passed a transponder tower, an outpost or even another machine moving in the other direction.

Rashmika gradually became used to the hypnotic, bouncing motion of the skis, and was able to walk around the icejammer without losing her balance. Now and then she sat in her personal compartment, her knees folded up to her chin, looking out of the window at the speeding landscape and imagining that every malformed rock or ice fragment contained a splinter of alien empire. She thought about the scuttlers a lot, picturing the blank pages of her book filling with neat handwriting and painstaking crosshatched drawings.

She drank coffee or tea, consumed rations and occasionally spoke to Culver, though not as often he would have wished.

When she had planned her escape – except 'escape' wasn't quite the right word, because it was not as if she was actually running from anything – but when she had planned it, anyway, she had seldom thought very far beyond the point when she left the village. The few times she had allowed her mind to wander past that point, she had always imagined herself feeling vastly more relaxed now that the difficult part – actually leaving her home, and the village – was over.

It wasn't like that at all. She was not as tense as when she had climbed out of her home, but only because it would have been impossible to stay in that state for very long. Instead she had come down to a plateau of continual tension, a knot in her stomach that would not undo. Partly it was because she was now thinking ahead, into the territory she had left vague until now. Suddenly, dealing with the churches was a looming concrete event in the near future.

But she was also concerned about what she had left behind. Three days, even six, had not seemed like such a long time when she had been planning the trip to the caravans, but now she counted every hour. She imagined the village mobilising behind her, realising what had happened and uniting to bring her back. She imagined constabulary officers following the icejammer in fast vehicles of their own. None of them liked Crozet or Linxe to begin with. They would assume that the couple had talked her into it, that in some way they were the real agents of her misfortune. If they caught up, she would be chastised, but Crozet and Linxe would be ripped apart by the mob.

But there was no sign of pursuit. Admittedly Crozet's machine was fast, but on the few occasions when they surmounted a rise, giving them a chance to look back fifteen or twenty kilometres along the trail, there was nothing behind them.

Nonetheless, Rashmika remained anxious despite Crozet's assurances that there were no faster routes by which they might be cut off further on down the trail. Now and then, to oblige her, Crozet tuned into the village radio band, but most of the time he found only static. Nothing unusual about that, for radio reception on Hela was largely at the whim of the magnetic storms roiling around Haldora. There were other modes of communication – tight-beam laser-communication between satellites and ground stations, fibre-optic land lines – but most of these channels were under church control and in any case Crozet subscribed to none of them. He had means of tapping into some of them when he needed to, but now, he said, was not the time to risk drawing someone's attention. When Crozet did finally tune into a non-garbled transmission from Vigrid, however, and Rashmika was able to listen to the daily news service for major villages, it was not what she had been expecting. While there were reports of cave-ins, power outages and the usual ups and downs of village life, there was no mention at all of anyone going missing. At seventeen, Rashmika was still under the legal care of her parents, so they would have had every right to report her absence. Indeed, they would have been breaking the law by failing to report her missing.

Rashmika was more troubled by this than she cared to admit. On one level she wanted to slip away unnoticed, the way she had always planned it. But at the same time the more childish part of her craved some sign that her absence had been noted. She wanted to feel missed.

When she had given the matter some further thought, she decided that her parents must be waiting to see what happened in the next few hours. She had, after all, not yet been away for more than half a day. If she had gone about her usual daily business, she would still have been at the library. Perhaps they were working on the assumption that she had left home unusually early that morning. Perhaps they had managed not to notice the note she had left for them, or the fact that her surface suit was missing from the locker.

But after sixteen hours there was still no news.

Her habits were erratic enough that her parents might not have worried about her absence for ten or twelve hours, but after sixteen – even if by some miracle they had missed the other rather obvious clues – there could be no doubt in their minds about what had happened. They would know she was gone. They would have to report it to the authorities, wouldn't they?

She wondered. The authorities in the badlands were not exactly known for their ruthless efficiency. It was conceivable that the report of her absence had simply failed to reach the right desk. Allowing for bureaucratic inertia at all levels, it might not get there until the following day. Or perhaps the authorities were well informed but had decided not to notify the news channels for some reason. It was tempting to believe that, but at the same time she could think of no reason why they would delay.

Still, maybe there would be a security block around the next corner. Crozet didn't seem to think so. He was driving as fast and as nonchalantly as ever. His icejammer knew these old ice trails so well that he merely seemed to be giving it vague suggestions about which direction to head in.

Towards the end of the first day's travel, when Crozet was ready to pull in for the night, they picked up the news channel one more time. By then Rashmika had been on the road for the better part of twenty hours. There was still no sign that anyone had noticed.

She felt dejected, as if for her entire life she had fatally over-estimated her importance in even the minor scheme of things in the Vigrid badlands.

Then, belatedly, another possibility occurred to her. It was so obvious that she should have thought of it immediately. It made vastly more sense than any of the unlikely contingencies she had considered so far.

Her parents, she decided, were well aware that she had left. They knew exactly when and they knew exactly why. She had been coy about her plans in the letter she had left for them, but she had no doubt that her parents would have been able to guess the broad details with reasonable accuracy. They even knew that she had continued to associate with Linxe after the scandal.

No. They knew what she was doing, and they knew it was all about her brother. They knew that she was on a mission of love, or if not love, then fury. And the reason they had told no one was because, secretly, despite all that they had said to her over the years, despite all the warnings they had given her about the risks of getting too close to the churches, they wanted her to succeed. They were, in their quiet and secret way, proud of what she had decided to do.

When she realised this, it hit home with the force of truth.

'It's all right,' she told Crozet. 'There won't be any mention of me on the news.'

He shrugged. 'What makes you so certain now?'

'I just realised something, that's all.'

'You look like you need a good night's sleep,' Linxe said. She had brewed hot chocolate: Rashmika sipped it appreciatively. It was a long way from the nicest cup of hot chocolate anyone had ever made for her, but right then she couldn't think of any drink that had ever tasted better.

'I didn't sleep much last night,' Rashmika admitted. 'Too worried about making it out this morning.'

'You did grand,' Linxe said. 'When you get back, everyone will be very proud of you.'

'I hope so,' Rashmika said.

'I have to ask one thing, though,' Linxe said. 'You don't have to answer. Is this just about your brother, Rashmika? Or is there more to it than that?'

The question took Rashmika aback. 'Of course it's only about my brother.'

'It's just that you already have a bit of a reputation,' Linxe said. 'We've all heard about the amount of time you spend in the digs, and that book you're making. They say there isn't anyone else in the villages as interested in the scuttlers as Rashmika Els. They say you write letters to the church-sponsored archaeologists, arguing with them.'

'I can't help it if the scuttlers interest me,' she said.

'Yes, but what exactly is it you've got such a bee in your bonnet about?'

The question was phrased kindly, but Rashmika couldn't help sounding irritated when she said, 'I'm sorry?'

'I mean, what is it you think everyone else has got so terribly wrong?'

'Do you really want to know?'

'I'm as interested in hearing your side of the argument as anyone else's.'

'Except deep down you probably don't care who's right, do you? As long as stuff keeps coming out of the ground, what does anyone really care about what happened to the scuttlers? All you care about is getting spare parts for your icejammer.'

'Manners, young lady,' Linxe admonished.

'I'm sorry,' Rashmika said, blushing. She sipped on the hot chocolate. 'I didn't mean it like that. But I do care about the scuttlers and I do think no one is very interested in the truth of what really happened to them. Actually, it reminds me a lot of the Amarantin.'

Linxe looked at her. 'The what?'

'The Amarantin were the aliens who evolved on Resurgam. They were evolved birds.' She remembered drawing one of them for her book – not as a skeleton, but as they must have looked when they were alive. She had seen the Amarantin in her mind's eye: the bright gleam of an avian eye, the quizzical beaked smile of a sleek alien head. Her drawing had resembled nothing in the official reconstructions in the other archaeology texts, but it had always looked more authentically alive to her than those dead impressions, as if she had seen a living Amarantin and they had only had bones to go on. It made her wonder if her drawings of living scuttlers had the same vitality.

Rashmika continued, 'Something wiped them out a million years ago. When humans colonised Resurgam, no one wanted to consider the possibility that whatever had wiped out the Amarantin might come back to do the same to us. Except Dan Sylveste, of course.'

'Dan Sylveste?' Linxe asked. 'Sorry – also not ringing any bells.'

It infuriated Rashmika: how could she not know these things? But she tried not to let it show. 'Sylveste was the archaeologist in charge of the expedition. When he stumbled on the truth, the other colonists silenced him. They didn't want to know how much trouble they were in. But as we know, he turned out to be right in the end.'

'I bet you feel a little affinity with him, in that case.'

'More than a little,' Rashmika said.

Rashmika still remembered the first time she had come across his name. It had been a casual reference in one of the archaeological texts she had uploaded on to her compad, buried in some dull treatise about the Pattern Jugglers. It was like lightning shearing through her skull. Rashmika had felt an electrifying sense of connection, as if her whole life had been a prelude to that moment. It was, she now knew, the instant when her interest in the scuttlers shifted from a childish diversion to something closer to obsession.

She could not explain this, but nor could she deny that it had happened.

Since then, in parallel with her study of the scuttlers, she had learned much about the life and times of Dan Sylveste. It was logical enough: there was no sense in studying the scuttlers in isolation, since they were merely the latest in a line of extinct galactic cultures to be encountered by human explorers. Sylveste's name loomed large in the study of alien intelligence as a whole, so a passing knowledge of his exploits was essential.

Sylveste's work on the Amarantin had spanned many of the years between 2500 and 2570. During most of that time he had either been a patient investigator or under some degree of incarceration, but even while under house arrest his interest in the Amarantin had remained steady. But without access to resources beyond anything the colony could offer, his ideas were doomed to remain speculative. Then Ultras had arrived in the Resurgam system. With the help of their ship, Sylveste had unlocked the final piece of the puzzle in the mystery of the Amarantin. His suspicions had turned out to be correct: the Amarantin had not been wiped out by some isolated cosmic accident, but by a response from a still-active mechanism designed to suppress the emergence of starfaring intelligence.

It had taken years for the news to make it to other systems. By then it was second- or third-hand, tainted with propaganda, almost lost in the confusion of human factional warfare. Independently, it seemed, the Conjoiners had arrived at similar conclusions to Sylveste. And other archaeological groups, sifting through the remains of other dead cultures, were coming around to the same unsettling view.

The machines that had killed the Amarantin were still out there, waiting and watching. They went by many names. The Conjoiners had called them wolves. Other cultures, now extinct, had named them the Inhibitors.

Over the last century, the reality of the Inhibitors had come to be accepted. But for much of that time the threat had remained comfortably distant: a problem for some other generation to worry about.

Recently, however, things had changed. There had long been unconfirmed reports of strange activity in the Resurgam system: rumours of worlds being ripped apart and remade into perplexing engines of alien design. There were stories that the entire system had been evacuated; that Resurgam was now an uninhabitable cinder; that something unspeakable had been done to the system's sun.

But even Resurgam could be ignored for a while. The system was an archaeological colony, isolated from the main web of interstellar commerce, its government a totalitarian regime with a taste for disinformation. The reports of what had happened there could not be verified. And so for several more decades, life in the other systems of human-settled space continued more or less unaffected.

But now the Inhibitors had arrived around other stars.

The Ultras had been the first to bring the bad news. Communications between their ships warned them to steer clear of certain systems. *Something* was happening, something that transgressed the accepted scales of human catastrophe. This was not war or plague, but something infinitely worse. It had happened to the Amarantin and – presumably – to the scuttlers.

The number of human colonies known to have witnessed direct intervention by Inhibitor machines was still fewer than a dozen, but the ripples of panic spreading outwards at the speed of radio communications were almost as effective at collapsing civilisations. Entire surface communities were being evacuated or abandoned, as citizens tried to reach space or the hopefully safer shelter of underground caverns. Crypts and bunkers, disused since the dark decades of the Melding Plague, were hastily reopened. There were, invariably, too many people for either the evacuation ships or the bunkers. There were riots and furious little wars. Even as civilisation crumbled, those with an eye for the main chance accumulated small, useless fortunes. Doomsday cults flourished in the damp, inviting loam of fear, like so many black orchids. People spoke of End Times, convinced that they were living through the final days.

Against this background, it was hardly any wonder that so many people were drawn to Hela. In better times, Quaiche's miracle would have attracted little attention, but now a miracle was precisely what people were looking for. Every new Ultra ship arriving in the system brought tens of thousands of frozen pilgrims. Not all of them were looking for a religious answer, but before very long, if they wanted to stay on Hela, the Office of Bloodwork got to them anyway. Thereafter, they saw things differently.

Rashmika could not really blame them for coming to Hela. Had she not been born here, she sometimes thought she might well have made the same pilgrimage. But her motives would have been different. It was truth she was after: the same drive that had taken Dan Sylveste to Resurgam; the same drive that had brought him into conflict with his colony and which, ultimately, had led to his death.

She thought back to Linxe's question. Was it really Harbin driving her towards the Permanent Way, or was Harbin just the excuse she had made up to conceal – as much from herself as anyone else – the real reason for her journey?

Her reply that it was all to do with Harbin had been so automatic and flippant that she had almost believed it. But now she wondered whether it was really true. Rashmika could tell when anyone around her was lying. But seeing through her own deceptions was another matter entirely.

'It's Harbin,' she whispered to herself. 'Nothing else matters except finding my brother.'

But she could not stop thinking of the scuttlers, and when she dozed off with the mug of chocolate still clasped in her hands, it was the scuttlers that she dreamed of, the mad permutations of their insectile anatomy shuffling and reshuffling like the broken parts of a puzzle.

Rashmika snapped awake, feeling a rumble as the icejammer slowed, picking up undulations in the ice trail.

'I'm afraid this is as far as we can go tonight,' Crozet said. 'I'll find somewhere discreet to hide us away, but I'm near my limit.' He looked drawn and exhausted to Rashmika, but then again that was how Crozet always looked.

'Move over, love,' Linxe said to Crozet. 'I'll take us on for a couple of hours, just until we're safe and sound. You can both go back and catch forty winks.'

'I'm sure we're safe and sound,' Rashmika said.

'Never you mind about that. A few extra miles won't hurt us. Now go back and try to get yourself some sleep, young lady. We've another long day ahead of us tomorrow and I can't swear we'll be out of the woods even then.'

Linxe was already easing into the driver's position, running her thick babylike fingers over the icejammer's timeworn controls. Until Crozet had mentioned pulling over for the night, Rashmika had assumed that the machine would keep travelling using some kind of autopilot, even if it had to slow down a little while it guided itself. It was a genuine shock to learn that they would be going nowhere unless someone operated the icejammer manually.

'I can do a bit,' she offered. 'I've never driven one of these before, but if someone wants to show me ...'

'We'll do fine, love,' Linxe said. 'It's not just Crozet and me, either. Culver can do a shift in the morning.'

'I wouldn't want . . .'

'Oh, don't worry about Culver,' Crozet said. 'He needs something else to occupy his hands.'

Linxe slapped her husband, but she was smiling as she did it. Rashmika finished her now-cold chocolate drink, dog-tired but glad that she had at least made it through the first day. She was under no illusions that she was done with the worst of her journey, but she supposed that every successful stage had to be treated as a small victory in its own right. She just wished she could tell her parents not to worry about her, that she had made good progress so far and was thinking of them all the time. But she had vowed not to send a message home until she had joined the caravan.

Crozet walked her back through the rumbling innards of the icejammer. It moved differently under Linxe's direction. It was not that she was a worse or even a better driver than Crozet, but she definitely favoured a different driving style. The icejammer flounced, flinging itself through the air in long, weightless parabolic arcs. It was all quite conducive to sleep, but a sleep filled with uneasy dreams in which Rashmika found herself endlessly falling.

She woke the next morning to troubling and yet strangely welcome news.

'There's been an alert on the news service,' Crozet said. 'The word's gone out now, Rashmika. You're officially missing and there's a search operation in progress. Doesn't that make you feel proud?'

'Oh,' she said, wondering what could have happened since the night before.

'It's the constabulary,' Linxe said, meaning the law-enforcement organisation that had jurisdiction in the Vigrid region. 'They've sent out search parties, apparently. But there's a good chance we'll make the caravan before they find us. Once we get you on the caravan, the constabulary can't touch you.'

'I'm surprised they've actually sent out parties,' Rashmika said. 'It's not as if I'm in any danger, is it?'

'Actually, there's a bit more to it than that,' Crozet said.

Linxe looked at her husband.

What did the two of them know that Rashmika didn't? Suddenly she felt a tension in her belly, a line of cold trickling down her spine. 'Go on,' she said.

'They say they want to bring you back for questioning,' Linxe said.

'For running away from home? Haven't they got anything better to do with their time?'

'It's not for running away from home,' Linxe said. Again she glanced at Crozet. 'It's about that sabotage last week. You know the one I mean, don't you?'

'Yes,' Rashmika said, remembering the crater where the demolition store had been.

'They're saying you did it,' Crozet said.

Hela, 2615

Out of orbit now, Quaiche felt his weight increasing as the *Daughter* slowed down to only a few thousand kilometres per hour. Hela swelled, its hectic terrain rising up to meet him. The radar echo – the metallic signature – was still there. So was the bridge.

Quaiche had decided to spiral closer rather than making a concerted dash for the structure. Even on the first loop in, still thousands of kilometres above Hela's surface, what he had seen had been tantalising, like a puzzle he needed to assemble. From deep space the rift had been visible only as a change in albedo, a dark scar slicing across the world. Now it had palpable depth, especially when he examined it with the magnifying cameras. The gouge was irregular: there were places where there was a relatively shallow slope all the way down to the valley floor, but elsewhere the walls were vertical sheets of ice-covered rock towering kilometres high, as smooth and foreboding as granite. They had the grey sheen of wet slate. The floor of the rift varied between the flatness of a dry salt lake to a crazed, fractured quilt of tilted and interlocking ice panels separated by hair-thin avenues of pure sable blackness. The closer he came, the more it indeed resembled an unfinished puzzle, tossed aside by a god in a tantrum.

Once every minute or so he checked the radar. The echo was still there, and the *Daughter* had detected no signs of imminent attack. Perhaps it was just junk after all. The thought troubled him, for it meant someone else must have come this close to the bridge without finding it remarkable enough to report to anyone else. Or perhaps they had meant to report it, but some subsequent misfortune had befallen them. He wasn't sure that was any less worrying, on balance.

By the time he had completed the first loop he had reduced his speed to five hundred metres a second. He was close enough to the surface now to appreciate the texturing of the ground as it changed from jagged uplands to smooth plains. It was not all ice; most of the moon's interior was rocky, and a great deal of fractured rocky material was embedded in the ice, or lying upon it. Ash plumes radiated away from dormant volcanoes. There were slopes of fine talus and up-rearing sharp-sided boulders as big as major space habitats; some poked through the ice, tipped at absurd angles like the sterns of sinking ships; others sat on the surface, poised on one side in the manner of vast sculptural installations.

The *Daughter*'s thrusters burned continuously to support it against Hela's gravity. Quaiche fell lower, edging closer to the lip of the rift. Overhead, Haldora was a brooding dark sphere illuminated only along one limb. Amused and distracted for a moment, Quaiche saw lightning storms play across the gas giant's darkened face. The electrical arcs coiled and writhed with mesmerising slowness, like eels.

Hela was still catching starlight from the system's sun, but shortly its orbit around Haldora would take it into the larger world's shadow. It was fortuitous, Quaiche thought, that the source of the echo had been on this face of Hela, or else he would have been denied the impressive spectacle of the gas giant looming over everything. If he had arrived later in the world's rotation cycle, of course, the rift would have been pointing away from Haldora. A difference of one hundred and sixty days and he would have missed this amazing sight.

Another lightning flash. Reluctantly, Quaiche turned his attention back to Hela.

He was over the edge of Ginnungagap Rift. The ground tumbled away with unseemly haste. Even though the pull of gravity was only a quarter of a standard gee, Quaiche felt as much vertigo as he would have on a heavier world. It made perfect sense, for the drop was still fatally deep. Worse, there was no atmosphere to slow the descent of a falling object, no terminal velocity to create at least an outside chance of a survivable accident.

Never mind. The *Daughter* had never failed him, and he did not expect her to start now. He focused on the thing he had come to examine, and allowed the *Daughter* to sink lower, dropping below the zero-altitude surface datum.

He turned, vectoring along the length of the rift. He had drifted one or two kilometres out from the nearest wall, but the more distant one looked no closer than it had before he crossed the threshold. The spacing of the walls was irregular, but here at the equator the sides of the rift were never closer than thirty-five kilometres apart.

The rift was a minimum of five or six kilometres deep, pitching down to ten or eleven in the deepest, most convoluted parts of the valley floor. The feature was hellishly vast, and Quaiche came to the gradual conclusion that he did not actually like being in it very much. It was too much like hanging between the sprung jaws of a trap.

He checked the clock: four hours before the *Dominatrix* was due to emerge from the far side of Haldora. Four hours was a long time; he expected to be on his way back well before then.

'Hang on, Mor,' he said. 'Not long now.'

But of course she did not hear him.

He had entered the rift south of the equator and was now moving towards the northern hemisphere. The fractured mosaic of the floor oozed beneath him. Measured against the far wall, the motion of his ship was hardly apparent at all, but the nearer wall slid past quickly enough to give him some indication of his speed. Occasionally he lost his grasp of scale, and for a moment the rift would become much smaller. These were the dangerous moments, for it was usually when an alien landscape became familiar, homely and containable that it would reach out and kill you.

Suddenly he saw the bridge coming over the horizon between the pinning walls. His heart hammered in his chest. No doubt at all now, if ever there had been any: the bridge was a made thing, a confection of glistening thin threads. He wished Morwenna were here to see it as well.

He was recording all the while as the bridge came closer, looming kilometres above him: a curving arc connected to the walls of the rift at either end by a bewildering filigree of supporting scrollwork. There was no need to linger. Just one sweep under the span would be enough to convince Jasmina. They could come back later with heavy-duty equipment, if that was what she wished.

Quaiche looked up in wonder as he passed under the bridge. The roadbed – what else was he meant to call it? – bisected the face of Haldora, glowing slightly against the darkness of the gas giant. It was perilously thin, a ribbon of milky white. He wondered what it would be like to cross it on foot.

The *Daughter* swerved violently, the gee-force pushing red curtains into his vision.

'What . . .' Quaiche began.

But there was no need to ask: the *Daughter* was taking evasive action, doing exactly what she was meant to. Something was trying to attack him. Quaiche blacked out, hit consciousness again, blacked out once more. The landscape hurtled around him, pulsing bright light back at him, reflected from the *Daughter's* steering thrusters. Blackout again. Fleeting consciousness. There was a roaring in his ears. He saw the bridge from a series of abrupt, disconnected angles, like jumbled snapshots. Below it. Above it. Below it again. The *Daughter* was trying to find shelter.

This wasn't right. He should have been up and out, no questions asked. The *Daughter* was supposed to get him away from any possible threat as quickly as possible. This veering – this indecision – was not characteristic at all.

Unless she was cornered. Unless she couldn't *find* an escape route.

In a window of lucidity he saw the situational display on the console. Three hostile objects were firing at him. They had emerged from niches in the ice, three metallic echoes that had nothing to do with the first one he had seen.

The *Scavenger's Daughter* shook herself like a wet dog. Quaiche saw the exhaust plumes of his own miniature missiles whipping away, corkscrewing and zigzagging to avoid being shot down by the buried sentries. Blackout again. This time when he came around he saw a small avalanche oozing down one side of the cliff. One of the attacking objects was now offline: at least one of his missiles had found its mark.

The console flickered. The hull's opacity switched to absolute black. When the hull cleared and the console recovered he was looking at emergency warnings across the board, scribbled in fiery red Latinate script. It had been a bad hit.

Another shiver, another pack of missiles streaking away. They were tiny things, thumb-sized antimatter rockets with kilotonne yields.

Blackout again. A sensation of falling when he came round.

Another little avalanche; one fewer attacker on the display. One of the sentries was still out there, and he had no more ordnance to throw at it. But it wasn't firing. Perhaps it was damaged – or maybe just reloading.

The *Daughter* dithered, caught in a maelstrom of possibilities.

'Executive override,' Quaiche said. 'Get me out of here.'

The gee-force came hard and immediately. Again, curtains of red closed on his vision. But he did not black out this time. The ship was keeping the blood in his head, trying to preserve his consciousness for as long as possible.

He saw the landscape drop away below, saw the bridge from above.

Then something else hit him. The little ship stalled, thrust interrupted for a jaw-snapping instant. She struggled to regain power, but something – some vital propulsion subsystem – must have taken a serious hit.

The landscape hung motionless below him. Then it began to approach again.

He was going down.

Fade to black.

Quaiche fell obliquely towards the vertical wall of the rift, slipping in and out of consciousness. He assumed he was going to die, smeared across that sheer cliff face in an instant of glittering destruction, but at the last moment before impact, the *Scavenger's Daughter* used some final hoarded gasp of thrust to soften the crash.

It was still bad, even as the hull deformed to soften the blow. The wall wheeled around: now a cliff, now a horizon, now a flat plane pressing down from the sky. Quaiche blacked out, came to consciousness, blacked out again. He saw the bridge wheel around in the distance. Clouds of ice and rubble were still belching from the avalanche points in the sides of the cliff where his missiles had taken out the attacking sentries.

All the while, Quaiche and his tiny jewel of a ship tumbled towards the floor of the rift.

Ararat, 2675

Vasko followed Clavain and Scorpio into the administration compound, Blood escorting them through a maze of underpopulated rooms and corridors. Vasko expected to be turned back at any moment: his Security Arm clearance definitely did not extend to this kind of business. But although each security check was more stringent than the last, his presence was accepted. Vasko supposed it unlikely that anyone was going to argue with Scorpio and Clavain about their choice of guest.

Presently they arrived at a quarantine point deep within the compound, a medical centre housing several freshly made beds. Waiting for them in the quarantine centre was a sallow-faced human physician named Valensin. He wore enormous rhomboid-lensed spectacles; his thin black hair was glued back from his scalp in brilliant waves, and he carried a small scuffed bag of medical tools. Vasko had never met Valensin before, but as the highest-ranking physician on the planet, his name was familiar.

'How do you feel, Nevil?' Valensin asked.

'I feel like a man overstaying his welcome in history,' Clavain said.

'Never one for a straight answer, were you?' But even as he was speaking Valensin had whipped some silvery apparatus from his bag and was now shining it into Clavain's eyes, squinting through a little eyepiece of his own.

'We ran a medical on him during the shuttle flight,' Scorpio said. 'He's fit enough. You don't have to worry about him doing anything embarrassing like dropping dead on us.'

Valensin flicked the light off. 'And you, Scorpio? Any immediate plans of your own to drop dead?'

'Make your life a lot easier, wouldn't it?'

'Migraines?'

'Just getting one, as it happens.'

'I'll look you over later. I want to see if that peripheral vision of yours has deteriorated any faster than I was anticipating. All this running around really isn't good for a pig of your age.'

'Nice of you to remind me, particularly when I have no choice in the matter.'

'Always happy to oblige.' Valensin beamed, popping his equipment away. 'Now, let me make a couple of things clear. When that capsule opens, no one so much as *breathes* on the occupant until I've given them an extremely thorough examination. And by thorough, of course, I mean to the limited degree possible under the present conditions. I'll be looking for infectious agents. If I do find anything, and if I decide that it has even a remote chance of being unpleasant, then anyone who came into contact with the capsule can forget returning to First Camp, or wherever else they call home. And by unpleasant I'm not talking about genetically engineered viral weapons. I mean something as commonplace as influenza. Our antiviral programmes are already stretched to breaking point.'

'We understand,' Scorpio said.

Valensin led them into a huge room with a high domed ceiling of skeletal metal. The room smelt aggressively sterile. It was almost completely empty, save for an intimate gathering of people and machines near the middle. Half a dozen white-clad workers were fussing over ramshackle towers of monitoring equipment.

The capsule itself was suspended from the ceiling, hanging on a thin metal line like a plumb bob. The scorched-black egg-shaped thing was much smaller than Vasko had been expecting: it almost looked too small to hold a person. Though there were no windows, several panels had been folded back to reveal luminous displays. Vasko saw numbers, wobbling traces and trembling histograms.

'Let me see it,' Clavain said, pushing through the workers to get closer to the capsule.

At this intrusion, one of the workers surrounding the capsule made the mistake of frowning in Scorpio's direction. Scorpio glared back at him, flashing the fierce curved incisors that marked his ancestry. At the same moment Blood signalled to the workers with a quick lateral stab of his trotter. Obediently they filed away, vanishing back into the depths of the compound.

Clavain gave no sign that he had even noticed the commotion. Still hooded and anonymous, he slipped between the obstructions and moved to one side of the capsule. Very gently he placed a hand near one of the illuminated panels, caressing the scorched matt hide of the capsule.

Vasko guessed it was safe to stare now.

Scorpio looked sceptical. 'Getting anything?'

'Yes,' Clavain said. 'It's talking to me. The protocols are Conjoiner.'

'Certain of that?' asked Blood.

Clavain turned away from the machine, only the fine beard hairs on his jaw catching the light. 'Yes,' he said.

Now he placed his other hand on the opposite side of the panel, bracing himself, and lowered his head until it lay against the capsule. Vasko imagined that the old man's eyes would be shut, blocking off outward distraction, concentration clawing grooves into his forehead. No one was saying anything, and Vasko realised that he was even making an effort not to breathe loudly.

Clavain tilted his head this way and that, slowly and deliberately, in the manner of someone trying to find the optimum orientation for a radio antenna. He locked at one angle, his frame tensing through the fabric of the coat.

'Definitely Conjoiner protocols,' Clavain said. He remained silent and perfectly still for at least another minute, before adding, 'I think it recognises me as another Conjoiner. It's not allowing me complete system access – not yet, anyway – but it's letting me query certain low-level diagnostic functions. It certainly doesn't *look* like a bomb.'

'Be very, very careful,' Scorpio said. 'We don't want you being taken over, or something worse.'

'I'm doing my best,' Clavain said.

'How soon can you tell who's in it?' Blood asked.

'I won't know for sure until it cracks open,' Clavain said, his voice low but cutting through everything else with quiet authority. 'I'll tell you this now, though: I don't think it's Skade.'

'You're absolutely sure it's Conjoiner?' Blood insisted.

'It is. And I'm fairly certain some of the signals I'm picking up are coming from the occupant's implants, not just from the capsule itself. But it can't be Skade: she'd be ashamed to have anything to do with protocols this old.' He pulled his head away from the capsule and looked back at the company. 'It's Remontoire. It has to be.'

'Can you make any sense of his thoughts?' Scorpio asked.

'No, but the neural signals I'm getting are at a very low level, just routine housekeeping stuff. Whoever's inside this is probably still unconscious.'

'Or not a Conjoiner,' Blood said.

'We'll know in a few hours,' Scorpio said. 'But whoever it is, there's still the problem of a missing ship.'

'Why is that a problem?' Vasko asked.

'Because whoever it is didn't travel twenty light-years in that capsule,' Blood said.

'But couldn't he have come into the system quietly, parked his ship somewhere we wouldn't see it and then crossed the remaining distance in the capsule?' Vasko suggested.

Blood shook his head. 'He'd still have needed an in-system ship to make the final crossing to our planet.'

'But we could have missed a small ship,' Vasko said. 'Couldn't we?'

'I don't think so,' Clavain said. 'Not unless there have been some very unwelcome developments.'

NINE

Hela Surface, 2615

Quaiche came around, upside down. He was still. Everything, in fact, was immensely still: the ship, the landscape, the sky. It was as if he had been planted here centuries ago and had only just opened his eyes.

But he did not think he could have been out for long: his memories of the terrifying attack and the dizzying fall were very clear. The wonder of it, really, was not that he remembered those events, but that he was alive at all.

Moving very gently in his restraints, he tried to survey the damage. The tiny ship creaked around him. At the limit of his vision, as far as he could twist his neck (which seemed not to be broken), he saw dust and ice still settling from one of the avalanche plumes. Everything was blurred, as if seen through a thin grey veil. The plume was the only thing moving, and it confirmed to him that he could not have been under for more than a few minutes. He could also see one end of the bridge, the marvellous eye-tricking complexity of scrolls supporting the gently curving roadbed. There had been a moment of anxiety, as he watched his ordnance rip away, when he had worried about destroying the thing that had brought him here. The bridge was huge, but it also looked as delicate as tissue paper. But there was no evidence that he had inflicted any damage. The thing must be stronger than it looked.

The ship creaked again. Quaiche could not see the ground with any clarity. The ship had come to rest upside down, but had it really reached the bottom of Ginnungagap Rift?

He looked at the console but couldn't focus on it properly. Couldn't – now that he paid attention to the fact – focus on much at all. It was not so bad if he closed his left eye. The gee-force might have knocked a retina loose, he speculated. It was precisely that kind of fixable damage that the *Daughter* was prepared to inflict in the interests of bringing him back alive.

With his right eye open he appraised the console. There was a lot of red there – Latinate script proclaiming systems defects – but also many blank areas where there should have been something. The *Daughter* had clearly sustained heavy damage, he realised: not just mechanical, but also to the cybernetic core of her avionics suite. The ship was in a coma.

He tried speaking. 'Executive override. Reboot.'

Nothing happened. Voice recognition might be one of the lost faculties. Either that or the ship was as alive as she was ever going to be.

He tried again, just to be on the safe side. 'Executive override. Reboot.'

But still nothing happened. *Close down that line of enquiry*, he thought.

He moved again, shifting an arm until his hand came into contact with one of the tactile control clusters. There was discomfort as he moved, but it was mostly the diffuse pain of heavy bruising rather than the sharpness of broken or dislocated limbs. He could even shift his legs without too much unpleasantness. A screaming jag of pain in his chest didn't bode well for his ribs, however, but his breathing seemed normal enough and there were no odd sensations anywhere else in his chest or abdomen. If a few cracked ribs and a detached retina were all he had suffered, he had done rather well.

'You always were a jammy sod,' he said to himself as his fingers groped around the many stubs and stalks of the tactile control cluster. Every voice command had a manual equivalent; it was just a question of remembering the right combinations of movements.

He had it. Finger there, thumb there. Squeeze. Squeeze again.

The ship coughed. Red script flickered momentarily into view where there had been nothing a moment before.

Getting somewhere. There was still juice in the old girl. He tried again. The ship coughed and hummed, trying to reboot herself. Flicker of red, then nothing.

'Come on,' Quaiche said through gritted teeth.

He tried again. Third time lucky? The ship spluttered, seemed to shiver. The red script appeared again, faded, then came back. Other parts of the display changed: the ship explored her own functionality as she came out of the coma.

'Nice one,' Quaiche said as the ship squirmed, reshaping her hull – probably not intentional, just some reflex adjustment back to the default profile. Rubble sputtered against the armour, dislodged in the process. The ship pitched several degrees, Quaiche's view shifting.

'Careful . . .' he said.

It was too late. The *Scavenger's Daughter* had begun to roll, keeling off the ledge where it had come to temporary rest. Quaiche had a glimpse of the floor, still a good hundred metres below, and then it was coming up to meet him, fast.

Subjective time stretched the fall to an eternity.

Then he hit the deck; although he didn't black out, the tumbling series of impacts felt as if something had him in its jaws and was whacking him against the ground until he either snapped or died.

He groaned. This time it seemed unlikely that he was going to get away so lightly. There was heavy pressure on his chest, as if someone had placed an anvil there. The cracked ribs had given in, most likely. That was going to hurt when he had to move. He was still alive, though. And this time the *Daughter* had landed right-way-up. He could see the bridge again, framed like a scene in a tourist brochure. It was as if Fate were rubbing it in, reminding him of just what it was that had got him into this mess in the first place.

Most of the red parts on the console had gone out again. He could see the reflection of his own stunned-looking face hovering behind the fragmented Latinate script, deep shadows cutting into his cheeks and eye sockets. He had seen a similar image, once: the face of some religious figure burned into the fabric of an embalming shroud. Just a sketch of a face, like something done in thick strokes of charcoal.

The indoctrinal virus grumbled in his blood.

'Reboot,' he said, spitting crunched tooth.

There was no response. Quaiche groped for the tactile input cluster, found the same sequence of commands, applied them. Nothing happened. He tried again, knowing that this was his only option. There was no other way to awaken the ship without a full diagnostic harness.

The console flickered. Something *was* still alive; there was still a chance. As he kept on applying the wake-up command, a few more systems returned from sleep each time, until, after eight or nine tries, there was no further improvement. He didn't want to continue for fear of draining the remaining avionics power reserves, or stressing the systems that were already alive. He would just have to make do with what he had.

Closing his left eye, he scanned the red messages: a cursory glance told him that the *Scavenger's Daughter* was going nowhere in a hurry. Critical flight systems had been destroyed in the attack, secondaries smashed during the collision with the wall and the long tumble to the ground. His beautiful, precious gem of a private spacecraft was ruined. Even the self-repair mechanisms would have a hard time fixing her now, even if he had months to wait while they worked. But he supposed he should be grateful that the *Daughter* had kept him alive. In that sense she had not failed him.

He examined the read-outs again. The *Daughter's* automated distress beacon was working. Its range would be restricted by the walls of ice on either side, but there was nothing to obstruct the signal from reaching upwards – except, of course, the gas giant he had positioned between himself and Morwenna. How long was it until she would emerge from the sunlit side of Haldora?

He checked the ship's one working chronometer. Four hours until the *Dominatrix* would emerge from behind Haldora.

Four hours. That was all right. He could last that long. The *Dominatrix* would pick up the distress signal as soon as she came out from behind Haldora, and would then need an hour or so to get down to him. Ordinarily he would never have risked bringing the other ship so close to a potentially dangerous site, but he had no choice. Besides, he doubted that the booby-trap sentries were anything to worry about now: he had destroyed two of three and the third looked to have run out of power; it would surely have taken another pot shot at him by now if it had the means.

Four hours, plus another one to reach him: five in total. That was all it would take until he was safe and sound. He would sooner have been out of the mess right now, this instant, but he could hardly complain, especially not after telling Morwenna that she had to endure six hours away from him. And that business about not sewing the relay satellites? He had to admit to himself now that he had been thinking less about Morwenna's safety and more about not wanting to waste any time. Well, he was getting a dose of his own medicine now, wasn't he? Better take it like a man.

Five hours. Nothing. *Piece of piss.*

Then he noticed one of the other read-outs. He blinked, opened both eyes, hoping that it was some fault of his vision. But there was no mistake.

The hull was breached. The flaw must be tiny: a hairline crack. Ordinarily, it would have been sealed without him knowing about it, but with so much damage to the ship, the normal repair systems were inoperable. Slowly – slowly enough that he had yet to feel it – he was losing air pressure. The *Daughter* was doing her best to top up the supply with the pressurised reserves, but it could not continue this indefinitely.

Quaiche did the sums. Time to exhaustion: two hours.

He wasn't going to make it.

Did it make any difference whether or not he panicked? He mulled this over, feeling that it was important to know. It was not simply the case that he was stuck in a sealed room with a finite amount of oxygen slowly being replaced by the carbon dioxide of his exhalations. The air was whistling out through a crack in the hull, and the leak was going to continue no matter how quickly he used up the oxygen by breathing. Even if he only drew one breath in the next two hours, there would still be no air left when he came to take the next. It wasn't depleting oxygen that was his problem, it was escaping atmosphere. In two hours he would be sucking on good hard vacuum, the kind some people paid money for. They said it hurt, for the first few seconds. But for him the transition to airlessness would be gradual. He would be unconscious – more than likely dead – long before then. Perhaps within the next ninety minutes.

But it probably wouldn't hurt *not* to panic, would it? It might make a slight difference, depending on the details of the leak. If the air was being lost as it made its way through the recycling system, then it would certainly help matters if he used it as slowly as possible. Not knowing where the crack was, he might as well assume that panic would make a difference to his life expectancy. Two hours might stretch to three ... three to four if he was really lucky and prepared to tolerate a bit of brain damage. Four might, just might, stretch to five.

He was kidding himself. He had two hours. Two and a half at the absolute limit. *Panic all you like*, he told himself. It was not going to make a shred of difference.

The virus tasted his fear. It gulped it up, feeding on it. It had been simmering until now, but as he tried to hold the panic at bay it rose in him, crushing rational thought.

'No,' Quaiche said, 'I don't need you now.'

But maybe he did. What good was clarity of mind if there was nothing he could do to save himself? At least the virus would let him die with the illusion that he was in the presence of something larger than himself, something that cared for him and was there to watch over him as he faded away.

But the virus simply did not care either way. It was going to flood him with immanence whether he liked it or not. There was no sound save his own breathing and the occasional patter of icy scree still raining down on him, dislodged from the high sides of the rift during his descent. There was nothing to look at except the bridge. But in the silence, distantly, he heard organ music. It was quiet now, but coming nearer, and he knew that when it reached its awesome crescendo it would fill his soul with joy and terror. And though the bridge looked much the way it had before, he could see the beginnings of stained-glass glories in the black sky beyond it, squares and rectangles and lozenges of pastel light starting to shine through the darkness, like windows into something vaster and more glorious.

'No,' Quaiche said, but this time without conviction.

An hour passed. Systems gave up the ghost, portions of the red script dropping off the console. Nothing that failed was going to make much difference to Quaiche's chances of survival. The ship was not going to put him out of his misery by blowing up, however painless and immediate that might have been. No, Quaiche thought: the *Scavenger's Daughter* would do all in her power to keep him alive until that last ragged breath. The sheer futility of the exercise was completely wasted on the machine. She was still sending out that distress signal, even though he would be two or three hours dead by the time the *Dominatrix* received it.

He laughed: gallows humour. He had always thought of the *Daughter* as a supremely intelligent machine. By the standards of most spacecraft – certainly anything that did not already have at least a gamma-level subpersona running it – that was probably the case. But when you boiled it down to essentials she was still a bit on the dim side.

'Sorry, ship,' he said. And laughed again, except this time the laughing segued into a series of self-pitying sobs.

The virus was not helping. He had hoped that it would, but the feelings it brought were too superficial. When he most needed their succour he could feel them for the paper-thin façades they were. Just because the virus was tickling the parts of his brain that produced feelings of religious experience didn't mean he was able to turn off the other parts of his mind that recognised these feelings as having been induced artificially. He truly felt himself to be in the presence of something sacred, but he also knew, with total clarity, that this was due to neuroanatomy. Nothing was really with him: the organ music, the stained-glass windows in the sky, the sense of proximity to something huge and timeless and infinitely compassionate were all explicable in terms of neural wiring, firing potentials, synaptic gaps.

In his moment of greatest need, when he most desired that comfort, it had deserted him. He was just a Godless man with a botched virus in his blood, running out of air, running out of time, on a world to which he had given a name that would soon be forgotten.

'I'm sorry, Mor,' he said. 'I screwed up. I really fucking screwed up.'

He thought of her, so distant from him, so unreachable ... and then he remembered the glass-blower.

He hadn't thought about the man for a long time, but then again it had been a long time since he had felt this alone. What was his name? Trollhattan, that was it. Quaiche had encountered him in one of the migrogravitic commercial atria of Pygmalion, one of Parsifal's moons, around Tau Ceti.

There had been a glass-blowing demonstration. The free-fall artisan Trollhattan had been an ancient Skyjack defector with plug-in limbs and a face with skin like cured elephant hide, cratered with the holes where radiation-strike melanomas had been inexpertly removed. Trollhattan made fabulous glass constructs: lacy, room-filling things, some of them so delicate that they could not withstand even the mild gravity of a major moon. The constructs were always different. There were three-dimensional glass orreries that stressed the eye with their aching fineness. There were flocks of glass birds, thousands of them, linked together by the tiniest mutual contact of wingtip against wingtip. There were shoals of a thousand fish, the glass of each fish shot through with the subtlest of colours, yellows and blues, the rose-tipped fins of a heartbreaking translucence. There were squadrons of angels, skirmishes of galleons from the age of fighting sail, fanciful reproductions of major space battles. There were creations that were almost painful to look at, as if by the very act of observation one might subtly unbalance the play of light and shade across them, causing some tiny latent crack to widen to the point where the structure became unsustainable. Once, an entire Trollhattan glasswork had indeed spontaneously exploded during its public unveiling, leaving no shard larger than a beetle. No one had ever been sure whether that had been part of the intended effect.

What everyone agreed on was that Trollhattan artefacts were expensive. They were not cheap to buy in the first place, but the export costs were a joke. Just getting one of the things off Pygmalion would bankrupt a modest Demarchist state. They could be buffered in smart packing to tolerate modest accelerations, but every attempt to ship a Trollhattan artefact between solar systems had resulted in a lot of broken glass. All surviving works were still in the Tau Ceti system. Entire families had relocated to Parsifal just to be able to possess and show off their own Trollhattan creation.

It was said that somewhere in interstellar space, a slow-moving automated barge carried hundreds of the artefacts, crawling towards another system (which one depended on which story you listened to) at a few per cent of light-speed, fulfilling a commission placed decades earlier. It was also said that whoever had the wit to intercept and pirate that barge – without shattering the Trollhattan artefacts – would be wealthy beyond the bounds of decency. In an era in which practically anything with a blueprint could be manufactured at negligible cost, handmade artefacts with watertight provenance were amongst the few 'valuable' things left.

Quaiche had considered dabbling in the Trollhattan market during his stay on Parsifal. He had even, briefly, hooked up with an artisan who believed he could produce high-quality fakes using miniature servitors to chew away an entire room-sized block of glass. Quaiche had seen the dry-runs: they were good, but not *that* good. There was something about the prismatic quality of a real Trollhattan that nothing else in the universe quite matched. It was like the difference between ice and diamond. In any case, the provenance part had been the killer. Unless someone killed off Trollhattan, there was no way the market would swallow the fakes.

Quaiche had been sniffing around Trollhattan when he saw the demonstration. He had wanted to see if there was any dirt he could use on the glass-blower, anything that might make him open to negotiation. If Trollhattan could be persuaded to turn a blind eye when the fakes started hitting the market – saying he didn't exactly remember making them, but didn't exactly remember *not* making them either – then there might still be some mileage to be had out of the scam.

But Trollhattan had been untouchable. He never said anything and he never moved in the usual artists' circles.

He just blew glass.

Dismayed, his enthusiasm for the whole thing waning in any case, Quaiche had lingered long enough to watch part of the demonstration. His cold, dispassionate interest in the practical matter of the value of Trollhattan's art had quickly given way to awe at what was actually involved.

Trollhattan's demonstration involved only a small work, not one of the room-filling creations. When Quaiche arrived, the man had already crafted a wonderfully intricate free-floating plant, a thing of translucent green stem and leaves with many horn-shaped flowers in pale ruby; now Trollhattan was fashioning an exquisite shimmering blue thing next to one of the flowers. Quaiche did not immediately recognise the shape, but when Trollhattan began to draw out the incredibly fine curve of a beak towards the flower, Quaiche saw the hummingbird. The arc of amber tapered to its point a finger's width from the flower, and Quaiche imagined that this would be it, that the bird and the plant would float next to one another without being connected. But then the angle of the light shifted and he realised that between the tip of the beak and the stigma of the plant was the finest possible line of blown glass, a crack of gold like the last filament of daylight in a planetary sunset, and that what he was seeing was the tongue of the hummingbird, blown in glass.

The effect had surely been deliberate, for the other onlookers noticed the tongue at more or less the same moment. No suggestion of emotion flickered on the parts of Trollhattan's face still nominally capable of registering it.

In that moment, Quaiche despised the glass-blower. He despised the vanity of his genius, judging that studied and total absence of emotion to be as reprehensible as any display of pride. Yet he also felt a vast upwelling of admiration for the trick he had just seen performed. How would it feel, Quaiche wondered, to import a glimpse of the miraculous into everyday life? Trollhattan's spectators lived in an age of miracles and wonders. Yet that glimpse of the hummingbird's tongue had clearly been the most surprising and wonderful thing any of them had seen in a long time.

It was certainly true for Quaiche. A sliver of glass had moved him to the core, when he was least expecting it.

He thought now of the hummingbird's tongue. Whenever he was forced to leave Morwenna, he always imagined a thread of stretching molten glass, tinged with gold and spun out to the exquisite thinness of the hummingbird's tongue, connecting himself to her. As the distance increased, so did the thinness and inherent fragility of the tongue. But as long as he was able to hold that image in mind, and consider himself still linked to her, his isolation did not seem total. He could still feel her through the glass, the tremors of her breathing racing along the thread.

But the thread seemed thinner and frailer now than he had ever imagined it, and he didn't think he could feel her breathing at all.

He checked the time: another half-hour had passed. Optimistically, he could not have much more than thirty or forty minutes of air left. Was it his imagination or had the air already begun to taste stale and thin?

Hela, 2727

Rashmika saw the caravan before the others did. It was half a kilo-metre ahead, merging on to the same track they were following, but still half-hidden by a low series of icy bluffs. It appeared to move very slowly compared to Crozet's vehicle, but as they got closer she realised that this was not true: the vehicles of the caravan were much larger, and it was only this size that made their progress seem at all ponderous.

The caravan was a string of perhaps four dozen machines stretch-ing along nearly a quarter of a kilometre of the trail. They moved in two closely spaced columns, almost nose-to-tail, with no more than a metre or two between the back of each vehicle and the front of the one behind it. In Rashmika's estimation, no two of them were exactly alike, although in a few cases it was possible to see that the vehicles must have started off identically, before being added to, chopped about or generally abused by their owners. Their upper structures were a haphazard confusion of jutting additions buttressed with scaffolding. Symbols of ecclesiastical affiliation had been sprayed on wherever possible, often in complicated chains denoting the shifting allegiances between the major churches. On the rooftops of many of the caravan machines were enormous tilted surfaces, all canted at the same precise angle by gleaming pistons. Vapour puffed from hundreds of exhaust apertures.

The majority of the caravan vehicles moved on wheels as tall as houses, six or eight under each machine. A few others moved on plodding caterpillar tracks, or multiple sets of jointed walking limbs. A couple of the vehicles used the same kind of rhythmic skiing motion as Crozet's icejammer. One machine moved like a slug, inching itself along via propulsive waves of its segmented mechanical body. She had no idea at all how a couple of them were propelled. But regardless of their mismatched designs, all the machines were able to keep exact pace with each other. The entire ensemble moved with such co-ordinated precision that there were walkways and tunnels thrown across the gaps between them. They creaked and flexed as the distances varied by fractions of a metre, but were never broken or crushed.

Crozet steered his icejammer alongside the caravan, using what remained of the trail, and inched forwards. The rumbling wheels towered above the little vehicle. Rashmika watched Crozet's hands on the controls with a degree of unease. All it would take would be a slip of the wrist, a moment's inattention, and they would be crushed under those wheels. But Crozet looked calm enough, as if he had done this kind of thing hundreds of times before.

'What are you looking for?' Rashmika asked.

'The king vehicle,' Crozet said quietly. 'The reception point – the place where the caravan does business. It's normally somewhere near the front. This is a pretty big lash-up, though. Haven't seen one like this for a few years.'

'I'm impressed,' Rashmika said, looking up at the moving edifice of machinery towering above the little jammer.

'Well, don't be too impressed,' Crozet said. 'A cathedral – a proper cathedral – is a bit bigger than this. They move slower, but they don't stop either. They can't, not easily. Like stopping a glacier. Near one of those mothers, even I get a bit twitchy. Wouldn't be half so bad if they didn't move ...'

'There's the king,' Linxe said, pointing through the gap in the first column. 'Other side, dear. You'll have to loop around.'

'Fuck. This is the bit I really don't like.'

'Play it safe and come up from the rear.'

'Nah.' Crozet flashed an arc of dreadful teeth. 'Got to show some bloody balls, haven't I?'

Rashmika felt her seat kick into the back of her spine as Crozet applied full power. The column slid past as they overtook the vehicles one by one. They were moving faster, but not by very much. Rashmika had expected the caravan to move silently, the way most things did on Hela. She couldn't exactly hear it, but she felt it – a rumble below audible sound, a chorus of sonic components reaching her through the ice, through the ski blades, through the complicated suspension systems of the icejammer. There was the steady rumble of the wheels, like a million booted feet being stamped in impatience. There was the *thud, thud, thud*, as each plate of the caterpillar tracks slammed into ice. There was the scrabble of picklike mechanical feet struggling for traction against frosty ground. There was the low, groaning scrape of the segmented machine, and a dozen other noises she couldn't isolate. Behind it all, like a series of organ notes, Rashmika heard the labour of countless engines.

Crozet's icejammer had gained some distance from the leading pair of machines, which had dropped back behind them by perhaps twice their own length. Batteries of floodlights shone ahead of the caravan, bathing Crozet's vehicle in harsh blue radiance. Rashmika saw tiny figures moving behind windows, and even on the top of the machines themselves, leaning against railings. They wore pressure suits marked with religious iconography.

The caravans were a fact of life on Hela, but Rashmika admitted to only scant knowledge of how they operated. She knew the basics, though. The caravans were the mobile agents of the great churches, the bodies that ran the cathedrals. Of course, the cathedrals moved – slowly, as Crozet had said – but they were almost always confined to the equatorial belt of the Permanent Way. They sometimes deviated from the Way, but never this far north or south.

The all-terrain caravans, however, could travel more freely. They had the speed to make journeys far from the Way and yet still catch up with their mother cathedrals on the same revolution. They split up and re-formed as they moved, sending out smaller expeditions and merging with others for parts of their journeys. Often, a single caravan might represent three or four different churches, churches that might have fundamentally different views on the matter of the Quaiche miracle and its interpretation. But all the churches shared common needs for labourers and component parts. They *all* needed recruits.

Crozet steered the icejammer into the central part of the path, immediately ahead of the convoy. They had encountered a slight upgrade now, and the slope was causing the icejammer to lose its advantage of speed compared to the caravan, which merely rolled on, oblivious to the change in level.

'Be careful now,' Linxe said.

Crozet flicked his control sticks and the rear of the icejammer swung to the other side of the procession. The nose followed, and with a thud the skis settled into older grooves in the ice. The gradient had sharpened even more, but that was all right now – Crozet no longer needed to keep ahead of the caravan. Slowly, therefore, but with the unstoppable momentum of land sliding past a ship, the lead machines caught up with them.

'That's the king, all right,' Crozet said. 'Looks like they're ready for us, too.'

Rashmika had no idea what he meant, but as they drew alongside, she saw a pair of skeletal cranes swinging out from the roof, dropping metal hooks. A jaunty pair of suited figures rode down on the cable lines, one standing on each hook. Then they passed out of view, and nothing happened for several further seconds until she heard heavy footsteps stomping around somewhere on the roof of the jammer. Then she heard the clunk of metal against metal, and a moment later the motion of the icejammer was dreamily absent. They were being winched off the ice, suspended to one side of the caravan.

'Cheeky sods do it every time,' Crozet said. 'But there's no point arguing with 'em. You either take it or leave it.'

'At least we can get off and stretch our legs for a bit,' Linxe said.

'Are we on the caravan now?' Rashmika asked. 'Officially, I mean?'

'We're on it,' Crozet said.

Rashmika nodded, relieved that they were now out of reach of the Vigrid constabulary. There had been no sign of the investigators, but in her mind's eye they had only ever been one or two bends behind Crozet's icejammer.

She still did not know what to make of the business of the constabulary. She had expected some fuss to be made if the authorities discovered she had run away. But beyond a request for people to keep a lookout for her – and to return her to the badlands if they found her – she had not expected any active efforts to be made to bring her back. It was worse than that, of course, since the constabulary had got it into their heads that she'd had something to do with the explosion in the demolition store. She guessed they were assuming that she was running away because she had done it, out of fear at being found out. They were wrong, of course, but in the absence of a better suspect she had no obvious defence.

Crozet and Linxe, thankfully, had given her the benefit of the doubt: either that or they just didn't care what she might have done. But she had still been worried about a constabulary roadblock bringing the icejammer to a halt before they reached the caravan.

Now she could stop worrying – about that, at least.

It only took a minute for a docking arrangement to be set up. Crozet appeared to have precious little say in the matter, for without him doing anything that Rashmika was aware of, the air in the vehicle gusted, making her ears pop slightly. Then she heard footsteps coming aboard.

'They like you to know who's boss,' Crozet told her, as if this needed explaining. 'But don't be afraid of anyone here, Rashmika. They put on a show of strength, but they still need us badlanders.'

'Don't worry about me,' Rashmika told him.

A man bustled into the cabin as if he had left on some minor errand only a minute earlier. His wide froglike face had a meaty complexion, the bridge of skin between the base of his flat nub of a nose and the top of his mouth glistening with something unpleasant. He wore a long-hemmed coat of thick purple fabric, the collars and cuffs generously puffed. A lopsided beret marked with a tiny intricate sigil sat lopsidedly on the red froth of his hair, while his fingers were encumbered by many ornate rings. He carried a compad in one hand, its read-out screen scrolling through columns of numbers in antique script. There was, Rashmika noticed, a kind of construction perched on his right shoulder, a jointed thing of bright green columns and tubes. She had no idea of its function, whether it was an ornament or some arcane medical accessory.

'Mr Crozet,' the man said by way of welcome. 'What an unexpected surprise. I really didn't think you were going to make it this time.'

Crozet shrugged. Rashmika could tell he was doing his best to look nonchalant and unconcerned, but the act needed some work. 'Can't keep a good man down, Quaestor.'

'Perhaps not.' The man glanced at the screen, pursing his lips in the manner of someone sucking on a lemon. 'You have, however, left things a tiny bit late in the day. Pickings are slim, Crozet. I trust you will not be too disappointed.'

'My life is a series of disappointments, Quaestor. I think I've probably got used to it by now.'

'One devoutly hopes that is the case. We must all of us know our station in life, Crozet.'

'I certainly know mine, Quaestor.' Crozet did something to the control panel, presumably powering down the icejammer. 'Well, are you open for business or not? You've really been working hard to polish that lukewarm welcome routine.'

The man smiled very thinly. 'This is hospitality, Crozet. A lukewarm welcome would have involved leaving you on the ice, or running you over.'

'I'd best count my blessings, then.'

'Who are you?' Rashmika asked suddenly, surprising herself.

'This is Quaestor . . .' Linxe said, before she was cut off.

'Quaestor Rutland Jones,' the man interrupted, his tone actorly, as if playing to the gallery. 'Master of Auxiliary Supplies, Superintendent of Caravans and other Mobile Units, Roving Legate of the First Adventist Church. And you'd be?'

'The First Adventists?' she asked, just to make sure she had heard him properly. There were many offshoots of the First Adventists, a number of them rather large and influential churches in their own right, and some of them had names so similar that it was easy to get them confused. But the First Adventist Church was the one she was interested in. She added, 'As in the oldest church, the one that goes all the way back?'

'Unless I am very mistaken about my employer, yes. I still don't believe you have answered my question, however.'

'Rashmika,' she said, 'Rashmika Els.'

'Els.' The man chewed on the syllable. 'Quite a common name in the villages of the Vigrid badlands, I believe. But I don't think I've ever encountered an Els this far south.'

'You might have, once,' Rashmika said. But that was a little unfair: though the caravan her brother had travelled on had also been affiliated to the Adventists, it was unlikely that it had been this one.

'I'd remember, I think.'

'Rashmika is travelling with us,' Linxe said. 'Rashmika is ... a clever girl. Aren't you, dear?'

'I get by,' Rashmika said.

'She thought she might find a role in the churches,' Linxe said. She licked her fingers and neatened the hair covering her birthmark.

He put down the compad. 'A role?'

'Something technical,' Rashmika said. She had rehearsed this encounter a dozen times, always in her imagination having the upper hand, but it was all happening too quickly and not the way she had hoped.

'We can always use keen young girls,' the quaestor said. He was digging in a chest pocket for something. 'And boys, for that matter. It would depend on your talents.'

'I have no *talents*,' Rashmika said, transforming the word into an obscenity. 'But I happen to be literate and numerate. I can program most marques of servitor. I know a great deal about the study of the scuttlers. I have ideas about their extinction. Surely that can be of use to someone in the church.'

'She wonders if she couldn't find a position in one of the church-sponsored archaeological study groups,' Linxe said.

'Is that so?' the quaestor asked.

Rashmika nodded. As far as she was concerned, the church-sponsored study groups were a joke, existing only to rubber-stamp current Quaicheist doctrine regarding the scuttlers; but she had to start somewhere. Her real goal was to reach Harbin, not to advance her study of the scuttlers. However, it would be much easier to find him if she began her service in a clerical position – such as one of the study groups – rather than with lowly work like Way repair.

'I think I could be of value,' she said.

'Knowing a great deal about the study of a subject is not the same as knowing anything about the subject itself,' the quaestor told her with a sympathetic smile. He pulled his hand from his breast pocket, a small pinch of seeds between forefinger and thumb. The jointed green thing on his shoulder stirred, moving with a curious stiffness that reminded Rashmika of something inflated, like a balloon-creature. It *was* an animal, but unlike any that Rashmika – in her admittedly limited experience – remembered seeing. She saw now that at one end of its thickest tube was a turretlike head, with faceted eyes and a delicate, mechanical-looking mouth. The quaestor offered his fingers to the creature, pursing his lips in encouragement. The creature stretched itself down his arm and attacked the pinch of seeds with a nibbling politeness. What was it? she wondered. The body and limbs were insectile, but the elongated coil of its tail, which was wrapped around the quaestor's upper arm several times, was more suggestive of a reptile. And there was something uniquely birdlike about the way it ate. She remembered birds from somewhere, brilliant crested strutting things of cobalt blue with tails that opened like fans. Peacocks. But where had she ever seen peacocks?

The quaestor smiled at his pet. 'Doubtless you have read many books,' he said, looking sidelong at Rashmika. 'That is to be applauded.'

She looked at the animal warily. 'I grew up in the digs, Quaestor. I've helped with the excavation work. I've breathed scuttler dust from the moment I was born.'

'Unfortunately, though, that's hardly the most unique of claims. How many scuttler fossils have you examined?'

'None,' Rashmika said, after a moment.

'Well, then.' The quaestor dabbed his forefinger against his lip, then touched it against the mouthpiece of the animal. 'That's enough for you, Peppermint.'

Crozet coughed. 'Shall we continue this discussion aboard the caravan, Quaestor? I don't want to have too great a journey back home, and we still have a lot of business to attend to.'

The creature – Peppermint – retreated back along the quaestor's arm now that its feast was over. It began to clean its face with tiny scissoring forelimbs.

'The girl's your responsibility, Crozet?' the quaestor asked.

'Not exactly, no.' He looked at Rashmika and corrected himself. 'What I mean is, yes, I'm taking care of her until she gets where she's going, and I'll take it personally if anyone lays a hand on her. But what she does with herself after that is none of my business.'

The quaestor's attention snapped back to Rashmika. 'And how old are you, exactly?'

'Old enough,' she said.

The green creature turned the turret of its head towards her, its blank faceted eyes like blackberries.

Quaiche slipped in and out of consciousness. With each transition, the difference between the two states became less clear cut. He hallucinated, and then hallucinated that the hallucinations were real. He kept seeing rescuers scrabbling over the scree, picking up their pace as they saw him, waving their gloved hands in greeting. The second or third time, it made him laugh to think that he had imagined rescuers arriving under exactly the same circumstances as the real ones. No one would ever believe him, would they?

But somewhere between the rescuers arriving and the point where they started getting him to safety, he always ended up back in the ship, his chest aching, one eye seeing the world as if through a gauze.

The *Dominatrix* kept arriving, sliding down between the sheer walls of the rift. The long, dark ship would kneel down on spikes of arresting thrust. The mid-hull access hatch would slide open and Morwenna would emerge. She would come out in a blur of pistons, racing to his rescue, as magnificent and terrible as an army arrayed for battle. She would pull him from the wreck of the *Daughter*, and with a dreamlike illogic he would not need to breathe as she helped him back to the other ship through a crisp, airless landscape of shadow and light. Or she would come out in the scrimshaw suit, somehow managing to make it move even though he knew the thing was welded tight, incapable of flexing.

Gradually the hallucinations took precedence over rational thought. In a period of lucidity, it occurred to Quaiche that the kindest thing would be for one of the hallucinations to occur just as he died, so that he was spared the jolting realisation that he had still to be rescued.

He saw Jasmina coming to him, striding across the scree with Grelier lagging behind. The queen was clawing out her eyes as she approached, banners of gore streaming after her.

He kept waking up, but the hallucinations blurred into one another, and the feelings induced by the virus became stronger. He had never known such intensity of experience before, even when the virus had first entered him. The music was behind every thought, the stained-glass light permeating every atom of the universe. He felt intensely observed, intensely loved. The emotions did not feel like a façade any more, but the way things really were. It was as if until now he had only been seeing the reflection of something, or hearing the muffled echo of some exquisitely lovely and heart-wrenching music. Could this really just be the action of an artificially engineered virus on his brain? It had always felt like that before, a series of crude mechanically induced responses, but now the emotions felt like an integral part of him, leaving no room for anything else. It was like the difference between a theatrical stage effect and a thunderstorm.

Some dwindling, rational part of him said that nothing had really changed, that the feelings were still due to the virus. His brain was being starved of oxygen as the air in the cabin ran out. Under those circumstances, it would not have been unusual to feel some emotional changes. And with the virus still present, the effects could have been magnified many times.

But that rational part was quickly squeezed out of existence.

All he felt was the presence of the Almighty.

'All right,' Quaiche said, before passing out, 'I believe now. You got me. But I still need a miracle.'

TEN

Hela, 2615

He woke. He was moving. The air was cold but fresh and there was no pain in his chest. *So this is it*, he thought. The last hallucination, perhaps, before his brain slid into the trough of cascading cell-death. *Just make it a good one, and try to keep it up until I die. That's all I'm asking for.*

But it felt real this time.

He tried looking around, but he was still trapped inside the *Daughter*. Yet his view of things was moving, the landscape bouncing and jolting. He realised that he was being dragged across the scree, down to the level part of the floor. He craned his neck and through his good eye he saw a commotion of pistons, shining limb joints.

Morwenna.

But it wasn't Morwenna. It was a servitor, one of the repair units from the *Dominatrix*. The spiderlike robot had attached adhesive traction plates to the *Scavenger's Daughter* and was hauling it across the ground, with Quaiche still in it. *Of course, of course, of course*: how else was it going to get him out of there? He felt stupid now. He had no suit and no airlock. For all intents and purposes, in fact, the ship *was* his vacuum suit. Why had this never occurred to him before?

He felt better: clear-headed and sharp. He noticed that the servitor had plugged something into one of the *Daughter's* umbilical points. Feeding fresh air back into it, probably. The *Daughter* would have told the servitor what needed to be done to keep her occupant alive. The air might even be supercharged with oxygen, to take the edge off his pain and anxiety.

He could not believe this was happening. After all the hallucinations, this really, genuinely felt like reality. It had the prickly texture of actual experience. And he did not think that servitors had featured in any of his hallucinations to date. He had never thought things through clearly enough to work out that a servitor would have to drag the ship to safety with him in it. Obvious in hindsight, but in his dreams it had always been people coming to his rescue.

That one neglected detail had to make it real, didn't it?

Quaiche looked at the console. How much time had passed? Had he really managed to make the air last for five hours? It had seemed doubtful before, but here he was, still breathing. Perhaps the indoctrinal virus had helped, putting his brain into some mysterious state of zenlike calm so that he used up the oxygen less quickly.

But there wouldn't have been any air left, let alone oxygen, not by the third or fourth hour. Unless the ship had made a mistake. This was a dismaying thought, given all that he had been through, but it was the only possible explanation. The air leak must not have been as serious as the *Daughter* had thought it was. Perhaps it had started off badly, but had sealed itself to some extent. Perhaps the auto-repair systems had not been totally destroyed, and the *Daughter* had been able to fix the leak.

Yes, that had to be it. There was simply no other explanation.

But the console said that only three hours had passed since his crash.

That wasn't possible. The *Dominatrix* was still supposed to be tucked away behind Haldora, out of communications range. It would be out of range for another sixty minutes! Many more minutes, even at maximum burn, before it could possibly reach him. And maximum burn was not an option either, was it? There was a person aboard the ship who had to be protected. At the very least, the *Dominatrix* would have been restricted to slowdown acceleration.

But it was sitting there, on the ice. It looked as real as anything else.

The time had to be wrong, he thought. The time had to be wrong, and the leak must have fixed itself. There was no other possibility. Well, there was, now that he thought about it, but it did not merit close examination. If the time was right, then the *Dominatrix* must have somehow received his distress signal before emerging from behind Haldora. The signal would have had to find its way around the obstruction of the planet. Could that have happened? He had assumed it was impossible, but with the evidence of the ship sitting before him, he was ready to consider anything. Had some quirk of atmospheric physics acted as a relay for his message, curving it around Haldora? He couldn't swear that something like that was impossible. If the clock was correct, what was the alternative? That the entire planet had ceased to exist just long enough for his message to get through?

Now *that* would have been a miracle. He had asked for one, but he hadn't really been *expecting* one.

Another servitor was waiting by the open dorsal lock. Co-operating, the two machines hoisted the *Daughter* into the *Dominatrix*. Once inside the bay, the machines nudged the *Daughter* until a series of clunking sounds resonated through the hull. Despite the damage it had sustained, the little ship was still more or less the right shape to be accommodated by the cradle. Quaiche looked down, watched the airlock sealing beneath him.

A minute later, another servitor – much smaller this time – was opening the *Daughter*, preparing to lift him out of it.

'Morwenna,' he said, finding the energy to talk despite the returning pain in his chest. 'Morwenna, I'm back. Bruised but intact.'

But there was no reply.

Ararat, 2675

The capsule was preparing to open. Clavain sat before it, his fingers laced together beneath his chin, his head bowed as if in prayer, or the remorseful contemplation of some recent and dreadful sin.

He had thrown back his hood; white hair spilled over the collar of his coat and on to his shoulders. He looked like an old man, of obvious stature and respectability, but he did not look much like the Clavain everyone thought they knew. Scorpio had little doubt that the workers would go back to their husbands and wives, lovers and friends and, despite express orders to the contrary, they would talk abut the elderly apparition that had materialised out of the night. They would remark on his uncanny similarity to Clavain, but how much older and frailer he looked. Scorpio was equally certain they would prefer the old man to turn out to be someone else entirely, with their leader really halfway around the world. If they accepted this old man as Clavain, it meant that they had been lied to, and that Clavain was nothing more than a grey ghost of himself.

Scorpio sat down in the vacant seat next to him. 'Picking something up?'

It was a while before Clavain answered, his voice a whisper. 'Not much more than the housekeeping stuff I already reported. The capsule blocks most of his neural transmissions. They're only coming through in shards, and sometimes the packets are scrambled.'

'Then you're certain it's Remontoire?'

'I'm certain that it isn't Skade. Who else can it be?'

'I'd say there are dozens of possibilities,' Scorpio whispered back.

'No, there aren't. The person inside this capsule is a Conjoiner.'

'One of Skade's allies, then.'

'No. Her friends were all cast from the same mould: new-model Conjoiners, fast and efficient and as cold as ice. Their minds feel different.'

'You're losing me, Nevil.'

'You think we're all alike, Scorp. We're not. We never were. Every Conjoiner I ever linked minds with was different. Whenever I touched Remontoire's thoughts it was like ...' Clavain hesitated for a moment, smiling slightly when the right analogy occurred to him. 'Like touching the mechanism of a clock. An old clock, good and dependable. The kind they had in churches. Something made of iron, something ratcheted and geared. I think to him I was something even slower and more mechanical ... a grindstone, perhaps. Whereas Galiana's mind ...'

He faltered.

'Easy, Nevil.'

'I'm all right. Her mind was like a room full of birds. Beautiful, clever songbirds. And they were singing – not in some mindless cacophony, not in unison, but to each other – a web of song, a shining, shimmering conversation, quicker than the mind could follow. And Felka ...' He hesitated again, but resumed his thread almost immediately. 'Felka's was like a turbine hall, that awful impression of simultaneous stillness and dreadful speed. She seldom let me see deep into it. I'm sure she thought I wouldn't be able to take it.'

'And Skade?'

'She was like a shining silver abattoir, all whirling and whisking blades, designed to slice and chop reality and anyone foolish enough to peer too far into her skull. At least, that's what I saw when she let me. It may not have had very much to do with her true mental state. Her head was like a hall of mirrors. What you saw in it was only what she wanted you to see.'

Scorpio nodded. He had met Skade on precisely one occasion, for a few minutes only. Clavain and the pig had infiltrated her ship, which was damaged and drifting after she had attempted, with the aid of dangerous alien machinery, to exceed the speed of light. She had been weakened then, and evidently disturbed by the things that she had seen after the accident. But even though he had not been able to see into her mind, he had come away from the meeting with a sure sense that Skade was not a woman to be trifled with.

Frankly, he did not very much mind that he would never be able to see into her skull. But he still had to assume the worst. If Skade was in the capsule, it was entirely possible that she would be disguising her neural packets, lulling Clavain into a false sense of security, waiting for the moment when she could claw her way into his skull.

'The instant you feel anything odd ...' Scorpio began.

'It's Rem.'

'You're absolutely certain of that?'

'I'm certain it isn't Skade. Good enough for you?'

'I suppose it'll have to do, pal.'

'It had better,' Clavain said, 'because ...' He fell silent and blinked. 'Wait. Something's happening.'

'Good or bad?'

'We're all about to find out.'

The glowing displays in the side of the egg had never been still since the moment it had been pulled from the sea, but now they were changing abruptly, flicking from one distinct mode to another. A pulsing red circle was now flashing several times a second rather than once every ten. Scorpio watched it, hypnotised, and then observed it stop flashing entirely, glaring at them with baleful intent. The red circle became green. Something inside the egg made a muffled series of clunks, making Scorpio think of the kind of old mechanical clock Clavain had described. A moment later the side of the capsule cracked open: Scorpio, for all that he was expecting something, jumped at the sudden lurch of movement. Cool steam vented out from under the widening crack. A large plaque of scorched metal folded itself back on smooth hinged machinery.

A jangle of smells hit the pig: sterilising agents, mechanical lubricants, boiling coolants, human effluvia.

The steam cleared to reveal a naked human woman packed inside the egg, bent into a foetal position. She was covered in a scum of protective green jelly; lacy black machinery curled around her, like vines wrapping a statue.

'Skade?' Scorpio said. She didn't look like his memories of Skade – her head was the right shape, for a start – but a second opinion never hurt.

'Not Skade,' Clavain said. 'And not Remontoire, either.' He stood back from the capsule.

Some automated system kicked in. The machinery began to unwind itself from around her, while pressure jets cleansed her skin of the protective green jelly. Beneath the matrix her flesh was a pale shade of caramel. The hair on her skull had been shaved almost to the scalp. Small breasts were tucked into the concave space between her legs and upper body.

'Let me see her,' Valensin said.

Scorpio held him back. 'Hold on. She's come this far on her own; I'm sure she can manage for a few more minutes.'

'Scorp's right,' Clavain said.

The woman quivered like some inanimate thing shocked into a parody of life. With stiff scrabbling movements she picked at the jelly with her fingers, flinging it away in cloying patches. Her movements became more frantic, as if she was trying to douse a fire.

'Hello,' Clavain said, raising his voice. 'Take it easy. You're safe and amongst friends.'

The seat or frame into which the woman had been folded pushed itself from the egg on pistons. Even though much of the enveloping machinery had unwrapped itself, a great many cables still vanished into the woman's body. A complex plastic breathing apparatus obscured the lower part of her face, giving her a simian profile.

'Anyone recognise her?' Vasko asked.

The frame was slowly unwinding the woman, pulling her out of the foetal position into a normal human posture. Ligaments and joints creaked and clicked unpleasantly. Beneath the mask the woman groaned and began to rip away the cables and lines that punctured her skin or were attached to it by adhesive patches.

'I recognise her,' Clavain said quietly. 'Her name's Ana Khouri. She was Ilia Volyova's sidekick on the old *Infinity*, before it fell into our hands.'

'The ex-soldier,' Scorpio said, remembering the few times he had met the woman and the little he knew of her past. 'You're right – it's her. But she looks different, somehow.'

'She would. She's twenty years older, give or take. They've also turned her into a Conjoiner.'

'You mean she wasn't one before?' Vasko asked.

'Not while we knew her,' Clavain said.

Scorpio looked at the old man. 'Are you sure she's one now?'

'I picked up her thoughts, didn't I? I could tell she wasn't Skade or one of Skade's cronies. Stupidly, I assumed that meant she had to be Remontoire.'

Valensin attempted to push past one more time. 'I'd like to help her now, if that's not too much of an inconvenience.'

'She's taking care of herself,' Scorpio said.

Khouri sat in what was almost a normal position, the way someone might sit while waiting for an appointment. But the moment of composure only lasted a few seconds. She reached up and pulled away the mask, tugging fifteen centimetres of phlegmy plastic tubing from her throat. At that point she let out a single bellowing gasp, as if someone had punched her unexpectedly in the stomach. Hacking coughs followed, before her breathing settled down.

'Scorpio . . .' Valensin said.

'Doc, I haven't hit a man in twenty-three years. Don't give me a reason to make an exception. Sit down, all right?'

'Better do as he says,' Clavain told him.

Khouri turned her head to face them. She held up a palm to shade the bloodshot slits of her eyes, blinking through the gaps between her fingers.

Then she stood, still facing them. Scorpio watched with polite indifference. Some pigs would have been stimulated by the presence of a naked human woman, just as there were some humans who were attracted to pigs. But although the points of physiological difference between a female pig and a female human were hardly extreme, it was precisely those differences that mattered to Scorpio.

Khouri steadied herself by holding on to the capsule with one hand. She stood with her knees slightly together, as if at any moment she might collapse. Yet she was able to tolerate the glare now, if only by squinting at them.

She spoke. Her voice was hoarse but firm. 'Where am I?'

'You're on Ararat,' Scorpio said.

'Where.' It was not phrased as a question.

'On Ararat will do for now.'

'Near your main settlement, I'm guessing.'

'As I said . . .'

'How long has it been?'

'That depends,' Scorpio said. 'A couple of days since we picked up the beacon from your capsule. How long you were under the sea, we don't know. Or how long it took you to reach the planet.'

'A couple of days?' The way she looked at him, it was as if he had said weeks or months. 'What exactly took you so long?'

'You're lucky we got to you as quickly as we did,' Blood said. 'And the wake-up schedule wasn't in our control.'

'Two days . . . Where's Clavain? I want to see him. Please don't anyone tell me you let him die before I got here.'

'You needn't worry about that,' Clavain said mildly. 'As you can see, I'm still very much alive.'

She stared at him for a few seconds with the sneering expression of someone who thought they might be the victim of a poorly executed hoax. 'You?'

'Yes.' He offered his palms. 'Sorry to be such a disappointment.'

She looked at him for a moment longer, then said, 'I'm sorry. It's just not ... quite what I was expecting.'

'I believe I can still make myself useful.' He turned to Blood. 'Fetch her a blanket, will you? We don't want her catching her death of cold. Then I think we'd better let Doctor Valensin perform a comprehensive medical examination.'

'No time for that,' Khouri said, ripping away a few adhesive patches she had missed. 'I want you to get me something that can cross water. And some weapons.' She paused, then added, 'And some food and water. And some clothes.'

'You seem in a bit of a hurry,' Clavain said. 'Can't it wait until morning? It's been twenty-three years, after all. There must be a great deal to talk about.'

'You have no fucking idea,' she said.

Blood handed Clavain a blanket. He stepped forward and offered it to Khouri. She wrapped it around herself without any real enthusiasm.

'We can do boats,' Clavain said, 'and guns. But I think it might help if we had some idea just why you need them right this moment.'

'Because of my baby,' Khouri said.

Clavain nodded politely. 'Your baby.'

'My daughter. Her name's Aura. She's here, on ... what did you say this place was called?'

'Ararat,' Clavain said.

'OK, she's here on Ararat. And I've come to rescue her.'

Clavain glanced at his companions. 'And where would your daughter be, exactly?'

'About eight hundred kilometres away,' Khouri said. 'Now get me those weps. And an incubator. And someone who knows field surgery.'

'Why field surgery?' Clavain asked.

'Because,' Khouri replied, 'you're going to have to get her out of Skade first.'

ELEVEN

Rashmika looked up at the scuttler fossil. A symbol of conspicuous wealth, it hung from the ceiling in a large atrium area of the caravan vehicle. Even if it was a fake, or a semi-fake botched together from incompatible parts, it was still the first apparently complete scuttler she had ever seen. She wanted to find a way to climb up there and examine it properly, taking note of the abrasion patterns where the hard carapacial sections slid against each other. Rashmika had only ever read about such things, but she was certain that with an hour of careful study she would be able to tell whether it was authentic, or at the very least exclude the possibility of its being a cheap fake.

Somehow she didn't think it was very likely to be either cheap or fake.

Mentally, she classified the scuttler body morphology. DK4V8M, she thought. Maybe a DK4V8L, if she was being confused by the play of dust and shadows around the trailing tail-shell. At least it was possible to apply the usual morphological classification scheme. The cheap fakes sometimes threw body parts together in anatomically impossible formations, but this was definitely a plausible assemblage of components, even if they hadn't necessarily come from the same burial site.

The scuttlers were a taxonomist's nightmare. The first time one had been unearthed, it had appeared to be a simple case of reassembling the scattered body parts to make something that looked like a large insect or lobster. The scuttler exhibited a complexity of body sections, with many different highly specialised limbs and sensory organs, but they had all snapped back together in a more or less logical fashion, leaving only the soft interior organs to be conjectured.

But the second scuttler hadn't matched the first. There were a different number of body sections, a different number of limbs. The head and mouth parts looked very dissimilar. Yet – again – all the pieces snapped together to make a complete specimen, with no embarrassing bits left over.

The third hadn't matched the first or second. Nor the fourth or fifth.

By the time the remains of a hundred scuttlers had been unearthed and reassembled, there were a hundred different versions of the scuttler body-plan.

The theorists groped for an explanation. The implication was that no two scuttlers were born alike. But two simultaneous discoveries shattered that idea overnight. The first was the unearthing of an intact clutch of infant scuttlers. Though there were some differences in body-plan, there *were* identical infants. Based on their frequency of occurrence, statistics argued that at least three identical adults should already have been discovered. The second discovery – which happened to explain the first – was the unearthing of a pair of adult scuttlers in the same area. They had been found in separated but connected chambers of an underground tunnel system. Their body parts were reassembled, providing another two unique morphologies. But upon closer examination something unexpected was discovered. A young researcher named Kimura had begun to take a particular interest in the patterns caused by the body sections scraping against each other. Something struck her as not quite right about the two new specimens. The scratch marks were inconsistent: a scrape on the edge of one carapace had no matching counterpart on the adjoining one.

At first, Kimura assumed the two clusters of body parts were hoaxes; there was already a small market for that kind of thing. But something made her dig a little deeper. She worried at the problem for weeks, convinced that she was missing something obvious. Then one night, after a particularly busy day examining the scratches at higher and higher magnifications, she slept on it. She dreamed feverish dreams, and when she woke she dashed back to her lab and confirmed her nagging suspicion.

There was a precise match for every scratch – but it was always to be found on the *other* scuttler. The scuttlers interchanged body parts with each other. That was why no two scuttlers were ever alike. They made themselves dissimilar: swapping components in ritualised ceremonies, then crawling away to their own little hollows to recuperate. As more scuttler pairs were unearthed, so the near-infinite possibilities of the arrangement became apparent. The exchange of body parts had pragmatic value, allowing scuttlers to adapt themselves for particular duties and environments. But there was also an aesthetic purpose to the ritualised swapping: a desire to be as atypical as possible. Scuttlers that had deviated far from the average body plan were socially successful creatures, for they must have participated in many exchanges. The ultimate stigma – so far as Kimura and her colleagues could tell – was for one scuttler to be identical to another. It meant that at least one of the pair was an outcast, unable to find a swap-partner.

Bitter arguments ensued among the human researchers. The majority view was that this behaviour could not have evolved naturally; that it must stem from an earlier phase of conscious bioengineering, when the scuttlers tinkered with their own anatomies to allow whole body parts to be swapped from creature to creature without the benefit of microsurgery and antirejection drugs.

But a minority of researchers held that the swapping was too deeply ingrained in scuttler culture to have arisen in their recent evolutionary history. They suggested that, billions of years earlier, the scuttlers had been forced to evolve in an intensely hostile environment – the evolutionary equivalent of a crowded lobster pot. So hostile, in fact, that there had been a survival value not just in being able to regrow a severed limb, but also in actually being able to reattach a severed limb there and then, before it was eaten. The limbs – and later, major body parts – had evolved in turn, developing the resilience to survive being ripped from the rest of the body. As the survival pressure increased, the scuttlers had evolved intercompatibility, able to make use not just of their own discarded parts but those of their kin.

Perhaps even the scuttlers themselves had no memory of when the swapping had begun. Certainly, there was no obvious allusion to it in the few symbolic records that had ever been found on Hela. It was too much a part of them, too fundamentally a part of the way they viewed reality, for them to have remarked upon it.

Looking up at the fantastic creature, Rashmika wondered what the scuttlers would have made of humanity. Very probably they would have found the human race just as bizarre, regarding its very immutability horrific, like a kind of death.

Rashmika knelt down and propped the family compad on the slope of her legs. She flipped it open and pulled the stylus from its slot in the side. It wasn't comfortable, but she would only be sitting like that for a few minutes.

She began to draw. The stylus scratched against the compad with each fluid, confident stroke of her hand. An alien animal took shape on the screen.

*

Linxe had been right about the caravan: no matter how frosty the reception had been, it still afforded them all the chance to get out of the icejammer for the first time in three days.

Rashmika was surprised at the difference it made to her general mood. It wasn't just that she had stopped worrying about the attention of the Vigrid constabulary, although the question of *why* they had come after her continued to nag at her. The air was fresher in the caravan, with interesting breezes and varying smells, none of which were as unpleasant as those aboard the icejammer.

There was room to stretch her legs, as well: the interior of just this one caravan vehicle was generously laid out, with wide, tall gangways, comfortable rooms and bright lights. Everything was spick-and-span and – compared at least to the welcome – the amenities were more than adequate. Food and drink were provided, clothes could be washed, and for once it was possible to reach a state of reasonable cleanliness. There were even various kinds of entertainment, even though it was all rather bland compared to what she was used to. And there were new people, faces she hadn't seen before.

She realised, after some reflection, that she had been wrong in her initial judgement of the relationship between the quaestor and Crozet. While there did not appear to be much love lost between them, it was obvious now that both parties had been of some use to each other in the past. The mutual rudeness had been a charade, concealing an icy core of mutual respect. The quaestor was fishing for titbits, aware that Crozet might still have something he could use. Crozet, meanwhile, needed to leave with mechanical spares or other barterable goods.

Rashmika had only intended to sit in on a few of the negotiation sessions, but she quickly realised that she could, in a small way, be of practical use to Crozet. To facilitate this she sat at one end of the table, a sheet of paper and a pen before her. She was not allowed to bring the compad into the room, in case it contained voice-stress-analysis software or some other prohibited system.

Rashmika noted down observations about the items Crozet was selling, writing and sketching with the neatness she had always taken pride in. Her interest was genuine, but her presence also served another purpose.

In the first negotiation session, there had been two buyers. Later, there was sometimes a third or fourth, and the quaestor or one of his deputies would always attend as an observer. Each session would begin with one of the buyers asking Crozet what he had to offer them.

'We aren't looking for scuttler relics,' they said the first time. 'We're simply not interested. What we want are artefacts of indigenous human origin. Things left on Hela in the last hundred years, not million-year-old rubbish. There's a declining market for useless alien junk, what with all the rich solar systems being evacuated. Who wants to *add* to their collection, when they're busy selling their assets to buy a single freezer slot?'

'What sort of human artefacts?'

'Useful ones. These are dark times: people don't want art and ephemera, not unless they think it's going to bring them luck. Mainly what they want are weapons and survival systems, things they think might give them an edge when whatever they're running from catches up with them. Contraband Conjoiner weapons. Demarchist armour. Anything with plague-tolerance, that's always an easy sell.'

'As a rule,' Crozet said, 'I don't do weapons.'

'Then you need to adapt to a changing market,' one of the men replied with a smirk.

'The churches moving into the arms trade? Isn't that a tiny bit inconsistent with scripture?'

'If people want protection, who are we to deny them?'

Crozet shrugged. 'Well, I'm all out of guns and ammo. If anyone's still digging up human weapons on Hela, it isn't me.'

'You must have something else.'

'Not a hell of a lot.' He made as if to leave at that point, as he did in every subsequent session. 'Best be on my way, I think – wouldn't want to be wasting anyone's time, would I?'

'You've absolutely nothing else?'

'Nothing that you'd be interested in. Of course, I have some scuttler relics, but like you said . . .' Crozet's voice accurately parodied the dismissive tones of the buyer. 'No market for alien junk these days.'

The buyers sighed and exchanged glances; the quaestor leaned in and whispered something to them.

'You may as well show us what you have,' one of the buyers said, reluctantly, 'but don't raise your hopes. More than likely we won't be interested. In fact, you can more or less guarantee it.'

But this was a game and Crozet knew he had to abide by its rules, no matter how pointless or childish they were. He reached under his chair and emerged with something wrapped in protective film, like a small mummified animal.

The buyers' faces wrinkled in distaste.

He placed the package on the table and unwrapped it solemnly, taking a maddening time to remove all the layers. All the while he maintained a spiel about the extreme rarity of the object, how it had been excavated under exceptional circumstances, weaving a dubious human-interest story into the vague chain of provenance.

'Get on with it, Crozet.'

'Just setting the scene,' he said.

Inevitably he came to the final layer of wrapping. He spread this layer wide on the table, revealing the scuttler relic cocooned within.

Rashmika had seen this one before: it was one of the objects she had used to buy her passage aboard the icejammer.

They were never very much to look at. Rashmika had seen thousands of relics unearthed from the Vigrid digs, had even been allowed to examine them before they passed into the hands of the trading families, but in all that time she had never seen anything that made her gasp in admiration or delight. For while the relics were undoubtedly artificial, they were in general fashioned from dull, tarnished metals or grubby unglazed ceramics. There was seldom any hint of surface ornamentation – no trace of paint, plating or inscription. Once in a thousand finds they uncovered something with a string of symbols on it, and there were even researchers who believed they understood what some of those symbols meant. But most scuttler relics were blank, dull, crude-looking. They resembled the dug-up leftovers of an inept bronze-age culture rather than the gleaming products of a starfaring civilisation – one that had certainly not evolved in the 107 Piscium system.

Yet for much of the last century there *had* been a market for the relics. Partly this was because none of the other extinct cultures – the Amarantin, for instance – had left behind a comparable haul of day-to-day objects. Those cultures had been so thoroughly exterminated that almost nothing had survived, and the objects that had were so valuable that they remained in the care of large scientific organisations like the Sylveste Institute. Only the scuttlers had left behind enough objects to permit private collectors to acquire artefacts of genuine alien origin. It didn't matter that they were small and unglamorous: they were still very old, and still very alien. And they were still tainted by the tragedy of extinction.

No two relics were ever quite alike, either. Scuttler furniture, even scuttler dwellings, exhibited the same horror of similarity as their makers. What had begun with their anatomies had now spread into their material environment. They had mass production, but it was a necessary end-stage of that process that every object be worked on by a scuttler artisan, until it was unique.

The churches controlled the sale of these relics to the outside universe. But the churches themselves had always been uncomfortable with the deeper question of what the scuttlers represented, or how they slotted into the mystery of the Quaiche miracle. The churches needed to keep up the drip-feed supply of relics so that they had something to offer the Ultra traders who visited the system. But at the same time there was always the fear that the next scuttler relic to be unearthed would be the one that threw a spanner into the midst of Quaicheist doctrine.

It was now the view of almost all the churches that the Haldoran vanishings were a message from God, a countdown to some event of apocalyptic finality. But what if the scuttlers had also observed the vanishings? It was difficult enough to decipher their symbols at the best of times, and so far nothing had been found that appeared to relate directly to the Haldora phenomenon. But there were a lot of relics still under Hela's ice, and even those that had been unearthed to date had never been subjected to rigorous scientific study. The church-sponsored archaeologists were the only ones who had any kind of overview of the entire haul of relics, and they were under intense pressure to ignore any evidence that conflicted with Quaicheist scripture. That was why Rashmika wrote them so many letters, and why their infrequent replies were always so evasive. She wanted an argument; she wanted to question the entire accepted view of the scuttlers. They wanted her to go away.

Thus it was that the buyers in the caravan affected an air of tolerant disapproval while Crozet turned on the hard sell.

'It's a plate cleaner,' Crozet said, turning a grey, cleft-tipped, bone-like object this way and that. 'They used it to scrape dead organic matter out of the gaps between their carapacial sections. We think they did it communally, the way monkeys pick ticks out of each other's hair. Must have been very relaxing for them.'

'Filthy creatures.'

'Monkeys or scuttlers?'

'Both.'

'I wouldn't be too harsh, mate. Scuttlers are paying your wages.'

'We'll give you fifty ecumenical credit units for it, Crozet. No more.'

'Fifty ecus? Now you're taking the piss.'

'It's a revolting object serving a revolting function. Fifty ecus is ... quite excessively generous.'

Crozet looked at Rashmika. It was only a glance, but she was ready for it when it came. The system they had arranged was very simple: if the man was telling the truth – if this really was the best offer he was prepared to make – then she would push the sheet of paper a fraction closer to the middle of the table. Otherwise, she would pull it towards her by the same tiny distance. If the man's reaction was ambiguous, she did nothing. This did not happen very often.

Crozet always took her judgement seriously. If the offer on the table was as good as it was going to get, he did not waste his energies trying to talk them up. On the other hand, if there was some leeway, he haggled the hell out of them.

In that first negotiating session, the buyer was lying. After a rapid-fire back and forth of offer and counter-offer, they reached an agreement.

'Your tenacity does you credit,' the buyer said with visible bad grace, before writing him out a chit for seventy ecus that was only redeemable within the caravan itself.

Crozet folded it neatly and stuffed it into his shirt pocket. 'Pleasure doing business, mate.'

He had other scuttler plate cleaners, as well as several things that might have served some entirely different function. Now and then he came back to the negotiation sessions with something that Linxe or Culver had to help him carry. It might be an item of furniture, or some kind of heavy-duty domestic tool. Scuttler weapons were rare, appearing to have had only ceremonial value, but they sold the best of all. Once, he sold them what appeared to be a kind of scuttler toilet seat. He only got thirty-five ecus for that: barely enough, Crozet said, for a single servo-motor.

But Rashmika tried not to feel too sorry for him. If Crozet wanted the best pickings from the digs, the kinds of relics that picked up three- or four-figure payments, then he needed to rethink his attitude towards the rest of the Vigrid communities. The truth of the matter was that he liked scabbing around on the perimeter.

It went on like that for two days. On the third, the buyers suddenly demanded that Crozet be alone during the negotiations. Rashmika had no idea if they had guessed her secret. There was, as far as she was aware, no law against being an adept judge of whether people were lying or not. Perhaps they had just taken a dislike to her, as people often did when they sensed her percipience.

Rashmika was fine with that. She had helped Crozet out, paid him back a little more in addition to the scuttler relics for the help he had given her. He had, after all, taken an extra, unforeseen risk when he found out about the constabulary pursuing her.

No: she had nothing bad on her conscience.

Ararat, 2675

Khouri protested as they took her away from the capsule into the waiting infirmary. 'I don't need an examination,' she said. 'I just need a boat, some weapons, an incubator and someone good with a knife.'

'Oh, I'm good with a knife,' Clavain said.

'Please take me seriously. You trusted Ilia, didn't you?'

'We came to an arrangement. Mutual trust never had much to do with it.'

'You respected her judgement, though?'

'I suppose so.'

'Well, she trusted me. Isn't that good enough for you? I'm not making excessive demands here, Clavain. I'm not asking for the world.'

'We'll consider your requests in good time,' he said, 'but not before we've had you examined.'

'There isn't *time*,' she said, but from her tone of voice it was clear she knew she had already lost the argument.

Within the infirmary, Dr Valensin waited with two aged medical servitors from the central machine pool. The swan-necked robots were a drab institutional green, riding on hissing air-cushion pedestals. Many specialised arms emerged from their slender chess-piece bodies. The physician would be keeping a careful eye on the machines while they did their work: left alone, their creaking circuits had a nasty habit of absent-mindedly switching into autopsy mode.

'I don't like robots,' Khouri said, eyeing the servitors with evident disquiet.

'That's one thing we agree on,' Clavain said, turning to Scorpio and lowering his voice. 'Scorp, we'll need to talk to the other seniors about the best course of action as soon as we have Valensin's report. My guess is she'll need some rest before she goes anywhere. But for now I suggest we keep as tight a lid on this as possible.'

'Do you think she's telling the truth?' Scorpio asked. 'All that stuff about Skade and her baby?'

Clavain studied the woman as Valensin helped her on to the examination couch. 'I have a horrible feeling she might be.'

After the examination, Khouri fell into a state of deep and apparently dreamless sleep. She awakened only once, near dawn, when she summoned one of Valensin's aides and again demanded the means to rescue her daughter. After that they administered more relaxant and she fell asleep for another four or five hours. Now and then she thrashed wildly and uttered fragments of speech. Whatever she was trying to say always sounded urgent, but the meaning never quite cohered. She was not properly awake and cognisant until the middle of the morning.

By the time Dr Valensin deemed that Khouri was ready for visitors, the latest storm had broken. The sky above the compound was a bleak powder-blue, marbled here and there by strands of feathered cirrus. Out to sea, the *Nostalgia for Infinity* gleamed shades of grey, like something freshly chiselled from dark rock.

They sat down on opposite sides of her bed – Clavain in one chair, Scorpio in another, but reversed so that he sat with his arms folded across the top of the backrest.

'I've read Valensin's report,' Scorpio began. 'We were all hoping he'd tell us you were insane. Unfortunately, that doesn't appear to be the case.' He pinched the bridge of his nose. 'And that gives me a really bad headache.'

Khouri pushed herself up in the bed. 'I'm sorry about your headache, but can we skip the formalities and get on with rescuing my daughter?'

'We'll discuss it when you're up on your feet,' Clavain said.

'Why not now?'

'Because we still need to know exactly what's happened. We'll also need an accurate tactical assessment of any scenario involving Skade and your daughter. Would you define it as a hostage situation?' Clavain asked.

'Yes,' Khouri replied, grudgingly.

'Then until we have concrete demands from Skade, Aura is in no immediate danger. Skade won't risk hurting her one asset. She may be cold-hearted, but she's not irrational.'

Guardedly, Scorpio observed the old man. He appeared as alert and quick-witted as ever, yet to the best of Scorpio's knowledge Clavain had allowed himself no more than two hours of sleep since returning to the mainland. Scorpio had seen that kind of thing in other elderly human men: they needed little sleep and resented its imposition by those younger than themselves. It was not that they necessarily had more energy, but that the division between sleep and waking had become an indistinct, increasingly arbitrary thing. He wondered how that would feel, drifting through an endless succession of grey moments, rather than ordered intervals of day and night.

'How much time are we talking about?' Khouri said. 'Hours or days, before you act?'

'I've convened a meeting of colony seniors for later this morning,' Clavain said. 'If the situation merits it, a rescue operation could be underway before sunset.'

'Can't you just take my word that we need to act *now*?'

Clavain scratched his beard. 'If your story made more sense, I might.'

'I'm not lying.' She gestured in the direction of one of the servitors. 'The doctor gave me the all-clear, didn't he?'

Scorpio smiled, tapping the medical report against the back of his chair. 'He said you weren't obviously delusional, but his examination raised as many questions as it answered.'

'You talk about a baby,' Clavain said before Khouri had a chance to interrupt, 'but according to this report you've never given birth. Nor is there any obvious sign of Caesarean surgery having been performed.'

'It wouldn't be obvious – it was done by Conjoiner medics. They can sew you up so cleanly it's as if it never happened.' She looked at each of them in turn, her anger and fear equally clear. 'Are you saying you don't believe me?'

Clavain shook his head. 'I'm saying we can't verify your story, that's all. According to Valensin there *is* womb distension consistent with you having very recently been pregnant, and there are hormonal changes in your blood that support the same conclusion. But Valensin admits that there could be other explanations.'

'They don't contradict my story, either.'

'But we'll need more convincing before we organise a military action,' Clavain said.

'Again: why can't you just trust me?'

'Because it's not only the story about your baby that doesn't make sense,' Clavain replied. 'How did you *get* here, Ana? Where's the ship that should have brought you? You didn't come all the way from the Resurgam system in that capsule, and yet there's no sign of any other spacecraft having entered our system.'

'And that makes me a liar?'

'It makes us suspicious,' Scorpio said. 'It makes us wonder if you're what you appear to be.'

'The ships are here,' she said, sighing, as if spoiling a carefully planned surprise. 'All of them. They're concentrated in the immediate volume of space around this planet. Remontoire, the *Zodiacal Light*, the two remaining starships from Skade's taskforce – they're all up there, within one AU of this planet. They've been in your system for nine weeks. That's how I got here, Clavain.'

'You can't hide ships that easily,' he said. 'Not consistently, not all the time. Not when we're actively looking for them.'

'We can now,' she said. 'We have techniques you know nothing about. Things we've learned ... things we've *had* to learn since the last time you saw us. Things you won't believe.'

Clavain glanced at Scorpio. The pig tried to guess what was going through the old man's mind and failed.

'Such as?' Clavain asked.

'New engines,' she said. 'Dark drives. You can't see them. *Nothing* sees them. The exhaust ... slips away. Camouflaging screens. Free-force bubbles. Miniaturised cryo-arithmetic engines. Reliable control of inertia on bulk scales. Hypometric weapons.' She shivered. 'I *really* don't like the hypometric weapons. They scare me. I've seen what happens when they go wrong. They're *not right*.'

'All that in twenty-odd years?' Clavain asked, incredulously.

'We had some help.'

'Sounds as if you had God on the end of the phone, taking down your wish list.'

'It wasn't God, believe me. I should know. I was the one who did the asking.'

'And who exactly did you ask?'

'My daughter,' Khouri said. 'She knows things, Clavain. That's why she's valuable. That's why Skade wants her.'

Scorpio felt dizzy: it seemed that every time they scratched back one layer of Khouri's story, there was something even less comprehensible behind it.

'I still don't understand why you didn't signal your arrival from orbit,' Clavain said.

'Partly because we didn't want to draw attention to Ararat,' Khouri said. 'Not until we had to. There's a war going on up there, understand? A major space engagement, with heavily stealthed combatants. Any kind of signalling is a risk. There's also a lot of jamming and disruption going on.'

'Between Skade's forces and your own?'

'It's more complicated than that. Until recently, Skade was fighting with us, rather than against us. Even now, aside from the personal business between Skade and myself, I'd say we're in what you might call a state of uneasy truce.'

'Then who the hell are you fighting?' Clavain asked.

'The Inhibitors,' Khouri said. 'The wolves, whatever you want to call them.'

'They're here?' Scorpio asked. 'Actually in this system?'

'Sorry to rain on your parade,' Khouri said.

'Well,' Clavain said, looking around, 'I don't know about the rest of you, but that certainly puts a dent in my day.'

'That was the idea,' Khouri said.

Clavain ran a finger down the straight line of his nose. 'One other thing. Several times since you arrived here you've mentioned a word that sounds like "hella". You even said we had to get there. The name means nothing to me. What is its significance?'

'I don't know,' she said. 'I don't even remember saying it.'

TWELVE

Hela, 2727

Quaestor Jones had been warned to expect a new guest aboard his caravan. The warning had come straight from the Permanent Way, with the official seals of the Clocktower. Shortly afterwards, a small spacecraft – a single-seat shuttle of Ultra manufacture shaped like a cockleshell – came sliding over the procession of caravan vehicles.

The ruby-hulled vehicle loitered on a spike of expertly balanced thrust, hovering unnervingly while the caravan continued on its way. Then it lowered, depositing itself on the main landing pad. The hull opened and a vacuum-suited figure stepped from the vehicle's hatch. The figure hesitated, reaching back into the cockpit for a walking stick and a small white case. Cameras tracked him from different viewpoints as he made his way down into the caravan, opening normally impassable doors with Clocktower keys, shutting them neatly behind him. He walked very slowly, taking his time, giving the quaestor the opportunity to exercise his imagination. Now and then he tapped his cane against some component of the caravan, or paused to run a gloved hand along the top of a wall, inspecting his fingers as if for dust.

'I don't like this, Peppermint,' the quaestor told the creature perched on his desk. 'It's never good when they send someone out, especially when they only give you an hour's warning. It means they want to surprise you. It means they think you're up to something.'

The creature busied itself with the small pile of seeds the quaestor had tipped on to the table. There was something engrossing about just watching it eat and then clean itself. Its faceted black eyes – in the right light they were actually a very dark, lustrous purple – shone like rare minerals.

'Who can it be, who can it be . . .' the quaestor said, drumming his fingers on the table. 'Here, have some more seeds. A *stick*. Who do we know who walks with a stick?'

The creature looked up at him, as if on the verge of having an opinion. Then it went back to its nibbling, its tail coiled around a paperweight.

'This isn't good, Peppermint. I can feel it.'

The quaestor prided himself on running a tight ship, as far as caravans went. He did what the church asked of him, but in every other respect he kept his nose out of cathedral business. His caravan always returned to the Way on time to meet its rendezvous, and he rarely came back without a respectable haul of pilgrims, migrant workers and scuttler artefacts. He took care of his passengers and clients without in any way seeking their friendship or gratitude. He needed neither: he had his responsibilities, and he had Peppermint, and that was all that mattered.

Things had not been as good lately as in the past, but that went for all the caravans, and if they were going to single anyone out for punishment, there were others who had far worse records than the quaestor. Besides, the church must have been largely satisfied with his work for them over the last few years, or else they would not have allowed his caravan to grow so large and to travel such important trade routes. He had a good relationship with the cathedral officials he dealt with, and – though none of them would ever have admitted it – a reputation for fairness when it came to dealing with traders like Crozet. So what was the purpose of this surprise visit?

He hoped it had nothing to do with blood. It was well known that the closer you got to cathedral business, the more likely you were to come into contact with the agents of the Office of Bloodwork, that clerical body which promulgated the literal blood of Quaiche. Bloodwork was an organ of the Clocktower, he knew that. But this far from the Way, Quaiche's blood ran thin and diluted. It was hard to live in the country, beyond the iron sanctuary of the cathedrals. You needed to think about icefalls and geysers. You needed detachment and clarity of mind, not the chemical piety of an indoctrinal virus. But what if there had been a change of policy, a broadening of the reach of Bloodwork?

'It's that Crozet,' he said, 'always brings bad luck. Shouldn't have let him aboard this late in the run. Should've sent him back with his tail between his legs. He's a lazy good-for-nothing, that one.'

Peppermint looked up at him. The little mouthparts said, 'Let he who is without sin cast the first stone.'

'Yes, thank you, Peppermint.' The quaestor opened his desk drawer. 'Now why don't you climb in there until we've seen our visitor? And keep your trap shut.'

He reached out for the creature, ready to fold it gently into a form that would fit within the drawer. But the door to his office was already opening, the stranger's passkey working even here.

The suited figure walked in, stopped and closed the door behind him. He rested the cane against the side of the table and placed the white case on the ground. Then he reached up and unlatched his helmet seal. The helmet was a rococo affair, with bas-relief gargoyles worked around the visor. He slid it over his head and set it down on the end of the table.

Rather to his surprise, the quaestor did not recognise the man. He had been expecting one of the usual church officials he dealt with, but this was truly a stranger.

'Might I have a wee word, Quaestor?' the man asked, gesturing towards the seat on his side of the desk.

'Yes, yes,' Quaestor Jones said hastily. 'Please sit down. How was your, um ...?'

'My journey from the Way?' The man blinked, as if momentarily narcotised by the utter dullness of the quaestor's question. 'Unremarkable.' Then he looked at the creature that the quaestor had not had time to hide. 'Yours, is it?'

'My Pep ... my Petnermint. My Peppermint. Pet. Mine.'

'A genetic toy, isn't it? Let me have a guess: one part stick insect, one part chameleon, one part something mammalian?'

'There's cat in him,' the quaestor said. 'Definitely cat. Isn't there, Peppermint?' He pushed some of the seeds towards the visitor. 'Would you like to, um ...?'

Again to the quaestor's surprise – and he wasn't quite sure why he had asked in the first place – the stranger took a pinch of the seeds and offered his hand up to Peppermint's head. He did it very gently. The creature's mandibles began to eat the seeds, one by one.

'Charming,' the man said, leaving his hand where it was. 'I'd get one for myself, but I hear they're very hard to come by.'

'Devils to keep healthy,' the quaestor said.

'I'm sure they are. Well, to business.'

'Business,' the quaestor said, nodding.

The man had a long, thin face with a very flat nose and a strong jaw. He had a shock of white hair sticking straight up from his brow, stiff as a brush and mathematically planar on top, as if sliced off with a laser. Under the room's lights it shone with a faint blue aura. He wore a high-collared side-buttoned tunic marked with the Clocktower insignia: that odd, mummylike spacesuit radiating light through cracks in its shell. But there was something about him that made the quaestor doubt that he was a cleric. He didn't have the smell of someone with Quaiche blood in them. Some high-ranking technical official, then.

'Don't you want to know my name?' the man asked.

'Not unless you want to tell me.'

'You're curious, though?'

'I was told to expect a visitor. That's all I need to know.'

The man smiled. 'That's a very good policy. You can call me Grelier.'

The quaestor inclined his head. There had been a Grelier involved in Hela's affairs since the very earliest days of the settlement, after the witnessing of the first vanishing. He presumed the Grelier family had continued to play a role in the church ever since, down through the generations. 'It's a pleasure to have you aboard the caravan, Mr Grelier.'

'I won't be here long. Just wanted, as I said, a wee word.' He stopped feeding Peppermint, dropping the remaining seeds on the floor. Then he bent down and retrieved the white case, setting it on his lap. Peppermint started cleaning itself, making prayerlike motions. 'Has anyone come aboard lately, Quaestor?'

'There are always people coming and going.'

'I mean lately, last few days.'

'Well, there's Crozet, I suppose.'

The man nodded and flipped open the lid of his case. It was, the quaestor saw, a medical kit. It was full of syringes, racked next to each other like little pointy-headed soldiers. 'Tell me about Crozet.'

'One of our regular traders. Makes his living in the Vigrid region, keeps himself to himself. Has a wife named Linxe, and a son, Culver.'

'They're here now? I saw an icejammer winched against your machine as I came in.'

'That's his,' the quaestor said.

'Anyone else come in on it?'

'Just the girl.'

The man raised his eyebrows. Like his hair, they were the colour of new snow under moonlight. 'Girl? You said he had a son, not a daughter.'

'She was travelling with them. Not a relative, a hitchhiker. Name of . . .' The quaestor pretended to rack his memory. 'Rashmika. Rashmika Els. Sixteen, seventeen standard years.'

'Had your eye on her, did you?'

'She made an impression. She couldn't *help* but make an impression.' The quaestor's hands felt like two balls of eels, sliding slickly against each other. 'She had a certainty about her, a determination you don't see very often, especially not in one her age. She seemed to be on a mission.'

The man reached into the case and took out a clear syringe. 'What was her relationship to Crozet? Everything above board?'

'As far as I know she was just his passenger.'

'You heard about the missing-persons report? A girl running away from her family in the Vigrid badlands? The local constabulary enquiring after a possible saboteur?'

'That was her? I didn't put two and two together, I'm afraid.'

'Good for you that you didn't.' He held the syringe up to the light, his face distorted through the glass. 'Or you might have sent her back where she came from.'

'That wouldn't have been good?'

'We'd rather she stayed on the caravan for now. She's of interest to us, you see. Give me your arm.'

The quaestor rolled up his sleeve and leant across the table. Peppermint eyed him, pausing in its ablutions. The quaestor could not refuse. The command had been issued so calmly that there could be no prospect of disobedience. The syringe was clear: he had come to take blood, not give it.

The quaestor forced himself to remain calm. 'Why does she have to stay on the caravan?'

'So she gets to where she has to get to.' Grelier slid the needle in. 'Any complaints from your usual acquisitions department, Quaestor?'

'Complaints?'

'About Crozet. About him making a bit more out of his scuttler junk than he normally does.'

'The usual mutterings.'

'This time there might be something in them. The girl sat in on his dealings, didn't she?'

The quaestor realised that his interrogator knew the answer to almost every question he had come to ask. He watched the syringe as it filled with his blood. 'She seemed curious,' he said. 'She says she's interested in scuttler relics. Fancies herself as a bit of a scholar. I didn't see any harm in letting her sit in. It was Crozet's decision, not mine.'

'I bet it was. The girl has a talent, Quaestor, a God-given gift: she can detect lies. She reads microexpressions in the human face, the subliminal signals most of us barely notice. They scream at her, like great neon signs.'

'I don't see . . .'

He pulled out the syringe. 'The girl was reading your acquisitions negotiators, seeing how sincere they were when they said they'd reached their limit. Sending covert signals to Crozet.'

'How do you know?'

'I was expecting her to show up. I listened for the signs. They brought me here, to this caravan.'

'But she's just a girl.'

'Joan of Arc was just a girl. Look at the bloody mess she left behind.' He put a plaster on the quaestor's arm, then slid the syringe into a special niche in the side of the case. The blood drained out as the plunger was pushed down by a mechanical piston. The case hummed and chugged to itself.

'If you want to see her . . .' the quaestor began.

'No, I don't want to see her. Not yet, at least. What I want is for you to keep her in your sight until you reach the Way. She mustn't return with Crozet. Your job is to make sure she stays aboard the caravan.'

The quaestor pulled down his sleeve. 'I'll do my best.'

'You'll do more than your best.' With the case still on his lap he reached over and picked Peppermint up, holding the stiff creature in the fist of one of his vacuum suit gauntlets. With the other hand he took hold of one of Peppermint's forelimbs and pulled it off. The creature thrashed wildly, emitting a horrid shrill whistle.

'Oh,' Grelier said. 'Now *look* what I've done.'

'No,' the quaestor said, frozen in shock.

Grelier placed the tormented animal back down on the table and flicked the severed arm to the floor. 'It's just a limb. Plenty more where that came from.'

Peppermint's tail writhed in agonised coils.

'Now let's talk particulars,' Grelier said. He reached into a pocket of his suit and pulled out a small metal tube. The quaestor flinched, one eye still on his mutilated pet. Grelier nudged the tube across the table. 'The girl is a problem,' he said. 'She has the potential to be useful to the dean, although he doesn't know it yet.'

The quaestor tried to hold his voice together. 'You actually know the dean?'

'On and off.'

'You'd know if he was alive, I mean?'

'He's alive. He just doesn't get out of the Clocktower very often.' Grelier looked at Peppermint again. 'Ask a lot of questions for a caravan master, don't you?'

'I'm sorry.'

'Open the tube.'

The quaestor did as he was told. Inside, tightly rolled, were two pieces of paper. He pulled them out gently and flattened them on the table. One was a letter. The other contained a series of cryptic markings.

'I don't know what I'm supposed to do with these.'

'That's all right, I'll tell you. The letter, you keep here. The markings, including the tube, you give to a man named Pietr.'

'I don't know anyone called Pietr.'

'You should. He's a pilgrim, already aboard your caravan. A wee bit on the unstable side.'

'Unstable?'

Ignoring him, Grelier tapped the case, which was still humming and gurgling to itself as it assayed the quaestor's blood. 'Most of the virus strains in circulation aren't particularly dangerous. They induce religious feelings or visions, but they don't directly meddle with the host's sense of self. What Pietr has is different. We call it DEUS-X. It's a rare mutation of the original indoctrinal virus that we've tried to keep a lid on. It places him at the centre of his own private cosmos. He doesn't always realise it, but the virus is rewiring his sense of reality such that he becomes his own God. He'll be drawn to the Way, to one or other of the orthodox churches, but he'll always feel in conflict with conventional doctrine. He'll bounce from one sect to another, always feeling himself on the verge of enlightenment. His choices will become more and more extreme, pushing him towards odder and odder manifestations of Haldora worship, like the Observers.'

The quaestor had never heard of DEUS-X, but the religious type Grelier had described was familiar enough to him. They were usually young men, usually very serious and humourless. There was something already in their brains that the virus latched on to. 'What does he have to do with the girl?'

'Nothing, yet. I just want him to come into possession of that tube and that piece of paper. It will mean something to him already, although he'll never have seen the markings written down that precisely. For him it will be like finding illuminated scripture, where before all he had were scratches on stone.'

The quaestor examined the paper again. Now that he looked closer, he thought he had seen the markings before. 'The missing vanishing?' he asked. 'I thought that was just an old wives' tale.'

'It doesn't matter if it's an old wives' tale or not. It'll be one of the fringe beliefs with which Pietr has already come into contact. He'll recognise it and it will spur him to act.' Grelier studied the quaestor very carefully, as if measuring his reliability. 'I have arranged for a spy to be present amongst the Observers. He will mention to Pietr something about a girl on a crusade, something already foretold. A girl born in ice, destined to change the world.'

'Rashmika?'

Grelier made a gun shape with his hand, pointed it at the quaestor and made a clicking sound. 'All you have to do is bring them together. Allow her to visit the Observers and Pietr will take care of the rest. He won't be able to resist passing on the knowledge he has gained.'

The quaestor frowned. 'She needs to see those markings?'

'She needs a reason to meet the dean. The other letter will help – it concerns her brother – but it may not be enough. She's interested in the scuttlers, so the missing vanishing will prick her curiosity. She'll have to follow it to its conclusion, no matter how badly her instincts tell her to stay away from the cathedrals.'

'But why don't I just give her the tube now? Why the need for this cumbersome charade with the Observers?'

Grelier looked at Peppermint again. 'You really don't learn, do you?'

'I'm sorry, I just ...'

'The girl is extraordinarily difficult to manipulate. She can read a lie instantly, unless the liar is completely sincere. She needs to be handled with a buffer of unquestioning, utterly delusional self-belief.' Grelier paused. 'Anyway, I need to know her limits. When I have studied her from a distance, she can be approached openly. But until then I want to guide her remotely. You are part of the buffer, but you will also be a test of her ability.'

'And the letter?'

'Give it to her personally. Say it came into your possession through a secret courier and that you know nothing beyond that. Observe her closely, and report on her reaction.'

'And what if she asks too many questions?'

Grelier smiled sympathetically. 'Have a bash at lying.'

The medical case chimed, its analysis complete. Grelier swung it around so that the quaestor could see the results. On the inside of the lid, histograms and pie charts had sprung into view.

'All clear?' the quaestor asked.

'Nothing you need worry about,' Grelier replied.

On his private cameras, the quaestor watched the ruby-hulled cockle-shell spacecraft lift off from the caravan. It flipped over, its main thrusters throwing wild shadows across the landscape.

'I'm sorry, Peppermint,' he said.

The creature was trying to clean its face, its one remaining forelimb thrashing awkwardly across its mouth-parts like a broken windscreen wiper. It looked at the quaestor with those blackcurrant eyes, which were not as uncomprehending as he might have wished.

'If I don't do what he wants, he'll come back. But whatever he wants with that girl isn't right. I can feel it. Can you? I didn't like him at all. I knew he was trouble the moment he landed.'

The quaestor flattened out the letter again. It was brief, written in a clear but childish script. It was from someone called Harbin, to someone called Rashmika.

Ararat, 2675

The flight to the *Nostalgia for Infinity* only took ten minutes, most of which was spent in the final docking phase, queued up behind the transports that had arrived earlier. There were a number of entry points into the towering ship, open apertures like perfectly rect-angular caves in the sides of the spire. The highest was more than two kilometres above the surface of the sea. In space they would have been the docking bays for small service craft, or the major airlocks that permitted access to the ship's cavernous internal chambers.

Scorpio had never really enjoyed trips to the *Infinity*, under any circumstances. Frankly, the ship appalled him. It was a perversion, a twisted mutation of what a mechanical thing should be like. He did not have a superstitious bone in his body, but he always felt as if he was stepping into something haunted or possessed. What really troubled him was that he knew this assessment was not entirely inaccurate. The ship *was* genuinely haunted, in the sense that its whole structural fabric had been inseparably fused with the residual psyche of its erstwhile Captain. In a time when the Melding Plague had lost some of its horror, the fate of the Captain was a shocking reminder of the atrocities it had been capable of.

The shuttle dropped off its passengers in the topmost docking bay, then immediately returned to the sky on some other urgent colonial errand. A Security Arm guard was already waiting to escort them down to the meeting room. He touched a communications earpiece with one finger, frowning slightly as he listened to a distant voice, then he turned to Scorpio. 'Room is secured, sir.'

'Any apparitions?'

'Nothing reported above level four hundred in the last three weeks. Plenty of activity in the lower levels, but we should have the high ship to ourselves.' The guard turned to Vasko. 'If you'd care to follow me.'

Vasko looked at Scorpio. 'Are you coming down, sir?'

'I'll follow in a moment. You go ahead and introduce yourself. Say only that you are Vasko Malinin, an SA operative, and that you participated in the mission to recover Clavain – and then don't say another word until I get there.'

'Yes, sir.' Vasko hesitated. 'Sir, one other thing?'

'What?'

'What did he mean about apparitions?'

'You don't need to know,' Scorpio said.

Scorpio watched them troop off into the bowels of the ship, waiting until their footsteps had died away and he was certain that he had the landing bay to himself. Then he made his way to the edge of the bay's entrance, standing with the tips of his blunt, childlike shoes perilously close to the edge.

The wind scrubbed hard against his face, although today it was not especially strong. He always felt in danger of being blown out, but experience had taught him that the wind usually blew into the chamber. All the same, he remained ready to grab the left-hand edge of the door for support should an eddy threaten to tip him over the lip. Blinking against the wind, his eyes watering, he watched the claw-shaped aircraft bank and recede. Then he looked down, surveying the colony that, despite Clavain's return, was still very much his responsibility.

Kilometres away, First Camp sparkled in the curve of the bay. It was too distant to make out any detail save for the largest structures, such as the High Conch. Even those buildings were flattened into near-insignificance by Scorpio's elevation. The happy, bustling squalor and grime of the shanty streets were invisible. Everything appeared eerily neat and ordered, like something laid out according to strict civic rules. It could have been almost any city, on any world, at any point in history. There were even thin quills of smoke rising up from kitchens and factories. Yet other than the smoke there was nothing obviously moving, nothing that he could point to. But at the same time the entire settlement trembled with a frenzy of subliminal motion, as if seen through a heat haze.

For a long time, Scorpio had thought that he would never adjust to life beyond Chasm City. He had revelled in the constant roaring intricacy of that place. He had loved the dangers almost as much as the challenges and opportunities. On any given day he had known that there might be six or seven serious attempts on his life, orchestrated by as many rival groups. There would be another dozen or so that were too inept to be worth bringing to his attention. And on any given day Scorpio might himself give the order to have one of his enemies put to sleep. It was never business with Scorpio, always personal.

The stress of dealing with life as a major criminal element in Chasm City might have appeared crippling. Many did crack – they either burned out and retreated back to the limited spheres of petty crime that had bred them, or they made the kind of mistake it wasn't possible to learn from.

But Scorpio had never cracked, and if he had ever screwed up it was one time only – and even then it had not exactly been his fault. It had been wartime by then, after all. The rules were changing so fast that now and then Scorpio had even found himself acting legally. Now *that* had been frightening.

But the one mistake he had made had been nearly terminal. Getting caught by the zombies, and then the spiders . . . and because of *that* he had fallen under Clavain's influence. And at the end of it a question remained: if the city had defined him so totally, what did it mean to him no longer to have the city?

It had taken him a while to find out – in a way, he had only really found the answer when Clavain had left and the colony was entirely in Scorpio's control.

He had simply woken up one morning and the longing for Chasm City was gone. His ambition no longer focused on anything as absurdly self-centred as personal wealth, or power, or status. Once, he had worshipped weapons and violence. He still had to keep a lid on his anger, but he struggled to remember the last time he had held a gun or a knife. Instead of feuds and scores, scams and hits, the things that crammed his days now were quotas, budgets, supply lines, the bewildering mire of interpersonal politics. First Camp was a smaller city – barely a city at all, really – but the complexity of running it and the wider colony was more than enough to keep him occupied. He would never have believed it back in his Chasm City days, but here he was, standing like a king surveying his empire. It had been a long journey, fraught with reversals and setbacks, but somewhere along the way – perhaps that first morning when he awoke without longing for his old turf – he had become something like a statesman. For someone who had started life as an indentured slave, without even the dignity of a name, it was hardly the most predictable of outcomes.

But now he worried that it was all about to slip away. He had always known that their stay on this world was only ever intended to be temporary, a port of call where this particular band of refugees would wait until Remontoire and the others were able to regroup. But as time went on, and the twenty-year mark had approached and then passed without incident, the seductive idea had formed in his mind that perhaps things might be more permanent. That perhaps Remontoire had been more than delayed. That perhaps the wider conflict between humanity and the Inhibitors was going to leave the settlement alone.

It had never been a realistic hope, and now he sensed that he was paying the price for such thinking. Remontoire had not merely arrived, but had brought the arena of battle with him. If Khouri's account of things was accurate, then the situation truly was grave.

The distant town glimmered. It looked hopelessly transient, like a patina of dust on the landscape. Scorpio felt a sudden visceral sense that someone dear to him was in mortal danger.

He turned abruptly from the open door of the landing deck and made his way to the meeting room.

THIRTEEN

Ararat, 2675

The meeting room lay deep inside the ship, in the spherical chamber that had once been the huge vessel's main command centre. The process of reaching it now resembled the exploration of a large cave system: there were cold, snaking warrens of corridor, spiralling tunnels, junctions and dizzying shafts. There were echoing sub-chambers and claustrophobic squeeze-points. Weird, unsettling growths clotted the walls: here a leprous froth, there a brachial mass horribly suggestive of petrified lung tissue. Unguents dripped constantly from ceiling to floor. Scorpio dodged the obstacles and oozing fluids with practised ease. He knew that there was nothing really hazardous about the ship's exudations – chemically they were quite uninteresting – but even for someone who had lived in the Mulch, the sense of revulsion was overpowering. If the ship had only ever been a mechanical thing, he could have taken it. But there was no escaping the fact that much of what he saw stemmed in some arcane sense from the memory of the Captain's biological body. It was a matter of semantics as to whether he walked through a ship that had taken on certain biological attributes or a body that had swollen to the size and form of a ship.

He didn't care which was more accurate: both possibilities revolted him.

Scorpio reached the meeting room. After the gloom of the approach corridors it was overwhelmingly bright and clean. They had equipped the ship's original spherical command chamber with a false floor and suitably generous wooden conference table. A refurbished projector hung above the table like an oversized chandelier, shuffling through schematic views of the planet and its immediate airspace.

Clavain was already waiting, garbed in the kind of stiff black dress uniform that would not have looked outrageously unfashionable at any point in the last eight hundred years. He had allowed someone to further tidy his appearance: the lines and shadows remained on his face, but with the benefit of a few hours' sleep he was at least recognisable as the Clavain of old. He stroked the neat trim of his beard, one elbow propped on the table's reflective black surface. His other hand drummed a tattoo against the wood.

'Something kept you, Scorp?' he asked mildly.

'I needed a moment of reflection.'

Clavain looked at him and then inclined his head. 'I understand.'

Scorpio sat down. A seat had been reserved for him next to Vasko, amid a larger group of colony officials.

Clavain was at the head of the table. To his left sat Blood, his powerful frame occupying the width of two normal spaces. Blood, as usual, managed to look like a thug who had gate-crashed a private function. He had a knife in one trotter and was digging into the nails of the other with the tip of the blade, flicking excavated dirt on to the floor.

In stark contrast was Antoinette Bax, sitting on Clavain's right side. She was a human woman Scorpio had known since his last days in Chasm City. She had been young then, barely out of her teens. Now she was in her early forties – still attractive, he judged, but certainly heavier around the face, and with the beginnings of crow's-feet around the corners of her eyes. The one constant – and the thing that she would probably take to her grave – was the stripe of freckles that ran across the bridge of her nose. It always looked as if it had just been painted on, a precisely stippled band. Her hair was longer now, pinned back from her forehead in an asymmetrical parting. She wore complex locally made jewellery. Bax had been a superb pilot in her day, but lately there had been few opportunities for her to fly. She complained about this with good humour, but at the same time knuckled down to solid colony work. She had turned out to be a very good mediator.

Antoinette Bax was married. Her husband, Xavier Liu, was a little older than her, his black hair now veined with silver, tied back in a modest tail. He had a small, neat goatee beard and he was missing two fingers on his right hand from an industrial accident down at the docks fifteen or so years ago. Liu was a genius with anything mechanical, especially cybernetic systems. Scorpio had always got on well with him. He was one of the few humans who genuinely didn't seem to see a pig when he talked to him, just another mechanically minded soul, someone he could really talk to. Xavier was now in charge of the central machine pool, controlling the colony's finite and dwindling reserve of functioning servitors, vehicles, aircraft, pumps, weapons and shuttles: technically it was a desk job, but whenever Scorpio called on him, Liu was usually up to his elbows in something. Nine times out of ten, Scorpio would find himself helping out, too.

Next to Blood was Pauline Sukhoi, a pale, spectral figure seemingly either haunted by something just out of sight, or else a ghost herself. Her hands and voice trembled constantly, and her episodes of what might be termed transient insanity were well known. Years ago, in the patronage of one of Chasm City's most shadowy individuals, she had worked on an experiment concerning local alteration of the quantum vacuum. There had been an accident, and in the whiplash of severing possibilities that was a quantum vacuum transition, Sukhoi had seen something dreadful, something that had pushed her to the edge of madness. Even now she could barely speak of it. It was said that she passed her time sewing patterns into carpets.

Then there was Orca Cruz, one of Scorpio's old associates from his Mulch days, one-eyed but still as sharp as a monofilament scythe. She was the toughest human he knew, Clavain included. Two of Scorpio's old rivals had once made the mistake of underestimating Orca Cruz. The first Scorpio knew of it was when he heard about their funerals. Cruz wore much black leather and had her favourite firearm out on the table in front of her, scarlet fingernails clicking against the ornamented Japanwork of its carved muzzle. Scorpio thought the gesture rather gauche, but he had never picked his associates for their sense of decorum.

There were a dozen other senior colony members in the room, three of them swimmers from the Juggler contact section. Of necessity they were all young baseline humans. Their bodies were sleek and purposeful as otters', their flesh mottled by faint green indications of biological takeover. They all wore sleeveless tunics that showed off the broadness of their shoulders and the impressive development of their arm muscles. They had tattoos worked into the paisley complexity of their markings, signifying some inscrutable hierarchy of rank meaningful only to other swimmers. Scorpio, on balance, did not much like the swimmers. It was not simply that they had access to a luminous world that he, as a pig, would never know. They seemed aloof and scornful of everyone, including the other baseline humans. But it could not be denied that they had their uses and that in some sense they were right to be scornful. They *had* seen things and places no one else ever would. As colonial assets, they had to be tolerated and tapped.

The nine other seniors were all somewhat older than the swimmers. They were people who had been adults on Resurgam before the evacuation. As with the swimmers, the faces changed when new representatives were cycled in and out of duty. Scorpio, nonetheless, made it his duty to know them all, with the intimate fondness for personal details he reserved only for close friends and blood enemies. He knew that this curatorial grasp of personal data was one of his strengths, a compensation for his lack of forward-thinking ability.

It therefore troubled him profoundly that there was one person in the room that he hardly knew at all. Khouri sat nearly opposite him, attended by Dr Valensin. Scorpio had no hold on her, no insights into her weaknesses. That absence in his knowledge troubled him like a missing tooth.

He was contemplating this, wondering if anyone else felt the same way, when the murmur of conversation came to an abrupt end. Everyone, including Khouri, turned towards Clavain, expecting him to lead the meeting.

Clavain stood, pushing himself up. 'I don't intend to say very much. All the evidence I've seen points to Scorpio having done an excellent job of running this place in my absence. I have no intention of replacing his leadership, but I will offer what guidance I can during the present crisis. I trust you've all had time to read the summaries Scorp and I put together, based on Khouri's testimony?'

'We've read them,' said one of the former colonists – a bearded, corpulent man named Hallatt. 'Whether we take any of it seriously is another thing entirely.'

'She certainly makes some unusual claims,' Clavain said, 'but that in itself shouldn't surprise us, especially given the things that happened to us after we left Yellowstone. These are unusual times. The circumstances of her arrival were bound to be a little surprising.'

'It's not just the claims,' Hallatt said. 'It's Khouri herself. She was Ilia Volyova's second-in-command. That's hardly the best recommendation, as far as I'm concerned.'

Clavain raised a hand. 'Volyova may well have wronged your planet, but in my view she also atoned for her sins with her last act.'

'*She* may believe she did,' Hallatt said, 'but the gift of redemption lies with the sinned-against, rather than the sinner. In *my* view she was still a war criminal, and Ana Khouri was her accomplice.'

'That's your opinion,' Clavain allowed, 'but according to the laws that we all agreed to live under during the evacuation, neither Volyova nor Khouri were to be held accountable for any crimes. My only concern now is Khouri's testimony, and whether we act upon it.'

'Just a moment,' Khouri said as Clavain sat down. 'Maybe I missed something, but shouldn't someone else be taking part in this little set-up?'

'Who did you have in mind?' Scorpio asked.

'The ship, of course. The one we happen to be sitting in.'

Scorpio scratched the fold of skin between his forehead and the upturned snout of his nose. 'I don't quite follow.'

'Captain Brannigan brought you all here, didn't he?' Khouri asked. 'Doesn't that entitle him to a seat at this table?'

'Maybe you weren't paying attention,' Pauline Sukhoi said. 'This isn't a ship any more. It's a landmark.'

'You're right to ask about the Captain,' Antoinette Bax said, her deep voice commanding immediate attention. 'We've been trying to establish a dialogue with him almost since the *Infinity* landed.' Her many-ringed fingers were knitted together on the table, her nails painted a bright chemical green. 'No joy,' she said. 'He doesn't want to talk.'

'Then the Captain's dead?' Khouri said.

'No ...' Bax said, looking around warily. 'He still shows his face now and then.'

Pauline Sukhoi addressed Khouri again. 'Might I ask something else? In your testimony you claim that Remontoire and his allies – *our* allies – have achieved significant breakthroughs in a range of areas. Drives that can't be detected, ships that can't be seen, weapons that cut through space-time ... that's quite a list.' Sukhoi's frail, frightened voice always sounded on the verge of laughter. 'All the more so given the very limited time that you've had to make these discoveries.'

'They weren't discoveries,' Khouri said. 'Read the summary. Aura gave us the clues to make those things, that's all. We didn't *discover* anything.'

'Let's talk about Aura,' Scorpio said. 'In fact, let's go right back to the beginning, from the moment our two forces separated around Delta Pavonis. *Zodiacal Light* was badly damaged, we know that much. But it shouldn't have taken more than two or three years for the self-repair systems to patch it up again, provided you fed them with enough raw material. Yet we've been waiting here for twenty-three years. What took you so long?'

'The repairs took longer than we anticipated,' Khouri replied. 'We had problems obtaining the raw materials now that the Inhibitors had so much of the system under their control.'

'But not twenty years, surely,' said Scorpio.

'No, but once we'd been there a few years it became clear we were in no immediate danger of persecution by the Inhibitors provided we stayed near the Hades object, the re-engineered neutron star. That meant we had more time to study the thing. We were scared at first, but the Inhibitors always kept clear of it, as if there was something about it they didn't like. Actually, Thorn and I had already guessed as much.'

'Tell us a bit more about Thorn,' Clavain said gently.

They all heard the crack in her voice. 'Thorn was the resistance leader, the man who made life difficult for the regime until the Inhibitors showed up.'

'Volyova and you struck up some kind of relationship with him, didn't you?' Clavain asked.

'He was our way of getting the people to accept our help to evacuate. Because of that I had a lot of involvement with Thorn. We got to know each other quite well.' She faltered into silence.

'Take your time,' Clavain said, with a kindness Scorpio had not heard in his voice lately.

'One time, stupid curiosity drew Thorn and I too close to the Inhibitors. They had us surrounded, and they'd even started pushing their probes into our heads, drinking our memories. But then something – some entity – intervened and saved us. Whatever it was, it appeared to originate around Hades. Maybe it was even an extension of Hades itself, another kind of probe.'

Scorpio tapped the summary before him. 'You reported contact with a human mind.'

'It was Dan Sylveste,' she said, 'the same self-obsessed bastard who started all this in the first place. We know he found a way into the Hades matrix all those years ago, using the same route that the Amarantin took to escape the Inhibitors.'

'And you think Sylveste – or whatever he had become by then – intervened to save you and Thorn?' Clavain asked.

'I know he did. When his mind touched mine, I got a blast of . . . call it remorse. As if the penny had finally dropped about how big a screw-up he'd been, and the damage he'd done in the name of curiosity. It was as if he was ready, in a small way, to start making amends.'

Clavain smiled. 'Better late than never.'

'He couldn't work miracles, though,' Khouri said. 'The envoy that Hades sent to Roc to help us was enough to intimidate the Inhibitor machines, but it didn't do more than hamper them, allowing us to make it back to Ilia. But it was a sign, at least, that if we stood a chance of doing something about the Inhibitors, the place to look for help was in Hades. Some of us had to go back inside.'

'You were one of them?' Clavain said.

'Yes,' she said. 'I did it the same way I'd done it before, because I knew that would work. Not via the front door inside the thing orbiting Hades, the way Sylveste did it, but by falling towards the star. By dying, in other words; letting myself get ripped apart by the gravitational field of Hades and then reassembled inside it. I don't remember any of that. I guess I'm grateful.'

It was clear to Scorpio that even Khouri had little idea of what had really happened to her during her entry into the Hades object. Her earlier account of things had made it clear that she believed herself to have been physically reconstituted within the star, preserved in a tiny, quivering bubble of flat space-time, so that she was immune to the awesome crush of Hades' gravitational field. Perhaps that had indeed been the case. Equally, it might have been some fanciful fiction created for her by her once-human hosts. All that mattered, ultimately, was that there was a way to communicate with entities running inside the Hades matrix – and, perhaps more importantly, a way to get back out into the real universe.

Scorpio was contemplating that when his communicator buzzed discreetly. As he stood up from the table, Khouri halted her monologue.

Irritated at the interruption, Scorpio lifted the communicator to his face and unspooled the privacy earpiece. 'This had better be good.'

The voice that came was thready and distant. He recognised it as belonging to the Security Arm guard that had met them at the landing stage. 'Thought you needed to know this, sir.'

'Make it quick.'

'Class-three apparition reported on five eighty-seven. That's the highest in nearly six months.'

As if he needed to be told. 'Who saw it?'

'Palfrey, a worker in bilge management.'

Scorpio lowered his voice and pressed the earpiece in more tightly. He was conscious that he had the full attention of everyone in the room. 'What did Palfrey see?'

'The usual, sir: not very much, but enough that we'll have a hard time persuading him to go that deep again.'

'Interview him, get it on record, make it clear that he speaks of this to no one. Understood?'

'Understood, sir.'

'Then find him another line of work.' Scorpio paused, frowning as he thought through all the implications. 'On second thoughts, I'd like a word with him as well. Don't let him leave the ship.'

Without waiting for a reply, Scorpio broke the link, spooled the earpiece back into the communicator and returned to the table. He sat down, gesturing at Khouri for her to continue.

'What was all that about?' she asked.

'Nothing that need worry you.'

'I'm worried.'

He felt a splinter of pain between his eyes. He had been getting a lot of headaches lately, and this kind of day didn't help. 'Someone reported an apparition,' he said, 'one of the Captain's little manifestations that Antoinette mentioned. Doesn't mean anything.'

'No? I show up, *he* shows up, and you think that doesn't mean something?' Khouri shook her head. 'I know what it means, even if you don't. The Captain understands there's some heavy stuff going down.'

The splinter of pain had become a little broken arrowhead. He pinched the bridge of skin between snout and forehead. 'Tell us about Sylveste,' he said with exaggerated patience.

Khouri sighed, but did as she was asked. 'There was a kind of welcoming committee inside the star, Sylveste and his wife, just as I'd last met them. It even looked like the same room – a scientific study full of old bones and equipment. But it didn't *feel* the same. It was as if I was taking part in some kind of parlour game, but I was the only one not in on it. I wasn't talking to Sylveste any more, if I ever had been.'

'An impostor?' Clavain asked.

'No, not that. I was talking with the genuine article ... I'm sure of that ... but at the same time it wasn't Sylveste, either. It was as if ... he was condescending to me, putting on a mask so that I'd have something familiar to talk to. I knew I wasn't getting the whole story. I was getting the comforting version, with the creepy stuff taken out. I don't think Sylveste thought I was *capable* of dealing with what he'd really become, after all that time.' She smiled. 'I think he thought he'd blow my mind.'

'After sixty years in the Hades matrix, he might have,' Clavain said.

'All the same,' Khouri said, 'I don't think there was any actual deception. Nothing that wasn't absolutely essential for the sake of my sanity, anyhow.'

'Tell us about your later visits,' Clavain said.

'I went in alone the first few times. Then it was always with someone else – Remontoire sometimes, Thorn, a few other volunteers.'

'But always you?' Clavain asked.

'The matrix accepted me. No one was willing to take the risk of going in without me.'

'I don't blame them.' Clavain paused, but it was apparent to all present that he had something more to say. 'But Thorn died, didn't he?'

'We were falling towards the neutron star,' she said, 'just the way we always did, and then something hit us. Maybe an energy burst from a stray weapon, we'll never know for sure; it might have been orbiting Hades for a million years, or it could have been something from the Inhibitors, something they risked placing that close to the star. It wasn't enough to destroy the capsule, but it was enough to kill Thorn.'

She stopped speaking, allowing an uncomfortable silence to invade the room. Scorpio looked around, observing that everyone had their eyes downcast; that no one dared look at Khouri, not even Hallatt.

Khouri resumed speaking. 'The star captured me alive, but Thorn was dead. It couldn't reassemble what was left of him into a living being.'

'I'm sorry,' Clavain said, his voice barely audible.

'There's something else,' Khouri said, her voice nearly as quiet.

'Go on.'

'Part of Thorn did survive. We'd made love on the long fall to Hades, and so when I went into the star, I took a part of him with me. I was pregnant.'

Clavain waited a decent while before answering, allowing her words to settle in, giving them the dignified space they warranted. 'And Thorn's child?'

'She's Aura,' Khouri said. 'The baby Skade stole from me. The child I came here to get back.'

FOURTEEN

Ararat, 2675

The room in which Palfrey had been told to wait for Scorpio was a small annexe off one of the larger storage areas used by bilge management, the branch of the administration tasked with keeping the lower levels of the ship as dry as possible. The curved walls of the little chamber were layered with a glossy grey-green plaque that had hardened into stringy, waxy formations. The smooth floor was sheet metal. Anchored to it with thick bolts was a small, battered desk from Central Amenities, upon which lay an ashtray, a half-empty beaker of something tarlike and the parts of several dismantled bilge pump assemblies. Bookended by the pump parts was what Scorpio took to be a vacuum helmet of antique design, silver paint peeling from its metal shell. Behind the desk, Palfrey sat chain-smoking, his eyes red with fatigue, his sparse black hair messed across the sunburned pink of his scalp. He wore khaki overalls with many pockets, and some kind of breathing apparatus hung around his neck on frayed cords.

'I understand you saw something,' Scorpio said, pulling up another chair, the legs squealing horribly against the metal, and sitting in it the wrong way around, facing the man with his legs splayed either side of the backrest.

'That's what I told my boss. All right if I go home now?'

'Your boss didn't give me a very clear description. I'd like to know a bit more.' Scorpio smiled at Palfrey. 'Then we can all go home.'

Palfrey stubbed out his current cigarette. 'Why? It's not as if you believe me, is it?'

Scorpio's headache had not improved. 'Why do you say that?'

'Everyone knows you don't believe in the sightings. You think we're just finding reasons to skive off the deep-level duties.'

'It's true that your boss will have to arrange a new detail for that part of the ship, and it's true that I don't believe all the reports that reach my desk. Many of them, however, I'm inclined to take seriously. Often they follow a pattern, clustering in one part of the ship, or moving up and down a series of adjacent levels. It's as if the Captain focuses on an area to haunt and then sticks with it until he's made his point. You ever seen him before?'

'First time,' Palfrey said, his hands trembling. His fingers were bony, the bright-pink knuckles like blisters ready to pop.

'Tell me what you saw.'

'I was alone. The nearest team was three levels away, fixing another pump failure. I'd gone down to look at a unit that might have been overheating. I had my toolkit with me and that was all. I wasn't planning to spend much time down there. None of us like working those deep levels, and definitely not alone.'

'I thought it was policy not to send anyone in alone below level six hundred.'

'It is.'

'So what were you doing down there by yourself?'

'If we stuck to the rules you'd have a flooded ship in about a week.'

'I see.' He tried to sound surprised, but he heard the same story about a dozen times a week, all over the colony. Individually, everyone thought they were on the only team being stretched past breaking point. Collectively, the whole settlement was lurching from one barely contained crisis to another. But only Scorpio and a handful of his lieutenants knew that.

'We don't fiddle the timesheets,' Palfrey volunteered, as if this must have been next thing on Scorpio's mind.

'Why don't you tell me about the apparition? You were down looking at the hot pump. What happened?'

'Out of the corner of my eye, I saw something move. Couldn't tell what it was at first – it's dark down there, and our lights don't work as well as they should. You imagine a lot of stuff, so you don't immediately jump out of your skin the first time you think you see something. But when I shone the light on it and looked properly, there was definitely something there.'

'Describe it.'

'It looked like machinery. Junk. Old pump mechanisms, old servitor parts. Wires. Cables. Stuff that must have been lying down there for twenty years.'

'You saw machinery and you thought that was an apparition?'

'It wasn't just machinery,' Palfrey said defensively. 'It was organised, gathered together, lashed into something larger. It was man-shaped. It just stood there, watching me.'

'Did you hear it approach?'

'No. As I said, it was just junk. It could have been there all along, waiting until I noticed it.'

'And when you did notice it – what happened then?'

'It looked at me. The head – it was made up of hundreds of little bits – moved, as if acknowledging me. And I saw something in the face, like an expression. It wasn't just a machine. There was a mind there. A distinct purpose.' Redundantly, he added, 'I didn't like it.'

Scorpio drummed the tips of his fingers against the seatback. 'If it helps, what you saw was a class-three apparition. A class one is a localised change in the atmospheric conditions of the ship: an unexplained breeze, or a drop in temperature. They're the commonest kind, reported almost daily. Only a fraction probably have anything at all to do with the Captain.'

'We've all experienced those,' Palfrey said.

'A class two is a little rarer. We define it as a recognisable speech sound, a word or sentence fragment, or even a whole statement. Again, there's an element of uncertainty. If you're scared and you hear the wind howl, it's easy to imagine a word or two.'

'It wasn't one of those.'

'No, clearly not. Which brings us to a class-three manifestation: a physical presence, transient or otherwise, manifesting either via a local physical alteration of the ship's fabric – a face appearing in a wall, for instance – or the co-opting of an available mechanism or group of mechanisms. What you saw was clearly the latter.'

'That's very reassuring.'

'It should be. I can also tell you that despite rumours to the contrary no one has ever been harmed by an apparition, and that very few workers have ever seen a class three on more than one occasion.'

'You're still not getting me to go down there again.'

'I'm not asking you to. You'll be reassigned to some other duty, either in the high ship levels or back on the mainland.'

'The sooner I'm off this ship, the better.'

'Good. That's sorted, then.' Scorpio moved to stand up, the chair scraping against the floor.

'That's it?' Palfrey asked.

'You've told me everything I need to know.'

Palfrey poked around in the ashtray with the dead stub of his last cigarette. 'I see a ghost and I get interviewed by one of the most powerful men in the colony?'

Scorpio shrugged. 'I just happened to be in the area, thought you'd appreciate my taking an interest.'

The man looked at him with a critical expression Scorpio seldom saw in pigs. 'Something's up, isn't it?'

'Not sure I follow you.'

'You wouldn't interview someone from bilge management unless something was going down.'

'Take it from me, something's always going down.'

'But this must be more than that.' Palfrey smiled at him, the way people smiled when they thought they knew something you'd have preferred them not to know, or when they imagined they had figured out an angle they weren't supposed to see. 'I listen. I hear about all the other apparitions, not just the ones on my shift.'

'And your conclusion is?'

'They've been growing more frequent. Not just in the last day or so, but over the last few weeks or months. I knew it was only a matter of time before I saw one for myself.'

'That's a very interesting analysis.'

'The way I see it,' Palfrey said, 'it's as if he – the Captain – is getting restless. But what would I know? I'm just a bilge mechanic.'

'Indeed,' Scorpio said.

'You know something's happening, though, don't you? Or you wouldn't be taking so much interest in a single sighting. I bet you're interviewing everyone these days. He's really got you worried, hasn't he?'

'The Captain's on our side.'

'You hope.' Palfrey sniggered triumphantly.

'We all hope. Unless you have some other plans for getting off this planet, the Captain's our only ticket out of here.'

'You're talking as if there's some sudden urgency to leave.'

Scorpio considered telling him that there might well be, just to mess with his mind. He had decided that he did not very much like Palfrey. But Palfrey would talk, and the last thing Scorpio needed now was a wave of panic to deal with in addition to Khouri's little crisis. He would just have to deny himself that small, puissant pleasure.

He leaned across the table, Palfrey's stench hitting him like a wall. 'A word of this meeting to anyone,' he said, 'and you won't be working in effluent management any more. You'll be part of the problem.'

Scorpio pushed himself up from the chair, intending to leave Palfrey alone with his thoughts.

'You haven't asked me about this,' Palfrey said, offering Scorpio the battered silver helmet.

Scorpio took it from him and turned it in his hands. It was heavier than he had expected. 'I thought it belonged to you.'

'You thought wrong. I found it down there in the junk, when the apparition had gone. I don't think it was there before.'

Scorpio took a closer look at the helmet. Its design appeared very old. Above the small rectangular porthole of the faceplate were many rectangular symbols containing blocks of primary colour. There were crosses and crescents, stripes and stars.

The pig wondered what they meant.

Hela, 2727

Now that she had time on her hands, Rashmika used it to explore the caravan. Although there was a great deal of space to investigate inside, she quickly found that one compartment in the caravan was much like another. Wherever she went she encountered the same bad smells, the same wandering pilgrims and traders. If there were variations on these themes they were too dull and nuanced to interest her. What she really wanted was to get outside, on to the roof of the procession.

It was many months since she had seen Haldora, and now that the gas giant had finally crept above the horizon as the caravan narrowed the distance to the cathedrals of the Way, she was struck by a desire to go outside, lie on her back and just look at the huge planet. But the first few times she tried to find a way to the roof, none of the doors would open for her. Rashmika tried different routes and times of the day, hoping to slip through a gap in the caravan's security, but the roof was well protected, presumably because there was a lot of sensitive navigation equipment up there.

She was backtracking from one dead end when she found her way blocked by the quaestor. He had his little green pet with him, squatting on his shoulder. Was it Rashmika's imagination or was there something wrong with one of its forelimbs? It ended in a green-tipped stump that she did not remember seeing before.

'Can I help you, Miss Els?'

'I was just exploring the caravan,' she said. 'That's allowed, isn't it?'

'Within certain restrictions, yes.' He nodded beyond her, to the door she had found blocked. 'The roof, naturally, is one of the places that are out of bounds.'

'I wasn't interested in the roof.'

'No? Then you must be lost. This door only leads to the roof. There's nothing up there to interest you, take my word for it.'

'I wanted to see Haldora.'

'You must have seen it many times before.'

'Not recently, and never very far above the horizon,' she said. 'I wanted to see it at the zenith.'

'Well, you'll have to wait for that. Now ... if you don't mind.' He pushed past her, his bulk pressing unpleasantly against her in the narrow squeeze of the corridor.

The green creature tracked her with his faceted eyes. 'Let he who is without sin cast the first stone,' it intoned.

'Where are you going, Quaestor? You're not wearing a suit.'

'Run along now, Miss Els.'

He did something that he obviously did not want her to see, reaching into a shadowed alcove next to the door that a casual visitor would never have noticed. He tried to be quick about it, to hide the gesture. She heard a low click, as if some hidden mechanism had just snapped open.

The door worked for him. He stepped through. In the red-lit space beyond she glimpsed emergency equipment and several racked vacuum suits.

She came back several hours later, when she was certain that the quaestor had returned inside the caravan. She carried her own surface suit in a collapsed bundle, sneaking it through the rumbling innards of the caravan. She tried the door: it was still blocked to her. But when she slipped her hand into the alcove that the quaestor had not wanted her to see she found a concealed control. She applied pressure and heard the click as the locking mechanism relaxed. Presumably there was some further fail-safe that would have prevented the inner door from opening if the outer one was also open. That was not the case now, however, and the door yielded to her as it had to the quaestor. She slipped into the lock, secured the inner door behind her and changed into her own suit. She checked the air, satisfying herself that there was enough in the reservoir, and feeling a moment of *déjà vu* as she remembered making the same check before leaving her home.

She recalled how the reservoir had not been completely full, as if someone had used her suit recently. She had thought little of it at the time, but now a cluster of thoughts arrived in quick, uneasy succession. There had been footprints in the ice around the surface lock, suggesting that someone had used the lock as well as the suit.

The prints had been small enough to belong to her mother, but they could just as easily have belonged to Rashmika.

She remembered the constabulary, too, and their suspicion that she had had something to do with the sabotage. She hadn't helped her case by running away shortly afterwards, but they wouldn't have come after her unless they had some additional evidence to link her to the act.

What did it mean? If she had been the one who had blown up the store of demolition charges, surely she'd have some memory of doing it. More to the point, why would she have done such a pointless thing? No, she told herself, it couldn't have been her. It was just an unfortunate set of coincidences.

But she could not dismiss her doubts that easily.

Ten minutes later she was standing under airless sky astride the back of the huge machine. The business with the sabotage still troubled her, but with an effort of will she forced her thoughts on to more immediate matters.

She thought back to what had happened in the corridor, when the quaestor had found her. Convenient, that. Of all the possible entrances to the roof he had bumped into her at precisely the one she had been trying. More than likely he had been spying on her, observing her peregrinations through his little rolling empire. When he had spoken to her he had been hiding something. She was certain of that: it had been written on his face, in the momentary elevation of his eyebrows. His own guilt at spying on her? She doubted that he had the chance to spy on many girls her age, so he was probably making the most of it, him and that horrible pet of his.

She didn't like the idea of him watching her, but she would not be on the caravan for very long and all she really cared about now was exploring the roof. If he had been observing her, then he would have had plenty of chances to stop her when she was changing into her own suit and finding the steps that led up to the roof. No one had come, so perhaps his attention had been elsewhere, or he had decided it was not worth his bother to stop her going where she wanted.

Quickly she forgot all about him, thrilled to be outside again.

Rashmika had never seen a vanishing. Two had occurred in her lifetime, once when Haldora was visible from the badlands, but she had been in classes at the time. Of course, she knew that the chances of seeing anything were tiny, even if one had the extreme good fortune to be out on the ice when it happened. The vanishings lasted for only a fraction of a second. By the time you knew one had happened, it was always too late. The only people who had ever seen one happen – with the exception of Quaiche, of course, who had started it all – were those who made it their duty to observe Haldora at every possible moment. And even then they had to pray that they did not blink or look away at that critical instant. Deprived of sleep by drugs and elective neurological intervention, they were half-mad to begin with.

Rashmika could not imagine that kind of dedication, but then she had never felt the slightest inclination to join a church in the first place. She wanted to observe a vanishing because she still clung to the notion that it was a rational natural phenomenon rather than evidence of divine intervention on the cosmic scale. And in Rashmika's view it would be a shame not to be able to say one had seen something so rare, so wondrous. Consequently, ever since she was small, and whenever Haldora was high, she would try to devote some time each day to watching it. It was nothing compared to the endless hours of the cathedral observers, and the statistical odds against seeing anything did not bear contemplation, but she did it anyway, cheerfully ignoring such considerations while chiding those who did not share her particular brand of scientific rationalism.

The caravan's roof was a landscape of treacherous obstructions. There were crouching generator boxes, radiator grilles and vanes, snaking conduits and power lines. It all looked very old, patched together over many years. She made her way from one side to the other, following the course of a railed catwalk. When she reached the edge she looked over, appalled at how far down the ground was and how slowly it now appeared to move. There was no one else up here, at least not on this particular machine.

She looked up, craning her neck as far as the awkward articulation of the helmet joint permitted. The sky was full of counter-moving lights. It was as if there were two celestial spheres up there, two crystal globes nested one within the other. As always the effect was immediately dizzying. Normally the sense of vertigo was little more than a nuisance, but this high up it could easily kill her.

Rashmika tightened her grip on the railing and looked back down at the horizon again. Then, steeled, she looked up once more.

The illusion that she stood at the centre of two spheres was not entirely inaccurate. The lights pinned to the outermost sphere were the stars, impossibly distant; pinned to the innermost sphere were the ships in orbit around Hela, the sunlight glinting off the polished perfection of their hulls. Occasionally one or other would flicker with the hard gemlike flash of steering thrust as the Ultra crews trimmed their orbits or prepared for departure.

At any one time, Rashmika had heard, there were between thirty and fifty ships in orbit around Hela, always coming and going. Most were not large vessels, for the Ultras distrusted Haldora and preferred to hold their most valuable assets much further out. In general those she saw were in-system shuttles, large enough to hold frozen pilgrims and a modest team of Ultra negotiators. The ships that flew between Hela and orbit were usually even smaller, for the churches did not allow anything large to approach Hela's surface.

The big ships, the starships – the lighthuggers – made only very rare visits to Hela's orbit. When they did, they hung in the sky like ornaments, sliding along invisible tracks from horizon to horizon. Rashmika had seen very few of those in her lifetime; they always impressed and scared her at the same time. Her world was a froth of ice lathered around a core of rubble. It was fragile. Having one of those vessels nearby – especially when they made main-drive adjustments – was like holding a welding torch close to a snowball.

The vertigo returned in waves. Rashmika looked back towards the horizon, easing the strain on her neck. The old suit was dependable, but it was not exactly engineered for sightseeing.

Here, instead, was Haldora. Two-thirds of it had risen above the horizon now. Because there was no air on Hela, nothing to blur features on the horizon, there were very few visual cues to enable one to discriminate between something a few dozen kilometres away and something nearly a million kilometres beyond that. The gas giant appeared to be an extension of the world on which she stood. It looked larger when it was near the horizon than the zenith, but Rashmika knew that this was an illusion, an accidental by-product of the way her mind was wired together. Haldora loomed about forty times larger in the sky of Hela than the Moon did in the skies of Earth. She had always wondered about this, for it implied that the Moon was really not a very impressive thing compared to Haldora, in spite of the Moon's prominence in Earth literature and mythology.

From the angle at which she saw it, Haldora appeared as a fat crescent. Even without the suit's contrast filters slid down, she made out the bands of equatorial coloration that striped the world from pole to pole: shades of ochre and orange, sepia and buff, vermilion and amber. She saw the curlicues and flukes where the colour bands mingled or bled; the furious scarlet eye of a storm system, like a knot in wood. She saw the tiny dark shadows of the many smaller moons that wheeled around Haldora, and the pale arc of the world's single ring.

Rashmika crouched down until she was sitting on her haunches. It was as uncomfortable as trying to look up, but she held the posture for as long as she was able. At the same time she kept on looking at Haldora, willing it, daring it to vanish, to do that which had brought them all here in the first place. But the world simply hung there, seemingly anchored to the landscape, close enough to touch, as real as anything she had ever seen in her life.

And yet, she thought, it *does* vanish. That it happened – that it continued to happen – was not disputed, at least not by anyone who had spent any significant time on Hela. Look at it long enough, she thought, and – unless you are unlucky – you *will* see it happen.

It just wasn't her turn today.

Rashmika stood up, then made her way past the point where she had emerged, towards the rear of the vehicle. She was looking back along the procession of the caravan now, and she could see the other machines rising and falling in waves as they moved over slight undulations in the trail. The caravan was even longer than when she had first arrived: at some point, without any fanfare, a dozen more units had tagged on to the rear. It would keep growing until it reached the Permanent Way, at which point it would fragment again as various sections were assigned to specific cathedrals.

She reached the limit of the catwalk, at the back of the vehicle. There was an abyss between her and the next machine, spanned only by a flimsy-looking bridge formed from many metal slats. It had not been apparent from the ground, but now she saw that the distance – vertical and horizontal – was changing all the while, making the little bridge lash and twist like something in pain. Instead of the stiff railings she now held, there were only metal wires. Down below, halfway to the ground, was a pressurised connector that puffed in and out like a bellows. That looked much safer.

Rashmika supposed that she could go back inside the caravan and find her way to that connector. Or she could pretend that she had done enough exploring for one day. The last thing she needed to do was start making enemies this early in her quest. There would be plenty of time for that later on, she was certain.

Rashmika stepped back, but only for a moment. Then she returned to the bridge and spread her arms apart so that each hand could grip one of the wire lines. The bridge writhed ahead of her, the metal plates slipping apart, revealing an awful absence. She took a step forwards, planting one booted foot on the first plate.

It did not feel safe. The plate gave beneath her, offering no hint of solidity.

'Go on,' she said, goading herself.

She took the next step, and both feet were on the bridge. She looked back. The lead vehicle pitched and yawed. The bridge squirmed under her, throwing her from one side to the other. She held on tightly. She wanted desperately to turn back, but a small, quiet voice told her she must not. The voice told her that if she did not have the courage to do this one simple thing, then she could not possibly have the courage to find her brother.

Rashmika took another step along the bridge. She began to cross the gap. It was what she had to do.

FIFTEEN

Ararat, 2675

Blood bustled into the conference room, a huge number of rolled-up maps tucked beneath his arms. He placed the maps on the table and then spread one of them wide, the map flattening itself obediently. It was a single sheet of thick creamy paper as wide as the table, with the slightly mottled texture of leather. At a command from Blood, topographic features popped into exaggerated relief, then shaded themselves according to the current pattern of daylight and darkness on that part of Ararat. Latitude and longitude appeared as thin glowing lines, labelled with tiny numerals.

Khouri leant across, studying the map for a moment. She turned it slightly, then pointed to one small chain of islands. 'Near here,' she said, 'about thirty kilometres west of that strait, eight hundred kilometres north of here.'

'Is this thing updated in real time?' Clavain asked.

'Refresh time is about every two days on average,' Scorpio said. 'It can take a bit longer. Depends on the vagaries of satellite positions, high-altitude balloons and cloud cover. Why?'

'Because it looks as if there's something more or less where she said there would be.'

'He's right,' Khouri said. 'It has to be Skade's ship, doesn't it?'

Scorpio leant in to inspect the tiny white dot. 'That's no ship,' he said. 'It's just a speck of ice, like a small iceberg.'

'You're sure about that?' Clavain asked.

Blood jabbed his trotter at the point Khouri had indicated. 'Let's be certain. Map: magnify, tenfold.'

The surface features of the map crawled away to the edges. The speck of ice swelled until it was the size of a fingernail. Blood told the map to apply an enhancement filter, but there was no obvious increase in detail save for a vague suggestion that the iceberg was bleeding into the surrounding sea, extending fine tendrils of whiteness in all directions.

'No ship,' Scorpio said.

Clavain sounded less certain. 'Ana, the craft Skade came down in – you said in your report that it was a heavy corvette, correct?'

'I'm no expert on ships, but that's what I was told.'

'You said it was fifty metres long. That would be about right for a moray-class corvette. The funny thing is, that iceberg looks about the same size. The proportions are consistent – maybe a bit larger, but not much.'

'Could be coincidence,' Blood said. 'You know there are always bits of iceberg drifting down into those latitudes. Sometimes they even make it as far south as here.'

'But there are no other icebergs in the surrounding area,' Clavain pointed out.

'All the same,' Scorpio said, 'there can't be a ship in that thing, can there? Why would it have ended up covered in ice? If anything, ships come in hot, not cold. And why wouldn't the ice have melted by now?'

'We'll find out when we get there,' Clavain said slowly. 'In the meantime, let's stick to practicalities. We won't want to alarm Skade into doing something rash, so we'll make sure our approach is slow and obvious.' He indicated a spot on the map, to the south of the iceberg. 'I suggest we take a shuttle out to about here; Antoinette can fly us. Then we'll drop two or three boats and make the rest of the crossing by sea. We'll carry surgical equipment and close-quarters arms, but nothing excessive. If we need to destroy the ship we can always call in an air-strike from the mainland.' He looked up, his finger still pressing down on the map. 'If we leave this afternoon, we can time our arrival at the iceberg for dawn, which will give us a whole day in which to complete negotiations with Skade.'

'Wait a moment,' said Dr Valensin, smiling slightly. 'Before we get too carried away – are you telling me that you're actually taking any of this seriously?'

'You mean you're not?' Clavain asked.

'She's my patient,' Valensin said, looking sympathetically at Khouri. 'I'll vouch for the fact that she's isn't *obviously* insane. She has Conjoiner implants, and if her child had them as well they could have communicated with each other while the child was still in her womb. It would have been unorthodox, but Remontoire could have put those implants in her unborn child using microsurgical remotes. Given Conjoiner medicine, too, it's not inconceivable that Skade could have removed Khouri's child without evidence of surgery. But the rest of it? This whole business about a space war taking place on our doorstep? It's a bit of a stretch, wouldn't you say?'

'I'm not so sure,' Clavain said.

'Please explain,' Valensin said, looking to his colleagues for support.

Clavain tapped the side of his skull. 'Remember, I'm a Conjoiner as well. The last time I was able to check, all the machinery in my head was still working properly.'

'I could have told you as much,' Valensin said.

'What you forget is how sensitive it is. It's designed to detect and amplify ambient fields, signals produced by machines or other Conjoiners. Two Conjoiners can share thoughts across tens of metres of open space even if there aren't any amplifying systems in the environment. The hardware translates those fields into patterns that the organic part of the brain can interpret, harnessing the basic visual grammar of the perceptual centre.'

'This isn't news to me,' Valensin said.

'So consider the implications. What if there really was a war going on out there – a major circumsolar engagement, with all sorts of weapons and countermeasures being deployed? There'd be a great deal of stray electromagnetic noise, much more powerful than normal Conjoiner signals. My implants might be picking up signals they can't interpret properly. They're feeding semi-intelligible patterns into my meat brain. The meat does its best to sort out the mess and ends up throwing shapes and faces into the sky.'

'He told me he'd been seeing things,' Scorpio said.

'Figures, signs and portents,' Clavain said. 'It only began in the last two or three months. Khouri said the fleet arrived nine weeks ago. That's too much of a coincidence for me. I thought that perhaps I was going mad, but it looks as if I was just picking up rumours of war.'

'Like the good old soldier you always were,' Scorpio said.

'It just means I'm inclined to take Khouri seriously,' Clavain said, 'no matter how strange her story.'

'Even the part about Skade?' Valensin asked.

Clavain scratched his beard. His eyes were slit-lidded, almost closed, as if viewing a vast mental landscape of possibilities. '*Especially* the part about Skade,' he replied.

Hela, 2727

Rashmika looked straight ahead. She had nearly reached the other machine. In the distance she could see suited figures moving about on errands, clambering from one catwalk to another. Cranes swung out, burdened by pallets of heavy equipment. Servitors moved with the eerie, lubricated glide of clockwork automata. The vast single machine, the sum of many parts that was the caravan, needed constant care. It was, Rashmika suspected, a little like a cathedral in microcosm.

She stood again on the relatively firm ground of another vehicle. The motion of this one depended on legs rather than wheels, so instead of rumbling steadily, the metal surface beneath her feet drummed a slow rhythm, a series of timed thuds as each piston-driven mechanical foot hit ice. The gap she had crossed looked trivial now, a matter of metres, but she did not doubt that it would be just as unnerving on the way back.

Now she looked around. There was something very different about the layout of this roof: it was more ordered, lacking any of the obvious mechanical clutter of the last one. The few equipment boxes had been neatly stowed around the edges of the roof, with the conduits and power lines routed likewise.

Occupying much of the central area was a tilted surface, angled up from the roof on a set of pistons; she'd seen it during the approach in Crozet's icejammer, and she'd also seen something like it in her village: an array of solar collectors forming part of the reserve power supply in case the main generators failed. The array had been a precise mosaic of small, square photovoltaic cells that spangled emerald and blue as they caught the light. But here there were no cells; instead the surface was covered by ranks of dark cruciform objects. Rashmika counted them: there were thirty-six cruciform shapes, arranged six across and six high, and every one of the objects was about the same size as a human being.

She walked closer, but with trepidation. There really were people shackled to the tilted surface, held in place by clasps around their wrists, their heels supported by small platforms. As near as she could tell they were dressed identically. Each one wore a hooded, foot-length gown of chocolate-brown material, cinched around the waist by a braided white rope. The cowl of each hood framed the curved mirror of a vacuum suit visor. She saw no faces, just the warped reflection of the slowly crawling landscape, herself an insignificant part of it.

They were looking at Haldora. It was obvious now: the tilt of the platform was just right for observation of the rising planet. As the caravan approached the Way and the cathedrals that ran on it, the platform would approach the horizontal, until the thirty-six watchers were all flat on their backs, staring at the zenith.

They were pilgrims, she realised. They had been picked up by the caravan during its deviation away from the equatorial settlements. She had been stupid not to realise that there were bound to be some along for the ride. There was an excellent chance that some of them had even come down from the badlands, perhaps even from her village.

She looked up at them, wondering if they were somehow aware of her presence. She hoped that their attentions were too thoroughly fixed on Haldora for them to take any notice of her. That was the point of them being up there, after all: half-crucified, lashed to an iron raft, forced to stare into the face of the world they considered miraculous.

The thing that she found most disturbing was the speed with which these pilgrims had taken their faith to this limit. It was likely that they had only left their homes in the last few weeks. Until then, they would have had very little choice but to act like normal members of a secular community. They were welcome to their beliefs, but the necessary duties of functioning in the badlands precluded taking religious observations as seriously as this. They would have had to fit into families and work units, and to smile at the jokes of their colleagues. But here, now, they were free. Very likely there was already Quaicheist blood in their veins.

Rashmika looked back along the winding line of the caravan. There were other tilted surfaces. Assuming that they each held about the same number of pilgrims, there could easily have been two hundred just on this one caravan. And at any one time there were many other caravans on Hela. It amounted to thousands of pilgrims being transported to the shining Way, with thousands more making the journey on foot, step by agonising step.

The futility of it, the sheer miserable waste of finite human life, made her indignant and filled with self-righteous anger. She wanted to climb on to the rack herself to wrench one of the pilgrims away from the sight that transfixed them, to rip back the cowl from their helmet, to press her own face against that blank mirror and try to make contact – before it was too late – with whatever fading glimmer of human individuality remained. She wanted to drive a rock into the faceplate, shattering faith in an instant of annihilating decompression.

And yet she knew that her anger was horribly misdirected. She knew that she only loathed and despised these pilgrims because of what she feared had happened to Harbin. She could not smash the churches, so she desired instead to smash the gentle innocents who were drawn towards them. At this realisation she felt a secondary sort of revulsion directed towards herself. She could not recall ever feeling a hatred of this intensity. It was like a compass needle turning inside her, looking for a direction in which to settle. It both awed and frightened her that she had the capacity for such animus.

Rashmika forced a kind of calm upon herself. In all the time that she had been watching them, the figures had never stirred. Their dark-brown cloaks hung about their suited figures in reverential stillness, as if the various folds and twists in the fabric had been chiselled from the hardest granite by expert masons. Their mirrored faces continued to reflect the slow ooze of the landscape. Perhaps it was a kindness that she could not see the individuals behind the glass.

Rashmika turned from them, and then began to make her way back towards the bridge.

SIXTEEN

Ararat, 2675

The shuttle came to a halt, hovering a few metres above the water. The rescue team assembled in the rear bay, waiting as the first boat – still tethered to the shuttle – was lowered gently on to the surface of the water. The sea was vast and dark in all directions, but also calm, apart from the area immediately within the thermal footprint of the shuttle. There was no wind, nor any indication of unusual Juggler activity, and the sea currents in this region were at their usual seasonal ebb. The iceberg would barely have moved between updates from the mapping network.

Once the boat had stabilised, the first three members of the team were lowered individually on to its decking. Scorpio went down first, followed by a male Security Arm officer called Jaccottet, with Khouri completing the trio. Rations, weapons and equipment were lowered down in scuffed metal boxes, then quickly stowed in waterproof hatches along the sides of the boat. The last thing to go in was the portable incubator, a transparent box with an opaque base and carrying handle. This was secured with particular care, almost as if it already held a child.

The first boat was then unhitched, allowing Scorpio to steer it clear of the shuttle. The whine of its battery-driven motor cut across the loud simmer of the hovering shuttle. The second boat was then lowered down and allowed to settle. Vasko watched as another Security Arm officer – a woman named Urton – was lowered down into it, followed by Clavain. The old man teetered at first, but quickly found his sea legs. Then it was Vasko's turn to be lowered down, helped by Blood. Vasko had expected that the other pig would be joining them on the operation, but Scorpio had ordered him to return to First Camp, to take care of things there. Scorpio's only concession had been to let Blood come this far, to help with the loading of the boats.

The final boxes of equipment were lowered down, causing the boat to sink even more worryingly low in the water. The instant it was unhitched, the Security Arm woman had it speeding over to join Scorpio's craft. The hulls chafed and squealed together. Minutes of whispered activity followed while items were transferred from craft to craft, until they were evenly trimmed.

'You ready for this?' Urton asked Vasko. 'It's not too late to back out, you know.'

She had been on his case from the moment they had met, during mission-planning sessions back on the *Nostalgia for Infinity*. Before that, their paths had barely crossed: like Jaccottet, she had only ever been another Arm operative to Vasko, with a few years of seniority on him.

'You seem to have a particular problem with me being on this mission,' he said, as calmly as he could. 'Is it something personal?'

'Some of us have earned the right to be here,' she said. 'That's all.'

'And you think I haven't?'

'You did a small favour for the pig,' she said, keeping her voice low. 'Because of that you ended up embroiled in something bigger than you. That doesn't mean you automatically earn my undying respect.'

'I'm not really interested in your respect,' Vasko said. 'What I'm interested in is your professional co-operation.'

'You needn't worry about that,' she said.

He started to say something, but she had already turned away, levering a heavy Breitenbach cannon into locking stanchions set along one side of the boat.

Vasko did not know what he had done to earn her hostility. Was it simply the fact that he was younger and less experienced? Sighing, he busied himself by helping to check and stow the equipment. It was not pleasant work: all the delicate tackle – the weapons, navigation and communication devices – had been lathered in a revolting opaque grey mucous layer of protective unguent. It kept getting all over his hands, breaking free in sticky ropes.

Swearing under his breath, wiping the muck off on to his knees, he barely noticed as the shuttle yawed away, leaving them alone at sea.

They slid across kilometres of mirror-flat water. The cloud layer had broken up in patches, opening ragged windows in the deep black sky. There were stars visible now, but it was one of those comparatively rare nights when none of Ararat's moons were above the horizon. Lamps provided their only illumination. The boats kept within metres of each other, scudding side by side, the whine of their motors not quite loud enough to hinder conversation. Vasko had decided early in the expedition that his best course of action – having apparently won the grudging approval of Clavain – would be to say as little as possible. Besides, he had plenty to think about. He sat near the back of the second boat, squatting on the gunwale, loading and unloading a weapon in a kind of mindless loop, burning the action into the muscle memory of his hands so that it would happen without thought when he needed it to. For the hundredth time since they had set out, he wondered if it would actually come to violence. Perhaps the whole thing would be revealed to be a colossal misunderstanding, nothing more.

In Vasko's opinion, however, that was rather unlikely.

They had all read Khouri's testimony; had all sat in on the session while she was cross-examined. Much of what had been discussed had meant little to Vasko, but as the argument and interrogation had continued, a picture had begun to form in his mind.

What was clear was this: Ana Khouri had returned from the computational matrix of the Hades neutron star with Thorn dead and his unborn child in her belly. Even then, she had known what Aura signified: that the unborn girl was not merely her child, but an agent of the ancient minds – human and alien – trapped within the sanctuary of the Hades matrix. Aura was a gift to humanity, her mind loaded with information capable of making a difference in the war against the Inhibitors. In Sylveste's case – and it seemed likely that she carried some of his memories in addition to the reserves of knowledge – she was an act of atonement.

Khouri knew also that Aura's information had to be accessed as quickly as possible if it was going to mean anything. They did not have time to wait for her to be born, let alone for her to grow up and begin talking.

With Khouri's permission, therefore, Remontoire had sent droves of surgical remotes into the heads of mother and child while Aura was still inside Khouri's womb. The drones had established Conjoiner-type implants in both Aura and Khouri, enabling them to share thoughts and experiences. Khouri had become Aura's mouthpiece and eyes: she had found herself dreaming Aura's dreams, unwilling or unable to define precisely where Aura ended and she began. Her child's thoughts were leaking into her own, permeating them to the point where no concrete division existed.

But the thoughts and experiences had remained difficult to interpret. Khouri's daughter was still an unborn child; the structures of her mind were tentative and half-formed, her mental model of the external universe necessarily vague. Khouri had done her best to interpret the signals, but despite her efforts only a fraction of the things she was picking up were intelligible. But even that fraction had turned out to be of vital importance. Following clues from Aura – sifting jewel-like nuggets from a slurry of confusing signals – Remontoire had made drastic improvements to his arsenal of weapons and instruments. If nothing else, Aura's potential significance was becoming obvious.

But that was when Skade had entered the affair.

She had arrived in the Delta Pavonis system long after the Inhibitors had completed their torching of Resurgam and the other planets. Quickly she had established lines of negotiation with the human elements still present after the departure of the *Nostalgia for Infinity*. Her ultimate objective remained the recovery of as many of the old Conjoiner-built cache weapons as possible. But with her own fleet damaged, and with the Inhibitors themselves gathering *en masse*, Skade was in no position to take what she wanted by brute force.

By then, the *Zodiacal Light* had completed its self-repairs and the human exploration of the Hades object had reached its logical conclusion. As Remontoire and his allies moved out of the system, therefore, Skade had shadowed them. Tentative communications ensued, and Skade had deployed her existing assets to protect the evacuees from the pursuing Inhibitor elements. The gesture was calculated and risky, but nothing else would convince Remontoire that she was to be trusted.

But Skade had wanted nothing more than to be trusted. She had seen the evidence of Remontoire's new technologies and had realised that she was now at a tactical disadvantage. She had originally come to take the cache weapons – but the new ones would do equally well.

What had really interested her, however, was Aura.

Over months of shiptime, as the *Zodiacal Light* and the other two Conjoiner ships raced towards Ararat, Skade had played a delicate game of insinuation. She had gained Remontoire's confidence, making conspicuous sacrifices, trading intelligence and resources. She had played on his old loyalties to the Mother Nest, convincing him that it was in their mutual best interests to co-operate. When, finally, Remontoire had allowed some of Skade's fellow Conjoiners aboard his ship, it had merely seemed like the latest cordial step in a thawing *détente*.

But the Conjoiners had turned out to be a snatch-team. Killing dozens in the process, they had located Khouri, drugged her and taken her back to Skade's ship. There, Skade's surgeons had operated on Khouri to remove Aura. The foetus, still only in its sixth month of development, had then been reintroduced into another womb. A biocybernetic support construct of living tissue, the womb had then been installed in the new body Skade had grown for herself after discarding her old, damaged one in the Mother Nest. The implants in Aura's head were meant to communicate only with their counterparts in Khouri, but Skade's infiltration routines had quickly undone Remontoire's handiwork. With Aura now growing inside her, Skade had tapped into the same flow of data that had already given Remontoire his new weapons.

She had her prize, but even then Skade was clever. *Too* clever, perhaps. She should have killed Khouri then and there, but in Khouri she had seen another means of obtaining leverage over Remontoire. Even after her child had been ripped from her, Khouri was still useful as a potential hostage. Following negotiations, Skade had returned her to Remontoire in return for even more technological trade-offs. Aura would have given her these things sooner or later, but Skade had been in no mood to wait.

By then, the Inhibitors were almost upon them.

When the ships eventually arrived around Ararat, the battle had entered a new and silent phase. As the humans had escalated their conflict to include the use of novel, barely understood weaponry, the Inhibitors had retaliated with savage new strategies of their own. It was a war of maximum stealth: all energies were redirected into undetectable wavebands. Phantom images were projected to confuse and intimidate. Matter and force were thrown around with abandon. Day by day, skirmish by skirmish, even hour by hour, the human factions had fallen in and out of co-operation, depending on minute changes in battle projections. Skade had only wanted to aid Remontoire if the alternative was her own guaranteed annihilation. Remontoire's reasoning had not been so very far removed.

But a week ago, Skade had changed her tactics. A corvette had left one of her two remaining heavy ships. Remontoire's side had tracked the swiftly moving ship to Ararat at it slipped between the major battle fronts. Analysis of its acceleration limits suggested that it was carrying at least one human occupant. A small detachment of Inhibitor forces had chased the corvette, cutting much closer to the planet than they usually did. It was as if the machines had realised that something significant was at stake, and that the corvette must be stopped at all costs.

They had failed, but not before damaging the Conjoiner ship.

Again, Remontoire and his allies had managed to track the limping spacecraft as its stealth systems shifted in and out of functionality. They had watched the ship ditch in Ararat's atmosphere, making a barely controlled landing in the sea. There was no sign that anyone on Ararat had even noticed.

A few days later, Khouri had followed. Remontoire had refused to commit a larger force, not when there was so little chance of making it past the Inhibitors to the surface. But they had agreed that a small capsule might stand a slim chance. In addition, someone really needed to let the people on Ararat know what was going on, and sending Khouri would kill two birds with one stone.

Vasko thought about the strength of mind that it must have taken for Khouri to come down here on her own, with no guarantee of rescue, let alone of being able to save her daughter. He wondered what the stronger emotion was: her love for her daughter, or the hatred she must have felt towards Skade.

The more he considered it, the less likely it seemed that this situation was the result of any kind of misunderstanding. And he very much doubted that any of this was going to be resolved by negotiation. Skade might have stolen Aura from Khouri, but she had had the element of surprise, and she would have lost nothing if her attempt had resulted in the death of either mother or baby. But that wasn't true now. And Skade – if she was still alive and if the baby was still alive inside her – would be expecting them.

What would it take to make her give up Aura?

In the lamp-light, Vasko saw a flicker of silver-grey from Clavain's direction, and watched as the old man examined the knife he had brought with him from his island retreat.

Hela, 2727

Rashmika had arranged a private meeting with Quaestor Jones. It took place immediately after a trading session, in the same windowless room she had visited with Crozet. Behind his desk, the quaestor waited for her to say something, hands folded across his generous paunch, his lips conveying suspicion mingled with faint prurient interest. Now and then he popped a morsel of food into the jaws of his pet, which squatted on the desk like a piece of abstract sculpture moulded from bright-green plastic.

As she studied him, Rashmika wondered how good he was at telling truth from lies. It was difficult to tell with some people.

'She's a persistent little madam, Peppermint,' the quaestor said. 'Warned her away from the roof, and there she was, not two hours later. What do you think we should do with her, eh?'

'If you don't want people up on the roof, you ought to make it a bit harder to get up there,' Rashmika said. 'In any case, I don't particularly like being spied on.'

'I have an obligation to protect my passengers,' he said. 'If you don't like that, you're very welcome to leave when Mr Crozet returns to the badlands.'

'Actually, I want to stay aboard,' Rashmika said.

'You mean you wish to make the pilgrimage to the Way?'

'No.' She hid her distaste at the thought of the people on the racks. She had learned that they were called Observers. 'Not that. I want to travel to the Way and to find work there. But pilgrimage hasn't got anything to do with it.'

'Mm. We've already been over your skills profile, Miss Els.'

It did not please her that he remembered her name. 'We barely discussed it, Quaestor. I don't think you can really make an honest assessment of my skills based on one short conversation.'

'You informed me you were a scholar.'

'Correct.'

'So return to the badlands and continue your scholarship.' He made an effort to look and sound reasonable. 'What better place to further your study of the scuttlers than at the very site where their relics are being unearthed?'

'It isn't possible to study there,' she said. 'No one cares what the relics signify as long as they're able to get good money for them. No one's interested in the bigger picture.'

'And you are, I take it?'

'I have theories concerning the scuttlers,' she said, fully aware of how precocious she sounded, 'but to make further progress I need access to proper data, the kind in the possession of the church-sponsored archaeological groups.'

'Yes, we all know about those groups. But aren't they in a position to form theories of their own? Begging your pardon, Miss Els, but why do you imagine that you – a seventeen-year-old – are likely to bring a fresh perspective to the matter?'

'Because I have no vested interest in maintaining the Quaicheist view,' Rashmika said.

'Which would be?'

'That the scuttlers are an incidental detail, unrelated to the deeper matter of the vanishings, or at best a reminder of what's likely to happen to us if we don't follow the Quaicheist route to salvation.'

'There's no doubt that they were denied salvation,' the quaestor said, 'but then so were eight or nine other alien cultures. I forget what the latest count is. There's clearly no particular mystery here. Local details about this particular vanished species, their history and society and so on, still need to be researched, of course, but what happened to them in the end isn't in doubt. We've all heard those pilgrims' tales from the evacuated systems, Miss Els, the stories about machines emerging from the dark between the stars. Now, it seems, it's our turn.'

'The supposition being that the scuttlers were wiped out by the Inhibitors?' she asked.

He popped a crumb into the intricate little mouth of his animal. 'Draw your own conclusions.'

'That's all I've ever done,' she said. 'And my conclusion is that what happened here was different.'

'Something wiped them out,' the quaestor said. 'Isn't that enough for you?'

'I'm not sure it was the same thing that wiped out the Amarantin, or any of those other cultures. If the Inhibitors had been involved, do you think they'd have left this moon intact? They might have compunctions about destroying a world, a place with an established biosphere, but an airless moon like Hela? They'd have turned it into a ring system, or a cloud of radioactive steam. Yet whoever or whatever finished off the scuttlers wasn't anywhere near that thorough.' She paused, fearful of revealing too much of her cherished thesis. 'It was a rush job. They left behind too much. It's almost as if they wanted to leave a message, maybe a warning.'

'You're invoking an entirely new agency of cosmic extinction, is that it?'

Rashmika shrugged. 'If the facts demand it.'

'You're not greatly troubled by self-doubt, are you, Miss Els?'

'I know only that the vanishings and the scuttlers must be related. So does everyone else. They're just too scared and intimidated to admit it.'

'And you're not?'

'I was put on Hela for a reason,' she said, the words tumbling out of her mouth as if spoken by someone else.

The quaestor looked at her for a long, uncomfortable moment. 'And this crusade,' he said, 'this quest to uncover the truth no matter how many enemies it makes you – is that why you're so intent on reaching the Permanent Way?'

'There's another reason,' she said, quietly.

The quaestor appeared not to have heard her. 'You have a particular interest in the First Adventists, don't you? I noticed it when I mentioned my role as legate.'

'It's the oldest of the churches,' Rashmika said. 'And one of the largest, I'd imagine.'

'*The* largest. The First Adventist order runs three cathedrals, including the largest and heaviest on the Way.'

'I know they have an archaeological study group,' she said. 'I've written to them. Surely there'd be some work for me there.'

'So you can advance your theory and rub everyone up the wrong way?'

She shook her head. 'I'd work quietly, doing what was needed. It wouldn't stop me examining material. I just need a job, so that I can send some money home and make some enquiries.'

He sighed, as if the world and all its troubles were now his responsibility. 'What exactly do you know of the cathedrals, Miss Els? I mean in the physical sense.'

She sensed that the question, for once, was a sincere one. 'They are moving structures,' she said, 'much larger than this caravan, much slower . . . but machines, all the same. They travel around Hela on the equatorial road we call the Permanent Way, completing a revolution once every three hundred and twenty standard days.'

'And the point of this circumnavigation?'

'Is to ensure that Haldora is always in the sky, always at the zenith. The world moves beneath the cathedrals, but the cathedrals cancel out that motion.'

A smile ghosted the quaestor's lips. 'And what do you know about the motion of the cathedrals?'

'It's slow,' she said. 'On average, the cathedrals only have to move at a baby's crawl to complete a circuit of Hela in three hundred and twenty days. A third of a metre a second is enough.'

'That doesn't seem fast, does it?'

'Not really, no.'

'I assure you it does when you have a few hundred vertical metres of metal sliding towards you and you have a job to do that involves stepping out of the way at the last possible moment, before you fall under the traction plates.' Quaestor Rutland Jones leant forwards, compressing the bulk of his belly against the table and lacing his fingers before him. 'The Permanent Way is a road of compacted ice. With one or two complications, it encircles the planet like a ribbon. It is never wider than two hundred metres, and is frequently much narrower than that. Yet even a small cathedral may be fifty metres across. The largest of them – the Lady Morwenna, for instance – are double that. And since the cathedrals all wish to situate themselves under the mathematically exact spot on the Way that corresponds to Haldora being precisely at the zenith, directly overhead, there is a certain degree of . . .' His voice became mockingly playful. '. . . competition for the available space. Between rival churches, even those bound by the ecumenical protocols, it can be surprisingly fierce. Sabotage and trickery are not unheard of. Even amongst cathedrals belonging to one church, there is still a degree of playful jockeying.'

'I'm not sure I see your point, Quaestor.'

'I mean that damage to the Way – deliberately inflicted vandalism – is not unusual. Cathedrals may leave obstacles in their wake, or they may tamper with the integrity of the Way itself. And Hela itself does its share of harm. Rock blizzards . . . ice-flows . . . volcanic eruptions . . . all these can render the Way temporarily impassable. That is why cathedrals have Permanent Way gangs.' He looked at Rashmika sharply. 'The gangs work ahead of the cathedrals. Not too far ahead, or they risk their good work being exploited by rivals, but just far enough to enable their tasks to be completed before their cathedrals arrive. I'll make no bones about it: the work is difficult and dangerous. But it is work that requires some of the skills you have mentioned.' He tapped pudgy fingers against the table. 'Working under vacuum, on ice. Using cutting and blasting tools. Programming servitors for the most hazardous tasks.'

'That's not the kind of work I had in mind,' Rashmika said.

'No?'

'Like I said, I think my skills would be put to far better use in a clerical context, such as one of the archaeological study groups.'

'That may be so, but vacancies in those groups are rare indeed. On the other hand, by the very nature of the work, vacancies do tend to keep opening up in clearance gangs.'

'Because people keep dying?'

'It's tough work. But it *is* work. And there are degrees of risk even in clearance duty. It shouldn't be too difficult to find you something slightly less hazardous than fuse-laying, something where you might not even have to wear a surface suit all day long. And it might keep you occupied until something opens up in one of the study groups.'

Rashmika read the quaestor's face. He had not lied to her so far. 'It's not what I wanted,' she said, 'but if it's all that's on offer, I'll have to take it. If I said I was prepared to do such work, could you find me a vacancy?'

'If I felt I could live with myself afterwards ... then yes, I dare say I could.'

'I'm sure you'd sleep fine at night, Quaestor.'

'And you are certain that this is what you want?'

She nodded, before her own doubt began to show. 'If you could start making the arrangements, I would be grateful.'

'There are always favours that can be called in,' he said. 'But there is something I need to mention. There are people looking for you, from the Vigrid badlands. The constabulary can't touch you here, but your absence has been noted.'

'That doesn't surprise me.'

'There has been speculation about the purpose of your mission. Some say it has something to do with your brother.' The green creature looked up, as if taking a sudden interest in the conversation. It was definitely missing one of its forelimbs, Rashmika noted. 'Harbin Els,' the quaestor continued. 'That's his name, isn't it?'

There was clearly no point pretending otherwise. 'My brother went to look for work on the Way,' she said. 'They lied to him about what would happen, said they wouldn't put the dean's blood in him. We never saw him again.'

'And now you feel the need to find out what became of him?'

'He was my brother,' she said.

'Then perhaps this may be of interest to you.' The quaestor reached under his desk and produced a folded sheet of paper. He pushed it towards her. The green creature watched it slide across the desk.

She took the letter, rubbing her thumb against the red wax seal that held it closed. Embossed on the seal was a spacesuit, arms spread like a crucifix, radiating shafts of light. The seal had been broken; it only loosely adhered to the paper on one side of the join.

'What is it?' she asked, looking at his face very carefully.

'It came through official channels, from the Lady Morwenna. That's a Clocktower seal.'

That part was true, she thought. Or at least the quaestor sincerely believed that was the case. 'When?'

'Today.'

But that was a lie.

'Addressed to me?'

'I was told to make sure you saw it.' He looked down, not wanting to meet her eyes. It made his face harder to read.

'By whom?'

'No one . . . I . . .' Again, he was lying. 'I looked at it. Don't think ill of me – I look at all correspondence that passes through the caravan. It's a matter of security.'

'Then you know what it says?'

'I think you should read it for yourself,' he said.

SEVENTEEN

Hela, 2727

The ticking of his cane marked the surgeon-general's progress through the iron heart of the cathedral. Even in the parts of the cathedral where the engines and traction mechanisms were audible, they heard him coming long before he arrived. His footsteps were as measured and regular as the beats of a metronome, the tap of his cane punctuating the rhythm, iron against iron. He moved with a deliberate arachnoid slowness, giving the nosy and the idle time to disperse. Occasionally he was aware of watchers secreted behind metal pillars or grilles, spying on him, thinking themselves discreet. More often than not he knew with certainty that he went about his errands unobserved. In the long years of his service to Quaiche, one thing had been made clear to the cathedral populace: Grelier's business was not a matter for the curious.

But sometimes those who fled from him were doing so for reasons other than the edict to keep their noses out of his work.

He reached a spiral staircase, a helix of skeletal iron plunging down into the clanking depths of Motive Power. The staircase was ringing like a struck tuning fork. Either it was picking up a vibration from the machines below or someone had just employed it to get away from Grelier.

He leant over the balustrade, peering down the corkscrewing middle of the staircase. Two turns below, pudgy fingers slipped urgently along the handrail. Was that his man? Very probably.

Humming to himself, Grelier unlatched the protective gate that allowed entry to the stairwell. He flipped it shut with the sharp end of his cane and began to descend. He took his time, allowing each pair of footfalls to echo before proceeding down to the next step. He let the cane *tap, tap, tap* against the balusters, informing the man that he was coming and that there was no conceivable avenue of escape. Grelier knew the innards of Motive Power as intimately as he knew the innards of every section of the cathedral. He had sealed all the other stairwells with the Clocktower key. This was the only way up or down, and he would be sure to seal it once he reached the bottom. His heavy medical case knocked against one thigh as he descended, in perfect synchrony with the tapping of the cane.

The machines in the lower levels sang more loudly as he approached them. There was no part of the cathedral where you couldn't hear those grinding mechanisms, if there were no other sounds. But in the high levels the noise from the motors and traction systems had to compete with organ music and the permanently singing voices of the choir. The mind soon filtered out that faint background component.

Not here. Grelier heard the shrill whine of turbines, which set his teeth on edge. He heard the low clank and thud of massive articulated cranks and eccentrics. He heard pistons sliding, valves opening and closing. He heard relays chattering, the low voices of technical staff.

He descended, cane tapping, medical kit ready.

Grelier reached the lowest turn of the spiral. The exit gate squeaked on its hinges: it hadn't been latched. Someone had been in a bit of a hurry. He stepped through the doorframe and placed his medical kit between his shoes. He took the key from his breast pocket and locked the gate, preventing anyone from ascending from this level. Then he picked up the medical kit and resumed his leisurely progress.

Grelier looked around. There was no sign of the fugitive, but there were plenty of places where a man might hide. This did not concern Grelier: in time, he was bound to find the pudgy-fingered absconder. He could allow himself a few moments to look around, take a break from his usual routine. He did not come down here all that often, and the place always impressed him.

Motive Power occupied one of the largest chambers of the cathedral, on the lowest pressurised level. The chamber ran the entire two-hundred-metre length of the moving structure. It was one hundred metres wide and fifty metres from floor to magnificently arched ceiling. Machinery filled much of the available volume, except for a gap around the walls and another of a dozen or so metres below the ceiling. The machinery was immense: it lacked the impersonal, abstract vastness of starship mechanisms, but there was something more intimate and therefore more personally threatening about it. Starship machinery was vast and bureaucratic: it just didn't notice human beings. If they got on the wrong side of it they simply ceased to exist, annihilated in a painless instant. But as huge as the machinery in Motive Power was, it was also small enough to notice people. If they got in the way of it they were liable to find themselves maimed or crushed.

It wouldn't be painless and it wouldn't be instantaneous.

Grelier pushed his cane against the pale-green carapace of a turbine. Through the cane he felt the vigorous thrum of trapped energies. He thought of the blades whisking round, drawing energy from the superheated steam spewing from the atomic reactor. All it would take was a flaw in one of the blades and the turbine could blow apart at any instant, bringing whirling, jagged death to anyone within fifty metres. It happened now and then; he usually came down to clean up the mess. It was all rather thrilling, really.

The reactor – the cathedral's atomic power plant – was the largest single chunk of machinery in the chamber, housed in a bottle-green dome at the rear end of the room. The kindest thing you could say about it was that it worked and it was cheap. There was no nuclear fuel to be mined on Hela, but the Ultras provided a ready supply. Dirty and dangerous, maybe, but more economical than antimatter and easier to work with than a fusion power plant. They had done the calculations: refining local ice to provide fusion fuel would have required a pre-processing plant as large as the entire existing Motive Power assembly. But the cathedral had already grown as big as it ever could, given the dimensions of the Way and the Devil's Staircase. Besides, the reactor worked and supplied all the power that the cathedral required, and the reactor workers didn't get sick all that often.

From the reactor's apex sprouted a tangle of high-pressure steam pipes. The gleaming silver intestines traversed the entire chamber, subject to inexplicable hairpin bends and right angles. They fed into thirty-two turbines, stacked atop one another in two rows, each row eight turbines long. Catwalks, inspection platforms, access tunnels, ladders and equipment elevators caged the whole humming mass. The turbines were dynamos, converting the rushing steam into electrical power. They fed the electrical energy into the main traction motors, twenty-four of them squatting atop the turbines in two rows of twelve. The traction motors in turn converted the electrical energy into mechanical force, propelling the great cranked and hinged mechanisms that ultimately moved the cathedral along the Way. At any one time only ten of the twelve motors on one side were doing any work: the spare set was idling, ready to be connected into use if another motor or set of motors needed to be taken offline for overhaul.

The mechanisms themselves passed overhead, extending from the traction motors to the walls on either side. They penetrated the walls via pressure-proofed gaskets positioned at the precise rocking points of the main coupling rods. The gaskets were troublesome, Grelier gathered: they were always failing and having to be replaced. But somehow or other the mechanical motion generated inside the Motive Power chamber had to be conveyed beyond the walls, into vacuum.

Above him, with a dreamlike slowness, the coupling rods swept back and forth and up and down in orchestrated waves, beginning at the front of the chamber and working back. A complicated arrangement of smaller cranks and eccentrics connected the rods to each other, synchronising their movements. Aerial catwalks threaded between the huge spars of thrusting metal, allowing workers to lubricate joints and inspect failure points for metal fatigue. It was risky work: one moment of inattention and there'd be lubrication of entirely the wrong sort.

There was more to Motive Power, of course. A lot more. Somewhere there was even a small foundry, working day and night to fabricate replacement parts. The largest components had to be made in Wayside plants, but it always took time to procure and deliver such replacements. The artisans in Motive Power took great pride in their ingenuity when it came to fixing something at short notice, or pressing a part into service for a different function than intended. They knew what the bottom line was: the cathedral had to keep moving, no matter what. No one was asking the world of them – it only had to move a third of a metre a second, after all. You could crawl faster than that, easily. The point was not the speed, but that the cathedral must never, ever stop.

'Surgeon-General, might I help you?'

Grelier tracked the voice to its source: someone was looking down at him from one of the catwalks above. The man wore the grey overalls of Motive Power, and was gripping the handrail with oversized gloves. His bullet-shaped scalp was blue with stubble, a filthy neckerchief around his collar. Grelier recognised the man as Glaur, one of the shift bosses.

'Perhaps you could come down here for a moment,' Grelier said.

Glaur complied immediately, traversing the catwalk and vanishing back into the machinery. Grelier tapped his cane idly against the cleated metal floor, waiting for the man to make his way down.

'Something up, Surgeon-General?' Glaur asked when he arrived.

'I'm looking for someone,' Grelier told him. No need to say why. 'He won't belong down here, Glaur. Have you seen anyone unexpected?'

'Like who?'

'The choirmaster. I'm sure you know the fellow. Pudgy hands.'

Glaur looked back up to the slowly threshing coupling rods. They moved like the oars of some biblical galleon, manned by hundreds of slaves. Grelier imagined that Glaur would much rather be up there working with the predictable hazards of moving metal than down here navigating the shifting treacheries of cathedral politics.

'There was someone,' Glaur offered. 'I saw a man move through the hall a few minutes ago.'

'Seem in a bit of a rush, did he?'

'I assumed he was on Clocktower business.'

'He wasn't. Any idea where I might find him now?'

Glaur glanced around. 'He might have taken one of the staircases back up to the main levels.'

'Not likely. He'll still be down here, I think. In which direction was he moving when you saw him?'

A moment of hesitation, which Grelier duty noted. 'Towards the reactor,' Glaur said.

'Thank you.' Grelier tapped his cane smartly and left the shift boss standing there, his momentary usefulness over.

He followed his quarry's path towards the reactor. He resisted the temptation to pick up his pace, maintaining his stroll, tapping the cane against the floor or any suitably resonant thing he happened to pass. Now and then he stepped over a glassed, grilled window in the floor, and paused awhile to watch the faintly lit ground crawl beneath him, twenty metres below. The cathedral's motion was rock steady, the jerky walking motion of the twenty buttressed treads smoothed out by the skill of engineers like Glaur.

The reactor loomed ahead. The green dome was surrounded by its own rings of catwalks, rising to the apex. Heavily riveted viewing windows were set with thick dark glass.

He caught sight of a sleeve vanishing around the curve of the second catwalk from the ground.

'Hello,' Grelier called. 'Are you there, Vaustad? I'd like a wee word.'

No reply. Grelier circled the reactor, taking his time. From above, its originator always out of sight, came a metallic scamper. He smiled, dismayed at Vaustad's stupidity. There were a hundred places to hide in the traction hall. Simian instinct, however, had driven the choirmaster to head for higher ground, even if that meant being cornered.

Grelier reached the gated access point to the ladder. He stepped through it and locked the gate behind him. He could not climb and carry the medical kit and the cane, so he left the medical kit on the ground. He tucked the cane into the crook of his arm and made his way upwards, one rung at a time, until he reached the first catwalk.

He walked around it once, just to unnerve Vaustad further. Humming quietly to himself, he looked over the edge and took in the scenery. Occasionally he rapped the cane against the curving metal sides of the reactor, or the black glass of one of the inspection portholes. The glass reminded him of the tarlike chips in the cathedral's front-facing stained-glass window, and he wondered for a moment if it was the same material.

Well, on to business.

He reached the ladder again and ascended to the next level. He could still hear that pathetic lab-rat scampering.

'Vaustad? Be a good fellow and come here, will you? It'll all be over in a jiffy.'

The scampering continued. He could feel the man's footfalls through the metal, transmitted right around the reactor.

'I'll just have to come over to you myself, then, won't I?'

He began to circumnavigate the reactor. He was on a level with the coupling rods now. There were none close to him, but – seen in foreshortened perspective – the moving spars of metal threshed like scissor blades. He saw some of Glaur's technicians moving amongst that whisking machinery, oiling and checking. They appeared imprisoned in it, yet magically uninjured.

The hem of a trouser leg vanished around the curve. The scampering increased in pace. Grelier smiled and halted, leaning over the edge. He was close now. He took the top end of his cane and twisted the head one quarter turn.

'Up or down?' he whispered to himself. 'Up or down?'

It was up. He could hear the clattering rising above him, to the next level of the catwalk. Grelier didn't know whether to be pleased or disappointed. Down, and the hunt would be over. The man would find his escape blocked, and Grelier would have had no difficulty pacifying him with the cane. With the man docile, it would only take a minute or two to inject him with the top-up dose. Efficient, but where was the fun in that?

At least now he was getting a run for his money. The end result would still be the same: the man cornered, no way out. Touch him with the cane and he'd be putty in Grelier's hands. There would be the problem of getting him down the ladder, of course, but one of Glaur's people could help with that.

Grelier climbed to the next level. This catwalk was smaller in diameter than the two below, set back towards the apex of the reactor dome. There was only one more level, at the apex itself, accessed by a gently sloping ramp. Vaustad was moving up the ramp as Grelier watched.

'There's nothing for you up there,' the surgeon-general said. 'Turn around now and we'll forget all about this.'

Would he hell. But Vaustad was beyond reason in any case. He had arrived at the apex and was taking a moment to look back at his pursuer. Pudgy hands, mooncalf face. Grelier had his man all right, not that there had ever been much doubt.

'Leave me alone,' Vaustad shouted. 'Leave me alone, you bloody ghoul!'

'Sticks and stones,' Grelier said with a patient smile. He tapped his cane against the railing and began to ascend the ramp.

'You won't get me,' Vaustad said. 'I've had enough. Too many bad dreams.'

'Oh, come now. A little prick and it'll all be over.'

Vaustad grabbed hold of one of the silver steam pipes erupting from the top of the reactor dome, wrapping himself around it. He began to scramble up it, using the pipe's metal ribs for grip. There was nothing graceful or speedy about his progress, but it was steady and methodical. Had he planned this? Grelier wondered. It had been a mistake to forget about the steam pipes.

But where would he go, ultimately? The pipes would only take him back along the hall towards the turbines and the traction motors. It might prolong the chase, but it was still futile in the long run.

Grelier reached the reactor's apex. Vaustad was a metre or so above his head. He held up the cane, trying to tap Vaustad's heels. No good; he had made too much height. Grelier turned the head of the cane another quarter turn, increasing the stun setting, and touched it against the pipework. Vaustad yelped, but kept moving. Another quarter turn of the cane: maximum-discharge setting, lethal at close quarters. He kissed the end of the cane against the metal and watched Vaustad hug the pipe convulsively. The man clenched his teeth, moaned, but still managed to hold on to the pipe.

Grelier dropped the cane, the charge exhausted. Suddenly this wasn't proceeding quite the way he had planned it.

'Where are you going?' Grelier asked, playfully. 'Come down now, before you hurt yourself.'

Vaustad said nothing, just kept crawling.

'You'll do yourself an injury,' Grelier said.

Vaustad had reached the point where his pipe curved over to the horizontal, taking it across the hall towards the turbine complex.

Grelier expected him to stop at the right-angled turn, having made his point. But instead Vaustad wriggled around the bend until he was lying on the upper surface of the pipe with his arms and legs wrapped around it. He was now thirty metres from the ground.

The scene was drawing a small audience. About a dozen of Glaur's men were standing in the hall below, looking up at the spectacle. Others had paused in their work amongst the coupling rods.

'Clocktower business,' Grelier said warningly. 'Go back to your jobs.'

The workers drifted away, but Grelier was aware that most of them were still keeping one eye on what was happening. Had the situation reached the point where he needed to call in additional assistance from Bloodwork? He hoped not; it was a matter of personal pride that he always took care of these house calls on his own. But the Vaustad call was turning messy.

The choirmaster had made about ten metres of horizontal distance, carrying him beyond the perimeter of the reactor. There was only floor below him now. Even in Hela's reduced gravity, a fall from thirty metres on to a hard surface was probably not going to be survivable.

Grelier looked ahead. The pipe was supported from the ceiling at intervals, hanging by thin metal lines anchored to enlarged versions of the ribs. The nearest line was about five metres in front of Vaustad. There was no way he would be able to get around that.

'All right,' Grelier said, raising his voice above the din of the traction machinery. 'You've made your point. We've all had a bit of a laugh. Now turn around and we'll talk things over sensibly.'

But Vaustad was beyond reason now. He had reached the supporting stay and was trying to wriggle past it, shifting much of his weight to one side of the pipe. Grelier watched, knowing with numbing inevitability that Vaustad was not going to make it. It would have been a difficult exercise for an agile young man, and Vaustad was neither. He was curled around the obstacle now, one leg hanging uselessly over the side, the other trying to act as a balance, one hand on the metal stay and the other fumbling for the nearest rib on the other side. He stretched, straining to reach the rib. Then he slipped, both legs coming off the pipe. He hung there, one hand taking his weight while the other thrashed around in midair.

'Stay still!' Grelier called. 'Stay still and you'll be all right. You can hold yourself there until we get help if you stop moving!'

Again, a fit young man could have held himself up there until rescue arrived, even hanging from one hand. But Vaustad was a large, soft individual who had never had to use his muscles before.

Grelier watched as Vaustad's remaining hand slipped from the metal stay. He watched Vaustad fall down to the floor of the traction hall, hitting it with a thump that was nearly muffled by the constant background noise. There had been no scream, no gasp of shock. Vaustad's eyes were closed, but from the expression on his upturned face it was likely that the man had died instantly.

Grelier collected his cane, stuffed it into the crook of his arm and made his way back down the series of ramps and ladders. At the foot of the reactor he retrieved his medical kit and unlocked the access door. By the time he reached Vaustad, half a dozen of Glaur's workers had gathered around the body. He considered shooing them away, then decided against it. Let them watch. Let them see what Bloodwork entailed.

He knelt down by Vaustad and opened the medical kit. It gasped cold. It was divided into two compartments. In the upper tray were the red-filled syringes of top-up doses, fresh from Bloodwork. They were labelled for serotype and viral strain. One of them had been intended for Vaustad and would now have to go to a new home.

He peeled back Vaustad's sleeve. Was there still a faint pulse? That would make life easier. It was never a simple business, drawing blood from the dead. Even the recently deceased.

He reached into the second compartment, the one that held the empty syringes. He held one up to the light, symbolically.

'The Lord giveth,' Grelier said, slipping the syringe into one of Vaustad's veins and starting to draw blood. 'And sometimes, unfortunately, the Lord taketh away.'

He filled three syringes before he was done.

Grelier latched the gate to the spiral staircase behind him. It was good, on reflection, to escape the aggressive stillness of the traction hall. Sometimes it seemed to him that the place was a cathedral within a cathedral, with its own unwritten rules. He could control people, but down there – amid machines – he was out of his element. He had tried to make the most of the business with Vaustad, but everyone knew that he had not come to take blood, but to give it.

Before ascending further he stopped at one of the speaking points, calling a team down from Bloodwork to deal with the body. There would be questions to answer, later, but nothing that would cost him any sleep.

Grelier moved through the main hall, on his way to the Clocktower. He was taking the long way around, in no particular hurry to see Quaiche after the Vaustad debacle. Besides, it was his usual custom to make at least one circumnavigation of the hall before going up or down. It was the largest open space in the cathedral, and the only one – save for the traction hall – where he could free himself from the mild claustrophobia that he felt in every other part of the moving structure.

The hall had been remade and expanded many times, as the cathedral itself grew to its present size. Little of that history was evident to the casual eye now, but having lived through most of the changes, Grelier saw what others might have missed. He observed the faint scars where interior walls had been removed and relocated. He saw the tidemark where the original, much lower ceiling had been. Thirty or forty years had passed since the new one had been put in – it had been a mammoth exercise in the airless environment of Hela, especially since the old space had remained occupied throughout the whole process and the cathedral had, of course, kept moving the entire time. Yet the choir had not missed a note during the entire remodelling, and the number of deaths amongst the construction workers had remained tolerably low.

Grelier paused awhile at one of the stained-glass windows on the right-hand side of the cathedral. The coloured edifice towered dozens of metres above him. It was framed by a series of divided stone arches, with a rose window at the very top. The cathedral's architectural skeleton, traction mechanisms and external cladding were necessarily composed largely of metal, but much of the interior was faced with a thin layer of cosmetic masonry. Some of it had been processed from indigenous Hela minerals, but the rest of it – the subtle biscuit-hued stones and the luscious white-and-rose marbles – had been imported by the Ultras. Some of the stones, it was said, had even come from cathedrals on Earth. Grelier took that with a large pinch of salt: more than likely they'd come from the nearest suitable asteroid. It was the same with the holy relics he encountered during his tour, tucked away in candlelit niches. It was anyone's guess how old they really were, whether they'd been hand-crafted by medieval artisans or knocked together in manufactory nano-forges.

But regardless of the provenance of the stonework that framed it, the stained-glass window was a thing of beauty. When the light was right, it not only shone with a glory of its own but transmitted that glory to everything and everyone within the hall. The details of the window hardly mattered – it would still have been beautiful if the chips of coloured, vacuum-tight glass had been arranged in random kaleidoscopic patterns – but Grelier took particular note of the imagery. It changed from time to time, following dictates from Quaiche himself. When Grelier sometimes had difficulty reading the man directly (and that was increasingly the case) the windows offered a parallel insight into Quaiche's state of mind.

Take now, for instance: when he had last paid attention to this window, it had focused on Haldora, showing a stylised view of the gas giant rendered in swirling chips of ochre and fawn. The planet had been set within a blue backdrop speckled with the yellow chips of surrounding stars. In the foreground there had been a rocky landscape evoked in contrasting shards of white and black, with the gold form of Quaiche's crashed ship parked amid boulders. Quaiche himself was depicted outside the ship, robed and bearded, kneeling on the ground and raising an imploring hand to the heavens. Before that, Grelier recalled, the window had shown the cathedral itself, pictured descending the zigzagging ramp of the Devil's Staircase, looking for all the world like a tiny storm-tossed sailing ship, all the other cathedrals lagging behind, and with a slightly smaller rendition of Haldora in the sky.

Before that, he couldn't be sure, but he thought it might have been a more modest variation on the theme of the crashed ship.

The images that the window showed now were clear enough, but their significance to Quaiche was much more difficult to judge. At the top, worked into the rose window itself, was the familiar banded face of Haldora. Below that were a couple of metres of starlit sky, shaded from deep blue to gold by some artifice of glass tinting. Then, taking up most of the height of the window, was a toweringly impressive cathedral, a teetering assemblage of pennanted spires and buttresses, lines of converging perspective making it clear that the cathedral sat immediately below Haldora. So far so good: the whole point of a cathedral was for it to remain precisely below the gas giant, just as depicted. But the cathedral in the window was obviously larger than any to be found on the Permanent Way; it was practically a citadel in its own right. And – unless Grelier was mistaken – it was clearly portrayed as being an outgrowth of the rocky foreground landscape, as if it had foundations rather than traction mechanisms. There was no sign of the Permanent Way at all.

The window puzzled him. Quaiche chose the content of the windows, and he was usually very literal-minded in his selections. The scenes might be exaggerated, might even have the taint of unreality (Quaiche outside his ship without a vacuum suit, for instance) but they usually bore at least some glancing relationship to actual events. But the present content of the window appeared to be worryingly metaphorical. That was all Grelier needed, Quaiche going all metaphorical on him. But what else was he to make of the vast, grounded cathedral? Perhaps it symbolised the fixed, immobile nature of Quaiche's faith. Fine, Grelier told himself: you think you can read him now, but what if the messages start getting even foggier?

He shook his head and continued his journey. He traversed the entire left-hand wall of the cathedral, not seeing any further oddities amongst the windows. That was a relief, at least. Perhaps the new design would turn out to be a temporary aberration, and life would continue as normal.

He moved around to the front of the cathedral, into the shadow of the black window. The chips of glass were invisible; all he could see were the ghostly arcs and pillars of the supporting masonry. The design in that window had undoubtedly changed since the last time he had seen it.

He moved back across to the right-hand side and proceeded along half the length of the cathedral until he arrived at the base of the Clocktower.

'Can't put it off any longer,' Grelier said to himself.

Back in her quarters on the caravan, Rashmika opened the letter, breaking the already weakened seal. The paper sprung wide. It was good-quality stuff: creamy and thick, better than anything she had handled in the badlands. Printed inside, in neat but naïve handwriting, was a short message.

She recognised the handwriting.

Dear Rashmika,

I am very sorry not to have been in touch for so long. I heard your name on the broadcasts from the Vigrid region, saying you had run away from home. I had a feeling that you would be coming after me, trying to find out what had happened to me since my last letter. When I found out that there was a caravan coming towards the Way, one that you might have been able to reach with help, I felt certain you would be on it. I made an enquiry and found out the names of the passengers and now I am writing this letter to you.

I know you will think it strange that I have not written to you or any of the family for so long. But things are different now, and it would not have been right. Everything that you said was true. They did not tell the truth to start with, and they gave me the dean's blood as soon as I arrived at the Way. I am sure you could tell this from the letters I sent to begin with. I was angry at first, but now I know that it was all for the best. What's done is done, and if they had been honest it wouldn't have happened this way. They had to tell a lie for the greater good. I am happy now, happier than I have ever been. I have found a duty in life, something bigger than myself. I feel the dean's love and the love of the Creator beyond the dean. I don't expect you to understand or like any of this, Rashmika. That's why I stopped writing home. I didn't want to lie, and yet I also didn't want to hurt anyone. It was better to say nothing.

It is kind and brave of you to come after me. It means more than you can imagine. But you must go home now, before I bring you any more hurt. Do this for me: go home, back to the badlands, and tell everyone that I am happy and that I love them all. I miss them terribly, but I do not regret what I have done. Please. Do that for me, will you? And take my love as well. Remember me as I was, as your brother, not as what I have become. Then it will all be for the best.

With love,

Your brother, Harbin Els.

Rashmika read it one more time, scrutinising it for hidden meaning, and then put it down. She closed it, but the seal would no longer hold the edges tight.

Grelier liked the view, if little else. Two hundred metres above the surface of Hela, Quaiche's room was a windowed garret at the very top of the Clocktower. From this vantage point one could see nearly twenty kilometres of the Way in either direction, with the cathedrals strung along it like artfully placed ornaments. There were only a few of them ahead, but to the rear they stretched back far over the horizon. The tops of distant spires sparkled with the unnatural clarity of things in vacuum, tricking the eye into the illusion that they were much nearer than they actually were. Grelier reminded himself that some of those spires were nearly forty kilometres behind. It would take them thirty hours or more to reach the spot now immediately beneath the Lady Morwenna, the better part of a Hela day. There were some cathedrals so far behind that even their spires were not visible.

The garret was hexagonal in plan, with high armoured windows on all six sides. The slats of metal jalousies were ready to tilt into position at a command from Quaiche, blocking light in any direction. For now the room was fully illuminated, with stripes of light and shade falling on every object and person within it. There were many mirrors in the room, arranged on pedestals, sight-lines and angles of reflection carefully chosen. When Grelier entered, he saw his own shattered reflection arriving from a thousand directions.

He placed the cane into a wooden rack by the door.

Aside from Grelier, the room contained two people. Quaiche, as usual, reclined in the baroque enclosure of his medical support couch. He was a shrivelled, spectral thing, seemingly less substantial in the full glare of daylight than in the half-shuttered darkness that prevailed in the garret. He wore oversized black sunglasses that accentuated the morbid pallor and thinness of his face. The couch ruminated to itself with thoughtful hums and clicks and gurgles, occasionally delivering a dose of medicine into its client. Most of the distasteful medical business was tucked away under the scarlet blanket that covered his recumbent form to the ribcage, but now and then something pulsed along one of the feedlines running into his forearms or the base of his skull: something chemical-green or electric-blue, something that could never be mistaken for blood. He did not look a well man. Appearances, in this case, were not deceptive.

But, Grelier reminded himself, this was how Quaiche had looked for decades. He was a very old man, pushing the envelope of available life-prolongation therapies, testing them to their limit. But the limit was always slightly out of reach. Dying seemed to be a threshold that he lacked the energy to cross.

They had both, Grelier reflected, been more or less the same physiological age when they had served under Jasmina aboard the *Gnostic Ascension*. Now Quaiche was by far the older man, having lived through all of the last hundred and twelve years of planetary time. Grelier, by contrast, had experienced only thirty of those years. The arrangement had been simple enough, with generous benefits where Grelier was concerned.

'I don't really like you,' Quaiche had told him, back aboard the *Gnostic Ascension*. 'If that wasn't already obvious.'

'I think I got the message,' Grelier said.

'But I need you. You're useful to me. I don't want to die here. Not just now.'

'What about Jasmina?'

'I'm sure you'll think of something. She relies on you for her clones, after all.'

It had been shortly after Quaiche's rescue from the bridge on Hela.

As soon as she received data on the structure, Jasmina had turned the *Gnostic Ascension* around and brought it into the 107 Piscium system, swinging into orbit around Hela. There had been no more booby traps on the surface: later investigation showed that Quaiche had triggered the only three sentries on the entire moon, and that they had been placed there and forgotten at least a century before by an earlier and now unremembered discoverer of the bridge.

Except that was almost but not quite true. There *was* another sentry, but only Quaiche knew about it.

Fixated by what he had seen, and stunned by what had happened to him – the miraculous nature of his rescue combined inseparably and punishingly with the horror of losing Morwenna – Quaiche had gone mad. That was Grelier's view, at least, and nothing in the last hundred and twelve years had done anything to reverse his opinion. Given what had happened, and given the perception-altering presence of the virus in Quaiche's blood, he thought Quaiche had got off lightly with only a mild kind of insanity. He still had some kind of grip on reality, still understood – with a manipulative brilliance – all that was going on around him. It was just that he saw the world through a gauze of piety. He had sanctified himself.

Rationally, Quaiche knew that his faith had something to do with the virus in his blood. But he also knew that he had been rescued because of a genuinely miraculous event. Telemetry records from the *Dominatrix* were clear on this: his distress signal had only been intercepted because, for a fraction of a second, Haldora had ceased to exist. Responding to that signal, the *Dominatrix* had raced to Hela, desperate to save him before his air ran out.

The ship had only been doing its duty by racing at maximum thrust to reach Hela as quickly as possible. The acceleration limits that would have applied had Quaiche been aboard were ignored. But the dull intelligence of the ship's mind had neglected to take Morwenna into consideration.

When Quaiche found his way back aboard, the scrimshaw suit was silent. Later, in desperation – part of him already knowing that Morwenna was dead – he had cut through the thick metal of the suit. He had reached inside, caressing the pulped red atrocity within, weeping even as she flowed through his fingers.

Even the metal parts of her had been mangled.

Quaiche had lived, therefore, but at a terrible cost. His options, at that point, had seemed simple enough. He could find a way to discard his faith, some flushing therapy that would blast all traces of the virus from his blood. He would then have to find a rational, secular explanation for what had happened to him. And he would have to accept that although he had been saved by what appeared to be a miracle, Morwenna – the only woman he had truly loved – was gone for ever, and that she had died so that he might live.

The other choice – the path that he had eventually chosen – was one of acceptance. He would submit himself to faith, acknowledging that a miracle had indeed occurred. The presence of the virus would, in this case, simply be a catalyst. It had pushed him towards faith, made him experience the feelings of Holy presence. But on Hela, with time running out, he had experienced emotions that felt deeper and stronger than any the virus had ever given him. Was it possible that the virus had merely made him more receptive to what was already there? That, as artificial as it had been, it had enabled him to tune in to a real, albeit faint, signal?

If that was the case, then everything had meaning. The bridge meant something. He had witnessed a miracle, had called out for salvation and been granted it. And the death of Morwenna must have had some inexplicable but ultimately benign function in the greater plan of which Quaiche was himself only a tiny, ticking, barely conscious part.

'I have to stay here,' he had told Grelier. 'I have to stay on Hela until I know the answer. Until it is revealed unto me.'

That was what he had said: 'revealed unto me.'

Grelier had smiled. 'You can't stay here.'

'I'll find a way.'

'She won't let you.'

But Quaiche had made a proposal to Grelier then, one that the surgeon-general had found difficult to dismiss. Queen Jasmina was an unpredictable mistress. Her moods, even after years of service, were largely opaque to him. His relationship with her was characterised by intense fear of disapproval.

'In the long run, she'll get you,' Quaiche had said. 'She's an Ultra. You can't read her, can't second-guess her. To her, you're just furniture. You serve a need, but you'll always be replaceable. But look at me – I'm a baseline human like yourself, an outcast from mainstream society. She said it herself: we have much in common.'

'Less than you think.'

'We don't have to worship each other,' Quaiche had said. 'We just have to work together.'

'What's in it for me?' Grelier had asked.

'Me not telling her your little secret, for one. Oh, I know all about it. It was one of the last things Morwenna found out before Jasmina put her in the suit.'

Grelier had looked at him carefully. 'I don't know what you mean.'

'I mean the body factory,' Quaiche had said, 'your little problem with supply and demand. There's more to it than just meeting Jasmina's insatiable taste for fresh bodies, isn't there? You've also got a sideline in body usage yourself. You like them small, undeveloped. You take them out of the tanks before they've reached adulthood – sometimes even before they've reached childhood – and you *do* things to them. Vile, vile things. Then you put them back in the tanks and say they were never viable.'

'They have no minds,' Grelier had said, as if this excused his actions. 'Anyway, what exactly are you proposing – blackmail?'

'No, just an incentive. Help me dispose of Jasmina, help me with other things, and I'll make sure no one ever finds out about the factory.'

Quietly, Grelier had said, 'And what about my needs?'

'We'll think of something, if that's what it takes to keep you working for me.'

'Why should I prefer you as my master in place of Jasmina? You're as insane as each other.'

'Perhaps,' Quaiche had said. 'The difference is, I'm not murderous. Think about it.'

Grelier had, and before very long had decided that his short-term best interests lay beyond the *Gnostic Ascension*. He would co-operate with Quaiche for the immediate future, and then find something better – something less submissive – at the earliest opportunity.

Yet here he was, over a century later. He had underestimated his own weakness to a ludicrous degree. For in the Ultras, with their ships crammed full of ancient, faulty reefersleep caskets, Quaiche had found the perfect means of keeping Grelier in his service.

But Grelier had known nothing of this future in the earliest days of their liaison.

Their first move had been to engineer Jasmina's downfall. Their plan had consisted of three steps, each of which had to be performed with great caution. The cost of discovery would be huge, but – Grelier was certain now – in all that time she had never once suspected that the two former rivals were plotting against her.

That didn't mean that things had gone quite according to plan, however.

First, a camp had been established on Hela. There were habitation modules, sensors and surface rovers. Some Ultras had come down, but as usual their instinctive dislike of planetary environments had made them fidgety, anxious to get back to their ship. Grelier and Quaiche, by contrast, had found it the perfect venue in which to further their uneasy alliance. And they had even made a remarkable discovery, one that only aided their cause. It was during their earliest scouting trips away from the base, under the eye of Jasmina, that they had found the very first scuttler relics. Now, at last, they had some idea of who or what had made the bridge.

The second phase of their plan had been to make Jasmina unwell. As master of the body factory, it had been a trivial matter for Grelier. He had tampered with the clones, slowing their development, triggering more abnormalities and defects. Unable to anchor herself to reality with regular doses of self-inflicted pain, Jasmina had grown insular. Her judgement had become impaired, her grasp on events tenuous.

That was when they had attempted the third phase: rebellion. They had meant to engineer a mutiny, taking over the *Gnostic Ascension* for their own ends. There were Ultras – former friends of Morwenna – who had showed some sympathy to Quaiche. During their initial explorations of Hela, Quaiche and Grelier had located a fourth fully functional sentry of the same type that had downed the *Scavenger's Daughter*. The idea had been to exploit Jasmina's flawed judgement to drag the *Gnostic Ascension* within range of the remaining sentry weapon. Ordinarily, she would have resisted bringing her ship within light-hours of a place like Hela, but the spectacle of the bridge, and the discovery of the scuttler relics, had overridden her better instincts.

With the expected damage from the sentry – ultimately superficial, but enough to cause panic and confusion amongst her crew – the ship would have been ripe for takeover.

But it hadn't worked. The sentry had attacked with greater force than Quaiche had anticipated, inflicting fatal, spreading damage on the *Gnostic Ascension*. He had wanted to cripple the ship and occupy it for his own purposes, but instead the vessel had blown up, waves of explosions stuttering away from the impact points on her hull until the wavefront of destruction had reached the Conjoiner drives. Two bright new suns had flared in Hela's sky. When the light faded, there had been nothing left of Jasmina, or of the great lighthugger that had brought Quaiche and Grelier to this place.

Quaiche and Grelier had been stranded.

But they were not doomed. They'd had all they needed to survive on Hela for years to come, courtesy of the surface camp already established. They had begun to explore, riding out in the surface rovers. They had collected scuttler parts, trying to fit the weird alien fossils together into some kind of coherent whole, always failing. To Quaiche it had become an obsessive enterprise. Above him, the puzzle of Haldora. Below, the maddening taxonomic jigsaw of the scuttlers. He had thrown himself into both mysteries, knowing that somehow they were linked, knowing that in finding the answer he would understand why he had been saved and Morwenna sacrificed. He had believed that the puzzles were tests from God. He had also believed that only he was truly capable of solving them.

A year had passed, then another. They circumnavigated Hela, using the rovers to carve out a rough trail. With each circumnavigation, the trail became better defined. They had made excursions to the north and south, veering away from the equator to where the heaviest concentrations of scuttler relics were to be found. Here they had mined and tunnelled, gathering more pieces of the jigsaw. Always, however, they had returned to the equator to mull over what they had found.

And one day, in the second or third year, Quaiche had realised something critical: that he must witness another vanishing.

'If it happens again, I have to see it,' he had told Grelier.

'But if it does happen again – for no particular reason – then you'll know it isn't a miracle.'

'No,' Quaiche had said, emphatically. 'If it happens twice, I'll know that God wanted to show it to me again for a reason, that he wanted to make sure there could be no doubt in my mind that such a thing had already happened.'

Grelier had decided to play along. 'But you have the telemetry from the *Dominatrix*. It confirms that Haldora vanished. Isn't that enough for you?'

Quaiche had dismissed this point with a wave of his hand. 'Numbers in electronic registers. I didn't see it with my own eyes. This means something to me.'

'Then you'll have to watch Haldora for ever.' Hastily, Grelier had corrected himself. 'I mean, until it vanishes again. But how long did it disappear for last time? Less than a second? Less than an eyeblink? What if you miss it?'

'I'll have to try not to.'

'For half a year you can't even see Haldora.' Grelier had pointed out, sweeping his arm overhead. 'It rises and falls.'

'Only if you don't follow it. We circled Hela in under three months the first time we tried; under two the second time. It would be easier still to travel slowly, keeping pace with Haldora. One-third of a metre a second, that's all it would take. Keep up that pace, stay close to the equator, and Haldora will always be overhead. It'll just be the landscape that changes.'

Grelier had shaken his head in wonderment. 'You've already thought this through.'

'It wasn't difficult. We'll lash together the rovers, make a travelling observation platform.'

'And sleep? And blinking?'

'You're the physician,' Quaiche had said. 'You figure it out.'

And figure it out he had. Sleep could be banished with drugs and neurosurgery, coupled with a little dialysis to mop up fatigue poisons. He had taken care of the blinking as well.

'Ironic, really,' Grelier had observed to Quaiche. 'This is what she threatened you with in the scrimshaw suit: no sleep and an unchanging view of reality. Yet now you welcome it.'

'Things changed,' Quaiche had said.

Now, standing in the garret, the years collapsed away. For Grelier, time had passed in a series of episodic snapshots, for he was only revived from reefersleep when Quaiche had some immediate need of him. He remembered that first slow circumnavigation, keeping pace with Haldora, the rovers lashed together like a raft. A year or two later another ship had arrived: more Ultras, drawn by the faint flash of energy from the dying *Gnostic Ascension*. They were curious, naturally cautious. They kept their ship at a safe distance and sent down emissaries in expendable vehicles. Quaiche traded with them for parts and services, offering scuttler relics in return.

A decade or two later, following trade exchanges with the first ship, another had arrived. They were just as wary, just as keen to trade. The scuttler relics were exactly what the market wanted. And this time the ship was willing to offer more than components: there were sleepers in its belly, disaffected émigrés from some colony neither Quaiche nor Grelier had ever heard of. The mystery of Hela – the rumours of miracle – had drawn them across the light-years.

Quaiche had his first disciples.

Thousands more had arrived. Tens of thousands, then hundreds. For the Ultras, Hela was now a lucrative stopover on the strung-out, fragile web of interstellar commerce. The core worlds, the old places of trade, were now out of bounds, touched by plague and war. Lately, perhaps, by something worse than either. It was difficult to tell: very few ships were making it out to Hela from those places now. When they did, they brought with them confused stories of things emerging from interstellar space, fiercely mechanical things, implacable and old, that ripped through worlds, engorging themselves on organic life, but which were themselves no more alive than clocks or orreries. Those who came to Hela now came not only to witness the miraculous vanishings, but because they believed that they lived near the end of time and that Hela was a point of culmination, a place of final pilgrimage.

The Ultras brought them as paid cargo in their ships and pretended to have no interest in the local situation beyond its immediate commercial value. For some, this was probably true, but Grelier knew Ultras better than most and he believed that lately he had seen something in their eyes – a fear that had nothing to do with the size of their profit margins and everything to do with their own survival. They had seen things as well, he presumed. Glimpses, perhaps: phantoms stalking the edge of human space. For years they must have dismissed these as travellers' tales, but now, as news from the core colonies stopped arriving, they were beginning to wonder.

There were Ultras on Hela now. Under the terms of trade, their lighthugger starships were not permitted to come close to either Haldora or its inhabited moon. They congregated in a parking swarm on the edge of the system, dispatching smaller shuttles to Hela. Representatives of the churches inspected these shuttles, ensuring that they carried no recording or scanning equipment pointed at Haldora. It was a gesture more than anything, one that could have been easily circumvented, but the Ultras were surprisingly pliant. They wanted to play along, for they needed the business.

Quaiche was completing his dealings with an Ultra when Grelier arrived in the garret. 'Thank you, Captain, for your time,' he said, his ghost of a voice rising in grey spirals from the life-support couch.

'I'm sorry we weren't able to come to an agreement,' the Ultra replied, 'but you appreciate that the safety of my ship must be my first priority. We are all aware of what happened to the *Gnostic Ascension*.'

Quaiche spread his thin-boned fingers by way of sympathy. 'Awful business. I was lucky to survive.'

'So we gather.'

The couch angled towards Grelier. 'Surgeon-General Grelier ... might I introduce Captain Basquiat of the lighthugger *Bride of the Wind*?'

Grelier bowed his head politely at Quaiche's new guest. The Ultra was not as extreme as some that Grelier had encountered, but still odd and unsettling by baseline standards. He was very thin and colourless, like some desiccated weather-bleached insect, but propped upright in a blood-red support skeleton ornamented with silver lilies. A very large moth accompanied the Ultra: it fluttered before his face, fanning it.

'My pleasure,' Grelier said, placing down the medical kit with its cargo of blood-filled syringes. 'I hope you had a nice time on Hela.'

'Our visit was fruitful, Surgeon-General. It wasn't possible to accommodate the last of Dean Quaiche's wishes, but otherwise, I believe both parties are satisfied with proceedings.'

'And the other small matter we discussed?' Quaiche asked.

'The reefersleep fatalities? Yes, we have around two dozen brain-dead cases. In better times we might have been able to restore neural structure with the right sort of medichine intervention. Not now, however.'

'We'd be happy to take them off your hands,' Grelier said. 'Free up the casket slots for the living.'

The Ultra flicked the moth away from his lips. 'You have a particular use for these vegetables?'

'The surgeon-general takes an interest in their cases,' Quaiche said, interrupting before Grelier had a chance to say anything. 'He likes to attempt experimental neural rescripting procedures, don't you, Grelier?' He looked away sharply, not waiting for an answer. 'Now, Captain – do you need any special assistance in returning to your ship?'

'None that I am aware of, thank you.'

Grelier looked out of the east-facing window of the garret. At the other end of the ridged roof of the main hall was a landing pad, on which a small shuttle was parked. It was the bright yellow-green of a stick insect.

'Godspeed back to the parking swarm, Captain. We await transhipment of those unfortunate casket victims. And I look forward to doing business with you on another occasion.'

The captain turned to walk out, but paused before leaving. He had noticed the scrimshaw suit for the first time, Grelier thought. It was always there, standing in the corner of the room like a silent extra guest. The captain stared at it, his moth fluttering orbits around his head, then continued on his way. He could have no idea of the dreadful significance it represented to Quaiche: the final resting place of Morwenna and an ever-present reminder of what the first vanishing had cost him.

Grelier waited until he was certain the Ultra was not coming back.

'What was all that about?' he asked. 'The extra stuff he "couldn't accommodate"?'

'The usual negotiations,' Quaiche said, as if the matter was beneath him. 'Count yourself lucky that you'll get your vegetables. Now – Bloodwork, eh? How did it go?'

'Wait a moment.' Grelier moved to one wall and worked a brass-handled lever. The jalousies folded shut, admitting only narrow wedges of light. Then he bent down over Quaiche and removed the sunglasses. Quaiche normally kept them on during his negotiations: partly to protect his eyes against glare, but also because without them he was not a pretty sight. Of course, that was precisely the reason he sometimes chose not to wear them, as well.

Beneath the eyeshades, hugging the skin like a second pair of glasses, was a skeletal framework. Around each eye were two circles from which radiated hooks, thrusting inwards to keep the eyelids from closing. There were little sprays built into the frames, blasting Quaiche's eyes with moisture every few minutes. It would have been simpler, Grelier said, to have removed the eyelids in the first place, but Quaiche had a penitential streak as wide as the Way, and the discomfort of the frame suited him. It was a constant reminder of the need for vigilance, lest he miss a vanishing.

Grelier took a small swab from the garret's medical locker and cleaned away the residue around Quaiche's eyes.

'Bloodwork, Grelier?'

'I'll come to that. Just tell me what that business with the Ultra was all about. Why did you want him to bring his ship closer to Hela?'

Visibly, Quaiche's pupils dilated. 'Why do you think that's what I wanted of him?'

'Isn't it? Why else would he have said that it was too dangerous?'

'You presume a great deal, Grelier.'

The surgeon-general finished cleaning up, then slotted the top pair of glasses back into place. 'Why do you want the Ultras closer, all of a sudden? For years you've worked hard to keep the bastards at arm's-reach. Now you want one of their ships on your doorstep?'

The figure in the couch sighed. He had more substance in the darkness. Grelier opened the slats again, observing that the yellow-green shuttle had departed from the landing pad.

'It was just an idea,' Quaiche said.

'What kind of idea?'

'You've seen how nervous the Ultras are lately. I trust them less and less. Basquiat seemed like a man I could do business with. I was hoping we might come to an arrangement.'

'What sort of arrangement?' Grelier returned the swabs to the cabinet.

'Protection,' Quaiche said. 'Bring one group of Ultras here to keep the rest of them away.'

'Madness,' Grelier said.

'Insurance,' his master corrected. 'Well, what does it matter? They weren't interested. Too worried about bringing their ship near to Hela. This place scares them as much as it tantalises them, Grelier.'

'There'll always be others.'

'Perhaps . . .' Quaiche sounded as if the whole business was already boring him, a mid-morning fancy he now regretted.

'You asked about Bloodwork,' Grelier said. He knelt down and picked up the case. 'It didn't go swimmingly, but I collected from Vaustad.'

'The choirmaster? Weren't you supposed to be administering?'

'Wee change of plan.'

Bloodwork: the Office of the Clocktower dedicated to the preservation, enrichment and dissemination of the countless viral strains spun off from Quaiche's original infection. Almost everyone who worked in the cathedral carried some of Quaiche in their blood now. It had reached across generations, mutating and mingling with other types of virus brought to Hela. The result was a chaotic profusion of possible effects. Many of the other churches were based on, or had in some sense even been caused by, subtle doctrinal variants of the original strain. Bloodwork operated to tame the chaos, isolating effective and doctrinally pure strains and damping out others. Individuals like Vaustad were often used as test cases for newly isolated viruses. If they showed psychotic or otherwise undesirable side-effects, the strains would be eliminated. Vaustad had earned his role as guinea pig after a series of regrettable indiscretions, but had grown increasingly fearful of the results of each new test jab.

'I hope you know what you're doing,' Quaiche said. 'I need Bloodwork, Grelier, more so now than ever. I'm losing my religion.'

Quaiche's own faith was subject to horrible lapses. He had developed immunity to the pure strain of the virus, the one that had infected him before his time aboard the *Gnostic Ascension*. One of the principle tasks of Bloodwork was to isolate the new mutant strains that were still able to have an effect on Quaiche. Grelier didn't advertise the fact, but it was getting harder and harder to find them.

Quaiche was in a lapse now. Out of them, he never spoke of losing his religion. It was just there, solidly a part of him. It was only during the lapses that he found it possible to think of his faith as a chemically engineered thing. These interludes always worried Grelier. It was when Quaiche was at his most conflicted that he was at his least predictable. Grelier thought again of the enigmatic stained-glass window he had seen below, wondering if there might be a connection.

'We'll soon have you right as rain,' he said.

'Good. I'll need to be. There's trouble ahead, Grelier. Major icefalls reported in the Gullveig Range, blocking the Way. It will fall to us to clear them, as it always does. But even with God's Fire I'm still worried that we'll lose time on Haldora.'

'We'll make it up. We always do.'

'Drastic measures may be called for if the delay becomes unacceptably large. I want Motive Power to be ready for whatever I ask of them – even the unthinkable.' The couch tilted again, its reflection breaking up and reforming in the slowly moving mirrors. They were set up to guide light from Haldora into Quaiche's field of view: wherever he sat, he saw the world with his own eyes. 'The unthinkable, Grelier,' he added. 'You know what I mean by that, don't you?'

'I think so,' Grelier said. And then thought of blood, and also of bridges. He also thought of the girl he was bringing to the cathedral and wondered if perhaps – just perhaps – he had set in motion something it would no longer be possible to stop.

But he won't do it, he thought. *He's insane, no one doubts that, but he isn't* that *insane. Not so insane that he'd take the Lady Morwenna across the bridge, over Absolution Gap.*

EIGHTEEN

Ararat, 2675

The internal map of the *Nostalgia for Infinity* was a long scroll of scuffed, yellowing paper, anchored at one end by Blood's knife and at the other by the heavy silver helmet Palfrey had found in the junk. The scroll was covered with a dense crawl of pencil and ink lines. In places it had been erased and redrawn so many times that the paper had the thin translucence of animal skin.

'Is this the best we've got?' Blood asked.

'It's better than nothing,' Antoinette said. 'We're doing our best with very limited resources.'

'All right.' The pig had heard that a hundred times in the last week. 'So what does it tell us?'

'It tells us that we have a problem. Did you interview Palfrey?'

'No. Scorp took care of that.'

Antoinette fingered the mass of jewellery packed into her earlobes. 'I had a little chat with him as well. I wanted to see how the land was lying. Turns out practically everyone in bilge management is convinced that the Captain is changing his haunt patterns.'

'And?'

'Now that we've got the last dozen or so apparitions plotted, I'm beginning to think they're right.'

The pig squinted at the map, his eyes poorly equipped for discerning the smoke-grey pencil marks in the low light of the conference room. Maps had never really been his thing, even during his days under Scorpio in Chasm City. There, it had hardly mattered. Blood's motto had always been that if you needed a map to find your way around a neighbourhood, you were already in trouble.

But this map was important. It depicted the *Nostalgia for Infinity*, the very sea-spire in which they were sitting. The ship was a tapering cone of intricate vertical and horizontal lines, an obelisk engraved with crawling, interlocked hieroglyphics. The lines showed floor levels, interconnecting shafts and major interior partitions. The ship's huge internal storage bays were unmarked cavities in the diagram.

The ship was four kilometres tall, so there was no space on the map for detail at the human scale. Individual rooms were usually not marked at all unless they had some strategic importance. Mostly, mapping it was a pointless exercise. The ship's slow processes of interior reorganisation – utterly outside the control of its human occupants – had rendered all such efforts nearly useless within a handful of years.

There were other complications. The high levels of the ship were well charted. Crews were always moving around in these areas, and the constant presence of human activity seemed to have dissuaded the ship from changing itself too much. But the deep levels, and especially those that lay below sea level, were nowhere near as well visited. Teams only went down there when they had to, and when they did they usually found that the interior failed utterly to conform to their expectations. And the transformed parts of the ship – warped according to queasy, biological archetypes – were by their very nature difficult to map with any accuracy. Blood had been down into some of the most severely distorted zones of the deep ship levels. The experience had been akin to the exploration of some nightmarish cave system.

It was not only the interior of the ship that remained uncertain. Before descending from orbit, the lighthugger had prepared itself for landing by flattening its stern. In the chaos of that descent, very few detailed observations of the changes had been possible. And since the lower kilometre of the ship – including the twin nacelles of the Conjoiner drives – was now almost permanently submerged, there had been little opportunity to improve matters in the meantime. Divers had explored only the upper hundred metres of the submerged parts, but even their reports had revealed little that was not already known. Sensors could probe deeper, but the cloudy shapes that they returned showed only that the basic form of the ship was more or less intact. The crucial question of whether or not the drives would ever work again could not be answered. Through his own nervous system of data connections the Captain presumably knew the degree of spaceworthiness of the ship. But the Captain wasn't talking.

Until, perhaps, now.

Antoinette had marked with annotated red stars all recent and reliable apparitions of John Brannigan. Blood peered at the dates and comments, the handwritten remarks which gave details of the type of apparition and the associated witness or witnesses. He dabbed at the map with his knife, scraping the blade gently against it, scything arcs and feints against the pencil marks.

'He's moving up,' Blood observed.

Antoinette nodded. A lock of hair had come loose, hanging across her face. 'That's what I thought, too. Judging by this, I'd say Palfrey and his friends have a point.'

'What about the dates? See any patterns there?'

'Only that things looked pretty normal until a month or so ago.'

'And now?'

'Draw your own conclusions,' she said. 'Me, I think the map speaks for itself. The hauntings have changed. The Captain's suddenly become restless. He's increased the range and boldness of his haunts, showing up in parts of the ship where we've never seen him before. If I included the reports I didn't think were entirely trustworthy, you'd see red marks all the way up to the administration levels.'

'But you don't believe those, do you?'

Antoinette pushed back the stray strands of hair. 'No, right now I don't. But a week ago I wouldn't have believed half of the others, either. Now all it'd take is one good witness above level six hundred.'

'And then what?'

'All bets would be off. We'd have to accept that the Captain's woken up.'

In Blood's view this was already a given. 'It can't be down to Khouri, can it? If the Captain had started behaving differently today, then I could believe it. But if this is real, it started weeks ago. She wasn't here then.'

'But they'd arrived in-system by then,' Antoinette pointed out. 'The battle was already here. How do we know the Captain wasn't sensitive to that? He's a *ship*. His senses reach out for light-hours in all directions. Being anchored to a planet doesn't change that.'

'We don't know that Khouri was telling the truth,' Blood said.

Antoinette used her red marker to add another star, one that corresponded to Palfrey's report. 'I'd say we do now,' she said.

'All right. One other thing. If the Cap's woken up . . .'

She looked at him, waiting for him to finish the sentence. 'Yes?'

'Do you think it means he wants something?'

Antoinette picked up the helmet, causing the map to roll back on itself with a snapping sound. 'Guess one of us is going to have to ask him,' she replied.

Two hours before dawn something twinkled on the horizon.

'I see it, sir,' Vasko said. 'It's the iceberg, like we saw on the map.'

'I don't see anything,' Urton said, after peering into the distance for half a minute.

'I do,' Jaccottet said, from the other boat. 'Malinin's right, I think. There's something there.' He reached for binoculars and held them to his eyes. The wide cowl of the lenses stayed rigidly fixed on target even as the rest of the binoculars wavered in Jaccottet's hands.

'What do you see?' Clavain asked.

'A mound of ice. At this range, that's about all I can make out. Still no sign of a ship, though.'

'Good work,' Clavain said to Vasko. 'We'll call you Hawkeye, shall we?'

On Scorpio's order the boats slowed to half their previous speed, then veered gradually to port. They commenced a long encirclement of the object, viewing it from all sides in the slowly changing dawn light.

Within an hour, as the boats spiralled nearer, the iceberg had become a small round-backed hummock. There was, in Vasko's opinion, something deeply odd about it. It sat on the sea and yet seemed a part of it as well, surrounded as it was by a fringe of white that extended in every direction for perhaps twice the diameter of the central core. It made Vasko think of an island, the kind that consisted of a single volcanic mountain, with gently sloping beaches reaching the sea on all sides. He had seen a few icebergs, when they drifted down to the latitude of First Camp, and this was unlike any iceberg in his experience.

The boats circled closer. Now and then, Vasko heard Scorpio speaking to Blood via his wrist radio. The western sky was a bruised purple, with only a scattering of bright stars showing. In the east it was a bleak shade of rose. Against either backdrop the pale mound of the iceberg threw back subtly distorted variations of the same hues.

'We've circled it twice,' Urton reported.

'Keep it up,' Clavain instructed. 'Reduce our distance by half, but slow to half our present speed. She may not be alert, and I don't want to startle her.'

'Something's not right about that iceberg, sir,' Vasko said.

'We'll see.' Clavain turned to Khouri. 'Can you sense her yet?'

'Skade?' she asked.

'I was thinking more of your daughter. I wondered if there might be some remote cross-talk between your mutual sets of implants.'

'We're still a long way out.'

'Agreed, but let me know the instant you feel anything. My own implants may not pick up Aura's emissions at all, or not until we're much nearer. And in any case you *are* her mother. I am certain you'll recognise her first, even if there is nothing unusual about the protocols.'

'I don't need reminding that I'm her mother,' Khouri said.

'Of course. I just meant . . .'

'I'm listening for her, Clavain. I've been listening for her from the moment you pulled me out of that capsule. You'll be the first to hear if I pick up Aura.'

Half an hour later they were close enough to make out more detail. It was clear to all of them now that this was no ordinary iceberg, even if one discounted the way it infiltrated the water around it. Indeed, it appeared increasingly unlikely that the thing was any kind of iceberg at all.

Yet it *was* made of ice.

The sides of the floating mass were weird and crystalline. Rather than facets or sheets, they consisted of a thickening tangle of white spars, a briar formed from interleaved spikes of ice. Stalagmites and stalactites daggered up and down like icy incisors. Vertical spikes bristled like rapiers. At the root of each spike was a flourish of smaller growths thrusting out in all directions, intersecting and threading through their neighbours. In all directions, the spikes varied in size. Some – the major trunks and branches of the structure – were as wide across as the boat. Others were so thin, so fine, that they formed only an iridescent haze in the air, as if the merest breeze would shatter them into a billion twinkling parts. From a distance, the berg had appeared to be a solid block. Now the mound seemed to be formed from a huge haphazardly tossed pile of glass needles. Unthinkable numbers of glass needles. It was a glistening cavity-filled thicket, as much hollow space as ice.

It was easily the most unsettling thing Vasko had ever seen in his life.

They circled closer.

Of all of them, only Clavain seemed unimpressed by the utter strangeness of what lay before them. 'The smart maps were accurate,' he said. 'The size of this thing . . . by my reckoning, you could easily hide a moray-class corvette inside it.'

Vasko raised his voice. 'You still think there might be a ship inside that thing, sir?'

'Ask yourself a question, son. Do you really think Mother Nature had anything to do with this?'

'But why would Skade surround her ship with all this strange ice?' Vasko persisted. 'I wouldn't have thought it was much use as armour, and all it's done so far is make her ship more visible on the maps.'

'What makes you so sure she had any choice, son?'

'I don't follow, sir.'

Scorpio said, 'He's suggesting that all this might mean there's something wrong with Skade's ship. Isn't that right?'

'That's my working hypothesis,' Clavain said.

'But what . . .' Vasko abandoned his question before he got himself into even deeper water.

'Whatever's inside,' Clavain said, 'we still have to reach it. We don't have tunnelling equipment or anything that can blast through thick ice. But if we're careful, we won't have to. We just have to locate a route through to the middle.'

'What if Skade spots us, sir?' Vasko asked.

'I'm hoping she does. The last thing I want is to have to knock on her front door. Now take us closer. Nice and slowly does it.'

Bright Sun rose. In the early minutes of dawn, the iceberg took on an entirely different character. Against the soft violet of the sky the whole structure seemed magical, as delicate as some aristocrat's confection. The briar spikes and icy spars were shot through with gold and azure, the colours refracted with the untainted dazzle of cut diamond. There were glorious halos, shards and jangles of chromatic purity, colours Vasko had never seen in his life. Instead of shadows, the interior shone turquoise and opal with a radiance that groped and fingered its way to the surface through twisting corridors and canyons of ice. And yet within that shining interior there was a shadowy kernel, a hint of something cocooned.

The two boats had come within fifty metres of the outer edge of the island's fringe. The water had been calm for much of their journey, but here in the immediate vicinity of the iceberg it moved with the languor of some huge sedated animal, as if every ripple cost the sea great effort. Closer to the edge of the fringe, the sea was already beginning to freeze. It had the slick blue-grey texture of animal hide. Vasko touched his fingers just beneath the surface of the water by the boat and then pulled them back out immediately. Even here, this far from the fringe, the water was much colder than it had been when they had left the shuttle.

'Look at this,' Scorpio said. He had one of the smart maps rolled out before him. Khouri was studying it, too, obviously agreeing with something Scorpio was saying to her as he pointed out features with the blunt-trottered stub of one hand.

Clavain opened his own map. 'What is it, Scorp?'

'An update just came through from Blood. Take a look at the iceberg: it's larger.'

Clavain made his map display the same coordinates. The iceberg leapt into view. Vasko peered over the old man's shoulder, searching for the pair of boats. There was no sign of them. He assumed that the update had taken place before sunset the previous evening.

'You're right,' Clavain said. 'What would you say ... thirty, forty per cent larger, by volume?'

'Easily,' Scorpio said. 'And this *isn't* real-time. If it's growing this rapidly, it could be ten or twenty per cent larger again by now.'

Clavain folded his map: he had seen enough. 'It certainly seems to be refrigerating the surrounding water. Before very long, where we're sitting will be frozen as well. We're lucky we arrived when we did. If we'd left it a few more days, we'd never have stood a chance. We'd be looking at a mountain.'

'Sir,' Vasko said, 'I don't understand how it can be getting larger. Surely it should be shrinking. Icebergs don't last at these latitudes.'

'I thought you said you didn't know much about them,' Clavain replied.

'I said we don't see many in the bay, sir.'

Clavain looked at him shrewdly. 'It's not an iceberg. It never was. It's a shell of ice around Skade's ship. And it's growing because the ship is making it grow by cooling the sea around it. Remember what Khouri said? They have ways of making their hulls as cold as the cosmic microwave background.'

'But you also said you didn't think Skade had any control over this.'

'I'm not sure she has.'

'Sir ...'

Clavain cut him off. 'I think something may have gone wrong with the cryo-arithmetic engines that keep the hull cold. What, I don't know. Perhaps Skade will tell us, when we find her.'

Until a day ago Vasko had never heard of cryo-arithmetic engines. But the phrase had cropped up in Khouri's testimony – it was one of the technologies that Aura had helped Remontoire and his allies to perfect as they raced away from the ruins of the Delta Pavonis system.

In the hours that followed, Vasko had done his best to ask as many questions as possible, trying to fill in the most embarrassing voids in his knowledge. Not all of his questions had met with ready answers, even from Khouri. But Clavain had told him that the cryo-arithmetic engines were not completely new, that the basic technology had already been developed by the Conjoiners towards the end of their war against the Demarchists. At that time, a single cryo-arithmetic engine had been a clumsy thing the size of a mansion, too large to be carried on anything but a major spacecraft. All efforts to produce a miniaturised version had ended in disaster. Aura, however, had shown them how to make engines as small as apples.

But they were still dangerous.

The cryo-arithmetic principle was based on a controlled violation of thermodynamic law. It was an outgrowth from quantum computation, exploiting a class of algorithms discovered by a Conjoiner theorist named Qafzeh in the early years of the Demarchist war. Qafzeh's algorithms – if implemented properly on a particular architecture of quantum computer – led to a net heat loss from the local universe. A cryo-arithmetic engine was in essence just a computer, running computational cycles. Unlike ordinary computers, however, it got colder the faster it ran. The trick – the really difficult part – was to prevent the computer from running even faster as it chilled, spiralling into a runaway process. The smaller the engine, the more susceptible it was to that kind of instability.

Perhaps that was what had happened to Skade's ship. In space, the engines had worked to suck heat away from the corvette's hull, making the ship vanish into the near-zero background of cosmic radiation. But the ship had sustained damage, perhaps severing the delicate web of control systems monitoring the cryo-arithmetic engines. By the time it hit Ararat's ocean it had become a howling mouth of interstellar cold. The water had begun to freeze around it, the odd patterns and structures betraying the obscene violation of physical law taking place.

Could anyone still be alive inside it?

Vasko noticed something then. It was possible that he was the first. It was a keening sound at the very limit of his hearing, a sensation so close to ultrasound that he barely registered it as noise at all. It was more like a kind of data arriving by a sensory channel he had never known he possessed.

It was like singing. It was like a million fingers circling the wet rims of a million wine glasses.

He could barely hear it, and yet it threatened to split his skull open.

'Sir,' Vasko said, 'I can hear something. The iceberg, sir, or whatever it is – it's making a noise.'

'It's the sun,' Clavain said, after a moment. 'It must be warming the ice, stressing it in different ways, making it creak and shiver.'

'Can you hear it, sir?'

Clavain looked at him with an odd expression on his face. 'No, son, I can't. These days, there are a lot of things I can't hear. But I'm taking your word for it.'

'Closer,' Scorpio said.

Through dark, dank corridors of the great drowned ship, Antoinette Bax walked alone. She held a torch in one hand and the old silver helmet in the other, her fingers tucked through the neck ring. Lolloping ahead of her with the eagerness of a hunting dog, the wandering golden circle of torchlight defined the unsettling sculptural formations that lined the walls: here an archway that appeared to be made from spinal vertebrae, there a mass of curled and knotted intestinal tubes. The crawling shadows made the tubes writhe and contort like copulating snakes.

A steady damp breeze blew up from the lower decks, and from some unguessable distance Antoinette heard the clanging report of a hesitant, struggling mechanism – a bilge pump, maybe, or perhaps the ship itself remaking a part of its own fabric. Sounds propagated unpredictably through the ship, and the noise could just as easily have originated mere corridors away as from some location kilometres up or down the spire.

Antoinette hitched high the collar of her coat. She would have preferred company – any company – but she knew that this was the way it had to be. On each of the very few occasions in the past when she had elicited anything from the Captain that might be construed as a meaningful response, it had always been when she was alone. She took this as evidence that the Captain was prepared to reveal himself to her, and that there was an element of trust – however small – in their relationship. True or not, Antoinette had always believed that she stood a better chance of communicating with the Captain than her peers did. It was all about history. She had owned a ship herself once, and although that ship had been much smaller than the *Nostalgia for Infinity*, in some sense it, too, had been haunted.

'Talk to me, John,' she had said on previous occasions. 'Talk to me as someone you can trust, as someone who appreciates a little of what you are.'

There had never been an unequivocal answer, but if she looked at all the instances when she had drawn some response, however devoid of content, it appeared to her that the Captain was more likely to do *something* in her presence than not. Taken together, none of these apparitions amounted to any kind of coherent message. But what if the recent spate of manifestations pointed to him emerging from some dormant state?

'Captain,' she said now, holding aloft the helmet, 'you left a calling card, didn't you? I've come to give it back. Now you have to keep your side of the bargain.'

There was no response.

'I'll be honest with you,' she said. 'I really don't like it down here. Matter of fact, it scares the hell out of me. I like my ships small and cosy, with décor I chose myself.' She cast the torch beam around, picking out an overhanging globular mass filling half the corridor. She stooped under the shock-frozen black bubbles, brushing her fingers against their surprising warmth and softness. 'No, this isn't me at all. But I guess this is your empire, not mine. All I'm saying is that I hope you realise what it takes to bring me down here. And I hope you're going to make it worthwhile for me.'

Nothing happened. But she had never expected success at first bite.

'John,' she said, deciding to risk familiarity, 'we think something may be happening in the wider system. My guess is you may have some suspicions about this as well. I'll tell you what we think, anyway – then you can decide for yourself.'

The character of the breeze changed. It was warmer now, with an irregularity about it that made her think of ragged breathing.

Antoinette said, 'Khouri came back. She dropped out of the sky a couple of days back. You remember Khouri, don't you? She spent a lot of time aboard, so I'd be surprised if you didn't. Well, Khouri says there's a battle going on around Ararat, something that makes the Demarchist–Conjoiner war look like a snowball fight. If she isn't lying, we've got two squabbling human factions up there, plus a really frightening number of wolf machines. You remember the wolves, don't you, Captain? You saw Ilia throw the cache weapons at them, and you saw what good it did.'

There it was again. The breeze had become a faint suction.

In Antoinette's estimation that already made it a class-one apparition. 'You're here with me, aren't you?'

Another shift in the wind. The breeze returned, sharpened to a howl. The howl ripped her hair loose, whipping it in her eyes.

She heard a word whispered in the wind: *Ilia*.

'Yes, Captain. Ilia. You remember her well, don't you? You remember the Triumvir. I do, too. I didn't know her for long, but it was long enough to see that she isn't the kind of woman you'd forget in a hurry.'

The wind had died down. All that remained was a nagging suction.

A small, sane voice warned Antoinette to stop now. She had achieved a clear result: a class one by anyone's definition, and almost certainly (if she had not imagined the voice) a class two. That was enough for one day, wasn't it? The Captain was nothing if not temperamental. According to the records she had left behind, Ilia Volyova had pushed him into a catatonic sulk many times by trying to coax just one more response from him. Often it had taken the Captain weeks to emerge from one of those withdrawals.

But the Triumvir had had months or years to build up her working relationship with the Captain. Antoinette did not think she had anywhere near as much time.

'Captain,' she said, 'I'll lay the cards on the table. The seniors are worried. Scorpio's so worried he's pulled Clavain back from his island. They're taking Khouri seriously. They've already gone to see if they can get her baby back for her. If she's right, there's a Conjoiner ship already in our ocean, and it was damaged by the wolves. They're here, Captain. It's crunch time. Either we sit here and let events happen around us, or we think about the next move. I'm sure you know what I mean by that.'

Abruptly, as if a door or valve had slammed shut somewhere, the suction stopped. No breeze, no noise, only Antoinette standing alone in the corridor with the small puddle of light from her torch.

'Holy shit,' Antoinette said.

But then, ahead of her, a cleft of light appeared. There was a squeal of metal and part of the corridor wall hinged aside. A new sort of breeze hit her face, a new concoction of biomechanical smells.

Through the cleft she saw a new corridor, curving sharply down towards underlying decks. Golden-green light, firefly pale, oozed up from the depths.

'I guess I was right about the calling card,' she said.

NINETEEN

Ararat, 2675

The boats rammed through the thickening water on the periphery of the fringe, and then into the fringe itself. A blizzard of ice shards sprayed away on either side of the hulls. The boats surged forwards for ten or twelve metres and then scraped to a grinding halt, electric motors howling.

The rectangular hulls had cut neat channels into the fringe, but the oily grey water had no sooner stopped sloshing than it began to turn suspiciously immobile and pearly. Scorpio thought of coagulating blood, the way it turned sticky and viscid. In a few minutes, he estimated, the channels would be frozen solid again.

The two Security Arm people were the first out of the craft, establishing that the ice was firm enough to take the weight of the party. The others followed a minute later, carrying what weapons and equipment they could manage but leaving much else – including the incubator – in the boats. The firm part of the fringe formed a belt of land, five or six metres wide in most places, around the main peak of the iceberg. The huge crystalline structure rose up, steepsided, above them. Scorpio, stiff-necked, found it awkward to look at the top for more than a few moments.

He waited for Clavain to disembark, then moved over to him. They stood shivering, stamping their feet up and down. The ice beneath them had a braided texture, thick tuberous strands woven together into a kind of matting. It was treacherous, both slippery and uneven. Every footfall had to be taken with caution.

'I was expecting a welcome by now,' Scorpio said. 'The fact that we haven't had one is starting to worry me.'

'Me, too.' Clavain kept his voice very low. 'We haven't discussed the possibility, but Skade could well be dead. I just don't think ...' He trailed off, eyeing Khouri. She was sitting on her haunches, assembling the remaining parts of the Breitenbach cannon. 'I just don't think *she* is quite ready to deal with that yet.'

'You believe everything she's said, don't you?'

'I'm sure we'll find a ship in here. But she had no reason to believe that Skade survived the crash.'

'Skade's a survivor type,' Scorpio said.

'There is that, but I never thought I'd find myself wishing it were the case.'

'Sirs?'

They followed the voice. It was Vasko. He had made his way some distance around the fringe, until he was almost about to vanish around the corner.

'Sirs,' he said again, eyeing Scorpio and Clavain in turn, 'there's an opening here. I saw it from the sea. I think it's the largest one all the way around.'

'How deep does it go?' Scorpio asked.

'Don't know. More than a few metres, at least. I could easily squeeze through, I think.'

'Wait,' Scorpio said. 'Let's take this one step at a time, shall we?'

They followed Vasko to the gap in the ice. As they neared the wall, it was necessary to duck under and between the jutting horizontal spikes, shielding their eyes and faces with the backs of their arms. Some instinct made Scorpio loath to harm any part of the structure. It was next to impossible not to, for even as he stepped cautiously around one spike, protecting himself against the rapierlike tip of another, he shattered half a dozen smaller ones. They tinkled as they broke into pieces, and set off a cascade of secondary fractures metres away.

'Is it still singing to you?' he asked Vasko.

'No, sir,' he said, 'not the way it was just now. I think that was only when the sun was coming up.'

'But you can still hear something?'

'I don't know, sir. It's lower, much lower. It comes in waves. I might be imagining it.'

Scorpio could not hear a thing. He had not been able to hear the iceberg singing, either. Nor had Clavain. Clavain was an old man, with an old man's ailing faculties. Scorpio was a pig, with faculties about as good as they had ever been.

'I'm ready to squeeze inside, sir.'

The opening that Vasko had found was merely a larger-than-usual pocket between the ragged weave of interthreading ice branches and needle-pointed spurs. It began at chest height: a vaguely oval widening, with the hint of a larger clearing beyond it. It was impossible to tell how far in they could reach.

'Let me see,' Khouri said. She carried the cannon on a shoulder strap, slung down her back, its weight shifted on to one hip.

'There are other ways in,' Vasko said, 'but I think this is the easiest.'

'We'll take it,' Khouri said. 'Stand aside. I'm going first.'

'Wait,' Clavain said.

Her lip curled. 'My daughter's in there. Someone go fetch the incubator.'

'I know how you feel,' Clavain said.

'Do you?'

His voice was marvellously calm. 'Yes, I do. Skade took Felka once. I went in after her, just the way you're doing. I thought it was the right way to proceed. I see now that it was foolish and that I came very close to losing her. That's why you shouldn't be the first one in. Not if you want to see Aura again.'

'He's right,' Scorpio said. 'We don't know what we'll find in that thing, or how Skade will react when she knows we're here. We might lose someone. The one person we can't afford to lose is you.'

'You can still fetch the incubator.'

'No,' Scorpio said. 'It stays out here, out of harm's way. I don't want it getting smashed in a firefight. And if it turns out that we can negotiate our way through this, there'll be time to come back and get it.'

Khouri appeared to see the sense in his argument, even though she didn't look very happy about it. She stepped back from the side of the berg. 'I'm going in second,' she said.

'I'll lead,' Scorpio said. He turned to the two Security Arm officers. 'Jaccottet, you follow Khouri. Urton, stay here with Vasko. Keep an eye on the boats and watch out for anything emerging from any other part of the ice. The instant you see something unusual . . .' He paused, noticing the way his companions were looking around. 'The instant you see something *really* unusual . . . let us know.'

He would let Clavain decide for himself what he did.

Scorpio negotiated the forest of impaling spikes. Daggers and fronds shattered with every movement, every breath. The air was a constant iridescent haze of crystals. With great effort he pulled himself through the aperture, his short stature and limbs making it more difficult for him than for any of the others. The tip of an icy blade kissed his skin, not quite breaking it but scraping painfully along the surface. He felt another push into his thigh.

Then he was through, landing on his feet on the other side. He dusted himself off and looked around. Everywhere, the ice gleamed with a neon-blue intensity. There were almost no shadows, just different intensities of that same pastel radiance. The spikes were here in abundance, as well as the rootlike structures that composed the fringe. They thrust through underfoot, thick as industrial pipes. He reminded himself that nothing here was static: the iceberg was growing, and this inclusion might only have existed for a few hours.

The air was as cold as steel.

Behind him, Khouri crunched to the ground. The muzzle of the Breitenbach cannon pulverised a whole fan of miniature stalactites as it swung around. Other weapons, too numerous to list, hung from her belt like so many shrunken trophies.

'What Vasko said ...' she began. 'The low noise. I can hear it as well. It's like a throbbing.'

'I don't hear it, but that doesn't mean it isn't real,' Scorpio acknowledged.

'Skade's here,' she said. 'I know what you think: that she might be dead. But she's alive. She's alive and she knows we've landed.'

'And Aura?'

'I can't feel her yet.'

Clavain emerged into the chamber, picking his way through the opening with the methodical slowness of a tarantula. His thin dark-clad limbs seemed built for precisely this purpose. Scorpio noticed that he managed to enter without breaking any of the ornamentation. He also noticed that the only weapon that Clavain appeared to be carrying was the short-bladed knife he had taken from his tent. He had it clutched in one hand, the blade vanishing when he turned it edge-on.

Behind Clavain came Jaccottet, much less stealthily. The Security Arm man stopped to brush the ice shards from his uniform.

Scorpio lifted his sleeve, revealing his communicator. 'Blood, we've found a way inside the iceberg. We're going deeper. I'm not sure what will happen to comms, but stay alert. Malinin and Urton are staying outside. If all else fails, we may be able to relay communications through them. I'm guessing we might be inside this thing for a couple of hours, maybe more.'

'Be careful,' Blood said.

What was this, Scorpio wondered: concern from Blood? Things were truly worse than he had feared. 'I will be,' he said. 'Anything else I need to know?'

'Nothing immediately related to your mission. Reports of

enhanced Juggler activity from many of the monitoring stations, but that might just be a coincidence.'

'Right now I'm not sure if *anything* is a coincidence.'

'And – uh – just to cheer you up – some reports of lights in the sky. Not confirmed.'

'Lights in the sky? It gets better.'

'Probably nothing. If I were you, I'd put it all out of your mind. Concentrate on the job in hand.'

'Thanks. Sterling advice. All right, pal, speak to you later.'

Clavain had heard the conversation. 'Lights in the sky, eh? Maybe next time you'll believe an old man.'

'I didn't not believe you for one instant.' Scorpio reached down to his own belt and pulled out a gun. 'Here, take this. I can't stand to see you walking around with just that silly little knife.'

'It's a very good knife. Did I mention that it saved my life once?'

'Yes.'

'It's a wonder I've held on to it all this time. Honestly, don't you think there's something very *chivalrous* about a knife?'

'Personally,' Scorpio said, 'I think it's time to stop thinking chivalry and start thinking artillery.'

Clavain took the gun the way one took a gift out of politeness, a gift of which one did not entirely approve.

They moved deeper into the iceberg, following the path of least resistance. The texture of the ice, braided and tangled like a wildly overgrown wood, made Scorpio think of some of the buildings in the Mulch layers of Chasm City. When the plague had hit them, their repair and redesign systems had produced something of the same organic fecundity. Here, it seemed, the growth of the ice was driven entirely by weird localised variations in temperature and air flow. Between one step and the next, the air shifted from lung-crackingly frigid to merely chilly, and any attempt to navigate by means of the draughts was doomed to failure. More than once he had the feeling he was inside a huge, cold, respiring lung.

But their path was always clear: away from the daylight, into the pastel blue core.

'It's music,' Jaccottet said.

'What?' Scorpio asked.

'Music, sir. That low noise. There were too many echoes before. I couldn't make sense of it. But I'm sure it's music now.'

'Music? Why the *fuck* would there be music?'

'I don't know, sir. It's faint, but it's definitely there. Advise caution.'

'I can hear it, too,' Khouri said. 'And I advise hurrying the fuck up.'

She removed one of the weapons from her belt and shot at the thickest spar in front of her. It exploded into white marble dust. She stepped through the ruins and raised the gun towards another obstruction.

Clavain did something to his knife. It began to hum, just at the limit of Scorpio's hearing. The blade became a blur. Clavain swept it through one of the smaller spars, severing it neatly and cleanly.

They moved on, further from the light. In waves, the air became colder still. They huddled deeper into their clothes and spoke only when it was strictly necessary. Scorpio had been grateful for his gloves, but now it felt as if he had forgotten to wear them at all. He had to keep looking down to remind himself they were still in place. It was said that hyperpigs felt the cold more acutely than baseline humans: some quirk of pig biochemistry that the designers had never seen any compelling reason to rectify.

He was thinking about that when Khouri spoke excitedly. She had pushed ahead of them all despite their best efforts to hold her back.

'There's something ahead,' she said, 'and I think I can feel Aura now. We must be near.'

Clavain was immediately behind her. 'What can you see?'

'The side of something dark,' she said. 'Not like the ice.'

'Must be the corvette,' Clavain said.

They advanced another ten or twelve metres, taking at least two minutes to gain that distance. The ice was so thick now that Clavain's little knife could only hack and pare away insignificant parts of it, and Khouri was wise enough not to use her weapon so close to the heart of the iceberg. Around them, the ice formations had taken on an unsettling new character. Jaccottet's torch beam glanced off conjunctions resembling thigh bones or weird sinewy articulations of bone and gristle.

Then the density of the obstructions thinned out. They were suddenly in the core of the iceberg. A sort of roof folded over them, veined and buttressed by enormous trunks of scaly ice rising up from the floor below. The thick weavelike tangle was also visible on the far side of the chamber.

In the middle was the ruin of a ship.

Scorpio did not consider himself any kind of an expert on Conjoiner spacecraft, but from what he did know, the moray-class corvette ought to have been a sleek ultra-black chrysalis of a vessel.

It should have been flanged and spined like some awful instrument of interrogation. There should have been no hint of a seam in the light-sucking surface of its hull. And the ship should most certainly not have lain on one side, broken-backed, splayed open like a dissected specimen, its guts frozen in mid-explosion. The gore of machine entrails should not have surrounded the corpse, and nor should bits of the hull, as sharp and irregular as glass shards, have been lying around the wreck like so many toppled gravestones.

That wasn't the only thing wrong with the ship. It was throbbing, making staccato purring noises at the low-frequency limit of Scorpio's hearing. He felt it in his belly more than he heard it. It was the music.

'This isn't good,' Clavain said.

'I can still feel Aura,' Khouri said. 'She's in there, Clavain.'

'There isn't much of it left for her to be in,' he told her.

Scorpio saw that for an instant the muzzle of Khouri's Breitenbach cannon tipped towards Clavain, sweeping across him. It was only for an instant, and there was nothing in Khouri's expression to suggest that she was on the point of losing control, but it still gave him pause for thought.

'There's still a ship here,' Scorpio said. 'It may be a wreck, Nevil, but someone could be aboard it. And something's making that music. We shouldn't give up yet.'

'No one was about to give up,' Clavain said.

'The cold's coming from the ship,' Khouri said. 'It's pouring out of it, as if it's *bleeding* cold.'

Clavain smiled. 'Bleeding cold? You can say that again.'

'Sorry?'

'Old joke. One that doesn't work too well in Norte.'

Khouri shrugged. They walked towards the wreck.

At the foot of the sloping green-lit corridor down which she had been invited, Antoinette found an echoing chamber of indistinct proportions. She estimated that she had descended five or six levels before the corridor flattened out, but there was no point attempting to plot her position on the pocket blow-up of the main ship map. It had already proven itself to be hopelessly out of date even before the apparitions had summoned her down here.

She halted, keeping the torch on for now. Green light poked through gill-like slats in the ceiling. Wherever she aimed the beam she found machinery, huge rusting piles of it reaching as far away as the torchlight penetrated. The metallic junk ranged from curved scabs of hull plating taller than Antoinette to thumb-sized artefacts covered in brittle green corrosive fur. In between were bronze pump parts and the damaged limbs and sensory organs of shipboard servitors, tossed into loose, teetering piles. The effect was exactly as if she had stumbled into the waste room of a mechanical abattoir.

'Well, Captain,' Antoinette said. Gently, she put the helmet down in front of her. 'Here I am. I presume you've brought me here for a reason.'

The machinery stirred. One of the heaps moved as if being pushed by an invisible hand. The slurry of mechanical parts flowed and gyred, animated by the still-working servitor parts that lay embedded in the charnel pile. The articulated limbs twitched and flexed with a mesmerising degree of co-ordination. Antoinette held her breath. She supposed that she had been expecting something along these lines – a fully fledged class-three apparition, exactly as Palfrey had described – but the actuality of it was still unnerving. This close, the potential dangerousness of the machinery was stark. There were sharp edges that could cut or shear, hinged parts that could crush and maim.

But the machinery did not lurch towards her. Instead it continued to shuffle and organise itself. Bits dropped to the floor, twitching stupidly. Detached limbs flexed and grasped. Eye parts goggled and blinked. The red scratches of optical lasers rammed from the pyre, sliding harmlessly over Antoinette's chest.

She was being triangulated.

The pile collapsed. A layer of useless slurry had avalanched away to reveal the thing that had been assembling at its core. It was a machine, an accumulation of junk parts in the schematic shape of a man. The skeleton – the main armature of the thing – was composed of perhaps a dozen servitor limbs, grasping each other by their manipulators. It stood expertly balanced on the scuffed metal bulbs of ball-and-socket joints. Cables and feedlines were wrapped around it like tinsel, lashing the looser parts together. The head was a ramshackle conglomeration of sensor parts, stacked in a way that vaguely suggested the proportions of a human skull and face. In places, the cables were still sparking from intermittent short circuits. The smell of hot soldered metal hit her, slamming her back to times when she had worked on the innards of *Storm Bird* under the watchful supervision of her father.

'I suppose I should say hello,' Antoinette said.

There was something in one of the Captain's hands. She hadn't noticed it before. The limb whipped towards her and the thing arced through the air, describing a graceful parabola. A reflex made her reach out and snatch the thing from the air.

It was a pair of goggles.

'I guess you want me to put these on,' Antoinette said.

The broken black hull loomed above them. There was a tall rent in the side, a gash fringed by a scurf of something black and crystalline. Scorpio watched silently as Jaccottet knelt down and examined it. The white pulse of his breath was as crisp as a vapour trail against the ruined armour. His gloved fingers touched the froth, tracing its peculiar angularity. It was a growth of dice-sized black cubes, arranged into neatly stepped structures.

'Be careful,' Khouri said. 'I think I recognise that stuff.'

'It's Inhibitor machinery,' Clavain said, his own voice barely a breath.

'Here?' Scorpio asked.

Clavain nodded gravely. 'Wolves. They're here, now, on Ararat. I'm sorry, Scorp.'

'You're absolutely sure? It couldn't just be something weird that Skade was using?'

'We're sure,' Khouri said. 'Thorn and I got a dose of that stuff around Roc, in the last system. I haven't seen it up close since then, but it's not something you forget in a hurry. Scares the hell out of me just to see it again.'

'It doesn't seem to be doing much,' Jaccottet said.

'It's inert,' Clavain said. 'Has to be. Galiana met this stuff as well, in deep space. It ripped through her ship, assembling itself into attack machinery. Took out her entire crew, section by section, until only Galiana was left. Then it got to her as well. Trust me: if it was functional, we'd be dead by now.'

'Or we'd be having our skulls sucked dry of data,' Khouri said. 'And trust *me* as well, that's not the preferred option.'

'We're all agreed on that,' Clavain said.

Scorpio approached the gash after the others, making sure that they were not leaving themselves unprotected from the rear. The black crust of Inhibitor machinery had clearly erupted through the hull from the inside, haemorrhaging out under pressure. Perhaps it had happened before Skade's ship had hit the surface, after the corvette was attacked in space.

Khouri began to squeeze through into the deeper blackness of the hull. Clavain reached out and touched her sleeve. 'I wouldn't rush this,' he said. 'For all we know, there's active wolf machinery just inside.'

'What other options have we got, guy? From where I'm standing they look a bit thin on the ground.'

'None of the weapons we brought with us will be worth a damn against active Inhibitor machinery,' Clavain said. 'If that stuff wakes, it'd be like trying to put out a forest fire with a water pistol.'

'At least it'll be quick,' Jaccottet said.

'Actually, the one thing it won't be is quick,' Khouri said, with what sounded like malicious pleasure. 'Because you probably won't be allowed to die. It suits the machinery to keep you alive while it drinks your skull dry. So if you have any doubts about whether you want to put yourself through that, I suggest you keep back one round for yourself. If you're lucky, you can beat the black stuff before it hits your brain and hijacks motor control. After that, you're fucked.'

'If it's so bad,' Jaccottet said, 'how did you get away from it?'

'Divine intervention,' Khouri replied. 'But if I were you, it's not something I'd put a lot of faith in.'

'Thanks for the tip.' Jaccottet's hand moved involuntarily to a small weapon on his belt.

Scorpio knew what he was thinking: would he be fast enough, if the moment came? Or would he wait that fatal instant too long?

Clavain moved, his knife humming in his hand. 'We'll have to trust that the stuff remains dormant,' he said.

'It's stayed dormant this long,' Jaccottet said. 'Why would it wake up now?'

'We're heat sources,' Clavain said. 'That *might* make a tiny bit of difference.'

Khouri pushed through into the belly of the ruined ship. Her torchlight bounced back through the gash, picking out the stepped edges of the froth. Under a fine patina of ice the machinery gleamed like freshly hewn coal. Where Jaccottet had rubbed his fingers across it, however, the stuff was pure black, lacking any highlights or lustre.

'There's more of the shit in here,' she said. 'It's spread over everything, like black vomit.' The torchlight played around again, their shadows wheeling over the walls like stalking ogres. 'But it doesn't seem to be any more active than the stuff outside.'

'All the same,' Clavain said, 'don't touch it, just to be on the safe side.'

'It wasn't on my to-do list,' Khouri replied.

'Good. Anything else?'

'The music's louder. It comes in blasts, speeded up. It's almost as if I recognise it.'

'I do recognise it,' Clavain said. 'It's Bach – Passacaglia and Fugue in C Minor, if I'm not mistaken.'

Scorpio turned to his Security Arm man. 'I want you to stay out here. I can't afford to leave this exit uncovered.'

Jaccottet knew better than to argue.

Scorpio and Clavain climbed in after Khouri. Clavain played his torch around the mangled interior of this part of the corvette, pausing now and then as the beam alighted on some recognisable but damaged structure. The black invasion resembled a prolific fungal growth that had all but consumed the fabric of the spacecraft.

The hull, Scorpio realised, was a shattered ruin, barely holding itself together. He watched where he put his feet.

'It subsumes,' Clavain said quietly, as if wary – despite the intermittent pulses of music – of alerting the machinery. 'It only takes one element to invade a whole ship. Then it eats its way through the entire thing, converting as it goes.'

'What are those little black cubes made of?' asked Scorpio.

'Almost nothing,' Clavain told him. 'Just pure force maintained by a tiny mechanism deep inside, like the nucleus of an atom. Except we never got a look at the mechanism.'

'I take it you had a go?'

'We removed some cubic elements from Galiana's crew by mechanical force, breaking the inter-cube bonds. They just shrank away to nothing, leaving a tiny pile of grey dust. We presumed that was the machinery, but by then there wasn't a lot it could tell us. Reverse engineering wasn't really an option.'

'We're in a lot of trouble, aren't we?' Scorpio said.

'Yes, we're in trouble,' Khouri said. 'You're right about that part. Matter of fact, we probably don't know how much trouble we really are in. But understand one thing: we're not dead, not yet, and not while we have Aura.'

'You think she'll make that much of a difference?' Clavain asked.

'She made a difference already, guy. We wouldn't have made it to this system if she hadn't.'

'Do you still think she's here?' Scorpio asked her.

'She's here. Just can't say where.'

'I'm picking up signals as well,' Clavain said, 'but they're fractured and confused. Too many echoes from all the half-functioning systems in this ship. I can't say if it's one source or several.'

'So what do we do?' Scorpio asked.

Clavain angled his torch into the gloom. The beam knifed against fabulous crenellations and castellations of frozen black cubes. 'Back there should be the propulsion systems compartment,' he said. 'Not a very likely place to look for survivors.' He swung around, hunting with the beam, squinting at the unfamiliarity of it all. 'Through here, I think. It seems to be the source of the music, as well. Careful, it'll be a tight squeeze.'

'Where will that take us?' Scorpio said.

'Habitat and flight deck. Assuming we recognise any of it when we get there.'

'It's colder that way,' Khouri said.

They stepped towards the part of the ship Clavain had indicated. There was a gap ahead, the remains of a bulkhead. The air felt as if it was only a breath away from freezing solid altogether. Scorpio glanced back, his mind playing tricks on him, conjuring languid ripples and waves of motion in the black tar of the wolf machinery.

Instead, something moved ahead. A section of shadow detached itself from the wall, black against black.

Khouri's gun tipped towards it.

'No!' Clavain shouted.

Scorpio heard the click of the Breitenbach cannon's trigger. He flinched, steeling himself for the energy discharge. It was not really the weapon of choice for close-quarters combat.

Nothing happened. Khouri lowered the weapon's muzzle an inch. She had pulled back on the trigger, but not enough to fire.

Clavain's knife trembled in his hand like an elver.

The black presence became a person in black vacuum armour. The armour moved stiffly, as if rusted into seizure. It clutched a dark shape in one hand. The figure took another step and then keeled towards them. It hit the ground with a crack of metal against ice. Black cubes splintered away in all directions, frosted with ice. The weapon – or whatever it was – skidded away and knocked against the wall.

Scorpio knelt down to pick it up.

'Careful,' Clavain said again.

Scorpio's trotters closed on the rounded contours of the Conjoiner side arm. He tried to close his hand around the grip in such a way that he could still depress the trigger. It wasn't possible. The grip had never been engineered for use by pigs.

In fury he tossed it to Clavain. 'Maybe you can get this thing to work.'

'Easy, Scorp.' Clavain pocketed the weapon. 'It won't work for me, either, not unless Skade was very careless with her defences. But we can keep it out of harm's way, at least.'

Khouri shouldered the cannon and lowered herself down next to the crashed armour of the figure. 'It ain't Skade,' she said. 'Too big, and the helmet crest isn't the right shape. You picking up anything, Clavain?'

'Nothing intelligible,' he said. He stilled the shivering blade of his knife and slipped it back into one of his pockets. 'But let's get that helmet off and see where we are, shall we?'

'We don't have time to waste,' Scorpio said.

Clavain started working the helmet seals. 'This will only take a moment.'

The extremities of Scorpio's hands were numb, his co-ordination beginning to show signs of impairment. He did not doubt that Clavain was suffering much the same thing; it must be taking real strength and precision to unlock the intricate mechanism of the helmet seal.

There was a latching sound, then a scrape of metal against metal and a gasp of equalising air pressure. The helmet popped off, trapped between Clavain's trembling fingertips. He placed it gently on to the ice, rim down.

The face of a young female Conjoiner looked back at them. She had something of the same sleekly sculpted look as her mentor, but she was clearly not Skade. Her face was wide and flat-featured, her bloodless skin the colour of static on a monitor. Her neural crest – the heat-dissipating ridge of bone and cartilage running from the very top of her forehead to the nape of her neck – was less extravagant than the one Scorpio remembered seeing on Skade, and was almost certainly a much less useful indicator of her state of mind. It probably incorporated a more advanced set of neural mechanisms, with lower heat-dissipation burdens.

Her lips were grey and her eyebrows pure chrome white. She opened her eyes. In the torchlight her irises were a metallic blue-grey.

'Talk to me,' Clavain said.

She coughed and laughed at the same time. The appearance of a human expression on that stiff mask shocked them all.

Khouri leaned closer. 'I'm only picking up mush,' she said.

'There's something wrong with her,' Clavain replied quietly. Then he held the woman's head from behind, supporting it off the ice. 'Listen to me carefully. We don't want to hurt you. You've been injured, but if you help us we will take care of you. Can you understand me?'

The woman laughed again, a spasm of delight creasing her face. 'You ...' she began.

Clavain leaned closer. 'Yes?'

'Clavain.'

Clavain nodded. 'Yes, that's me.' He looked back at the others. 'Damage can't be too severe if she remembers me. I'm sure we'll be able ...'

She spoke again. 'Clavain. Butcher of Tharsis.'

'That was a long time ago.'

'Clavain. Defector. *Traitor.*' She smiled again, coughed, and then hacked a mouthload of saliva into his face. 'Betrayed the Mother Nest.'

Clavain wiped the spit from his face with the back of his glove. 'I didn't betray the Mother Nest,' he said, with an alarming lack of anger. 'It was actually Skade who betrayed it.' He corrected her with avuncular patience, as if putting right some minor misapprehension about geography.

She laughed and spat at him again. The power of it surprised Scorpio. It caught Clavain in the eye and made him hiss in pain.

Clavain leant closer to the woman, keeping a hand over her mouth this time. 'We have some work to do, I think. A little bit of re-education. A little bit of attitude adjustment. But that's all right, I've got plenty of time.'

The woman coughed again. Her titanium-grey eyes were bright and joyful, even as she struggled for breath. There was something idiotic about her, Scorpio realised.

The armoured body started convulsing. Clavain kept hold of her head, his other hand still across her mouth.

'Let her breathe,' Khouri said.

He released the pressure across her mouth for an instant. The woman kept smiling, her eyes wide, unblinking. Something black squeezed between Clavain's fingers, forcing its way through the gaps like some manifestation of demonic foulness. Clavain flinched back, letting go of the woman, dropping her head against the floor. The black stuff pulsed out of her mouth, out of her nostrils, the flows merging into a horrible black beard which began to engulf her face.

'Live machinery,' Clavain said, falling back. His own left hand was covered in ropes of the black stuff. He swatted it against the ice, but the black ooze refused to dislodge. The ropes combined into a coherent mass, a plaque covering his fingers to the knuckle. It was composed of hundreds of smaller versions of the same cubes they had seen elsewhere. They were swelling perceptibly, enlarging as they consolidated their hold on his hand. The black growth progressed towards his wrist in a series of convulsive waves, cubes sliding over each other.

From behind, something lit up the entire cavity of the wrecked ship. Scorpio risked a glance back, just long enough to see the barrel of Khouri's cannon glowing cherry-red from a minimum-yield discharge. Jaccottet was aiming his own weapon at the corpse of the Conjoiner, but it was obvious that nothing more remained of the organic part of the Inhibitor victim. The emerging machines appeared totally unaffected: the blast had dispersed some of them from the main mass, but there was no sign that the energy had harmed them in any way whatsoever.

Scorpio had only glanced away for a second, but when he returned his attention to Clavain, he was horrified to see Clavain slumped back against the wall, grimacing.

'They've got me, Scorp. It hurts.'

Clavain closed his eyes. The black plaque had now taken his hand to the wrist. At the finger end it had formed a rounded stump which was creeping slowly back as the wrist end advanced.

'I'll try to lever it off,' Scorpio said, fumbling in his belt for something thin and strong, but not so sharp that it would damage Clavain's hand.

Clavain opened his eyes. 'It won't work.'

With his good hand he reached into the pocket where he had put the knife. A moment earlier his face had been a grey testament to pain, but now there was an easing there, as if the agony had abated.

It hadn't, Scorpio knew. Clavain had merely dulled off the part of his brain that registered it.

Clavain had the knife out. He held it by the haft, trying to make the blade come alive. It wasn't happening. Either the control could never be activated single-handedly, or Clavain's other hand was too numb from the cold to do the job. In error or frustration, the knife tumbled from his grip. He groped towards it, then abandoned the effort.

'Scorp, pick it up.'

He took the knife. It felt odd in his trotter, like something precious he had stolen, something he had never been meant to handle. He moved to give it back to Clavain.

'No. You have to do it. Activate the blade with that stud. Be careful: she kicks when the piezo-blade starts up. You don't want to drop it. She'll cut through hyperdiamond like a laser through smoke.'

'I can't do this, Nevil.'

'You have to. It's killing me.'

The black caul of Inhibitor machinery was eating back into his hand. There was no room in that thing for his fingertips, Scorpio realised. It had devoured them already.

He pressed the activation stud. The knife twisted in his hand, alive and eager. He felt the high-frequency buzz through the hilt. The blade had become a blur of silver, like the flicker of a hummingbird's wing.

'Take it off, Scorp. Now. Quickly and cleanly. A good inch above the machinery.'

'I'll kill you.'

'No, you won't. I'll make it through this.' Clavain paused. 'I've shut down pain reception. Bloodstream implants will handle clotting. You've nothing to worry about. Just do it. *Now.* Before I change my mind, or that stuff finds a short cut to my head.'

Scorpio nodded, horrified by what he was about to do but knowing that he had no choice.

Making sure that none of the machinery touched his own flesh, Scorpio supported Clavain's damaged arm at the elbow. The knife buzzed and squirmed. He held the locus of the blur close to the fabric of the sleeve.

He looked into Clavain's face. 'Are you sure about this?'

'Scorp. Now. As a friend. *Do it.*'

Scorpio pushed the knife down. He felt no resistance as it ghosted through fabric, flesh and bone.

Half a second later the work was done. The severed hand – Scorpio had cut it off just above the wrist – dropped to the ice with a solid whack. With a moan Clavain slumped back against the wall, losing whatever strength he had mustered until then. He'd told Scorpio that he had blocked all pain signals, but some residual message must have reached his brain: either that or what Scorpio heard was a moan of desperate relief.

Jaccottet knelt down by Clavain, unhitching a medical kit from his belt. Clavain had been right: there was very little in the way of blood loss from the wound. He held the truncated forearm against his belly, pressing it tight, while Jaccottet prepared a dressing.

There was a rustle of movement from the hand. The black machines were detaching themselves, breaking free of the remaining flesh. They moved hesitantly, as if sapped of the energy they had drawn from the warmth of living bodies. The mass of cubes oozed away from the hand, slowed and then halted, becoming just another part of the dormant growth that filled the ship. The hand lay there, the flesh a contused landscape of recent bruises and older age spots, yet still largely intact save for the eroded stubs of the fingertips, which had been consumed down to the first joint.

Scorpio made the knife stop shivering and put it on the ground. 'I'm sorry, Nevil.'

'I've lost it once already,' Clavain said. 'It really doesn't mean that much to me. I'm grateful that you did what you had to do.' Then he leant back against the wall and closed his eyes for another few seconds. His breathing was sharply audible and irregular. It sounded like someone making inexpert saw cuts.

'Are you going to be all right?' Scorpio asked Clavain, eyeing the severed hand.

Clavain did not respond.

'I don't know enough about Conjoiners to say how much shock he can take,' Jaccottet said, keeping his voice low, 'but I know this man needs rest and a lot of it. He's old, for a start, and no one's been around to fine-tune all those machines in his blood. It might be hitting him a lot worse than we think.'

'We have to move on,' Khouri said.

'She's right,' Clavain said, stirring again. 'Here, someone help me to my feet. Losing a hand didn't stop me last time; it won't now.'

'Wait a moment,' Jaccottet said, finishing off the emergency dressing.

'You need to stay here, Nevil,' Scorpio said.

'If I stay here, Scorp, I *will* die.' Clavain groaned with the effort of trying to stand up on his own. 'Help me, God damn you. Help me!'

Scorpio eased him to his feet. He stood unsteadily, still holding the bandaged stump against his belly.

'I still think you'd be better off waiting here,' Scorpio said.

'Scorp, we're all staring hypothermia in the face. If I can feel it, so can you. Right now the only thing that's holding it off is adrenalin and movement. So I suggest we *keep moving*.' Then Clavain reached down and picked up the knife from where Scorpio had put it down. He slipped it back into his pocket. 'Glad I brought it with me now,' he said.

Scorpio glanced down at the ground. 'What about the hand?'

'Leave it. They can grow me a new one.'

They followed the draught of cold towards the front portion of Skade's wrecked ship.

'Is it me,' Khouri said, 'or has the music just changed?'

'It's changed,' Clavain said. 'But it's still Bach.'

TWENTY

Hela, 2727

Rashmika watched the icejammer being winched down to the rolling ribbon of road. There was a scuff of ice as the skis touched the surface. On the icejammer's roof, the two suited men unhitched the hooks and rode them up to the top of the winches, before being swung back on to the top of the caravan vehicle. Crozet's tiny-looking vehicle bobbed and yawed alongside the caravan for several hundred metres, then allowed itself to be slowly overtaken by the rumbling procession. Rashmika watched until it was lost to view behind the grinding wheels of one of the machines.

She stepped back from the inclined viewing window. That was it, then: all her bridges burned. But her resolve to continue remained as strong as ever. She was going onwards, no matter what it took.

'I see you've made your mind up, then.'

Rashmika turned from the window. The sound of Quaestor Jones's voice shocked her: she had imagined herself alone.

The quaestor's green pet cleaned its face with its one good forelimb, its tail wrapped tight as a tourniquet around his upper arm.

'My mind didn't need making up,' she said.

'I had hoped that the letter from your brother would knock some sense into your head. But it didn't, and here you are. At least now we have a small treat for you.'

'I'm sorry?' Rashmika asked.

'There's been a slight change in our itinerary,' he said. 'We'll be taking a little longer to make our rendezvous with the cathedrals than planned.'

'Nothing serious has happened, I hope.'

'We've already incurred delays that we can't make up by following our usual route south. We had intended to traverse the Ginnungagap Rift near Gudbrand Crossing, then move south down the Hyrrokkin Trail until we reached the Way, where we'd meet the cathedrals. But that simply isn't possible now, and in any case, there's been a major icefall somewhere along the Hyrrokkin Pass. We don't have the gear to shift it, not quickly, and the nearest caravan with ice-clearing equipment is stuck at Glum Junction, pinned down by a flash glacier. So we'll have to take a short cut, if we aren't to be even later.'

'A short cut, Quaestor?'

'We're approaching the Ginnungagap Rift.' He paused. 'You know about the rift, of course. Everything has to cross it at some point.'

Rashmika visualised the laceration of the Rift, a deep sheer-sided ice canyon slicing diagonally across the equator. It was the largest geological feature on the planet, the first thing Quaiche had named on his approach.

'I thought there was only one safe crossing,' she said.

'For the cathedrals, yes,' he allowed. 'The Way deviates a little to the north, where the walls of the Rift have been tiered in a zigzag fashion to allow the cathedrals to descend to the floor. It's a laborious process, costs them days, and then they have to repeat the process climbing up the far side. They need a good head start on Haldora if they aren't to slip behind. They call that route the Devil's Staircase, and every cathedral master secretly dreads it. The descent is narrow and collapses aren't uncommon. But we don't have to take the Staircase: there's another way across the Rift, you see. A cathedral can't make it, but a caravan doesn't weigh anywhere near as much as a cathedral.'

'You're talking about the bridge,' Rashmika said, with a shiver of fear and anticipation.

'You've seen it, then.'

'Only in photos.'

'What did you think?'

'I think it looks beautiful,' she said, 'beautiful and delicate, like something blown from glass. Much too delicate for machines.'

'We've crossed it before.'

'But no one knows how much it can take.'

'I think we can trust the scuttlers in that regard, wouldn't you say? The experts say it's been there for millions of years.'

'They say a lot of things,' Rashmika replied, 'but we don't know for sure how old it is, or who built it. It doesn't look much like anything else the scuttlers left behind, does it? And we certainly don't know that it was ever meant to be crossed.'

'You seem unnaturally worried about what is – in all honesty – a technically simple manoeuvre, one that will save us many precious days. Might I ask why?'

'Because I know what they call that crossing,' she said. 'Ginnungagap Rift is what Quaiche named the canyon, but they have another name for it, don't they? Especially those who decide to cross the bridge. They call it Absolution Gap. They say you'd better be free from sin before you begin the crossing.'

'But of course, you don't believe in the existence of sin, do you?'

'I believe in the existence of reckless stupidity,' Rashmika replied.

'Well, you needn't worry yourself about that. All you have to do is enjoy the view, just like the other pilgrims.'

'I'm no pilgrim,' she said.

The quaestor smiled and popped something into his pet's mouth. 'We're all either pilgrims or martyrs. In my experience, it's better to be a pilgrim.'

Ararat, 2675

Antoinette put on the goggles. The view through them was like a smoky counterpart of the real room, with red Canasian numerals tumbling in her right visual field. For a moment nothing else changed. The haphazard skeletal machine – the class-three apparition – continued to stand amid the discarded slurry of junk from which it had been birthed, one limb frozen in the act of tossing her the goggles.

'Captain . . .' she began.

But even as she spoke the apparition and its detritus were merging into the background, losing sharpness and contrast against the general clutter of the chamber. The goggles were not working perfectly, and in one square part of her visual field the skeletal machine remained unedited, but elsewhere it was vanishing like buildings into a wall of sea fog.

Antoinette did not like this. The machinery had not threatened her, but it troubled her not to have a good idea of where it was. She was reaching up for the goggles, ready to slip them off, when a voice buzzed in her ear.

'Don't. Keep them on. You need them to see me.'

'Captain?'

'I promise I won't hurt you. Look.'

She looked. Something was emerging now, being slowly edited into her visual field. A human figure – utterly real, this time – was forming out of thin air. Antoinette took an involuntary step backwards, catching her torch against an obstruction and dropping it to the floor.

'Don't be alarmed,' he told her. 'This is what you came for, isn't it?'

'Right now I'm not sure,' she breathed.

The human figure had stepped out of history. He wore a truly ancient space suit, a baggy, bulging affair of crinkled rust-orange fabric. His boots and thick-fingered gloves were clad in the same tawny material, ripped here and there to reveal a laminated mesh of underlying layers. He wore a dull silver belt festooned with numerous tools of unclear function. A rugged square box hung on the chest region of his suit, studded with chunky plastic-sealed controls large enough to be worked despite the handicap of the gloves. An even larger box sat on his back, rising above his neck. Moulded from bright red plastic, a thick ribbed hose dangled from the backpack over his left shoulder, its open end resting against the upper shelf of the chest-pack. The silver band of the suit's neck ring was a complexity of locking mechanisms and black rubberised seals. Between the neck ring and the upper part of the suit were many unrecognisable logos and insignia.

He wore no helmet.

The Captain's face looked too small for the suit. On his scalp – which appeared shaven – he wore a padded black and white cap veined with monitor wires. In the smoky light of the goggles she couldn't guess at the shade of his skin. It was smooth, stretched tight over his cheekbones, shadowed with a week's growth of patchy black beard. He had very fine razor-cut eyebrows, which arched quizzically above wide-set, doglike eyes. She could see the whites of those eyes between the pupil and the lower eyelid. He had the kind of mouth – thin, straight, perfect for a certain superciliousness – that she might find either fascinating or untrustworthy, depending on her mood. He did not look like a man much inclined to small talk. Usually that was all right with Antoinette.

'I brought this back,' she said. She stooped down and picked up the helmet.

'Give it to me.'

She moved to throw it.

'No,' he said sharply. 'Give it to me. Walk closer and hand it to me.'

'I'm not sure I'm ready to do that,' she said.

'It's called a gesture of mutual trust. You either do it or the conversation ends here. I've already said I won't hurt you. Didn't you believe me?'

She thought of the machinery that the goggles had edited out of her vision. Perhaps if she took them off, so that she saw the apparition as it really was . . .

'Leave the goggles on. That's also part of the deal.'

She took a step closer. It was clear that she had no choice.

'Good. Now give me the helmet.'

Another step. Then one more. The Captain waited with his hands at his sides, his eyes encouraging her forwards.

'I understand that you're scared,' he said. 'That's the point. If you weren't frightened, there'd be no show of trust, would there?'

'I'm just wondering what you're getting out of this.'

'I'm trusting you not to let me down. Now pass me the helmet.'

She held it out in front of her, as far as her arms would stretch, and the Captain reached out to take it from her. The goggles lagged slightly, so that a flicker of machinery was briefly visible as his arms moved. His gloved fingers closed around the helmet. She heard the rasp of metal on metal.

The Captain took a step back. 'Good,' he said, approvingly. He rolled the helmet in his hands, inspecting it for signs of wear. Antoinette noticed now that there was a vacant round socket in one side, into which the red umbilical was meant to plug. 'Thank you for bringing this down to me. The gesture is appreciated.'

'You left it with Palfrey. That wasn't an accident, was it?'

'I suppose not. What did you say it was – a "calling card"? Not far from the truth, I guess.'

'I took it as a sign that you were willing to talk to someone.'

'You seemed very anxious to talk to me,' he said.

'We were. We are.' She looked at the apparition with a mixture of fear and dangerous, seductive relief. 'Do you mind if I ask you something?' She took his silence to indicate assent. 'What shall I call you? "Captain" doesn't seem quite right to me, not now that we've been through the mutual-trust thing.'

'Fair point,' he conceded, not sounding entirely convinced. 'John will do for now.'

'Then, John, what have I done to deserve this? It wasn't just my bringing back the helmet, was it?'

'Like I said, you seemed anxious to talk.'

Antoinette bent down to pick up her torch. 'I've been trying to reach you for years, with no success at all. What's changed?'

'I feel different now,' he said.

'As if you were asleep but have finally woken up?'

'It's more as if I *need* to be awake now. Does that answer your question?'

'I'm not sure. This might sound rude, but . . . who am I talking to, exactly?'

'You're talking to me. As I am. As I was.'

'No one really knows who you were, John. That suit looks pretty old to me.'

A gloved hand moved across the square chest-pack, tracing a pattern from point to point. To Antoinette it looked like a benediction, but it might equally have been a rote-learned inspection of critical systems. *Air supply, pressure integrity, thermal control, comms, waste management ...* she knew that litany herself.

'I was on Mars,' he said.

'I've never been there,' she said.

'No?' He sounded disappointed.

'Fact of the matter is, I really haven't seen all that many worlds. Yellowstone, a bit of Resurgam, and this place. But never Mars. What was it like?'

'Different. Wilder. Colder. Savage. Unforgiving. Cruel. Pristine. Bleak. Beautiful. Like a lover with a temper.'

'But this was a while back, wasn't it?'

'Uh huh. How old do you think this suit is?'

'It looks pretty damn antique to me.'

'They haven't made suits like this since the twenty-first century. You think Clavain's old, a relic from history. I was an old man before he took a breath.'

It surprised her to hear him mention Clavain by name. Clearly the Captain was more aware of shipboard developments than some gave him credit for. 'You've come a long way, then,' she said.

'It's been a long, strange trip, yes. And just look where it's brought me.'

'You must have some stories to tell.' Antoinette reckoned that there were two safe areas of conversation: the present and the very distant past. The last thing she wanted was to have the Captain dwelling on his recent sickness and bizarre transformation.

'There are some stories I don't want told,' he said. 'But isn't that true for us all?'

'No argument from me.'

His thin slit of a mouth hinted at a smile. 'Dark secrets in your own past, Antoinette?'

'Nothing I'm going to lose any sleep over, not when we have so much else we need to worry about.'

'Ah.' He rotated the helmet in his gloved hands. 'The difficult matter of the present. I am aware of things, of course, perhaps more than you realise. I know, for instance, that there are other agencies in the system.'

'You feel them?'

'It was their noises that woke me from long, calm dreams of Mars.' He regarded the icons and decals on the helmet, stroking them with the stubby tip of one gloved finger. Antoinette wondered about the memories they stirred, preserved across five or six hundred years of experience. Memories thick with the grey dust of centuries.

'We thought that you were waking,' she said. 'In the last few weeks we've become more aware of your presence. We didn't think it was coincidence, especially after what Khouri told us. I know you remember Khouri, John, or you wouldn't have brought me down here.'

'Where is she?'

'With Clavain and the others.'

'And Ilia? Where is Ilia?'

Antoinette was sweating. The temptation to lie, to offer a soothing platitude, was overwhelming. But she did not doubt for one instant that the Captain would see through any attempt at deception. 'Ilia's dead.'

The black and white cap bowed down. 'I thought I might have dreamed it,' he said. 'That's the problem now. I can't always tell what's real and what's imagined. I might be dreaming you at this very moment.'

'I'm real,' she said, as if her assurance would make any difference, 'but Ilia's dead. You remember what happened, don't you?'

His voice was soft and thoughtful, like a child remembering the significant events in a nursery tale. 'I remember that she was here, and that we were alone. I remember her lying in a bed, with people around her.'

What was she going to tell him now? That the reason Ilia had been in a bed in the first place was because she had suffered injuries during her efforts to thwart the Captain's own suicide attempt, when he had directed one of the cache weapons against the hull of the ship. The scar he had inflicted on the hull was visible even now, a vertical fissure down one side of the spire. She was certain that on some level he knew all this but also that he did not need to be reminded of it now.

'She died,' Antoinette said, 'trying to save us all. I gave her the use of my ship, *Storm Bird*, after we'd used it to rescue the last colonists from Resurgam.'

'But I remember her being unwell.'

'She wasn't so unwell that she couldn't fly a ship. Thing is, John, she felt she had something to atone for. You remember what she did to the colonists, when your crew were trying to find Sylveste? Made them think she'd wiped out a whole settlement in a fit of pique? That's why they wanted her for a war criminal. Towards the end, I wonder whether she didn't start believing it herself. How are we to know what went through her head? If enough people hate you, it can't be easy not to start thinking they might be right.'

'She wasn't a particularly good woman,' the Captain said, 'but she wasn't what they made her out to be. She only ever did what she thought right for the ship.'

'I guess that makes her a good woman in my book. Right now the ship is about all we have, John.'

'Do you think it worked for her?' he asked.

'What?'

'Atonement, Antoinette. Do you think it made the slightest difference, in the end?'

'I can't guess what went through her mind.'

'Did it make any difference to the rest of you?'

'We're here, aren't we? We got out of the system alive. If Ilia hadn't taken her stand, we'd probably all be smeared over a few light-hours of local solar space around Resurgam.'

'I hope you're right. I did forgive her, you know.'

Antoinette knew that it had been Ilia who had allowed the Captain's Melding Plague to finally engulf the ship. At the time she did it, it had seemed the only way to rid the ship of a different kind of parasite entirely. Antoinette did not think that Ilia had taken the decision lightly. Equally – based on her very limited experience of the woman – she did not think consideration of the Captain's feelings had had very much influence on her decision.

'That's pretty generous of you,' she said.

'I realise that she did it for the ship. I realise also that she could have killed me instead. I think she wanted to, after she learned what I had done to Sajaki.'

'Sorry, but that's way before my time.'

'I murdered a good man,' the Captain said. 'Ilia knew. When she did this to me, when she made me what I am, she knew what I'd done. I would have sooner she'd killed me.'

'Then you've paid for whatever you did,' Antoinette said. 'And even if you hadn't then, even if she hadn't done whatever she did, it doesn't matter. What counts is that you saved one hundred and sixty thousand people from certain death. You've repaid that one crime a hundred thousand times over and more.'

'You imagine that's the way the world works, Antoinette?'

'It's good enough for me, John, but what do I know? I'm just a space pilot's daughter from the Rust Belt.'

There was a lull. Still holding the helmet, the Captain took the end of the ribbed red umbilical and connected it to the socket in the side of the helmet. The interface between the real object and the simulated presence was disturbingly seamless.

'The trouble is, Antoinette, what good was it to save those lives, if all that happens is that they die now, here on Ararat?'

'We don't know that anyone's going to die. So far the Inhibitors haven't touched us down here.'

'All the same, you'd like some insurance.'

'We need to consider the unthinkable, John. If the worst comes to the worst, we'll need to leave Ararat. And you're going to have to be the man with the plan.'

He slipped the helmet on to his neck ring, twisting it to and fro to engage the latching mechanisms. The faceplate glass was still up. The whites of his eyes were two bright crescents in the shadowed map of his face. Green and red numerals were back-reflected on to his skin.

'It took some guts to come down here on your own, Antoinette.'

'I don't think this is a time for cowards,' she said.

'It never was,' he said, beginning to slide down the faceplate glass. 'About what you want of me?'

'Yes?'

'I'll give the matter some thought.'

Then he turned around and walked slowly into the darkness. A skirl of red-brown dust swelled up to block him from view. It was like a sandstorm on Mars.

Hela, 2727

The Ultra captain was called Heckel, his ship the *Third Gazometric*. He had come down in a red-hulled shuttle of very ancient design – a triad of linked spheres with large, stylised tarantula markings.

Even by recent standards, Heckel struck Quaiche as a very strange individual. The mobility suit in which he came aboard the Lady Morwenna was a monstrous contraption of leather and brass, with rubberised accordion joints and gleaming metal plates secured by rivets. Behind the tiny grilled-over eyeholes of his helmet, wiper blades flicked back and forth to clear condensation. Steam vented from poorly maintained joints and seals. Two assistants had accompanied him: they were constantly opening and closing hatches in the suit, fiddling with brass knobs and valves. When Heckel spoke, his voice emerged from a miniature pipe organ projecting from the top of his helmet. He had to keep making adjustments to knobs in his chest area to stop the voice becoming too shrill or deep.

Quaiche understood none of Heckel's utterances, but that was all right: Heckel had also brought along a baseline interpreter. She was a small doe-eyed woman dressed in a more modern spacesuit. Her helmet had folded back on itself, retracting like a cockatoo's crest so that everyone could see her face.

'You're not an Ultra,' Quaiche remarked to the interpreter.

'Does it matter?'

'I just find it amusing, that's all. It's where I started, doing the same line of work as you.'

'That must have been a long time ago.'

'But they still don't find it any easier to negotiate with the likes of us, do they?'

'Us, Dean?'

'Baseline humans, like you and me.'

She hid it well, but he read her amused reaction. He saw himself from her point of view: an old man reclining on a couch, deathly frail, surrounded by an audience of moving mirrors, his eyes peeled open like fruits. He was not wearing the sunglasses.

Quaiche moved a hand. 'I wasn't always like this. I could pass for a baseline human, once, move in normal society with no one so much as batting an eyelid. I was taken into the employment of Ultras, just as you have been. Queen Jasmina, of the *Gnostic Ascension* . . .'

Heckel adjusted his chest knobs, then piped out something incomprehensible.

'He says Jasmina did not have the best of reputations, even amongst other Ultras,' the interpreter said. 'He says that even now, in certain Ultra circles, mentioning her name is considered the height of bad taste.'

'I didn't know Ultras even recognised bad taste as a concept,' Quaiche replied archly.

Heckel piped back something shrill and peremptory.

'He says there is a lot you need to remember,' the interpreter said. 'He also says he has other business he needs to attend to today.'

Quaiche fingered the edge of his scarlet blanket. 'Very well, then. Just to clarify . . . you would be willing to consider my offer?'

The interpreter listened to Heckel for a moment, then addressed

Quaiche. 'He says he understands the logic of your proposed security arrangement.'

Quaiche nodded enthusiastically, forcing the mirrors to nod synchronously. 'Of course, it would work to the benefit of *both* parties. I would gain the protection of a ship like the *Third Gazometric*, insurance against the less scrupulous Ultra elements we all know are out there. And by agreeing to provide that security – for a fixed but not indefinite period, naturally – there would be compensations in terms of trading rights, insider information, that sort of thing. It could be worth both our whiles, Captain Heckel. All you'd have to do is agree to move the *Third Gazometric* closer to Hela, and to submit to some very mild mutual friendship arrangements . . . a small cathedral delegation on your ship and – naturally – a reciprocal party on the Lady Morwenna. And then you'd have immediate access to the choicest scuttler relics, before any of your rivals.' Quaiche looked askance, as if seeing enemies in the garret's shadows. 'And we wouldn't have to be looking over our shoulders all the time.'

The captain piped his reply.

'He says he understands the benefits in terms of trading rights,' the interpreter said, 'but he also wishes to emphasise the risk he would be taking by bringing his ship closer to Hela. He mentions the fate that befell the *Gnostic Ascension* . . .'

'And there was me thinking it was bad taste to mention it.'

She ignored him. 'And he wishes to have these beneficial trading arrangements clarified before any further discussion takes place. He wishes also to specify a maximum term for the period of protection, and . . .' She paused while Heckel piped out a series of rambling additions. 'He also wishes to discuss the exclusion from trade of certain other parties currently in the system, or approaching it. Parties to be excluded would include, but not be limited to, the trade vessels *Transfigured Night*, *Madonna of the Wasps*, *Silence Under Snow* . . .'

She continued until she noticed Quaiche's raised hand. 'We can discuss these things in good time,' he said, his heart sinking. 'In the meantime, the cathedral would – of course – require a full technical examination of the *Third Gazometric*, to ensure that the ship poses no hazard to Hela or its inhabitants . . .'

'The captain wonders if you doubt the worthiness of his ship,' the interpreter said.

'Not at all. Why should I? He made it this far, didn't he? On the other hand, if he has nothing to hide . . .'

'The captain wishes to retire to his shuttle to consider matters.'

'Of course,' Quaiche said with sudden eagerness, as if nothing was too much to ask. 'This is a serious proposal, and nothing should be agreed in haste. Sleep on it. Talk to some other parties. Get a second opinion. Shall I call an escort?'

'The captain can find his own way back to the shuttle,' she said.

Quaiche spread his fingers in farewell. 'Very well, then. Please convey my best wishes to your crew ... and consider my offer *very* seriously.'

The captain swung around, his assistants continuing to adjust the control valves and levers in his ludicrous kettle of a suit. With a mad rhythmic clanking he began to locomote towards the door. His departure was as painfully slow as his arrival had been, the suit appearing incapable of moving more than an inch at a time.

The captain paused, then laboriously turned around. The wiper blades flicked back and forth. The pipe organ chimed out another sequence of notes.

'Begging your pardon,' the interpreter said, 'but the captain has another question. Upon his approach to the Lady Morwenna, he made an unscheduled excursion from the usual flight path due to a technical problem with the shuttle.'

'A technical problem? Now there's a surprise.'

'In the process of this deviation he witnessed significant excavation work taking place a little to the north of the Permanent Way, near the Jarnsaxa Flats. He saw what appeared to be a partially camouflaged dig. Investigating with the shuttle's radar, he detected a sloping cavity several kilometres in length and at least a kilometre deep. He assumed that the dig was related to the unearthing of scuttler relics.'

'That may be the case,' Quaiche said, affecting an uninterested tone.

'The captain was puzzled. He admits to being no expert on Hela affairs, but he was given to understand that most significant scuttler relics have been unearthed in the circumpolar regions.'

'Scuttler relics are found all over Hela,' Quaiche said. 'It's just that due to quirks of geography they're easier to get at in the polar regions. I don't know what this dig was that you saw, or why it was camouflaged. Most of the digging work takes place outside the direct administration of the churches, alas. We can't keep tabs on everyone.'

'The captain thanks you for your most helpful response.'

Quaiche frowned, and then corrected his frown to a tolerant smile. What was that: sarcasm, or had she just not hit quite the right note? She was a baseline human, like himself, the kind of person he had once been able to read like a diagram. Now she and her kind – not just women, but almost everyone – lay far beyond the boundaries of his instinctive understanding. He watched them leave, smelling something hot and metallic trailing in the captain's wake, waiting impatiently while the room cleared of the noxious steam.

Soon, the tapping of a cane announced Grelier's arrival. He had not been far away, listening in on the proceedings via concealed cameras and microphones.

'Seems promising enough,' the surgeon-general ventured. 'They didn't dismiss you out of hand, and they do have a ship. My guess is they can't wait to make the deal.'

'That's what I thought as well,' Quaiche said. He rubbed a smear of condensation from one of his mirrors, restoring Haldora to its usual pinpoint sharpness. 'In fact, once you stripped away Heckel's not very convincing bluster I got the impression they needed our arrangement very badly.' He held up a sheet of paper, one that he had held tightly to his chest throughout the negotiations. 'Technical summary on their ship, from our spies in the parking swarm. Doesn't make encouraging reading. The bloody thing's falling to bits. Barely made it to 107 P.'

'Let me see.' Grelier glanced at the paper, skimming it. 'You can't be certain this is accurate.'

'I can't?'

'No. Ultras routinely downplay the worthiness of their ships, often putting out misinformation to that effect. They do it to lull competitors into a false sense of superiority, and to dissuade pirates interested in stealing their ships.'

'But they always overstate their defensive capabilities,' Quaiche said, wagging a finger at the surgeon-general. 'Right now there isn't a ship in that swarm that doesn't have weapons of some kind, even if they're disguised as innocent collision avoidance systems. They're scared, Grelier, all of them, and they all want their rivals to know they have the means to defend themselves.' He snatched back the paper. 'But this? It's a joke. They need our patronage so they can fix their ship first. It should be the other way around, if their protection is to have any meaning to us.'

'As I said, where the intentions of Ultras are concerned nothing should be taken at face value.'

Quaiche crumpled the paper and threw it across the room. 'The problem is I can't *read* their bloody intentions.'

'No one could be expected to read a monstrosity like Heckel,' Grelier said.

'I don't mean just him. I'm talking about the other Ultras, or the normal humans that come down with them, like that woman just now. I couldn't tell if she was being sincere or patronising, let alone whether she really believed what Heckel was having her say.'

Grelier kissed the head of his cane. 'You want my opinion? Your assessment of the situation was accurate: she was just Heckel's mouthpiece. He wanted to do business very badly.'

'Too bloody badly,' Quaiche said.

Grelier tapped the cane against the floor. 'Forget the *Third Gazometric* for the time being. What about the *Lark Descending*? The third-party summaries suggested a very useful weapons allocation, and the captain seemed willing to do business.'

'The summaries also mentioned an instability in her starboard drive. Did you miss that bit?'

Grelier shrugged. 'It's not as though we need them to take us anywhere, just to sit in orbit around Hela intimidating the rest of them. As long as the weapons are sufficient for that task, what do we care if the ship won't be capable of leaving once the arrangement is over?'

Quaiche waved a hand vaguely. 'To be honest, I didn't really like the fellow they sent down. Kept leaking all over the floor. Took weeks to get rid of the stain after he'd left. And a drive instability isn't the mild inconvenience you seem to assume. The ship we come to an agreement with will be sitting within tenths of a light-second of our surface, Grelier. We can't risk it blowing up in our faces.'

'Back to square one, in that case,' Grelier said, with little detectable sympathy. 'There are other Ultras to interview, aren't there?'

'Enough to keep me busy, but I'll always come back to the same fundamental problem: I simply cannot *read* these people, Grelier. My mind is so open to Haldora that there isn't room for any other form of observation. I cannot see through their strategies and evasions the way I once could.'

'We've had this conversation before. You know you can always seek my opinion.'

'And I do. But – no insult intended, Grelier – you know a great deal more about blood and cloning than you do about human nature.'

'Then ask others. Assemble an advisory council.'

'No.' Grelier, he realised, was quite right – they had been over this many times. And always it came round to the same points. 'These negotiations for protection are, by their very nature, extremely sensitive. I can't risk a security leak to another cathedral.' He motioned for Grelier to clean his eyes. 'Look at me,' he went on, while the surgeon-general opened the medicine cabinet and prepared the antiseptic swabs. 'I'm a thing of horror, in many respects, bound to this chair, barely able to survive without it. And even if I had the health to leave it, I would remain a prisoner of the Lady Morwenna, still enmeshed in the optical sightlines of my beloved mirrors.'

'Voluntarily,' Grelier said.

'You know what I mean. I cannot move amongst the Ultras as they move amongst us. Cannot step aboard their ships the way other ecumenical emissaries do.'

'That's why we have spies.'

'All the same, it limits me. I need someone I can trust, Grelier, someone like my younger self. Someone able to move amongst them as I used to. Someone they wouldn't dare to suspect.'

'Suspect?' Grelier dabbed at Quaiche's eyes with the swabs.

'I mean someone they would automatically trust. Someone not at all like you.'

'Hold still.' Quaiche flinched as the stinging swab dug around his eyeball. It amazed him that he had any nerve endings there at all, but Grelier had an unerring ability to find those that remained. 'Actually,' Grelier said, musingly, 'something did occur to me recently. Perhaps it's worth mentioning.'

'Go ahead.'

'You're aware I like to know what's happening on Hela. Not just the usual business with the cathedrals and the Way, but in the wider world, including the villages.'

'Oh, yes. You're always on the hunt for uncatalogued strains, reports of interesting new heresies from the Hauk settlements, that sort of thing. Then out you ride with your shiny new syringes, like a good little vampire.'

'I won't deny that Bloodwork plays a small role in my interest, but along the way I do pick up all sorts of interesting titbits. *Keep still.*'

'And you keep out of my sightlines! What sort of titbits?'

'The last but one time I was awake was a two-year interval, between ten and eight years ago. I remember that revival very well: it was the first occasion on which I found myself needing this cane. Towards the end of that period awake I made a long trip north, following leads on those uncatalogued strains you just mentioned. On the return journey I rode with one of the caravans, keeping my eyes peeled – sorry – for anything else that might take my fancy.'

'I remember that trip,' Quaiche said, 'but I don't recall you saying that anything of significance happened during it.'

'Nothing did. Or at least nothing *seemed* to, at the time. But then I heard a news bulletin a few days ago and it reminded me of something.'

'Are you going to drag this out much longer?'

Grelier sighed and began returning the equipment to its cabinet. 'There was a family,' he said, 'from the Vigrid badlands. They'd travelled down to meet the caravan. They had two children: a son and a younger daughter.'

'Fascinating, I'm sure.'

'The son was looking for work on the Way. I sat in on the recruitment interview, as I was permitted to do. Idle curiosity, really: I had no interest in this particular case, but you never know when someone interesting is going to show up.' Grelier snapped shut the cabinet. 'The son had aspirations to work in some technical branch of Way maintenance – strategic planning, something like that. At the time, however, the Way had all the pencil-pushers it needed. The only vacancies available were – shall we say – at the sharp end?'

'Beggars can't be choosers,' Quaiche said.

'Quite. But in this case the recruiting agent decided against a full and frank disclosure of the relevant facts. He told the son that there would be no difficulty in finding him a safe, well-paid job in the technical bureau. And because the work would be strictly analytical, requiring a clear-headed coolness of mind, there would be no question whatsoever of viral initiation.'

'If he'd told the truth, he'd have lost the recruit.'

'Almost certainly. He was a clever lad, no doubt about that. A waste, really, to throw him straight into fuse laying or something with an equally short life-expectancy. And because the family was secular – they mostly are, up in the badlands – he definitely didn't want your blood in his veins.'

'It isn't my blood. It's a virus.'

Grelier raised a finger, silencing his master. 'The point is that the recruiting agent had good reason to lie. And it was only a *white* lie, really. Everyone knew those bureau jobs were thin on the ground. Frankly, I think even the son knew it, but his family needed the money.'

'There's a point to this, Grelier, I'm sure of it.'

'I can barely remember what the son looked like. But the daughter? I can see her now, clear as daylight, looking through all of us as if we were made of glass. She had the most astonishing eyes, a kind of golden brown with little flecks of light in them.'

'How old would she have been, Grelier?'

'Eight, nine, I suppose.'

'You revolt me.'

'It wasn't like that,' Grelier said. 'Everyone there felt it, I think, especially the recruiting agent. She kept telling her parents he was lying. She was certain. She was visibly *affronted* by him. It was as if everyone in that room was playing a game and she hadn't been told about it.'

'Children behave oddly in adult environments. It was a mistake to have her there.'

'She wasn't behaving oddly at all,' Grelier said. 'In my view, she was behaving very rationally. It was the adults who weren't. They all knew that the recruiting agent was lying, but she was the only one who wasn't in denial about it.'

'I expect she overheard some remark before the interview, something about how the recruiting agents always lie.'

'She may have done, but even at the time I thought it went a little deeper than that. I think she just knew that the recruiter was lying simply by looking at him. There are people, individuals, who have that ability. They're born with it. Not more than one in a thousand, and probably even fewer who have it to the extent of that little girl.'

'Mind-reading?'

'No. Just an acute awareness of the subliminal information already available. Facial expression, primarily. The muscles in your face can form forty-three distinct movements, which enable tens of thousands in combination.'

Grelier had done his homework, Quaiche thought. This little digression had obviously been planned all along.

'Many of these expressions are involuntary,' he continued. 'Unless you've been very well trained, you simply can't lie without revealing yourself through your expressions. Most of the time, of course, it doesn't matter. The people around you are none the wiser, just as blind to those microexpressions. But imagine if you had that awareness. Not just the means to read the people around you when they don't even know they're being read, but the self-control to block your own involuntary signals.'

'Mm.' Quaiche could see where this was heading. 'It wouldn't be much use against something like Heckel, but a baseline negotiator ... or something with a *face* ... that's a different matter. You think you could teach me this?'

'I can do better than that,' Grelier said. 'I can bring you the girl. She can teach you herself.'

For a moment, Quaiche regarded the hanging image of Haldora, mesmerised by a writhing filament of lightning in the southern polar region.

'You'd have to bring her here first,' he said. 'Not easy, if you can't lie to her at any point.'

'Not as difficult as you think. She's like antimatter: it would only be a question of handling her with the right tools. I told you something jogged my memory a few days ago. It was the girl's name. Rashmika Els. She was mentioned in a general news bulletin originating from the Vigrid badlands. There was a photo. She's eight or nine years older than when I last saw her, obviously, but it was her all right. I wouldn't forget those eyes in a hurry. She'd gone missing. The constabulary were in a fuss about her.'

'No use to us, then.'

Grelier smiled. 'Except I found her. She's on a caravan, heading towards the Way.'

'You've met her?'

'Not exactly. I visited the caravan, but didn't reveal myself to Miss Els. Wouldn't want to scare her off, not when she can be so useful to us. She's very determined to find out what happened to her brother, but even she will be wary of getting too close to the Way.'

'Mm.' For a moment the beautiful conjunction of these events caused Quaiche to smile. 'And what exactly *did* happen to her brother?'

'Died in clearance work,' Grelier said. 'Crushed under the Lady Morwenna.'

TWENTY-ONE

Ararat, 2675

Skade lay half-cocooned in ice and the frozen black froth of Inhibitor machinery. She was still alive. This much was clear as they squeezed through the narrow, crimped opening of the crushed bulkhead. From the control couch in which she still lay, Skade's head tilted slightly in their direction, the merest glaze of interest troubling the smooth composure of her face. The fingers of one white-gauntleted hand hovered above a portable holoclavier propped in her lap, the fingers becoming a blur of white in time with the gunlike salvos of music.

The music stopped as her hand moved away from the keyboard. 'I was beginning to wonder what had kept you.'

'I've come for my child, bitch,' Khouri said.

Skade showed no sign of having heard her. 'What happened, Clavain?'

'A little mishap.'

'The wolves took your hand. How unfortunate.'

Clavain showed her the knife. 'I did what had to be done. Recognise this, Skade? Today wasn't the first time it's saved my life. I used it to cut the membrane around the comet, when you and I had that little disagreement over the future policy of the Mother Nest. You *do* remember, don't you?'

'There's been a lot of water under the bridge since I last saw that knife. I still had my old body then.'

'I'm sorry about what happened, but I only did what I had to do. Put me back there now, I'd do the same thing again.'

'I don't doubt it for a moment, Clavain. No matter what people say, you always were a man of conviction.'

'We've come for the child,' he said.

She acknowledged Khouri with the tiniest of nods. 'I had gathered.'

'Are you going to hand her over, or is this going to become tedious and messy?'

'Which way would you prefer it, Clavain?'

'Listen to me, Skade. It's over. Whatever happened between you and me, whatever harm we did each other, whatever loyalties we believed in, none of that matters any more.'

'That's exactly what I told Remontoire.'

'But you did negotiate,' Clavain said. 'We know that much. So let's take it to the limit. Let's join forces again. Give Aura back to us and we'll share everything she tells us. It'll be better for all of us in the long run.'

'What do I care about the long run, Clavain? I'm never going to see the outside of this ship again.'

'If you're hurt, we can help you.'

'I really don't think so.'

'Give me Aura,' Khouri demanded.

Scorpio stepped closer, taking a better look at the injured Conjoiner. She wore armour of a very pale shade, perhaps even white. Chameleoflage armour, probably: the outer integument had tuned itself to match the colour of the ice that had condensed or ruptured through into the cabin before the lighting failed. The suit was styled in the manner of medieval armour, with bulbous sliding plates covering the limb joints and an exaggerated breastplate. There was a cinched, feminine waist above a skirtlike flaring. The rest of the body – below the waist – Scorpio could not see at all. It vanished into ice that pinned Skade neatly in place like a doll for sale.

All around her, in little aggregations of blackness, were warty clumps of Inhibitor machinery. But none were touching Skade, and none appeared active at the moment.

'You can have Aura,' she said. 'At, of course, a price.'

'We're not paying for her,' Clavain said. His voice was faint and hoarse, stripped of strength.

'You're the one who mentioned negotiation,' Skade said. 'Or were you thinking more along the lines of a threat?'

'Where is she?'

Skade moved one of her arms. The armour creaked as it budged, dislodging curtains of frost. She tapped the hard plate covering her abdomen. 'She's here, in me. I'm keeping her alive.'

Clavain glanced back at Khouri, his eyes conveying the admission that, finally, everything she had told them had turned out to be true. 'Good,' he said, turning his attention back to Skade. 'I'm grateful. But now her mother needs her back.'

'As if you care about her mother,' Skade said, mocking him with an adversarial smile. 'As if you truly care about the fate of a child.'

'I came all this way for that child.'

'You came all this way for an asset,' Skade corrected.

'And I suppose the child means vastly more to you than that.'

'Enough,' Scorpio interrupted. 'We haven't got time for this. We came for Khouri's child. Fuck the reasons. Just hand her over.'

'Hand her over?' Now Skade laughed at the pig. 'Did you honestly think it was going to be that easy? The child is *in* me. It's in my womb, wired into my circulatory system.'

'*She*,' Khouri insisted. 'Aura isn't an "it", you heartless piece of shit.'

'She isn't human either,' Skade said, 'no matter what you might think.' Her head tracked back towards Clavain. 'Yes, I had Delmar culture me another body, just as he'd always intended. I'm all flesh from the neck down. Even the womb is more organ than machine. Face it, *Nevil*: I'm more alive than you are, now that you've lost that hand.'

'You were always a machine, Skade. You just didn't realise it.'

'If you're saying I only ever did my duty, then I accept that. Machines do have a certain dignity: they're not capable of betrayal or disloyalty. They're not capable of treason.'

'I didn't come here for a lesson in ethics.'

'Aren't you curious about what happened to my ship? Don't you like my fabulous palace of ice?' She gestured around her, as if inviting commentary on her choice of décor. 'I made it especially for you.'

'Actually, I think something went wrong with your cryo-arithmetic engines,' Clavain said.

Skade pouted. 'Go ahead, dismiss my efforts.'

'What happened?' Scorpio asked quietly.

She sighed. 'Don't expect to understand. The finest minds in the Mother Nest barely grasped the underlying principles. You don't even have the intelligence of a baseline human. You're just a pig.'

'I'd really appreciate it if you didn't call me that.'

'Or you'll do what? You can't hurt me; not while I'm carrying Aura. I die, she dies. It's that simple.'

'Nice hostage setup,' Clavain said.

'I'm not saying it was easy. Our respective immune systems needed a great deal of tinkering before we stopped rejecting each other.' Skade's eyes flashed to Khouri. 'Don't even think about taking her back into your womb now. I'm afraid the two of you just aren't remotely compatible.'

Khouri started to say something, but Clavain quickly raised his good hand, talking over her. 'Then you are willing to negotiate,' he said, 'or else you wouldn't have needed to warn her about compatibility.'

Skade's attention remained on Khouri. 'You can walk out of here with Aura. There should still be functional surgical tools aboard this ship. I can talk you through the Caesarean. Otherwise, I'm sure you can improvise. After all, it's not *brain* surgery.' She looked at Clavain. 'You did bring a life-support unit, didn't you?'

'Of course.'

'Then we're all set. I still have neural connections with Aura's mind. I can put her into a temporary coma until the surgery is over.'

'I've found a surgical box,' Jaccottet said, shoving a heavy black case across the ruined floor. A bas-relief caduceus stood out from its surface, rimed with frost. 'Even if this doesn't work, we've probably got all the tools we need in our own emergency kits.'

'Open it,' Clavain said. There was something hollow about his voice, as if he grasped something that everyone else was missing.

The box sprung open, seals hissing, divesting itself of many cunningly packed trays. Surgical instruments made of matt-white metal sat in neat foam inlays. The instruments – all looped fingerholes and precisely hinged mechanisms – made Scorpio think of some weird alien cutlery. They were all made of dumb matter, designed to be used in field surgery situations where rogue nanomachinery might corrupt smarter, more subtle instruments.

'Need some help?' Skade asked.

Jaccottet's gloved fingers lifted one of the instruments from its nest. His hand trembled. 'I'm not really a surgeon,' he said. 'I've had Security Arm medical training, but that didn't stretch to field operations.'

'No matter,' Skade said. 'As I said, I can talk you through it. It has to be you, you see. The pig lacks the necessary dexterity, and Khouri has far too much of an emotional investment. And Clavain ... well, that's obvious, isn't it?'

'It isn't just because of my hand,' Clavain said.

'No, not just that,' Skade agreed.

'Tell them,' Clavain said.

'Clavain can't do the procedure,' Skade said, addressing the other three as if Clavain were not present at all, 'because he won't be alive: not by the end of it, anyway. This is the arrangement: you walk out of here with Aura, and Clavain dies, here and now. No negotiation, no argument over the terms. It either happens this way or it doesn't happen at all. It's entirely up to you.'

'You can't do this,' Scorpio said.

'Perhaps you didn't hear me. Clavain dies. Aura lives. You walk out of here with what you came for. How can that not be a satisfactory result?'

'Not this way,' Khouri said. 'Please, not this way.'

'I'm afraid I've already given the matter a great deal of consideration. I am dying, you see. This palace will also be my mausoleum. The options – for me, at least – are remarkably restricted. If I die, I take Aura with me. Humanity – whatever *that* means – will lose whatever gifts she carries. But if I give her to you, those gifts may be put to some practical use. In the long run it may not be the difference between extinction and survival, but it may be the difference between extinction now, this century, and extinction a few thousand years down the line. Not much of a stay of execution, really . . . but human nature being what it is, I'm sure we'll take what we're given.'

'She might make more of a difference than that,' Clavain said.

'Well, that's not something you or I will ever know, but I take your point. Aura's value is – as yet – indeterminate. That's why she remains such a prized asset.'

'So give her up,' Khouri said. 'Give her up and do something good for once in your fucking existence.'

'Brought her along to help oil the negotiations, did you?' Skade asked, winking at Clavain. For an agonising moment they might have been old friends sharing a humorous recollection.

'It's all right,' Clavain said to Khouri. 'We'll get Aura back for you.'

'No, Clavain, not this way,' she said.

'This is the only way it's going to happen,' he said. 'Trust me, I know Skade. Once she's made her mind up, it stays made up.'

'I'm glad you understand that,' Skade said. 'And you're right. There is no flexibility in my position.'

'We could kill her,' Khouri said. 'Kill her and operate quickly.'

'Worth a try,' Scorpio said. Often in Chasm City – for the purposes of deterrence – he had been called upon to kill people with maximum slowness. He thought now of all the swift ways he knew to end the life of a sentient being. Those methods had their uses, too: mercy executions, button jobs. Some of them were very swift indeed. The only drawback was that he had never knowingly tried any of his methods on a Conjoiner. He had certainly never killed a Conjoiner carrying a hostage in their womb.

'She won't let it happen,' Clavain said soothingly. He touched Khouri's arm. 'She'd find a way to kill Aura before we got to her. But it's all right, this is the way it has to be.'

'No, Clavain,' Khouri repeated.

He shushed her. 'I came here to secure Aura's release. That's still my mission objective.'

'I don't want you to die.'

Scorpio saw a smile crinkle the skin at the corners of Clavain's eyes. 'No, I doubt that you do. Frankly, I don't want to, either. Funny how these things seem a lot less attractive when it's someone else doing the deciding for you. But Skade's made up her mind, and this is how it's going to happen.'

'I suggest we get a move on,' Skade interrupted.

'Wait,' Scorpio said. The words had an unreality in his head as he marshalled what he was about to say. 'If we give you Clavain . . . and you kill him . . . what's to stop you reneging on your part of the deal?'

'She's thought of that,' Clavain said.

'Of course I have,' Skade answered. 'And I've also considered the opposite scenario: what's to prevent you from taking Clavain away if I give you Aura first? Clearly our mutual trust is an insufficient guarantee of compliance. So I've devised a solution I believe both parties will find entirely satisfactory.'

'Tell them,' Clavain said.

Skade gestured at Jaccottet. 'You – security man – will perform the Caesarean.' Then her attention flicked to Scorpio. 'You – pig – will perform the execution of Clavain. I will direct both procedures, incision by incision. They will take place in parallel, step by step. One must last precisely as long as the other.'

'No,' Scorpio gasped, as the horror of her words slammed home.

'The message isn't getting through, is it?' Skade asked. 'Shall I kill her now, and be done with it?'

'No,' Clavain said. He turned to his friend. 'Scorp, you have to do this. I know you have the strength to do it. You've already shown me that a thousand times. Do it, friend, and end this.'

'I can't.'

'It's the hardest thing anyone's ever asked you to do, I know that. But I'm still asking.'

Scorpio could only say the same thing again. 'I can't.'

'You must.'

'No,' said another voice. 'He doesn't have to. I'll do it.'

All of them, including Skade, followed the voice to its source. There, framed in the ruined bulkhead, was Vasko Malinin. He had a gun in his hand and looked as cold and bewildered as the rest of them.

'I'll do it,' he repeated. He had obviously been standing there for some time, unnoticed by those present.

'You were given orders to stay outside,' Scorpio said.

'Blood countermanded them.'

'Blood?' Scorpio repeated.

'Urton and I heard gunfire. It sounded as if it was coming from inside here. I contacted Blood and he gave me permission to investigate.'

'Leaving Urton alone outside?'

'Not for long, sir. Blood's sending a plane. It'll be here in under an hour.'

'That isn't the way it's supposed to happen,' Scorpio said.

'Pardon, sir, but Blood's view was that once shooting started, it was time to tear up the rules.'

'You can't argue with that,' Clavain said.

Scorpio nodded, still burdened by the vast weight of what lay before him. He could not let Vasko do it, no matter how devoutly he wished to abdicate this particular responsibility. 'Anything else to report?' he asked.

'The sea's funny, sir. It's greener, and there are mounds of biomass appearing all around the iceberg, as far as the eye can see.'

'Juggler activity,' Clavain said. 'Blood already told us it was hotting up.'

'That's not all, sir. More reports of things in the sky. Eyewitnesses even say they've seen things re-entering.'

'The battle's coming closer,' Clavain said, with something close to anticipation. 'Well, Skade, I don't think any of us really want to delay things now, do we?'

'Wiser words were never spoken,' she said.

'You tell us how you want it done. I presume we'll need to get that armour off you first?'

'I'll deal with that,' she said. 'In the meantime, make sure you have the incubator ready.'

Scorpio made a shooting gesture in Vasko's direction. 'Return to the boat. Inform Blood that we are in the process of delicate negotiations, then bring the incubator back through the iceberg.'

'I'll do that, sir. But seriously, I know how hard it is for you to ...' Vasko could not complete his sentence. 'What I mean is, I'm willing to do it.'

'I know,' Scorpio said, 'but I'm his friend. The one thing I know is that I wouldn't want anyone else to have this on their conscience.'

'There'll be nothing on your conscience, Scorp,' Clavain said.

No, Scorpio thought. There'd be nothing on his conscience. Nothing save the fact that he had tortured his best friend – his only genuine human friend – to death, slowly, in return for the life of a child he neither knew nor cared for. So what if he had no choice in the matter? So what if it was only what Clavain wanted him to do? None of that made it any easier to do, or would make it any easier to live with in times to come. Because he knew that what happened in the next half hour – he did not think the procedure could last much longer than that – would surely be burned into his memory as indelibly as the self-inflicted scar on his shoulder, the one that covered his original emerald-green tattoo of human ownership.

Perhaps it would be faster than that. And perhaps Clavain would really suffer very little. After all, he had managed to block most of the pain when he lost the hand. Presumably it was within his power to establish a more comprehensive set of neural barricades, nulling the agony Skade sought to inflict.

But she would know that, wouldn't she?

'Go. Now,' he said to Vasko. 'And don't return immediately.'

'I'll be back, sir.' Vasko hesitated at the bulkhead, studying the little tableau as if committing it to memory. Scorpio read his mind. Vasko knew that when he returned, Clavain would not be amongst the living.

'Son,' Clavain said, 'do as the man says. I'll be all right. I appreciate your concern.'

'I wish I could do something, sir.'

'You can't. Not here, not now. That's another of those difficult lessons. Sometimes you can't do the right thing. You just have to walk away and fight another day. Tough medicine, son, but sooner or later we all have to swallow it.'

'I understand, sir.'

'I haven't known you that long, but it's been long enough for me to form a reasonable impression of your abilities. You're a good man, Vasko. The colony needs you and it needs others like you. Respect that need and don't let the colony down.'

'Sir,' Vasko said.

'When this is done, we'll have Aura again. First and foremost, she's her mother's daughter. Don't ever let anyone forget that.'

'I won't, sir.'

'But she's also ours. She'll be fragile, Vasko. She'll need protecting as she grows up. That's the task I'm giving you and your generation. Take care of that girl, because she may be the last thing that matters.'

'I'll take care of her, sir.' Vasko looked at Khouri, as if seeking permission. 'We'll all take care of her. That's a promise.'

'You sound as if you mean it. I can trust you, can't I?'

'I'll do my best, sir.'

Clavain nodded, weary, resigned, facing an abyss the depth of which only he could comprehend. 'That's all I've ever done, too. Mostly, it's been good enough. Now go, please, and give my regards to Blood.'

Vasko hesitated again, as if there was something more he wished to say. But whatever words he intended remained unsaid. He turned and was gone.

'Why did you want to get rid of him?' Scorpio asked, after a few seconds had passed.

'Because I don't want him to see one moment of this.'

'I'll make it as quick as she'll let me,' Scorpio said. 'If Jaccottet works fast, I can work fast as well. Isn't that right, Skade?'

'You'll work as fast as I dictate, and no faster.'

'Don't make this any harder than it has to be,' Scorpio said.

'It won't hurt him, will it?' Khouri asked. 'He can turn off the pain, can't he?'

'I was coming to that,' Skade said, with an obvious reptilian delight in her own cunning. 'Clavain – explain to your friends what you will allow to happen, please.'

'I have no choice, do I?'

'Not if you want this to go ahead.'

Clavain scratched at his brow. It was pale with frost, his eyebrows pure ermine white. 'Since I entered this room, Skade has been trying to override my neural barricades. She's been launching attack algorithms against my standard security layers and firewalls, trying to hijack deeper control structures. Take my word for it, she's very good. The only thing stopping her is the antiquated nature of my implants. For her, it's like trying to hack into a clockwork calculator. Her methods are too advanced for the battleground.'

'So?' Khouri said, squinting as if she were missing something obvious.

'If she could penetrate those layers,' Clavain said, 'she could override any pain-blocks I cared to install. She could open them all one by one, like water-release valves in a dam, letting the pain flow through.'

'But she can't get at them, can she?' Scorpio asked.

'Not unless I let her. Not unless I invite her in and give her complete control.'

'But you'd never do that.'

'I wouldn't,' he said, 'unless, of course, she demanded it of me.'

'Skade, please,' Khouri said.

'Lower those blockades,' Skade said, ignoring the woman. 'Lower them and let me in. If you don't, the deal's off. Aura dies now.'

Clavain closed his eyes for a moment fractionally longer than a blink. It was only an instant, but for Clavain it must have involved the issuing of many intricate, rarely used neural management commands, rescinding standard security states that had probably remained frozen for decades.

He opened his eyes. 'It's done,' he said. 'You have control.'

'Let's make sure, shall we?'

Clavain made a noise somewhere between a moan and a yelp. He clutched at the bandaged stump of his left hand, his jaw stiffening. Scorpio saw the tendons in his neck stand out like guylines.

'I think you have it,' Clavain said, teeth clenched.

'I'm locked in now,' Skade told her audience. 'He can't throw me out or block my commands.'

'Get this over with,' Clavain said. Again, there was an easing in his expression, like the change of light on a landscape. Scorpio understood. If Skade was going to torture him, she would not want to ruin her carefully orchestrated efforts with an extraneous pain source. Especially one that had never been part of her plan.

Skade reached down to her belly with both gauntleted hands. No seam had been visible in her armour before, but now the curved white plate that covered her abdomen detached itself from the rest of the suit. Skade placed it next to her, then returned her hands to her sides. Where the armour had been opened, a bulge of soft human flesh moved under the thin, crosshatched mesh of a vacuum suit inner layer.

'We're ready,' she said.

Jaccottet moved towards her and knelt down, one knee resting on the mound of fused ice that covered Skade's lower half. The black box of white surgical instruments sat splayed open at his side.

'Pig,' she said, 'take a scalpel from the lower compartment. That will do for now.'

Scorpio's trotter poked at the snugly embedded instrument. Khouri reached over and pulled it out for him. She placed it delicately in his grasp.

'For the last time,' Scorpio said, 'don't make me do this.'

Clavain sat down next to him, crossing his legs. 'It's all right, Scorp. Just do what she says. I've a few tricks up my sleeve she doesn't know about. She won't be able to block all my commands, even if she thinks she can.'

'Tell him that if you think it makes it easier for him,' Skade said.

'He's never lied to me,' Scorpio said. 'I don't think he'd start now.'

The white instrument sat in his hand, absurdly light, an innocent little surgical tool. There was no evil in the thing itself, but at that moment it felt like the focus of all the inchoate badness in the universe, its pristine whiteness part of the same sense of malignity. Titanic possibilities were balanced in his palm. He could not hold the instrument the way its designers had intended. All the same, he could still manipulate it well enough to do harm. He supposed it did not really matter to Clavain how skilfully the work was done. A certain imprecision might even help him, dulling the white-hot edge of the pain Skade intended.

'How do you want me to sit?' Clavain asked.

'Lie down,' Skade said. 'On your back. Hands at your sides.'

Clavain positioned himself. 'Anything else?'

'That's up to you. If you have anything you want to say, now would be a good time. In a little while, you might find it difficult.'

'Only one thing,' Clavain said.

Scorpio moved closer. The dreadful task was almost upon him. 'What is it, Nevil?'

'When this is over, don't waste any time. Get Aura to safety. That's really all I care about.' He paused, licked his lips. Around them the fine growth of his beard glistened with a haze of beautiful white crystals. 'But if there's time, and if it doesn't inconvenience you, I'd ask you to bury me at sea.'

'Where?' Scorpio asked.

'Here,' Clavain said. 'As soon as you can. No ceremony. The sea will do the rest.'

There was no sign that Skade had heard him, or cared what he had to say. 'Let's start,' she said to Jaccottet. 'Do exactly as I tell you. Oh, and Khouri?'

'Yes?' the woman asked.

'You really don't have to watch this.'

'She's my daughter,' she said. 'I'm staying right here until I get her back.' Then she turned to Clavain, and Scorpio sensed a vast private freight of communication pass between them. Perhaps it was more than just his imagination. After all, they were both Conjoiners now.

'It's all right,' Clavain said aloud.

Khouri knelt down and kissed him on the forehead. 'I just wanted to say thank you.'

Behind her, Skade's hand moved over the holoclavier again.

Outside the iceberg, on the spreading fringe of whiteness, Urton looked at Vasko the way a teacher would look at a truant child. 'You took your time,' she said.

Vasko fell to his knees. He vomited. It came from nowhere, with no warning. It left him feeling excavated, husked out.

Urton knelt down on the ice next to him. 'What is it? What's happening?' Her voice was urgent.

But he couldn't speak. He wiped a smear of vomit from his chin. His eyes stung. He felt simultaneously ashamed and liberated by his reaction, as if in that awful admission of emotional weakness he had also found an unsuspected strength. In that moment of hollowing, that moment in which he felt the core of himself evacuated, he knew that he had taken a step into the adult world that Urton and Jaccottet thought was theirs alone.

Above, the sky was a purple-grey bruise. The sea roiled, grey phantasms slipping between the waves.

'Talk to me, Vasko,' she said.

He pushed himself to his feet. His throat was raw, his mind as clear and clean as an evacuated airlock.

'Help me with the incubator,' he said.

TWENTY-TWO

p Eridani 40, 2675

Battle raged in the immediate volume of space around the Pattern Juggler planet. Near the heart of the engagement itself, and close to the geometric centre of his vast ship *Zodiacal Light*, Remontoire sat in a posture of perfect zenlike calm. His expression betrayed only mild interest in the outcome of current events. His eyes were closed; his hands were folded demurely in his lap. He looked bored and faintly distracted, like a man about to doze off in a waiting room.

Remontoire was not bored, nor was he about to doze off. Boredom was a condition of consciousness he barely remembered, like anger or hate or the thirst for mother's milk. He had experienced many states of mind since leaving Mars nearly five hundred years earlier, including some that could only be approximated in the flat, limiting modalities of baseline human language. Being bored was not amongst them. Nor did he expect it to play a significant role in his mental affairs in the future, most certainly not while the wolves were still around. And he wasn't very likely to experience sleep, either.

Now and then some part of him – his eyelids, or even his entire head – twitched minutely, betraying something of the extreme state of non-boredom he was actually experiencing. Tactical data surged incessantly through his mind with the icy clarity of a mountain torrent. He was actually running his mind at a dangerously high clock-rate, just barely within the cooling parameters of his decidedly old-fashioned Conjoiner mental architecture. Skade would have laughed at him now as he struggled to match a thought-processing rate that would – to her – have barely merited comment. Skade could think this fast and simultaneously fragment her consciousness into half a dozen parallel streams. And she could do it while moving around, exerting herself, whereas Remontoire had to sit in a state of trancelike stillness so as not to put additional loads on his already stressed body and mind. They really were creatures of different centuries.

But although Skade had been in his thoughts much of late, she was of no immediate concern now. He considered it likely she was dead. His suspicions had been strong enough even before he had permitted Khouri to descend into the planet's atmosphere, following after Skade's downed corvette, but he had been careful not to make too much of them. For if Skade was dead, then so was Aura.

Something changed: a tick and a whirr of the great dark orrery of war in which he floated. For hours the opposed forces – the baseline humans, Skade's Conjoiners, the Inhibitors – had wheeled around the planet in a fixed formation, as if they had finally settled into some mathematical configuration of maximum stability. The other Conjoiners were cowed: for weeks they had been gaining an edge over Remontoire's loose alliance of humans, pigs and Resurgam refugees. They had stolen Aura, and through her they had learned many of the secrets that had enabled Remontoire and his allies to outflank the Inhibitor forces around Delta Pavonis. Later, Remontoire had given them even more in return for Khouri. But since Skade's disappearance the other Conjoiners had become confused and directionless, far more than would have been the case with an equivalent grouping from Remontoire's generation. Skade had been too powerful, too effective at manipulation. During the war against the Demarchists (which seemed now, to Remontoire, like an innocently remembered childhood diversion) the ruthlessly democratic structure of Conjoiner politics had been gradually partitioned, with the creation of security layers: the Closed Council, the Inner Sanctum, even – perhaps – the rumoured Night Council. Skade was the logical end product of that process of compartmentalisation: highly skilled, highly resourceful, highly knowledgeable, highly adept at manipulating others. In the pressure of the war against the Demarchists, his people had – unwittingly – made a tyrant for themselves.

And Skade had been a very good tyrant. She had only wanted the best for her people, even if that meant extinction for the rest of humanity. Her single-mindedness, her willingness to transcend the limits of the flesh and the mind, had been inspirational even to Remontoire. He had very nearly chosen to fight on her side rather than Clavain's. It was no wonder those Conjoiners around her had forgotten how to think for themselves. In thrall to Skade, there had never been any need.

But now Skade was gone, and her army of swift, brilliant puppets didn't know what to do next.

In the last ten hours, Remontoire's forces had intercepted twenty-eight thousand separate invitations to negotiation from the remaining Conjoiner elements, squirted through the brief windows in the sphere of jammed communications afflicting the entire theatre of battle. After all the betrayals, after all the fragile alliances and spiteful enmities, they still thought he was a man they could do business with. There was, he thought, something else as well: hints that they were worried about something he had yet to identify. It might have been a gambit to snare his attention and encourage him to talk to them, but he wasn't sure.

He had decided to keep them waiting just a little bit longer, at least until he had some concrete data from the surface.

Now, however, something *had* changed. He had detected the alteration in the disposition of battle forces one-fifteenth of a second earlier; in the ensuing time nothing had happened to suggest that it was anything but real.

The Inhibitors were moving. A clump of wolf machines – they moved in clumps, aggregations, flickering clouds, rather than ordered squadrons or detachments – had left its former position. Between ninety-five and ninety-nine per cent of the wolf assets around p Eridani 40 – estimated by mass, or volume (it was difficult to be sure *how much* wolf machinery had actually followed them from Delta Pavonis) – held station, but according to the sensor returns, which could not always be trusted, the small aggregate – between one and five per cent of the total force – was on its way to the planet.

It accelerated smoothly, leaving physics squirming in its wake. When Inhibitor machinery moved, it did so without any hint of Newtonian reaction. The recent modifications to the Conjoiner drives had approximated something of the same effect by making the exhaust particles undergo rapid decay into a non-observable quantum state. But the wolves used a different principle. Even up close, there was no hint of any thrusting medium. The best guess – and guess it was – was that the Inhibitor drives employed a form of the quantum Casimir effect, using the unbalanced vacuum pressure on two parallel plates to skip themselves through space-time. The fact that the machines accelerated several trillion times faster than theory allowed was deemed slightly less embarrassing than having no theory at all.

He ran a simulation, predicting the flight path of the aggregate. It might fracture into smaller elements, or combine with another, but if it continued on its present course, it was destined to skim the planet's immediate airspace.

This troubled Remontoire. So far the alien machines had avoided coming that close. It was as if, scripted deep into their controlling routines, was an edict, a fundamental command to avoid unnecessary contact with Pattern Juggler worlds.

But humans had taken the battle to the waterlogged planet. How deep did that edict run? Perhaps the visible downing of Skade's corvette had tripped some switch, the damage already done. Perhaps Inhibitor machinery had already entered the biosphere. In which case even this Juggler planet might not be safe for very much longer.

The aggregate had been underway for nearly a second, from Remontoire's point of view. Assuming the usual acceleration curves, it would reach the planet's airspace in under forty minutes. In his present state of consciousness, that would seem like an eternity. But Remontoire knew better than to believe that.

Remontoire's trident-shaped ship departed from the parking bay in the side of the *Zodiacal Light*. Almost immediately he felt the spinal compression as the main drive came on, as hard and unforgiving as a fall on to concrete. The hull creaked and protested as the acceleration ramped up through five, six, seven gees. The single outrigger-mounted engine was a microminiature Conjoiner drive, engineered with watchmaker precision, every component squeezed down to neurotic tolerances. It would have made Remontoire nervous, had he permitted himself to feel nervousness.

He was the only living thing aboard the recently manufactured ship. Even he seemed something of an afterthought, crammed into a tiny eyelike hollow in the long carbon-black needle of the hull. There were no windows, and only the bare minimum of sensor apertures, but through his implants Remontoire barely perceived the little craft, sensing it only as a glassy extension of his personal space. Beyond the hard boundaries of the ship was a less tangible sphere of sensor coverage: passive and active contacts tickling the part of his brain associated with the proprioceptive knowledge of his own body image.

The thrust levelled out at eight gees. There was no inertial protection against that acceleration, even though bulk control of inertia had been within the reach of Conjoiner technology for more than half a century. It couldn't be allowed. The other technology that the ship carried – the glittering, tinsel-like machinery of the hypometric weapon – was highly intolerant of alterations to the local metric. The hypometric weapons were difficult enough to use in nearly flat, unmolested space-time. But within the influence of inertial technology they became malevolently unpredictable, like spiteful imps. Remontoire would have liked to have accelerated even harder, but above eight gees there was a real danger of shifting the weapon's tiny components out of alignment.

The weapon itself wasn't much to look at from the outside. Shrouded in a cigar-shaped nacelle flung out as an extension from the same outrigger that held the drive, there was no muzzle, no exhaust, no surface detailing of any kind. The only design constraint had been to arrange for the weapon to be as far from the human occupant as possible. It was, Remontoire thought, a measure of the device's threatening glamour that he actually felt *safer* with the dangerous, unstable miniature Conjoiner drive between him and the quixotic weapon.

He checked the progress of the Inhibitor aggregate, neither gratified nor disappointed to see that it was exactly where he had predicted it would be. Something had changed, though: his departure from the *Zodiacal Light* had drawn the attention of the other protagonists. One of Skade's former allies was moving on an intercept trajectory with his ship at a higher acceleration than he could sustain. The other Conjoiner craft would engage him within fifteen minutes. Five or six minutes after that, a second aggregate would have reached him.

Remontoire allowed himself a flicker of disquiet, just enough to pump some adrenalin into his blood. Then he blocked it, the way one slammed the door on a boisterous party.

He knew, rationally, that the logical thing would have been to remain on the *Zodiacal Light*, where his co-ordination and insight were most valued. He could have programmed a beta-level simulation of himself to fly this ship, or asked for a volunteer. There would have been dozens of willing candidates, some of whom had been equipped with Conjoiner implants of their own. But he had insisted on taking the ship himself. It wasn't just because he had spent more time than most of them learning the ways of the hypometric weapon. There was also a sense of obligation: it was something he had to do.

It was, he knew, because of Ana Khouri. He had made a mistake in letting her travel down to the planet on her own. From a military perspective it had been exactly the right thing to do: no point committing already overstretched resources when there was every likelihood that Aura was already dead. More than that, he thought, when there was every chance that Aura had already been as useful to them as she was ever going to be. Also, nothing much larger than an escape capsule had stood a chance of reaching the surface anyway, with the Inhibitor blockade in maximum effect.

But Clavain wouldn't have seen it that way. Nine times out of ten he had based his decisions upon the strict application of military sense. He wouldn't have lived through five hundred years otherwise. But one time out of ten he would disregard the rules entirely and do something that made no sense except on a humane level.

Remontoire thought it likely that this would have been one of those occasions. No matter that Skade and Aura were probably both dead: Clavain would have gone down with Khouri even if the rescue attempt itself was almost guaranteed to end in their deaths.

Time and again over the years Remontoire had examined the minutiae of Clavain's life, the critical points, trying to work out if those irrational acts had helped or hindered his old friend. He reviewed Clavain's decisions once more while he waited for the Conjoiner ship to meet him. As always he arrived at no satisfactory answer. But he had decided that this was a time when he needed to live by Clavain's rules rather than the rigid gamesmanship of tactical analysis.

A clock rang in his brain. His fifteen minutes were up.

There had been no point thinking about the approaching Conjoiner ship before it arrived: a quick review of the options had shown him that nothing would be gained by deviating from his present course.

The other ship pushed through his concentric sensor boundaries like a fish nosing through sharply defined sea currents. In his mind's eye it became a tangible thing rather than a vague hint in the sensor data.

It was a moray-class corvette like Skade's craft, just as light-suckingly black as Remontoire's ship, but shaped more like a weirdly barbed fish-hook than the trident form of his own machine. Even at close range, the spectral whisper of its highly stealthed drives was barely detectable. On average, its hull radiated at a chill 2.7 kelvin above absolute zero. Up close, in the microwave spectrum, it was a quilt of hot and cold spots. He mapped the emplacement of cryo-arithmetic engines; observed those that were functioning less efficiently than their neighbours; observed also those that were running worryingly cold, teetering on the edge of algorithmic-cycle runaway. The occasional blue flicker sparked as one of the nodes dropped below 1 kelvin, before being dragged back into lockstep with its cohorts.

Ships could be made arbitrarily cold, and could therefore be made to blend in with the background radiation of the early universe, which was still shining after fifteen billion years. But the background map was not smooth: cosmic inflation had magnified tiny flaws in the expanding universe to produce subtle variations in the background, depending on which way one looked. They were deviations from true anisotropy: wrinkles in the face of creation. Unless they could adjust their hull temperatures to match those fluctuations, ships could only achieve an imperfect match with the background spectrum. Under some circumstances, hunting for those tiny signs of mismatch was the only way to detect enemy ships at all.

But the Conjoiner ship was maintaining the coldness of its hull purely as camouflage against Inhibitor forces in the vicinity. It was making no real effort to hide itself from Remontoire. In fact, it was even trying to speak to him.

There was one thing about Conjoiners that even the non-augmented had to admire: they didn't give up. Twenty-eight thousand unanswered requests for negotiation wouldn't deter a twenty-eight thousand and first.

Remontoire allowed the narrow line of the message laser to scribe against his hull until it found one of the few sensor patches.

He examined the transmission through copious layers of mental fire-walling. Eventually, after many seconds of cogitation, he decided that it was safe to unpack the transmission into the most sensitive parts of his own mind. The message format was in natural language rather than any of the high-level Conjoiner protocols. Nicely insulting touch, he thought: from the perspective of Skade's allies, it was the Conjoiner equivalent of baby talk.

[Remontoire? It's you, isn't it? Why won't you talk to us?]

He composed a thought in the same format. *Why are you so certain I'm Remontoire?*

[You were always more fond of wild gestures than you'd ever admit. This is straight out of Clavain's book of daring escapades.]

Someone has to do it.

[It's a brave effort, Remontoire, but it's pointless worrying about those people on the planet. Nothing we can do can help them now. They're not even relevant to the future outcome of the war.]

We'd best let them hang, then. That'd be Skade's way, wouldn't it?

[Skade would do what she could for them if she thought they were going to make a difference. But you're only making things worse. Don't take the battle down there. Don't stretch things up here when we most need to consolidate our forces.]

Another plea for co-operation? Skade must be turning in her grave.

[She was a pragmatist, Remontoire, much like yourself. She would have seen that now is the time to amalgamate our parties, to pool our knowledge-base and inflict real damage on the enemy machines.]

What you mean is that you've achieved all you can through deception and theft. You know I'll never trust you that way again. Now you have nothing to lose by negotiating.

[With regret, we acknowledge that tactical errors were made. But now that Skade is – as you have alluded – very probably dead . . .]

The ducklings are waddling around looking for a new mother duck.

[Adopt the analogy of your choice, Remontoire. We only offer the outstretched hand of friendship. The situation here is more complex than we've hitherto realised. You must have seen this for yourself: the teasing hints in the data, the scraps – too small and insignificant on their own – but which add up to a clear conclusion. We're not just dealing with wolves, Remontoire. There is something else.]

I've seen nothing I couldn't explain.

[Then you haven't been looking hard enough. Here, Remontoire: examine *our* data, if you doubt us. See if that changes your opinion. See if that makes it any clearer to you.]

The data nugget was scripted into his head. An instinct told him to delete it still compressed, still unread. But he decided to leave it there for the time being.

You're suggesting a partnership?

[Disunited, we'll never beat them. Together, we could make a difference.]

Perhaps. But it's not me you really want, is it?

[Of course not, Remontoire.]

He smiled: Skade's Conjoiners might have been leaderless, might even have been driven towards him by some instinctive imperative to fill that void, but mainly it was the hypometric weapon. It was the one technology they hadn't managed to steal or reverse-engineer, despite Skade's theft of Aura. All that they needed was one prototype; it didn't even have to be intact, so long as they could reconstruct its working configuration.

Thanks for the offer, but I'm actually a tiny bit preoccupied at the moment. Why don't we chat about this later? Say, in a few months?

[Remontoire . . . don't make us do this.]

He applied lateral thrust, veering rudely away from the other ship. He mapped areas of brain function dropping in and out as the blood sloshed through his skull. A moment later the corvette shadowed him, mimicking his vicious moves with a finesse verging on the sarcastic.

[We need that weapon, Remontoire.]

So I guessed. Why didn't you just come out and say it at the beginning?

[We wanted to give you the chance to see things our way.]

I suppose I should be grateful, in that case.

He felt his ship judder. His head lit up with damage reports, bright and geometric as a migraine. They had hit him with multiple hull-penetrating slugs targeted for ship-critical functions. It was very surgical: they wanted to leave him drifting, ripe for theft, rather than to blow his ship apart. Whether they cared about his survival was another matter entirely.

[Surrender the weapon now, Rem, and we'll leave you with enough flight-capability to escape that wolf aggregate closing in on us.]

Sorry, but that's not really in my plans for today.

His vessel rattled again: more vital functions faltered or dropped out of service. The ship was already trying to find work-arounds, doing its best to keep flying, but there was a limit to the damage it could soak up. He considered retaliating, but he was keen to save his conventional ordnance for the aggregates. That left the hypometric weapon itself, barely tested since its laborious calibration.

He issued the mental command that caused it to spin up to activation energy, compensating for the drift in the ship's vector as angular momentum transferred to the shining innards of the weapon. Externally, there was no evidence of any change in the device at all. He wondered what kind of sensors the corvette had trained on him, and whether they were good enough to pick up the subtle signatures of activation.

It was a small weapon with a correspondingly limited precision and radial volume of effect (conventional terminology – things like 'range' and 'accuracy' – were only vaguely applicable to hypometric weapons). But it also spun up very quickly. He tuned its scale of effect, found the solution in the complex topography of weapon parameters that corresponded to a specific point in the three-dimensional volume of surrounding space.

He re-established a communications channel to the corvette. *Pull back.*

[Again, don't make us do this, Remontoire.]

The weapon discharged. In the microwave-frequency map of the corvette's cold spots, a wound had suddenly appeared: a perfectly hemispherical bite in the side of the hull. The cryogenic temperature gradients flowed like water around a sinkhole, gyring and wheeling as they tried to find a new equilibrium. Pairs of cooling nodes locked into unstable oscillation modes.

The weapon spun up again. He put another hole in the corvette's hull, deeper this time, so that the wound was concave.

The corvette responded. Reluctantly, he parried the ship-to-ship munitions with a spread of countermeasures while still holding some back for the Inhibitor machines.

The weapon spun up a third time. He concentrated, forcing himself to examine the solution from every angle. An error now could be fatal for all involved.

Discharge. His third attack was not visible at all. If he had done his sums correctly he had just put a spherical hole inside the ship without touching the hull. It would not have touched any vital internal systems. And – his *coup de grâce* – the centre of the final hole would be exactly in line with the centres of the last two, to micron accuracy.

He waited a moment for the precision – and essential restraint – of his attack to sink in before contacting them again. *The next one takes out your life-system. Got the message?*

The corvette hesitated. Seconds oozed by, time for Skade's acolytes to examine thousands of possible response scenarios, toying with them the way children toyed with building blocks, constructing huge, wobbling edifices of event and counter-event. Almost certainly they had not expected him to turn the weapon against them. Their best intelligence would never have suggested he had *that* degree of control over the weapon's effects. Even if it had – and even if they had considered the possibility of an attack – they must have assumed he would strike at their ship's drive core, taking it out in an instant of blinding light.

Instead, he had let them off with a warning. This wasn't, Remontoire had thought to himself, a time to be making new enemies.

There was no further transmission. He watched, fascinated, as the cryo-arithmetic engines smoothed out the temperature gradients around the two exterior wounds, doing their best to camouflage the damage. Then the corvette flipped over, pushed its thrust to the limit and made itself scarce.

Remontoire allowed himself a miserly instant of self-congratulation. He had played that one well. His ship was still spaceworthy despite the damage it had sustained. And all he had to worry about now was the approaching aggregate of Inhibitor machines. The machines would arrive in three minutes.

Two thousand kilometres, then a thousand, then five hundred. Closer, his sensors struggled to deal with the clump of Inhibitor machines as a single entity, throwing back wildly conflicting estimates for distance, scale and geometric disposition. The best he could do was to focus his efforts on the larger nodes, refining his hull-camouflaging to provide a better line-of-sight match with the cosmic background. He adjusted his thrust vectoring, losing some acceleration but steering his ship's exhaust beams away from the shifting concentrations of enemy machines. The exhausts were invisible, all but undetectable via the methods available to Remontoire. He hoped the same disadvantage applied to the aliens, but it paid not to take chances.

The clumps reorganised, shifting nearer. They were still too far away and too vaguely dispersed to make an effective target for the hypometric weapon. He was also wary of using it against them except as a tool of last resort. There was always the danger that he'd show it to them too many times, giving them enough data to conjure up a response. It had already happened with other weapons: time and again the Inhibitors had evolved effective defences against human technologies, including some of those already bequeathed by Aura. It was possible that the alien machines were not evolving them at all, but simply retrieving countermeasures from some ancient, jumbled racial memory. This conjecture alarmed Remontoire more than the idea that they might have developed their adaptations and responses through intelligent thinking. There was always the hope that one kind of intelligence could be beaten by the application of another kind, or that intelligence – self-regarding, prone to doubt – might even conspire in its own downfall. But what if there was no intelligence in the Inhibitor activities, just a process of archival retrieval, an utterly mindless bureaucracy of systematised extinction? The galaxy was a very old place and it had seen many clever ideas. More than likely, the Inhibitors already possessed ancient data on the humans' new weapons and technologies. If they had not yet developed effective responses, it was only because that retrieval system was slow, the archive itself vastly distributed. What that meant was that there was *nothing* the humans could do, in the long run. No way to outgun the Inhibitors, except on a very local scale. Think galactically, think beyond the immediate handful of solar systems, and it was already over.

But through the channel of her mother, Aura had told them that it *wasn't* over, not yet. According to Aura there was a means of buying time, if not outright victory, over the Inhibitors.

Snatches, fragments: that was all they could glean from Aura's confused messages. But out of the noise had emerged hints of a signal. Time and again a cluster of words had appeared.

Hela. Quaiche. Shadows.

These were shards broken loose from a larger whole that Aura had been too young to articulate. All Remontoire could do was guess at the shape of that bigger picture, using what they had learned before Skade had kidnapped her. Skade and Aura were both gone now, he believed, but he still had those shards. They had to mean something, no matter how unlikely it appeared. And there was, tantalisingly, a clear link between two of them. Hela and Quaiche: the words meant something in association. But of the Shadows he knew nothing at all.

What were they, and what difference would they make?

The aggregate was very close now. It had begun to grope horns around either side of his ship, dark pincers flickering with buried violet lightning. Hints of cubic symmetries could now be glimpsed in sheared edges and stepped curves. He reviewed his options, taking account of the systems damaged in the Conjoiner attack. He wasn't willing to use the hypometric weapon just yet, and doubted that he'd be able to spin up for a second attack before the undamaged elements took him out.

Ahead, the planet had grown noticeably larger. He had pushed the other aggregate from his mind, but it was still ahead of him, still skimming towards the fragile Juggler biosphere and its human parasites. Half the world was in darkness, the rest a marbled turquoise speckled by white clouds and swirling storm systems.

Remontoire made up his mind: it would have to be the bladder-mines.

In a fraction of a second, apertures popped open along the habitat hull of his trident-shaped ship. In another fraction of a second, launchers flung half a dozen melon-sized munitions in all directions. The hull clanged as the weapons were deployed.

Then there was silence.

An entire second passed, then the munitions detonated in an exactly choreographed sequence. There was no stutter of blinding-white flashes; these were not fusion devices or antimatter warheads. They were, in fact, only bombs in the very loosest sense of the word. Where each munition had detonated there was, suddenly, a twenty-kilometre-wide sphere of *something* just sitting there, like a rapidly inflated barrage balloon. The surface of each sphere was wrinkled, like the skin of a shrivelling fruit, shaded a purple-black and prone to nauseating surges of colour and boundary radius. Where two spheres happened to intersect – because their munitions had been closer than twenty kilometres apart when they detonated – the merged boundaries twinkled with sugary emanations of violet and pastel-blue.

The mechanisms inside the bladder mines were as intricate and unfathomable as those inside the hypometric weapon. There were even weird points of correspondence between the two technologies – odd parts that looked vaguely similar, suggesting that, perhaps, they had originated from the same species, or the same epoch of galactic history.

Remontoire's suspicion was that the bladder-mines represented an early step towards the metric-engineering technology of the Shrouders. Whereas the Shrouders had learned how to encase entire stellar-sized volumes of space in shells of re-engineered space-time (with its own uncanny defensive properties), the bladder-mines produced unstable shells a mere twenty kilometres wide. They decayed back to normal space-time within a few seconds, popping out of existence in a shiver of exotic quanta. Where they had been, the local properties of the metric showed tiny indications of earlier stress. But the shells could never be made larger or more permanent, at least not by using the technology Aura had given them.

His spread of munitions was already decaying. The spheres popped away one by one, in random sequence.

Remontoire surveyed the damage. Where the shells had detonated, the intersected Inhibitor machinery had been ripped out of existence. There were curved mathematically smooth wounds in the groping aggregation of cubic elements. The lightning was arcing through the ruined structure, its mad flickering suggesting nothing so much as pain and rage.

Hit them when they're down, Remontoire thought. He issued the mental command that would fling a final spread of bladder-mines into the surrounding machinery.

This time, nothing happened. Error messages stormed his brain: the launcher mechanism had failed, succumbing to damage from the earlier attack. He had been fortunate that it had worked once.

For the first time, Remontoire permitted himself more than an instant of real, blood-freezing fear. His options were now seriously diminished. He had no hull-armouring: that was another alien technology they had gleaned from Aura, but like inertial suppression it did not work well in proximity with the hypometric weapon. The hull-armouring came from the grubs; the h-weapon and the bladder-mines from a different culture. There were, unfortunately, compatibility issues. All he had left was the hypometric weapon and his conventional armaments, but there was still no clear focus for an attacking move.

The hull shuddered as his conventional mines were released from their hatches. Fusion detonations painted the sky. He felt the electromagnetic backwash play havoc with his implants, strobing abstract shapes through his visual field.

The Inhibitors were still there. He fired two Stinger missiles, watching them slam away on hundred-gee intercepts. Nothing happened: they hadn't even detonated properly. He had no beam weapons, nothing more to offer.

Remontoire became very calm. His experience told him that nothing would be gained by using the hypometric weapon other than giving the machines another chance to study its operational function. He also knew that the wolves had yet to capture one of the weapons, and that he could not allow it to happen today.

He prepared the suicide command, visualising the coronet of fusion mines packed into the nacelle of the alien weapon. They would make a spectacular flash as they went off, almost as bright as the one that would follow an instant later when the Conjoiner drive went the same way. There was, he thought, very little chance that either would be appreciated by spectators.

Remontoire adjusted his state of mind so that he felt no fear, no apprehension about his own death. He felt only a tingle of irritation that he would not be around to see how events unfurled. In every significant respect he approached the matter of his own demise with the bored acceptance of someone waiting to sneeze. There were, he thought, some consolations to being a Conjoiner.

He was about to execute the command when something happened. The remaining machinery began to pull away from his ship, retreating with surprising speed. Beyond the machinery, his sensors picked up suggestions of weapons discharges and a great deal of moving mass – bladder-mine detonations, the signatures subtly different from the ones he had used. Antimatter and fusion warhead bursts followed, then the streaking exhaust plumes of missiles, and finally a single massive explosion that had to be a crustbuster device.

None of it would have made much difference ordinarily, but he had weakened the Inhibitor machinery with his own assault. The mass sensor teased out the signature of a single small ship, consistent, he realised now, with a Conjoiner moray-class corvette.

He guessed that it was the same ship he had spared. They had turned around, or perhaps had shadowed him all along. Now they were doing their best to draw the Inhibitor machinery away from him. Remontoire knew, beyond any shadow of a doubt, that the gesture was suicidal: they couldn't hope to make it back to their faction in the engagement. Yet they had taken a decision to help him, even after their earlier attack and his refusal to hand over the hypometric weapon. Typical Conjoiner thinking, he reflected: they would not hesitate to shift tactics at the last minute if that shift was deemed beneficial to the long-term interests of the Mother Nest. They had no capacity for frustration, no capacity for shame.

They had tried to negotiate with him, and when that had failed they had tried to take what they wanted by force. That hadn't worked either, and to rub it in he had made a show of sparing them. Was this a demonstration of their gratitude? Perhaps, he thought, but it was likely to be more for the benefit of those observing the battle, for Remontoire's allies and the other Conjoiner factions, than for himself: let them see the brave sacrifice they had made here. Let them see the wiping clean of the slate. If twenty-eight thousand and one offers to share resources had failed, perhaps this gesture would be the thing that made a difference.

Remontoire didn't know: not yet. He had other matters on his mind.

His ship pulled away from the entanglement of wolf and Conjoiner assets. Behind, naked energy and naked force strove to gore matter down to its fundamentals. Something absurdly bright lit up the sky, something so intense that he swore a glimmer of it reached him through the black hull of his ship.

He turned his attention to the other aggregate, the one that was now very close to the planet. At extreme magnification he saw a black mass squatting a few hours into the dayside of the planet, hovering above a specific point on the surface. It was doing something.

TWENTY-THREE

Hela, 2727

Quaiche was alone in his garret, save for the scrimshaw suit. He heard only his own breathing and the attentive sounds of the couch on which he rested. The jalousies were half-drawn, the room scribed with parallel lines of fiery red.

He could feel, very faintly – and only because he had learned to feel it – the tiny residual side-to-side and back-to-front lurching of the Lady Morwenna as it progressed along the Way. Far from annoying him, the swaying was a source of reassurance. The instant the cathedral became rock steady, he would know that they were losing ground on Haldora. But the cathedral had not stopped for more than a century, and then only for a matter of hours during a reactor failure. Ever since then, even as it had grown in size, doubling and then quadrupling in height, it had kept moving, sliding along the Way at the exact speed necessary to keep Haldora fixed directly above, and therefore transmitted via the mirrors into his pinned-open, ever-watchful eyes. No other cathedral on the Way had such a record: the Lady Morwenna's nearest rival, the Iron Lady, had failed for an entire rotation fifty-nine years earlier. The shame of that breakdown – having to wait in the same spot until the other cathedrals came around again after three hundred and twenty days – still hung heavy six decades later. Every other cathedral, including the Lady Morwenna, had a stained-glass window in commemoration of that humiliation.

The couch propelled him to the westerly window, tipping up slightly to improve his view. As he moved, the mirrors shuffled around him, maintaining sight-lines. No matter which way he steered the couch, Haldora was the predominant object reflected back to him. He was seeing it after multiple reflections, the light jogged through right angles, reversed and inverted again, magnified and diminished by achromatic lenses, but it was still *the light* itself, not some second- or third-hand image on a screen. It was always there, but the view was never quite the same from hour to hour. For one thing, the illumination of Haldora changed throughout the forty-hour cycle of Hela's orbit: from fully lit face, to crescent, to storm-racked nightside. And even during any given phase the details of shading and banding were never quite the same from one pass to the next. It was enough, just, to stave off the feeling that the image had been branded into his brain.

It was not all that he saw, of course. Surrounding Haldora was a ring of black shading to silver grey, and then – packed into a band of indistinct detail – his immediate surroundings. He could look to one side and shift Haldora into his peripheral vision, for the mirrors were focusing the image on to his eyes, not just his pupils. But he did not do this very often, fearful that a vanishing would happen when the planet did not have his full attention.

Even with Haldora looming head-on, he had learned how to make the most of his peripheral vision. It was surprising how the brain was able to fill in the gaps, suggesting details that his eyes were really not capable of resolving. More than once it had struck Quaiche that if human beings really grasped how synthetic their world was – how much of it was stitched together not from direct perception, but from interpolation, memory, educated guesswork – they would go quietly mad.

He looked at the Way. In the far easterly distance, in the direction that the Lady Morwenna was headed, there was a distinct twinkling. That was the northern limit of the Gullveig Mountains, the largest range in Hela's southern hemisphere. It was the last major geological feature to be crossed before the relative ease of the Jarnsaxa Flats and the associated fast run to the Devil's Staircase. The Way cut through the northern flanks of the Gullveig Range, pushing through foothills via a series of high-walled canyons. And that was where an icefall had been reported. It was said to be a bad one, hundreds of metres deep, completely blocking the existing alignment. Quaiche had personally interviewed the leader of the Permanent Way repair team earlier that day, a man named Wyatt Benjamin who had lost a leg in some ancient, unspecified accident.

'Sabotage, I'd say,' Benjamin had told him. 'A dozen or so demolition charges placed in the wall during the last crossing, with delayed timing fuses. A spoiling action by trailing cathedrals. They can't keep up, so they don't see why anyone else should.'

'That would be quite a serious allegation to make in public,' Quaiche had said, as if the very thought had never occurred to him. 'Still, you may be right, much as it pains me to admit it.'

'Make no mistake, it's a stitch-up.'

'The question is, who's going to clear it? It would need to be done in – what, ten days at the maximum, before we reach the obstruction?'

Wyatt Benjamin had nodded. 'You may not want to be that close when it's cleared, however.'

'Why not?'

'We're not going to be chipping this one away.'

Quaiche had absorbed that, understanding exactly what the man meant. 'There was a fall of that magnitude three, four years ago, wasn't there? Out near Glum Junction? I seem to remember it was cleared using conventional demolition equipment. Shifted the lot in fewer than ten days, too.'

'We could do this one in fewer than ten days,' Benjamin told him, 'but we only have about half of our usual allocation of equipment and manpower.'

'That sounds odd,' Quaiche had replied, frowning. 'What's wrong with the rest?'

'Nothing. It's just that it's all been requisitioned, men and machines. Don't ask me why or who's behind it. I only work for the Permanent Way. And I suppose if it was anything to do with Clocktower business, you'd already know, wouldn't you?'

'I suppose I would,' Quaiche had said. 'Must be a bit lower down than Clocktower level. My guess? Another office of the Way has discovered something they should have fixed urgently already, a job that got forgotten in the last round. They need all that heavy machinery to get it done in a rush, before anyone notices.'

'Well, we're noticing,' Benjamin had said. But he had seemed to accept the plausibility of Quaiche's suggestion.

'In that case, you'll just have to find another means of clearing the blockage, won't you?'

'We already have another means,' the man had said.

'God's Fire,' Quaiche had replied, forcing awe into his voice.

'If that's what it takes, that's what we'll have to use. It's why we carry it with us.'

'Nuclear demolitions should only ever be used as the absolute final last resort,' Quaiche had said, with what he hoped was the appropriate cautioning tone. 'Are you quite certain that this blockage can't be shifted by conventional means?'

'In ten days with the available men and equipment? Not a sodding hope.'

'Then God's Fire it will have to be.' Quaiche had steepled the twigs of his fingers. 'Inform the other cathedrals, across all ecumenical boundaries. We'll take the lead on this one. The others had better draw back to the usual safe distance, unless they've improved their shielding since last time.'

'There's no other choice,' Wyatt Benjamin had agreed.

Quaiche had placed a hand on his shoulder. 'It's all right. What has to be done, has to be done. God will watch over us.'

Quaiche snapped out of his reverie and smiled. The Permanent Way man was gone now, off to arrange the rare and hallowed deployment of controlled fusion devices. He was alone with the Way and the scrimshaw suit and the distant, alluring twinkle of the Gullveig Range.

'You arranged for that ice, didn't you?'

He turned to the scrimshaw suit. 'Who told you to speak?'

'No one.'

He fought to keep his voice level, betraying none of the fear he felt. 'You aren't supposed to talk until I make it possible.'

'Clearly this is not the case.' The voice was thin, reedy: the product of a cheap speaker welded to the back of the scrimshaw suit's head, out of sight of casual guests. 'We hear everything, Quaiche, and we speak when it suits us.'

It shouldn't have been possible. The speaker was only supposed to work when Quaiche turned it on. 'You shouldn't be able to do this.'

The voice – it was like something produced by a cheaply made woodwind instrument – seemed to mock him. 'This is only the start, Quaiche. We will always find a way out of any cage you build around us.'

'Then I should destroy you now.'

'You can't. And you shouldn't. We are not your enemy, Quaiche. You should know that by now. We're here to help you. We just need a little help in return.'

'You're demons. I don't negotiate with demons.'

'Not demons, Quaiche. Just shadows, as you are to us.'

They had had this conversation before. Many times before. 'I can think of ways to kill you,' he said.

'Then why not try?'

The answer popped unbidden into his head, as it always did: because they might be useful to him. Because he could control them for now. Because he feared what would happen if he killed them as much as if he let them live. Because he knew there were more where this lot came from.

Many more.

'You know why,' he said, sounding pitiable even to himself.

'The vanishings are increasing in frequency,' the scrimshaw suit said. 'You know what that means, don't you?'

'It means that these are the end times,' Quaiche said. 'No more than that.'

'It means that the concealment is failing. It means that the machinery will soon be evident to all.'

'There is no machinery.'

'You saw it for yourself. Others will see it, too, when the vanishings reach their culmination. And sooner or later someone will want to do business with us. Why wait until then, Quaiche? Why not deal with us now, on the best possible terms?'

'I don't deal with demons.'

'We are only shadows,' the suit said again. 'Just shadows, whispering across the gap between us. Now help us to cross it, so that we can help you.'

'I won't. Not ever.'

'There is a crisis coming, Quaiche. The evidence suggests it has already begun. You've seen the refugees. You know the stories they tell, of machines emerging from the darkness, from the cold. Engines of extinction. We've seen it happen before, in this very system. You won't beat them without our help.'

'God will intervene,' Quaiche said. His eyes were watering, blurring the image of Haldora.

'There is no God,' the suit said. 'There is only us, and we don't have limitless patience.'

But then it fell silent. It had said its piece for the day, leaving Quaiche alone with his tears.

'God's Fire,' he whispered.

Ararat, 2675

When Vasko returned to the heart of the iceberg there was no more music. With the light bulk of the incubator hanging from one hand he made his way through the tangle of icy spars, following the now well-cleared route. The ice tinkled and creaked around him, the incubator knocking its way through obstructions. Scorpio had told him not to rush back to the ruined ship, but he knew that the pig had only been trying to spare him any unnecessary distress. He had made the call to Blood, told Urton what was happening and then returned with the incubator as fast as he dared.

But as he neared the gash in the ship's side he knew it was over.

There was a pillar of light ramming down from the ceiling of ice, where someone had blasted a metre-wide hole through to the sky. Scorpio stood in the circle of light at the foot of the pillar, his features sharply lit from above as if in some chiaroscuro painting. He was looking down, the thick mound of his head sunk into the wide yoke of his shoulders. His eyes were closed, the fine-haired skin of his forehead rendered blue-grey in the light's dusty column. There was something in his hand, speckling red on to the ice.

'Sir?' Vasko asked.

'It's done,' Scorpio said.

'I'm sorry you had to do that, sir.'

The eyes – pale, bloodshot pink – locked on to him. Scorpio's hands were shaking. When he spoke his perfectly human voice sounded thin, like the voice of a ghost losing its grip on a haunt. 'Not as sorry as I am.'

'I would have done it, if you'd asked me.'

'I wouldn't have asked you,' Scorpio said. 'I wouldn't have asked it of anyone.'

Vasko fumbled for something else to say. He wanted to ask Scorpio how merciful Skade had allowed him to be. Vasko thought that he could not have been away for more than ten minutes. Did that mean, in some abhorrent algebra of hurting, that Skade had given Clavain some respite from the prolonged death she had promised? Was there any sense in which she could have been said to have shown mercy, if only by shaving scant minutes from what must still have been unutterable agony?

He couldn't guess. He wasn't sure he really wanted to know.

'I brought the incubator, sir. Is the child . . .'

'Aura's all right. She's with her mother.'

'And Skade, sir?'

'Skade is dead,' Scorpio told him. 'She knew she couldn't survive much longer.' The pig's voice sounded dull, void of feeling. 'She'd diverted her own bodily resources to keep Aura alive. There wasn't much of Skade left when we opened her up.'

'She wanted Aura to live,' Vasko said.

'Or she wanted a bargaining position when we came with Clavain.'

Vasko held up the light plastic box, as if Scorpio had not heard him properly. 'The incubator, sir. We should get the child into it immediately.'

Scorpio leaned down, wiping the blade of the scalpel against the ice. The red smear bled away into the frost in patterns that made

Vasko think of irises. He thought Scorpio might discard the knife, but instead the pig slipped it into a pocket.

'Jaccottet and Khouri will put the child into the incubator,' he said. 'Meanwhile, you and I can take care of Clavain.'

'Sir?'

'His last wish. He wanted to be buried at sea.' Scorpio turned to step back into the ship. 'I think we owe him that much.'

'Was that the last thing he said, sir?'

Scorpio turned slowly back to face Vasko and studied him for a long moment, his head tilted. Vasko felt as if he was being measured again, just as the old man had measured him, and the experience induced exactly the same feeling of inadequacy. What did these monsters from the past want of him? What did they expect him to live up to?

'It wasn't the last thing he said, no,' Scorpio replied quietly.

They laid the body bag down on the fringe of ice surrounding the iceberg. Vasko had to keep reminding himself that it was still only the middle of the morning: the sky was a wet grey, clouds jammed in from horizon to horizon, like a ceiling scraping the top of the iceberg. A few kilometres out to sea was a distinct and threatening smudge of wet ink in that same ceiling, like a black eye. It seemed to move against the wind, as if looking for something below. On the horizon, lightning scribed chrome lines against the tarnished silver of the sky. Distant rain came down in slow sooty streams.

Around the iceberg, the sea roiled in sullen grey shapes. In all directions, the surface of the water was being constantly interrupted by slick, moving phantasms of an oily turquoise-green colour. Vasko had seen them earlier: they broke the surface, lingered and then vanished almost before the eye had time to focus. The impression was that a vast shoal of vague whale-like things was in the process of surrounding the iceberg. The phantasms bellied and gyred between waves and spume. They merged and split, orbited and submerged, and their precise shape and size was impossible to determine. But they were not animals. They were vast aggregations of micro-organisms acting in a coherent manner.

Vasko saw Scorpio looking at the sea. There was an expression on the pig's face that he hadn't seen before. Vasko wondered if it was apprehension.

'Something's happening, isn't it?' Vasko asked.

'We have to carry him beyond the ice,' Scorpio said. 'The boat's still good for a few hours. Help me get him into it.'

'We shouldn't take too long over it, sir.'

'You think it makes the slightest difference how long it takes?'

'From what you've said, sir, it made a difference to Clavain.'

They heaved the bag into the black carcass of the nearest boat. In daylight the hull already looked far rougher than Vasko remembered it, the smooth metal surface pocked and pitted with spots of local corrosion. Some of them were deep enough to put his thumb into. Even as they lifted the bag over the side, bits of the boat came off in metallic scabs where Vasko's knee touched it.

The two of them climbed aboard. Urton, who was to remain on the iceberg's ledge, helped them on their way with a shove. Scorpio turned on the motor. The water fizzed and the boat inched back towards the sea, retreating along the channel it had cut into the fringe.

'Wait.'

Vasko followed the voice. It was Jaccottet, emerging from the iceberg. The incubator hung from his wrist, obviously heavier than when Vasko had carried it in.

'What is it?' Scorpio called, idling the engine.

'You can't leave without us.'

'No one's leaving.'

'The child needs medical attention. We must get her back to the mainland as soon as possible.'

'That's just what's going to happen. Didn't you hear what Vasko said? There's a plane on its way. Sit tight here and everything will be all right.'

'In this weather the plane might take hours, and we don't know how stable this iceberg is.'

Vasko felt Scorpio's anger. It made his skin tingle, the way static electricity did. 'So what are you saying?'

'I'm saying we should leave now, sir, in both boats, just as we came in. Head south. The plane will pick us up by transponder. We're bound to save time that way, and we don't have to worry about this thing collapsing under us.'

'He's right, sir, I think,' Vasko said.

'Who asked you?' Scorpio snapped.

'No one, sir, but I'd say we all have a stake in this now, don't we?'

'You have no stake in anything, Malinin.'

'Clavain seemed to think I did.'

He expected the pig to kill him there and then. The possibility loomed in his mind even as his gaze drifted to that deep black eye in the clouds. It was closer now – no more than a kilometre from the iceberg – and it was bellying down, beginning to reach something nublike towards the sea. It was a tornado, Vasko realised: just what they needed.

But Scorpio only snarled and powered up the engine again. 'Are you with me or not? If not, get out and wait on the ice with the others.'

'I'm with you, sir,' Vasko said. 'I just don't see why we can't do it the way Jaccottet says. We can leave with both boats and bury Clavain on the way.'

'Get out.'

'Sir?'

'I said get out. It isn't up for negotiation.'

Vasko started to say something. Time and again, when he replayed the incident in his mind, it would never be clear to him just what he intended to say to the pig at that moment. Perhaps he already knew he had crossed the line at that point, and that nothing he could say or do would ever unmake that crossing.

Scorpio moved with lightning speed. He let go of the engine control, seized Vasko with both trotters and then levered him over the side. Vasko felt the top inch of the metal side of the boat crumble under his thigh, like brittle chocolate. Then his back hit a thin and equally brittle skein of ice, and finally he sank into water colder than anything he had ever imagined, the bitter chill ramming up his spine like a gleaming piston of shock and pain. He couldn't breathe. He couldn't cry out or reach for anything solid. He could hardly remember his name, or why drowning was such a bad thing after all.

He saw the boat slide away into the sea. He saw Jaccottet place the incubator on the ground, Khouri stepping up behind him, and start walking quickly but carefully towards him.

Above, the sky was a blank cerebral grey, except for the shadowy focus of the stormy eye. The nub of blackness had almost reached the surface of the water. It was curling to one side, towards the iceberg.

Scorpio brought the boat to a standstill. It rocked in a metre-high swell, not so much floating in water now as resting on a moving raft of blue-green organic matter. The raft reached away in all directions for many dozens of metres, but it was thickest at its epicentre, which appeared to be precisely where the boat had come to rest. Surrounding it was a dark charcoal band of relatively uncontaminated water, and beyond that lay several other distinct islands of Juggler matter. Beneath the surface of the water, glimpsed intermittently between waves and foam, were suggestions of frondlike tentacular structures, thick as pipelines. They bobbed and swayed, and occasionally moved with the slow, eerie deliberation of pre-hensile tails.

Scorpio rummaged in the boat for something to wrap around his face. The smell was drilling into his brain. Humans said it was bad, or at least overwhelmingly strong and potent. It was the smell of rotting kitchen waste, compost, ammonia, sewage, ozone. For pigs it was unbearable.

He found a covering in a medical kit and wrapped it twice around his snout, leaving his eyes free. They were stinging, watering incessantly. There was nothing he could do about that now.

Standing up, careful not to overbalance himself or the boat, he took hold of the body bag. The fury he had felt when he had thrown Vasko overboard had sapped what little strength he had managed to conserve. Now the bag felt three times as heavy as it should, not twice. He gripped it, trotters either side of the head end, and began to inch backwards. He did not want to risk dropping the body over one of the sides, fearful that the boat would capsize with the weight of two adults so far from the midline. If he dragged the body to the front or the back, he might be safe.

He slipped. His trotters lost their grip. He went flying backwards, landing on the calloused swell of his buttocks, the body bag thumping down against the decking.

He wiped the tears from his eyes, but that only made matters worse. The air was clotted with micro-organisms, a green haze hovering above the sea, and all he had done was force that irritation deeper into himself.

He stood up again. He noticed, absently, the trunk of blackness reaching down from the sky. He grasped the bag once more and started to heave it towards the stern. The organic shapes congealed around the boat in a constant procession of disturbing effigies, bottle-green silhouettes forming and dissolving like the work of mad topiarists. When he looked at them directly, the shapes had no meaning, but from the corner of his eye he saw hints of alien anatomy: a menagerie of strangely joined limbs, oddly arranged faces and torsos. Mouths gaped wide. Multiple clusters of eyes regarded him with mindless scrutiny. Articulated wing parts spread open like fans. Horns and claws erupted from the greenery, lingering for an instant before collapsing back into formlessness. The constant changes in the physical structure of the Juggler biomass was accompanied by a warm, wet breeze and a rapid slurping and tearing sound.

He turned around so that the bag lay between him and the stern. Leaning over the bag, he grasped it near the shoulders and levered it on to the metal side of the stern. He blinked, trying to focus. All around him, the green frenzy continued unabated.

'I'm sorry,' he said.

It was all meant to happen differently. In his imagination, Scorpio had often considered the possible circumstances of Clavain's death. Assuming he would live long enough to witness it himself, he had always seen Clavain's burial in heroic terms, some solemn fire-lit ceremony attended by thousands of onlookers. He had always assumed that if Clavain died it would be gently and in the belly of the colony, his last hours the subject of loving vigils. Failing that, in some courageous and unexpected action, going out heroically the way he had almost done a hundred times before, pressing a hand to some small, innocent-looking chest wound, his face turning the colour of a winter sky, holding on to breath and consciousness just long enough to whisper some message to those who would have to go on without him. In his imagination, it had always been Scorpio who passed on that valediction.

There would be dignity in his death, a sense of rightful closure. And his burial would be a thing of wonder and sadness, something to be talked about for generations hence.

That was not how it was happening.

Scorpio did not want to think about what was in the bag, or what had been done to it. He did not want to think about the enforced slowness of Clavain's death, or the vital part he had played in it. It would have been bad enough to have been a spectator to what took place in the iceberg. To know that he had been a participant was to know that some irreplaceable part of himself had been hollowed out.

'I won't let them down,' he said. 'When you were away on your island, I always tried to do things the way you would have done them. That doesn't mean I ever thought I was your equal. I know that won't ever be true. I have trouble planning beyond the end of my nose. Like I always say, I'm a hands-on type.'

His eyes stung. He thought about what he had just said, the bitter irony of it.

'I suppose that was the way it was, right to the end. I'm sorry, Nevil. You deserved better than this. You were a brave man and you always did the right thing, no matter what it cost you.'

Scorpio paused, catching his breath, quashing the vague feeling of absurdity he felt in talking to the bag. Speeches had never been his thing. Clavain would have made a much better job of it, had their roles been reversed. But he was here and Clavain was the dead man in the bag. He just had to do the best he could, fumbling through, the way he had done most things in his life.

Clavain would forgive him, he thought.

'I'm going to let you go now,' Scorpio said. 'I hope this is what you wanted, pal. I hope you find what you were looking for.'

He gave the bag one last heave over the side. It vanished instantly into the green raft that surrounded the boat. In the moments after the bag had gone there was a quickening in the activity of the Juggler forms. The constant procession of alien shapes became more frenzied, shuffling towards some excited climax.

In the sky, the questing black trunk had curved nearly horizontal, groping towards the iceberg. The tip of the thing was no longer a blunt nub: it had begun to open, dividing into multiple black fingers that were themselves growing and splitting, writhing their way through the air.

There was nothing he could do about that now. He looked back at the play of Juggler shapes, thinking for an instant that he had even seen a pair of female human faces appear in the storm of images. The faces had been strikingly alike, but one possessed a maturity that the other lacked, a serene and weary resignation. It was as if entirely too much had been witnessed, entirely too much imagined, for one human life. Eyeless as statues, they stared at him for one frozen moment, before dissolving back into the flicker of masks.

Around him, the raft began to break up. The changing wall of shapes slumped, collapsing back into the sea. Even the smell and the stinging miasma had begun to lose something of their astringency. He supposed that meant he had done his duty. But above the sea, the black thing continued to push its branching extremities towards the iceberg.

He still had work to do.

Scorpio turned the boat around. By the time he reached the iceberg the other craft was already afloat: Vasko, Khouri, the incubator and the two Security Arm people were visible within it, the adults crouching down against the spray, the hull sinking low in the water. The Jugglers had redoubled their activity after the lull when the ocean received Clavain. Scorpio was certain now that it had something to do with the thing reaching down from the sky. The Jugglers didn't like it: it was making them agitated, like a colony of small animals sensing the approach of a snake.

Scorpio didn't blame them: it was no kind of weather phenomenon he had ever experienced. Not a tornado, not a sea-spout. Now that the swaying multi-armed thing was directly overhead, its artificial nature was sickeningly obvious. The entire thing – from the thick trunk descending down through the cloud layer to the thinnest of the branching extremities – was composed of the same cubic black elements they had seen in Skade's ship. It was Inhibitor machinery, wolf machinery – whatever you wanted to call it. There was no guessing how much of it hovered above them, hidden behind the cloud deck. The trunk might even have reached all the way down through Ararat's atmosphere.

It made him feel ill just to look at it. It simply wasn't *right*.

He steered towards the other boat. Now that he had dealt with Clavain he felt a clarity of mind he'd lacked a few minutes before. It had probably been wrong to leave them on the iceberg with just that one boat for escape, but he had not wanted anyone else with him when he buried his friend. Selfish, perhaps, but it hadn't been any of them doing the cutting.

'Hold tight,' he told them via the communicator. 'We'll even out the load as soon as I'm close enough.'

'Then what?' Vasko asked, looking fearfully up at the thing stretched across the sky.

'Then we run like hell.'

The thing's attention lingered over the iceberg. With slow, python-like movements it pushed a cluster of tentacles into the roof of the frozen structure, the needles and jags of ice shattering as the machinery forced its way through. Perhaps, Scorpio thought, it sensed the presence of other pieces of Inhibitor machinery, dormant or dead within the wreckage of the corvette. It needed to be reunited with them. Or perhaps it was after something else entirely.

The iceberg quivered. The sea responded to the movement, slow, shallow waves oozing away from the fringe. From somewhere within the structure came crunching sounds, like the shattering of bone. Flaws opened wide in the outer layer of the ice, exposing a lacy marrow of fabulously differentiated colour: pinks and blues and ochres.

Black machinery forced its way through the cracks. A dozen tentacles emerged from the iceberg, coiling and writhing, sniffing the air, splitting into ever-smaller components as they pushed outwards.

Scorpio's boat kissed the hull of the other craft. 'Give me the incubator,' he shouted, above the screaming of the engine.

Vasko stood up, leaning between the boats, steadying himself with one hand on Scorpio's shoulder. The young man looked pale, his hair plastered to his scalp. 'You came back,' he said.

'Things changed,' Scorpio said.

Scorpio took the incubator, feeling the weight of the child within it, and jammed it safely between his feet. 'Now Khouri,' he said, offering a hand to the woman.

She crossed over to his boat; he felt it sink lower in the water as she boarded. She met his gaze for a moment, seemed about to say something. He turned back to Vasko before she had a chance.

'Follow me. I don't want to hang around here a moment longer than necessary.'

The cracks in the iceberg had widened to plunging abysses, rifts that cut deep into its heart. The black machinery forced more of itself into the ice, insinuating itself in eager surges. More extremities emerged from the perimeter, waving and extending. The iceberg began to break up into distinct chunks, each as large as a house. Scorpio gunned his boat's engine harder, slamming across the waves, but could not tear his attention from what was happening behind him. Chunks of the iceberg calved away, jagged pieces tipping into the sea with a powdery roar of displaced water. Now he could see a writhing tangle of black tentacles flexing and coiling around the ruined corvette. Not much remained of the iceberg now, just the ship that had grown it.

The machinery pulled the ship into the air. The black shapes forced themselves through the gaps in the hull, their movements delicate and thoughtful and vaguely apprehensive, like someone removing the last layer of wrapping from a present.

The other boat was lagging: it was slower in the water, with three adults aboard.

The corvette broke into sharp black pieces, all but the smallest of them still suspended in the sky. Coils and bows of perfect blackness wheeled around the parts.

It's looking for something, Scorpio thought.

The coils loosened their grip. Tentacles and sub-tentacles withdrew in a flurry of contracting motion. Layers of black cubes flowed across each other, swelling and shrinking in queasy unison. Scorpio only saw the details in the edges, where the machinery met the grey backdrop of the sky.

The pieces of the corvette – all of them, now – splashed into the sea.

But it still held something: a tiny, white, star-shaped form hung limply in the air. It was Skade, Scorpio realised. The machinery had found her in the wreckage, wrapped part of itself around her waist and plunged another, more delicate part of itself into her head. It was interrogating her, retrieving neural structures from her corpse.

It might, for a moment, feel like being alive again.

The black machinery pushed a new trunk of itself towards the fleeing boats. With that, something tightened in Scorpio's stomach: some instinctive visceral response to the approach of a slithering predator. *Get away from it.* He tried to push the boat harder. But the boat was already giving him all it had.

He saw motion in the other boat: the glint as a muzzle was trained towards the sky. An instant later, the blinding electric-pink discharge of a Breitenbach cannon lit the grey sky. The beam lanced up towards the looming mass of alien machinery. It should have speared right through it, etching a searing line into the cloud deck. Instead, the beam veered around the machinery like a firehose.

Vasko kept firing, but the beam squirmed away from any point where it might have done damage.

The black machinery followed the thick trunk. The whole mass still hung from the sky, multi-armed, like some obscene chandelier.

It was taking a particular interest in the second boat.

The cannon sputtered out. Scorpio heard the crackle of small-arms fire.

None of it was going to make any difference.

Suddenly he felt a lancing pain in his ears. All around him, in the same instant, the sea bellied up three or four metres, as if a tremendous suction effect had pulled it into the sky. There was a thunderclap louder than anything he had ever heard. He looked up, his ears still roaring, and saw ... something – a hint, for a fraction of a second, of a circular absence in the sky, a faint demarcation between the air and something within it. The circle was gone almost immediately, and as it ceased to exist he felt the same pain in his ears, the same sense of suction.

A few seconds later, it happened again.

This time, the circle intersected the main black mass of the hovering Inhibitor machinery. A huge misshapen clot of it fell towards the waves, severed from the rest. Even more of the mass had simply ceased to exist: it was as if everything within the spherical region above him had winked out of existence – not just air, but the Inhibitor machinery occupying the same volume. The limbs attached to the falling chunk thrashed wildly even as it fell. Scorpio sensed it slowing as it neared the surface of the water, but the rate of arrest was not sufficient to bring it to a halt. It hit, submerged, rebounded to the surface. The limbs continued to whip around the main core, threshing the sea.

Khouri leaned towards him. Her lips moved, but her voice was lost under the blood-tide roaring in his ears. He knew what she was saying, though: the three syllables were unmistakable. 'Remontoire.'

He nodded. He didn't need to know the details: it was enough that he had intervened. 'Thank you, Rem,' he said, hearing his own voice as if underwater.

The grey-green mass of the Juggler material was coalescing around the floating, thrashing mass of black machinery. Above, the intruder had begun to pull itself back into the cloud deck, the curved surfaces of its wounds still obvious. Scorpio was beginning to wonder about the other part – whether it would repair itself, shrug off the Juggler biomass and continue to cause them trouble – when it and the Jugglers and an entire hundred-metre-wide hemispherical scoop of sea vanished. He watched as the sloping, seamless wall of water around the absence seemed to freeze there, as if unwilling to reclaim the volume taken away from it. Then it crashed in, a tower of dirty green surging into the air above the epicentre, and an ominous ramp of water sped towards them.

Scorpio tightened his grip on both the boat and the incubator. 'Hold on,' he shouted to Khouri.

TWENTY-FOUR

Ararat, 2675

That night, strange lights appeared in the skies over Ararat. They were vast and schematic, like the blueprints of forbidden constellations. They were unlike any aurorae that the settlers had ever seen.

They began to appear in the twilight hour that followed sundown, in the western sky. There were no clouds to hide the stars, and the moons remained almost as low as they had during the long crossing to the iceberg. The solitary spire of the great ship was a wedge of deeper blackness against the purple twilight, like a glimpse into the true stellar night beyond the veil of Ararat's atmosphere.

No one had any real idea what was causing the lights. Conventional explanations, involving beam weapons interacting with Ararat's upper atmosphere, had proven utterly inadequate. Observations captured by camera from different locations on Ararat established parallactic distances for the shapes of whole fractions of a light-second, well beyond Ararat's ionosphere. Now and then there was something more explicable: the flash of a conventional explosion, or a shower of exotic particles from the grazing lash of some stray beam weapon; occasionally the hard flicker of a drive exhaust or missile plume, or an encrypted burst of comms traffic. But for the most part the war above Ararat was being waged with weapons and methods incomprehensible in their function.

One thing was clear, however: with each passing hour, the lights increased in brightness and complexity. And in the water around the bay, more and more dark shapes crested the waves. They shifted and merged, changing form too rapidly to be fixed by the eye. No sense of purpose was apparent, merely an impression of mindless congregation. The Juggler contact swimmer corps specialists watched nervously, unwilling to step into the sea. And as the lights above became more intense, the changes more frequent, so the shapes in the sea responded with their own quickening tempo.

Ararat's natives, too, were aware that they had visitors.

Grelier took his position in the great hall of the Lady Morwenna, in one of the many seats arranged before the black window. The hall was dim, external metal shutters having been pulled down over all the other stained-glass windows. There were a few electric lights to guide the spectators to their seats, but the only other source of illumination came from candles, vast arrays of them flickering in sconces. They threw a solemn, painterly cast on the proceedings, rendering every face noble, from the highest Clocktower dignitary to the lowliest Motive Power technician. There was, naturally, nothing to be seen of the black window itself, save for a faint suggestion of surrounding masonry.

Grelier surveyed the congregation. Apart from a skeleton staff taking care of essential duties, the entire population of the cathedral must now be present. He knew many of the five thousand people here by name – more than many of them would ever have suspected. Of the others, there were only a few hundred faces that he was not passingly familiar with. It thrilled him to see so many in attendance, especially when he thought of the threads of blood that bound them all. He could almost see it: a rich, red tapestry of connections hanging above the congregation, drapes and banners of scarlet and maroon, simultaneously complex and wondrous.

The thought of blood reminded him of Harbin Els. The young man, as Grelier had told Quaiche, was dead, killed in clearance duties. Their paths had never crossed again after that initial interview on the caravan, even though Grelier had been awake during part of Harbin's period of work in the Lady Morwenna. The Bloodwork processing that Harbin had indeed gone through had been handled by Grelier's assistants rather than the surgeon-general himself. But like all the blood that was collected by the cathedral, his sample had been catalogued and stored in the Lady Morwenna's blood vaults. Now that the girl had re-entered his life, Grelier had taken the expedient step of recalling Harbin's sample from the library and running a detailed assay on it.

It was a long shot, but worth his trouble. A question had occurred to Grelier: was the girl's gift a learned thing, or innate? And if it was innate, was there something in her DNA that had activated it? He knew that only one in a thousand people had the gift for recognising and interpreting microexpressions; that fewer still had it to the same degree as Rashmika Els. It could be learned, certainly, but people like

Rashmika didn't need any training: they just knew the rules, with absolute conviction. They had the observational equivalent of perfect pitch. To them, the strange thing was that everyone else failed to pick up on the same signs. But that didn't mean the gift was some mysterious superhuman endowment. The gift was socially debilitating. The afflicted could never be told a consoling lie. If they were ugly and someone told them they were beautiful, the gap between intention and effect was all the more hurtful because it was so obvious, so stingingly sarcastic.

He had searched the cathedral's records, scanning centuries-old medical literature for anything on genetic predisposition to the girl's condition. But the records were frustratingly incomplete. There was much on cloning and life-extension, but very little on the genetic markers for hypersensitivity to facial microexpression.

Nonetheless, he had still gone to the trouble of analysing Harbin's blood sample, looking for anything unusual or anomalous, preferably in the genes that were associated with the brain's perceptual centres. Harbin could not have had the gift to anything like the same degree as his sister, but that in itself would be interesting. If there were no significant differences in their genes beyond the normal variations seen between non-identical siblings, then Rashmika's gift would begin to look like something acquired rather than inherited. A fluke of development, perhaps, something in her early environment that nurtured the gift. If something did show up, on the other hand, then he might be able to map the mismatched genes to specific areas of brain function. The literature suggested that people with brain damage could acquire the skill as a compensatory mechanism when they lost the ability to process speech. If that was the case, and if the important brain regions could be identified, then it might even be possible to introduce the condition by surgical intervention. Grelier's imagination was freewheeling: he was thinking of installing neural blockades in Quaiche's skull, little valves and dams that could be opened and closed remotely. Isolate the right brain regions – make them light up or dim, depending on function – and it might even be possible to turn the skill on and off. The thought thrilled him. What a gift for a negotiator, to be able to choose when you wished to see through the lies of those around you.

But for now he only had a sample from the brother. The tests had revealed no striking anomalies, nothing that would have made the sample stand out had he not already had a prior interest in the family. Perhaps that supported the hypothesis that the skill was acquired. He would not know for certain until he had some blood from Rashmika Els.

The quaestor had been useful, of course. With the right persuasion, it wouldn't have been difficult to find a way to get a sample from Rashmika. But why risk derailing a process that was already rolling smoothly towards its conclusion? The letter had already had precisely the desired effect. She had interpreted it as a forgery, designed to warn her off the trail. She had seen through the quaestor's fumbling explanation for the letter's existence. It had only strengthened her resolve.

Grelier smiled to himself. No; he could wait. She would be here very shortly, and then he would have his blood.

As much of it as he needed.

At that moment a hush fell on proceedings. He looked around, watching Quaiche slide down the aisle in his moving pulpit. The upright black structure made a faint trundling sound as it approached. Quaiche remained in his life-support couch, tilted nearly to vertical and carried atop the pulpit. Even as he moved down the aisle, the light from Haldora was still reaching his eyes. An elaborate system of jointed tubes and mirrors conveyed it all the way down from the Clocktower. Robed technicians followed behind the pulpit, adjusting the tubes with long clawed poles. In the dim light, Quaiche's sunglasses were gone, revealing the painful framework of the eye-opener.

For many of those present – certainly those who had arrived in the Lady Morwenna in the last two or three years – this might well be the first time they had ever seen Quaiche in person. It was very rare for him to descend from the Clocktower these days. Rumours of his death had been circulating for decades, barely checked by each increasingly infrequent appearance.

The pulpit swung around and moved along the front of the congregation before coming to a halt immediately below the black window. Quaiche had his back to it, facing the audience. In the candlelight he appeared to be a chiselled outgrowth of the pulpit itself. In bas-relief, vacuum-suited saints supported him from below.

'My people,' he said, 'let us rejoice. This is a day of wonders, of opportunity in adversity.' His voice was the usual smoky croak, but amplified and enhanced by hidden microphones. From high above, the organ provided a rumbling, almost subsonic counterpoint to Quaiche's oration.

'For twenty-two days we have been approaching the impasse in the Gullveig canyon, slowing our speed, allowing Haldora to slip ahead of us, but never actually stopping. We had hoped that the blockage would be cleared twelve or thirteen days ago. If it had, we would have lost no ground. But the obstruction proved more challenging than we had feared. Conventional clearance measures proved ineffective. Good men died surveying the problem, and yet more lives were lost in planting the demolition charges. I need hardly remind anyone present that this is a delicate business: the Way itself must remain substantially undamaged once the main obstruction is cleared.' He paused, the circular frames around his eyes catching the candlelight and flaring the colour of brass. 'But now the dangerous work is done. The charges are in place.'

At that moment, the choir and the organ swelled in unison. Grelier's hand was tight on the head of his cane. He squinted, knowing exactly what was coming.

'Behold God's Fire,' Quaiche intoned.

The black window flared with wonderful light. Through each chip and facet of glass rammed a tangible shaft of colour, each shaft so intense and pure that it slammed Grelier back to a nursery world of bright shapes and colours. He felt the chemical seepage of joy into his brain, struggling to resist it even as he felt his resolve crumbling.

Before the window, Quaiche stood silhouetted on the pulpit. His arms were raised, spindly as branches. Grelier narrowed his eyes even more, trying to make out the pattern revealed in the black window. He was just beginning to tease it out when the shockwave hit, making the whole cathedral shake. Candles fluttered and died, the suspended chandeliers swaying.

The window faded to black. An afterimage remained, however: a rendering of Quaiche himself, kneeling before the iron monstrosity of the scrimshaw suit. The suit was hinged open along the once-welded seam. Quaiche's hands were cupped before him, lathered in a cloying red mass that extended tendrils and ropes back into the cavity of the scrimshaw suit. It was as if he had reached into the suit and drawn out that sticky red mess. Quaiche's face was turned to heaven, to the banded globe of Haldora.

But it wasn't Haldora as Grelier had ever seen it portrayed.

The afterimage was fading. Grelier began to wonder if he would have to wait until the next blockage to see the window again, but another demolition burst followed the first, again revealing the design. Worked into the face of Haldora, conspiring to look as if it was shining through the atmospheric bands of the gas giant, was a geometric pattern. It was very complicated, like the intricate wax seal of an emperor: a three-dimensional lattice of silver beams. At the heart of the lattice, radiating beams of light, was a single human eye.

Another shockwave came through, rocking the Lady Morwenna. One final detonation followed and then the show was over. The black window was again black, its facets too opaque to be illuminated by anything other than the nuclear brilliance of God's own Fire.

The organ and the choir subsided.

'The Way may now be cleared,' Quaiche said. 'It will not be easy, but we will now be able to proceed at normal Way speeds for several days. There may even have to be more demolition charges, but the bulk of the obstacle no longer exists. For this we thank God. But the time we have lost cannot be easily recovered.'

Grelier's hand was again tight on the cane.

'Let the other cathedrals attempt to make up lost time,' Quaiche said. 'They will struggle. Yes, the Jarnsaxa Flats lie before us, and the race there will be to the swift. The Lady Morwenna is not the fastest cathedral on the Way, nor has it ever sought that worthless accolade. But what is the point of trying to make up lost ground on the Flats when the Devil's Staircase lies just beyond it? Normally we would be trying to have time in hand at this point, pulling ahead of Haldora in preparation for the slow and difficult navigation of the Staircase. This time we do not have that luxury. We have lost critical days when we can least afford to lose them.'

He waited a moment, knowing that he had the congregation's terrified attention. 'But there is another way,' Quaiche said, leaning forwards in the pulpit, almost threatening to topple out of the support couch. 'One that will require daring, and faith. We do not have to take the Devil's Staircase at all. There is another route across Ginnungagap Rift. You all know, of course, of what I speak.'

All around the cathedral, transmitted through its armoured fabric, Grelier heard the rattling as the external shutters were drawn up. The ordinary stained-glass windows were being reopened, light flooding through them in sequenced order. Ordinarily he would have been duly impressed, but the memory of the black window was still there, its afterimage still ghosting his vision. When you had seen nuclear fire through welding glass, all else was as pale as watercolour.

'God gave us a bridge,' Quaiche said. 'I believe it is time we used it.'

Rashmika found herself drawn to the roof of the caravan again, crossing between the vehicles until she reached the tilted rack of the

Observers. The identical smooth mirrors of their faces, neatly spaced and ranked, had taken on a peculiar abstract quality. They made her think of the bottoms of stacked bottles in a cellar, or the arrayed facets of one of the gamma-ray monitoring stations out near the edge of the badlands. She did not know whether she found this more or less comforting than the realisation that each was a distinct human being – or had been, at least, until their compulsion to gaze at Haldora had scoured the last stubborn trace of personality from their minds.

The caravan rocked and rolled, negotiating a stretch of road that had only recently been reclaimed from icefalls. Now and then – more often, it seemed, than a day or so before – they swerved to steer past a group of pilgrims making the journey on foot. The pilgrims looked tiny and stupid, so far below. The fortunate ones had closed-cycle vacuum suits that permitted long journeys across the surface of a planet. Some of the suits even tended to ailments, healing minor wounds or soothing arthritic joints. Certainly those were the lucky ones. The rest had to make do with suits that had never been designed for travelling more than a few kilometres unassisted. They trudged beneath the weight of bulky home-made backpacks, like peasants carrying all their possessions. Some of them had ended up with such grotesque contraptions that they had no choice but to haul their belongings and their makeshift life-support systems behind them, on skis or treads. The suits, helmets, backpacks and towed contraptions were all augmented with religious totems, often of a cumbersome nature. There were golden statues, crosses, pagodas, demons, snakes, swords, armoured knights, dragons, sea monsters, arks and a hundred other things Rashmika did not trouble herself to recognise. Everything was done by muscle power, without the succour of mechanical assistance. Even in Hela's moderate gravity the pilgrims were bent double with the effort, every sliding footstep a study in exhaustion.

Something drew her eye, far to what she judged to be the south. She looked sharply in that direction, but caught only a fading nimbus: a blue-violet glow retreating behind the nearest line of hills.

A moment later, she saw another flash in the same direction. It was as sharp and quick as an eye-blink, but it left the same dying aura.

A third. Then nothing.

She had no definite idea of what the flashes had been, but she guessed that the direction she was looking in could not be far from the position on the Permanent Way currently occupied by the cathedrals. Perhaps she had witnessed part of the clearing operation of which the quaestor had spoken.

Now something else was happening, but this time much nearer. The rack on which the Observers were mounted was tilting, lowering itself down towards the horizontal. At an angle of about thirty degrees it halted, and with one eerily smooth movement the Observers all sat up, their shackles unlocked. The suddenness of the motion quite startled Rashmika. It was like the co-ordinated rising of an army of somnambulists.

Something brushed past her – not forcefully, but not exactly gently either. Then another something.

She was being passed by a procession of the same hooded pilgrims. She looked back and saw that there was a long line of them approaching the rack. They were emerging from a trapdoor in the roof of the caravan, one she had not noticed earlier. At the same time, the ones that had been on the rack were filing off it one row at a time, stepping down the gentle slope with synchronised movements. As they reached the roof of the caravan they made their own line, winding back around the rack and vanishing down another trapdoor. Even before the rack was fully vacated, the new batch of Observers were taking their positions: lying flat on their backs, buckling in. The entire shift change took perhaps two minutes, and was executed with such a degree of manic calm that it was difficult to see how it could have been completed any more quickly. Rashmika had the impression that blood had been spilled over every second of that shift change, for here was a hiatus during which Haldora remained unobserved. This was not quite true, she realised then, for she saw no sign of similar activity anywhere else along the caravan: the other racks were still tilted at their usual observation angles. Doubtless the shift changes were staggered so that at least one group of Observers would be sure to witness a Haldora vanishing.

Until now, it had not occurred to her that the Observers would spend any time off the rack. But here they were, filing obediently back into the caravan. She wondered if this was because there were too many Observers to go around, or whether they needed to be taken off the rack now and then for their own health.

Doubtless the sequence of distant flashes had been a coincidence, but it had served to underscore the shift change in a way that Rashmika found faintly unsettling. The last time she had been up here she had felt as if she was spying on a sacred ceremony. Now she felt as if she had been caught in the middle of it, and had in some way marred the sanctity of the ritual.

The last of the new batch of Observers had assumed their positions on the rack. Though they had bustled past her, there was no obvious sign that she had spoiled their timing. Now the rack itself was tilting back to the same slope as the others along the line of the caravan, angling to face Haldora.

Rashmika turned around to watch the last of the old shift vanish back into the machine. There were three left, then two, and then the last one disappeared down into the hole. Where the new shift had emerged the trapdoor was now sealed, but the other one remained open.

Rashmika looked up at the Observers on the rack. They seemed utterly indifferent to her presence now, if indeed they had really noticed her at all. Perhaps they had only registered her as a minor obstacle on the way to their duty.

She began to make her way to the open trapdoor. All the while she kept an eye on the rack, but at its present angle it would have been almost impossible for anyone on it to see her at all, even in peripheral vision, and especially not given the fact that they were wearing helmets and hoods.

She had no intention of going down the trapdoor. At the same time she was hugely curious to see what was below. A glimpse would suffice. She might see nothing, just a laddered tube leading somewhere else, perhaps to an airlock. Or she might see ... well, her imagination drew a blank. But she could not help but picture rows of Observers, hooked into machines, being refreshed in time for another shift.

The caravan swayed and bumped. She steadied herself on a railing, expecting any moment that the trapdoor would be tugged shut from within. She hesitated to go any nearer. The Observers had appeared docile so far, but how would they react to an invasion of their territory? She knew next to nothing about their sect. Maybe they had an elaborate series of death penalties lined up for those who violated their secrets. A thought crossed her mind: what if Harbin had done exactly what she was about to do? She was a lot like her brother. She could easily imagine Harbin killing time by wandering around the caravan, stumbling into the same shift change, being driven by his natural curiosity to see what was down below. Another thought, even less welcome, chased the first: what if one of the Observers was Harbin?

She pushed forwards until she reached the lip of the trapdoor. It still had not closed. Warm red light spilled up from the depths.

Rashmika steadied herself again, making certain she could not fall over the edge if the caravan made another sharp swerve. She peered into the shaft and saw a simple ladder descending as far as her angle of vision allowed her to see. To look deeper, she would have to lean further out.

Rashmika stretched, letting go of her hand-hold to make the move. She could see a little further into the hole now. The ladder terminated against grilled flooring. There was a hatch or doorway leading further into the caravan – one end of an airlock, perhaps, unless the Observers spent their entire lives in vacuum.

The caravan lurched. Rashmika felt herself tip forwards. She flailed, reaching back for the support railing. Her fingers clasped empty space. She tilted further forwards. The hole yawned bigger, the shaft suddenly appearing much wider and deeper than it had an instant ago. Rashmika started to cry out, certain that she was about to fall in. The ladder was on the wrong side; there was no way she was going to be able to grab it.

But suddenly she was still. Something – someone – held her. The person pulled her gently back from the edge of the trapdoor. Rashmika's heart was in her throat. She had never understood what people meant when they said that, but now the expression made perfect sense to her.

Looking up into the face of her benefactor, she saw her own mirrored faceplate reflected back at her, and a smaller reflection in that, dwindling all the way to some vague, not too distant vanishing point. Behind the hooded mirror, faintly visible, was a suggestion of a young man's face. Cheekbones, caught sharply in the light. Slowly, but unmistakably, he shook his head.

Almost as soon as this realisation had dawned, Rashmika was on her own again. The Observer moved around to the side of the shaft where the ladder was and slipped nimbly over the side and then down. Still catching her breath after the shock of nearly falling, Rashmika moved sluggishly to the edge, arriving just in time to see the Observer operate some lever-driven mechanism that brought the trapdoor down. Once snugly in its frame, the door twisted through ninety degrees.

She was on her own again.

Rashmika stood up, shaky on her feet. She felt foolish and irresponsible. How careless she had been to allow herself to be saved by one of the pilgrims. And how unwise to assume that they did not perceive her at all. It was obvious now, crushingly so. They had always been aware of her but had simply chosen to ignore her as best they could. When, finally, she had done something that could not be ignored – something idiotic, it had to be said – they had intervened quickly and sternly, the way adults did around children. She had been put right without reprimand or caution, but the sense of indignity remained. Rashmika had little experience with rebuke, and the sensation was both novel and unpleasant.

Something snapped in her then. She knelt down on the armoured trapdoor and pounded it with her fists. She wanted the Observer to come back up and make some explanation for why he had shaken his head. She wanted him to apologise, to make her feel as if she had done nothing wrong by spying on their ritual. She wanted him to purge her guilt, to take it upon himself. She wanted absolution.

She kept knocking on the door, but nothing happened. The caravan rumbled on. The racked Observers maintained their tireless scrutiny of Haldora. Finally, humbled and humiliated, feeling even more foolish than she had when the man had saved her, Rashmika stood up and went back across the roof of the machine to her own part of the caravan. Inside her helmet she cried at her own weakness, wondering why she had ever imagined she had the strength or courage to see her quest through to the end.

Ararat, 2675

'Do you believe in coincidences?' asked the swimmer.

'I don't know,' Vasko said. He stood at a window in the High Conch, a hundred metres above the grid of night-time streets. His hands were laced neatly behind his back, his booted feet set slightly apart, his spine straight. He had heard that there was to be a meeting here, and that he would not be prevented from attending. No one had explained why it was taking place in the conch structure rather than the supposedly more secure environment of the ship.

He looked out beyond the land to the ribbon of water between the shore and the dark spire of the ship. The Juggler activity had not lessened, but there was, strangely, a swathe of calm water reaching out into the bay like a tongue. The shapes festered on either side of it, but between them the water had the smooth cast of molten metal. The moving lanterns of boats meandered away from land, navigating that strip. They were sailing in the direction of the ship, strung out in a ragged, bobbing procession. It was as if the Jugglers were giving them clear passage.

'Rumours spread fast,' the swimmer said. 'You've heard, haven't you?'

'About Clavain and the girl?'

'Not just that. The ship. They say it's started to come alive again. The neutrino detectors – you know about those?' She didn't wait for his answer. 'They're registering a surge in the engine cores. After twenty-three years, they're warming. The ship's thinking about leaving.'

'No one told it to.'

'No one has to. It's got a mind of its own. Question is, are we better off being on it when it leaves, or halfway around Ararat? We know there's a battle going on up there now, even if we didn't all believe that woman's story at first.'

'Not much doubt about it now,' Vasko said, 'and the Jugglers seem to have made up their minds as well. They're letting those people reach the ship. They *want* them to reach safety.'

'Maybe they just don't want them to drown,' the swimmer said. 'Maybe they're simply humouring whatever decision we make. Maybe none of it matters to them.'

Her name was Pellerin and he knew her from the earlier meeting aboard the *Nostalgia for Infinity*. She was a tall woman with the usual swimmer's build. She had a handsome, strong-boned face with a high brow, and her hair was slicked back and glossy with perfumed oils, as if she had just emerged from the sea. What he took at first glance to be freckles across her cheeks and the bridge of her nose were in fact pale-green fungal markings. Swimmers had to keep an eye on those markings. They indicated that the sea was taking a liking to them, invading them, breaking down the barriers between vastly different organisms. Sooner or later, it was said, the sea would snatch them as a prize, dissolving them into the Pattern Juggler matrix.

Swimmers made much of that. They liked to play on the risks they took each time they entered the ocean, especially when they were senior swimmers like Pellerin.

'It's quite possible they do want them to make it to safety,' Vasko said. 'Why don't you swim and find out for yourselves?'

'We never swim when it's like this.'

Vasko laughed. 'Like this? It's *never* been like this, Pellerin.'

'We don't swim when the Jugglers are so agitated,' she said. 'They're not predictable, like one of your scraping machines. We've lost swimmers before, especially when they've been wild, like they are now.'

'I'd have thought the circumstances outweighed the risks,' he said. 'But then what do I know? I just work in the food factories.'

'If you were a swimmer, Malinin, you'd certainly know better than to swim on a night like this.'

'You're probably right,' he said.

'Meaning what?'

He thought of the sacrifice that had been made today. The scale of that gesture was still too large for him to take in. He had begun to map it, to comprehend some of its essential vastness, but there were still moments when abysses opened before him, reaching into unsuspected depths of courage and selflessness. He did not think a lifetime would be enough to diminish what he had experienced in the iceberg.

Clavain's death would always be there, like a piece of shrapnel buried inside him, its sharp foreign presence felt with every breath.

'Meaning,' he said, 'that if I were more concerned about my own wellbeing than the security of Ararat ... then, yes, I might have second thoughts about swimming.'

'You insolent little prick, Malinin. You have no idea.'

'You're wrong,' he said, with sudden venom, 'I have every idea. What I witnessed today is something you can thank God you didn't have to experience. I know what it means to be brave, Pellerin. I know what it means and I wish I didn't.'

'I heard it was Clavain who was the brave one,' she said.

'Did I say otherwise?'

'You make it sound as if it was you.'

'I was there,' he said. 'That was enough.'

There was a forced calm in her voice. 'I'll forgive you this, Malinin. I know you all went though something awful out there. It must have messed with your mind pretty badly. But I've seen my two best friends drown before my eyes. I've watched another two dissolve into the sea and I've seen six end up in the psychiatric camp, where they spend their days drooling and scratching marks on to the walls with the blood from their fingertips. One of them was my lover. Her name is Shizuko. I visit her there now and when she looks at me she just laughs and goes back to her drawings. I have about as much personal significance for her as the weather.' Pellerin's eyes flashed wide. 'So don't give me a lecture about bravery, all right? We've all seen things we'd sooner forget.'

Her calm had undermined his own furious sense of self-right-eousness. He was, he realised, shaking. 'I'm sorry,' he said quietly. 'I shouldn't have said that.'

'Just get over it,' she said. 'And never, ever tell me that we don't have the guts to swim when you don't know a damned thing about us.'

Pellerin left him. He stood alone, his thoughts in turmoil. He could still see the line of boats, each lantern now fractionally further out from the shoreline.

TWENTY-FIVE

Ararat, 2675

Vasko slipped an anonymous brown coat over his Security Arm uniform, descended the High Conch and walked unobserved into the night.

As he stepped outside he felt a tension in the air, like the nervous stillness that presaged an electrical storm. The crowds moved through the narrow, twisting defiles of the streets in boisterous surges. There was a macabre carnival atmosphere about the lantern-lit assembly, but no one was shouting or laughing; all that he heard was the low hum of a thousand voices, seldom raised above a normal speaking level.

He did not much blame them for their reaction. Towards the end of the afternoon there had been only one curt official statement on the matter of Clavain's death, and it now seemed unlikely that there was any part of the colony that hadn't heard that news. The surge of people into the streets had begun even before sundown and the arrival of the lights in the sky. Rightly, they sensed that there was something missing from the official statement. There had been no mention of Khouri or the child, no mention of the battle taking place in near-Ararat space, merely a promise that more information would be circulated in the fullness of time.

The ragtag procession of boats had begun shortly afterwards. Now there was a small braid of bobbing lights at the very base of the ship, and more boats were continually leaving the shore. Security Arm officers were doing their best to keep the boats from leaving the colony, but it was a battle they could not hope to win. The Arm had never been intended to cope with massive civil disobedience, and the best that Vasko's colleagues could do was impede the exodus. Elsewhere, there were reports of disturbances, fires and looting, with the Arm regulars having to make arrests. The Juggler activity – whatever it signified – continued unabated.

Vasko was grateful to find himself relieved of any scheduled duties. Wandering through the crowds, his own part in the day's events not yet revealed, he listened to the rumours that were already in circulation. The simple kernel of truth – that Clavain had been killed in an ultimately successful action to safeguard a vital colonial asset – had accreted many layers of speculation and untruth. Some of the rumours were extraordinary in their ingenuity, in the details they posited for the circumstances of the old man's death.

Pretending ignorance, Vasko stopped little groups of people at random and asked them what was going on. He made sure no one saw his uniform and also that none of the groups contained people likely to recognise him from work or his social circles.

What he heard disgusted him. He listened earnestly to graphic descriptions of gunfights and bomb plots, subterfuge and sabotage. It amazed and appalled him to discover how easily these stories had been spun out of nothing more than the fact of Clavain's death. It was as if the crowd itself was manifesting a sly, sick collective imagination.

Equally distressing was the eagerness of those listening to accept the stories, bolstering the accounts with their own interjected suggestions for how events had probably proceeded. Later, eavesdropping elsewhere, Vasko observed that these embellishments had been seamlessly embroidered into the main account. It did not seem to bother anyone that many of the stories were contradictory, or at best difficult to reconcile with the same set of events. More than once, with incredulity, he heard that Scorpio or some other colony senior had died alongside Clavain. The fact that some of those individuals had already appeared in public to make short, calming speeches counted for nothing. With a sinking feeling, a cavernous resignation, Vasko realised that even if he were to start recounting events exactly as they had happened, his own version would have no more immediate currency than any of the lies now doing the rounds. He hadn't actually witnessed the death himself, so even if he told the truth of things it would still only be from his point of view, and his story would of necessity have a damning taint of second-hand reportage about it. It would be dismissed, its content unpalatable, the details too vague.

Tonight, the people wanted an unequivocal hero. By some mysterious self-organising process of story creation, that was precisely what they were going to get.

He was shouldering his way through the lantern-carrying mob when he heard his own name called out.

'Malinin.'

It took him a moment to locate the source of the voice in the crowd. A woman was standing in a little circle of stillness. The rabble flowed around her, never once violating the immediate volume of private space she had defined. She wore a long-hemmed black coat, the collar an explosion of black fur, the black peak of an unmarked cap obscuring the upper part of her face.

'Urton?' he asked, doubtfully.

'It's me,' she said, stepping nearer to him. 'I guess you got the night off as well. Why aren't you at home resting?'

There was something in her tone that made him defensive. In her presence he still felt that he was continually being measured and found wanting.

'I could ask you the same question.'

'Because I know there wouldn't be any point. Not after what happened out there.'

Provisionally, he decided to go along with this pretence at civility. He wondered where it was going to lead him. 'I did try to sleep this afternoon,' he said, 'but all I heard were screams. All I saw was blood and ice.'

'You weren't even in there when it happened.'

'I know. So imagine what it must be like for Scorpio.'

Now that Urton was next to him he shared the same little pocket of quiet that she had defined. He wondered how she did it. He did not think it very likely that the people flowing around them had any idea who Urton was. They must have sensed something about her: an electric prickle of foreboding.

'I feel sorry for what he had to do,' Urton said.

'I'm not sure how he's going to take it, in the long run. They were very close friends.'

'I know that.'

'It wasn't just any old friendship,' Vasko replied. 'Clavain saved Scorpio's life once, when he was due to be executed. There was a bond between them that went right back to Chasm City. I don't think there was anyone else on this planet that Clavain respected quite as much as Scorpio. And Scorpio also knew that. I went with him to the island where Clavain was waiting. I saw them talking together. It wasn't the way I'd imagined it to be. They were more like two old adventurers who'd seen a lot of the same things, and knew no one else quite understood them.'

'Scorpio isn't that old.'

'He is,' Vasko said. 'For a pig, anyway.'

Urton led him through the crowd, towards the shore. The crowd began to thin out, and a warm night breeze salted with brine made his eyes tingle. Overhead, the strange lights etched arcane motifs from horizon to horizon. It was less like a firework display or aurora and more like a vast, painstaking geometry lesson.

'You're worried it'll have done something to him, aren't you?' Urton asked.

'How would you take it if you had to murder your best friend in cold blood? And slowly, with an audience?'

'I don't think I'd take it too well. But then I'm not Scorpio.'

'What's that supposed to mean?'

'He's led us competently while Clavain was away, Vasko, and I know that you think well of him, but that doesn't make him an angel. You already said that the pig and Clavain went all the way back to Chasm City.'

Vasko watched lights slide across the zenith, trailing annular rings like the pattern he sometimes saw when he pressed his fingertips against his own closed eyelids. 'Yes,' he said, grudgingly.

'Well, what do you think Scorpio was doing in Chasm City in the first place? It wasn't feeding the needy and the poor. He was a criminal, a murderer.'

'He broke the law in a time when the law was brutal and inhuman,' Vasko said. 'That's not quite the same thing, is it?'

'So there was a war on. I've studied the same history books as you have. Yes, the emergency rule verged on the Draconian, but does that excuse murder? We're not just talking about self-preservation or self-interest here. Scorpio killed for sport.'

'He was enslaved and tortured by humans,' Vasko said. 'And humans made him what he is: a genetic dead end.'

'So that lets him off the hook?'

'I don't quite see where you're going with this, Urton.'

'All I'm saying is, Scorpio isn't the thin-skinned individual you like to think. Yes, I'm sure he's upset by what he did to Clavain ...'

'What he was *made* to do,' Vasko corrected.

'Whatever. The point is the same: he'll get over it, just like he got over every other atrocity he perpetrated.' She lifted the peak of her cap, scrutinising him, her eyes flicking from point to point as if alert for any betraying facial tics. 'You believe that, don't you?'

'Right now I'm not sure.'

'You have to believe it, Vasko.' He noticed that she had stopped calling him Malinin. 'Because the alternative is to doubt his fitness for leadership. You wouldn't go that far, would you?'

'No, of course not. I've got total faith in his leadership. Ask anyone here tonight and you'll get the same answer. And guess what? We're all right.'

'Of course we are.'

'What about you, Urton? Do you doubt him?'

'Not in the slightest,' she said. 'Frankly, I doubt that he'll have lost much sleep at all over anything that happened today.'

'That sounds incredibly callous.'

'I want it to be callous. I want *him* to be callous. That's the point. It's exactly what we want – what we need – in a leader now. Don't you agree?'

'I don't know,' he said, feeling a huge weariness begin to slide over him. 'All I know is that I didn't come out here tonight to talk about what happened today. I came out here to clear my head and try to forget some of it.'

'So did I,' Urton said. Her voice had softened. 'I'm sorry. I didn't mean to rake over what happened. I suppose talking about it is my way of coping with it. It was pretty harrowing for all of us.'

'Yes, it was. Are you done now?' He felt his temper rising, a scarlet tide lapping against the defences of civility. 'For most of yesterday and today you looked as if you couldn't stand to be in the same hemisphere as me, let alone the same room. Why the sudden change of heart?'

'Because I regret the way I acted,' she said.

'If you don't mind my saying, it's a little late in the day for second thoughts.'

'It's the way I cope, Vasko. Cut me some slack, all right? There was nothing personal about it.'

'Well, that makes me feel a lot better.'

'We were going into a dangerous situation. We were all trained for it. We all knew each other, and we all knew we could count on each other. And then you show up at the last minute, someone I don't know, yet whom I'm suddenly expected to trust with my life. I can name a dozen SA officers who could have taken your position in that boat, any one of whom I'd have felt happier about covering my back.'

Vasko saw that she was leading him towards the shore, where the crowd thinned out. The dark shapes of boats blocked the gloom between land and water. Some were moored ready for departure, some were aground.

'Scorpio chose to include me in the mission,' Vasko said. 'Once that decision was taken, you should have had the guts to live with it. Or didn't you trust his judgement?'

'One day you'll be in my shoes, Vasko, and you won't like it any more than I did. Come and give me a lecture about trusting judgement then, and see how convincing it sounds.' Urton paused, watching the sky as a thin scarlet line transected it from horizon to horizon. She had evaded his question. 'This is all coming out wrong. I didn't pick you out of the crowd to start another fight. I wanted to say I was sorry. I also wanted you to understand why I'd acted the way I did.'

He kept the lid on his anger. 'All right.'

'And I admit I was wrong.'

'You weren't to know what was about to happen,' he said.

She shrugged and sighed. 'No, I don't suppose I was. No matter what they say, he walked the walk, didn't he? When it came to putting his life on the line, he went and did it.'

They had reached the line of boats. Most of those still left on land were wrecks: their hulls had gaping holes in them near the waterline, where they had been consumed by seaborne organisms. Sooner or later they would have been hauled away to the smelting plant, to be remade into new craft. The metalworkers were fastidious about reusing every possible scrap of recyclable metal. But the amount recovered would never have been equal to that in the original boats.

'Look,' Urton said, pointing across the bay.

Vasko nodded. 'I know. They've already encircled the base of the ship.'

'That's not what I mean. Look a bit higher, Hawkeye. Can you see them?'

'Yes,' he said after a moment. 'Yes. My God. They'll never make it.'

They were tiny sparks of light around the base of the ship, slightly higher than the bobbing ring of boats Vasko had already noticed. He estimated that they could not have climbed more than a few dozen metres above the sea. There were thousands of metres of the ship above them.

'How are they climbing?' Vasko said.

'Hand over hand, I guess. You've seen what that thing looks like close-up, haven't you? It's like a crumbling cliff wall, full of handholds and ledges. It's probably not that difficult.'

'But the nearest way in must be hundreds of metres above the sea, maybe more. When the planes come and go they always land near the top.' Again he said, 'They'll never make it. They're insane.'

'They're not insane,' Urton said. 'They're just scared. Really, really scared. The question is, should we be joining them?'

Vasko said nothing. He was watching one of the tiny sparks of light fall back towards the sea.

They stood and watched the spectacle for many minutes. Nobody else appeared to fall, but the other climbers continued their relentless slow ascent undaunted by the failure that many of them had doubtless witnessed. Around the sheer footslopes, where the boats must have been rocking and crashing against the hull, new climbers were beginning their ascent. Boats were returning from the ship, scudding slowly back across the bay, but progress was slow and tension was rising amongst those waiting on the shoreline. The Security Arm officials were increasingly outnumbered by the angry and frightened people who were waiting for passage to the ship. Vasko saw one of the SA men speaking urgently into his wrist communicator, obviously calling for assistance. He had almost finished talking when someone shoved him to the ground.

'We should do something,' Vasko said.

'We're off duty, and two of us aren't enough to make a difference. They'll have to think of something different. It's not as if they're going to be able to contain this for much longer. I don't think I want to be here any more.' She meant the shoreline. 'I checked the reports before I came out. Things aren't so bad east of the High Conch. I'm hungry and I could use a drink. Do you want to join me?'

'I don't have much of an appetite,' Vasko said. He had actually been starting to feel hungry again until he saw the person fall into the sea. 'But a drink wouldn't go amiss. Are you sure there'll be somewhere still open?'

'I know a few places we can try,' Urton said.

'You know the area better than me, in that case.'

'Your problem is you don't get out enough,' she said. She pulled up the collar of her coat, then crunched down her hat. 'Come on. Let's get out of here before things turn nasty.'

She turned out to be right about the zone of the settlement east of the Conch. Many Arm members lodged there, so the area had always had a tradition of loyalty to the administration. Now there was a sullen, reproachful calm about the place. The streets were no busier than they usually were at this time of night, and although many premises were closed, the bar Urton had in mind was still open.

Urton led him through the main room to an alcove containing two chairs and a table poached from Central Amenities. Above the alcove a screen was tuned to the administration news service, but at the moment all it was showing was a picture of Clavain's face. The picture had been taken only a few years earlier, but it might as well have been centuries ago. The man Vasko had known in the last couple of days had looked twice as old, twice as eroded by time and circumstance. Beneath Clavain's face was a pair of calendar dates about five hundred years apart.

'I'll fetch us some beers,' Urton said, not giving him a chance to argue. She had removed her coat and hat, piling them on the chair opposite his.

Vasko watched her recede into the gloom of the bar. He supposed she was a regular here. On their way to the alcove he had seen several faces he thought he half-recognised from SA training. Some of them had been smoking seaweed – the particular variety which when dried and prepared in a certain way induced mild narcotic effects. Vasko remembered the stuff from his training. It was illegal, but easier to get hold of than the black market cigarettes which were said to originate from some dwindling cache in the belly of the *Nostalgia for Infinity*.

By the time Urton returned, Vasko had removed his coat. She put the beers down in front of him. Cautiously Vasko tasted his. The stuff in the glass had an unpleasant urinal tint. Produced from another variety of seaweed, it was only beer in the very loosest sense of the word.

'I talked to Draygo,' she said, 'the man who runs this place. He says the Security Arm officers on duty just went and punched holes in all the boats on the shore. No one else is being allowed to leave, and as soon as a boat returns, they impound it and arrest anyone on board.'

Vasko sipped at his beer. 'Nice to see they haven't resorted to heavy-handed tactics, then.'

'You can't really blame them. They say three people have already drowned just crossing the bay. Another two have fallen off the ship while climbing.'

'I suppose you're right, but it seems to me that the people should have the right to do what they like, even if it kills them.'

'They're worried about mass panic. Sooner or later someone is bound to try swimming it, and then you might have hundreds of people following after. How many do you think would make it?'

'Let them,' Vasko said. 'So what if they drown? So what if they contaminate the Jugglers? Does anyone honestly think it makes a shred of difference now?'

'We've maintained social order on Ararat for more than twenty years,' Urton said. 'We can't let it go to hell in a handcart in one night. Those people using the boats are taking irreplaceable colony property without authorisation. It's unfair on the citizens who don't want to flee to the ship.'

'But we're not giving them an alternative. They've been told Clavain's dead, but no one's told them what those lights in the sky are all about. Is it any wonder they're scared?'

'You think telling them about the war would make things any better?'

Vasko wiped his mouth with the back of his hand, where the seaweed beer had left a white rime. 'I don't know, but I'm fed up with everyone being lied to just because the administration thinks it's in our best interests not to know all the facts. The same thing happened with Clavain when he disappeared. Scorpio and the others decided we couldn't deal with the fact that Clavain was suicidal, so they made up some story about him going around the world. Now they don't think the people can deal with knowing *how* he died, or what it was all for in the first place, so they're not telling anyone anything.'

'You think Scorpio should be taking a firmer lead?'

'I respect Scorpio,' Vasko said, 'but where is he now, when we need him?'

'You're not the only one wondering that,' Urton said.

Something caught Vasko's eye. The picture on the screen had changed. Clavain's face was gone, replaced for a moment by the administration logo. Urton turned around in her seat, still drinking her beer.

'Something's happening,' she said.

The logo flickered and vanished. They were looking at Scorpio, surrounded by the curved rose-pink interior of the High Conch. The pig wore his usual unofficial uniform of padded black leather, the squat dome of his head a largely neckless outgrowth of his massive barrelled torso.

'You knew this was going to happen, didn't you?' Vasko asked.

'Draygo told me he'd heard that there was an announcement scheduled for around this time. But I don't know what it'll be about and I didn't know Scorpio was going to show his face.'

The pig was speaking. Vasko was about to find a way to make the screen louder when Scorpio's voice rang out loudly throughout the maze of alcoves, piped through on some general-address system.

'Your attention, please,' he said. 'You all know who I am. I speak now as the acting leader of this colony. With regret, I must again report that Nevil Clavain was killed today while on a mission of maximum importance for the strategic security of Ararat. Having participated in the same operation, I can assure you that without Clavain's bravery and self-sacrifice the current situation would be enormously more grave than is the case. As things stand, and despite Clavain's death, the mission was successful. It is my intention to inform you of what was accomplished in that operation in due course. But first I must speak about the current disturbances in all sectors of First Camp, and the actions that the Security Arm is taking to restore social order. Please listen carefully, because all our lives depend on it. There will be no more unauthorised crossings to the *Nostalgia for Infinity*. Finite colony resources cannot be risked in this manner. All unofficial attempts to reach the ship will therefore be punished by immediate execution.'

Vasko glanced at Urton, but he couldn't tell if her expression was one of disgust or quiet approval.

The pig waited a breath before continuing. Something was wrong with the transmission, for the earlier image of Clavain had begun to reappear, overlaying Scorpio's face like a faint nimbus. 'There will, however, be an alternative. The administration recommends that all citizens go about their business as usual and do not attempt to leave the island. Nonetheless it recognises that a minority wish to relocate to the *Nostalgia for Infinity*. Beginning at noon tomorrow, therefore, and continuing for as long as necessary, the administration will provide safe authorised transportation to the ship. Designated aircraft will take groups of one hundred people at a time to the *Infinity*. As of six a.m. tomorrow, rules of conveyance, including personal effects allocations, will be available from the High Conch and all other administrative centres, or from uniformed Security Arm personnel. There is no need to panic about being on the first available transport, since – to repeat – the flights will continue until demand is exhausted.'

'They had no choice,' Vasko said quietly. 'Scorp's doing the right thing.'

But the pig was still talking. 'For those who wish to board the *Infinity*, understand the following: conditions aboard the ship will be atrocious. For the last twenty-three years, there have seldom been more than a few dozen people aboard it at any one time. Much of the ship is now uninhabitable or simply unmapped. In order to accommodate an influx of hundreds, possibly even thousands, of refugees, the Security Arm will have to enforce strict emergency rule. If you think the crisis measures in the First Camp are Draconian, you have no idea how much worse things will be on the ship. Your sole right will be the right of survival, and we will dictate how that is interpreted.'

'What does he mean by that?' Vasko asked, while Scorpio continued with the arrangements for the transportation.

'He means they'll have to freeze people,' Urton said. 'Squeeze them into those sleep coffins, like they did when the ship came here in the first place.'

'He should tell them, in that case.'

'Obviously he doesn't want to.'

'Those reefersleep caskets aren't safe,' Vasko said. 'I know what happened the last time they used them. A lot of people didn't make it out alive.'

'It doesn't matter, does it?' Urton said. 'He's still giving them better odds than if they try to make the journey themselves – even without that execution order.'

'I still don't understand. Why provide that option at all, if the administration doesn't think it's the right thing to do?'

Urton shrugged. 'Because maybe the administration isn't sure what to do. If they declare a general evacuation to the ship, they'll really have a panic on their hands. Looking at it from their point of view, how do they know whether it's better for the people to evacuate to the ship or remain on the ground?'

'They don't,' he said. 'Whichever they choose, there'll always be a risk that it might be the wrong decision.'

Urton nodded emphatically. She had nearly finished her beer. 'At least this way Scorpio gets to split the difference. Some people will end up in the ship, some will chose to stay at home. It's the perfect solution, if you want to maximise the chances of *some* people surviving.'

'That sounds very heartless.'

'It is.'

'In which case I don't think you need worry about Scorpio not being the callous leader you said we needed.'

'No. He's callous enough,' Urton agreed. 'Of course, we could be misreading this entirely. But assuming we aren't, does it shock you?'

'No, I suppose not. And I think you're right. We do need someone strong, someone prepared to think the unthinkable.' Vasko put down his glass. It was only half-empty, but his thirst had gone the same way as his appetite. 'One question,' he said. 'Why are you being so nice to me all of a sudden?'

Urton inspected him the way a lepidopterist might examine a

pinned specimen. 'Because, Vasko, it occurred to me that you might be a useful ally, in the long run.'

Hela, 2727

The scrimshaw suit said, 'We've heard the news, Quaiche.'

The sudden voice startled him, as it always did. He was alone. Grelier had just finished seeing to his eyes, swabbing an infected abscess under one retracted eyelid. The metal clamp of the eye-opener felt unusually cruel to him today, as if, while Quaiche was sleeping, the surgeon-general had covertly sharpened all its little hooks. Not while he was really sleeping, of course. Sleep was a luxury he remembered in only the vaguest terms.

'I don't know about any news,' he said.

'You made your little announcement to the congregation down-stairs. We heard it. You're taking the cathedral across Absolution Gap.'

'And if I am, what business is it of yours?'

'It's insanity, Quaiche. And your mental health is very much our business.'

He saw the suit in blurred peripheral vision, around the sharp central image of Haldora. The world was half in shadow, bands of cream and ochre and subtle turquoise plunging into the sharp terminator of the nightside.

'You don't care about me,' he said. 'You only care about your own survival. You're afraid I'll destroy you when I destroy the Lady Morwenna.'

'"When", Quaiche? Frankly, that's a little disturbing to us. We were hoping you still had some intention of actually succeeding.'

'Perhaps I do,' he conceded.

'Where nobody has done so before?'

'The Lady Morwenna isn't any old cathedral.'

'No. It's the heaviest and tallest on the Way. Doesn't that give you some slight pause for thought?'

'It will make my triumph all the more spectacular.'

'Or your disaster, should you topple off the bridge or bring the entire thing crashing down. But why now, Quaiche, after all these revolutions around Hela?'

'Because I feel that the time is right,' he said. 'You can't second-guess these things. Not the work of God.'

'You truly are a lost cause,' the scrimshaw suit said. Then the cheaply synthesised voice took on an urgency it had lacked before. 'Quaiche, listen to us. Do what you will with the Lady Morwenna. We won't stop you. But first let us out of this cage.'

'You're scared,' he said, pulling the stiff tissue of his face into a smile. 'I've really put the wind up you, haven't I?'

'It doesn't have to be this way. Look at the evidence, Quaiche. The vanishings are increasing in frequency. You know what that means, don't you?'

'The work of God is moving towards its culmination.'

'Or, alternatively, the concealment mechanism is failing. Take your pick. We know which interpretation we favour.'

'I know all about your heresies,' he said. 'I don't need to hear them again.'

'You still think we are demons, Quaiche?'

'You call yourselves shadows. Isn't that a bit of a giveaway?'

'We call ourselves shadows because that is what we are, just as you are all shadows to us. It's a statement of fact, Quaiche, not a theological standpoint.'

'I don't want to hear any more of it.'

It was true: he had heard enough of their heresies. They were lies, engineered to undermine his faith. Time and again he had tried to purge them from his head, but always to no avail. As long as the scrimshaw suit remained with him – as long as the thing inside the scrimshaw suit remained – he would never be able to forget those untruths. In a moment of weakness, a lapse that had been every bit as unforgivable as the one twenty years earlier that had brought them here in the first place, he had even followed up some of their heretical claims. He had delved into the Lady Morwenna's archives, following lines of enquiry.

The shadows spoke of a theory. It meant nothing to him, yet when he searched the deep archives – records carried across centuries in the shattered and corrupted data troves of Ultra trade ships – he found something, glints of lost knowledge, teasing hints from which his mind was able to suggest a whole.

Hints of something called brane theory.

It was a model of the universe, an antique cosmological theory that had enjoyed a brief interlude of popularity seven hundred years in the past. So far as Quaiche could tell, the theory had not been discredited so much as abandoned, put aside when newer and brighter toys came along. At the time there had been no easy way of testing any of these competing theories, so they had to stand and fall on their strict aesthetic merit and the ease with which they could be tamed and manipulated with the cudgels and barbs of mathematics.

Brane theory suggested that the universe the senses spoke of was but one sliver of something vaster, one laminate layer in a stacked ply of adjacent realities. There was, Quaiche thought, something alluringly theological in that model, the idea of heavens above and hells below, with the mundane substrate of perceived reality squeezed between them. As above, so below.

But brane theory had nothing to do with heaven and hell. It had originated as a response to something called string theory, and specifically a conundrum within string theory known as the hierarchy problem.

Heresy again. But he could not stop himself from delving deeper.

String theory posited that the fundamental building blocks of matter were, at the smallest conceivable scales, simply one-dimensional loops of mass-energy. Like a guitar string the loops were able to vibrate – to *twang* – in certain discrete modes, each of which corresponded to a recognisable particle at the classical scale. Quarks, electrons, neutrinos, even photons, were all just different vibrational modes of these fundamental strings. Even gravity turned out to be a manifestation of string behaviour.

But gravity was also the problem. On the classical scale – the familiar universe of people and buildings, ships and worlds – gravity was much weaker than anyone normally gave it credit for. Yes, it held planets in their orbits around stars. Yes, it held stars in their orbits around the centre of mass of the galaxy. But compared to the other forces of nature, it was barely there at all. When the Lady Morwenna lowered one of its electromagnetic grapples to lift some chunk of metal from a delivery tractor, the magnet was resisting the entire gravitational force of Hela – everything the world could muster. If gravity had been as strong as the other forces, the Lady Morwenna would have been crushed into an atom-thick pancake, a film of collapsed metal on the perfectly smooth spherical surface of a collapsed planet. It was only gravity's extreme weakness on the classical scale that allowed life to exist in the first place.

But string theory went on to suggest that gravity was really very strong, if only one looked closely enough. At the Planck scale, the smallest possible increment of measurement, string theory predicted that gravity ramped up to equivalence with the other forces. Indeed, at that scale reality looked rather different in other respects as well: curled up like dead woodlice were seven additional dimensions –

hyperspaces accessible only on the microscopic scale of quantum interactions.

There was an aesthetic problem with this view, however. The other forces – bundled together as a single unified electroweak force – manifested themselves at a certain characteristic energy. But the strong gravity of string theory would only reveal itself at energies ten million billion times greater than for the electroweak forces. Such energies were far beyond the grasp of experimental procedure. This was the hierarchy problem, and it was considered deeply offensive. Brane theory was one attempt to resolve this glaring schism.

Brane theory – as far as Quaiche understood it – proposed that gravity was really as strong as the electroweak force, even on the classical scale. But what happened to gravity was that it leaked away before it had a chance to show its teeth. What was left – the gravity that was experienced in day-to-day life – was only a thin residue of something much stronger. Most of the force of gravity had dissipated *sideways*, into adjoining branes or dimensions. The particles that made up most of the universe were glued to a particular braneworld, a particular slice of the laminate of branes that the theory referred to as the bulk. That was why the ordinary matter of the universe only ever saw the one braneworld within which it happened to exist: it was not free to drift off into the bulk. But gravitons, the messenger particles of gravity, suffered no such constraint. They were free to drift between branes, sailing through the bulk with impunity. The best analogy Quaiche had been able to come up with was the printed words on the pages of a book, each confined for all eternity to one particular page, knowing nothing of the words printed on the next page, only a fraction of a millimetre away. And then think of book-worms, gnawing at right angles to the text.

But what of the shadows? This was where Quaiche had to fill in the details for himself. What the shadows appeared to be hinting at – the heart of the heresy – was that they were messengers or some form of communication from an adjacent braneworld. That braneworld might have been completely disconnected from our own, so that the only possible means of communication between the two was through the bulk. There was another possibility, however: the two apparently separate braneworlds might have been distant portions of a single brane, one that was folded back on itself like a hairpin. If that were the case – and the shadows had said nothing on the matter either way – then they were messengers not from another reality but merely from a distant corner of the familiar universe, unthinkably remote in both space and time. The light and energy from their region of space could only travel along the brane, unable to slip across the tiny gap between the folded surfaces. But gravity slipped effortlessly across the bulk, carrying a message from brane to brane. The stars, galaxies and clusters of galaxies in the shadow brane cast a gravitational shadow on our local universe, influencing the motions of our stars and galaxies. By the same token, the gravity caused by the matter in the local part of the brane leaked through the bulk, into the realm of the shadows.

But the shadows were clever. They had decided to communicate across the bulk using gravity as their signalling medium.

There were a thousand ways they might have done it. The specifics didn't matter. They might have manipulated the orbits of a pair of degenerate stars to produce a ripple of gravitational waves, or learned how to make miniature black holes on demand. The only important thing was that it could be done. And – equally importantly – that someone would be able to pick up the signals on this side of the bulk.

Someone like the scuttlers, for instance.

Quaiche laughed to himself. The heresy made a repulsive kind of sense. But then what else would he have expected? Where there was the work of God, would there not also be the work of the Devil, insinuating himself into the schemes of the Creator, trying to robe the miraculous in the mundane?

'Quaiche?' the suit asked. 'Are you still here?'

'I'm still here,' he said. 'But I'm not listening to you. I don't believe what you say to me.'

'If you don't, someone else will.'

He pointed at the scrimshaw suit, his own bony-fingered hand hovering in his peripheral vision like some detached phantasm. 'I won't let anyone else be poisoned by your lies.'

'Unless they have something you want very badly,' the scrimshaw suit said. 'Then, of course, you might change your mind.'

His hand wavered. He felt cold suddenly. He was in the presence of evil. And it knew more about his schemes than it had any right to.

He pressed the intercom control on his couch. 'Grelier,' he snapped. 'Grelier, come here this instant. *I need new blood.*'

TWENTY-SIX

Hela, 2727

The next day Rashmika got her first view of the bridge.

There was no fanfare. She was inside the caravan, in the forward observation deck of one of the two leading vehicles, having forsworn any further trips to the roof after the incident with the mirror-faced Observer.

She had been warned that they were now very close to the edge of the fissure, but for all the long kilometres of the approach there had been no change in the topography of the landscape. The caravan – longer than ever now, having picked up several more sections along the way – was winding its ponderous way through a sheer-sided ice canyon. Occasionally the moving machines scraped against the blue-veined canyon walls, which were twice as high as the tallest vehicle in the procession, dislodging tonnes of ice. It had always been hazardous for the walkers making their way to the equator on foot, but now that they had to traverse the same narrow defile as the caravan, it must have been downright terrifying. There was no room for the caravan to steer around them now, so they had to let it roll over them, making sure they were not aligned with the wheels, treads or stomping mechanical feet. If the machines didn't get them, the falling ice-boulders probably would. Rashmika watched with a mingled sense of horror and sympathy as the parties vanished from view beneath the huge hull of the caravan. There was no way to tell if they made it out the other side, and she doubted that the caravan would stop if there was an accident.

There came a point where the canyon made a gentle curve to the right, blocking any view of the oncoming scenery for several minutes, and then suddenly there was an awful, heart-stopping absence in the landscape. She had not realised how used she had become to seeing white crags stepping into the distance. Now the ground fell away and the deep black sky dropped much lower than it had before, like a curtain whose tangled lower hem had just unfurled to its fullest extent. The sky bit hungrily into the land.

The road emerged from the canyon and ran along a ledge that skirted one wall of Ginnungagap Rift. To the left of the road, the sheer-sided canyon wall lurched higher; to the right, there was nothing at all. The road was just broad enough to accommodate the two-vehicle-wide procession, with the right-hand sides of the right-hand vehicles never more than two or three metres from the very edge. Rashmika looked back along the extended, motley train of the caravan – which was now thrillingly visible in its entirety as it had never been before – and saw wheels, treads, crawler plates, piston-driven limbs and flexing carapacial segments picking their way daintily along the edge, scuffing tonnes of ice into the abyss with each misplaced tread or impact. All along the caravan, the individual masters were steering and correcting like crazy, trying to navigate the fine line between smashing against the wall on the left and plunging over the side on the right. They couldn't slow down because the whole point of this short cut was to make up valuable lost time. Rashmika wondered what would happen to the rest of the caravan if one of the elements got it wrong and went over the side. She had seen the inter-caravan couplings, but had no idea how strong they were. Would that one errant machine take the whole lot with it, or fall gallantly alone, leaving the others to close up the gap in the procession? Was there some nightmarish protocol for deciding such things in advance: a slackening of the couplings, perhaps?

Well, she was up front. If anywhere was safe, it had to be up at the front where the navigators had the best view of the terrain.

After several minutes during which no calamity occurred, she began to relax, and for the first time was able to pay due attention to the bridge, which had been looming ahead all the while.

The caravan was moving in a southerly direction, towards the equator, along the eastern flank of Ginnungagap Rift. The bridge was still some way south. Perhaps it was her imagination, but she thought she could see the curvature of the world as the high wall of the Rift marched into the distance. The top was jagged and irregular, but if she smoothed out those details in her mind's eye, it appeared to follow a gentle arc, like the trajectory of a satellite. It was very difficult to judge how distant the bridge was, or how wide the Rift was at this point. Although Rashmika recalled that the Rift was forty kilometres wide at the point where the bridge spanned it, the ordinary rules of perspective simply had no application: there were no visual cues to assist her; no intermediate objects to offer a sense of diminishing scale; no attenuation of detail or colour due to atmosphere. Although the bridge and the far wall looked vast and distant, they could as easily have been five kilometres away as forty.

Rashmika judged the bridge to be still some fifty or sixty kilometres away as the crow flies – more than two-hundredths of the circumference of Hela – but the road along the ledge took many twists and turns getting there. She could easily believe they had another hundred kilometres of travel to go before they arrived at the eastern approach to the bridge.

Still, at least now she could see it – and it was everything she had ever imagined. Everyone said that photographs could not even remotely convey the true essence of the structure. Rashmika had always doubted that, but now she saw that the common opinion was quite correct: to appreciate the bridge, it was necessary to see it.

What people appeared to find most dismaying about the bridge, Rashmika knew, was its very *lack* of strangeness. Disregarding its scale and the materials that had been used to build it, it looked like something transplanted from the pages of human history, something built on Earth, in the age of iron and steam. It made her think of lanterns and horses, duels and courtships, winter palaces and musical fountains – except that it was vast and looked as if it had been blown from glass or carved from sugar.

The upper surface of the bridge described a very gentle arc as it crossed from one side of the Rift to the other, and was at its highest in the middle. Apart from that it was perfectly flat, unencumbered by any form of superstructure. There were no railings on either side of the road bed, which was breathtakingly shallow – from her present angle it looked like a rapier-thin line of light. It appeared broken in places, until she moved her head slightly and the illumination shifted. Fifty kilometres away, and the movement of her head was enough to affect what she could see of the delicate structure! The span was indeed unsupported for most of its width, but at either end – reaching out to a distance of five or six kilometres from the walls – was a delicate tracery of filigreed stanchions. They were curled into absurd spirals and whorls, scroll-like flourishes and luscious organic involutes catching the light and throwing it back to her, not in white and silver, but in a prismatic shimmer of rainbow hues. Every tilt of her head shifted the colours into some new configuration of glories.

The bridge looked evanescent, as if one ill-judged breath might be sufficient to blow it away.

Yet they were actually going to cross it.

As soon as he had washed and breakfasted, Vasko set off to report for duty at the nearest Security Arm centre. He had slept for little more than four hours, but the alertness he had felt the night before was still there, stretched a little thinner and tighter. First Camp was deceptively quiet; the streets were littered with debris, some premises and dwellings had been damaged and the evidence of fires smouldered here and there, but the vast numbers of people he had seen the night before seemed to have vanished. Perhaps they had responded to Scorpio's pronouncement after all and returned to their homes, having grasped how unpleasant it was going to be on the *Nostalgia for Infinity*.

Vasko realised his error as soon as he turned the corner next to the Security Arm compound. A huge grey mob was pressed up against the building, many hundreds of people crushed together with their belongings piled at their feet. A dozen or so SA guards were keeping order, standing on railed plinths with small weapons presented but not aimed directly at the crowd. Other Arm personnel, in addition to unarmed administration officials, were manning tables that had been set up outside the two-storey conch structure. Paperwork was being processed and stamped; personal effects were being weighed and labelled. Most of the people had obviously decided not to wait for the official rules: they were here, now, ready to depart, and very few of them looked as if they were having second thoughts.

Vasko made his way through the crowd, doing his best not to push and shove. There was no sign of Urton, but this was not her designated Arm centre. He stopped at one of the tables and waited for the officer manning it to finish processing one of the refugees.

'Are they still planning to start flying them out at noon?' Vasko asked quietly.

'Earlier,' the man replied, his voice low. 'The pace has been stepped up. Word is we're still going to have trouble coping.'

'There's no way that ship can accommodate all of us,' Vasko said. 'Not now. It'd take months to get us all into the sleep caskets.'

'Tell that to the pig,' the man said and went back to his work, stamping a sheet of paper almost without looking at it.

Sudden warmth kissed the back of Vasko's neck. He looked up and squinted against the blinding-bright underside of a machine, an aircraft or shuttle sliding across the square. He expected it to slow and descend, but instead the machine curved away, heading beyond the shore, towards the spire. It slid under the clouds like a bright ragged flake of daylight.

'See, they've already begun moving 'em out,' the man said. 'As if that's going to make everyone else calmer ...'

'I'm sure Scorpio knows what he's doing,' Vasko said. He turned away before the man was able to answer.

He pushed beyond the processing tables, through the rest of the crowd, and into the conch structure. Inside, it was the same story: people squeezed in everywhere, holding paperwork and possessions aloft, children crying. He could feel the panic increasing by the minute.

He passed through into the part of the building reserved for SA personnel. In the small curved chamber where he usually received his assignments, he found a trio of people sitting around a low table drinking seaweed tea. He knew them all.

'Malinin,' said Gunderson, a young woman with short red hair. 'To what do we owe the pleasure?'

He didn't care for her tone. 'I came for my duties,' he said.

'I didn't think you mixed with the likes of us these days,' she sneered.

He reached across the tea-drinkers to rip the assignment sheet from the wall. 'I mix with whoever I like,' he said.

The second of the trio, a pig named Flenser, said, 'We heard you were more likely to be hanging around with administration stiffs.'

Vasko looked at the docket. He couldn't see his name against any of the regular duties. 'Like Scorpio, you mean?'

'I bet you know a lot more than we do about what's going on,' Gunderson said. 'Don't you?'

'If I did, I'd hardly be in a position to talk about it.' Vasko pinned the sheet back on the wall. 'Truthfully, I don't know very much more.'

'You're lying,' the third one – a man named Cory – said. 'You want to climb that ladder, Malinin, you'd better learn how to lie better than that.'

'Thanks,' he said, smiling, 'but I'll settle for learning how to serve this colony.'

'You want to know where to go?' Gunderson asked him.

'It would help.'

'They told us to pass you a message,' she said. 'You're expected in the High Conch at eight.'

'Thank you,' he said. 'You've been very helpful.' He turned to leave.

'Fuck you, Malinin,' he heard her say to his back. 'You think you're better than us, is that it?'

'Not at all,' he replied, surprised by his calmness. He turned back to face her. 'I think my abilities are average. I just happen to feel a sense of responsibility, an obligation to serve Ararat to the best of my abilities. I'd be astonished if you felt differently.'

'You think that now Clavain's out of the picture, you can slime your way to the top?'

He looked at Gunderson with genuine surprise. 'That thought never crossed my mind.'

'Well, that's good, because if it had, you'd be making a serious mistake. You don't have what it takes, Malinin. None of us have got what it takes, but you *especially* don't have it.'

'No? And what exactly is it that I don't have?'

'The balls to stand up against the pig,' she said, as if this should have been obvious to all present.

In the High Conch, Antoinette Bax was already seated at the table, a compad open in front of her. Cruz, Pellerin and several other colony seniors had joined her, and now Blood came in, swaggering like a wrestler.

'There'd better be a good reason for this,' he said. 'It's not as if I haven't got a shitload of other things I really need to be taking care of.'

'Where's Scorpio?' she asked.

'In the infirmary, checking on mother and daughter. He'll be here as soon as he can,' Blood replied.

'And Malinin?'

'I had someone leave a message for him. He'll get here eventually.' Blood collapsed into a seat. Reflexively, he took out his knife and began to scrape the blade against his chin. It made a thin, insectile noise.

'Well, we've got a problem,' Antoinette said. 'In the last six hours, the neutrino flux from the ship has about trebled. If the flux increases another ten, fifteen per cent, that ship's going to have nowhere to go but *up*.'

'There's no exhaust yet?' asked Cruz.

'No,' Antoinette replied, 'and I'm pretty worried about what will happen when those drives do start thrusting. No one was living around the bay when she came down. We need to think seriously about an evacuation to inland areas. I'd recommend moving everyone to the outlying islands, but I know that's not possible given the existing load on aircraft and shuttles.'

'Yeah, dream on,' Blood said.

'All the same, we have to do something. When the Captain decides to take off, we're going to have tidal waves, clouds of superheated steam, noise so loud it will deafen everyone within hundreds of kilometres, all kinds of harmful radiation spewing out . . .' Antoinette trailed off, hoping she had made her point. 'Basically, this isn't going to be the kind of environment you want to be anywhere near unless you're inside a spacesuit.'

Blood buried his face in his hands, making a mask of his stubby pig fingers. Antoinette had seen Scorpio do something similar when crises pressed on him from all sides. With Clavain gone and Scorpio absent, Blood was experiencing the responsibility he had always craved. Antoinette doubted that the novelty of command had lasted for more than about five minutes.

'I can't evacuate the town,' he said.

'You have no choice,' Antoinette insisted.

He lowered his hands and jabbed a finger at the window. 'That's *our* fucking ship. We shouldn't be speculating about what it's going to do. We should be giving it orders, where and when it suits us.'

'Sorry, Blood, but that isn't how it works,' Antoinette said.

'There'll be panic,' Cruz said. 'Worse than anything we've seen. All the processing stations will have to be closed down and relocated. It'll delay exodus flights to the *Infinity* by at least a day. And where are those relocated people going to sleep tonight? There's nothing for them inland – just a bunch of rocks. We'd have hundreds dead of exposure by daybreak.'

'I don't have all the answers,' Antoinette said. 'I'm just pointing out the difficulties.'

'There must be something else we can do,' Cruz said. 'Damn, we should have had contingencies in place for this.'

'Should haves don't count,' Antoinette said. It was something her father had always told her. It had annoyed her intensely, and she was dismayed to hear the same words coming out of her mouth before she could stop them.

'Pellerin,' Blood said, 'what about swimmer corps intervention? Ararat seems to be on our side, or it wouldn't have made a channel for the boats to reach the ship. Anything you can offer?'

Pellerin shook her head. 'Sorry. Not now. If the Jugglers show signs of returning to normal activity patterns, we might sanction an exploratory swim, but not before then. I'm not sending someone to their death, Blood, not when there's so little chance of a useful outcome.'

'I understand,' the pig said.

'Wait,' Cruz said. 'Let's turn this around. If it's going to be such a bad thing to be anywhere near the ship when it lifts, maybe we should be looking at ways to speed up the exodus.'

'We're already moving 'em out as fast as we can,' Blood said.

'Then cut back on the bureaucracy,' Antoinette said. 'Just move them and worry about the details later. And don't take all day doing it. We may not have that much time left. Shit, what I wouldn't give for *Storm Bird* now.'

'Perhaps there is something you can do for us,' Cruz said, gazing straight at her.

Antoinette returned the one-eyed woman's stare. 'Name it.'

'Go back aboard the *Infinity*. Reason with the Captain. Tell him we need some breathing space.'

It was not what she wanted to hear. She had, if anything, become even more frightened of the Captain since their conversation; the thought of summoning him again filled her with renewed dread.

'He may not want to talk,' she said. 'Even if he does, he may not want to hear anything I have to say.'

'You might still buy us time,' Cruz said. 'In my book, that's got to be better than nothing.'

'I guess,' Antoinette agreed, reluctantly.

'So you may as well try it,' Cruz said. 'There's no shortage of transport to the ship, either. With administration privileges, you could be aboard in half an hour.'

As if this was meant to encourage her.

Antoinette was staring at her fingers, lost in the metal intricacies of her home-made jewellery and hoping for some remission from this duty, when Vasko Malinin entered the room. He was flushed, his hair glistening with rain or sweat. Antoinette thought he looked terribly young to be sitting amongst these seniors; it seemed unfair to taint him with such matters. The young were still entitled to believe that the world's problems always had clear solutions.

'Have a seat,' Blood said. 'Anything I can get you – coffee, tea?'

'I had trouble collecting my orders from my duty station,' Vasko said. 'The crowds are getting quite heavy. When they saw my uniform, they wouldn't let me leave until I'd more or less promised them seats on one of those shuttles.'

The pig played with his knife. 'You didn't, I hope.'

'Of course not, but I hope everyone understands the severity of the problem.'

'We've got a rough idea, thanks,' Antoinette said. Then she stood up, pulling down the hem of her formal blouse.

'Where are you going?' Vasko asked.

'To have a chat with the Captain,' she said.

In another part of the High Conch, several floors below, a series of partially linked, scalloplike chambers had been opened out of the conch matter with laborious slowness and much expenditure of energy. The chambers now formed the wards of the main infirmary for First Camp, where the citizenry received what limited medical services the administration could provide.

The doctor's two green servitors budged aside as Scorpio entered, their spindly jointed limbs clicking against each other. He pushed between them. The bed was positioned centrally, with an incubator set on a trolley next to it on one side and a chair on the other.

Valensin stood up from the chair, placing aside a compad he had been consulting.

'How is she?' Scorpio asked.

'Mother or daughter?'

'Don't be clever, doc. I'm not in the mood.'

'Mother is fine – except, of course, for the obvious and predictable side effects of stress and fatigue.' Milky-grey daylight filtered into the room from one high slit of a window, which was actually a part of the conch material left unpainted; the light flared off the glass in Valensin's rhomboid spectacles. 'I do not believe she requires any particular care other than time and rest.'

'And Aura?'

'The child is as well as can be expected.'

Scorpio looked at the small thing in the incubator. It was surprisingly shrivelled and red. It twitched like some beached thing struggling for air.

'That doesn't tell me much.'

'Then I'll spell it out for you,' Valensin said. Highlights in the doctor's slicked-back hair gleamed cobalt blue. 'The child has already undergone four potentially traumatic procedures. The first was Remontoire's insertion of the Conjoiner implants to permit communication with the child's natural mother. Then the child was surgically kidnapped, removed from her mother's womb. Then she was implanted inside Skade, perhaps following another period in an incubator. Finally, she was removed from Skade under less than optimal field surgical conditions.'

Scorpio assumed Valensin had heard the full story of what happened in the iceberg. 'Take my word for it: there wasn't a lot of choice.'

Valensin laced his fingers. 'Well, she is resting. That's good. And there do not appear to be any immediate and obvious complications. But in the long run? Who can tell? If what Khouri tells us is true, then it isn't as if she was ever destined for a normal development.' Valensin lowered himself back down into the seat. His legs folded like long hinged stilts, the crease in his trousers razor-sharp. 'On a related matter, Khouri had a request. I thought it best to refer it to you first.'

'Go on.'

'She wants the girl put back into her womb.'

Scorpio looked again at the incubator and the child within it. It was a larger, more sophisticated version of the portable unit they had taken to the iceberg. Incubators were amongst the most valued technological artefacts on Ararat, and great care was taken to keep them running.

'Could it be done?' he asked.

'Under ordinary circumstances, I would never contemplate such a thing.'

'These aren't ordinary circumstances.'

'Putting a child back inside a mother isn't like putting a loaf of bread back into an oven,' Valensin said. 'It would require delicate microsurgery, hormonal readjustment ... a host of complex procedures.'

Scorpio let the doctor's condescension wash over him. 'But it could be done?'

'Yes, if she wants it badly enough.'

'But it would be risky?'

Valensin nodded after a moment, as if until then he had considered only the technical hurdles, rather than the hazards. 'Yes. To mother and child both.'

'Then it doesn't happen,' Scorpio said.

'You seem rather certain.'

'That child cost the life of my friend. Now that we've got her back, I'm not planning on losing her.'

'I hope you'll be the one to break the news to the mother, in that case.'

'Leave it to me,' Scorpio said.

'Very well.' Scorpio had the feeling that the doctor was disappointed. 'One other thing: she mentioned that word again, in her sleep.'

'What word?'

'Hella,' Valensin said. 'Or something like it.'

Hela, 2727

Rashmika's estimate turned out to have been optimistic. She had expected another two or three hours of travel before the caravan reached the eastern side of the bridge, but after four hours they appeared only to have made up half the distance. There had been many frustrating periods where the caravan doubled back on itself, following sinuous reverse-loops in the walls. There were times when they had to squeeze through tunnels in the cliff, moving at little more than walking pace while the ice scraped against either side of the procession. Two or three times they had come to a complete halt while some technical matter was attended to – no explanation was ever forthcoming. She had the impression that the drivers tried to make up time after these delays, but the subsequent recklessness – which caused the vehicles to bounce and swerve perilously close to the edge – only added to her anxiety. When the quaestor had told her that they would be taking the bridge she had felt great apprehension, but now she was inclined to think it preferable to the many hazards of the ledge traverse. The road along the ledge was a human artefact: it had been blasted or cut into the cliffs within the last century and had probably been repaired and realigned several times since then. Doubtless bits of it had collapsed over the years, and many vehicles must have taken the long, ballistic plunge to the bottom of the Rift. But the bridge was surely older than that. Now that she had given the matter some thought, it struck her as highly unlikely that it would choose her lifetime in which to come crashing down. It would actually be a remarkable *privilege* were that to happen.

Even so, she would still be glad when they reached the other side.

She was looking out of the viewing window when she saw another quick succession of flashes, like those she had observed from the roof. They were brighter now – she was undoubtedly closer to the source of whatever they were – and they left hemispherical purple after-images on her eyes, even when she blinked.

'You're wondering what they are,' a voice said.

She turned. She was expecting to see Quaestor Jones, but the voice did not quite have his timbre. It was the voice of a younger man, with an accent from somewhere in the badlands.

Harbin, she wondered for an instant? Could it possibly be Harbin? But it wasn't her brother.

She didn't recognise the man at all. He was taller than her and a little older, she guessed, although there was something in his expression – something in his eyes, now that she narrowed it down – that made him appear to be a *lot* older. He was not really bad-looking, she supposed. He had a thin, serious face, with prominent cheekbones and a jawline so sharp it hurt. His hair was cut very short, shorter than she liked it, so that she could see the exact shape of his skull: a phrenologist's dream date. He had small ears that stuck out more than he might have wished. His neck was thin and his Adam's apple was prominent in a way that always alarmed her in men, as if something inside his neck had popped out of alignment and needed to be pushed back before harm was done.

'How do you know what I'm wondering?' Rashmika asked.

'Well, you are, aren't you?'

She half-scowled. 'And you'd know all about them, I suppose?'

'They're charges,' he said amicably, as if he was accustomed to this kind of rudeness. 'Nuclear demolition charges. They're being used by Permanent Way teams clearing the road ahead of the cathedrals. God's Fire.'

She had already guessed that the explosions had something to do with the Way. 'I didn't think they ever used anything like that.'

'Mostly they don't. I haven't been keeping up with the news, but they must have hit some unusually heavy obstructions. They could clear it with conventional charges and digging, if they had all the time in the world. But of course that's the one thing they never have, not when those cathedrals are coming closer all the while. My guess is it was a rearguard spoiler action.'

'Oh, do please enlighten me.'

'It's what happens when the cathedrals at the back begin to lose ground. Sometimes they sabotage the Way behind them to cause trouble for the leading cathedrals when they come round again on the next loop. Of course, it's nothing anyone can ever prove . . .'

She studied his clothing: trousers and a high-collared loose-sleeved shirt; light, flat-soled shoes; everything grey and nondescript. No indication of rank, status, wealth or religious affiliation.

'Who are you?' Rashmika asked. 'You're talking to me as if we've already met, but I don't know you at all.'

'But you do know me,' the young man said.

His face said that he was telling the truth, or at least not believing himself to be lying. His certainty made her all the less willing to give ground, irrational as that was.

'I think you're mistaken.'

'What I mean is, we have met. And I believe you owe me a debt of gratitude.'

'Do I, now?'

'I saved your life – when you were on the roof, looking down the access shaft. You nearly fell, and I caught you.'

'That wasn't you,' she said. 'That was ...'

'An Observer? Yes, it was. But that doesn't mean it wasn't me.'

'Don't be silly,' Rashmika said.

'Why don't you believe me? Did you see my face?'

'Not clearly, no.'

'Then you have no reason to think it *wasn't* me, either. Yes, I know it could have been anyone up there. But who else saw what happened?'

'You can't be an Observer.'

'No, not now I can't.'

She did not want his company. Not specifically his company, but company in general. She wanted only to observe the slow approach to the bridge, to compose her thoughts as they made the crossing, mentally mapping the difficult terrain that lay ahead of her. She did not want idle conversation or distraction, most certainly not with the sort of person he claimed to be.

'What do you mean by that?' she asked. 'Are you an Observer or aren't you?'

'I was, but now I'm not.'

She felt a flicker of sympathy. 'Because of what happened on the roof?'

'No. That didn't help, certainly, but my doubts had already set in before that happened.'

'Oh.' Then her conscience was clear.

'I can't say you didn't play a small part in it, though.'

'What?'

'I saw you the first time you came up. I was on the viewing platform, with the others. We were supposed to be concentrating on Haldora, blocking out all external distractions. They could make it easy for us by physically restricting our view, forcing our eyes to stay locked on the planet, but that's not the way it's done. There has to be an element of discipline, an element of self-control. We're supposed to look at Haldora for every instant of the day, despite the distractions. There are devices in the helmets that monitor how well we do that, recording every twitch of the eye. And I saw you. Only in my peripheral vision, to begin with. My eye made an involuntary movement to bring you into focus and I lost contact with Haldora for a fraction of a second.'

'Naughty,' she said.

'Naughtier than you think. There would have been a disciplinary measure for just that violation. It's not so much the fact that I looked away as that I was occupying a space on the roof that might have been used by someone more vigilant. That was the sin, because in that instant there was always a chance – no matter how small – that Haldora might vanish. And someone else would have been denied the chance of witnessing that miracle because I had the weakness of mind to look away.'

'But it didn't vanish. You're off the hook.'

'I assure you that isn't the way they see it.' He looked down, sheepishly, she thought. 'Anyway, it's academic: I made things a lot worse. I didn't look back towards Haldora even when I was consciously aware that I'd lost contact. I just watched you, straining to hold you in focus, not daring to move any part of my body. I couldn't see your face, but I could see the way you moved. I knew you were a woman, and when I realised that it just made it worse. It wasn't idle curiosity any more. I wasn't simply being distracted by some oddity in the landscape.'

When he said 'woman' she felt a quiet thrill that she hoped did not show in her face. When had anyone ever called her that before without prefacing it with 'young', or something equally diminishing?

She blushed. 'You can't possibly have known who I was, though.'

'No,' he said, 'not for certain. But when you came up again, I thought, "She must be a very independent-minded person." Nobody else had come up on to the roof the whole time I was there. And when you nearly had your accident . . . well, then I did see your face. Not clearly, but enough to know I'd recognise you again.' He paused, and for a moment watched the rolling view himself. 'I did have my doubts,' he said, 'even when I saw you here. But when I saw the flashes, I knew I had to take the chance. I'm glad I did. You seem like a nice person, and now you've as good as admitted you were the same person I helped up on the roof. Do you mind if I ask your name?'

'Provided you tell me yours.'

'Pietr,' he said. 'Pietr Vale. I'm from Skull Cliff, in the Hyrrokkin lowlands.'

'Rashmika Els,' she said guardedly. 'From High Scree, in the Vigrid badlands.'

'I thought I recognised the accent. I guess I'm not really a badlander myself, but we're not from places so very far apart, are we?'

Rashmika felt torn between politeness and hostility. 'I think you'll find we're a lot further apart than you realise.'

'Why do you say that? We're both going south, aren't we? Both taking the caravan towards the Way. How different can we be?'

'Very,' Rashmika said. 'I'm not on a pilgrimage. I'm on an ... enquiry.'

He smiled. 'Call it what you will.'

'I'm on personal business. Personal secular business. Business that has nothing to do with your religion – which, incidentally, I do *not* believe in – but which has everything to do with right and wrong.'

'I was right. You really are a serious and determined person.'

She didn't like that. 'Shouldn't you be getting back to your friends?'

'They won't let me back,' he said. 'They might have tolerated a moment of inattention; they might even have forgiven me a lapse of the kind I mentioned before. But once you leave them, that's it. You're poisoned. There is no way back.'

'Why did you leave?'

'Because of you, as I said. Because seeing you up there opened a glint of doubt in my armour. I don't suppose it was ever very secure, or I wouldn't have noticed you in the first place. But by the second occasion, when you nearly fell, I was already doubting that I had the conviction to continue.' At that, Rashmika started to say something, but he held up his hand and continued. 'You shouldn't blame your-self. Really, it could have been anyone up there. My faith was never as strong as the others'. And when I thought about what lay ahead, what I was setting myself up for, I knew I didn't have the strength to go through with it.'

She knew what he meant. The rigours of this part of the pilgrimage were as nothing compared to what would happen when Pietr reached the cathedral that was his destination. There, his faith would be irreversibly consolidated by chemical means. And as an Observer he would be surgically and neurologically adapted to enable him to witness Haldora for every instant of his existence. No sleep, no inattention, not even the respite of blinking.

Only mute observance, until he died.

'I wouldn't have the strength either,' she said. 'Even if I believed.'

'Why don't you?'

'Because I believe in rational explanations. I do not believe planets simply cease to exist without good reason.'

'But there is a good reason. The best possible reason.'

'The work of God?'

Pietr nodded. Fascinated, she watched the bob of his Adam's apple pushing against the high edge of his collar. 'What better explanation can you ask for?'

'But why here, why now?'

'Because these are End Times,' Pietr said. 'We've had human war and human plagues. Then we had stranger plagues and reports of stranger wars. Don't you wonder where the refugees come from? Don't you wonder why they come *here*, of all places? They know it. They know this is the place where it will begin. This is the place where it will happen.'

'I thought you said you weren't a believer.'

'I said I wasn't sure of the strength of my faith. That isn't quite the same thing.'

'I think if God wanted to make a point, He'd find a better way to do it than through the random vanishing of a gas-giant planet light-years from Earth.'

'But it isn't random,' Pietr countered, evading the rest of her point. 'That's what everyone thinks, but it isn't true. The churches know it, and those who take the time to study the records know it, too.'

Now, despite herself, she found that she wanted to hear what he had to say. Pietr was correct: the vanishings of Haldora were always spoken of by the churches as if they were random events, subject to inscrutable divine scheduling. And the shameful thing was that she had always taken this information at face value, without questioning it. She had never stopped to think that the truth might be more complex. She had been far too preoccupied with her academic study of the scuttlers to look further afield.

'If it isn't random,' she asked, 'then what is it?'

'I don't know what you'd call it if you were a mathematician or a scholar. I'm neither. I only know what such people have told me. It's true that you can never predict when a vanishing will occur – in that sense they *are* random. But the average gap between vanishings has been growing shorter ever since Quaiche witnessed the first one. It's just that until recently no one could see it clearly. Now you can't miss it, if you study the evidence.'

The back of Rashmika's neck prickled. 'Then show me the evidence. I want to see it.'

The caravan swerved sharply as it entered another of the tunnels bored through the side of the cliff.

'I can show you evidence,' he said, 'but whether it's the right evidence or not is another matter entirely.'

'You're losing me, Pietr.'

The caravan scraped and gouged its way through the narrow confines of the tunnel. Rashmika heard thumps as dislodged ceiling materials – rocks and ice – hammered against the roof. She thought of the Observers up there and wondered what it was like for them.

'We'll reach the bridge in four or five hours,' he said. 'When we're halfway across, meet me on the roof, where we were before. I'll have something interesting to show you.'

'Why would I want to meet you on the roof, Pietr? Can I trust you?'

'Of course,' he said.

But she only accepted his word because she knew that he believed what he said.

Ararat, 2675

Khouri awoke. Scorpio was with her when she opened her eyes, sitting in the seat next to her bed where Valensin had been earlier. Another hour had passed, and he had missed the meeting in the High Conch. He considered this an acceptable trade-off.

The woman blinked and rubbed sleep gum from her eyes. Her lips were caked in the stringy white residue of dried saliva. 'How long have I been out?'

'It's the morning of the day after we rescued Aura. You've been out for most of it. Doc says it's just fatigue catching up with you. That whole time you were with us, you must have been running on vapour.'

Khouri's head turned to the other side of the bed. 'Aura?'

'Doc says she's doing OK. Like you, she just needs rest. Considering all the crap she's been through, she's doing pretty well.'

Khouri closed her eyes. She sighed. In that moment Scorpio saw tension flood out of her. It was as if the whole time she had been with them, ever since they had pulled her out of the capsule, she had been wearing a mask. Now the mask had been discarded.

She opened her eyes again. They were like windows into a younger woman. He remembered, forcefully, the way Khouri had been before the two ships had separated in the Resurgam system. Half his life ago.

'I'm glad she's safe,' she said. 'Thank you for helping me. And I'm sorry for what happened to Clavain.'

'So am I, but there was no choice. Skade had us. She set the trap, we walked into it. Once she knew she couldn't benefit from holding on to Aura, she was ready to give her back to us. But she wasn't going to let us leave without paying. She felt Clavain still owed her.'

'But what she did to him ...'

Scorpio touched her head gently. 'Don't think about it now. Don't ever think about it, if you can help it.'

'He was your friend, wasn't he?'

'Guess so. Inasmuch as I've ever had friends.'

'I think you've had friends, Scorp. I think you still have friends. Two more now, if you want them.'

'Mother and daughter?'

'We both owe you.'

'I'll take it under advisement.'

She laughed. It was good to hear someone laugh. Khouri was the last one he'd have expected it from. Before the trip to the iceberg she had struck him as monomanically driven, like a purposeful preprogrammed weapon sent down from the heavens. But he understood now that she was as fragile and human as the rest of them. Whatever 'human' meant for a pig.

'Mind if I ask you something?' he said. 'If you're sleepy, I can come back in a little while.'

'Fetch me that water, will you?'

He brought her the beaker of water she'd indicated. She drank half of it down, then wiped the white scurf from her moistened lips. 'Go on, Scorp.'

'You have a link to Aura, don't you? A mental connection, via the implants Remontoire put in both of you?'

'Yes,' she said, guardedly.

'Do you understand everything that comes through it?'

'How do you mean?'

'You said that Aura speaks through you. Fine, I think I understand that. But do you ever pick up unintentional stuff?'

'Like what?'

'You know the leakage we have from the wolf war? Stuff slipping through the defences? Do you ever get leakage from Aura, things that cross over the gap between you, but which you can't process?'

'I wouldn't know.' She sounded less happy now than she had a minute earlier. She was frowning. The windows had slammed shut again. 'What sort of thing were you thinking of, exactly?'

'Not sure,' he said. He pinched the bridge of his nose. 'It's just a shot in the dark. When we pulled you out of that capsule, Valensin hit you with sedatives because you wouldn't let us examine you. Knocked you out good and cold. But in your sleep you still kept saying something.'

'I did, did I?'

'The word was "Hella", or something like that. It appeared to mean something to you, but when we asked you about it, you gave me what I'd call a plausible denial. I'm inclined to believe you were telling the truth, that the word doesn't mean anything to you. But I'm wondering if it might mean something to Aura.'

She looked at him with suspicion and interest. 'Does it mean anything to you?'

'Not that I'm aware of. Certainly doesn't mean anything to anyone on Ararat. But in the wider sphere of human culture? Could mean almost anything. Lot of languages out there. Lot of people, lot of places.'

'Still can't help you.'

'I understand. But the thing is, while I was sitting here waiting for you to wake up, you said something else.'

'What did I say?'

'Quaiche.'

She lifted the beaker to her lips and finished what remained of the water. 'Still doesn't mean anything to me,' she said.

'Pity. I was hoping it might ring some bells.'

'Well, maybe it means something to Aura. I don't know, all right? I'm just her mother. Remontoire wasn't a miracle worker. He linked us together, but it's not as if everything she thinks is accessible to me. I'd go mad if that was the case.' Khouri paused. 'You've got databases and things. Why don't you query them?'

'I will, when things quieten down.' Scorpio pushed himself up from the seat. 'One other thing: I understand you communicated a particular desire to Doctor Valensin?'

'Yeah, I talked to the doc.' She said it in a lilting voice, parodying his earlier tone. '"I understand why you want that to happen. I respect your wish and sympathise with you. If there was a safe way . . ."'

She closed her eyes. 'She's my baby. They stole her from me. Now I want to give birth to her, the way it was meant to happen.'

'I'm sorry,' he said, 'but I just can't allow it.'

'There's no room for argument, is there?'

'None at all, I'm afraid.'

She did not reply, did not even turn away from him, but there was a withdrawal and the sliding down of a barrier he didn't have to see to feel.

Scorpio turned from the bed and walked slowly out of the room. He had expected her to weep when he broke the news. If not weeping, then hysterics or insults or pleading. But she remained still, silent, as if she had always known it would happen this way. As he walked away, the force of her dignity made the back of his neck tingle. But it changed nothing.

Aura was a child. But she was also a tactical asset.

TWENTY-SEVEN

Ararat, 2675

In the deep cloisters of the ship, Antoinette halted. 'John?' she said. 'It's me again. I've come down to talk to you.'

Antoinette knew he was nearby. She knew that he was watching her, alert to her every gesture. When the wall moved, pushing itself into the bas-relief image of a spacesuited figure, she controlled her natural instinct to flinch. It was not quite what she had been expecting, but it was still an apparition.

'Thanks,' she said. 'Good to see you again.'

The figure was a suggestion rather than an accurate sketch. The image shimmered, the wall's deformations undergoing constant and rapid change, fluttering and rippling like a flag in a stiff gale. When the image occasionally broke up, fading back into the rough texture of the wall, it was as if the figure was being hidden by scarves of windblown Martian dust cutting horizontally across the field of view.

The figure gestured to her, raising an arm, touching one gloved hand to the narrow visor of its space helmet.

Antoinette raised her own hand in greeting, but the figure on the wall merely repeated the gesture, more emphatically this time.

Then she remembered the goggles that the Captain had given her the time before. She slipped them from her pocket and settled them over her eyes. Again the view through the goggles was synthetic, but this time – for now, at least – nothing was being edited out of her visual field. This reassured her. She had not enjoyed the feeling that large and possibly dangerous elements in her vicinity were being masked from her perception. It was shocking to think that for centuries people had accepted such manipulation of their environment as a perfectly normal aspect of life, regarding such perceptual filtering as no more remarkable than the wearing of sunglasses or earmuffs. It was even more shocking to think that they had allowed the machinery controlling that filtering to creep into their skulls, where it could make the trickery even more seamless. The Demarchists – and, for that matter, the Conjoiners – truly were strange people. She was sad about many things, but not the fact that she had been born too late to participate in such reality-modifying games. She liked to reach out for something and know it was really there.

But the goggles were a necessary evil. In the Captain's realm, she had to consent to his rules.

The bas-relief image took a definite step towards her and then emerged from the wall, solid now, taking on form and detail, exactly as if a physical person had stepped out of a highly localised sand-storm.

Now she did flinch, for the illusion of presence was striking. She could not help but take a step backwards.

There was something different about the manifestation this time. The space helmet was not quite as ancient as the one she remembered, and it was covered in different symbols. The suit, while still of an old design, was not as utterly archaic as the first he had worn. The chest-pack was more streamlined, and the whole suit fitted its wearer more tightly. Antoinette was no expert, but she judged that the new suit must be fifty-odd years ahead of the one he had worn last time.

She wondered what *that* meant.

She was on the point of taking another step backwards when the Captain halted his approach and again raised a gloved hand. The gesture served to calm her, which was probably the intention. Then he began to work the mechanism of his visor, sliding it up with a conspicuous hiss of equalising air pressure.

The face inside the helmet was instantly recognisable, but it was also the face of an older man. There were lines where there had been none before, grey in the stubble that still shadowed his cheeks. There were wrinkles around his eyes, which appeared more deeply set. The cast of his mouth was different, too, curving downwards at the corners.

His voice, when he spoke, was both deeper and more ragged. 'You don't give up easily, do you?'

'As a rule, no. Do you remember the last chat we had, John?'

'Adequately.' With one hand he punched a matrix of controls set into the upper surface of the chest-pack, keying in a chain of commands. 'How long ago was it?'

'Do you mind if I ask you how long ago you think it was?'

'No.'

She waited. The Captain looked at her, his expression blank.

'How long ago do you think it was?' she asked, eventually.

'A couple of months. Several years of shiptime. Two days. Three minutes. One point one eight milliseconds. Fifty-four years.'

'Two days is about right,' she said.

'I'll take your word for it. As you'll have gathered, my memory isn't quite the razor-sharp faculty it once was.'

'Still, you did remember that I'd come before. That counts for something, doesn't it?'

'You're a very charitable person, Antoinette.'

'I'm not surprised that your memory works in funny ways, John. But it's enough for me that you remembered my name. Do you remember anything else we talked about?'

'Give me a clue.'

'The visitors, John? The presences in the system?'

'They're still here,' he said. For a moment he was again distracted by the functions of his chest-pack. He looked more vigilant than concerned. She saw him tap the little bracelet of controls that encircled one wrist, then nod as if satisfied with some subtle change in the suit's parameter settings.

'Yes,' she said.

'They're also closer. Aren't they?'

'We think so, John. That's what Khouri told us was happening, and everything she's said has checked out so far.'

'I'd listen to her, if I were you.'

'It's not just a question of listening to Khouri now. We have her daughter. Her daughter knows things, or so we've been led to believe. We think we may have to start listening to what she tells us to do.'

'Clavain will guide you. Like me, he understands the reach of historical time. We're both phantoms from the past, hurtling into futures neither of us expected to see.'

Antoinette bit her lower lip. 'I'm sorry, but I've got some bad news. Clavain's dead. He was killed saving Khouri's daughter. We have Scorpio, but . . .'

The Captain was a long time answering. She wondered if the news of Clavain's death had affected him more than she had anticipated. She had never thought of Clavain and the Captain as having any kinship, but now that the Captain put it like that, the two had a lot more in common with each other than with most of their peers.

'You don't have absolute faith in Scorpio's leadership?' he asked.

'Scorpio's served us well. In a crisis, you couldn't ask for a better leader. But he'd be the first to admit that he doesn't think strategically.'

'Then find another leader.'

Something happened then that surprised her. Unbidden, she had a flashback to the earlier meeting in the High Conch. She saw Blood swaggering in at the start of it and then she saw Vasko Malinin arriving late for the same meeting. She saw Blood reprimanding him for his lateness and Vasko shrugging off that same reprimand as an irrelevance. And she realised, with hindsight, that she had accepted the young man's insouciance as a necessary correlative to what he was and what he would become, and that she had, on some level, found it admirable.

She had seen a gleam of something shining through, like steel.

'This isn't about leaders,' Antoinette said hastily. 'It's about you, John. Are you intending to leave?'

'You suggested I should give the matter some thought.'

She recalled those elevating neutrino levels. 'You seem to be giving it a bit more than thought.'

'Perhaps.'

'We need to be careful,' she said. 'We may well need to get into space at short notice, but we have to think about the consequences for those around us. It will take days to get everyone loaded aboard, even if everything goes without a hitch.'

'There are thousands aboard now. Their survival will have to be my main priority. I'm sorry about the others, but if they don't get here in time they may have to be left behind. Does that sound callous to you?'

'I'm not the one to judge. Look, some people will choose to stay behind anyway. We may even encourage them, just in case leaving Ararat turns out to be a mistake. But if you leave now, you'll kill everyone not already aboard.'

'Have you considered moving them aboard faster?'

'We're doing what we can, and we've begun to make plans to relocate a limited number of people away from the bay. But by this time tomorrow there'll still be at least a hundred thousand people we haven't moved.'

For a moment the Captain faded back into the dust storm. Antoinette stared at the rough leathery texture of the wall. She thought she had lost him and was about to turn away. Then he emerged again, stooping against an imagined wind.

He raised his voice over something only he could hear. 'I'm sorry, Antoinette. I understand your concerns.'

'Does that mean you've listened to a word I said, or are you just going to leave when it suits you, regardless?'

He reached up to lower his visor. 'You should do all that you can to get the others to safety, whether it's aboard the ship or further from the bay.'

'That's it, then, is it? Those that we haven't moved will just have to take their chances?'

'None of this is easy for me.'

'It wouldn't kill you to wait until we can get everyone to safety.'

'But it might, Antoinette. It might do exactly that.'

Antoinette turned away in disgust. 'Remember what I told you last time? I was wrong. I see it now, even if I didn't then.'

'What was that exactly?'

She looked back at him. She felt spiteful and reckless. 'I said you'd paid for your crimes. I said you'd done it a hundred thousand times over. Nice dream, John, but it wasn't true, was it? You didn't care a damn about those people. It was only ever about saving yourself.'

The Captain did not answer her. He pulled down the visor and vanished back into the storm, still angling his body against the tremendous lacerating force of that invisible wind. And Antoinette began to wonder whether this visit hadn't after all been a grave mistake, exactly the sort of reckless behaviour that her father had always warned her about.

'No joy,' she told her companions back in the High Conch.

Around the table sat a quorum of colony seniors. She did not notice any obvious absences except for Pellerin, the swimmer. Even Scorpio was now present. It was the first she had seen of him since Clavain's death, and there was, Antoinette thought, something in his gaze that she had never seen there before. Even when he looked directly at her his eyes were focused on something distant and almost certainly hostile – a glint on some imagined horizon, an enemy sail or the gleam of armour. She had seen that look somewhere else recently, but it took her a moment to remember where. The old man had been sitting in the same place at the table, fixated on the same remote threat. It had taken years of pain and suffering to bring Clavain to that state, but only days to do it to the pig.

Antoinette knew that something awful had happened in the iceberg. She had flinched from the details. When the others had told her she did not need to know – that she was much better off *not* knowing – she had decided to believe them. But although she had never been very good at reading the expressions of pigs, in Scorpio's face half the story was already laid out for her inspection, the horror anatomised if only she had the wit to read the signs.

'What did you tell him?' Scorpio asked.

'I told him we'd be looking at tens of thousands of casualties if he decided to lift off.'

'And?'

'He more or less said "too bad". His only immediate concern was for the people already aboard the ship.'

'Fourteen thousand at the last count,' Blood commented.

'That doesn't sound too bad,' Vasko said. 'That's – what? Not far off a tenth of the colony already?'

Blood toyed with his knife. 'You want to come and help us squeeze in the next five hundred, son, you're more than welcome.'

'It's that difficult?' Vasko asked.

'It gets worse with every consignment. We might manage to get it up to twenty thousand by dawn, but only if we start treating them like cattle.'

'They're human beings,' Antoinette said. 'They deserve better treatment than that. What about the freezers? Aren't they helping?'

'The caskets aren't working as well as they used to,' Xavier Liu said, addressing his wife exactly as he would any other colony senior. 'Once they're cooled down they're OK, but putting someone under means hours of supervision and tinkering. There's no way to process them fast enough.'

Antoinette closed her eyes and pressed her fingertips against her eyelids. She saw turquoise rings, like ripples in water. 'This is about as bad as things can get, isn't it?' Then she reopened her eyes and tried to shake some clarity into her head. 'Scorp – any contact with Remontoire?'

'Nothing.'

'But you're still convinced he's up there?'

'I'm not convinced of anything. I'm merely acting on the best intelligence I have.'

'And you think we'd have seen a sign by now, some attempt to communicate with us, if he were up there.'

'Khouri was that sign,' Scorpio said.

'Then why haven't they sent down someone else?' Antoinette replied. 'We need to know, Scorp: do we sit tight or get the hell off Ararat?'

'Believe me, I'm aware of the options.'

'We can't wait for ever,' Antoinette said, frustration seeping into her voice. 'If Remontoire loses the battle, we'll be looking at a sky full of wolves. No way out once that happens, even if they don't touch Ararat. We'll be locked in.'

'As I said, I'm aware of the options.'

She had heard the menace in his voice. Of course he was aware. 'I'm sorry,' she said. 'I just . . . don't know what else we can do.'

No one spoke for a while. Outside, an aircraft swept low overhead, curving away with another consignment of refugees. Antoinette did not know if they were being taken to the ship or the far side of the island. Once the need to get people to safety had been recognised, the evacuation effort had been split down the middle.

'Did Aura offer anything useful?' Vasko asked.

Scorpio turned to him, the leather of his uniform creaking. 'What sort of thing were you thinking of?'

'It wasn't Khouri that was the sign,' Vasko said, 'it was Aura. Khouri may know things, but Aura is the hotline. She's the one we really need to talk to, the one who might know the right thing to do.'

'I'm glad you've given the matter so much consideration,' Scorpio said.

'Well?' Vasko persisted.

Antoinette stiffened. The atmosphere in the meeting room had never exactly been relaxed, but now it made the hairs on the back of her hands tingle. She had never dared speak to Scorpio like that, and she did not know many who had.

But Scorpio answered calmly. 'She – Khouri – said the word again.'

'The word?' Vasko repeated.

'Hela. She's said it several times since we revived her, but we didn't know what it meant, or even if it had any particular significance. But there was another word this time.' Again the leather creaked as he shifted his frame. For all that he appeared disconnected from events in the room, the violence of which he was capable was a palpable thing, waiting in the wings like an actor.

'The other word?' Vasko asked.

'Quaiche,' Scorpio replied.

The woman walked to the sea. Overhead the sky was a brutal, tortured grey and the rocks under her feet were slippery and unforgiving. She shivered, more in apprehension than cold, for the air was humid and oppressive. She looked behind her, along the shoreline towards the ragged edge of the encampment. The buildings on the fringe of the settlement had a deserted and derelict air to them. Some of them had collapsed and never been reoccupied. She thought it very unlikely that there was anyone around to notice her presence. Not, of course, that it mattered in the slightest. She was entitled to be here, and she was entitled to step into the sea. The fact that she would never have asked this of her own swimmers did not mean that her actions were in any way against colony rules, or even the rules of the swimmer corps. Foolhardy, yes, and very probably futile, but that could not be helped. The pressure to do something had grown inside her like a nagging pain, until it could not be ignored.

It had been Vasko Malinin who had tipped her over the edge. Did he realise the effect his words had had?

Marl Pellerin halted where the shoreline began to curve back around on itself, enclosing the waters of the bay. The shore was a vague grey scratch stretching as far as the eye could see, until it became lost in the mingled wall of sea-mist and cloud that locked in the bay in all directions. The spire of the ship was only intermittently visible in the silvery distance, and its size and remoteness varied from sighting to sighting as her brain struggled to cope with the meagre evidence available to it. Marl knew that the spire reached three kilometres into the sky, but at times it looked no larger than a medium-sized conch structure, or one of the communications antennae that ringed the settlement. She imagined the squall of neutrinos streaming out from the spire – actually from the submerged part of it, of course, where the engines lay underwater – as a shining radiance, a holy light knifing through her. The particles sang through her cell membranes, doing no damage as they sprinted for interstellar space at a hair's breath below the speed of light. They meant that the engines were gearing up for starflight. Nothing organic could detect those squalls, only the most sensitive kinds of machine. But was that really true? The Juggler organisms – taken as a single planet-spanning entity – constituted a truly vast biomass. The Juggler organisms on a single planet outweighed the cumulative mass of the entire human species by a factor of a hundred. Was it so absurd to think that the Jugglers in their entirety might not be as oblivious to that neutrino flux as people imagined? Perhaps they, too, sensed the Captain's restlessness. And perhaps in their slow, green, nearly mindless fashion they comprehended something of what his departure would mean.

At the sea's edge something caught Marl's eye. She walked over to examine it, skipping nimbly from rock to rock. It was a lump of metal, blackened and twisted like some melted sugar confection, strange folds and creases marring its surface. Smoke coiled up from it. The thing buzzed and crackled, and an articulated part resembling the sectioned tail of a lobster twitched horribly. It must have come down recently, perhaps in the last hour. All around Ararat, wherever there were human observers, one heard reports of things falling from the sky. There were too many near these outposts to be accidental.

Efforts were being concentrated above centres of human population. Someone – or something – was trying to get through. Occasionally, some small shard succeeded.

The thing disturbed her. Was it alien or human? Was it friendly-human or Conjoiner-human? Was anyone still making that kind of distinction?

Marl walked past the object and stopped at the water's edge. She disrobed. Preparing to enter the sea, she had a weird flash of herself from the sea's perspective. Her vision seemed to bob up and down from the water. She was a thin, naked thing, a pale upright starfish on the shore. The smashed object pushed a quill of smoke into the sky.

Marl wet her hands in water that had gathered in a rockpool. She splashed her face, wetting back her hair. The water stung her eyes, made them blur with tears. Even the water in the pools was fetid with Juggler life. Pellerin's skin itched, especially in the band across her face where she already showed signs of Juggler takeover. The two colonies of micro-organisms – the one in the water and the one buried in her face – were recognising each other, fizzing with excitement.

Those who monitored such things considered Marl a marginal case. Her signs of takeover were by no means the worst anyone had ever seen. On statistical grounds, she ought to be safe for another dozen swims, at the very least. But there were always exceptions. Sometimes the sea consumed those who had only very slight indications of takeover. Rarely, it took complete newcomers the first time they swam.

That was the point about the Pattern Jugglers. They were alien. *It*, the Juggler biomass, was alien. It would not succumb to human analysis, to neatly circumscribed cause and effect. It was as quixotic and unpredictable as a drunkard. You could guess how it might behave given certain parameters, but once in a while you might be terribly, terribly wrong.

Marl knew this. She had never pretended otherwise. She knew that any swim brought risks.

She had been lucky so far.

She thought of Shizuko, waiting in the psychiatric section for one of Marl's visits – except she wasn't really waiting in the usual sense of the word. Shizuko might have been aware that Marl was due to arrive, and she might have varied her activities accordingly. But when Marl showed up, Shizuko merely looked at her with the distracted passing interest of someone who has seen a crack in a wall that they did not remember, or a fleeting suggestion of meaningful shape in a cloud. The flicker of interest was waning almost as soon as Marl had noticed it. Sometimes Shizuko would laugh, but it was an idiot's laugh, like the chime of small, stupid bells.

Shizuko would then return to her scratching, her fingers always bleeding under the nails, ignoring the crayons and chalks offered to her as substitutes. Marl had stopped visiting some months ago. Once she had acknowledged and accepted that she now meant nothing to Shizuko, there had been an easing. Counter-pointing it, however, had also been a dispiriting sense of betrayal and weakness.

She thought now of Vasko. She thought of his easy certainties, his conviction that the only thing that stood between the swimmers and the sea was fear.

She hated him for that.

Marl took a step into the water. A dozen or so metres out, a raft of green matter twirled in response, sensing that she had entered its realm. Marl took in a deep breath. She was impossibly scared. The itch across her face had become a burn. It made her want to swoon into the water.

'I'm here,' she said. And she stepped towards the mass of Juggler organisms, submerging up to her thighs, up to her waist, then deeper. Ahead, the biomass formed shapes with quickening intensity, the breeze of its transformations blowing over her. Alien anatomies shuffled through endless permutations. It was a pageant of monsters. The water too deep now to walk through, she kicked off from the bed of rocks and began to swim towards the show.

Vasko looked at the others present. 'Quaiche? That doesn't mean anything more to me than the first word.'

'They meant nothing to me either,' Scorpio said. 'I wasn't even sure of the spelling of the first word. But now I'm certain. The second word locks it. The meaning is unambiguous.'

'So are you going to enlighten us?' Liu asked.

Scorpio gestured to Orca Cruz.

'Scorp's right,' she said. 'Hela means nothing significant in isolation. Query the databases we brought with us from Resurgam or Yellowstone and you'll find thousands of possible explanations. Same if you try variant spellings. But put in Quaiche and Hela and it's a different kettle of fish. There's really only one explanation, bizarre as it seems.'

'I'm dying to hear it,' Liu said. Next to him, Vasko nodded in agreement. Antoinette said nothing and conveyed no visible interest, but her curiosity was obviously just as strong.

'Hela is a world,' Cruz said. 'Not much of one, just a medium-sized moon orbiting a gas giant named Haldora. Still not ringing any bells?'

No one said anything.

'What about Quaiche?' Vasko asked. 'Another moon?'

Cruz shook her head. 'No. Quaiche is actually a man, the individual who assigned the names to Hela and Haldora. There's no entry for Quaiche or his worlds in the usual nomenclature database, but we shouldn't be too surprised about that – it's been more than sixty years since it was updated by direct contact with other ships. But ever since we've been on Ararat, we've been picking up the occasional stray signal from other Ultra elements. A lot, recently – they're using long-range wide-beam transmissions far more than they ever did in the past, and occasionally one of those signals sweeps over us by accident.'

'Why the change in tactics?' Vasko asked.

'Something's got them scared,' Cruz said. 'They're becoming nervous, unwilling to do face-to-face trade. Some Ultras must have met something they didn't like, and now they're spreading the word, switching to long-range trading of data rather than material commodities.'

'No prizes for guessing what's spooked them,' Vasko said.

'It works to our advantage, though,' Cruz said. 'They may not be authoritative transmissions, and half of those we do intercept are riddled with errors and viruses, but over the years we've been able to keep our databases more up to date than we could ever have hoped given our lack of contact with external elements.'

'So what do we know about Quaiche's system, then?' Vasko asked.

'Not as much as we'd like,' Cruz said. 'There were no conflicts with prior assignments, which means that the system Quaiche was investigating must have been very poorly explored prior to his arrival.'

'So whatever Aura is referring to happened – what – fifty, sixty years ago?' Vasko asked.

'Easily,' Cruz said.

Vasko stroked his chin. It was clean-shaven, smooth as sand-papered wood. 'Then it can't mean much to us, can it?'

'Something happened to Quaiche,' Scorpio said. 'Accounts vary. Seems he was doing scoutwork for Ultras, getting his hands dirty exploring planetary environments they weren't happy around. He witnessed something, something to do with Haldora.' Scorpio looked at them all, one by one, daring anyone – especially Vasko – to interrupt or quibble. 'He saw it vanish. He saw the planet just cease to exist for a fraction of a second. And because of that he started up a kind of religion on Hela, Haldora's moon.'

'That's it?' Antoinette asked. 'That's the message Aura came all this way to give us? The address of a religious lunatic?'

'There's more,' Scorpio said.

'I sincerely hope there is,' she replied

'He saw it happen more than once. So, apparently, did others.'

'Why am I not surprised?' she said.

'Wait,' Vasko said, holding up a hand. 'I want to hear the rest. Go on, Scorp.'

The pig looked at him with an utter absence of expression. 'Like I need your permission?'

'That's not how I meant it to sound. I just . . .' Vasko looked around, perhaps wondering whom he might solicit for support. 'I just think we shouldn't be too quick to dismiss anything we learn from Aura, no matter how little sense it seems to make.'

'No one's dismissing anything,' Scorpio said.

'Please tell us what you learned,' Antoinette interrupted, sensing that things were about to get out of hand.

'Not much happened for decades,' Scorpio continued. 'Quaiche's miracle drew a few people to Hela. Some of them signed up for the religion, some of them became disillusioned and set up shop as miners. There are alien artefacts on Hela – nearly useless junk, but they export enough to sustain a few settlements. Ultras buy the junk off them and sell it on to curio collectors. Someone probably makes a bit of money out of it, but you can guess that it isn't the poor idiots who dig the stuff out of the ground.'

'There are alien artefacts on a bunch of worlds,' Antoinette said. 'I'm guessing this lot went the same way as the Amarantin and a dozen or so other civilisations, right?'

'The databases didn't have much on the indigenous culture,' Scorpio said. 'The people who run Hela don't exactly encourage free-thinking scientific curiosity. But yes, reading between the lines, it looks as though they met the wolves.'

'And they're extinct now?' she asked.

'So it would seem.'

'Help me out here, Scorp,' Antoinette said. 'What do you think all this *might* mean to Aura?'

'I have no idea,' he said.

'Perhaps she wants us to go there,' Vasko said.

They all looked at him. His tone of voice had been reasonable, as if he was merely voicing something the rest of them were taking for granted. Perhaps that was even true, but hearing someone articulate it was like a small, quiet profanity in the most holy of audiences.

'Go there?' Scorpio said, frowning, the skin between his snout and forehead crinkling into rolls of flesh. 'You mean actually *go there*?'

'If we conclude that she's suggesting it would help us, then yes,' Vasko said.

'We can't just go to this place on the basis of a sick woman's delirious ramblings,' said Hallatt, one of the colony seniors from Resurgam who had never trusted Khouri.

'She isn't sick,' said Dr Valensin. 'She has been tired, and she has been traumatised. That's all.'

'I hear she wanted the baby put back inside her,' Hallatt said, a revolted sneer on his face, as if this was the most debased thing anyone had ever imagined.

'She did,' Scorpio said, 'and I vetoed it. But it wasn't an unreasonable request. She is the child's mother, and the child was kidnapped before she could give birth to her. Under the circumstances, I thought it was an entirely understandable desire.'

'But you still turned her down,' Hallatt said.

'I couldn't risk losing Aura, not after the price we paid for her.'

'Then you were cheated,' Hallatt said. 'The price was too high. We lost Clavain and all we got back was a brain-damaged child.'

'You're saying Clavain died in vain?' Scorpio asked him, his voice dangerously soft.

The moment stalled, elongated, like a fault in a recording. Antoinette realised with appalling clarity that she was not the only one who did not know what had happened in the iceberg. Hallatt, too, must be ignorant of the actual events, but his ignorance was of an infinitely more reckless kind, trampling and transgressing its own boundaries.

'I don't know how he died. I don't care and I don't need to know. But if Aura was all it was about then no, it wasn't worth it. He died in vain.' Hallatt locked his fingers together and pursed his lips in Scorpio's direction. 'You might not want to hear it, but that's the way it is.'

Scorpio glanced at Blood. Something passed between them: an interplay of minute gestures too subtle, too familiar to each participant, ever to be unravelled by an outsider. The exchange only lasted for an instant. Antoinette wondered if anyone else even noticed it, or whether she had simply imagined it.

But another instant later, Hallatt was looking down at something parked in his chest.

Languidly, as if standing up to adjust a picture hung at a lopsided angle, Blood eased to his feet. He strolled towards Hallatt, swaying from side to side with the slow, effortless rhythm of a metronome.

Hallatt was making choking sounds. His fingers twitched impotently against the haft of Blood's knife.

'Get him out of here,' Scorpio ordered.

Blood removed his knife from Hallatt, cleaned it against his thigh, sheathed it again. A surprisingly small amount of blood leaked from the wound.

Valensin moved to stand up.

'Stay where you are,' Scorpio said.

Blood had already called for a pair of SA aides. They arrived within the minute, reacting to the situation with only a momentary jolt of surprise. Antoinette gave them top marks for that. Had she walked into the room and found someone bleeding to death from an obvious knife wound, she would have had a hard time staying conscious, let alone calm.

'I'm going after him,' Valensin said, standing up again as the SA aides removed Hallatt.

'I said, stay put,' Scorpio repeated.

The doctor hammered a fist on the table. 'You just killed a man, you brutal little simpleton! Or at least you will have if he doesn't get immediate medical attention. Is that something that you really want on your conscience, Scorpio?'

'Stay where you are.'

Valensin took a step towards the door. 'Go ahead, then. Stop me, if it really means that much to you. You have the means.'

Scorpio's face twisted into a mask of fury and hatred that Antoinette had never seen before. It astonished her that pigs had the necessary facial dexterity to produce such an extreme expression.

'I'll stop you, trust me on that.' Scorpio reached into a pocket or sheath of his own – whatever it was lay hidden under the table – and removed his knife. It was not one Antoinette had seen before. The blade, at some command from the pig, grew blurred.

'Scorpio,' she said, standing up herself, 'let him do it. He's a doctor.'

'Hallatt dies.'

'There've been enough deaths already,' Antoinette said. 'One more isn't going to make anything better.'

The knife quivered in his grasp, as if not quite tamed. Antoinette expected it to leap from his hand at any moment.

Something chimed. The unexpected noise seemed to catch the pig unawares. His fury slipped down a notch. He looked for the source of the sound. It had come from his communications bracelet.

Scorpio quietened the knife. It grew solid again, and he returned it to the sheath or pocket where it had originated.

He looked at Valensin and said one word. 'Go.'

The doctor nodded curtly – his own face still angry – and scurried after the aides who had carried the wounded man away.

Scorpio lifted the bracelet to his ear and listened to some small, shrill, distant voice. After a minute he frowned and asked the voice to repeat what it had said. As the message was reiterated his frown lessened, but did not entirely vanish.

'What is it?' Antoinette asked.

'The ship,' he said. 'Something's happening.'

Within ten minutes a shuttle had been commandeered and diverted from the ongoing evacuation effort. It came down within a block of the High Conch, descending between buildings, a Security Arm retinue clearing the area and providing safe access for the small party of colony seniors. Vasko was the last aboard, after Scorpio and Antoinette Bax, while Blood and the others remained on the ground as the plane hauled itself aloft once more. The shuttle threw hard white light against the sides of the buildings, the citizens below shielding their eyes but unwilling to look away. There was now no one in First Camp who did not urgently wish to be somewhere else. There was only room for the three who had just boarded because the shuttle's bay was already loaded to near-capacity with evacuees.

Vasko felt the machine accelerate. He hung on to a ceiling hand-hold, hoping that the flight would be brief. The evacuees looked at him with stunned faces, as if waiting for an explanation he was in no position to give.

'Where are they supposed to be heading?' he asked the foreman in charge.

'The outlands,' he said quietly, meaning the sheltered ground, 'but now they'll be taken to the ship instead. We can't afford to waste valuable time.'

The cold efficiency of this decision stunned Vasko. But he also found himself admiring it.

'What if they don't like it?' he asked, keeping his voice low.

'They can always lodge a complaint.'

The journey did not take very long. They had a pilot this time; some of the evacuation flights were being handled by autonomous craft, but this one had been deemed too unusual. They kept low, heading out to sea, and then executed a wide turn around the base of the ship. Vasko was lucky enough to be by the wall. He had made a window in it, peering into silvery mist. Around him, the evacuees crowded forwards for a better look.

'Close the window,' Scorpio said.

'What?'

'You heard me.'

'I'd do it if I were you,' Antoinette said.

Vasko closed the window. If ever there was a day not to argue with the pig, he thought, then this was it. He had seen nothing in any case, just a hint of the ship's looming presence.

They climbed, presumably continuing the spiralling flight path around the spire, and then he felt the shuttle slow and touch solid ground. After a minute or so a crack of light signalled the opening of the escape door and the evacuees were ushered out. Vasko did not get a good look at what lay beyond, in the reception area. He had only a brief glimpse of Security Arm guards standing alertly, shepherding the newcomers with an efficiency that went way beyond polite urgency. He had expected the people to show some anger when they realised they had been taken to the ship instead of the safe haven on the surface, but all he saw was docile acceptance. Perhaps they did not yet realise that this was the ship, and not some ground-level processing area on the other side of the island. If so, he did not care to be around when they learned about the change of plan.

Soon the shuttle was empty of evacuees. Vasko half-expected to be ushered off as well, but instead the three of them remained aboard with the pilot. The loading door closed again and the plane departed from the bay.

'You can open the window now,' Scorpio said.

Vasko made a generous window in the hull, large enough for the three of them to look out of, but for the moment there was nothing to see. He felt the shuttle lurch and yaw as it descended from the reception bay, but he could not tell if they were staying near the *Nostalgia for Infinity* or returning to First Camp.

'You said something was happening with the ship,' Vasko said. 'Is it the neutrino levels?'

Scorpio turned to Antoinette Bax. 'How are they looking?'

'Higher than the last time I reported,' she said, 'but according to our monitor stations they haven't been climbing at quite the same rate as before. Still going up, but not as fast. Maybe my little chat with John did some good after all.'

'Then what's the problem?' Vasko asked.

Scorpio gestured at something through the window. 'That,' he said.

Vasko followed the pig's gaze. He saw the spire of the ship emerging from the silver sea haze. They had descended rapidly and were looking at the place where the ship thrust out of the water. It was here, only the night before, that Vasko had seen the ring of boats and the climbers trying to ascend to the ship's entrance points. But everything had changed since then. There were no climbers, no boats. Instead of a ring of clear water around the base of the spire, the ship was hemmed by a thick, impenetrable layer of solid Juggler biomass. It was a fuzzy green colour, intricately textured. The layer reached out for perhaps a kilometre in all directions, connecting with other biomass clusters via floating bridges of the same verdant material. But that was not the whole of it. The layer around the ship was reaching up around the hull, forming a skin of biomass. It must have been tens of metres thick in places, dozens more where it flared upwards near the base. At that moment, by Vasko's estimate, it had reached two or three hundred metres up the side of the ship. The uppermost limit was not a neatly regular circle but a ragged, probing thing, extending questing tendrils and fronds higher and higher. Faint green veins were already visible at least a hundred metres above the main mass. The whole sheath was moving even as he watched, creeping inexorably upwards. The main mass must have been moving at close to a metre a second. Assuming it could sustain that rate, it would have encased the entire ship within the hour.

'When did this start happening?' Vasko asked.

'Thirty, forty minutes ago,' Scorpio said. 'We were alerted as soon as the concentration began to build up around the base.'

'Why now? I mean, after all the years that ship's been parked here, why would they start attacking it now, of all days?' Vasko said.

'I don't know,' Scorpio replied.

'We can't be certain that it's an attack,' Antoinette said quietly.

The pig turned to her. 'So what does it look like to you?'

'It could be anything,' she replied. 'Vasko's right – an attack doesn't make any sense. Not now, after all these years. It has to be something else.' She added, 'I hope.'

'You said it,' Scorpio replied.

The plane continued to circle the spire. All around it was the same story. It was like watching an accelerated film of some enormous stone edifice being covered in moss, or a statue with verdigris – purposeful, deliberate verdigris.

'This changes things,' Antoinette said. 'I'm worried, Scorp. It might not be an attack, but what if I'm wrong? What about the people already aboard?'

Scorpio lifted up his bracelet and spoke in hushed tones.

'Who are you calling?' Antoinette asked.

He cupped a hand over the microphone. 'Marl Pellerin,' he said. 'I think it's time the swimmer corps found out what's going on.'

'I agree,' Vasko said. 'I thought they should have swum already, as soon as the Juggler activity started up. Isn't that what they're for?'

'You wouldn't say that if it was you that had to swim out there,' Antoinette said.

'It isn't me. It's them, and it's their job.'

Scorpio continued to speak softly into the bracelet. He kept saying the same thing over and over again, as if repeating himself to different people. Finally he shook his head and lowered his sleeve.

'No one can find Pellerin,' he said.

'She must be somewhere,' Vasko said. 'On stand-by or something, waiting for orders. Have you tried the High Conch?'

'Yes.'

'Leave it,' Antoinette said, touching the pig's sleeve. 'It's chaos back there. I'm not surprised that the lines of communication are breaking down.'

'What about the rest of the swimmer corps?' Vasko asked.

'What about them?' Scorpio asked.

'If Pellerin can't be bothered to do her job, what about the others? We're always hearing about how vital they are to the security of Ararat. Now's their chance to prove it.'

'Or die trying,' Scorpio said.

Antoinette shook her head. 'Don't ask any of them to swim, Scorp. It isn't worth it. Whatever's happening out there is the result of a collective decision taken by the biomass. A couple of swimmers aren't going to make much difference now.'

'I just expected better of Marl,' Scorpio said.

'She knows her duty,' Antoinette said. 'I don't think she'd let us down, if she had any choice. Let's just hope she's safe.'

Scorpio moved away from the window and started towards the front of the aircraft. Even as the plane pitched, responding to the unpredictable thermals that spiralled around the huge ship, the pig remained rooted to the ground. Low and wide, he was more comfortable on his feet in the turbulent conditions than either of his human companions.

'Where are you going?' Vasko asked.

The pig looked back. 'I'm telling him to change our flight plan. We're supposed to be going back to pick up more evacuees.'

'And we're not?'

'Afterwards. First, I want to get Aura into the air. I think the sky might be the safest place right now.'

TWENTY-EIGHT

Ararat, 2675

Vasko and Scorpio handled the incubator, carrying it gently into the empty belly of the shuttle. The sky was darkening now, and the thermal matrix of the shuttle's heating surface glowed an angry cherry red, the elements hissing and ticking. Khouri followed them warily, stooping against the oppressive blanket of warm air trapped beneath the shuttle's downcurved wings. She had said nothing more since waking, moving in a dreamlike state of wary compliance. Valensin followed behind his patients, sullenly accepting the same state of affairs. His two medical servitors trundled after him, tied to their master by inviolable bonds of obedience.

'Why aren't we going to the ship?' Valensin kept asking.

Scorpio hadn't answered him. He was communicating with someone via the bracelet again, most likely Blood or one of his deputies. Scorpio shook his head and snarled out an oath. Whatever the news was, Vasko doubted it was welcome.

'I'm going up front,' Antoinette said, 'see if the pilot needs any help.'

'Tell him to keep it slow and steady,' Scorpio ordered. 'No risks. And be prepared to get us up and out if it comes to that.'

'Assuming this thing still has the legs to reach orbit.'

They took off. Vasko helped the doctor and his mechanical aides to secure the incubator, Valensin showing him how the shuttle's interior walls could be persuaded to form outgrowths and niches with varying qualities of adhesion. The incubator was soon glued down, with the two servitors standing watch over its functions. Aura, visible as a wrinkled *thing* within the tinted plastic, bound up in monitors and tubes, appeared oblivious to all the fuss.

'Where are we going?' Khouri asked. 'The ship?'

'Actually, there's a bit of a problem with the ship,' Scorpio said. 'C'mon, take a look. I think you'll find it interesting.'

They circled the ship again, at the same altitude as before. Khouri stared at the view with wide, uncomprehending eyes. Vasko did not blame her in the slightest. When he had seen the ship himself, only thirty minutes earlier, it had been in the earliest stages of being consumed by the Juggler biomass. Because the process had only just begun, it had been easy enough to assimilate what was going on. But now the ship was *gone*. In its place was a towering, irregular fuzzy green spire. He knew that there was a ship under the mass, but he could only guess at how strange the view must look to someone who hadn't seen the early stages of the Juggler envelopment.

But there was something else, wasn't there? Something that Vasko had noticed almost immediately but had dismissed as an optical illusion, a trick of his own tilted vantage point within the shuttle. But now that he was able to see the horizon where it poked through rents in the sea mist, it was obvious that there was no illusion, and that what he saw had nothing to do with his position.

The ship was tilting. It was a slight lean, only a few degrees away from vertical, but it was enough to inspire terror. The edifice that had for so long been a solid fixture of the landscape, seemingly as ancient as geography itself, was leaning to one side.

It was being pulled over by the collective biomass of the Pattern Juggler organisms.

'This isn't good,' Vasko said.

'Tell me what's happening,' Khouri said, standing next to him.

'We don't know,' Scorpio said. 'It started an hour or so ago. The sea thickened around the base, and the ring of material started swallowing the ship. Now it looks as if the Jugglers are trying to topple it.'

'Could they?'

'Maybe. I don't know. The ship must weigh a few million tonnes. But the mass of all that Juggler material isn't exactly negligible. I wouldn't worry about the ship toppling, though.'

'No?'

'I'd be more worried about it snapping. That's a lighthugger. It's designed to tolerate one or more gees of acceleration along its axis. Standing on the surface of a planet doesn't impose any more stress on it than normal starflight. But they don't build those ships to handle lateral stresses. They're not designed to stay in one piece if the forces are acting sideways. A couple more degrees and I'll start worrying. She might come down.'

Khouri said, 'We need that ship, Scorp. It's our only ticket out of here.'

'Thanks for the newsflash,' he said, 'but right now I'd say there isn't a lot I can do about it – unless you want me to start fighting the Pattern Jugglers.'

The very notion was extreme, almost absurd. The Pattern Jugglers were harmless to all but a few unfortunate individuals. Collectively, they had never indicated any malicious intentions towards humanity. They were archives of lost knowledge, lost minds. But if the Pattern Jugglers were trying to destroy the *Nostalgia for Infinity*, what else could the humans do but retaliate? That simply could not be allowed to happen.

'Do you have weapons on this shuttle?' Khouri asked.

'Some,' Scorpio said. 'Light ship-to-ship stuff, mainly.'

'Anything you could use against that biomass?'

'Some particle beams which won't work too well in Ararat's atmosphere. The rest? Too likely to take chunks out of the ship as well. We could try the particle beams . . .'

'No!'

The voice had come from Khouri's mouth. But it had emerged explosively, like a vomit of sound. It almost didn't resemble her voice at all.

'You just said . . .' Scorpio began.

Khouri sat down suddenly, falling – as if exhausted – into one of the couches that the shuttle had provided. She pressed a hand to her brow.

'No,' she said again, less stridently this time. 'No. Leave. Leave alone. Help us.'

Wordlessly, Vasko, Scorpio, Valensin – and Khouri too – turned to look at the incubator, where Aura lay entombed in the care of machines. The tiny red-pink form within was moving, writhing gently against those restraints.

'Help us?' Vasko asked.

Khouri answered, but again the words seemed to emerge without her volition. She had to catch her breath between them. 'They. Help us. Want to.'

Vasko moved over to the incubator. He had one eye on Khouri, another on her daughter. Valensin's machines shuffled agitatedly. They did not know what to do, and their jointed arms were jerking with nervous indecision.

'They?' Vasko asked. 'They as in the Pattern Jugglers?'

The pink form kicked her little legs, the tiny, perfectly formed nub of a fist clenched in front of the miniature scowl of her face. Aura's eyes were sealed slits.

'Yes. They. Pattern Jugglers,' Khouri said.

Vasko turned to Scorpio. 'I think we've got this all wrong,' he said.

'You do?'

'Wait. I need to talk to Antoinette.'

He went forward to the bridge without waiting for the pig's permission. In the shuttle's cockpit he found Antoinette and the pilot strapped into their command couches. They had turned the entire cockpit transparent, so that they appeared to be floating in midair, accompanied only by various disembodied read-out panels and controls. Vasko took a dizzy step back and then collected himself.

'Can we hover?' he asked.

Antoinette looked at him over her shoulder. 'Of course.'

'Then bring us to a stop. Do you have any ranging equipment? Anticollision sensors, that sort of thing?'

'Of course,' she said again, as if both questions were amongst the least intelligent she had heard in a long while.

'Then shine something on the ship.'

'Any particular reason, Vasko? We can all see that the damned thing's tilting.'

'Just do it, all right?'

'Yes, sir,' she said. Her small hands, clinking with jewellery, worked the controls floating above her couch. Vasko felt the ship nudge to a halt. The view ahead rotated, bringing the leaning tower directly in front of them.

'Hold it there,' Vasko said. 'Now get that ranging thing – whatever it is – on to the ship. Somewhere near the base if you can manage it.'

'That isn't going to help us figure out the tilt angle,' Antoinette said.

'It's not the tilt I'm interested in. I don't think they're really trying to topple it.'

'You don't?'

Vasko smiled. 'I think it's just a by-product. They're trying to move it.'

He waited for her to set up the ranging device. A pulsing spherical display floated in front of her, filled with smoky green structures and numbers. 'There's the ship,' she said, pointing to the thickest return in the radar plot.

'Good. Now tell me how far away it is.'

'Four hundred and forty metres,' she said, after a moment. 'That's an average. The green stuff is changing in thickness all the while.'

'All right. Keep an eye on that figure.'

'It's increasing,' the pilot said.

Vasko felt hot breath on his neck. He turned around to see the pig looking over his shoulder.

'Vasko's on to something,' Antoinette said. 'Distance to the spire is now ... four hundred and fifty metres.'

'You're drifting,' Scorpio said.

'No, we're not.' She sounded the tiniest bit affronted. 'We're rock steady, at least within the errors of measurement. Vasko's right, Scorp – the ship's moving. They're dragging it out to sea.'

'How fast is it moving?' Scorpio asked.

'Too soon to say with any certainty. A metre, maybe two, per second.' Antoinette checked her own communicator bracelet. 'The neutrino levels are still going up. I'm not sure exactly how long we have left, but I don't think we're looking at more than a few hours.'

'In which the case the ship isn't going to be more than a few kilometres further away when it launches,' Scorpio said.

'That's better than nothing,' Antoinette said. 'If they can at least get it beyond the curve of the bay, so that we have some shelter from the tidal waves ... that's got to be better than nothing, surely?'

'I'll believe it when I see it,' the pig replied.

Vasko felt a thrilling sense of affirmation. 'Aura was right. They don't want to hurt us. They only want to save us, by getting the ship away from the bay. They're on our side.'

'Nice theory,' Scorpio said, 'but how did they know we were in this mess in the first place? It's not as if anyone went down into the sea and explained it to them. Someone would have had to swim for that.'

'Maybe someone did,' Vasko said. 'Does it matter now? The ship's moving. That's all that counts.'

'Yeah,' Scorpio said. 'Let's just hope it isn't too late to make a difference.'

Antoinette turned to the pilot. 'Think you can get us close to that thing? The green stuff doesn't seem too thick near the top. It might still be possible to get into the usual landing bay.'

'You're joking,' the pilot said, incredulously.

Antoinette shook her head. She was already assigning full control back to the regular pilot. ''Fraid not, fella. If we want John to hold his horses until the ship's clear of the bay, someone's going to have go down and talk to him. And guess who just drew *that* straw?'

'I think she's serious,' Vasko said.

'Do it,' Scorpio said.

The caravan threaded cautiously through tunnels and inched along ridiculously narrow ledges. It twisted and turned, at points doubling back on itself so that the rear parts advanced while the lead machines retreated. Once, navigating a rising hairpin, engines and traction limbs labouring, part of the caravan passed over itself, letting Rashmika look down on the racked Observers.

All the while the bridge grew larger. When she had first seen it, the bridge had the appearance of something lacy and low-relief, painted on a flat black backdrop in glittering iridescent inks. Now, slowly, it was taking on a faintly threatening three-dimensional solidity. This was not some mirage, some peculiar trick of lighting and atmospherics, but a real object, and the caravan was really going to cross it.

The three-dimensionality both alarmed and comforted Rashmika. The bridge now appeared to be more than just an assemblage of infinitely thin lines, and although many of its structural parts were still very fine in cross section, now that she was seeing them at an oblique angle the structural components didn't look quite so delicate. If the bridge could support itself, surely it could support the caravan. She hoped.

'Miss Els?'

She looked around. This time it really was Quaestor Jones. 'Yes,' she said, unhappy at his attention.

'We'll be over it before very long. I promised you that the experience would be spectacular, didn't I?'

'You did,' she said, 'but what you didn't explain, Quaestor, was why everyone doesn't take this short cut, if it's as useful as you claim.'

'Superstition,' he said, 'coupled with excessive caution.'

'Excessive caution sounds entirely appropriate to me where this bridge is involved.'

'Are you frightened, Miss Els? You shouldn't be. This caravan weighs barely fifty thousand tonnes, all told. And by its very nature, the weight is distributed along a great length. It isn't as if we're taking a *cathedral* across the bridge. Now that *would* be folly.'

'No one would do that.'

'No one sane. And especially not after they saw what happened last time. But that needn't concern us in the slightest. The bridge will hold the caravan. It has done so in the past. I would have no particular qualms about taking us across it during every expedition away from the Way, but the simple truth is that most of the time it wouldn't help us. You've seen how laborious the approach is. More often than not, using the bridge would cost us more time than it would save. It was only a particular constellation of circumstances that made it otherwise on this occasion.' The quaestor clasped his hands decisively. 'Now, to business. I believe I have secured you a position in a clearance gang attached to an Adventist cathedral.'

'The Lady Morwenna?'

'No. A somewhat smaller cathedral, the Catherine of Iron. Everyone has to start somewhere. And why are you in such a hurry to reach the Lady Morwenna? Dean Quaiche has his foibles. The Catherine's dean is a good man. His safety record is very good, and those who serve under him are well looked after.'

'Thank you, Quaestor,' she said, hoping her disappointment was not too obvious. She had still been hoping he might be able to find her a solid clerical job, something well away from clearance work. 'You're right. Something is better than nothing.'

'The Catherine is amongst the main group of cathedrals, moving towards the Rift from the western side. We will join them when we have completed our crossing of the bridge, shortly before they begin their descent of the Devil's Staircase. You are privileged, Miss Els: very few people get the chance to cross Absolution Gap twice in one year, let alone within a matter of days.'

'I'll count myself lucky.'

'Nonetheless, I will repeat what I said before: the work is difficult, dangerous and poorly rewarded.'

'I'll take what's available.'

'In which case you will be transferred to the relevant gang as soon as we reach the Way. Keep your nose clean, and I am sure you will do very well.'

'I will certainly bear that in mind.'

He touched a finger to his lips and made to turn away, as if remembering some other errand, then halted. The eyes of his green pet – it had been on his shoulder the whole time – remained locked on to her, blank as gun barrels.

'One other matter, Miss Els,' the quaestor said, looking back at her over his shoulder.

'Yes?'

'The gentleman you were speaking to earlier?' His eyes narrowed as he studied her expression. 'Well, I wouldn't, if I were you.'

'You wouldn't what?'

'Have anything to do with his sort.' The quaestor stared vaguely into the distance. 'As a rule, it's never wise to circulate amongst Observers, or any other pilgrims of a similarly committed strain of faith. But in my general experience it is *especially* unwise to associate with those who are vacillating between faith and denial.'

'Surely, Quaestor, it is up to me who I talk to.'

'Of course, Miss Els, and please don't take offence. I offer only advice, from the bottomless pit of goodness which is my heart.' He popped a morsel into the mouthpiece of his pet. 'Don't I, Peppermint?'

'Let he who is without sin cast the first stone,' the creature observed.

The caravan surmounted the eastern approach to the bridge. A kilometre from the eastern abutment, the road had veered back into the side of the cliff, ascending a steep defile that – via scraping hairpins, treacherous gradients and brief interludes of tunnel and ledge – brought it to the level of the bridge deck. Behind them, the landscape was an apparently impassable chaos of ice boulders. Ahead, the road deck stretched away like a textbook example of perspective, straight as a rifle barrel, unfenced on either side, gently cambered towards the middle, gleaming with the soft diamond lustre of starlit ice.

Gathering speed now that it was on a level surface with no immediate worry of obstructions, the caravan sped towards the point where the ground fell away on either side. The road beneath the procession became smoother and wider, no longer furrowed or interrupted by rock-falls or man-deep fissures. And here there were, finally, very few pilgrims to be avoided. Most of them did not take the bridge, and so there was minimal risk of any unfortunates being trundled to death beneath the machines.

Rashmika's grasp of the scale of the structure underwent several ratchetting revisions. She recalled that, from a distance, the deck of the bridge had formed a shallow arc. From this approach, however, it appeared flat and straight, as if aligned by laser, until the point where it vanished into convergence, far ahead. She was trying to resolve this paradox when she realised – dizzyingly – that at that moment she must only be seeing a small fraction of the distance along the deck. It was like climbing a dome-shaped hill: the summit was always tantalisingly out of reach.

She walked to another viewing point and looked back. The first half-dozen vehicles of this flank of the caravan were now on the bridge proper, and the sheer walls of the cliff were dropping back to the rear, offering her the first real opportunity to judge the depth of the Rift.

It fell away with indecent swiftness. The cliff walls were etched and gouged with titanic geological clawmarks, here vertical, there horizontal, elsewhere diagonal or curled and folded into each other in a display of obscene liquidity. The walls sparkled and spangled with blue-grey ice and murkier seams of darker sediment. The ledge that the caravan had traversed, visible now to the left, appeared far too narrow and hesitant to be used as a road, let alone by something weighing fifty thousand tonnes. Beneath the ledge, Rashmika now saw, the cliff often curved in to a worrying degree. She had never exactly felt safe during the traverse, but she had convinced herself that the ground beneath them continued down for more than a few dozen metres.

She did not see the quaestor again during the rest of the crossing. Within an hour she judged that the opposite wall of the Rift looked only slightly further away than the one that was receding behind them. They must be nearing the midpoint of the bridge. Quickly, therefore, but with the minimum of fuss, Rashmika put on her vacuum suit and stole up through the caravan to its roof.

From the top of the vehicle things looked very different from the sanitised, faintly unreal scene she had observed from the pressurised compartment. She now had a panoramic view of the entire Rift, and it was much easier to see the floor, which was a good dozen kilometres below. From this perspective, the Rift floor almost appeared to be creeping forwards as the flat ribbon of the road bed streaked backwards beneath the caravan. This contradiction made her feel immediately dizzy, and she was gripped by an urgent desire to flatten herself on the roof of the machine, spread-eagled so that she could not possibly topple over the edge. But although she bent her knees, lowering her centre of gravity, Rashmika managed to screw up the courage to remain standing.

The road bed appeared only slightly wider than the caravan. They were moving down the middle of it, only occasionally veering to one side or the other to avoid a patch of thickened ice or some other obstruction. There were rocks on the frozen surface of the road, deposited there from volcanic plumes elsewhere on Hela. Some of them were half as high as the caravan's wheels. The fact that they had managed to smash on to the road without shattering the bridge gave her a tiny flicker of reassurance. And if the road bed was just wide enough to accommodate the two rows of vehicles that made up the caravan, then it was clearly absurd to think of a cathedral making the same journey.

That was when she noticed something down in the floor of the Rift. It was a huge smear of rubble, kilometres across. It was dark and star-shaped, and as far as she could tell the epicentre of the smear lay almost directly beneath the bridge. Near the centre of the star were vague suggestions of ruined structures. Rashmika saw what she thought might be the uppermost part of a spire, leaning to one side. She made out sketchy hints of smashed machinery, smothered in dust and debris.

So someone *had* tried to cross the bridge with a cathedral.

She moved between the vehicles, focusing dead ahead as she made her own personal crossing. The Observers were still on their racks, tilted towards the swollen sphere of Haldora. Their mirrored face-plates made her think of dozens of neatly packed titanium eggs.

Then she saw another suited figure waiting on the next vehicle along, resting against a railing on one side of the roof. It became aware of her presence at about the same time that she noticed it, for the figure turned to her and beckoned her onwards.

She moved past the Observers, then crossed another swaying connection. The caravan swerved alarmingly to negotiate the chicane between two rockfalls, then bounced and crunched its way over a series of smaller obstructions.

The other figure wore a vacuum suit of unremarkable design. She had no idea whether it was the same kind that the Observers wore, since she had never seen beneath their habits. The mirrored silver visor gave nothing away.

'Pietr?' she asked, on the general channel.

There was no response, but the figure still urged her on with increased urgency.

What if this was a trap of some kind? The quaestor had known about her conversation with the young man. It was quite likely that he also knew about her earlier assignation on the roof. Rashmika had little doubt that she would be making enemies during the course of her investigations, but she did not think she had made any yet, unless one counted the quaestor. But since he had now arranged work for her in the clearance gang, she imagined that he had a vested interest in seeing her safely delivered to the Permanent Way.

Rashmika approached the figure, weighing possibilities all the while. The figure's suit was a hard-shelled model, closely fitting the anatomy of its wearer. The helmet and limb parts were olive green, the accordion joints gleaming silver. Unlike the suits she had seen being worn by the walking pilgrims, it was completely lacking in any ornamentation or religious frippery.

The faceplate turned to her. She saw highlights glance off a face behind the glass, the hard shadow beneath well-defined cheekbones.

Pietr extended an arm and with the other hand folded back a flap on the wrist of the outstretched arm. He unspooled a thin optical fibre and offered the other end to Rashmika.

Of course. Secure communication. She took the fibre and plugged it into the corresponding socket on her own suit. Such fibres were designed to allow suit-to-suit communications in the event of a radio or general network failure. They were also ideal for privacy.

'I'm glad you made it,' Pietr said.

'I wish I understood the reason for all the cloak-and-dagger stuff.'

'Better safe than sorry. I shouldn't really have talked to you about the vanishings at all, at least not down in the caravan. Do you think anyone overheard us?'

'The quaestor came and had a quiet word with me when you had gone.'

'That doesn't surprise me in the least,' Pietr said. 'He's not really a religious man, but he knows which side his bread's buttered on. The churches pay his salary, so he doesn't want anyone rocking the boat with unorthodox rumours.'

'You were hardly calling for the abolition of the churches,' Rashmika replied. 'From what I remember, all we discussed was the vanishings.'

'Well, that's dangerous enough, in some people's views. Talking of which – views, I mean – isn't this something else?' Pietr pivoted around on his heels, illustrating his point with an expansive sweep of his free hand.

Rashmika smiled at his enthusiasm. 'I'm not sure. I'm not really one for heights.'

'Oh, c'mon. Forget all that stuff about the vanishings, forget your enquiry – whatever it is – just for now. Admire the view. Millions of people will never, ever see what you're seeing now.'

'It feels as if we're trespassing,' Rashmika said, 'as if the scuttlers built this bridge to be admired, but never used.'

'I don't know much about them. I'd say we haven't a clue what they thought, if they even built this thing. But the bridge is here, isn't it? It seems an awful shame not to make some use of it, even if it's only once in a while.'

Rashmika looked down at the star-shaped smear. 'Is it true what the quaestor told me? Did someone once try to take a cathedral across this thing?'

'So they say. Not that you'll find any evidence of it in any ecumenical records.'

She grasped the railing tighter, still beguiled by the remoteness of the ground so far below. 'But it did happen, all the same?'

'It was a splinter sect,' Pietr said. 'A one-off church, with a small cathedral. They called themselves the Numericists. They weren't affiliated to any of the ecumenical organisations, and they had very limited trading agreements with the other churches. Their belief system was ... odd. It wasn't just a question of being in doctrinal conflict with any of the other churches. They were polytheists, for a start. Most of the churches are strictly monotheistic, with strong ties to the old Abrahamic religions. Hellfire and brimstone churches, I call them. One God, one Heaven, one Hell. But the ones who made that mess down there ... they were a lot stranger. They weren't the only polytheists, but their entire world view – their entire cosmology – was so hopelessly unorthodox that there was no possibility of interecumenical dialogue. The Numericists were devout mathematicians. They viewed the study of numbers as the highest possible calling, the only valid way to approach the numinous. They believed there was one God for every class of number: a God of integers, a God of real numbers, a God of zero. They had subsidiary gods: a lesser god of irrational numbers, a lesser god of the Diophantine primes. The other churches couldn't stomach that kind of weirdness. So the Numericists were frozen out, and in due course they became insular and paranoid.'

'Not surprising, under the circumstances.'

'But there's something else. They were interested in a statistical interpretation of the vanishings, using some pretty arcane probability theories. It was tricky. There hadn't been so many vanishings at that time, so the data was sparser – but their methods, they said, were robust enough to be able to cope. And what they came up with was devastating.'

'Go on,' Rashmika said. She finally understood why Pietr had wanted her to come up on to the roof midway through the crossing.

'They were the first to claim that the vanishings were increasing in frequency, but it was statistically difficult to prove. There was already anecdotal evidence that they occurred in closely spaced clusters, but now, or so the Numericists claimed, the spaces between the clusters were growing shorter. They also claimed that the vanishings themselves were growing longer in duration, although they admitted that the evidence for that was much less "significant", in the statistical sense.'

'But they were right, weren't they?'

Pietr nodded, the reflected landscape tilting in his helmet. 'At least for the first part. Now even crude statistical methods will show the same result. The vanishings are definitely becoming more frequent.'

'And the second part?'

'Not proven. But all the new data hasn't disproved it, either.'

Again Rashmika risked a glance down at the smear. 'But what happened to them? Why did they end up down there?'

'No one really knows. As I said, the churches don't even admit that an attempt at a crossing ever took place. Dig a little deeper and you'll find grudging acknowledgement that the Numericists once existed – paperwork relating to rare trade dealings, for instance – but you won't find anything about them ever crossing Absolution Gap.'

'It happened, though.'

'They tried it, yes. No one will ever know why, I think. Perhaps it was a last-ditch attempt to steal prestige from the churches that had frozen them out. Perhaps they'd worked out a short cut that would bring them ahead of the main procession without ever losing sight of Haldora. It doesn't matter, really. They had a reason, they tried to make the crossing, and they failed. Why they failed, that's something else.'

'The bridge didn't give way,' Rashmika said.

'No – doesn't look as if it did. Their cathedral was small, by the standards of the main ones. From the position of the impact point we can tell they made it a good way across the bridge before sliding off, so it wasn't a question of the bridge buckling. My guess is it was always a delicate balancing act, with the cathedral extending either side of the road, and that midway over they lost navigational control just long enough to topple over. Who knows?'

'But you think there's another possibility.'

'They hadn't made themselves popular, what with all that statistical stuff about the vanishings. Remember what I said about the other churches not wanting to know about the increasing frequency?'

'They don't want the world to change.'

'No, they don't. They've got a nice arrangement as it stands. Keep circling Hela, keep monitoring Haldora, make a living exporting scuttler relics to the rest of human space. In the high church echelons, things are fine as they are, thank you very much. They don't want any rumours of apocalypse upsetting their gravy train.'

'So you think someone destroyed the Numericists' cathedral.'

'Like I said, don't go trying to prove anything. Of course, it could have been an accident. No one has ever said that taking a cathedral across Absolution Gap was a *wise* course of action.'

'Despite all that, Pietr, you still have faith?' She saw his fist close tighter on the rail.

'I believe that the vanishings are a message in a time of crisis. Not just a mute statement of Godlike power, as the churches would have it – a miracle for a miracle's sake – but something vastly more significant. I believe that they are a kind of clock, counting down, and that zero hour is much closer than anyone in authority will have us believe. The Numericists knew this. Do I believe that the churches are to be trusted? By and large, with one or two exceptions, no. I trust them about as far as I can piss in a vacuum. But I still have my faith. That hasn't changed.'

She thought he sounded as if he was telling the truth, but without a clear view of his face, her guess was as good as anyone's.

'There's something else though, isn't there? You said the churches couldn't possibly conceal all evidence of the changing vanishings.'

'They can't. But there *is* an anomaly.' Pietr let go of the railing long enough to pass something to Rashmika. It was a little metal cylinder with a screw top. 'You should see this,' he said. 'I think you will find it interesting. Inside is a piece of paper with some markings on it. They're not annotated, since that would make them more dangerous should anyone in authority recognise them for what they are.'

'You're going to have to give me a little more to go on than that.'

'In Skull Cliff, where I come from, there was a man named Saul Tempier. I knew him. He was an old hermit who lived in an abandoned scuttler shaft on the outskirts of the town. He fixed digging machines for a living. He wasn't mad or violent, or even particularly antisocial; he just didn't get on well with the other villagers and kept out of their way most of the time. He had an obsessive, methodical streak that made other people feel slightly ill at ease. He wasn't interested in wives or lovers or friends.'

'And you don't think he was particularly antisocial?'

'Well, he wasn't actually rude or inhospitable. He kept himself clean and didn't – as far as I am aware – have any genuinely unpleasant habits. If you visited him, he'd always make you tea from a big old samovar. He had an ancient neural lute which he played now and then. He'd always want to know what you thought of his playing.' She caught the flash of his smile through the faceplate.

'Actually, it was pretty dreadful, but I never had the heart to tell him.'

'How did you come to know him?'

'It was my job to keep our stock of digging machinery in good order. We'd do most of the repairs ourselves, but whenever there was a backlog or something we just couldn't get to work properly, one of us would haul it over to Tempier's grotto. I suppose I visited him two or three times a year. I never minded it, really. I actually quite liked the old coot, bad lute playing and all. Anyway, Tempier was getting old. On one of our last meetings – this would have been eleven or twelve years ago – he told me there was something he wanted to show me. I was surprised that he trusted me that much.'

'I don't know,' Rashmika said. 'You strike me as the kind of person someone would find it quite easy to trust, Pietr.'

'Is that intended as a compliment?'

'I'm not sure.'

'Well, I'll take it as one, in that case. Where was I?'

'Tempier said there was something he wanted to show you.'

'It's actually the piece of paper I've just given you, or, rather, the paper is a careful copy of the original. Tempier, it turned out, had been keeping a record of the vanishings for most of his life. He had done a lot of background work – comparing and contrasting the public records of the main churches, even making visits to the Way to inspect those archives that were not usually accessible. He was a very diligent and obsessive sort, as I've said, and when I saw his notes I realised that they were easily the best personal record of the vanishings I'd ever seen. Frankly, I doubt there's a better amateur compilation anywhere on Hela. Alongside each vanishing was a huge set of associated material – notes on witnesses, the quality of those witnesses, and any other corroborative data sets. If there was a volcanic eruption the day before, he'd note that as well. Anything unusual – no matter how irrelevant it appeared.'

'He found something, I take it. Was it the same thing that the Numericists discovered?'

'No,' Pietr said. 'It was more than that. Tempier was well aware of what the Numericists had claimed. His own data didn't contradict theirs in the slightest. In fact, he regarded it as rather obvious that the vanishings were growing more frequent.'

'So what did he discover?'

'He found out that the public and official records don't quite match.'

Rashmika felt a wave of disappointment. She had expected more than that. 'Big deal,' she said. 'It doesn't surprise me that the Observers might occasionally spot a vanishing when everyone else misses it, especially if it happened during some other distracting . . .'

'You misunderstand,' Pietr said sharply. For the first time she heard irritation in his voice. 'It wasn't a case of the churches claiming a vanishing that everyone else had missed. This was the other way around. Eight years earlier – which would make it twenty-odd years ago now – there was a vanishing which did not enter the official church records. Do you understand what I'm saying? A vanishing took place, and it was noted by public observers like Tempier, but according to the churches no such thing happened.'

'But that doesn't make any sense. Why would the churches expunge knowledge of a vanishing?'

'Tempier wondered exactly the same thing.'

So perhaps her trip up on to the roof had not been entirely in vain after all. 'Was there anything about this vanishing that might explain why it wasn't admitted into the official record? Something that meant it didn't quite meet the usual criteria?'

'Such as what?'

She shrugged. 'I don't know. Was it very brief, for instance?'

'As a matter of interest – if Tempier's notes are correct – it was one of the longest vanishings ever recorded. Fully one and one-fifth of a second.'

'I don't get it, in that case. What does Tempier have to say on the matter?'

'Good question,' Pietr said, 'but not one likely to be answered any time soon. I'm afraid Saul Tempier is dead. He died seven years ago.'

'I'm sorry. I get the impression you liked him. But you said it yourself: he was getting old.'

'He was, but that didn't have anything to do with his death. They found him electrocuted, killed while he was repairing one of his machines.'

'All right.' She hoped she did not sound too heartless. 'Then he was getting careless.'

'Not Saul Tempier,' Pietr said. 'He didn't have a careless bone in his body. That was the bit they got wrong.'

Rashmika frowned. 'They?'

'Whoever killed him,' he said.

They stood in silence for a while. The caravan surmounted the brow of the bridge, then began the long, shallow descent to the other side of the Rift. The far cliffs grew larger, the folds and seams of tortured geology becoming starkly obvious. To the left, on the south-western face of the Rift, Rashmika made out another winding ledge. It appeared to have been pencilled tentatively along the wall, a hesitant precursor for the proper job that was to follow. Yet that *was* the ledge. Very soon they would be on it, the crossing done. The bridge would have held, and all would be well with the world – or at least as well as when they had set out.

'Is that why you came here, in the end?' she asked Pietr. 'To find out why they killed that old man?'

'That makes it sound like just another of your secular enquiries,' he replied.

'What is it, then, if it isn't that?'

'I'd like to know why they murdered Saul, but more than that, I'd like to know why they feel the need to lie about the word of God.'

She had asked him about his beliefs already, but she still felt.the need to probe the limits of his honesty. There had to be a chink, she thought: a crack of uncertainty in the shield of his faith. 'So that's what you believe the vanishings are?'

'As firmly as I believe anything.'

'In which case . . . if the true pattern of vanishings is different from the official story, then you believe that the true message is being suppressed, and the word of God isn't being communicated to the people in its uncorrupted form.'

'Exactly.' He sounded very pleased with her, grateful that some vast chasm of understanding had now been spanned. She had the sense that a burden had been taken from him for the first time in ages. 'And my mistake was to think I could silence those doubts by immersing myself in mindless observation. But it didn't work. I saw you, standing there in all your fierce independence, and I realised I had to do this on my own.'

'That's . . . something like the way I feel.'

'Tell me about your enquiry, Rashmika.'

She did. She told him about Harbin, and how she thought he had been taken away by one of the churches. More than likely, she said, he had been forcibly indoctrinated. This was not something she really wanted to consider, but the rational part of her could not ignore the possibility. She told him how the rest of her family had accepted Harbin's faith some time ago, but that she had never been able to let him slip away that easily. 'I had to do this,' she said. 'I had to make this pilgrimage.'

'I thought you weren't a pilgrim.'

'Slip of the tongue,' she said. But she wasn't sure if she really meant it any more.

Ararat, 2675

The upper decks of the *Nostalgia for Infinity* were crammed with evacuees. Antoinette wanted to avoid thinking of them as so many cattle, but as soon as she hit the main cloying mass of bodies and found her own progress blocked or impeded, frustration over-whelmed her. They were human beings, she kept reminding herself, ordinary people caught up as she was in the ebb of events they barely comprehended. In other circumstances she could easily have been one of them, just as frightened and dazed as they were. Her father had always emphasised how easy it was to find oneself on the wrong side of the fence. It wasn't necessarily a question of who had the quickest wits or the firmest resolve. It wasn't always about bravery or some shining inner goodness. It could just as easily be about the position of your name in the alphabet, the chemistry of your blood, or whether you were fortunate enough to be the daughter of a man who happened to own a ship.

She forced herself not to push through the crowds of people waiting to be processed, doing her best to ease forward politely, making eye contact and apologies, smiling at and tolerating those who did not immediately step out of her way. But the mob – she could not help but think of them as such in spite of her best intentions – was so large, so collectively stupid, that her patience only lasted for about two decks. Then something inside her snapped and she was pushing through with all her strength, teeth gritted, oblivious to the insults and the spitting that followed in her wake.

She finally made it through the crowds and descended three bliss-fully deserted levels using interdeck ladders and stairwells. She moved in near darkness, navigating from one erratic light source to the next, cursing herself for not bringing a torch. Then her shoes sloshed through an inch of something wet and sticky she was glad she couldn't see.

Finally she found a functioning main-spine elevator and operated the control to summon it. The ship's lean was disturbingly apparent – it was part of the problem for the continued processing of the immigrants – but so far main ship functions did not appear to have been affected. She heard the elevator thundering towards her, clattering against its inductance rails, and took a moment to check the neutrino levels on her wrist unit. Assuming that the planetwide monitors could still be trusted, the ship was now only five or six per cent from drive criticality. Once that threshold was reached, the ship would have enough bottled energy to lift itself from the surface of Ararat and into orbit.

Only five or six per cent. There had been times when the neutrino flux had jumped that much in only a few minutes.

'Take your time, John,' she said. 'None of us are in that much of a hurry.'

The elevator was slowing. It arrived in a self-important flutter of clanking mechanisms. The doors opened, fluid sluicing down the shaft as Antoinette stepped into the waiting emptiness of the elevator car. Again, why had she forgotten to bring a light with her? She was getting sloppy, taking it as read that the Captain would usher her into his realm like a familiar house guest. *Come on in. Put your feet up. How're things?*

What if, this time, he was not so enthusiastic about having company?

None of the elevator voice-control systems worked properly. With practised ease Antoinette unlatched an access panel, exposing the manual controls. Her fingers dithered over the options. They were annotated in antiquated script, but she was familiar enough with them by now. This elevator would only take her part of the way down to the Captain's usual haunts. She would have to change to another at some point, which would mean a cross-ship trek of at least several hundred metres, assuming no blockades had materialised along the way since her last visit. Would it be better to go up first, and take a different spine track down? For a moment the possibilities branched, Antoinette acutely aware that this time, literally, a minute here or there might make all the difference.

But then the elevator started moving. She had done nothing to it.

'Hello, John,' she said.

TWENTY-NINE

Ararat, 2675

The shuttle loitered over First Camp.

The sun was almost down. In the last, miserly light of the day, Vasko and his companions watched the green-clad spire slip beyond the headland. The towering thing had cast its own slanted shadow in the final minutes of daylight, a shadow that moved not just with the descent of the sun but also with the changing position and tilt of the ship. The movement was almost too slow to make out from moment to moment. It was like watching the hour hand of a clock: the movement was only really apparent when you looked away for a minute or two. But the ship *was* moving, being dragged along by that cloak of biomass, and now a tongue of land stood between the ship and the bay. It was not much of a tongue, just the last hundred metres of headland, and surely not enough to completely deflect the anticipated tidal waves; but it was bound to make some difference, and as the ship moved further along its course the sheltering effect would become larger and larger.

'Did she make it aboard?' Khouri asked, her eyes wide and unfocused. Aura seemed to be sleeping again, Khouri once more speaking for herself alone.

'Yes,' Vasko said.

'I hope she can talk some sense into him.'

'What happened back there ...' Vasko said. He looked at her, waiting for her to say something, but nothing came. 'When Aura spoke to us ... ?'

'Yes?'

'That was really her, right?'

Khouri looked at him, one eye slightly narrowed. 'Does that bother you? Does my daughter disturb you?'

'I just want to know. She's sleeping now, isn't she?'

'She isn't in my head, no.'

'But she was?'

'Where are you going with this, Malinin?'

'I want to know how it works,' he said. 'I think she might be useful to us. She's already helped us, but that's only the start, isn't it?'

'I told you already,' Khouri said, 'Aura knows stuff. We just have to listen.'

Hela, 2727

Rashmika sat alone in her room, the night after the caravan had crossed the bridge. She opened the little metal canister that Pietr had given her with trembling hands, fearing – despite herself – some deception or trick. But there was nothing in the canister except a rolled-up spool of thin yellow paper. It slid into her hands, the colour of tobacco. She flattened it carefully, and then inspected the faint sequences of grey marks on one side of the paper.

To the untrained eye they meant precisely nothing. At first they reminded her a little of something, and she had to think for a while before it came to her. The spaced vertical dashes – clustered and clumped, but sliding closer and closer together as her eye panned from left to right – brought to mind a diagram of the chemical absorption lines in a star's spectrum, bunching closer and closer towards a smeared continuum of states. But these lines represented individual vanishings, and the smeared continuum lay in the future. But what exactly did it signify? Would the vanishings become the norm, with Haldora stuttering in and out of reality like a defective light fitting? Or would the planet just vanish, popping out of existence for evermore?

She examined the paper again. There was a second sequence of marks above the other. They agreed closely, except at one point where the lower sequence had an additional vertical mark where none was present above it.

Twenty-odd years ago, Pietr had said.

Twenty-odd years ago, Haldora had winked out of existence for one and one-fifth of a second. A long cosmic blink. Not just a moment of divine inattention, but a fully-fledged deific snooze.

And during that absence, something had happened that the churches did not like. Something that might even have been worth the life of a harmless old man.

She looked at the paper again, and for the first time it occurred to Rashmika to wonder why Pietr had given it to her, and what she was meant to do with it.

The elevator had been descending for several minutes when Antoinette felt a lurch as it shifted from its usual track. She cried out at first, thinking the elevator was about to crash, but the ride continued smoothly for a dozen seconds before she felt another series of jolts and swerves as the car switched routes again. There was no guessing where she was, only that she was deep inside the ship. Perhaps she was even below the waterline, in the last few hundred metres of the submerged hull. Any maps she might have brought along with her – not that she had, of course – would have been totally useless by now. It was not only that these dank levels were difficult to access from the upper decks, but that they were prone to convulsive and confusing changes of local architecture. For a long time it had been assumed that the elevator lines remained stable when all else changed, but Antoinette knew that this was not the case, and that it would be futile to attempt to navigate by apparently familiar reference points. If she'd brought an inertial compass and a gravito-meter she might have been able to pinpoint her position to within a few dozen metres in three-dimensional space ... but she hadn't, and so she had no choice but to trust the Captain.

The elevator arrived at its destination. The door opened and the last dregs of fluid spilled out. She tapped her shoes dry, feeling the unpleasant wetness of her trouser hems against the skin of her calves. She was really not dressed for a meeting with the Captain. What would he think?

She looked out and had to suppress an involuntary gasp of surprise and delight. For all that she knew every moment was precious, it was impossible not to be moved by the view she was seeing. Deep in the ship as she was, she had been expecting another typically gloomy, damp enclosure. She had been assuming that the Captain would manifest via the manipulation of local junk or one of the distorting wall surfaces. Or something else, but qualitatively similar.

But the Captain had brought her somewhere else entirely. It was a huge chamber, a place that at first glance appeared not to have any limits at all. There was an endless sky above her, shaded a rich, heraldic blue. In all directions she saw only stepped tiers of trees reaching away into blue-green infinity. There was a lovely fragrant breeze and a cackle of animal life from the high branches of the nearest trees. Below her, accessed by a meandering rustic wooden staircase, was a marvellous little glade. There was a pool off to one side being fed by a hissing waterfall. The water in the pool, except where it was stirred into creamy whiteness under the waterfall, was the exquisite black of space. Rather than suggesting taintedness, the blackness of the water made it look wonderfully cool and inviting. A little way in from the water's edge, resting on the perfectly tended lawn, was a wooden table. On either side of the table, forming benches, were long logs.

She had taken an involuntary step from the elevator. Behind her, the door closed. Antoinette saw no alternative but to make her way down the ambling stairs to the floor of the glade, where the grass shimmered with all the shades of green and yellow she had ever imagined.

She had heard about this place. Clavain had spoken about it once, she recalled. A glade within the *Nostalgia for Infinity*. Once, its location had been well mapped, but after the great ship had been emptied in the days following its landing on Ararat, no one had ever been able to find the glade again. Parties had scoured the areas of the ship where it was supposed to be, but they had found nothing.

The glade was enormous. It was astonishing that you could lose a place this large, but the *Nostalgia for Infinity* was vast. And if the ship itself didn't want something to be found ... well, the Captain certainly had the means to hide whatever he wanted. Access corridors and elevator lines could be rerouted. The entire place – the entire chamber, glade and all – could even have been moved around in the ship, the way one heard about old bullets making slow, meandering journeys through people, years after they had been shot.

Antoinette didn't think she would ever find out exactly where this was. The Captain had brought her here on his own strict terms, and maybe she would never be allowed to see it again.

'Antoinette.' The voice was a hiss, a modulation of the waterfall's sibilance.

'Yes?'

'You've forgotten something again, haven't you?'

Did he mean the torch? No, of course not. She smiled. Despite herself, she hadn't been quite as forgetful as she had feared.

She slipped on the goggles. Through them she saw the same glade. The colours, if anything, were even brighter. Birds were in the air, moving daubs of red and yellow against the blue backdrop of the sky. Birds! It was great to see birds again, even if she knew they were being manufactured by the goggles.

Antoinette looked around and realised with a jolt that she had company. There were people sitting at the table, on the logs placed either side of it.

Strange people. *Really* strange people.

'Come on over,' one of them said, inviting her to take the one vacant place. The man beckoning her was John Brannigan; she was certain of that immediately. But yet again he was manifesting in a slightly different form.

She thought back to the first two apparitions. Both had evoked Mars, she thought. In the first, he had been wearing a spacesuit so elderly that she had half-expected it to have an opening where you fed in coal. The second time the suit had been slightly more up to date: not modern, by any stretch of the imagination, but at least a generation beyond the first. John Brannigan had looked older then as well – by a good decade or two, she had judged. And now she was looking at an even older counterpart of him, wearing a suit that again skipped fashions forwards another half-century or so.

It was barely a suit at all, really, more a kind of cocoon of something resembling silver-grey insect spit that had been neatly lathered around him. Through the transparent material of the suit she glimpsed a vague tightly packed complexity of organic-looking mechanisms: kidney-shaped bulges and purple lunglike masses; things that pulsed and throbbed. She saw lurid-green fluids scurrying through miles of zigzagging intestinal piping. Beneath all this the Captain was naked, the vile mechanics of catheters and waste-management systems laid out for her inspection. The Captain appeared oblivious. She was looking at a man from a very remote century; one that – on balance – seemed more distant and strange than the earlier periods she had glimpsed in the first two apparitions.

The suit left his head uncovered. He looked older now. His skin appeared to have been sucked on to his skull by some vacuum-forming process, so that it hugged every crevice. She could map the veins beneath his skin with surgical precision. He looked delicate, like something she could crush in her hands.

She sat down, taking the place she had been offered. The other people around the table were all wearing the same kind of suit, with only minor variations in detail. But they were not all alike. Some of them were missing whole chunks of themselves. They had cavities in their bodies which the suits had invaded, cramming them with the same intricacy of organic machinery and bright-green tubing that she could see inside the Captain's suit. One woman was missing an arm. In its place, under the spit-layer of the suit, was a glass moulding of an arm filled with a tentative structure of bone and meat and nerve fibre. Another one, a man this time, had a glass face, living tissue pressed against its inner surface. Another looked more or less normal at first glance, except that the body had two heads: a woman's emerging at more or less the right place and a second one – a young man's – attached above her right shoulder.

'Don't mind them,' the Captain said.

Antoinette realised she must have been staring. 'I wasn't . . .'

John Brannigan smiled. 'They're soldiers. Forward deployment elements in the Coalition for Neural Purity.'

If that had ever meant anything to Antoinette, it was history she had forgotten a long time ago. 'And you?' she asked.

'I was one, for a while. While it suited my immediate needs. We were on Mars, fighting the Conjoiners, but I can't say my heart was entirely in it.'

Antoinette leaned forwards. The table, at least, was completely real. 'John, there's something we really need to talk about.'

'Oh, don't be such a spoilsport. I've only just started shooting the breeze with my soldier buddies.'

'All these people are dead, John. They died – oh, conservative estimate? – three or four hundred years ago. So snap out of the nostalgia trip, will you? You need to get a fucking good grip on the immediate here and now.'

He winked at her and bobbed his head towards one of the people along the table. 'Do you see Kolenkow there? The one with two heads?'

'Difficult to miss,' Antoinette said, sighing.

'The one on her shoulder's her brother. They signed up together. He took a hit, got zeroed by a spider mansweeper. Immediate decap. They're brewing a new body for him back in Deimos. They can hook your head up to a machine in the meantime, but it's always better if you're plumbed into a proper body.'

'I'll bet. Captain . . .'

'So Kolenkow's carrying her brother's head until the body's ready. They might even go into battle like that. I've seen it happen. Isn't much that scares the hell out of spiders, but two-headed soldiers might do the trick, I reckon.'

'Captain. John. Listen to me. You need to focus on the present. We have a situation here on Ararat, all right? I know you know about it – we've talked about it already.'

'Oh, that stuff,' he said. He sounded like a child being reminded of homework on the first day of a holiday.

Antoinette thumped the table so hard that the wood bruised her fist. 'I know you don't want to deal with this, John, but we have to talk about it all the same. You cannot leave just when you feel like it. You may save a few thousand people, but many, many more are going to die in the process.'

The company changed. She was still sitting at a table surrounded by soldiers – she even recognised some of the faces – but now they all looked as if they had been through a few more years of war. Bad war, too. The Captain had a clunking prosthetic arm where there had been a good arm before. The suits were no longer made of insect spit, but were now sliding assemblages of lubricated plates. They were hyper-reflective, like scabs of frozen mercury.

'Fucking Demarchists,' the Captain said. 'Let us keep all that fancy biotech shit until the moment we really needed it. We were really kicking the spiders. Then they pulled the licenses, said we were violating terms of fair use. All that neat squirmy stuff just fucking *melted* overnight. Bioweps, suits – gone. Now look what we've got to work with.'

'I'm sure you'll do fine,' Antoinette said. 'Captain, listen to me. The Pattern Jugglers are moving the ship to safety. You have to give them time.'

'They've had time,' he said. It was a heartening moment of lucidity, a connection to the present.

'Not enough,' she said.

The steel fist of his new arm clenched. 'You don't understand. We have to leave Ararat. There are windows opening above us.'

The back of her neck tingled. 'Windows, John?'

'I sense them. I sense a lot of things. I'm a *ship*, for fuck's sake.'

Suddenly they were all alone. It was just the Captain and Antoinette. In the bright lustre of his reflective armour she saw a bird traverse the sky.

'You're a ship. Good. So stop whining and start acting like one, beginning with a sense of responsibility to your crew. That includes me. What are these windows?'

He waited a while before answering. Had she just got through to him, or sent him scurrying ever deeper into labyrinths of regression?

'Opportunities for escape,' he said eventually. 'Clear channels. They keep opening, and then closing.'

'You could be mistaken. It would be really, really bad if you were mistaken.'

'I don't think I am.'

'We've been waiting, hoping, for a sign,' Antoinette said. 'Some message from Remontoire. But there hasn't been one.'

'Maybe he can't get a message through. Maybe he's been trying, and this is the best you're going to get.'

'Give us a few more hours,' she said. 'That's all we're asking for. Just enough time to move the ship to a safe distance. Please, John.'

'Tell me about the girl. Tell me about Aura.'

Antoinette frowned. She remembered mentioning the girl, but she did not think she had ever told the Captain her name. 'Aura's fine,' she said, guardedly. 'Why?'

'What does she have to say on the matter?'

'She thinks we should trust the Pattern Jugglers,' Antoinette said.

'And beyond that?'

'She keeps talking about a place – somewhere called Hela. Something to do with a man named Quaiche.'

'That's all?'

'That's all. It may not even mean anything. It's not even Aura speaking to us directly – it's all coming via her mother. I don't think Scorpio takes it that seriously. Frankly, I'm not sure I do either. They really, really want to think that Aura is something valuable because of what she cost them. But what if she isn't? What if she's just a kid? What if she knows a little, but nowhere near as much as everyone wants her to?'

'What does Malinin think?'

This surprised her. 'Why Malinin?'

'They talk about him. I hear them. I heard about Aura the same way. All those thousands of people inside me, all their whispers, all their secrets. They need a new leader. It could be Malinin; it could be Aura.'

'There hasn't even been an official announcement about the existence of Aura,' Antoinette said.

'You seriously believe that makes any difference? They know, all of them. You can't keep a secret like that, Antoinette.'

'They have a leader already,' she said.

'They want someone new and bright and a little frightening. Someone who hears voices, someone they'll allow to lead them in a time of uncertainties. Scorpio isn't that leader.' The Captain paused, caressed his false hand with the scarred fingers of the other. 'The windows are still opening and closing. I sense a growing urgency. If Remontoire is behind this, he may not be able to offer us many more opportunities for escape. Soon, very soon, I shall have to make my move.'

She knew she had wasted her time. She had thought at first that in showing her this place he was inviting her to a new level of intimacy, but his position had not changed at all. She had stated her case, and all he had done was listen.

'I shouldn't have bothered,' she said.

'Antoinette, listen to me now. I like you more than you realise. You have always treated me with kindness and compassion. Because of that I care for you, and I care for your survival.'

She looked into his eyes. 'So what, John?'

'You can leave. There is still time. But not much.'

'Thanks,' she said. 'But – if it's all right with you – I think I'll stay for the ride.'

'Any particular reason?'

'Yeah,' she said, looking around. 'This is about the only decent ship in town.'

Scorpio moved through the shuttle. He had turned almost all the fuselage surfaces transparent, save for a strip which marked the floor and a portion where Valensin waited with Khouri and her child. With all nonessential illumination turned down, he saw the outside world almost as if he were floating in the evening air.

With nightfall it had become obvious that the space battle was now very close to Ararat. The clouds had broken up, perhaps because of the excessive energies now being dumped into Ararat's upper atmosphere. Reports of objects splashing down were coming in too rapidly to be processed. Gashes of fire streaked from horizon to horizon every few minutes as unidentified objects – spacecraft, missiles, or perhaps things for which the colonists had no name – knifed deep into Ararat's airspace. Sometimes there were volleys of them; sometimes things moved in eerie lock-step formation. The trajectories were subject to violent, impossible-looking hairpins and reversals. It was clear that the major protagonists of the battle were deploying inertia-suppressing machinery with a recklessness that chilled Scorpio. Aura had already told them as much, through the mouthpiece of her mother. Clearly the appropriated alien technology was a little more controllable than it had been when Clavain and Skade had tested each other's nerves with it on the long pursuit from Yellowstone to Resurgam space. But there were still people who told horror stories of the times when the technology had gone wrong. Pushed to its unstable limits, the inertia-suppressing machinery did vile things to both the flesh and the mind. If they were using it as a routine military tool – just another toy in the sandpit – then he dreaded to think what was now considered dangerous and cutting edge.

He thought about Antoinette for a moment, hoping that she was getting somewhere with the Captain. He was not greatly optimistic that she would succeed in changing the Captain's mind once it was made up. But it still wasn't absolutely clear whether or not he intended to take the ship up. Perhaps the revving-up of the Conjoiner drive engines was just his way of making sure they were in good working order, should they be needed at some point in the future. It didn't have to mean that the ship was going to leave in the next few hours.

That kind of desperate, yearning optimism was foreign to Scorpio even now, and would have been quite alien during his Chasm City years. He was a pessimist at heart. Perhaps that was why he had never been very good at forward planning, at thinking more than a few days ahead. If you tended to believe on an innate level that things were always going to go from bad to worse, what was the point of even trying to intervene? All that was left was to make the best of the immediate situation.

But here he was hoping – in spite of plenty of evidence to the contrary – that the ship was going to stay on Ararat. Something had to be wrong for him to start thinking that way. Something had to be playing on his mind. He didn't have far to look for it, either.

Only a few hours earlier he had broken twenty-three years of self-imposed discipline. In Clavain's presence, he had made every effort to live up to the old man's standards. For years he had hated baseline humans for what they had done to him during his years of indentured slave service. And if that was not enough to spur his animosity, he only had to think of the thing that he was: this swaying, comedic mongrel of human and pig, this compromise that had all the flaws of both and none of the advantages of either. He knew the litany of his disadvantages. He couldn't walk as well as a human. He couldn't hold things the way they could. He couldn't see or hear as well as they did. There were colours he would never know. He couldn't think as fluidly as they did and he lacked a well-developed capacity for abstract visualisation. When he listened to music all he heard was complex sequential sounds, lacking any emotional component. His predicted lifespan, optimistically, was about two-thirds that of a human who had received no longevity therapy or germline modifications. And – so some humans said, when they didn't think they were in earshot of pigs – his kind didn't even *taste* the way nature intended.

That hurt. That *really* fucking hurt.

But he had dared to think that he had put all that resentment behind him. Or if not behind him, then at least in a small, sealed mental compartment which he only ever opened in times of crisis.

And even then he kept the resentment under control, used it to give him strength and resolve. The positive side was that it had forced him to try to be better than they expected. It had made him delve inside himself for qualities of leadership and compassion he had never suspected he possessed. He would show them what a pig was capable of. He would show them that a pig could be as statesmanlike as Clavain; as forward-thinking and judicial; as cruel and as kind as circumstances merited.

And for twenty-three years it had worked, too. The resentment had made him better. But in all that time, he now realised, he had still been in Clavain's shadow. Even when Clavain had gone to his island, the man had not really abdicated power.

Except that now Clavain was gone, and only a few dozen hours into this new regime, only a few dozen hours after stumbling into the hard scrutiny of real leadership, Scorpio had failed. He had lashed out against Hallatt, against a man who in that instant of rage had personified the entire corpus of baseline humanity. He knew it was Blood who had thrown the knife, but his own hand had been on it just as surely. Blood had merely been an extension of Scorpio's intent.

He knew he had never really liked Hallatt. Nothing about that had changed. The man was compromised by his involvement in the totalitarian government on Resurgam. Nothing could be proved, but it was more than likely that Hallatt had at least been aware of the beatings and interrogation sessions, the state-sanctioned executions. And yet the evacuees from Resurgam had to be represented in some form. Hallatt had also done a lot of good during the final days of the exodus. People that Scorpio judged to be reasonable and trustworthy had been prepared to testify on his behalf. He was tainted, but he wasn't incriminated. And – when one looked at the data closely – there was something unfortunate in the personal history of just about everyone who had come from Resurgam. Where did one draw the line? One hundred and sixty thousand evacuees had come to Ararat from the old world, and very few of them had lacked some association with the government. In a state like that, the machinery of government touched more lives than it left alone. You couldn't eat, sleep or breathe without being in some small way complicit in the functioning of the machine.

So he didn't like Hallatt. But Hallatt wasn't a monster or a fugitive. And because of that – in that instant of incandescent rage – he had struck out against a fundamentally decent man that he just happened not to like. Hallatt had pushed him to the edge with his under-standable scepticism about the matter of Aura, and Scorpio had allowed that provocation to touch him where it hurt. He had struck at Hallatt, but it could have been anyone. Even, had the provocation been severe enough, someone that he actually liked, like Antoinette, Xavier Liu or one of the other human seniors.

What almost made it worse was the way the rest of the party had reacted. When the rage had died, when the enormity of what he had done had begun to sink in, he had expected mutiny. He had at least expected some open questioning of his fitness for leadership.

But there had been nothing. It was almost as if they had all just turned a blind eye, regretting what he had done but accepting that this flash of madness was part of the package. He was a pig, and with pigs you had to tolerate that kind of thing.

He was sure that was what they were all thinking. Even, perhaps, Blood.

Hallatt had survived. The knife had touched no major organs. Scorpio didn't know whether to put this down to spectacular accuracy on Blood's behalf, or spectacular inaccuracy instead.

He didn't want to know.

As it turned out, no one else really liked Hallatt either. The man's days as a colony senior were over, his avowed distrust of Khouri not helping his case. But since the Resurgam representatives were cycled around anyway, Hallatt's enforced standing-down was not the dra-matic thing it might have been. The circumstances of his resignation would be kept secret, but something would inevitably filter out. There would be rumours of violence, and Scorpio's name would surely feature somewhere in the telling.

Let it happen. He could live with that easily enough. There had been violent episodes in the past, and the rumours of those had become suitably exaggerated as they did the rounds. They had done him no real harm in the long run.

But those violent episodes had been justified. There had been no hatred behind them, no attempt to redress the sins visited upon Scorpio and his kind by their human elders. They had been necessary gestures. But what he had done to Hallatt had been personal, nothing whatsoever to do with the security of the planet.

He had failed himself, and in that sense he had also failed Ararat.

'Scorp? Are you all right?'

It was Khouri, sitting in the darkened portion of the shuttle. Valensin's servitors were still monitoring Aura's incubator, but Khouri was keeping her own vigil. Once or twice he had heard her talking softly to the child, even singing to her. It seemed odd to him, given that they were already bonded on a neural level.

'I'm fine,' he said.

'You look preoccupied. Is it what happened in the iceberg?'

Her remark surprised him. Most of the time, his expressions were completely opaque to outsiders. 'Well, there's the small business of the war we're caught up in, and the fact that I'm not sure any of us are going to make it into next week, but other than that . . .'

'We're all bothered by the war,' she said, 'but with you there's something else. I didn't see it before we went to find Aura.'

He had the shuttle form a chair for him, something at pig-height, and sat down next to her. He noticed that Valensin was snoozing, his head bobbing up at periodic intervals as he tried to stay awake. They were all exhausted, all functioning at the limits of endurance.

'I'm surprised that you want to talk to me,' he said.

'Why shouldn't I?'

'Because of what you asked of me, and what I refused to give you.' In case his point was not obvious to her, he gestured at Aura. 'I thought you'd hate me for that. You'd have had every right.'

'I didn't like it, no.'

'Well, then.' He offered her his palms, accepting his fate.

'But it wasn't *you*, Scorp. You didn't stop me taking her back inside me. It was the situation, the mess we're in. You simply acted in the only way that made sense to you. I'm not over it, but don't cut yourself up about it, all right? This is war. Feelings get hurt. I can cope. I still have my daughter.'

'She's beautiful,' Scorpio said. He didn't believe it, but it seemed the right sort of thing to say under the circumstances.

'Really?' she asked.

He looked at the wrinkled, pink-red child. 'Really.'

'I was worried you'd hate her, Scorp, because of what she cost.'

'Clavain wouldn't have hated her,' he said. 'That's good enough for me.'

'Thanks, Scorp.'

They sat in silence for a minute or so. Above, through the transparent hull, the light show continued. Something – some weapon or device in near-Ararat space – was scribing lines across the sky. There were arcs and angles and straight lines, and each mark took a few seconds to fade into the purple-black background. There was something nagging him about those lines, Scorpio thought, some sense that there was a meaning implicit in them, if only he had the quickness of mind to tease it out.

'There's something else,' he said, quietly.

'Concerning Aura?'

'No. Concerning me, actually. You weren't there, but I hurt a man today.' Scorpio looked down at his small, childlike shoes. He had misjudged the height of the seat slightly, so that his toes did not quite reach the floor.

'I'm sure you had your reasons,' Khouri said.

'That's the problem: I didn't. I hurt him out of blind rage. Something inside me snapped, something I'd kidded myself that I had under control for the last twenty-three years.'

'We all have days like that,' she said.

'I try not to. For twenty-three years, all I've ever tried to do is get through the day without making that kind of mistake. And today I failed. Today I threw it all away, in one moment of weakness.'

She said nothing. He took that as permission to continue.

'I used to hate humans. I thought I had good enough reasons.' Scorpio reached up and undid the fastenings on his leather tunic, exposing his right shoulder. Three decades of ageing – not to mention the slow accretion of later, fresher wounds – had made the scar less obvious now. But still it made Khouri avert her eyes for an instant, before she looked back unflinchingly.

'They did that to you?'

'No. I did it to myself, using a laser.'

'I don't understand.'

'I was burning away something else.' He traced the coastline of the scar, obedient to every inlet and peninsula of raised flesh. 'There was a tattoo there, a green scorpion. It was a mark of ownership. I didn't realise that at first. I thought it was a badge of honour, something to be proud of.'

'I'm sorry, Scorp.'

'I hated them for that, and for what I was. But I paid them back, Ana. God knows, I paid them back.'

He began to do up the tunic again. Khouri leaned over and helped with the fastenings. They were large, designed for clumsy fingers.

'You had every right,' she said.

'I thought I was over it. I thought I'd got it out of my system.'

She shook her head. 'That won't ever happen, Scorp. Take it from me, you won't ever lose that rage. What happened to me can't compare with what they did to you – I'm not saying that. But I do know what it's like to hate something you can't ever destroy, something that's always out of reach. They took my husband from me, Scorp. Faceless army clerks screwed up and ripped him away from me.'

'Dead?' he asked.

'No. Just out of reach, at the wrong fucking end of a thirty-year starship crossing. Same thing, really. Except worse, I suppose.'

'You're wrong,' he said. 'That's as bad as anything they did to me.'

'Maybe. I don't know. It isn't for me to make those comparisons. But all I know is this: I've tried to forgive and forget. I've accepted that Fazil and I will never see each other again. I've even accepted that Fazil's probably long dead, wherever he really ended up. I have a daughter by another man. I suppose that counts as moving on.'

He knew that the father of her child was dead as well, but that was not obvious in the tone of her voice when she mentioned him.

'Not moving on, Ana. Just staying alive.'

'I knew you'd understand, Scorp. But you also understand what I'm saying about forgiving and forgetting, don't you?'

'That it ain't gonna happen,' he said.

'Never in a million years. If one of those people came into this room – one of those fools who screwed up my life with one moment of inattention – I don't think I'd be able to stop myself. What I'm saying is, the rage doesn't go away. It gets smaller, but it also gets brighter. We just pack it deep down and kindle it, like a little fire we're never going to let die. It's what keeps us going, Scorp.'

'I still failed.'

'No, you didn't. You did damn well to keep it bottled up for twenty-three years. So you lost it today.' Suddenly she was angry. 'So what? So fucking *what*? You went through something in that iceberg that I wouldn't wish on any one of those clerks, Scorp. I know what Clavain meant to you. You went through hell on Earth. The wonder of it isn't that you've lost it once, but that you've managed to keep your shit together at all. Honestly, Scorp.' Her anger shifted to insistence. 'You've got to go easy on yourself, man. What happened out there? It wasn't a walk in the park. You earned the right to throw a few punches, OK?'

'It was a bit more than a punch.'

'Is the guy going to pull through?'

'Yes,' he said, grudgingly.

Khouri shrugged. 'Then chill out. What these people need now is a leader. What they don't need is someone moping around with a guilty conscience.'

He stood up. 'Thank you, Ana. Thank you.'

'Did I help, or did I just screw things up even more?'

'You helped.'

The seat melted back into the wall.

'Good. Because, you know, I'm not the most eloquent of people. I'm just a grunt at heart, Scorp. A long way from home, with some weird stuff in my head, and a daughter I'm not sure I'll ever understand. But really, I'm still just a grunt.'

'It's never been my policy to underestimate grunts,' he said. Now, inevitably, it was his turn to feel ineloquent. 'I'm sorry about what happened to you. I hope one day . . .' He looked around, noticing that Vasko was moving down the opaque line of the floor towards Aura's niche. 'Well, I don't know. Just that you find something to make that rage a little smaller and brighter. Maybe when it gets small and bright enough it will just pop away.'

'Would that be a good thing?'

'I don't know.'

She smiled. 'Me neither. But I guess you and I are the ones who'll find out.'

'Scorpio?' Vasko said.

'Yes?'

'You should see this. You, too, Ana.'

They woke Valensin. Vasko ushered them to a different part of the shuttle, then made some modifications to the hull to increase the visibility of the night sky, calling bulkheads into existence and enhancing the brightness of the transmitted light to compensate for the reflected glare from the shuttle's wings. He did so with an ease that suggested he had been working with such systems for half his life, rather than the few days that was actually the case.

Above, Scorpio saw only the same appearing and fading scratches of light that he had noticed earlier. The nagging feeling that they meant something still troubled him, but the scratches made no more sense to him now than they had before.

'I'm not seeing it, Vasko.'

'I'll have the hull add a latency, so that the marks take longer to fade out.'

Scorpio frowned. 'Can you do that?'

'It's easy.' Vasko patted the cold, smooth surface of the inner fuselage. 'There's almost nothing these old machines won't do, if you know the right way to ask.'

'So do it,' Scorpio said.

All four of them looked up. Even Valensin was fully awake now, his eyes slits behind his spectacles.

Above, the scratches of light took longer to fade. Before, only two or three had ever been visible at the same time. Now dozens lingered, bright as the images scorched on to the retina by the setting sun.

And now they most definitely meant something.

'My God,' Khouri said.

THIRTY

Ararat, 2675

In the glade, everything changed. The sky above had turned mid-night-black; no birds moved from tree to tree now, and the trees themselves formed only a darker frame to the night sky, looming in on all sides like encroaching thunder clouds. The animals had fallen silent, and Antoinette could no longer hear the simmering hiss of the waterfall. Perhaps it had never been real.

When she turned her attention back to the Captain, he was sitting alone at the table. Again he had slipped forward some years, reiterating another slice from his history. The last time she had seen him, in the silver armoured suit, one of his arms had been mechanical. Now the process of mechanisation had marched on even more. It was difficult to judge how much of him had been replaced by prosthetic components because of the suit, but she could at least see his head since the helmet was resting in front of him on the table. His scalp was completely bald, his face hairless save for a moustache that drooped on either side of his mouth. It was the same mouth she remembered from the first apparition: compact, straight, probably not much given to small talk. But that was about the only point of reference she recognised. She couldn't see his eyes at all. They were lost under a complicated-looking band of some sort that reached from one side of his face to the other. Optics twinkled beneath the band's pearly coating. The skin across his scalp was quilted with fine white lines. Glued tight to his skull, it revealed irregular raised plates just under the skin.

'Something's wrong, isn't it?' Antoinette asked.

'Look up.'

She complied, and saw immediately that something had changed in the few scant minutes during which she had been studying the Captain's latest manifestation. Scratches of light cut across the sky. She thought of someone making quick, neat, butcherlike gashes in soft skin. The scratches looked random at first, but then she began to discern the emergence of a pattern.

'John . . .'

'Keep looking.'

The scratches increased in frequency. They became a flicker, then a frenzy, then something that almost appeared permanent.

The scratches formed letters.

The letters formed words.

The words said: LEAVE NOW.

'I just wanted you to know,' John Brannigan said.

That was when she felt the entire floor of the glade rumble. She had barely had time to register this when she felt her own weight increasing. She was being pressed into the roughly formed wooden seat. It was a gentle pressure, but that was no surprise. A ship with a mass of several million metric tonnes didn't just leap into space. Especially not when it had been sitting in a kilometre of water for twenty-three years.

Across the bay, lighting up the sea and land all the way to the horizon, a temporary day had come to Ararat. At first, all that Vasko could see was a mountain of steam, a scalding eruption of superheated water engulfing first the lower flanks of the ship and then the entire green-clad structure. A blue-white light shone out through the steam, like a lantern in a mound of tissue paper. It was painfully bright even through the darkening filter of the shuttle's fuselage. It shaded to violet and left jagged pink shadows on his retinae. Even far away from the edge of the steam column, the water shone a luminous turquoise. It was beautiful and strange, like nothing he had seen in his twenty years of existence.

He saw now that the water was bellying up around the ship, the surface rising many hundreds of metres. Frightful energies were being released underwater, creating swelling bubbles of superdense, superhot plasma.

The wall of elevated water surged away from the *Nostalgia for Infinity* in two concentric waves.

'Did they get far enough beyond the headland?' he asked.

'We're about to find out,' Scorpio said.

The surface of the water was crusted with a scum of stiff green biomass. They watched it crack into disjointed plates, unable to flex fast enough to match the distortion as the wave passed. It was moving at hundreds of metres per second. In only a few moments it would hit the bay's low rock shields.

Vasko looked back towards the source of the tidal wave. The ship was beginning to climb now, its nose emerging from the steam layer.

The movement was awesomely smooth, almost as if he was seeing a fixed landmark – an ancient storm-weathered spire on a high promontory, perhaps – being revealed by the retreat of morning fog.

He watched the top kilometre of the *Nostalgia for Infinity* push clear of the steam, holding up a hand to shade his eyes from the brightness. The ship was almost clean of Juggler biomass: he saw only a few green strands still attached to the hull. Now the next kilometre came out. Ropy strands of biomass – thicker than houses – were slithering free, losing traction against the accelerating space-craft.

The glare became intolerable. The hull of the shuttle darkened, protecting its occupants. The entire ship was now free of the ocean. Through the almost opaque shuttle fuselage, Vasko saw only two hard points of radiance, rising slowly.

'No going back now,' he observed.

Scorpio turned to Khouri. 'I'm going to follow it, unless you disagree.'

Khouri eyed her daughter. 'I'm not getting anything from Aura, Scorp, but I'm certain Remontoire's behind this. He always said there'd be a message. I don't think we have any choice but to trust him.'

'Let's just hope it is Remontoire,' Scorpio said.

But it was clear that his mind was already made up. He told them all to make seats for themselves and prepare for whatever they might find in Ararat orbit. Vasko went back to arrange his seat, but before he settled in he noticed that the floor of the fuselage was now transparent again. Down below, lit by the rising flare of the ship, he saw First Camp laid out in hallucinatory detail, the grid of streets and buildings picked out in monochrome clarity. He saw the small moving shadows of people running between buildings. Then he looked out towards the bay. The ramp of water had dashed against the barrier of the headland, dissipating much of its strength, but it had not been completely blocked. With an agonising sense of detachment he watched the remnant of the tidal wave cross the bay, slowing and gaining height as it hit the rising slope of the shallows. Then it was swallowing the shoreline, redefining it in an instant, overrunning streets and buildings. The flood lingered and then retreated, pulling debris with it. In its wake it left rubble and rect-angular absences where entire buildings had simply vanished. Large conch structures, inadequately ballasted or anchored, were being carried along on the surface, claimed back by the sea.

Within the bay the tidal wave echoed back on itself, creating several smaller surges, but none did as much damage as the first. After a minute or so, all was quite still again. But Vasko judged that a quarter of First Camp had simply ceased to exist. He just hoped that most of the citizens from those vulnerable shoreline properties had been prioritised in the evacuation effort.

The glare was fading. The ship was already far above them now, picking up speed, clawing towards rarefied atmosphere and, ultimately, space. The bay, robbed of that single landmark, looked unfamiliar. Vasko had lived here all his life, but now it was foreign territory, a place he barely recognised. He was certain it could never feel like home again. But it was easy for him to feel that way, wasn't it? He was in the privileged position of not having to go back and rebuild his life amongst the ruins. He was already leaving, already saying goodbye to Ararat, farewell to the world that had made him what he was.

He nestled into his newly formed seat, allowing the hull to squirm intimately tighter around him, conforming to his precise shape. Almost as soon as he was settled he felt the shuttle commence its own steep climb.

It did not take long for them to catch up with the *Nostalgia for Infinity*. He remembered what Antoinette Bax had told him, when he had asked her if the Captain was really capable of leaving Ararat. She had said that it could be done, but it would not be a fast departure. Like most ships of its kind, the great lighthugger was designed to sustain one gravity of thrust, all the way up to the bleeding edge of the speed of light. But at sea level Ararat's own gravity was already close to one standard gee. At normal cruise thrust, the ship was just capable of balancing itself against that force, hovering at a fixed altitude. Landing had not been a problem, therefore: it had simply been a question of letting gravity win, albeit in a slow, controlled fashion. Taking off was different: now the ship had to beat both gravity and air resistance. There was some power in reserve for emergency manoeuvres – up to ten gees or more – but that reserve capacity was designed only for seconds of use, not the many minutes that would be needed to reach orbit or interplanetary escape velocity. To leave Ararat, therefore, the engines had to be pushed just beyond the normal one-gee limit, giving a slight excess thrust, but not enough to overload them. The excess equalled about one-tenth of a gee of acceleration.

It would be a slower departure than the most primitive chemical rocket, Antoinette had said, slower even than the glorified firework that had carried the first astronaut (she had said that his name was Neal Gagarin and Vasko had believed her) into orbit. But the *Nostalgia for Infinity* weighed several thousand times more than the heaviest chemical rocket. And the old chemical rockets had to reach escape velocity very quickly, because they only had enough fuel for a few minutes of thrust. The *Nostalgia for Infinity* could sustain thrust for years and years.

Air resistance lessened as the ship climbed. It began to accelerate a little harder, but still the shuttle had no difficulty keeping up. The escape felt leisurely and dreamlike. This, Vasko knew, was probably a dangerous misconception.

When he had satisfied himself that the ride was likely to be smooth and predictable, at least for the next few minutes, he left his niche and went forward. Scorpio and the pilot were in the control couches.

'Any transmissions from the *Infinity*?' Vasko asked.

'Nothing,' the pilot replied.

'I hope Antoinette's all right,' he said. Then he remembered the other people – fourteen thousand by the last count – who had already been loaded into the ship.

'She'll cope,' Scorpio said.

'I guess in a few minutes we'll find out if that message really was from Remontoire. Are you worried?'

'No,' Scorpio said. 'And you know why? Because there isn't anything you or I or anyone else can do about it. We couldn't stop that ship going up and we can't do anything about what's up there waiting for it.'

'We have a choice about whether we follow it or not,' Vasko said.

The pig looked at him, eyes narrowed either in fatigue or disdain. 'No, you're wrong,' he said. '*We* have a choice, yes – that's me and Khouri. But you don't. You're just along for the ride.'

Vasko thought about going back to his seat, but decided to stick it out. Although it was night, he could clearly see the curve of Ararat's horizon now. He was going into space. This was what he had always wanted, for much of his life. But he had never imagined it would be like this, or that the destination itself would contain such danger and uncertainty. Instead of the thrill of escape he felt a knot of tension in his stomach.

'I've earned the right to be here,' he said, quietly, but loud enough for the pig to hear. 'I have a stake in Aura's future.'

'You're keen, Malinin, but you're way out of your depth.'

'I'm also involved.'

'You were embroiled. It isn't the same thing.'

Vasko started to say something, but there was a flicker of static across all the display read-outs hovering around the pilot. He felt the shuttle lurch.

'Picking up interference on all comms frequencies,' the pilot reported. 'We've lost all surface transponder contacts and all links to First Camp. There's a lot of EM noise out here – more than we're used to. There's stuff the sensors can't even interpret. Avionics are responding sluggishly. I think we're entering some kind of jamming zone.'

'Can you keep us close to the *Infinity*?' Scorpio asked.

'I'm more or less flying this thing manually. I guess if I still have the ship as a reference, we're not going to get lost. But I'm not making any promises.'

'Altitude?'

'One hundred and twenty klicks. We must be entering the lower sphere of battle about now.'

Above, the view had not changed dramatically since the departure of the ship. The scratches of light had faded, perhaps because Remontoire was aware that the message had been received and acted upon. There were still flashes of light, expanding spheres and arcs, and the occasional searing passage of an atmosphere-skimming object, but other than the darkness becoming a more intense, deeper shade of black, there was no real difference compared to the surface view.

Khouri came through to join them. 'I'm hearing Aura,' she said. 'She's awake now.'

'Good,' Scorpio began.

'There's more. I'm seeing things. So's Aura. I think it must be the same kind of thing Clavain and I saw before things got really serious – leakage from the war. It's getting through again.'

'We must be close,' Vasko said. 'I guess the wolves blocked those signals when they could, to stop Remontoire sending a message through that easily. Now that we're getting so close they can't stop all of them.'

From somewhere, Vasko heard a noise he didn't recognise. It was shrill, ragged, pained. It was muffled by plastic. He realised it was Aura, crying.

'She doesn't like it,' Khouri said. 'It's painful.'

'Contacts,' the pilot announced. 'Radar returns, incoming. Fifty klicks and closing. They weren't there a moment ago.'

The shuttle lurched violently, throwing Vasko and Khouri to one side. The walls deformed to soften the impact, but Vasko still felt the wind knocked out of him. 'What's happening?' he asked, breathless.

'The *Infinity* is making evasive manoeuvres. She's seen the same radar echoes. I'm just trying to keep up.' The pilot glanced at a read-out again. 'Thirty klicks. Twenty and slowing. Jamming is getting worse. This isn't good, folks.'

'Do your best,' Scorpio said. 'Everyone else – secure yourselves. It's going to get rough.'

Vasko and Khouri went back to where Valensin and his machines were continuing their vigil over Aura. She was still moving, but had at least stopped crying. Vasko wished that there was something he could do to help her, some way to temper the voices screaming into her head. He could not imagine what it must be like for her. By rights she should not even have been born yet; should barely have had any sense of her own individuality or the wider world in which she existed. Aura was not an ordinary baby, that much was clear – she already had the language skills of a two- or three-year-old child, in Vasko's estimation – but it was also unlikely that all parts of her mind were developing at the same accelerated rate. There was only room in that tiny wrinkled head for a certain amount of complexity; she must still have had an infant's view of many things. When he had been two years older than Aura, Vasko's own grasp of the world had barely reached further than the handful of rooms that made up his home. Everything else had been hazy, unimportant, subject to comic misapprehension.

The *Nostalgia for Infinity* was now further away from the shuttle than it had been: tens of kilometres distant, easily. The shuttle's hull had still not turned fully transparent again, but in the light from its engines he caught the reflections of *things* moving closer. Not just moving, but fluttering, swirling, splintering and reforming, retreating and advancing in pulsing waves.

They came closer. Now the glare of the engines revealed hints of stepped structures: tiers, contours, zigzag edges. It was the same machinery they had found in Skade's ship, the same stuff that had reached down from the clouds and ripped the corvette apart, but this time the scale was immeasurably larger – these cubes were almost as large as houses, forming structures hundreds of metres across. The wolf cubes were in constant, sliding motion: slithering across each other, swelling and contracting, larger structures organising and dissipating with hypnotic fluidity. Filaments of cubes spanned the larger structures; clusters of them fluttered from point to point like messengers. The scale was still difficult to judge, but the cubes were converging from nearly all sides and it seemed to Vasko that they had already formed a loose shell around both the shuttle and the *Nostalgia for Infinity*. What *was* certain was that the shell was tightening, the gaps becoming smaller.

'Ana?' Vasko asked. 'You've seen these things before, haven't you? They attacked your ship. Is this how it begins?'

'We're in trouble,' she confirmed.

'What happens next, if we can't escape?'

'They come inside.' Her voice was hollow, like a cracked bell. 'They invade your ship and then they invade your head. You don't want that to happen, Vasko. Trust me on this one.'

'How long will we have, if they reach the ship?'

'Seconds, if we're lucky. Maybe not even that.' Then she convulsed, a whiplash movement that had her body slamming against the restraining surface that the ship had fashioned around her. Her eyes closed and then reopened, her pupils raised to the ceiling, the whites bright and frightening. 'Kill me. Now.'

'Ana?'

'Aura,' she said. 'Kill me. Kill us *both*. Now.'

'No,' he said. He looked at Valensin, hoping for some explanation.

The doctor simply shook his head. 'I won't do it,' he said. 'No matter what she wants. I won't take a life.'

'Listen to me,' she insisted. 'What I know – too important. They can't find out. Will read our minds. Cannot allow that to happen. Kill us now.'

'No, Aura. I won't do it. Not now. Not ever,' Vasko said.

Valensin's servitors moved nearer to the incubator. Their jointed limbs twitched, clicking against their drab bodies. One of the machines extended a manipulator towards the incubator, grasping it. The servitor then backed away, trying to tug the incubator away from the niche.

Vasko leapt forwards and wrestled the machine away from the baby. The machine was lighter than it looked, but much stronger than he had anticipated. The many limbs thrashed against him, hard articulated metal pressing into his skin.

'Valensin!' he shouted. 'Do something!'

'They're beyond my control,' Valensin said, calmly, as if all that followed was out of his hands.

Vasko sucked in his chest, making a cavity between his body and the machine in an attempt to avoid the swiping pass of a sharp-bladed manipulator. He wasn't fast enough. He felt a nick through his clothing, the instant cold that told him he had been wounded. He fell back, hitting the wall, and tried to kick out at the wide base of the servitor. The machine toppled, clattering against its companion. The thrashing limbs entwined, knives sparking against knives.

He touched his chest, fingering through the gashed fabric. His hand came back lathered in blood. 'Get Scorpio,' he said to Valensin.

But Scorpio was already on his way. Something gleamed in his right hand: a humming blur of metal, a knife-shaped smear of silver. He saw the machines, saw Vasko with blood on his fingers. The servitors had disentangled themselves and the one still standing had begun to pick at the base of the incubator, trying to claw it open. Scorpio snarled and slid the knife into the machine's armour. The knife sailed through the drab green carapace as if it wasn't there at all. There was a fizzle of shorting circuitry, a thrashing whirr of damaged mechanisms. The knife howled and twisted out of Scorpio's grip, hitting the floor, where it continued to buzz and whirr.

The servitor had broken down. It remained frozen in place, limbs still extended but now immobile.

Scorpio knelt down and retrieved the piezo-knife, stilled the blade and returned it to its sheath.

Outside the shuttle, the wall of Inhibitor machinery looked close enough to touch. Jags of blue-pink lightning flickered and danced between different portions of it.

'Someone mind telling me what just happened?' Scorpio snapped.

'Aura,' said Vasko. He wiped his bloody hand against his trouser leg. 'Aura tried to turn the servitors against herself.' He was breathing hard, forcing out each word between ragged gulps of air. 'Trying to kill herself. She doesn't want the cubes to reach her while she's still alive.'

Khouri coughed. Her eyes were like a trapped animal's. 'Kill me, Scorp. Not too late. You have to do it.'

'After all we've been through?' he said.

'You have to go to Hela,' she said. 'Find Quaiche. Negotiate with shadows. *They* will know.'

'Fuck,' Scorpio said.

Vasko watched as the pig pulled the knife from its sheath once more. Scorpio stared at the now-still blade, his lips curled in disgust. Did he really mean to use it, or was he simply thinking about throwing it away, before circumstances once again forced him to wield it against someone or something he cared for?

Despite himself, despite the fact that he felt his own strength draining away, Vasko reached out and took hold of the pig's sleeve. 'No,' he said. 'Don't do it. Don't kill them.'

The pig's expression was something beyond fury. But Vasko had him. Scorpio couldn't activate the knife one-handed; his anatomy wouldn't allow it.

'Malinin. Let go now.'

'Scorp, listen to me. There has to be another way. The price we paid for her ... we can't just throw her away now, no matter how much *she* wants it.'

'You think I don't know what she cost us?'

Vasko shook his head. He had no idea what else to say. His strength was very nearly gone. He did not think he had been seriously injured, but the wound was still deep, and he was already desperately tired.

Scorpio tried to fight him. They were eye to eye. The pig had the advantage in strength, Vasko was sure, but Vasko had leverage and dexterity.

'Drop the knife, Scorp.'

'I'll kill you, Malinin.'

'Wait,' Valensin said mildly, taking off his spectacles and polishing them on the hem of his tunic. 'Both of you, wait. You should look outside, I think.'

Still struggling over control of the knife, they did as he suggested.

Something was happening, something that in the heat of the struggle they had missed completely. The *Nostalgia for Infinity* was starting to fight back. Weapons had emerged from its hull, poking out through the intricate accretion of detail that marked the Captain's transformations. These were not the cache weapons, Vasko realised, not the major Conjoiner ordnance that the ship carried deep inside it. Instead these were the conventional armaments that it had carried for much of its lifetime, designed primarily to intimidate trading customers and to warn off potential rivals or pirates. The same weapons that had been used against the colony on Resurgam, when the colony had been slow in handing over Dan Sylveste.

Scorpio relaxed his grip on Vasko, and slowly returned the knife to its sheath. 'That won't make much difference,' he said.

'It's buying time,' Vasko said. He let go of the pig. The two of them glowered at each other. Vasko knew he had just crossed yet another line, one that could never be traversed in the opposite direction.

So be it. He had been serious in his promise to Clavain to protect Aura.

Lines of fire were stabbing out from the *Nostalgia for Infinity*, sweeping around and scything into the closing wall of wolf machinery. They were very high above Ararat now and there was little atmosphere left to make the beam weapons – or whatever they were – visible for more than few dozen metres along their course. Vasko guessed that the great ship, after so long in an atmosphere, was still bleeding trapped air and water from pockets in the folds and crevices of its hull. He watched the dark clots of wolf machinery squirm away from the impact points of the beams, like specks of iron being repelled by a magnet. The beams moved quickly, but the cubes moved faster, slipping from one point to another with dizzying rapidity. Vasko realised, dejectedly, that Scorpio was right. It was a gesture of defiance, nothing more. Everything they had learned about the wolves, in all the glancing contacts to date, had taught them that conventional human weapons had almost no effect on them whatsoever. They might slow the closing of the shell, but no more than that.

Perhaps Aura was right all along. Better for her to die now, before the machines drained every last scrap of knowledge from her head. She had told them that Hela was significant. Perhaps no one would survive to act on that knowledge. But if anyone did, they would at least be able to act without the wolves knowing their exact intentions.

He looked at the sheath where the pig kept his knife.

No. There had to be another way. If they started murdering children to gain a tactical advantage, the Inhibitors might as well win the war now.

'They're backing off,' Valensin said. 'Look. Something's hurting them. I don't think it's the *Infinity*.'

The wall of machines was peppered with gaping, irregular holes. Carnations of colourless white light flashed from the cores of the cube structures. Chunks of cubic machinery veered into each other or dropped out of sight entirely. Tentacles of cubes thrashed purposelessly. The lightning pulsed in ugly, spavined shapes. And, suddenly, dashing through the gaps, machines appeared.

Vasko recognised the smooth, melted, muscular lines of spacecraft much like their shuttle. They moved like projections rather than solid objects, slowing down in an eyeblink.

'Remontoire,' Khouri breathed.

Beyond the ragged shell of Inhibitor machines, Vasko glimpsed a much wider battle, one that must have been encompassing many light-seconds of space around Ararat. He saw awesome eruptions of light, flashes that grew and faded in slow motion. He saw purple-black spheres simply appear, visible only when they formed against some brighter background, lingering for a few seconds, their wrinkled surfaces undulating, before popping out of existence.

Vasko faded out. When he came to, Valensin was inspecting his wound. 'It's clean and not too deep, but it will need treating,' he said.

'But it isn't serious, is it?'

'No. I don't think Aura really wanted to hurt you.'

Vasko felt some of the tension drain from his body. Then he realised that Scorpio had said very little since their scuffle over the knife. 'Scorp,' he began, 'we couldn't just kill her like that.'

'It's easy to say that now. It's what she wanted of us that matters.'

Valensin dabbed at his wound with something that stung. Vasko drew in a sharp breath. 'What did she mean when she spoke? She said something about shadows.'

Scorpio's expression gave nothing away. As calm as he now appeared, Vasko did not think it likely that the pig had forgiven him for the struggle.

'I don't know,' Scorpio said, 'except I didn't like the sound of it very much.'

'What matters is Hela,' Khouri said. She sighed, rubbed at the fatigue-darkened skin under her eyes. Vasko thought it safe to assume that they were dealing with Ana rather than Aura now.

'And the other thing – the business with shadows?'

'We'll find out when we get there.'

There was a call from the flight deck. 'Incoming transmission from the *Nostalgia for Infinity*,' said the pilot. 'We're being invited aboard.'

'By whom?' Scorpio asked.

'Antoinette Bax,' the pilot said, his voice trailing off hesitantly. 'With – um – the compliments of Captain John Brannigan.'

'Good enough for me,' Scorpio said.

Vasko felt the shuttle turn, arrowing towards the much larger vessel. At the same time, one of the small, sleek human-controlled ships detached from its neighbours and accompanied them, making an almost painful effort not to outpace them there.

One further incident stuck in Rashmika's mind before the caravan arrived at the Permanent Way. It was a day after the crossing of the bridge, and the caravan had finally climbed out of the Rift on to the bone-white level plateau of the Jarnsaxa Flats. To the north, the southern limits of the Western Hyrrokkin Uplands were visible as a roughness on the horizon, while to the east, Rashmika knew, lay the complex volcano fields of the Glistenheath and Ragnarok complexes, all currently dormant. By contrast, the Jarnsaxa Flats were mirror smooth and geologically stable. There were no scuttler digs in this area – whatever geological process had created the Flats had also erased or subducted any scuttler relics in this part of Hela – but there were still many small communities that made a direct living from their proximity to the Way. Now and then the caravan passed one of these dour little hamlets of surface bubbletents, or barrelled past a roadside shrine commemorating some recent but unspecified tragedy. Occasionally they saw pilgrims hauling their penitential life-support systems across the ice. To Rashmika they looked like returning hunters in some brown-hued painting by Brueghel, sledges topheavy with winter foodstock.

The buildings, shrines and figures slipped from horizon to horizon with indecent speed. With a broad, straight road ahead of it, the caravan had been able to move at maximum velocity for several hours, and now it seemed to have settled into a rhythm, an unstoppable stampede of machinery. Wheels rolled, tracks whirled around, traction limbs disappeared in a blur of pistoning motion. Visibly, Haldora moved closer to the zenith, until – by Rashmika's estimation – they could not be more than a few tens of kilometres from the Way.

Very soon the cathedrals would be visible, their spires clawing above the horizon.

But before she saw the cathedrals she saw other machines. They began as dots in the distance, throwing up pure white ballistic plumes from their rumbling wheels and treads. For many minutes they did not appear to move at all. Rashmika wondered if the caravan was simply catching up with similar processions arriving at the Way from elsewhere on Hela. This seemed reasonable, for many roads had joined up with the one they were on since they had climbed out of the Rift.

But then she realised that the vehicles were actually racing towards them. Even this did not strike her as particularly noteworthy, but then she felt the caravan slow and begin to oscillate from one side of the road to the other, as if uncertain which side it ought to be on. The swerves made her feel nauseous. She had the viewing area largely to herself, but the few caravan personnel that she saw also appeared ill at ease with developments.

The other machines continued to sweep towards them. In a few moments they had swelled to enormous size. They were much larger than any of the caravan's components. Rashmika saw a blur of treads and wide meshwork road wheels, with a superstructure of vicious ice-and-rock-moving machinery. The machines were painted a dusty yellow, with bee-stripes and rotating warning beacons. Many of the components were half-familiar to her: massively scaled-up counterparts of the heavy excavation equipment her fellow villagers used in the scuttler digs.

She recognised the function, even if the size was daunting. There were toothed claws and gaping lantern-jawed dragline buckets. There were grader blades and mighty percussive hammers. There were angled conveyor belts like the ridged spines of dinosaurs. There were rotating shield drills: huge toothed discs as wide as any one of the caravan's vehicles. There were fusion torches, lasers, bosers, high-pressure water cutters, steam-borers. There were tiny cabins jacked high on articulated gantries. There were vast ore hoppers and grilled, chimneyed machines she couldn't even begin to identify. There were generators, equipment carriers and accommodation cabins painted the same dusty yellow.

All of it rolled by, machine after machine, hogging the road while the caravan bounced along in a rut on one side of it.

She sensed grinding humiliation.

Later, when the caravan was on the move again, she tried to find out what had happened. She thought Pietr might know, but he was nowhere to be found. Quaestor Jones, when she tracked him down, dismissed the matter as one of trifling importance. But he still did not tell her what she wanted to know.

'That wasn't a caravan like ours,' she said.

'Your powers of observation do you credit.'

'So might I ask where it was going?'

'I would have thought that was obvious, especially given your chosen intention to work on the Permanent Way. Very evidently, those machines were part of a major Way taskforce. Doubtless they were on their way to clear a blockage, or to make good a defect in the infrastructure.' Quaestor Rutland Jones folded his arms, as if the matter was settled.

'Then they'd be affiliated to a church, wouldn't they? I may not know much, but I know that all the gangs are tied to specific churches.'

'Most certainly.' He drummed his fingers on the desk before him.

'In which case, what church was it? I watched every one of those machines go past and I didn't see a single clerical symbol on any of them.'

The quaestor shrugged, a little too emphatically for Rashmika's tastes. 'It's dirty work – as you will soon discover. When the clock is against a team, I doubt that touching-up painted insignia is very high on the list of priorities.'

She recalled that the excavation machines had been dusty and faded. What the quaestor said was undoubtedly true in a general sense, but in Rashmika's opinion, not one of those machines had ever carried a clerical symbol – not since they were last painted, at least.

'One other thing, Quaestor.'

'Yes,' he said, tiredly.

'We're heading down towards the Way because we took a short cut across Absolution Gap. We'd come from the north. It seems to me that if those machines really were on their way to clear a blockage, they'd hardly be taking the same route we did, even in reverse.'

'What are you suggesting, Miss Els?'

'It strikes me as much more likely that they were headed somewhere else entirely. Somewhere that has nothing to do with the Way.'

'And that's your considered opinion, is it? Based on all your many years of experience with matters of the Way and the operational complexities of its maintenance?'

'There's no call for sarcasm, Quaestor.'

He shook his head and reached for a compad, making an exaggerated show of finding his place in whatever work he had been engaged in before her interruption. 'Based on my own limited experience, you will do one of two things, Miss Els. You will either go very far, or you will shortly meet a very unfortunate end in what on the face of it might resemble a regrettable accident out on the ice. One thing I am certain about, however: in the process of reaching either outcome, you will still manage to irritate a great many people.'

'Then at least I'll have made a difference,' she said, with vastly more bravado than she felt. She turned to go.

'Miss Els.'

'Quaestor?'

'Should you at any point decide to return to the badlands ... would you do me a singular favour?'

'What?' she asked.

'Find some other mode of transport to take you back,' the quaestor said, before returning to his duties.

THIRTY-ONE

Near Ararat, 2675

Scorpio cycled through the airlock as soon as the shuttle had engaged with its docking cradle, latching itself securely into place in the reception bay. The other ship that had accompanied them – it was much smaller and sleeker – was a wedge of darkness parked alongside. All he could see was its silhouette, a flint-shaped splash of ink like one of the random blots sometimes used in a psychological examination. It just sat there, hissing, its smell sharp and antiseptic, like a medicine cabinet. It looked completely two-dimensional, as if stamped from a sheet of thin black metal.

It looked like something you could cut yourself on.

Security Arm militia had already cordoned off both craft. They recognised the shuttle, but they were wary of the other arrival. Scorpio assumed it had received the same invitation, but the guards were still taking no chances. He stood most of them down, keeping only a couple handy just in case the ship really did contain an unpleasant surprise.

He raised his sleeve and spoke into his communicator. 'Antoinette? You around?'

'I'm on my way up, Scorp. Be there in a minute or so. Do you have our guest?'

'I'm not sure,' he said.

He moved over to the black ship. It was not much larger than the capsule Khouri had come down in. Room in it for one or two people at the very most, he estimated. He rapped a knuckle against the black surface. It was cold to the touch. The hairs on his knuckle tingled with shock.

A dogleg of pink light split the black machine down the middle and a section of the hull slid aside, revealing a dim interior. A man was already extricating himself from the prison of an acceleration couch and fold-around controls. It was Remontoire, just as Scorpio had suspected. He was a little older than Scorpio remembered, but still fundamentally the same: a very thin, very tall, very bald man, dressed entirely in tight black clothes that served only to emphasise his arachnoid qualities. His skull was a peculiar shape: elongated, like a teardrop.

Scorpio leaned into the cavity to help him out.

'Mr Pink, I presume,' Remontoire said.

Scorpio hesitated a moment. The name meant something, but the association was buried decades in the past. He tugged at the strands of his memory until one came loose. He recalled the time when Remontoire and he had travelled incognito through the Rust Belt and Chasm City, pursuing Clavain when he had first defected from the Conjoiners. Mr Pink had been the name Scorpio had travelled under. What had Remontoire called himself? Scorpio tried to remember.

'Mr Clock,' he said at last, just at the point when the pause would have become uncomfortable.

They had hated each other's guts back then. It had been inevitable, really. Remontoire did not like pigs (there had been something unpleasant in his past, some incident in which he had been tortured by one of them) but had been forced to employ Scorpio because of his useful local knowledge. Scorpio did not like Conjoiners (no one did, unless they were already Conjoiners) and he particularly did not like Remontoire. But he had been blackmailed into assisting them, promised his freedom if he did. To refuse meant being handed over to the authorities, who had a nice little pre-scripted show trial planned for him.

No; they hadn't exactly started out as friends, but the hatred had gradually evaporated, aided by their mutual respect for Clavain. Now Scorpio was actually glad to see the man, a reaction that would have stunned and appalled his younger self.

'We're quite a pair of relics, you and I,' Remontoire said. He stood up, stretching his limbs, turning them this way and that as if ascertaining that none of them had become dislocated.

'I'm afraid I have some bad news,' Scorpio said.

'Clavain?'

'I'm sorry.'

'I guessed, of course. The moment I saw you, I knew he must be dead. When did it happen?'

'A couple of days ago.'

'And how did he die?'

'Very badly. But he died for Ararat. He was a hero to the end, Rem.'

For a moment Remontoire was somewhere else, wandering

through a landscape of mental reflection accessible only to Conjoiners. He closed his eyes, remained that way for perhaps ten seconds and then opened them again. They were now gleaming with bright alertness, no trace of sorrow visible.

'Well, I've grieved,' he said.

Scorpio knew better than to doubt Remontoire's word; that was just how Conjoiners did things. It was a measure of Remontoire's respect for his old friend and ally that he had even deemed a period of grieving necessary in the first place. It would have been trivial for him to edit his own mind into a state of serene acceptance. By going through the motions of grief he had paid a great, humbling tribute to Clavain. Even if it had only taken ten or twelve seconds.

'Are we safe?' Scorpio asked.

'For now. We planned your escape carefully, creating a major diversion using the remaining assets. We knew the wolves would be able to reallocate some of their resources to bring you down, but our forecasts showed that we could handle them, provided you left exactly on schedule.'

'You can beat the wolves?'

'No, not beat them, Scorpio.' Remontoire's tone was schoolmasterly, gently reproachful. 'We can overwhelm a small number of wolf machines in a specific location by using a deliberate concentration of power. We can inflict some damage, push them back, force them to regroup. But really, it's like throwing pebbles at pack dogs. Against a large grouping, there is still little we can do. And in the longer term – so our forecasts tell us – we will lose.'

'But you've survived until now.'

'With the weapons and techniques Aura gave us, yes. But that well is nearly dry now. And the wolves have shown a remarkable propensity for matching us.' Remontoire's eyes sparkled with admiration. 'They are very efficient, these machines.'

Scorpio laughed. After everything that he had been through, this was the outcome Remontoire was spelling out? 'Then we're screwed, right?'

'In the long run, at least according to the current forecasts, the prognosis is not good.'

Behind Remontoire, the black ship sealed itself, becoming once again a sharp-edged chunk of shadow.

'Then why don't we just give up now?'

'Because there is a chance – albeit a small one – that the forecasts may be badly wrong.'

'I think we need to talk,' Scorpio said.

'And I know just the place,' said Antoinette Bax, stepping into the bay. She inclined her head towards Remontoire, as if they had seen each other only minutes earlier. 'Follow me, you two. I think you're going to love this.'

Hela, 2727

Rashmika saw the cathedrals.

It was not how she had imagined it, when she had rehearsed in her head her arrival at the Way. In her mind's eye she was always simply *there*, with no approach, no opportunity to see the cathedrals small and neat in the distance, perched like ornaments on the horizon. But here they were, still a dozen or more kilometres away, yet clearly visible. It was like looking at the sailing ships of olden days, the way their topgallants came over the horizon long before their hulls. She could reach out her hand, open her fist and trap any one of those cathedrals in the curve between finger and thumb. She could close one eye so that the lack of perspective made the cathedral appear like a small and lovely toy, a thing of magical jewelled delicacy.

And she could just as easily imagine closing her fist on it.

There were too many of them to count. Thirty, forty, easily. Some were bunched up into tight clusters, like galleons exchanging close-quarters cannon fire. When they were so close, it was not easy to separate the resulting confusion of towers and spires into individual structures. Some cathedrals were single-spired or single-towered; others resembled whole city parishes joined together and set adrift. There were elbowed towers and lavish minarets. There were spires – barbed, flanged and buttressed. There were stained-glass windows hundreds of metres tall. There were rose windows wide enough to fly a ship through. There were glints of rare metals, acres of fabulous alloys. There were things like barnacles climbing halfway up the skins of some of the cathedrals, things whose scale she completely misjudged until she was close enough to realise that they were actually buildings in their own right, piled higgledy-piggledy atop one another.

Again, she thought of Brueghel.

As the caravan continued its approach to the Way, a greater proportion of each cathedral gradually became visible. Yet more sailed over the horizon, far to their rear, but this was the main group, Rashmika knew: the vanguard of the procession.

Above, Haldora sat perfectly at the zenith, at the apex of the celestial dome.

She had nearly arrived.

Near Ararat, 2675

Scorpio sat on the wooden table in the glade. He looked around, anxious to absorb every detail, but at the same time hoping not to appear too overwhelmed. It was really like no place he had ever been. The sky was a pure corneal blue, richer and deeper than anything he recalled from Ararat. The trees were amazingly intricate, shimmering with detail. They breathed. He had only ever seen pictures of trees, but the pictures had failed utterly to convey the enormous dizzying complexity of the things. It was like the first time he had seen the ocean: the gulf between expectation and reality was vast and nauseating. It wasn't simply a question of scaling up some local, familiar thing, like a cup of water. There was a whole essence of *seaness* that he could never have predicted.

Frankly, the trees alarmed him. They were so huge, so alive. What if they decided they didn't like him?

'Scorp,' Antoinette said. 'Put these on, will you?'

He took the goggles, frowning at them. 'Any particular reason why?'

'So you can talk to John. Those of us without machines in our heads can't see him most of the time. Don't worry, you won't be the only one looking silly.'

He fixed the goggles in place. They were designed for people, not pigs, but they were not too uncomfortable when he adjusted them for the shape of his face. Nothing happened when he looked through them.

'John'll be here in a moment,' Antoinette reassured him.

This meeting had been convened very quickly. Around the table, in addition to Antoinette and himself, sat Vasko Malinin, Ana Khouri and her daughter – still inside a portable incubator, which Khouri rested on her lap – Dr Valensin and three low-ranking colony representatives. The three representatives were simply the most senior of the fourteen thousand or so citizens who were already aboard the *Nostalgia for Infinity*. The usual senior members – Orca Cruz, Blood, Xavier Liu, amongst others – were still on Ararat. Remontoire took the place opposite Scorpio, leaving only one vacant position.

'This will have to be brief,' Remontoire said. 'In less than an hour I must be on my way.'

'You won't be staying for lunch?' Scorpio asked, remembering belatedly that Remontoire had no sense of humour.

The Conjoiner shook the delicately veined egg that was his head. 'I'm afraid not. The *Zodiacal Light* and the other Conjoiner assets will remain in this system, at least until you are into clear interstellar space. We will draw the Inhibitors away from you. Some elements may follow you, but they will almost certainly not constitute the main force.' He had made a thin-boned church of his fingers. 'You should be able to handle them.'

'It sounds a lot like self-sacrifice to me,' Antoinette said.

'It isn't. I am pessimistic, but not totally without hope. There are still weapons we haven't used and a number we haven't even manufactured yet. Some of them may make a small difference, locally at least.' He paused and reached into an invisible pocket in his tunic. His fingers vanished into the fabric, as if executing a conjuring trick, and then emerged clutching a small slate-grey sliver, which he placed on the table and then tapped with his forefinger. 'Before I forget: schematics for several militarily useful technologies. Some of these Aura or Khouri may already have mentioned. We owe them all to Aura, of course, but while she showed us the way forward and gave us clues to the basic principles, there was still much that we had to work out from scratch. These files should be compatible with standard manufactory protocols.'

'We have no manufactories,' Antoinette said. 'They all stopped working years ago.'

Remontoire pursed his lips. 'Then we will provide you with new ones, good against most plague variants. I'll have them dropped off before you leave the system, along with medical supplies and reefersleep components. Feed them the files and they will make weapons and devices. If you have any queries, phrase them appropriately to Aura and she should be able to help you.'

'Thanks, Rem,' said Antoinette.

'This is a gift,' he said. 'We give it freely, just as we are happy for you to take Aura. She is yours now. But there *is* something that you can give us in return.'

'Name it,' Antoinette told him.

But Remontoire said nothing. He looked over his shoulder at a figure crunching towards them through the grass.

'Hello, John,' Antoinette said.

Scorpio sat back stiffly on the bench as the figure approached. At first glance it barely looked like a human being at all. It walked, and it had arms and legs and a head, but that was where the resemblance ended. One half of the man's body – one arm and one leg, and one half of the torso – was, so far as he could tell, approximately flesh and blood. But the other half was hulking and mechanical, grotesquely so, with no effort having been expended to create an illusion of symmetry. There were pistons and huge articulated hinge points, sliding metal gleaming from constant polishing and lubrication. The arm on the mechanical side hung down to knee-level, terminating in a complex multi-purpose tool-delivery system. The effect was as if a piece of earth-moving equipment had collided with a man at brutal speed, fusing them together in the process.

His head, by contrast, was almost normal. But only by contrast. Red multifaceted cameras were crammed into the orbits of his eyes. Tubes emerged from his nostrils, curving back around the side of his face to connect to some unseen mechanism. An oval grille covered his mouth, stitched into the flesh of his face. His scalp was bald save for a dozen or so matted locks emerging from the crown. They were tied back, knotted into a single braid that hung down the back of his neck. He had no ears. In fact, Scorpio realised, he had no visible orifices at all. Perhaps he had been redesigned to tolerate hard vacuum without the protection of a space helmet.

His voice appeared to emerge from the grille. It was small, tinny, like a broken toy. 'Hey. The gang's all here.'

'Have a seat, John,' Antoinette said. 'Do you need to be brought up to speed? Remontoire was just explaining a technical trade-off. He's giving us some cool new toys.'

'In return for something else, I gather.'

'No,' Remontoire said. 'The technical blueprints and the other items really are a gift. But if you are willing to consider offering us a reciprocal gift, we have something in mind.'

John Brannigan assumed his seat, lowering himself into place with a hiss and chuff of contracting pistons. 'You want the remaining cache weapons,' he said.

Remontoire dignified the remark with a nod. 'You guess our desires well.'

'Why do you want them?' John Brannigan asked.

'Our forecasts show that we will need them if we are to create a useful diversion. There is, necessarily, an element of uncertainty. Not all the weapons have known properties. But we can make some useful guesses.'

'We will be running from the machines as well,' Scorpio said. 'Who's to say we won't need the weapons ourselves?'

'No one,' Remontoire replied. As always he was unflappable, like an adult suggesting parlour games for children. 'You may very well need them. But you will be running *from* the wolves, not already engaged with them. If you are sensible, you will avoid further encounters for as long as possible.'

'You said we might still have wolves on our tail,' Antoinette reminded him. 'What do we do about them? Ask them nicely to go away?'

Remontoire again tapped the data recording he had placed on the table. 'This will show you how to construct a hypometric weapon system. Our forecasts indicate that three of these devices will be sufficient to disperse a small wolf pursuit element.'

'And if your forecasts turn out to be wrong?' Scorpio asked.

'You will have other resources.'

'Not good enough,' the pig said. 'Those cache weapons were the whole reason we went all the way out to the Resurgam system in the first place. They're what got us into this steaming pile of shit. And now you're saying we should just give them up?'

'I am still your ally,' Remontoire said. 'I am merely proposing that the weapons be reassigned to their point of maximum usefulness.'

'I don't get this,' Antoinette said, nodding at the data sliver. 'You have the means to make stuff we can't even dream of yet, and you still want those mouldy old cache weapons?'

'We cannot underestimate the cache weapons,' Remontoire said. 'They were a gift from the future. Until they have been exhaustively tested, we cannot assume that they are inferior to anything Aura has given us. You must agree with this reasoning as well.'

'Guy's got a point, I suppose,' Antoinette said.

John Brannigan's projected form moved with a hiss of locomotive systems. It must have been Scorpio's imagination, but he thought he smelled lubricant. The Captain spoke again in his tinny voice. 'He may well have a point, but Aura's capabilities are equally untested. We have at least deployed a number of cache weapons and found them functional. I cannot sanction handing the rest of them over.'

'Then we'll have to arrive at a compromise position,' Remontoire said.

The Captain looked at him, his grille-mouthed face expressionless. 'I'm all ears,' he said.

'Our forecasts show a reduced but still statistically significant chance of success with only a subset of the available cache weapons.'

'So you get some of 'em, but not all of 'em, right?' Antoinette asked.

Remontoire dipped his head once. 'Yes, but don't assume that this position is arrived at lightly. With a reduced range of cache weapons at our disposal, it may not be possible to prevent a larger pursuit element coming after you.'

'Yeah,' Antoinette said, 'but then we'll have more to throw at them, right?'

'Correct,' Remontoire said, 'but don't underestimate the risk of failure.'

'We'll take that risk,' Scorpio said.

'Wait,' Khouri said. She trembled, one hand steadying the incubator on her lap, the other gripping the wooden table with her fingernails. 'Wait. I ... Aura ...' Her eyes became all whites, the muscles in her neck pulling taut. 'No,' she said. 'No. Definitely no.'

'No what?' Scorpio asked.

'No. *No no no.* Do what Remontoire says. Give all the weapons. *Will* make a difference. Trust him.' Her fingernails gouged raw white trails into the wood.

Vasko leant forwards and spoke for the first time during the meeting. 'Aura might be right,' he said.

'I am right,' Khouri said.

'We should listen to her,' Vasko said. 'She seems pretty clear on this.'

'How would she know?' Scorpio said. 'She knows some stuff, I'll buy that. But no one said anything about her seeing the future.'

The seniors nodded as one.

'I'm with Scorp on this one,' Antoinette said. 'We can't give Rem all those weapons. We've got to keep some back for ourselves. What if we can't get the manufactories to work? What if the stuff they make doesn't work either?'

'They will work,' Remontoire said, still utterly calm and relaxed, even though vast destinies hung in the balance.

Scorpio shook his head. 'Not good enough. We'll give you some of the cache weapons, but not all of them.'

'Fine,' said Remontoire, 'as long as we're agreed.'

'Scorpio ...' Vasko said.

The pig had had enough. This was his colony, his ship, his crisis. He reached up and ripped away the goggles, breaking them in the process. 'It's decided,' he snapped.

Remontoire spread his fingers wide. 'We'll make the arrangements, then. Cargo tugs will be sent to assist in the transfer of the weapons.

Another shuttle will arrive with the new manufactories and some prefabricated items. Conjoiners will arrive to help with the installation of the hypometric weapons and the other new technologies. Is it necessary to airlift any remaining personnel from the surface?'

'Yes,' Antoinette said.

'A major evacuation is out of the question,' Remontoire said. 'We can open safe passage to and from the surface on one, possibly two further occasions – enough for a couple of shuttle flights, but no more than that.'

'That'll do,' Antoinette said.

'What about the rest of them?' asked one of the seniors.

'They had their chance,' Scorpio said.

Remontoire smiled primly, as if someone had committed a *faux pas* in polite company. 'They aren't necessarily in immediate peril,' he said. 'If the Inhibitors wished to destroy Ararat's biosphere, they could have done so already.'

'But they'll be prisoners down there,' Antoinette said. 'The wolves won't ever let them leave.'

'But they will still be alive,' Remontoire said. 'And we may stand a chance of reducing the wolf presence around Ararat. Without access to the full complement of cache weapons, however, that cannot be guaranteed.'

'Could you guarantee it if you had all the weapons?' Scorpio asked.

After a moment's consideration Remontoire shook his head. 'No,' he said. 'No guarantees, not even then.'

Scorpio looked around at the assembled delegates, realising for the first time that he was the only pig amongst them. Where the Captain had been sitting only a vacant space now remained, a focus towards which everyone else's attention was being subtly attracted. The Captain was still there, Scorpio thought. He was still there, still listening. He even thought he could still smell the lubricant.

'Then I'm not going to lose any sleep over it,' Scorpio said.

Antoinette came to see Scorpio after the meeting. He had taken the elevator back upship, to assist with the ongoing efforts to process the evacuees. There were people everywhere, huddled into filthy, dank, winding corridors as far as the eye could see.

He walked along one of these corridors, absorbing the frightened faces, fielding questions when he was able to, but saying nothing about the wider plans for the ship and its passengers. He told them only that they would be taken care of, that some of them would be frozen, but that every effort would be taken to make the process as painless and safe as possible. He believed it, too, for a while. But then it dawned on him, after navigating one corridor, that he had seen only a few hundred evacuees out of the thousands supposedly aboard.

He met Antoinette in a junction, where Security Arm militia were directing people to functioning elevators that would take them to different processing centres much further down the ship.

'It's going to be all right, Scorp,' she said.

'Am I that easy to read?'

'You look worried, as if you've got the weight of the world on your shoulders.'

'Funny, but that's more or less how I feel.'

'You'll hack it. Do you remember how it was with Clavain, when we were in the Mademoiselle's Château?'

'That was a while back.'

'Well, I remember even if you don't. He looked just the way you look now, Scorp, as if his whole life had been a sequence of errors, culminating in that one moment of absolute failure. He nearly lost it then. But he *didn't*. He kept it together. And it worked out. In the end, that sequence of errors turned out to be exactly the right set of choices.'

He smiled. 'Thanks for the pep talk, Antoinette.'

'I just thought you should know. Things are getting complicated, Scorp, and I know you sometimes don't think that's exactly your ideal milieu, if you get my drift. But you're wrong. Your kind of leadership is just what we need now: blunt and to the point. You're not a politician, Scorp. Thank God for that. Clavain would have agreed, you know.'

'You think so?'

'I *know* so. I'm just asking you not to have a crisis on us. Not now.'

'I'll try not to.'

She sighed and punched him playfully on the arm. 'I just wanted you to know that before I leave.'

'Leave?'

'I've made my mind up: I'm going back down to Ararat on one of Remontoire's shuttles. Xavier's down there.'

'That'll be risky,' he warned. 'Why not just let Remontoire bring Xavier back up here? He's already agreed to bring Orca back from Ararat. I hate to be blunt – sorry – but at least that way we'd only lose one of you if the wolves take out the shuttle.'

'Because I'm not coming back,' she said. 'I'm going down to Ararat and I'm staying there.'

It took a moment for that to sink in. 'But you made it out,' he said.

'No, Scorp, I came up with the *Infinity* because I didn't have a lot of choice in the matter. But my responsibilities are down there, with the thousands we'll be leaving behind. Oh, they don't really need me, I suppose, but they definitely need Xavier. He's about the only one who knows how to fix anything when it goes wrong.'

'I'm sure you'll make yourself useful,' Scorpio said, smiling.

'Well, if they let me fly something now and then, I guess I won't go totally insane.'

'We could still use you up here. I could use an ally any time of the day.'

'You've got allies, Scorp; you just don't know it yet.'

'You're doing a brave thing,' he said.

'It's not such a dreadful place,' she replied. 'Don't make me out to be too much of a martyr. I never really minded Ararat. I liked the sunsets. I guess I've even developed a taste for seaweed tea after all these years. All I'm really doing is staying at home.'

'We'll miss you,' he said.

She looked down. He had the feeling that she could not look at his face. 'I don't know what's going to happen now, Scorp. Maybe you'll take this ship to Hela, like Aura says. Maybe you'll go somewhere else. But I've a feeling we won't ever meet again. It's a big universe out there, and the chances of our paths ever crossing again ...'

'It's a big place,' he said, 'but on the other hand, I guess that also makes it big enough for a few coincidences.'

'For some people, maybe, but not for the likes of you and me, Scorp.' She looked up then, staring hard into his eyes. 'I was scared of you when I met you, I don't mind admitting that now. Scared and ignorant. But I'm glad everything happened the way it did. I'm glad I got to know you for a few years.'

'It was half my life.'

'They were good years, Scorp. I won't forget them.' Once more she looked down. He wondered if she was looking at his small, childlike shoes. Suddenly he felt self-conscious, wishing he was larger, more human, less like a pig and more like a man. 'Remontoire's going to have that shuttle ready soon,' she said. 'I'd better be going. Take care of yourself, all right? You're a good man. A good pig.'

'I try,' Scorpio said.

She hugged him, then kissed him.

Then she was gone. He never saw her again.

THIRTY-TWO

Hela, 2727

The caravan sidled up to the kerb of the Way, overtaking one cathedral after another. Monstrous machinery loomed over Rashmika. She was too overwhelmed to take it all in, retaining only a blurred impression of great dark-grey mechanisms, projected to an inhuman scale. As the caravan wormed between them, the cathedrals appeared to remain completely still, as fully rooted to the landscape as the buildings she had seen on the Jarnsaxa Flats. Except, of course, that these buildings were true skyscrapers, jagged fingers clawing across the face of Haldora. And that stillness, Rashmika knew, was only an illusion born of the caravan's speed. Were they to stop, one or other of the cathedrals would be rolling over them within a few minutes.

It was said that the cathedrals never stopped. It was also said that they seldom deviated from their paths unless a given obstacle was too large to be safely crushed beneath their traction mechanisms.

The Way was much narrower than she had expected. She recalled what Quaestor Jones had said: that it was never more than two hundred metres wide, and usually much less than that. Distances were difficult to judge in the absence of any familiar landmarks, but she did not think the Way was more than one hundred metres wide at any point along this stretch. Some of the larger cathedrals were almost that wide themselves, squatting across the full width of the Way like mechanical toads. The smaller cathedrals were able to travel two abreast, but only by allowing parts of their superstructures to lean out over the edges of the Way. Here, it did not really matter: the Way was just a smoothed and cleared strip across the otherwise flat and unobstructed expanse of the Flats. Any one of the cathedrals could have diverted off the path prepared ahead of it, taking its chances on the slightly rougher ground on either side. But clearly no such risk-taking was on the cards today, and the relative order of the procession looked set to remain unchallenged for the time being. This was the normal way of things: the jockeying, jousting and general dirty tricks that one heard about in the badlands were very much the exception rather than the rule, and such stories, Rashmika had long suspected, enjoyed a degree of exaggeration as they travelled north.

For now, therefore, the flotillas of cathedrals would creep along the Way in a more or less fixed formation. If she thought of them as city-states, then now would be a period of trade and diplomacy rather than war. Doubtless there would be espionage and subtle gamesmanship, and doubtless plans were continually being drawn up for future contingencies. But for the moment what prevailed was a state of genteel cordiality, with all the strained courtesies one customarily expected between historical rivals.

This suited Rashmika: it would be difficult enough fitting in with the repair gang without having to deal with additional crises and complications.

She had been given orders to collect her belongings – such as they were – and remain in one vehicle of the caravan. The reason soon became obvious, as the caravan fissioned into many smaller components. Rashmika watched as the quaestor's workers hopped from vehicle to vehicle, unhooking umbilicals and couplings with cool indifference to the obvious risks.

Some of these sub-caravans were still several vehicles in length, and she watched as they peeled away to rendezvous with the larger cathedrals or cathedral-clusters. To her disappointment, however, the vehicle to which she had been assigned departed on its own. She was not alone in it – there were a dozen or so pilgrims and migrant workers waiting with her – but any hope that the Catherine of Iron might turn out to be amongst the larger cathedrals was quickly dashed, if it only merited one portion of the caravan.

Well, she had to start somewhere, as the quaestor had said.

Quickly the vehicle nosed away from the major cathedrals, bouncing and jinking over the ruts and potholes they had left in their wake.

'You lot,' she said, addressing the other travellers, standing in front of them with arms akimbo. 'Which one of those is the Lady Morwenna?'

One of her companions wiped a smear of mucus from his upper lip. 'None of them, love.'

'One of them has to be,' she said. 'That's the main gathering. The sweet spot is right there.'

'That's the main gathering all right, but no one said the Lady Mor was part of it.'

'Now you're being oblique for the sake of it.'

'Hark at her,' someone else said. 'Right stuck-up little cow.'

'All right,' she countered. 'If the Lady Morwenna isn't there, where is it?'

'Why are you so interested?' the first one asked.

'It's the oldest cathedral on the Way,' she said. 'I think it'd be a little strange *not* to want to see it, don't you?'

'All we want is work, love. Doesn't matter which one doles it out. It's still the same fucking *ice* you have to shovel out the way.'

'Well, I'm still interested,' she said.

'It isn't any of those cathedrals,' another voice said, bored but not unreasonable. She saw a man at the back of the gathering, lying down on a couch with a cigarette in one hand and the other tucked deep into his trousers, where it rummaged and scratched. 'But you can see it.'

'Where?'

'Over here, little girl.'

She stepped towards the man.

'Watch him,' another voice said. 'He'll be on you like a rash.'

She hesitated. The man waved her over with his cigarette. He pulled his hand free from his trousers. It ended in a crude-looking metal claw. He transferred the cigarette to it and beckoned her over with his undamaged hand. 'It's all right. I stink a bit, but I don't bite. Just want to show you the Lady Mor, that's all.'

'I know,' she said. She stepped through the jumble of other bodies.

The man pointed to a small scuffed window behind him. He wiped it clean with his sleeve. 'Look through there. You can still see the top of her spire.'

She looked. All she saw was landscape. 'I'm not ...'

'There.' The man nudged her chin until she was looking in exactly the right direction. He smelled like vinegar. 'Between those bluffs, do you see something sticking up?'

'There's something sticking up all right,' someone else said.

'Shut up,' Rashmika snapped. There must have been something in the tone of her voice because it had exactly the desired effect.

'See it now?' the man asked.

'Yes. What's it doing all the way out there? It can't be on the Permanent Way at all.'

'It is,' the man said. 'Just not on the part we usually follow.'

'Doesn't she know?' said another voice.

'If I did, I wouldn't be asking,' Rashmika replied tartly.

'The Way branches near here,' the man said, explaining it to her the way you would explain something to a child. She decided that she did not really like him after all. He was helping her, but the manner in which he was helping mattered, too. Sometimes refusal was better than grudging assistance. 'Splits in two,' he said. 'One route is the one the cathedrals normally follow. Takes them all the way down to the Devil's Staircase.'

'I know about that,' she said. 'Zigzag ramps cut into the side of the Rift. The cathedrals follow them down to the bottom of the Rift, then up the other side again after they've crossed it.'

'Right. Care to have a guess where the other route takes them?'

'I'm assuming it crosses the bridge.'

'You're a clever little girl.'

She pulled away from the window. 'If there's a branch of the Way from the bridge to here, why didn't we follow it?'

'Because for a caravan it isn't the quickest route. Caravans can cut corners, go up slopes and around tight bends. Cathedrals can't. They have to take the long way around anything they can't blast through. Anyway, the route to the bridge doesn't see much maintenance. You might not have noticed it was a part of the Way even if you were on it.'

'Then the Lady Morwenna will pull further and further away from the main gathering of cathedrals,' she said. 'Doesn't that mean Haldora won't be overhead any more?'

'Not exactly, no,' he said. He scratched at the side of his face with his claw, metal rasping against stubble. 'But the Devil's Staircase isn't bang on the equator, either. They had to dig it where they could dig it, not where it should have gone. Another thing, too: you go down the Devil's Staircase, you've got overhanging ice to contend with. Not good for Observers: blocks their view of the planet. And the Staircase is where cathedrals stand the best chance of pulling ahead of each other. But if one of them ever managed to cross the bridge, it'd be so far ahead of the pack it'd have to stop to let the others catch up with it. After that, nothing would ever get ahead of them. They could build themselves as wide as they liked. Never mind the glory in having crossed the bridge. They'd rule the Way.'

'But no cathedral has ever crossed the bridge.' She remembered the cratered ruins she had seen from the roof of the caravan. 'I know that one did try it once, but . . .'

'No one said it wasn't madness, love, but that's old pop-eyed Dean Quaiche for you. You should be glad you're ending up on the Iron Katy. They say the rats have already started leaving the Lady Mor.'

'The dean must think he has a good chance of making it,' she said.

'Or he's insane.' The man grinned at her, his yellow teeth like chipped tombstones. 'Take your pick.'

'I don't have to,' she said, then added, 'Why did you call him pop-eyed?'

They all laughed at her. One of them made goggles of his fingers around his eyes.

'Girl's got a lot to learn,' someone said.

The Catherine of Iron was one of the smaller cathedrals in the procession, travelling alone several kilometres to the rear of the main pack. There were others further behind it, but these were little more than spires on the horizon. Almost certainly they were struggling to catch up with the others, determined to bring themselves as close as possible to the abstract moving point on the Way that corresponded to Haldora sitting precisely overhead. The ultimate shame, from a cathedral's point of view, was to fall so far back that even the casual observer became aware that Haldora was not quite at the zenith. Worse than that – unspeakably worse – was the stigma that went beyond shame that was the fate suffered by any cathedral that lost sight of Haldora altogether. That was why the work of the Permanent Way gangs was taken so seriously. A day's delay here or there was nothing, but many such delays could have a catastrophic effect on a cathedral's progress.

Rashmika's vehicle slowed as it approached the Catherine of Iron, then looped around to the rear. The partial circumnavigation afforded her an excellent view of the place that was to be her new home. Small though her assigned cathedral undoubtedly was, it was not an untypical example of their general style.

The flat base of the cathedral was a rectangle thirty metres wide and perhaps one hundred in length. Above this base towered the superstructure; below it – partially hidden by metal skirts – lay the rude business of engines and traction systems. The cathedral inched along the Way by dint of many parallel sets of caterpillar tracks. Currently, on one side, an entire traction unit had been hauled ten or so metres above the ice. Suited workers were lashed to the immobile underside of one of the tread plates, their welding and cutting torches flashing a pretty blue-violet as they effected some repair. Rashmika had never asked herself how the cathedrals dealt with that kind of overhaul, and the sheer bloody-minded *ruthlessness* of the solution – fixing part of the traction machinery while the cathedral was still moving – rather impressed her.

All around the cathedral, now that she noticed it, was more such activity; traceries of scaffolding covered much of the superstructure. Small figures were working everywhere she looked. The way they popped in and out of hatches, high above ground, made her think of clockwork automata.

Above the flat base, the cathedral conformed more or less to the traditional architectural expectations. Seen from above, the cathedral was an approximate cruciform shape, made up of a long nave with two stubbier transepts jutting out on either side and a smaller chapel at the head of the cross. Rising from the intersection of the nave and its transepts was a square-based tower. It rose for one hundred metres – about equal to the length of the cathedral – before tapering into a four-sided spire which was another fifty metres higher. The ridges of the spire were serrated, and at the very top of the spire was an assemblage of communications dishes and semaphoric signalling mirrors. Rising from the traction base and angling inwards to connect with the top part of the nave were a dozen or so flying buttresses formed from skeletal girderwork. One or two were obviously missing or incomplete. Much of the cathedral, in fact, had a haphazard look, with various parts of the architecture sitting in only approximate harmony with each other. There were whole sections that appeared to have been replaced in great haste, or at minimal expense, or some combination of the two. The spire appeared to lean at a small angle away from the true vertical. It was propped up on one side by scaffolding.

She didn't know whether to be saddened or relieved. At this point, knowing what she now knew about Dean Quaiche's plans for the Lady Morwenna, she was glad not to have been assigned to it. She could entertain all the fantasies she liked, but there was no chance of rescuing her brother before the Lady Morwenna reached the bridge. She would be lucky to have infiltrated any level of the cathedral's hierarchy by then.

The notion of infiltration chimed in her head. It was as if it had resonated with something intimate and personal, something that ran as deep within her as bone marrow. Why did the idea suddenly have such grave and immediate potency? She supposed that her entire mission had been a form of infiltration, from the moment she left her village and set about joining the caravan. The work of ascending through the cathedral until she located Harbin was only a later, more dangerous aspect of an enterprise upon which she had already embarked. She had taken the first step weeks ago, when she first heard of the caravan passing so close to the badlands.

But it had begun earlier than that, really.

Very much earlier.

Rashmika felt dizzy. She had glimpsed something there, a moment of clarity that had opened and closed in an instant. She herself had jammed it shut, the way one slammed a door on a loud noise or a bright light. She had glimpsed a plan – a scheme of infiltration – which stood outside the one she thought she knew. Outside and beyond, enveloping it in its entirety. A scheme of infiltration so huge, so ambitious, that even this trek across Hela was but one chapter in something much longer.

A scheme in which she was not simply a puppet, but also the puppeteer. One thought shone through with painful clarity: *you brought this on yourself.*

You wanted it to happen this way.

She tore her mind away from that line of thinking. With an effort of will she forced it back on to the immediate business of the cathedrals. A lapse now, a moment of inattention, could make all the difference.

A shadow fell on the vehicle. It was under the Catherine of Iron, moving between those great rows of crawler tracks. Wheels and treads moved with an unstoppable, inexorable slowness. Never mind her own lapses: it was the driver she had to trust now.

She moved to the other side of the cabin. Ahead, folding down from the underside of the cathedral, was a ramp, its edges marked with pulsing red lights. The lower end of the ramp scraped against the ground, leaving a smooth trail in its wake. The sub-caravan pushed itself on to the slope, wheels spinning for a moment to gain traction, and then its whole length surmounted the ramp. Rashmika grabbed for a handhold as the vehicle began to climb the steep slope. She could feel the labouring grind of the transmission through the metal framing of the cabin.

Soon they reached the top. The sub-caravan righted itself, emerging in a barely lit reception area. There were a couple of other vehicles parked there, as well as a great amount of unfathomable and elderly-looking equipment. Figures moved around wearing vacuum suits. Three of them were fixing an airlock umbilical to the side of the sub-caravan, puzzling over the interconnectors as if this was something they had never had to do before.

Presently Rashmika heard thumps and hisses, then voices. Her companions began to gather themselves and their possessions, edging towards the airlock. She collected her own bundle of belongings and stood ready to join them. For a while nothing happened. She heard the voices getting louder, as if some dispute was taking place. Standing by the window, she had a better view of what was going on outside. Within the depressurised part of the chamber was a figure, standing, doing nothing. She caught a glimpse of a man's face through the visor of his rococo helmet: the expression was blank, but the face was not entirely unfamiliar.

Whoever it was stood watching the proceedings, with one hand resting on a cane.

The commotion continued unabated for a few more moments. Finally it died down and Rashmika's companions began to shuffle out through the airlock, donning the helmets of their vacuum suits as they entered it. They all looked a lot less lively than they had five minutes ago. The actuality of arriving at the Catherine of Iron had brought them to the end of their journey. Judging by their expressions, this dim, grimy-looking enclosure filled with derelict junk and bored-looking workers was not quite what they had imagined when they had set out. She remembered what the quaestor had said, however: that the dean of the Iron Katy was a fair man who treated his workers and pilgrims well. They should all count themselves lucky, in that case. Better a down-at-heel cathedral run by a good man than the doomed madhouse of the Lady Morwenna, even if she did have to get to the Lady Mor eventually.

She had reached the door when a hand touched her chest, preventing her from going any further. She looked into the eyes of a fat-faced Adventist official.

'Rashmika Els?' the man said.

'Yes.'

'There's been a change of plan,' he said. 'You're to stay on the caravan, I'm afraid.'

They took her away from the Catherine of Iron, away from the smooth road of the Permanent Way. She was the only passenger in the sub-caravan apart from the suited man with the cane. He just sat there, his helmet still on, tapping the cane against the heel of his boot. Most of the time she could not see his face.

The vehicle bounced over ruts of ice for many minutes, the main gathering of cathedrals falling into the distance.

'We're going to the Lady Morwenna, aren't we?' Rashmika asked, not really expecting an answer.

None arrived. The man merely tightened the grip on his cane, tilting his head just so, the reflected lighting making a perfect blank mask of his visor. Rashmika felt sick by the time they hit smoother ground and drew alongside the cathedral. It was not only the motion of the caravan sub-unit that made her feel ill, but also a nauseating sense of entrapment. She had wanted to come to the Lady Morwenna. She had not wanted the Lady Morwenna to draw her into it, against her will.

The vehicle pulled alongside the slowly moving mountain of the cathedral. Whereas the Catherine of Iron crawled around Hela on caterpillar tracks, the Lady Morwenna actually walked, shuffling along on twenty vast trapedozoidal feet. There were two parallel rows of ten of them, each row two hundred metres long. The entire mass of the main structure, towering far above, was connected to the feet by the huge telescoping columns of the cathedral's flying buttresses. They were not really buttresses at all, but rather the legs of the feet: complex, brutishly mechanical things, sinewy with pistons and articulation points, veined by thick segmented cables and power lines. They were driven by moving shafts thrusting through the walls of the main structure like the horizontal oars of a slave-powered galleon. In turn, each foot was elevated three or four metres from the surface of the Way, allowed to move forwards slightly, and then lowered back down to the ground. The result was that the entire structure slid smoothly along at a rate of one-third of a metre per second.

It was, she knew, very old. It had grown from a tiny seed sown in the earliest days of Hela's human settlement. Everywhere Rashmika looked she saw indications of damage and repair, redesign and expansion. It was less like a building than a city, one that had been subjected to grandiose civic projects and urban improvement schemes, each throwing out the blueprint of the old. In amongst the machinery, coexisting with it, was a crawling population of sculptural forms: gargoyles and gryphons, dragons and demons, visages of carved masonry or welded metal. Some of these were animated, drawing their motion from the moving mechanisms of the legs, so that the jaws of the carved figures gaped wide and snapped closed with each step taken by the cathedral.

She looked higher, straining to see the vehicle's windows. The great hall of the cathedral reached far above the point where the articulated buttresses curved in to join it. Enormous stained-glass windows towered above her, pointing towards the face of Haldora. There were outflung prominences of masonry and metal capped by squatting gryphons or other heraldic creatures. And then there was the Clocktower itself, shaming even the hall, a tapering, teetering finger of iron thrusting higher than any structure Rashmika had ever seen. She could see the history of the cathedral in the tower, the strata of growth periods laid bare, showing how the vast structure had expanded to its present size. There were follies and abandoned schemes; out-jutting elbows that went nowhere. There were strange levellings-off where it looked as if the spire had been tapering towards a conclusion, before deciding to continue upwards for another hundred metres. And somewhere near the very top – difficult to see from this angle – was a cupola in which burned the unmistakable yellow lights of habitation.

The caravan vehicle swerved closer to the line of slowly stomping feet. There was a clang, and then they floated free of the ground, winched off the surface just as Crozet's icejammer had been by the caravan.

The man in the vacuum suit began undoing his helmet clasp. He did it with a kind of manic patience, as if the act itself was a necessary penitence.

The helmet came off. The man riffled one gloved hand through the white shock of his hair, making it stand straight up from his scalp. The top was mathematically flat. He looked at her, his face long and flat-featured, making her think of a bulldog. She was certain, then, that she had seen the man somewhere before, but for now that was all she remembered.

'Welcome to the Lady Morwenna, Miss Els,' he said.

'I don't know who you are, or why I'm here.'

'I'm Surgeon-General Grelier,' he said. 'And you're here because we want you to be here.'

Whatever that meant, he was telling the truth.

'Now come with me,' he said. 'There is someone you need to see. Then we can discuss terms of employment.'

'Employment?'

'It's work you came for, isn't it?'

She nodded meekly. 'Yes.'

'Then we may have something right up your alley.'

THIRTY-THREE

Near Ararat, 2675

Scorpio had hoped for some rest. But the days immediately following Antoinette's departure were as tiring as any that had preceded them. He stayed awake nearly all the time, watching the arrival and departure of shuttles and tugs, supervising the processing of new evacuees and the comings and goings of Remontoire's technical personnel.

He felt stretched beyond breaking point, never certain that he was more than one or two breaths from collapsing. And yet he kept functioning, sustained by Antoinette's words and his own stubborn refusal to show the slightest glimmer of weakness around the humans. It was becoming difficult. More and more it seemed to him that they had an energy that he lacked; that they were never as close to exhaustion or complete breakdown as he was. It had been different in his younger days. He had been the unstoppable powerhouse then, stronger not only than the humans who made up part of his coterie but also many of the pigs. He had been foolish to imagine that this would be the pattern for the whole of his life, that he would always have that edge. He had never quite noticed the moment when parity occurred; it might have happened months or years in the past, but now he was quite sure that the humans had pulled ahead of him. In the short term he still had a furious, impulsive strength that they lacked, but what use was thuggish immediacy now? What mattered were slow-burning, calculated strength, endurance and presence of mind. The humans were quicker-minded than he was, much less prone to making mistakes. Did they realise that? he wondered. Perhaps not immediately, for he was working hard to compensate for this intrinsic weakness. But sooner or later the effort would take its toll and then they would start to notice his failings. Many of them – the allies Antoinette had spoken of – would do their best to ignore his increasing inadequacy, making excuses for his failings. But again, that process could only continue for so long. Inevitably there would come a time when his enemies would pick up on that creeping weakness and use it against him. He wondered if he would have the courage to step down first, before it became so obvious. He didn't know. It was too hard to think about that, because it cut too close to the essence of what he was, and what he could never be.

Antoinette had not meant to be cruel when she had talked of their time on Ararat as being 'good years'. She had meant it sincerely, and twenty-three years was no small chunk out of anyone's life. But Antoinette was a human. True enough, she did not have access to all the life-extension procedures that had been commonplace a couple of hundred years earlier. Nobody did nowadays. But Antoinette still had advantages that Scorpio lacked. The genes she had inherited had been modified many hundreds of years earlier, weeding out many of the commoner causes of death. She could expect to live about twice as long as she would have had her ancestors never undergone those changes. A one-hundred-and-fifty-year lifespan was not unthinkable for her. Given exceptional luck, she might even see two hundred. Long enough, perhaps, to witness and maybe even benefit from a resurgence in the other kinds of life-extending medicine, the kinds that had been in short supply since the Melding Plague. Granted, the present crisis didn't make that likely, but it was still a remote possibility, still something she could hope for.

Scorpio was fifty now. He would be lucky to see sixty. He had never heard of a pig living longer than seventy-five years, and the oldest pig he had ever met had been seventy-one years old. That pig had died one year later, as a constellation of time-bomb illnesses had ripped him apart over a period of a few months.

Even if, by some stroke of luck, he found a medical facility that still had access to the old rejuvenation and life-extension treatments, they would be useless to him, too finely tuned to human bio-chemistry. He had heard about pigs who had tried such things, and their efforts had invariably been unsuccessful. More often than not they had died prematurely, as the procedures triggered fatal iatrogenic side effects.

It wasn't an option. The only option, really, was to *die*, in about ten to fifteen years' time. Twenty if he was astonishingly lucky. Less time, even then, than he had already spent on Ararat.

'It was half my life,' he had told her. But he didn't think she had understood exactly what that meant. Not just half the life he had lived to date, but a decent fraction of the life he could ever hope to live. The first twenty years of his life barely counted, anyway. He hadn't really been born until he turned the laser on his shoulder and burned the green scorpion into scar tissue. The humans were making plans for decades to come. He was thinking in terms of years, and even then counting on nothing.

The question was, did he have the courage to acknowledge this? If he stepped down now and made it clear that it was because of his genetic inheritance – because of the encroachment of premature death that was part and parcel of the pig package – no one would criticise him. They would understand, and he would have their sympathy. But what if he was wrong to relinquish power now, just because he felt the shadow on him? The shadow was still faint. He thought it likely that only he had seen it clearly. Surely it was a kind of cowardice to give up now, when he still had five or ten more years of useful service in him. Surely he owed Ararat – or Ararat's refugees – more than that. He was many things – violent, stubborn, loyal – but he had never been a coward.

He thought, then, of Aura. It came to him with crystal clarity: she would be followed. She was a child who spoke of things beyond her reach. She had, in a way, already saved thousands of lives by preventing Scorpio from attacking the Jugglers as they tried to haul the *Infinity* to a safe distance from First Camp. She had known what the right thing to do was.

She was just a small thing now, encased in the transparent crib of the incubator, but she was growing. In ten years, what would she be like? It hurt him to have to think so far ahead. He did it anyway. He saw a flash of her then, a girl who looked older than her years, the expression on her face hovering somewhere between serene certainty and the stiff mask of a zealot, untroubled by the smallest flicker of doubt. She would be beautiful, in human terms, and she would have followers. He saw her wearing Skade's armour – the armour as it had been when they had found Skade in the crashed ship, tuned to white, its chameleoflage permanently jammed on that one setting.

She might be right, he thought. She might know exactly what had to be done to make a difference against the Inhibitors. Given what she had already cost them, he desperately hoped that this would be the case. But what if she was wrong? What if she was a weapon, implanted in their midst? What if her one function was to lead them all to extinction, by the most efficient means?

He didn't really think that likely, though. If he had, he would have killed her already, and then perhaps himself. But the chance was still there. She might even be innocent, but still *wrong*. In some respects that was an even more dangerous possibility.

Vasko Malinin had already sided with her. So, Scorpio thought, had a number of the seniors. Others were uncommitted, but might turn either way in the coming days. Against this, against what would surely be the magnetic charisma of the girl, there had to be a balance, something stolid and unimaginative, not much given to crusades or the worship of zealots. He couldn't step down. It might wear him out even sooner, but – somehow or other – he had to be there. Not as Aura's antagonist, necessarily, but as her brake. And if it came to a confrontation with Aura or one of her supporters (he could see them now, rallying behind the white-armoured girl) then it would only vindicate his decision to stay.

The one thing Scorpio knew about himself was that when he made a decision it stayed made. In that respect, he thought, he had much in common with Clavain. Clavain had been a better forward-thinker than Scorpio, but at the end – when he had met his death in the iceberg – all his life had amounted to was a series of dogged stands.

There were, Scorpio concluded, worse ways to live.

'You're quite happy with this?' Remontoire asked Scorpio.

They were sitting alone in a spider-legged inspection saloon, a pressurised cabin clutching the sheer clifflike face of the accelerating starship. From an aperture below them – a docking gate framed by bony structures that resembled fused spinal vertebrae – the cache weapons were being unloaded. It would have been a delicate operation at the best of times, but with the *Nostalgia for Infinity* continuing to accelerate away from Ararat, following the trajectory Remontoire and his projections had specified, it was one that required the utmost attention to detail.

'I'm happy,' Scorpio said. 'I thought you'd be the one with objections, Rem. You wanted all of these things. I'm not letting you have them all. Doesn't that piss you off?'

'Piss me off, Scorp?' There was a faint, knowing smile on his companion's face. Remontoire had prepared a flask of tea and was now pouring it into minuscule glass tumblers. 'Why should it? The risk is shared equally. Your own chance of survival – according to our forecasts, at least – is now significantly reduced. I regret this state of affairs, certainly, but I can appreciate your unwillingness to hand over all the weapons. That would require an unprecedented leap of faith.'

'I don't do faith,' Scorpio said.

'In truth, the cache weapons may not make very much difference in the long run. I did not want to say this earlier, for fear of dispiriting our associates, but the fact remains that our forecasts may be too optimistic. When Ilia Volyova rode *Storm Bird* into the heart of the wolf concentration around Delta Pavonis, the cache weapons she deployed made precious little impact.'

'As far as we know. Maybe she did slow things down a bit.'

'Or perhaps she did not deploy the weapons in the most effective manner possible – she was ill, after all – or perhaps those were not the most dangerous weapons in the arsenal. We shall never know.'

'What about these other weapons,' Scorpio asked, 'the ones that they're making for us now?'

'The hypometric devices? They have proven useful. You saw how the wolf concentration around your shuttle and the *Nostalgia for Infinity* was dispersed. I also used a hypometric weapon against the wolf aggregate that was causing you difficulties on the surface of Ararat.'

Scorpio sipped at his tea, holding the little tumbler – it was barely larger than a thimble – in the clumsy vice of his hands. He felt as if at any minute he was going to shatter the glass. 'These are the weapons Aura showed you how to make?'

'Yes.'

'And you still don't really know how any of it works?'

'Let's just say that theory is lagging some distance behind practice, shall we?'

'All right. It's not as if I'd be able to understand it even if you knew. But one thing does occur to me. If this shit is so useful, why aren't the wolves using it against us?'

'Again, we don't know,' Remontoire admitted.

'Doesn't that worry you? Doesn't it concern you that maybe there's some kind of long-term problem with this new technology that you don't know about?'

Remontoire arched an eyebrow. 'You, thinking ahead, Scorpio? Whatever next?'

'It's a legitimate point.'

'Conceded. And yes, it does, amongst other things, give me pause for concern. But given the choice between extinction now and dealing with an unspecified problem at a later point ... well, it's not much of a contest, is it?' Remontoire peered through the amber belly of his tiny glass, one eye looming large in distortion. 'Anyway, there's another possibility. The wolves may not have this technology.'

Beyond the observation spider, framed by the brass-ringed eye of one of its portholes, Scorpio saw one of the cache weapons emerge. The weapon – it was all bronze-green lustre and art deco flanges, like an old radio or cinema – was encased in a cradle studded with steering jets. The cradle, in turn, was being grasped by four tugs of Conjoiner manufacture.

'Then where did this technology come from?'

'The dead. The collective memories of countless extinct cultures, gathered together in the neutron-crust matrix of the Hades computer. Clearly it wasn't enough to make a difference to those extinct species; maybe none of the other techniques Aura has given us will make a difference to our eventual future. But perhaps they have served to slow things down. It might be that all we need is time. If there is something else out there – something more significant, something more potent than the wolves – then all we need is time to discover it.'

'You think it's Hela, don't you?'

'Doesn't it intrigue you, Scorpio? Don't you want to go there and see what you find?'

'We looked it up, Rem. Hela is an iceball, home to a bunch of religious lunatics tripping on the tainted blood of an indoctrinal virus carrier.'

'Yet they speak of miracles.'

'A planet that disappears. Except no one you'd trust to fix a vac-suit seal has ever *seen* it happen.'

'Go there and find out. One-oh-seven Piscium is the system. The Inhibitors haven't reached it yet, by all accounts.'

'Thanks for the information.'

'It will be your decision, Scorpio. You already know what Aura will recommend, but you don't have to be swayed by that.'

'I won't.'

'But keep this in mind: one-oh-seven Piscium is an outlying system. Reports of wolf incursions into human space are fragmentary at best, but you can be certain that *when* they move in, the core colonies – the worlds within a dozen or so light years of Earth – will be the first to fall. That's how they work: identify the hub, attack and destroy it. Then they pick off the satellite colonies and anyone trying to flee deeper into the galaxy.'

Scorpio shrugged. 'So nowhere's safe.'

'No. But given your responsibilities – given the seventeen thousand individuals now in your care – it would be far safer to head outwards than to dive back towards those hub worlds. But I sense that you may feel otherwise.'

'I have unfinished business back home,' Scorpio replied.

'You don't mean Ararat, do you?'

'I mean Yellowstone. I mean the Rust Belt. I mean Chasm City and the Mulch.'

Remontoire finished his tea, consuming the last drop with the fastidious neatness of a cat. 'I understand that you still have emotional ties to that place, but don't overestimate the danger of returning there. If the wolves have gathered any intelligence on us, it won't have taken them very long to identify Yellowstone as a critical hub. It will be high on their list of priorities. They may already be there, building a Singer, as they did around Delta Pavonis.'

'In which case there'll be a lot of people needing to get out.'

'You can't make enough of a difference to justify the risk,' Remontoire told him.

'I can try.' Scorpio gestured through the window of the inspection spider, towards the looming presence of the ship. 'The *Infinity* brought one hundred and sixty thousand people from Resurgam. I may not be much of a mathematician, but with only seventeen thousand aboard her now, that means we have some spare capacity.'

'You will be risking all the lives we have already saved.'

'I know,' he replied.

'You will be squandering any advantage you gain in the next few days, as we draw the machines away from you.'

'I know,' he said again.

'You will also be risking your own life.'

'I know that as well, and it isn't going to make one damned bit of difference, Rem. The more you try to talk me out of it, the more I know I'm going to do it.'

'If you have the backing of the seniors.'

'They either back me or sack me. It's their choice.'

'You'll also need the ship to agree to it.'

'I'll ask nicely,' Scorpio said.

The tugs had dragged the cache weapon to a safe distance from the ship. He expected to see their main drives flick on, bright spears of scattered light from plasma exhausts, but the whole assembly just accelerated away, as if moved by an invisible hand.

'I don't agree with your stance,' Remontoire said, 'but I respect it. You remind me of Nevil, in some ways.'

Scorpio recalled the ludicrously brief episode of 'grieving' Remontoire had undergone. 'I thought you were over him now.'

'None of us are over him,' Remontoire said curtly. Then he gestured to the flask again and his mood lightened visibly. 'More tea, Mr Pink?'

Scorpio didn't know what to say. He looked at the bland-faced man and shrugged. 'If you don't mind, Mr Clock.'

Hela, 2727

The surgeon-general ushered Rashmika through the labyrinthine Lady Morwenna. It was clearly not a sightseeing trip. Though she dawdled when she was able – slowing down to look at the windows, or something of equal interest – Grelier always chivvied her on with polite insistence, tapping his cane against the walls and floor to emphasise the urgency of his mission. 'Time is of the essence, Miss Els,' he kept saying. That and, 'We're in a wee bit of a hurry.'

'It would help if you told me what all this is about,' she said.

'No, it wouldn't,' he replied. 'Why would it help? You're here and we're on our way.'

He had a point, she supposed. She just didn't like it very much.

'What happened with the Catherine of Iron?' she asked, determined not to give up too easily.

'Nothing that I'm aware of. There was a change of assignment. Nothing significant. You're still being employed by the First Adventist Church, after all. We've just relocated you from one cathedral to another.' He tapped the side of his nose, as if sharing a grand confidence. 'Frankly, you've done rather well out of it. You don't know how difficult it is to get into the Lady Mor these days. Everyone wants to work in the Way's most historic cathedral.'

'I was given to understand that its popularity had taken a bit of a knock lately,' she said.

Grelier looked back at her. 'Whatever do you mean, Miss Els?'

'The dean is taking it over the bridge. At least, that's what people are saying.'

'And if that were the case?'

'I wouldn't be too surprised if people aren't all that keen to stay aboard. How far from the crossing are we, Surgeon-General?'

'Navigation's not really my thing.'

'You know exactly how far away we are,' she said.

He flashed a smile back at her. She decided that she did not like his smile at all. It looked altogether too feral. 'You're good, Miss Els. As good as I'd hoped.'

'Good, Surgeon-General?'

'The lying thing. The ability to read faces. That's your little stock in trade, isn't it? Your little party trick?'

They had arrived at what Rashmika judged to be the base of the Clocktower. The surgeon-general pulled out a key, slipped it into a lock next to a wooden door and admitted them into what was obviously a private compartment. The walls were made of trellised iron. Inside he pressed a sequence of brass knobs and they began to rise. Through the trelliswork, Rashmika watched the walls of the elevator shaft glide by. Then the walls became stained glass, and as they ascended past each coloured facet the light changed in the compartment: green to red, red to gold, gold to a cobalt blue that made the surgeon-general's shock of white hair glow as if electrified.

'I still don't know what this is about,' she persisted.

'Are you frightened?'

'A bit.'

'You needn't be.' She saw that he was telling the truth, at least as he perceived it. This calmed her slightly. 'We're going to treat you very well,' he added. 'You're too valuable to us to be treated otherwise.'

'And if I decide I don't want to stay here?'

He looked away from her, glancing out of the window. The light traced the outline of his face with dying fire. There was something about him – a muscular compactness to his body, that bulldog face – that made her think of circus performers she had seen in the badlands, who were actually unemployed miners touring from village to village to supplement their income. He could have been a fire-eater or an acrobat.

'You can leave,' he said, turning back to her. 'There'd be no point keeping you here without your permission. Your usefulness to us depends entirely on your good will.'

Perhaps she was reading him incorrectly, but she did not think he was lying about that, either.

'I still don't see . . .' she said.

'I've done my homework,' he told her. 'You're a *rara avis*, Miss Els. You have a gift shared by fewer than one in a thousand people. And you have the gift to a remarkable degree. You're off the scale. I doubt that there's anyone else quite like you on the whole of Hela.'

'I just see when people lie,' she said.

'You see more than that. Look at me now.' He smiled at her again. 'Am I smiling because I am genuinely happy, Miss Els?'

It was the same feral smile she had seen before. 'I don't think so.'

'You're right. Do you know why you can tell?'

'Because it's obvious,' she said.

'But not to everyone. When I smile on demand – as I did just then – I make use of only one muscle in my face: the zygomaticus major. When I smile spontaneously – which I confess does not happen very often – I flex not only my zygomaticus major but I also tighten the orbicularis oculi, pars lateralis.' Grelier touched a finger to the side of his temple. 'That's the muscle that encircles the eye. The majority of us cannot tighten that muscle voluntarily. I certainly can't. By the same token the majority of us cannot stop it tightening when we are genuinely pleased.' He smiled again; the elevator was slowing. 'Many people do not see the difference. If they notice it, they notice it subliminally, and the information is lost in the welter of other sensory inputs. The crucial data is ignored. But to you these things come screaming through. They sound trumpets. You are incapable of ignoring them.'

'I remember you now,' she said.

'I was there when they interviewed your brother, yes. I remember the fuss you made when they lied to him.'

'Then they did lie.'

'You always knew it.'

She looked at him: square in the face, alert to every nuance. 'Do you know what happened to Harbin?'

'Yes,' he replied.

The trelliswork carriage rattled to a halt.

Grelier led her into the dean's garret. The six-sided room was alive with mirrors. She saw her own startled expression jangling back at her, fragmented like a cubist portrait. In the confusion of reflections she did not immediately notice the dean himself. She saw the view through the windows, the white curve of Hela's horizon reminding her of the smallness of her world, and she saw the suit – the strange, roughly welded one – that she recognised from the Adventist insignia. Rashmika's skin prickled: just looking at the suit disturbed her. There was something about it, an impression of evil radiating from it in invisible lines, flooding the room; a powerful sense of presence, as if the suit itself embodied another visitor to the garret.

Rashmika walked past the suit. As she neared it the impression of evil became perceptibly stronger, almost as if invisible rays of malevolence were boring into her head, fingering their way into the private cavities of her mind. It was not like her to respond so irrationally to something so obviously inanimate, but the suit had an undeniable power. Perhaps, buried inside it, was a mechanism for inducing disquiet. She had heard of such things: vital tools in certain spheres of negotiation. They tickled the parts of the brain responsible for stimulating dread and the registering of hidden presences.

Now that she thought she could explain the suit's power she felt less disturbed by it. All the same, she was glad when she reached the other side of the garret, into full view of the dean. At first she thought he was dead. He was lying back on his couch, hands clasped across his blanketed chest like a man in the repose of the recently deceased. But then the chest moved. And the eyes – splayed open for examination – were horribly alive within their sockets. They trembled like little warm eggs about to hatch.

'Miss Els,' the dean said. 'I hope your trip here was an enjoyable one.'

She couldn't believe she was in his presence. 'Dean Quaiche,' she said. 'I heard ... I thought ...'

'That I was dead?' His voice was a rasp, the kind of sound an insect might have manufactured by the deft rubbing of chitinous surfaces. 'I have never made any secret of my continued existence, Miss Els ... for all these years. The congregation has seen me regularly.'

'The rumours are understandable,' Grelier said. The surgeon-general had opened a medical cabinet on the wall and was now fishing through its innards. 'You don't show your face outside of the Lady Morwenna, so how are the rest of the population expected to know?'

'Travel is difficult for me.' Quaiche pointed with one hand towards a small hexagonal table set amid the mirrors. 'Have some tea, Miss Els. And sit down, take the weight off your feet. We have much to talk about.'

'I have no idea why I am here, Dean.'

'Didn't Grelier tell you anything? I told you to brief the young lady, Grelier. I told you not to keep her in the dark.'

Grelier turned from the wall and walked towards Quaiche, carrying bottles and swabs. 'I told her precisely what you asked me to tell her: that her services were required, and that our use for her depended critically on her sensitivity to facial microexpressions.'

'What else did you tell her?'

'Absolutely nothing.'

Rashmika sat down and poured herself some tea. There appeared little point in refusing. And now that she was being offered a drink she realised that she was very thirsty.

'I presume you want me to help you,' she ventured. 'You need my skill, for some reason or other. There is someone you're not sure if you trust or not.' She sipped at the tea: whatever she thought of her hosts, it tasted decent enough. 'Am I warm?'

'You're more than warm, Miss Els,' Quaiche remarked. 'Have you always been this astute?'

'Were I truly astute, I'm not sure I'd be sitting here.'

Grelier leant over the Dean and began dabbing at the exposed whites of his eyes. She could see neither of their faces.

'You sound as if you have misgivings,' the dean said. 'And yet all the evidence suggests you were rather keen on reaching the Lady Morwenna.'

'That was before I found out where it was going. How close are we to the bridge, Dean? If you don't mind my asking.'

'Two hundred and fifty-six kilometres distant,' he said.

Rashmika allowed herself a moment of relief. She sipped another mouthful of the tea. At the crawling pace the cathedrals maintained, that was sufficiently far away not to be of immediate concern. But even as she enjoyed that solace, another part of her mind quietly informed her that it was really much closer than she feared. A third of a metre a second did not sound very fast, but there were a lot of seconds in a day.

'We'll be there in ten days,' the dean added.

Rashmika put down her tea. 'Ten days isn't very long, Dean. Is it true what they say, that you'll be taking the Lady Morwenna over Absolution Gap?'

'God willing.'

That was the last thing she wanted to hear. 'Forgive me, Dean, but the one thing I didn't have in mind when I came here was dying in some suicidal folly.'

'No one's going to die,' he told her. 'The bridge has been proven able to take the weight of an entire supply caravan. Measurements have never detected an ångström of deflection under any load.'

'But no cathedral has ever crossed it.'

'Only one has ever tried, and it failed because of guidance control, not any structural problem with the bridge.'

'You think you'll be more successful, I take it?'

'I have the finest cathedral engineers on the Way. And the finest cathedral, too. Yes, we'll make it, Miss Els. We'll make it and one day you'll tell your children how fortunate you were to enter my employment at such an auspicious time.'

'I sincerely hope you're right.'

'Did Grelier tell you that you could leave at any time?'

'Yes,' she said, hesitantly.

'It was the truth. Go now, Miss Els. Finish your tea and go. No one will stop you, and I will make arrangements for your employment in the Catherine. Good work, too.'

She was about to ask: the same good work you promised my brother? But she stopped herself. It was too soon to go barging in with another question about Harbin. She had come this far, and either extraordinary luck or extraordinary misfortune had propelled her into the heart of Quaiche's order. She still did not know exactly what they wanted of her, but she knew she had been granted a chance that she must not throw away with one idle, ill-tempered question. Besides, there was another reason not to ask: she was frightened of what the answer might be.

'I'll stay,' she said, adding quickly, 'For now. Until we've talked things over properly.'

'Very wise, Miss Els,' Quaiche said. 'Now, would you do me a small favour?'

'That would depend,' she said.

'I only want you to sit there and drink your tea. A gentleman is going to come into this room and he and I are going to have a little chat. I want you to observe the gentleman in question – carefully, but not obtrusively – and report your observations to me when the gentleman has departed. It won't take long, and there's no need for you to say anything while the man is present. In fact, it would be better if you didn't.'

'Is that what you want me for?'

'That is part of it, yes. We can discuss terms of employment later. Consider this part of your interview.'

'And if I fail?'

'It isn't a test. You've already been tested on your basic skills, Miss Els. You came through with flying colours. In this instance, I just want honest observation. Grelier, are you done yet? Stop fussing around. You're like a little girl playing with her dolly.'

Grelier began to put away his swabs and ointments. 'I'm done,' he said curtly. 'That abscess has nearly stopped weeping pus.'

'Would you care for more tea before the gentleman arrives, Miss Els?'

'I'm fine with this,' she said, holding on to her empty cup.

'Grelier, make yourself scarce, then have the Ultra representative shown in.'

The surgeon-general locked the medical cabinet, said goodbye to Rashmika and walked out of the room by a different door than the one through which they had entered. His cane tapped into the distance.

Rashmika waited. Now that Grelier had gone she felt uncomfortable in Quaiche's presence. She did not know what to say. She had never wanted to reach him specifically. She found the very idea distasteful. It was his order she had wanted to infiltrate, and then only to the point necessary to find Harbin. It was true that she did not care how much damage she did along the way, but Quaiche himself had never been of interest to her. Her mission was selfish, concerned only with the fate of her brother. If the Adventist church continued to inflict misery and hardship on the population of Hela, that was their problem, not hers. They were complicit in it, as much a part of the problem as Quaiche. And she had not come to change any of that, unless it stood in her way.

Eventually the representative arrived. Rashmika observed his entry, remembering that she had been told to say nothing. She presumed that extended to not even greeting the Ultra.

'Come in, Triumvir,' Quaiche said, his couch elevating to something approximating a normal sitting position. 'Come in and don't be alarmed. Triumvir, this is Rashmika Els, my assistant. Rashmika, this is Triumvir Guro Harlake of the lighthugger *That Which Passes*, recently arrived from Sky's Edge.'

The Ultra arrived in a shuffling red mobility contraption. His skin had the smooth whiteness of a baby reptile's, faintly tattooed with scales, and his eyes were partially concealed behind slitted yellow contacts. His short white hair fell over his face in a stiff, foppish fringe. His fingernails were long, green, vicious as scythes, and they kept clicking against the armature of his mobility device.

'We were the last ship out during the evacuation,' the Triumvir said. 'There were ships behind us, but they didn't make it.'

'How many systems have fallen so far?' Quaiche asked.

'Eight ... nine. Maybe more by now. News takes decades to reach us. They say Earth is still intact, but there have been confirmed attacks against Mars and the Jovian polities, including the Europan Demarchy and Gilgamesh Isis. No one has heard anything from Zion or Prospekt. They say every system will fall eventually. It'll just be a matter of time until they find us all.'

'In which case, why did you stop here? Wouldn't it have been better to keep moving outwards, away from the threat?'

'We had no choice,' the Ultra said. His voice was deeper than Rashmika had expected. 'Our contract required that we bring our passengers to Hela. Contracts mean a great deal to us.'

'An honest Ultra? What is the world coming to?'

'We're not all vampires. Anyway, we had to stop for another reason, not just because our sleepers wanted to come here as pilgrims. We had shield difficulties. We can't make another interstellar transit without major repairs.'

'Costly ones, I'd imagine,' Quaiche said.

The Triumvir bowed his head. 'That is why we are having this conversation, Dean Quaiche. We heard that you had need of the services of a good ship. A matter of protection. You feel yourself threatened.'

'It's not a question of feeling threatened,' he said. 'It's just that in these times ... we'd be foolish not to want to protect our assets, wouldn't we?'

'Wolves at the door,' the Ultra said.

'Wolves?'

'That's what the Conjoiners named the Inhibitor machines, just before they evacuated human space. That was a century ago. If we'd had any sense we'd all have followed them.'

'God will protect us,' Quaiche said. 'You believe that, don't you? Even if you don't, your passengers do, otherwise they wouldn't have embarked upon this pilgrimage. They know something is going to happen, Triumvir. The series of vanishings we have witnessed here is merely the precursor – the countdown – to something truly miraculous.'

'Or something truly cataclysmic,' the Ultra said. 'Dean, we are not here to discuss the interpretation of an anomalous astronomical phenomenon. We are strict positivists. We believe only in our ship and its running costs. And we need a new shield very badly. What are your terms of employment?'

'You will bring your ship into close orbit around Hela. Your weapons will be inspected for operational effectiveness. Naturally, a party of Adventist delegates will be stationed aboard your ship for the term of the contract. They will have complete control of the weapons, deciding who and what constitutes a threat to the security of Hela. In other respects, they won't get in your way at all. And as our protectors, you will be in a very advantageous position when it comes to matters of trade.' Quaiche waved his hand, as if brushing away an insect. 'You could walk away from here with a lot more than a new shield if you play your cards right.'

'You make it sound very tempting.' The Ultra drummed his fingernails against the chest-plate of his mobility device. 'But don't underestimate the risk that we perceive in bringing our ship close to Hela. We all know what happened to the ...' He paused. 'The *Gnostic Ascension*.'

'That's why our terms are so generous.'

'And the matter of Adventist delegates? You should know how unusual it is for anyone to be permitted aboard one of our ships. We could perhaps accommodate two or three hand-picked representatives, but only after they had undergone extensive screening ...'

'That part isn't negotiable,' Quaiche said abruptly. 'Sorry, Triumvir, but it all boils down to one thing: how badly do you want that shield?'

'We'll have to think about it,' the Ultra said.

Afterwards, Quaiche asked Rashmika for her observations. She told him what she had picked up, restricting her remarks to the things she was certain she had detected rather than vague intuitions.

'He was truthful,' she said, 'right up to the point where you mentioned his weapons. Then he was hiding something. His expression changed, just for a moment. I couldn't tell you what it was, exactly, but I do know what it means.'

'Probably a contraction of the zygomaticus major,' Grelier said, sitting with his fingers knitted together before his face. He had removed his vacuum suit while he was away and now wore a plain grey Adventist smock. 'Coupled with a depressing of the corners of the lips, using the risorius. Some flexion of the mentalis – chin elevation.'

'You saw all that, Surgeon-General?' Rashmika asked.

'Only by slowing down the observation camera and running a tedious and somewhat unreliable interpretive routine on his face. For an Ultra he was rather expressive. But it wasn't in real-time, and even when the routine detected it, I didn't see it for myself. Not viscerally. Not the way you saw it, Rashmika: instantly, written there as if in glowing letters.'

'He was hiding something,' she said. 'If you'd pushed him on the topic of the weapons, he'd have lied to your face.'

'So his weapons aren't what he makes them out to be,' Quaiche said.

'Then he's no use to us,' Grelier said. 'Tick him off the list.'

'We'll keep him on just in case. The ship's the main thing. We can always augment his weapons if we decide we have to.'

Grelier looked up at his master, peering over the steeple of his fingers. 'Doesn't that rather defeat the purpose?'

'Perhaps.' Quaiche seemed irritated by his surgeon's needling. 'In any case, there are other candidates. I have two more waiting in the cathedral. I take it, Rashmika, that you'd be willing to sit through another couple of interviews?'

She poured herself some more tea. 'Send them in,' she said. 'It's not as if I have anything else to do.'

THIRTY-FOUR

Interstellar Space, Near p Eridani 40, 2675

Scorpio had been walking through the ship for hours. It was still chaotic in the high levels, where the latest arrivals were being processed. There were smaller pockets of chaos at a dozen other locations. But the *Nostalgia for Infinity* was a truly enormous spacecraft, and it was remarkable how little evidence there was of the seventeen thousand newcomers once he moved away from the tightly policed processing zones. Throughout much of the ship's volume, things were as empty and echoing as they had ever been, as if all the newcomers had been imagined spectres.

But the ship was not completely deserted, even away from the processing zones. He paused now at a window that faced on to a deep vertical shaft. Red light bathed the interior, throwing a roseate tint on the metallic structure taking form within it. The structure was utterly unfamiliar. And yet it reminded him, forcefully, of something – one of the trees he had seen in the glade. Only this was a tree made from countless bladelike parts, foil-thin leaves arranged in spiralling ranks around a narrow core that ran the length of the shaft. There was too much detail to take in; too much geometry; too much perspective. His head hurt to look at the treelike object, as if the whole sculptural form was a weapon designed to shatter perception.

Servitors scuttled amongst the leaves like black bugs, their movements methodical and cautious, while black-suited human figures hung from harnesses at a safe distance from the delicate convolutions of the forming structure. The servitors carried metal-foil parts on their backs, slotting them into precisely machined apertures. The humans – they were Conjoiners – appeared to do very little except hang in their harnesses and observe the machines. But they were undoubtedly directing the action at a fundamental level, their concentration intense, their minds multitasking with parallel thought threads.

These were just some of the Conjoiners aboard the ship. There were dozens more. Hundreds, even. He could barely tell them apart.

Except for minor variations in skin tone, bone structure and sex, they all appeared to have stepped from the same production line. They were of the crested kind, advanced specimens from Skade's own taskforce. They said nothing to each other and were uncomfortable when forced to talk to the non-Conjoined. They stuttered and made elementary errors of pronunciation, grammar and syntax: things that would have shamed a pig. They functioned and communicated on an entirely non-verbal level, Scorpio knew. To them, verbal communication – even when speeded up by mind-to-mind linkage – was as primitive as communication by smoke signal. They made Clavain and Remontoire look like grunting Stone-Age relics. Even Skade must have felt some itch of inadequacy around these sleek new creatures.

If the wolves lost, Scorpio thought, but the only people left to celebrate were these silent Conjoiners, would it have been worth it?

He had no easy answer.

Beyond their silent strangeness, their stiffly economical movements and utter absence of expression, the thing that most chilled him about the Conjoiner technicians was the blithe ease with which they had shifted loyalty to Remontoire. At no point had they acknowledged that their obedience to Skade had been in error. They had, they said, only ever been following the path of least resistance when it came to the greater good of the Mother Nest. For a time, that path had involved co-operation with Skade's plans. Now, however, they were content to align themselves with Remontoire. Scorpio wondered how much of that had to do with the pure demands of the situation and how much with respect for the traditions and history of the Nest. With Galiana and Clavain now dead, Remontoire was probably the oldest living Conjoiner.

Scorpio had no choice but to accept the Conjoiners. They were not a permanent fixture in any case; in fewer than eight days they would have to leave if they wanted to return home to the *Zodiacal Light* and their other remaining ships. There were already fewer of them than there had been at first.

They had helped to reinstall nanotechnological manufactories, plague-hardened so that they would continue to function even in the contagious environment of the *Infinity*. Primed with blueprints and raw matter, the forges spewed out gleaming new technologies of mostly unfamiliar function. The same blueprints showed how the newly minted components were to be assembled into even larger – yet equally unfamiliar – new shapes. In evacuated shafts running the length of the *Nostalgia for Infinity* – just like the one he was looking into now – these contraptions grew and grew. The thing that looked like an elongated silver tree – or a dizzyingly complicated turbine, or some weird alien take on DNA – was a hypometric weapon. Perhaps sensing their value, the Captain tolerated the activity, although at any moment he could have remade his interior architecture, crushing the shafts out of existence.

Elsewhere, Conjoiners crawled through the skin of the ship, installing a network of cryo-arithmetic engines. Tiny as hearts, each limpetlike engine was a sucking wound in the corpus of classical thermodynamics. Scorpio recalled what had happened to Skade's corvette when the cryo-arithmetic engines had gone wrong. The runaway cooling must have begun with a tiny splinter of ice, smaller than a snowflake. But it had been growing all the while, as the engines locked into manic, spiralling feedback loops, destroying more heat with every computational cycle, the cold feeding the cold. In space, the ship would simply have cooled down to within quantum spitting distance of absolute zero. On Ararat, however, with an ocean at hand, it had grown an iceberg around itself.

Other Conjoiners were crawling through the ship's original engines, tinkering with the hallowed reactions at their core. More were out on the hull, tethered to the encrusted architecture of the Captain's growth patterns. They were installing additional weapons and armouring devices. Still more – secluded deep within the ship, far from any other focus of activity – were assembling the inertia-suppression devices that had been tested during the *Zodiacal Light's* chase from Yellowstone to Resurgam. This was alien technology, Scorpio knew, machinery that humans had appropriated without Aura's assistance. But they had never been able to get it to work reliably. By all accounts, Aura had shown them how to modify it for relatively safe operation. Skade, in desperation, had attempted to use the same technology for faster-than-light travel. Her effort had failed catastrophically, and Aura had refused to reveal any secrets that might make another attempt possible. Amongst the gifts she was giving them, there was to be no superluminal technology.

He watched the servitors slip another blade into place. The device had looked finished a day ago, but since then they had added about three times more machinery. Yet, strangely, the structure looked even more lacy and fragile than it had before. He wondered when it would be done – and what exactly it would *do* when it was done – and then began to turn from the window, apprehension lying heavy in his heart.

'Scorp.'

He had not been expecting company, so was surprised to hear his own name. He was even more surprised to see Vasko Malinin standing there.

'Vasko,' he said, offering a noncommittal smile. 'What brings you down here?'

'I wanted to find you,' he said. Vasko was wearing a stiff, fresh-looking Security Arm uniform. Even his boots were clean, a miracle aboard the *Nostalgia for Infinity*.

'You managed.'

'I was told you'd probably be down here somewhere.' Vasko's face was lit from the side by the red glow spilling from the hypometric weapon shaft. It made him look young and feral by turns. Vasko glanced through the window. 'Quite something, isn't it?'

'I'll believe it works when I see it do something other than sit there looking pretty.'

'Still sceptical?'

'Someone should be.'

Scorpio realised now that Vasko was not alone. There was a figure looming behind him. He would have been able to see the person clearly years ago; now he had difficulty making out detail when the light was gloomy.

He squinted. 'Ana?'

Khouri stepped into the pool of red light. She was dressed in a heavy coat and gloves, enormous boots covering her legs up to her knees – they were much dirtier than Vasko's – and she was carrying something, tucked into the crook of her arm. It was a bundle, a form wrapped in quilted silver blanketing. At the top end of the bundle, near the crook of her arm, was a tiny opening.

'Aura?' he said, startled.

'She doesn't need the incubator now,' Khouri said.

'She might not *need* it, but ...'

'Dr Valensin said it was holding her back, Scorp. She's too strong for it. It was doing more harm than good.' Khouri angled her face down towards the open end of the bundle, her eyes meeting the hidden eyes of her daughter. 'She told me she wanted to be out of it as well.'

'I hope Valensin knows what he's doing,' Scorpio said.

'He does, Scorp. More importantly, so does Aura.'

'She's just a child,' he said, keeping his voice low. 'Barely that.'

Khouri stepped forwards. 'Hold her.'

She was already offering the bundle to him. He wanted to say no. It wasn't just that he did not quite trust himself with something as precious and fragile as a child. There was something else: a voice that warned him not to make this physical connection with her. Another voice – quieter – reminded him that he was already bound to her in blood. What more harm could be done now?

He took Aura. He held her against his chest, just tight enough to feel that he had her safely. She was astonishingly light. It stunned him that this girl – this asset they had lost their leader to recover – could feel so insubstantial.

'Scorpio.'

The voice was not Khouri's. It was not an adult voice; barely a child's. It was more a gurgling croak that half-approximated the sound of his name.

He looked down at the bundle, into the opening. Aura's face turned towards his. Her eyes were still tightly closed gummy slits. There was a bubble emerging from her mouth.

'She didn't just say my name,' he said incredulously.

'I did,' Aura said.

He felt, for a heartbeat, as if he wanted to drop the bundle. There was something *wrong* lying there in his arms, something that had no right to exist in this universe. Then the shameful reflex passed, as quickly as it had come. He looked away from the tiny pink-red face, towards her mother.

'She can't even see me,' he said.

'No, Scorp,' Khouri confirmed, 'she can't. Her eyes don't work yet. But mine do. And that's all that matters.'

Throughout the ship, Scorpio's technicians worked day and night laying listening devices. They glued newly manufactured microphones and barometers to walls and ceilings, then unspooled kilometres of cables, running them through the natural ducts and tunnels of the Captain's anatomy, splicing them at nodes, braiding them into thickly entwined trunk lines that ran back to central processing points. They tested their devices, tapping stanchions and bulkheads, opening and closing pressure doors to create sudden draughts of air from one part of the ship to another. The Captain tolerated them, even, it seemed, did his best to make their efforts easier. But he was not always in complete control of his reshaping processes. Fibre-optic lines were repeatedly severed; microphones and barometers were absorbed and had to be remade. The technicians accepted this stoically, going back down into the bowels of the ship to re-lay a kilometre of line that they had just put in place; even, sometimes, repeating the process three or four times until they found a better, less vulnerable routing.

What they did not do, at any point, was ask why they were doing this. Scorpio had told them not to, that they did not want to know, and that if they were to ask, he would not tell them the truth. Not until the reason for their work was over, and things were again as safe as they could be.

But he knew why, and when he thought about what was going to happen, he envied them their ignorance.

Hela, 2727

The interviews with the Ultras continued. Rashmika sat and made her observations. She sipped tea and watched her own shattered reflection swim in the mirrors. She thought about each hour bringing her more than a kilometre closer to Absolution Gap. But there were no clocks in the garret, hence no obvious means of judging their progress.

After each interview, she told Quaiche what she thought she had seen, taking care neither to embroider nor omit anything that might have been crucial. By the end of the third interview, she had formed an impression of what was happening. Quaiche wanted the Ultras to bring one of their ships into close orbit around Hela, to act as bodyguard.

Exactly what he feared, she could not guess. He told the Ultras that he desired protection from other spacefaring elements, that he had lately thwarted a number of schemes to seize control of Hela and wrest the supply of scuttler relics from the Adventist authorities. With a fully armed lighthugger in orbit around Hela, he said, his enemies would think twice about meddling in Hela's affairs. The Ultras, in return, would enjoy favoured trader status, a necessary compensation for the risk entailed in bringing their valuable ship so close to the world that had destroyed the *Gnostic Ascension*. She could smell their nervousness: even though they only ever came down to Hela in shuttles, leaving their main spacecraft parked safely on the system's edge, they did not want to spend a minute longer than necessary in the Lady Morwenna.

But there was, Rashmika suspected, something more to Quaiche's plan than mere protection. She was certain that Quaiche was hiding something. It was a hunch this time, not something she saw in his face. He was, to all intents and purposes, unreadable. It was not just the mechanical eye-opener, hiding all those nuances of expression she counted on. There was also a torpid, masklike quality to his face, as if the nerves that operated his muscles had been severed or poisoned. When she stole glances at him she saw a vacuity of expression. The faces he made were stiff and exaggerated, like the expressions of a glove puppet. It was ironic, she thought, that she had been brought in to read people's faces by a man whose own face was essentially closed. Almost deliberately so, in fact.

Finally the interviews for the day were over. She had reported her findings to Quaiche and he had listened appreciatively to what she had to say. There was no guessing where his own intuitions lay, but at no point did he question or contradict any of her observations. He merely nodded keenly, and told her she had been very helpful.

There would be more Ultras to interview, she was assured, but that was it for the day.

'You can go now, Miss Els. Even if you leave the cathedral now, you will still have been very useful to me and I will see to it that your efforts are rewarded. Did I mention a good position in the Catherine of Iron?'

'You did, Dean.'

'That is one possibility. Another is for you to return to the Vigrid region. You have family there, I take it?'

'Yes,' she said, but even as the word left her mouth, her own family suddenly felt distant and abstract to her, like something she had only been told about. She could remember the rooms of her house, the faces and voices of her parents, but the memories felt thin and translucent, like the facets in the stained-glass windows.

'You could return with a nice bonus – say, five thousand ecus. How does that sound?'

'That would be very generous,' she replied.

'The other possibility – the preferred one from my point of view – is that you remain in the Lady Morwenna and continue to assist me in the interviewing of Ultras. For that I will pay you two thousand ecus for every day of work. By the time we reach the bridge, you will have made double what you could have taken back to your home if you'd left today. And it doesn't have to stop there. For as long as you are willing, there will always be work. In a year's service, think what you could earn.'

'I'm not worth that much to anyone,' she said.

'But you are, Miss Els. Didn't you hear what Grelier said? One in a thousand. One in a million, perhaps, with your degree of receptivity.

I'd say that makes you worth two thousand ecus per day of anyone's money.'

'What if my advice isn't right?' she asked. 'I'm only human. I make mistakes.'

'You won't get it wrong,' he said, with more certainty than she liked. 'I have faith in few things, Rashmika, beyond God Himself. But you are one of them. Fate has brought you to my cathedral. A gift from God, almost. I'd be foolish to turn it away, wouldn't I?'

'I don't feel like a gift from anything,' she said.

'What do you feel like, then?'

She wanted to say, like an avenging angel. But instead she said, 'I feel tired and a long way from home, and I'm not sure what I should do.'

'Work with me. See how it goes. If you don't like it, you can always leave.'

'Is that a promise, Dean?'

'As God is my witness.'

But she couldn't tell if he was lying or not. Behind Quaiche, Grelier stood up with a click of his knee-joints. He ran a hand through the electric-white bristles of his hair. 'I'll show you to your quarters, then,' he said. 'I take it you've agreed to stay?'

'For now,' Rashmika said.

'Good. Right choice. You'll like it here, I'm sure. The dean is right: you are truly privileged to have arrived at such an auspicious time.' He reached out a hand. 'Welcome aboard.'

'That's it?' she said, shaking his hand. 'No formalities? No initiation rituals?'

'Not for you,' Grelier said. 'You're a secular specialist, Miss Els, just like myself. We wouldn't want to go clouding your brain with all that religious claptrap, would we?'

She looked at Quaiche. His metal-goggled face was as unreadable as ever. 'I suppose not.'

'There is just one thing,' Grelier said. 'I'm going to have to take a bit of blood, if you don't mind.'

'Blood?' she asked, suddenly nervous.

Grelier nodded. 'Strictly for medical purposes. There are a lot of nasty bugs going around these days, especially in the Vigrid and Hyrrokkin regions. But don't worry.' He moved towards the wall-mounted medical cabinet. 'I'll only need a wee bit.'

Energies pocked the space around Ararat. Scorpio watched the distant, receding battle from the spider-shaped observation capsule, secure in the warm, padded plush of its upholstery.

Carnations of light bloomed and faded over many seconds, slow and lingering as violin chords. The lights were concentrated into a tight, roughly spherical volume, centred on the planet. Around them was a vaster darkness. The slow brightening and fading, the pleasing randomness of it, stirred some memory – probably second-hand – of sea creatures communicating in benthic depths, throwing patterns of bioluminescence towards each other. Not a battle at all but a rare, intimate gathering, a celebration of the tenacity of life in the cold lightlessness of the deep ocean.

In the early phases of the space war in the p Eridani A system, the battle had been fought under a ruling paradigm of maximum stealth. All parties, Inhibitor and human, had cloaked their activities by using drives, instruments and weapons that radiated energies – if they radiated *anything* – only into the narrow, squeezed blind spots between orthodox sensor bands. The way Remontoire had described it, it had been like two men in a dark room, treading silently, slashing almost randomly into the darkness. When one man took a wound, he could not cry out for fear of revealing his location. Nor could he bleed, or offer tangible resistance to the passage of the blade. And when the other man struck, he had to withdraw the blade quickly, lest he signal his own position. A fine analogy, if the room had been light-hours wide, and the men had been human-controlled spacecraft and wolf machines, and the weapons had kept escalating in size and reach with every feint and parry. Ships had darkened their hulls to the background temperature of space; masked the emissions from their drives; used weapons that slid undetected through darkness and killed with the same discretion.

Yet there had come a point, inevitably, when it had suited one or other of the combatants to discard the stealth stratagem. Once one abandoned it, the others had to follow suit. Now it was a war not of stealth but of maximum transparency. Weapons, machines and forces were being tossed about with abandon.

Watching the battle from the observation capsule, Scorpio was reminded of something Clavain had said on more than one occasion, when viewing some distant engagement: war was beautiful, when you had the good fortune not to be engaged in it. It was sound and fury, colour and movement, a massed assault on the senses. It was bravura and theatrical, something that made you gasp. It was thrilling and romantic, when you were a spectator. But, Scorpio reminded himself, they *were* involved. Not in the sense that they were participants in the engagement around Ararat, but because their own fate depended critically on its outcome. And to a large extent he was responsible for that. Remontoire had wanted him to hand over all the cache weapons, and he had refused. Because of that, Remontoire could not guarantee that the covering action would be successful.

The console chimed, signifying that a specific chip of gravitational radiation had just swept past the *Nostalgia for Infinity*.

'That's it,' Vasko said, his voice hushed and businesslike. 'The last cache weapon, assuming we haven't lost count.'

'He wasn't meant to use them up this quickly,' Khouri said. She was sitting with him in the observation capsule, with Aura cradled in her arms. 'I think something's gone wrong.'

'Wait and see,' Scorpio said. 'Remontoire may just be changing the plan because he's seen a better strategy.'

They watched a beam of *something* – bleeding visible light sideways so that it was evident even in vacuum – reach out with elegant slowness across the theatre of battle. There was something obscene and tonguelike about the way it extended itself, pushing towards some invisible wolf target on the far side of the battle. Scorpio did not like to think about how bright that beam must have been close-up, for it was visible now even without optical magnification or intensity enhancement. He had turned down all the lights in the observation capsule, dimming the navigation controls so that they had the best view of the engagement. Shields had been carefully positioned to screen out the glare and radiation from the engines.

The capsule lurched, something snapping free of the larger ship. Scorpio had learned not to flinch when such things happened. He waited while the capsule reoriented itself, picking its way to a new place of rest with the unhurried care of a tarantula, following the dictates of some ancient collision-avoidance algorithm.

Khouri looked through one of the portholes, holding Aura up to the view even though the baby's eyes were still closed.

'It's strange down here,' she said. 'Like no other part of the ship. Who did this? The Captain or the sea?'

'The sea, I think,' Scorpio replied, 'though I don't know whether the Jugglers had anything to do with it or not. There was a whole teeming marine ecology below the Jugglers, just as on any other aquatic planet.'

'Why are you whispering?' Vasko asked. 'Can he hear us in here?'

'I'm whispering because it's beautiful and strange,' Scorpio said. 'Plus, I happen to have a headache. It's a pig thing. It's because our skulls are a bit too small for our brains. It gets worse as we get older. Our optic nerves get squeezed and we go blind, assuming macular degeneration doesn't get us first.' He smiled into darkness. 'Nice view, isn't it?'

'I only asked.'

'You didn't answer his question,' Khouri said. 'Can he hear us in here?'

'John?' Scorpio shrugged. 'Don't know. Me, I'm inclined to give him the benefit of the doubt. Only polite, isn't it?'

'I didn't think you "did" polite,' Khouri said.

'I'm working on it.'

Aura gurgled.

The capsule stiffened its legs, pushing itself closer to the hull with a delicate clang of contacting surfaces. It hung suspended beneath the flattened underside of the great ship, where the *Nostalgia for Infinity* had come to rest on Ararat's seabed. All around it, seen in dim pastel shades, were weird coral-like formations. There were grey-green structures as large as ships, forests of gnarled, downward-pointing fingers, like stone chandeliers. The growths had all formed during the ship's twenty-three years of immersion, forming a charming rock-garden counterpoint to the brutalist transformations inflicted on the hull by the captain's own plague-driven reshaping processes. They had remained intact even as the Jugglers had moved the *Infinity* to deeper water, and they had survived both the departure from Ararat and the subsequent engagement with wolf forces. Doubtless John Brannigan could have removed them, just as he had redesigned the ship's lower extremities to permit it to land on Ararat in the first place. The entire ship was an externalisation of his psyche, an edifice chiselled from guilt, horror and the craving for absolution.

But there was no sign of any further transformations taking place here. Perhaps, Scorpio mused, it suited the Captain to carry these warts and scabs of dead marine life, just as it suited Scorpio to carry the scar on his shoulder, where he had effaced the scorpion tattoo. Remove evidence of that scar, and he would have been removing part of what made him Scorpio. Ararat, in turn, had changed the Captain. Scorpio was certain of that, certain also that the Captain felt it. But how had it changed him, exactly? Shortly, he thought, it would be necessary to put the Captain to the test.

Scorpio had already made the appropriate arrangements. There was a fistful of bright-red dust in his pocket.

Vasko stirred, the upholstery creaking. 'Yes, it might pay to be polite to him,' he said. 'After all, nothing's going to happen around here without his agreement. I think we all recognise that.'

'You talk as if you think there's going to be a clash of wills,' Scorpio said. He kept one eye on the extending beam of the cache weapon, watching as it scribed a bright scratch across the volume of battle. The scratch was now of a finite length, inching its way across space. Where the cache weapon had been was only a fading smudge of dying matter. The weapon had been a one-shot job, a throwaway.

'You think there won't be?' Vasko asked.

'I'm an optimist. I think we'll all see sense.'

'You won the battle over the cache weapons,' Vasko said. 'Remontoire went along with it, and so did the ship. I'm not surprised about that: the ship felt safer with the weapons than without them. But we still don't know that it was the right thing to do. What about next time?'

'Next time? I don't see any disputes on the horizon,' Scorpio said.

But he did, and he felt isolated now that Remontoire and Antoinette had gone. Remontoire and the last of the Conjoiners had departed a day ago, taking with them their servitors, machines and the last of the negotiated number of cache weapons. In their place they had left behind working manufactories and the vast shining things Scorpio had watched them assemble. Remontoire had explained that the weapons and mechanisms had only been tested in a very limited fashion. Before they could be used they would require painstaking calibration, following a set of instructions the Conjoiner technicians had left behind. The Conjoiner technicians could not stay aboard and complete the calibrations: if they waited any longer, their small ships would be unable to return to the main battle group around Ararat. Even with inertia-suppressing systems, they were still horribly constrained by the exigencies of fuel reserves and delta-vee margins. Physics still mattered. It was not their own survival they cared about, but their usefulness to the Mother Nest. And so they had left, taking with them the one man Scorpio felt would have had the will to oppose Aura, if the circumstances merited it.

Which leaves me, he thought.

'I can foresee at least one dispute in the very near future,' Vasko said.

'Enlighten me.'

'We're going to have to agree about where we go – whether it's out, to Hela, or back to Yellowstone. We all know what you think about it.'

'It's "we" now, is it?'

'You're in the minority, Scorp. It's just a statement of fact.'

'There won't necessarily be a confrontation,' Khouri said. Her voice was low and soothing. 'All Vasko means to say is that the majority of seniors believe Aura has privileged information, and that what she tells us ought to be taken seriously.'

'That doesn't mean they're right. It doesn't mean we'll find anything useful when we get to Hela,' Scorpio argued.

'There must be something about that system,' Vasko said. 'The vanishings ... they must mean *something*.'

'It means mass psychosis,' Scorpio said. 'It means people see things when they're desperate. You think there's something useful on that planet? Fine. Go there and find out. And explain to me why it didn't make one damned bit of difference to the natives.'

'They're called scuttlers,' Vasko said.

'I don't care what they're called. They're fucking *extinct*. Doesn't that tell you something even slightly significant? Don't you think that if there was something useful in that system they'd have used it already and still be alive?'

'Maybe it isn't something you use lightly,' Vasko said.

'Great. And you want to go there and see what it was they were too scared to use even though the alternative was extinction? Be my guest. Send me a postcard. I'll be about twenty light-years away.'

'Frightened, Scorpio?' Vasko asked.

'No, I'm not frightened,' he said, with a calm that even he found surprising. 'Just prudent. There's a difference. You'll understand it one day.'

'Vasko only meant to say that we can't take a guess at what really happened there unless we visit the place,' Khouri said. 'Right now we know almost nothing about Hela or the scuttlers. The churches won't allow orthodox scientific teams anywhere near the place. The Ultras don't poke their noses in too deeply because they make a nice profit exporting useless scuttler relics. But we need to know more.'

'More,' Aura said, and then laughed.

'If she knows we need to go there, why doesn't she tell us why?' Scorpio said. He nodded towards the vague milky-grey shape of the child. 'All this stuff has to be in there somewhere, doesn't it?'

'She doesn't know,' Khouri said.

'Do you mean she won't tell us yet, or that she'll never know?'

'Neither, Scorp. I mean it hasn't been unlocked for her yet.'

'I don't understand,' he said.

'I told you what Valensin said: every day he looks at Aura, and every day he comes up with a different guess as to her developmental state. If she were a normal child she wouldn't be born yet. She wouldn't be talking. She wouldn't even be breathing. Some days it's as if she has the language skills of a three-year-old. Other days, she's barely past one. He sees brain structures come and go like clouds, Scorp. She's changing even while we're sitting here. Her head's like a furnace. Given all that, are you really surprised that she can't tell you exactly why we need to go to Hela? It's like asking a child why they need food. They can tell you they're hungry. That's all.'

'What did you mean about it being locked?'

'I mean it's all in there,' she said, 'all the answers, or at least everything we'll need to know to work them out. But it's encoded, packed too tightly to be unwound by the brain of a child, even a two- or three-year-old. She won't begin to make sense of those memories until she's older.'

'You're older,' he said. 'You can see into her head. You unwind them.'

'It doesn't work like that. I only see what she understands. What I get from her – most of the time, anyway – is a child's view of things. Simple, crystalline, bright. All primary colours.' In the gloom Scorpio saw the flash of her smile. 'You should see how bright colours are to a child.'

'I don't see colours that well to begin with.'

'Can you put aside being a pig for five minutes?' Khouri asked. 'It would really help if everything didn't keep coming back to that.'

'It keeps coming back to that for me. Sorry if it offends you.'

He heard her sigh. 'All I'm saying, Scorp, is that we can't begin to guess how significant Hela is unless we go there. And we'll have to go there carefully, not barging in with all guns blazing. We'll have to find out what we need before we ask for it. And we'll have to be ready to take it if necessary, and to make sure we do it right the first time. But first of all we have to *go* there.'

'And what if going there is the worst thing we could do? What if all of this is a setup, to make the job easier for the Inhibitors?'

'She's working for us, Scorp, not them.'

'That's an assumption,' he said.

'She's my daughter. Don't you think I have some idea about her intentions?'

Vasko interrupted them, touching Scorpio's shoulder. 'I think you need to see this,' he said.

Scorpio looked at the battle, seeing immediately what Vasko had noticed. It was not good. The beam of the cache weapon was being bent away from its original trajectory, like a ray of light hitting water. There was no sign of anything at the point where the beam changed direction, but it did not take very much imagination to conclude that it was some hidden focus of Inhibitor energy that was throwing the beam off course. There was no weapon left to re-aim and refire; all that could be done now was to sit back and watch what happened to the deviated beam.

Somehow Scorpio knew that it wasn't just going to sail off into interstellar space, fading harmlessly as it fell into the night.

That was not how the enemy did things.

They did not have long to wait. Seen in magnification, the beam grazed the edge of Ararat's nearest moon, cleaving its way through hundreds of kilometres of crust and then out the other side. The moon began to come apart like a broken puzzle. Red-hot rocky gore oozed from the wound with dreamlike slowness. It was like the time-lapse opening of some red-hearted flower at dawn.

'That's not good,' Khouri said.

'You still think this is going according to plan?' Vasko asked.

The stricken moon was extending a cooling tentacle of cherry-red slurry along the path of its orbit. Scorpio looked at it in dismay, wondering what it would mean for the people on Ararat's surface. Even a few million tonnes of rubble hitting the ocean would have dreadful consequences for the people left behind, but the amount of debris from the moon would be far, far worse than that.

'I don't know,' Scorpio said.

A little while later, there was a different chime from the console.

'Encrypted burst from Remontoire,' Vasko said. 'Shall I put him on?'

Scorpio told him to do it, watching as a fuzzy, pixellated image of Remontoire appeared on the console. The transmission was highly compressed, subject to jolting gaps and periods when the image froze while Remontoire continued speaking.

'I'm sorry,' he said, 'but it hasn't worked quite as well as I'd hoped.'

'How bad?' Scorpio mouthed.

It was as if Remontoire had heard him. 'A small aggregate of Inhibitor machines appears to be pursuing you,' he said. 'Not as large as the pack that followed us from Delta Pavonis, but not something you can ignore, either. Have you completed testing the hypometric weaponry? That should be a priority now. And it might not be a bad idea to get the rest of the machinery working as well.' Remontoire paused, his image breaking up and reassembling. 'There's something you need to know,' he continued. 'The failure was mine. It had nothing to do with the number of cache weapons in our arsenal. Even if you had given all of them to me, the outcome would have been the same. As a matter of fact, it was good that you didn't. Your instincts served you well, Mr Pink. I'm glad of that little conversation we had just before I left. You still have a chance.' He smiled: the expression looked as forced as ever, but Scorpio welcomed it. 'You may be tempted to respond to this transmission. I recommend that you do nothing of the sort. The wolves will be trying to refine their positional fix on you, and a clear signal like that would do you no favours at all. Goodbye and good luck.'

That was it: the transmission was over.

'Mr Pink?' Vasko said. 'Who's Mr Pink?'

'We go back a way,' Scorpio said.

'He didn't say anything about himself,' Khouri said. 'Nothing about what he's going to do.'

'I don't think he considered it relevant,' Scorpio said. 'There's nothing we can do to help them, after all. They've done what they could for us.'

'But it wasn't good enough,' Malinin said.

'Maybe it wasn't,' Scorpio said, 'but it was still a lot better than nothing, if you ask me.'

'The conversation he mentioned,' Khouri said. 'What was that about?'

'That was between me and Mr Clock,' Scorpio replied.

Hela, 2727

After the surgeon-general had taken her blood, he showed her to her quarters. It was a small room about a third of the way up the Clocktower. It had one stained-glass window, a small, austere-looking bed and a bedside table. There was an annexe containing a washbasin and a toilet. There was some Quaicheist literature on the bedside table.

'I hope you weren't expecting the height of luxury,' Grelier said.

'I wasn't expecting anything,' she said. 'Until a few hours ago I expected to be working in a clearance gang for the Catherine of Iron.'

'Then you can't complain, can you?'

'I wasn't intending to.'

'Play your cards right and we'll sort out something a little larger,' he said.

'This is all I need,' Rashmika said.

Grelier smiled and left her alone. She said nothing as he left. She had not liked him taking her blood, but had felt powerless to resist. It was not simply the fact that the whole business of the churches and blood made her feel queasy – she knew too much about the indoctrinal viruses that were part and parcel of the Adventist faith – but something else, something that related to her own blood and the fact that she felt violated when he sampled it. The syringe had been empty before he drew the sample, which meant – assuming that the needle was sterile – that he had not tried to put the indoctrinal virus into her. That would have been a violation of a different order, but not necessarily worse. The thought that he had taken her blood was equally distressing.

But why, she wondered, did it bother her so much? It was a reasonable thing to do, at least within the confines of the Lady Morwenna. Everything here ran on blood, so it was hardly objectionable that she had been made to supply a sample. By rights, she should have been grateful that it had stopped there.

But she was not grateful. She was frightened, and she did not exactly know why.

She sat by herself. In the quiet of the room, bathed in the sepulchral light from the stained-glass window, she felt desperately alone. Had all this been a mistake? she wondered. Now that she had reached its roaring heart, the church did not seem like such a distant, abstract entity. It felt more like a machine, something capable of inflicting harm on those who strayed too close to its moving parts. Though she had never specifically set out to reach Quaiche, it had seemed evident to her that only someone very high up in the Adventist hierarchy would be able to reveal the truth about Harbin. But she had also envisaged that the path there would be treacherous and time-consuming. She had been resigned to a long, slow, will-sapping investigation, a slow progress through layers of administration. She would have begun in a clearance gang, about as low as it was possible to get.

Instead, here she was: in Quaiche's direct service. She should have felt elated at her good fortune. Instead she felt unwittingly manipulated, as if she had set out to play a game fairly and someone had turned a blind eye, letting her win by fiat. On one level she wanted to blame Grelier, but she knew that the surgeon-general was not the whole story. There was something else, too. Had she come all this way to find Harbin, or to meet Quaiche?

For the first time, she was not completely certain.

She began to flick through the Quaicheist literature, looking for some clue that would unlock the mystery. But the literature was the usual rubbish she had disdained since the moment she could read: the Haldora vanishings as a message from God, a countdown to some vaguely defined event, the nature of which depended on the function of the text in which it was mentioned.

Her hand hesitated on the cover of one of the brochures. Here was the Adventist symbol: the strange spacesuit radiating light as if seen in silhouette against a sunrise, with the rays of light ramming through openings in the fabric of the suit itself. The suit had a curious welded-together look, lacking any visible joints or seams. There was no doubt in her mind now that it was the same suit that she had seen in the dean's garret.

Then she thought about the name of the cathedral: the Lady Morwenna.

Of course. It all snapped into her head with blinding clarity. Morwenna had been Quaiche's lover, before he came to Hela. Everyone who read their scripture knew that. Everyone also knew that something awful had happened to her, and that she had been imprisoned inside a strange welded-up suit when it happened. A suit that was itself a kind of punishment device, fashioned by the Ultras Quaiche and Morwenna had worked for.

The same suit she had seen in the garret; the same one that had made her feel so ill at ease.

She had rationalised away that fear at the time, but now, sitting all alone, the mere thought of being in the same building as the suit frightened her. She wanted to be as far away from it as possible.

There's something in it, she thought. Something more than just a mechanism to put the jitters on rival negotiators.

A voice said, [Yes. Yes, Rashmika. We are inside the suit.]

She dropped the booklet, letting out a small gasp of horror. She had not imagined that voice. It had been faint, but very clear, very precise. And its lack of resonance told her that it had sounded inside her head, not in the room itself.

'I don't need this,' she said. She spoke aloud, hoping to break the spell. 'Grelier, you bastard, there was something on that needle, wasn't there?'

[There was nothing on the needle. We are not a hallucination. We have nothing to do with Quaiche or his scripture.]

'Then who the hell are you?' she said.

[Who are we? You know who we are, Rashmika. We are the ones you came all this way to find. We are the shadows. You came to negotiate with us. Don't you remember?]

She swore, then pummelled her head against the pillow at the end of the bed.

[That won't do any good. Please stop, before you hurt yourself.]

She snarled, smashing her fists against the sides of her skull.

[That won't help either. Really, Rashmika, don't you see it yet? You aren't going mad. We've just found a way into your head. We speak to Quaiche as well, but he doesn't have the benefit of all that machinery in his head. We have to be discreet, whispering aloud to him when he's alone. But you're *different*.]

'There's no machinery in my head. And I don't know anything about any shadows.'

The voice shifted its tone, adjusting its timbre and resonance until it sounded exactly as if there was a small, quiet friend whispering confidences into her ear.

[But you *do* know, Rashmika. You just haven't remembered yet. We can see all the barricades in your head. They're beginning to come down, but it will take a little while yet. But that's all right. We've waited a long time to find a friend. We can wait a little longer.]

'I think I should call Grelier,' she said. Before he left, the surgeon-general had shown her how to access the cathedral's pneumatic intercom system. She leant over the bed, towards the bedside table. There was a grilled panel above it.

[No, Rashmika,] the voice warned. [Don't call him. He'll only look at you more closely, and you don't want that, do you?]

'Why not?' she demanded.

[Because then he'll find out that you aren't who you say you are. And you wouldn't want that.]

Her hand hesitated above the intercom. Why not press it, and summon the surgeon-general? She didn't like the bastard, but she liked voices in her head even less.

But what the voice had said reminded her of her blood. She visualised him taking the sample, drawing the red core from her arm.

[Yes, Rashmika, that's part of it. You don't see it yet, but when he analyses that sample he'll be in for a shock. But he may leave it at that. What you don't want is him crawling over your head with a scanner. Then he'd really find something interesting.]

Her hand still hovered above the intercom, but she knew she was not going to press the connecting button. The voice was right: the one thing she did not want was Grelier taking an even deeper interest in her, beyond her blood. She did not know why, but it was enough to know it.

'I'm scared,' she said, moving her hand away.

[You don't have to be. We're here to help you, Rashmika.]

'Me?' she said.

[All of you,] the voice said. She sensed it pulling away, leaving her alone. [All we ask of you is a little favour in return.]

Afterwards, she tried to sleep.

Interstellar space, 2675

Scorpio looked over the technician's shoulder. Glued to one wall was a large flexible screen, newly grown by the manufactories. It showed a cross-section through the ship, duplicated from the latest version of the hand-drawn map that had been used to track the Captain's apparitions. Rather than the schematic of a spacecraft, it resembled a blow-up of some medieval anatomy illustration. The technician was marking a cross next to a confluence of tunnels, near to one of the acoustic listening posts.

'Any joy?' Scorpio asked.

The other pig made a noncommittal noise. 'Probably not. False positives from this area all day. There's a hot bilge pump near this sector. Keeps clanging, setting off our 'phones.'

'Better check it out all the same, just to be on the safe side,' Scorpio advised.

'There's a team already on their way down there. They've never been far away.'

Scorpio knew that the team would be going down in full vacuum-gear, warned that they might encounter a breach at any point, even deep within the ship. 'Tell them to be careful,' he said.

'I have, Scorp, but they could be even more careful if they knew what they needed to be careful about.'

'They don't need to know.'

The pig technician shrugged and went back to his task, waiting for another acoustic or barometric signal to appear on his read-out.

Scorpio's thoughts drifted to the hypometric weapon moving in its shaft, a corkscrewing, meshing, interleaving gyre of myriad silver blades. Even immobile, the weapon had felt subtly *wrong*, a discordant presence in the ship. It was like a picture of an impossible solid, one of those warped triangles or ever-rising staircases; a thing that looked plausible enough at first glance but which on closer inspection produced the effect of a knife twisting in a particular part of the brain – an area responsible for handling representations of the external universe, an area that handled the mechanics of what did and didn't work. Moving, it was worse. Scorpio could barely look at the threshing, squirming complexity of the operational weapon. Somewhere within that locus of shining motion, there was a point or region where something sordid was being done to the basic fabric of space-time. It was being abused.

That the technology was alien had come as no surprise to Scorpio. The weapon – and the two others like it – had been assembled according to instructions passed to the Conjoiners by Aura, before Skade had stolen her from Khouri's womb. The instructions had been precise and comprehensive, a series of unambiguous mathematical prescriptions, but utterly lacking any context – no hint of how the weapon actually functioned, or which particular model of reality had to apply for it to work. The instructions simply said: just build it, calibrate it in this fashion, and it will work. But do not ask how or why, because even if you were capable of understanding the answers, you would find them *upsetting*.

The only other hint of context was this: the hypometric weapon represented a general class of weakly acausal technologies usually developed by pre-Inhibitor-phase Galactic cultures within the second or third million years of their starfaring history. There were layers of technology beyond this, Aura's information had implied, but they could certainly not be assembled using human tools. The weapons in that theoretical arsenal bore the same abstract relationship to the hypometric device as a sophisticated computer virus did to a stone axe. Simply grasping how such weapons were in some way disadvantageous to something loosely analogous to an enemy would have required such a comprehensive remapping of the human mind that it would be pointless calling it human any more.

The message was: make the most of what you have.

'Teams are there,' the other pig said, pressing a microphone into the little pastrylike twist of his ear.

'Found anything?'

'Just that pump playing up again.'

'Shut it down,' Scorpio said. 'We can deal with the bilge later.'

'Shut it down, sir? That's a schedule-one pump.'

'I know. You're probably going to tell me it hasn't been turned off in twenty-three years.'

'It's been turned off, sir, but always with a replacement unit standing by to take over. We don't have a replacement available now, and won't be able to get one down there for days. All service teams are tied up following other acoustic leads.'

'How bad would it be?'

'About as bad as it gets. Unless we install a replacement unit, we'll lose three or four decks within a few hours.'

'Then I guess we'll have to lose them. Is your equipment sophisticated enough to filter out the sounds of those decks being flooded?'

The technician hesitated for a moment, but Scorpio knew that professional pride would win out in the end. 'That shouldn't be a problem, no.'

'Then look on the bright side. Those fluids have to come from somewhere. We'll be taking the load off some other pumps, more than likely.'

'Yes, sir,' the pig said, more resigned than convinced. He gave the order to his team, telling them to sacrifice those levels. He had to repeat the instruction several times before the message got through that he was serious and that he had Scorpio's authorisation.

Scorpio understood his reservations. Bilge management was a serious business aboard the *Nostalgia for Infinity*, and the turning off of pumps was not something that was ever done lightly. Once a deck had been flooded with the Captain's chemical humours and exudations, it could be very difficult to reclaim it for human use. But what mattered more now was the calibration of the weapon. Turning off the pump made more sense than turning off the listening devices in that area. If losing three or four decks meant having a realistic hope of defeating the pursuing wolves, it was a small price to pay.

The lights dimmed; even the constant background churn of bilge pumps became muted. The weapon was being discharged.

As the weapon rotated up to speed, it became a silent columnar blur of moving parts, a glittering whirlwind. In vacuum, it moved with frightening speed. Calculations had shown that it would only take the failure of one tiny part of the hypometric weapon to rip the *Nostalgia for Infinity* to pieces. Scorpio remembered the Conjoiners putting the thing together, taking such care, and now he understood why.

They followed the calibration instructions to the letter. Because their effects depended critically on atomic-scale tolerances, Remontoire had said, no two versions of the weapon could ever be exactly alike. Like handmade rifles, each would have its own distinct *pull*, an unavoidable effect of manufacture that had to be gauged and then compensated for. With a hypometric weapon it was not just a case of aiming-off to compensate – it was more a case of finding an arbitrary relationship between cause and effect within a locus of expectations. Once this pattern was determined, the weapon could in theory produce its effect almost anywhere, like a rifle able to fire in any direction.

Scorpio had already seen the weapon in action. He didn't have to understand how it worked, only what it did. He had heard the sonic booms as spherical volumes of Ararat's atmosphere were deleted from existence (or, conceivably, shifted or redistributed somewhere else). He had seen a hemispherical chunk of water removed from the sea, the memory of those inrushing walls of water – even now – making him shiver at the sheer wrongness of what he had witnessed.

The technology, Remontoire had told him, was spectacularly dangerous and unpredictable. Even when it was properly constructed and calibrated, a hypometric weapon could still turn against its maker. It was a little like grasping a cobra by the tail and using it to lash out against enemies while hoping that the snake didn't coil around and bite the hand that held it.

The trouble was, they needed that snake.

Thankfully, not all aspects of the h-weapon's function were totally unpredictable. The range was limited to within light-hours of the weapon itself, and there was a tolerably well-defined relationship between weapon spin-rate (as measured by some parameter Scorpio didn't even want to think about) and radial reach in a given direction. What was more difficult to predict was the direction in which the extinction bubble would be launched, and the resulting physical size of the bubble's effect.

The testing procedure required the detection of an effect caused by the weapon's discharge. On a planet, this would have presented no real difficulties: the weapon's builders would simply tune the spin-rate to allow the effect to show itself at a safe distance, and then make some guess as to the size of the effect and the direction in which it would occur. After the weapon had been fired, they would examine the predicted zone of effect for any indication that a spherical bubble of space-time – including all the matter within it – had simply winked out of existence.

But in space it was much more difficult to calibrate a hypometric weapon. No sensors in existence could detect the disappearance of a few atoms of interstellar gas from a few cubic metres of vacuum. The only practical solution, therefore, was to try to calibrate the weapon within the ship itself. Of course, this was scarily dangerous: had the bubble appeared within the core of one of the Conjoiner drives, the ship would have been destroyed instantly. But the mid-flight calibration procedure had been done before, Remontoire had said, and none of his ships had been destroyed in the process.

The one thing they didn't do was immediately select a target within the ship. They were aiming for an effect on the skin of the vessel, safely distant from any critical systems. The procedure, therefore, was to set the weapon's initial coordinates to generate a small, unobserved extinction bubble beyond the hull. The weapon would then be fired repeatedly, with the spin-rate adjusted by a tiny amount each time, decreasing the radial distance and therefore drawing the bubble closer and closer to the hull. They couldn't see it out there; they could only imagine it approaching, and could never be sure whether it was about to nibble the ship's hull or was still hundreds of metres distant. It was like summoning a malevolent spirit to a seance: the moment of arrival was a thing of both dread and anticipation.

The test area around the weapon had been sealed off right out to the skin of the ship, save for automated control systems. Everyone not already frozen had been moved as far away from the weapon as possible. After each firing – each squirming, rebounding collapse of the threshing mechanisms – Scorpio's technicians pored over their data to see if the weapon had generated an effect, scanning the network of microphones and barometers to see if there was any hint that a spherical chunk of the ship a metre in diameter had just ceased to exist. And so the calibration process continued, the technicians tuning the weapon time and again and listening for results.

The lights dimmed again.

'Getting something,' the technician said, after a moment. Scorpio saw a cluster of red indicators appear on his read-out. 'Signals coming in from . . .'

But the technician did not complete his sentence. His words were drowned out by a rising howl, a noise unlike anything Scorpio had ever heard aboard the *Nostalgia for Infinity*. It was not the shriek of air escaping through a nearby breach, nor the groan of structural failure. It was much closer to a low, agonised vocalisation, to the sound of something huge and bestial being hurt.

The moan began to subside, like the dying after-rumble of a thunder-clap.

'I think you have your effect,' Scorpio said.

He went down to see it for himself. It was much worse than he had feared: not a one-metre-wide nibble taken out of the ship, but a gaping fifteen-metre-wide wound, the edges where bulkheads and floors had been sheared gleaming a bright, untarnished silver. Greenish fluids were raining down through the cavity from severed feed-lines; an electrical cable was thrashing back and forth in the void, gushing sparks each time it contacted a metallic surface.

It could have been worse, he told himself. The volume of the ship nipped out of existence by the weapon had not coincided with any of the inhabited parts, nor had it intersected critical ship systems or the outer hull. There had been a slight local pressure loss as the air inside the volume ceased to exist, but, all told, the weapon had had a negligible effect on the ship. But it had unquestionably had an effect on the Captain. Some part of his vaguely mapped nervous system must have passed through this volume, and the weapon had evidently caused him pain. It was difficult to judge how severe that pain must have been, whether it had been transitory or was even now continuing. Perhaps there was no exact analogue for it in human terms. If there was, Scorpio was not certain that he really wished to know, because for the first time a disturbing thought had occurred to him: if this was the pain the Captain felt when a tiny part of the ship was harmed, what would it be like if something much worse happened?

Yes, it could have been worse.

He visited the technicians who were calibrating the weapon, taking in their nervous expressions and gestures. They were expecting a reprimand, at the very least.

'Looks like it was a bit larger than one metre,' he said.

'It was always going to be uncertain,' their leader flustered. 'All we could do was take a lucky guess and hope—'

Scorpio cut her off. 'I know. No one ever said this was going to be easy. But knowing what you know now, can you adjust the volume down to something more practical?'

The technician looked relieved and doubtful at the same time, as if she could not really believe that Scorpio had no intention of punishing her.

'I think so ... given the effect we've just observed ... of course, there's still no guarantee ...'

'I'm not expecting one. I'm just expecting the best you can do.'
She nodded quickly. 'Of course. And the testing?'
'Keep it up. We're still going to need that weapon, no matter how much of a bastard it is to use.'

THIRTY-FIVE

Hela, 2727

The dean had called Rashmika to his garret. When she arrived, she was relieved to find him alone in the room, with no sign of the surgeon-general. She had no great affection for the dean's company, but even less for the skulking attentions of his personal physician. She imagined him lurking somewhere else in the Lady Morwenna, busy with his Bloodwork or one of the unspeakable practices he was rumoured to favour.

'Settling in nicely?' the dean asked her as she took her appointed seat in the middle of the forest of mirrors. 'I do hope so. I've been very impressed with your acumen, Miss Els. It was an inspired suggestion of Grelier's to have you brought here.'

'I'm glad to have been of service,' Rashmika said. She prepared herself a small measure of tea, her hands shaking as she held the china. She had no appetite – the mere thought of being in the same room as the iron suit was enough to unsettle her nerves – but it was necessary to maintain the illusion of calm.

'Yes, a bold stroke of luck,' Quaiche said. He was nearly immobile, only his lips moving. The air in the garret was colder than usual, and with each word she saw a jet of exhalation issue from his mouth. 'Almost too lucky, one might say.'

'I beg your pardon, Dean?'

'Look at the table,' he said. 'The malachite box next to the tea service.'

Rashmika had not noticed the box until then, but she was certain it had not been there during any of her earlier visits to the garret. It sat on little feet, like the paws of a dog. She picked it up, finding it lighter than she had expected, and fiddled with the gold-coloured metal clasps until the lid popped open. Inside was a great quantity of paper: sheets and envelopes of all colours and bonds, neatly gathered together with an elastic band.

'Open them,' the dean said. 'Have a gander.'

She took out the bundle, slipped the elastic band free. The

paperwork spilled on to the table. At random, she selected a sheet and unfolded it. The lilac paper was so thin, so translucent that only one side had been written on. The neatly inked letters, seen in reverse, were already familiar to her before she turned it over. The dark-scarlet script was hers: childish but immediately recognisable.

'This is my correspondence,' she said. 'My letters to the church-sponsored archaeological study group.'

'Does it surprise you to see them gathered here?'

'It surprises me that they were collected and brought to your attention,' Rashmika said, 'but I'm not surprised that it *could* have happened. They were addressed to a body within the ministry of the Adventist church, after all.'

'Are you angered?'

'That would depend.' She was, but it was only one emotion amongst several. 'Were the letters ever seen by anyone in the study group?'

'The first few,' Quaiche replied, 'but almost all the others were intercepted before they reached any of the researchers. Don't take it personally: it's just that they receive enough crank literature as it is; if they had to answer it all they'd never get anything else done.'

'I'm not a crank,' Rashmika said.

'No, but – judging by the content of these letters – you *are* coming from a slightly unorthodox position on the matter of the scuttlers, wouldn't you agree?'

'If you consider the truth to be an unorthodox position,' Rashmika countered.

'You aren't the only one. The study teams receive a lot of letters from well-meaning amateurs. The majority are really quite worthless. Everyone has their own cherished little theory on the scuttlers. Unfortunately, none of them has the slightest grasp of scientific method.'

'That's more or less what I'd have said about the study teams,' Rashmika said.

He laughed at her temerity. 'Not greatly troubled by self-doubt, are you, Miss Els?'

She gathered the papers into an untidy bundle, stuffed them back in the box. 'I've broken no rules with this,' she said. 'I didn't tell you about my correspondence because I wasn't asked to tell you about it.'

'I never said you had broken any rules. It just intrigued me, that's all. I've read the letters, seen your arguments mature with time.

Frankly, I think some of the points you raise are worthy of further consideration.'

'I'm very pleased to hear it,' Rashmika said.

'Don't sound so snide. I'm sincere.'

'You don't care, Dean. No one in the church cares. Why should they? The doctrine disallows any other explanation except the one we read about in the brochures.'

He asked, playfully, 'Which is?'

'That the scuttlers are an incidental detail, their extinction unrelated to the vanishings. If they serve any theological function it's only as a reminder against hubris, and to emphasise the urgent need for salvation.'

'An extinct alien culture isn't much of a mystery these days, is it?'

'Something different happened here,' Rashmika said. 'What happened to the scuttlers wasn't what happened to the Amarantin or any of the other dead cultures.'

'That's the gist of your objection, is it?'

'I think it might help if we knew what happened,' she said. She tapped her fingernails against the lid of the box. 'They were wiped out, but it doesn't bear the hallmarks of the Inhibitors. Whoever did this left too much behind.'

'Perhaps the Inhibitors were in a hurry. Perhaps it was enough that they'd wiped out the scuttlers, without worrying about their cultural artefacts.'

'That's not how they work. I know what they did to the Amarantin. Nothing survived on Resurgam unless it was under metres of bedrock, deliberately entombed. I know what it was like, Dean: I was there.'

The light flared off his eye-opener as he turned towards her. 'You were *there*?'

'I meant,' she said hastily, 'that I've read so much about it, spent so much time thinking about it, it's *as if* I was there.' She shivered: it was easy to gloss over the statement in retrospect, but when she had said it she had felt a burning conviction that it was completely true.

'The problem is,' Quaiche said, 'that if you remove the Inhibitors as possible agents in the destruction of Hela, you have to invoke another agency. From a philosophical standpoint, that's not the way we like to do things.'

'It may not be elegant,' she said, 'but if the truth demands another agency – or indeed a third – we should have the courage to accept the evidence.'

'And you have some idea of what this other agency might have been, I take it?'

She could not help but glance towards the welded-up space suit. It was an involuntary shift in her attention, unlikely to have been noticed by the dean, but it still annoyed her. If only she could control her own reactions as well as she read those of others.

'I don't,' she said. 'But I do have some suspicions.'

The dean's couch shifted, sending a wave of accommodating movement through the mirrors. 'The first time Grelier told me about you – when it seemed likely that you might prove of use to me – he said that you were on something of a personal crusade.'

'Did he?'

'In Grelier's view, it had something to do with your brother. Is that true?'

'My brother came to the cathedrals,' she said.

'And you feared for him, anxious because you had heard nothing from him for a while, and decided to come after him. That's the story, isn't it?'

There was something about the way he said 'story' that she did not care for. 'Why shouldn't it be?'

'Because I wonder how much you really care about your brother. Was he really the reason you came all this way, Rashmika, or did he just legitimise your quest by making it seem less intellectually vain?'

'I don't know what you mean.'

'I think you gave up on your brother years ago,' the dean said. 'I think you knew, in your heart, that he was gone. What you really cared about was the scuttlers, and your ideas about them.'

'That's preposterous.'

'That bundle of letters says otherwise. It speaks of a deep-rooted obsession, quite unseemly in a child.'

'I came here for Harbin.'

He spoke with the calm insistence of a Latin tutor emphasising some subtlety of tense and grammar. 'You came here for *me*, Rashmika. You came to the Way with the intention of climbing to the top of the cathedral administration, convinced that only I had the answers you wanted, the answers you craved, like an addict.'

'I didn't invite myself here,' she said, with something of the same insistence. 'You brought me here, from the Catherine of Iron.'

'You'd have found your way here sooner or later, like a mole burrowing its way to the surface. You'd have made yourself useful in one of the study groups, and from there you'd have found a connection to me. It might have taken months; it might have taken years. But Grelier – bless his sordid little heart – expedited something that was already running its course.'

'You're wrong,' she said, her hands trembling. 'I didn't want to see you. I didn't want to come here. Why would that have meant so much to me?'

'Because you've got it into your head that I know things,' the dean said. 'Things that might make a difference.'

Her hands fumbled for the box. 'I'll take this,' she said. 'It's mine, after all.'

'The *letters* are yours. But you may keep the box.'

'Is it over, now?'

He seemed surprised. 'Over, Miss Els?'

'The agreement. My period of employment.'

'I don't see why it should be,' he said. 'As you pointed out, you were never obliged to mention your interest in the scuttlers. No crimes have been committed; no trust betrayed.'

Her hands left sweaty imprints on the box. She had not expected him to let her keep it. All that lost correspondence: sad, earnest little messages from her past self to her present. 'I thought you'd be displeased,' she said.

'You still have your uses. I'm expecting more Ultras very shortly, as a matter of fact. I'll want your opinions on them, your peculiar insights and observations, Miss Els. You can still do that for me, can't you?'

She stood up, clutching the box. From the tone of his voice it was clear that her audience with the dean was at an end. 'Might I ask one thing?' she enquired, nearly stammering over her words.

'I've asked you enough questions. I don't see why not.'

She hesitated. Even as she made her request, she had meant to ask him about Harbin. The dean must have known what had happened to him: it wouldn't have cost him anything to uncover the truth from cathedral records, even if he'd never set eyes on her brother. But now that the moment was here, now that it had arrived and the dean had granted her permission to ask her question, she knew that she did not have the strength of mind to go through with it. It was not simply that she was frightened of hearing the truth. She already suspected the truth. What frightened her was finding out how she would react when that truth was revealed. What if she turned out not to care about Harbin as much as she claimed? What if everything the dean had said was true, about Harbin just being the excuse she gave for her quest?

Could she take that?

Rashmika swallowed. She felt very young, very alone. 'I wanted to ask if you had ever heard of the shadows,' she said.

But the dean said nothing. He had never, she realised, promised her an answer.

Interstellar space, 2675

Three days later, the Inhibitor aggregate had moved within range of the weapon. The technicians still felt they had more calibration to do, more parameter space to explore. Every now and then the weapon did something weird and frightening, taking a nibble out of something local when it was supposed to be tuned for a target several AU distant. Sometimes, most frighteningly of all, its effects seemed only loosely coupled to any input. It was weakly acausal, after all: a weapon that undercut both time and space, and did so according to rules of Byzantine and shifting complexity. It was no wonder that the wolves had nothing analogous to it in their own arsenal. Perhaps they had decided that, all told, it was more trouble than it was worth. The same logic probably applied to Skade's faster-than-light drive. A great many things were possible in the universe, far more than appeared so at first glance. But many of them were unhealthy, on both the individual and the species/galactic culture level.

But the lights kept dimming, and the weapon kept operating, and Scorpio's private sense of self continued, unperturbed. The weapon might be doing grotesque things to the very foundations of reality, but all he cared about was what it did to the wolves. Slowly, it was taking chunks out of the pursuing swarm.

He wasn't winning. He was surviving. That was good enough, for now.

Aura was wrapped in her customary quilted silver blanket, supported on her mother's lap. Scorpio still found her frighteningly small, like a doll designed to sit inside a cabinet rather than be subjected to the damaging rough-and-tumble of the outside world. But there was something else, too: a quiet sense of invulnerability that made the back of his neck tingle. He only felt it now that her eyes were fully open. Focused and bright, like the eyes of some hunting bird, she absorbed everything that took place around her. Her eyes were golden-brown, flecked with glints of gold and bronze and some colour closer to electric blue. They didn't simply look around. They probed and extracted. They *surveilled*.

Scorpio and the other seniors had gathered in the usual meeting room, facing each other around the dark mirror of the table. He studied his companions, mentally listing his allies and adversaries and those who had probably still to make up their minds. He could have counted on Antoinette, but she was back on Ararat now. He was sure that Blood would also have seen things his way, not because Blood would necessarily have thought things through, but because it took imagination to think of disloyalty, and imagination had never been Blood's strong point. Scorpio missed him already. He had to keep reminding himself that his old deputy was not in fact dead, just out of reach.

It was two weeks since they had left Ararat. The *Nostalgia for Infinity* had pushed its way out of Ararat's system at a steady one-gee acceleration, slipping between the meshing gear-teeth of the battle. In the first week, the *Infinity* had put twelve AU between itself and Ararat, reaching a fiftieth of the speed of light. By the end of the second week it had reached a twenty-fifth of light speed and was now nearly fifty AU from Ararat. Scorpio felt that distance now: looking back, Ararat's Bright Sun, p Eridani A – the one that had warmed them for the last twenty-three years – was now only a very bright star, one hundred thousand times fainter than when seen from the planet's surface. It looked no brighter now than its binary companion, Faint Sun or p Eridani B; they were two amber eyes falling behind the lighthugger, pulling together as the ship headed further and further out into interstellar space. He couldn't see the wolves – only the sensors could even begin to pick them out of the background, and then with only limited confidence – but they were there. The hypometric weapons – there were three of them online now – had been chewing holes in the pursuing elements, but not all of the wolves had been destroyed.

There was no going back. But until this moment their course had been dictated solely by Remontoire's plan, his trajectory designed merely to get them away from the wolves with the lowest probability of interception. It was only now, after two weeks, that they had the option to steer on a new heading. The pursuing wolves had no bearing on that decision: Scorpio had to assume that they would eventually be destroyed, long before the ship reached its final destination.

He stood up and waited for everyone to fall silent. Saying nothing himself, he pulled Clavain's knife from its sheath. Without turning it on, he leant across the table and made two marks, one on either side of the centre line, each requiring only three scratches of the blade. One was a 'Y', the other an 'H'. In the dark lacquer of the wood the scratches were the colour of pigskin.

They all watched him, expecting him to say something. Instead he returned the knife to its sheath and sat back down in his seat. Then he meshed his hands behind his neck and nodded at Orca Cruz.

Cruz was his only remaining ally from his Chasm City days. She looked at them all in turn, fixing everyone with her one good eye, black fingernails rasping against the table as she made her points.

'The last few weeks haven't been easy,' she began. 'We've all made sacrifices, all seen plans upturned. Some of us have lost loved ones or seen our families ripped apart. Every certainty that we had a month ago has been pulverised. We are deep into unfamiliar territory, and we don't have a map. Worse, the man we had come to trust, the man who would have seen the right way forward, isn't with us any more.' She fixed her gaze on Scorpio, waiting until everyone else was looking at him as well. 'But we still have a leader,' she continued. 'We still have a damned *good* leader, someone Clavain trusted to run things on Ararat when he wasn't around. Someone we should trust to lead us, more now than ever. Clavain had faith in his judgement. I think it's about time we took a leaf from the old man's book.'

Urton, the Security Arm woman, shook her head. 'This is all well and good, Orca. None of us has a problem with Scorpio's leadership.' She gave the last word a heavy emphasis, leaving everyone to draw their own conclusions about just what problems they might have with the pig. 'But what we want to hear now is where *you* think we should go.'

'It's very simple,' Orca Cruz replied. 'We have to go to Hela.'

Urton tried unsuccessfully to hide her surprise. 'Then we're in agreement.'

'But only after we've been to Yellowstone,' Cruz said. 'Hela is ... speculative, at best. We don't really know what we'll find there, if anything. But we know that we can do some good around Yellowstone. We have the capacity to take tens of thousands more sleepers. Another hundred and fifty thousand, easily. Those are human lives, Urton. They're people we can save. Fate gave us this ship. We have to do something with it.'

'We've already evacuated the Resurgam system,' Urton said. 'Not to mention seventeen thousand people from this one. I'd say that wipes the slate clean.'

'This slate is never wiped clean,' Cruz said.

Urton waved her hand across the table. 'You're forgetting something. The core systems are crawling with Ultras. There are dozens, hundreds of ships with the sleeper capacity of *Infinity*, in any system you care to name.'

'You'd trust lives to Ultras? You're dumber than you look,' Orca said.

'Of course I'd trust them,' Urton said.

Aura laughed.

'Why did she do that?' Urton asked.

'Because you lied,' Khouri told her. 'She can tell. She can *always* tell.'

One of the refugee representatives – a man named Rintzen – coughed tactically. He smiled, doing his best to seem conciliatory. 'What Urton means is that it simply isn't our job. The motives and methods of the Ultras may be questionable – we all know that – but it is a simple fact that they have ships and a desire for customers. If the situation in the core systems does indeed reach a crisis point, then – might I venture to suggest – all we'd have is a classic case of demand being met by supply.'

Cruz shook her head. She looked disgusted. If Scorpio had walked in at that moment and only had her face to go by, he would have concluded that someone had just deposited a bowel movement on the table.

'Remind me,' she said. 'When you came aboard this ship from Resurgam – how much did it cost you?'

The man examined his fingernails. 'Nothing, of course ... but that's not the point. The situation was totally different.'

The lights dimmed. It was happening every few minutes now, as the weapons were spun up and discharged; often enough that everyone had stopped remarking on it, but that didn't mean that the dimming went unnoticed. Everyone knew that it meant the wolves were still out there, still creeping closer to the *Nostalgia for Infinity*.

'All right,' Cruz said when the lights flicked back up to full strength. 'Then what about this time, when you were evacuated from Ararat? How much did you cough up for the privilege?'

'Again, nothing,' Rintzen conceded. 'And again, the two things can't be compared ...'

'You revolt me,' Cruz said. 'I dealt with some slime down in the Mulch, but you'd have been in a league of your own, Rintzen.'

'Look,' said Kashian, another of the refugee representatives, 'no one's saying it's right for the Ultras to make a profit out of the wolf emergency, but we have to be pragmatic. Their ships will always be better suited than this one to the task of mass evacuation.' She looked around, inviting the others to do likewise. 'This room may seem normal enough, but it's hardly representative of the rest of the ship. It's more like a hard, dry pearl in the slime of an oyster. There are still vast swathes of this ship that are not even mapped, let alone habitable. And let's not forget that things are significantly worse than they were during the Resurgam evacuation. Most of the seventeen thousand who came aboard two weeks ago still haven't been processed properly. They are living in unspeakable conditions.' She shivered, as if experiencing some of that squalor by osmosis.

'You want to talk about unspeakable conditions,' Cruz said, 'try death for a few weeks, see how it suits you.'

Kashian shook her head, looking in exasperation at the other seniors. 'You can't negotiate with this woman. She reduces everything to insult or absurdity.'

'Might I say something?' asked Vasko Malinin.

Scorpio shrugged in his direction.

Vasko stood up, leaning forwards across the table, his fingers splayed for support. 'I won't debate the logistics of helping the evacuation effort from Yellowstone,' he said. 'I don't believe it makes any difference. Irrespective of the needs of those refugees, we have been given a clear direction not to go there. We have to listen to Aura.'

'She didn't say we shouldn't go to Yellowstone,' Cruz interjected. 'She just said we should go to Hela.'

Vasko's expression was severe. 'You think there's a difference?'

'Yellowstone could be our first priority, as I said. It doesn't preclude a visit to Hela once the evacuation is complete.'

'It will take decades to do that,' Vasko said.

'It'll take decades whatever we do,' Cruz said, smiling slightly. 'That's the nature of the game, kid. Get used to it.'

'I know the nature of the game,' Vasko told her, his voice low, letting her know that she had made a mistake in addressing him that way. 'I'm also aware that we've been given a clear instruction about reaching Hela. If Yellowstone formed part of Aura's plans, don't you think she'd have told us?'

They all looked at the child. Sometimes Aura spoke: by now they had all become accustomed to her small, half-formed, liquid croak. Yet there were still days when she said nothing at all, or made only childlike noises. Then, as now, she appeared to have switched into some mode of extreme receptivity, taking in rather than giving out. Her development was accelerated, but it was not progressing smoothly: there were leaps and bounds, but there were also plateaux and unaccountable reversals.

'She means for us to go to Hela,' Khouri said. 'That's all I know.'

'What about the other part?' Scorpio asked. 'The bit about negotiating with shadows?'

'It was something that came through. Maybe a memory that came loose, but which she couldn't interpret.'

'What else came through at the same time?'

She looked at him, hesitating on the edge of answering. It was a lucky guess, but his question had worked. 'I sensed something that frightened me,' she said.

'Something about these shadows?'

'Yes. It was like the chill from an open door, like a draught of terror.' Khouri looked down at the hair on her baby's head. 'She felt it as well.'

'And that's all you can tell me?' Scorpio asked. 'We have to go to Hela and negotiate with something that frightens both of you to death?'

'It was just that the message carried a warning,' Khouri said. 'It said proceed with caution. But it also said it's what we have to do.'

'You're sure of that?' Scorpio persisted.

'Why shouldn't I be?'

'Maybe you interpreted the message wrongly. Maybe the "draught of terror" was there for a different reason. Maybe it was there to indicate that on no account should we have anything to do with ... whatever these shadows are.'

'Maybe, Scorp,' Khouri said, 'but in that case, why mention the shadows at all?'

'Or Hela, for that matter,' Vasko added.

Scorpio looked at him, drawing out the moment. 'You done?' he asked.

'I guess so,' Vasko said.

'Then I think the decision needs to be taken,' the pig said. 'We've heard all the arguments, either way. We can go to Hela on the off chance that there might be something there worth our effort. Or we can take this ship to Yellowstone and save some lives, guaranteed. I think you all know my feelings on the matter.' He nodded at the letters he had gouged into the table using Clavain's old knife. 'I think you also know what Clavain would have done, under the same circumstances.'

No one said anything.

'But there's a problem,' Scorpio said. 'And the problem is that it isn't our choice to make. This isn't a democracy. All we can do is present our arguments and let Captain John Brannigan make up his mind.'

He reached into a pocket in his leather tunic and pulled out the small handful of red dust he had carried there for days.

It was finely graded iron oxide, collected from one of the machine shops – as close to Martian soil as it was possible to get, twenty-seven light-years from Mars. It trailed between the short stubs of his fingers even as he stood up and held it over the centre of the table, between the Y and the H.

This was it, he knew: the crux moment. If nothing happened – if the ship did not immediately signal its intentions by making the dust point unambiguously to one letter or other, he was over. No matter how much he wanted to see things through, he would have made a mockery of himself. But Clavain had never shirked from these moments. His whole life had lurched from one point of maximum crisis to another.

Scorpio looked up. The dust was beginning to run out.

'Your call, John.'

Hela, 2727

At night, in her room, the voice returned. It always waited until Rashmika was alone, until she was away from the garret. She had hoped, the first time, that it might turn out to be some temporary delusion, the effect, perhaps, of Quaicheist viral agents somehow entering her system and playing havoc with her sanity. But the voice was too rational for that, entirely too quiet and calm, and what it said was specifically directed at Rashmika and her predicament, rather than some ill-defined generic host.

[Rashmika,] it said, [listen to us, please. The time of crisis grows near, in more ways than one.]

'Go away,' she said, burying her head in the pillow.

[We need your help now,] the voice said.

She knew that if she did not answer the voice it would keep pestering her, its patience endless. 'My help?'

[We know what Quaiche intends to do with this cathedral, how he plans to drive it over the bridge. He won't succeed, Rashmika. The bridge won't take the Lady Morwenna. It wasn't ever meant to take something like a cathedral.]

'And you'd know, would you?'

[The bridge wasn't made by the scuttlers. It's a lot more recent than that. And it won't withstand the Lady Mor.]

She sat up in her narrow cot of a bed and turned the shutters to admit stained-glass light. She felt the rumble and sway of the cathedral's progress, the distant churning of engines. She thought of the bridge, shining somewhere ahead, delicate as a dream, oblivious to the vast mass sliding slowly towards it.

What did the voice mean, that it was a lot more recent?

'I can't stop it,' she said.

[You don't have to stop it. You just have to get us to safety, before it's too late.]

'Ask Quaiche.'

[Don't you think we've tried, Rashmika? Don't you think we've spent hours trying to persuade him? But he doesn't care about us. He'd rather we didn't exist. Sometimes, he even manages to convince himself that we don't. When the cathedral falls from the bridge, or the bridge collapses, we'll be destroyed. He'll let that happen, because then he doesn't have to think about us any more.]

'I can't help you,' she said. 'I don't want to help you. You scare me. I don't even know what you are, or where you've come from.'

[You know more than you imagine,' the voice said. 'You came here to find *us*, not Quaiche.]

'Don't be silly.'

[We know who you are, Rashmika, or rather we know who you aren't. That machinery in your head, remember? Where did all that come from?]

'I don't know about any machinery.'

[And your memories – don't they sometimes seem to belong to someone else? We heard you talking to the dean. We heard you talk about the Amarantin, and your memories of Resurgam.]

'It was a slip,' she said. 'I didn't mean ...'

[You meant every word of it, but you just don't realise it yet. You are vastly more than you think, Rashmika. How far back do your memories of life on Hela really stretch? Nine years? Not much more, we suspect. So what came before?]

'Stop talking like that,' she said.

The voice ignored her. [You aren't what you seem. These memories of life on Hela are a graft, nothing more. Beneath them lies something else entirely. For nine years they've served you well, allowing you to move amongst these people as if born to them. The illusion was so perfect, so seamless, that you didn't even suspect it yourself. But all along your true mission was at the back of your mind. You were waiting for something: some conjunction of events. It brought you from the badlands, down to the Permanent Way. Now, nearing the end of your quest, you are coming out of the dream. You are starting to remember who you really are, and it thrills and terrifies you in equal measure.]

'My mission?' she asked, almost laughing at the absurdity of it.

[To make contact with us,] the voice said, [the shadows. Those you were sent to negotiate with.]

'Who are you?' she asked quietly. '*Please* tell me.'

[Go to sleep, little girl. You'll dream of us, and then you'll know everything.]

Rashmika went to sleep. She dreamed of shadows, and more. She dreamed the kinds of dream she had always associated with shallow sleep and fever: geometric and abstract, highly repetitive, filled with inexplicable terrors and ecstasies. She dreamed the dream of a hunted people.

They were far away, so far away that the distance separating them from the familiar universe – in both space and time – was incomprehensibly large, beyond any sensible scheme of measurement. But they *were* people, of a kind. They had lived and dreamed, and they had a history that was itself a kind of dream: unimaginably far-reaching, unimaginably complex, an epic now grown too long for the telling. All that it was necessary for her to know – all that she *could* know, now – was that they had reached a point where their memory of interstellar colonisation on the human scale was so remote, so faded and etiolated by time, that it almost seemed to merge with their earliest prehistory, barely separable from a faint ancestral recollection of fire-making and the bringing down of game.

They had colonised a handful of stars, and then they had colonised their galaxy, and then they had colonised much more than that, leap-frogging out into ever-larger territories, dancing from one hierarchical structure to the next. Galaxies, then groups of galaxies, then sprawling superclusters of tens of thousands of galaxy-groups, until they called across the starless voids between superclusters – the largest structures in creation – like apes howling from one tree-top to the next. They had done wonderful and terrible things. They had reshaped themselves and their universe, and they had made plans for eternity.

They had failed. Across all that dizzying history, from one leap of scale to the next, there had never been a time when they were not running from something. It wasn't the Inhibitors, or anything very like them. It *was* a kind of machinery, but this time more like a blight, a transforming, ravening disease that they themselves had let loose. The dream's details were vague, but what she understood was this: in their very earliest history they had made something, a tool rather than a weapon, its intended function peaceful and utilitarian, but which had slipped from their control.

The tool neither attacked the people nor showed any great evidence of recognising them. What it did – with the mindless efficiency of wildfire – was rip matter apart, turning worlds into floating clouds of rubble, shells of rock and ice surrounding entire stars. Mirrors in the swarms of machinery gathered starlight, focusing life-giving energy on to the grains of rubble; transparent membranes trapped that energy around each grain and allowed tiny bubble-like ecologies to grow. Within these warm emerald-green pockets the people were able to survive, if they chose. But that was their only choice, and even then only a certain kind of existence was possible. Their only other option was flight: they could not stop the advancement of the transforming machines, only keep running from the leading edge of the wave. They could only watch as the transforming fire swept through their vast civilisation in a mere flicker of cosmic time, as the great swarms of machine-stimulated living matter turned stars into green lanterns.

They ran, and they ran. They sought solace in satellite galaxies, and for a few million years they thought they were safe. But the machines eventually reached the satellites, and began the same grindingly slow process of stellar consumption. The people ran again, but it was never far enough, never fast enough. No weapons worked: they either did more damage than the blight, or helped spread it faster. The transforming machines evolved, becoming steadily more agile and clever. Yet one thing never changed: their central task remained the smashing of worlds, and the remaking of them into a billion bright-green shards.

They had been created to do something, and that was what they were going to do.

Now, at the tail end of their history, the people had run as far as it was possible to run. They had exhausted every niche. They could not go back, could not make an accommodation with the machines. Even the transformed galaxies were now uninhabitable, their chemistries poisoned, the ecological balance of stellar life and death upset by the swarming industry of the machines. Out-of-control weapons, designed originally to defeat the machines, were themselves now as much of a hazard as the original problem.

So the people turned elsewhere. If they were being squeezed out of their own universe, then perhaps it was time to consider moving to another.

Fortunately, this was not as impossible as it sounded.

In her dream, Rashmika learned about the theory of braneworlds. There was a hallucinatory texture to it: velvety curtains of light and darkness rippled in her mind with the languor of auroral storms. What she understood was this: everything in the visible universe, everything that she saw – from the palm of her hand to the Lady Morwenna, from Hela itself out to the furthest observable galaxy – was necessarily trapped on one brane, like a pattern woven into a sheet of fabric. Quarks and electrons, photons and neutrinos – everything that constituted the universe in which she lived and breathed, including herself, was forced to travel along the surface of this one brane alone.

But the brane itself was only one of many parallel sheets floating in the higher-dimensional space that was called the bulk. The sheets were stacked closely together; were even, perhaps, joined at their edges, like the folded musical programme of some vast cosmic orchestrion. Some of the sheets had very different properties from others: although the same fundamental rules of nature applied in each, the strengths of the coupling constants – and hence the properties of the macroscopic universe – depended on where a particular brane lay within the bulk. Life within those distant branes was bizarre and strange, assuming that the parochial physics even allowed anything as complex as life. Elsewhere, some sheets were brushing against each other, the glancing impact of their collisions generating primordial events in each brane that looked very much like the Big Bangs of traditional cosmology.

If the local brane was connected to another, then the fold point – the crease – lay at a cosmological distance beyond even the Hubble length scale. But there was nothing to prevent matter and radiation making the journey around that fold, given time. If one travelled far enough along the surface of one of these connected branes – through countless megaparsecs, far enough through the conventional universe of matter and light – one would eventually end up on the next closest brane in the multidimensional void of the bulk.

Rashmika could not see the topological relationship between her brane and the brane of the shadows. Were they joined, or separate? Were the shadows deliberately withholding this information, or was it just not known to them?

It probably didn't matter.

What did matter – the *only* thing that mattered – was that there was a way to signal across the bulk. Gravity was not like the other elements of her universe: it was only imperfectly bound to a particular brane. It could take the long way around – oozing along an individual brane like a slowly spreading wine stain – but it could also leak through, taking the short cut across the bulk.

The people – the shadows, she now realised – had used gravity to send messages across the bulk, from brane to brane. And with their usual patience – for they were nothing if not patient – they had waited until someone answered.

Finally, someone had. They were the scuttlers: a starfaring species in their own right. Their history was much shorter than that of the shadows; only a few million years had passed since they had emerged from their birth world, in some lost corner of the galaxy. They were a peculiar species, with their strange habit of swapping body parts and their utter abhorrence of similarity and duplication. Their culture was impenetrably weird: nothing about it made any sense to any other species that the scuttlers ever met. Because of this they had established few trading partners, made few allegiances, and accumulated very little knowledge from other societies. They lived on cold worlds, favouring the moons of gas giants. They kept themselves to themselves, and had no ambitions beyond the modest settlement of a few hundred systems in their local galactic sector. Because of their solitary habits, it took them a while to draw down the attentions of the Inhibitors.

It made no difference. The Inhibitors didn't distinguish between the meek and aggressive: the rules applied equally to all. By the time the scuttlers had made contact with the shadows, they had been pushed to the edge of extinction. They were, needless to say, ready to consider anything.

The shadows learned of the scuttlers' travails. They listened, amused, at the stories of entire species being wiped out by the swarming black machines.

We can help, they said.

At that time, all they could do was transmit messages across the bulk, but with the co-operation of the scuttlers, they could do much more than that: the vast gravitational signal receiver constructed by the scuttlers to collect the shadows' messages had the potential to allow physical intervention. At its heart was a mass-synthesiser, a machine capable of constructing solid objects according to transmitted blueprints. Like the receiver itself, the mass-synthesiser was old galactic-level technology. It fed itself on the metal-rich remains of the gas-giant planet that had been stripped apart to make the receiver in the first place. But for all its simplicity, the mass-synthesiser was versatile. It could be programmed to build receptacles for the shadows: vacant, near-immortal machine bodies into which they could transmit their personalities. For the shadows, already embodied in machines on their side of the bulk, it was no great sacrifice.

But the scuttlers – nothing if not a cautious species – had installed clever safeguards, mindful of the danger in permitting physical intervention from one brane to another. The mass-synthesiser couldn't be activated remotely, from the shadows' side of the bulk. Only the scuttlers could turn it on, and allow the shadows to start colonising this side of the bulk. The shadows weren't interested in taking over the entire galaxy, or so they said, merely in establishing a small, independent community away from the dangers that were making their own braneworld uninhabitable.

In return, they promised, they would supply the scuttlers with the means to defeat the Inhibitors.

All the scuttlers had to do was turn on the mass-synthesiser and allow the shadows to reach across the bulk.

Rashmika awoke. It was bright daylight outside, and the stained-glass window threw tinted lozenges across the damp hummock of her pillow. For a moment she lay there, anointed in colours, lulled by the sway of the Lady Morwenna. She felt as if she had been deeply asleep, but at the same time she also felt drained, in desperate need of a few hours of dreamless oblivion. The voice was gone now, but she did not doubt that it would return. Nor was there any doubt in her mind that the voice had been real, and its story essentially true.

Now, at least, she understood a little more. The scuttlers had been offered a chance to escape extinction, but the price of that deal had been opening the door to the shadows. They had come so very close to doing it, too, but at the final moment they had not been able to make that leap of faith. The shadows had remained on their side of the bulk; the scuttlers had been wiped out.

With that realisation she felt a groaning sense of failure. She had been wrong to doubt that the scuttlers were destroyed by the Inhibitors. Everything she had worked for over the last nine years, every pious certainty she had allowed herself to indulge in, had been undermined by that one revelatory dream. The shadows had put her right. What did her opinions matter, when set against actual testimony from another alien intelligence?

She had already considered the alternative: that the shadows had wiped out the scuttlers. But that made even less sense than the Inhibitor hypothesis. If the scuttlers had let the shadows through, and if the shadows had organised themselves enough to do that much damage, then where were they now? It was unthinkable that they would have pulverised Hela, wiping out the scuttlers, and then crawled quietly back into their own universe. Nor was it likely that they had crossed the gap, done that damage, and then vanished into some solitary corner of this one, because – or so the voice had told her – they still needed to make the crossing. That was why they were speaking to her.

They wanted humanity to have the courage that the scuttlers had lacked.

Haldora, she now understood, was the signalling mechanism: the great receiver that the scuttlers had built. They had taken the former gas giant, smashed it down to its essentials and woven the remains into a world-sized gravitational antenna with a mass-synthesiser at its heart.

What the Observers saw when they looked into the sky – the illusion of Haldora – was just a form of projected camouflage. The scuttlers were gone, but their receiver remained. And now and then, for a fraction of a second, the camouflage failed. In the vanishings, what the Observers glimpsed was not some shining citadel of God but the mechanism of the receiver itself.

A door in the sky, waiting to be unlocked.

That only left one question. It was, perhaps, the hardest of all. If everything the shadows had told her was true, then she also had to accept what the shadows told her about herself.

That she wasn't who she thought she was.

Interstellar space, 2675

Five days later, technicians plumbed Scorpio into the reefersleep casket. It was a surgical procedure: a ritual of incisions and catheters, anaesthetic swabs, sterilising balms.

'You don't have to watch,' he told Khouri, who was standing at the foot of the casket with Aura in her arms.

'I want to see you go under safely,' she said.

'You mean you want to see me safely out the picture.' He knew even as he said it that it was cruel and unnecessary.

'We still need you, Scorp. We might not agree with you about Hela, but that doesn't make you any less useful.'

The child watched fascinatedly as the technicians fumbled a plastic shunt into Scorpio's wrist. He could still see the scar where the last one had been removed, twenty-three years earlier.

'It hurts,' Aura said.

'Yeah,' he said. 'It hurts, kid. But I can handle it.'

The reefersleep casket sat in a room of its own. It was the same one that had brought him to Ararat all those years ago. It was very old and very unsophisticated: a brutish black box with squared-off edges and the heavy, wrought-iron look of some artefact of medieval jurisprudence.

But it also had a perfect operational record, a flawless history of preserving its human occupants in frozen stasis during the years of relativistic travel between stars. It had never killed anyone, never brought anyone back to life with anything other than the full spectrum of mental faculties. It incorporated the minimum of nanotechnology. The Melding Plague had never touched it, nor had the Captain's own transforming influences. A baseline human contemplating a spell in the casket could have been quietly confident of revival. The transitions to and from the cryogenic state were slow and uncomfortable compared to the sleeker, more modern units. There would be discomfort, both physical and mental. But there would be little doubt that the unit would work as intended, and that the occupant would wake again at the other end of the journey.

The only problem was, none of this applied to pigs. The caskets were tuned to baseline human physiology on the unforgiving level of cell chemistry. Scorpio had made it through reefersleep before, but each time had been a gamble. He told himself that the odds didn't get any worse each time he submitted himself to a casket, that he was no more likely to die in this unit than in the first one he had used. But that wasn't strictly true. He was much older now. His body was intrinsically weaker than the last time he had been through the process. Everyone was being very coy about the hard numbers – whether it was a ten or twenty or even a thirty per cent chance of him not making out – but their very refusal to discuss the matter alarmed him more than a cold assessment of the risk would ever have done. At least then he could have compared the risks of taking the casket and staying awake for the entire trip. Five or six years of shiptime, making him fifty-five or fifty-six, against a thirty per cent chance of not making it there at all? It wouldn't have been an easy decision – as a pig, he had no guarantee of making it to sixty under normal circumstances. But at least full disclosure of the facts would have enabled him to make a considered choice. Instead, what drove him to the casket was a simple desire to skip over the intervening time. Damn the odds; he had to get the waiting over with. He had to know if it was worth their while making it to Hela.

And before that, of course, he had to know if he had made a terrible mistake by persuading the ship to travel to Yellowstone first.

He thought of the dust leaking from his hand, spilling on to the table, the trail drifting towards the Y he had marked rather than the H. Within minutes it had been confirmed: the ship was executing a slow turn, steering for Epsilon Eridani rather than the dim, unfamiliar star of 107 Piscium.

He had been pleased with the Captain's decision, but it also frightened him. The Captain had followed the minority view rather than the democratic wish of the seniors. It had suited Scorpio, but he wondered how he would have felt if the Captain had sided with the others. It was one thing to know that he had an ally in John Brannigan. It would be quite another to feel himself the prisoner of the ship.

'It's not too late,' Khouri said. 'You can stop now, spend the trip awake.'

'Is that what you're planning to do?'

'At least until Aura is older,' she said.

The girl laughed.

'I can't take the risk,' Scorpio said. 'I may not last the journey if they don't freeze me. Five or six years might not be much to you, but it's a big chunk out of my life.'

'It might not be that long if they can get the new machines to work. Our subjective time to Yellowstone might only be a couple of years.'

'Still too long for my liking.'

'It worries you that much? I thought you said you never thought much about the future.'

'I don't. Now you know why.'

She came closer to the black cabinet, lowering down on one knee, presenting Aura to him. 'She thinks this is the wrong thing to do,' Khouri said. 'I feel it coming through. She really thinks we should be going straight to Hela.'

'We'll get there eventually,' he said. 'John willing.' He directed his attention to Aura, looking into her golden-brown eyes. He expected her to flinch, but she held his gaze, barely blinking.

'Shadows,' she said, in her liquid gurgle, a voice that always seemed on the edge of hilarity. 'Negotiate with shadows.'

'I don't believe in negotiation,' Scorpio said. 'All it gets you into is a world of pain.'

'Maybe it's time you changed your opinion,' Khouri said.

Khouri and Aura left him alone with the technicians. He had been glad of the visit, but he was also glad to have a moment to marshal his thoughts, making sure that he did not forget the important things. One thing in particular assumed particular importance in his mind. He had still not told either of them about the private conversation he had had with Remontoire just before the Conjoiner's departure. The conversation had not been recorded, and Remontoire had given little more than his words: no data, no written evidence, just a shard of translucent white material small enough to fit in his pocket.

Now that omission was beginning to weigh upon him. Was it right to keep Remontoire's doubts from Aura and her mother? Remontoire had left the final decision to him, in the end: a measure of the extent to which he trusted Scorpio.

Now, in the casket, Scorpio could have done with a bit less of that trust.

He didn't have the shard with him now. It was with his personal effects, awaiting his revival. It had no intrinsic worth in its own right, and had anyone else found it, it was more than likely that they would have left it undisturbed, assuming only that it was some personal trinket or totem of purely sentimental value. What mattered was where Remontoire had found it. And aboard the ship, to the best of his knowledge, Scorpio was the only one who knew.

'I don't know what to make of it,' Remontoire said, handing him the curved white shard. Scorpio examined it, immediately disappointed at what he had been given. He could see through it. The edges were sharp enough to be dangerous, and it was too hard to flex or break. The thing looked like a dinosaur's toenail clipping.

'I know what it is, Rem.'

'You do?'

'It's a piece of conch material. We found it all the time on Ararat, washed up after storms or floating out at sea. Much bigger than this piece.'

'How big?' Remontoire asked, steepling his fingers.

'Large enough to use for dwellings, sometimes. Sometimes even for major administrative structures. We didn't have enough metal or plastic to go around, so we were always trying to make the best use of local resources. We had to anchor the conch pieces down, because otherwise they blew away in the first storm.'

'Difficult to work with?'

'We couldn't cut them with anything other than torches, but that's not saying much. You should have seen the state of our tools.'

'What did you make of the conch pieces, Scorp? Did you have a theory about them?'

'We didn't have much time for theories about anything.'

'You must have had an inkling.'

Scorpio shrugged and passed the fragment back to him. 'We assumed they were the discarded shells of extinct marine creatures, bigger than anything now living on Ararat. The Jugglers weren't the only organism in that ocean; there was always room for other kinds of life, maybe relics of the original inhabitants, before the Juggler colonisation.'

Remontoire tapped a finger against the shard. 'I don't think we're dealing with marine life, Scorp.'

'Does it matter?'

'It might do, especially given the fact that I found this in space, around Ararat.' He handed it back to the pig. 'Interested now?'

'I might be.'

Remontoire told him the rest. During the last phase of the battle around Ararat, he had been contacted by a group of Conjoiners from Skade's party. 'They knew she was dead. Without a leader, they were devolving into a directionless squabble. They approached me, hoping to steal the hypometric technology. They'd learned much already, but that was the one thing they didn't have. I resisted, fought them off, but I also let them go with a warning. I considered it rather late in the day to be making new enemies.'

'And?'

'They came back to help me when the wolf aggregate was about to finish me off. A suicidal move on their part. I think it convinced me and my associates to accept terms of co-operation from Skade's people. But there was something else.'

'The shard?'

'Not the shard itself, but data pertaining to the same mystery. I viewed it with suspicion, as I still do. I can't rule out the possibility that it may have been a piece of disinformation sown by Skade when she knew her days were numbered. Just like her to throw a posthumous spanner into our works, wouldn't you say?'

'I wouldn't put it past her for a second,' Scorpio replied. Now that he knew it had some deeper significance, the piece of conch material felt like some holy relic in his hands. He held it with reverential care, as if he might damage it. 'What did the data tell you?'

'Before they transmitted the data, they spoke of the situation around Ararat being more complicated than we had assumed. I didn't admit it at the time, but what they said chimed with my own observations. There had, for some time, been hints of something else in the game. Not my people, nor Skade's, not even the Inhibitors, but another party, lurking on the very edge of events, like spectators. Of course, in the confusion of battle it was easy to dismiss such speculation: ghost returns from mass sensors, vague phantom forms glimpsed during intense energy bursts. There *was* a great deal of deliberate confusion.'

'And the data?'

'It only confirmed those fears. Added to my own observations, the conclusion was inescapable: we were being watched. Something else – neither human nor Inhibitor – had followed us to Ararat. It may even have been there before us.'

'How do you know they weren't part of the Inhibitors? We know so little about them.'

'Because their movements suggested they were as wary of the Inhibitors as we were. Not to the same degree, but cautious none-theless.'

'Then who are they?'

'I don't know, Scorp. I only have this shard. It was recovered after an engagement during which one of their vehicles may have been damaged by drifting too close to the battle. It is a piece of debris, Scorp. The same applies, I think, to every piece of conch material you have ever found on Ararat. They are the remains of ships, fallen into the sea.'

'Then who made them?'

'We don't know.'

'What do they want with us?'

'We don't know that, either, only that they have taken an *interest*.'

'I'm not sure I like the sound of that.'

'I'm not sure I like it either. They haven't contacted us directly, and everything they've done suggests they have no intention of making their presence known. They're more advanced than us, that's for sure. They may skulk in the darkness, slinking around the Inhibitors, but they've survived. They're still out there, when we're on the brink of extinction.'

'They could help us.'

'Or they could turn out to be as bad for us as the Inhibitors.'

Scorpio looked into the old Conjoiner's face: so maddeningly calm, despite the vast implications of their conversation. 'You sound as if you think we're being judged,' he said.

'I wonder if that isn't the case.'

'And Aura? What does she have to say?'

'She has never made any mention of another party,' Remontoire said.

'Perhaps these are the shadows, after all.'

'Then why go to Hela to make contact with them? No, Scorp: these aren't the shadows. They're something else, something she either doesn't know about, or chooses not to tell us.'

'Now you're making me nervous.'

'That, Mr Pink, was very much the idea. Someone has to know this, and it might as well be you.'

'If she doesn't know about the other party, how can we be sure the rest of her information's correct?'

'We can't. That's the difficulty.'

Scorpio fingered the shard. It was cool to the touch, barely heavier than the air it displaced. 'I could talk to her about it, see if she remembers.'

'Or you could keep the information to yourself, because it is too dangerous to reveal to her. Remember: it may be misinformation created by Skade to destroy our confidence in Aura. If she were to deny knowledge of it, will you be able to trust her any more?'

'I'd still like the data,' Scorpio said.

'Too dangerous. If I passed it to you, it might find its way into her head. She's one of us, Scorp: a Conjoiner. You'll have to make do with the shard – call it an *aide-mémoire* – and this conversation. That should suffice, should it not?'

'You're saying I shouldn't tell her, ever?'

'No, I'm merely saying you must make that decision for yourself, and that it should not be taken lightly.' Remontoire paused, and then offered a smile. 'Frankly, I don't envy you. Rather a lot may depend on it, you see.'

Scorpio pushed the shard into his pocket.

Hela, 2727

[Help us, Rashmika,] the voice said, when she was alone. [Don't let us die when the cathedral dies.]

'I can't help you. I'm not even sure I want to.'

[Quaiche is unstable,] the voice insisted. [He will destroy us, because we are a chink in the armour of his faith. That cannot be allowed to happen, Rashmika. For your sakes – for the sake of all your people – don't make the same mistake as the scuttlers. Don't close the door on us.]

She thrashed her head into the damp landscape of her pillow, smelling her own days-old sweat worked into the yellowing fabric during sleepless, voice-tormented nights such as this. All she wanted was for the voice to silence itself; all she wanted was a return to the old simplicities, where all she had to worry about was the imposition of her own self-righteous convictions.

'How did you get here? You still haven't told me. If the door is closed—'

[The door was opened, briefly. During a difficult period with the supply of the virus, Quaiche endured a lapse of faith. In that crisis he began to doubt his own interpretation of the vanishings. He arranged for the firing of an instrument package into the face of Haldora, a simple mechanical probe crammed with electronic instrumentation.]

'And?'

[He provoked a response. The probe was injected into Haldora during a vanishing. It caused the vanishing to last longer than usual, more than a second. In that hiatus, Quaiche was granted a glimpse of the machinery the scuttlers made to contact us across the bulk.]

'So was everyone else who happened to see it.'

[That's why that particular vanishing had to be stricken from the public record,] the voice said. [It couldn't be *allowed* to have happened.]

She remembered what the shadows had told her about the mass-synthesiser. 'Then the probe allowed you to cross over?'

[No. We are still not physically embodied in this brane. What it did re-establish was the communication link. It had been silenced since the last time the scuttlers spoke to us, but in the moment of Quaiche's intervention it was reopened, briefly. In that window we transmitted an aspect of ourselves across the bulk, a barely sentient ghost, programmed only to survive and negotiate.]

So that was what she was dealing with: not the shadows themselves, but their stripped-down minimalist envoy. She did not suppose that it made very much difference: the voice was clearly at least as intelligent and persuasive as any machine she had ever encountered.

'How far did you get?' Rashmika asked.

[Into the probe, as it fell within the Haldora projection. From there – following the probe's telemetry link – we reached Hela. But no further. Ever since then, we have been trapped within the scrimshaw suit.]

'Why the suit?'

[Ask Quaiche. It has some deeply personal significance for him, irrevocably entwined with the nature of the vanishings and his own salvation. His lover – the original Morwenna – died in it. Afterwards, Quaiche couldn't bring himself to destroy the suit. It was a reminder of what had brought him to Hela, a spur to keep looking for an answer, for Morwenna's memory. When it came time to send the probe into Haldora, Quaiche filled the suit with the cybernetic control system necessary to communicate with the probe. That is why it has become our prison.]

'I can't help you,' she said again.

[You *must*, Rashmika. The suit is strong, but it will not survive the destruction of the Lady Morwenna. Yet without us, you will have lost your one channel of negotiation. You might establish another, but you cannot guarantee it. In the meantime, you will be at the mercy of the Inhibitors. They're coming closer, you know. There isn't much time left.]

'I can't do this,' she said. 'You're asking too much of me. *You're just a voice in my head.* I won't do it.'

[You will if you know what's good for you. We don't know all that we would like to know about you, Rashmika, but one thing is clear: you are most certainly not who you claim to be.]

She pulled her face from the pillow, brushed lank, damp hair from her eyes. 'So what if I'm not?'

[It would probably be for the best if Quaiche didn't find out, don't you think?]

The surgeon-general sat alone in his private quarters in the Office of Bloodwork, high in the middle levels of the Clocktower. He hummed to himself, happy in his environment. Even the faint swaying motion of the Lady Morwenna – exaggerated now that she was moving over the rough ground of the ungraded and potholed road that led to the bridge – was pleasing to him, the sense of continuing motion spurring him to work. He had not eaten in many hours and his hands trembled with anticipation as he waited for the assay to finish. The task of prolonging Quaiche's life had offered many challenges, but he had not felt this sense of intellectual excitement since his days in the service of Queen Jasmina, when he was the master of the body factory.

He had already pored over the results of Harbin's blood analysis. He had been looking for some explanation in his genes for the gift that had been so strongly manifested in his sister. There had never been any suggestion that Harbin had the same degree of hyper-sensitivity to expressions, but that might simply mean that the relevant genes had only been activated in his sister's case. Grelier did not know exactly what he was looking for, but he had a rough idea of the cognitive areas that ought to have been affected. What she had was a kind of inverse autism, an acute sensitivity to the emotional states of the people around her, rather than blank indifference. By comparing Harbin's DNA against Bloodwork's genetic database, culled not just from the inhabitants of Hela but from information sold to him by Ultras, he had hoped to see something anomalous. Even if it was not immediately obvious, the software ought to be able to tease it out.

But Harbin's blood had turned out to be stultifyingly normal, utterly deficient in anything anomalous. Grelier had gone back into the library and found a back-up sample, just in case there had been a labelling error. It was the same story: there was nothing in Harbin's blood that would have suggested anything unusual in his sister.

So perhaps, Grelier reasoned, there was something uniquely anomalous in her blood, the result of some statistical reshuffling of her parents' genes that had somehow failed to manifest in Harbin. Alternatively, her blood could turn out to be just as uninteresting. In that case he would have to conclude that her hypersensitivity had in some way been learned, that it was a skill anyone could acquire, given the right set of stimuli.

The analysis suite chimed, signalling that it had finished its assay. He leant back in his chair, waiting for the results to be displayed. Harbin's analysis – histograms, pie charts, genetic and cytological maps – were already up for inspection. Now the data from Rashmika Els's blood appeared alongside it. Almost immediately the analysis software began to search for correlations and mismatches. Grelier crackled his knuckles. He could see his own reflection, the ghostly white nimbus of his hair floating in the display.

Something wasn't right.

The correlation software was struggling. It was throwing up red error messages, a plague of them appearing all over the read-out. Grelier was familiar with this: it meant that the software had been told to hunt for correlations at a statistical threshold far above the actual situation. It meant that the two blood samples were far less alike than he had expected.

'But they're siblings,' he said.

Except they weren't. Not according to their blood. Harbin and Rashmika Els did not appear to be related at all.

In fact, it looked rather unlikely that Rashmika Els had even been born on Hela.

THIRTY-SIX

Interstellar Space, Near Epsilon Eridani, 2698

In the instant of awakening he assumed there had been a mistake. He was still in the black cabinet. Only a moment earlier the technicians had been cutting him open, stuffing tubes into him, pulling pieces out, examining and replacing them like children looking for treats. Now they were here again, white-hooded forms shuffling around him in a gauzy haze of vapour. He found it difficult to focus on them, the white forms blurring and joining like clouds.

'What ...' he started to say. But he couldn't speak. There was something packed into his mouth, chafing his throat with sharp edges.

One of the technicians leant into his field of view. The blur of white relaxed into a face framed in a hood, the lower half concealed behind a surgical mask.

'Easy, Scorp, don't try talking for a moment.'

He made a sound that was both furious and interrogative. The technician appeared to understand. He pushed back his hood and lowered the mask, revealing a face that Scorpio almost recognised. A man, like the older brother of someone he knew.

'You're safe,' the man said. 'Everything worked.'

He grunted another question. 'The wolves?'

'We took care of them. In the end they evolved – or deployed – some defence against the hypometric weaponry. It just stopped working against them. But we still had the cache weapons we didn't give to Remontoire.'

'How many?' he signalled.

'We used all but one finishing off the wolves.'

For a moment none of these things meant anything to Scorpio. Then the memories budged into some kind of order, some kind of sense. There was a feeling of dislocation, of standing on one side of a rift that was widening, gaping open to geological depths. The land that had seemed immediately in reach a second or two ago was racing away into the distance, forever inaccessible. The memory of the technicians pushing lines into him suddenly felt ancient, something from a second- or third-hand account, as if it had happened to someone else entirely.

They pulled the breather assembly from his throat. He took ragged breaths, each inhalation feeling as if finely ground glass had been stuffed into his pleural cavity. Was it ever this bad for humans, he wondered, or was reefersleep a special kind of hell for pigs? He guessed no one would ever know for sure.

It was enough to make him laugh. One weapon left. *One fucking weapon*, out of the nearly forty they had begun with.

'Let's hope we saved the best until last,' he said, when he felt he could manage a sentence. 'What about the hypometrics? Are you saying they're just so much junk?'

'Not yet. Maybe in time, but the local wolves don't seem to have evolved the defence that the others used. We still have a window of usefulness.'

'Oh, good. You said "local". Local to where?'

'We've reached Yellowstone,' the man said. 'Or rather, we've reached the Epsilon Eridani system, but it isn't good. We can't slow down to system speeds, just enough to make the turn for Hela.'

'Why can't we slow down? Is something wrong with the ship?'

'No,' the man replied. Scorpio had realised by then that he was talking to an older version of Vasko Malinin. Not a young man now, a man. 'But there is something wrong with Yellowstone.'

He didn't like the sound of that. 'Show me,' Scorpio said.

Before they showed him, he met Aura. She walked into the reefersleep chamber with her mother. The shock of it nearly floored him. He didn't want to believe it was her, but there was no mistaking those golden-brown eyes. Glints of embedded metal threw prismatic light back at him like oil in water.

'Hello,' she said. She held her mother's hand, standing hip-high against Khouri's side. 'They said they were waking you, Scorpio. Are you all right?'

'I'm all right,' he replied, which was as much as he was prepared to commit. 'It was always a risk, going in that thing.' *Understatement of the century*, he thought. 'How are you, Aura?'

'I'm six,' she said.

Khouri gripped her daughter's hand. 'She's having one of her child days, Scorp, when she acts more or less the way you'd expect a six-year-old to act. But she isn't always like this. I just thought you should be prepared.'

He studied the two of them. Khouri looked a little older, but not dramatically so. The lines in her face had a little more definition, as if an artist had taken a soft-edged sketch of a woman and gone over it with a sharp pencil, lovingly delineating each crease and fold of skin. She had grown her hair to shoulder length, parted it to one side, clasping it there with a small slide the colour of ambergris. There were veins of white and silver running through her hair, but these served only to emphasise the blackness of the rest of it. Folds of skin he didn't remember marked her neck, and her hands were somehow thinner and more anatomical. But she was still Khouri, and had he no knowledge that six years had passed he might not have noticed these changes.

The two of them wore white. Khouri was dressed in a floor-length ruffled skirt and a high-collared white jacket over a scoop-necked blouse. Her daughter wore a knee-length skirt over white leggings, with a simple long-sleeved top. Aura's hair was a short, tomboyish black crop, the fringe cut straight above her eyes. Mother and daughter stood before him like angels, too clean to be a part of the ship he knew. But perhaps things had changed. It had been six years, after all.

'Have you remembered anything?' he asked Aura.

'I'm six,' she said. 'Do you want to see the ship?'

He smiled, hoping it wouldn't frighten the child. 'That would be nice. But someone told me there was something else I had to deal with first.'

'What did they tell you?' Khouri asked.

'That it wasn't good.'

'Understatement of the century,' she replied.

But Valensin would not let him out of the reefersleep chamber without a full medical examination. The doctor made him lie back on a couch and submit to the silent scrutiny of the green medical servitors. The machines fussed over his abdomen with scanners and probes while Valensin peeled back Scorpio's eyelids and shone a migraine-inducing light into his head, tutting to himself as if he had found something slightly sordid hidden away inside.

'You had me asleep for six years,' Scorpio said. 'Couldn't you have made your examinations then?'

'It's the waking that kills you,' Valensin said breezily. 'That and the immediate period after revival. Given the antiquity of the casket you just came out of and the unavoidable idiosyncrasies of your anatomy, I'd say you have no more than a ninety-five per cent chance of making it through the next hour.'

'I feel fine.'

'If you do, that's quite some achievement.' Valensin held up a hand, flicking his fingers around Scorpio's face. 'How many?'

'Three.'

'Now?'

'Two.'

'And now?'

'Three.'

'And now?'

'Three. Two. Is there a point to this?'

'I'll need to run some more exhaustive tests, but it looks to me as if you're exhibiting a ten or fifteen per cent degradation in your peripheral vision.' Valensin smiled, as if this was exactly the sort of news Scorpio needed: just the ticket for getting him off the couch and putting a spring in his step.

'I've just come out of reefersleep. What do you expect?'

'More or less what I'm seeing,' Valensin said. 'There was some loss of peripheral vision before we put you under, but it has definitely worsened now. There may be some slight recovery over the next few hours, but I wouldn't be at all surprised if you never get back to where you were.'

'But I haven't aged. I was in the casket all the time.'

'It's the transitions,' Valensin said, spreading his hands apologetically. 'In some respects, they're as hard on you as staying awake. I'm sorry, Scorp, but this technology just wasn't made for pigs. The best I can say is that if you'd stayed awake, the loss in vision would have been five to ten per cent worse.'

'Well, that's fine, then. I'll bear it in mind next time. Nothing I like better than having to choose between two equally fucked-up options.'

'Oh, you made the right decision,' Valensin said. 'From a hard-nosed statistical viewpoint, it was your best chance of surviving through the last six years. But I'd think very carefully about the "next time", Scorp. The same hard-nosed statistical viewpoint gives you about a fifty per cent chance of surviving another reefersleep immersion. After that, it drops to about ten per cent. Throughout your body, your cells will be putting their affairs in order, settling their debts and making sure their wills are up to date.'

'What does that mean? That I've got one more shot in that thing?'

'About that. You weren't planning on going back in there in a hurry, were you?'

'What, with your bedside manner to cheer me up? I'd be mad to.'

'It's the lowest form of wit,' Valensin said.

'It beats a kick in the teeth.'

Scorpio pushed himself off the couch, sending Valensin's robots scurrying for cover. *Check-out time for the pig*, he thought.

Symbols floated in the sphere of a holographic display, resolving into suns, worlds, ships and ruins. Scorpio, Vasko, Khouri and Aura stood before it, their reflections looming spectrally in the sphere's glass. With them were half a dozen other ship seniors, including Cruz and Urton.

'Scorp,' Khouri said, 'take it easy, all right? Valensin's a certified prick, but that doesn't mean you should ignore what he said. We need you in one piece.'

'I'm still here,' he said. 'Anyway, you woke me for a reason. Let's get the bad news over with, shall we?'

It was worse than anything he could have anticipated.

Wolves had reached Epsilon Eridani, the Yellowstone system. The evidence from departing ships suggested that their depredations had begun only recently. Three light-months from Yellowstone, expanding outwards in all directions, was a ragged shell of lighthuggers: the leading edge of an evacuation wave. He saw them in the display when the scale was adjusted to include the entire volume of surrounding space to a light-year out from Epsilon Eridani. The ships, each marked with its own colourfully annotated symbol – ship ID and vector – looked like startled fish racing in radial lines away from some central threat. Some had pulled slightly ahead of the rest, some were lagging, but the one-gee acceleration ceiling of their drives guaranteed that the shell was only now beginning to lose its symmetry.

On either side of the wave there were hardly any ships. Those few vessels further out must have left Yellowstone before the wolves arrived. They were on routine trade routes. Some of them were travelling so fast that it would be years before news of the crisis caught up with them. Further in, there were a handful of ships – the last to leave, or perhaps they had been unable to maintain their usual acceleration rate for some reason. Closer to Epsilon Eridani, within a light-week of the system, there was no outbound traffic at all. If there were any starships left down in the still-hot ruins, they were not going anywhere in a hurry. There was no indication of in-system traffic, and nor were there any signals being received from the system's colonies or navigation beacons. Those few ships that had been on approach patterns when the crisis erupted were now engaged in wide, lazy turnarounds. They had heard the warnings and seen the evacuees streaming out in the other direction; now they were trying to head back into interstellar space.

It had taken the wolves a year to sterilise every world around Delta Pavonis. Here, Scorpio doubted that more than half a year had passed since the onset of the cull.

This, however, was a different kind of cull from that which had obliterated Resurgam and its fellow worlds. Around Delta Pavonis, an earlier cull – a million years previously – had already failed, so the Inhibitor elements tasked with the current clean-up operation had gone to extraordinary lengths to make sure the job was done properly this time. They had ripped worlds apart, mining them for raw materials to be assembled into an engine that murdered stars. They had turned it on Delta Pavonis, stabbing deep to the star's heart and unleashing an arterial gush of core material at fusion temperatures and pressures. They had sprayed this hellfire across the face of Resurgam, incinerating every organism unfortunate enough not to be shielded beneath hundreds of kilometres of crust. If life was ever to arise again on Resurgam, it would have to start almost from scratch. Faced with the unambiguous evidence of two prior extinctions, even other starfaring cultures would want to give the place a wide berth.

But that was not the Inhibitors' usual *modus operandi*. Felka had revealed to Clavain that the wolves were not programmed simply to wipe intelligent life out of existence. They were more cunning and purposeful than that, and their task was ultimately more difficult than wholesale extermination. They were designed to hold back the eruption of starfaring life, to keep the galaxy in a state of bucolic pastoralism for the next three billion years. Life, confined to individual worlds, would be shepherded through an unavoidable cosmic crisis in what the wolves viewed as only the moderately distant future. Then, and only then, could it be allowed to teem unchecked. But the preservation of life on the planetary scale was just as much a part of the wolves' plan as its desire to control expansion on the interstellar scale. To this end, the sterilisation of fertile systems like Delta Pavonis was a tool of last resort. It was a marker of local incompetence. Wolf packs vied for prestige, competing with each other to demonstrate their subtle control over emergent life. Having to destroy first worlds and then a star was a sign of slippage, an unforgivable lapse in attention. It was the sort of thing that might result in a group of wolves being ostracised, denied the latest tips in extinction management.

Around Epsilon Eridani, events were taking place on a more subtle, surgical scale. The attacking efforts were concentrated around the infrastructure of human presence rather than on the worlds themselves. There was no need to sterilise Yellowstone: the planet had never been truly inhabitable in the first place, and the only native life was microscopic. The human colonies on its surface were tenuous, domed affairs. They drew minerals and warmth from the planet, but this was only an expediency: had those resources not existed, the colonies could have been as totally self-sufficient as space habitats. It was enough for the wolves to target them and leave the rest of Yellowstone intact. Where Ferrisville had been, and Loreanville and Chasm City, all that now remained were glaring, molten craters of radioactivity. They winked through the thick yellow smog of the planet's atmosphere. No one could have survived. No *thing* could have survived.

It was the same around the planet. Before the Melding Plague, the Glitter Band had been the local name for the twinkling swarm of orbital habitats encircling the planet. Ten thousand jewelled city-states had swung around Yellowstone, nose-to-nose, many with populations in the millions. The Melding Plague had taken the shine off that glory, but Scorpio had only ever known the Glitter Band in its post-plague days, when they renamed it the Rust Belt. Many of the habitats had been airless shells by then, but there were still hundreds more that had managed to hold on to their ecologies, each a festering little microkingdom with its own laws and uniquely tasty opportunities for criminal adventuring. Scorpio hadn't been greedy. The Rust Belt had been more than sufficient for his needs, especially when he had access to Chasm City as well. But now there was no Rust Belt. A glowing ring system now hung around Yellowstone, a bracelet of cherry-red ruins. There was nothing left larger than a boulder. Every single human artefact had been pulverised. It was horrifying and beautiful.

Not just the Rust Belt, either, but all the way out. The Inhibitor machines had smashed and sterilised all the other human habitats in near-Yellowstone space. Scorpio identified their ruins from their orbits. No Haven, now. No Idlewild. Even Marco's Eye, the planet's moon, had been pruned. There was no sign that any structure larger than an igloo had ever existed on its surface. No cities, no spaceports, just a local enhancement in radioactivity and a few interesting trace elements to puzzle over.

Elsewhere in the system, the same story: nothing remained. No habitats. No surface encampments. No ships. No transmitters.

Scorpio wept.

'How many got out?' he said, when he could face reality again. 'Count the ships, tell me how many survivors they could have carried.'

'It doesn't matter,' Vasko said.

'What the fuck do you mean, *it doesn't matter*? It matters to *me*. That's why I'm asking you the fucking question.'

Khouri frowned at him. 'Scorpio ... she's only six.'

He looked at Aura. 'I'm sorry.'

'You don't understand,' Vasko said softly. He nodded at the holographic sphere. 'It's not real-time, Scorp.'

'What?'

'It's a snapshot. It's the way things were two months ago.' Vasko looked at him with his too-adult eyes. 'Things got worse, Scorp. Let me show you what I'm talking about, and then you'll understand why it doesn't make much difference how many got out.'

Vasko ran the holographic display forwards in time. Timecode numerals, logged to worldtime, tumbled in one corner. Scorpio saw the date and felt a lurch of disorientation: 04/07/2698. The numerals were meaningless, too far removed from his own days in Chasm City to have any emotional impact. *I wasn't made for these times*, he thought. He had been yanked from the ordinary flow of time and now he was adrift, unmoored from history. He realised, with a shudder of comprehension, that it was precisely this sense of dislocation that shaped the psychologies of Ultras. How much worse must it have been for Clavain?

He watched the ragged shell of the migration wave increase in size, becoming a little less spherical as the distances between the ships increased. And then, one by one, the ships began to disappear. Their icons flashed red and vanished, leaving nothing behind.

Urton was speaking now, her hands folded across her chest. 'The Inhibitors had already locked on to those escaping ships,' she said. 'From the moment the attack began, they didn't have a hope. The Inhibitors caught up, smothered them, stripped the ships down to make more Inhibitors.'

'We can even track them mathematically,' Vasko elaborated, 'with models based on the mass of raw material in each ship. Each captured vessel becomes the seed for a new wolf expansion sphere.'

The shell was breaking up. There had been hundreds of ships to begin with; now there could not be more than three dozen left. Even some of these last remaining sparks were vanishing from the display.

'No,' he said.

'There was nothing we could do,' Vasko said. 'It's the end of the world, Scorp. That's all it was ever going to be.'

'Run it forwards, to the end.'

Vasko complied. The numerals blurred, the scale of the display lurching wider. There were still some ships left: maybe twenty. Scorpio didn't have the heart to count them. At least a third of them had been the ones that had been approaching Yellowstone when the crisis started. Of the ships in the evacuation wave, not many more than a dozen had made it out this far.

'I'm sorry,' Vasko said.

'You woke me for this?' Scorpio said. 'Just to rub my snout in it? Just to show me the utter fucking futility of coming all this way?'

'Scorpio,' Aura said chidingly. 'Please. I'm only six.'

'We woke you because you ordered us to wake you when we got here,' Vasko said.

'We never got anywhere,' Scorpio said. 'You said it yourself. We're turning around, just like those other fortunate sons of bitches. I'll ask you again: why did you wake me, if it wasn't to show me this?'

'Show him,' Khouri said.

'There was another reason,' Vasko said.

The image in the tank wobbled and stabilised. Something new appeared. It was fuzzy, even after the enhancement filters had been applied. The computers were guessing details into existence, constantly testing their assumptions against the faint signal rising above the crackle of background noise. The best that the high-magnification cameras could offer was a rectangular shape with vague suggestions of engine modules and comms blisters.

'It's a ship,' Vasko said. 'Not a lighthugger. Something smaller, like an in-system shuttle or freighter. It's the only human spacecraft within two light-months of Epsilon Eridani.'

'What the hell is it doing out there?' Scorpio asked.

'What everyone else was doing,' Khouri said. 'Trying to get away from there as quickly as possible. It's sustaining five gees, but it won't be able to keep that up for very long.' She added, 'If it's really what it looks like.'

'What do you mean?'

'She means that we backtracked its point of origin,' Vasko said. 'Of course, there's some guesswork, but we think this is more or less what happened.'

He cut back to the main display showing the shell of expanding lighthuggers. Now the numerals tumbled in reverse. The icon of the shuttle zoomed back into the heart of the expansion, coinciding with a lighthugger that had just popped into existence. Vasko ran the scenario back a little more, then let it run forwards in accelerated time. Now the lighthugger was moving away from Yellowstone, following its own escape trajectory. Scorpio read the ship's name: *Wild Pallas*.

The icon winked out. At that same moment the separate emblem of the shuttle raced away from the point where the lighthugger had been.

'Someone got out,' Scorpio said, marvelling. 'Used the shuttle as a lifeboat before the wolves got them.'

'Not many, if that lighthugger was carrying hundreds of thousands of sleepers,' Vasko said.

'If we save a dozen we've justified our visit. And that shuttle could easily be carrying thousands.'

'We don't know that, Scorp,' Khouri said. 'It isn't transmitting, or at least not along a line of sight we can intercept. No distress codes, nothing.'

'They wouldn't be transmitting if they thought the space around them was swarming with wolves,' Scorpio said, 'but that doesn't mean we shouldn't save the poor bastards. That *is* why you woke me, isn't it? To decide whether we rescue them or not?'

'Actually,' Vasko said, 'the reason we woke you was to let you know that the ship's within range of the hypometric weapons. We think it may be safer to destroy it.'

THIRTY-SEVEN

Interstellar Space, Epsilon Eridani, 2698

Scorpio toured the ship. It distracted his mind from dwelling on what had happened to Yellowstone. He kept hoping all this would turn out to be a bad dream, one of those plausible nightmares that sometimes happened during a slow revival from reefersleep. Any moment now this layer of reality was going to peel back and they would be pulling him out of the casket again. The news would be bad: the wolves would still be on their way, but they would not yet have reached Yellowstone. There would still be time to warn the planet – still time to make a difference. If the system had just one more month, millions might be saved. The wolves would still be out there, of course, but any prolongation of life was better than immediate extinction. He had to believe that, or else everything was futile.

But he kept not waking up. This nightmare into which he had woken had the stubborn texture of reality.

He was going to have to get used to it.

Aboard the ship, a great many things had changed while he had been sleeping. Time dilation had compressed the twenty-three-year journey between Ararat and the Yellowstone system into six years of shiptime, with many of the crew staying awake for a significant portion of that time. Some had spent the entire trip warm, unwilling to submit to reefersleep when the future was so uncertain. They had coaxed and nursed the new technologies into life – not just the hypometric weapons, but the other gifts that Remontoire had left. When Scorpio's companions took him beyond the hull in the observation capsule, they traversed a landscape darker and colder than space itself. Nested in the outer layer of the hull, the cryo-arithmetic engines conjured heat out of existence by a sleight of quantum computation. A technician had tried to explain how the cryo-arithmetic engines worked, but some crucial twist had lost him halfway through. In Chasm City he had once hired an accountant to make his finances disappear from the official scrutiny of the Canopy financial regulators. He had experienced a similar feeling when his accountant explained the devious little principle that underpinned his patented credit-laundering technique: some detail that made his head hurt. Scorpio just couldn't grasp it. Similarly, he simply couldn't grasp the paradox of quantum computation that allowed the engines to launder heat away from under the noses of the universe's thermal regulators.

Just as long as they kept working, just as long they didn't spiral out of control like they had on Skade's ship: that was all he cared about.

There was more. The ship was under thrust, but there was no sign of exhaust glare from the Conjoiner drives. The ship slid through space on a wake of darkness.

'They tweaked the engines,' Vasko said, 'did something to the reaction processes deep inside them. The exhaust – the stuff that gives us thrust – doesn't interact with this universe for very long. Just enough time to impart momentum – a couple of ticks of Planck time – and then it decays away into something we can't detect. Maybe something that isn't really there at all.'

'You've learned some physics while I was sleeping.'

'I had to keep up. But I don't pretend to understand it.'

'All that matters is that it's something the wolves can't track,' Khouri said. 'Or at least not very easily. Maybe if they had a solid lock on us, they could sniff out something. But they'd have to get close for that.'

'What about the neutrinos coming from the reaction cores?' Scorpio asked.

'We don't see them any more. We think they've been shifted into some flavour no one knew about.'

'And you hope the wolves don't know about it either.'

'The one way to find out, Scorp, would be to get too close.'

She meant the shuttle. They knew a little more about it now: it was a blunt-hulled in-system vehicle with no transatmospheric capability, one example of what must have been tens of thousands of similar ships operating in Yellowstone space before the arrival of the wolves. Although a large ship by the standards of shuttles, it was still small enough to have been carried within the lighthugger. There was no guessing how much time the crew and passengers had had to board it, but a ship like that could easily have carried five or six thousand people; more if some of them were frozen or sedated in some way.

'I'm not turning my back on them,' Scorpio insisted.

'They could be wolves,' Vasko said.

'They don't look like wolves to me. They look like people scared for their lives.'

'Scorp, listen to me,' Khouri said. 'We picked up transmissions from some of those lighthuggers before they vanished. Omnidirectional distress broadcasts to anyone who was listening. The early ones, the first to go? They talked about being attacked by the wolves as we know them – machines made from black cubes, like the ones that brought down Skade's ship. But the ships that went later, they said something different.'

'She's right,' Vasko said. 'The reports were sketchy – understandable, given that the ships were being overrun by wolf machines – but what came through was that the wolves don't always *look* like wolves. They learn camouflage. They learn how to move amongst us, disguising themselves. Once they'd ripped apart one lighthugger, they began to learn how to make themselves look like our ships. They mimicked shuttles and other transports; made exhaust signatures and put out identification signals. It wasn't perfect – you could tell the difference close up – but it was enough to fool some lighthuggers into staging rescue attempts. They thought they were being good Samaritans, Scorp. They thought they were helping other evacuees.'

'That's fine, then,' Scorpio said. 'Just gives us an excuse not even to think about rescuing those poor bastards, right?'

'If they're wolves, everything we've done so far will have been wasted.' Vasko lowered his voice, as if afraid of disturbing Aura. 'There are seventeen thousand people on this ship. They're relatively safe. But you'd be gambling those seventeen thousand lives against the vague chance of saving only a few thousand more.'

'So we should just let them die, is that it?'

'If you knew there were only a few dozen people on that ship, what would you do then? Still take that risk?' Vasko argued.

'No, of course not.'

'Then where do you draw the line? When does the risk become acceptable?'

'It never does,' Scorpio said. 'But this is where *I* draw the line. Here. Now. We're saving that shuttle.'

'Maybe you should ask Aura what she thinks,' Vasko said, 'because it's not just about those seventeen thousand lives, is it? It's about the millions of lives that might depend on Aura's survival. It's about the future of the human species.'

Scorpio looked at the little girl, at her white dress and neat hair, the absurdity of the situation pressing in on him like a concrete shroud. No matter her history, no matter what she had already cost them, no matter what else was going on inside her head, it all boiled down to this: she was still a six-year-old girl, sitting there with her mother, speaking when she was spoken to. And now he was going to consult her about a tactical situation upon which depended the lives of thousands.

'You have an opinion on the matter?' he asked her.

She looked to her mother first for approval. 'Yes,' she said. Her small, clear voice filled the capsule like a flute. 'I have an opinion, Scorpio.'

'I'd really like to hear it.'

'You shouldn't rescue those people.'

'You mind if I ask why not?'

'Because they won't be people any more,' she said. 'And neither will we.'

Scorpio sat in an oversized command chair, in a windowless room that in the days of the old Triumvirate had formed part of the *Nostalgia for Infinity*'s gunnery-control complex. He felt like a child in an adult's world of huge furniture, his feet not even touching the chair's grilled footrest.

He was surrounded by screens showing the cautious approach of the shuttle. Lasers picked it out of the darkness, scribing the boxy blunt-nosed rectangle of its hull. Three-dimensional realisations grew more detailed with each passing second. He could see docking gear, comms antennae, thrusters' venturi tubes, airlock panels and windows.

'Be ready, Scorp,' Vasko said.

'I'm ready,' he replied, gripping the makeshift trigger he had ordered installed on the armrest of the command chair. It had been shaped for his trotters, but it still felt alien in his hand. One squeeze, that was all it would take. The three hypometric weapons had been spun up to discharge speed, corkscrewing even now in their shafts and ready for their first shot. They were locked on to the moving target of the shuttle, ready to attack if he squeezed the trigger. So was the one remaining cache weapon and all the other hull-mounted defences. Scorpio hoped that the cache weapon would make some difference if the shuttle suddenly revealed itself to be a wolf machine, but he doubted that the hull-mounted defences would have any effect at all, other than giving the wolves something conspicuous to retaliate against. But there seemed little sense in underplaying his hand. Full-spectrum dominance, that was what Clavain had always said.

But even the hypometric weapons could not be relied upon at such short range. There was a savage, shifting relationship between the size of the target region and the certainty with which its radial distance and direction from the ship could be predetermined. When a target was distant – light-seconds away or further – the target volume could be made large enough to destroy a ship in one go. When the target was closer – when it was only hundreds of metres away, as was now the case – the degree of unpredictability increased vastly. The target volume had to be kept very small, mere metres across, so that it could be positioned with some reliability. The hypometric weapons each needed several seconds to spin up to their discharge speeds after firing, so the best Scorpio could hope for was to inflict an early, crippling wound. He doubted that he would have the chance to spin up and refire the hypometric weapons a second time.

But he hoped it was not going to come to that. When the shuttle was still at a safe distance, there had been talk of sending out one of their own vessels to meet it, so that a crew could verify that it was really what it appeared to be. But Scorpio had vetoed the idea. It would have taken too much time, delaying the rescue of the shuttle long enough for the other wolves to come dangerously close. And even if a human crew got aboard the shuttle and reported back that it was genuine, there would have been no way of knowing for sure that they had not been co-opted by the wolves, their memories sucked dry for codewords. By the same token, he could place no real reliance on the voices and faces of the shuttle's crew that had been transmitted to the *Infinity*. They had seemed genuine enough, but the wolves had had millions of years to learn the art of expert, swift mimicry. Doubtless the crews of the lighthuggers had been certain that they were receiving friendly evacuees as well. No, there were only two choices, really: abandon it (probably destroying it to be on the safe side) or stake everything upon it being real. No half-measures. He was certain Clavain would have agreed with this analysis. The only thing he wasn't certain of was which choice Clavain would have taken in the end. He could be a cold-hearted bastard when the situation demanded it.

Well, so can I, Scorpio thought to himself. But this wasn't the time.

'Two hundred metres,' Vasko called, studying the laser ranger. 'Getting close, Scorp. Are you certain you don't have second thoughts?'

'I'm certain.'

He became aware, joltingly, of Aura's presence next to him. She appeared less childlike with each apparition. 'This is too dangerous,' she said. 'You mustn't take this risk, Scorpio. There's too much to be lost.'

'You don't know any more about that shuttle than I do,' he said.

'I know that I don't like it,' she said.

He gritted his teeth. 'This isn't one of your little girl days, is it? This is one of your scary prophet days.'

'She's only telling us how she feels,' Khouri said, sitting on Scorpio's opposite side. 'She has that right, doesn't she, Scorp?'

'I got the message already,' he said.

'Destroy it now,' Aura said, golden-brown eyes aflame with authority.

'One-fifty metres,' Vasko said. 'I think she means it, Scorp.'

'I think she'd better shut up.' But involuntarily his hand tightened on the trigger. He was one twitch away from doing it himself. He wondered how much warning the other ships had received before it was too late to do anything about it.

'One-thirty. She's within floodlight range now, Scorp.'

'Light her up. Let's see what happens.'

The view shuffled, making way for the grab from the optical cameras, the scene now illuminated by the floods. The shuttle was veering, turning end over end as it made its final approach. The light caught the texture of the hull: battered metal and ceramics, hyperdiamond viewing blisters, scratched and scuffed surface markings, glints of bare metal along the edges of panel lines, spirals of vapour from attitude jets. It looked terribly real, Scorpio thought. Too real, surely, to be the product of wolf camouflage. A wolf machine would only look human from a distance; up close, surely, it would reveal itself to be no more than a crude approximation shaped from myriad black cubes rather than metals and ceramics. There would be no smooth curves, no subtlety of detail, no uneven coloration or signs of damage and repair ...

'One-ten,' Vasko said. 'Ten metres closer and I'll be disarming the cache weapon. You fine with that, Scorp?'

'Copacetic.'

This had always been part of the plan. Any closer and the cache weapon stood a better than average chance of doing real damage to the *Nostalgia for Infinity* as well as the shuttle. Of course, if they needed the cache weapon in the first place ... but Scorpio did not want to think about that.

'Disarmed,' Vasko said. 'Ninety-five metres. Ninety.'

The shuttle's slow tumble brought its tail-parts into view. Scorpio saw gaping exhaust nozzles packed together like multiple gunbarrels. They were still cooling down from operation, sliding down through the spectrum. Retracted tail-mounted landing gear, for dropping down on airless worlds, became visible. Blisters and pods of unguessable function. And something else: scabrous, black encrustations, stepped along geometric lines.

'Wolf,' Vasko said, his voice barely a whisper.

Scorpio looked at the ship, his heart frozen. Vasko was right. The black growths were exactly what they had seen around Skade's ship, in the iceberg.

His hand tightened on the trigger. He could almost feel the hypometric weapons squirming in anticipation.

'Scorp,' Vasko said. 'Kill it. Now.'

He did nothing.

'Kill it!' Vasko shouted.

'It isn't an impostor,' Scorpio said. 'It's just been infect—'

Vasko seized the hypometric trigger from his hands, snapping it from the seat-rest. It trailed cables behind it. For a drawn-out moment, Vasko fumbled with it, struggling to get his fingers around the weird pig-specific trigger design. Scorpio fought back, leaning over in the seat until he was able to reach Vasko's hand and wrestle the trigger under his own control once more. He plunged his hand into the complexity of the grip, using his other arm to hold Vasko back.

'You'll fucking pay for that,' he snarled.

But the young man just said, 'Kill it. Kill it now and deal with me later. It's seventy-five fucking metres away, Scorp!'

Scorpio felt something cold press against the side of his neck. He whipped his head around, and there was Urton. She was holding something against him. All he could see was a blur of silver in her hand. A gun, or a knife, or a hypodermic – it didn't make much difference.

'Drop it, Scorp,' she said. 'It's over.'

'What is this?' he asked calmly. 'A mutiny?'

'No, nothing that dramatic. Just a regime change.'

Vasko took back the trigger, forced his hand into the guard. 'Sixty-five metres,' he whispered, and closed the trigger.

The lights dimmed.

He was allowed to watch the off-loading of the shuttle's refugees.

The shuttle had been brought into one of the smaller docking bays and the occupants were now filing off, marshalled by SA guards who were taking down their personal details. Some of the people did not seem entirely certain who they were, or who they were meant to be. Some of them looked relieved to have been rescued. Others just looked weary, as if sensing that this rescue was unlikely to be anything other than a temporary reprieve.

There were about twelve hundred of them, all told, including two dozen crew. None of them had been frozen: the shuttle had not carried reefersleep caskets, and when the wolf takeover of the lighthugger had commenced, there had barely been time to get those thousand-odd people aboard. Several hundred thousand people had been left behind on the lighthugger, to be reprocessed into wolf components. Mercifully, most of them had been frozen when it happened. The wolves might have sunk probes into their heads, but at least most of them would have been unconscious. And perhaps by that point the wolves had gathered all the tactical data they needed. Perhaps by then humans were really only useful to them for the trace elements contained in their bodies.

Interviewing the crew and passengers, they heard horror stories. Some of them had brought documentary recordings with them: first-hand evidence of the wolf onslaught – habitats being ripped apart in an orgy of transformative destructions, spewing out new wolf machines even as the structures crumbled to rubble; shots of Chasm City's newly rebuilt domes being breached, life and property being sucked into the cold, rushing atmosphere of Yellowstone in spiralling vortices of escaping air; the wolf machines descending into the ruins of the city like clouds of purposeful ink, oblivious to gravity, coalescing around and copulating with the city's warped and wizened buildings; the buildings swelling, engorged with wolf spawn. They didn't use killing energy when a process of grinding assimilation was just as efficient.

But when humans fought back, the Inhibitors lashed out with fire ripped from the vacuum itself.

The evacuees spoke of the chaos in the Rust Belt as people tried to get aboard the few remaining starships. Thousands had died in the panic, in the desperate, crowding rush for reefersleep slots. Towards the end, some survivors had been cutting their way into the hulls of lighthuggers, infesting them, hoping to find some liveable niche in the machine-crammed interior. Overwhelmed by the surge of evacuees, the Ultras had either fought back with their own weapons or let their ships be stormed. There had been no checking of documentation, no questions about names or medical histories. Whole identities had been discarded, lives flung aside in a moment of desperation. People carried only their own memories. But reefersleep did terrible things to memories.

They had allowed him to come down here and watch the unloading before he was taken away. He was not bound or cuffed – they had at least allowed him that dignity – but he was under no illusions. They felt that they owed him nothing. It was a privilege to be allowed to witness this process, and he was not going to be allowed to forget it.

The guards were processing an older man who appeared to have forgotten who he was. At some recent point in time he must have been thawed from reefersleep too hastily, perhaps during a transfer of frozen assets from one ship to another. He was gesticulating at the SA officials, trying to make them understand something that was obviously dearly important to him. The man had a grey-white moustache and a thick head of grey-white hair, combed back from his brow in neat grooves. For a moment he looked in Scorpio's direction and their eyes met. There was something pleading in his expression, a burning desire to reach out and connect with one other living creature capable of understanding his predicament. He desperately wanted someone, somewhere, to understand him. Not to help him, necessarily – there was something in his expression that spoke clearly of tremendous self-reliance and dignity, even now – but just, for one moment, to acknowledge what he felt and share that emotional burden.

Scorpio looked away, knowing he could not give the man what he wanted. When he looked back the man had been processed, moved through the connecting door into the rest of the ship, and the SA officials were working on another lost soul. There were already seventeen thousand sleepers aboard the *Infinity*, he thought. It was very unlikely that their paths would ever cross again.

'Seen enough, Scorpio?' Vasko asked.

'Guess I have,' he said.

'Still haven't changed your mind?'

'I guess not.'

'You were right, Scorp. No one doubts that.' Vasko looked at the people being processed. 'We can all see that now. But it was still the wrong thing to do. It was still too much of a risk.'

'That's not what the Captain seemed to think. Surprised you, didn't he?'

Vasko's hesitation told him everything he needed to know. In truth, he had been as surprised as anyone else. When Vasko had fired the hypometric weapon, it had discharged on schedule. But the targeting had been altered. Rather than destroying the shuttle, the weapon had surgically excised the part where the wolf machinery had established a foothold. The Captain had agreed with Scorpio: the shuttle was not a wolf impostor, just a human ship that happened to have suffered a small degree of Inhibitor infestation. The initial seed must have been tiny, or else the entire shuttle would have been consumed by the time they reached it. But there had still been hope, the Captain had recognised. And in changing the target-setting of the weapon he had revealed that his control over the internal processes of the ship was far more developed than anyone had suspected.

Vasko shrugged. 'We'll just have to factor it into our long-term planning. It's nothing we can't deal with. The ship's still headed for Hela, isn't it? Even the Captain sees that's the right place to go now.'

'Just make sure you keep on his right side,' Scorpio said. 'Place could get a little uncomfortable otherwise.'

'The Captain isn't a problem.'

'Nor am I, now.'

'It doesn't have to be this way. It's your call, Scorp.'

Yes, his call: whether to stand down from command on the grounds of medical unsuitability, or save his dignity by going back into the casket. What was it Valensin had told him? He had a fifty-fifty chance of making it out alive next time. But even if the casket didn't kill him he would be a wreck, surviving only by a kind of chemical momentum. One more trip into the casket after that and he'd be pushing the statistics to breaking point.

'You're still not going to admit this is mutiny?' he asked.

'Don't be ridiculous,' Vasko said. 'We still value your input as a colony senior. No one has ever said otherwise. You'll still be nominally in charge. It's just that your role will become more of a consultative one.'

'Rubber-stamping whatever you and Urton and the rest of your gang decide is the next policy decision?'

'That sounds terribly cynical.'

'I should have drowned you when I had the chance,' Scorpio said.

'You shouldn't say that. I've learned as much from you as I did from Clavain.'

'You knew Clavain for about a day, kid.'

'And how long did you know him, Scorp? Twenty, thirty years? That still wasn't a scratch against his lifetime. You think it really makes any difference? If you want to make a point of it, then neither of us knew him.'

'Maybe I didn't know *him*,' Scorpio said, 'but I know he'd have let that shuttle in, just the way I did.'

'You're probably right,' Vasko said, 'but it would still have been a mistake. He wasn't infallible, you know. They didn't call him the Butcher of Tharsis for nothing.'

'You'd have deposed him as well, is that what you're saying?'

Vasko considered the point and then nodded. 'He'd have been getting old as well. Sometimes you just have to cut out the dead wood.'

Aura came to see him before they put him under again. She stood in front of her mother, knees together, hands together. Khouri was straightening her daughter's hair, fussing her fringe into shape. They both wore white.

'I'm sorry, Scorpio,' Aura said. 'I didn't want them to get rid of you.'

He felt like saying something angry, something that would hurt her, but the words stalled in his mouth. He knew, on some fundamental level, that none of this was Aura's fault. She had not asked for the things that had been put in her head.

'It's all right,' he said. 'They're not getting rid of me. I'm just going to go back to sleep again until they remember how useful I am.'

'It won't take them long,' Khouri said. She knelt down so that her head was at the same level as her daughter's. 'You were right,' she said. 'No matter what advice Aura gave you, and no matter what the others said, it was the right thing to do. The brave thing. The day we forget that is the day we might as well start calling ourselves wolves as well.'

'That's the way I saw it,' Scorpio said. 'Thanks for your support. It's not that I don't have allies, I just don't have as many as I need.'

'None of us are going anywhere in a hurry, Scorp. We'll still be around when you wake up.'

He acknowledged that with a nod, but kept his thoughts to himself. She knew as well as he did that there was nothing certain about his chances of waking up again.

'What about you?' he asked. 'Planning to sleep this one out?'

He had expected Khouri to answer: the question had been addressed at her. But it was Aura who spoke. 'No, Scorpio,' she said. 'I'm going to stay awake. I'm six now. I want to be older when we reach Hela.'

'You have it all worked out, don't you?'

'Not all of it,' she said, 'but I'm remembering more and more each day.'

'About the shadows?' he asked.

'They're people,' she said. 'Not exactly like us, but closer than you'd think. They just live on the other side of something. But it's very bad there. Something's gone wrong with their home. That's why they can't live there any longer.'

'Sometimes she speaks of brane worlds,' Khouri said, 'mumbles mathematics in her sleep, stuff about folded branes and gravitic signalling across the bulk. We think the shadows are entities, Scorp: the inhabitants of an adjacent universe.'

'That's quite a leap.'

'It's all there, in the old theories. They might only be a few millimetres away, in the hyperspace of the bulk.'

'And what does this have to do with us?'

'Like Aura says, they can't live there any longer. They want out. They want to come across the gap, into this brane, but they need help from someone on this side to do it.'

'Just like that? Would there be something in it for us, as well?'

'She's always talked about negotiation, Scorp. I think what she meant was that the shadows might be able to help us out with our own local problem.'

'Provided we let them cross the gap,' Scorpio said.

'That's the idea.'

'You know what?' he said, as the technicians began to plumb him in. 'I think I'm going to have to sleep on this one.'

'What are you holding in your hand?' Khouri asked.

He opened his fist, showing her the shard of conch material Remontoire had given him. 'It's for luck,' he said.

THIRTY-EIGHT

Hela, 2727

Rashmika was on her way to the Clocktower when Grelier emerged from the shadows between two pillars. She wondered how long he had been skulking there, waiting on the off chance that she would select this particular route from her quarters.

'Surgeon-General,' she said.

'Like a wee word, if that won't take too much of your time.'

'I'm on my way to the garret. The dean has a new Ultra delegation to interview.'

'This won't take a moment. I understand how useful you've become to him.'

Rashmika shrugged: clearly she was going nowhere until Grelier was done with her. 'What is it?' she asked.

'Nothing much,' he said, 'just a small anomaly in your bloodwork. Thought it worth mentioning.'

'Then mention it,' she said.

'Not here, if you don't mind. Loose lips, and all that.'

She looked around. There was no one else in sight. There was, now that she thought about it, almost never anyone else in sight when the surgeon-general was in the vicinity. He made witnesses melt into the architecture, especially when he did his rounds with the medical case and its arsenal of loaded syringes. Today all he carried was the cane, the head of which he tapped against the bottom of his chin as he spoke.

'I thought you said it would only take a moment,' Rashmika said.

'It will, and it's on your way. We'll just make a stop in Bloodwork, and then you can go about your duty.'

He escorted her to the nearest Clocktower elevator, slid the trellis-work door closed and set the carriage in motion. Outside it was daytime. The coloured light from the stained-glass windows slid tints across his face as they rose.

'Enjoying your work here, Miss Els?'

'It's work,' she said.

'You don't sound sparklingly enthusiastic. I'm surprised, frankly. Given what you might have ended up with – dangerous work in a clearance gang – haven't you landed on your feet?'

What could she tell him? That she was scared to death by the voices that she had started hearing?

No. That wasn't necessary at all. She had enough rational fears to draw from without invoking the shadows.

'We're seventy-five kilometres from Absolution Gap, Surgeon-General,' she said. 'In just under three days this cathedral is going to be crossing that bridge.' She mimicked his tone of voice. 'Frankly, there are places I'd rather be.'

'Alarms you, does it?'

'Don't tell me that you're thrilled at the prospect.'

'The dean knows what he's doing.'

'You think so?'

Green and pink light chased each other across his face. 'Yes,' he said.

'You don't believe it,' she said. 'You're as scared as I am, aren't you? You're a rational man, Surgeon-General. You don't have his blood in your veins. You know this cathedral can't be taken over the bridge.'

'There's a first time for everything,' he said. Self-conscious of her attention, he was trying so hard to control his expression that a muscle in the side of his temple had started twitching.

'He has a death wish,' Rashmika said. 'He knows that the vanishings are heading towards a culmination. He wants to mark the occasion with a bang. What better way than to smash the cathedral to dust and make a holy martyr of himself in the process? He's the dean now, but who's to say he doesn't have his mind set on sainthood?'

'You're forgetting something,' Grelier said. 'He's thinking beyond the crossing. He wants the long-term protection of Ultras. That isn't the desire of a man planning suicide in three days. What other explanation is there?'

Unless she was reading him badly, Grelier believed that himself. She began to wonder just how much Grelier really knew about what Quaiche had in mind.

'I saw something odd when I was on my way here,' Rashmika said.

Grelier neatened his hair. His usually impeccably tidy white bristle-cut showed signs of distress. It was getting to him, Rashmika thought. He was as scared as everyone else, but he could not let it show.

'Saw something?' he echoed.

'Towards the end of the caravan trip,' she said, 'after we'd crossed the bridge and were on our way to meet the cathedrals, we passed a huge fleet of machines moving north – excavating equipment, the sort they use to open out the largest scuttler seams. Whatever it was, it was on its way somewhere.'

Grelier's eyes narrowed. 'Nothing strange in that. They'd have been on their way to fix a problem with the Permanent Way before the cathedrals got there.'

'They were moving in the wrong direction for that,' Rashmika said. 'And whatever they were doing, the quaestor didn't want to talk about them. It was as if he'd been given orders to pretend they didn't exist.'

'This has nothing to do with the dean.'

'But something on that scale could hardly take place without him knowing about it, surely,' Rashmika said. 'In fact, he probably authorised it. What do you think it is? A new scuttler excavation he doesn't want anyone to know about? Something they've found that can't be left to the usual settlement miners?'

'I have no idea.' The twitch in the side of his temple had set up camp. 'I have no idea and I don't care. My responsibility is to Bloodwork and the dean's health. That's all. I have enough on my plate without worrying about interecumenical conspiracies.' The carriage shuddered to a halt, Grelier shrugging with evident relief. 'Well, we're here, Miss Els. And now, if you don't mind, it's my turn to ask the questions.'

'You said it would only take a wee moment.'

He smiled. 'Well, that may well have been a wee *fib*.'

He sat her down in Bloodwork and showed her the results of her blood analysis, which had been correlated against some other sample he had not deigned to identify.

'I was interested in your gift,' Grelier said, resting his chin on the head of his cane, looking at her with heavy-lidded, heavily bagged eyes. 'Wanted to know if there was a genetic component. Fair enough, eh? I'm a man of science, after all.'

'If you say so,' Rashmika replied.

'Problem was, I hit a block even before I could start looking for any peculiarities.' Affectionately, Grelier tapped his medical kit. It was resting on a bench. 'Blood's my thing,' he said. 'Always has been, always will be. Genetics, cloning, you name it – but it all boils down to good old blood in the end. I dream about the stuff. Torrential, haemorrhaging rivers of it. I'm not what you'd call a squeamish man.'

'I'd never have guessed.'

'The thing is, I take a professional pride in understanding blood. Everyone who comes near me gets sampled sooner or later. The archives of the Lady Morwenna contain a comprehensive picture of the genetic make-up of this world, as it has evolved over the last century. You'd be surprised at how distinctive it is, Rashmika. We haven't been settled in piecemeal fashion, over many hundreds of years. Almost everyone who now lives on Hela is descended from the colonists of a handful of ships, right back to the *Gnostic Ascension*, all from single points of origin, and all of *those* worlds have very distinct genetic profiles. The newcomers – the pilgrims, the evacuees, the chancers – make very little difference at all to the gene pool. And of course even their blood is sampled and labelled at their point of entry.' He took a vial from the case and shook it, inspecting the frothy raspberry-red liquid within. 'All of which means that – unless you happen to have just arrived on Hela – I can predict what your blood will look like, to a high degree of precision. Even more accurately if I know where you live, so that I can factor in interbreeding. The Vigrid region's one of my specialities, actually. I've studied it a lot.' He tapped the vial against the side of the display showing the unidentified blood sample. 'Take this fellow, for instance. Classic Vigrid. Couldn't be mistaken for the blood of someone from any other place on Hela. He's so typical it's almost frightening.'

Rashmika swallowed before speaking. 'That blood is from Harbin, isn't it?' she asked.

'That's what the archives tell me.'

'Where is he? What happened to him?'

'This man?' Grelier made a show of reading fine print at the bottom of his display. 'Dead, it looks like. Killed during clearance work. Why? You weren't going to pretend he was your brother, were you?'

She felt nothing yet. It was like driving off a cliff. There was an instant when her trajectory carried on normally, as if the world had not been pulled from under her.

'You know he was my brother,' she said. 'You saw us together. You were there when they interviewed Harbin.'

'I was there when they interviewed *someone*,' Grelier said. 'But I don't think he could have been your brother.'

'That's not true.'

'In the strict genetic sense, I'm afraid it must be.' He nodded at the display, inviting her to draw her own conclusion. 'You're no more related to him than you are to me. He was not your brother, Rashmika. You were never his sister.'

'Then one of us was adopted,' she said.

'Well, funny you should say that, because it crossed my mind as well. And it struck me that perhaps the only way to get to the bottom of this whole mess was to pop up there myself and have a bit of a nose around. So I'm off to the badlands. Won't keep me away from the cathedral for more than a day. Any messages you'd like me to pass on, while I'm up there?'

'Don't hurt them,' she said. 'Whatever you do, don't hurt them.'

'No one said anything about hurting anyone. But you know how it is with those communities up there. Very secular. Very closed. Very suspicious of interference from the churches.'

'You hurt my parents,' she said, 'and I'll hurt you back.'

Grelier placed the vial back in the case, snapped shut its lid. 'No, you won't, because you need me on your side. The dean's a dangerous man, and he cares very much about his negotiations. If he thought for one moment that you weren't what you said you were, that you might in any way have compromised his discussions with the Ultras ... well, I wouldn't want to predict what he might do.' He paused, sighed, as if they had simply got off on the wrong foot and all he needed to do was spool back to the start of the conversation and everything would be fine. 'Look, this is as much my problem as yours. I don't think you're everything you say you are. This blood of yours looks suspiciously foreign. It doesn't look as though you ever had ancestors on Hela. Now, there may be an innocent explanation for this, but until I know otherwise, I have to assume the worst.'

'Which is?'

'That you're not at all who or what you say you are.'

'And why is that a problem for you, Surgeon-General?' She was crying now, the truth of Harbin's death hitting her as hard as she had always known it would.

'Because,' he said, snarling his answer, 'I brought you here. It was my bright idea to bring you and the dean together. And now I'm wondering *what the hell* I've brought here. I'm also assuming I'll be in nearly as much trouble as you if he ever finds out.'

'He won't hurt you,' Rashmika said. 'He needs you to keep him alive.'

Grelier stood up. 'Well, let's just hope that's the case, shall we? Because a few minutes ago you were trying to convince me he had a death wish. Now dry your eyes.'

Rashmika rode the elevator alone, up through strata of stained-glass light. She cried, and the more she tried to stop crying the worse the tears became. She wanted to think it was because of the news she had just learned about Harbin. Crying would have been the decent, human, sisterly response. But another part of her knew that the real reason she was crying was because of what she had learned about herself, not her brother. She could feel layers of herself coming loose, peeling away like drying scabs, revealing the raw truth of what she was, what she had always been. The shadows had been right: of that she no longer had any doubt. Nor was there was any reason for Grelier to have lied about her blood. He was as disturbed by the discovery as she was.

She felt sorry for Harbin. But not as sorry as she felt for Rashmika Els.

What did it mean? The shadows had spoken of machines in her head; Grelier thought it unlikely that she had even been born on Hela. But her memories said she had been born to a family in the Vigrid badlands, that she was the sister of someone named Harbin. She looked back over her past, examining it with the raptorial eye of someone inspecting a suspected forgery, attentive to every detail. She expected a flaw, a faint disjunction where something had been pasted over something else. But her recent memories flowed seamlessly into the past. Everything that she recalled had the unmistakable grain of lived experience. She didn't just see her past in her mind's eye: she heard it, smelt it, felt it, with the bruising, tactile immediacy of reality.

Until she looked back far enough. Nine years, the shadows had said. And then things became less certain. She had memories of her first eight years on Hela, but they felt detached: a sequence of anonymous snapshots. They could have been her memories; they could equally well have belonged to someone else.

But perhaps, Rashmika thought, that was what childhood always felt like from the perspective of adulthood: a handful of time-faded moments, as thin and translucent as stained glass.

Rashmika Els. It might not even be her real name.

The dean waited in his garret with the next Ultra delegation, sunglasses covering the eye-opener. When Rashmika arrived the air had a peculiar stillness, as if no one there had spoken for several minutes. She watched the shattered components of herself prowl through the confusion of mirrors, trying to reassemble the expression on her own face, anxious that there should be no indication of the upsetting conversation she had just had with the surgeon-general.

'You're late, Miss Els,' the dean observed.

'I was detained,' she told him, hearing the tremble in her voice. Grelier had made it clear she was to make no mention of her visit to Bloodwork, but some excuse seemed necessary.

'Have a seat, drink some tea. I was just having a chat with Mr Malinin and Miss Khouri.'

The names, inexplicably, meant something to her. She looked at the two visitors and felt another tingle of recognition. Neither of them looked much like Ultras. They were too normal; there was nothing obviously artificial about either of them, no missing or augmented bits, no suggestion of genetic reshaping or chimeric fusion. He was a tall, slim, dark-haired man, about ten years older than her. Handsome, even, in a slightly self-regarding way. He wore a stiff red uniform and stood with his hands behind his back, as if at attention. He watched her as she sat down and poured herself some tea, taking more interest in her than any of the other Ultras had done. To them she had only ever been part of the scenery, but from Malinin she sensed curiosity. The other one – the woman called Khouri – looked at her with something of the same inquisitiveness. Khouri was a small-framed older woman, sad eyes dominating a sad face, as if too much had been taken from her and not enough given back.

Rashmika thought she had seen both of them before. The woman, in particular.

'We haven't been introduced,' the man said, nodding towards Rashmika.

'This is Rashmika Els, my advisor,' the dean said, the tone of his voice indicating that this was all he was prepared to say on the matter. 'Now, Mr Malinin ...'

'You still haven't properly introduced us,' he said.

The dean reached out to adjust one of his mirrors. 'This is Vasko Malinin, and this is Ana Khouri,' he said, gesturing to each of them in turn, 'the human representatives of the *Nostalgia for Infinity*, an Ultra vessel recently arrived in our system.'

The man looked at her again. 'No one mentioned anything about advisors sitting in on negotiations.'

'You have a particular problem with that, Mr Malinin? If you do, I can ask her to leave.'

'No,' the Ultra said, after a moment's consideration. 'It doesn't matter.'

The dean invited the two visitors to sit down. They took their seats opposite Rashmika, on the other side of the little table where she poured tea.

'What brought you to our system?' the dean asked, directing his question to the male Ultra.

'The usual. We have a belly full of evacuees from the inner systems. Many of them specifically wanted to be brought here, before the vanishings reach culmination. We don't question their motives, so long as they pay. The others want to be taken further out, as far away from the wolves as possible. We, of course, have our own technical needs. But we don't plan on staying very long.'

'Interested in scuttler relics?'

'We have a different incentive,' the man said, pressing a crease from his suit. 'We're interested in Haldora, as it happens.'

Quaiche reached up and unclipped his sunglasses. 'Aren't we all?'

'Not in the religious sense,' the Ultra replied, apparently unfazed by Quaiche lying there with his splayed-open eyelids. 'But it's not our intention to undermine anyone's belief system. However, since this system was discovered, there's been almost no scientific investigation into the Haldora phenomenon. Not because no one has wanted to examine it, but because the authorities here – including the Adventist church – have never permitted close-up examinations.'

'The ships in the parking swarm are free to use their sensors to study the vanishings,' Quaiche said. 'Many have done so, and have circulated their findings to the wider community.'

'True,' the Ultra said, 'but those long-distance observations haven't been taken very seriously beyond this system. What's really needed is a detailed study, using physical probes – instrument packages fired into the face of the planet, that kind of thing.'

'You might as well spit in the face of God.'

'Why? If this is a genuine miracle, it should withstand investigation. What do you have to fear?'

'God's ire, that's what.'

The Ultra examined his fingers. Rashmika read his tension like a book. He had lied once, when he told the dean about the ship being full of evacuees who wanted to witness the vanishings. There might be a host of mundane reasons for that. Beyond that he had told the truth, so far as she was able to judge. Rashmika glanced at the woman, who had said nothing yet, and felt another electric shock of recognition. For a moment their eyes met, and the woman held the gaze for a second longer than Rashmika found comfortable. It was Rashmika who looked away, feeling the blood rush to her cheeks.

'The vanishings are reaching culmination,' the Ultra said. 'No one disputes this. But it also means that we do not have much time to study Haldora as it is now.'

'I can't allow it.'

'It has happened once before, hasn't it?'

The light caught the frame of his eye-opener as he turned towards the man. 'What has?'

'The direct probing of Haldora,' the Ultra said. 'On Hela, so far as we can gather, there are rumours of an unrecorded vanishing, one that happened about twenty years ago. A vanishing that lasted longer than the others, but which has now been stricken from the public record.'

'There are rumours about everything,' Quaiche said, sounding peevish.

'It's said that the prolonged event was the result of an instrument package being sent into the face of Haldora at the moment of an ordinary vanishing. Somehow it delayed the return of the normal three-dimensional image of the planet. Stressed the system, perhaps. Overloaded it.'

'The system?'

'The mechanism,' the Ultra said. 'Whatever it is that projects an image of the gas giant.'

'The mechanism, my friend, is God.'

'That's one interpretation.' The Ultra sighed. 'Look, I didn't come here to irritate you, only to state our position honestly. We believe that an instrument package has already been sent into the face of Haldora, and that it was probably done with Adventist blessing.' Rashmika thought again about the scratchy markings Pietr had shown her, and what she had been told by the shadows. It was true, then: there really had been a missing vanishing, and it was in that moment that the shadows had sent their bodiless envoy – their agent of negotiation – into the scrimshaw suit. The same suit they wanted her to remove from the cathedral, before it was dashed to pieces on the floor of Ginnungagap Rift.

She forced her attention back to the Ultra, for fear of missing something crucial. 'We also believe that no harm can come from a second attempt,' he said. 'That's all we want: permission to repeat the experiment.'

'The experiment that never happened,' Quaiche said.

'If so, we'll just have to be the first.' The Ultra leaned forwards in his seat. 'We'll give you the protection you require for free. No need to offer us trade incentives. You can continue to deal with other Ultra parties as you have always done. In return, all we ask for is the permission to make a small study of Haldora.'

The Ultra leant back. He glanced at Rashmika and then looked out of one of the windows. From the garret, the line of the Way was clearly visible, stretching twenty kilometres into the distance. Very soon they would see the geological transitions that marked the approach of the Rift. The bridge could not be far below the horizon.

Fewer than three days, she thought. Then they'd be on it. But it wouldn't be over quickly, even then. At the cathedral's usual crawl it would take a day and a half to make the crossing.

'I do need protection,' Quaiche said, after a great silence. 'And I suppose I am prepared to be flexible. You have a good ship, it seems. Heavily armed, and with a sound propulsion system. You'd be surprised how difficult it has been to find a ship that can meet my requirements. By the time they get here, most ships are on their last legs. They're in no fit state to act as a bodyguard.'

'Our ship has some idiosyncrasies,' the Ultra said, 'but yes, it is sound. I doubt that there's a better-armed ship in the parking swarm.'

'The experiment,' Quaiche said. 'It wouldn't be anything more than the dropping of an instrument package?'

'One or two. Nothing fancy.'

'Sequenced with a vanishing?'

'Not necessarily. We can learn a great deal at any time. Of course, if a vanishing chooses to happen . . . we'll be sure to have an automated drone stationed within response distance.'

'I don't like the sound of any of this,' Quaiche said. 'But I *do* like the sound of protection. I take it you have studied the rest of my terms?'

'They seem reasonable enough.'

'You agree to the presence of a small Adventist delegation on your ship?'

'We don't really see why it's necessary.'

'Well, it is. You don't understand the politics of this system. It's no criticism: after only a few weeks here, I wouldn't expect you to. But how are you going to know the difference between a genuine threat and an innocent transgression? I can't have you shooting at everything that comes within range of Hela. That wouldn't do at all.'

'Your delegates would take those decisions?'

'They'd be there in an advisory capacity,' Quaiche said, 'nothing more. You won't have to worry about every ship that comes near Hela, and I won't have to worry about your weapons being ready when I need them.'

'How many delegates?'

'Thirty,' Quaiche said.

'Too many. We'll consider ten, maybe twelve.'

'Make it twenty, and we'll say no more on the matter.'

The Ultra looked at Rashmika again, as if it was her advice that he sought. 'I'll have to discuss this with my crew,' he said.

'But in principle, you don't have any strong objections?'

'We don't like it,' Malinin said. He stood up, straightened his uniform. 'But if that's what it takes to get your permission, we may have no choice but to accept it.'

Quaiche bobbed his head emphatically, sending a sympathetic ripple through his attendant mirrors. 'I'm so pleased,' he said. 'The moment you came through that door, Mr Malinin, I knew you were someone I could do business with.'

THIRTY-NINE

Hela Surface, 2727

When the Ultras' shuttle had departed, Quaiche turned to her and said, 'Well? Are they the ones?'

'I think they are,' she said.

'The ship looks very suitable from a technical standpoint, and they certainly want the position very badly. The woman didn't give us much to go on. What about the man: did you sense that Malinin was hiding anything?'

This was it, she thought: the crux moment. She had known that Vasko Malinin meant something important as soon as she heard his name: it had felt like the right key slipping into a lock after so many wrong ones, like the sequenced falling of well-oiled tumblers.

She had felt the same thing when she had heard the woman's name.

I know these people, she thought. They were older than she remembered them, but their faces and mannerisms were as familiar to her as her own flesh and blood.

There had been something in Malinin's manner, too: he knew her, just as she knew him. The recognition went both ways. And she had sensed, too, that he was hiding something. He had lied blatantly about his motive for coming to Hela, but there had been more to it than that. He wanted more than just the chance to make an innocent study of Haldora.

This was it: the crux moment.

'He seemed honest enough,' Rashmika said.

'He did?' the dean asked.

'He was nervous,' she replied, 'and he was hoping you wouldn't ask too many questions, but only because he wants his ship to get the position.'

'It's odd that they should show such an interest in Haldora. Most Ultras are only interested in trade advantages.'

'You heard what he said: the market's crashed.'

'Still doesn't explain his interest in Haldora, though.'

Rashmika sipped at her tea, hoping to hide her own expression. She was nowhere near as successful at lying as she was adept at its detection.

'Doesn't really matter, does it? You'll have your representatives aboard their ship. They won't be able to get up to anything fishy with a bunch of Adventists breathing down their necks.'

'There's still something,' Quaiche said. With no visitors to intimidate he had replaced his sunglasses, clipping them into place over the eye-opener. 'Something I just can't put my finger . . . I know, did you see the way he kept looking at you? And the woman, too? Odd, that. The others have barely looked at you.'

'I didn't notice,' she said.

Hela Orbit, 2727

Vasko felt his weight increase as the shuttle pushed them back towards orbit. As the vessel altered its course, he saw the Lady Morwenna again, looking tiny and toylike compared to when they had first approached it. The great cathedral sat alone on its own diverging track of the Permanent Way, so far from the others that it appeared to have been cast into the icy wilderness for some unspeakable heresy, excommunicated from the main family of cathedrals. He knew it was moving, but at this distance the cathedral might as well have been fixed to the landscape, turning with Hela. It took ten minutes to travel its own length, after all.

He looked at Khouri, sitting next to him. She had said nothing since they left the cathedral.

An odd thought occurred to him, popping into his mind from nowhere. All this trouble that the cathedrals went to – the great circumnavigation of Hela's equator – was undertaken to ensure that Haldora was always overhead, so that it could be observed without interruption. And that was because Hela had not quite settled into synchronous rotation around the larger planet. How much simpler it would have been had Hela reached that state, so that it always kept the same face turned towards Haldora. Then all the cathedrals could have gathered at the same spot and set down roots. There would have been no need for them to move, no need for the Permanent Way, no need for the unwieldy culture of support communities that the cathedrals both depended upon and nurtured. And all it would have taken was a tiny adjustment in Hela's rotation. The planet was like a clock that almost kept time. It only needed a tiny nudge to fall into absolute, ticking synchrony. How much? Vasko ran the numbers in his head, not quite believing what they told him. The length of Hela's day would only have to be changed by one part in two hundred. Just twelve minutes out of the forty hours.

He wondered how any of them could keep their faith knowing that. For if there was anything miraculous about Haldora, why would the Creator have slipped up over a matter of twelve minutes in forty hours when arranging Hela's diurnal rotation? It was a glaring omission, a sign of cosmic sloppiness. Not even that, Vasko corrected himself. It was a sign of cosmic obliviousness. The universe didn't know what was happening here. It didn't know and it didn't care. It didn't even *know* that it didn't know.

If there was a God, he thought, then there wouldn't be wolves. They weren't part of anyone's idea of heaven and hell.

The shuttle banked away from the cathedral. He could see the rough, ungraded surface of the Permanent Way stretching ahead of the Lady Morwenna. But it did not stretch very far before meeting the dark, shadowed absence of Ginnungagap Rift. Vasko knew exactly what the locals called it.

The Way appeared to end at the edge of Absolution Gap. On the far side of the Rift, forty kilometres from the near side, the road continued. There appeared to be nothing in between but forty kilometres of empty space. It was only when the shuttle had climbed a little higher that a particular angle of the light picked out the absurdly delicate filigree of the bridge, as if it had been breathed into being just at that moment.

Vasko looked at the bridge, then back to the cathedral. It still appeared to be stationary, but he could see that the landmarks that had been next to it a few minutes earlier were now just behind it. The crawl was slug-slow, but there was also an inevitability about it.

And the bridge did not look remotely capable of carrying the cathedral to the other side of the rift.

He opened the secure channel to the larger shuttle waiting in orbit, the one that would relay his signal to the *Nostalgia for Infinity*, which was still waiting in the parking swarm.

'This is Vasko,' he said. 'We've made contact with Aura.'

'Did you get anything?' asked Orca Cruz.

He looked at Khouri. She nodded, but said nothing.

'We got something,' Vasko said.

Scorpio came to consciousness knowing that this sleep had been even longer than the one before. He could feel the messages of chemical protestation from his cells flooding his system as they were cajoled back towards the grudging labour of metabolism. They were picking up tools like disgruntled workers, ready to down them for good at the slightest provocation. They had had enough mistreatment for one lifetime. *Join the club*, Scorpio thought. It was not as if the management was enjoying it, either.

He groped back into memory. He recalled, clearly enough, the episode of waking in the Yellowstone system. He remembered seeing the evidence of the wolves' handiwork, Yellowstone and its habitats reduced to ruins, the system gutted. He remembered also the part he had played in the dispute over the evacuees. He had won that particular battle – the shuttle had been allowed aboard – but it seemed that he had lost the war. The choice had been his: surrender command and submit to a passive role as an observer, or go into the freezer again. Practically, the two amounted to the same thing: he would be out of the picture, leaving the running of the ship to Vasko and his allies. But at least if frozen he would not have to stand there watching it happen. It was a small compensation, but at his point in life it was the small compensations that mattered.

And now at last he was being awoken. His position aboard the ship might be just as compromised as before he went under, but at least he would have the benefit of some different scenery.

'Well?' he asked Valensin, while the doctor ran his usual battery of tests. 'Ducked the odds again, didn't I?'

'You always had an even chance of surviving it, Scorpio, but that doesn't make you immortal. You go into that thing again, you won't come out of it.'

'You said I had a ten per cent chance of survival the next time.'

'I was trying to cheer you up.'

'It's worse than that?'

Valensin pointed at the reefersleep casket. 'You climb into that box one more time, we might as well paint it black and put handles on it.'

But the true state of his current health, even when he filtered out Valensin's usual tendency to put a positive spin on things, was still bad. In some respects it was as if he had not been in the casket at all; as if the flow of time had operated on him with stealthy disregard for the supposed effects of cryogenic stasis. His vision and hearing had degenerated further. He could barely see anything in his peripheral vision now, and even in full view, things that had been sharp before now appeared granular and milky. He kept having to ask Valensin to speak up above the churn of the room's air conditioners. He had never had to do that before. When he walked around he found himself tiring quickly, always looking for somewhere to rest and catch his breath. His heart and lung capacities had weakened. Pig cardiovascular systems had been engineered by commercial interests for maximum ease of transgenic transplantation. The same interests hadn't been overly concerned about the longevity of their products. Planned obsolescence, they called it.

He had been fifty when he left Ararat. To all intents and purposes he was still fifty: he had lived through only a few subjective weeks of additional time. But the transitions to and from reefersleep had put another seven or eight years on the clock, purely because of the battering his cells had taken. It would have been worse if he had stayed awake, living through all those years of shiptime, but not by very much.

Still, he was alive. He had lived through more years of worldtime than most pigs. So what if he was pushing the envelope of pig longevity? He was weakened, but he wasn't on his back just yet.

'So where are we?' he asked Valensin. 'I take it we're around 107 Piscium. Or did you just wake me up to tell me how bad an idea it was to wake me up?'

'We're around 107 Piscium, yes, but you still need to do a little catching up.' Valensin helped him off the examination couch, Scorpio noticing that the two old servitors had finally broken down and been consigned to new roles as coat racks, standing guard on either side of the door.

'I don't like the sound of that,' Scorpio said. 'How long has it been? What's the year?'

'Twenty-seven twenty-seven,' Valensin said. 'And no, I don't like the sound of that any more than you do. One other thing, Scorpio.'

'Yes?'

Valensin handed him a curved white shard, like a flake of ice. 'You were holding this when you went under. I presumed it had some significance.'

Scorpio took the piece of conch material from the doctor.

*

There was something wrong, something that no one was telling him. Scorpio looked at the faces around the conference table, trying to see it for himself. Everyone that he would have expected to be there was present: Cruz, Urton, Vasko, as well as a good number of seniors he did not know so well. Khouri was also there. But now that he saw her he realised the obvious, screaming absence. There was no sign of Aura.

'Where is she?' he asked.

'She's all right, Scorp,' Vasko said. 'She's safe and well. I know because I've just seen her.'

'Someone tell him,' Khouri said. She looked older than last time, Scorpio thought. There were more lines on her face, more grey in her hair. She wore it short now, combed across her brow. He could see the shape of her skull shining through the skin.

'Tell me what?' he asked.

'How much did Valensin explain?' Vasko asked him.

'He told me the date. That was about it.'

'We had to take some difficult decisions, Scorp. In your absence, we did the best we could.'

In my absence, Scorpio thought: as if he had walked out on them, leaving them in the lurch when they most needed him; making him feel as if he was the one at fault, the one who had shirked his responsibilities.

'I'm sure you managed,' he said, pinching the bridge of his nose. He had woken up with a headache. It was still there.

'We arrived here in 2717,' Vasko said, 'after a nineteen-year flight from the Yellowstone system.'

The back of Scorpio's neck prickled. 'That's not the date Valensin just gave me.'

'Valensin didn't lie,' Urton said. 'The local system date is 2727. We arrived around Hela nearly ten years ago. We'd have woken you then, but the time wasn't right. Valensin told us we'd only get one shot. If we woke you then, you'd either be dead now or frozen again with only a small chance of revival.'

'This is the way it had to happen, Scorp,' Vasko said. 'You were a resource we couldn't afford to squander.'

'You've no idea how good that makes me feel.'

'What I mean is, we had to think seriously about when would be the best time to wake you. You always told us to wait until we'd arrived around Hela.'

'I did, didn't I?'

'Well, think of this as our proper arrival. As far as the system authorities are concerned – the Adventists – we've only shown up in the last few weeks. We left and came back again, making a loop through local interstellar space.'

'Why?' he asked.

'Because of what had to happen,' Vasko said. 'When we got here ten years ago, we realised that the situation in this system was vastly more complex than we'd anticipated. The Adventists controlled access to Haldora, the planet that keeps vanishing. You had to deal with the church to get near Hela, and even then you weren't allowed to send any probes anywhere near the gas giant.'

'You could have shot your way in, taken what you wanted by force.'

'And risked a bloodbath? There are a million innocent civilians on Hela, not to mention all the tens of thousands of sleepers in the ships parked in this system. And it's not as if we knew exactly what we were looking for. If we'd come in with guns blazing, we might have destroyed the very thing we needed, or at the very least made sure that we'd never get our hands on it. But if we could get close to Quaiche, then we could get at the problem from the inside.'

'Quaiche is still alive?' Scorpio asked.

'We know that for sure now – Khouri and I met him today,' Vasko said. 'But he's a recluse, kept alive with faltering longevity therapies. He never leaves the Lady Morwenna, his cathedral. He doesn't sleep. He's had his brain altered so that he doesn't need to. He doesn't even blink. He spends every waking instant of his life staring at Haldora, waiting for *it* to blink instead.'

'He's insane, then.'

'In his situation, wouldn't you be? Something awful happened to him down there. It pushed him over the edge.'

'He has an indoctrinal virus,' Cruz said. 'It's always been in his blood, since before he came to Hela. Now there's a whole industry down there, fractioning it off, splicing it into different grades, mixing it with other viruses brought in by the evacuees. They say he has moments of doubt, when he realises that everything he's created here is a sham. That deep down inside he knows the vanishings are a rational phenomenon, not a miracle. That's when he has a new strain of the indoctrinal virus pumped back into his blood.'

'Difficult man to get to know, sounds like,' Scorpio observed.

'More difficult than we anticipated,' Vasko said. 'But Aura saw the way. It was her plan, Scorp, not ours.'

'And the plan was?'

'She went down there nine years ago,' Khouri said, looking straight at him, as if the two of them were alone in the room. 'She was eight years old, Scorp. I couldn't stop her. She knew what she'd been sent out into the world to do, and it was to find Quaiche.'

He shook his head. 'You didn't send an eight-year-old girl down there alone. Tell me you didn't do it.'

'We had no choice,' Khouri said. 'Trust me. I'm her mother. Trying to stop her from going down there was like trying to stop a salmon swimming upriver. It was going to happen whether we liked it or not.'

'We found a family,' Vasko said. 'Good people, living in the Vigrid badlands. They had a son, but they'd lost their only daughter in an accident a couple of years earlier. They didn't know who or what Aura was, only that they weren't to ask too many questions. They were also told to treat her exactly as if she'd always been with them. They fell into the role very easily, telling her stories of things that their other daughter had done when she was younger. They loved her very much.'

'Why the pretence?'

'Because she didn't remember who she really was,' Khouri said. 'She buried her own memories, suppressing them. She's halfway to being a Conjoiner. She can arrange her own head the way the rest of us arrange furniture. It wasn't all that difficult for her to do, once she realised it had to happen.'

'Why?' he asked.

'So that she'd fit in without her whole life becoming an act. If she believed she'd been born on Hela, so would the people she met.'

'That's horrific.'

'You think it was any easier for me, Scorp? I'm her mother. I was with her the day she decided to forget me. I walked into the same room as her and she barely noticed me.'

He gradually learned the rest of the story, doing his best to ignore the sense of unreality he felt. More than once he had to examine his surroundings, convincing himself that this was not just another revival nightmare. He felt foolish, having slept through all these machinations. But their story, or at least what he had been told of it, was seamless. It also had, he was forced to admit, a brutal inevitability. It had taken the *Nostalgia for Infinity* decades to reach Hela: more than forty years just travelling from Ararat via the Yellowstone system. But Aura's mission had begun long before that, when she was hatched within the matrix of the Hades neutron star. Given all the time that she had been on her way, an extra nine years was really not all that serious an addition. Yes: now that he put it like that, it all made a horrid kind of sense. But only if you chose not to view the universe through the eyes of a pig close to the end of his life.

'She didn't really forget anything,' Vasko said. 'It was just buried subconsciously, planted there to bubble up as she grew older. We knew that sooner or later she would start to be compelled by those hidden memories, even if she didn't know exactly what was going on herself.'

'And?' Scorpio asked.

'She sent us a signal. It was to warn us that she was on her way to meet Quaiche. That was our cue to start making approaches to the Adventists. By the time we got through to him, Aura had already worked her way into his confidence.'

The leather of Scorpio's jacket creaked as he folded his arms across his chest. 'She just strolled into his life?'

'She's his advisor,' Vasko said. 'Sits in on his dealings with Ultras. We don't know exactly what she's doing there, but we can guess. Aura had – has – a gift. We saw it even when she was a baby.'

'She can read our faces better than we can,' Khouri said, 'can tell if we're lying, if we're sad when we say we're happy. It doesn't have anything to do with her implants, and it won't have gone away just because she hid those memories of herself.'

'She must have drawn attention to herself,' Vasko said, 'made herself irresistible to Quaiche. But that was really just a short cut to his attention. Sooner or later she'd have found her way there, no matter what the obstacles. It was what she was born to do.'

'Did you talk to her?' Scorpio asked.

'No,' Vasko said. 'It wasn't possible. We couldn't let Quaiche suspect that we'd ever met. But Khouri has the same implants, with the same compatibilities.'

'I was able to dig into her memories,' Khouri said, 'once we were in the same room. It was close enough for direct contact between our implants without her suspecting anything.'

'You revealed yourself to her?' Scorpio asked.

'No. Not yet,' Khouri said. 'She's too vulnerable. It's safer if she doesn't remember everything straight away. That way she can continue to play the role Dean Quaiche expects of her. If he suspects she's an Ultra spy, she's in as much trouble as we are.'

'Let's hope no one takes too close an interest in her, then,' Scorpio said. 'How long are we looking at before she remembers everything on her own?'

'Days,' Khouri said. 'No more than that. Maybe less. The cracks must already be showing.'

'About these talks with the dean,' Scorpio said. 'Would you mind telling me exactly what was discussed?'

Vasko told him what he had talked about with the dean. Scorpio could tell that he was glossing over details, omitting anything not strictly essential. He learned of the dean's request for a ship to provide local defence duties for Hela, orbiting the planet, sponsored by the Adventists. He learned that many Ultras were unwilling to accept the contract even with the sweeteners Quaiche had offered. They were frightened that their ships would be damaged by whatever had destroyed the *Gnostic Ascension*, the ship that had originally brought Quaiche to Hela.

'But that isn't a problem for us,' Vasko said. 'The risk is probably overstated in any case, but even if something does take a pot shot at us, we're not exactly lacking defences. We've kept all the new technologies hidden ever since we approached the system, but that doesn't mean we can't turn them on again if we need them. I doubt that we'd have much to worry about from a few buried sentry weapons.'

'And for that protection, Quaiche is willing to let us take a closer look at Haldora?'

'Grudgingly,' Vasko said. 'He still doesn't like the idea of anyone poking sticks into the face of his miracle, but he wants that protection very badly.'

'Why is he so scared? Have other Ultras been causing trouble?'

Vasko shrugged. 'The occasional incident, but nothing serious.'

'Sounds like an overreaction, in that case.'

'It's his paranoia. There's no need to second-guess him, so long as it gives us a licence to get close to Haldora without firing a gun.'

'Something isn't right,' Scorpio said, his headache returning, having gone away and sharpened itself.

'You're naturally cautious,' Vasko said. 'There's no fault in that. But we've waited nine years for this. This is our one chance. If we don't take it, he'll make the contract with another ship.'

'I still don't like it.'

'Maybe you'd feel differently if it was your plan,' Urton said. 'But it's not. You were sleeping while we put this together.'

'That's all right,' he said, obliging her with a smile. 'I'm a pig. We don't do long-term plans anyway.'

'What she means is,' Vasko said, 'try to see it from our side. If you'd lived through all the years of waiting, you'd see things differently.' He leant back in his seat and shrugged. 'Anyway, what's done is done. I told Quaiche that we'd have to discuss the issue of the delegates, but other than that, all we're waiting for is the agreement to come through from his side. Then we can go on in.'

'Wait,' Scorpio said, raising his hand. 'Did you say delegates? What delegates?'

'Quaiche insists on it,' Vasko said. 'Says he'll need to station a small party of Adventists on the ship.'

'Over my dead body.'

'It's all right,' Urton said. 'The arrangement is reciprocal. The church sends up a party, we send one down to the cathedral. It's all above board.'

Scorpio sighed. What point was there in arguing? He was already tired, and all he had done was sit in on this discussion. This discussion in which everything was already agreed, and he was – to all intents and purposes – relegated to the role of passive observer. He could object all he wanted, but for all the difference he made he might as well have stayed in the reefersleep casket.

'You're making a serious mistake,' he said. 'Trust me on this.'

Hela Surface, 2727

Captain Seyfarth was a slight, unsmiling man with a small thin-lipped mouth ideally evolved for the registering of contempt. In fact, beyond his neutral calm, Quaiche had never known the captain of the Cathedral Guard to show any other emotion. Even Seyfarth's contempt was deployed sparingly, like a very expensive, difficult to procure item of military ordnance. It was usually in connection with his opinion of someone else's security arrangements. He was a man who liked his work very much, and little else. He was, in Quaiche's opinion, the perfect man for the job.

Standing in the garret, he wore the highly polished armour of the Guard, with his pink-plumed ceremonial vacuum helmet tucked under his arm. The ostentatiously flanged and recurved armour was the deep maroon of arterial blood. Many medals and ribbons had been painted on the chest-plate, commemorating the actions Sey-farth had led in defence of the Lady Morwenna's interests. Officially, they had all been above board and within the generally accepted rules of Way behaviour. He had fought off raiding parties of disgruntled villagers; he had repelled hostile actions by rogue trading elements, including small parties of Ultras. But there had been covert operations as well, matters too delicate to commemorate: pre-emptive sabotage of both the Permanent Way and other cathedrals; the discreet removal from the church hierarchy of progressive elements hostile to Quaiche. Assassination was too strong a word, but that, too, was within Seyfarth's repertoire of possible effects. He had the kind of past best left unmentioned. It included wars and war crimes.

But he remained fiercely loyal to Quaiche. In thirty-five years of service, there had been enough opportunities for Seyfarth to betray his master in return for personal advancement. It had never happened; all he cared about was the excellence with which he discharged his duty as Quaiche's protector.

It had still been a risk, all the same, for Quaiche to let him know of his plans in advance. Everyone else involved – even the master of holdfast construction – needed to know only certain details. Grelier knew nothing at all. But Seyfarth required an overview of the entire scheme. He was the one, after all, who was going to have to take the ship.

'It's going to happen, then,' Seyfarth said. 'I wouldn't have been called here otherwise.'

'I've found a willing candidate,' Quaiche said. 'More importantly, one that also suits *my* needs.' He passed Seyfarth a picture of the starship, captured by spy remotes. 'What do you think? Can you do the business?'

Seyfarth took his time studying the picture. 'I don't like the look of it,' he said. 'All that gothic ornamentation ... it looks like a chunk of the Lady Morwenna, flying through space.'

'All the more appropriate, then.'

'My objection stands.'

'You'll have to live with it. No two Ultra ships look alike, and we've seen stranger. Anyway, the holdfast can accommodate any hull profile, within reason. This won't pose any problems. And it's what's inside that really matters.'

'You've managed to put a spy aboard?'

'No,' Quaiche said. 'Too little time. But it doesn't matter. They've more or less agreed to accept a small party of Adventist observers. That's all we need.'

'And the condition of the engines?'

'Nothing to cause alarm. We observed her approach: everything looked clean and stable.'

Seyfarth was still studying the picture, his lips signalling the contempt Quaiche recognised so well. 'Where had she come from?'

'Could have been anywhere. We didn't see her until she was very near. Why?'

'There's something about this ship that I don't like.'

'You'd say that no matter which one I offered you. You're a born pessimist, Seyfarth: that's why you're so good at your work. But the matter is closed. The ship's already been selected.'

'Ultras aren't to be trusted,' he said. 'Now more than ever. They're as scared as everyone else.' He flicked the picture, making it crack. 'What is it *they* want, Quaiche? Have you asked yourself that?'

'What I'm giving them.'

'Which is?'

'Favoured trading incentives, first refusal on relics, that kind of thing. And . . .' He left the sentence unfinished.

'And what?'

'They're mainly interested in Haldora,' Quaiche said. 'They have some studies they'd like to make.'

Seyfarth watched him inscrutably; Quaiche felt as if he was being peeled open like a fruit. 'You've always denied anyone that kind of access in the past,' he said. 'Why the sudden change of heart?'

'Because,' Quaiche said, 'it doesn't really matter now. The vanishings are heading towards some sort of conclusion anyway. The word of God is about to be revealed whether we like it or not.'

'There's more to it than that.' Idly, Seyfarth ran one red gauntlet through the soft pink plume of his helmet. 'You don't care now, do you? Not now that your triumph is so close at hand.'

'You're wrong,' Quaiche said. 'I do care, more than ever. But perhaps this is God's way after all. The Ultras may even hasten the end of the vanishings by their interference.'

'The word of God revealed, on the eve of your victory? Is that what you're hoping for?'

'If that's the way it's meant to happen,' Quaiche said, with a fatalistic sigh, 'then who am I to stand in the way?'

Seyfarth returned the picture to Quaiche. He walked around the garret, his form sliced and shuffled by the intervening mirrors. His armour creaked with every footstep, his gauntleted fists opening and closing in neurotic rhythm.

'The advance party: how many delegates?'

'They agreed to twenty. Seemed unwise to try to talk them up. You can make do with twenty, can't you?'

'Thirty would have been better.'

'Thirty begins to look too much like an army. In any case, the twenty will only be there to make sure the ship's really worth taking. Once they've started softening things up, you can send in as many Cathedral Guard as you can spare.'

'I'll need authorisation to use whatever weapons I see fit.'

'I don't want you murdering people, Captain,' Quaiche said, raising a forbidding finger. 'Reasonable resistance may be dealt with, yes, but that doesn't mean turning the ship into a bloodbath. Pacify the security elements, by all means, but emphasise that we only want the loan of the ship: we're not stealing it. Once our work is done, they can have it back, with our gratitude. I need hardly add that you'd better make sure you deliver the ship to me in one piece.'

'I only asked for permission to use weapons.'

'Use whatever you see fit, Captain, provided you can smuggle it past the Ultras. They'll be looking for the usual: bombs, knives and guns. Even if we had access to anti-matter, we'd have a hard time getting it past them.'

'I've already made all the necessary arrangements,' Seyfarth said.

'I'm sure you have. But – please – show a modicum of restraint, all right?'

'And your magic advisor?' Seyfarth asked. 'What did she have to say on the matter?'

'She concluded there was nothing to worry about,' Quaiche said.

Seyfarth turned around, latching his helmet into place. The pink plume fell across the black strip of his faceplate. He looked both comical and fearsome, which was exactly the intended effect.

'I'll get to work, then.'

Nostalgia for Infinity, *Parking Swarm, 107 Piscium, 2727*

An hour later there was an official transmission from the Clocktower of the Lady Morwenna. The arrangement had been accepted by the Adventist party. Subject to the installation of twenty clerical observers aboard the *Nostalgia for Infinity*, the lighthugger was free to move into near-Hela space and commence the defence watch. Once the observers had come aboard and inspected the weapons setup, the crew would be permitted to make a limited physical study of the Haldora phenomenon.

The reply was sent back within thirty minutes. The terms were acceptable to the *Nostalgia for Infinity*, and the Adventist party would be welcomed aboard as the ship made its approach-spiral to Hela orbit. At the same time, an Ultra delegation would proceed by shuttle to the landing stage of the Lady Morwenna.

Thirty minutes after that, with a flicker of main drive thrust, the *Nostalgia for Infinity* broke station from the parking swarm.

FORTY

The threshing machinery of Motive Power seemed to salute Captain Seyfarth as he strode through the chamber, his gloved hands tucked behind his back. As the leader of the Cathedral Guard, he never counted on a warm welcome from the mechanically minded denizens of the propulsion department. While they had no instinctive dislike for him, they did have long memories: it was always Seyfarth's people who put down any rebellions within the Lady Morwenna's technical workforce. There were surprisingly few workers in the chamber now, but in his mind's eye Seyfarth sketched in the fallen bodies and injured victims of the last 'arbitration action', as the cathedral authorities had referred to the matter. Glaur, the shift boss he was looking for now, had never been directly linked to the rebellion, but it was clear from their infrequent dealings that Glaur had no love for either the Cathedral Guard or its chief.

'Ah, Glaur,' he said, catching sight of the man next to an open access panel.

'Captain. What a pleasure.'

Seyfarth made his way to the panel. Wires and cables hung from its innards, like disembowelled vitals. Seyfarth pulled the access hatch down so that it hung half-opened over the dangling entrails. Glaur started to say something – some useless protestation – but Seyfarth silenced him by touching a finger to his own lips. 'Whatever it is, it can wait.'

'You have no . . .'

'Bit quiet in here, isn't it?' Seyfarth said, looking around the chamber at the untended machines and empty catwalks. 'Where is everyone?'

'You know exactly where everyone is,' Glaur said. 'They got themselves off the Lady Mor as soon as they could. By the end of it they were charging a year's wages for a surface suit. I'm down to a skeleton crew now, just enough lads to keep the reactor sweet and the machines greased.'

'Those who left,' Seyfarth mused. It was happening all over the cathedral: even the Guard was having trouble stopping the exodus. 'They'd be in violation of contract, wouldn't they?'

Glaur looked at him incredulously. 'You think they give a damn about that, Captain? All that they care about is getting off this thing before we reach the bridge.'

Seyfarth could smell the man's fear boiling off him like a heat haze. 'You mean they don't think we'll make it?'

'Do you?'

'If the dean says we'll make it, who are we to doubt him?'

'I doubt him,' Glaur said, his voice a hiss. 'I know what happened the last time, and we're bigger and heavier. This cathedral isn't going to cross that bridge, Captain, no matter how much blood the surgeon-general pumps into us.'

'Fortunate, then, that I won't be on the Lady Morwenna when it happens,' Seyfarth said.

'You're leaving?' Glaur asked, suddenly keen.

Did he imagine, Seyfarth thought, that he was actually proposing rebellion? 'Yes, but on church business. Something that'll keep me away until the bridge is either crossed ... or it isn't. What about you?'

Glaur shook his head, stroking the filthy handkerchief he kept knotted around his neck. 'I'll stay, Captain.'

'Loyalty to the dean?'

'Loyalty to my machines, more like.'

Seyfarth touched him on the shoulder. 'I'm impressed. You wouldn't be tempted, not even once, to steer the cathedral from the Way, or to sabotage the motors?'

Glaur's teeth flashed. 'I'm here to do a job.'

'It'll kill you.'

'Then maybe I'll leave at the last moment. But this cathedral's staying on the Way.'

'Good man. We'd better make sure of that, all the same.'

Glaur looked into his eyes. 'I'm sorry, Captain?'

'Walk me to the lock-out controls, Glaur.'

'No.'

Seyfarth seized him by the neckerchief, lifted him half his height from the ground. Glaur choked, flailing his fists uselessly against Seyfarth's chest.

'Walk me to the lock-out controls,' Seyfarth repeated, his voice still calm.

*

The surgeon-general's private shuttle made its own approach, squatting down on a stiletto of fusion thrust. The landing pad Grelier had selected was a small, derelict affair on the outskirts of the Vigrid settlement. His red cockleshell of a ship came to rest with a pronounced lean, the pad's surface subsiding into the ground. The pad clearly saw very little traffic: it might easily have been decades since anything larger than a robot supply drone had landed on it.

Grelier gathered his belongings and exited his ship. The pad was decrepit, but the walkway leading away from it was still more or less serviceable. Tapping his cane against the fractured craquelure of the concrete surface, he made his way to the nearest public entrance point. The airlock, when he tried it, refused to open. He resorted to the all-purpose Clocktower key – it was supposed to open just about any door on Hela – but that didn't work either. Gloomily he concluded that the door was simply broken, its mechanism failed.

He followed the trail for another ten minutes, casting around until he found a lock that actually worked. He was near the centre of the little buried hamlet now; the topside was a confusion of parked vehicles, abandoned equipment modules, scorched and broken-faceted solar collectors. This was all very well, but the closer he was to the heart of the settlement, the more likely he was to be discovered going about his business.

No matter: it had to be done, and he had exhausted the alternatives. Still suited, he cycled through the airlock and then descended a vertical ladder. This brought him into a dimly lit tunnel network, with corridors radiating in five different directions. Fortunately, they were colour-coded, indicating the residential and industrial districts they led to. Except districts wasn't really the right word, Grelier thought. This tiny community, though it might have enjoyed social ties with others in the badlands, was smaller in population than one floor of the Lady Morwenna.

He hummed as he walked. As bothered as he was by recent events, he always enjoyed being on Clocktower business. Even if, as now, the business was verging on the personal, a mission the precise reason for which Grelier had not told the dean.

Fair enough, he said to himself. If the dean kept secrets from him, then he would keep secrets from the dean.

Quaiche was up to something. Grelier had suspected as much for months, but the girl's remarks about witnessing the construction fleet had clinched it. Although Grelier had done his best to dismiss her observation, it had continued to gnaw at him. It chimed with other odd things that he had noticed lately. The skimping on Way maintenance, for instance. They had got stuck behind the ice block-age precisely because Way maintenance lacked the usual resources to clear it. Quaiche had been forced to deploy nuclear demolition charges: God's Fire.

At the time, Grelier had put it down to nothing more than a happy coincidence. But the more he thought about it, the less likely that seemed. Quaiche had wanted to make his announcement about taking the Lady Morwenna over the bridge with the maximum fanfare. What better way to underline his words than with a dose of God's Fire shining through his newly installed stained-glass window?

The use of God's Fire had only been justified because Way main-tenance was already stretched. But what if Way maintenance was stretched precisely because Quaiche had ordered the diversion of its equipment and manpower?

Another thought occurred to Grelier: the blockage itself might even have been orchestrated. Quaiche had blamed it on sabotage by another church, but Quaiche could easily have arranged it himself. It would only have been a question of laying fuses and explosives the last time the Lady Mor went through.

A year earlier.

Did he honestly think Quaiche had been planning something all that time? Well, perhaps. People who built cathedrals tended to take the long view, after all.

Grelier still couldn't see where all this was heading. All he knew – with a growing conviction – was that Quaiche was keeping some-thing from him.

Something to do with the Ultras?

Something to do with the bridge crossing?

Events did after all seem to be rushing towards some grand cul-mination. And then there was the girl. Where did she fit into all this? Grelier could have sworn he had picked her, not the other way around. But now he was not so certain. She had made herself conspicuous to him, that much was true. It was like that trick they did with cards, suggesting the one you were meant to take from the spread.

Of course, he'd have had no suspicions if her blood had checked out.

'It's a wee bit of a puzzle,' he said to himself.

He stopped suddenly, for in his cogitations he had walked straight past the address he was looking for. He backtracked, grateful that no one else seemed to be about at this hour. He had no idea what the local time was, whether everyone was asleep, or down at the scuttler mines.

Didn't care, either.

He opened his helmet visor, ready to introduce himself, and then rapped his cane smartly against the outer door of the Els residence. And then waited, humming to himself, until he heard the door opening.

Hela Orbit, 2727

The Adventist delegates had arrived at the *Nostalgia for Infinity*. There were twenty of them, all seemingly stamped from the same production mould. They came aboard with apparent trepidation, their politeness exaggerated to the point of insolence. They wore hard-shelled scarlet vacuum suits marked with the cruciform spacesuit insignia of their church, and they all carried their pink-plumed helmets tucked under the same arm.

Scorpio studied their leader through the window in the inner airlock door. He was a small man with a cruel, petulant slot of a mouth seemingly cut into his face as an afterthought.

'I'm Brother Seyfarth,' the man announced.

'Glad to have you aboard, Brother,' Scorpio said, 'but before we let you into the rest of the ship, we're going to have to run some decontamination checks.'

The man's voice rattled through the speaker grille. 'Still concerned about plague traces? I thought we all had other things to worry about these days.'

'Can't be too careful,' Scorpio said. 'It's nothing personal, of course.'

'I wouldn't dream of complaining,' Brother Seyfarth replied.

In truth, they had been scanned from the moment they entered the *Infinity's* airlock. Scorpio had to know whether there was anything hidden under that armour, and if there was, he had to know what it was.

He had studied the *Nostalgia for Infinity's* history. Once, when the ship had been under the command of its old triumvirate, they had made the mistake of allowing someone aboard with a tiny anti-matter device implanted in the mechanism of their artificial eyes. That pin-sized weapon had enabled the entire ship to be hijacked. Scorpio didn't blame Volyova and the others for having made that mistake: such devices were both rare and exquisitely difficult to manufacture, and you didn't encounter them very often. But it was not the kind of mistake he was going to allow on his watch, if there was anything he could do to stop it.

Elsewhere in the ship, Security Arm officers examined the spectral images of the scanned delegates, peering through smoky grey-green layers of armour to the flesh, blood and bone beneath. There were no obvious concealed weapons: no guns or knives. But that didn't surprise Scorpio. Even if the delegates had ill intentions, they'd have known that even a cursory scan would pick up normal weapons. If they had anything, it was going to be a lot less obvious.

But perhaps they had nothing at all. Perhaps they were what they said they were, and nothing more. Perhaps he was only objecting to the delegates because he had not been consulted before they were allowed aboard.

But there was something about Brother Seyfarth that he didn't like, something in the cruel set of his mouth that made him think of other violent men he had known. Something in the way he kept clenching and unclenching the metal fists of his gloves as he waited to be processed through the airlock.

Scorpio touched his earpiece. 'Clear on concealed weapons,' he heard. 'Clear on chemical traces for explosives, toxins or nerve agents. Clear on standard nanotech filters. Nothing pre-plague here, and no plague traces either.'

'Look for implants,' he said, 'any mechanisms under those suits that don't serve an obvious function. And check the ones that do, as well. I don't want hot dust within a light-year of this ship.'

He was asking a lot of them, he knew. They couldn't risk annoying the delegates by subjecting them to an obvious invasive examination. But – again – this was *his* watch. He had a reputation to live up to. It hadn't been him who had invited the fuckers aboard.

'Clear on implants,' he heard. 'Nothing large enough to contain a standard pinhead device.'

'Meaning that none of the delegates have implants of any kind?'

'Like I said, sir, nothing large enough ...'

'Tell me about *all* the implants. We can't assume anything.'

'One of them has something in his eye. Another has a prosthetic hand. A total of half a dozen very small neural implants spread throughout the whole delegation.'

'I don't like the sound of any of that.'

'The implants aren't anything we wouldn't expect to see in a random sample of Hela refugees, sir. Most of them look inactive, anyway.'

'The one with the eye, the one with the hand – I want to know for sure that there isn't any nasty stuff inside those things.'

'Going to be tricky, sir. They might not like it if we start bombarding them with protons. If there *is* anti-matter in those things, there'll be local cell damage from the spallation products . . .'

'If there is anti-matter in those things, they're going to have a lot more than cancer to worry about,' Scorpio said.

Trouble was, so would he.

He waited as the man sent a mantislike servitor into the airlock, a bright-red stick-limbed contraption equipped with a proton beam generator. Scorpio told the delegates it was just a more refined form of the plague scanners they had already used, designed to sniff out some of the less common strains. They probably knew this was a lie, but agreed to go along with it for the sake of avoiding a scene. Was that a good sign? he wondered.

The proton beam drilled through flesh and bone, too narrow to hurt major bodily structures. At worst, it would inflict some local tissue damage. But if it touched anti-matter, even a microgram nugget of anti-matter suspended in vacuum in an electromagnetic cradle, it would induce a burst of proton–antiproton reactions.

The servitor listened for the back-scatter of gamma rays, the incriminating sizzle of annihilation.

It heard nothing: not from the hand, not from the eye.

'They're clean, sir,' the SA operative announced into Scorpio's earpiece.

No, he thought, they weren't. At least, he couldn't be sure of it. He'd ruled out the obvious, done what he could. But the proton beam might have missed the cradles: there hadn't been time to make an exhaustive sweep of either the hand or the eye. Or the cradles themselves might have been surrounded with deflection or absorption barriers: he'd heard of such things. Or the nuggets could be in the neural implants, hidden behind too many centimetres of bone and tissue for non-surgical scanning.

'Sir? Permission to let them through?'

Scorpio knew that there was nothing else he could do except keep a close watch on them.

'Open the door,' he said.

Brother Seyfarth stepped through the aperture and stood eye to eye with Scorpio. 'Don't trust us, sir?'

'Got a job to do,' Scorpio said. 'That's all.'

The leader nodded gravely. 'Don't we all? Well, no hard feelings. I take it you didn't find anything suspicious?'

'I didn't *find* anything, no.'

The man winked at him, as if the two of them were sharing a joke. The other nineteen delegates bustled through, Scorpio's distorted reflection gleaming back at him in the buffed and polished plates of their armour. He looked worried.

Now that they were aboard he had to keep them where he wanted them. They didn't need to see the whole of the ship, just the parts that related to their specific areas of interest. No tour of the cache weapon chambers, no tour of the hypometric weapon shafts or any of the other modifications installed after their departure from Ararat. He'd be careful to keep the delegates away from the weirder manifestations of the Captain's transforming illness, too, although some of the changes were always going to be apparent. They bobbed along behind him like twenty ducklings, showing emphatic interest in everything he stopped to point out.

'Interesting interior design you have here,' the leader said, fingering – with vague distaste – a riblike extrusion sticking out from a wall. 'We always knew that your ship looked a little odd from the outside, but we never imagined you'd have extended the theme all the way through.'

'It grows on you,' Scorpio said.

'I don't suppose it makes very much difference, from our point of view. As long as the ship does what you've claimed it can, who are we to care about the décor?'

'What you really care about is our hull defences and long-range sensors, I imagine,' Scorpio said.

'Your technical specifications were very impressive,' Brother Seyfarth said. 'Naturally, we'll have to double-check. The security of Hela depends on our knowing that you can deliver the protection you promised.'

'I don't think you need lose any sleep over that,' Scorpio said.

'You're not offended, I hope?'

The pig turned back to him. 'Do I look like someone easily offended?'

'Not at all,' Seyfarth said, his fists clenching.

They were uneasy around him, Scorpio realised. He doubted that they saw many pigs on Hela. 'We're not great travellers,' he elaborated. 'We tend to die on the way.'

'Sir?' asked one of the other delegates. 'Sir, if it isn't too much bother, we'd really like to see the engines.'

Scorpio checked the time. They were on schedule. In fewer than six hours he would be able to launch the two instrument packages into Haldora. They were simply modified automated drones, hardened slightly to tolerate passage into the atmosphere of a gas giant. No one was exactly certain what they would encounter when they hit the visible surface of Haldora, but it seemed prudent to take every precaution, even if the planet popped like a soap bubble.

'You want to see the engines?' he said. 'No problem. No problem at all.'

The light from Hela's sun was low on the horizon, casting the cathedral's great gothic shadow far ahead of it. It was more than two days since Vasko and Khouri had first visited Quaiche, and in the intervening time the Lady Morwenna had nearly reached the western edge of the rift. The bridge lay before it: a sparkling, dreamlike confection of sugar-ice and gossamer. Now that they were so close to it, the cathedral looked heavier, the bridge less substantial, the very idea of taking one across the other even more absurd.

A thought occurred to Vasko: what if the bridge didn't exist any more? It was a foolhardy thing to take the Lady Morwenna across such a fragile structure, but in Quaiche's mind there must have been at least a glimmer of hope that he might succeed. But if the bridge was destroyed, surely he wouldn't take the cathedral over the edge, to certain destruction?

'How far?' Khouri asked.

'Twelve, thirteen kilometres,' Vasko said. 'She travels about a kilometre per hour, which gives us around half a day before it really wouldn't be a good idea to be aboard any more.'

'That doesn't give us much time.'

'We don't need much time,' he said. 'Twelve hours should be more than enough time to get in and out. All we have to do is find Aura, and whatever we need from Quaiche. How difficult can it be?'

'Scorpio needs time to drop those instrument packages into Haldora,' she said. 'If we break our side of the agreement before he's done, there's no telling how much trouble we'll be in. Things could start getting messy. That's exactly what we spent nine years trying to avoid.'

'It'll be all right,' Vasko said. 'Trust me on this, it'll be all right.'

'Scorp didn't like the idea of those delegates,' she said.

'They're church dignitaries,' Vasko said. 'How much of a problem can they be?'

'In these matters,' Khouri said, 'I'm inclined to trust Scorpio's judgement. Sorry, but he's got a bit more mileage on him than you have.'

'I'm getting there,' Vasko said.

Their shuttle picked its way down to the cathedral. It grew from something small and delicate, like an ornate architectural model, to something huge and threatening. Something more than a building, Vasko thought: more like a pinnacled chunk of the landscape that had decided to make a slow circumnavigation of its world.

They landed. Suited Adventist officials were there to usher them deep into the iron heart of the Lady Morwenna.

FORTY-ONE

Hela, 2727

At long last, Quaiche could see the bridge for himself. The spectacle sent a shiver of excitement through him. There was less ground to cover to reach it now than the span of the bridge itself. Everything he had planned, everything he had schemed into existence, was now tantalisingly close to fruition.

'Look at it, Rashmika,' he said, inviting the girl to stand by the garret window and admire the view for herself. 'So ancient, yet so sparklingly ageless. From the moment I announced that we were to cross the rift, I've been counting every second. We're not there yet, but at least now I can see it.'

'Are you really going to do it?' she asked.

'You think I've come all this way just to back down now? Not likely. The prestige of the church is at stake, Rashmika. Nothing matters more to me than that.'

'I wish I could read your face,' she said. 'I wish I could see your eyes and I wish Grelier hadn't deadened all your nerve endings. Then I'd know if you were telling the truth.'

'You don't believe me?'

'I don't know what to believe,' she said.

'I'm not asking you to believe anything,' he said, turning his couch around so that all the mirrors had to adjust their angles. 'I've never asked you to submit to faith, Rashmika. All I've ever asked of you is honest judgement. What troubles you, all of a sudden?'

'I need to know the truth,' she said. 'Before you take this thing over the bridge, I want some answers.'

His eyes quivered in their sockets. 'I've always been open with you.'

'Then what about the vanishing that never happened? Was that you, Dean? Did *you* make that happen?'

'Make that happen?' he echoed, as if her words made no sense at all.

'You had a lapse of faith, didn't you? A crisis during which you began to think that there was a rational explanation for the van-ishings after all. Maybe you'd developed immunity to whatever was the strongest indoctrinal virus Grelier could offer you that week.'

'Be very, very careful, Rashmika. You're useful to me, but you're far from indispensable.'

She gathered her composure. 'What I mean is, did you decide to test your faith? Did you arrange for an instrument package to be dropped into the face of Haldora, at the moment of a vanishing?'

His eyes became quite still, regarding her intently. 'What do you think?'

'I think you sent something into Haldora – a machine, a probe of some kind. Perhaps some Ultras sold it to you. You hoped to glimpse something in there. What, I don't know. Maybe something you'd already glimpsed years earlier, but which you didn't want to admit to yourself.'

'Ridiculous.'

'But you succeeded,' she said. 'The probe *did* something: it caused the vanishing to be prolonged. You threw a spanner in, Dean, and you got a reaction. The probe encountered something when the planet vanished. It made contact with whatever the planet was meant to conceal. And whatever it was had precious little to do with miracles.' He started to say something, tried to cut her off, but she forced herself to continue, speaking over him. 'I have no idea whether the probe came back or not, but I do know that you're still in contact with something. You opened a window, didn't you?' Rashmika pointed at the welded metal suit, the one that had disturbed her so much on her first visit to the garret. 'They're in there, trapped within it. You made a prison of the same suit in which Morwenna died.'

'Why would I do that?' Quaiche asked.

'Because,' she said, 'you don't know if they're demons or angels.'

'And you do know, I take it?'

'I think they might be both,' she said.

Hela Orbit, 2727

Scorpio whisked back a heavy metal shutter, revealing a tiny oval porthole. The scuffed and scratched glass was as thick and dark as burned sugar. He pushed himself away from the window.

'You'll have to take turns,' he said.

They were in a zero-gravity section of the *Infinity*. It was the only way to view the engines while the ship was in orbit, since the rotating sections of the ship that provided artificial gravity were set too deeply back into the hull to permit observation of the engines. Had the engines themselves been pushed up to their usual one-gee of thrust – providing the illusion of gravity by another means throughout the entire ship – the orbit around Hela could not have been sustained.

'We'd like to see them fire up, if that's possible,' Brother Seyfarth said.

'Not exactly standard procedure while we're holding orbit,' Scorpio said.

'Just for a moment,' Seyfarth said. 'They don't have to operate at full capacity.'

'I thought it was the defences you were interested in.'

'Those as well.'

Scorpio spoke into his cuff. 'Give me a burst of drive, counteracted by the steering jets. I don't want to feel this ship move *one inch*.'

The order was implemented almost instantly. Theoretically, one of his people had to send the command into the ship's control system, whereupon Captain Brannigan might or might not choose to act upon it. But he suspected that the Captain had made the engines fire before the command had ever been entered.

The great ship groaned as the engines lit up. Through the dark glass of the porthole, the exhaust was a scratch of purple-white – visible only because the stealthing modifications to the drives had been switched off during the *Nostalgia for Infinity*'s final approach to the system. At the other end of the hull, multiple batteries of conventional fusion rockets were balancing the thrust from the main drives. The ancient hull creaked and moaned like some vast living thing as it absorbed the compressive forces. The ship could take a lot more punishment than this, Scorpio knew, but he was still grateful when the drive flame flicked out. He felt a tiny lurch, evidence of the minutest lack of synchrony between the shutting down of the fusion rockets and the drives, but then all was motionless. The great, saurian protestations of stressed ship fabric died away like diminishing thunder.

'Good enough for you, Brother Seyfarth?'

'I think so,' the leader said. 'They seem to be in excellent condition. You wouldn't believe how difficult it is to find well-maintained Conjoiner drives now that their makers are no longer with us.'

'We do our best,' Scorpio said. 'Of course, it's the weapons you're really interested in, isn't it? Shall I show them to you, and then we can call it a day? There'll be plenty of time for a more detailed examination later.' He was fed up with small talk, fed up with showing the twenty intruders around his empire.

'Actually,' Brother Seyfarth said, when they were safely back inside one of the rotating sections, 'we're more interested in the engines than we admitted.'

There was an itch at the back of Scorpio's neck. 'You are?'

'Yes,' Seyfarth said, nodding to the nineteen others.

In one smoothly choreographed blur, the twenty delegates touched parts of their suits, causing them to fly apart in irregular scablike pieces, as if spring-loaded. The hard-shelled components rained down around them, clattering in untidy piles at their feet. Beneath the suits, as he already knew from the scans, they wore only flimsy inner layers.

He wondered what he had missed. There were still no obvious weapons; still no guns or knives.

'Brother,' he said, 'think very carefully about this.'

'I've already thought about it,' Seyfarth replied. Along with the other delegates, he knelt down and – his hands still gloved – rummaged with quick efficiency through the pile of sloughed suit parts.

His fist rose clutching something sharp-edged and aerodynamically formed. It was a shard of suit, viciously curved along its leading edge. Seyfarth raised himself on one knee and flicked his wrist. Tumbling end over end, the projectile wheeled through the air towards Scorpio. He heard it coming: the *chop, chop, chop* of its whisking approach. The fraction of a second of its flight stretched to a subjective eternity. A small, plaintive voice – lacking any tone of recrimination – told him it had been the suits all along. He had been looking so hard *through* them, so convinced they had to be hiding something, that he had missed the suits themselves.

The suits were the weapons.

The tumbling thing speared into his shoulder, the brutality of its impact knocking him against the slick, ribbed side of the corridor. It pinned him, through leather and flesh, to the wall itself. He thrashed in pain, but the shard had anchored itself firmly.

Seyfarth stood up, a bladed weapon in each hand. There was nothing accidental about them: their lines were too spare and deliberate for that. The suits must have been primed to fall apart along precise flaw lines etched into them with ångström precision.

'I'm sorry I had to do that,' he said.

'You're a dead man.'

'And you'd be a dead pig if I'd intended to kill you.' Scorpio knew it was true: the casual way Seyfarth had tossed the weapon towards him had betrayed an easy fluency in its use. It would have cost him no more effort to sever Scorpio's head. 'But instead I've spared you. I'll spare all your crew if we have the co-operation we request.'

'No one's co-operating with anything. And you won't get far with knives, no matter how clever you think you are.'

'It's not just knives,' Seyfarth said.

Behind him, two of the other Adventist delegates stood up. They were holding something between them: a rig containing the lashed-together parts of their air-tanks. One of them was pointing the open nozzle of a hose in Scorpio's direction.

'Show him,' Seyfarth said, 'just so he gets the picture.'

Fire roared from the nozzle, jetting five or six metres beyond the pair of Adventists. The curving plume of the flame scythed against the corridor wall, blistering the surface. Again the ship groaned. Then the flames died, the only sound the hiss of fuel escaping from the nozzle.

'This is a bit of a surprise,' Scorpio said.

'Do what we say and no one will come to any harm,' Seyfarth said. Behind him, the other delegates were looking around: they had heard that groan as well. Perhaps they thought the ship was still settling down after the drive burn, creaking like an old house after sunset.

The moment stretched. Scorpio felt strangely calm. Perhaps, he thought, that was what being old did to you. 'You've come to take my ship?' he asked.

'Not *take* it,' Seyfarth said, with urgent emphasis. 'We just want to borrow it for a while. When we're finished, you can have it back.'

'I think you picked the wrong ship,' Scorpio said.

'On the contrary,' Seyfarth replied, 'I think we picked exactly the right ship. Now stay there, like a good pig, and we'll all come away from this as friends.'

'You can't seriously expect to take my ship with just twenty of you.'

'No,' Seyfarth said. 'That would be silly, wouldn't it?'

Scorpio tried to free himself. He could not move his arm enough to bring the communicator up to his face. The weapon had pinned him too tightly. He shifted, the pain of movement like so many shards of glass twisting within his shoulder. It was *that* shoulder: the one he had burned.

Seyfarth shook his head. 'What did I say about being a good pig?' He knelt down, examined another weapon, something like a dagger this time. He walked slowly over to Scorpio. 'I've never been overly fond of pigs, truth be told.'

'Suits me.'

'You're quite an old one, aren't you? What are you – forty, fifty years old?'

'Young enough to take the shine off your day, pal.'

'We'll see about that.'

Seyfarth stabbed the dagger in, impaling Scorpio through the other shoulder in more or less the corresponding position. Scorpio yelped in pain: a high-pitched squeal that sounded nothing like a human scream.

'I can't claim an exhaustive knowledge of pig anatomy,' Seyfarth said. 'All being well, I haven't severed anything I shouldn't have. But if I were you, I'd play it safe and not wriggle about too much.'

Scorpio tried to move, but gave up before the tears of pain blocked his view. Behind Seyfarth, another pair of delegates test-fired their makeshift flame-thrower. Then the whole party split into two groups and moved away into the rest of the ship, leaving Scorpio alone.

FORTY-TWO

Hela, 2727

A rapture of black machines climbed from the surface of Hela. They were small shuttles for the most part: surface-to-orbit vehicles bought, stolen, impounded and purloined from Ultras. Most had only chemical drives; a very few had fusion motors. The majority carried only one or two members of the Cathedral Guard, packed into armoured bubbles within their stripped-down skeletal chassis. They lifted from orthodox landing stages along the Way, or from concealed bunkers in the ice itself, dislodging plaques of surface frost as they fled. Some even departed from the superstructures of the Adventist cathedrals, including the Lady Morwenna. What had appeared to be small subsidiary spires or elbowed out-jutting towers were suddenly revealed as long-concealed spacecraft. Shells of mock architecture fell away like dead grey foliage. Complex cantilevered gantries swung the ships away from delicate masonry and glass before their drives lit. Domes and cupolas opened along ridge-lines, revealing ships packed tightly within, now rising on hydraulic launch platforms. When the ships hauled themselves aloft, the glare of their motors etched bright highlights and pitch-dark shadows into the ornate frippery of the architecture. Gargoyles seemed to turn their heads, their jaws lolling in wonderment and surprise. Below, the cathedrals trembled at the violent departure of so much mass. But when the ships had gone, the cathedrals were still there, little changed.

In seconds, the ships of the Guard had reached orbit; in several more seconds they had identified and signalled their brethren who were already parked around Hela. From every direction, drives flicked on to engagement thrust. The ships grouped into formations, stacked themselves into assault waves and commenced their run towards the *Nostalgia for Infinity*.

Even as the ships of the Cathedral Guard were leaving Hela, another spacecraft settled on to the pad of the Lady Morwenna, parking alongside the larger shuttle that had brought the Ultra delegates down from their lighthugger.

Grelier sat inside the cockpit for several minutes, flicking ivory-tipped toggle switches and making sure that vital systems would continue to tick over even in his absence. The cathedral was alarmingly close to the bridge now, and he had no plans to stay aboard once it had commenced the crossing. He would find an excuse to leave: Clocktower duty, something to do with Bloodwork. There were dozens of likely reasons he could give. And if the dean decided that he would much rather have the surgeon-general's company for the crossing, then Grelier would just have to do a runner and smooth things over later. If, of course, there turned out to *be* a later. But the one thing he did not want to have to wait for was for his ship to go through its pre-flight cycle.

He snapped his helmet on, gathered his belongings and cycled through the airlock. Outside, standing on the pad, he had to admit that the view was awesome. He could see the point where the land just ended, that vast cliff edge towards which they were sliding. Unstoppable now, he thought. Under any circumstances even slowing the progress of the Lady Morwenna was a matter of labyrinthine bureaucratic procedure. It could take many hours for the paperwork to filter down to the Motive Power technicians who actually had their hands on the motor controls. More often than not, conditioned to believe that the cathedral should never slow, they queried their orders, sending the paperwork echoing back up through the chain of command, resulting in more hours of delay. And what the cathedral needed now was not to slow down but to come to a complete standstill. Grelier shuddered: he didn't want to think about how long it would take for *that* to happen.

Something caught his eye. He looked up, seeing countless sparks zip across the sky. Dozens – no, hundreds – of ships. What was going on?

Then he looked towards the horizon and saw the much larger bulk of the lighthugger, a small but visibly elongated sliver of twinkling iron-grey. The other ships were obviously heading towards it.

Something was up.

Grelier turned from the shuttle, anxious to make his way indoors and find out what was happening. Then he noticed the smudge of red on the end of his cane. He thought he had cleaned it thoroughly before leaving the settlement in the Vigrid region, but evidently he had been remiss.

Tutting to himself, he wiped the end of the cane against the frost-covered surface of the landing pad, leaving smears of pink.

Then he set off to find the dean, for he had interesting news to deliver.

Orca Cruz saw the two Adventists before the rest of her party. They were at the end of a wide, low-ceilinged corridor, one against each wall, moving towards her with the measured pace of sleepwalkers.

Cruz turned to the three Security Arm officers behind her. 'Minimum necessary force,' she said quietly. 'Bayonets and stun-prods only. This lot don't have a flame-gun, and I'd really like to do some questioning.'

The Arm unit nodded in unison. They all knew what Cruz meant by that.

She started towards the Adventists, pushing the sharp blade of her weapon before her. The Adventists had little armour now. Garbled reports from the other elements of the Security Arm – the same messages that had warned her about the flame-throwers – had suggested that they had removed their vacuum suits, but she had not been prepared to believe it until she saw it with her own eye. But they hadn't discarded the armour entirely: they carried jagged bits of it in their hands, and had lashed large curved parts to their chests. They still wore their metal gloves and pink-plumed helmets.

She admired the thinking behind their strategy. Once a boarding party had reached this far inside a lighthugger, armour was largely superfluous. Ultras would be very unwilling to deploy energy weapons against boarders even if they knew themselves to be safely distant from vacuum or ship-critical systems. The instinct not to harm their own ship was just too deeply ingrained, even when the ship was under threat of takeover. And aboard a ship like the *Nostalgia for Infinity* – with every inch of the ship's fabric wired into the Captain's nervous system – that instinct was all the stronger. They had all seen what happened when some accident inflicted a wound in the ship; they had all felt the Captain's pain.

Cruz advanced down the corridor. 'Put down your weapons,' she called. 'You know you can't succeed.'

'Put down *your* weapons,' one of the Adventists replied, chidingly. 'We only want your ship. No one will be harmed, and the ship will be returned to you.'

'You could have asked nicely,' Cruz said.

'Would you have been likely to agree?'

'Not very,' she said, after a moment's reflection.

'Then I think we have nothing else to say to each other.'

Cruz's party moved forwards to within ten metres of the Adventists. She noticed that one of them was not in fact wearing a gauntlet at all; his hand was artificial. She remembered him: Scorpio had gone to extra pains to make sure the hand did not contain an anti-matter bomb.

'Final warning,' she said.

The other Adventist flung a bladed weapon towards her. It gyred through the air; Cruz threw herself back against the wall and felt the sharp, brief breeze as the weapon whisked past her throat and buried itself in the wall. Another weapon spun through the air; she heard it glance against body armour without finding a weak spot.

'All right, game over,' Cruz said. She gestured to her people. 'Pacification strength. Take 'em down.'

They pushed ahead of her, bayonets and snub-nosed stun-prods at the ready. The Adventist with the artificial hand pointed it in Cruz's direction, like an admonition. It didn't worry her: Scorpio's examination had been thorough; the hand couldn't possibly contain a concealed projectile or beam weapon.

The tip of the index finger came off. It detached from the rest of the finger, but instead of dropping to the ground it just floated there, slowly drifting away from the hand like a spacecraft on a lazy departure.

Cruz watched it, stupidly transfixed. The tip accelerated, travelled ten, twenty centimetres. It approached her party, bobbing slightly, and then yawed to the right as the hand moved, as if still connected to it by an invisible thread.

Which, she realised, it was.

'Monofilament scythe,' she shouted. 'Fall back. *Fall the fuck back!*'

Her party got the message. They retreated from the Adventists even as the tip of the finger began to move in a vertical circle, seemingly of its own volition. The man's hand was making tiny, effortless movements. The circle widened, the tip of the finger becoming a blurred grey ring a metre wide. In Chasm City, Orca Cruz had seen the grotesque results of scythe weapons. She had seen what happened when people blundered into static scythe defence lines, or moving scythes like the one being demonstrated here. It was never pretty. But what she remembered, more than the screams, more than the hideously sculpted and segregated corpses left behind, was the expression she always saw on the faces of the victims an instant after they'd realised their mistake. It was less fright, less shock, more acute embarrassment: the realisation that they were about to make a terrible, sickening spectacle of themselves.

'Fall back,' she repeated.

'Permission to fire,' one of her party said.

Cruz shook her head. 'Not yet,' she said. 'Not until we're cornered.'

The whisking blur of the scythe advanced further down the corridor, emitting a high-pitched quavering note that was almost musical.

Scorpio tried again, shifting his weight as much as he was able, to prise himself away from the wall. He had given up calling for help and had long since stopped paying attention to his own yelps and squeals. The Adventist delegates had not returned, but they were still out there: intermittently, the muffled sounds of battle reached him through the echoing labyrinth of corridors, ducts and elevator shafts. He heard shouts and screams, and very occasionally he heard the basso groan of the ship itself, responding to some niggling internal injury. Nothing that the delegates did – either with their cutting tools or their flame-throwers – could possibly inflict any real harm upon the Captain. The *Nostalgia for Infinity* had survived a direct attack by one of its own cache weapons, after all. But even a tiny splinter could become an irritation out of all proportion to its physical size.

He thrashed again, feeling savage fire in both shoulders. There: something was beginning to give, wasn't it? Was it him or the throwing weapons?

He tried again, and blacked out. He came around seconds or possibly minutes later, still pinned to the wall, an unpleasant metallic taste in his mouth. He was still alive, and – pain aside – he didn't feel much worse than when Seyfarth had stuck him here. He supposed there must have been something in Seyfarth's boast about not damaging any of his internal organs. But there was no guarantee that Scorpio wouldn't start bleeding all over the place as soon as the weapons were removed. Why were the Security Arm taking so long to find him?

Twenty soldiers, he thought. That was enough to make trouble, no doubt about it, but they couldn't possibly hope to take the entire ship. They had known all along that they could not smuggle serious firepower aboard the *Nostalgia for Infinity*, not in these hair-trigger times. But Seyfarth had struck him as a man who knew what he was doing, very unlikely to have volunteered for a futile suicide mission.

Scorpio groaned: not with pain, this time, but with the realisation that he had made a dreadful mistake. He couldn't be blamed for letting the delegates aboard: he had been overruled on that one, and if he had missed the true nature of their armour, it was only because he had never heard of anyone using that particular trick before. Anyway, he *had* scanned the armour – even if he'd been looking through, rather than at it – and he'd seen nothing suspicious. The armour would have to have been removed and examined in a lab before the microscopic flaws and weak points would have revealed themselves. No: that wasn't his mistake either. But he really shouldn't have turned on the engines. Why had the Adventists needed to see them? They'd already observed the ship making its approach to the system, if that was what they were interested in.

What they were really interested in, if he read them rightly, was something else entirely: they had been using the engines to send a signal to Hela. The burst of thrust meant they were in place – that they had passed through his security arrangements and were ready to begin the takeover operation.

It was a signal to send in reinforcements.

Even as that thought crystallised in his head, he heard the ship groan again. But it was a different kind of groan this time. It was more like the sonorous off-key tolling of a very large, very cracked bell.

Scorpio closed his eyes: he knew exactly what that sound was. It was the hull defences: the *Nostalgia for Infinity* was under attack from outside as well as from within. *Great*, he thought. This was really shaping up to be one of those days when he should have stayed inside the reefersleep casket. Or, better still, should never have survived thawing in the first place.

A moment later, the entire fabric of the ship trembled. He felt it through the sharp-edged things pinning him to the wall. He screamed and blacked out again.

What woke him was pain – more than he had felt so far. It was hard and strangely rhythmic, as if he had been convulsing in his sleep. But he was making no conscious movements at all. Instead, the wall against which he was pinned was bellowing in and out, like a huge breathing lung.

Suddenly, anticlimactically, he popped loose. He hit the deck, sprawling, his lower jaw in the filthy, stinking overflow of ship effluent. The two bladed weapons clattered to the ground beside him. He experimented with pushing himself to his knees, and – to his surprise – found he was able to exert pressure on his arms without the pain becoming more than two or three times as intense. Nothing was broken, then – or at least nothing that had much to do with either arm.

Scorpio struggled to his feet. He touched the first wound, then the second. There was a lot of blood, but it wasn't jetting out under arterial pressure. Presumably it was the same story with the two exit wounds. No telling about internal bleeding, but he'd cross that bridge when it became a problem.

Still unsure exactly what had happened to him, he knelt down again and picked up one of the bladed things. It was the first one: the boomerang weapon. He could see the curve of the original armour, the larger form implied by the fragment. He threw it away, kicked the other one aside. Then he reached down to his belt, through waves of pain, and found the haft of Clavain's knife. He removed it from its sheath and flicked on the piezo-electric effect, feeling the hum transmitted to his palm.

In the gloom of the corridor ahead of him, something moved.

'Scorpio.'

He squinted, half-expecting it to be another Adventist, hoping it was someone from the Security Arm. 'Took your time,' he said, which seemed to cover either possibility.

'We've got trouble, Scorp. *Big* trouble.'

The figure stepped out of the gloom. Scorpio flinched: it was no one he had been expecting. 'Captain,' he breathed.

'I thought you needed some help to get free of that wall. Sorry it took me so long.'

'Better late than never,' Scorpio said.

It was a class-three apparition. No, Scorpio thought, strike that: this apparition demanded a new category all of its own. It was more than just a local alteration of the ship's fabric, a remodelling of a wall or the temporary reassignment of some servitor parts. This thing was real and distinct from the ship itself. It was a physical artefact: a spacesuit, a huge, lumbering golemlike servo-powered affair. And it was empty. The faceplate was cranked up: there was only darkness within the helmet. The voice he heard came through the speaker grille beneath the helmet's chin that was normally used for audio communications in a pressurised environment.

'Are you all right, Scorp?'

He dabbed at the blood again. 'I'm not down yet. Doesn't look as if you are, either.'

'It was a mistake to let them aboard.'

'I know,' Scorpio said, looking down at his shoes. 'I'm sorry.'

'It wasn't your fault,' the Captain said. 'It was mine.'

Scorpio looked up at the apparition again. Something forced him to direct his attention into the darkness within the helmet: it seemed impolite not to. 'So what now? They're bringing reinforcements, aren't they?'

'That's their plan. Ships have begun to attack. I've parried most of them, but a handful have slipped through my hull defences. They've begun to drill into the hull. They're hurting me, Scorp.'

He echoed the Captain's earlier question: 'Are you all right?'

'Oh, I'm all right, it's just that I'm beginning to get a little *pissed off*. I think they've had enough fun for one day, don't you?'

Though it hurt him, Scorpio nodded vigorously. 'They picked the wrong pig to fuck with.'

The vast suit bowed towards him, then turned, its huge boots sending sluggish wakes through the effluent. 'They did more than pick the wrong pig. They picked the wrong ship. Now, shall we go and do some damage?'

'Yes,' Scorpio said, smiling wickedly. 'Let's do some damage.'

Orca Cruz and her party had retreated as far as they could go. The two Adventists had pushed her group to a major nexus of corridors and shafts, something like a heart valve in the Captain's anatomy, from which point it would be possible to reach any other part of the *Nostalgia for Infinity* with comparative ease. Cruz knew that she could not allow the Adventists such access. There were only twenty of them, maybe fewer now – it was unthinkable that they could ever gain more than a transient, faltering control over very small districts of the ship – but it was still her duty to limit their nuisance value. If that meant inflicting some small, local hurt on John Brannigan, then that was what she had to do.

'All right,' she said. 'Disarm them. Short, controlled bursts. I want *something* at the end to interrogate.'

Her last few words were drowned out by the sudden, enraged roar of her soldiers' slug-firing automatic weapons. Tracers sliced bright convergent lines down the corridor. The Adventist with the false hand fell down, his right leg peppered with bullet holes. The whirling demon of the scythe bit an arc into the floor, then fell silent. Some retraction mechanism inched the fingertip back to the rest of the hand as the line spooled itself in.

The other Adventist lay on his side, his chest bloody despite the protection of the armour pieces.

The ship groaned.

'I did warn you,' Cruz said. Her own weapon lay cold in her hand. She hadn't fired a shot.

The second Adventist moved, clawing at his face with his hand, like a man trying to remove a bee.

'Don't move,' Cruz said, approaching him cautiously. 'Don't move and you might make it through the day.'

He kept clawing at his face, concentrating his efforts around his eye. He dug his fingers into the socket, popping something loose. He held it between thumb and forefinger for a moment: a perfect human eye, glassily solid, bloodied like some horrid raw delicacy.

'I said—' Orca Cruz began.

He crunched his fingers down on the eye, shattering it. Something chrome-yellow emerged in smoky wisps. A moment later Cruz felt the nerve agent infiltrate her lungs.

No one had to tell her it would be fatal.

From the safe vantage point of his garret, the dean studied the progress of his takeover effort. Cameras around Hela offered him continuous real-time imagery of the Ultras' ship, no matter where its orbit took it. He had seen the telling flicker of drive flame: Seyfarth's message that the first phase of the acquisition operation had been successful. He had seen – indeed, felt – the departure of the massed ships of the Cathedral Guard, and he had also seen the gathering and co-ordination of the squadrons above Hela. Tiny, flimsy ships, to be sure, but many of them. Crows could mob a man to death.

He had no data about the ensuing activities within the ship. If Seyfarth had followed his own plan, then the twenty members of the spearhead unit would have begun their attack shortly after the signal was returned to Hela. Seyfarth was a brave man: he must have known that his chances of surviving until the arrival of reinforcements were not excellent. He was also, it had to be remembered, a career survivor. More than likely Seyfarth had lost some of his squad by now, but Quaiche very much doubted that Seyfarth himself was amongst the casualties. Somewhere on that ship he was still fighting, still surviving.

The dean craved, desperately, some means of divining what was happening in the ship at this moment. After all the planning, all the years of dreaming and scheming this mad folly into existence, it struck him as the height of unfairness not to be able to see whether events were unfolding as planned. He had always skipped over this hiatus in his imagination: it was either successful or it wasn't, and there had been little point dwelling on the agony of uncertainty it represented.

But now he had doubts. The squadrons were meeting unexpected resistance from the ship's hull defences. The imagery showed the ship to be surrounded by a spangling halo of explosions, like a dark and foreboding castle throwing a fireworks display. Most Ultra craft had defences of some kind, so Quaiche had not been greatly surprised to see them deployed here. His cover story had even demanded that the ship have the means to defend itself. But the scale of the defences and the speed and efficiency with which they had reacted: that *had* taken him aback. What if the forces within the ship were encountering the same unexpected resistance? What if Seyfarth was dead? What if everything was going slowly, catastrophically wrong?

His couch chimed: an incoming message. Shaking, his hand worked the control. 'Quaiche,' he said.

'Report from Cathedral Guard,' said a muffled voice, lashed by static. 'Report successful incursion of relief units three and eight. Hull has been breached; no significant airloss. Reinforcement squads are now aboard the *Nostalgia for Infinity*. Attempting to rendezvous with elements of spearhead.'

Quaiche sighed, disappointed in himself. Of course it was going according to plan, and of course it was turning out to be a little more difficult than anticipated. That was the nature of worthy tasks. But he should never have doubted its ultimate success.

'Keep me posted,' he said.

The two mismatched figures – the Captain's hulking, vacant suit and the childlike form of the pig – sloshed their way towards the scene of battle. They moved through corridors and passages that had never been fully reclaimed for human habitation: rat-ridden, rank with effluent and other toxins, crypt-dark save for the occasional weak and stuttering light source. When the Adventists had turned on him, Scorpio had known exactly where he was. But since then he had been following the Captain, allowing himself to be led into areas of the ship that were completely unfamiliar. As the tour progressed, and as the Captain ushered him through obscure hatchways and hidden apertures, he was struck by the increasing absence of the usual markers of shipwide authority: the jury-rigged electrical and hydraulic systems, the painted, luminescent direction arrows. There was only anatomy. They were navigating parts of the ship known only to the Captain, he realised: private corridors he must have haunted alone. It was his flesh and blood, Scorpio thought: up to him what he did with it.

The pig was under no illusion that he was actually in the Captain's physical presence. The suit was just a focus for his attention; in every other respect the Captain was as omnipresent as ever, surrounding him in every sinew of the architecture. But for all that Scorpio would have preferred something with a face to talk to rather than the empty suit, it was a lot better than being on his own. He knew that he had been hurt badly by the Adventist leader, and that sooner or later he was going to feel the delayed shock of those injuries. How hard it would hit him, he couldn't say. He'd have shrugged off the wounds twenty years ago. Now, shrugging off anything seemed unlikely. Yet while he had some form of companion, he felt he could keep delaying that moment of accounting. *Just give me a few hours*, he thought, *just long enough to sort out this mess.*

A few hours were all he needed; all he wanted.

'There's something we need to discuss, Scorp. You and me. Before it's too late.'

'Captain?'

'I need to do something before it becomes impractical. We came here on Aura's instructions, in the hope that we'd find something that might make a difference against the Inhibitors. Quaiche and the scuttlers were always the key, which is why we sent Aura into Hela society nine years ago. She was to gather information, to infiltrate the cathedrals through the back door, without anyone ever suspecting her connection to us. That was a good plan, Scorp. It was the best we had at the time. But we mustn't neglect Haldora itself.'

'No one's neglecting it,' Scorpio said. 'Aura already thinks she's made contact with the shadows, via that suit. Isn't that good enough for now?'

'It might have been if the Adventists hadn't betrayed us. But we don't control that suit: Quaiche does, and he's no longer a man we can trust. It's time to up the ante, Scorp. We can't put all our faith in that one line of negotiation.'

'So we launch the instrument packages, just like we always planned.'

'The packages were only ever intended as a precursor. More than likely, they'd have told us nothing we haven't already learned from Aura. Sooner or later we'd have had to bring in the big guns.'

For a moment Scorpio had forgotten his pain. 'So what have you got in mind?'

'We need to know what's inside Haldora,' the Captain said. 'We need to break through the camouflage, and we can't afford to sit around waiting for a vanishing.'

'The cache weapon,' Scorpio said, guessing his companion's intentions. 'You want to use it, don't you? Fire it into the face of that planet, and see what happens?'

'Like I said, it's time to bring out the big guns.'

'It's the last one we've got. Make it count, Captain.'

The suit studied him with the blank aperture of its faceplate. 'I'll do my best,' it said.

Presently, the suit slowed its pace. The pig halted, using the wide bulk of the suit for cover.

'There's something ahead, Scorp.'

Scorpio looked into darkness. 'I don't see anything.'

'I sense it, but I need the suit to take a closer look. I don't have cameras here.'

They rounded a slight bend, easing their way through a knuckle of interconnected corridors. Suddenly they were back in a part of the ship Scorpio thought he recognised – one of the corridors he had taken the Adventists down earlier that day. Dull sepia light dribbled from sconces in the wall.

'There are bodies here, Scorp. It doesn't look good.'

The suit strode ahead, sloshing through unspeakable fluids. The bodies were shadowed lumps, half-submerged in the muck. The suit's head-light flicked on, playing over the forms. Feral janitor rats fled from the glare.

'They're not Adventists,' Scorpio said.

The suit knelt down next to the closest of the bodies. 'Do you recognise them?'

Scorpio squatted on his haunches, grimacing at the twin spikes of pain on either side of his chest. He touched the body nearest to the Captain, turning it over so that he could see the face. He fingered the rough leather of an eyepatch.

'It's Orca Cruz,' he said.

His own voice sounded detached, matter-of-fact. *She's dead*, he thought. *This woman who was loyal to you for more than thirty years of your life is dead; this woman who aided you, protected you, fought for you and made you laugh with her stories, is dead, and she died because of your mistake, your stupidity in not seeing through the Adventists' plans. And all you feel now is that something you own has been stepped on.*

There was a hiss of pistons and servo-mechanisms. The monstrous gauntlet of the Captain's suit touched him gently on the back. 'It's all right, Scorp. I know how you feel.'

'I don't feel anything.'

'That's what I mean. It's too soon, too sudden.'

Scorpio looked at the other bodies, knowing that they were all members of the Security Arm. Their weapons were gone, but there was no obvious indication of injury on any of them. But he wouldn't forget the expression on Cruz's face in a hurry.

'She was good,' he said. 'She stuck by me when she could have carved out a little empire of her own in Chasm City. She didn't deserve this. None of them deserved this.'

He forced himself to his full height, steadying himself against the wall. First Lasher, on the trip to Resurgam. Then he'd had to say goodbye to Blood, probably for ever. Now Cruz was gone: his last, precious link to that half-remembered life in Chasm City.

'I don't know about you, Captain,' he said, 'but I'm about ready to start taking things personally.'

'I've already started,' the empty suit said.

Battle continued to rage within the *Nostalgia for Infinity*. Slowly, however, the tide was turning against the Adventist boarders. Around the ship, the last elements of the Cathedral Guard had either tunnelled through to the interior or were being picked off by the hull-mounted defences. Damage had been sustained: fresh craters and scars gouged into the already treacherous landscape of the starship's hull. The tiny ships that had reached the hull and anchored themselves in place – with projectile barbs, epoxy-pads, rocket grapples and drilling equipment – resembled mechanical ticks half-embedded in the flesh of some monstrous animal. Elsewhere, the mashed corpses of other ships lay entangled in the crevices and folds of the *Nostalgia for Infinity*'s architecture, quills of escaping air and fluid bleeding into space. Other ships had been ripped apart before they got close to the lighthugger, their hot, mangled wreckage trailing the larger vessel as it orbited Hela. No additional reinforcements had been launched from the moon: the assault had been designed to be total and overwhelming, and only a handful of Cathedral Guard units had not been mobilised during the first wave.

The few elements still trying to make their boarding approach must have known that their chances were not excellent. The resistance had been greater than expected: for the first time, a group of Ultras had actually downplayed the effectiveness of their defences. But the regular soldiers of the Cathedral Guard were blood-loyal to the Adventist order, Quaicheist doctrine running thick and true in their veins, and for them retreat was literally unthinkable. They did not have to know the purpose of their mission to understand that it was of the utmost importance to the dean.

Preoccupied with the matter of finding a safe route to the hull, none of them observed the opening of a space-door in the side of the *Nostalgia for Infinity*, a chink of golden-yellow light amidst the complexity of the Captain's transformations. The door looked tiny, but that was only because of the dizzying scale of the ship itself.

Something emerged, moving with the smooth, unhesitating autonomy of a machine. It did not look very much like a spacecraft, even the ungainly sort used for ship-to-ship operations. It resembled a strange abstract ornament: a surreal juxtaposition of flanged bronze-green shapes, windowless and seamless, as if carved from soap or marble, the whole thing encased in a skeletal black harness, a geodesic framework stubbed with docking latches, thrusters and navigation and aiming devices.

It was a cache weapon. There had been forty of the hell-class devices once; now only this unit remained. The science that had made it, the engineering principles embodied in its construction, were almost certainly less advanced than those in the latest additions to the *Infinity*'s arsenal, like the bladder-mines or the hypometric weapons. No one would ever know for sure. But one thing was clear: the new weapons were instruments of surgical precision rather than brute force, so the cache weapon still had its uses.

It cleared the space-door. Around the skeletal framework of the harness, thrusters sparked blue-white. The glare lit the *Nostalgia for Infinity*, throwing hard radiance across the black shapes of the last few ships of the Cathedral Guard.

No one noticed.

The cache weapon wheeled around, the harness aligning itself with the looming face of Haldora. Then it accelerated, climbing away from the *Nostalgia for Infinity*, away from the battle, away from the scratched face of Hela.

Vasko and Khouri stepped into the mirror-filled room of the garret. Vasko looked around, satisfying himself that the room was much as they had left it. The dean was still sitting in the same couch, in the same part of the chamber. Rashmika was seated at the table in the middle of the room, watching their arrival. She had a tea set before her: a neat china service. Vasko observed her reactions carefully, wondering how much of her memory she had recovered. Even if she had not recalled everything, he could not believe that the sight of her mother's face would not elicit some reaction. There were certain things that cut through memory, he thought.

But if there was a flicker of reaction from Rashmika, he missed it.

She simply inclined her head towards them, the way she would have to greet any arriving visitors.

'Just the two of you?' Dean Quaiche asked.

'We're the advance party,' Vasko said. 'There didn't seem to be any need to send down dozens of us, not until we've assessed the facilities.'

'I told you there were many rooms available,' he said, 'for as many delegates as you cared to send.'

Rashmika spoke up. 'They're not mad, Dean. They know what's going to happen in a few hours.'

'The crossing concerns you?' he asked the Ultras, as if the very thought was ludicrous.

'Let's just say we'd rather observe it from a distance,' Vasko said. 'That's fair enough, isn't it? There was nothing in our agreement that said we absolutely had to remain aboard the Lady Morwenna. The disadvantage is on our side if we choose not to have delegates present.'

'I'm disappointed, all the same,' Quaiche said. 'I'd hoped you would want to share it with me. The spectacle won't be anywhere near as impressive from a distance.'

'I don't doubt that for a moment,' Vasko said. 'All the same, we'll leave you in peace to enjoy it first-hand.' He looked at Khouri, choosing his words carefully. 'We wouldn't want to interfere with a sacred event.'

'You wouldn't be interfering,' the dean said. 'All the same, if that's what you wish . . . I can hardly stop you. But we're still twelve hours from the crossing. There's no need to get nervous just yet.'

'Are you nervous?' Khouri asked him.

'Not in the slightest,' he said. 'That bridge was put there for a reason. I've always believed that.'

'There's the wreckage of another cathedral at the bottom of the rift,' Vasko said. 'Doesn't that worry you at all?'

'It tells me that the dean of that cathedral lacked faith,' Quaiche said.

Vasko's communicator chimed. He lifted the bracelet to his ear, listened carefully. He frowned, then turned and whispered something into Khouri's ear.

'Something the matter?' Quaiche asked.

'There's some trouble on the ship,' Vasko said. 'I'm not sure exactly what it is, but it seems to have something to do with your delegates.'

'My delegates? Why would they be causing trouble?'

'It seems they're trying to take over the ship,' Vasko said. 'You wouldn't know anything about that, would you?'

'Well, now that you mention it—' Quaiche made a very poor imitation of a smile '—I might have an inkling.'

One of the doors to the garret swung open. Six red-uniformed Adventist guards walked in, carrying weapons and looking as if they knew what to do with them.

'I'm sorry it's come to this,' Quaiche said, as the guards motioned for Vasko and Khouri to sit down opposite Rashmika. 'But I really need your ship, and – let's be honest – there was never much chance of you just giving it to me, was there?'

'But we had an agreement,' Vasko said, one of the guards prodding him on the shoulder. 'We offered you protection.'

'The trouble was, it wasn't protection I was after,' Quaiche said. The rim of his eye-opener flashed polished brass. 'It was propulsion.'

FORTY-THREE

Rashmika had a premonitory sense that something was about to trespass into her head. In the moments before the shadows spoke to her, she had learned to identify a specific sensation: a faint tingle of neural intrusion, like the feeling that somewhere in a huge and rambling old house a door had just opened.

She steeled herself: aware of the proximity of the scrimshaw suit, conscious of the ease with which the shadows were able to slip in and out of her skull.

But the voice was different this time.

[Rashmika. Listen to me. Don't react. Don't pay any more attention to me than you would to a stranger.]

Rashmika shaped an answer, without speaking. It was as if she had been born to it, as if the skill had always been there. *Who are you?*

[I'm the only other woman in this room.]

Despite herself, Rashmika glanced towards Khouri. The woman's face was impassive: not hostile, not even unkind, but utterly blank of any kind of expression. It was as if she were looking at a wall, rather than Rashmika.

You?

[Me, Rashmika. Yes.]

Why are you here?

[To help you. How much do you remember? All of it, or only some of it? Do you remember anything at all?]

Aloud, Vasko said, 'Propulsion, Dean? Are you saying you want our ship to take you somewhere?'

'Not exactly, no,' Quaiche replied.

Rashmika tried not to look at the woman, keeping her attention focused on the men instead. *I don't remember much, only that I don't belong here. The shadows already found me out. Do you know about the shadows, Khouri?*

[A little. Not as much as you.]

Can you answer any of my questions? Who sent me here? What was I supposed to do?

[We sent you here.] In her peripheral vision Rashmika saw the woman's head nod by the slightest of degrees: silent, discreet affirmation that it was really her voice Rashmika was hearing. [But it was your decision. Nine years ago, Rashmika, you told us we had to put you on Hela, in the care of another family.]

Why?

[To learn things, to find out as much as you could about Hela and the scuttlers, from the inside. To reach the dean.]

Why?

[Because the dean was the only way of reaching Haldora. We thought Haldora was the key: the only route to the shadows. We didn't know he'd already used it. You told us that, Rashmika. You found the short cut.]

The suit?

[That's what we came for. And you, of course.]

Whatever your plan was, it's going wrong. We're in trouble, aren't we?

[You're safe, Rashmika. He doesn't know you have anything to do with us.]

If he finds out?

[We'll protect you. *I'll* protect you, no matter what happens. You have my word on that.]

She looked into the woman's face, daring Quaiche to notice. *Why would you care about me?*

[Because I'm your mother.]

Look into my eyes. Say it again.

Khouri did. And though Rashmika watched her face intently for the slightest indication of a lie, there was none. She supposed that meant Khouri was telling the truth.

There was shock, a stinging sense of denial, but it was not nearly as great as Rashmika might have expected. She had, by then, already begun to doubt much of what passed for her assumed history. The shadows – and, of course, Surgeon-General Grelier – had already convinced her that she had not been born on Hela, and that the people in the Vigrid badlands could not be her real parents. So what remained was a void waiting to be filled with facts, rather than one truth waiting to be displaced by another.

So here it was. There was still much she needed to remember for herself, but the essence was this: she was an agent of Ultras – *these* Ultras, specifically – and she had been put on Hela on an intelligence-gathering mission. Her actual memories had been suppressed, and in their place she had a series of vague, generic snapshots of early life on Hela. They were like a theatrical backdrop: convincing enough to pass muster provided they were not the object of attention themselves. But when the shadows had told her about her false past, she had seen the early memories for what they were.

The woman said she was Rashmika's mother. She had no reason to doubt her – her face had conveyed no indication of a lie, and Rashmika already knew that her supposed mother in the badlands was only a foster parent. She felt sadness, a sense of loss, but no sense of betrayal.

She shaped a thought. *I think you* must *be my mother.*

[Do you remember me?]

I don't know. A little. I remember someone like you, I think.

[What was I doing?]

You were standing in a palace of ice. You were crying.

Hela Orbit, 2727

Ribbons of grey-blue smoke twisted in the corridor, writhing with the shifts of air pressure. Fluid sluiced from weeping wounds in the walls and ceiling, raining down in muddy curtains. From some nearby part of the ship, Captain Seyfarth heard shouts and the rattle of automatic slug-guns, punctuated by the occasional bark of an energy weapon. He stepped through an obstacle course of bodies, his booted feet squashing limbs and heads into the ankle-deep muck that seemed to flood every level of the ship. One gauntleted hand gripped the rough handle of a throwing knife formed from the armour he had been wearing upon his arrival. The knife was already bloodied – by Seyfarth's estimate he had killed three Ultras so far, and left another two with serious injuries – but he was still looking for something better. As he passed each body he kicked it over, checking the hands and belt for something promising. All he needed was a slug-gun.

Seyfarth was alone, the rest of his group either dead or cut off, wandering some other part of the ship. He had anticipated nothing less. Of the twenty units of the first infiltration team, Seyfarth would have been surprised if more than half a dozen survived to see the taking of the ship. Of course, he counted himself amongst the likely survivors, but based on past experience that was only to be expected. It was not, never had been, a suicide mission: just an operation with a low survival probability for most of those involved. The infiltration squad wasn't required to survive, just to signal the fitness of the ship for the full takeover effort, using the massed ships of the Cathedral Guard. If the infiltrators were able to disrupt the defensive activities aboard the ship, creating pockets of internal confusion, then all the better. But once that signal had been sent to the surface, the survival or otherwise of Seyfarth's unit had no bearing on subsequent events.

Given that, he thought, things were actually going tolerably well. There had been reports – fragmented, not entirely trustworthy – that the massed assault had met more resistance than expected. Certainly, the Cathedral Guard had appeared to suffer greater losses than Seyfarth had ever planned. But the massed assault had been overwhelming in scale for precisely the reason that it needed to be able to absorb huge losses and still succeed. It was shock and awe: no one needed to lecture Seyfarth on that particular doctrine. And the reports of weapons fire from elsewhere in the ship confirmed that elements of the second wave had indeed reached the *Nostalgia for Infinity*, together with the slug-guns they could never have smuggled past the pig.

His foot touched something.

Seyfarth knelt down, grimacing at the smell. He pushed the body over, bringing a sodden hip out of the brown muck in which it lay. He spied the tarnished gleam of a slug-gun.

Seyfarth pulled the weapon from the belt of the dead Cathedral Guardsman, shaking loose most of the muck. He checked the clip: fully loaded. The slug-gun was crudely made, mass-produced from cheap metal, but there were no electronic components in it, nothing that would have suffered from being immersed in the shipboard filth. Seyfarth tested it anyway, releasing a single slug into the nearest wall. The ship groaned as the slug went in. Now that he paid attention to it, it occurred to Seyfarth that the ship had been groaning rather a lot lately – more than he would have expected if the groans were merely structural noises. For a moment this troubled him.

Only for a moment, though.

He threw the knife away, grateful for the weighty heft of the slug-gun. It had taken nerve to come aboard the ship with only knives and a few concealed gadgets, but he had always known that if he made it this far – to the point where he had a real gun in his hand – he would make it all the way through.

It was like the end of a bad dream.

'Going somewhere?'

The voice had come from behind him. But that simply wasn't possible: he had been checking his rearguard constantly, and there had been no one coming along the corridor behind him when he knelt down to recover the slug-gun. Seyfarth was a good soldier: he never left his back uncovered for more than a few seconds.

But the voice sounded very near. Very familiar, too.

The safety catch was still off. He turned around slowly, holding the slug-gun at waist level. 'I thought I took care of you,' he said.

'I need a lot of taking care of,' the pig replied. He stood there, unarmed, not even a slug-gun to his name. Looming behind him, like an adult above an infant, stood the hollow shell of a spacesuit. Seyfarth's lip twisted in a sneer of incomprehension. The pig, just possibly, could have hidden in the darkness, or even pretended to be a body. But the hulking spacesuit? There was no conceivable way he had walked past that without noticing it. And it didn't seem very likely that the suit could have sprinted from the far end of the corridor in the few seconds during which he'd had his back turned.

'This is a trick,' Seyfarth said, 'isn't it?'

'I'd put down that gun if I were you,' the pig said.

Seyfarth's finger squeezed the trigger. Part of him wanted to blow the snout-faced abortion away. Another part wanted to know why the pig thought he had the *right* to speak to him in that kind of tone.

Didn't the pig know his place?

'I hung you out to dry,' Seyfarth said. He wasn't mistaken: this *was* the same pig. He could even see the wounds from where he had pinned him to the wall.

'Listen to me,' the pig said. 'Put down the gun and we'll talk. There are things I want you to tell me. Like what the hell Quaiche wants with my ship.'

Seyfarth touched one finger to his helmeted head, as if scratching an itch. 'Which one of us is holding the gun, pig?'

'You are.'

'Right. Just felt that needed clearing up. Now step away from the suit and kneel in the shit, where you belong.'

The pig looked at him, the sly white of an eye catching the light. 'Or what?'

'Or we'll be looking at pork.'

The pig made a move towards him. It was only a flinch, but it was enough for Seyfarth. There were questions he'd have liked answered, but they would all have to wait for now. Once they had taken the ship, there would be all the time in the world for a few forensic investigations. It would actually give him something to do.

He made to squeeze the trigger. Nothing happened. Furious,

imagining that the slug-gun had jammed after all, Seyfarth glanced down at the weapon.

It wasn't the weapon that was the problem. The problem was his arm. Two spikes had appeared through it: they had shot out from one wall, speared his forearm and emerged on the other side, their sharp tips a damp ruby-red.

Seyfarth felt the pain arrive, felt the spikes grinding against bone and tendon. He bit down on the agony, sneering at the pig. 'Nice ...' he tried to say.

The spikes slid out of his arm, making a slick, slithery sound as they retracted. Seyfarth watched, fascinated and appalled, as they vanished back into the smooth wall.

'Drop the gun,' the pig said.

Seyfarth's arm quivered. He raised the barrel towards the pig and the suit, made one last effort to squeeze the trigger. But there was something badly amiss with the anatomy of his arm. His forefinger merely spasmed, tapping pathetically against the trigger like a worm wriggling on a hook.

'I did warn you,' the pig said.

All around Seyfarth, walls, floor and ceiling erupted spikes. He felt them slide into him, freezing him in place. The gun fell from his hand, clattering to the ground through the labyrinth of interlaced metal rods.

'That's for Orca,' the pig said.

It went quickly after that. The Captain's control over his own local transformations seemed to grow in confidence and dexterity with each kill. It was, at times, quite sickening to watch. How much more terrible it must have been for the Adventists, to suddenly have the ship itself come alive and turn against them. How shocking, when the supposedly fixed surfaces of walls and floors and ceilings became mobile, crushing and pinning, maiming and suffocating. How distressing, when the fluids that ran throughout the ship – the fluids that the bilge pumps strove to contain – suddenly became the liquid instruments of murder, gushing out at high pressure, drowning hapless Adventists caught in the Captain's hastily arranged traps. Growing up on Hela, drowning probably hadn't been amongst the ways they expected to die. But that, Scorpio reflected, was life: full of nasty little surprises.

The tide had been turning against the Adventists, but now it was in full ebb. Scorpio felt his strength redouble, tapping into some last, unexpected reserve. He knew he was going to pay for it later, but for now it felt good to be pushing the enemy back, doing – as the Captain had promised – some actual damage. The slug-gun wasn't designed for a pig, but that didn't stop him finding a way to fire it. Sooner or later he was able to trade up for a shipboard boser pistol, pig-issue. Then, as he had always liked to say in Chasm City, he was really cooking.

'Do what you have to do,' the Captain told him. 'I can take a little pain, for now.'

Pushing through the ship, following the Captain's lead, he soon met up with surviving members of the Security Arm. They were shell-shocked, confused and disorganised, but on seeing him they rallied, realising that the ship had not yet fallen to the Adventists. And when word began to spread that the Captain was assisting in the effort, they fought like devils. The nature of the battle changed from minute to minute. Now it was no longer a question of securing control of their ship, but of mopping up the few outstanding pockets of Adventist resistance holed up in volumes of the ship where the Captain had only limited control.

'I could kill them now,' he told Scorpio. 'I can't reshape those parts of me, but I can depressurise them, or flood them. It will just take a little longer than usual. I could even turn the hypometric weapon against them.'

'Inside yourself?' Scorpio asked, remembering the last time that had happened, during the calibration exercise.

'I wouldn't do it lightly.'

Scorpio tightened his grip on the boser pistol. His heart was hammering in his chest, his eyesight and hearing no better than when he had been revived.

None of that mattered.

'I'll deal with them,' he said. 'You've done your bit for the day, Captain.'

'I'll leave things to you, then,' the suit said, stepping back into a perfectly formed aperture that had just appeared in the wall. The wall resealed itself. It was as if the Captain had never been with him.

Beyond the *Nostalgia for Infinity*, the Captain's manifold attention was at least partly occupied by the progress of the cache weapon. Even as the battle raged within him, even as the ship was brought slowly back under orthodox control, he was mindful of the weapon, anxious that it should not be wasted. For years he had carried the forty hell-class weapons within him, treasuring them against the predations of theft and damage. His degree of transformation had been much less than it was now, but he still felt an intense bond of care towards the weapons that had played such a central role in his recent history. Besides, the weapons themselves had been the beloved playthings of the old Triumvir, Ilia Volyova. He still had fond thoughts for the Triumvir, despite what she had done to him. As long as he remembered Ilia – who had always found time to speak to the Captain, even when he had been at his least communicative – he was not going to let her down by misusing the last of those dark toys.

Telemetry from the cache weapon reached him through multiply secure channels. The Captain had already sewn tiny spysat cameras around himself during the fiercest phase of the Cathedral Guard assault. Now that same swarm of eyes permitted continuous communication with the weapon, even as the *Nostalgia for Infinity* swung around the far side of Hela.

Haldora, from the cache weapon's perspective, now swallowed half the sky. The gas giant was a striped behemoth of primal cold oozing exotic chemistries, its bands of colour so wide that you could drown a rocky world in them. It looked very real: every sensor on the cache weapon's harness reported exactly what would have been expected this close to a gas giant. It sniffed the cruel strength of its magnetic field, felt the hard sleet of charged particles entrained by that field. Even at extreme magnification, the whorls and flurries of the atmosphere looked absolutely convincing.

The Captain had listened to the conversations of the humans in his care, to their speculations concerning the nature of the Haldora enigma. He knew what they expected to find behind this mask of a world: a mechanism for signalling between adjacent realities, entire universes fluttering there like ribbons, adjacent braneworlds in the higher-dimensional reality of the bulk: a kind of radio, capable of tuning into the whisper of gravitons. The details, as yet, didn't matter. What they needed, now, was to make contact with the entities on the other side as quickly as possible. The suit in the Lady Morwenna was one possible means – perhaps the easiest, since it was already *open* – but it couldn't be relied upon. If Quaiche destroyed it, then they would need to find another way to contact the shadows. Quaiche had waited until a vanishing occurred before sending his probe into the planet. They didn't have time for that.

They needed to provoke a vanishing, to expose the machinery for themselves.

The weapon began to slow, taking up its firing posture. Within it, grave preparations were being made. Arcane physical processes began to occur: sequences of reactions, tiny at first, but growing towards an irreversible cascade. The commanding sentience of the device had settled into a state of calm acceptance. After so many years of inaction, it was now going to do the thing for which it had been created. The fact that it would die in the process did not alarm it in the slightest. It felt only a microscopic glimmer of regret that it was the last of its kind, and that no other cache weapons would be around to witness its furious proclamation.

That was the one thing their human masters had never grasped: cache weapons were intensely vain.

Scorpio sat at the conference table, scowling. He was alone except for a handful of seniors. Valensin was tending to his wounds: there was a small museum's worth of antiquated medical equipment spread out on a bloodstained sheet before the pig, including bandages, scalpels, scissors, needles and various bottled ointments and sterilising agents. The doctor had already cut away part of his tunic, exposing the twin wounds where the Adventist's throwing knives had pinned him to the wall.

'You're lucky,' Valensin said, when he had cleaned away most of the blood and began sealing the entrance and exit wounds with an adhesive salve. 'He knew what he was doing. You probably weren't meant to die.'

'And that makes me lucky? It wasn't remotely *unlucky* to end up impaled on a wall in the first place? Just a thought.'

'All I'm saying is, it could have been worse. It looks to me as if they were under orders to minimise casualties, as far as possible.'

'Tell that to Orca.'

'Yes, the nerve gas was unfortunate. At some point, obviously, they were prepared to kill, but in general it appears that they considered themselves to be on holy business, like Crusaders. The sword was to be used only as an instrument of last resort. But they must have known some blood would be shed.'

Urton leant across the table. Her arm was in a sling and there was a vivid purple bruise across her right cheek, but she was otherwise unhurt. 'The question is, what now? We can't just sit here and not react, Scorp. We have to take this back to Quaiche.'

The pig winced as Valensin tugged two folds of skin together, drawing a slug of adhesive across them. 'That thought's crossed my mind, believe me.'

'And?' Jaccottet asked.

'I'd like nothing more than to target all our hull defences on that cathedral and turn the fucker into a smouldering pile of rubble. But that isn't an option, not while we've got people aboard it.'

'If we could get a message to Vasko and Khouri,' Urton said, 'they could start doing some damage themselves. At the very least, they could find their way to safety.'

Scorpio sighed. Of all of them, why did it fall to him – the one who had the least-developed capacity for forward thinking – to point out the problems?

'This isn't about revenge,' he said. 'Believe me, I'm big on revenge. I wrote the book on retribution.' He paused, catching his breath while Valensin started fussing around with another wound, snipping away at leather and scabbed blood. 'But we came here for a reason. I don't know what Quaiche wanted with our ship, and it doesn't look as if any of the surviving Adventists have much of an idea either. My guess is we just got caught up in some local power game, something that probably has damn all to do with the shadows. As tempting as it might be to take revenge now, it'd be the worst thing we could do in terms of our mission objective. We still have to make contact with the shadows, and our quickest route to them is inside a metal spacesuit inside the Lady Morwenna. That, people, is what we need to focus on, not on giving Quaiche the kicking he so richly deserves because he betrayed us. We can do that later, once we've established contact with the shadows. Believe me, I'll be the first in line. And I won't be operating on a minimum-casualties basis, either.'

No one said anything for a moment. There was a hiatus, a stillness in the room. It reminded him of something, but it took a while to remember what it was. When he did, he almost flinched away from the memory: Clavain. There had been a similar pause whenever the old man had finished one of his rabble-rousing monologues.

'We could still storm the cathedral,' Urton said, her voice low. 'There's time. We've taken losses, but we have operational shuttles. How about it, Scorp: a precision raid on the Lady Morwenna, in and out, snatch the suit and our people?'

'It'd be dangerous,' said another of the Security Arm people. 'We don't just have Khouri and Malinin to worry about. There's Aura. What if Quaiche suspects she's one of us?'

'He won't,' Urton said. 'There's no reason for him to do that.'

Scorpio wrestled away from Valensin long enough to lift up his sleeve and inspect the plastic and metal ruin of his communicator. He did not remember when he had damaged it, just as he did not recall where all the additional bruises and cuts had come from.

'Someone get me a line to the cathedral,' he said. 'I want to talk to the man in charge.'

'You never used to think much of negotiation,' Urton said. 'You said all it ever got you was a world of pain.'

'Trouble is,' Scorpio acknowledged ruefully, 'sometimes that's the best you can hope for.'

'You're wrong about this,' Urton said. 'This isn't the way to handle things.'

'Like I was wrong about letting those twenty Adventists aboard the ship? That wasn't my bright idea, the last time I checked.'

'They slipped past your security checks,' Urton said.

'You wouldn't let me examine them as thoroughly as I'd have liked.'

Urton glanced at her fellows. 'Look, we're grateful for your help in regaining control. *Deeply* grateful. But now that the situation is stable again, wouldn't it be better if—'

The ship moaned. Someone else slid a communicator across the polished gloss of the table. Scorpio reached for it, snapped it around his wrist, and called Vasko.

Hela Surface, 2727

Grelier stepped into the garret and took a moment to adjust to the scene that met his eyes. Superficially, the room was much as he had left it. But now it had extra guests – a man and an older woman – detained by a small detachment of the Cathedral Guard. The guests – they were from the Ultra ship, he realised – looked at him as if expecting an explanation. Grelier merely brushed a hand through the white shock of his hair and placed his cane by the door. There was a lot he wanted to get off his chest, but the one thing he couldn't do was explain what was happening here.

'I go away for a few hours and all hell breaks loose,' he commented.

'Have a seat,' the dean said.

Grelier ignored the suggestion. He did what he usually did upon his arrival in the garret, which was to attend to the dean's eyes. He opened the wall cabinet and took out his usual paraphernalia of swabs and ointments.

'Not now, Grelier.'

'Now is as good a time as any,' he said. 'Infection won't stop spreading merely because it is inconvenient to treat it.'

'Where have you been, Grelier?'

'First things first.' The surgeon-general leant over the dean, inspecting the points where the barbs of the eye-opener hooked into the delicate skin of Quaiche's eyelids. 'Might be my imagination, but there seemed to be a wee bit of an atmosphere when I came in here.'

'They're not too thrilled about my taking the cathedral over the rift.'

'Neither am I,' Grelier said, 'but you're not holding me at gunpoint.'

'It's rather more complicated than that.'

'I'll bet it is.' More than ever, he was glad that he had left his shuttle in a state of immediate flight-readiness. 'Well, is someone going to explain? Or is this a new parlour game, where I have twenty guesses?'

'He's taken over our ship,' the man said.

Grelier glanced back at him, continuing to dab at the dean's eyes. 'I'm sorry?'

'The Adventist delegates were a trick,' the man elaborated. 'They were sent up there to seize control of the *Nostalgia for Infinity*.'

'*Nostalgia for Infinity*,' Grelier said. 'Now there's a name that keeps coming up.'

Now it was the man's turn to be puzzled. 'I'm sorry?'

'Been here before, haven't you? About nine years ago.'

The two prisoners exchanged glances. They did their best to hide it, but Grelier had been expecting some response.

'You're ahead of me,' Quaiche said.

'I think we're all ahead of each other in certain respects,' Grelier said. He scooped his swab under an eyelid, the tip yellow with infection. 'Is it true what he said, about the delegates taking over their ship?'

'I don't think he'd have any reason to lie,' Quaiche said.

'You set that up?'

'I needed their ship,' Quaiche said. He sounded like a child explaining why he had been caught stealing apples.

'We know that much. Why else did you spend all that time looking for the right one? But now that they've brought the ship, what's the problem? You're better off letting them run it, if protection's what you want.'

'It was never about protection.'

Grelier froze, the swab still buried under the dean's eyelid. 'It wasn't?'

'I wanted a ship,' Quaiche said. 'Didn't matter which one, so long as it was in reasonably good condition and the engines worked. It wasn't as if I was planning on taking it very far.'

'I don't understand,' Grelier said.

'I know why,' the man said. 'At least, I think I have a good idea. It's about Hela, isn't it?'

Grelier looked at him. 'What about it?'

'He's going to take our ship and land it on this planet. Somewhere near the equator, I'd guess. He's probably already constructed something for docking – a cradle of some kind.'

'A cradle?' Grelier said blankly.

'A holdfast,' Quaiche said, as if that explained everything. Grelier thought about the diverted Permanent Way resources, the fleet of construction machines Rashmika had described to him. Now he knew exactly what they were for. They must have been on their way to the holdfast – whatever that was – to put the finishing touches to it.

'Just one question,' Grelier said. 'Why?'

'He's going to land the ship sideways,' the man replied. 'Lie it down on Hela with the hull aligned east-west, parallel to the equator. Then he'll lock it in place, so that it can't move.'

'There's a point to all this?' Grelier said.

'There will be when I start the engines,' Quaiche said, unable to contain himself. 'Then you'll see. Then everyone will see.'

'He's going to change the spin rate of Hela,' the man said. 'He's going to use the ship's engines to lock Hela into synchronous rotation around Haldora. He doesn't have to change the length of the day by much – twelve minutes will do the trick. Won't they, Dean?'

'One part in two hundred,' Quaiche said. 'Sounds trivial, doesn't it? But worlds – even small ones like Hela – take a lot of shifting. I always knew I'd need a lighthugger to do it. Think about it: if those engines can push a million tonnes of ship to within a scratch of the speed of light, I think they can change Hela's day by twelve minutes.'

Grelier retrieved the swab from under Quaiche's eyelid. 'What God failed to put right, you can fix. Is that it?'

'Now don't go giving me delusions of grandeur,' Quaiche chided.

Vasko's bracelet chimed. He looked at it, not daring to move.

'Answer it,' Quaiche said eventually. 'Then we can all hear how things are going.'

Vasko did as he was told. He listened to the report very carefully, then snapped the bracelet from his wrist and passed it to Grelier. 'Listen to it yourself,' he said. 'I think you'll find it very interesting.'

Grelier examined the bracelet, his lips pursed in suspicion. 'I'll take this call, I think,' he said.

'Suits me either way,' Vasko said.

Grelier listened to the voice coming out of the bracelet. He spoke into it carefully, then listened to the answers, nodding occasionally, raising his snow-white eyebrows in mock astonishment. Then he shrugged and passed it back to Vasko.

'What?' Quaiche said.

'The Cathedral Guard have failed in their attempt to take the ship,' he said. 'They've been cut to shreds, including the reinforcements. I had a nice chat with the pig in command of ship operations. Seemed a very reasonable fellow, for a pig.'

'No,' Quaiche breathed. 'Seyfarth gave me his promise. He told me he had the men to do it. It can't have failed.'

'It did.'

'What happened? What did they have on that ship that Seyfarth didn't know about? A whole army?'

'That's not what the pig says.'

'The pig's right,' Vasko said. 'It was the ship that ruined your plans. It's not like other ships, not inside. It has ideas of its own. It didn't take very kindly to your intruders.'

'This wasn't how it was meant to happen,' Quaiche moaned.

'You're in a spot of bother, I think,' Grelier said. 'The pig mentioned something about taking the cathedral by force.'

'They set me up,' Quaiche said, realisation dawning.

'Oh, don't think ill of them. They just wanted access to Haldora. It wasn't their fault they stumbled into your scheme. They'd have left you alone if you hadn't tried to use them.'

'We're in trouble,' Quaiche said quietly.

'Actually,' Grelier said, as if remembering something important, 'things aren't quite as bad as you think.' He leant closer to the dean, then looked back at the three people sitting around the table. 'We still have a bit of leverage, you see.'

'We do?' Quaiche said.

'Give me the bracelet,' he told Vasko.

Vasko passed it to him. Grelier smiled and spoke into it. 'Hello, is that the pig? Nice to speak to you again. Got a bit of news for you. We have the girl. If you want her back in one piece, I suggest you start taking instructions.'

Then he handed the bracelet to the dean. 'You're on,' he said.

FORTY-FOUR

Scorpio struggled to hear the whispery, paper-thin voice of Dean Quaiche. He held up a hand to silence his companions, screwing his eyes closed against the tight, nagging discomfort of his sealed wounds. His work finished, Valensin began wrapping up the soiled blood-red bundle of surgical tools and ointments.

'I don't know about any girl,' Scorpio said.

The dean's answer was like a scratch of nails against tin. 'Her name is Rashmika Els. Her real name, I neither know nor care. What I do know is that she arrived on Hela from your ship nine years ago. We've established the connection beyond any doubt. And so much else suddenly tumbles into place.'

'It does?'

The voice changed: it was the other man again, the surgeon-general. 'I don't know exactly how you did it,' he said, 'but I'm impressed. Buried memories, autosuggestion . . . what was it?'

'I have no idea what you're talking about.'

'The business with the Vigrid constabulary.'

Again, 'I'm sorry?'

'The girl had to be primed to emerge from her shell. There must have been a trigger. Perhaps after eight or nine years she knew, on a subconscious level, that she had spent enough time amongst the badland villagers to begin the next phase of her infiltration: penetrating the highest level of our very order. Why, I don't yet know, although I'm a wee bit inclined to think *you* do.'

Scorpio said nothing. He let the man continue speaking.

'She had to wait until a means arrived to reach the Permanent Way. Then she had to signal to you that she was on her way, so that you would know to bring your ship in from the cold. It was a question of timing: your successful dealings with the dean obviously depended on internal intelligence fed to you by the girl. There are machines in her head – they rather resemble Conjoiner implants – but I doubt that you could read them from orbit. So you needed another sign, something you couldn't possibly miss. The girl sabotaged a store of demolition charges, didn't she? She blew it up, drawing down the attention of the constabulary. I doubt that she even knew she had done it herself: it was probably more like sleepwalking, acting out buried commands. Then she felt an inexplicable need to leave home and journey to the cathedrals. She concocted a motive for herself: a search for her long-lost brother, even though every rational bone in her body must have told her he was already dead. You, meanwhile, had your signal. The sabotage was reported on all the local news networks; doubtless you had the means to intercept them even far beyond Hela. I imagine there was something unambiguous about it – the time of day, perhaps – that made it absolutely clear that it was the work of your spy.'

Scorpio saw that there was no further point in bluffing. 'You've done your homework,' he said.

'Bloodwork, really, but I take your point.'

'Touch her, and I'll turn you to dust.'

He heard the smile in the surgeon-general's voice. 'I think touching her is the last thing any of us have in mind. I don't think we intend to harm a hair on her head. On that note, why don't I put you back on to the dean? I think he has an interesting proposition.'

The whispery voice again, like someone blowing through driftwood: 'A proposition, yes,' the dean said. 'I was prepared to take your ship by force because I never imagined I'd have any leverage over you. Force, it seems, has failed. I'm surprised: Seyfarth assured me he had every confidence in his own abilities. Frankly, it doesn't matter now that I have the girl. Obviously she means something to you. That means you're going to do what I want, without a single one of my agents lifting a finger.'

'Let's hear your proposition,' Scorpio said.

'I told you I wanted the loan of your ship. As a gesture of my good faith – and my extremely forgiving nature – that arrangement still stands. I will take your ship, use it as I see fit, and then I shall return it to you, its occupants and infrastructure largely intact.'

'Largely intact,' Scorpio said. 'I like that.'

'Don't play games with me, pig. I'm older and uglier, and that's really saying something.'

Scorpio heard his own voice, as if from a distance. 'What do you want?'

'Take a look at Hela,' Quaiche said. 'I know you have cameras spotted all around your orbit. Examine these co-ordinates; tell me what you see.'

It took a few seconds to acquire an image of the surface. When the picture on the compad stabilised, Scorpio found himself looking at a neatly excavated rectangular hole in the ground, like a freshly prepared grave. The co-ordinates referred to a part of Hela that was in daylight, but even so the sunken depths of the hole were in shadow, relieved by strings of intense industrial floodlights. The overlaid scale said that the trench was five kilometres long and nearly three wide. Three of the sides were corrugated grey revetments, sloping steeply, slightly outwards from their bases, carved with ledges and sloping access ramps. Windows shone in the two-kilometre-high walls, peering through plaques of industrial machinery and pressurised cabins. Around the upper edges of the trench, Scorpio saw retracted sheets, serrated to lock together. In the shadowed depths, sketchy, floodlit suggestions of enormous mechanisms were barely visible, things like grasping lobster claws and flattened molars: the movable components of a harness as large as the *Nostalgia for Infinity*. He could see the tracks and piston-driven hinges that would enable the harness to lock itself around almost any kind of light-hugger hull, within limits.

Only three walls of the trench were sheer. The fourth – one of the two short sides – provided a much shallower transition to the level of the surrounding plain. From the fall of surface shadows it was obvious that the trench was aligned parallel to Hela's equator.

'Got the message?' Quaiche asked.

'I'm getting it,' Scorpio said.

'The structure is a holdfast: a facility for supporting the mass of your ship and preventing her escape, even while she is under thrust.'

Scorpio noted how the rear parts of the cradle could be raised or lowered to enable adjustment of the angle of the hull by precise increments. In his mind's eye he already saw the *Nostalgia for Infinity* down in that trench, pinned there as he had been pinned to the wall.

'What is it for, Dean?'

'Haven't you grasped it yet?'

'I'm a little slow on the uptake. It comes with my genes.'

'Then I'll explain. You're going to slow Hela for me. I'm going to use your ship as a brake, to bring this world into perfect synchronisation with Haldora.'

'You're a madman.'

Scorpio heard a dry rattle of laughter, like old twigs being shaken in a bag. 'I'm a madman with something you want very badly. Shall we do business? You have sixty minutes from now. In exactly one hour, I want your ship locked down in that holdfast. I have an approach trajectory already plotted, one that will minimise lateral hull stresses. If you follow it, the damage and discomfort will be minimalised. Would you like to see it?'

'Of course I'd like to . . .'

But even before he had finished the sentence he felt a lurch, the impulse as the ship broke from orbit. The other seniors reached instinctively for the table, clawing at it for support. Valensin's bundle of medical tools slid to the floor. Groans and bellows of protest from the ship's fabric were like the creaking of vast old trees in a thunderstorm.

They were going down. It was what the Captain wanted.

Scorpio snarled into the communicator, 'Quaiche: listen to me. We can work this out. You can have your ship – we're already on our way – but you have to do something for me in return.'

'You can have the girl when the ship has finished its business.'

'I'm not expecting you to hand her over right now. But do one thing: stop the cathedral. Don't take it over the bridge.'

The whisper of a voice said, 'I'd love to, I really would, but I'm afraid we're already committed.'

In the core of the cache weapon, the cascade of reactions passed an irreversible threshold. Exotic physical processes simmered, rising like boiling water. No conceivable intervention could now prevent the device from firing, short of the violent destruction of the weapon itself. Final systems checks were made, targeting and yield cross-checked countless times. The spiralling processes continued: something like a glint became a spark, which in turn became a little marble-sized sphere of naked, swelling energy. The fireball grew larger still, swallowing layer after layer of containment mechanisms. Microscopic sensors, packed around the expanding sphere, recorded squalls of particle events. Space-time itself began to curl and crisp, like the edge of a sheet of parchment held too close to a candle flame. The sphere engulfed the last bastion of containment and kept growing. The weapon sensed parts of itself being eaten from within: glorious and chilling at the same time. In its last moments it reassigned functions from the volume around the expanding sphere, cramming more and more of its control sentience into its outer layers. Still the sphere kept growing, but now it was beginning to deform, elongating in one direction in exact accordance with prediction. A spike of annihilating force rammed forwards, blasting through a marrow of abandoned machine layers. The weapon felt it as a cold steel impalement. The tip of the spike reached beyond its armour, beyond the harness, towards the face of Haldora.

The expanding sphere had now consumed eighty per cent of the cache weapon's volume. Shockwaves were racing towards the gas giant's surface: in a matter of nanoseconds, the weapon would cease to exist except as a glowing cloud at one end of its beam.

It had nearly run out of viable processing room. It began to discard higher sentience functions, throwing away parts of itself. It did so with a curious discrimination, intent on preserving a tiny nugget of intelligence until the last possible moment. There were no more decisions to be made; nothing to do except await destruction. But it had to know: it had to cling to sentience long enough to know that it had done some damage.

Ninety-five per cent of the cache weapon was now a roiling ball of photo-leptonic hellfire. Its thinking systems were smeared in a thin, attenuated crust on the inside of the weapon's skin: a crust that was itself beginning to break up, sundered and riven by the racing shockwave of the explosion. The machine's intelligence slid down the cognitive ladder until all that remained was a stubborn, bacterial sense of its own existence and the fact that it was there to do something.

The light rammed through the last millimetre of armour. By then, the first visual returns were arriving from Haldora. The cameras on the cache weapon's skin relayed the news to the shrinking puddle of mind that was all that remained of the once-sly intelligence.

The beam had touched the planet. And something was happening to it, spreading away from the impact point in a ripple of optical distortion.

The mind shrivelled out of existence. The last thing it allowed itself was a dwindling thrill of consummation.

In the depths of the Lady Morwenna – in the great hall of Motive Power – several things happened almost at once. An intense flash of light flooded the hall through the narrow colourless slits of the utilitarian windows above the coupling sleeves. Glaur, the shift boss, was just blinking away the afterimages of the flash – the propulsion systems etched into his retinae in looming pink-and-green negative forms – when he saw the machinery lose its usual keen synchronisation: the scissoring aerial intricacy of rods and valves and compensators appearing, for a heart-stopping moment, to be about to work loose, threshing itself and anyone nearby into a bloody amalgam of metal and flesh.

But the instant passed: the governors and dampers worked as they were meant to, forcing the motion back into its usual syncopated rhythm. There were groans and squeals of mechanical protestation – deafening, painful – as hundreds of tonnes of moving metal struggled against the constraints of hinge-point and valve sleeve, but nothing actually worked loose, or came flying through the air towards him. Glaur noticed, then, that the emergency lights were flashing on the reactor, as well as on the servo-control boxes of the main propulsion assembly.

The wave of unco-ordinated motion had been damped and controlled within the Motive Power hall, but these mechanisms were only part of the chain: the wave itself was still travelling. In half a second it passed through the airtight seals in the wall and out into vacuum. An observer, watching the Lady Morwenna from a distance, would have seen the usual smooth movements of the flying buttresses slip out of co-ordination. Glaur didn't need to be outside: he knew exactly what was about to happen, saw it in his imagination with the clarity of an engineering blueprint. He even reached for a handhold before he had made a conscious decision to do so.

The Lady Morwenna stumbled. Huge reciprocating masses of moving machinery – normally counterweighted so that the walking motion of the cathedral was experienced as only the tiniest of sways even at the top of the Clocktower – were now appallingly unbalanced. The cathedral lurched first to one side, then to the other. The effect was catastrophic and predictable: the lurch sent a fresh shudder through the propulsion mechanisms, and the entire process began again even before the first lurch had been damped out.

Glaur gritted his teeth and hung on. He watched the floor tilt by entire, horrifying degrees. Klaxons tripped automatically; red emergency lights flashed from the chamber's vaulted heights.

A voice sounded on the pneumatic speaker system. He reached for the mouthpiece, raising his own voice above the racket.

'This is the surgeon-general. What, exactly, is happening?'

'Glaur, sir. I don't know. There was a flash . . . systems went berserk. If I didn't know better I'd say someone just let off a very powerful demolition charge, hit our 'tronics boxes.'

'It wasn't a nuke. I meant, what is happening with your control of the cathedral?'

'She's on her own now, sir.'

'Will she topple?'

Glaur looked around. 'No, sir. No.'

'Will she leave the Way?'

'No sir, not that either.'

'Very well. I just wanted to be certain.' Grelier paused: in the gap between his words Glaur heard something odd, like a kettle whistling. 'Glaur . . . what did you mean by "she's on her own"?'

'I mean, sir, that we're on automatic control, like we're supposed to be during times of emergency. Manual control is locked out on the twenty-six-hour timer. Captain Seyfarth made me do it, sir: said it was on Clocktower authority. So we don't stop, sir. So we *can't* stop.'

'Thank you,' Grelier said quietly.

Above them all, something was very wrong with Haldora. Where the beam from the weapon had struck the planet, something like a ripple had raced out, expanding concentrically. The weapon itself was gone now; even the beam had vanished into Haldora, and only a dispersing silvery-white cloud remained at the point where the device had been activated.

But the effects continued. Within the circular interior of the expanding ripple, the usual swirls and bands of gas-giant chemistry were absent. Instead there was just a ruby-red bruise, smooth and undifferentiated. In seconds it grew to encompass the entire planet. What had been Haldora was now something like a bloodshot eye.

It stayed like that for a few seconds, staring balefully down at Hela. Then hints of patterning began to appear in the ruby-red sphere: not the commas and horsetails of random chemical boundaries, not the bands of differentiated rotation belts, not the cyclopean eyes of major storm foci. These patterns were regular and precise, like designs worked into carpets. They sharpened, as if being worked and neatened by an invisible hand. Then they shifted: now a tidily manicured ornamental labyrinth, now a suggestion of cerebral folds. The colour flicked from ruby-red to bronze to a dark silver. The planet erupted forth a thousand spikes. The spikes lingered, then collapsed back into a sea of featureless mercury. The mercury became a chequerboard; the chequerboard became a spherical cityscape of fantastic complexity; the cityscape became a crawling Armageddon.

The planet returned. But it wasn't the same planet. In a blink, Haldora became another gas giant, then another – the colouring and banding different each time. Rings appeared in the sky. A garland of moons, orbiting in impossible procession. Two sets of rings, intersecting at an angle, passing through each other. A dozen perfectly square moons.

A planet with a neat chunk taken out of it, like a half-eaten wedding cake.

A planet that was a reflected mirror of stars.

A dodecahedral planet.

Nothing.

For a few seconds there was only a black sphere up there. Then the sphere began to wobble, like a balloon full of water.

At last the great concealment mechanism was breaking down.

FORTY-FIVE

Quaiche clawed at his eyes, making a faint screaming sound, the words *I'm blind, I'm blind* his pitiful refrain.

Grelier put down the pneumatic speaking tube. He leant over the dean, pulling some gleaming ivory-handled optical device from his tunic pocket and peering into the trembling horror of Quaiche's exposed eyes. With the other hand he cast shadows over them, watching the reactions of the twitching irises.

'You're not blind,' he said. 'At least, not in both eyes.'

'The flash—'

'The flash damaged your right eye. I'm not surprised: you were staring straight at the face of Haldora when it happened, and you have no blink reflex, of course. But we happened to lurch at the same moment: whatever caused that flash also upset Glaur's machines. It was enough to perturb the optical light path from the collecting apparatus above the garret. You were spared the full effect of it.'

'I'm blind,' Quaiche said again, as if he had heard nothing that Grelier had told him.

'You can still see me,' Grelier said, moving his finger, 'so stop snivelling.'

'Help me.'

'I'll help you if you tell me what just happened – and also why the hell the Lady Mor is on automatic control.'

Quaiche's voice regained a semblance of calm. 'I don't know what happened. If I'd been expecting that, do you think I'd have been looking at it?'

'I imagine it was your friends the Ultras. They professed an interest in Haldora, didn't they?'

'They said they were going to send in instrument packages.'

'I think they fibbed,' Grelier replied.

'I trusted them.'

'You still haven't told me about the automatic control. Glaur says we can't stop.'

'Twenty-six-hour lockout,' Quaiche said, as if reciting from a technical manual. 'To be used in the event of a complete collapse of cathedral authority, ensuring that the Lady Mor continues to move along the Way until order is restored. All manual control of the reactor and propulsion systems is locked out on sealed, tamper-proof timing systems. Guidance cameras detect the Way; gyroscopes prevent drift even if there's a loss of all visual cues; multiply redundant star-trackers come online for celestial navigation. There's even a buried inductance cable we can follow, if all else fails.'

'When was the lockout instigated?'

'It was the last thing Seyfarth did before departing for the *Infinity*.'

Many hours ago, Grelier thought, but fewer than twenty-six. 'So she's going over that bridge, and nothing can stop it, short of sabotage?'

'Have you *tried* sabotaging a reactor lately, Grelier? Or a thousand tonnes of moving machinery?'

'Just wondering what the chances were.'

'The chances are, Surgeon-General, that she's going over that bridge.'

It was a tiny surface-to-orbit ship, barely larger than the re-entry capsule that had brought Khouri to Ararat. It slipped from the belly of the *Nostalgia for Infinity*, impelled by the merest whisper of thrust. Through the transparent patches in the cockpit armour, Scorpio watched the huge old ship fall slowly away, more like a receding landscape than another vessel. He gasped: at last he could see the changes for himself.

Wonderful and frightening things were happening to the *Nostalgia for Infinity*. As she made her slow approach to the surface holdfast, vast acres of the hull were peeling away, sheets of biomechanical cladding and radiation shielding breaking loose like flakes of sloughed skin. As the ship approached Hela, the pieces stretched behind her, forming a dark, jostling tail, like a comet's. It was the perfect camouflage for Scorpio, permitting him to make his departure undetected.

None of it, Scorpio knew, was unintentional. The ship wasn't breaking up because of the unbalanced stresses of its sidelong approach to Hela. It was breaking up because the Captain was choosing to fling away entire parts of himself. Where the skin cladding had gone, the ship's innards were revealed in all their bewildering intricacy. And even there – in the solid depths of the *Nostalgia for Infinity* – great changes were afoot. The Captain's ordinary transformative processes had been accelerated. The former maps of the ship were now utterly useless – no one had the slightest idea how to navigate through those deep districts. Not that it mattered: the living crew were crammed into a tiny, stable district near the nose, and if anyone was alive and warm down in the parts of the ship that were changing, they were only the last, wandering elements of the Cathedral Guard. In Scorpio's opinion, it was unlikely that they'd be alive and warm for very much longer.

No one had told the Captain to do this, just as no one had told him to lower himself towards Hela. Even if there had been a rebellion – even if some of the seniors had decided to abandon Aura – it wouldn't have made the slightest difference. Captain John Brannigan had made up his mind.

When he was clear of the tumbling cloud of sloughed parts, Scorpio told the ship to accelerate harder. It had been a long time since he had sat behind the controls of a spacecraft, but that didn't matter: the little machine knew exactly where it needed to go. Hela rolled below: he saw the diagonal scratch of the rift, and the even fainter scratch of the bridge spanning it. He turned up the magnification, steadied the image and tracked back from the bridge until he made out the tiny form of the Lady Morwenna, creeping towards the edge of the plain. He had no idea what was going on aboard it now: since the appearance of the Haldora machinery, all attempts to communicate with Quaiche or his hostages had failed. Quaiche must have destroyed or disabled all the communication channels, no longer wishing to be distracted by outside parties now that he had finally seized effective control of the *Nostalgia for Infinity*. All Scorpio could do was assume that Aura and the others were still safe, and that there was still some measure of rationality in Quaiche's mind. If he could not be contacted by conventional means, then he would have to be sent a very obvious and compelling signal to stop.

Scorpio's ship aimed itself for the bridge.

The pressure of thrust, mild as it was, made Scorpio's chest hurt. Valensin had told him he was a fool even to think about riding a ship down to Hela after what he had been through in the last few years.

Scorpio had shrugged. A pig had to do what a pig had to do, he'd said.

Grelier attended to Quaiche, dribbling solutions into the blinded eye. Quaiche flinched and moaned at each drop, but gradually his moans became intermittent whimpers, signifying irritation and disappointment more than pain.

'You still haven't told me what she's doing here,' Quaiche said, finally.

'That wasn't my job,' Grelier replied. 'I established that she wasn't who she said she was, and I established that she had arrived on Hela nine years ago. The rest you'll have to ask her yourself.'

Rashmika stood up and walked over to the dean, brushing the surgeon-general aside. 'You don't have to ask,' she said. 'I'll tell you myself. I came here to find you. Not because I was particularly interested in *you*, but because you were the key to reaching the shadows.'

'The shadows?' Grelier asked, screwing the lid on to a thumb-sized bottle of blue fluid.

'He knows what I'm talking about,' Rashmika said. 'Don't you, Dean?'

Even through the masklike rigidity of his face, Quaiche managed to convey his sense of awful realisation. 'But it took you nine years to find me.'

'It wasn't just about finding you, Dean. I always knew where you were: no one ever made a secret of that. A lot of people thought you were dead, but it was always clear where you were *meant* to be.'

'Then why wait all this time?'

'I wasn't ready,' she said. 'I had to learn more about Hela and the scuttlers, otherwise I couldn't be sure that the shadows were the right people to talk to. It was no good trusting the church authorities: I had to learn things for myself, make my own deductions. And, of course, I had to have a convincing background, so you'd trust me.'

'But nine years,' Quaiche said again, marvelling. 'And you're still just a child.'

'I'm seventeen. And it's been a lot more than nine years, believe me.'

'The shadows,' Grelier said. 'Will one of you please do me the courtesy of explaining who or what they are?'

'Tell him, Dean,' Rashmika said.

'I don't know what they are.'

'But you know they exist. They talk to you, don't they, just the way they talk to me. They asked you to save them, to make sure they aren't destroyed when the Lady Morwenna goes over the bridge.'

Quaiche raised a hand, dismissing her. 'You're quite deluded.'

'Just like Saul Tempier was deluded, Dean? He knew about the missing vanishing, and he didn't believe the official denials. He also knew that the vanishings were due to end, just like the Numericists did.'

'I've never heard of Saul Tempier.'

'Perhaps you haven't,' Rashmika said, 'but your church had him killed because he couldn't be allowed to speak of the missing vanishing. Because you couldn't face the fact that it had happened, could you?'

Grelier's fingers shattered the little blue vial. 'Tell me what this is about,' he demanded.

Rashmika turned to him, cleared her throat. 'If he won't tell you, I will. The dean had a lapse of faith during one of those periods when he began to build up immunity to his own blood viruses. He began to question the entire edifice of the religion he'd built around himself, which was painful for him, because without this religion the death of his beloved Morwenna becomes just another meaningless cosmic event.'

'Be careful what you say,' Quaiche said.

She ignored him. 'During this crisis, he felt compelled to test the nature of a vanishing, using the tools of scientific enquiry normally banned by the church. He arranged for a probe to be fired into the face of Haldora during a vanishing.'

'Must have called for some careful preparations,' Grelier said. 'A vanishing's so brief—'

'Not this one,' Rashmika said. 'The probe had an effect: it prolonged the vanishing by more than a second. Haldora is an illusion, nothing more: a piece of camouflage to hide a signalling mechanism. The camouflage has been failing, lately – that's why the vanishings have been happening in the first place. The dean's probe added additional stress, prolonging the vanishing. It was enough, wasn't it, Dean?'

'I have no . . .'

Grelier pulled out another vial – a smoky shade of green, this time – and held it over his master, pinched tight between thumb and forefinger. 'Let's stop mucking about, shall we? I'm convinced that she knows more than you'd like the rest of us to know, so will you please stop denying it?'

'Tell him,' Rashmika said.

Quaiche licked his lips: they were as pale and dry as bone. 'She's right,' he said. 'Why deny it now? The shadows are just a distraction.' He tilted his head towards Vasko and Khouri. 'I have your ship. Do you think I give a damn about anything else?'

The skin of Grelier's fingers whitened around the vial. 'Tell us,' he hissed.

'I sent a probe into Haldora,' Quaiche said. 'It prolonged the vanishing. In that extended glimpse I saw ... *things* – shining machinery, like the inside of a clock, normally hidden within Haldora. And the probe made contact with something. It was destroyed almost instantly, but not before that *something* – whatever it was – had managed to transmit itself into the Lady Morwenna.'

Rashmika turned and pointed towards the suit. 'He keeps it in that.'

Grelier's eyes narrowed. 'The scrimshaw suit?'

'Morwenna died in it,' Quaiche said, picking his way through his words like someone crossing a minefield. 'She was crushed in it when our ship made an emergency sprint to Hela, to rescue me. The ship didn't know that Morwenna couldn't tolerate that kind of acceleration. It pulped her, turned her into red jelly, red jelly with bone and metal in it. *I* killed her, because if I hadn't gone down to Hela ...'

'I'm sorry about what happened to her,' Rashmika said.

'I wasn't like this before it happened,' Quaiche said.

'No one could have blamed you for her death.'

Grelier sneered. 'Don't let him fool you. He wasn't exactly an angel before that happened.'

'I was just a man with something bad in his blood,' Quaiche said defensively, 'just a man trying to make his way.'

Quietly, Rashmika said, 'I believe you.'

'You can read my face?' he asked.

'No,' she said. 'I just believe you. I don't think you were a bad man, Dean.'

'And now, after all that I've made happen? After what happened to your brother?' There was, she heard, an audible crack of hope in his voice. This late in the day, this close to the crossing, he still craved absolution.

'I said that I believed you, not that I was in a forgiving mood,' she said.

'The shadows,' Grelier said. 'You still haven't told me what they are, or what they have to do with the suit.'

'The suit is a holy relic,' Rashmika said, 'his one tangible link with Morwenna. In testing Haldora, he was also validating the sacrifice she'd made for him. That was why he put the receiving apparatus inside the suit: so that when the answer came, when he discovered whether or not Haldora was a miracle, it would be Morwenna who told him.'

'And the shadows?' Grelier asked.

'Demons,' Quaiche said.

'Entities,' Rashmika corrected. 'Sentient beings trapped in a different universe, adjacent to this one.'

Grelier smiled. 'I think I've heard enough.'

'Listen to the rest,' Vasko said. 'She's not lying. They're real, and we need their help very badly.'

'Their help?' Grelier repeated.

'They're more advanced than us,' Vasko said, 'more advanced than any other culture in this galaxy. They're the only things that are going to make a difference against the Inhibitors.'

'And in return for this help, what do *they* want?' Grelier asked.

'They want to be let out,' Rashmika said. 'They want to be able to cross over into this universe. The thing in the suit – it's not really the shadows, just a negotiating agent, like a piece of software – it knows what we have to do to let the rest of them through. It knows the commands we need to send to the Haldora machinery.'

'The Haldora machinery?' the surgeon-general asked.

'Take a look for yourself,' the dean said. The arrangement of mirrors had locked on to him again, beaming a shaft of focused light into his one good eye. 'The vanishings have ended, Grelier. After all this time, I can see the holy machinery.'

Glaur was alone, the only member of the technical staff left in the vaulted hall of Motive Power. The cathedral had recovered from the earlier disturbance; the klaxon had silenced, the emergency lights on the reactor had dimmed, and the motion of the rods and spars above his head had fallen back into their usual hypnotic rhythm. The floor swayed from side to side, but only Glaur had the hard-won acuity of balance to detect that. The motion was within normal limits, and to someone unfamiliar with the Lady Morwenna the floor would have felt rock steady, as if anchored to Hela.

Breathing heavily, he made his way around one of the catwalks that encircled the central core of turbines and generators. He felt the breeze as the whisking spars moved just above his head, but years of familiarity with the place meant that he no longer ducked unnecessarily.

He reached an anonymous, unremarkable-looking access panel. Glaur flipped the toggles that held the panel shut, then hinged it open above his head. Inside were the gleaming silver-blue controls of the lockout system: two enormous levers, with a single keyhole beneath each. The procedure had been simple enough: well rehearsed in many exercises using the dummy panel on the other side of the machine.

Glaur had inserted a key into one lock. Seyfarth had inserted his key into the corresponding hole. The keys had been engaged simultaneously, and then the two of them had pulled the levers as far as they would travel, in one smooth, synchronised movement. Things had clunked and whirred. All around the chamber there had been the chatter of relays as the normal control inputs were disconnected. Behind this one panel, Glaur knew, was an armoured clock ticking down the seconds from the moment the levers had been pulled. The levers had now moved through half of their travel: there were another twelve or thirteen hours before the relays would chatter again, restoring manual control.

Too long. In thirteen hours, there probably wouldn't be a Lady Morwenna.

Glaur braced himself against the catwalk handrail, then positioned both gloved hands on the left-side handle. He squeezed down, applying as much force as he could muster. The handle didn't budge: it felt as solid as if it had been welded into place, at exactly that angle. He tried the other, and then tried to pull both of them down at the same time. It was absurd: his own knowledge of the lockout system told him that it was engineered to resist a lot more interference than this. It was built to withstand a rioting gang, let alone one man. But he had to try, no matter how unlikely the chances of success.

Sweating, his breathing even more laboured, Glaur returned to the floor of Motive Power and gathered some heavy tools. He climbed back up to the catwalk, found the panel again and began attacking the levers with the instruments he had chosen. The clanging rang out across the hall, audible above the smooth churning of the machinery.

That didn't work either.

Glaur collapsed in exhaustion. His hands were too sweaty to hold anything made of metal, his arms too weak to lift even the lightest hammer.

If he couldn't force the lockout mechanism to skip forwards to the end of its twenty-six-hour run, what else could he do? He only wanted to stop the Lady Morwenna or steer it off course, not destroy it. He could damage the reactor – there were plenty of access ports still accessible to him – but it would take hours for his actions to have any effect. Sabotaging the propulsion machinery was no more realistic: the only way to do it would be to jam something into it, but it would have to be something huge. There might be chunks of metal in the repair shops – entire spars or rods removed for refurbishment or meltdown – but he could never lift one on his own. It would be asking a lot of him to throw a spanner at the moment.

Glaur had considered his chances of sabotaging or fooling the guidance systems: the cameras watching the Way, the star-trackers scanning the sky, the magnetic field sensors sniffing for the signature of the buried cable. But those systems were all multiply redundant, and most of them were situated beyond the pressurised areas of the cathedral, high above ground or in difficult-to-access parts of the substructure.

Face it, he told himself: the engineers who had designed the lockout controls hadn't been born yesterday. If there was an obvious way to stop the Lady Morwenna, they would have taken care of it.

The cathedral wasn't going to stop, and it wasn't going to deviate from the Way. He had told Seyfarth that he would stay aboard until the last minute, tending his machines. But what was there to tend now? His machines had been taken from him, taken out of his hands as if he couldn't be trusted with them.

From the catwalk, Glaur looked down at the floor, at one of the observation windows he had often walked over. He could see the ground sliding below, at one-third of a metre per second.

Scorpio's little ship touched down, its retractile skids crunching into the hardening slush of just-melted ice. The ship rocked as he unstrapped himself and fussed with his vacuum-suit connections, verifying that all was well. He was having trouble concentrating, clarity of mind fading in and out like a weak radio signal. Perhaps Valensin had been right, after all, and he should have stayed on the ship, deputising someone else to come down to Hela.

Fuck that, Scorpio thought.

He checked the helmet indicators one final time, satisfying himself that all the telltales were in the green. No point spending any more time worrying about it: the suit was either ready or it wasn't, and if it didn't kill him, something else was probably waiting around the corner.

He groaned in pain as he twisted around to release the exit latch. The side door popped away, splatting silently into the slush. Scorpio felt the slight tug as the last whiff of air in the cabin found its way into space. The suit seemed to be holding: none of the green lights had changed to red.

A moment later he was out on the ice: a squat, childlike figure in a metallic-blue vacuum suit designed for pigs. He waddled around to the rear of the ship, keeping away from the cherry-red exhaust vents, and opened a cargo recess. He reached into it, grunting against pain, and fumbled around with the clumsy two-fingered gauntlets of his suit. Pig hands were not exactly masterpieces of dexterity to begin with, but put them in a suit and they were not much better than stumps. But he'd been practising. He'd had a lifetime of practice.

He removed a pallet: a thing the size of a dinner-tray. Nestling in it, like Fabergé eggs, were three bladder-mines. He took one mine out, handling it with instinctive caution – even though the one thing a bladder-mine wasn't very likely to do was go off by accident – and walked away from the parked ship.

He walked one hundred paces from it: far enough that there was no chance of the ship's exhaust washing over the mine. Then he knelt down and used Clavain's knife to carve out a little cone-shaped depression in the surface frost. He pressed the bladder-mine firmly down into the depression until only the top part was showing. Then he twisted a knurled dial on the mine's surface through thirty degrees. His gloves kept slipping, but eventually he managed it. The dial clicked into place. A tiny red indicator shone in the upper pole of the bladder-mine: it was armed. Scorpio stood up.

He paused: something had caught his eye. He looked up into the face of Haldora. The planet was gone now; in its place, occupying a much smaller part of the sky, was a kind of mechanism. It had the look of some unlikely diagram from medieval cosmology, something crafted in the ecstatic grip of a vision: a geometric, latticelike structure, a thing of many finely worked parts. Around its periphery, distinct twinkling spars crisscrossed each other, radiating away from linking nodes. Towards the middle it became far too complicated to take in, let alone to describe or memorise. He retained only a sense of vertiginous complexity, like a glimpse of the clockwork mind of God. It made his head hurt. He could feel the swarming, tingling onset of a migraine, as if the thing itself was defying him to look at it for one moment longer.

He turned away, kept his eyes on the ground and trudged back to the ship. He placed the two remaining mines back inside the cargo recess, then climbed aboard, leaving the hull door lying on the ground. No need to repressurise now: he would just have to trust the suit.

The ship bucked into the air. Through the open part of the hull he watched the deck of the bridge drop away until the sides came into view. Below: the distant floor of Absolution Gap. He felt a lurch of dizziness. When he had been standing on the bridge, laying the mine, it had been easy to forget how far from the ground he really was.

He wouldn't have that comfort the next time.

The holdfast readied itself below the *Nostalgia for Infinity*. The ship was close now, or at least what remained of it. During his descent from orbit, the Captain had committed himself to a series of terminal transformations, intent on protecting those in his care while doing what was necessary to safeguard Aura. He had shed much of his hull cladding around the midsection, revealing the festering complexity of his innards: structural spars and bulkhead partitions larger than many medium-sized spacecraft, the gristlelike tangle of densely packed ship systems, grown wild and knotted as strangler vines. As he discarded these protective sections he felt a chill of nakedness, as if he was exposing vulnerable skin where once he had been armoured. It had been centuries since these internal regions had last been open to vacuum.

He continued his transformation. Within him, major elements of ship architecture were reshuffled like dominos. Umbilical lines were severed and reconnected. Parts of the ship that had relied on others for the supply of life-giving power, air and water were now made self-sufficient. Others were allowed to die. The Captain felt these changes take place within him with a queasy sense of abdominal movement: pressure and cold, sharp pains and the sudden, troubling absence of any sensation whatsoever. Although he had instigated and directed the alterations, he still felt an unsettling sense of self-violation.

What he was doing to himself could not be easily undone.

He lowered closer to Hela, correcting his descent with bursts of docking thrust. Gravitational gradients stressed the geometry of his hull, soft fingers threatening to rip him apart.

He fell further. The landscape slid beneath him – not just ice and crevasses now, but an inhabited territory pocked with tiny hamlets and scratched with lines of communication. The maw of the holdfast was a golden cleft on the horizon.

He convulsed, like something giving birth. All the preparations were complete. From his midsection, neatly separated chunks of himself detached from the hull, leaving geometric holes. They trailed thousands of severed connections, like the pale roots beneath blocks of uprooted turf. The Captain had dulled the pain where it was possible, but ghost signals still reached him where cables and feed-lines had been ripped in two. *This*, the Captain thought, *is how it feels to be gored*. But he had expected the pain and was ready for it. In a way, it was actually quite bracing. It was a reminder that he was alive, that he had begun his thinking existence as a creature of flesh and blood. As long as he felt pain, he could still think of himself as distantly human.

The twenty chunks fell with the *Nostalgia for Infinity*, but only for a moment. Once they were safely clear of each other, the tiny sparks of steering rockets boosted them away. The rockets were not capable of pushing the chunks beyond Hela's gravitational influence, but they were sufficient to lift them back into orbit. There, they would have to take care of themselves. He had done what he could for his eighteen thousand sleepers – he had brought many of them all the way from Ararat, and some from Yellowstone – but now they were safer outside him than within.

He just hoped someone else would arrive to take care of them.

The holdfast loomed much larger now. Within it, the waiting cradles and harnesses were moving, preparing to lock themselves around his gutted remains.

'What do you want with the scrimshaw suit?' Quaiche asked.

'I want to take it with me,' Rashmika said, with a forcefulness that surprised her. 'I want to remove it from the Lady Morwenna.'

Vasko looked at Khouri, then at Rashmika. 'You remember it all now?' he asked.

'I remember more than I did,' she said, turning to her mother. 'It's coming back.'

'She means something to you?' Quaiche asked.

'She's my mother,' Rashmika said. 'And my name isn't Rashmika. That was the name of the daughter they lost. It's a good name, but it isn't mine. My real name is something else, but I don't quite remember it yet.'

'It's Aura,' Khouri said.

Rashmika heard the name, considered it, and then looked her mother in the eye. 'Yes. I remember now. I remember you calling me that.'

'I was right about the blood,' Grelier said, unable to suppress a smirk of satisfaction.

'Yes, you were right,' Quaiche said. 'Happy now? But you brought her here, Surgeon-General. You brought this viper into our nest. It was your mistake.'

'She'd have found her way here in the end,' Grelier replied. 'It was what she came to do. Anyway, why should you worry?' Grelier indicated the video capture of the descending ship. 'You've got the thing you wanted, haven't you? You've even got your holy machinery looking down at you in congratulation.'

'Something's happened to the ship,' Quaiche said, raising a trembling hand towards the image. He snapped a look at Vasko. 'What is it?'

'I have no idea,' he replied.

'The ship will still work,' Khouri said. 'You only needed it for its engines. You've got that much. Now let us leave with the scrimshaw suit.'

He appeared to consider her request. 'Where will you take it, without a ship?'

'Anywhere other than the Lady Morwenna would be a good start,' Khouri said. 'You may have suicidal inclinations, Dean, but we don't.'

'If I had the slightest inclination towards suicide, do you think I'd have lived as long as I have?'

Khouri looked at Malinin, then at Rashmika. 'He has a way off this thing. You were never planning on staying aboard, were you?'

'It's a question of timing,' Quaiche said. 'The ship is nearly in the holdfast. That's the moment of triumph. That's the moment when everything on Hela changes. The moment – indeed – when Hela itself changes. Nothing will be the same again, you see. There will be no more Permanent Way, no more procession of cathedrals. There will be only one spot on Hela that is precisely beneath Haldora, and that spot will no longer be moving. And there will only be one cathedral occupying it.'

'You haven't built it yet,' Grelier said.

'There's time, Surgeon-General. All the time in the world, once I stake my claim. I *choose* where that spot falls, understand? I have my hand on Hela. I can spin this world like a globe. I can stop it with my finger.'

'And the Lady Morwenna?' Grelier asked.

'If this cathedral crosses the bridge, so be it. If it doesn't, it will only emphasise the end of one era and the start of another.'

'He doesn't want it to succeed,' Vasko whispered. 'He never did.'

On the dean's couch something started chiming.

Scorpio stood his ground even though every instinct told him to run backwards. The wrinkled purple-black sphere of the nearest bladder-mine detonation had raced towards him in an eyeblink, an unstoppable wall threatening to engulf him and the portion of the bridge on which he stood. But he had placed the three charges carefully, and he knew from Remontoire's specifications that the bladder-mines were highly predictable in their effects, assuming that they worked in the first place. There was no air on Hela, so no shockwave to consider; all he had to worry about was the limiting radius of the nearest expanding sphere. With a small margin of error to allow for undulations in the surface, he would be safe only a few hundred metres beyond the nominal boundary.

The bridge was forty kilometres wide; he had arranged the charges in a row with their centres seven kilometres apart, the middle one situated at the highest point of the span. The combined effect of the overlapping spheres would take out the central thirty-four kilometres of the bridge, leaving only a few intact kilometres at either side of the rift. When he detonated the charges, Scorpio had still been standing more than a kilometre and a half out over open space.

The boundary of the sphere was nearly a kilometre away, but it looked as if it was just beyond his nose. It rippled and bulged, wrinkles and blisters rising and falling on its shrivelled surface. The nearest part of the bridge still plunged into the wall: in his mind's eye it was impossible not to imagine it continuing across the gap. But the bridge was already gone: nothing material would be left behind when the sphere evaporated.

It vanished. The middle one had already gone, and the furthest one popped out of existence a moment later.

He started walking to the edge. The tongue of bridge beneath his feet felt as steady as ever, even though it was no longer connected to the other side. He slowed as he neared the point where the tongue ended, mindful that this part might be a lot less stable than the portion nearer the cliff. It had been within metres of the edge of the bladder-mine detonation, where all sorts of peculiar quantum effects were to be expected. The atomic properties of the bridge's material might have been altered, fatal flaws introduced. Time for a person – even a pig – to tread carefully.

Vertigo gripped him as he approached the edge. The cut was miraculously clean. The surgical neatness of it, and the complete absence of debris from the intervening section, made it look as if the bridge was merely under construction. It made him feel less like a vandal than a spectator, anticipating something yet to be finished.

He turned around. In the distance, beyond the crouched form of his parked ship, he saw the Lady Morwenna. From his point of view the cathedral looked as if it had virtually reached the edge of the cliff. He knew that it still had some way to travel, but it would not be long before it arrived there.

Now that the bridge was gone, though, they would have no choice but to stop. There was no longer any question of degrees of risk, any question of just possibly being able to cross Absolution Gap. He had removed any doubt from the situation. There would be no glory, only devastation.

If they were sane, they'd stop.

A flashing pink light came on inside his helmet, synchronised with a shrill alarm tone. Scorpio halted, wondering at first if there was something wrong with his suit. But the pink light meant only that the suit was receiving a powerful modulated radio signal, outside of the usual assigned communications bands. The suit was asking him if he wanted to have the signal interpreted and passed through to him.

He looked at the cathedral again. It had to be from the Lady Morwenna.

'Do it,' Scorpio said.

The radio signal, the suit told him, was a repeating one: it was cycling through a short prerecorded transmission. The format was audio/holographic.

'Let me see it,' he said, less sure now that it had anything to do with the cathedral.

A figure appeared on the ice a dozen metres from him. It was nobody he had been expecting; in fact, it was nobody he even recognised. The figure wore no spacesuit and had the odd, asymmetrical anatomy of someone who spent most of their existence in free fall. He had plug-in limbs and a face like a planetary surface after a small nuclear exchange. An Ultra, Scorpio thought; but then, after a moment's consideration, he decided that the man probably wasn't an Ultra at all, but a member of that other, less social spacefaring human faction: the Skyjacks.

'You couldn't leave it alone, could you?' the figure asked. 'You couldn't just live with it; couldn't tolerate the existence of something so beautiful and yet so enigmatic. You had to know what it was. You had to know what its limits were. My lovely bridge. My beautiful, delicate bridge. I made it for you, placed it here like a gift. But that wasn't enough for you, was it? You had to test it. You had to destroy it. You had to fucking *ruin* it.'

Scorpio walked through the figure. 'Sorry,' he said. 'Not interested.'

'It was a thing of beauty,' the man said. 'It was a thing of fucking beauty.'

'It was in my way,' Scorpio said.

None of them could see the report Quaiche was accessing, sent through to the private display of his couch. But Rashmika watched his lips move and observed the barest crease of a frown as he reread the summary, as if he had made a mistake the first time.

'What is it?' Grelier asked.

'The bridge,' Quaiche answered. 'It doesn't seem to be there any more.'

Grelier leant closer to the couch. 'There must be some mistake.'

'There doesn't seem to be one, Surgeon-General. The inductance cable – the line we use for emergency navigation – is quite clearly severed.'

'So someone cut the cable.'

'I'll have surface imagery in a moment. Then we'll know.'

They all turned to the screen that had been showing the descent of the *Nostalgia for Infinity*. The image flickered with ghostly colours, then stabilised around a familiar view captured by a static camera that must have been mounted on the wall of Ginnungagap Rift itself.

The dean was right: there was no longer any bridge. All that remained were the extremities of the span: those curlicued fancies of scrolled sugar and icing flung out from either cliff as if to suggest the rest of the bridge by a process of elegant mathematical extrapolation. But most of the span was simply not there. Nor was there any hint of wreckage down on the floor. In her mind's eye, Rashmika had thought of the bridge collapsing time and again, ever since she had known she would have to cross it. But always she had seen it coming down in an avalanche of splintering shards, forming a jewelled, glinting scree that was in itself a thing of wonder: an enchanted glass forest you could lose yourself in.

'What happened?' the dean asked.

Rashmika turned to him. 'Does it matter? It's gone: you can see for yourself. Crossing it isn't an issue now. There's no reason not to stop the cathedral.'

'Weren't you listening, girl?' he asked. 'The cathedral doesn't stop. The cathedral *cannot* stop.'

Khouri stood up, followed by Vasko. 'We can't stay aboard any longer. You'll come with us, Aura.'

Rashmika shook her head. She was still not used to being called by that name. 'I'm not leaving without the thing I came for.'

'She is right,' said a new voice, thin and metallic.

No one said anything. It was not the intrusion of a new voice that alarmed them, but its obvious point of origin. As one, they all turned to look at the scrimshaw suit. Outwardly, nothing about it had changed: it was exactly the same brooding silver-grey form, crawling with manic detail and the blistered seams of crude welding.

'She is right,' the suit continued. 'We must leave now, Quaiche. You have your ship, the thing you wanted so badly. You have your means of stopping Hela. Now let us go. We are of no consequence to any of your plans.'

'You never spoke except when I was alone before,' Quaiche said.

'We spoke to the girl, when you wouldn't listen. She was easier: we could see straight into her head. Couldn't we, Rashmika?'

Bravely, she said, 'I'd rather you called me Aura now.'

'Aura it is, then. It changes nothing, does it? You came all this way to find us. Now you have. And there's nothing to prevent the dean from giving us to you.'

Grelier shook his head, as if he alone were the victim of an extended joke. 'The suit is talking. The suit is talking and you're all just standing around as if this happens every day.'

'For some of us,' Quaiche said, 'it does.'

'These are the shadows?' Grelier asked.

'An envoy of the shadows,' the suit said. 'The distinction need not detain us. Now, please, we must be removed from the Lady Morwenna immediately.'

'You'll stay here,' Quaiche said.

'No,' Rashmika said. 'Dean – give us the suit. It doesn't matter to you, but it means everything to us. The shadows are going to help us survive the Inhibitors. But that suit is our only direct line of communication with them.'

'If they mean that much to you, send another probe into Haldora.'

'We don't know that it will work twice. Whatever happened to you may have been a fluke. We can't gamble everything on the off chance that it might happen again.'

'Listen to her,' the suit said urgently. 'She is right: we are your only guaranteed contact with the shadows. You must safeguard us, if you wish our assistance.'

'And the price of this assistance?' Quaiche asked.

'Nothing compared to the price of extinction. We wish only to be allowed to cross over from our side of the bulk. Is that so much to ask? Is that so great a cost to pay?'

Rashmika faced the others, feeling as if she had been appointed as witness for the shadows. 'They can cross over provided that the matter-synthesiser is allowed to function. It's a machine at the heart of the Haldora receiver. It will make them bodies, and their minds will slip across the bulk and inhabit them.'

'Machines, again,' Vasko said. 'We run from one group, and now we negotiate with another.'

'If that's what it takes,' Rashmika said. 'And they're only machines because they had no choice, after everything they'd lived through.' She remembered, in hypnagogic flashes, the vision she had been granted of life in the shadow universe: of entire galaxies stained green with the marauding blight; suns like emerald lanterns. 'They were a lot like us once,' she added. 'Closer than we realise.'

'They're demons,' Quaiche said. 'Not people at all. Not even machines.'

'Demons?' Grelier asked tolerantly.

'Sent to test my faith, of course. To undermine my belief in the miracle. To pollute my mind with fantasies of other universes. To make me doubt that the vanishings are the word of God. To cause me to stumble, in the hour of my greatest testing. It's no coincidence, you know: as my plans for Hela grew towards culmination, so the demons increased their taunting of me.'

'They were scared you'd destroy them,' Rashmika said. 'The mistake they made was to deal with you as a rational individual. If only they had pretended to be demons or angels they might have got somewhere.' She leant over him, until she could smell his breath: old and vinegary, like a disused wine cellar. 'They may be demons to you, Dean, I won't deny it. But don't deny *them* to us.'

'They are demons,' he said. 'And that's why I can't let you have them. I should have had the courage to destroy them years ago.'

'Please,' Rashmika said.

Something else chimed on his couch. Quaiche pursed his lips, his eyes watering against the metal harness that held them open.

'It's done,' he said. 'The ship's in the holdfast. I have what I wanted.'

The viewscreen showed them everything. The *Nostalgia for Infinity* lay lengthwise in the pen Quaiche had prepared for it, like some captured sea creature of monstrous, mythic proportions. The clasps and supports of the cradle clutched the hull in a hundred places, expertly conforming to its irregularities and architectural flourishes. The damage that the ship had wrought upon itself during its descent – the shedding of the hull around the midsection and the disgorging of so many internal parts – was obvious now, and for a moment Quaiche wondered if his prize would be too weakened to serve his needs. But the doubt vanished immediately: the ship had withstood the stresses of the approach to the holdfast and the final, brutal mating procedure as it came to a crunching stop in the cradle. The harness machinery had been engineered to dampen the impact of that moving mass, but the instant of collision had still sent all the stress indicators into the red. Yet the harness had held – enough of it, anyway – and so had the ship. The lighthugger had not broken her back; her engines had not been ripped away from their outriggers. It had survived the hardest part of its journey, and nothing else that he asked of it would put quite the same load on it as the capture. It was everything that he had anticipated.

Quaiche signalled his audience closer. 'Look at it. See how the rear of the ship is being elevated to align the exhaust away from Hela's surface. A slight angle, but critical nonetheless.'

'As soon as the engines are fired,' Vasko said, 'she'll rip her way out of your holdfast.'

Quaiche shook his head. 'No, she won't. I didn't just pick the first place on the map, you know. This is a region of extreme geological stability. The holdfast itself is anchored deep into Hela's crust. It won't budge. Trust me: after all the effort I went to getting my hands on that ship, do you think I'd forget geology?' Another chime. Quaiche bent a speaking stalk towards his lips and whispered something to his contact in the holdfast. 'She's elevated now,' he said. 'No reason not to begin firing. Mr Malinin?'

Vasko spoke into his communicator. He asked for Scorpio, but it was another senior who answered.

'Request that the ship fire its engines,' Vasko said.

But even before he had finished his sentence they saw the engines light. Twin spikes of purple-edged white lanced from the Conjoiner drives, their brilliance overloading the camera. The ship crept forwards in the harness, like a last, weakened effort at escape by a captured sea creature. But the holding machines flexed, absorbing the shock of drive activation, and the ship gradually returned to its earlier position. The engines burned clean and steady.

'Look,' Grelier said, pointing to one of the garret's windows. 'We can see it.'

The exhaust beams were two scratches of fading white, probing over the horizon like searchlights.

A moment later, they felt a tremble run through the Lady Morwenna.

Quaiche summoned Grelier, gestured at his eyes. 'Take this monstrosity off my face. I don't need it any more.'

'The eye-opener?'

'Remove it. *Gently.*'

Grelier did as he was told, carefully levering the metal frame away from its subject.

'Your eyelids will take a while to settle back,' Grelier told him. 'In the meantime, I'd keep the glasses on.'

Quaiche held the shades to his face, like a child playing with an adult's spectacles. Without the eye-opener, they were much too large to stay in place.

'Now we can leave,' he said.

*

Scorpio loped back to the squat pebble of his ship, climbed in through the open doorframe and took the little craft away from the remains of the bridge. The gashed landscape wheeled below him, myriad sharp black shadows stretching across it like individual ink-spills. One wall of the Rift was now as dark as night, while the other was illuminated only near its top. Some part of him wanted the bridge to still be there; wanted his last act to have been revoked so that he could have more time to consider its consequences. He had always felt that way after he hurt someone or something. He always regretted his impulsiveness, but the one thing about the regret was that it never lasted.

The experts had been wrong about the bridge, he now knew. It was a human artefact, not something made by the scuttlers at all. It had certainly been here for more than a century, but it might not have been very much older than that. But until it was shattered, broken open, its origin – its very nature – had remained unknown. It was a thing of advanced science, but it was the advanced science of the Demarchist era rather than the vanished aliens'. He thought of the man who had appeared on the ice, his sense of anguish that his beautiful, pointless creation had been destroyed. But it was a recording, not a live transmission. It must have been made when the bridge was made, designed to activate when the structure was damaged or destroyed. It meant that the man had always considered this possibility; had even perhaps anticipated it. To Scorpio he had sounded very much like someone being vindicated.

The ship pulled away from the side of the Rift. He was over solid ground now, with the roughly defined track of the Way visible below him. There, no more than three or four kilometres away, was the Lady Morwenna, throwing its own shadow far back along the route it had travelled, dragging it like a great black wedding train. He pushed the bridge and its maker from his mind. Everything he wanted, everything that mattered now, was in that cathedral. And he had to find a way to get inside it.

He took his ship closer, until he could make out the slow, inching crawl of the great walking machine. There was something hypnotic and calming about the sequenced movements of the flying buttresses. It was not his imagination, then: the Lady Morwenna was still moving, seemingly oblivious to the nonexistence of any safe crossing ahead of it.

He hadn't expected that.

Perhaps it would start slowing any moment now, as forward

sensors detected the interruption in its route. Or perhaps it was simply going to keep walking towards the edge, exactly as if the bridge still existed. A thought occurred to him for the first time: what if stopping *really* wasn't an option, and not just bluster on Quaiche's part?

He slid the ship to within five hundred metres of the cathedral, approximately level with the top of its main tower. All he needed was a landing stage, or something he could improvise as one, and some means of accessing the interior of the cathedral from there. The main landing pad was too crowded; he couldn't put his ship down on it without risking a collision with one of the other two craft already occupying it. One of them was an unfamiliar red cockleshell; the other was the shuttle Vasko and Khouri had brought from the *Nostalgia for Infinity*. The shuttle was the only ship capable of getting all of them – including Aura and the suit – back into orbit, so he was anxious not to damage it or push it from the landing stage.

But there were other possibilities, and a landing on the designated pad would have lacked the element of surprise. He circled the cathedral, tapping the thruster stud to hold his altitude steady, watching the stuttering glare flicker against the Lady Morwenna like midsummer lightning. The shadows and highlights moved with him, making the architectural features appear to slide and ooze against each other, as if the cathedral were yawning, waking from some tremendous sleep of stone and metal. Even the gargoyles joined in the illusion of movement, their gape-jawed heads seeming to track him with the smooth, oiled malevolence of weapons turrets.

It wasn't an illusion.

He saw a flash of fire from one of the gargoyles, and then felt his ship shudder and lurch. In his helmet, alarms rang. The console lit up with emergency icons. He saw the cathedral and the landscape tilt alarmingly and felt the ship begin a sharp, barely controlled descent. The thrusters fired urgently, doing their best to stabilise the falling craft, but there was no hope of getting away from the Lady Morwenna, let alone of reaching orbit. Scorpio pulled hard on the controls, trying to steer the damaged ship away from the gargoyle defence systems. His chest hurt as he applied maximum pressure to the steering stick, making him groan and bite his bottom lip. He tasted his own blood. Another head vomited red fire towards him. The ship lurched and fell even more swiftly. He braced for the impact; it came an instant later. He stayed conscious as the ship slammed into the ice, but cried out with the pain – a pure meaningless roar of rage and indignation. The ship rolled, finally coming to rest on its side. The open door was above him, neatly framing the revealed heart of Haldora.

He waited for at least a minute before moving.

FORTY-SEVEN

The detachment of Cathedral Guard kept watch over their prisoners while Grelier left the garret with whispered orders from Quaiche buzzing in his ear. When he returned he brought with him a suit of approximately the right size for Rashmika: a blood-red Adventist model rather than the one she had worn during her journey aboard the caravan.

Grelier dropped the pieces of the suit into her lap. 'Put it on,' he said. 'And don't take an eternity doing it. I want to get off this thing as much as you do.'

'I'm not leaving without the scrimshaw suit,' she said, before glancing at her mother. 'Or my friends. They're coming with me, both of them.'

'No,' Quaiche said. 'They're staying here, at least until you and I reach the safety of the ship.'

'Which ship?' Vasko asked.

'Your ship, of course,' Quaiche said, as if this should have been obvious. 'The *Nostalgia for Infinity*. There's still rather a lot I don't know about it. The ship even appears to have something of a mind of its own. Mysteries, mysteries: doubtless we'll get to the bottom of them all in good time. What I do know is this: I don't trust that ship not to do something stupid like making itself blow up.'

'There are people aboard it,' Vasko said.

'A fully armed squad of Cathedral Guard will be attempting occupation from the holdfast even as I speak. They will have the weapons and armour denied to the earlier infiltration units, and they won't need to wait for back-up from spaceborne elements. I assure you: they'll have that ship flushed clean in a matter of hours, no matter what tricks it tries to play on them. In the meantime, it seems to me that the one thing guaranteed to stop that ship from doing anything foolish would be the presence of Rashmika – apologies, *Aura* – herself. After all, it practically threw itself into my holdfast as soon as I declared my position.'

'I won't save you,' Rashmika said. 'With me or without me, Dean, you're a dead man unless you give me the shadows.'

'The shadows stay here, with your friends.'

'That's murder.'

'No, merely prudence.' He beckoned one of the Cathedral Guard officers closer to his couch. 'Haken, keep them here until you have news of my safe arrival in the holdfast. I should be there within thirty minutes, but you are not to act without my word. Understood?'

The guard acknowledged him with a nod. 'And if we don't hear from you, Dean?'

'The cathedral won't reach the western limit of the bridge for another four hours. In three hours and thirty minutes, you may release your prisoners and make your own escape. Regroup at the holdfast at your earliest convenience.'

'And the suit, sir?' Haken asked.

'It goes down with the Lady Mor. The cathedral will take its demons with it when it dies.' Quaiche directed his attention towards Grelier, who was helping Rashmika with the final details of the Adventist suit. 'Surgeon-General? Would you happen to have your medical kit, by any chance?'

Grelier looked affronted. 'I never leave home without it.'

'Then open it. Find a syringe containing something potent, like DEUS-X. That should be sufficient encouragement, don't you agree?'

'Find your own way of controlling the girl,' Grelier said. 'I'm leaving on my own. I think it's about time you and I went our separate ways.'

'We can talk about that later,' Quaiche said, 'but for the time being I think you need me as much as I need you. I guessed that you and I might be headed for a slight crisis in our relationship, so I had Haken's men disable your ship.'

'I'm not fussed. I'll take the other one.'

'There isn't another one. Haken's men took care of the Ultra shuttle at the same time.'

'Then we're all stuck aboard the cathedral, is that it?' Grelier asked.

'No. I *said* we were going to the holdfast, didn't I? Have some faith, Surgeon-General. Have some faith.'

'Bit late in the day for that, I think,' Grelier said. But even as he spoke he began rummaging in his case, flipping it open to reveal the ranked sets of syringes.

Rashmika finished putting on the suit by herself. There was no helmet: they were keeping that from her for the moment. She looked at her mother, then at Vasko. 'You can't leave them here. They have to come with us.'

'They'll be allowed to leave in good time,' Quaiche said.

Rashmika felt the cold pressure of the syringe against her neck.

'Ready to move?' Grelier asked.

'I'm not leaving them here,' Rashmika insisted.

'We'll be all right,' Khouri said. 'Just go with him and do what he says. You're the one that matters now.'

She breathed heavily, accepting it, knowing she had no other choice. 'Let's get this over with,' Rashmika said.

Glaur allowed himself one last look at the throbbing empire of Motive Power before he left it for ever. He felt an unconscionable twinge of pride: the machines were performing flawlessly even though they had been running without human assistance ever since Seyfarth and he had turned their dual keys in the lockout console, thereby putting the Lady Morwenna on autonomic control. It was the feeling a headmaster might have experienced upon spying into a classroom of diligent scholars, busy with their studies even in the absence of authority. Given time, the lack of human attention would make its mark: warning lights would begin to appear on the reactor, and the turbines and their associated mechanisms would begin to overheat from the lack of lubrication and adjustment. But that was many hours in the future: far beyond the likely lifetime of the Lady Morwenna. Glaur was no longer concerned about the probability of the cathedral sustaining a crossing of the bridge. He knew from the telltale indicators on the main navigation board that the inductance cable had been broken some distance ahead of the cathedral. It could have been at any point within a hundred kilometres of the Lady Mor's present position, but Glaur knew, with absolute conviction, that it was because the bridge itself had been taken down. He couldn't say how, or who had done it. A rival cathedral, most likely, intent on robbing the dean of even this one foolhardy shot at glory. It must have been quite a thing to see, though. Almost as spectacular a sight as the one the cathedral herself would make very shortly.

He turned from the machines and began to ascend the spiral staircase that accessed the next level of the cathedral. He trudged from tread to tread, awkward in the emergency vacuum suit he had retrieved from the repair shop. He had the faceplate raised, but shortly he expected to be out on Hela's surface, retracing the cathedral's footsteps back towards the orthodox route of the Way. Many had already left: if he maintained a brisk pace, he was sure to catch up with one of the parties before very long. There might even be a vehicle he could take from the garage deck, if they hadn't all been used.

Glaur neared the top. Something was wrong: his usual exit was obstructed, blocked by grilled metal. It was the protective gate: normally open, only rarely locked by members of the Clocktower when they were on sensitive duties.

He had been locked into Motive Power.

Glaur backed away from the gate. There were other stairwells, but he was certain that he would find similar obstructions at the top of them. Why go to the trouble of blocking one route, and not all the rest?

Glaur panicked. He grabbed the gate, rattling it on its hinges. It shuddered, but there was no way that he was going to be able to open it with brute force. There was no lock on this side, even if he'd had a key. He would need cutting tools to make his escape into the rest of the Lady Morwenna.

He forced calm: there was still plenty of time. In all likelihood he had been locked down in Motive Power by mistake, by someone thinking the hall was unattended and that it might as well be secured against possible sabotage attempts, no matter how ineffective they were likely to be.

All he needed was cutting equipment. That, fortunately, wasn't a problem. Not down in Motive Power.

Keeping his head, forcing himself not to rush down the stairs, Glaur began to descend again. In his mind's eye he was already rummaging through the tools of the repair shop, selecting the best for the task.

FORTY-EIGHT

From their newly constructed garrisons in the steep walls of the holdfast, detachments of Cathedral Guard stormed the downed hulk of the *Nostalgia for Infinity*. This time they were prepared: they had sifted the intelligence reports from the earlier attack and had some idea of what to expect. They knew that they were entering an active and hostile environment – not just because of the resistance they could expect from the Ultras, but because this ship had the means to turn against them, crushing and impaling, drowning and suffocating. None of this needed explanation, however: that was someone else's problem. All that concerned the Guard units was the appropriate response.

Now they carried heavy-duty flame-throwers and energy weapons, massive high-penetration slug-guns and hyperdiamond-tipped drilling rigs. They carried hydraulic bulwarks to shore up corridors and bulkheads against collapse or unwanted closure. They carried shock-hardening epoxy sprays to freeze changing structures into shape. They carried explosives and nerve agents. They carried outlawed nanotechnologies.

Their mandate was still the same: they were to take the ship with minimum casualties. But the strict interpretation of that mandate was to be left at the discretion of the commanding officers. And any damage to the ship itself – while regrettable – was not as serious an issue as it had been while the *Nostalgia for Infinity* was still in orbit. The dean had promised the Ultras that they could have their ship back, but – given all that had happened since the last attempt at takeover – it appeared very unlikely that the ship would ever be leaving Hela's surface. It had, perhaps, ceased even to be a ship.

The Cathedral Guard made swift progress. They swarmed through the vessel, neutralising resistance with maximum force. Surrender was always an option, but it was never one that Ultras took.

So be it. If the minimum of casualties meant the death of every remaining crew member, then that was the way it would have to be.

The ship groaned around them as they gouged and cleaved and burned their way through it. It fought back, taking some of their number, but its efforts were becoming sporadic and misdirected. As the Cathedral Guard declared more and more of the ship to be under their secure control, it struck them that the ship was dying. It didn't matter: all the dean had ever wanted was the engines. The rest of it was an unnecessary complication.

He knew that he was dying. There was a place of rest for all things, and after all the centuries, all the light-years, all the changes, he began to think that he had found his final destination. He supposed that he had known it even before he saw the holdfast; even, perhaps, before he had gutted himself to save the sleepers he had carried from Ararat and Yellowstone. Perhaps he had known it from the moment he slowed from interstellar space into this place of miracle and pilgrimage, nine years earlier. There had been a weariness in him ever since he had been woken from his sleep in the ocean of Ararat, drawn to bad-tempered alertness by the newcomers and the urgent need to evacuate. Like Clavain, brooding alone on his island, he had really only wanted rest and solitude and an ease from his own unresolved burden of sins. Had none of that happened, he thought he would have been very content to remain in that bay, rusting into history, becoming part of the geography, no longer even haunting himself, fading into a final, mindless dream of flight.

He felt the Cathedral Guards enter his body, their violent progress at first no worse than pins and needles, but gradually becoming more unpleasant – an intense, fiery indigestion which in turn became a prickling agony. He could not guess their number, whether there were a hundred or a thousand of them. He could not guess at the weapons they used against him, or the damage they left behind. They burned his nerve endings and blinded his eyes. They left trails of numbness behind them. The lack of pain where they had passed – the lack of any sensation whatsoever – was the worst thing of all. They were reclaiming the dead machinery of the ship from the temporary grasp of his living infection. It had been a nice dream, what he had become. Now it was coming to an end.

When he was gone, when they had cleansed him, everything essential would remain. Even if the engines faltered as his mind ceased to control them, the people in the holdfast would find a way to make them fire again. They would make his corpse work for them, jerking him into a twitching parody of life. It would not be the work of days to bring Hela into synchronisation with Haldora, but something like the building of a cathedral itself. They would run his corpse until that work was done, and then, perhaps, enshrine or sanctify him.

The Guards were pushing deeper. The numbness that they left behind them was no longer confined to the narrow, winding routes they had taken into him, but had enlarged to consume entire districts of his anatomy. He had felt a similar sense of absence when he released the sleepers into orbit, but that wounding had been self-inflicted, and he had wrought no more harm upon himself than absolutely necessary. Now, the damage was indiscriminate, and the absence of sensation all the more terrifying. In a little while – a few hours, perhaps – the voids would have swallowed everything. He would be gone, then, leaving only the autonomic processes behind.

There was still time to act. He was becoming blind to himself, but his own body formed only the tiny, glittering kernel of his sphere of consciousness. Even as he rested in the cradle of the holdfast, he was still in receipt of data from the drones he had already released around Hela. He apprehended everything that was happening on the planet, his view synthesised and enhanced from the patchwork impressionism of the cameras.

And in his belly, yet to be reached by the Cathedral Guard, he still had the three hypometric weapons. They were excruciatingly delicate things: it had been difficult enough using them under normal conditions of thrust, let alone when he was lying on his side. It was anyone's guess as to how the threshing machinery would react if he started it now; how long it would function before ripping itself and everything around it to shreds.

But he thought it likely they would work at least once. All he needed was a target, some means of making a difference.

His view of Hela changed emphasis. With an effort of will he focused on the streams of data that included imagery of the cathedral, shot from a variety of angles and elevations. For a moment, the effort of assembling these faint, fuzzy, multispectral moving views into a single three-dimensional picture was sufficiently taxing that he forgot all about the Cathedral Guards and what they were doing to him. Then, in his mind's eye, with the unnatural clarity of a vision, he saw the Lady Morwenna. He felt his ever-shifting spatial relationship to the cathedral, as if a taut iron chain bound them together. He knew how far away it was. He knew in which direction it lay.

High on the flat surface of one tower, tiny figures moved like clockwork marionettes.

*

They had reached the Lady Morwenna's landing stage. Two spacecraft waited there: the vehicle that the Ultras had arrived in, and the red cockleshell that Rashmika recognised as belonging to the surgeon-general. Both ships were peppered with the scorched holes of impact points where they had been shot at close range. Given time, Rashmika thought, the ships might have been able to repair themselves enough to leave the cathedral. But the one thing they didn't have now was time.

Grelier had the syringe pressed hard against the outer integument of her suit. She didn't know if the needle would be able to penetrate that layer and reach through to her skin, but she was certain that she did not want to take the chance. She had heard of DEUS-X; she knew what it could do. There might be a cure, and maybe the virus's effects would even begin to fade after a while as her body developed its own immune response. But the one thing everyone agreed on where indoctrinal viruses were concerned was that once you'd had one in your blood, you were never quite the same again.

'Look,' Grelier said, with the cheerfulness of someone pointing out beautiful scenery, 'you can still see the exhaust beams.' He directed Rashmika's attention to the double-edged sliver of light, like a highway in the sky. 'Say what you like about our dean, but once he makes a plan, he sticks to it. It's just such a shame he couldn't bear to tell me about it first.'

'I'd worry about that ship if I were you,' Rashmika said. 'It's close enough to make trouble, even now. Are you sure you feel safe, Surgeon-General?'

'They won't try anything,' Quaiche said. 'Too much risk of hurting you. That's why we've got you with us.'

Unlike Grelier and Rashmika, the dean was not wearing any kind of vacuum suit. He still travelled in his mobility couch, but now a transparent blister had been fitted into place around the couch's upper surface, providing the necessary amenities of life-support. They heard his voice through their helmet speakers: it sounded just as thin and papery as usual.

'We can't all fit in my ship,' Grelier said. 'And I'm certainly not taking the risk of getting into their shuttle. We don't know what booby traps might be aboard it.'

'That's all right,' Quaiche said. 'I've thought of that.'

Light hit their faces. Despite Grelier's hold on her, Rashmika looked around. A third ship – one she had not seen before – was holding station on the side of the ramp. It was long and thin, like an arrow. It held itself upright, balancing on a single spike of thrust. Where had it come from? Rashmika was quite certain she would have noticed if another ship had approached the cathedral from any direction.

'It was here all along,' Quaiche said, as if reading her mind, 'built into the architecture below us. I always knew I'd need it one day.' She noticed now that he had something in his lap: a portable control deck of some kind. The bony tips of his fingers were skating over it, like a spiritualist's over a Ouija board.

'Your ship?' Rashmika asked.

'It's the *Dominatrix*,' Grelier interjected, as if this was supposed to mean something to her. 'The ship that brought him to Hela in the first place. The one that rescued him when he got into trouble poking his nose into things that didn't concern him.'

'So it has history,' Quaiche said. 'All right, let's get aboard. We haven't got time to stand around admiring things. I told Haken we'd be at the holdfast within half an hour. I want to be there when the Guards declare her secured.'

'You'll never take the *Infinity*,' Rashmika said.

A door opened in the side of Quaiche's ship, exactly aligned with the side of the ramp. Quaiche steered his couch towards it, obviously intent on being the first aboard his private craft. Rashmika felt a tingle of apprehension: was he going to leave without them? She supposed anything was possible now: all the talk of safeguards, of having her along for the ride, might have been lies. As he had said in the garret, one era was ending and another beginning. Old loyalties – and possibly even rationality itself – could not be counted upon.

'Wait for us,' Grelier said.

'Of course I'll wait for you! Who else is going to keep me alive?'

The ship yawed away from the landing pad, leaving a metre-wide gap. Rashmika saw Quaiche's fingers skate with panicked speed over the control board. The stabilising jets from the waiting ship stammered out in different directions: rapiers of purple-edged fire lasting a fraction of a second.

Glaur reached the repair shop. It was a lavish grotto of possible escape tools, all sparklingly clean and neatly racked. He could cut his way out of anything, given the equipment at hand. His only problem would be manhandling whatever he chose all the way back up the spiral staircase to the locked gate. And he would need space to use it safely, without injuring himself: not so simple given the tight spiral of the stairs. He appraised the tools: even given that constraint, there were still adequate possibilities. It would just take a little time, that was all. His gloved hands dithered over one tool, then another. Make the right choice: the one thing he didn't want to have to do was come back down the stairs again, especially not while wearing the suit.

He looked back across the floor of Motive Power. Now that the idea of cutting his way out had occurred to him, he realised that he had no need to ascend the stairs at all. His only objective was to leave the Lady Morwenna by the quickest possible means: he had no possessions worth saving, no loved ones he needed to find and rescue, and there was – now that he thought about it properly – very little chance of finding a vehicle on the garage deck.

He could cut his way out right here, right now.

Glaur gathered the tools of his choice and walked across the floor to one of the transparent panels set into it. The ground was still oozing below: almost a twenty-metre drop, but that was a lot more palatable than going all the way back up to the next level and finding his way out by other means. He could cut through the glass and its associated grillework easily: all he needed was a means to lower himself to the ground.

He went back to the repair shop and found a spool of wire cabling. There was probably some rope somewhere, but he didn't have time to hunt for it. The wire would have to do. He wouldn't be asking very much of it, not in Hela's gravity.

Back at the window in the floor, Glaur looked around for the nearest solid piece of machinery. There: the support stanchion for one of the catwalks, bolted solidly to the floor. There was more than enough cable to reach it.

He looped the line around the stanchion, then walked back to the glass panel. One end of the cable formed a convenient loop: he undid his suit utility belt and passed the loop through from one end, then refastened the belt securely.

He judged that the line would drop him to within three or four metres of the surface. The crudity of the arrangement offended Glaur's engineering sensibilities, but he did not want to spend one minute longer than was absolutely necessary aboard the doomed cathedral.

He closed his helmet faceplate and made sure that the air was chugging in correctly. Then he sat on the floor, the glass panel between his legs, and turned on the cutter. Glaur plunged the blinding stiletto of the beam into the glass, and almost immediately saw the cold jet of escaping gas on the other side of the panel. Very shortly it would be a gale as all the air in the hall was sucked away. Emergency shutters would seal off the rest of the cathedral, but anyone still up there was probably on borrowed time already. It was possible, Glaur reflected, that he was the last man aboard the Lady Morwenna. The thought thrilled him: he had never expected fate to lay that kind of significance upon his life.

He carried on cutting, thinking of the stories he would tell.

FORTY-NINE

The Cathedral Guard had finished securing an entire district of the *Nostalgia for Infinity*. The bodies of dead Ultras lay all around them, smoking from weapons hits. There were one or two Cathedral Guard, but they were far outnumbered by the victims from the crew.

The Guards picked their way through the dead, poking them with the cherry-red muzzles of slug-guns and boser rifles. Lights burned from sconces in the corridor walls, casting a solemn ochre sheen on the fallen. On balance, the victims did not look very much like the usual image of Ultras. The majority were unaugmented: autopsies might reveal buried implants, but there was little sign of the flamboyant display of mechanical parts usually associated with Ultra crews. Most of these people, in fact, appeared to be baseline humans, just like the Cathedral Guard themselves. The only difference was that there were, amongst the dead, an unusual number of pigs. The Guards poked and prodded the pigs with particular interest: they did not see very many of them on Hela. What had they been doing, fighting alongside these humans, often in the same uniform? It was yet another mystery to add to the pile. Yet another problem for someone else to worry about.

'Perhaps we'll find Scorpio,' one of the officers said to a colleague.

'Scorpio?'

'The pig that was running things when Seyfarth's unit came aboard. They say there's a special reward for the one who brings his body out of the ship. It'll be difficult to miss: Seyfarth impaled him, here and here.' He gestured to his collar bones.

The other officer kicked one of the pigs over, grateful for the helmet that meant he did not have to smell the carnage. 'Let's keep an eye out, then.'

The lights in the wall faded. The Cathedral Guard stepped through the bodies, only their helmet markers penetrating the darkness. Another part of the ship must have died; it was a wonder, really, that the lights had kept burning as long as they had.

But then they flickered back on again, as if to mock that assumption.

Something was wrong.

'The ship's losing control,' Quaiche said. 'This shouldn't be happening.'

His private vessel nudged closer to the pad. The gap was only a few centimetres.

'No,' Grelier said, with sudden insistence. 'Don't risk it. There's obviously something wrong . . .'

But Quaiche had seen his moment. He sped his couch towards the waiting airlock, pushing its speed to the maximum. For a long, lingering moment the spacecraft held perfect station. It looked as if he might make it, even if he had to cross a hand's width of empty space. But then the *Dominatrix* lurched back again, its control jets firing chaotically. The gap enlarged: not centimetres now, but a good fraction of a metre. Quaiche began to slow down, realising his mistake. His hands worked like demons. But the gap was widening, and his couch was not going to stop in time.

The *Dominatrix* was now five or six metres from the landing stage, still desperately trying to orientate itself. It began to rotate, turning the open aperture of the airlock away from view.

By then it didn't matter. Quaiche screamed. His couch passed over the edge.

'Fool,' Grelier said, before Quaiche's scream had finished.

Rashmika looked at the ship. It had turned its rear-facing side back into view. Now, finally, they saw that the ship was terribly damaged, the smoothness of its hull ruined by a series of strange wounds. They were perfectly circular openings, revealing near-spherical interiors filled with the bright, clean metal of sheared surfaces. It was as if blisters had opened in the hull itself, bursting to reveal mathematically precise apertures.

'Something attacked it,' Grelier said.

The ship fell back, losing altitude, its corrective gestures becoming more frantic and ineffectual with each second.

'Get down,' Grelier said. He pushed her to the deck, falling beside her at the same instant. He flattened himself as efficiently as he could, one hand urging Rashmika to do likewise.

'What . . .' she began.

'Close your eyes.'

The warning came a fraction too late. She caught the beginning of the blast as the damaged ship hit the surface of Hela. The glare of it reached through her eyelids, a light like a hot needle pushed into her optic nerve. Through her body she felt the entire structure of the cathedral shake.

When the gale of escaping air had died down, Glaur judged that it was safe to make his escape. He had cut himself a man-sized hole in both the glass panel and the protective grille beneath it. Below were vacuum and – about twenty metres further down – the endlessly scrolling surface of Hela.

He checked his safety line once more, then heaved his lower half over the edge and pushed his legs through the hole. The edges of the glass were softly rounded where they had melted: there was no danger of them ripping any part of his suit. For a moment he lingered, his upper body still inside Motive Power, his lower half dangling into space. This was it: the final moment of surrender. Then he gave himself a valiant shove and became temporarily weightless. He fell for a second, retaining only an impression of blurred machinery rushing past. Then the line arrested his fall, snagging him sharply. The belt dug into his waist; he came to a halt on his back, with his head and shoulders at a slight angle to the ground.

He looked down: four, maybe five metres. The ground slid by beneath him. It was further than he had planned, and it would probably knock the wind out of him when he hit, but he should still be able to dust himself off and get up. Even if he was knocked out by the fall, the cathedral would just pass harmlessly over his fallen body: the huge, stomping plates of the traction feet were arranged in rows on either side of him. One set of feet would pass much nearer to him than the other, but still too far away to cause him any real anxiety.

The belt was beginning to grow uncomfortable. *Now or never*, Glaur thought. He reached up, fiddled with the catch, and suddenly he was falling.

He hit the ice. It was bad – he had never fallen from such a distance before – but he took the brunt of it on his back and after he had lain still for a minute he had the strength to roll over and think about standing up. The intricate machinery-filled underbelly of the Lady Morwenna had been sliding over him all the while, like a sky full of angular clouds.

Glaur stood up. To his relief, all his limbs seemed unbroken. Nor had the fall damaged his air supply: the helmet indicators were all in the green. There was enough air in the suit for another thirty hours of vigorous activity. He'd need it, too: he was going to have to hike all the way back along the Way until he met with other evacuees, or a rescue party sent out by another cathedral. It would be close, he thought, but he would far rather be walking than waiting aboard the Lady Morwenna, anticipating the first sickening lurch as she went over the edge.

Glaur was about to start walking when a vacuum-suited figure emerged from the cover of the nearest line of traction feet. The figure sprinted towards him – except it was more of a concentrated waddle than a sprint. Despite himself, Glaur laughed: there was something ludicrous about the way the childlike form moved. He racked his memory of the cathedral's inhabitants, wondering who this dwarflike survivor could possibly be, and what he might want of Glaur.

Then he noticed the glint of a knife in the figure's odd two-fingered gauntlet – a knife that shimmered and flickered, like something that could not decide what shape it wanted to be – and suddenly Glaur's sense of humour deserted him.

'I was worried that might happen,' Grelier said. 'Are you all right? Can you see?'

'I think so,' she said. She was dazed from the explosion of the dean's ship, but still basically able to function.

'Then stand up. We don't have much time.' Again Rashmika felt the needle squeeze against the outer layer of her suit.

'Quaiche was wrong,' she said, not moving. 'You were never safe.'

'Shut up and walk.'

His presence must have alerted it. The red cockleshell-shaped spacecraft blinked two green lights in acknowledgement. A small door opened in one side.

'Get in,' Grelier said.

'Your ship's no good,' Rashmika said. 'Didn't you hear Quaiche? He had his men shoot it up.'

'It doesn't have to get us very far. Just getting off this cathedral would be a start.'

'And then where, assuming it even takes off? Not the holdfast, surely?'

'That was Quaiche's plan, not mine.'

'Where, then?'

'I'll think of something,' he said. 'I know a lot of places to hide on this planet.'

'You don't have to take me with you.'

'You're useful, Miss Els, too useful to throw away just this moment. You do understand, don't you?'

'Let me go. Let me go back and save my mother. You don't need me now.' She nodded at his waiting spacecraft. 'Take it, and they'll assume I'm with you. They won't attack you.'

'Wee bit risky,' he said.

'Please . . . just let me save her.'

He took a step towards the waiting ship, then halted. It was as if he had remembered something he had forgotten, something that meant he would have to go back into the Lady Morwenna.

But instead he just looked at her, and made a horrible sound.

'Surgeon-General?' she said.

The pressure of the needle was gone. The syringe hit the deck in silence. The surgeon-general twitched, and then sagged to his knees. He made that sound again: a pained gurgling she hoped never to hear again.

She stood up, still unsteady on her feet. She did not know whether it was due to the after-effects of the explosion or the relaxation of the fear she had felt with the syringe pressed against her all that time.

'Grelier?' she said quietly.

But Grelier said nothing. She looked down at him, realising then that there was something very, very wrong with him. The abdomen of his suit had caved in, as if an entire part of him had been scooped away from within.

Rashmika reached down, fumbling through the surgeon-general's belongings until she found the Clocktower key. She stood up, stepping back from the body, and watched as it suddenly disintegrated, spheres of nothingness chewing into it until all that remained was a kind of frozen interstitial residue.

'Thank you, Captain,' she said, without quite knowing why.

She looked ahead, towards the broken bridge. Not much time now.

Alone, Rashmika rode an elevator back down into the Lady Morwenna, closing her eyes against the stained-glass light, forcing concentration. Thoughts crashed through her head: Quaiche was dead; the surgeon-general was dead. Quaiche had ordered the Cathedral Guard not to let anyone leave until he reached the holdfast, or until thirty minutes before the Lady Morwenna was due to fall over the western limit of the bridge. And the scrimshaw suit was to remain aboard: he had been very specific about that. But the suit was heavy and cumbersome: even if the guards could be persuaded to let them take it, they would need more than thirty minutes to get it off the cathedral. They might even need more time than the handful of hours they had left before the cathedral ceased to exist.

Perhaps, she thought, it was time to make a deal with the shadows, here and now. Even they must see that she had no other choice, no way of saving their envoy. She had done the best she could, hadn't she? If they had information regarding what Rashmika and her allies needed to do to allow the other shadows to cross over, then they would lose nothing by giving it to her now.

The elevator came to a clanging halt. Gingerly, Rashmika slid aside the trellised gate. She still had to move through the interior of the cathedral, retracing the route along which Grelier and the dean had brought her. Then she would have to find the other elevator that would take her to the high levels of the Clocktower. And she would have to do all this while avoiding any contact with the remaining elements of the Cathedral Guard.

She stepped out of the elevator. Anxious to conserve suit air for when she really needed it, she slid up her visor. The cathedral had never been this quiet before. She could still hear the labouring of the engines, but even that seemed muted now. There was no choir, no voices raised in prayer, no solemn processions of footsteps.

Her heart quickened. The cathedral was already deserted. The Cathedral Guard must have left already, during the commotion on the landing stage. If that was the case, all she had to do was find her mother and Vasko and hope that the scrimshaw suit was still in a communicative frame of mind.

She orientated herself using the designs in the stained-glass windows as a reference, and set off towards the Clocktower. But she had barely taken a step when two officers of the Cathedral Guard emerged from an annexe, pointing weapons at her. They had their helmets on, visors down, pink plumes hanging from their crests.

'Please,' Rashmika said, 'let me through. All I want is to reach my friends.'

'Stay where you are,' said one of the guards, training his gun on the flickering indices of her life-support tabard. He nodded to his partner. 'Secure her.'

His companion shouldered his gun and reached for something on his belt.

'The dean is dead,' Rashmika said. 'The cathedral is about to be smashed to pieces. You should leave, now, while you still can.'

'We have orders,' the guard said, while his partner pushed her against a slab of stonework.

'Don't you understand?' she asked. 'It's all over now. Everything has changed. It doesn't matter.'

'Bind her. And if you can shut her up, do that as well.'

The guard moved to slide her visor down. Rashmika started to protest, wanting to fight but knowing she didn't have the strength. But even as she struggled, she saw something lurch from the shadows behind the guard holding the gun.

A flicker of a moving blade flashed through her peripheral vision. The guard made a guttural sound, his gun dropping to the floor.

The other one started to react, springing away from Rashmika and making an effort to bring his own weapon around. Rashmika kicked him, her boot catching him in the knee. He stumbled back into the masonry, still fumbling for the gun. The vacuum-suited pig crossed the distance to him, slid the silver gleam of his knife into the man's abdomen and then dragged it upwards through his sternum in one smooth arc.

Scorpio killed the knife, slipped it back into its sheath. Firmly but gently, he pushed Rashmika into the shadows, where the two of them crouched together.

She pushed her visor up again, surprised at the harshness of her own breathing.

'Thanks, Scorp.'

'You know who I am? After all this time?'

'You left your mark,' she said, between breaths. She reached and touched his hand with hers. 'Thanks for coming.'

'Had to drop in, didn't I?'

She waited until her breathing had settled down. 'Scorp – was that you, with the bridge?'

'Had my trademark on it, did it?' He pushed his own visor up and smiled. 'Yes. How else was I going to get them to stop this thing?'

'I understand,' she said. 'It was a good idea, too. Shame about the bridge, but—'

'But?'

'The cathedral can't stop, Scorp. It's going over.'

He seemed to take this as only a minor adjustment to his world view. 'Then we'd better get off it as soon as we can. Where are the others?'

'Up the Clocktower, in the dean's garret. They're under guard.'

'We'll get them out,' he said. 'Trust me.'

'And the suit, Scorp? The thing I came all this way to find?'

'We need to have a word about that,' he said.

FIFTY

They rode the elevator up to the garret, the low sun sliding colours across their faces.

Scorpio reached into his suit pocket. 'Remontoire gave me this,' he said.

Rashmika took the piece of conch material, examined it with the cautious, critical eye of someone who has lived amongst fossils and bones and who knows that the slightest scratch can speak volumes – both truthful and false.

'I don't recognise it,' she said.

He told her everything that he had learned from Remontoire, everything that Remontoire had guessed or conjectured.

'We're not alone in this,' Scorpio said. 'There's someone else out there. We don't even have a name for them. We only know them from the wreckage they leave behind.'

'They left this behind on Ararat?'

'And around Ararat,' he said. 'And elsewhere, you can bet. Whoever they are, they must have been out there a long time. They're clever, Aura.' He used her real name deliberately. 'They'd have to be, to have lived with the Inhibitors for so long.'

'I don't understand what they have to do with us.'

'Maybe nothing,' he said. 'Maybe everything. It depends on what happened to the scuttlers. That's where you come in, I think.'

Her voice was flat as she said, 'Everyone knows what happened to the scuttlers.'

'Which is?'

'They were destroyed by the Inhibitors.'

He watched the colours paint her face. She looked radiant and dangerous, like an avenging angel in an illuminated heretical gospel. 'And what do you think?'

'I don't think the Inhibitors had anything to do with the extinction of the scuttlers. I never have: not since I started paying attention, at least. It didn't look like an Inhibitor cull to me. Too much was left behind. It was thorough, don't get me wrong, but not thorough enough.' She paused, cast her face down as if embarrassed. 'That was what my book was about: the one I was working on when I lived in the badlands. It was a thesis, proving my hypothesis through the accumulation of data.'

'No one would have listened to you,' he said. 'But if it's any consolation, I think you're right. The question is: what did the shadows have to do with any of this?'

'I don't know.'

'When we came here, we thought it was simple. The evidence pointed to one conclusion: that the scuttlers had been wiped out by the Inhibitors.'

'That's what the scrimshaw suit told me,' Rashmika said. 'The scuttlers built the mechanism to receive the signals from the shadows. But they didn't take the final step: they didn't allow the shadows to cross over to help them.'

'But now we have the chance not to make the same mistake,' Scorpio said.

'Yes,' Rashmika said, sounding wary of a trap. 'But you don't think we should do it, do you?'

'I think the mistake the scuttlers made was to contact the shadows,' Scorpio said.

Rashmika shook her head. 'The shadows didn't wipe out the scuttlers. That doesn't make any sense, either. We know that they're at least as powerful as the Inhibitors. They wouldn't have left a trace behind here. And if they had crossed over, why would they still be pleading for the chance to do so?'

'Exactly,' Scorpio said.

Rashmika echoed him. 'Exactly?'

'It wasn't the Inhibitors that annihilated the scuttlers,' he said. 'And it wasn't the shadows, either. It was whoever – or whatever – made that shard of conch material.'

She gave it back to him, as if the thing were in some way tainted. 'Do you have any proof of this, Scorp?'

'None whatsoever. But if we were to dig around on Hela – really dig – I wouldn't be surprised if we eventually turned up something like this. Just a shard would do. Of course, there's another way to test my theory.'

She shook her head, as if trying to clear it. 'But what did the scuttlers do that meant they had to be wiped out of existence?'

'They made the wrong decision,' he said.

'Which was?'

'They negotiated with the shadows. That was the test, Aura, that was what the conch-makers were waiting for. They knew that the one thing the scuttlers shouldn't do was open the door to the shadows. You can't beat one enemy by doing a deal with something worse. We'd better ensure that we don't make the same mistake.'

'The conch-makers don't sound much better than the shadows – or the Inhibitors – in that case.'

'I'm not saying we have to climb into bed with them, just that we might want to take them into consideration. They're here, Aura, in this system. Just because we can't see them doesn't mean they aren't watching our every move.'

The elevator ascended in silence for several more seconds. Eventually Rashmika said, 'You haven't actually come for the scrimshaw suit at all, have you?'

'I had an open mind,' Scorpio said.

'And now?'

'You've helped me make it up. It isn't leaving the Lady Morwenna.'

'Then Dean Quaiche was right,' Rashmika said. 'He always said the suit was full of demons.'

The elevator slowed. Scorpio placed the shard of conch material back in his belt pouch, then retrieved Clavain's knife. 'Stay here,' he said. 'If I don't come back out of that room in two minutes, take the elevator down to the surface. And then get the hell out of the cathedral.'

The four of them stood on the ice: Rashmika and her mother, Vasko and the pig. They had walked with the Lady Morwenna since leaving it, following the immense thing as it continued its journey towards the attenuated stump of the bridge thrusting out from the edge of the cliff. They were actually standing on that last part of the bridge, a good kilometre out from the cliff wall.

It seemed very unlikely that there was anyone left alive aboard the cathedral now, but Scorpio had resigned himself to never knowing that for certain. He had swept the main spaces looking for survivors, but there were almost certainly dozens of pressurised hiding places he would never have found. It was, he thought, enough that he had tried. In his present weakened state, even that had been more than anyone could have expected.

In other respects, nothing very much about the Lady Morwenna had changed. The lower levels had been depressurised, as he had discovered when he climbed aboard using the line that the technician had dropped down from the propulsion chamber. But the great machines evidently worked as well in vacuum as in air: there had been no hesitation in the cathedral's onward march, and the subsystems of electrical generation had not been affected. High up in the garret of the Clocktower, lights still burned. But no one moved up there, nor in any of the other windows that shone in the moving edifice.

'How far now?' Scorpio asked.

'Two hundred metres to the edge,' Vasko said, 'near as I can judge.'

'Fifteen minutes,' Rashmika said. 'Then the front half of her will be over thin air – assuming that the remaining part of the bridge holds her that far.'

'I think it'll hold,' Scorpio said. 'I think it would have held all the way over, to be honest.'

'That would have been something to see,' Khouri said.

'I guess we'll never know what made the bridge,' Vasko said. Next to him, one of the huge feet was hoisted into the air by the complex machinery of the flying buttress. The foot moved forwards, then descended silently on to the ice.

Scorpio thought of the message he had intercepted via his suit. 'One of life's mysteries,' he said. 'It wasn't the scuttlers, though. We can be sure of that.'

'Not them,' Rashmika agreed. 'Not in a million years. They'd never have left behind anything that marvellous.'

'It's not too late,' Vasko said.

Scorpio turned to him, catching the distorted reflection of his own face in the man's helmet. 'Not too late for what, son?'

'To go back inside. Fifteen minutes. Say, thirteen or fourteen, to be on the safe side. I could get to the garret in time.'

'And haul that suit down the stairs?' Khouri asked. 'It won't fit in the elevator.'

'I could smash the window of the garret. With two of us, we ought to be able to push the suit over the side.'

'I thought the idea was to save it,' Scorpio said.

'It's a lot less of a drop from the garret to the ice than from the bridge to the bottom of the Gap,' Rashmika said. 'It would probably survive, with some damage.'

'Twelve minutes, if you want to play safe,' Khouri said.

'I could still do it,' Vasko said. 'What about you, Scorp? Could you make it, if we had to?'

'I probably could, if I didn't have anything planned for the rest of my life.'

'I'll take that as a no, then.'

'We made a decision, Vasko. Where I come from, we tend to stick with them.'

Vasko craned his neck to take in the highest extremities of the Lady Morwenna. Scorpio found himself doing the same thing, even though it made him dizzy to look up. Against the fixed stars over Hela, the cathedral hardly seemed to be moving at all. But it was not the fixed stars that were the problem: it was the twenty bright new ones strung in a ragged necklace around the planet. They couldn't stay up there for ever, Scorpio thought. The Captain had done the right thing by protecting his sleepers from the uncertainties of the holdfast, even if it had been a kind of suicide. But sooner or later someone was going to have to do something about those eighteen thousand sleeping souls.

Not my problem, Scorpio thought. Someone else could take care of that one. 'I didn't think I'd make it this far,' he said under his breath.

'Scorp?' Khouri asked.

'Nothing,' he said, shaking his head. 'Just wondering what the hell a fifty-year-old pig is doing this far from home.'

'Making a difference,' Khouri said. 'Like we always knew you would.'

'She's right,' Rashmika agreed. 'Thank you, Scorpio. You didn't have to do what you did. I'll never forget it.'

And I'll never forget the screams of my friend as I dug into him with that scalpel, Scorpio thought. But what choice had he had? Clavain had never blamed him; had, in fact, done everything in his power to absolve him of any feelings of guilt. The man was about to die horribly, and the only thing that really mattered to him was sparing his friend any emotional distress. Why couldn't Scorpio honour Clavain's memory by letting go of the hatred? He had just been in the wrong place at the wrong time. It wasn't the pig's fault. It hadn't been Clavain's, either. And the one person whose fault it definitely hadn't been was Aura.

'Scorp?' she asked.

'I'm glad you're safe,' he said.

Khouri put an arm around his shoulder. 'I'm glad you made it as well, Scorp. Thank you for coming back, for all of us.'

'A pig's got to do . . .' he said.

They stood in silence, watching the cathedral narrow the distance between itself and the edge of the bridge. For more than a century it had kept moving, never once losing the endless race with Haldora. One-third of a metre per second, for every second of every day, every day of every year. And now that same clocklike inevitability was sending it to its destruction.

'Scorp,' Rashmika said, breaking the spell, 'even if we destroy the scrimshaw suit, what do we do about the machinery in Haldora? It's still there. It's still just as capable of letting them through.'

'If we had one more cache weapon . . .' Khouri said.

'If wishes were horses,' Scorpio answered. He stamped his feet to keep warm: either there was something wrong with the suit, or there was something wrong with him. 'Look, we'll find a way to destroy it, or at least throw a spanner into it. Or else they'll show us.'

'They?' she asked.

'The ones we haven't met yet. But they're out there, you can count on that. They've been watching and waiting, taking notes.'

'What if we're wrong?' Khouri asked. 'What if they're waiting to see if we're clever enough to contact the shadows? What if *that's* the right thing to do?'

'Then we'll have added a new enemy to the list,' Scorpio said. 'And hey, if that happens . . .'

'What?'

'It's not the end of the world. Trust me on this: I've been collecting enemies since I drew my first breath.'

For another minute no one said anything. The Lady Morwenna continued its crunching advance towards oblivion. The twin fire trails of the *Nostalgia for Infinity* continued to bisect the sky, like the first tentative sketch towards a new constellation.

'So what you're saying is,' Vasko said, 'we should just do what we think is right, even if they don't like it?'

'More or less. Of course, it may be the right thing as well. All depends on what happened to the scuttlers, really.'

'They certainly pissed someone off,' Khouri said.

'Amen to that,' Scorpio replied, laughing. 'My kind of species. We'd have got on famously.'

He couldn't help himself. *Here I am*, he thought: *critically injured, most likely more than half-dead, having in the last day lost both my ship and some of my best friends. I've just killed my way through a cathedral, murdering anyone who had the insolence to stand in my way. I'm about to watch the utter destruction of something that might – just might – be the most important discovery in human history, the only thing capable of standing between us and the Inhibitors. And I'm standing here laughing, as if the only thing at stake is a good night out.*

Typical pig, he concluded: *no sense of perspective*. Sometimes, occasionally, it was the one thing in the universe he was most grateful for.

Too much perspective could be bad for you.

'Scorp?' Khouri said. 'Do you mind if I ask you something, before we get separated again?'

'I don't know,' he said. 'Ask, and find out.'

'Why did you save that shuttle, the one from the *Wild Pallas*? What stopped you firing on it, even when you saw the Inhibitor machines? You saved those people.'

Did she know? he wondered. He had missed so much during the nine extra years for which he had been frozen. It was possible that she had found out, confirmed that which he had only suspected.

He remembered something that Antoinette Bax had said to him just before they had parted. She had wondered if they would ever meet again. It was a big universe, he had said: big enough for a few coincidences. Maybe for some people, Antoinette had replied, but not for the likes of Scorpio and her. And she had been right, too. He knew that they were never going to meet each other again. Scorpio had smiled to himself: he knew exactly what she meant. He didn't believe in miracles either. But where exactly did you draw the line? But he knew now, with absolute confidence, that she had also been wrong. It didn't happen for the likes of Scorpio and Antoinette. But for other people? Sometimes things like that just *happened*.

He knew. He had seen the names of all the evacuees on the shuttle they had rescued from the Yellowstone system. And one name in particular had stood out. The man had even made an impression on him, when he had seen the shuttle being unloaded. He remembered his quiet dignity, the need for someone to share what he felt, but not to take that load from him. The man had – like all the other passengers – probably been frozen ever since.

He would now be amongst the eighteen thousand sleepers who were orbiting Hela.

'We have to find a way to get to those people,' he told Khouri.

'I thought we were talking about—'

'We were,' he said, leaving at it that. Let her wait a little longer: she'd waited this long, after all.

For a while, no one spoke. The cathedral looked as if it would last for another thousand years. It had, in Scorpio's opinion, no more than five minutes left.

'I could still make it up there,' Vasko said. 'If I ran ... if we ran, Scorp ...' He trailed off.

'Let's go,' Scorpio said.

They all looked at him, then at the cathedral. Its front was a good seventy metres from the end of the bridge; there were still another three or four minutes before it began to push out into empty space. Then what? At least another minute, surely, before the awesome mass of the Lady Morwenna began to overbalance.

'Go where, Scorp?' Khouri asked.

'I've had enough,' he said, decisively. 'It's been a long day and we've all got a long walk ahead of us. The sooner we make a start on it, the better.'

'But the cathedral—' Rashmika said.

'I'm sure it will be very impressive. You're welcome to tell me all about it.'

He turned around and started walking back along what remained of the bridge. The sun was low behind him, pushing his own comical shadow ahead of him. It waddled before him, swaying from side to side like a poorly worked puppet. He was colder now: it was a peculiar, intimate kind of coldness, a coldness that felt as if it had his name on it. Maybe this is it, he thought: the end of the line, just as they had always warned him. He was a pig; he shouldn't expect the world. He'd already made more of a dent in it than most.

He walked faster. Presently, three other shadows began to loom around his. They said nothing, walking together, mindful of the difficult journey ahead of them. When, after another few minutes, the ground rumbled – as if a great fist had just struck Hela in fury – none of them paused or broke their pace. They just kept walking. And when, eventually, he saw the smallest of the shadows begin to lose its footing, he watched the others rush towards it and hold it up.

After that, he didn't remember very much.

EPILOGUE

She issues another command and the mechanical butterflies disengage their interlaced wings, shattering the temporary screen they have formed. The butterflies reassemble themselves into the lacy, fluttering fabric of her sleeve. When she looks into the sky she sees only a handful of stars: those bright enough to shine through the moonlight and the sparkling river of the ring. Of the green star that the butterflies have revealed there is no longer any sign. But she knows it is still there, just too faint to be seen. Once revealed, it is not something that can ever be forgotten.

She knows that there is nothing actually wrong with the star. Its fusion processes have not been unbalanced; its atmospheric chemistry has not been perturbed. It shines as hot as it did a century ago, and the neutrinos spilling from its core attest to normal conditions of pressure, temperature and nucleotide abundance. But something very wrong has happened to the system that once orbited the star. Its worlds have been unmade, stripped back to raw atoms, then reassembled into a cloud of glassy bubbles: air-and-water-filled habitats, countless numbers of them. Vast mirrors – forged in the same orgy of demolition and reconstruction – trap every outgoing photon of starlight and pump it into the swarm of habitats. Nothing is wasted; nothing is squandered. In the bubbles, the sunlight feeds complex, teetering webs of closed-cycle biochemistry. Plants and animals thrive in the swarm, machines tending to their every need. People are welcome: indeed, it was people for whom the swarm was made in the first place.

But people were never asked.

This green-stained sun is not the first, nor will it be the last. There are dozens more stained suns out there. The transforming machines that make the swarms of habitats can hop from system to system with the mindless efficiency of locusts. They arrive, make copies of themselves and then they start to dismantle. All attempts to contain their spread have failed. It only takes one to start the process, although they arrive by the million.

They are called greenfly.

No one knows where they came from, or who made them. The best guess is that they are a rogue terraforming technology: something developed almost a thousand years earlier, in the centuries before the Inhibitors came. But they are obviously much more than revenant machines. They are too quick and strong for that. They are something that has spent a long time learning to survive by itself, growing fierce and feral in the process. They are something opportunistic: something that has hidden in the woodwork, waiting for its moment.

And, she thinks, *we gave them that moment.*

While humanity was under the heel of the Inhibitors, nothing like this outbreak could ever have been allowed to happen. The Inhibitors – themselves a form of spacefaring replicating machinery – would never have tolerated a rival. But the Inhibitors were gone now; they had not been seen for more than four hundred years. Not that they had exactly been beaten: that wasn't how it had happened. But they had been pushed back, frontiers and buffer-zones established. Much of the galaxy, presumably, still belonged to them. But the attempt to exterminate humanity – this local cull – had failed.

It had nothing to do with human cleverness.

It had everything to do with circumstance, luck, cowardice. Collectively, the Inhibitors had been failing for millions of years. Sooner or later, an emergent species was bound to break loose. Humanity would probably not have been that species, even with the assistance from the Hades matrix. But the matrix had pointed them in the right direction. It had sent them to Hela, and there they had made the correct decision: not to invoke the shadows, but to petition the assistance of the Nestbuilders. It was they who had annihilated the scuttlers, when the scuttlers had made the mistake of negotiating with shadows.

And we almost made the same one, she thinks. They came so close that even now she turns cold at the thought of it.

The white armour of her butterflies shuffles closer.

'We should leave now,' her protector says, calling from the end of the jetty.

'You gave me an hour.'

'You've used most of it, stargazing.'

It doesn't seem possible. Perhaps he's exaggerating, or perhaps she really did spend that long picking out the green star. Sometimes she slipped into a reverie of self-remembrance, and the moments oozed into hours, the hours into decades. She is so old that sometimes she even frightens herself.

'A little longer,' she says.

The Nestbuilders (she thinks back to the earlier, now-forgotten name for the symbionts: the conch-makers) had long practised a strategy of skulking. Rather than confront the Inhibitors head-on, they preferred to slip between the stars, avoiding contact wherever possible. They were experts in stealth. But after acquiring some of their weapons and data, humanity had pursued a tactic of pure confrontation. They had cleansed local space of the Inhibitors. The Nestbuilders hadn't liked this: they had warned of the dangers in upsetting equilibria. Some things, no matter how bad, were always better than the alternative.

This wasn't what humanity wanted to hear.

Maybe it was all worth it, she thinks. *For four hundred years we had a second Golden Age. We did wonderful things, left wonderful marks on time. We had a blast. We forgot the old legends and made better ones, new fables for new times. But all the while, something else was waiting in the woodwork. When we took the Inhibitors out of the equation, we gave greenfly its chance.*

It isn't the end of everything. Worlds are being evacuated as the greenfly machines sweep through their systems. But after the catastrophic mismanagement of the first few evacuations, things move more smoothly now. The authorities are ahead of the wave. They know all the tricks of crowd-control.

She looks out into darkness again. The greenfly machines move slowly: there are still colonies out there that won't fall victim to them for hundreds, even thousands of years. There is still time to live and love. Rejuvenation, even for an old demi-Conjoiner, has its allure. They say there are settled worlds in the Pleiades now. From there, the wave of green-stained suns must seem pretty remote, pretty unthreatening.

But by the time she gets to the Pleiades, she will be another four hundred years downstream from her birth.

She thinks, as she often does, about the messages from the shadows. They had also spoken of being harried by machines that turned stars green. She wonders, not for the first time, if that could really be a coincidence. Under the ruling paradigm of brane theory, the message must have come from the present, rather than the distant future or the distant past. But what if the theory was wrong? What if all of it – the shadow branes, the bulk, the gravitational signalling – was just a convenient fiction to dress up an even stranger truth?

She doesn't know. She doesn't think she ever will know.

She isn't sure she wants to.

She turns from the sky, directing her attention to the ocean. It was here that they died, back when this place was called Ararat. No one calls it that now: no one even remembers that Ararat was ever its name. But she remembers.

She remembers seeing that moon being shattered as the Inhibitors deflected the energy of the cache-weapon while the *Nostalgia for Infinity* made its escape.

Inhibitors. Cache-weapon. *Nostalgia for Infinity*: they are like the incantations of a childhood game, forgotten for years. They sound faintly ridiculous, yet also freighted with a terrible significance.

She hadn't really seen the moon being shattered, if truth be told. It was her mother who had seen it. But her memories made no great distinction between the one and the other. She had been a witness, even if she had seen things through another's eyes.

She thinks of Antoinette, Xavier, Blood and the others: all the people who – by choice or compulsion – had remained on Ararat while the starship made its escape. None of them could have survived the phase of bombardment when the pieces of the ruined moon began to hit the ocean. They would have drowned, as tsunamis washed away their fragile little surface communities.

Unless, she thinks, they chose to drown before then. What if the sea welcomed them? The Pattern Jugglers had already co-operated in the departure of the ship. Was it such a leap of imagination to think of them saving the remaining islanders?

People had been living here for four hundred years, swimmers amongst them. Sometimes, the records said, they spoke of encountering ghost impressions: other, older minds. Were the islanders amongst them, preserved in the living memory of the sea after all these years?

The glowing smudges in the water now surround the jetty. She had made a decision even before she descended the transit stalk: she will swim, and she will open her mind to the ocean. And she will tell the ocean everything that she knows: everything that is going to happen to this place when the terraformers arrive. No one knows what will happen when the greenfly machines touch the alien organism of a Juggler sea, which one will assimilate the other. It is an experiment that has not yet been performed. Perhaps the ocean will absorb the machines harmlessly, as it has absorbed so much else.

Perhaps there will be a kind of stalemate. Or perhaps this world, like dozens before it, will be ripped apart and remade, in a fury of reorganisation.

She does not know what that will mean for the minds now in the ocean. On some level, she is certain, they already know what is about to happen. They cannot have failed to pick up the nuances of panic as the human population made its escape plans. But she thinks it unlikely that anyone has swum with the specific purpose of telling the world what is to come. It might not make any difference. On the other hand, quite literally, it might make all the difference in the world.

It is, she supposes, a matter of courtesy. Everything that happens here, everything that will happen, is her responsibility.

She issues another command to the butterflies. The white armour dissipates, the mechanical insects fluttering in a cloud above her head. They linger, not straying too far, but leaving her naked on the jetty.

She risks a glance back towards her protector. She can just see his silhouette against the milky background of the sky, his childlike form leaning against a walking stick. He is looking away, his head bobbing impatiently. He wants to leave very much, but she doesn't blame him for that.

She sits on the edge of the jetty. The water roils around her in anticipation. Things move within it: shapes and phantasms. She will swim for a little while, and open her mind. She does not know how long it will take, but she will not leave until she is ready. If her protector has already departed – she does not think this is very likely, but it must still be considered – then she will have to make other plans.

She slips into the sea, into the glowing green memory of Ararat.

Alastair Reynolds was born in Barry, South Wales, in 1966, and studied at Newcastle and St Andrews Universities. He has a PhD in astronomy and works part-time as an astrophysicist for the European Space Agency. His 'Revelation Space' series, *Revelation Space*, shortlisted for the Arthur C. Clarke and the BSFA Awards, *Redemption Ark* and *Absolution Gap*, shortlisted for the British Science Fiction Award, and his SF thrillers, *Chasm City*, winner of the British Science Fiction Award, and *Century Rain*, are all Gollancz bestsellers.